MEMORIES OF
SORROW

BY KEISHA CONES

DORRANCE
PUBLISHING CO
EST. 1920
PITTSBURGH, PENNSYLVANIA 15238

Dorrance Publishing Co
585 Alpha Drive
Suite 103
Pittsburgh, PA 15238
Visit our website at *www.dorrancebookstore.com*

ISBN: 979-8-88729-015-7
eISBN: 979-8-88729-515-2

MEMORIES OF

SORROW

This book is dedicated to my father, who always believed in me, and to my mother, for her endless compassion. Their encouragement made this book possible.

CHAPTER ONE

Below the glow of a yard light, a large rabbit appeared out of the darkness and shuffled across the dead grass. When he was close to the light pole he paused, his nose taking in the scents around him. Something made him listen for danger. His ears turned outward, his nose twitched intensely, and for several seconds he remained still frozen. The threat – real or perceived – was dismissed by the rabbit and he continued his nocturnal habits.

Ava Reid sat at the window seat on the second floor of her house, her knees drawn up to her bare chest, her arms wrapped around her legs. Her brunette hair cascaded down her shoulders and back in thick layers. With her forehead leaning against the wall, she watched the rabbit. Her breath left a little patch of fog on the glass.

The rabbit's antics were a welcomed distraction. Ava had a pleasant view of the creature from the decorative window, which she had noticed immediately when she saw the property for sale online. The day after moving in, she had constructed the bench seat and floor-to-ceiling bookcases to make this area a reading nook. By day, natural light streamed through the large window the nook had been built around. Ava rarely sat still for long, but when she did, she read.

At three in the morning, however, with the house full of shadows around her, the nook was where she sat as she waited for sleep to return.

A scream had woken her this early morning. Cacophonous in the silence of the house, it broke through her subconscious mind easily and sent her rolling smoothly from bed into a crouch on the floor, ready to defend herself. After listening for a moment or two, letting her eyes adjust and making sure no one was moving around in her bedroom, she began to check each room for an intruder.

She knew better.

Shortly after moving into this house, she had increased the security by adding high grade electronic door locks to the front and back doors in addition to the standard locks already in place. Every night she confirmed each lock was secure on the windows and doors throughout the house. She was confident she had not skipped last night's routine. The house was locked and tidy, just as she left it before bed. Strangers were not inside her house playing tricks or trying to steal from her. No intruders were walking around in her home, invading her sanctuary.

Yet she had heard the scream as clearly as she was seeing the rabbit below her in the yard. It was followed by sobbing that trailed off into silence.

This was not the first time a scream woke her from sleep.

The rabbit had left the circle of visibility cast by the yard light. Now Ava could only see a patch of dead grass.

The ground was bare. This winter had brought almost no snow at all, a rarity for south central Wisconsin. Ava had witnessed several people around town favoring the lack of snow while they fussed about the cold. When summer arrived, those same people would complain about the heat and humidity. No matter where she lived, people seemed to obsess about the weather. She thought it ridiculous to complain about outside stimuli they had no control over.

Her eyelids became heavy. By the time a red fox darted through the glow of the yard light, following the scent of the rabbit, she had relaxed against the nook wall. Too exhausted now from lack of sleep, Ava dropped off into unconsciousness.

She didn't hear the whisper-soft slap of bare feet walking toward her on the hardwood floor.

$$\bullet \quad \bullet \quad \bullet \quad \bullet \quad \bullet$$

The young girl appeared out of nowhere. Just a face materializing where once there was none. She looked to be around ten or eleven years old. Her eyes were the color of medium wash blue jeans, and there was laughter in them.

They were the first attribute anyone noticed about her; so many times, people had told her she had beautiful eyes. She was used to hearing it by now. She was smiling, not showing her teeth but clearly amused. One long braid, draped over her left shoulder, held back brown hair.

A thick trickle of blood oozed down her left temple.

Ava jerked against the wall of the reading nook. Squinting against the onslaught of morning light, she propped her elbow on her knee and shaded her eyes with her hand.

She hadn't made it back to bed after watching the rabbit. Slouching against the wall for hours had given her a headache. The muscles in her back and neck were sore. Her morning workout and a warm shower afterwards would help to loosen her up and get her blood flowing. Tonight, she would take an Epsom salt bath to help with any residual stiffness.

Intent on starting her day, she started to swing her legs over the edge of the bench. What she saw made her shove herself back against the wall, flinging her arms out. Instinct told her to go through every room of the house again, check every window and door lock to make sure no one had broken in. A break in was the only explanation for how a blanket was covering her that had not been on her at three thirty this morning when she fell asleep in the reading nook.

The blanket someone had covered her with had dropped onto the floor when Ava startled. It was one David, her foster father, had given her when she moved out. His wife, Ruth, made it before she died. Ava knew she had not arisen again this morning, walked to the closet where she kept the blanket, and returned to the reading nook to cover herself with it. Had she stirred enough to stand up, she would have returned to her bed.

Just as she knew every lock was engaged and no one had broken into her house.

Turning, she set her feet on the cold hardwood floor. She picked up the blanket and methodically folded it, set it beside her on the bench.

She stood slowly to get her bearings. Since she slept naked, that was how she left her bed earlier this morning to investigate the scream. She didn't worry about being seen from the large window she currently stood in front of. The isolation of this property was high on the list of reasons why she had chosen it.

Taking a deep breath, she held it, let it out slowly. She inhaled again, held it. Bending forward, she exhaled and laid her palms flat on the floor, keeping her legs straight. She held the stretch for several moments, breathing slowly, before gradually returning upright. She rotated her shoulders forward and backward, moved her head from side to side. As she stretched, she thought of someone or something covering her with a blanket and what that act implied.

At first glance, compassion. A selfless act meant to ease the suffering of others. Ava understood compassion to be a bribe for future obligations expected in return. Whoever had covered her to keep her warm had done so to get something from her in return.

Glancing down at the blanket, she wondered what that something was. No matter: she had not asked for help. She never put herself in a position to be obligated to anyone.

As she dressed for her workout, she thought about the young girl with the braid. The face was familiar. Since moving to Langdon six months ago, she had dreamed of the girl several times. Nothing of consequence happened in the dreams; Ava simply saw the face and awoke shortly after. The blood on the temple was new.

Ava twisted a band through her hair as she walked downstairs. She stopped in the kitchen for a glass of water before heading to the basement, where she would put in two and a half hours of various activity that would push her body to its limits. Jogging afterwards would round out her morning routine. The exertion would keep her mind from wondering about a child she had never met.

•   •   •   •   •

A man named Stan did not own Stan's Grocery. As far as Gabriel Harris knew, no one name Stan had ever owned or operated the business, and Gabriel had never figured out where the name originated. The store was, however, the largest in Langdon and the prices were only a few cents higher than any chain in Madison. Gabriel liked to support local businesses, and he preferred the calm atmosphere of Stan's to a corporation bustling with half-dressed trailer trash and screaming kids.

It wasn't unusual for him to wait until the last minute to remember he needed something and run to the store before he started work. Working from home afforded him that luxury. So did getting a late start to his day because starting work before nine, in his opinion, was criminal.

Today it was razor blades. He could have let it go if he didn't already have a couple days' worth of stubble. It was making his skin crawl like a son of a bitch. He tried the blade already in his razor and it cut the shit out of his neck. After letting out a string of curses, he wiped off the shaving cream and admitted he would have to go to the store.

Filling his travel mug with coffee, he headed to Stan's.

It was an unpleasant drive. The morning was frigid, and the afternoon was supposed to warm up only marginally. Gabriel always did his best work when he could open the garage up and smell nature, especially during the creative process. He still had at least a month, probably more, before that happened.

Snow had barely made an appearance this year. The trees still had that dead, dry look they took on during the winter. At least he would be able to hear birds again soon. He hated the silence and isolation of winter, even though he wasn't the biggest fan of crowds.

He parked his truck and walked toward the building, longing for summer. Everybody was at this time of the year, when the daily high temperatures were starting to climb toward warmer weather, but mornings still caused frost. The days were gradually getting longer. Mother Nature loved to tease in Wisconsin.

Entering a quiet store, Gabriel picked up a basket and headed for the discount aisle. He might as well see if there were any bargains while he was here. The sale items were strategically placed in the first aisle, so the customer saw them instantly upon entering the store. Gabriel browsed, saw nothing helpful to his cupboards, and moved on.

He started going over his plan for the day's workload as he walked. He had passed a couple aisles before remembering he was running low on coffee. He turned back and headed for the coffee.

As he was skimming the shelves, wishing they would quit changing the location of products so he could find his damn weekly staples from one week to the next, his stomach suddenly felt hollow, like he was long past needing to eat. He rubbed his stomach absently. Coffee was his usual breakfast; he didn't eat solid food until close to noon most days. Something seemed to tug at him like the nagging sensation that he had to be somewhere but couldn't remember where. When he glanced to the left in search of his brand of coffee, he noticed a woman was standing a few feet away. A partially filled cart sat a few inches from her.

Gabriel twitched. Damn, she was close enough he should have heard her approach, especially since she was pushing a cart.

He had seen her around town the past few months, always at a distance from people, always by herself. People in small towns talked, and people in Langdon were saying she was odd and quiet, but polite. Many had theories, but she hadn't given anyone a chance to talk to her. Even now she kept a deliberate distance from him.

Gabriel took a moment to watch her out of the corner of his eye. Dark blue jeans showed off long, slender legs. She wore boots with thick, solid heels. They were not something from the season's latest fashion; they were the ass-kicking kind similar to what military personnel wore. Instead of a purse, she carried a miniature backpack slung over one shoulder. The coat she wore was light green, unfortunately covering a rear end that promised to be killer if her legs were any indication.

Thick auburn hair that looked almost black flowed halfway down her back in a long, layered cut. Gabriel couldn't tell the color of her eyes standing beside her, but the woman was vigilant. She appeared to be intently scanning coffee flavors, but her head was tilted at an angle so she could study her surroundings.

Who did she think was going to come after her?

Spotting his brand, Gabriel picked up a bag of coffee and dropped it into his basket. He gave her a wide berth as he passed her to leave the aisle because everything about her said STAY BACK. He noticed she tensed as he walked by and wondered if she expected him hurt her.

Was she on the run from an abusive spouse or boyfriend? Is that why she was so cautious?

Not in a particular hurry to go back out into the glacial morning, Gabriel continued roaming the aisles for a few more minutes. Finally, he considered his shopping done. He could no longer procrastinate; eventually, he would have to leave the store. The bitter wind and eye-watering cold was waiting for another victim.

Only one checkout counter was open this early in the morning. Gabriel started setting his items on the belt.

"Good morning, Mr. Harris." Megan, a girl just out of high school, began scanning his items. She tucked a strand of her shoulder-length, mousy brown hair behind her ear. "What are you building today?"

He didn't bother telling her she could call him Gabriel. While still in school, she had been working at Stan's during nights and on weekends for the past few years. During the summers she picked up even more hours, until she graduated last year and became a full-time employee. She had never once used his first name. It made him feel old.

"Kitchen cabinets." Gabriel dug in his wallet for his credit card. He found himself glancing around for the woman in the green coat. He hadn't passed her in the aisles since their first encounter.

"That seems like a waste of your talent." Megan swiped items across the scanner quickly, bagging as she went. Her Stan's smock, a disturbing pale pink color, hung loosely off her willowy frame.

"It all pays the bills," Gabriel said amiably.

"My mom still talks about you restoring Gran's antique dresser. She still gets misty-eyed when she tells people about it." There was amusement in Megan's tone, but pride as well. Gabriel wondered if she would eventually inherit the piece.

"It was a solid piece, well taken care of," Gabriel said, touched, as always, by a customer's strong reaction to something that came naturally to him. Megan's mother had given him a staggering tip after he delivered the dresser to her house, even though he'd argued with her for days about it. "I just uncovered what was already there."

Megan smiled, hitting buttons on the register. Her aqua nail polish was mostly chipped off. She had an eyebrow piercing, which surprised him every time he saw it. How did she wear a hat during Wisconsin winters?

Rattling off his total, she finished bagging the rest of his items as he punched in his card information.

"I'm so done with winter," Megan said, her hand poised as she waited for his receipt to print out. "How do you get any work done?"

"Heated garage," he said, smiling as he pocketed his wallet. "But I'm definitely ready for summer."

Megan handed him his grocery sack. "You have a good day, Mr. Harris. Try not to get frostbite."

7

"You, too, Megan."

Carrying his paper sack out into the parking lot, Gabriel mumbled a few profanities at the cold and walked to his truck. He glanced around the parking lot. The woman in green was loading groceries into a Chevy Equinox a few cars down from his. Somehow, she had finished filling half a cart, checked out, and was loading her vehicle before he had left the store with a few items in a small basket.

He set his bag on the front seat of his truck and walked toward her. "Do you need some h-"

He began asking while he was still several feet away and hadn't finished before she whirled on him. She planted her feet and positioned her hands in a defensive gesture, with one balled into a fist at her side and the other aimed at Gabriel with her fingers slightly spread.

"Sorry, I didn't mean to scare you," he said calmly, holding up his hands with his palms out. "I'm just being friendly. I've seen you around Langdon and thought I'd introduce myself. Gabriel Harris."

He held out his hand.

The woman stared at it as if it held a glob of dog shit. She didn't relax her guarded position.

"You did not scare me," she said tonelessly. "I do not shake hands."

Lowering his hand, Gabriel could see she was more annoyed than startled. The way her jaw was set, and her eyes bored into his, he would have guessed she was irritated that he felt obligated to be polite. She returned to loading groceries in her vehicle. His initial thought that she was fleeing an abusive relationship didn't make sense. The woman wasn't nervous around him. She hadn't cowered in submission and fear when Gabriel approached her. She'd stood her ground and let him know he was intruding in her space.

"Do you want some help with that?" he asked, watching her lift a heavy bag.

"No."

She efficiently finished with the rest of the bags and shut the door, turning back to her cart to find him still there. From her expression, she wasn't pleased about it and had no compunctions about showing her feelings with a frown.

"I do woodworking and restoration." He took off his glove and reached into his back pocket for his wallet. The woman instantly became more focused, her eyes locking on his face and her body leaned slightly forward, ready to defend herself.

Slowly, he pulled out his business card. He looked closely at her face for the first time.

Gray, he thought. Her eyes are gray.

Right now, they were watching him intently, the color of a storm waiting to erupt. Color rose in her cheeks. Gabriel wondered if that was from the cold or him. Or both. She wasn't wearing makeup, he noticed with appreciation.

"You are soliciting your business," she said. "You are not being friendly."

Though her tone showed no inflection one way or the other, Gabriel was sure she felt he had lied to her and was disgusted by the thought. She rested her hands on the handle of the cart. The skin on her knuckles paled as she deliberately squeezed.

"I didn't plan on offering my card." He dropped his hand. "It's an icebreaker for most people. I didn't mean to offend you."

The woman's attention was suddenly diverted to a point several feet to Gabriel's right. Her eyes seemed to be following the movement of someone in the parking lot.

Gabriel turned to see what she was looking at but saw nothing. She was an odd one, he had to admit. The people of Langdon had been right about that. She was absolutely beautiful, and there was something intriguing about her. Something had drawn him to her that had nothing to do with her beauty.

Cautiously, she reached out.

Gabriel offered his business card again. Though he had left plenty of room for her to take it without touching him, her fingers brushed lightly against his. He was surprised when she didn't snatch the card and instantly pull back. She looked down at the point where their fingers met. Watching her stare with such an intense expression, Gabriel couldn't help but look at their hands. He didn't understand why she was gazing at them with such interest. He had given his card to hundreds, if not thousands of people, and never had this reaction before.

After a long moment, she raised her head as if hypnotized, her movements sleepy. Her stormy eyes were out of focus.

Damn, he thought. Those eyes could knock a guy right on his ass.

"Such sadness," she whispered, and Gabriel felt as if someone had jabbed him with a cattle prod. A jolt had his body shuddering all over. He broke into a sweat even though the temperature hadn't reached twenty degrees.

"Excuse me?"

She seemed to be looking through him. Sometime during the past few seconds, she had taken his wrist with her other hand. Now she held him in a powerful grip with both of her hands. Her pupils were the size of dimes, making her eyes look black.

He felt mesmerized by those large, dark eyes. How could they appear to be staring into his very soul and simultaneously sucking him into their blind voids? Gabriel could feel his heartbeat thudding madly in his chest, the blood pumping through his veins as if filled with ice, and his feet seemed rooted to the blacktop parking lot.

"Blue, the color of denim," she said suddenly. Her voice sounded deafening in the empty parking lot.

A coldness swept up his spine that had nothing to do with the weather. He couldn't look away from those blank, black eyes. Something heavy was pressing against his chest, making it impossible to breathe.

"Your eyes are the same color of blue. That's why it still hurts so much."

"What did you say?" he finally managed.

The woman pulled her hands back with considerable effort. The business card fluttered toward the ground. Still watching Gabriel, she shot her hand out and snatched the card from the air so quickly, Gabriel only saw a pale blur. Her eyes came into focus again and she appeared momentarily depleted. What was visible of her irises now looked almost silver.

"Excuse me," she said. She put the card in her coat pocket before pushing the cart past him toward the corral.

"Sure," Gabriel said, turning to watch her. "I'll see you around."

She didn't answer.

He felt strange as hell. The encounter had left him unsettled. Tucking his wallet back in his pocket, he pulled his glove back on.

Walking back to his truck, Gabriel could still feel the slam of energy that had coursed through his body when they had been touching. His body gave an involuntary shiver.

• • • • •

Ava found herself distracted before she reached the highway heading out of town toward home. During the short drive, she tried several times to slow her breathing and gain control of her emotions. She was exhausted from the episode at Stan's. A headache had started behind her right eye. Both made concentrating harder. If she couldn't concentrate, she couldn't focus her energy on breathing.

That's an excuse. She heard Sensei's voice in her head. Her teacher's voice was just as matter of fact in her thoughts as it was when she was in his class. You're using your physical weakness as a crutch to get out of doing something your mind doesn't want you to do.

Her mind didn't want to replay the events at the grocery store.

Once she was parked in her driveway, she sat for a moment in her car, staring at the steering wheel. She lifted her right hand, holding it flat, palm down, at eye level. Her hand shook noticeably. Her entire body felt drained.

The man (Gabriel his name is Gabriel) had no reason to think she needed his help. Ava didn't allow herself to get into situations where she needed anything. If she had a problem, she took care of it on her own. Never in her life had she reached out to anyone, certainly not for something as mundane as loading groceries into her car. Yet he had offered anyway. His behavior was strange.

Her own behavior puzzled her even more. She usually wasn't so careless. Keeping her distance from people came naturally to her. When proximity to humans was unavoidable, she made sure to wear gloves or avoid direct contact. She hadn't realized the man (Gabriel) had taken his glove off until it was too late. Accepting anything from him was a mistake – one she should have been able to avoid. That was the problem; without wearing gloves, her hands acted without her consent and always found their target. That they could get her in so much trouble was one of the reasons she steered clear of people.

How could she have missed the signs of a connection when she'd stood next to him in the coffee aisle? When her temples had begun to throb dully and a wave of dizziness hit her, she should have realized she was in the presence of someone in mourning. Proximity to a person in that state made her vulnerable. Avoidance was the best solution.

You missed it because he hides it.

That should not have mattered. Ava was not easily fooled by dishonesty and pretenses. Yet the sorrow had not presented itself until she touched him, and it flooded over her. And then she had looked into his eyes, and the pain there had been so obvious. Simply paying attention, taking a moment to observe his face, would have told her all she needed to know to avoid today's incident.

As if all that were not bad enough, he caught her looking at something he was unable to see in the parking lot. Before she had taken his card, the girl with the braid had appeared, standing behind him. Once Ava had spotted her, the girl had started walking across the parking lot and Ava automatically followed her progress. The man (Gabriel) had witnessed it in the movement of her eyes. Usually, she had more common sense than that and easily masked her visions in public.

Leaning back against the driver's seat, she closed her eyes and began deep breathing exercises. The inability to immediately regain control was stupefying her. This overreaction was causing her physical issues and could make her work suffer, which she would not tolerate. She refused to let a stranger's seemingly altruistic gesture and her subsequent vision tarnish her professional reputation. And she would absolutely not allow her errors to weaken her body and her ability to take care of herself.

The moment at Stan's was over. She could do nothing to change it now. Moving forward, she would keep her distance from the man (Gabriel) if she saw him again, which was highly probable in a small town. She was used to keeping her distance from people. She would manage, as she had done in the past. Around people in general, she would have to remember to pay closer attention, listen to her instincts, and read them better.

Breathe in for four seconds, hold breath for seven seconds, exhale over a period of eight seconds. In through the nose, out through the mouth.

She repeated the exercise until her full attention was on her body. In her mind, she took an inventory of herself to redirect her energy. Starting at her feet, she thought about how they felt against her shoes, if they were cold or hot, did they ache from this morning's workout? She moved to her ankles asking herself the same questions, then her calves, and all the way up her body. When she reached her wrists, she realized they were sore. She had walked on her hands this morning simply to practice it. Because they were sore, she decided she had waited too long since the last time she practiced the exercise and needed to put the activity into her rotation.

She continued the breathing and awareness exercise, working her way up her neck, into her head, until she was aware of every single part of her body and how it was feeling.

Finally, she opened her eyes, raised her flat hand to eye level again.

It was unwavering.

•   •   •   •   •

During her martial arts class that afternoon, though she was no longer shaking, Ava was distracted. While she warmed up, she couldn't keep her mind focused. Her timing was off as she mimicked her teacher's movements, making it difficult to keep up with him. Even after they had been stretching for five minutes, she was still breathing heavy and couldn't seem to get it under control.

Her teacher noticed, of course.

"You're thinking of something else," Ward Sensei said as he leaned to the side in the revolved triangle pose.

"Hai, Sensei. Sumi maisen," she panted in Japanese. Yes, teacher, please excuse me.

"A mugger isn't going to care if you're having a bad day," Sensei said with a wry smile. "He won't take it easy on you. I won't either."

"Hai, Sensei. Arrigato, gozaimashita." Yes, teacher, thank you.

He lowered the hand stretched toward the ceiling to the floor next to his foot. She did the same. "Having said that, is there anything you want to talk about?"

Ava contemplated her answer as they continued to stretch. "Hai, Sensei. Onegai shimasu." Yes, teacher, please teach me. "Since you have been training, have you ever lost the ability to control your body?"

Sensei thought about that. "Twice. The first time, I was feeling invincible after I passed my black belt test for Ninpo. I went out to celebrate with some friends and we... well, let's just say there was no point during the evening that I was without a drink in each hand. By the end of the night, I couldn't even lift my head. My friends had to carry me into my apartment."

Ava couldn't imagine Sensei being so reckless, or his body not responding to his commands.

"Pick your jaw up off the mat, Ava. I am human." He grinned. "I had to train again early the next morning with the worst hangover I'd ever had. My body wasn't fully recovered so my response time was slow. I was uncoordinated. My Sensei was not forgiving of my foolishness. It was the most brutal training I've ever had to endure. I considered quitting."

Ava leaned to the side and lay her torso along her right leg, stretching both her side muscles and her thigh muscles. Sensei did the same with only slightly less ease. Even at thirty-eight, he could do things most younger men couldn't because of his daily training.

"Is that why you do not drink alcohol now?" she asked, her face next to her knee as she stretched.

"One of many reasons."

"So, the lesson is to avoid putting myself in a position where I do not have control?" Ava asked.

"That's one way to look at it."

"I do not allow myself to get out of control in that way, Sensei. I do not drink alcohol or take mind-altering substances."

"Control is not always possible, even with strict discipline. Some medical conditions don't allow people to be in full control of their bodies. People with epilepsy or multiple sclerosis, for example, can't always control what their bodies are doing, no matter how disciplined the individual."

She was listening intently now, even as she continued to stretch and monitor her breathing. She had finally gained control over it and was no longer panting. They both leaned to the left and rested their torsos along their left legs now.

"If you cannot avoid losing control, what do you do? How do you accept not being in control?"

Sensei raised into a sitting position once more. She did the same. "In the case of a medical issue, one would have to wait out the episode. The second time I didn't have control was because of a medical situation. I had surgery on my hip three years ago. Between the surgery and the pain medication, my body movements were restricted. That took almost a year to heal."

They both spread their legs to their sides and leaned forward, arms extended in front of them. Ava's chest touched the floor. Daniel Ward had always been impressed with how fluid her movements were.

"When Vincent took over training for two months?" Ava asked, surprised. She had not asked questions when Sensei had taken a leave. It was not her business.

He nodded. They relaxed that stretch and paused for a moment.

"Vincent trained with me during every session instead of just on Thursdays," Ava remembered. "You used a cane for a while when you came back."

"Yes. During the first few weeks, I relied heavily on my family, friends, and a physical therapist while I rebuilt my body. My years of training helped speed up the recovery time, but as far as changing my medical diagnosis, I still needed surgery. After surgery, I still needed time to recover. In that case, I would say that's what family and friends are for. To help you mentally, physically, and emotionally when you can't help yourself."

Ava frowned as she bent her right knee, placed her left elbow on the outside of it, and turned away from her chest. It was a half spinal twist pose used in Yoga. Her back cracked and a flood of relief ran through her body.

"I do not have any friends."

From the same stretch across from her, Sensei looked at her curiously. "Is that by choice?"

"Hai, Sensei. I do not seek out the company of others."

"What about your father?" Mirroring Ava, Sensei switched legs, so his left knee was propped up now and he was twisting to the left. "Is this something David can help with?"

"David lives an hour away. I do not know what he could do, even if he were here."

"What causes this loss of control?" Sensei asked, relaxing the pose slowly and bringing his feet together in front of him. Ava did the same. "Is it a medical issue?"

Ava shifted on the mat.

"You've been training with me for about fifteen years, right?" Sensei asked, perceiving her discomfort. They both leaned forward, each stretching their arms past their feet.

"Sixteen, Sensei."

"Sixteen years," he said thoughtfully. He exhaled, held the stretch for several moments in silence. "If you have a medical condition that requires I adjust your training, I need to know."

"Hai, Sensei. It is not a medical condition. It has not affected my training so far."

"Then it's not my business until you tell me it is. We've known each other long enough for me to know you don't like asking for help. You want to remain completely self-sufficient without imposing on anyone for anything."

"Hai, Sensei."

They both sat up.

"After my surgery, for the first time in my life, I was limited in what I could do physically. It was hard to accept that my body couldn't withstand the training I did before the surgery, no matter how much my mind wanted it. I would have destroyed my body if I pushed it that far. I was depressed, angry, afraid my body had failed me. It took some time to deal with that. I had to ask for help. I had to trust people I love to give me support."

Ava stretched in silence for several seconds, mimicking Sensei's movements. He let her think about what he said before continuing.

"People need each other," Sensei went on. He sat in a butterfly pose, feet touching, hands around his feet, and leaned forward, keeping his back straight. "It's the nature of our species. I'll admit you are different from any person I've ever met, but you also show more self-discipline than most people. If you're finding times when you lack control, it must be serious. Whatever causes these episodes, having family and friends around to help you through them could make them a lot easier."

Ava inhaled deeply, pushing herself to stretch deeper. When she spoke, her tone was resolute. "People are unreliable."

• • • • •

Gabriel finished work for the day feeling unproductive and frustrated. He hadn't been able to concentrate all day. Images of the young woman from Stan's kept interrupting his workflow, messing with his coordination, and annoying the hell out of him. He was forced to redo simple tasks, making errors he hadn't made since he was ten years old helping his grandfather.

Something about what she said kept nagging at him, but he couldn't place what it was or why it was bothering him. She hadn't been making any sense, really. A brief meeting and a couple offhand comments didn't really warrant such contemplation.

She never told me her name.

Even her reaction to him offering a handshake was odd. That intrigued him. Gabriel had watched enough action movies to recognize she had studied some style of fighting. He wasn't educated enough to tell the difference between Karate and Tae Kwan Do, but he understood the way she had moved wasn't street fighting. She had been trained.

The way her eyes followed every move he made and constantly watched her surroundings made him wonder about her motivation for moving to Langdon. Was she running from her past?

He did a quick sketch of her as he sat at the bench in his heated garage, finished with the cabinets for the day. He would be able to concentrate better tomorrow, and the project would be completed on time. He was never late finishing a job and he never had to ask for an extension.

When his cell phone rang, he jerked and glanced around as if he had something to feel guilty about. He began filling in details of The Woman in Green's face as he answered his sister's call.

"Hey, Isabel." His voice was indifferent as he thought of the woman's intense, alert gaze. Those beautiful eyes that had been so hypnotic. They had looked almost inhuman, like storms were building in the shades of gray.

"Beth and Mom want me to go with them to Hayden's on Wednesday. They know you probably won't be there."

"I always visit Hayden on her birthday. I just don't like a crowd."

Something about her eyes, he thought as his hand moved over the paper, creating the image of the woman from memory. They were so...fearless.

"I had a feeling you did," Isabel was saying in his ear. "I'd rather go alone, but I don't know how to tell them that without causing an emotional shit storm. Anyway, they're also planning something for Sunday, the eleventh. Like a memorial or something, I don't know what, exactly."

"Why?" He didn't really care. He could go along with whatever was planned. He thought of the woman's fingers brushing against his, the feeling it gave him, like a live wire being held against his skin.

"Mom's always more sentimental at this time of year and now Beth's trying to get pregnant and they're both big wailing balls of vaginas." The desperation in Isabel's voice was evident even through her sarcasm.

"Christ, Iz." He added shadowing to give depth to The Woman in Green's hair. A couple strokes to outline her shoulders, though he wanted to focus on her face.

"They're driving me insane," Isabel continued. "You get a break because you have a dick. They don't talk to you because they know guys don't want to hear this shit. I don't want to hear this shit. They both call me about it and I'm going to go postal. It's the only time they actually include me in anything."

"I'll talk to them, see if I can get them to tone it down. I can't promise anything." He would probably forget.

"Thank you. But they still want everyone at Mom and Dad's the eleventh."

"We're all there, every Sunday." Isabel's voice was tugging him into the present; her stress, though she tried to hide it, was dragging him out of his fog. Was she on the verge of tears? He lifted his gaze from the drawing to the black screen of his laptop monitor.

"I know, just... expect a lot of crying because it's going to be some memorial kind of shit. And don't bail on me. I won't make it through this alone. Dad's no help."

"I won't bail. It'll take more than women crying to scare me away. I was raised with three sisters. How are you doing besides feeling matricidal?" Her voice was more real, somewhat louder than seconds ago when he had only been half-listening.

Isabel sighed. "Besides that, fine. I love Mom and Beth, really. I didn't mean to call you up just to bitch."

"I know." Gabriel tossed his sketch of The Woman in Green onto his work bench. He needed a shower - maybe a cold one. That woman was stunningly beautiful.

"Or maybe I did. It's just... every damn year they go through the same thing... it's been sixteen years. I wish they'd stop torturing themselves. It doesn't do any good. Does that make me horrible?"

Gabriel thought of camping as a kid, of staying up late and roasting marshmallows. He thought of an early morning so still he could hear his own heartbeat, and that morning suddenly being filled with his mother's screams.

"No, Iz," he said, his voice gentle now. "You're not horrible and you don't love Hayden any less for wanting to move on."

Isabel was silent for several moments. When she spoke, her voice was thick with grief. "Mom has more than one kid."

"I know."

"She doesn't," she snapped, unable to keep the bitterness at bay. "The only important one died and the rest of us are... leftovers."

"She doesn't mean to make you feel that way." He didn't know why he was defending his mother. He knew exactly how Isabel felt. He'd also learned long ago that anger at their mother's grief was a waste of time.

"I know." Isabel sniffed. "That's just what naturally happens when a parent picks one child to obsess about. The rest of us are left behind."

Gabriel wasn't sure what to say to that. How many times had his life taken a back burner because some memory of Hayden had thrown his mother into a depression? How many times had it pissed him off when his mother couldn't watch his high school football game or join in the family activities because she was sobbing in her bedroom? As time had passed, dealing with her daughter's absence had seemed to come easier, except for a couple times a year when anniversaries just made it too painful. But that didn't take away the anger of what was already lost.

"Hey," he said, making an instant decision. "Why don't you stop by tonight? We'll have dinner at this little restaurant in town. We've been caged all winter."

"I'm sorry. It just kind of hit me." She let out a shaky laugh. "I didn't realize I was holding all that in. I need a therapist, not a pity dinner."

"I'm serious. Come over. We haven't hung out, just the two of us, for months. Unload on Mom and Beth if you need to. You know I don't snitch."

"Really?" Her voice sounded hopeful. "You don't have plans?"

"If we can't cheer ourselves up, we can always get shitfaced."

•   •   •   •   •

Ava continued to towel dry her hair as she descended the stairs, walking to the kitchen for a glass of water. She'd spent too much time working out after training, and ordering dinner was going to be a hassle.

Still, she had too much work to do to stop and make a meal. With her mind wandering over the exchange at the grocery store, she hadn't worked as fast as she normally did, putting her behind schedule.

She called her order in to one of the restaurants in town – the other did not serve much healthy food – and was given an estimated time it would be ready. That gave her twenty minutes to get some work done before she had to leave.

•　•　•　•　•

"We picked the wrong night to have dinner," Isabel said as she was bumped from behind. She had to raise her voice to be heard over the conversations of the people milling around them. When they'd first arrived, she'd felt a stab of panic. They had to wait to be seated. The lobby wasn't very crowded at the time, but it quickly filled up five minutes later and now Isabel was ready to toss a grenade into the bunch to clear a path.

"It usually isn't this busy," Gabriel said, staring at the group of people waiting to be seated. I didn't think Langdon had this many people."

"So much for small town living." Isabel was feeling claustrophobic. It wasn't as bad with Gabriel with her, but he had told her this diner was never busy when he came here. It was the only reason she agreed to come. Even if they were able to finally get a table, it would be too noisy and crowded. The ability to carry on a conversation would be impossible. She was going to have a breakdown if she didn't get some fresh air.

Behind them, an icy blast blew through as the door opened. They both tried to move to the side to make room for more customers. Gabriel glanced up and was surprised to see the woman from Stan's in the doorway, her eyes roaming over the people waiting in the lobby.

"Hey, close the door!" a dark-haired woman with horribly blunt bangs snapped, barely looking up from her cell phone. Her fake nails tapped across her screen. "It's freezing out there."

The woman seemed to briefly contemplate her options before stepping just inside the door and letting it close behind her. She stayed in the corner as far as she could from the line of people waiting to be seated.

"That's weird," Isabel said, glancing at her. Someone pushed past her elbow on the way to the restrooms. "She can come in more than that. There's room." A customer on his way out knocked into her shoulder, earning him a glare. "Barely," she added.

"I ran into her at Stan's, where I get my groceries," Gabriel said, taking Isabel by the shoulder and moving her back a step so the person in front of her wouldn't fall into her. "She seems to prefer keeping a distance from people."

"I know the feeling. Listen, Gabriel-"

But he had already turned his attention back to the woman in the corner. He was trying not to be obvious in his appraisal. The woman was wearing the same green coat as earlier, carrying the same mini backpack. She had braided her hair at the temples and then tied it back with the rest in a loose ponytail, looking casual yet still attractive. He imagined that under the impassive expression on the woman's face, distaste was boiling.

A waitress, Lindsey, came up to them. Her face was creased with lines of worry and stress. Several strands of hair were sticking out of her loose ponytail. Gabriel had gone to school with her a lifetime ago.

"I'm so sorry, Gabriel." She touched his arm.

"What's taking so long?" someone complained loudly. A male, someone closer than Gabriel to being seated, wondering why Lindsey was talking to him.

She blew the other guy off and turned back to Gabriel.

"We suddenly got slammed and we're a waitress down. There's a huge party in the back that called fifteen minutes before they arrived. The backup waitress is on her way, but it's going to be a few minutes yet. If these guys don't kill me first." She glanced at the rest of the people waiting. Several were talking, more were glued to their cell phones.

"We were just thinking of leaving, Lindsey," Gabriel said after a quick glance at Isabel. He unzipped his coat a few inches. He was roasting in it.

Lindsey's eyes clouded. "Oh no!"

He gave her shoulder an affectionate squeeze. "We don't want to add to the chaos. We'll be back another time."

Isabel was relieved she didn't have to stay. She glanced around at all the people waiting and her stomach rolled lazily. Too close, she thought. They are standing too fucking close.

Lindsey's eyes flicked to the woman in the corner. "Oh, damn." She was already stepping toward the woman when she called back to Gabriel: "Come back soon, and I'll comp your meal. I'm really sorry."

"Ava!" she called over the noise. "You're order's up! Come on up, you don't have to wait!" She motioned for the woman in the corner to move forward toward the register. As she turned to walk back toward the counter, she tried to cajole the irritated people waiting to be seated.

Ava, Gabriel thought. So that's her name.

Ava stepped forward into the crowd of people and started following Lindsey. Her strides were long, her body radiating confidence and purpose. Gabriel watched as people stepped aside to give her room without seeming to realize they were doing it. As she approached Gabriel, their eyes locked.

Isabel, too busy trying to remain calm to hear Lindsey call out to the woman, closed her eyes tight, opened them. She was hitching in her breath. She yelled at Gabriel to take her out of here, but it was only in her head. Drowning, she thought. I'm drowning in flesh.

Ava reached out as she was walking past and took Isabel's hand, squeezed it firmly but briefly. Isabel raised her head and found herself staring into the other woman's eyes. She didn't have time to react before the woman released her hand and passed by. Shocked, Isabel stared at the woman's retreating back for a full five seconds before forcing herself to pay attention to what was going on in the restaurant – and realized her breathing had returned to normal.

Gabriel watched Ava move through the crowd and regretted another missed opportunity to check out her ass. His thoughts were interrupted by a voice as grating as razor wire on ceramic.

"Hey, we were here first!" the woman with the bad bangs and the cell phone whined, finally glancing up. Gabriel had gone to school with her, too. Peggy Combs, thirty-one years old and still trying to dress like a teenager. She had her jacket draped over her arm, revealing a shirt cut so low her breasts almost spilled out her push-up bra. Her skinny jeans were so tight the small flabby pouch of skin leftover from her love of fast food spilled over the waist. She was covered with more makeup than four women could fit on their faces.

She reached out and grabbed at Ava as the younger woman started past her.

Gabriel watched as Ava slapped Peggy's hand off her shoulder, took one small step away at an angle to create space between them, and spun around to face her. In the crowded area, Ava managed to maneuver herself quickly and efficiently out of Peggy's reach. She raised her hands, ready to defend herself.

"You will not touch me."

Her voice was low, but Gabriel heard her clearly. He raised an eyebrow, and when he glanced at Isabel, hers was raised as well. Everyone surrounding the two women were now watching them, their conversations stopped.

"We were here first," Peggy fumed.

"That is not my problem." Ava turned and continued toward the register.

Gabriel grinned. There was nothing sexier than a woman capable of handling herself.

"Tyson!" Peggy yelled to a man in a Vikings hat who was walking toward her from the bathroom. The guy was tall, with wide shoulders and hips that were probably once used for an offensive tackle on a high school football team. Peggy narrowed her eyes and started after Ava again.

Bad idea, Gabriel thought. Peggy had never known when to keep her mouth shut or walk away.

He remembered how Ava had reacted to him trying to shake her hand in the grocery store parking lot and was thankful he hadn't pressed the issue.

Peggy pulled on Ava's shoulder to get her attention. "Don't you -"

This time Ava batted Peggy's hand off her as she spun around. Peggy's cell phone went flying, almost hitting an older man watching the show. Her coat dropped to the floor. She let out a squeal of surprise as Ava gripped her shirt at the chest and yanked her forward.

"I'm sorry," Peggy whispered.

Ava shoved Peggy back until she was holding her at arm's length and pulled her right fist back to strike.

The people surrounding the two women, including Gabriel and Isabel, were silent. The exchange had only taken seconds; Gabriel felt like they had been standing there, staring, for several minutes.

Ava's fist moved. The crowd gave a collective gasp. Peggy squealed again and closed her eyes.

A moment passed. Another.

Peggy opened her eyes and crossed them as she stared at the knuckles poised one inch away from her nose.

"You will not touch me." Ava released Peggy with another small shove and turned to continue to the register.

Lindsey had disappeared between the kitchen's swinging doors to get Ava's food. Ava reached the counter and stood waiting for her to return.

Peggy had straightened, crying with loud, dramatic gasps. When Tyson reached her, he tried to comfort her. She blubbered something in his ear.

"Hey!" Tyson called, pushing through the crowd toward Ava. "Don't you hit her!"

Buddy, Gabriel thought, you're about to find out what a real hit feels like. Instinctively, he stepped forward, but he was wasting his time.

"What the fuck did you do?" Tyson seethed, slamming a meaty hand into Ava's shoulder.

Ava turned, sweeping the man's arm to the side, and jabbing forward with her other hand. The hand that struck looked like a partially curled fist and delivered a precise blow to the Viking's fan's throat. Tyson gagged. His mouth began opening and closing, his eyes bulging, his Adam's apple bobbing as he struggled to catch his breath. The stunned look on his face was satisfying and a little entertaining to Gabriel and Isabel, who were still staring.

Lindsey carried a plastic bag out of the swinging doors of the kitchen. Her head was down as she checked the food with what was written on the ticket. Her mouth moved as she silently verified the order was correct.

"Tyson? Honey?" Peggy whined, hanging on the Viking's fan's arm.

Lindsey finally looked up. "I'm sorry, Ava, here's your order." She brushed a strand of hair behind her ear. She began to enter the information into the register.

Ava set her backpack on the counter and pulled out her wallet. "How much?"

Seeing the man behind her gaping like a fish and Peggy staring at her, Lindsey glanced back at Ava. "Is everything okay?"

Tyson made another gargling noise. Peggy's whines were quieter as she turned him toward the door. Ava spared a glance over her shoulder, her eyes expressionless.

"Come on, baby, let's go eat somewhere else," the woman murmured, picking up her coat and phone. Her legs were wobbly. Dark smears ran down her cheeks in twin lines. Somehow, her lipstick had smeared, leaving a large red swath across her upper lip. Grabbing the Viking's fan's arm and pulling him toward the exit, she gave Ava a final glance, her eyes wide, as she helped him walk up the three steps to the door.

Ava lifted her eyes from the bills she'd pulled from her wallet. "How much?"

• • • • •

"Holy shit," Isabel said as they walked out of the restaurant a moment later. "Did you see that? I mean... that was delicious!"

She was laughing so hard she had to hang onto him to stay upright. They stopped outside the entrance, stepping to the side so they weren't blocking the door. Isabel couldn't stop laughing as she struggled with her coat. Between shivering from the cold and snorting, she was having trouble getting her arms into the sleeves.

"That was impressive," Gabriel agreed, his lip curving slightly. "I don't think that asshole's going to be able to talk for a week."

"I think Peggy shit her pants. Like, literally, shit her pants." Isabel clutched her stomach with one hand. "Oh, it hurts! I haven't laughed this hard in years!"

Gabriel couldn't help but smile at his sister as she jabbed one hand into the sleeve of her jacket. She had cheered up considerably since their phone call earlier.

"Come on, you fucking jack wagon!" she blurted, turning circles as she tried to find her other sleeve. Gabriel held the coat so she could slip into it. "Thanks. Are you sure Lindsey's going to be okay? She looked heartbroken that we decided not to eat there." Isabel zipped up her coat and dug in her pocket for her gloves. "Where are my fucking gloves?"

"I'll make sure she gets a huge tip the next time," Gabriel said, mildly amused as he watched her dig in the many pockets her coat had. "That gives you and I an excuse to hang out again."

"Hey, I think that woman did something to m-"

The door opened and Ava stepped out holding the bag with her order. She glanced at them warily as she walked toward the parking lot.

"Hi," Isabel said loudly. "I'm Isabel. This is my brother, Gabriel."

Ava looked at her for a moment before saying, "Hello."

Isabel waited a moment, then said, "What's your name?"

Raising his hand behind her, Gabriel tugged not so gently on Isabel's hair. She slapped halfheartedly at him.

"Ava."

"That was nuts in there," Iz continued, motioning toward the restaurant. "You really knocked those two idiots down a notch."

Ava said nothing, only continued to stare at them.

Isabel finally said, "Are you new in town?"

Ava hesitated, nodded.

"Gabriel's lived here for years. If you need help with anything, he's your guy."

Gabriel tilted his head pointedly toward her. She pretended to ignore him, so he jabbed his elbow into her back. She grunted and fell forward a step, smirking.

Ava stiffened when Iz fell toward her. "I am fine on my own."

Ava's cool gaze shifted to the space just over Gabriel's left shoulder. He saw realization flood into her eyes. The bag of food dropped from her hand. Even as he knelt to pick it up for her, as Isabel said something she could not hear over the pounding of her heart, Ava took a step back. The girl with the denim blue eyes was hovering beside Isabel.

"Your sister," she breathed, as the girl reached toward Isabel, who did not feel the small hand pass through her shoulder. "She's your sister."

"What?" Isabel's head snapped up, intent on Ava.

Gabriel stood, brushing off the plastic bag. "Hopefully, this isn't too beat up," he said, holding it out to her.

Ava did not move. The young girl captured all her attention. Clothed in what looked like a blue nightgown, her hair in a single long braid, the girl's head and chest looked as solid as the two people she hovered next to. She was less visible midway through her body, at her stomach, and completely gone just before her knees. She hovered above the ground, looking up at her sister. Had she been older than Isabel when she died? Younger?

Older. Hayden turned to look at Ava. The voice had come clearly in her mind.

Ava jolted.

"Hey," Gabriel said, reaching for her arm.

Instinct kicked in. Ava was moving forward before she fully realized it, ready to strike. The girl was suddenly between her and Gabriel. Coldness spread out from the presence, making Ava reverse, her body recoiling to avoid contact with that eternal frost. The few seconds of broken concentration was enough to allow her to realize Gabriel was trying to help. His eyes were full of concern, not malice. She took a deep breath, reached through the frigid vision of the girl, and snatched her bag of food from Gabriel.

"Thank you for picking up my food," she said stiffly. Her wrist was cold where it had passed through the girl. She wanted to shiver, fought the urge. "Y-you will have a nice evening."

Gabriel watched her walk to her SUV. When he turned back to Isabel, he saw the blood had drained from his sister's face.

"Isabel," Gabriel murmured, tugging on her shoulder. "It's freezing out here. Let's go."

"Did you hear what she said?" Isabel didn't budge. She watched Ava drive away.

"You're turning into an Iz-cicle," he said, nudging her toward his vehicle. Prepared to heave her over his shoulder, he was relieved when she reluctantly started moving in the direction of his truck. When they were inside, where it was still warm, Gabriel looked at her.

"What were you saying?" He started the truck.

"She said something about our sister," Isabel said, her stomach clenching. "'She's your sister.' Something like that. I don't know. It doesn't make sense, I guess, but it gave me a weird feeling."

"She's a strange little ass kicker," Gabriel agreed. "She kind of zoned out when I saw her earlier today at the grocery store."

"In the restaurant, I swear she did something to me," Isabel said. "I was having trouble with all the people-"

"I'm sorry I didn't pick up on it sooner."

"Shut up and listen. I was freaking out. She took my hand as she was going to the counter to get her food. Before that idiot got her and her boyfriend's asses kicked."

"She touched you?" That sounded weird. The woman he'd met didn't seem to like being touched, even for a handshake. Then again if she had been abused... maybe she just didn't like contact with men. "Maybe she could tell you were freaked out intuitively. Maybe it's a woman thing."

Isabel contemplated that. "Maybe I'm just hungry. It felt so weird when it happened. Now it just sounds silly."

"Nothing food and drink can't fix," he decided. He put the truck in reverse and backed out of the parking space. "Pizza and beer at my place? Well, whiskey for you."

"Perfect. If I don't eat soon, things are going to get ugly."

• • • • •

Ava drove toward her house, her sanctuary, feeling nauseous. The smell of her dinner on the passenger seat wasn't helping. The drive home, which usually took ten minutes, seemed to be dragging on forever. The yellow lines on the road kept blurring. Lights from oncoming traffic were too bright, blinding her.

Getting out of the vehicle seemed a monumental task. Carrying her food to the front porch, she fumbled with the key – something she never did. She found her hands weren't quite steady as she tried to match the shape of the key to the hole in the lock. Inside, she took off her boots and coat.

Had she ever had such an engaging encounter with a spirit and their loved ones? Most of Ava's apparitions were instigated through dreams, by touching objects, or touching people. Because she avoided people, she had never been around them long enough to watch an interaction between the deceased and the loved one. Before Gabriel and Isabel, Ava had never spoken with people connected to a spirit she saw. After ignoring a spirit for so long, they stopped appearing to her. The little girl was the only one that had not left after several months.

The only chance she had to witness the interaction between the dead and living was tonight, and she had frozen. Seeing the young girl's expression of love as she watched her brother and sister, feeling it, had overwhelmed Ava. The conversations of all three, playing and laughing as children, filled her head, paralyzing her. An ache started in her chest as she felt the loss begin to grow. She had almost let Gabriel touch her again.

Why had it been so hard to walk away tonight? Ava thought as she set the food on the counter. Was it the loss she saw in Gabriel's and Isabel's eyes that tore at her as she looked at their sister, a child they could no longer see? Was it the affection she witnessed in the girl's eyes that was aimed at her living siblings? Or the war she felt Isabel constantly fight within herself but tried to never let show?

It does not matter. You owe them nothing.

Ava believed that, but tonight the knowledge did not seem to assuage the curiosity. Something bothered her about this trio. She would have to think about it at length.

Sliding the container of food back on the counter, she sighed. She no longer had an appetite.

•　　•　　•　　•　　•

CHAPTER TWO

The strong, frenzied drum beat of "Fuel" from Metallica drove Gabriel along the trail, pushing him deeper into the woods. Under his light jacket, sweat ran down his back and soaked under his arms. His hair was damp despite the cool March evening. His lungs were on fire and the muscles in his legs were screaming at him, but he continued to jog.

Stalling, he thought. Avoiding. Today was Hayden's birthday, and he was going to visit her grave. He didn't want to. He would anyway.

He finally had to stop before he made himself vomit. Pacing the trail, he greedily inhaled oxygen like a man who had almost drowned. Somewhere among the thoughts of soreness and edginess, he wondered how Iz had done at the cemetery earlier this evening. He should have called her to see if she was okay. A good brother would have; he knew she was anxious about it, and he should have followed up. He decided he would do that as soon as he returned to his truck.

When something rushed past a few feet away on his right, he wheeled around, catching a flash of black in the thick brush before it was gone.

"What the hell?" he wheezed.

Whatever it was had barely made a sound. Something had moved through undergrowth and trees so quickly he barely saw its shape or heard its passage. Langdon was too far south for bears, which lacked either ability anyway. The color was off for a cougar, which was rare in this area. And if he hadn't been mistaken, whatever it was had moved upright.

"Great," he said under his breath. "I've just spotted Bigfoot."

He continued pacing the trail, forcing himself to go slow. Turning the music off, he put his phone in his pocket and listened. He should have brought his water bottle. He knew better than to push himself without staying hydrated, but he had needed to expend the energy before he punched something. He felt itchy knowing the hours were counting down until he would stand at the empty grave meant to symbolize Hayden's resting place. Sometimes the only thing to do when he was in that kind of a mood was to go running.

He felt closer to Hayden during his time in the woods. The family had been camping when Hayden disappeared, so of course he did. Even in the winter he tried to hike as much as he could. It was never the same as in the summer, but it helped. Hayden and Isabel loved the outdoors and spent every moment they could outside. They used to bug the hell out of him and his friends when they set up tents in the back yard and camped overnight. Finally, their parents allowed the girls to set up their own tents on the opposite side of the lawn, as long as Gabriel checked on them a couple times during the night.

Another flash, this time to his left, had Gabriel jerking to a stop. He saw just enough fabric to understand it was a person. Someone was running off trail, faster than Gabriel ran on the trail that was devoid of dead logs, dense brush, and layers of leaves packed down by seasons of rain. Whoever it was must be a professional athlete; he put Gabriel's energy and speed to shame.

"Son of a bitch," Gabriel breathed.

Maybe it was a member of military keeping in shape. Whoever it was, he barely made a sound.

He had his breath back. Feeling better now that he had expended some of the restlessness and had the high from the endorphin rush of exercising, he started slowly back the way he had come. He wasn't sure how long he had been in the woods, but the cool air and physical exertion had helped. He wondered if he should set up some time to hike with Isabel and see if it helped her, too. They used to hike together at least twice a week before he moved to Langdon and the distance between them had made it less convenient.

A few yards ahead, someone exited the woods at a dead run. The person was at a forty-five-degree angle to Gabriel, and barely made a sound in the woods or on the trail. Had to be military, he thought, watching the person slow gradually to a quick walk. An arm came up to the back of the head. After a few seconds, Gabriel was shocked to see a long mane of thick hair fall halfway down a woman's back.

He wasn't the most athletic male. His exercise consisted of daily jogs and weekly strength training to stay healthy. But with longer legs, therefore a naturally longer stride, and an easier course, he should have had no problem keeping up with a woman running through untamed woods.

She had literally run circles around him.

. . . . .

"Again."

"Hai, Sensei."

Ava returned to her position across from Ward Sensei and took her stance. He mirrored her position.

They were currently working on Sensei's technique, which meant Ava only had to do a simple strike she had learned early on in her training. Ava made a sharp sound – a kiai - and started toward him, striking out with her right fist.

He easily blocked the punch and pivoted in toward her for his first strike. Instead of tilting her head back as if his elbow had actually struck her philtrum, Ava froze. Her mouth dropped open, and a flood of water gushed out.

Daniel Ward was already committed to the strike. Because she hadn't tilted her head back and out of the way, her face was where his elbow followed through. As soon as he realized she was frozen, he pulled the jab, but she still took most of the hit just below her nose.

The force of the blow caused her head to rock back. Stunned, Ava stood for a moment, wide-eyed, before she started to tip backward, straight legged, onto the mat. Daniel pivoted again so he could slip his arm around her waist before she collapsed. He eased her down to the mat, avoiding the pool of water she had just expelled.

"Are you okay?" He glanced around at the water, baffled. "What just happened?"

"It's freezing." Her voice was raw, as if she had been screaming for hours.

She began shivering, though she was wearing a heavy, long-sleeved uniform and they had been exercising rigorously for over forty minutes. He could feel her sweat beneath his hands; could feel the heat radiating off her from their training.

"Ava." Daniel unhooked his arm from under hers. She was unresponsive. A quick examination of her face led him to believe she was in shock. In spite of the sweat, her skin was clammy. The pulse beneath his fingertips was accelerated, and she was inhaling shallow breaths that would soon make her hyperventilate. The pupils of her eyes were dilated, the gaze distant. She had just vomited, although Daniel had never heard of or experienced someone in shock vomiting only water before.

"C-cold." Her teeth chattered.

Blinking slowly, she coughed. The sound was wet and raspy.

"Ava." He snapped his fingers in front of her eyes. She didn't flinch or blink.

Ava opened her mouth, and another gush of water came out, spilling down her shirt and pants, splashing across the mat. Daniel pressed his hand against the back of her head and leaned her gently forward so she wouldn't choke on the water. Where was it coming from? How could she have that much water inside her?

She made a gargling sound in her throat.

Daniel took her arm and rolled her onto her side to prevent drowning. Water soaked into the knees of his uniform, cold even though it had come out of her body. A mixture of smells came with it... wet grass, dead leaves, burnt wood, smoke, and something sickly sweet.

"I-I'm s-sorry," Ava whispered. "I s-s-s-shouldn't have..."

Her voice was childlike.

He pressed the backs of his fingers to her cheek. Her skin was still frigid, her lips turning blue. When she exhaled, he could see her breath. Tears were streaming from the corners of both eyes. A trickle of blood oozed down the side of her face. Daniel held the hem of his uniform with his fingers and pressed his covered wrist to her temple to stop the bleeding.

After a few seconds where she didn't vomit, Daniel turned her onto her back with his hand under her head. Lifting her upper lip, he saw blood smeared on her teeth and gums from his strike.

Gradually, color began returning to her skin. The discolored hue faded from her lips. She coughed again, then moved her head slowly as she looked around. Blinking, she seemed to become aware of her surroundings again. She jerked violently against him.

"Don't move," he soothed, leaning back to give her space. "Are you back?"

It took her a moment to respond. "Hai, Sensei." She glanced down at her soaked uniform and the wet mat. She still seemed dazed, but her pupils were no longer dilated, and she knew where she was.

"Let me help." He had to bark the order, or she wouldn't have stopped and may have hurt herself. Daniel took her arm and helped her ease into a sitting position.

"Can you sit a minute while I get towels?" Sensei asked.

She nodded mutely. He stood and walked off the mat into the back changing room. A moment later he returned with several towels, some of which he dropped on the floor to soak up the water. He held out a smaller one to her.

"You're bleeding," he said, when she looked curiously at him. He indicated his temple.

"It is not mine," she said, her voice dull. She pressed the towel to her temple.

Sensei began wiping up the water on the mat. When the towels had absorbed all they could, he picked them up and carried them to the back room again. He came back and laid more out to soak up the remaining water. He handed her another one, this one full size.

"Your uniform is wet."

Flushing, she pressed it to her chest to soak up some of the excess water. He noticed that once she had cleaned the blood off her temple, no more flowed. He could see no wound.

It was not hers, she had said.

But the blood in her mouth from his strike was. She ran her tongue over her teeth, winced at the metallic taste of blood. The inside of her lip stung where it had smacked against her teeth and split open.

He produced a bottle of water she had not realized he carried in. "Rinse with that, spit into the towel."

She did as she was told. It made her feel like a young child, having to be told how to take care of herself.

"This must be the loss of control we talked about," Daniel said, keeping his voice casual.

"Hai, Sensei." She was mortified.

"Explain it to me."

"Sometimes..." Struggling to describe what happened, she concentrated on pressing the water out of her uniform. "I sometimes experience things... I think they have happened to other people. The effects fade after a few moments."

"Are you talking about psychic ability?"

Her nod was hesitant. "People bother me," she said bluntly. She was too busy drying her uniform to catch Sensei's smile. "After they die, they... hover."

"You see spirits?"

"Hai, Sensei. I cannot control it."

"How has this never come up before? You've trained with me for over a decade."

She used the towel to wipe the tears from her cheeks. "It is worse than before. I recently bought a house so it might be stress. Or the town I moved to may have... someone who is reaching out."

Sensei was quiet for several moments. Ava felt her entire body stiffening as she prepared to be told she could not train with him anymore, that he thought she was a liar, that such things as ghosts did not exist, and she needed to seek professional help. She had a deep respect for her teacher, and she did not know if she could face his disapproval.

"Congratulations on buying a house."

Stunned, it took her a moment to say, "Arrigato, gozaimashita. I am sorry I made a mess in your dojo," she added.

"Do you want my help learning to control it?"

Her head jerked up. "You believe me?"

He smiled. "You're the most honest person I know, Ava. Your body was physically reacting just now. Your pupils were dilated, your voice changed, and you were coughing up more water than your body can physically hold. There was blood on your face but no cut. I'd have to be pretty obtuse to ignore all that."

She felt the tension drain from her body.

"Even if I could, I can't ignore the fact that those towels we just used to soak up more than a gallon of water are perfectly dry."

She looked at the mats, at the towels that had been drenched with water only moments before. The water was gone. The towels lay spread on the mats, dry. Ava's uniform was damp with sweat but nothing else.

"I don't know much about psychic ability," Sensei admitted. "Let me do some studying and educate myself first. I'll have a plan the next time we meet. We're going to need to meet a couple times more a week, outside our normal training sessions."

"Hai, Sensei."

"That's enough training for now. You need to let your body rest."

• • • • •

Isabel Harris walked into her apartment in a rotten mood. Along the wall in the entryway, she dropped her keys in a bowl on the little decorative table Gabriel had built for her. She let her purse fall unceremoniously to the floor. Above the table were pictures of her and her family. The largest, and the focal point of the arrangement, was Hayden. In the picture, she was wearing a crown made of dandelions, smiling at the camera in that way that showed no teeth and made her cheeks puff up. Isabel gazed at the picture for several seconds.

Maybe you were the lucky one, she thought.

She exhaled, rubbing her hands down her face. What a horrible thing to think. She was an asshole.

She kicked off her flats and walked immediately to the refrigerator. Leaning over to gaze in at her stock of alcohol, she considered her choices.

She couldn't shake off the events of the day.

Why the hell was she allowing her job to rule her life? Working her ass off for a boss pretending to be more important than his position allowed for only stressed her out and damaged her health. She remained stuck in an office overrun by petty squabbles that no longer served the clients it was created for. And the worst part was that if she quit, if she just told Jeff Watson to fuck himself and walked out, she had no idea what she would choose instead.

If she had something to look forward to, maybe work wouldn't bog her down. Music used to be her outlet. But when all she did was write and sing depressing songs, it was no longer a release; it was adding to the problem.

Family was important. Knowing she could leave work to spend time with her family would help wash work off at the end of the day. Instead, she had to visit her dead sister with a couple of weeping, hormone-crazed psychos who took too many hits of caffeine and were feeding off each other's angst. She should have stayed at work and gotten paid to be miserable. She tried to remind herself that they were grieving. She tried to find compassion.

The anger and frustration were too strong for iced tea or a soda. She shut the refrigerator door and reached into the cabinet to the side of it instead. A couple fingers of whiskey would take the edge off. Walking with her glass to the recliner in the living room, she sat sideways on the chair so she could drape her legs over the side. She loved sitting like this on her worn secondhand furniture. It was comfortable to dangle her feet and read a book or take a nap. Or drink.

Family. They used guilt to make you do things and then tears to excuse their own behavior when they pushed you to the limits.

And work – God! Without her boss breathing down her neck every day, expecting her to run his life for him, Isabel would have so much free time to... what? Look for another meaningless job? Work her ass off for yet another asshole so he could take credit for all the work she put in? She guaranteed the lives of her manager and everyone under him ran smoothly, and yet she was treated like the cleaning lady, Madelyn. If she changed jobs, it would be the same story with a different job title and a different asshole boss. So, what was the point?

The problem wasn't the job.

The problem was the life.

Careful, she thought to herself as she sipped her whiskey. Thoughts like that can lead you down a dark, dark hole. Get out of your own head.

Family was supposed to support each other. She set her drink on the end table and ran her hands through her hair, gripping the sides of her head. If the people in her family were always too busy needing to be taken care of, where did that leave her? It wasn't fair. She couldn't always be strong, dammit.

When tears slid down her cheeks, she angrily wiped them away with her sleeves.

She had really enjoyed hanging out with Gabriel the other night. Before Monday, she hadn't hung out with him, really spent time with him, for months. Probably because of the weather. Who wanted to travel in freezing temperatures and deep snow? The thought of warming up her car and bundling up, just to get wet feet and freeze anyway, for a couple hours' worth of chatting seemed like too much work. Winter was a time to hibernate for Isabel. The only exception was the obligatory Sunday dinner with her family.

Isabel instantly felt guilty for these thoughts. Every effort should be made to be with family, even if some members were drama queens. No one was guaranteed time – Isabel and her family knew that better than many.

She would see Gabriel this weekend, and he always cheered her up. He never really meant to; he just did. They were close, and her brother always said the right thing to make her laugh. The laughter, no matter how small, was enough to help her claw her way back out of the hole.

When she stood to refill her drink, she checked the clock on the stove. After seven. Gabriel would be going to the cemetery by now, visiting Hayden in private.

"Good luck, Gabe," Isabel whispered.

He would need it.

•　•　•　•　•

She exhaled water.

Gasping, Ava pushed herself up from the kitchen table and flailed to fight off possible danger. Her arm bumped the glass of water sitting next to her. Instinctively, her hand reached out and righted the glass before she was fully aware of what was going on.

She coughed forcefully, still feeling the water in her throat. Pressing both palms flat on the table, she inhaled, held her breath. Relax. You are awake. She exhaled slowly. Continuing the breathing exercises, she reminded herself of what she had been doing to get to where she was. Closing her eyes helped her to visualize.

Exhaustion had overcome her as she had been doing the accounts side of her business. She'd dozed off. She was in her house, safe, sitting at her kitchen table in front of her laptop in a brightly lit room. She was not coughing up water. She was not alone in the dark.

Slowly, the feeling of drowning receded. She exhaled slowly, opened her eyes. The young girl with the denim blue eyes was sitting across the table from her.

•　•　•　•　•

Gabriel turned his truck into Hope Hill Cemetery's parking lot, relieved to see it was empty of other vehicles. He preferred coming here alone. His visits to Hayden were private, moments he shared only with her. He didn't want to include his family in case he decided to say a few words to his sister. His mother

39

and Beth had always taken center stage on their grief for Hayden, making him feel as if he didn't have the right to mourn her. As he grew older, he decided his grief was his alone, and no one else was allowed to see it. Only Isabel, in a rare moment, caught a glimpse of it, usually manifesting as anger.

He blew out a breath and got out of the truck. The lily of the valley flowers he had brought lay on the passenger seat. He leaned back in and took them out tenderly, making sure no bulbs fell off. The action was silly; in this cold, the flowers would die very quickly.

As he crossed the parking lot, he caught sight of an SUV parked at the far end of the lot, initially hidden by the dumpster. Someone else was here after all. The odds of him running into the person was slim, so he didn't feel it was a problem.

Once or twice a month, he visited Hayden's grave. As the time grew closer to her birthday, he came more often. The anniversary of her disappearance was in August, and he visited the grave more often then, too. If asked, he couldn't have put into words why he made the trips.

He walked through the cemetery, garden-like in the summer but cold and brittle now. Because of the cold, he hurried to get blood flowing in his stiff legs. Tonight, the temperature was fifteen degrees. Even with a hat and gloves the cold was penetrating, seeping into his bones.

The cemetery was peaceful, beautiful even in winter, but also a reminder that his younger sister was no longer with him. She had gone missing over sixteen years ago, her body never found. Gabriel's parents had finally had her declared dead after eight years so they could have a ceremony and a place to mourn her. As if holding a funeral would bring any type of closure when everyone knew there was no body in the casket.

As he neared the area where the stone marker sat, he noticed a shadow crouched among the graves. He tried to be quiet and respectful but found himself drawing closer to the person to get to Hayden's marker. Even in the poor glow from a post light, Gabriel realized the person was at his destination.

Who the hell is that? he wondered. Whoever it was had her hands over her ears. Dark hair rustled in the slight but arctic wind, eliminating Gabriel's initial thought that it might be Isabel. She was supposed to come with their mom and Beth, but Gabe thought she might have stayed behind or come back for some privacy. Isabel had blonde hair, however, and it was shorter than the person kneeling at Hayden's grave.

As he neared, Gabriel recognized the green jacket.

Ava, he thought, surprised when that thought relieved some of the dread he'd been feeling.

Her body stiffened as he came closer. She lowered her hands from her ears. When he was still a few feet away, she stood. Turning toward him, she took a step back to put more distance between them. For a moment, her eyes scanned from left to right as if he'd brought a gang with him. Gabriel was surprised when she winced.

Gabriel shoved his free hand in his pocket. He held the delicate white bulbs in his other hand, against his chest, against the cold.

She was shivering slightly, her arms held stiffly at her sides. Her eyes were filled with sorrow and compassion. Gabriel noticed she was wearing ear buds.

What an odd place to listen to music, he thought.

Reaching into her pocket, she pulled out her phone and tapped something on her screen. After another tap to the screen, the buzzing he heard in her ear buds was silenced. She took the buds out and wrapped the cord around her phone.

"I did not mean to intrude, Gabriel." She took another step back.

He stepped forward. Her expression changed from sympathetic to guarded, and he remembered the way she handled people she judged were standing too close to her. "I'm not going to hurt you."

"I know."

She said it so bluntly, as if the thought of him being capable of hurting her was ludicrous. He almost let out a bark of nervous laughter. Again, her eyes drifted to him, then to his right, then left. A shiver ran through her as she shoved her phone into her pocket, forcing her eyes down at the ground.

"Why are you at my sister's grave?"

Now her gaze was direct, patient. "I was taking a walk. Excuse me."

She started to back away from the marble marker. Confusion swirled in Gabriel's head. If she was taking a walk, why had she knelt at Hayden's grave? He felt a sense of urgency he couldn't explain, and a thin slice of panic that she was going to disappear too soon.

"Wait," he said, reaching out.

"No." She put her hands up, ready to defend herself. The left rested palm up at her side, just below her breast. The other was aimed at him from an outstretched arm, the palm facing down and fingers stiff, in an obvious back off pose.

Different than the way she stood at Stan's, he thought. Both equally conveying the same message – back the fuck off.

Instantly he pulled his hand back. "I'm sorry." He raked his hand down the back of his neck. "I'm not trying to get in your face. Just, please, stop running off."

She watched him, studied his eyes. Even in the darkness with only a distant post light to see by Gabriel could see the spark of anger.

"I run from nothing." She lowered her hands, but the guarded expression remained, with a ridge of heat underneath.

Hit a nerve, he thought.

"Did you know my sister?"

Ava shook her head.

Asking questions was getting him nowhere. Frustrated, Gabriel raked his hand down the back of his neck again. He looked down at Hayden's headstone. He suddenly felt old, and unbearably sad.

"Today is her birthday." His voice sounded quiet and small.

"How can it be her birthday if she is dead?"

Gabriel narrowed his eyes but realized the question was innocent. There was no malice in her tone, no teasing glint in her eyes. It was as if she were a different species that didn't share the human concept of grief.

"Birthdays are anniversaries of the day we were born," he explained. He looked at the stone again. "Every year we remember the day she was born, whether she's still with us or not. Haven't you ever lost someone?"

He gazed at her, and she at him.

"I'm sorry. I shouldn't have asked you that."

Finally, her eyes dropped. "I have no one to lose. You want to be alone. Excuse me."

"No," Gabriel said, forcing himself not to reach out or step toward her. "I-"

He swallowed hard, unable to rationalize how her presence had a calming effect on him. How could he explain something he didn't understand himself?

From the moment he'd realized who was standing at Hayden's marker, he'd felt a loosening in his chest, a lightening of his spirit at her innate strength.

"Please don't go." He could barely raise his voice above a whisper.

The soft tone of his voice and destroyed look on his face as he stood over the grave caused Ava to hesitate. Why did he want comfort from someone he did not know? She did not know what to say. She did not understand what it was to have a sister. But she did understand what it felt like to reach for someone, and that horrible, empty feeling when someone never reached back.

Ava turned so she was facing the stone and politely folded her hands together in front of her like she had seen her foster father do at his wife's funeral. She bowed her head.

Gabriel knelt in front of the grave and carefully placed the lilies on the ground among the other flowers his family had brought earlier. Lily of the valley were Hayden's favorite, but she also loved orange Tiger lilies and daisies. Both were at her grave now, as well as roses and poppies.

Despite his glove, he knew the stone below his hand was cold. Its iciness bothered him. Why did people use such a frigid material to memorialize someone who brought such warm memories? How did such an archaic tradition stay in practice? Every year he grew farther from Hayden, from her memory, and every year he forgot more of her. Would he one day have to look at a picture of her just to recollect her face?

He didn't know how long he stayed that way, his mind a blur of childhood images and thoughts, but when he became aware of his surroundings again his hands were numb. He was startled by how lost he let himself get. He couldn't remember a single thought as he had knelt there.

As he stood, his knees cracked in protest. He could barely move his lips. His eyes felt like they were embedded in sand, and the skin on his cheeks felt like dried leather. He felt disoriented and full of sorrow. He turned to walk back to his truck and his heart lunged.

Ava was still standing with her hands folded and her head down.

"You stayed," he said. Jesus, he had forgotten she was there.

"You asked me to." She raised her head to look at him.

"How long was I-"

"Fifty-two minutes."

"Christ, you must be freezing." Instinctively, he reached out to touch her arm. She stiffened and brought a fist up. He took a step back. "Sorry, I was just trying to help."

He put his hands in his pockets so he wouldn't be tempted to reach out to her again. He hadn't realized how often people touched each other until now. A light bump of elbows, a friendly punch, a handshake, an arm around the shoulder. All were natural gestures between people. Except for this one.

"You were close."

Gabriel lifted his head at the unexpected sound of her voice.

"You were close with your sister."

He nodded.

Ava took a step closer to him and reached out. Startled, Gabriel hesitated only a moment before taking her hand. Even through his thick work glove and her leather one, he felt that odd physical connection as she led him through the cemetery toward the parking lot. A vibrating sensation coursed through him, as if he were holding onto a speaker while it played a song with heavy bass.

The Equinox she drove was closer than his truck. Ava surprised him by opening the passenger front door and nudging him toward it. Expecting him to simply obey, she continued to the driver's side and climbed in, starting the car, and cranking the heat.

It wasn't blowing the warmest of air yet, but it was warmer than outside. Ava took off her gloves and held her hands up to the vents. Gabriel did the same. His hands were shaking. The walk had gotten his heart rate up, but his extremities were still cold after so much time motionless as he kneeled at Hayden's grave. He flexed his fingers to stimulate the blood flow.

This evening was turning out to be strange, to say the least.

Ava reached for him again, hesitated, took his fingers. Even through his shocked spasm at her sudden contact, she felt how frigid his skin was. She tried not to notice the way his large hand fit exactly right against hers as she brought their hands closer to her chest. A moment or two passed.

No clear thoughts came from Gabriel. Only emotions – sorrow, guilt, aching, anger. They radiated off him so powerfully that Ava felt nauseous sitting so close to him. She closed her eyes, breathed deep, centered herself. When she raised her head and looked into his eyes, she saw all those emotions and more staring back.

"What made you decide to move to Langdon?" he asked, his voice not quite steady. He needed to take his mind off death. He needed to take his mind off thoughts of Ava that had nothing to do with shock and everything to do with lust.

The truck was starting to really warm up, and Gabriel was shaking less. His skin wasn't as cold as when he first sat down, but she sensed that he felt better when she touched him, so she continued to hold his hand.

"The house suits my needs," she answered him.

"That's it?"

His eyes, though full of sorrow, were such a stunning shade of blue. In spite of everything else she saw in them their color was the first thing she noticed about him.

"Is that not enough?" she asked. She rested their hands on the center console. After a moment, she turned in her seat and shifted hands, casually curling her fingertips across the underside of his wrist to check his pulse without alarming him.

"Sure, I guess." She was not good at small talk, he thought. He glanced around the vehicle. "Nice stereo system."

"I would not know." Ava noted his racing heartbeat and tried to breathe a little louder than she normally did so he would subconsciously copy her breathing pattern.

Raising an eyebrow, Gabriel looked at the touch screen system, which was in pristine condition. There were no fingerprints on it. "Did you just buy it?"

"I have owned the vehicle for twenty-one months. I do not listen to music."

"Who doesn't listen to music?" he asked rhetorically.

"I do not."

Ava tilted her head to the side when he cocked that eyebrow again. That tickled him. It reminded him of a puppy trying to figure out a new high-pitched sound.

"Ever?"

She shook her head.

"Not any kind – country, rock, alternative, classical?"

"No."

"Why not?"

"It is... busy." She closed her eyes briefly, grimaced. "It is too loud."

"But you were wearing ear buds at Hayden's grave..."

She didn't answer this. Her eyes shifted away from him as if she had become bored with the subject.

His pulse was slowing as his breathing became more regulated. Ava's idea of him mirroring her behavior had worked. Occasionally throughout their conversation, she caught him glancing down at their joined hands, as if he could not believe what he was seeing.

"I miss my sister," Gabriel sighed. "She was such a pain in my ass."

Ava studied him. Now his eyes were full of affection, but his words did not match up to what his body was projecting.

"If she was a... pain in your ass, why do you miss her?" she asked.

Letting out a bark of laughter, Gabriel rubbed his eyes with his free hand. "Because that's how siblings are."

"I do not have siblings."

Still nothing from touching him. Ava was hoping to get some kind of reading from him, anything that would give him peace, give him just enough to feel better and move on so she could be left alone. She could manipulate the phrasing, so it did not sound extrasensory if she needed to. But nothing was coming through. For the first time in her life, she wanted to get a reading and her ability was failing her.

"I cannot help you," she muttered, irritated with herself. "It is in the dark."

Why did it happen anytime she did not want to help someone, but when she tried to call on it, it disappeared?

Not sure if he heard her correctly, Gabriel gently pulled his hand out of her grasp. Her attitude had changed, and though he didn't know her well enough to understand how, exactly, he understood she was disturbed now.

"Thank you for staying," he said. A shaky exhale escaped him. "It was harder than usual to visit Hayden's grave today. I don't know why."

Because I am here now, she thought. The energy your sister is using to try to communicate is draining you.

"It is because of me," she said. "My presence has made it more difficult for you to grieve."

"I don't understand."

"You do not have to," Ava said. She turned down the blower so they could hear each other more easily.

"You say the strangest things."

She regarded him without speaking. She had the most direct gaze, unwavering, unapologetic.

"Can I buy you a drink?" he offered. "It's the least I can do after you waited out here in the cold with me."

"I do not drink alcohol."

"What about dinner?" He wanted to thank her, to make her understand just how much her presence meant to him. Even if he didn't exactly understand how, she had helped him.

"I must leave. I am sorry your sister is dead."

She doesn't use contractions, he suddenly realized. That's why her speech sounds strange. Her words are deliberate. She is one of few people, Gabriel thought, who thinks before she speaks.

"It was nice to see you again, Ava. Thank you again for staying."

For a long moment, she looked at him. Then she nodded, once.

Gabriel exited the car and watched her drive around the curvy cemetery driveway before he started toward his vehicle.

Somehow a stranger had made visiting his sister's grave more bearable.

• • • • •

Isabel played her guitar as she sang the haunting lyrics to Damien Rice's "9 Crimes" for the fourth time. The song sounded better on the piano, but she didn't have one in her apartment. Gabriel was the better piano player, anyway; she had always found the guitar came more naturally to her. The song was a duet, so it should be sung with a male partner. She didn't have one of those in her apartment, either.

She couldn't stop playing it. It was one of her and Gabriel's favorites to play on Sundays at their parent's house. The song was a little dark for a family gathering, but the notes and the harmony of male and female voices were so beautiful that they played it anyway. When Beth left her attitude at home and joined in with her violin, it was amazing.

But for now, it was just Isabel and her guitar, sounding soulful and alone.

She played for a little while longer before putting her guitar away and pouring another drink. That was three tonight. How many drinks, how often did it take, to make one an alcoholic? she wondered. She didn't drink every night, but the frequency of days during the week she drank was increasing.

What was the point? Everyone kept asking why she didn't switch jobs. As if a different asshole boss would make such a difference. As if the new location of a bunch of gossiping coworkers would change her entire outlook on life. No one seemed to understand that all jobs had the same problems: dicks for bosses, no room for moral or intellectual growth, and too many office politics to get anything constructive done. People were assholes no matter where she worked.

The hole was becoming too deep. If she didn't get help, she would watch the dirt fall on top of her and she wouldn't be unable to pull herself out until the cycle of depression worked its way through her system and passed on its own. That could take months. She was too tired to fight for months.

Picking up her cell phone, she tapped Gabriel's contact. The call went straight to voicemail. He was already on another call. Damn.

She pressed her fingers between her eyes. A headache was throbbing at her forehead and temples. If she called Beth, she would only end up feeling worse. Her mother would be too depressed about Hayden on her birthday to want to talk and her father wasn't much of a talker at all. They would spend most of their time in awkward silence.

"Think, Iz," she muttered. "You can't depend on other people all the time."

Glancing at her empty tumbler, she considered refilling it.

She tried Gabriel's number again.

• • • • •

Gabriel paced the living room thoughtfully, his hands shoved deep in the pockets of his jeans. His heart was still racing, though it had been an hour since he visited Hayden's grave.

He looked at the floor as he walked, avoiding the pictures hanging on the wall over the fireplace. He didn't want to think about Hayden right now.

Ava.

How was she still distracting him an hour later? The kindness she had shown him by staying at Hayden's grave for almost an hour was unexpected. Everything about her up until that moment had been deliberate, her demeanor reserved. In the few instances Gabriel had seen her, she had shown she not only despised human contact but was willing to physically defend herself against it.

Yet she stood next to him in thirty-degree weather for nearly an hour while he zoned out thinking about his sister.

His thoughts roamed to the time he had knelt in front of Hayden's grave. He tried to remember the barrage of thoughts running through his head, but there had been so many... so many. He couldn't recall a single one.

He was wound up about his sister's birthday, he supposed. What he couldn't understand was why. Usually, it was a day like any other. After work, he visited her grave, left flowers. He did it the same this year as he did every other year. So why did his stomach feel like it was riding a roller coaster while he was still standing on the ground? Why did his skin feel as if centipedes were crawling just under it? Was he sympathizing with Isabel's irritation at Beth and their mother?

His cell phone rang. Pulling it out of his jacket pocket, Gabriel frowned at the name on the display. Rachel Hampton. He had obviously forgotten to remove her from his Contacts after they had broken up over seven months ago.

"What?" His voice wasn't quite steady. The fireplace was empty. He knelt and began setting it up, one handed, to light a fire.

"Hey, Gabriel."

"Rachel," he said uncertainly. He cleared his throat. "What's going on?"

"It's been a while. I was wondering how you're doing... if you're okay." Her voice sounded different somehow.

"Why wouldn't I be?"

"Is that a joke?" There was a beat of silence. "You're serious. You're always restless this time of year."

"What are you talking about?" The question came out sharper than he had meant and sounded too loud in the empty house. He suddenly realized how alone he felt.

"Come on, Gabe. We were together for three years. Did you think I didn't notice how fidgety you became? You stopped sleeping, staying out in your garage all night. Our sex marathons were epic every March and August. Your temper became volatile."

Was all that true? Had he really been reacting this way every year without knowing it? Had he used sex to divert his attention? What the hell had he done before he was old enough to have sex?

A flush crept up his neck as the obvious hit him - he did what every teenage boy did alone in his bedroom before sex with a partner is an option.

"I didn't realize."

"I shouldn't be surprised," Rachel said wryly. "Everyone in your family retreats into their own little world when it comes to Hayden."

Gabriel didn't think she had any right to speak about his family, but he didn't say so. He didn't trust himself when it came to Rachel. "I didn't know I was taking it out on you that way."

"I had no complaints in the bedroom. I was always fascinated by your drive. But I do want to know you're okay. I know it's hard for you now and at the end of summer when she disappeared. I still care about you."

Gabriel started into the kitchen for a beer. Pacing was not helping. "I'm not your problem anymore, but thanks."

"No," she said carefully, "but you could have been pretty vindictive after we broke up, and you weren't. I appreciate that. You treated me better than I deserved."

After they hung up, Gabriel stared at his phone a few seconds before putting it back in his pocket. That had been an insight he hadn't expected. He wanted to talk to Isabel and ask her if she noticed his behavior change every year. He would talk to her about it Saturday. Maybe he was the only one who didn't realize he was a complete dick. Although, after everything that happened with Rachel, he didn't feel particularly guilty about the way he had apparently treated her.

When Disturbed's cover of "Sound of Silence" rang out from his pocket, he was back in the living room, pacing. He pulled his cell out again, thankful to be hearing from his sister.

"Iz. What's up?"

"Hey. Are you busy? Can I come over for a little bit?"

Gabriel instantly recognized the underlying despair hiding in her carefully neutral tone.

"Sure," he said without hesitation.

"Really? I'm not interrupting anything?"

"No, you're doing me a favor. I'm going batshit crazy with my own thoughts tonight."

He heard the relief in her voice as she thanked him and hung up and was pleased that she'd called. He wouldn't have to waste the rest of the night trying to fill the time or being unable to concentrate because he was thinking about Rachel's call.

·   ·   ·   ·   ·

Forty minutes later, Isabel was sitting at his breakfast bar with a glass of whiskey. Her complexion was pale, her eyes hollow. She gripped the tumbler of whiskey tightly, as if it alone anchored her to reality.

"I'm sorry," she said immediately.

"Why?"

To Isabel, he looked stable, laid back. The past few months, he had looked wounded, and it was nice to see him finally recovering from a bitch not worth wasting his time on.

"For crashing in on you tonight." She took a sip of whiskey. "I had a shitty day and just wanted to brood with someone who wouldn't judge me."

"Like Mom?" he said, raising his left eyebrow.

She did the same, and they both laughed.

Pulling a beer out of the fridge, he reached for a Bic lighter off the top of the refrigerator and angled the butt end between the cap and neck of the bottle. He pushed down on the lighter, using it as a lever, prying off the cap with a clear pop! The cap flew off, hit the ceiling, and bounced somewhere behind Isabel.

Iz grinned. "A bottle opener is just too damn ordinary for you."

"This way amuses me." He took a long pull. "Rachel called me just before you did."

Isabel set her glass of whiskey down, hard. "What did that little cu-" She paused, held her breath, let it out slowly. "What did she want?"

Gabriel gave her one of his lazy, one-sided smiles, where the right corner barely curved upward. "Actually, she gave me some insight. She said I become agitated around Hayden's birthday and the day she disappeared, in August. Apparently, I don't sleep much and I... well."

Isabel frowned. "You what?"

He looked at her over his beer bottle. "I had a habit of marathon fucking her around those two times every year."

Isabel choked on her drink of whiskey. She put a hand over her mouth to contain the spray. "Hit it, son."

"Do you notice a change in me every year?" he asked.

"Well, you and I don't engage in sex, Gabe, so I can't really say if we do more of it at this time or not."

He leaned over and punched her in the shoulder. "I mean, is my attitude different? Have I been this way for years and not known it?"

Isabel thought back. "Mom and Beth are so dramatic that I've never really had time to think of how it affected you. It sounds horrible, but they take up so much of my time calling me and whining about it that I don't have time to think about anyone else's grief. You're more of a subtle person. I guess it makes sense that you would be, though."

"Huh."

"Am I different?" Isabel asked.

"Let's sit in the living room."

As they walked, Gabriel said, "You get quiet, withdraw into yourself. It's like you're always thinking about something. I guess you get agitated more easily, like you want to kick someone's ass. So, I guess you're like normal, but more of it. I never really thought about it, either."

"How did we not realize this before? How is it that a superficial, cheating whore actually had a helpful insight? That pisses me off."

"We're too close to it, I guess. She also said everyone in the family goes into their own world when it comes to Hayden."

"Well, not everyone can reach out and fuck someone," Iz said bitterly.

Gabriel smirked. He nudged her with his elbow before settling in the recliner. Isabel chose the sofa. She set her whiskey on the end table.

"Why do you hate her so much, Iz?" he asked her.

Isabel's dark green eyes were like slits of rain-soaked leaves in the middle of summer. "Is that supposed to be funny?"

Taking a sip of his beer, he eyed her. "I remember her always being polite to you."

Isabel picked up her tumbler of whiskey to give her hands something to do. With her index finger, she traced the design on the glass.

"Did she say something to you that I'm not aware of?" Gabriel watched with curiosity and awe as his sister's anger rose the more she thought about his ex-girlfriend. Her jaw set and her body became rigid. She pursed her lips.

"No," she said, looking at him. "She fucked someone that you weren't aware of, then almost ruined your life when her thug fuck buddy tried to send you to jail. Are we remembering the same Rachel?"

"She's ultimately the reason I'm not in jail," he reminded her. "Regardless, I made sure nothing she did to me could come back to hurt you or the rest of the family."

"You're an idiot," Iz said softly, downing the rest of her drink. "I need a refill."

She stood and started toward the kitchen. Gabriel was up instantly. He grasped her by arm as if she were made of butterfly wings.

"Hey," he said, keeping his tone light. "What's going on? I can barely drum up disinterest for her."

As she raised her dark green eyes to his, Gabriel was startled to see them brimming with tears. He was shocked at the amount of emotion Iz was showing for a woman who was no longer in his life, who hadn't been much of a part of Isabel's. Rachel had come to a few Sunday dinners, and they had hung out together at Gabe's a few times, but Isabel was a loner. She hadn't shown much interest in getting to know any of his girlfriends.

"Isabel, what did she do to you?" he coaxed, taking both her shoulders now.

"She almost took my brother away from me." A tear slid down first her right cheek, then her left. "I need a fucking damn refill."

Backing out of his grasp, she turned and walked to the kitchen.

Gabriel stood for several seconds, stunned. He had no idea Isabel had been so affected by his relationship with Rachel. How the hell had he missed that? Touched, he was speechless with affection for her loyalty. They had always been close, even before Hayden's death. To see her have his back so completely, without mercy, was humbling.

She came back with a double for her and another beer for him. He was still standing where she left him. She handed him the bottle and was about to walk past him when he wrapped his arms around her, careful not to tip his bottle.

"Hey," he said, squeezing tight. "I'm sorry. I didn't know she upset you so much."

Iz buried her face in his chest, returning the hug while trying not to spill her drink. "Everything she did to you, she did to our family. If I ever run into her, I'll kick her in the vag."

Gabriel snickered, hugging her tighter. "Thanks, Iz."

She pulled back, taking a drink of her whiskey. Punched him on the shoulder before she returned to the couch.

"Of course, her vagenitals are probably like burlap with how much she gets pounded, so it might not do any good."

"Vagenitals?" Gabriel laughed, sitting in the recliner. His mood had improved significantly since she came over. He reached into the drawer of the end table and pulled out a lighter to open his beer. This time the cap flew across the room and almost landed in the fireplace.

Isabel watched its trajectory. "Good one."

"Thanks, Iz," Gabriel repeated. He was smiling at her with obvious affection.

"For what?"

"For having my back. For cheering me up."

Isabel grinned. She had crawled to the rim of the abyss as well, and Gabriel had reached the rest of the way in and pulled her out. "Back at you, bro."

Neither of them mentioned Hayden's birthday again.

CHAPTER THREE

"Get back here, you little shit! I'm not finished with you!"

Something crashed onto the floor behind her. She felt the whoosh of air as whatever it was almost hit her foot. Terrified, she clawed her way across the stained brown carpet toward the door. If she could make it to the door, she could run to the woods and wait him out. Soon the alcohol would take over and he wouldn't be able to chase her.

"I said come back here!"

He sounded closer.

Biting her lower lip until she tasted blood, she pushed herself forward, hitting chipped tile a moment later. A wave of relief rolled through her as she jumped up, not daring to turn and look. Not even a peek, because she knew if she did, he would get her. She pushed through the screen door and sprinted toward the woods.

Dead grass bit into her bare feet as she ran across the yard. She was only wearing tee shirt and underpants; he had ripped off her shorts before she was able to get away. Pressing on, she made it to the trees and kept going until she could no longer see the trailer. Then she ran a few seconds more before she collapsed on the ground.

Pine needles and leaves cushioned her fall. Struggling for air, she stayed on the ground with her hair a mess around her and her arms and legs cut, wondering if today would be the day that she died.

Ava's body twitched as she rose from sleep. She was standing next to the stairs, one arm bent above her head, one hand resting on the wall next to her face while she tapped her index finger in a random pattern. Slowly, as the dream cleared, she became aware that her naked body was pressed against the wall. She had been sleepwalking again.

Not just sleepwalking, she thought. Memories of her childhood often resurfaced as dreams, and each time, she relived them. Her heart was still racing, and she felt the fear as she had at five years old, not the controlled indifference she normally had toward her foster parents.

Stepping away from the wall, Ava felt disoriented and shaken. She was downstairs. The living room was at her back, the kitchen and dining room to her left. Early morning light was just starting to crest the eastern horizon. Ava hugged her arms, trying to warm herself. The chill she felt was not from the morning.

The only way to rid herself of the horrible feelings inside her after a dream like that was to keep her mind and body distracted with something else. She climbed the stairs and started to dress in preparation for a workout. The dream would linger all day, but she could keep the negative aftermath at bay with a vigorous workout if she pushed herself hard.

Letting her abusers win by wallowing in self-pity was not an option.

•   •   •   •   •

Isabel knelt in front of the granite marker and stared at the engraving spelling out her sister's name. She traced the "H" with her index finger. The granite marker was frigid.

She found herself coming here more often, not just on her sister's birthday or the anniversary of her disappearance. During warmer weather she visited several times a week. A cemetery was a peaceful place. Sometimes she wrote song lyrics. Other times she just sat among the graves, thinking. To prove to herself that she wasn't disappearing, Isabel often talked to Hayden as if she had grown up and was sitting beside Iz, listening without judgment. She talked about her day, about work, about anything she could think of just to hear the sound of a voice - any voice – out loud.

Today's visit was a silent one. After yesterday's sob-a-thon with her mother and Beth, she needed a palate cleanser. She felt she had more of a connection to her dead sister and wasn't competing to see who was grieving the most when she was here alone.

Whenever she was around Beth, Iz felt her older sister was trying too hard to show her grief. As if someone would think she forgot her sister was dead, or she wasn't sad enough. Why did Beth care what other people thought? Why couldn't she just feel what she felt honestly, and not have to announce some pretend version of her feelings to the world?

Fifteen minutes and several curses regarding the cold later, she was walking into the grocery store, trying to figure out what to buy for dinner. She pulled a small cart from the rack and started toward the second set of automatic doors. A woman in front of her suddenly stopped, staring down at her phone.

That's a great place to stop, Isabel thought, thankful she hadn't run her cart into the inconsiderate woman's ass. Did she think she was the only damn person out in public?

After a moment, the woman glanced up and continued through the door as if she had every right to block the entrance. Iz shook her head and entered the produce section, wondering if she should just broil some vegetables for dinner. She wasn't hungry. Her appetite had been nonexistent the past couple weeks. Maybe Gabriel was right, and her appetite suffered around Hayden's birthday.

A headache was already forming, and it kicked up a notch when a toddler threw a fit over by the organic section. He let out a piercing shriek that made Isabel grind her teeth. The boy's mother was trying to placate him by bribing him with fruit.

Mom never would have tolerated that, Iz thought, picking up an apple and checking it for bruises. She certainly wouldn't have rewarded the behavior.

A woman hurried past her, her heels clicking briskly on the floor. Her cart bumped into Isabel's, knocking it to the side. The woman glared at her as she hurried away.

"Yeah, that was my fault, you inconsiderate bitch," Iz muttered under her breath incredulously. She set the apple down. "What is with people today?" Everyone seemed especially selfish and rushed.

She walked over to the fresh lettuce and considered her options. She should have said something to that woman. No one had the right to shove into her without apologizing. People should watch where they were going and apologize when they made a mistake.

A middle-aged man pulled a cucumber from the stack. He had chosen one toward the middle of the pile and four or five others fell off the stack, rolling across the floor. The man glanced around, shoving his single cucumber into his produce bag, and started walking quickly away.

"Really?!" Isabel said, her hand on the romaine she was just about to pick up. "You're seriously going to leave that mess you just made?"

The man didn't glance around. He walked faster.

Oh my God, get out of here, girl. You're going to lose it.

Isabel rubbed her forehead. "Nobody sees me," she said, laughing humorlessly. She sounded a little hysterical. "Nobody sees anyone." Her hands were shaking.

She pushed her cart to a refrigerator with bagged lettuces and placed the first bag of romaine she saw in her cart without checking it for freshness. She would eat something that didn't require any preparation. She needed to get the bare minimum of groceries and get the hell out of this store before she yelled at someone. Her heart was pounding against her rib cage.

Iz walked out of the produce area and headed toward the dairy section. She was grinding her teeth persistently now. Each breath felt like she was swallowing razor blades.

She should have picked up the cucumbers even though she hadn't made the mess. That would have been the good thing to do, the right thing. Or spoken louder and called that idiot out on his asinine behavior. Apparently, he was used to mommy always cleaning up after him, if he thought he could get away with that in the middle of the grocery store.

He did get away with it. People will always get away with their selfish behavior.

That was the problem. People were assholes everywhere, and they all got away with it. No one was held accountable for their actions anymore.

She was almost to the dairy section when a tall man in a leather duster coat stepped out of the aisle inches in front of her, causing her to stop so suddenly she almost fell forward into her cart. She had to pull her cart abruptly to the side to avoid running into him. It slammed into an end cap instead. A jug of laundry detergent fell off the far end and hit the floor. The man took no notice. He turned to his right, away from Isabel, and moseyed away from her.

"What am I, fucking invisible?" She did not mumble or mutter under her breath this time. She enunciated every word at top volume.

The man glanced up, looked around, and turned back toward her. "I beg your pardon?"

"It's going to take more than begging, shit-bird," Isabel fumed. She pulled the cart away from the end cap. "Why don't you pay attention when you're out in public?"

Isabel felt like her entire body was crawling with fire ants. Every customer in the vicinity was staring at her. A middle-aged man previously studying dryer sheets down one aisle was placidly gazing at her. A large woman with a box of brownie bites was staring with her considerable mouth hanging open. In the bakery, a boy of four or five standing in a cart had paused jumping to turn his large eyes on her.

"Mommy, that lady said the 'f' word," he said, his voice filled with awe.

The man Isabel had confronted walked back toward her and her cart. Picking up the jug of laundry soap from the floor, he held it out toward her. Somehow it hadn't broken open.

"My apologies," he said. Isabel caught an English accent. "Did you want to purchase this?"

"No. I knocked it off the shelf trying not to ram it up your oblivious ass."

He set the jug back on the shelf.

Unable to help herself, Isabel snapped, "You know, it helps to remove your head from your asshole before you go out in public. The air quality's better, too."

The corners of his mouth twitched. "Many thanks for not... ah... ramming your cart up my oblivious ass, as you put it. I'm having a rather bad day and-"

"Who isn't?!" she fumed. "That doesn't give you the right to clomp through life without regard to anyone else, Captain A-hole."

The boy previously jumping in the cart started giggling.

At least someone is entertained, Isabel thought.

"I've upset you. I'm terribly sorry." The man's tone was full of pity, and that made her even angrier. He was treating her like she needed to be handled, like a crazy person or a rabid dog.

The shoppers around them had already lost interest and continued their business, and that infuriated her even more. What had to happen for people to acknowledge each other?

Iz pressed her fingers between her eyes. She felt a wave of dizziness rush over her and had to lean on her cart for support. She had placed her coat in her shopping cart earlier to keep from sweating as she wandered around the store. Now her body was suddenly so cold she was close to shuddering.

The man reached out and touched her arm. Despite her anger at him, Isabel almost burst into tears at the contact. His hand was warm even through her thick sweater. When was the last time someone had touched her for something as simple as to make sure she felt okay?

"Are you alright?"

"No." She had mistaken his accent. Australia? New Zealand? What the hell do you care what his accent is, get out of here, she thought to herself. "I'm leaving. Feel free to barge in front of someone else."

He smiled. It was a dazzling smile. Dammit. "Point taken. But I'm not leaving you like this. You look like you're going to pass out."

She exhaled sharply. "I don't need your help. Run along." She wiggled her fingers in a dismissive gesture.

Turning her cart down a random aisle, she started toward the self-checkout. She was too tired and shaky to complete her list of groceries. Lettuce would have to do. She had no idea if she had salad dressing at home that hadn't expired and didn't care. She would eat the lettuce leaves plain like a damn rabbit if she had to.

When she reached the self-checkout, she noticed the guy was still following her. "Are you waiting to be adopted?" she asked, scanning her purchase. She hit the pay button and slipped into her coat as she waited for it to process.

"I want to make sure you're okay."

He smiled again. He had perfect teeth.

"Oh, please." Iz rolled her eyes as she dug in her purse for her wallet. "I said I'm fine. Just because no one ever calls you pretty boys out when you're behaving like dicks, doesn't mean there must be something wrong with me." She swiped her debit card.

The man cocked his head to the side. "You think I'm pretty?" He wiggled his eyebrows.

Iz blushed. She hated herself for it.

"That's what you took away from what I said?" She was glad when she could distract herself by following the instructions on the card reader.

He laughed. "I'm Griffin Turner." He held out his hand.

Despite not wanting to let him off the hook so easily, Iz hated being rude to other people. Especially since she had just given him so much hell for doing the same. She gave him a firm shake and appreciated that he did the same. Limp handshakes pissed her off.

"Isabel."

For a moment she was able to get a better look at him. His light brown wavy hair had a slightly windblown look. His eyes were the color of honey. Looking into those eyes was like looking into the eyes of a lion. Isabel didn't think she had ever known anyone with eyes that color.

His coat was opened to reveal a button-down shirt with tie and slacks, probably tailored, since he was so tall and lean. Isabel knew the look of expensive clothing, even if she would never be able to afford wearing it. Wonderful. She was dealing with a man of privilege. No wonder he thought he was entitled.

"Have a nice evening, Griffin."

She put her wallet back in her purse and took her lettuce, pushing the cart one-handed in front of her toward the door. Griffin stepped up beside her and took the cart, setting his empty basket inside for convenience.

"You're not having a good day, are you?" he asked.

"No shit, Sherlock. Did the Ivy league education mommy and daddy paid for teach you those brilliant skills of deduction? Quantico must be waiting to scoop you up."

She tried, hard, to be furious at the sound of his laughter, but was unsuccessful. Needing to stay angry, needing the anger to take control until she had a moment alone to fall apart, she snapped at him.

"I think I can handle a miniature shopping cart."

She reached out to take it back, but he gently took her hand and moved it away. He continued pushing it beside her and returned it to the bank of carts in between the inner and outer sets of sliding doors. Lifting the basket out, he stacked it with the others. As Isabel put her gloves on, he buttoned his coat.

They walked out into the March evening. Iz stepped to the side of the automatic doors and dug in her purse to find her keys. She took a deep breath of chilly air.

"I had to deal with rude clients all day that yelled at me for being late with their work, even though they made last minute changes that made me late with their work. What's your excuse?"

"I visited my sister's grave."

She promptly burst into tears.

Griffin gently took her arm and directed her to one of the colossal decorative pillars at the store overhang, so they were out of the bustling line of human traffic. She leaned her butt against the pillar and put her hands on her knees to steady herself.

"Well, now I really feel like a bloody asshole." Griffin rested his hand on her back. Somehow it felt as heavy as an anvil but gave her great comfort.

"I'm sorry," Iz said. Her laugh was high pitched, on the verge of hysterical. Hearing the sound of that laugh made her afraid she was actually losing her grip on reality. "My sister died sixteen years ago. I should be over it. I am over it. Yesterday was her birthday, and t-that's always hard. And I c-came here and I'm inv-visible."

"I don't think grief has a statute of limitations," Griffin said calmly.

She raked her hand across her eyes angrily. Her tears were quickly drying on her face because of the cold. People were glancing at her as they entered the store.

Great job, Iz, she thought. Next time you should stream your mental breakdown live on social media so the entire world can see it.

She stood up, no longer needing the column for support. "I'm not making any sense. I need to go home."

"I think being alone is the last thing you need," Griffin said. Unzipping his coat a few inches, he reached into his inner jacket pocket and pulled out a crisp handkerchief. He held it out to her.

Isabel stared at it for a moment before accepting it. Who carried one of those around in this era? She dabbed her eyes dry and blew her nose.

"Why do you assume I live alone?" she asked.

Griffin picked up a hand tiller sitting in a large bin of garden supplies. He turned it to the left and right as if he had never seen one before. Spring was two months away, and already stores were stocking up for gardening.

"If you didn't, you'd be home right now, getting comforted by some lucky gentleman instead of stressing out in a supermarket. You're not invisible. I see you."

Isabel watched him use the gardening tool to scratch his knee as he studied her. Right now, in this moment, he did see her. He was decent enough to take a few minutes out of his day to make sure she was okay. Even if pity were the motivation, she'd take it. It was a kind gesture. People weren't kind enough to each other anymore.

She nodded, sniffed. The tears had stopped. She took a few shaky breaths.

Holding up the tiller, he asked, "Do you need your back scratched?"

Isabel snorted.

"Will you come with me somewhere?" Griffin asked. "We can walk. You don't have to get into my car or be alone with me at any point."

She raised an eyebrow, skeptical.

He flashed his perfect teeth. "I have a quick exercise that is guaranteed to alter your mood, and it won't impede your ability to drive home afterwards. I swear."

Intrigued, she picked up her purse and the bag of lettuce she had dropped. "We can walk?"

"Yeah, it's right in this strip mall. There are people everywhere. You'll be perfectly safe the entire time." He tossed the hand tiller back into the wooden bin, where it made a mild clanging sound among its crowd.

"What about my lettuce?"

"It'll be fine in your car. This won't take long and it's a cool enough evening to keep it fresh."

When he stood with her in front of Target a few minutes later, Isabel gave him a withering look. "You must be fucking joking."

"It's a specific kind of therapy. It doesn't matter which store; this one just happened to be within walking distance, so you felt safe. And we're not as likely to get kicked out of here as we would be at a high-end store."

Isabel reluctantly followed him inside, cringing at the amount of people plodding around. The after-work crowd here was even worse than the little grocery store. Griffin didn't explain, only led her to the Home Decor department. His long strides were hard to keep up with. Isabel found herself almost jogging to stay close. She also noticed a couple favorable looks from women as they passed him.

"How are you feeling?" he asked as they walked toward a bin of decorative throw pillows. "Physically, I mean. Are you feeling better?"

Absently, Isabel glanced around, spotting a pair of candle sticks she might like to purchase. They were a rustic wooden pair with a white finish that would go nicely on her bookcase.

"Okay, I guess. The walk and fresh air hel-"

Wham!

Iz gasped as a pillow slapped her across the face. Her hair whipped up, statically charged, clinging to her skin. She blinked, brushing her hair out of her face. Griffin was staring at her, holding a square pillow with a monkey swinging from a palm tree on it.

"What the actual fuck?" Iz said. She pulled her gloves off, which were making the static in her hair worse. Getting her hair to obey her hands now that it wanted to rise into the air of its own free will made her want to throttle Griffin.

He turned back to the bin and dug around. He pulled out a fuzzy blue square pillow and tossed it to her. Dropping her purse to catch it, Isabel gaped at him. Strands of her hair floated back to her cheek, tickling like tiny insects.

"This is your solution? A pillow fight in the middle of a crowded store?"

Griffin took a step forward and smacked her across the face again, a little harder this time. He stared at her smugly, trying not to grin.

Isabel bent down and picked up her purse. She pulled a hairband out, tucked the fuzzy pillow under her arm, dropped her purse again, and wound her hair into a tight ponytail. Shrugging out of her coat, she draped it over the bin of pillows. She gazed coldly at him.

"Oh, you're dead."

•　•　•　•　•

Daniel watched Ava and Vincent practice for several seconds before stopping them. He instructed each of them on the finer points of their techniques before releasing them to start again. He called out a correction to Ava as they continued. They continued practicing, even as Ava said a "Hai, Sensei," since he had not given the order to stop. Walking around them to get the full view of their progress, Daniel saw Ava had listened to his advice and incorporated it into her next punch.

"Good, Ava," he said.

She thanked him in Japanese. They continued sparring. They worked well together, putting all their energy into their techniques, and holding nothing back. Each move was executed as if they were in an actual confrontation, and they needed to defend their lives.

Yet tonight, she seemed distant. She was hiding it well, but Daniel sensed rage underneath each strike and kick. Even her blocks were hostile, causing discomfort to Vincent instead of simply defending Ava's body.

Later, while he was changing, Ava sat on the mat and stretched. Sensei sat across from her, observing. She had been silent tonight, only speaking in response to his instruction. Usually, she had questions for him and spoke with her partner as they practiced. Daniel knew Vincent had noticed the change, too.

Just as he knew Vincent could handle any angry assault Ava threw at him. She'd needed to work something out tonight and had used her training to do so.

The past couple weeks she had been off. Her timing, technique, and attitude were all just a little less than what Daniel was used to seeing from her. Under normal circumstances, she would openly address any issues she had, but for some reason, she hadn't been talking lately. He wondered if working on meditation, the first step in learning to control her psychic ability, had anything to do with it.

Vincent came out of the changing room and Ava stood. She responded when Vincent said good night before leaving and slipped into the changing room to gather her things.

On her way back across the mat to put on her shoes, Sensei gave her one more chance to disclose her issues if she so chose.

"Is everything alright, Ava?"

Sitting on the bench along the front window, she slipped her sneakers on. "Hai, Sensei."

The response was mechanical. Daniel bit down on disappointment.

"We'll work more on that other issue Monday after class," Sensei said. "Have a good night."

Ava opened the door to the dojo. "Hai, Sensei." She thanked him in Japanese and bowed before she left.

In silence, she made her way to her SUV. The cool night air chilled the sweat on her forehead. The temperature had dropped considerably since entering the dojo two hours earlier. Ava felt the isolation of winter pressing down upon her.

Winter had always been worse at the trailer. Always colder, with nowhere to run. The snow seemed to insulate her screams and kill her hope of ever escaping.

Opening the door to her vehicle, Ava tossed her bag onto the passenger's seat.

"Ava."

She spun around. Vincent was standing behind her, far enough she couldn't reach him with a startled strike. Of course, they both knew if he had been an attacker, she would have closed the distance easily.

"I thought you had left," she said. Her voice wavered, upsetting her even more.

"Something's wrong," he said, reaching out to rest his hand on hers. She gripped the top of the Chevy's door like a vise.

There was not much light in this parking lot, but Ava knew he was studying her intently.

"Would you like to follow me home?"

After a moment, she nodded.

His apartment was close. The drive took less than ten minutes at this time of night, long after peak traffic hours. Ava left her gym bag and reached into the back seat to pick up the bag she kept there for this very occasion. The bag had a clean change of clothes, her hairbrush, toiletries.

They showered together to save time and resources. Ava was grateful to be able to clean up so quickly. Tonight's class had been draining. She felt like she wasn't quite getting the techniques down and her body was exhausted. Had she driven all the way home, the drained, unclean feeling would have stuck with her for over an hour as she traveled, then showered. Vincent lived much closer, so she only had to deal with it for a few minutes.

Tonight, she did not want to feel dirty any longer than she had to.

The dojo had a small shower room, but Ava preferred showering at Vincent's or at home. That activity left her vulnerable; she hated to do it in public even though she trusted Sensei.

Some classes left her feeling as if she could train for several more hours, executing every technique perfectly. And sometimes, like tonight, she felt as if every minute were dragging by, and she wouldn't be able to make it through the entire class. She felt The Monster lurking, that mindless beast inside her that fought its way to the surface when she dropped her guard and thought about her childhood. The Monster had saved her when she was a child, but now, as an adult who no longer needed it, she couldn't seem to get rid of it.

Vincent remained quiet as they showered. They had known each other for years and he could tell when she did not want to talk.

After she first came to the dojo, Sensei knew better than to pair her with other children around her age. She was like a wild animal. Only Sensei worked with her for the first year, six days a week, always supervised by David or Ruth. During her second year, Sensei worked with her individually on four days, and one day he had her work with a stocky woman named Tammy. The middle-aged woman had several years' experience already. She could easily overpower Ava if she needed to and was strong enough to take any punches and kicks the little girl was able to get passed her. By then, Ava had settled down enough to trust Sensei, and since Sensei told her to work with Tammy, she trusted his decision. Tammy was her primary partner for two years, until she was disciplined enough to work with other students.

For the first six months of her third year, her partners rotated. Ava did not understand why Sensei kept having different students of different ages come in on Thursdays to train with her. She only knew that she felt safe in the presence of only one – Vincent.

Vincent knew when to speak and when to be silent.

She was ten and he was thirteen when Vincent first started rotating into her Thursday classes. When she was almost eleven, he became her only partner besides Tammy. They had been training together ever since. Tammy had moved nine years ago, and Ava did not know if she continued to train.

Vincent finished drying off before her and left the bathroom. Ava slowly towel-dried her hair, staring at the sink without seeing it. Where was her mind? Instead of racing so fast she could not keep up with coherent thought, she seemed incapable of thinking at all. She felt numb, both in body and in spirit. It was as if she was encased in thick mud and every movement was a struggle. The Monster lurked nearby. She could hear it breathing.

Vincent had dimmed the lights in the bedroom, not for seduction but for meditation. Ava walked into the room naked to find him sitting on the floor in the lotus position at the foot of the bed. He was dressed in black, as usual.

Wearing black made his eyes look even darker, more sinister. Ava had watched strangers grow uncomfortable in his presence because of his eyes. If she had that ability, she would use it to keep people at even more of a distance than she already did.

Exhausted, Ava lay down on her back on his neatly made bed and closed her aching eyes. Some kind of flute music was playing softly in the background, also for meditation. She tried to let it soothe her. The Monster panted in her ear. She tried to shut it out. She felt its claws on her shoulders as it waited for her to give it free reign of her emotions.

Release me, it whispered.

She raised her hands to her ears to shut out its slobbering, raspy breathing.

After several minutes, Vincent stood and walked to the bed, laying on his side next to her.

"What do you need?" he asked.

The Monster grinned in the darkness, its fangs dripping with spit. Even as it wanted to break free of the confines of her body, she felt its claws digging into her skin, trying to burrow.

Ava said, "Make The Monster go away."

After that, no words were needed.

•　•　•　•　•

"Ow."

Isabel had reached up to take the refilled cup of coffee Griffin offered as he sat across from her, and her stomach muscles protested.

"I feel like I just did too much on ab day at the gym."

Griffin smiled. "You'll be really sore for a day or two."

They had smacked each other with pillows for twenty minutes. By the end, Isabel had been laughing so hard she tripped over her own feet and would have fallen on her face if Griffin hadn't caught her. When customers seemed to be getting annoyed, they moved through the aisles in the toy section, beating each other with foam swords.

Isabel's stomach and face hurt from laughing. What was it about being pummeled silly by a pillow that made a person giggle uncontrollably? Isabel hadn't laughed that hard since she was a young child.

"You're an asshole." Stirring creamer into her coffee, she glared at him.

"I'm an asshole?" He took a sip of his coffee. She had been very enthusiastic smacking him, putting everything she had into each swing. She was going to feel it more tomorrow.

"No, I just wanted to hear you say 'ahsshole'." She mimicked his accent. "Actually, yes, yes, you are. My ribs are going to explode out of my chest."

The small coffee shop was almost empty this late at night. That suited Isabel just fine. She would have trouble sleeping tonight as punishment for drinking coffee so late, but she didn't care. For once, she didn't mind the company she was with.

After Target, they had walked to a diner across the street from the strip mall for dinner. Now they were in an all-night coffee shop, back in the same strip mall where they had started. Isabel wasn't alone with him at any point and didn't have to get into his car. It was smart on her part; considerate on his part to respect her enough to suggest it.

After eating, Iz found herself in a much better mood. That had been a while ago and they had been talking ever since.

"I told you it would alter your mood." Griffin grinned.

"It altered my entire body composition."

He smiled his gorgeous smile. "Are you feeling better, then?"

"My stress level has dropped significantly, yes. Thank you."

"Happy to help."

He pulled out his phone and began pressing buttons.

Great, Iz thought. I'm already boring him.

But he handed her his phone. "Add your information to my Contacts," he said. "In case you need to get smacked by a pillow in the future."

Stunned, Iz added her name and cell number and saved it. "Can I... have your number?"

She had never asked for anyone's phone number before. Certainly not from a man.

"Absolutely." He glanced at her contact information on his phone. "Nice to meet you, Isabel Harris."

He was so casual about exchanging their information. Isabel felt like she had suddenly been thrown in with the popular kids at school. She pulled up the Contacts screen on her phone and handed it to him.

A thought struck her as his long fingers flew over her screen. She eyed him suspiciously. "Are you a therapist?"

He handed her phone back. "Graphic designer."

Iz took a sip of her coffee to avoid her awkwardness. "Good. I rank therapists right up there with child molesters and fuck shits who run dog fighting rings."

"Bollocks." Griffin watched her stir her coffee, her face hardening. "Don't sugar coat it for me. Tell me how you really feel."

Blushing, Iz ducked her head. "Sorry. You've probably already figured out the filter between my brain and my mouth is broken."

"And here I thought you were just an honest person."

She snorted. "Give it time. You won't enjoy my 'honesty' so much when I say something you don't want to hear."

"I'm a good listener, if you want to talk about it."

"I wouldn't know where to start." Isabel moved the empty plastic creamer containers to the edge of the table. "I need more creamer."

You need a distraction, he thought, noting the full creamers still on the table.

"Let's start with something a little less intimidating," Griffin said, resting his hand on top of hers before she bolted. "What's your shoe size?"

Isabel gave him an incredulous look. When he squeezed her hand, she glanced down at it curiously.

"I'm a thirteen. I have big feet."

"Shoe size? What the actual fuck?" Isabel blurted. She covered her mouth with her free hand. "Sorry."

Griffin grinned. "No worries. It's next to impossible to make me blush. Would you rather get straight to the deep, intimate details of our lives? I figured you'd be more comfortable if we got to know each other first."

He lazily moved his thumb back and forth across her wrist as he talked.

"I suppose that makes more sense," Iz said. "I'm a size nine. My feet are also big for a woman. You know what they say about women with big feet. They have smart vaginas."

Griffin almost choked on the coffee he had been drinking. Isabel leaned back in case some went flying.

"I don't think that's how that saying goes," Griffin said, wiping his mouth off with a napkin. "Sorry about that."

She smiled. "I have that effect on people. You... ah..." She motioned near her mouth. "You missed some..."

"Here?" He wiped his upper lip. When she shook her head, he tried again, missing completely. Isabel reached over and took the napkin from him. Gently, as if afraid her touch would maim him, she dabbed around his chin.

"Thank you," he said.

"I'd make an excellent maid."

"You should try stand-up comedy," Griffin said. "Your sarcasm is funny."

"Most people are put off by it. Besides, I don't like crowds."

"That's personal." Griffin stirred his coffee thoughtfully. "I'll respond in kind. Let's see... Sometimes I don't wear underwear to work. It helps keep me awake in the afternoons."

She snorted. "Ever try a cup of coffee?"

"That's too boring for me."

"So, you free ball it and risk sitting on a nut? You live dangerously."

Grinning, Griffin began stacking the single cups of creamer on each other. "It's a bit tricky to navigate my zipper, but the anticipation keeps me at the top of my game all day."

He kept making her laugh. "Why did you invite me out for a pillow fight and coffee after I reamed your ass in the grocery store? Most people would have run the other way by now."

"I deserved your tongue lashing. I was being an inconsiderate jerk."

"As if anyone takes responsibility for their own actions. I'd bet a paycheck society would still view me as the bitch. Seriously, why? I called you an asshole."

Griffin studied Isabel with his amber eyes. "Captain A-Hole, I believe you said. You needed the pillow fight. That was a selfless act of valor on my part."

Iz snickered.

"You had the balls to call me out on my behavior. That intrigued me. When we were having the pillow fight, you were laughing so hard, tears were running down your face. You could barely stand up. I want to get to know a person who is so passionate about every single emotion she has."

"Bipolar chicks do it for you, huh? Or you need a charity case, and I came by at the right time, so you didn't have to waste time looking."

Amused, he half-smiled. "I don't think you're bi-polar. I think you're very generous with your emotions without giving a shit what other people think. I like knowing people who don't lie as a way of life."

"You must not have many friends."

"I have plenty of acquaintances. They probably think they're my friends. But close friends, the real kind I can talk to about anything, that will call me out on my bullshit when I need it, are harder to find. When I find someone as honest as you, I seek her out."

Isabel tilted her head, trying to gauge his sincerity. Nothing in his eyes made her think he was trying to deceive her. His body language was friendly, approachable. He wasn't trying to impress her. He didn't seem to have an ulterior motive to becoming her friend.

"What are you thinking?" he asked. "You went away for a moment there."

She blinked. Despite the coffee, she was exhausted. The most excitement she usually had on a work night was treating herself to a chocolate sundae in the park during the summer. The opportunity to be able to do that was still months away. She'd been talking for hours now, something she never did.

"I was just trying to figure out if you're being honest," she said. "I hate putting effort into a friendship that's one-dimensional."

Discussing emotions seemed to make her wary. Griffin noticed she was more comfortable with sarcasm and raunchy humor, so he chose to lighten the mood.

"Feel free to kick me in the nuts if I'm lying."

This time she almost choked on her coffee. She grabbed a napkin and shoved it against her nose and mouth, afraid it would spurt out of every orifice.

Griffin gave her a smile, showing off his perfect teeth. God, she loved his mouth. She wondered what it would be like to run her lips over his.

Blushing, Isabel took another drink of her coffee and hoped he hadn't noticed.

Griffin glanced at his phone. "I should get you back to your car. It's getting late."

Isabel glanced down at her watch and was surprised to find it was after midnight. They had been talking for over three hours after dinner. Where the hell had the time gone?

"I am going to be dragging ass tomorrow at work," she grumbled. She stood, slipping into her coat.

Griffin pulled on his coat and left a generous tip on the table. "Don't wear underwear. You'd be surprised at how every movement gives a little tickle at the oddest of times. It will keep you awake."

"Is that the Griffin Method?" she asked as they walked out into the freezing early morning air.

"Tried and true." As they walked back toward the grocery store, Griffin asked if she had a remote start on her vehicle.

When she shook her head, he pulled out his keys and pressed a couple buttons. "We can sit in mine while yours is warming up. Unless you're not comfortable with that."

Isabel inhaled deeply, sighed. "If you were going to kill me, you would have done it by now. We can wait in your car."

They stopped at her car first so she could start it. Isabel didn't think too much about it until they neared Griffin's vehicle and suddenly her own car seemed like something dug out of a salvage yard. Griffin's vehicle, a newer model Range Rover Sport, was humongous. Isabel caught a flash of dark blue before Griffin opened the passenger door for her.

The inside of his colossus was only a little less than frigid after so many hours sitting still. Isabel tucked her hands between her thighs even though she was wearing gloves. Griffin stuck the key in but turned the blower to low while the motor warmed up. Isabel thought she could easily fit her bathroom into the front seat.

"I should have hit the remote start sooner," he said. "Sorry about that."

"How do you feel about not wearing underwear now?" she asked. Her teeth began chattering loudly. She hunched over on the seat, trying to stay warm. "You could fit an underdeveloped country in this thing."

He laughed. Leaning down, he felt along the outside of his seat. "You can turn on the heated seats. The button is-"

Isabel had begun feeling around as soon as she heard "heated seats."

"Found it." Her butt instantly felt the difference as the warmth started on impact and spread quickly throughout her body. "How have I gone my entire life without these?"

"That should help until the rest of the car warms up."

"I'm surprised you didn't have a driver waiting for you with the car already running," Isabel said dryly. "You remind me of someone with a driver named Jeeves."

Laughing, he put the Jeep in gear. When she stiffened beside him, he said, "I'll park by your car, so you don't have to walk in the cold."

He turned up the blower, driving through the parking space toward her tiny Malibu. Her car looked like a miniature Hot Wheels toy when he parked next to it.

Seeing her shiver, he turned in the seat.

"Bugger." He leaned over and rubbed a hand up and down her arm.

"I don't think that actually works when I'm wearing a coat," she said.

"A minor technicality."

That made her giggle. Her teeth finally stopped chattering, even if it was because of her proximity to him more than the warm seats.

"Sorry, Rover takes a bit to warm up because of his size."

After a moment, what he said caught up to her. "Rover?"

Grinning, he said, "I call my car Rover."

"As in, it's a Jeep Range Rover?"

"As in."

"You're a dope." She smirked.

Rover's seat was nicely heating her ass, making the rest of her toasty. Isabel thought she definitely needed a vehicle with heated seats when she traded in her car in a year or two. Or twelve, at the rate she was going.

"I've kept you out too late and made you get into a frozen vehicle. Not very gentlemanly of me." Griffin checked the heat and turned up the blower even more.

"I'll survive."

"Next time, I'll plan better."

Isabel smiled, savoring the moment. It had been so long since she felt this comfortable around another human being. Already she was forgetting about the cold.

She kept hearing his words repeated in her head.

Next time.

•   •   •   •   •

Nearing one in the morning, Ava lifted her head and turned, letting her eyes roam over Vincent's naked torso. Odd, she thought, that he slept on his back. Ava couldn't imagine being comfortable sleeping like that. His lips were slightly parted, and she thought of how they had roamed her body hours before. Those lips knew when to please, when to tease. What she wanted, what she needed.

When she was twenty, she had asked Vincent to introduce her to sex. He was there when she needed him and gone when she did not. The only one she had ever trusted her body to in that way, he had taught her so much.

Reaching over, she took his hand, squeezed.

Vincent inhaled deeply, turned his head toward her, opened his eyes. After a moment, his eyes cleared, and he lifted his head. "Are you leaving?"

She nodded.

He squeezed her hand back. His head hit the pillow heavily. "You can stay. It's late."

Sitting up, she let the blanket fall away from her body without shame. "I need to go home."

Ava never stayed overnight. Theirs was not that kind of relationship.

Vincent sat up, rotated the heel of his hand in his eye. His body was well muscled but not bulky; those who did not know him mistook him for being lanky. That ignorance would give him an advantage if he were ever in a confrontation.

Considering, Ava moved to the edge of the bed. "Vincent?"

"Yes?"

"If you find someone, or if I no longer please you sexually, you can tell me. We can stop this if it no longer suits you."

Giving her a sleepy smile, he rolled onto his side to face her. "I haven't found anyone. The same goes for you. If you find someone."

"I will not find anyone. But thank you."

She leaned over and picked up her bra. Vincent watched her put it on, stand and slip into her panties. She thought she had everything figured out. She raised her hands over her head, bent back until her torso was perpendicular to the floor, then rotated counterclockwise to stretch. She repeated the exercise, this time rotating clockwise. When she knelt to pick up her jeans, she saw Vincent watching her.

"Why are you looking at me?"

The sweater she wore was loose enough to keep from feeling constricting. It still complemented her shape and brought out the gray in her eyes.

He sat up, pulling his feet up so he was sitting cross legged. "You're beautiful. You know that."

"I know people have said that to me."

Vincent watched her expression shift from curious to uncomfortable. She didn't understand beauty the way most people did; she certainly didn't think of herself as a beautiful person. Compliments embarrassed her.

Sitting on the side of the bed, she began lacing up her black boots.

"You know I say what I mean."

Finished with her boots, she pulled the hems her jeans over them. She turned back to him, squeezed his hand again.

"Thank you for making The Monster go away."

Vincent nodded once, slowly. "I would do much more if you'd let me, Ava."

She gazed at him, unblinking, and stood.

"Good night, Vincent."

•   •   •   •   •

Gabriel walked into Spencer's Bar and Grill just after eight o'clock Friday night with a headache pounding so hard, he was scowling. He didn't want to be in public tonight.

Beth had called earlier, crying about having another period, which meant she still wasn't pregnant. Gabriel could have done without the details. When he tried to make her feel better, she started sobbing and hung up on him, which prompted a phone call from his mother to bitch at him for not being more sensitive toward her "in her condition." As if he and Beth couldn't sort things out like adults once they both cooled off. Instead, she had to bring their mother into it like she had when they were children. Then again, she hadn't really acted like an adult during their conversation, so it shouldn't have surprised him.

Greg and Tom were sitting at their usual table. Gabriel walked over and took his normal seat. "Where's Jeremy?"

"The pisser," Tom said. "You look like shit."

"Thanks."

"Bad week." It wasn't a question.

Gabriel glanced at Tom and wondered if he was the only one who hadn't realized his own odd behavior regarding Hayden.

"Yeah, apparently I get 'restless' around this time of year," he said shortly. "No one bothered to tell me until now."

"'Restless?'" Greg said, taking a sip of his beer. "I would have said you're being a dick."

Gabriel scoffed. "You could have said it years sooner, man. A few things would have made more sense."

Tom shrugged. "Guys don't talk about stuff like that. We drink our problems away."

"Here, here," Greg said, raising his glass.

Gabriel had been friends with Greg, Jeremy, and Tom since grade school. Friday nights were exclusively for the guys. They shot pool at the local bar for a few hours, sometimes played Darts, and always gave each other a tough time. There was no exception to their Friday nights short of medical emergencies or certain life events. Tom Anderson was the only one that was married so they had managed to miss very few nights.

They met most often at Spencer's Bar and Grill because it was fairly quiet and had a wide variety of local beers. They could sit in the back, away from the loud drunks, and Karen would serve them as long as they didn't get obnoxious.

"I'm coming!" Karen called, rushing over with a bottle for Gabriel and an extra she set on the table in Jeremy's spot. "I didn't forget you." She winked at Gabriel.

"How's it going, Karen?" he asked, feeling the tension in his shoulders lessen a bit.

"Mitch is driving me nuts," she said, laughing. "I can't wait until this weather warms up so all you boys can get outside and give us women a break."

"Here, here!" Greg said again, and the guys drank to that.

"Thanks, Karen," Gabriel, tipping his beer in her direction.

"Anytime, handsome."

Jeremy came up behind her, giving her a kiss on the cheek before he walked to his seat.

"You flirt," she scolded. "I'm old enough to be your-"

"Slightly older girlfriend." He grinned.

She blushed. "If I were fifteen years younger and not happily married, I would be another heartbroken notch on your belt, young man."

She left them to their beers.

"Let's play a game," Gabriel said to Greg, nodding toward the pool table.

They walked over to the old six-foot table that had been there as long as Gabriel could remember. Dropping coins into the slot, Greg released the balls and they both began setting them on the table. Greg lined them up in the rack, switching them until they were in the right order. Behind them, the others had come over and set up at the nearby table so they could watch.

"Your break," Greg said, shoving them forward, then back to make them tight. He pulled the rack off.

Gabriel chalked his cue and leaned over the table, lining up the shot. The equipment was old and worn, but he had been playing pool here since he was eight years old and the smell of the chalk and felt lining was as familiar to him as his mother's cooking.

He took his shot. The cue ball shot across the table and hit the group, scattering them in an ear-splitting cacophony. Balls were sent clacking into each other and thudding into pockets. After a moment of thuds, he said mildly, "Solids."

"Any big plans this weekend?" Jeremy asked as soon as the racket from the balls settled down.

Gabriel lined up another shot. "Nope."

The ball landed nicely in the corner pocket.

"Fuck." Greg took a drink of his beer.

Tom stretched his legs out, eyeing the placement of the pool balls. "We're taking the kids to Abby's parents."

Greg let out a string of expletives when Gabriel made another shot.

"Language!" Tom said in a disapproving tone.

Gabriel gave him a lopsided smile.

Greg watched another ball sink easily into a pocket. "Cocksucker. Speaking of which, how is Rachel?"

Preparing to take a drink, Gabriel set his beer bottle down, hard. He picked up his pool cue and studied the table.

Tom picked up a sugar packet and threw it at Greg. "You buy the next round."

"Shit. Sorry, man. I forgot."

Gabriel put so much force behind the next shot that the cue ball bounced off the edge of the table and almost hit Greg in the crotch. Greg yelped and scooted out of the way.

"I said I'm sorry!" he said.

Gabriel shrugged. "I guess I missed the shot."

"Greg?" Jeremy asked. "What are you doing this weekend?"

Greg was glaring at the pool table. "I'm going to meet Charity's parents."

The group grew silent. Glances were exchanged.

"Sorry, man," Tom said.

"No, it's a good thing," Greg said. "We're going to have dinner. I'm sure they'll love me."

He took a shot and missed. Gabriel began running the table again.

"What about you?" Gabriel asked Jeremy after a long, uncomfortable pause.

"I'm going skiing with... Jennifer or Julia... or maybe it's Savannah. I can't remember who I'm hooked up with right now."

Gabriel scoffed. Another ball slid gracefully into a side pocket.

"Dick," Greg complained halfheartedly.

Gabriel missed his next shot.

"Finally," Greg said.

Karen stopped at the table a few feet from the pool table. "Are you guys ready for refills?"

"I've got your refill right here, Karen," Jeremy grinned.

She burst out laughing.

"We'll take refills," Tom said, glaring at Jeremy. "And a double order of cheese curds, please."

"Coming up, sugar. Jeremy, you slut." She was still laughing as she walked away.

"Is there anyone you won't flirt with?" Gabriel asked, leaning back against the table while Greg took a shot.

Jeremy gave him a wry smile. "You're not a notch on my belt."

"Boundaries, man!" Greg said, groaning.

"'Boundaries?'" Tom said. "What the hell kind of talk is that?"

Greg cleared his throat. "Sorry. Charity says I should set some 'boundaries' in my... ah... interpersonal relationships."

Jeremy gave him a sideways glance, then pointed at Gabriel. "There's one. I haven't flirted with that crazy bi-"

"Hey!" Greg said. "Come on, she's my girlfriend. Speaking of which... I have to leave by ten tonight."

Tom, Gabriel, and Jeremy stared at him.

"What are you talking about?" Tom asked. "It's Friday night."

Greg shifted in his seat, scraping at the label on his beer bottle with his thumb nail. "I know, I know. Tonight, I have to cut it a little short. It's no big deal."

"The hell it isn't," Jeremy said. "You said Charity wasn't going to be an issue."

"Maybe she isn't the issue."

The table fell silent. Gabriel took a long drink of his beer, wishing for the first time on a Friday night that he was anywhere but with his friends. None of them liked Charity. She was always trying to drive a wedge between Greg and the rest of them. She was jealous of their friendship. She tried to control every aspect of Greg's life and each of them had tried to tell him as gently as they could. She used her psychology degree to manipulate people and Gabriel thought that was the worst kind of bitch.

Karen came over with a fresh round for everyone. "Looks like I'm a little late," she said, eyeing their empty bottles. She began handing out the new round.

"Not at all," Jeremy said. The humor had left his tone. "We're just drinking heavy tonight."

"Celebrating or lamenting?" she asked, collecting their empties.

"Every night's a celebration with you, sweetheart."

She noted his usual cockiness was not behind the comment and wondered what had suddenly changed the mood. Still, this group was her favorite tab on Friday nights. She tried to lighten the tension that had suddenly surrounded the area.

She swatted at Jeremy. "One day love's going to bite you in the butt, and I hope it gets a good chunk."

When they were alone again, Tom said, "I think I'll take off after this one. I'm not feeling very social tonight."

Jeremy nodded.

"I hear that," Gabriel agreed.

"Come on, you guys," Greg said. "You can still hang out after I leave. It doesn't have to ruin everyone's night."

"Fridays are about the guys," Tom said. "We've done this since we were kids camping out in Gabe's parents' backyard, before we were old enough to do anything else. If that's not important enough a tradition for you to keep, Greg, it does ruin everyone's night."

•　　•　　•　　•　　•

Something was not right.

Isabel couldn't quite put her finger on it. She played the first few chords on her guitar, trying to find where the problem was, humming the tune softly, but she still couldn't figure out what was bugging her about that particular part in the song she was writing. Was it the key she was playing it in, or was she unsatisfied with the lyrics?

She played the succession of keys without singing, tilting her head to listen carefully. The progression sounded okay. She thought. She played it again and was convinced the chords worked well together and worked in the key she was singing.

Next, she sang the lyrics without the music.

She was happy with the lyrics.

She started singing one line before the two that were giving her trouble, adding the music. When she reached the end of the third line, she winced, stopped playing.

"Damn it!" she said loudly. Then louder: "DAMN IT!"

The music wasn't going well with the lyrics, the melody, or the key she was singing in. She couldn't tell which, only that she was having an issue with one of the three.

"FUCK!"

She stood and walked to the guitar stand near the patio door. Setting her guitar roughly in its place, she crossed her arms and stared out at the twilight sky. She wished the evening was warmer so she could sit out on her pitiful excuse for a balcony and work on her song. Inspiration was always better when she was outside. Being stuck inside all winter had made her itchy, and what should have been a simple strum session to work out a kink was turning into an unsatisfying hair-pulling experience.

The soft trill of an old-fashioned rotary phone diverted her attention long enough to keep her from heaving her guitar through a window. Iz crossed to the coffee table and frowned down at the screen on her phone. Griffin had used her phone to take a selfie at the coffee shop last night. He then linked it in her phone so his smiling face would pop up with his phone number when he called her. He was grinning at her as her phone rang.

"Hello?"

"Do you feel better after our therapy last night?" he asked.

"Therapy?" Isabel knew she sounded ignorant, but her mind was still reeling. When he put his information in her phone, she hadn't actually expected him to call.

"The pillow fights. You've forgotten already? It was quite memorable for me."

"Whatever happened to people offering a greeting when they answer the phone? Is that a little too pleasant for today's culture? A little too appropriate?"

"Another rough day?" Amusement was obvious in his tone.

She walked back to the patio door. God, she felt caged.

"Yes. No. I'm fine. I'm working on a song and it's driving me bug shit. I can't figure out what's wrong with it. I just know it's wrong. Whatever. It's not your fault."

She was rambling but couldn't seem to stop herself.

"You need more pillow therapy, then. So soon. My God, woman, you're a hot mess."

She couldn't help it; she smiled. "It's so cute when you act like a grown up."

"Ooh, shots fired! What do you mean, you're working on a song?"

"It's not important. Did you call to invite me to another pillow fight? I think Target's going to call the police this time."

"I wanted to see how you're doing. Obviously, it's a good thing I called if you're frustrated so early after our first session. I need to devise a more aggressive plan of action."

Hearing her own laughter felt good. "It's going to take more than a few soft taps from a pillow with a monkey on it to knock out all the shit in my head."

"Challenge accepted."

Having someone to talk to, to vent her frustration instead of letting it fester, was foreign to her. The immediate relief made her feel giddy. Usually, she saved it all during the week and unleashed it on Gabriel on Sunday at their parent's house when they had a moment alone. Or she kept it to herself, not wanting to burden him with it. Griffin was just so damn easy to talk to. She ended up blurting everything she usually kept inside.

"Do you want to take a break from what you're doing and meet me somewhere?"

Isabel paused. "Where?"

"I don't know. Pick a place."

"Helga's House of Pain."

"Oh, my. You do have some frustrations to work out. Is that actually a place?"

Isabel snorted. "Not that I know of. At least not around here."

"Where do you usually hang out?"

"In my apartment. I don't go out much." She walked into her kitchen, wondering what she was going to have for dinner. Her appetite lately had dwindled down to nothing, but she knew she had to feed the machine. Opening random cupboards, she found nothing interested her. Microwave popcorn was her go-to. It was easy and light enough to eat while she read a book or wrote more on her song.

"Not even on Friday night?" Griffin was asking.

"Not even."

"Have you had dinner?"

"No."

"Do you want to?"

This sounds like an interrogation, Iz thought, almost giggling. "Sure... okay. As long as wherever we go isn't crowded."

"Are you craving a particular cuisine? Thai? Italian? Mongolian? American?"

"I don't like spicy, and I don't like big crowds. Other than that, I don't have a preference."

Thank God, she thought, closing her cupboard, and walking toward her coat. I can get dinner taken care of and have a few laughs with a nice guy. I don't have to think anym-

"Well, you say that now, but if I suggest a place, you won't like it, but you won't want to pick a place yourself, so we'll-"

"Griffin," Isabel snapped, clenching her teeth, and yanking her coat off the hanger in her closet, "Pick a place you know won't be too busy that serves a dish that won't shoot fire from my asshole if I eat it. Text me the address. I'll meet you there."

She pulled the phone away from her ear and hit the red button on her screen to hang up. As she was putting her coat on, the notification sound went off on her phone. Griffin had sent her an address. She copied it, opened her map app, and pasted it to get directions. The stoic voice of the GPS narrator began instructing her.

Isabel grabbed her keys.

• • • • •

Come here. I'll tell you a secret.

The whisper echoed through the room, causing Ava to look up from her paperwork and glance around her office for the source.

Come play with me.

Ava rubbed her eyes. How long had she been working on this document? She glanced down and saw she was still at the beginning of the document and only the first paragraph had red edit marks on it. The past forty-five minutes while she had been sitting here, she had completed one paragraph of work.

She barely remembered the time passing. Every part of her – mind, body, soul – felt as if she had been asleep and just woken. Yet her eyes had been open the entire time. They were dry, gritty. Her hand was resting to the side of her laptop, on the legal notepad she kept near for notes and questions for her clients as she worked. Apparently, she had been in the middle of writing down a question when she zoned out. The pen she used for notes remained in her hand. Sometime during her blackout, she had gripped it so tightly she had snapped it in half. A shard of the plastic was sticking out of her index finger. Dried blood circled the entry wound and dribbled down her finger.

Slowly, Ava opened her right hand. The pieces of pen moved with her, separating from itself, and following whichever finger the piece was sealed to with blood. She used her left hand to pull the fragment out of her finger, which made it start bleeding again. Looking down at her desk, she noticed something she had not noticed before – the legal pad was filled with red scribbling.

I'll tell you a secret I'll tell you a secret   I'll tell you a secret
I'll tell you a secret I'll tell you a secret   I'll tell you a secret
I'll tell you a secret I'll tell you a secret   I'll tell you a secret

The handwriting was not hers.

She tore the page off, crumpling it, and leaned over to toss it in her recycle bin. When she looked down, several yellow pages were already tossed haphazardly into the bin, almost filling it. She lifted out a couple sheets and saw the same red ink on each of the pages in handwriting that was not hers.

I'll tell you a secret

Each page was filled, front and back, with the same phrase, repeated. Ava had no recollection of the past forty-five minutes. The muscles in her right hand ached severely, and as she wrote she had held her red pen so hard that she broke it. Pieces of it had been embedded in her hand and she had not realized it until she came out of whatever stupor she had been in.

She tossed the rest of the pages into the recycle bin, the bits of pen into the garbage. Saving the full document on her laptop, Ava closed the program and shut down her computer. She made sure the pad of paper and coaster were neatly returned to their proper place on her desk. All writing utensils were returned to their stations. The laptop was set back, out of the way, and plugged into the docking station.

Tonight was Friday. She did not have to keep working on a project that was not due until the end of next week.

Lowering her head, she pressed her palms to her temples and instantly froze. Her fingers registered something odd; her hair was different. Something had felt off when she came out of whatever semi-consciousness she had been in, but she had attributed it to the state of mind she had been in. Now, she gingerly moved her fingers over her head, feeling the odd pattern her hair was in. A few strands hung down by her temples. The rest of it was bound, wrapped around her head.

Ava stood and walked to the half bath, flipping on the light, and standing in front of the mirror. Staring, she reached up and touched the sides of her head again.

Someone had styled her hair.

One long braid had been wrapped around her head, creating a crown-like effect.

Her ear was bleeding.

Ava was used to her ear bleeding; that happened anytime she visited The Interval. The braid was new. Who had paid her a visit while she was taking a hiatus?

She splashed water over her face. She scrubbed the dried blood off her ear, jaw, and hand. She was done thinking of this for now. Too much time had been wasted on wondering who had invaded her space and played with her hair.

And she did not have the energy to think about what it meant that she had possibly stepped outside herself for almost an hour and let someone else take her place.

She decided to run.

•　　•　　•　　•　　•

Griffin stood leaning against his car in his leather coat, his arms crossed over his chest. Isabel pulled up beside him – his Rover was hard to miss - and parked her tiny Malibu. Getting out of the car, she was struck again by how good-looking he was, even with his wind-ruffled hair. He had to have a girlfriend. Why the hell was he here with her?

"It's good to see you," he said, by way of greeting. He leaned in and pressed his mouth to hers. Shocked, Isabel's body stilled. It was a direct kiss, warm and firm, but he pulled back almost instantly and followed it up with a brief hug. Isabel was unsure how to react. What was that? A friendly greeting? Something like her family's hugs every Sunday? Surely it was simply a more intimate greeting than she was used to, nothing more. Even if she were to dream for a moment that she could ever land a guy like Griffin, she had met him yesterday. He hadn't kissed her last night or made any moves in that direction.

Unsure how to respond, she said simply, "H-hi."

For the first time since arriving, she looked around. She had been so focused on Griffin that she hadn't even paid attention to where he wanted her to meet him.

The diner was set back away from the street in a parking lot that had seen better days. Currently the lot had three other vehicles. The building looked like it could fit neatly into Griffin's Rover; it was small and square and only one level. Through the large glass windows, Iz could see three customers sitting inside. It was the kind of restaurant where you seated yourself and the cheap menus were always on the table between the napkin holder and condiment holders.

No other businesses were on the road. She had driven out of Madison to an unincorporated township she'd already forgotten the name of to get here. The diner was only a mile from an Interstate, so it was open 24/7. Truckers frequented the truck stop just off the Interstate but most of them preferred a home cooked meal to the fast-food chains connected the gas station.

"Sorry I'm late," she said, glancing around. "This place is in bum-fuck Egypt."

He grinned. "You wanted private. On Friday night around Madison, you have to travel a bit to miss the crowds. I found this place years ago when I needed some quiet late at night. Shall we?"

"We shall."

Inside, they hung their coats before Griffin led her to a corner booth. Isabel wanted to hug him. Corner booths offered more privacy. After they ordered, he settled back in the booth and studied her.

"What? Do I have static cling?" Iz ran a hand down her hair.

"You sounded snippy on the phone," he said, but he was smiling. When she looked confused, he added, "When I asked if you were sure about me picking the restaurant."

She took a drink of the ice water the waitress had brought when she came to take their order. "I didn't want to spend all night arguing on the phone. Pick a place and be done with it."

"What if you don't find something you liked here?"

Isabel snorted. "Every restaurant has a salad or toast. I can always find sustenance."

"Wow. In my experience, I nearly starve to death while I argue about where to go with a girlfriend. We decide to go out, I ask where she wants to go, she says she doesn't care – pick a place. So, I mention a place and she doesn't want to go there. So, I pick another place, and so on. Agreeing on a restaurant usually takes half an hour."

"Tell her you've decided, and she can join you or wait in the damn car," Isabel said. "Why do people put up with so much shit from each other?"

Griffin grinned.

She rested her chin on her hand, glancing around the restaurant. An older man was working on a crossword puzzle at the counter, nursing a cup of coffee. His mostly gray beard grew all the way down to his chest. Isabel wondered if he liked beards or if he just grew it during the Wisconsin winters as insulation.

One of the patrons had left just after she and Griffin sat down, a young black female with a laptop and a notebook, probably a college student. She appeared so elegant, her slender fingers jotting notes from her laptop occasionally, chewing on her lower lip. If Isabel had beauty like her, what would she do with it?

The waitress returned with two coffees and a small tin pitcher of milk. Isabel started doctoring hers. Griffin ignored his.

"So, is she sick or something? Is that why you're out with me instead?"

"Who?" He pulled out a napkin from the dispenser and dug in his shirt pocket for a black pen. Picking up one of the menus, which looked to be nothing more than a printed piece of paper cheaply laminated, he set the napkin on it at an angle and began to sketch.

"Your girlfriend. Why aren't you arguing with her about where to eat instead of sitting here with me?"

"I don't currently have one." His eyes were focused now, his hand steady and sure. Like Gabriel when he was designing furniture, his eyes took on a clarity and intensity while he worked, as if he were transported to another place. Isabel always loved watching Gabriel when he had that look in his eyes, and she unabashedly studied Griffin now, knowing he wasn't paying much attention to her.

"You just gave me an entire lecture about arguing with your girlfriend about where to eat. Who the hell were you talking about?" she asked.

Griffin glanced up at her absently before returning to his drawing. "I meant, you know, in the past. In general."

"So, you're bored, and I was available to kill a couple hours on a Friday. That's delicious."

The wry comment had an undertone of hurt, Griffin noted, but didn't let on that he caught it. He continued working, glancing at Isabel while her eyes darted around the restaurant. She masked insult under sarcasm, a deeper pain over an aloof veneer. He was utterly intrigued by her. Who had hurt her?

Whatever he was drawing was more important than their conversation. Isabel thought it was rude as hell. So was hanging out with her because he had nothing better to do. Iz didn't have a social life, but that didn't mean the time she had was worthless. She opened her mouth to say so when his voice stopped her.

"I wasn't bored. I wanted to see you again." He didn't seem as distracted as before.

That stopped her from ripping into him about ignoring her while he played Rembrandt. Unsure how to answer, she sat quietly, grateful when Griffin raised his head and studied the drawing a moment.

"Sorry," he suddenly said, making her jump. He set the menu down with a slap that made her jump again and held the drawing out to her. "I had to get that out of my system."

Isabel took the napkin, frowning. He had drawn her in black ink with her chin on her hand, her eyes a little sad, staring off into the distance. Every detail, down to strands of her hair and the stripes on her sweater, was in the exact right spot. He had done all this, included all those technicalities, in minutes. His ability took her breath away.

"Griffin," she said, "this is... amazing."

"Beautiful," he said. "Just like the subject."

She scoffed. The person in the drawing looked real enough to walk out of it and shake her hand. That person looked beautiful... like Isabel, but beautiful.

"Not hardly," she replied. "But you have enough talent to turn a real live ugly duckling into a swan on paper." She ran her index finger delicately over the ink. "Wow."

She was bent over the table as she studied it, so she didn't notice the flash of irritation flicker across his face.

"The detail is impressive. You even put in the little snag on the arm of my sweater." Her voice was filled with awe. Griffin liked the sound of her voice when she was so overwhelmed, so delighted. It was softer.

Reluctantly, she held it out to him.

"It's yours." Griffin finally added two packets of sugar to his mug and took a drink of his coffee.

"Really?" Her eyes lit up. Then she scowled. "You didn't sign it. What kind of artist are you?"

Amused now, he took the napkin back and signed his autograph in the loopy, artistic signature he used to sign all his art. When he handed it back, he swore he saw stars in Isabel's eyes.

The waitress made her rounds and refilled their coffee.

"Ballin'." Isabel added her milk and sugar to her coffee, staring at the sketch as she worked. "I'm going to frame it and hang it in my apartment. Sorry, I'm totally going stalker crazy on you."

"Not at all." He grinned. "It's flattering. I haven't had anyone so excited about my work in years. Most of what I do is design for businesses, so I don't get back to drawing as much as I'd like to."

"Have you ever sold anything just as art? Instead of as a graphic designer?" Isabel asked, digging in her purse. She frowned as she pulled up items, set them aside. No makeup, Griffin noticed, no mirrors. Just her phone, wallet, lip balm, a pen.

Finally, she pulled out a small, worn notebook.

"You mean a painting or a drawing instead of branding? Sure."

As he watched her slide the napkin between two blank pages of the notebook so it wouldn't get wrinkled, he saw handwriting filled a good portion of the worn book. She gently set it back in her purse before tossing the rest of the items in carelessly.

"I don't usually do that in the middle of a conversation," he said. "It's incredibly rude. Sorry about that. You looked so calm for just a moment, and happy, and I wanted to capture that."

"Normally, I would agree it's rude," Isabel said. She waited while the waitress brought their food out, asked if they needed anything else, and disappeared into the back again. "But I understand needing to get creativity down on paper as soon as possible."

Griffin added salt and pepper to his rib eye, raising his eyebrows. "Speaking from experience?"

He wondered about the notebook in her purse.

"My brother has some artistic talent. He has to do sketches for clients."

She set aside the sour cream and salsa that came with the quesadilla appetizer she'd asked to have brought with the meal and picked up a triangle.

Griffin chewed a piece of steak and watched her take a small bite of her quesadilla. When she glanced up at him, he raised his eyebrows again.

"Don't." Isabel took a drink of coffee.

"Don't what?"

"I'm not one of them, so don't."

"One of them?" Griffin continued to eat and watch her while Iz squinted at him.

"You think I'm one of those women who refuses to eat in front of men because I'm worried you'll think I'm a pig. I'm not. I don't give two shits what you think of my eating habits."

He almost choked on the bite in his mouth and had to take a drink of water. "You only ordered an appetizer."

"And I probably can only eat half of it. So what?"

"Are you worried about paying for it? I invited you, it's only polite for me to pay."

Isabel dropped the triangle on her plate and wiped her hands on her napkin. "It has nothing to do with paying, although I can pay for myself." She took another drink of coffee, followed it with a sip of water. "Eating is a necessity, so I do it. The truth is, if scientists could invent a pill that gave people all the nutrition a body needs and none of the extra shit like trans-fat and cholesterol that it doesn't need, I'd rather take it. Having to stop what I'm doing and take the time to eat is annoying as fuck. It's a chore."

Amusement lit his eyes as he listened to her.

She sighed. "What? Why are you looking at me like that?"

"I've never heard anyone describe eating in quite that way before. I like listening to you. You have a beautiful voice."

"You should hear me sing on Saturday nights," she murmured absently, picking up a piece of quesadilla and taking a huge bite to make it go away faster. She was already tired of chewing.

His eyes narrowed. "You sing in public?"

Isabel froze, her mouth full. Shit. "Mmm hmmm."

Still chewing, Isabel looked everywhere but at him. Damn it. She felt as if her entire body had been set on fire; she was blushing so hard. She hadn't meant to let that slip. Singing at The Raz wasn't something she told people about; she did it for fun, and for practice. She did it in front of strangers.

"Do you write your own songs?"

She swallowed, hard. "Sometimes."

"That's how you understand getting creativity down on paper when it strikes."
Feeling like her throat was full of ash, she gulped down water. Nodded.

"Does that notebook in your purse have your work?"

Her eyes were large, the eyes of prey caught in a corner. Griffin watched them dart away from him and back again before she nodded. She wasn't a sulky artist, he thought, but she didn't like people knowing she was creative.

Intriguing, he thought again.

"I would love to hear you sing," he said. "You sing tomorrow?"

"Yes. Every other Saturday at The Raz, I play guitar and sing."

"Can I join you?"

"Oh. Well. I wasn't expecting you to say that." She took a drink of coffee.

Those eyes were studying her intently, hopeful she would agree. How the hell could she say no to those wonderful golden eyes? Shit.

"Okay." Her coffee was cold now, but she guzzled the rest of it anyway. If only it had Bailey's liquor in it.

"This is marvelous," he said, grinning. "I can't wait."

Unable to continue eating, Isabel pushed her plate back. She no longer had an appetite.

•　•　•　•　•

Something stirred in the woods to his left. The rustling was loud in the surrounding stillness as Gabriel paused on the trail. He could see his breath and remaining motionless wasn't helping his already cold hands.

A possum hobbled onto the trail. Gabriel watched the odd creature make its way across the dirt at its own slow pace, staying silent so he wouldn't startle it. In the darkness he couldn't make out its iconic hairless tail, hand-like feet, and unattractive face, but that possum waddle was unmistakable.

Gabriel waited several seconds after the animal had disappeared into the woods on the other side of the trail before he continued walking. He flexed his fingers to promote blood flow. Tonight, he should have still been knocking back a few beers at Spencer's, not freezing his ass off in the woods, trying to take his mind off his friend's idiocy.

Greg's insistence on dating Charity was pissing him off. Greg had witnessed her treat every single one of his friends like shit, yet he chose her over his friends. Twenty-odd years of friendship meant absolutely nothing over a piece of ass. On top of that, she didn't treat him any better, so why the hell was he following her like a damn puppy? He had no respect for himself or his friends.

He was so deep in thought that he didn't notice the figure walking toward him. Head down, fists clenched in anger, he didn't notice when the figure stop abruptly a few feet away. An owl hooted, startling him. He glanced around and his heart galloped.

Ava had stopped at the side of the trail and was staring at him. Her hair was pulled back from her face in a ponytail. Instead of wearing a coat, she was wearing layers that made her torso appear thicker than it was. The top layer was a sweatshirt.

Gabriel hadn't heard her approach.

"Hi," he managed, suddenly feeling incredibly shy. He tucked his hands in the pockets of his coat.

"Hello." Though her voice was soft, her gaze sharpened when he put his hands in his pockets, as if she were waiting for him to pull out a weapon. Gabriel took his hands back out to make her feel more at ease.

"Out for a jog?" His mind was scrambling to find something halfway intelligent to say. He wanted to hear her voice and be in her company.

"I am training."

That's a strange thing to say, he thought. He remembered the other night when someone had run circles around him off trail. "Do you do that a lot? Train here?"

The way she studied him was uncanny, as if she was sizing him up, expecting him to attack her. Those distinct gray eyes seemed to catalog every detail of his body and every nuance of their surroundings.

"Every night."

"Someone was running in the woods the other night when I was jogging. Wednesday. Was that you?"

She nodded without arrogance.

"I know guys in the military who aren't as fast as you."

Gabriel walked toward her and pretended not to notice when she tensed. He noticed her hair wasn't just in a ponytail; she had done something to it at the temples that he couldn't quite see clearly in the dark. Those strange eyes studied him.

She remained silent.

"I would like to buy you a cup of coffee sometime," he said, without realizing he was going to say it.

"I am financially capable of purchasing my own coffee."

That made him smile, just a slight curve of the edges of his lips. She found that appealing and her interest disconcerted her.

"That's not why I want to do it." Gabriel's hands were getting chilly, but he didn't want the conversation to end. He flexed his fingers and noticed Ava moved ever so slightly forward, her eyes sharpening. Did she think he had a weapon on him? What happened in this woman's past that she thought everyone was an enemy?

She frowned. "Then why?"

The conversation was so strange. Ava seemed truly perplexed that he would want to buy her coffee for any reason other than she couldn't afford it on her own.

"Because..." He found himself baffled. How could he explain his interest if she wasn't picking up on it? A woman as beautiful as her must have been hit on before now. "Because I want to."

She tilted her head, studying him. Her confusion toward him seemed genuine. "I need to finish my training."

"Knock yourself out."

She walked slowly past him. He caught the scent of her, a light hint of vanilla, green tea, and sweat, and found it appealing. As she started up the trail, her head was tilted slightly as if she was listening for something. After a moment she turned back.

"Alright."

"Alright?" He raised one eyebrow. Her eyes jerked to that one eyebrow in fascination.

"You may purchase a cup of coffee for me sometime."

"What are you doing tomorrow morning?"

"I will be ready for coffee by seven o'clock."

"Seven o'clock. Where do you want to meet?" Seven was early for him, but he had a feeling she was worth losing a couple hours' sleep.

"There is a cafe on the way out of Langdon called Willows."

"I know it. I'll see you there at seven."

"Yes."

She began jogging up the trail.

Gabriel watched her until she wound around a bend, out of sight.

•   •   •   •   •

"So, what's the weirdest thing you've ever eaten?"

Isabel thought about that as she used her fork to push her quesadilla around on her plate. Stabbing the tortilla, she said, "Calamari from the Olive Garden. Not very exciting. How about you?"

Griffin added butter and sour cream to his baked potato. "Gan guo tu tou."

"I thought they found a cure for that."

He laughed. "It's rabbit head."

The waitress made her rounds and topped off their coffee.

Isabel covered her mouth with her hand. The drink of coffee she was trying to swallow had almost flown out. "Just the head? That seems wasteful."

"It's popular in China. I never thought about what they do with the body."

She watched him devour the steak and potato. How the hell could he eat so much? He was built like Ichabod Crane, but he was shoveling the food in like a homeless dog. She glanced at his covered arms, which were slight but toned. Not really Ichabod, but not Dwayne Johnson, either.

"What did it taste like?" Iz asked, not sure if she wanted to know. She adjusted on the bench, slid a foot under her butt to get more comfortable.

"Quite a bit like duck. The brain is sort of like the yolk of a hardboiled egg."

"What did Bugs Bunny ever do to you?"

Griffin grinned. "It was offered to me, so I tried it. I couldn't get past the presentation; the teeth are still in it. Sorry. I probably shouldn't have mentioned that."

Iz shrugged. "It'll take more than headless Thumper to make me sick."

He smirked. "I probably would have preferred calamari at the Olive Garden."

"Bambi will forever be traumatized by your poor life choices."

She was a riot, he thought, blurting out whatever came to mind.

"Are you originally from Wisconsin? Does your family live in the area?" Griffin set his empty plate to the side.

She nodded. "My parents have a house out in Langdon that's been in the family for years. My brother bought a house out there a few years ago. My sister and I live here in Madison. Are you close with your family? Any siblings?"

"Not really. My parents travel a lot, so I only see them three or four times a year."

"Bummer."

He shrugged. "I can't miss what I've never known. Are you close with your family?"

Isabel fidgeted with the rim of her coffee cup. "With my brother, Gabriel. We tell each other everything. Not really with my oldest sister or parents. My dad's okay, but Mom and my sister are close. They tend to push everyone else out when they're in the middle of one of their many dramas."

Appearing suddenly, the waitress asked if they need any boxes as she topped off their coffees. Isabel nodded.

"Who was the last person to die in your family?" she asked when they were alone again. "Close enough that you attended the funeral?"

"My dear sweet Grandma Mavis, may she rest in peace." Griffin put his hands together as if in prayer and rolled his eyes upward.

"That blows."

"She was 95 and ready to go. I was closer to her than my parents. It was a couple years ago. Why are you single?"

This time Isabel did spit out her coffee – all over table. Droplets flew left and right.

"Shit!" Isabel hissed, fighting with the napkin dispenser to wipe up the mess. "Sorry. I'm an idiot."

"No worries." He smiled at her, watching with amusement as she moved plates and cups around. Griffin helped her, stacking dishes they were done with and setting them at the edge of the table. He set the one with the quesadilla aside.

His grin widened. "You didn't answer my question."

"How do you know I'm single?" She dropped the wet wad on top of the dirty dishes and pulled out a couple more napkins, dipping them in her water. Taking extra care and avoiding looking at him, she wiped the coffee off her hands.

"Because you're here with me instead of out with him."

"I can have male friends whether I'm dating or not." She sighed. "Fine. I'm single."

Isabel swallowed. Tossing the rest of the napkins onto the dirty dishes, she leaned against the back of the booth with her coffee. She tried not to stare at the way his eyes always seemed to be smiling, even when his mouth wasn't.

"I don't like crowds. Staying home doesn't give me much opportunity to meet people."

"It's my luck then that we both needed groceries when we did," he said, raising his coffee cup in a toast. "Is that all?"

"I'm kind of... I don't connect well with people. They want to talk about their jobs, or new shoes, or football. That shows no more depth of character than a tomato can. I want to ask questions that tell me their story."

Griffin was watching her thoughtfully. "Asking me about the weirdest thing I've ever eaten tells you my story?"

"You asked me that first," she reminded him, finishing her coffee, and setting her cup at the edge of the table. "And my head is always wondering random things. But eating Thumper's head tells me you travel and aren't afraid to try new things."

"Interesting."

"What about you? Why don't you have women falling all over you?" she asked to distract herself. She used her spoon to grab some ice. Her mouth was dry despite the coffee she had been drinking.

"Women do seem to love the Australian accent," he admitted. "But I've avoided latching onto anyone in a serious way. A good portion of people out there are really shallow."

"Yes, they are." Isabel could attest to that.

"I'm sure I'll know when the right one comes along."

Hours had passed as they sat talking. She glanced at the clock over the coffee machine and was startled to see it was nearing one in the morning. There hadn't been a lull in the conversation, an awkward moment, any point that she felt anxious or claustrophobic. Having a conversation with Griffin came so naturally. That never happened with her.

"I've kept you out all night again." Griffin tugged lightly on the sleeve of her sweater.

"What?" She startled.

"You just yawned."

"Did I?" She hadn't realized. She hoped she at least had the decency to hide it behind her hand. "I'm sorry. I'm not bored."

"Are you going to be okay to drive home?"

"Um..." She glanced around, trying to get her bearings. "Yeah, I think so."

"You're going to have to do better than that." Griffin picked up his fob, hit the remote start to warm up Rover. "It's a long drive back to Madison."

"I'll take an Uber," she said, smiling. She drew out the u, her lips forming into a circle and stretching out from her face.

Griffin laughed. "I can give you a ride and we can pick up your car tomorrow morning."

She yawned again, keeping her mouth closed this time and covering her mouth with the back of her hand. Her eyes watered. "I don't like having to depend on other people."

"I've noticed. No point paying for an Uber – if they even come this far out. I'm already warming up the car, so it'll be nice and toasty when you get in."

She was too tired to argue.

He paid for the meal. Isabel took her quesadilla and they walked to the hallway where they'd hung their coats. Griffin helped her into hers.

"I talked to you more tonight that I usually do in a month," she said, her head feeling like it was full of helium.

"I'm a good listener," he said easily, holding the door for her. "Anytime."

She exhaled ice. Even with her gloves and hat on, the bitter cold surprised her. They hurried to Griffin's Rover and climbed into warmth and comfort. Isabel held her hands to her cheeks for a moment. It didn't take long for the heater to warm her up.

Isabel gave him her address to put in the GPS on his phone. She didn't remember much more until she was drifting up from semi-consciousness. Griffin was gently shaking her shoulder.

"Hey. We're here."

She had rested her chin on her hand during the drive so she would startle herself awake if her head became unbalanced. Completely falling asleep would have been unwise since she hardly knew Griffin. Several times during the ride, she jerked alert. Now she raised her head and picked up her purse. She wanted to bury herself under the blankets and pass out.

Griffin opened the passenger door, almost making her yelp. She hadn't realized he'd already gotten out of the vehicle. He held his hand out. When Iz took it and stepped out, she stumbled a little and he caught her by the waist with his other hand.

"Okay?" he asked, setting her purse back on her shoulder.

She nodded. Her eyelids were weighed down with lead ingots. "I'll see you tomorrow at The Raz." She was so tired she was mumbling. With a hearty pat to his shoulder, she started toward her building. "Thank you."

"Which flat do you live in?" he asked, opening the door.

"What?"

"Sorry; my mum's influence. What's your apartment number?"

"3F. I can manage now."

"Are your keys in your purse?"

She felt the pockets of her coat. "In my pockets." Jangling them in front of his face, she yawned loudly.

"Don't wake the neighbors," he snickered, helping her into the elevator and pushing the button to close the door.

Isabel pushed the button for her floor, dropping the keys. When she knelt to pick them up, she put her hand on his leg for support. She kept her hand against him on her way back up to make sure the dizziness didn't take over. The upward motion of the elevator made her feel like she was drugged.

The last time she had stayed out too late was years ago when she and Gabriel had finished a twenty-four pack of beer at Hayden's grave. They had walked back to Gabriel's house, and she passed out on his couch, too drunk and drained to change out of her clothes or get a blanket. Gabriel hadn't made it to his bedroom; he ended up in the doorway between the dining room and kitchen, a rag in one hand and a bottle of cleaner in the other. Apparently, he had just cleaned something up when he passed out. Neither he nor Isabel could remember what the mess he had to clean up was.

Griffin unlocked the flat for her. He shuffled Iz inside and tugged on her hand just inside the door so she wouldn't keep walking.

"Are you coherent enough to lock the door when I leave?" He handed her the keys and held onto her hand.

Yawning again, Isabel wiped her bloodshot eyes. "I'm good." She smiled. "Thanks for listening to me ramble."

"I like listening to you ramble. See you tomorrow?"

She nodded. "I start singing at nine. I try to be there by... eight thirty to make sure my guitar's tuned and I have an idea what I'm playing. I guess you don't have to be there that early, but-"

"We'll figure it out tomorrow when you'll remember what we plan. I'll text you tomorrow morning about your car." Grinning, Griffin looped his arm around her and gave her a hug and a quick kiss. "Good night, Isabel. Lock the door."

"Good night."

She stood as she was a moment, blinking.

"Lock the door behind me, Isabel."

He closed it and waited until he heard the lock engage.

•　•　•　•　•

CHAPTER THREE

"Uhhh."

That was all Isabel could manage just before seven o'clock on a Saturday morning. The second ring of her cell phone brought her just enough out of sleep to react. Flailing her arm to the side, her hand finally found her cell phone and snatched it off the bedside table. She fumbled it, dropped it, and dragged herself over to the side of the bed to pick it up off the floor. She didn't bother trying to see who was calling through her sleepy, half-slit eyes. She tapped her index finger repeatedly on the screen.

"What do you want, douche flute?!" she snarled into the phone. Her voice sounded like sandpaper scraping across a metal file; her throat hurt even worse.

"Did I knock you up, mate?" The mild voice on the other end of the line infuriated her.

"Since I haven't had sex in over three years, I highly doubt that. Who is this and what the fuck do you want?"

"My apologies. I forgot that means something different in America. Did I wake you up?"

"Yes. Start talking." The fog wasn't lifting yet. She couldn't place the voice. Her only interest in doing so was to pulverize the person responsible for interrupting her sleep so early. Whoever it was would pay.

"Bloody hell... you're as cross as a frog in a sock. I don't want to bother y-"

"You're already bothering me. Speak!" she barked. She was still lying sideways on her bed and her head was hanging over the side. To talk, she had to raise her head, so her chin wasn't smashed against the mattress. Raising her head took more effort than she cared for.

"I thought we might get together this morning, maybe have breakfast. Or coffee."

"Coffee," she croaked, the only word that sounded appealing. The fog was finally clearing, allowing some of the pieces to come together. The voice finally made sense. The accent. "Fuck. Griffin?"

"Yeah." She heard laughter in his voice. "Who'd you think it was?"

"I can't really think when I get woken up at the ass crack of dawn. What time is it?"

"Just about seven."

"Holy balls." She lifted her body with one arm, rolling until she could flop down on her back and stare at the ceiling. "It's too God damn early in the morning." She dropped the phone and rolled over.

"I can ring you back later, if you'd prefer." His voice was distant since her phone lay behind her now. "Hello?"

His accent was starting to break through the mush, stirring her. She rolled back, picked up the phone.

"I'm going to unlock my door and text you my address. If I'm awake by the time you get here, we can go to breakfast."

She hung up without waiting for a reply. Dragging herself out of the comfort of her bed was brutal, but she unlocked the door as she texted him the address. She snuggled back into bed and let the comforter swallow her.

Dreams floated just beyond her reach. She didn't remember anything memorable about them, just that she was sleeping deep and content when she became partially aware of something brushing against her arm. At first, she reached up and scratched at it absently. When it happened again, the touch was slightly firmer, so it didn't tickle so much as entice.

Letting out a little moan, Isabel rolled onto her back. Something from her dream swirled in her conscience. An image, a sound. She couldn't quite catch it.

Griffin watched Isabel and grinned. A fan of dark blonde hair spread away from her face, splayed on the pillow. Forcing himself to stop staring, he touched her shoulder, gave it a gentle shake.

She moaned again. Her eyes remained closed. Her fingers began to twitch.

"Isabel," he said gently, trying not to laugh. "Time to wake up."

Isabel frowned in her sleep.

Griffin rubbed his hand up and down her arm. "Isabel."

She lifted a hand, rubbed her eye. Then her arm relaxed slightly, her fist still on her eye, her elbow in the air. Her arm hovered for a second or two and then fell like lead against her chest. She grunted.

Unable to hide a laugh, Griffin shook her shoulder a little harder. "Isabel," he said, more insistent. "Time for coffee."

Isabel's eyes sluggishly opened. She let out a string of curses when she saw Griffin sitting on the edge of her bed and scooted back, pulling the blankets up to her chest.

"Christ." Closing her eyes, she rubbed her palms over them. She squinted at him. "Why the fuck... Who gets up this early in the morning?"

"Millions of people." He poked at her. She kicked at him, but it was futile; her foot was buried under a mountain of bedding. "Well, anyway... good morning."

She grunted as a greeting. "Did you even try knocking on my door?" she asked, running a hand through her hair.

"Of course. You sleep like a coma patient. I assume you said you would unlock the door because it was okay to come in. Did I overstep?"

"No. I'm bitchy when I first wake up." Bitchy was putting it mildly. She wanted the fires of hell to punish all those who bothered her this early.

"You're also daft. You texted me your address, but I knew it from last night."

"Right," she mumbled. Trying to get her mind to wake up, she raised her hands over her head and stretched, tilting left and right slightly. She kept her mouth closed as she yawned.

"Okay. Okay. I'm... conscious. Give me a few minutes." She threw the blankets back but remembered she was only wearing a tee shirt and underwear. Instantly she drew them up to her chest again. "I need to get dressed."

Wiggling his eyebrows, Griffin stood and started toward the door. At least he got a glimpse of those lovely legs out of the deal, even if they ended up not going to breakfast. "Can I make some coffee for you?"

"I can wait until we figure out breakfast." She thought that was damn altruistic of her. "Unless you need some now."

The sun was too damn bright. What the hell was it doing awake this early, anyway? It wasn't even eight o'clock yet. Isabel walked to the curtains and yanked one to the side, so it overlapped the other, closing off the thin streak of sunlight it had been letting in.

Fucking sun.

She moved around her room, getting jeans and underwear from her dresser and a shirt from the closet. Sitting on the edge of the bed, she somehow managed to get dressed with a minimal amount of swearing. She ran a brush through her hair and glowered at it for being straight and unimaginative.

Griffin was sitting at her tiny kitchen table when she emerged carrying her shoes. He'd draped his coat over the back of the chair and was wearing a brown thermal Henley shirt that brought out the color of his eyes. He gave her a smile as she sat across from him.

"What's a better time to ring you in the morning?" he asked.

"Cheerful morning people bug me to fuck and gone. I'll work on it." Leaning over, she slid her shoes on and began the meticulous chore of tying them.

"You're so cute when you're half awake."

"Fuck off." But she managed a small smile. Slowly, she was thawing out. Finished with her shoes, she sat up. "So, breakfast. You want to go somewhere?"

"We don't have to, if it buggers up your entire schedule."

Now she gave him an authentic entertained smile and mimicked his voice. "Oh, it so buggers up my entire schedule."

He poked her arm. "Are you mocking me?"

"Every chance I get." She ran a hand through her hair, glancing around her kitchen. "Let me brush my teeth and I'll be ready."

•   •   •   •   •

Ava was prompt, of course.

When Gabriel pulled into the parking lot of Willow's, Ava's SUV was already parked and empty. He found her standing just inside the door, waiting for him.

She's an odd one, he thought, not for the first time. She smelled like a forest just after a fresh snowfall.

"Good morning," he said, pulling off his gloves.

"Good morning."

"Shall we?" He motioned toward the counter.

She stayed where she was, indicating she wanted him to go first.

Gabriel raised an eyebrow but walked ahead toward the counter, feeling rather rude. The early morning geezer crowd was chatting near one of the windows. A group of middle-aged women in yoga pants was sitting to the right of the door, each one talking in animated fashion. Gabriel was glad the conversations weren't too loud; he wanted to be able to hear Ava when she spoke.

"Welcome to Willow's," the young man behind the counter said. His name tag read Marco. "What can I get you?"

Gabriel stepped aside and turned to Ava. She took a step forward and a little to the right so she could put some distance between her and Gabriel.

"Hey, Ava." Marco smiled as he recognized her.

"Hello."

"You want your usual?"

She nodded.

"Regular coffee for me," Gabriel added. "Both for here."

"Coming up," Marco said, punching in the order on the iPad. He rattled off the total and went to get a mug while Gabriel pulled out his wallet. When he came back, he set the mug on the counter and took Gabriel's card.

"Thanks, man." Gabriel turned to Ava. "Do you want to find a seat and I'll bring the drinks?"

She started walking toward a booth at the back, her strides long and confident. Gabriel watched her walk to the last booth, farthest from the front door, settled against the wall. She began unzipping her coat. He noted that she sat with her back against the wall, facing the rest of the dining area. No other patrons were close, and he had a feeling that was the point of her choosing that booth.

"Here's the venti mocha with no whip," Marco said, setting it on the counter. He hooked his finger. "Coffee is on that table. Each urn is labeled. The tables and booths have creamer and sugar."

"Thank you."

Gabriel chose a strong brew for himself. He put a spoon in both his and Ava's drink and brought them over to the table. Sitting across from her, he set her drink in front of her.

"Thank you."

He pulled off his coat and tossed it into the booth beside him before sitting down.

Ava reached for the sweetener caddy at the same time as Gabriel. Their fingers almost brushed against each other. She jerked back as if electrocuted. He slid the caddy toward her so she could use it first.

"What would have happened?" he asked.

She frowned, pulling out raw sugar. Her eyes were so direct. He had never known anyone to gaze so candidly at him before. And that unique shade of gray, so metallic they were like steel.

"If we had touched, what are you afraid would have happened?"

"I am not afraid of anything."

"Call it whatever you like." He tore open a sugar packet. "You just did everything you could to keep us from bumping into each other."

"I do not like to be touched."

"That's sad," he said with so much sincerity she paused in the middle of pouring sugar into her coffee.

"Why?"

"Every living being should be touched. Studies have shown babies, puppies, plants, adults, all benefit from physical contact."

"I have done fine without it." She looked at him doubtfully.

"Is that so?" His tone was curious. He reached slowly across the table. She put her hands up, close to her chest, in a 'don't touch' gesture. The doubt was gone from her eyes, replaced with determined caution. "May I?"

He kept his hand half curled but relaxed, hovering halfway across the table. His palm was turned up slightly to show he meant no harm. Slowly, she lowered her hands until they were flat on the table. Her eyes never left his as she cautiously reached out to him with her left hand.

Gabriel lightly touched his palm to the back of her hand, keeping his fingers straight. She was trembling, he noticed. From fear? Anticipation? Was it so hard for her to relinquish control?

He kept his movements slow and easy. His hand closed over hers and rolled it over, so it was palm up. Rubbing his thumb over her palm, he massaged the muscles, working the tension out of her. He worked for several seconds, taking his time, allowing her to relax at her own pace.

"No matter how disciplined you are," he said in a conversational tone, "your body benefits from contact. That's just how we're built."

As he continued moving his hand over her palm, Ava started to move her fingers just a little against his wrist. Experimenting. Curious.

Gradually, he slowed the massage and pivoted his hand slightly, so they were palm to palm with his hand skimming hers. Ava was concentrating on their hands as if she were watching an experiment, intent and curious, as if she had never experienced this kind of contact before. Her long fingertips moved, exploring Gabriel's hand.

Her eyes were focused on their touching hands as if she was just as surprised by her actions as he was. In the cafe lighting they had looked almost silver earlier. Now they looked black. Her pupils were slowly expanding.

She abruptly yanked her hand back.

"Your body was reacting positively to it," he said, sitting back in the seat. "It's the nature of every living thing. There's nothing wrong with it."

She leveled her gaze at him. "I do not like to be touched."

Your body said otherwise, he thought, but didn't press the issue.

"I won't touch you again without your permission."

"I will not give it."

They were silent as they both added more sugar to their drinks. Gabriel used the time to study her, trying not to be obvious but certain she knew exactly what he was doing. Those eyes never stopped taking in everything around her.

Every move she made was graceful. Her slender hands wasted no time or space accomplishing what she wanted done.

When her coffee was sweetened to her liking, she looked at him silently.

Her eyes were unwavering. She drank her coffee and studied him without apprehension. Gabriel didn't think she would mind if they were silent during their entire visit.

He said the first thing that came to his mind.

"Do you own dogs?"

"No."

"You go to the dog park, but you don't have any dogs?"

"I use the trails and woods for exercise."

Like he did, he thought. Whether he had his parent's dogs or not, he used the park for jogging.

"You exercise a lot."

Ava said nothing to this. She took a sip of her coffee, her eyes flickering around the cafe.

Gabriel stirred his coffee nonchalantly. "So, you don't own dogs. Do you like them?"

"Yes."

"Maybe we could meet at the park on a Saturday."

"We were there yesterday."

He gave her an amused smile, just a slight curve of the right side of his lips. "I mean, to go for a walk with my parent's dogs. I pick them up Saturday afternoons."

"I do not walk."

"You hop like a rabbit?"

She gave him an incredulous look. Not big on humor, obviously. Because she had no sense of humor or because she didn't understand it?

"You shouldn't take life so seriously, Ava. So... what? You jog?" Getting information from her, even simple hobbies she enjoyed, was like drilling through cement using a wooden spoon.

Unsettled, Ava had to force herself to focus on the question. The sound of him saying her name had made her stomach feel funny; tense and loose and jumpy all at once. And he was unpredictable; his eyes showed great sadness, yet he easily slid into humor as if it was just as comfortable for him. He confused her.

"I use the terrain to run, climb, jump. It is training."

"Training for what? Do you run marathons?"

She shifted impatiently in her seat. "Dogs do not ask questions."

"How do you get to know someone if you don't ask questions?"

"People lie. If I have any inclination to get to know someone, his actions tell me who he is."

His left eyebrow shot up with a prominent arch. Ava's eyes darted to his eyebrow and widened. Her obvious curiosity at his ability amused him. It was a silly habit he and Isabel had taught themselves to do as young children. They'd watched a movie where the main actor did it and thought it hilarious. From then on, they practiced it until they perfected it and it became habit.

"Why agree to have coffee with me if you have no interest in getting to know me?" he asked Ava.

"I was coming here to have coffee whether you were here or not." Yet her attention had focused entirely on his lifted eyebrow. He kept it lifted a few seconds longer. Something about him intrigued her, he could tell.

"You can ask me something."

"If I want to know something about you, I'll touch-" She froze, the fingers on her coffee mug suddenly rigid. She glanced around the cafe as if trapped. "What are the names of your parent's dogs?"

"The black lab is Ozzie, and Maya is a Siberian husky. Is that really something you want to know?"

She shrugged. She knew their names already, but she was fumbling as she tried to fake her way through an acceptably normal conversation. Obviously, he knew her question about the dogs was shallow. How was she supposed to ask questions and pretend not to know the answers?

"Do you want to know why I asked to buy you a cup of coffee?"

Her gaze sharpened. "Yes."

That got her attention. He smiled. "You're suspicious of someone wanting to buy you a cup of coffee. That makes me wonder why. You're an attractive female with an excellent body. Any guy would be dying to introduce himself, buy you a drink at a bar-"

"I do not go to drinking establishments."

"-or a cup of coffee," he amended smoothly. "Yet it makes you very suspicious. Why is that?"

"People do not offer gifts or acts of kindness for free."

"That's a cynical way to look at things. Do you think I offered to buy you a five-dollar cup of coffee because I want something from you?"

"I do not know why you asked. I cannot see it..." She frowned, rubbed her forehead.

"Not everyone is out for himself."

The look she gave him told him she didn't believe that for a minute.

"You're a beautiful person, yet you feel no need to draw attention to it," he said softly. Her head whipped up and her eyes studied his. "No makeup, no perfume, no clothing that accents your feminine qualities. You don't give a damn if someone finds you attractive. You're satisfied to be on your own. I'm very curious to get to know you. That's why I asked if I could buy you a cup of coffee."

Despite her convictions, she was relieved that he spoke plainly to her without pretense. When he looked at her, it wasn't with the hunger she had seen from so many other men. The odd feeling that jolted through her when he touched her hand, the mix between a slap and a rush of heat, had felt both exhilarating and unsettling.

"Alright," she stated. He raised that eyebrow. That fascinated her as well, how just the one rose as if it had a mind of its own. "I accept your companionship."

He smiled, and she found she liked his smile, too. It was barely there, just a slight upward curve of the right side of his mouth. Ava found she enjoyed how simple the smile was; most people overindulged and grinned widely or laughed too loud. Life was full of overindulgences that sometimes made living too distracting. Gabriel smiled appropriately, quietly, she thought; just a curve of the lips to show amusement, nothing more.

That she found him pleasant company alarmed her.

"You say the strangest things," Gabriel said. "When I walked in here, you wanted me to go to the counter first. Why is that?"

"I do not like people directly behind me."

"Is that why you sit with your back to the wall?"

"Yes."

"Why don't you like people behind you?"

Something changed in her eyes. They went from neutral to alert instantly.

"Because they have the advantage if they are my enemies."

"Are you expecting an attack?"

"Always."

Gabriel glanced at the people left in the cafe. The geezers had left, leaving a couple women from the yoga class and a young man with ear buds in, bobbing his head to music. Gabriel didn't think anyone in the place would pose much of a threat. He decided to let that go for now.

"What are you training for at the dog park? Do you compete in races or run marathons?"

Her upper lip raised the slightest bit. "You people and your petty competitions." She sipped her coffee.

He laughed. "Okay, you don't compete. But you train."

"I survive."

He wanted to ask her more, so much more, but she was tiring from talking so much. If he pushed her too hard, she might stop talking altogether and refuse to meet with him again.

After a moment, he said, "Thank you, Ava."

Baffled, she stared at him. "Why are you thanking me?"

"For answering my questions and letting me get to know you. I'll give you a break."

She relaxed a little in her seat, but he was finding she never fully relaxed. She was always alert. Silence didn't bother her; she could sit and say nothing for long stretches at a time. Gabriel found this out as they sat for thirty minutes without talking. He stood to refill his coffee, and Ava ordered another mocha. Neither fidgeted nor tried to find something to say to fill the silence. Gabriel found it oddly comforting to be so relaxed in the company of another human being. He enjoyed not struggling to find something to fill the silence.

"I have three sisters," he suddenly said.

She raised her eyes to his. So much strength in those eyes, he thought, so much control and ability. Hiding so much pain. What had happened to her?

"Beth is older than me," he continued. "You were at Hayden's grave. She was younger."

She was fascinated by his soft, easy tone and by the fact that he was telling her about his family even though she did not ask. He was offering the information to put her at ease, to prove something to her. But she did not know what he wanted to prove. According to the standards of social interaction, asking about her family would have been natural after being so forthcoming with his own personal information. She knew this from reading about it and studying others during conversation. Yet he did not because he said he would not ask her any more questions. He kept his word. That mesmerized her.

"Hayden died when I was fifteen," he continued. "Isabel is the youngest."

"Why are you telling me about your family?" she asked. "I did not ask about them."

"It's known as conversation."

She looked at him, expressionless. Reaching up to tuck a strand of hair behind her ear, the sleeve of her sweater shifted slightly, just enough to expose a long scar curving around her wrist. Gabriel caught a glimpse of pale skin that was white against the rest of her skin tone before her sleeve moved back into place and covered it.

"I don't mean to annoy you by talking," he said. "I like the sound of your voice. I would like to hear it more."

No one had ever said that to her before. She wondered what the odd feeling in her chest and stomach was, why she was so aware of the thudding of her pulse. The sound of his voice was soothing, and she found she wanted to hear more of it, too. But she did not know how to keep a conversation going.

Most of all, she wondered why his dead sister was bothering her at her new house.

She moved her mug to the edge of the table and crossed her arms, resting them on the table. "I am done drinking coffee."

He tipped his cup and glanced in at the ring of dried mud at the bottom. "I guess I am, too."

Ava began gathering her purse and coat.

"I want to spend more time with you," Gabriel said. He set his mug at the edge of the table. "We don't have to talk if you don't want to."

She paused, her keys in one hand, the straps of her bag draped over one arm. Gabriel could tell she was contemplating, her gray eyes darting around.

"I have my parent's dogs for the day. Come over. Hang out with us."

"I do not know you."

"You're never going to if you don't spend time with me. We both know I'm not a threat since you can obviously take care of yourself."

Those eyes, so sincere as she studied him, never wavered from his. Her full lips were slightly parted, her head tilted just a bit.

"You stood at my sister's grave for an hour-"

"Fifty-two minutes." She frowned down at the table, still surprised she had done so.

He was pleased at both her precise detail and her memory. "I'm sure you can handle a couple hours at my house."

Raising her head, she gazed coldly at him. "I can handle anything," she said candidly.

"Then let's go."

• • • • •

"Why are you staring at me?" Isabel asked, five minutes after the waitress brought their breakfast over. She took a bite of bacon with her brow knitted.

They were sitting in a little mom-and-pop restaurant a few blocks from Isabel's apartment. She came here occasionally for breakfast on her days off and sometimes late at night if she suddenly craved fries or homemade chocolate cake. Iz liked the restaurant because she made sure to come when it wasn't crowded so it was quiet and peaceful. She was familiar with the staff, which helped her to be comfortable in public. And she could walk here from her apartment.

Griffin grinned. "You're so concentrated."

Blushing, Isabel set the bacon down and took a drink of coffee. "You can't just plow through bacon like you're at a pie eating contest. It's intense. You have to seduce it."

"Whoever figured out bacon should be canonized."

Isabel smiled, then grew serious as she picked the bacon up again. "I don't trust people who don't like bacon." She jabbed the bacon toward him to drive home her point. "There's something wrong there. Do you want a bite?"

"Sure."

She held out the piece. Instead of taking it from her, he leaned forward and bit a piece off. Isabel snorted.

"I thought eating was a chore for you."

The gold in his eyes was bright and clear. Iz loved the way the color in his shirt made his eyes pop, how her attention, no matter where she looked in his general direction, was immediately forced to his eyes. She wanted to buy him back ups of that shirt, so he never ran out of them.

"It is. Bacon is an exception. Consuming bacon is not ordinary eating, just as bacon isn't ordinary food."

"I shall forever remember your wisdom," he said, bowing his head, "and humbly ask your forgiveness for treating bacon as a paltry piece of food."

Isabel held up a fresh piece. "Don't apologize to me. Apologize to the bacon."

Snatching it from her fingers, Griffin stared at it seriously. "I humbly ask your forgiveness, bacon, for treating you as lowborn." He lowered his head again.

After a pause, he chomped a bite off the top of the piece.

Isabel's mouth fell open. "You just bit the head off your loyal subject."

Griffin grinned. "I wouldn't last long as a king. Do you want this back?" He held the other half of the slice of bacon out to her.

"He sacrificed his life for his king. Finish him off. How's your waffle?" she asked, laughing.

"Yummy. Do you want a bite?"

"Sure."

"Syrup, or no?"

"Drowned in syrup. If I don't get a cavity eating it, you're not doing it right."

He cut off a piece and held it over to her, holding the small side plate that had held his sausage patties underneath to catch the dripping syrup. Isabel leaned forward and took the bite.

"Belgian," she said around the mouthful. "Sweet."

"I never understood people who put fruit or whipped cream on these," he said, stuffing another bite in his mouth.

"Oh, my God," she said, holding her hand over her heart. "You're the perfect man. I agree. They don't need all that shit. Or chocolate chips. Who eats chocolate that early in the morning?"

Griffin toasted that sentiment with his coffee.

They ate in silence for a few seconds.

"So, were you bored this morning?" she asked after she swallowed a bite.

"What do you mean?"

Isabel set her coffee cup down. "Why did you call me to go to breakfast? Were you bored? Couldn't sleep?"

"I like spending time with you."

"Oh, right. You have to take me to my car." She felt foolish for believing, even for a second, that he was here because he wanted to be.

He tilted his head and gazed at her. "I want to spend time with you."

He wondered why that was so hard for her to believe. Something about her pulled at him. She was so strong, yet she had an underlying vulnerability about her. Sadness was written all over her face, but she was easily amused, too. She laughed without hesitation and found humor in most things.

Isabel took a sip of her coffee, wondering about his motives.

Why did he want to spend time with her? Not that she wasn't enjoying every minute of it, but what was he getting out of it? She was boring. She had nothing to offer anyone. Then it hit her: he was in between girlfriends, and she was filling the time until he found someone else.

"I didn't realize you weren't a morning person, or I would have waited until later to call," he said, adding even more syrup even though the waffle was already drowning in it.

"You caught me off guard. I haven't had to deal with mornings or people for years. I'll be ready next time. Not to presume there will be a next time."

"As long as you share your bacon, my heart belongs to you." He dramatically covered his heart with both hands.

"I could be persuaded to share." Her lips curved. "Or you could just buy your own instead of sausage next time."

"Everyone knows bacon tastes better as a gift."

"Sorry, I forgot. Not fully awake yet." She set her plate back with most of her hash browns uneaten and her toast untouched.

He grinned. "Are you busy today?"

"I'm not even awake yet. How can I be busy?"

"Do you want to go to a movie or a wine tasting?" Griffin wiggled his eyebrows above his coffee cup as he took a drink.

Isabel felt her stomach clench. "Do you mean stay in, stream Netflix, and open a bottle of wine or actually go out in public?"

His smile was so eager, so infectious. "We're out in public now."

"We're in a small diner with very few customers, which is the only reason I agreed."

"There's a local winery I frequent, and I need to restock my flat. They do tastings all day, and if we went after breakfast, no one else would be there. But if you get too uncomfortable, we can leave."

A flush crept up her neck and she felt a warmth spread in her stomach and chest. She had never talked to anyone about being nervous in public, and he had just accepted it easily, willing to work around it.

"Or I can restock later, and we can watch a movie at my flat, if you'd prefer," he continued. He lifted the last bite of waffle and turned the fork toward her, waving it seductively. "Want the last bite?"

She smiled and shook her head. "No, thank you." After a moment, she said thoughtfully, "I've never been to a wine tasting. It might be fun."

• • • • •

Gabriel lived on the edge of Langdon in a rather large country style house. Ava parked next to his truck in the driveway and took a moment to appreciate it. The wrap around porch was beautiful. Ava could imagine sitting right on the floor of the porch to read or meditate, listening to the sounds of nature around her, feeling the wind on her skin.

The dogs had been sleeping on the porch. They rose and Ozzie barked at the vehicles. Maya stared intently, her nose twitching, her tail raised.

The yard was large, with plenty of shade trees. From the driveway, she could see a wooded area stretching beyond the backyard and wondered what it would be like to train there.

Ava stared up at the second story windows. If this were her house, she would climb out those windows onto the porch roof and sit there on summer nights, staring at the sky. The vantage point would also work well if there was ever an intruder.

She exited her vehicle.

Ozzie ran to her and danced around her legs, pressing against her. Maya continued staring at her from the porch. Her icy blue eyes regarded the stranger, her pose stiff.

"Give her a break, Oz," Gabriel said to Ozzie, smirking at the lab's shameless attention seeking. He turned his attention to Ava. "Come on in."

Ava followed him up the stairs and practically detonated when he opened the door without unlocking it. How could he not protect his privacy? Stepping over the threshold, she glanced back at Maya, who quickly scooted inside. Ozzie walked in after them.

"Do you want something to drink?" Gabriel hung his jacket on a peg just inside the foyer.

She nodded. As she started to take off her coat, he stepped behind her and reached up to take it from her. Ava slipped her arms the rest of the way out of the coat as she spun around. Her fist was ready to strike as Gabriel caught her coat.

"I'll hang your coat," he said calmly. He draped it on the hook next to his.

How did he manage to make her feel like she had overreacted by preparing to defend herself?

Gabriel led her to the right of a beautiful staircase, down a hall to a large kitchen. As they walked, her eyes roamed, taking in doors, windows, furniture, appliances. Floor lamps could be used as weapons. Kitchen counters could put distance between them if needed. Kitchen chairs could be both a barrier and a weapon.

"Do you want juice? Soda? Tea? Coffee?" He leaned into the refrigerator, moved a couple things around.

Ava found herself looking at his butt. She tilted her head. The human body had never interested her before, not in the way she was looking at his now. Occasionally, during special training events, she would be impressed with another student's physique because it reflected his or her dedication to training. Many times, she had studied Sensei's body as he performed a technique to gauge what muscles he was utilizing. Vincent's body was adequate for sexual release because he was dedicated to martial arts, as she was. His muscle tone and endurance matched her needs. She trusted him enough to be vulnerable in his presence. When they were out in public, she saw the looks other women gave him and knew they considered him attractive. But Ava had never thought of Vincent that way. She never thought of anyone that way.

"What would you like to drink?" Gabriel had turned and was watching her.

"Water, please." She walked to the sink, taking in the breakfast room on the other side of the counter. A small table and chairs were set up next to large windows letting in the late morning sun. A view of a spacious back yard would make for an interesting view during breakfast, Ava thought, though Gabriel usually skipped breakfast and sat at the breakfast bar facing the kitchen if he sat in the morning at all. Usually once he got going, he didn't sit down.

She shook her head, trying to rid herself of the information that flooded in.

"Ice?" he asked her.

"Yes."

Gabriel put ice in pint glasses and made as much noise as he could as he stepped up next to her at the sink. "I need to use the tap here," he said in his patient, calm way, leaning forward and turning on the spout for the filtered water to fill her glass.

His arm brushed hers, but she didn't move away. She stood absolutely still beside him, registering his proximity even though she stared straight ahead. He could feel the tension vibrating off her. Gabriel thought that if he made a sound, she would snap like a worn guitar string. What in God's name had happened to this woman?

He turned off the spout and held out the glass.

She reached out. Her fingers settled over his. For a moment, it felt as if he had been given a small electric shock that coursed through his hand. Then her hand abruptly clamped down on the glass of water, with his fingers trapped under hers.

"It's cold," she rasped.

"You said you wanted ice," he answered, frowning. The physical contact was surprising, the cool feel of her skin even more so.

She turned her head, finally looked him. Her pupils appeared to be the size of dimes and pulsed against her eyes.

"So cold. It takes my breath away."

"I don't... Are you okay?" Gabriel tried to move his hand and couldn't. Her hand, so much smaller than his, was holding his so tight he couldn't break away.

"Or maybe it was the fall."

"Ava-"

She jolted, blinked rapidly. Glancing around the room, she squinted. She almost made him spill her water when she pulled her hand back.

He set the glass on the counter in front of her, though she had taken a step away from him.

Running a hand through her thick hair, Ava avoided looking at him. Did she have a medical condition? Was it a seizure? Gabriel reviewed the symptoms: uncontrollable body movement, blurting out nonsensical phrases, dilated pupils. Whatever it was seemed to embarrass her, so he decided to act as if nothing had happened. He began to fill his glass with filtered water.

"The main reason I bought this place was because of the natural views," he said. He motioned toward the Great Room, which had access to the southern sunroom. "Let's sit in the sunroom and enjoy them."

Wordlessly, she picked up her glass and followed him.

The room was warmed by the sunshine streaming through the floor-to-ceiling windows. Ava walked to a window panel and looked out at the yard. She raised her right hand and placed it gently against the glass.

Ozzie wagged his tail as he came up beside her. After a few moments, Maya entered the room and lay down in the sun by the east window.

Sitting in one of the chairs, Gabriel studied Ava. She was unique. Social interaction wasn't her strong point, which amused him. She was quiet and still and unlike anyone he'd ever met. What was that odd little episode she'd had in the kitchen? Maybe a seizure, but it didn't seem too bad. Could that be what kept her at a distance from others? Her embarrassment of a medical condition?

She was beautiful in such a natural way. The clothing she wore wasn't form fitting. She didn't dress like the Amish, but she didn't expose her breasts or accentuate her hips. Yet her figure was obvious anyway. She wore no makeup. Gabriel was sure her hair color was natural because he didn't think she would take the time or effort to change what she was naturally. To know a woman who was content to be completely natural thrilled him.

Still, he thought, gazing at her, she had made it clear she didn't like physical contact. When had that dislike started, he wondered? And why?

Who didn't like to be touched? Sure, he was a guy, and the obvious love of sex was in his DNA. But hugs were a family staple every Sunday at his parent's house, and he was always touching Isabel when they were together. They were either hugging or slugging each other, both as signs of affection. When he hung out with his guy friends, they constantly punched, shoved, and gave bro hugs. Hell, even at a store he sometimes had to touch someone on the shoulder or arm to move around him or her. People constantly touched. Getting change back at the grocery store, getting a haircut. Gabriel didn't think he could function if he suddenly were forbidden to have contact with people, especially those most important to him. Who the hell didn't like an occasional kiss, a hug, a touch on the arm?

Suddenly it occurred to him. Someone who had been touched when she hadn't wanted to be. Someone who hadn't given her permission. Had Ava's dislike begun as a child, or an adult? Either way was disgusting. Had she ever actually made love to a man by her own choice? From her reactions to even casual, platonic brushes, Gabriel thought not. And why would she want to if she'd been abused?

His stomach did a somersault.

He slowly came out of his own thoughts to find she had turned away from looking outside and was now studying him. How long had she been watching him? He hadn't heard her move, hadn't registered seeing it even as he apparently watched her do it.

Gabriel cleared his throat. "Do you have an apartment in Langdon?"

"I own a house." She took a sip of water.

"You didn't buy the Farley place, did you? A few months ago?"

She nodded. "Six months and ____ days ago."

"That was you. It was on the market for a couple years. Everyone was surprised when it finally sold."

She watched him. Those large gray eyes took in everything: the room, the furniture, the yard outside...him. She studied everything so avidly, as if seeing it for the first time.

Gabriel was rusty, but he was sure he was picking up on a vibe from her, the kind a woman reserved only for a man she was interested in.

"Do you like it?" he asked. "The house?"

"It serves my needs."

"Do you enjoy anything?" he asked. "I mean, are there things that make you happy?"

Ava bent her knees slowly and lowered herself until she was resting her butt on the backs of her ankles, her back against the glass. "I am content."

Ozzie stuck his face in hers, blocking Gabriel's view momentarily. Ava patiently but firmly brushed his head aside while she set her glass down. She took his head in both hands and began to massage his scalp. Ozzie groaned loudly, turning his head to make sure she reached all the good spots. Maya raised her head and watched them for a moment before resting her head on her paws.

"That's unfortunate," Gabriel said. "You deserve to be more than content."

"People worry too much about being happy," Ava said, never taking her eyes off Ozzie. "They demand instant gratification with every aspect of their lives. Promotions, money, sex. Always now, now. The more they get, the more they want."

Gabriel listened, surprised to hear her talk so much. "What do you want?"

She continued to massage Ozzie but looked at Gabriel. "I do not want anything."

"How old are you?"

The question caught her off guard. The space between her eyebrows creased briefly. "Twenty-two."

On its own, his mind did the math: he was seven years older than her. That difference in age seemed like a massive gulf of experience between them. His somehow still seemed to come up lacking.

"You're too young to be that cynical."

Ava gave Ozzie a pat on his chest and sat on the floor, stretching out her long legs. "It is not cynicism to be content. I do not want the same material items the majority of the population thinks it needs. That does not mean I am lacking anything."

"That's absolutely true," he said. When Ozzie made his rounds, he gave him a pet. "But I think you're settling for some things because you don't think you'll ever get others."

"You do not know me well enough to make that statement." And you never will, her tone clearly said.

Hit a sore spot, did I? he thought. He decided to change the subject, hoping to help her feel more comfortable. "I have another chair here."

For a moment, he thought she would refuse to sit beside him. Then she crossed her legs beneath her and pushed up without using her hands, gracefully rising as if she weighed no more than a feather. She picked up her water and crossed the room, sitting in the sturdy chair beside him with her legs curled under her. Leaning away from him, she rested her left elbow on the armrest, turning at an angle so she could watch him.

"Where did you live before Langdon?"

"You talk too much," she said shortly. Yet that vibe remained. That feeling that hovered between them like static electricity, bouncing between them in little shocks and jolts. It contradicted everything he saw in her eyes; the detachment, the discomfort at his proximity, the irritation at his attempts to engage her in conversation.

The right side of his mouth turned up slightly. "I'm just trying to get to know you."

"Why do you want to?" Now she sounded tired. She set her water on the table between the two recliners.

"I told you at Willow's. I find you interesting," Gabriel said. He hadn't been able to get her out of his mind since she stood with him at Hayden's grave.

"I wish you did not."

"It's not a choice I made. It just happened. Most people wouldn't stand in the cold for a complete stranger, especially at a place as disliked as a cemetery."

Ozzie walked over and sat in front of her, resting his head on the edge of the chair. He seemed endlessly drawn to her. Ava rubbed her hand over his head. Her brow was furrowed. "I am not most people."

"You certainly are not."

"I do not engage in interpersonal relationships. You can stop being nice to me."

His one eyebrow shot up. "I can be polite without an ulterior motive."

The look she gave him told him she highly doubted that.

Gabriel tried to remember she might be uncooperative because of previous abuse. Maybe every man in her life had betrayed her, and that made every man an enemy. If that was the case, Ava deserved the benefit of the doubt - and his kindness.

"So, you don't like talking about yourself," he said. "And you don't want to know anything about me. I guess I wasted your time inviting you here. I thought you might want a friend."

Ava looked flustered. "I have offended you. I am not good at this. I am better on my own."

"You just need practice," he said easily. "I'm in no hurry. It's friendship, Ava; I don't expect anything more. I'm not too horrible to be around, am I?"

Oddly, he wasn't. Ava did not enjoy the company of people in general. She preferred isolation or animals. Gabriel was different. He was quiet and calm, which she appreciated. So many people were always moving, speaking, taking up space and air without contributing to the world around them. In their presence, Ava always felt the need to get away, like an animal caught in a trap. Gabriel didn't make her feel trapped. He was comfortable with himself and therefore at ease, and the sense of calm radiated from him. It made her feel almost at peace in his presence.

Yet simultaneously, she felt like every one of her nerves was on fire. The sensation was intense and at times overwhelming and not entirely unpleasant. There was a deep sadness surrounding him that she was drawn to. She was sure it was caused from the death of his sister. Because Ava saw his sister's spirit, it stood to reason that was why she felt the odd connection to Gabriel. Whatever the reason for it, the feeling of connecting with him fascinated her.

Still, she held back. Every connection to another person created complications, obligations.

"I am getting used to your company," she said carefully.

He lifted one side of his mouth in a smile. She wanted to touch his face when he did that, feel the muscles move, examine how his face reflected his thoughts. When his eyebrow arched, she wanted to study it, rationalize it, touch it. She had never been interested in doing that to anyone before. No one had ever engaged her enough to want to look closer.

"Well," Gabriel said, gazing at the melting ice in his water, "that's something."

• • • • •

Griffin pulled up in front of an old building from the late 1800s and parked the car. Isabel studied the building, painted blue on the top half and white on the bottom half, with red trim.

They had driven to a small town forty minutes from Madison, and Iz thought the town was charming. Old buildings lined the "downtown" area – the town had less than one thousand people and Isabel didn't think they could legally claim having a downtown. Vintage style streetlights promised a beautiful evening reminiscent of Kinkade paintings, and hand-carved wooden benches with names and dates carved into them sat in front of several of the businesses. The entire town felt cozy, Isabel thought.

They entered the front door to a large, open floor plan with pine walls and large windows that let in natural light on the south and west sides. Immediately to their left, two tall round tables were set up with bar stool-type chairs. A dark gray microfiber couch sat across from two dark blue wingback chairs, with a pale gray rug under them and end tables placed around them. Black racks of merchandise – tee shirts, coasters, wine toppers – were set up throughout the area. Large racks of wine sorted by grape type, wine type, and style were set up away from the windows where they would be out of direct sunlight. On the far west wall, a bar ran two thirds the length of the room. Little bowls of oyster crackers had been set along the length of the table for nibbling on in between the wine tastings.

Isabel was charmed by the comfortable yet modern feel of the winery. Seeing no other customers instantly made her feel relaxed. Griffin nonchalantly took her hand as he guided her to the bar and pulled out a stool for her. They hung their coats on the backs of the stools as a middle-aged woman who couldn't have been more than five foot one came out from a back room.

"Griffin!" She smiled, little lines creasing around the corners of her eyes. Her gray-streaked blonde hair was pulled back into a high ponytail, and she was wearing too much make up.

"Vicki," Griffin said warmly, leaning over the counter to give her a hug. "How are the kids?"

She blew out a breath and laughed. "Handfuls, every damn one of 'em. But I love 'em, God help me."

"And Mike?"

"Back's getting better. He's at work now, so that helps."

"Good for him. He's doing better with the pain?"

Vicki gave him a bright smile. "He's so much better. It's almost completely gone now."

"Excellent."

Griffin sat back on his stool and touched Isabel on the shoulder. "This is Isabel. Isabel, Vicki. She's my wine dealer. I keep her in business, and she satisfies my every alcoholic need."

Vicki laughed. "You're such a philanderer. Pleasure to meet you, Isabel." She stuck her hand over the counter.

Isabel gave it a shake. "Nice to meet you."

Griffin kept his hand on her shoulder as he addressed Vicki. "I thought you could let us try some of your finest. I need a couple different bottles to take home with my usual stash."

"Is it too early to do a wine tasting?" Isabel asked, looking from Griffin to Vicki.

Griffin laughed. "Darling, this is Wisconsin. The only requirement for drinking is that you're conscious."

Vicki laughed as she set two small taster glasses on the counter. "Any ideas on what you want the new flavors to be like?"

"I'd like to try the Moscato and Summer Wine," Griffin said. "I've had my eye on those for a while." He turned to Isabel. "Anything you want to try?"

Her eyes were flying over the list sitting on the counter. She had no idea what to ask for. She didn't drink enough of a variety to know what she liked. "I'll try whatever you're drinking. I don't know dick about wine."

Her eyes widened. "Sorry," she said to Vicki.

The older woman waved her off. "You'll have to get pretty raunchy before you offend me."

She searched under the counter for the right bottles and set them on the counter, opening the Moscato first. Pouring a little in each taster, she slid them forward.

Griffin gently clinked his glass against Isabel's before he took a sip. Isabel liked the sweet taste that burst on her tongue when she drank. The wine was light, and she had a feeling she could drink an entire bottle if it was sitting within her reach.

"What do you think?" Griffin asked, popping a cracker into his mouth.

"I think I need to buy a couple bottles of that," Iz said, eating a couple crackers. "And be careful I don't drink them in one sitting."

"I agree," Griffin said. "Add six bottles to my usual order, Vic, and the lady will take two."

"I can see myself getting seriously fucked up on that," Isabel muttered, leaning closer to Griffin.

Only when he chuckled and squeezed her knee did she realize he was still touching her. His palm was warm on her jeans, and Isabel found that simple contact, no matter how silly, made her feel connected to the room and moment. Here were two people who saw her.

Vicki had jotted Griffin's request on a note pad. She poured a taster of Summer Wine.

"Sweet," Isabel said, taking another tiny sip. "Cherries. Not as good as Moscato, but good."

"I'll take two, Vic," Griffin said. "Are there any you want to try?" he asked Isabel.

She nibbled crackers to cleanse her pallet and read the descriptions of the wines. "Just Peachy," she said, pointing, then giggled. She nudged Griffin with her elbow. "Ha! Get it? Just Peachy!" She snorted. "I like peach flavored drinks, so I'll probably like that one."

Griffin looked amused at her silliness with the wordplay for the name. Vicki was already getting the bottle from under the counter.

Isabel started giggling. She snorted, covered her mouth, and snorted again.

"What are you on about?" Griffin asked, smiling at her. She was adorable, flushed, and embarrassed but unable to stop laughing.

"That one's called 'Raspberry Kind of You'! That's so ridiculous!"

"Do you want to try it?"

She nodded. "'Raspberry Kind of You'." She snorted again. "Sorry. I think they drink an entire bottle of each wine before they come up with these names. Only drunk people come up with that much silliness."

Vicki set out the peach and was getting the raspberry ready for them. Isabel picked up the taster with the peach in it and turned in the stool to clink her glass to Griffin's. He was staring at her, a slight smile on his face.

"What?" she asked, becoming self-conscious. She was suddenly aware of how close they were sitting and that she had turned her body into his knees. "What are you looking at?"

"You have a really beautiful laugh," he said softly. He reached up and tucked a strand of hair behind her ear. "You should do it more. It lights your whole face up."

Color rose in her cheeks, so bright and obvious it was a wonder she wasn't glowing.

Griffin touched his glass to hers. "Isn't this just peachy?" he asked, making her smirk.

"Ooh, I like this one, too."

Griffin held up four fingers to Vicki, who added it to the order.

"Alright, more crackers," he said, grabbing a handful. His hands, much bigger than hers, dropped so many crackers in her palm that some dropped on the floor. She scrambled to hold as many as she could.

"Griffin!" She leaned forward and tongued up a couple, afraid any hand movement would cause more to fall. "Jesus, a couple would do the job."

"I want to make sure you're not getting blitzed."

"On a couple sips of wine? Bitch, please." Still, to prove him wrong, she ate the entire handful of crackers. By the end, they were starting to stick to the roof of her mouth. Vicki reached under the counter and pulled out a bottle of water.

"Thank you," Isabel said around a mouth still full of crackers, holding her hand up to cover the mess. She chugged water and gulped the rest of the sticky ball of paste down.

Griffin had been popping crackers into his mouth as he watched her. "Are there any more you want to try?"

"I was considering the raspberry," she said, unable to hide the giggle, "but if you're worried about me being an alcoholic, we can skip it."

"I'm not worried. Vicki, we'll try the raspberry as our last taster."

Vicki poured.

"Then why did you give me a handful of crackers to cram in my mouth?"

"Obviously, I thought you would eat them slower," he said, resting his hand on her knee again. "I was wasting time so we could spend more time together."

"Jesus, Griffin." Isabel brushed crumbs off the bar and rubbed her hands together. "Why don't you just say, 'Hey, after this let's go for a walk?' or 'Gee, let's see a movie together.'"

"I suppose that makes more sense," he said, grinning. "When we're done here, do you want to hang out at my place and watch Netflix?"

"Sure." She snorted. "Raspberry Kind of You."

Vicki had slid the tasters across the counter toward them.

"Sweet Jesus. Let's see if the taste lives up to its humorous name."

They lifted their glasses. Isabel sipped, tilted her head, sipped again. She thought about different meals she ate and how the wine would pair with each one.

"I expected it to be jollier with a name like that, but it's good. This would go with the lamb my mom sometimes makes," Isabel said. She closed her eyes, breathed deep, and took another sip. Nodding, she finished it off.

Griffin held up three fingers to Vicki. "Add what we just tasted to my usual order, and we're all set, Vic," he said. He popped a couple crackers in his mouth.

Vicki disappeared to the back of the store.

Griffin turned so he was facing Isabel and leaned forward, bracing his hands on her knees. "What do you think? This wasn't too bad, was it?"

"I didn't realize I would be so entertained." Her heart was thudding painfully in her chest. All she could think about were Griffin's hands. What would it feel like if he cupped her breasts?

Blushing madly, Isabel lowered her eyes. She felt the heat rising in her cheeks. Why the hell would he ever do that? Jesus, she was losing it.

"I see those wheels turning," Griffin said, touching her temple. "What's going on up there?"

She smiled, blushing even more. She had to clear her throat before she could speak. "Nothing appropriate."

He grinned and wiggled his eyebrows. "Oh, you naughty girl."

"Do you ever have to figure out dorky names for clients like 'Just Peachy' or 'Raspberry Kind of You'?" she asked to distract herself. Her body was on fire, and not entirely from the wine. Good Lord.

"My design team does most of the foot work now. As the art director, I'm the liaison between the picky clients and my team. We work more for corporations, not smaller businesses. That's one of the things I want to change if I start my own business. I would also be able to be the only person do all the work, from start to finish."

Vicki came out from the back pushing a wheeled cart with several boxes stacked on it. "All boxed up, Griffin. Are you still driving that boat of an SUV?"

"Yes, dear. There's plenty of room." Griffin slipped into his coat and trotted to the door. "You can wait in here if you want," he said to Isabel.

"Gee," she said, "Raspberry kind of you."

• • • • •

After they moved to the living room, Gabriel lit the fireplace and watched Ava sit in front of it, mesmerized. She seemed to enjoy the sounds of the popping and snapping as the logs settled and the fire consumed wood. Gabriel watched her until Ozzie's persistent nose finally drove her to stand and investigate the room.

He moved to the couch, watching Ava walk the perimeter of the room and look at the few pictures he had on the walls. She scanned the books in a small bookcase, the family photos on the mantel above the fireplace.

"My family has been in this area for generations," he said. "They have this huge house in the country, where I grew up. I tried the big city while I went to college, but it just wasn't for me. So, I came back here a few years ago. I like the quiet."

At least they agreed on that. She thought about telling him so, then changed her mind. She did not want to encourage him or give him ammunition to use against her later.

"Have you always lived in this area?" He kept his voice casual.

"No."

It was obviously a touchy subject. So touchy she had momentarily lost her discipline long enough to outwardly show her disdain of him asking. Why would the places she grew up be a sore subject, he wondered?

"Where are you from?" He wanted to tread lightly, urging conversation without being too nosy. Doing so seemed to be a tedious balancing act.

"I do not know." Her words were clipped. She studied a picture of two girls and a boy, smiling up at the camera. One girl looked to be a young adult, seventeen or eighteen. The boy was around fifteen. The other girl was nine or ten. They were all lying on the floor on their stomachs with kittens their hands. Something was missing in their eyes, and the smiles were hesitant. It was taken after Hayden's death. Ava could read that as easily as if she had asked Gabriel outright, and she didn't have to be psychic.

"Well, obviously you don't remember being hatched, but -"

"I am adopted," Ava said stiffly. She closed her eyes, exhaled. Why had she told him that?

That could explain why she didn't connect with people. Gabriel had heard of some children having trouble trusting people if they were brought up in the system. But why would him knowing her childhood background upset her so much? Adoption was nothing to be ashamed of.

Gabriel motioned to the other side of the couch. "Have a seat."

Her body rigid, she sat on the sofa as far away from him as possible. She was pressed against the arm of the couch, facing him, her back straight as a yard stick and her knees drawn up to her chest.

Did she think he cared that she was adopted? Was she ashamed of it? Her family tree meant nothing to him. He wanted her to know it didn't matter.

"Did you grow up in Wisconsin?"

"I was moved around a lot when I was young."

Now he had information he could use against her. Ava hated that she had given him the opportunity. In trying to stop the questions, she had invited more. He was just so easy to talk to; words fell out of her mouth without her trying.

I was moved around she had said, Gabriel thought. Not I moved around, or we moved around. As if subconsciously, she detested how little control she had as a child.

"Are you close with them? Your foster parents?"

For several seconds, she only stared at him. Gabriel felt as if all the air had left the room. There was a tightness in his chest that hadn't been there before.

Ozzie snorted in his sleep.

"My foster parents," Ava said softly, her gaze unwavering, "liked the sound of my screams."

Gabriel watched an emotion he couldn't quite define flicker across her face and disappear.

He leaned forward slowly, resting his elbows on his knees, and turning his head to look at her. "What does that mean?"

Ava's gray eyes had darkened so they almost looked black. "It means I did not get along with my foster parents."

"Ava." He ran his hand down the back of his neck. He was only trying to get to know her, to hear her voice, to have a damn normal conversation. Why did everything turn into a nightmare with her?

Well fuck me sideways, Gabriel thought. Her face had remained emotionless as she said it except for that one flicker. So, she had been abused as a child. That explained so much. The idea that she was a virgin, at least by her own consent, fluttered through his mind again. Why would she want any man to ever touch her after what she had been through? Why would she trust anyone ever again?

His stomach rolled.

"I'm..." He had to clear his throat. "I'm sorry."

She looked confused. "It happened a long time ago."

Not long enough, he thought. Could a person recover from that?

He was still trying to get his mind around it. Ava seemed to have moved on from the conversation already. She drank her water and continued to look around the room. How the hell could she do that? Was she repressing memories? She had to be, for her to treat her horrific past so casually. Didn't she?

Yet she was opening up to him. He felt she was beginning to trust him, and that milestone gave him a glimmer of hope. If nothing else, he could show her that he wouldn't hurt her, that not all men had the evil inside them to pick on defenseless children or women.

He leaned toward her, reaching for her hand. Instantly, her attention was on him, and her body was alert. She didn't raise her hands to protect herself, but her muscles were ready if she needed to move, and her eyes watched him intently.

"Ava," he said, taking a chance and laying his palm flat on top of her hand so it was barely touching, "if you ever need to talk, I'm here."

She seemed genuinely confused. Her eyes grazed over him. "You are there, and I am here."

"I mean... I'm available if you need to talk about your... childhood." He let his fingers drop over her hand and shifted his, so it was loosely holding hers.

Her brow furrowed. "Why would I want to talk about something that happened sixteen years ago?"

As if in a trance, Ava stared down at their joined hands. She should have grabbed his hand the moment he moved toward her, injuring him in a way that reminded him she did not like to be touched. She had told him this many times now; she did not like to repeat herself. Yet she had not harmed him. She could not take her eyes off the contact their hands were making.

His skin was warm, rough from the woodwork he did daily. When he was deep in a project, he would work for hours without eating. His hands would keep running the tools over the wood until the shape beneath them matched the image in his head. Sometimes a piece would sit in his garage for days until he found what he was looking for; the perfect inlay or addition to the design that would make it belong to that client alone.

Ava shook her head, trying to block the images flashing through her head, the emotions that came with those images.

"I know you don't know me well, but I won't repeat anything you tell me." Gabriel hated this emotional shit. Isabel was better at it than he was. "Talking about it might make you feel better."

"I feel better when I punch things."

He smirked. "That works, too. I just want you to know I'm your friend. You can talk to me."

"I did not tell you to get sympathy," she said candidly.

"Why did you tell me?" he asked. He felt honored that she had opened up to him, that she had trusted him with that part of her life. From what he had heard around town and what he was learning about her, getting any information out of her was nearly impossible.

"I told you so you would shut up about my childhood."

So much for trust.

"You could have told me you don't want to talk about it," Gabriel said.

Ava opened her mouth to speak and glanced down at her hand. Her eyes widened. Gabriel's hand was still resting on hers. Instead of withdrawing into herself, she stared at their touching flesh for several seconds.

When she looked up at him, her eyes were filled with confusion and curiosity.

Always curious, Gabriel thought. As if she has never experienced the world until now.

"Warm," she said, her voice filled with awe.

"What?"

"People. I did not expect people to be so warm."

$$\bullet \quad \bullet \quad \bullet \quad \bullet \quad \bullet$$

After the wine tasting, they had returned to Griffin's apartment, where they binge watched Stranger Things for a few hours. The entire day still felt surreal to Isabel.

She was surprised she'd had so much fun trying different wines with him and talking. She hadn't talked that much since she was a young child. Her mouth was dry, her jaw sore. Her cheeks hurt from laughing so hard. Vicki had been friendly, nonjudgmental. Iz spent so much time laughing at the dorky names of the wines and enjoying something she had never done before that she forgot to be self-conscious after the first few minutes.

They had a couple hours left before she had to go home, shower, and get ready to drive to The Raz. Isabel was exhausted but also felt like she had done three lines of cocaine.

The pizza arrived as they were wrapping up the second season of Stranger Things. Griffin tipped the driver and brought the food to the coffee table. Sipping her wine, Iz wondered how it would taste with the pizza. It seemed so fancy. The only thing she ever drank with pizza was soda. Even whiskey was saved for after she ate.

It's that white trash mentality, she thought.

Griffin walked to the kitchen for plates. Isabel sneaked a look at his butt as he walked away. God, but he was adorable. She wanted to feed him pizza in bed. With just her teeth.

She almost spit out her wine. Wiping her mouth off, she snorted. Griffin was going to think she was having a breakdown if she didn't stop making herself laugh over ridiculous thoughts. She topped off her wine, so her hands had something to do. Griffin returned to the couch and handed her a plate and napkin.

"Did you say something?" he asked from the kitchen.

"Nope." Her answer was a little too quick, but he didn't say anything more, so she relaxed.

"Are we going to finish Stranger Things while we eat?" Isabel asked, setting a slice of pizza on her plate.

Griffin sat beside her on the couch. He seemed to be a little close. Maybe that was just her imagination. "I thought we'd get to know each other more. Much more interesting."

He wiggled his eyebrows.

She snickered and started on her pizza. The heat radiating off him was making her flush. Pushing up the sleeves of her sweater, she tried to think of something to say to start a conversation. Usually when she was nervous, she couldn't make herself shut up.

"What kind of music do you sing at The Raz?"

"Wow, you're still on this. Everything. Rock, classical, folk, rhythm and blues. My family is pretty musically inclined, actually. Everyone learned at least one instrument, and we all sing."

"What does everyone else play?"

"Beth, my older sister plays violin when she plays anything. Gabriel plays piano really well and does pretty well on acoustic guitar. I'm best on acoustic guitar, passable on piano. Gabriel and Beth play classical really well, but they also can rock Metallica and Avenged Sevenfold. My other sister, the one that died, she was really good on the piano. Amazingly good."

"What do you write?"

"Mostly... folk and rock, I guess. I've never really thought about quantifying it."

Griffin plucked a pepperoni off his slice of pizza and popped it into his mouth. "What's the real reason you're single?"

This time Isabel did spit out her wine – all over Griffin's shirt. It splattered on his chest and droplets flew left and right.

"Fuck!" Isabel said, using her napkin to dab at the cloth. "Shit, I'm sorry."

"It's a bum shirt, Isabel, no worries." He smiled at her, watching with amusement as she pressed her napkin to his chest.

"You're going to give that shirt to a bum?"

His grin widened. "I use it to bum around in. Answer the question."

He pulled the wet shirt over his head and tossed it to the side, revealing a crisp white tank underneath. Iz had a weakness for guys in muscle shirts. They accented a man's arms and shoulders and worked with tall and lean or muscular body types. She wasn't disappointed with Griffin.

She swallowed, leaned against the back of the couch with her wine, trying not to stare at the way his body filled out the shirt.

"I'm still trying to get used to being invited to someone's apartment."

Griffin tilted his head and gazed at her. "Why wouldn't people invite you over?"

She thought for a few seconds. "People used to invite me over. After I turned them down a few times, they stopped asking."

"Why did you turn them down?"

"I don't like casual relationships. Why would I agree to go to someone's house when I already know I'll be miserable? If you can't even tell me the truth about how you live – that your house is a mess because you just didn't feel like cleaning the damn thing up and your husband won't help– why would I trust you to tell you anything about my life? Then, if I just go along with your lie, I'm complicit in it, which makes me just as bad. We both know that stupid lie you told about your house being a mess because you were in a hurry this morning is just that, a lie, and we're both agreeing to feed that lie instead of just admitting the truth. I can't be something I'm not. I'm not Susie Homemaker, who can pretend to be polite with one face and talk behind people's backs with the other. I hate people who do that. Clean your damn house or don't, but don't make excuses for it."

She returned her empty wine glass to the coffee table. Griffin was gazing at her. "Why are you staring at me now?"

"I'm just listening. I like listening to you talk." Griffin shifted, scooting a little closer to her. Their knees bumped. "Do you want any more pizza?"

"I'm good, thanks. Where are you putting all that food?" She poked him in the stomach.

He nudged her with his elbow.

"You should bring your guitar over sometime and play for me." He had finally finished eating and brushed the crumbs off his fingertips. "I'll want to hear you more than just at the coffee shop."

Instantly her face lit up with embarrassment. "Back to that again." She hoped he'd forgotten about her singing at The Raz tonight. She was already starting to get nervous. "I suppose I can do that sometime."

Griffin closed the lid on the pizza. "I'll clean this up and then we can finish the show until you have to get ready."

·   ·   ·   ·   ·

The words on the page kept blurring. Ava reread the same paragraph and still could not remember a single thing that was happening in the book. She closed her eyes, shook her head. She tried another paragraph and finally gave up. Slamming the book shut, she set it on the coffee table and ran her fingers through her damp hair.

Leaning forward, she picked up her phone, pulled up the Internet to do a search, and typed in a business name. Gabriel Harris's name came up immediately, his phone number and business listed at the top of the page.

Dropping the phone angrily on the coffee table, Ava sat back on the couch. She let out a sharp exhale.

She had tried to meditate after she came home from Gabriel's house, but her thoughts kept returning to him. She had not been able to focus enough to meditate, let alone work on controlling visions.

Damn him.

She could not stop thinking about him. Why did he have to insist on buying her coffee, inviting her to his house? Why did he have to intrude on her life? With his endless questions coming at her, she had blurted out personal information without meaning to. She did not want to talk to him. She did not want a friend.

Don't you?

No. A friend would only let her down. People always did. A friend would mean taking time away from her routines, her schedules, to spend time with him, wasting time talking and answering questions instead of training.

Except the feeling in her head when he was around and that strange falling sensation in her stomach while the rest of her remained still had not been unpleasant. The sound of his deep voice was soothing, like a steady rain thrumming against glass. Feeling the warmth of his body when he was next to her had stirred something inside. Hearing him breathe calmed her.

During their time at the cafe, she had listened closely to him breathe. The simple, natural act had eased her distaste about being in public for an extended period of time with a stranger. She did not understand it. He asked too many questions. He invaded her thoughts when she was trying to focus on other matters.

Damn him.

She had no intention of rearranging her entire life to satisfy an emotional moment of weakness where she thought she wanted social acceptance.

She needed to give herself a task to divert her attention.

•   •   •   •   •

Isabel ran her index finger around the lip of her glass as she waited for her turn at the mic. Across the table from her, Griffin gave her what she was beginning to think of as his signature grin.

"Are you nervous? I thought you said you do this every other weekend."

She sucked as much liquid as she could from the bottom of her glass. All the alcohol was gone; the only thing left was a few dribbles from the ice starting to melt. "I do. You're usually not here."

"Pretend I'm a stranger."

"You practically are."

He was so attractive in his burgundy Henley shirt. Isabel wondered how he managed to make something casual look so effortless yet sexy. A sudden image flashed in her head: her coming out of his bedroom wearing only that Henley. Because his torso was so long, the shirt would go well past her ass.

She flushed to her roots, wondering where the hell her refill was.

Griffin didn't seem to notice. "What are you going to sing? Never mind, you'll probably say when you get up there. I've never known a real singer before." He took a sip of his wine.

"You still don't," she said wryly. "It's just a hobby."

"You're so modest. Now I'm really intrigued."

Isabel practically snatched her next whiskey from the waitress. "Can you bring me another, neat?"

"Sure," the waitress grinned. "No need to be nervous. Everyone loves your music."

"Thank you, Annie," Isabel said. She cursed the ice as she tried to chug the whiskey around it.

"I'm making you really nervous," Griffin said, studying her. "Why did you invite me if it upsets you so much?"

His accent was so adorable. And his hair... God, she wanted to run her hands through his tawny hair.

Focus, Isabel. Jesus, her thoughts were flying.

"You kind of invited yourself," she reminded him. She felt the whiskey course through her body, warming her stomach. Her cheeks flushed. She exhaled. "You're the only one who's ever come to see me sing. Except Gabe."

"I feel special."

"I'm up next," she said, turning back just as the waitress brought her third drink. She slammed it as soon as the waitress left. Exhaling what felt like fire, she took a sip of ice water. She stood and glanced at the crowd. It was a normal Saturday night crowd, no more, no less. Nothing was different. Except Griffin.

"If you make it through this alive, we can stop at Target afterward and have a pillow fight."

I'd rather have a pillow fight in your bed.

Griffin was looking at her seriously. She let out a bark of laughter. "You're an idiot."

He stood and took a step toward her, so their bodies were two inches apart. Hers wanted to respond to his immediately. She had to fight the urge to move toward him. He cupped her face in this large hands.

"You're amazing." He wouldn't look away from her. His golden eyes were calm. "So go up there and be amazing."

The whiskey was starting to relax her. She wanted to feel his hands on more than her face.

"I like how you say ah-mahy-zing," she said, smiling.

He grinned and nudged her toward the stage.

Isabel experienced a moment where her legs felt disconnected from her body. As she walked around the stage toward the back to pick up her guitar, she had to force herself to put one foot in front of the other. She had this feeling every time she prepared to go on stage. She had to remind herself repeatedly that this was just a hobby, that if no one liked her music she would simply stop playing at The Raz. She could enjoy creating music and songs in her own home and the world be damned because she wasn't doing it for everyone else. It was her outlet, her therapy.

She had already tuned her guitar so when the previous artist was finished and Isabel was announced, she carried it onto the stage and sat on the stool provided. She was surprised, as always, by the applaud from several of the patrons.

"Thank you," she said into the microphone. "I just took three shots of whiskey, so my voice is a little rough."

A guy gave her a cat call. Another one hollered. That relaxed her. They were regulars, and the normal routine helped to remind her that she had done this many times before.

No big deal.

Isabel straightened her shoulders and began to play.

• • • • •

Ava knew she shouldn't go shopping when she was agitated. Allowing herself to buy foods she never ate should have warned her immediately that she was using it as comfort, not nourishment. Nonetheless, she walked through the store with a purpose, having to search for the aisle she was going to use for the first time. She walked past it twice before she found it.

Ding Dongs, Andes mints, 3 Musketeers, Twix bars, and a handful of other garbage most people referred to as "food" made it into her cart. Adding Coke, she searched for the chips aisle and began dumping bags into her cart.

"Judging by all that junk food, I'm guessing you've had a bad day," a voice said to her right.

Ava raised her head, annoyed at the interruption. A man was standing a few feet away, carrying a small basket. His light hair was cut in the latest fashion and his predatory eyes were watching her with an amused look on his face.

Ava gritted her teeth. He was amused because he thought she would slide into bed with him, overwhelmed by his charm. This man was the type that jumped from bed to bed faster than Ava could do pushups. He was too pretty, too well kept, too particular about how he dressed and combed his hair. He kept up on the latest fashions to impress women so they would tumble into bed with him. Then he moved onto the next that caught his eye.

"My nutrition and my schedule are none of your business," she said, intent on ending the conversation before it started. She continued shoving junk food into her cart. She was going to watch movies and stuff all this food in her face.

She knew she should not let the uneasiness of a positive experience with a stranger get to her. Gabriel had invited her for coffee and to his house for a visit. The time with him had been pleasant, even enjoyable. Logically, she knew this was perfectly normal. She also understood that the sudden diversion from her normal schedule would cause a momentary vertigo to her system and to her disposition. She was not used to such a dramatic change in her lifestyle.

She knew all these things, but still she couldn't get Gabriel out of her head and that still vexed her.

Yet here she was, stocking up on poison she planned to introduce to her body instead of sticking to her regimen of healthy proteins and vegetables. And now this imbecile was bothering her. She wanted to bathe until she felt clean again.

"Come on, I'm just trying to be friendly." The man flashed a practiced smile.

"Well, stop it."

"My name's Jeremy."

"I do not care." She spotted a package of Sixlets candy and snatched them off the shelf. The man walked closer.

"What's your name?"

"None of your business."

Ava's hands gripped the shopping cart. She knew the moment he decided to touch her and was ready when he reached for her shoulder. Moving her right hand across her chest, she gripped his hand, jamming her thumb in between his index and middle fingers. Before he could react, she twisted the outer edge of his hand upward, simultaneously pulling it back across her chest to throw him off balance. She used her left palm to bear down on his elbow. He was driven to his knees immediately and let out a surprised curse. The shopping basket fell to the floor with a clatter. The technique caused him severe pain but did not take much effort on her part. She wanted him to know that.

She held the lock for several seconds. Breathing slowly, concentrating on each breath to gain control, she eased The Monster back toward its cage. It had damn near snapped this idiot's arm in a fit of rage.

An older man carrying a basket turned down the aisle and saw them. Ava looked at him over Jeremy's head. The twitch in her upper lip, a silent snarl, had the man quickly turning and racing back out of the aisle.

Ava's gaze returned to Jeremy. She could only see the back of his head from her position, but his entire body was shaking from the pain of the technique.

"Understand?" she asked.

The Monster struggled to get out, clawing and biting against the iron bars of the cage. Ava stepped back from it and turned her back.

Breathing normally again, she applied just a little more pressure to Jeremy's elbow to increase the pain. He groaned through gritted teeth.

"Do you understand?" she demanded.

"Yes," Jeremy gasped.

Because he had invaded her space as well as taking up her time, Ava held the arm lock a moment longer. "Tell me." The Monster banged its head against the bars, roaring in fury.

"I understand! Shit."

Ava released his arm and stepped around him.

"Son of a bitch, that hurt," Jeremy said, rubbing his elbow as he stood up. When he looked up, the woman was gone. The abandoned cart stood empty in the aisle.

Shit, Jeremy thought, picking up his basket. His wrist and elbow were throbbing. His ego was bruised. He had never been turned down by a woman before. Certainly not so absolutely or so physically.

His friends were going to give him so much shit about this. They would never let him live it down. He decided to keep it to himself.

•　•　•　•　•

"I told you," Griffin said, grinning widely. They sat across from each other at their original table. Griffin had pushed the sleeves of his shirt up, showing strong wrists and forearms. Iz was trying not to stare at them. "You were amazing."

"Thank you. You have perfect teeth." She was feeling great, the smile on her face natural for once.

He looked amused. "Your eyes are glassy. You're off your face, aren't you?"

"My face is right here."

He laughed. "You're drunk."

"Maybe a little tipsy. I'm surprised I remembered the chords."

"Your voice is sexy and smokey when you sing."

"Your eyes are amber, like a lion's. I've never met anyone with eyes that color." She gazed at them without inhibition, turning her head at different angles to watch how the light reflected in them.

Smiling, he watched her, keeping his head still but following her movement with his eyes like the old Felix the Cat clock her grandmother used to have in her kitchen. That made her giggle.

Isabel took a sip of ice water, trying to clear her head. God, she wanted to make out with him. She needed to get a hold of herself. What the hell had she been thinking, downing whiskey like water to calm her nerves? And the wine in the back room before and after her set... Shit. Alcohol made her extremely flirty. She was making a fool out of herself to someone not even remotely interested in her.

"Tell me something about yourself," she said, trying to focus. She blinked hard. The lights seemed brighter than usual tonight.

"What do you want to know?" He pushed his wine glass back, still mostly full, and took a drink of water. Isabel watched his mouth and wondered what it would feel like to kiss him.

Jesus.

"Your accent," she said. "You're Australian, right?"

"I'm American, born and raised. My mum is Australian, and my dad is American, and they moved here years before I was born. Since my mum was around more than my dad, I picked up her accent."

"Ha! Mum." Iz giggled.

"You're entertaining when you're tipsy. You're turn. Tell me something about you."

"I sing and play acoustic guitar." What was her sudden obsession with him? Now she was staring at his hands, wondering how they would feel on her body. She exhaled, her face burning. "Wow, I'm hot."

Isabel flagged down the waitress and ordered another shot of whiskey.

"Are you sure you want to do that?" Griffin asked.

"Fuck it," Iz said, gulping down more water. "If Mom and Beth want to hide behind their ovaries, I should be able to hide behind alcohol for one damn night. Maybe I'll finally get a good night's sleep."

"I have no idea what that means," Griffin said. Noting her hand on the table, he slid his over and rested it on top of hers. She was buzzing with energy, nerves and tension pulsing off her in waves.

"Never mind. Tell me something else... about... you." When his hand covered hers, her voice faded, and she gazed down at their connection.

"I'm addicted to black olives. I already knew the two things you told me. Cheater. You owe me three now. Get along with your mum and dad?"

"How about we change the subject?" Her tone was abruptly steel, her eyes like emeralds. The hand under his curled into a fist.

Annie brought Isabel's whiskey and set it down on the table. "I made it a double."

"I love you," Iz said, smiling. "Thank you."

When Annie walked away, Iz leaned toward Griffin conspiratorially. She nodded toward Annie's retreating backside. "If I was gay for a day, I'd totally tap that."

Griffin laughed. He watched Isabel sip the whiskey this time, which was better. "So, you don't like talking about family," he said. He casually hooked his fingers under hers and pried them open to keep her from making a fist. Her hand was warm in his as he brushed his thumb across the back of it. "Interesting."

"I really just want to fuck you in the back seat of your car."

"How about your job? Do you - Say what now?" His eyes sharpened as what she said sank in.

"Sorry, I didn't mean to say that out loud." Her face was absolutely scarlet now, her eyes wide. She rambled on, trying to forget the past few seconds had happened. "My job. Well, I work in the healthcare industry as an administrative assistant to the manager in the Claims department. Basically, I babysit the manager and everyone under him because, even though they're supposed to be adults, they can't push in their chairs, stop whining, play nice with each other, or survive even one day without me creating an itinerary with every detail of their day spelled out for them. Oh, and I get to clean up after them, because apparently, they don't know how to." She was talking fast and had to gulp in air when she finished.

Griffin was staring at her.

"So that's my job." She exhaled, hoping he would move on from her comment about his back seat.

He had a sly smile on his face. "Have you ever read books to dogs in shelters?"

Iz coughed, spilling a few drops of her drink. "Excuse me?"

"Reading to animals in shelters. It helps relieve their stress and it's therapeutic for the reader."

"This is like a Target pillow fight, isn't it? Where do you come up with these ideas?"

"I get paid a lot of money to be creative."

"Cre-ahye-tive," she mimicked. "I could listen to you talk for hours."

"I don't think you're going to last that long at the rate you're going." He squeezed her hand. She gazed at their hands again, blinking slowly.

"Nobody touches me. I like that you... you're not afraid to touch me."

"I enjoy touching you."

The smile she gave him was unencumbered and full of appreciation. Griffin watched as Isabel's eyes changed from bright and glassy to dull and unfocused. The smile slid from her face.

"And there she goes." He stood up, pulling his coat off the back of his stool.

"Oh. Fuck," she mumbled, falling heavily against the back of the stool. "I wanna go home."

"I'll drive you. Let me settle the tab."

A heavy haze settled over Iz. She glanced around the room, her eyes roaming so slow but not able to focus on any one thing. She could see people talking and laughing but the noise seemed to come from a long way off. Time seemed not to exist as she waited for Griffin.

Suddenly beside her, he took her hand to help her stand up.

"Annie said she'd lock up your guitar for the night. Come on, then."

Isabel slid off her stool. Her stomach lurched. Shit. She fought to get her hand to obey her head when she told it to go into the sleeve of her coat until Griffin helped her ease it on. He zipped it up gently, tucking it under her chin. Isabel raised her eyes to his, her lids heavy. Their faces were inches apart.

"I get obnoxious when I drink whiskey," she said, her voice repentant.

He gave her that dazzling smile. "That you do, love. And quite frisky. Come on. We'll come back tomorrow for your guitar and your car."

"Yes, let's come back tomorrow for my cah." She cackled. She leaned on him as he walked her through the cafe and opened the door to air that hit her like a wall made of ice. The fever that had enveloped her body just moments before turned to chills. Her feet didn't seem to be working right. Each step was like stumbling on stilts through quicksand.

"I think my feet are on backwards."

She lurched forward. Griffin reached over with his other hand to help steady her, accidentally brushing against her breast.

"Whoa," Isabel said. She reached up and took his arm. "I almost fell on my face."

"I've got you," he said easily, shifting so his hand and arm were away from her chest. "Put your arm around my waist. There you go."

He helped her to his vehicle, lifting her inside and leaning across her to engage the seat belt.

"That tickles," she laughed. Her head felt like it weighed a ton. She let it fall against the headrest. The darkness felt better to her eyes, which were sore from the lights of The Raz.

When Griffin leaned up, his amber eyes were inches from hers. Though her breath smelled like whiskey, he had to hold back the urge to press his mouth to hers.

"You should probably go see a doctor for that," Iz said somberly.

"What?" he asked, jiggling the belt to make sure it was snug across her body. He remained leaned over, bracing a hand on the console, staring into her beautiful jade eyes. She touched the side of his face with her fingertips.

"Your eyes are really beautiful, but I think they're making fun of your eyebrows."

Griffin couldn't help but chuckle. "Your mouth looks appetizing."

For some reason that made her giggle. "Like apples?"

"Hmm... Let's see."

His lips grazed hers, spreading warmth throughout her body. In her mind, she was sweeping her hands through his hair, but in reality, they were too heavy to lift. They lay like cement in her lap while she marveled over how gentle he was.

A pang of regret raced through her when he pulled back.

"Not apples," he said softly. "Much sweeter."

"Did my mouth work okay?" she looked worried. "I'm having trouble moving my lips."

Grinning, he ran his thumb across her lower lip and was satisfied when a shiver coursed through her. "They worked just fine."

"We aren't in the back seat," she said, her eyes dancing.

"Next time." Griffin rested his hand on her knee.

"Will you kiss me again? You're really good at it."

Smiling, he obliged her, keeping his hand on her knee, and skimming his other up her arm. He traced her shoulder and slid his hand under her hair, around the back of her head to knead the muscles in her neck. The small sound she made, somewhere between a sigh and a moan, had him struggling to go slow, keep it friendly.

Though it cost him, he raised his head.

"Whoa." Her voice was starting to drift, and her eye lids were getting heavy. Then: "Where's my car?"

"We'll pick it up tomorrow with your guitar."

When she didn't say anything more, he shut her door gently and walked around to the driver's side. "Do you want me to take you home or to my flat? Mine's closer."

Isabel's eyes were closed, her head turned away him. Her breathing had deepened.

"Isabel." He gave her a gentle shake. "Your flat is at least twenty-five minutes away. Do you think you can make it that far without puking?"

She groaned. Her head was lolling on the headrest.

"I'll take that as a hard no."

He drove carefully toward his place, easing into turns and stops so he wouldn't jostle her and upset her stomach. He wanted to get home as soon as possible to avoid vomit in the vehicle if he could.

"Bloody hell," he muttered when someone pulled out in front of him, and he had to tap his breaks a little too hard. Beside him, Isabel's body jerked against the seat belt, and she moaned again. He automatically reached out and pushed her back against the seat with his hand on her chest.

"Sorry, love. Almost there." Removing his hand instantly, he felt like a pervert. The guy in front of him flipped him the bird. Griffin muttered a string of obscenities to keep from chasing the guy down and beating him to a pulp.

"I'm sorry, Hayden."

Griffin glanced over at Isabel. Her eye lashes were damp.

"Please don't tell Gabriel."

He reached over and rested his hand on her knee. Because she seemed to need to hear it, he said, "I won't tell him."

His apartment complex came into view, and he sighed with relief as he pulled into the car park and eased into a space. The flat came with underground parking, but he didn't want to confuse Isabel with more stairs than necessary or an elevator ride that might make her nauseous. He thought the walk from the car to the building in the brisk air would help clear her head.

Isabel's head rolled toward him when he opened her door. Beads of sweat glistened on her forehead and upper lip. She inhaled deeply when he leaned toward her to unbuckle her.

"You smell good."

"Why, thank-"

She jerked forward and vomited all over his dashboard. Griffin barely had time to hop out of the way. Eyes wide, she turned to him. "I'm so sor-"

Another wave hit her, and she spewed all over the parking lot. She managed to lean out just enough to miss Rover with the second bout. The acrid smell of alcohol and bile hit them both.

"That's going take at least a couple sessions to get detailed," Griffin said cheerfully. "Good thing I know a guy."

He pulled a couple napkins out of the accessory compartment in the door so she could wipe her mouth.

"That tastes like straight-up ass," Isabel grumbled miserably. She wiped her mouth, grimacing. "It was probably the two glasses of wine I pounded before and after my set. I was so nervous with you there."

"I'm sure the whiskey had nothing to do with it," Griffin mused.

"I get obnoxious when I drink whiskey," she said, sounding sad again.

"You said." Shutting the door, he took her forearms and guided her around the vomit.

"I was so nervous with you there. I wanted you to like my music."

"I love your music. Your voice is like Bishop Briggs or ZZ Ward. Powerful, full of emotion."

She stopped abruptly. Looking up at him, he saw her eyes were brimming. "Really?"

"You're really good, Isabel."

He dipped his arm under hers and pulled her farther away from the vehicle. Magically, she had only gotten a little vomit on her jacket and a few drops on her shoes from where it dripped off the dashboard. Griffin had a friend that did great detailing for a decent price, but he was going to get hassled for this.

They started walking again. She grunted as she tripped over her own foot. Griffin lifted her slightly while she regained her balance.

"I'm not so ah-may-zing now, am I?" she asked as he helped her into the building.

"I'm still pretty smitten with you," he said, walking her toward the stairs. "We're taking the stairs. I think the elevator will make you nauseous."

They struggled up a few stairs, one at a time, before he spoke again.

"Who is Hayden?"

She stiffened in his arms but didn't have the muscular coordination at the moment to pull away from him. "My dead sister." She lifted her foot slowly, accomplished getting one step closer. Thank God he was only on the second floor.

"The one who's grave you visited the night we met in the grocery store."

"Yes." Another step. She was shaking now, the hand on his waist gripping his coat in a fist.

"Is today her birthday? Is that why you're thinking about her?"

"It was on the seventh." Another step. "I'm always thinking about her."

He shifted her as they stopped in front of his door. He bent forward to pull his keys out of his pocket while holding Iz up.

"This isn't my apartment. I don't know this door." Isabel was frowning. Tilting her head, she bumped it against Griffin's and giggled again. She liked the feel of him against her, so she kept her temple against his.

She pressed her palm against the door in wonder.

"This is my flat - apartment; yours was too far away. I tried to ask but you zoned out a bit."

"Are we on a date?"

"You're on a bender."

Her jerky movements were making it hard to use one hand to get the right key separated from the others. He finally had the one he needed and jangled the others down enough to get the key in the lock.

"I'm going to die."

"Everyone's going to die. In we go."

Griffin stepped sideways and half-walked, half-carried her in. With his free hand, he closed and locked the door behind him. He hobbled her to his kitchen, where he settled her on a stool at the island. Pulling a water bottle out of the refrigerator, he set it in front of her.

"Drink the entire thing, if you can."

He took off his coat, then helped her out of hers. Her arms didn't seem to work properly and stuck in the sleeves, but Griffin patiently and gently untangled them and eased the material off. He left her a moment to hang them in some magical place Isabel lost track of.

"You have a really big apartment," she said, taking a sip of water. The liquid was cool against her throat, which burned from the acidic vomit. She burped, long and low, and her entire mouth was full of the taste of bile.

"Ugh." She shook her head at the horrible taste, which made her dizzy. "Straight-up ass."

Griffin returned from the magic coat closet. "Are you going to be sick again?"

"M-maybe."

"Come on, then." He helped her off the stool and wrapped her arm around his waist, pressed her hand against his belt. "Hold on here."

She did as she was told, hoping the room would stop weaving in and out of focus. Griffin looped his arm around her shoulders. He had to stoop toward her to allow for the height difference. They walked-hobbled to the bathroom.

"Stand here just a moment."

Pulling a towel out of one of the cabinets, he partially unfolded it so she could kneel on it instead of the cold tile. The simple act of kindness made tears sting at the corners of her eyes. Even more so when he took her hand and helped ease her to the floor, his other hand on her back to keep her from tipping over. Having his hands on her helped her to feel steady both physically and emotionally. She wanted to tell him that but couldn't find the words.

He left her a moment to get two fresh wash cloths out of a drawer. One he left on the counter and the other he ran under cool water. Brushing her hair back from her face, he dabbed her cheeks and forehead with the rag.

"Push up your sleeves. There you go. What happened to Hayden?" he asked gently. He pulled her long, dark blonde hair back from her face, so it fanned out over her back.

"Nobody knows for sure." Her voice was dull. When she spoke next, her tone was emotionless, clinical. "My family used to go camping three or four times every summer. Dad would take time off work, and we'd all go for a few days during the week, when it wasn't as busy."

Her stomach was starting to feel queasy again. Iz braced her arms on the rim of the toilet – which seemed supernaturally clean for a single man's apartment – and leaned forward slightly to make sure she hit the mark if it came to that. Griffin set the rag on the counter behind him and gathered her hair again, making sure to keep it out of her face.

"That sounds like fun." He shifted her hair to one hand so he could rub her back with the other. "Sounds like you're close with your family."

Isabel dry heaved. Tears burned her eyes. Letting out a shaky breath, she nodded.

"We used to be. Mom and Beth didn't like it as much. Beth's the oldest. They're more for early mornings and reading magazines in the air-conditioned camper. But half the fun was teasing back and forth about how much we loved it and they hated it."

Griffin heard the affection in her voice, so different from the contempt he had heard when she talked about them earlier in The Raz.

"Anyway, she and Beth would go through magazines and talk school gossip and dates and all that bullshit. Gabriel, Hayden, and I would do things with Dad: hike in the woods, swim, fish, and look for reptiles and amphibians.

Hayden had these moleskin notebooks she used to keep information about all the animals we found in them. What we found, like a Bull frog or a toad: it's scientific name; a description of the location we found it in; it's length; color. It used to drive Gabe and I nuts because we wanted to look under the next rock or piece of bark, and she was still writing. She kept telling us to hold the 'species' still while she photographed and measured it. Like it would pose for us."

"Toads don't like getting their pictures taken?" Griffin asked. He kept rubbing her back steadily, not too slow, not too fast.

"Right?! Do you know what toads do to try to escape when you pick them up?" Isabel rested her head on her right arm and turned her face to look up at him. Though her eyes were bloodshot, and she obviously had an upset stomach, she gave him a lopsided smile.

"I'm afraid my knowledge of wild animals is quite limited."

"They piss."

"That's pleasant."

She smirked. "Yeah. So, I get to hold the toad while he gets his mugshot taken, and he's wetting himself. I have two handfuls of piss. What I wouldn't do for my sister."

She became quiet at the implication. Taking deep breaths, she tried to calm the horrible feeling in her stomach like she had swallowed something live, and it was eating its way out of her. She blinked back tears, feeling the familiar panic at the surge of emotions rushing through her.

"Anyway," she continued, trying to return to a dispassionate tone and failing, "the last trip we took was in late August of 2002. I was nine. The theory is she was kidnapped and probably murdered by a local pedophile who had just moved into the area. One morning we woke up and she was just gone. We n-never saw her again. Never f-found her b-body-"

She raised her head and violently hurled into the toilet. Griffin thought she was forcing out emotional pain as much as alcohol. He felt her muscles clench and her body convulse and winced at the force. He could only rest his hand on her back to let her know she wasn't alone while the sickness took its course.

When she was done, she rested her head on her arm, panting. Tears dripped into the bowl.

"That causes some tension between you and your family." Griffin pulled a few stray hairs back and grouped them with the others in his hand as a makeshift ponytail.

"Beth and my mom like to hold onto her death like it happened yesterday. It's been sixteen years. It's over. They shut everyone else out to wallow in their grief."

"Leaving you on your own to deal with your grief."

She leaned forward and threw up again. This time it wasn't as violent. Griffin held her hair, waited a beat, then stood and dampened the other washcloth. He gently wiped her mouth. She squeezed her eyes shut tight. More tears spilled over. Her lower lip was trembling.

"Thank you. I think I'm done."

She reached up and flushed the toilet. As the panting subsided, she used a wad of toilet paper to wipe her nose. Her skin was beaded with sweat. Her body was shaking from the effort of being sick and all the blood had drained from her face.

Griffin had run the first washcloth under water again and now he sat back down with it. He dabbed it around her feverish face again.

"I invited you to hear me sing, and I f-fucked it all up. I didn't mean to flake out on you." She shuddered. Blinking and miserable, she took the cloth from him and held it against her forehead.

"I invited myself, remember?" He rested his hand on the side of her head. "It's hard for you to let people in. Thank you for telling me about your music and your sister."

Isabel raked the back of her hand across her eyes. "I'm not used to... getting along with people."

"We get along just fine." He began to rub her back again.

The nausea was gone, replaced with a hollowed-out soreness.

"I like you. I feel like I won't disappear when I'm with you."

Invisible, she said in the grocery store the other day, Griffin thought. Disappear. The words danced in his head, filing into his mental storage so he could think about them later.

"Losing a sister so young, in such a horrible way, is going to leave scars."

"Now you know all my dark secrets," she said, suddenly very tired.

"I doubt that. I see more pillow fight therapy in your future."

She nodded somberly.

"Do you think you can gargle some Listerine? You'll feel better if you can."

She lifted her head. It felt as if it weighed seventy-five pounds. "Are you trying to politely tell me my breath stinks?"

"Your breath is festy; I won't lie."

"It's feisty?"

He smiled patiently. "Festy. It's Australian slang for disgusting. I know from experience if you don't taste bile and alcohol tomorrow on your tongue, you'll feel better than if you do."

Leaning up, he picked a small bottle of mouth wash off the sink.

"You're going to feel like shit in the morning. This will be one less thing making you feel that way."

She shifted on the floor. As she took a swig, she tried not to touch her mouth to the bottle. She handed it back to him. He took a swig as well. He stood up, offered her his hand. They gargled together over the sink. Iz had an insane urge to giggle.

What a hot mess I am, she thought. Hayden would roll over in her grave.

Except she doesn't have a grave. Not really.

Feeling like she was going to burst into tears, Iz leaned forward and spit. Then a couple more times. She was feeling a little better already but dinner at her family's house tomorrow was going to be even worse than it had been the past two weeks.

Griffin reached into a cabinet and pulled out a bottle of aspirin. Opening it for her, he poured three out and handed her the pills. From somewhere on the counter, he produced the water he had gotten for her in the kitchen. She hadn't even known he brought it in with them. Had she lost time? She couldn't quite remember walking into his apartment.

Obediently, she downed the pills and followed it with a large gulp of water. Then a second gulp. Her stomach was starting to settle, and the water was soothing to her raw throat.

"Do you want me to drive you home?" he asked. His hands were on her elbows, making sure she was steady. "Or do you feel safe enough to stay here?"

"I feel safe with you," she said. "I don't want to be in your way."

Griffin raised his arms to take her face in his hands. "You're not in my way, Izzie. Come on. I have a tee shirt and some shorts you can sleep in."

He took her by the hand as he had before, resting the other on her back. Guiding her, he walked to a door past the bathroom sink.

Beyond the bathroom was a walk-in closet. Griffin shut the bathroom door, locking it from the closet side. They continued to the master bedroom, where a king-sized bed faced a seventy-two-inch television across the room. Patio doors on the south wall opened onto a spacious balcony.

Griffin turned on a lamp on the bedside table.

"This place is huge," Isabel breathed.

"I told you, people pay me stupid amounts of money to be creative."

He turned down the bed and closed the curtains on the patio doors. When he turned back, she was lying on the bed, her long legs curled up to her chest, her hands curled under her chin. He walked to the bed, studying her outfit. She was wearing a long sweater, jeans, and boots. He carefully pulled the boots off, setting them on the floor. She didn't stir. She shouldn't sleep in her clothing, but he was reluctant to undress her.

He found a tee shirt and shorts with strings in his closet and set them next to her on the bed. She hadn't moved. He couldn't even hear her breathing.

"Isabel." He gave her a gentle shake. Her eyes fluttered open. "You need to put these on. You can't sleep in a sweater and jeans."

She sat up slowly, blinking. Griffin handed her the clothes and shifted on the bed, so he was turned away from her. He heard shuffling, and a moment later the sweater sailed over his head and hit the floor. More shuffling, some grunting, a couple of muttered curses, and her jeans joined the sweater. Another string of curses before the bra flew past his head and hit the TV, draping over the top of it. Then nothing.

"Are you finished?"

"Yeeaah," she drawled.

He turned around. Lying down in his massive bed made her look even smaller. She swam in his clothing - he was eight inches taller and outweighed her by almost one hundred pounds - but she was fully covered. She looked adorable.

Griffin stood. "If you need anything-"

"You're going out there alone?" An edge of panic laced her voice. She leaned up, her hands shooting out, her fingers digging into his wrists. Her eyes swam with terror. "You're going into the dark alone?"

Into the dark?

"I'll be right next door, on the sofa. That door locks so you know you're safe." He kept his tone patient and calm, pointing to the bedroom door as he spoke so she understood what he was saying. "The bathroom door is locked, too. You'll be safe here."

Her eyes filled with tears that seemed to take forever to spilled over. "Don't go. Don't leave me alone. I'm didn't mean to get drunk and ruin your car. I promise I'll pay for all of -"

"Okay. Okay. I won't leave you alone."

Sitting on the edge of the bed, he cupped her face in his hands. Her eyes were huge, swiping from left to right. She looked unbelievably fragile in that moment, more afraid than she should have been. Why was she afraid of him leaving the room? He wasn't sure she was awake.

Tremors rippled through her. He caressed her cheeks with his thumbs to dry the tears. Little by little, her grip on his wrists began to loosen.

"I'll be right back." Griffin said, pulling back. "I'm going to change."

"You shouldn't go out there alone," she said in a hushed tone. "It isn't safe."

"Isabel, I'm just going to change my clothes," he said, brushing her hair back from her face. She had broken out in a light sweat again. "I can't sleep in my jeans. I'll be right back."

He eased her back onto the bed and pulled the bedding up around her. Beneath his hands, her body was rigid. "I'll be right over there, changing into my shorts." He pointed to the closet.

Giving her a moment to understand, Griffin walked to the closet. He quickly pulled off his jeans and Henley shirt and put on a pair of shorts. He left his tee shirt on. Unlocking the bathroom door in case Isabel woke in the night to relieve herself or get sick, he shut off the light.

Back in the bedroom, sitting next to her on his side of the bed, he noticed with alarm that she was still shivering, goosebumps raised on her arms. Her eyelashes were soaked with fresh tears. Griffin pulled the blankets up higher around her. For a moment he simply watched her breathe, her eye lids flutter, her fingers twitch. Her breath was short and quick, as if she were afraid.

Griffin thought his entire purpose in life at that moment was to calm her fears.

But he wanted to know what had caused them. He needed to know.

Isabel's hand reached out across the bed, searching. Griffin took it and kissed the back, holding it against his chest to warm it up. At the contact, her body began to relax, her breathing returning to normal. She let out a soft little sigh.

"Stay close. We're stronger together," she mumbled. "Don't go into the dark alone."

Griffin stroked her hair thoughtfully. "I'm right here, love."

•　　•　　•　　•　　•

CHAPTER FOUR

Someone had swung a sledgehammer into her skull after driving ice picks into her temples. The pain woke her.

Isabel moved an arm that felt as heavy as a cinder block toward her face, pressed the heel of her hand to her forehead. The firm, steady pressure lessened the pain only slightly. The muscles around her eyes were sore, her stomach was rocking like it was riding the tide of the ocean, and her jaw felt as if it had come unhinged.

Sweet baby Jesus.

The sound of breathing was drilling into her ears. Had she taken her parent's dogs over night? No. She wouldn't have gotten so drunk while having them in her care. Besides, the sounds were too light. Ozzie snored like a chainsaw. Maya yipped and yowled in her sleep.

Isabel slowly opened her eyes. The room was mostly dark – thank God for light canceling curtains – so it took several seconds for her eyes to adjust. A foot from her face, Griffin lay sleeping on his side, his hair looking freshly tumbled. Isabel closed her eyes and pressed her fingers between them. When she opened them, she took in every detail of him to distract herself from the pain in her head.

His lips were slightly parted, making them look especially edible. One hand was tucked under his pillow. She hadn't noticed how long his eye lashes were before. His face was relaxed and flawless, the face of a man with endless compassion and patience.

Fragments of last night came back as she watched him sleep. Her being nervous about singing in front of him, the whiskey, the wine, more whiskey.

Her nervousness turning to grief over the loss of Hayden, turning to anger at her mother and sister for hoarding their grief. Didn't it always come back to that? She inwardly groaned.

Gently rolling over so she didn't wake him, she eased herself into a sitting position. She pressed her hands to the sides of her head, feeling as if they were barely holding her brain in. The pressure was agonizing.

"Oh my God," she mouthed.

She stood, walking to the bathroom with an unsteady gait. She knew better than to get drunk on whiskey, let alone adding wine to the mix. It took a moment for her fumbling fingers to unlock the door between the walk-in closet and the bathroom. She vaguely remembered Griffin locking it so she would know he couldn't take advantage of her while she slept. Such a sweet gesture. One she repaid by clinging to him like a damn barnacle.

Holding her head as she relieved herself, she exhaled slowly. She had made a complete ass out of herself last night and for what? Because she wasn't getting enough attention from mommy?

Give yourself a break, Gabriel often told her. It's not that simple and you know it.

That never made her feel any better, and it didn't now. She hated herself for becoming what she loathed in her mother and Beth – too weak to handle reality. Too selfish in her anxiety and depression to realize anyone else existed around her.

She washed her hands, then turned the water all the way to cold, splashing her face until she was gasping. Leaning over the sink, she took deep breaths until she was able to inhale without feeling as if she was going to burst into tears.

She didn't want to hide in alcohol. Sure, she liked the taste of whiskey. Downing five shots of whiskey (how many had been doubles?) and two full glasses of wine, however, was different than a drink of wine with dinner or slow sips from a glass in the evening as the sun went down. It made her feel tired, weak, and useless. She had her music and her brother. Hell, now she even had a new friend. Griffin seemed patient enough to tolerate her insanity. She wanted to be grateful for what she had instead of constantly wanting things she didn't have.

She sighed, feeling better.

Wiping her face and hands on the towel, she took a deep breath. "Okay."

She rinsed with mouth wash. Running her tongue over her teeth, she grimaced. She found toothpaste in the medicine cabinet and used some on her finger to brush the rest of the grime off her teeth. That made her feel better still.

Opening the cabinet she'd seen Griffin open last night, she pulled out the bottle of aspirin and took another three.

Back in the bedroom, she climbed onto the bed and slipped under the blankets. Propping herself up on an elbow, she gazed at him. Griffin's snoring had become a little louder. Biting her thumb nail, Iz worked up as much courage as she could. She reached out and brushed her fingers over his hair. It was soft, like holding a baby chick. Adding a little pressure, Iz touched his hair again. She imagined running her hands through it, letting it slip through her fingers. Heat instantly rose to her cheeks and loins. She snatched her hand back.

Griffin shifted slightly, turning his head. He began forcing the air out of the small opening in his mouth instead of breathing easily through his nose. Watching him, Isabel suddenly snorted with laughter. She clamped a hand over her mouth.

Griffin's eye lids fluttered open. He gazed at her sleepily. "Hello, beautiful."

She tried to hide her giggles behind her hand. His hair was adorably disheveled. Would he think she was insane if she asked if she could run her hands through it? Of course, he would. Any normal person would.

"What's so funny?" he asked, amused.

She snorted again. "You even snore with an Australian accent."

"Shut up." He gave her a lopsided grin.

She started laughing. It hurt her head, but she couldn't help it. He was endearing when he first woke up. She pressed the heel of her palm to her temple again until the worst of the pain lessened minutely.

"How are you feeling?" he asked, mirroring her pose by leaning up on an elbow.

"My head is killing me, but I'm not nauseous. I guess that's something."

"You look more relaxed than you did last night." He let out a yawn and ran a hand through his hair.

"I've decided whiskey and I are better friends than bed mates."

"That's probably a good decision."

"The hangover hurts like a bitch." She gazed into his walnut-colored eyes. "I borrowed some toothpaste."

"Oh? You're going to give it back, then?" He tugged affectionately on a strand of her hair.

She snickered. Before she realized it, she was reaching toward him. "Can I just-" She pulled back, her face crimson, and started fussing with the collar of the tee shirt she had borrowed. "Sorry."

"What?" He looked from her hand to her face. "What were you going to do?"

"Nothing. It's really strange and inappropriate. I wasn't thinking." Restless, she sat up, bringing her knees to her chest.

"Now you have to tell me." Amusement flickered across his face. He was constantly entertained at the way she acted before she thought.

Isabel twisted her fingers together to keep them from embarrassing her. "I have an insane urge to touch your hair. It's messed up. The urge, not your hair. Although your hair always has this messed up look to it, which is probably why I... you know what? Never mind." She was talking too fast, too much.

He grinned. "That's not inappropriate. I held your hair last night."

"You did?" Realization hit her and she groaned. "Right. While I was vomiting. Thanks for that."

"You can touch my hair, Izzie."

Her heart stuttered. No one called her that anymore. Hayden had, a long time ago. Ever since her sister's disappearance, Isabel had gone by her birth name or Iz.

"I don't really want to touch it," she admitted, before she could think about her sister too much. "I want to grab onto it like..." She fisted her hands without realizing it. When she became aware of what she was doing, she dropped her hands. "Anyway. It's a weird thing."

"Fist away."

Isabel let out a bark of laughter. "That could have been taken an entirely different way."

She reached out hesitantly. Her eyes intense. When her palms were beside his temples, Griffin lurched forward and let out a snarling, snapping growl.

Isabel jerked back, her eyes huge, lost her balance, and almost fell backward off the bed. Griffin grabbed her wrist and pulled her back up.

"You dick!" she yelled, punching his shoulder. Her face was scarlet, her heart springing around her rib cage like a rabbit. The pain in her head increased until she thought her head would simply blow up.

Griffin was laughing so hard he held his chest. "Totally worth it," he gasped.

"Fuck-stick!" Iz punched him in the shoulder again, sending more tremors through her body and into her head. "Ow."

He made an effort to keep a straight face. "Okay. Seriously. I won't do that again. I promise."

Suspicious, Isabel glared at him.

"I promise," he repeated, chuckling. He reached out, touched her hand before he withdrew. "You were concentrating so hard I couldn't help it. But I'll be good."

Isabel continued glaring at him while she reached out. When he behaved himself, she placed her fingers at his temples and moved them toward the back of his head. Griffin watched her expression soften. Her mouth was slightly open, her eyes bright and curious, as if she were standing at the edge of the Grand Canyon. She moved her hands slowly around his head, gripping his hair in her fists. An image of her raking her hands through his hair when he was inside her made her blush. She didn't realize her breath hitched, but Griffin heard it. He also noticed the flush burst across her cheeks and how her pupils dilated. Everything inside him tightened with lust.

"Thanks. For... humoring me," she said, pulling back quickly. She felt a little lightheaded.

Griffin looked delighted. "Happy to help."

As the fog was clearing from Isabel's head, her eyes slowly focused on his right shoulder. The sleeve of the shirt had pulled up slightly. Isabel's eyes rounded in surprise. "You have a tattoo."

His grin widened. "I had it when I was wearing this shirt last night, too."

Smiling, Iz lifted the sleeve higher to see it in its entirety. "I was a little preoccupied with all the vomiting."

It looked like high-quality ink, not the faded grayish green some people had. It was an intricate compass that had been fashioned out of gears. Instead of a single magnetic needle, there were four individual ones, each extending from a central cog. The needles created out of smaller gears looped together with an arrow at the end. The rim had tiny lines all the way around to indicate a degree dial. A chain came from the top of the compass, down his biceps, looping around his arm a couple times. The end of the chain had a larger link that seemed to grow into Griffin's skin. The four letters depicting the cardinal directions were done in script. It was a complex design, done all in black and gray hues. The artist had used his talent to make it look like the object was a part of Griffin's body. It was stunning.

"The tattoo artist took a discount off the charge since I came up with the design," Griffin said. "I kind of like the idea that no matter how lost I get, I always have a compass to find my way back."

"It's beautiful." Her voice turned soft and thoughtful. "I wish I had something to turn me in the right direction." She ran her index finger over the tattoo, thankful for the distraction while she owned up to her stupidity. She took a deep breath, let it out. "I'm sorry about last night."

"You said that."

"I thought I'd tell you now that I actually know what I'm saying."

"How much do you remember?"

"You liked my singing," Isabel said. "You said I sounded like Bishop Briggs, which I take as a major compliment. Thank you."

"You're most welcome." Isabel thought his smile was perfect even when his teeth weren't showing. She stopped playing with his ink and gave him her full attention.

"You said something about reading to dogs in animal shelters?"

He nodded.

"I think I had a lot of trouble walking. I remember you having to help me to your car, and into your building."

"It was similar to watching the Scarecrow from 'The Wizard of Oz' when he first gets down from the pole."

"Good Lord." Iz closed her eyes. "I think I may have mentioned having sex with Annie."

"Yes, yes you did. Thankfully, she had already walked away from our table and didn't hear you."

Isabel put her hand to her forehead. "Thank God. I have to pay to have your car cleaned. I threw up in it. Twice. Did I get you at all?"

"My catlike reflexes are legendary. I avoided all projectile vomit."

"Sorry."

"Do you remember what else you said about my car?"

She tried to think. Anything beyond 'coffee' was just too difficult right now. Shaking her head, she winced at the twinge of pain it caused her.

"You said you wanted to fuck me in the back seat of it. Your words, not mine."

Her eyes rounded. "Fuck."

"Exactly." He grinned.

Covering her mouth with her hands, she exhaled. "I turn everything into a sexual innuendo when I drink too much wine."

"Nah. You loosened up a little. No harm done."

"Jesus. Did I get combative? I can get really bitchy after too much whiskey. Was I a total bitch?"

"No. Quite the opposite. You were affectionate. Before you fell asleep, you were worried about me leaving the room alone, going out into the dark."

If he hadn't been paying close attention, he would have missed the slight shift in her eyes, the tensing of her muscles.

"I was?" Her tone was a little too casual.

"You didn't want me to sleep on the couch," he said, not letting on that he noticed a change. "That's why I slept in here. You kept saying, 'Don't go into the dark alone.'"

She didn't speak. Those dark green eyes had become distant. The shield had gone up. Griffin pondered that and tucked the information away for later contemplation.

"Do you know what that means?" he asked, touching her knee.

Jerking, she looked down at his hand. "What? I was so out of it; I don't remember most of what I said. I have to piss. Is there coffee?"

Not exactly a lie, but a pretty clear fuck off if one were listening closely, and he was.

Isabel was already off the bed and heading toward the bathroom, leaving him to wonder why she had been so afraid last night and why she didn't want to talk about it now.

He walked to the kitchen to make coffee, hearing the water running in the bathroom. When he returned to the bedroom, it was still running.

Sitting on the bed, he propped his pillow up against the headboard and leaned against it. What she had said last night made her nervous, not that he had stayed in the room in the same bed as her. When he told her what she'd said, she didn't want to continue talking about it. Interesting.

She returned looking slightly less spooked, sitting so she was leaning against the headboard, not directly facing him. She brought her knees to her chest. Her hairline was damp; she must have splashed water on her face.

"Is that okay?" Griffin asked, raising his eyebrows.

"Coffee is always okay."

"That I stayed in here with you last night."

As if suddenly realizing she should have been more modest about it, Iz flushed. Then shrugged. "I asked you to stay."

He nodded slowly. "You did."

"So... thanks." She lowered her legs and crossed them. "And I really am sorry."

"For what?"

"I wanted to share my music with you, something that's really important to me." She shifted so she was facing him, more comfortable with the subject matter. "Instead, I shared..."

"Gastrointestinal fluid?"

She snorted again, setting a hand on his chest, and giving him a playful shove. When she would have moved her hand away, he covered it with his and kept it pressed to his chest. She noticed his heart seemed to be thundering under her palm.

Feeling awkward, she began to ramble. "I promise, I'll pay to get your car cleaned. Professionally. As many times as it takes. I'm so sorry."

"You keep saying that."

"I've never been so drunk, especially when I'm going to sing." It was vital that he understood she didn't let herself lose it like that on a regular basis. "I put myself in a really stupid position, which you didn't take advantage of. Thank you, by the way. And now you think I'm a drunk-"

He leaned over and brushed his lips against hers. It was a light kiss, but her mouth instantly flooded with heat. Keeping her hand pressed firmly to his chest, Griffin eased back just enough to look into her eyes. Seeing surprise but also intense longing, he briefly touched his lips to hers again.

Years of distancing herself from people fought against the urges he was igniting.

When he pulled back, he finally released her hand.

Isabel was more than a little breathless and confused. "What was that for?"

"I wanted my toothpaste back."

She punched his shoulder.

"Minty fresh."

She punched him again. "I'm already confused enough about my behavior. I don't want to have to try to figure out yo-"

He cupped his hand around the back of her neck and pulled her in for the kiss this time, not so gentle. Though he was slow and thorough, he plunged like she was the very air he needed to breathe, making her stomach drop and her hands tingle. She whimpered against his mouth without meaning to, and the sound of her need aroused him even more. She reached for him, paused when her hand met his chest again. Wasn't this exactly what she had been avoiding?

Fantasizing about him was one thing. It was quite another to act on it. Acting on it meant pain down the road. Always the pain.

Fuck it, she thought. She would enjoy it while she had it.

She balled her hand into a fist, grasping his shirt, pulling him closer. Her body was trembling. For the first time in years, she let herself fall into the kiss, the overwhelming sensations rocketing through her. This was not a brotherly hug on Sunday during family dinner. This was honest-to-God, tongue-tangling passion. Isabel raised both hands and raked them through his hair, gripping it in her fists as she had done minutes before. The ache low in her belly twisted and clawed to break free.

Griffin's hand moved to her shoulder, down her arm to her elbow. Goosebumps rose where his fingertips trailed along her skin.

When he came up for air, her eyes were out of focus and her face was flushed. He rubbed his thumb gently over her cheek. "Is that less confusing?"

Her head was spinning now as well as throbbing. It took a moment to catch her breath.

"You want to... go out with me?" She couldn't keep the incredulity from her voice.

He laughed. "Can't get anything past you." Inside, his blood was raging, his heart straining against the confines of his body as it hammered, yearning for more contact with her. He had only meant to ease into a soft kiss, to test her interest. Not stir his body up beyond reason. That sound she had made, which spoke of deep loneliness and eagerness to be pleased, had damn near undone him.

"I threw up in your car," she reminded him. "Twice! Then in your apartment. The first time we met, I yelled at you in a crowded store."

"Nobody's perfect." His damn heart wouldn't slow down. He wanted her so bad his blood was screaming. "You're smart, strong, creative. Who wouldn't want to date you?"

"Plenty of guys," she muttered. Absently, she reached up and fidgeted with her ear lobe. Her face was still crimson, giving Griffin a little thrill.

"Plenty of assholes, maybe."

She snorted laughter. "Ahs-holes."

He flashed those perfect teeth in a smile. "I thought you were sending me signals. Did I misread your statement about fucking me in the back seat of my car? Was that a euphemism for going horseback riding or taking classes on becoming beekeepers?"

"Yes," she said, then when disappointment flashed across his face: "I mean, no, you didn't misread... I meant what I said about the back seat... what was the question?"

Flustered, she pressed her fingers to her forehead.

Griffin chuckled, pulling her hand down and kissing the back of it. "Do you want to give this a shot?"

She stared at their hands when he linked their fingers. "Yes."

For a moment, she simply marveled as they moved their fingers, exploring each other's hands. Iz loved the contrast; how Griffin's hands were much longer and wider and swallowed hers up. He could crush her with his hands but chose not to.

The thought of his gentleness brought the sting of tears to her eyes. She didn't deserve his kindness. To avoid tears, she did what she always did: she hid behind sarcasm.

"You must be running really low on options if I'm the best you can do."

· · · · ·

The white house with the burgundy shutters sat on an acre of land that included an adequate lawn and a patch of woods. The location had convinced Ava to buy it in spite of the house being smaller than she had originally wanted. It was located in a remote area a few miles from Langdon, making it unattractive to prospective buyers. In the winter, narrow winding roads made it hazardous to travel during bad weather. Ava worked from home so that aspect didn't bother her. She also owned an all-wheel drive vehicle.

The house's distance from town and any main streets was the primary reason Ava had chosen it. Having a section of trees that would keep nature close to her was a bonus.

The second reason, and one which she would not have compromised on, was the full unfinished basement. She needed space to set up a workout area with her treadmill, elliptical, and weights, as well as have plenty of space to put mats for martial arts training. Several mats were laid out in one area of the basement for practicing rolls and flips. She had a full body opponent bag, a speed bag, and a 150-pound body bag suspended from the ceiling rafters with a heavy chain.

The third reason she had chosen this property happened by accident. It wasn't until the real estate agent was showing her the house that she found out the previous owner had died here. The death made the property almost impossible to sell, especially with rumors of suicide, but it made the offer more attractive to Ava. If everyone in Langdon thought the man had killed himself in this house, they would stay away from it, and her. The property, already isolated, would be left alone. Ava put in an offer immediately once she did the initial walk through and found the house adequate for her needs.

As it turned out, the man hadn't committed suicide; he'd had a heart attack. He had been sad living here at times when he missed his wife, and a few times he had considered cutting his wrists in the bathtub. He had even gone as far as filling the tub with water and setting razor blades on the side of the tub before memories of his wife had pulled him back each time.

Ava found this out during the first month she lived in the house. Her bathtub had filled with water when she wasn't at home. Razor blades, which she did not own, suddenly appeared on the lip of the tub a time or two. She had never felt any malice in the house, but she did not need anyone invading her space, either.

She finally caught him standing on her front porch one day when she returned home. They simply looked at each other. Realizing she could see him and that it did not bother her, he had spoken. He told her about his wife, about how the sadness sometimes made him want to die to be with her. About how her love for him gave him the strength to die naturally. About how he was reunited with her, but the house still held his memories. Sometimes the strong emotions left behind caused an overexcitement of energy, resulting in a memory replaying or objects moving.

Now she might get an occasional door closing on its own or an object moving from one room to another, but her bathroom was usually left alone.

She was unable to describe what she felt for her new home. Some days she stood in a room and stared for several moments, caught up in how peaceful seeing her belongings in this new space made her feel. Previous apartments hadn't stirred these emotions in her. They had all been cells to sleep and eat in. This place was different. She had specifically chosen it to fit her lifestyle. She had not expected the sometimes-overwhelming sense of... something... that stole her breath when she sat on the front porch with a cup of hot coffee or curled on the bench seat in her reading nook. Her feelings confused her. She had no one to talk to about them.

As she finished her lunch and was cleaning up, she heard a vehicle pull into her driveway. She seethed, listening. She didn't have company over. Not once since moving in had she invited someone into her house.

When the visitor crossed her porch and knocked, she felt violated. Who thought he or she had the right to step foot on her property? The thought of purchasing a large dog to further dissuade visitors flitted through her mind and was gone. A dog would interfere with her schedule.

She closed the dishwasher and walked to the front door, keeping her expression neutral.

David stood on her porch. He was holding a plant, a philodendron with variegated leaves in a plain yet beautiful green and cream striped ceramic plant holder. "Hi, Ava."

"David," she said. For all her training, she was caught completely off guard. She could anticipate any attack, accommodate an immediate response to defend herself against any threat. Yet she was at a loss at how to deal with an unexpected visit from the man who had raised her. Instantly the feeling of being violated vanished, replaced by shame.

She stared at him, dressed in a button-down shirt and nice jeans instead of the worn jeans and work shirt clothing he usually wore around his farm. "I did not know you were coming."

"I thought I'd surprise you," David said. He looked embarrassed. "I should have known better. It was rude not to call first."

"Come in," she said hastily, finally remembering her manners. She opened the door wider and stepped aside. She should have invited him in sooner instead of making him stand on the porch. "You are my first visitor."

David stepped inside and looked at the spacious open layout of the first floor. He had entered a living room, with a dining room to his left, and the kitchen past that, all visible. No walls separated the rooms. Ava didn't like small rooms and tight spaces. To the right of the kitchen were the stairs, a hallway to the back door, and what looked like a utility room or bathroom.

The floor he was standing on was original hardwood, matching the window trim. Ava was a minimalist with decorating; she had bookcases filled and spaced around chairs and a couch in the living room, but nothing cluttered the floor. A couple prints hung on the walls, pictures of trees, a riverbed, a closeup of a sunflower. The entire space was open and inviting without being crowded.

"It's beautiful," he said. "You've really made it your own."

"Do you want something to drink?" she asked, trying to remember how he and Ruth had treated guests at their house when she was a child. She had mostly hidden in her bedroom during visits unless David told her to join them. Knowing she was uncomfortable around people he did not ask her to join them often.

"I have water or... milk..." She floundered, wishing she had stocked Sprecher's Root Beer. He loved root beer. She had not thought to put some in her refrigerator because she did not drink it. She had only been thinking of herself. On her next trip to the store, she would pick some up and make sure to always have it on hand.

"Water's just fine."

She walked to the kitchen and pulled two glasses from a cupboard. Hosting him gave her a sense of purpose, even though it was just getting a glass of water. An odd sensation filled her at the sight of him in her house, looking around. She did not understand it. She was glad he had come.

"I brought you a plant. I don't really know if you like flowers and... they die in a few days. You could have this for years."

"I prefer plants. I will put it in the living room, so it gets plenty of light. You can set it there for now." She pointed to the counter between the kitchen and the dining room. Filling their glasses with filtered water from the refrigerator, she felt guilty that she had not invited him over sooner.

"You're all settled in," David said. He took a drink of water, amazed at how she had everything set up in such a way.

"I unpacked the day the movers dropped everything off."

Of course, she did. David tried to hide his grin. "Do you mind showing me the rest of it?"

"Okay."

She left her glass of water on the counter and showed him the half-bath on the first floor, let him look around the dining room and living room some more, then led him upstairs. She showed him the master bedroom and bathroom, and the second bedroom that she used as an office for her freelance business. There was a second half-bath off that room. She was especially fond of the reading nook in between the two rooms, which looked out over the front yard. The padded window seat was very comfortable and offered a beautiful view across the road into a field. In the morning, the view must be gorgeous as the sun came up. A horizontal bookcase was filled along one side of the hallway leading to the nook.

"I watch thunderstorms from here," she stated as he gazed out over the beautiful view.

"I bet that's a hell of a sight."

He followed her to the basement, where she showed him her workout area and training set up. He looked at her training equipment for a long time.

"How is Ward Sensei?" he asked.

"He is doing well," she said.

"Let's go upstairs," David said. "It's been a while since we've talked."

When they had settled in the living room recliners with their glasses, David studied Ava. "Are you happy here?" he asked.

She stared at him. Ava didn't quite comprehend happiness like other people.

David laughed. "Are you glad you moved here, Ava? Do you enjoy being by yourself out in the middle of nowhere?"

She sipped her water. "I get a lot of work done. It is quieter than Madison. I do not have to talk to so many people."

That's as close to a happy definition as there is for her, he thought. "Do you miss anything about the city?"

"No." Her answer was instant and firm.

He gave her a smile. "Nothing soothes the soul like nature."

She turned in the recliner so she could face him and draped her legs over the arm.

"Have you made any friends?"

She looked around the room, avoiding his gaze. Then she brightened. "I spent an hour with someone in a public location."

"Good for you! Tell me about it."

His eyes sparkled when he was excited. She liked seeing that sparkle in his eyes. It reminded her of when he used to sneak up on Ruth when she was making breakfast. He would always look at Ava and press his index finger to his lips as he was slowly approaching Ruth's back, hoping to startle her into dropping a raw egg onto the floor, and he always had that sparkle in his eye. Ruth always knew he was there, of course, but she always made a big production of dropping the egg anyway. Their dog snatched it up happily. That dog was dead now.

Ava felt a twinge of something she could not explain at the memory of Ruth and the dead dog and shook her head slightly to clear her head.

"He was jogging in the park," she answered.

"You went for a run with someone in a park?"

"He was jogging. I was running. We were both in the park."

David bellowed out laughter. "Oh, Ava! Did he even know you were there?"

Ava averted her eyes again. "It took him the entire hour to figure it out."

He shook his head, chuckling. "I don't even understand how that's possible."

"He used the trails. I run in the woods. By the time he figured out I was there, I was almost done with my workout."

David looked amused. "How did it feel having him there? Was it better than running alone?"

She sipped her water, thoughtful. "He was pushing himself hard. That made me want to push myself harder, so it was beneficial."

He did not need to know that when she was near Gabriel, she felt like something in her stomach was blowing around, like a moth trapped in a net.

"That's progress, then. Good for you. Maybe some time, you can ask him if he wants to go running together and you'll make a friend."

She shifted, uncomfortable. "He invited me to have coffee with him."

David's eyebrow raised. "What did you say?"

"I accepted. He purchased my drink, even though I am fiscally capable. After, he invited me to his house. I met his parent's dogs."

Shocked, he tried not to show it. This was huge progress for Ava. He wondered why she'd agreed, what about this man made her willing to break out of her strict disciplined life to make time for him.

"That's really great, Ava. He must be quite a guy for you to spend time with him."

Uncomfortable again, she gulped water. She did not want to try to explain everything she felt when she was around Gabriel. Her feelings were illogical. David would think it strange if she explained the odd things her body did when she was near him.

"I went to a cemetery," she said hesitantly.

"To visit Ruth?"

She shifted on the chair again. "I was standing at a grave when the man from the park visited. He asked me to stay with him while he sat with his sister."

This subject was a little easier to talk about.

"A man you barely knew asked you to stand with him at the grave of his sister?" David asked. "Did you stay?"

Ava nodded. "He sat with her for 52 minutes."

"Why did you stay, Ava?"

She was silent for several seconds. "His sister led me to her grave."

"That's not really an answer."

"I wanted to help him."

The words sounded strange coming from her mouth.

"Do you feel obligated to this man now?"

Ava frowned, shifting once again. "I am obligated to no one. He asked me to stay."

"You could have said no."

"I wanted to help him," she repeated.

David leaned forward slightly. That was new. When Ava didn't elaborate, David asked, "Why? Have you read him?"

"I cannot... Some of it is in the dark. I get pieces."

"Has that ever happened before?"

She shook her head.

"You've never wanted to help anyone before," David said, watching her closely. "Why now? Is it because you've seen the person effected by the loss of the spirit visiting you? Does that make it more personal?"

"That is not why. I..." Her eyes darted around, as if she could find the right words hidden somewhere in the room. "I am trying to keep my distance, but he is always approaching me, always wanting to spend time with me. I am getting to know him because he has told me, not because..."

"Not because you've read it off him," David finished. "He sounds persistent."

She nodded. Suddenly, she wanted to tell him about this man that was evoking emotions in her, that was making her body react in ways she did not understand. If she spoke of it, maybe she could stop thinking about it. She had no one to talk to about such things.

Now sounding distressed, her words came out in a rush. "I feel something different around him. My heartbeat elevates. I have trouble catching my breath and cannot focus."

David took a long drink to hide his smile. "Do you think about him even when he's not around?"

Ava leaned up, alert. "Yes. Do you think his sister is trying to warn me of something?"

If he burst out laughing, it would offend her and ruin her trust in him. David took a moment to answer, pressing his lips tightly together. "I think you're attracted to him, Ava."

She all but recoiled. "I... do not know what that feels like."

"I know, honey," he answered patiently. "That's why I'm explaining it to you."

"Vincent satisfies my physical urges."

The statement was blunt and unapologetic. Ava had told David she was curious about sex, not understanding that mothers usually discussed it with their daughters, if at all. She told him she had a partner in mind. He was elated she had waited until she was a legal adult, but the father in him had cringed. Still, he knew she would proceed with or without his approval. He'd supported her and was grateful when she told him her training partner from the dojo, Vincent, was the person she wanted. Ruth was no longer around to ask questions, so it was David's responsibility to tell her about the possible pain, the responsibility of avoiding sexually transmitted diseases, and that initial confusion was normal. She had many questions after, which Vincent smoothly answered, thankfully.

Never, in all her talks with David, had Ava mentioned emotions toward Vincent, or toward sex. Her questions had been about physical changes. Sex was a physical outlet to release tension for her. It didn't involve an unsubstantiated emotion like love. But what did her future hold with a man she was attracted to? Was she capable of falling in love with this man?

"But you don't love Vincent like I love Ruth," he told her now. "Do you?"

She stared at him blankly. "I do not see what that has to do with this conversation."

Sweet Jesus, David thought, I wish Ruth were still around to explain this to her.

David wondered if Ava could comprehend love outside of the bond with her guardians. That she loved him, he had no doubt, although she had never said the words. She didn't quite understand the emotion; therefore, she didn't recognize it when she felt it. David knew it for what it was, and often saw it in her eyes when she looked at him. He had even seen it flash briefly around Ruth.

In the dojo, David had witnessed Ava's deep love for Daniel, a love she wasn't aware even existed. If asked, she would have said she respected him, but David knew it went deeper than that. Besides being a father figure, Daniel had saved her from remaining in the state she'd been in when she was being abused. Vincent, though she loved him and trusted him completely, had never caused her to brighten or get flustered when she spoke of him. She wasn't in love with Vincent.

"How is Buck?" Ava asked, sparing them both further discomfort regarding sex.

"Getting older, but still as playful as ever. I should have brought him. He'd love your yard."

There was no question as to whether he was welcome; Ava loved animals.

"Are you still having nightmares?" he asked.

"Yes."

She answered as pragmatic as if he'd asked her if she was a brunette. Ava never fished for sympathy. She never expected compassion or tenderness.

He sighed. "I wish I could do something to make them go away for you."

"That is illogical. You have no control over what happened to me before you met me."

"When it comes to my child, logic doesn't play a part," he said firmly. "You're my daughter, and I wish I had the ability to stop the pain."

She gazed at him for a long time. He could almost feel her trying to figure out what he meant, trying to understand the love he felt for her, the responsibility. Would she ever have children and understand that bond? Physically, she was incapable. The couple before he and Ruth had taken her had damaged her body so badly, she could never bear children of her own. That was a fact that still made David's blood boil. But would Ava consider adoption? Would she be able to have a healthy relationship with a man and raise children? Perhaps then she would understand that being a parent meant feeling responsible for every minute of that child's life, even when it was out of her hands.

"You have a beautiful house, Ava. I'm so proud of you."

She shifted. "Thank you."

They were silent for several moments. David drank his water and marveled at Ava's progress. Her house was beautiful, and it was hers. He wasn't upset she had never invited him to see it. The offer never would have occurred to her, and if it had, she wouldn't have wanted to inconvenience him with the drive.

In addition to a beautiful house, her freelance business had been going for over two years now, and her client base was steadily growing. Editing allowed her the ability to interact with people as little as possible, so it suited her. David was happy for her. And so proud.

"I would show her to you if I could," she said softly.

When he looked up, her eyes had darkened. She was staring straight ahead, her gaze unfocused. She was gripping her glass very tightly. Every muscle in her body was tense.

"I know," David said. "I know you would." He wanted to go to her, to give her a hug, but that wasn't her way.

"I should have seen it coming."

"You can't control it. Even if you had predicted it, there was nothing we could do."

"I should have tried harder."

"Ava." David leaned forward. "Every living thing will die. That is a fact. You know this, better than anyone."

She nodded thoughtfully. The blank expression was gone from her face, but she still seemed puzzled. "You miss her."

"Of course, I do," he said, smiling at her innocence. "We were married forty-four years. I will always miss her. My memories of her keep her alive. Knowing she's not in pain gives me peace."

"It feels different than the farm animals you had when I was growing up. I did not have this… emptiness when they died." Her fingers fluttered at her chest.

David nodded. "Losing a chicken or a calf is sad, but it's not the same as a person, is it?"

"Why not?" she asked, studying him intently. "One carbon-based form should not have more value than any other."

"But it does," he admitted. "Ruth was the closest thing you had to a mother. You may not have felt close to her, but she was a big part of your life in a maternal capacity."

"I do not understand."

David stood and patted her knee. "That's okay, Ava. Everything has its time and purpose. We don't always know what that purpose is right away. I have to get going. I have a long drive back."

·   ·   ·   ·   ·

Isabel pulled her car into her parent's driveway and drove back toward the garage. She parked behind Gabriel's truck. Beth's car was already here, too. Iz sat for a moment, trying to calm her nerves. Sunday dinners with her family were usually full of laughter, but she wasn't looking forward to this one.

"I am Thor, son of Odin!" Her phone's notification tone made her jump. She smirked. The ringtone told her Griffin had sent her a text. She pulled her phone out of her purse.

How's the family dinner going?

Not sure. Hiding in my car. Haven't gone in yet.

LOL. Get your bum in there. You'll be fine. Stop by my place after.

Isabel smiled. She even read his texts with an Australian accent.

I'll come over if I survive.

I'll file a missing person report if I don't hear from you in a few hours.

Feeling less irritable now that she had something to look forward to, Isabel put her phone back in her purse and stepped out of her car.

Her parent's house was huge. Isabel had grown up in this house and had loved it, but it was too big and impersonal for her. She preferred her little apartment to the huge wrap around porch and stone columns that adorned her childhood home. The inside was always perfectly cleaned, without a vase or a rug out of place. The backyard was beautifully landscaped to host family meals and parties in warmer weather. Sometimes the backyard had felt more like home than the interior of the house.

Iz walked to the back door and stepped inside the addition connecting the garage to the house. A load of towels was cycling in the dryer in the laundry area back here. Iz passed a half bath and the door to a screened porch before reaching the main part of the house. She slipped out of her shoes before walking into the kitchen, where Gabriel was sitting at the island in his socks. Their mother was pulling lamb out of the oven. Isabel set her purse next to her sister's in its usual place out of the way on a lesser used counter.

"Hey, sis," Gabriel said, punching her shoulder.

She punched him back. "Being helpful, as always."

"I know better than to get in Mom's way in the kitchen."

Allie set the lamb on trivets on the counter and pulled off her oven mitts. She turned to her daughter and gave her a hug, as she always did when she saw her. This hug lasted a beat longer than usual. When she pulled away her eyes were slightly glassy.

"Jesus, you've started already?" Isabel said, shooting a knowing glance at Gabriel.

"I haven't started anything," Allie said coolly. She turned back to the lamb. "Would you like something to drink?"

Her tone caught Isabel off guard. "I'll get it. Where's Dad and Beth?"

Gabriel poked her in the ribs, making her jump. "Jack's showing them something on the computer."

Beth and Jack had been married for seven years.

Isabel moved around her mother to get a pitcher of tea out of the refrigerator. Allie slid the lamb back in the oven. "Twenty more minutes should do it."

Feeling like she had walked in on a private conversation she wasn't part of Isabel said nothing, unwilling to upset her mother further. She poured herself a glass of tea and added a slice of lemon before hurrying out of the war zone.

Without speaking, afraid she would say something to make things worse, she walked toward the east end of the house. She passed the dining room, where the table was already set for dinner, and the living room, and didn't stop until she reached the solarium. Gabriel's house had two sunrooms, but her parent's house had a solarium. When Isabel had asked Gabriel what the hell the difference was, he told her several thousands of dollars. That made her laugh.

Gabriel's sunrooms didn't have a lot of furniture, but Allie and Josh's were top notch. A brick fireplace with a flat screen TV installed immediately caught the eye as the center piece. Furniture was set up everywhere, the kind that had the latest wooden trim and the finest cushions to ensure comfort. The floor was made of large bricks. The beams in the ceiling added a nice rustic touch. It was a gorgeous room. But Isabel didn't like showing off. She liked hiding in the corner, being quiet, doing things she liked where no one else would bother her. Her parent's house was too much.

She felt uneasy. Beth and her mother were close; Isabel had always felt like an outsider there. Beth and Jack had been trying to have children for the past three years and had begun discussing invitro fertilization. Getting tested to see if the problem was on his side or hers was the beginning of a long road. It was a sore subject for Beth, who excelled in every other aspect of her life.

Normally that fact didn't bother Iz since she was close with her brother and father. But lately her mother and Beth seemed to be sharing something she couldn't take part in. She was having more difficulty dealing with Hayden's death this year and she felt she couldn't go to them for support.

She heard the door open behind her and stiffened slightly.

"You okay?" Gabriel asked as he walked over to stand beside her at the far window. The windows were triple pane glass and standing next to the warmth of the fire while looking out at the frozen ground was like staring into an odd painting by Escher.

"I'm fine." The response was so automatic she almost believed it herself. She folded her arms across her chest.

"Right. We're all fine."

She looked at him sharply. "What's that supposed to mean?"

"It's okay if you're not, you know."

Isabel was quiet, thinking about that. "Yeah, I guess Mom and Beth aren't alone in that."

"They cry about it, and we get pissed off."

Iz grinned. "I prefer pissed off to crying all the time. How's Beth doing, really? Is she okay?"

Gabriel shrugged. "They haven't had the tests yet, so they don't know if the issue is on her end or his. They can't figure out a plan until they know that."

Isabel had her own ideas about the whole thing, but she kept them to herself. She didn't need more enemies than she already had.

Across the yard, dead grass seemed to go on forever. Would winter ever end?

"She wishes the baby could have your eyes," she said.

He gave her a sideways glance. "What?"

"You have such beautiful eyes. We've always been jealous. They're the color of denim, this beautiful shade of blu-"

"What did you just say?"

"I said-"

"The thing about the denim, say it again."

He was staring at her intently. The look in his eyes wasn't entirely rational. "Jesus, Gabriel. They remind us of blue jeans. What's your problem?"

"The color of denim," Gabriel muttered. "That's an odd description."

He seemed to be talking to himself now. He crossed his arms over his chest, his eyes vacant as he tossed something around in his head.

"What are you talking about?" Isabel asked. "You're not making any sense."

"Neither was she. At least I didn't think so at the time." Gabriel glanced at Isabel. "That woman at the restaurant, Ava, mentioned the color of my eyes. She said they're 'blue, the color of denim'. Exactly like that."

"Is she the one that kicked that guy's ass?"

"Yeah. She was acting weird, and it bothered me, but I couldn't figure out why. It's because of Hayden."

Isabel felt her stomach twist.

Gabriel wiped a hand down his face. "When we were really young, Mom used to say Hayden and I had eyes that are blue, the color of denim."

● ● ● ● ●

As if it was meant to be, Ava knew exactly where to put the plant from David.

Late evening sunlight swept through the living room window just right, and she knew she had to move the books on the top shelf and put David's plant there instead. She did not understand why that spot was the perfect place. She simply began moving the books off the shelf, stacking them on the coffee table until there was enough room to put the plant.

She walked to the kitchen to get it. As her hands wrapped around the beautiful ceramic pot, images flashed through her head: snow on the ground at David's farm; David standing in the library, where a very mature philodendron in a hanging pot flowed from a ceiling hook almost to the floor; David thinking about a young Ava lying on her stomach on the floor of the library while he read H. G. Wells and she filled in crossword puzzles.

Gasping, Ava bowed her head and shut her eyes tight, her grip on the pot so strong the skin on her fingers paled. The images continued, bombarding her like mental bullets.

David standing on a small ladder, taking a cutting from the stem just below a set of leaves of the plant, carrying it carefully to the kitchen, where he set it in a glass of water. Him entering the kitchen sometime later, changing out the water. Then again, entering the kitchen, glancing lovingly at the plant, where little tendrils of roots were floating in the water as the plant was beginning to thrive. Then David potting the cutting when it was big enough, in a small pot, patting the soil around it with his big hands, a smile on his face as he worked. Later, re-potting it as it grew too big for the small pot, and once more in the larger pot it was in today.

"Our baby's grown up," he said, resting his hand on the pot, but he was looking at the picture of Ruth hanging in the library. It was David's library, but the original plant had been one Ruth nurtured. The large, healthy philodendron Ava held in her hands right now had been a cutting taken from one of Ruth's plants, cared for lovingly by David. This gift had taken years to create.

Ava carefully set the plant back on the counter, exhaling. Backing away from the counter, she rested her hands on her knees, trying to breathe deeply. The emotions surrounding her were suffocating her. David had worked hard to cultivate this plant for her, to create the perfect gift for a housewarming present. It wasn't just any plant. He had not made a quick trip to a store to pick it up moments before giving it to her. It was part of a living entity he cared for greatly because it reminded him of his wife.

Ava didn't know what to do that information. She walked unsteadily to the drawer where her oven mitts were kept and pulled two out, slipping them on. With her hands covered, feeling as if her head was full of spikes, she picked the plant up and walked stiffly to the bookcase by the east window. She placed the philodendron on the top of the bookcase and stepped back.

Pulling off the oven mitts, she wiped a hand across her brow. Her head was pounding. Her temples throbbed. She could not slow her breathing, could not get a full breath of air. Every emotion David had felt while caring for this plant was inside her, filling her.

Forcing herself to move, she made it to the front door and burst through, staggering onto the front porch, and falling against the support beam by the stairs.

•　•　•　•　•

Later, after dinner, Isabel sat in the library, picking her guitar. Everything she said tonight seemed to start a confrontation with her family, so she finally stopped talking. Keeping her mouth closed when Beth or her mother brought up a memory of Hayden and then started crying was brutal, but she clenched her teeth and did it. She spoke only when spoken to and finished her meal as quickly as possible so she could get away. Hiding in the library was the only option because the living room was just off the dining room, and she didn't want to be that close to anyone.

What the hell was the matter with her? She didn't mean to be difficult. She didn't purposely try to pick fights. The things she said weren't meant to provoke her family.

I have Gabriel and I have Griffin, she thought, and that helped her muscles relax a little.

She plucked a few chords, turned them into a slow rhythm, softly sang a couple lines. Picking up her favorite guitar pick from the coffee table, Isabel started at the beginning of her favorite song, the one she could always relate to, the one that made her feel better.

It was an older song, Broken, by Seether and Amy Lee, and it was so hauntingly beautiful even as it tore at her heart.

Already lost in the song by the second line, Isabel jumped when Gabriel put his hand on her shoulder and began singing the male part with her. She backed off the lyrics; the first part was sung entirely by the male.

She continued playing the guitar and listened as his beautiful voice expressed the sorrow in the chorus.

The second verse had Isabel as lead singer as Gabriel walked over and sat on the couch, plugging an electric guitar. He turned on the amplifier.

As they both sang the chorus again, this time with a couple lines added, Jack entered the library from the foyer. He walked between the two and sat at the far end of the room in an overstuffed chair. A moment later, Josh entered from the kitchen side and stood next to Jack.

At the interlude, Gabriel began playing the electric guitar. Allie walked in to stand beside her husband. She felt a surge of pride as she watched her children. She was grateful when Beth entered the room and opened her violin case from near the fireplace. Beth didn't often play anymore. All three of her children were together in the same room, despite their differences, brought together by music.

At the end of the interlude, Beth eased progressively in with her violin. Isabel and Gabriel sang the chorus again, with all instruments playing. It was beautiful. Josh wrapped an arm around Allie as they listened. Jack was staring at his wife with obvious affection as her body seemed to have become one with the instrument. All the troubles from the past three years were gone as she closed her eyes and weaved with the music.

Gabriel and Isabel sang the last partial verse together.

With Beth's violin the most prevalent instrument, they ended the song on a mournful, soft tone.

The room was quiet for a few moments. Gabriel, Isabel, and Beth smiled at each other. They hadn't played together in years. Josh and Jack clapped their hands.

"That's my favorite song," Allie said, wiping away a tear.

Isabel didn't say anything. The song reminded her of the loss of her sister. She was afraid if she spoke, she would start crying.

"You guys play so well together," Jack said, hugging Beth. "I wish you would jump in there more often, Beth. That was... intense."

She smiled, and Jack saw none of the exhaustion she seemed to always carry. Isabel saw some of the old Beth hiding in her eyes. Beth should join in more often. Her talent on the violin was natural and beautiful. When they all played together, they were all as one, something they lacked in everyday life. It was the only time they all seemed to want the same thing.

"You should," Isabel agreed. "I love hearing you play."

Beth looked surprised. "Really?"

"Absolutely," Gabriel said. "We kick ass."

Beth looked at the two of them, surprised to see they were both serious. "Okay. I can dust this old thing off more."

"Wonderful," Allie said, smiling. "I love when all my children play nice together!"

Beth, Gabriel, and Isabel all looked at each other and burst out laughing.

• • • • •

Sweating profusely, Ava gave the body bag a final kick and considered her workout over for the morning. She needed to work on her front snap kicks more. Although each one sent the body bag straining the heavy chain it was attached to, she considered them weaker than her other kicks. The roundhouse technique was a favorite, so she practiced it more, which tended to leave the front snaps neglected. She would have to work on that.

She slung her towel over her shoulder and grabbed her water bottle before heading up the basement steps to take a shower. She was exhausted yet satisfied at the exercises she had completed this morning. Every type, whether cardio, strength training, or stretching, contributed to her well-being and excellent physical condition. She was not vain but keeping her body in shape was a point of pride for her. Doing so took discipline of both mind and body, and only positive rewards resulted from it.

She stopped by the counter to pick up her phone, which she never took with her while she was training. Her awareness of her surroundings at all times was paramount.

As she made her way upstairs, she pulled the hair band out of her hair and dropped it on the floor. Holding her phone, she had only one hand to strip with, making it tricky but not impossible. By the time she reached the bedroom, she had dropped her socks on the stairs and her shirt in the hallway.

Setting her phone on the vanity counter, she started the water in the shower. In her bedroom, she peeled off her sweaty yoga pants and underwear and used them to soak up some of the sweat, so she did not leave drops on the floor. She tossed the disgusting clothes on the floor at the end of the bed. Back in the bathroom, she left the door open. She needed to cool off. Her skin felt like a furnace. Little trails of sweat ran down body. Her hair hung limply down her back.

When her phone rang, she was just getting ready to step into the tub. It could be a client and she did not want them hearing the water in the background. Without paying attention to her phone, she shut the water off as she picked up her phone. She pressed the speaker button after she swiped to answer so she did not have to press the phone to her soggy head.

"Hello?" she said cautiously.

"Ava. I didn't wake you, did I?"

The thought was absurd; it was almost eight o'clock in the morning.

"Who is this?"

"It's Gabriel."

"No."

The word came automatically, and her tone was almost a whimper. That she made such a weak sound had her gritting her teeth.

"No?" he asked, but his tone was amused.

She had purposely steered clear of town for the past nine days, trying to bring herself back into focus, forcing herself to return to a sense of normality. Normality did not include Gabriel. The fact that the call was from him and not a client, a call she could have avoided, was irritating.

"Why are you calling me?" she asked, managing to make her voice sound stronger.

"I thought maybe you could stop by my house today. I have something to show you."

"What is it?"

"You'll just have to come by and see."

"I do not like games."

"It's not a game. It's just easier to show you than to tell you. Maybe we can watch a movie or something afterward."

"I do not watch television."

"That's where the 'or something' comes in."

She sighed. "Why are you doing this?"

There was a pause before he said, "I enjoyed our time the other day. I would like to see you again, and I have something here I think you'll enjoy."

"You do not know me well enough to know what I enjoy."

She was cooling off, but she was still dripping with perspiration. The feeling of hot liquid oozing down her body was making her itch. The need to wash off was strong.

"If my instincts are wrong, you can leave."

This unconditional patience was maddening. Ava lifted her palm and sent it toward the medicine cabinet mirror, regaining control at the last minute and pulling the strike. Still, the glass cracked beneath her palm, and she felt the sting of a cut on the meat of her thumb.

"What was that?" Gabriel's voice sounded like it was coming from a distance. "Are you okay?"

Ava forced herself back into the room, into the moment, where she was talking on the phone and her hand was pressed against the medicine cabinet with blood trickling down the mirror.

"It will be a while. I have to shower and pick up coffee at Willow's."

"I'll go get the coffee while you shower, and we'll meet at my place in forty-five minutes. How does that sound?"

"Tolerable." She all but barked the word.

After hanging up, she wondered if she had been too abrupt with him. He was offering her friendship, and she had not been very cooperative. Then again, she had not asked for his friendship. She did not want someone to butt into her life with his good intentions and his insistence in helping her be social. If she was irritated with him, she had every right to show it.

She showered off the sweat from the workout. Her muscles were sore, letting her know they had been used well. The water pummeled her body from the adjustable showerhead she had purchased, soothing the aches. Feeling the effects of a solid workout always made her feel wonderful, energized. Her mood improved as she washed her hair and ran the loofah over her skin. She continued standing in the shower for an extra five minutes to cool the rest of the way off in tepid water.

The temperature wasn't going to reach forty today, so she had to blow dry her hair. She hated to do it. Letting it dry naturally was what she usually did because it was healthier, but she had to change that since she was going outside.

Damn it.

Another thing she had to change because she was obligated to someone.

Agitated, she turned the blow dryer up to its highest setting and began the painstaking process. She had long, thick hair, and that took several minutes.

Gabriel just had to butt in. He had to insinuate himself into her life, messing up her schedules and taking up her time. Without realizing it, she began waving the dryer back and forth, as if that would make it dry her hair faster. She was furious that he had barged into her life and left a path of destruction. Everything was changed now.

She slammed the blow dryer on the counter and brushed out her hair. It would have to do. Forty-five minutes, he said, and she still needed time to drive there. Damn him for giving her a time frame, as if he owned her.

Pulling on her clean clothes quickly, snatching her bag off the counter, Ava stalked out of the house. She locked her door and all but stomped to her vehicle.

She was going to end this.

• • • • •

Gabriel returned home after picking up coffee at Willows with the dogs and still had seven minutes to spare before Ava was set to arrive. He had waited to go get it so it would still be hot for her. The dogs enjoyed the ride. Ozzie stuck his head out the window while Maya stood on the seat in the extended part of the cab, looking over Gabriel's shoulder as he drove.

He set the coffees on the kitchen counter and pulled his keys out of his pocket to join them. The ride had been nice even if brief. The weather was edging toward spring, allowing him to open his own window and enjoy the fresh air.

When the dogs signaled that company had arrived, he walked to the front door, opening it, and letting them charge out. Ava exited the vehicle as Ozzie ran up to her, but he hesitated when she slammed the door. Maya watched her warily from the top of the porch steps.

Taking a moment before turning to Ozzie, Ava knelt with her head tilted down slightly. Gabriel watched her murmur softly to him. He couldn't hear her at this distance, but whatever she said worked. Ozzie began wagging frantically and darted the rest of the way to her, wiggling happily and trying to get her to pet his favorite spots.

Gabriel wondered what had caused her to slam her car door. When she stood and walked toward him, her eyes had a hard edge to them that warned of temper.

"What's wrong?" he asked as she tromped up onto the porch. He opened the storm door for her. It took him a moment to realize he never heard her footsteps, yet she was practically stomping now.

Without speaking, she entered the house, walking briskly past him. She pulled her gloves off angrily.

He watched her for a moment. "Can I take your coat?"

She shed it quickly and pushed it toward him. No eye contact. He didn't like that. That meant she was mad at him. How could she be mad at him when they hadn't even seen each other yet?

"The coffee is in the kitchen."

She followed him and he could feel the anger emanating from her. He was surprised it didn't reach out and throttle him.

Handing her a cafe mocha with no whip cream, he leaned against the counter. "Are you going to tell me why you're so pissed, or do I have to guess?"

She set the coffee down on the counter beside her. "I told you I do not want friends. I do not like obligations."

He said nothing. Letting the silence spin out, he sipped his coffee and waited.

"Now you are calling me, interrupting my day, asking me to come over."

"You're upset because I want to spend time with you?"

"I had plans after I was done training. Now they are delayed because I am here. You keep doing pleasant things for me and I feel obligated to reciprocate."

"I'm not asking for anything in return."

"I feel obligated to reciprocate," she repeated, turning her coffee cup in slow circles on the counter.

"So... you're upset that I did something nice for you?" He was having trouble following her logic. "Or you're upset that me being nice makes you want to be nice back?"

"I am upset that you are taking up my time," she snapped. "Being nice creates obligations, which cause problems."

The dogs, sensing tension, stood from their beds in the breakfast room and trotted toward the great room.

Before he could think of something to say, Ava continued.

"Despite all my discipline, I am attracted to you. No matter how hard I try to block it, you are in my head. The more I try not to think of you, the more I want to. It is a distraction I do not need."

Gabriel kept his expression carefully neutral, but secretly he was enthused. Figuring her out was difficult; knowing she found him attractive helped his ego. He wanted to get to know her. That wouldn't happen unless she was interested as well. It also gave him hope that she would learn to trust him. She fought the attraction, so it would take time. He was willing to give her time, as he wasn't interested in jumping into anything too intense himself.

"I had to blow-dry my hair!" she blurted. She turned away from him, so she had time to calm down. "I would not have had to do that if you had just left me alone. You have changed everything."

"Is change so bad?"

"That is not the point." She paced a few feet away and back. "I had to blow-dry my hair because of you. I had to change my entire routine because you felt the need to interrupt my day. Now I have to allow for an entire new set of circumstances just to fix the mess you made by forcing me to be social."

Setting his coffee on the counter, Gabriel leveled his gaze at her.

"You were never a prisoner," he said, trying to keep the offense at what she said out of his tone. Being nice didn't mean he had to tolerate accusations of force or manipulation. "I'm sorry to have wasted your time. Enjoy your coffee."

Moving toward the front door to see her out, he took only one step before she raised her leg and swung it around as if to give him a roundhouse kick to the chest. Just before she made contact, she stopped, hovering at chest level. It happened so fast he barely had time to stop his momentum and almost ran into her boot.

He raised an eyebrow and looked over at her.

She was still upset, but she was no longer frantic. The physical effort caused her body to automatically take over her mind, allowing her time to snap out of her frustration and settle back into controlled mode.

Lowering her leg in a slow, deliberate manner, she studied him. Her head tilted to one side, then the other. She could not get a read on him. First, he wanted her here, then he did not. He pushed himself into her life and then backed off when she least expected it. Why did people act illogically, confusing her?

"Do you want to leave?"

Gabriel's blue eyes were fixed on hers, waiting patiently for her response. He seemed to enjoy looking at her, and not in the way most men stared at her with lust raging in their eyes and pheromones boiling under their skin. His exploration of her, at times, seemed to probe into her very soul, as if he was searching inside her for something he could not find in himself.

"I..." Flustered, Ava's direct gaze wavered slightly. "I do not know."

"Then stay until you figure it out."

Running her slender index finger around the lid of her coffee, she picked it up and took a hesitant sip. She blinked in surprise.

"You remember what I drink."

"I listen to what you say. And to what you don't say," he added, causing her to raise her head and narrow her eyes at him. He held out his hand to her. "Come with me. Bring your coffee."

"Where?"

"Trust me, Ava." Gabriel's tone was patient again. "For once, give me a chance."

Frowning, she hesitantly reached out and took his hand.

He turned and walked through the hall toward the stairs. "I asked you here to show you something I thought you would like."

He spoke over his shoulder as he walked, leading her up the stairs and down an open hallway. Ava was grateful the stairway was wide and open, with spindles. She was claustrophobic, especially when in the company of people.

"I'm not trying to be presumptuous, but you have to come into my bedroom."

The hand holding his twitched. Gabriel casually walked into the room. He let go of Ava's hand just inside the door to make his way around the bed to the window on the west side, facing the driveway.

This morning he had made sure his room was decent. He made the bed, a chore he usually skipped, and dragged all his dirty laundry to the basement. He wasn't incredibly messy, but when he really dug into a project, he could work fourteen hours a day until it was finished. His hamper ended up smelling like a locker room in a high school after football tryouts.

"I saw you staring at these when you came here," he said, opening the window. Beside it, on the top of his dresser, were two heavy throw blankets he had set out earlier in the morning. Now he picked them both up and set them and his coffee outside to the right on the roof, so they were out of the way. He turned back to Ava.

"I thought maybe it was because you were interested in sitting up on the roof. You said you climb trees. I figured you would like to sit out here and enjoy the view."

For a moment, Ava could only stand where she was. He had paid attention to how she reacted, something she had trained herself to do little of, and planned something nice for her. Only David and Ruth had ever done that for her before. A funny feeling churned in her stomach.

She walked across the room to where he stood. Hoisting himself up, Gabriel climbed onto the roof and reached back in to take her coffee. He set hers next to his before extending his hand to help her climb out with him.

The pitch was slight, so it was easy to walk on. Gabriel carried the blankets and Ava carried the coffees and followed him to the center bay (dormer?)

window. He sat down and unfolded a blanket, shaking it to get it positioned over him.

The view was breath taking. Trees stretched on for miles across the road. They were bare, but they were full of buds and soon they would have so many different leaves. For now, they could see squirrels' nests, a bird or two in the closer trees, a large crow coming in for a landing on a lower branch of a larger tree. The sun was out, warming them on what was otherwise a chilly day. Because of their height, they could see a bird soaring far off in a distant field, probably a hawk looking for rodents. Bluffs were visible above the trees that were out of sight at ground height.

After several moments of taking all this in, Ava crossed her ankles and sank down next to Gabriel, close enough that he bumped her while he was unfolding a blanket. Surprised that she was so close, he didn't let his delight show. He handed her the blanket. She spread it across her lap and pulled it over her arms, up to her chin.

"Are you warm enough?" he asked, settling the other blanket over his legs. He was so close he could see a small scar on her jawline, just a slight dip in the skin.

She nodded, staring out at the view. "Do you come out here every day?"

"Actually, this is my first time. It never occurred to me before. I'll damn sure be coming out a lot more."

"The sky must be beautiful at night from here," Ava said, in awe.

"Why don't you stick around and find out?"

He felt her tense against him.

"Stay here all day? With you?"

"Sure. Or you could go home if you needed to and come back later in the evening." His heart bucked at the thought of spending more time with her. He wanted to put his arm around her shoulders but didn't feel right about it. Not yet.

They sat quietly for several minutes, listening to the silence, and enjoying the view. Gabriel wondered if Ava was as aware of his proximity as he was of hers. He couldn't seem to stop thinking of her.

"If I leave," she said quietly, not looking at him, "I can come back later?"

"Of course." Let her say yes, he thought. Every single thought in my head leads back to her.

"We can sit out here… and watch the stars?"

"Absolutely." His body ached with the need to touch her, feel her beneath his hands. More than lust, his hands ached with the need to soothe her, to comfort her.

She could imagine the darkness surrounding her, the night sky looming above like a living being hovering over them, the feel of the chilly air against her face in contrast with the warmth of her body under the blanket. The peace darkness often brought.

The feel of Gabriel's body next to hers. That strange pulling feeling she had every time she was close, a feeling that drew her to him as she was simultaneously pummeled with little jolts like electric shocks.

What would it hurt to return later and allow herself to just feel the proximity of another human being? Just that, nothing more?

"You wish to sit up here and look at the sky? Nothing else?"

Her tone was cautious. Gabriel wondered if she'd ever had a friend before.

"Sure. Friends do that."

"That is why I do not have friends."

"Because they take up your time?"

Sighing, she frowned down at her knees, shifting. "Yes. And because everyone wants something in return."

Someone must have hurt her terribly, and his words wouldn't convince her that he wouldn't do the same. Only his actions could prove his credibility, and time.

"You'll either show up or you won't," he said. "No obligations, no timeframe. If you decide you want to come by, go ahead. Until then, let's enjoy the view."

He leaned back against the house, crossing his legs at the ankles.

After a moment, she settled against the house as well, though she wasn't quite relaxed. She closed her eyes and lifted her chin, breathing deep. Gabriel took the time to study her face.

Her skin was flawless but for a scar here or there, along her jaw, under her chin, along her ear, along the side of her neck. She wore no make up to cover any of the scars. He thought they were beautiful.

Gabriel wanted to frame her face with his hands and run his thumbs over her cheeks. Did she have any idea the effect she had on him?

Blinking, he snapped out of his reverie to find her staring at him thoughtfully. He had the feeling she knew exactly what he was thinking.

"Maybe," she said, shifting, her eyes avoiding his, "I will come back some other time to watch the stars."

"Okay."

"I do not spend time with people," she explained, finally making eye contact. "Today has been... exhausting."

His lips twitched.

"No problem. Friendship is a journey, not a race."

• • • • •

The next night, Ava sat across from Sensei in The Meditation Room. They were both in the lotus pose, facing each other. The room had no furniture and was lit only with soft lighting. A stereo was playing meditation music very quietly.

"The past two weeks we worked on taking meditation deeper than you usually go," Sensei said. "Have you practiced at home?"

"Hai, Sensei."

"Have you been able to get to the deeper state I taught you?"

"Hai, Sensei."

"Good. Tonight, I think you're ready to work on the psychic side and see if you can start to control the information coming in. Right now, you don't seem to be able to control when it comes or how much or what kind of information you receive, is that correct?"

"Hai, Sensei." Her palms were damp.

"The first obstacle is to overcome your fear of this ability."

Ava did not speak. It was impolite to argue with Sensei. She did not realize her body was tensing.

"You've been running from it your entire life," he continued. "You have to stop doing that or you'll never be able to gain control of it. To control it, you'll have to seek it out."

"Hai, Sensei."

Her teeth were clenched. Her tone had dropped. She tried to relax because that was the only way she would be able to get into a deeper meditative state.

In the many years since she had started coming to Sensei for guidance, she had rarely disagreed with him. When she did, she knew that he was wiser than she and that she would eventually understand the lesson he was teaching. She always had. This was different. Sensei did not know about this ability. He was telling her something about which he knew nothing. That he thought she was afraid made her furious.

"Relax, Ava," Sensei said, his voice soothing. "We're not in the dojo. Why did what I said make you angry?"

"I am not angry, Sensei," she said, her voice even. She kept her eyes unfocused at a point next to his heart, so she did not have to look at him. So hopefully he did not see what was in her eyes.

"Your fists are clenched so hard you're going to break your own fingers."

She glanced down. Unaware she had even moved her hands, which had been resting lightly on her knees, she uncurled them instantly.

"This won't work if you're not honest with me. Why are you angry?"

"I do not run from anything," she said, unable to relax her jaw. She was still grinding her teeth.

"You think that if you admit you avoid this ability, people will see that as weakness?" Sensei asked.

"I do not care what people think." Splotches of red were spreading in her cheeks. "I do not avoid my ability. I choose to ignore it."

He watched her try to control her anger. "Why?"

"They want something from me."

"Spirits?"

She nodded. "They want me to do things for them."

"You don't like helping people?"

He noticed she was trembling slightly.

"It is my life," she said urgently. "I do not do anything unless I choose to."

Sensei thought about that for several moments. He didn't think that was exactly what she meant to say. She was obviously struggling to find the right words.

"I am not afraid of them." Her hands were clenched again. "I refuse to do the bidding of others."

Now he understood. David had brought Ava to him as a tiny raging ball of fury. According to David, her previous foster parents were sadists that had abused her severely, making her perform unspeakable acts for their pleasure. Though the dojo uniforms kept her covered, while training Sensei often caught glimpses of scars on Ava's wrists and ankles when he was fine tuning a new technique, especially wrist locks. She didn't have control over what her foster parents had done to her as a child, and she didn't feel she had control over this ability she had been born with. She didn't want to be forced to do things for the spirits once she knew how to tell what they were coming to her for.

"No one's going to make you do anything you don't want to do," he told her. "You're here to get control over this so you can make the choice, Ava. The other day, you were completely out of control during the vision. I think once you gain control over this ability, you'll be able to decide if and when you have visions. You have the right to decide for yourself whether you help these entities or learn how to keep them at bay. I won't judge you either way."

"Hai, Sensei," she said softly. For a moment, she looked like the seven-year-old girl David had brought to him so many years ago.

"Okay. Help me understand. How does it work? Besides what happened during training the other day, is there any other way it manifests?"

"Sometimes I know things."

"Like what, for example?"

Ava's skin felt itchy. She licked her lips. "When I meet people for the first time, I know personal information before I am introduced. If someone is thinking about a particular subject obsessively, I... hear it in my head."

"Do you know things about me that I've never told you?"

Something was scratching at her skull, trying to make itself known. She shook her head. "I have never been able to get any information from you. I do not know why."

"That works in our favor. We should start with something safe before we move on to direct contact with an unknown entity. How do you usually get the information? What happens?"

She shrugged. "It comes to me. It is like tying my shoes. I do not remember learning how to do it; only that the knowledge is there."

"Try to get something from me. Relax, breathe, and just let whatever happens, happen."

Ava closed her eyes. She took deep breaths - in through her nose, out through her mouth. Whatever was trying to come through continued to tickle, ricocheting around her head, but it would not hold still long enough for her to see what it was. She waited. Nothing happened. She tried to be open to whatever came to her. After several moments, she opened her eyes.

"I am not getting anything," she said. "Sometimes..."

When she didn't continue, he coaxed, "Sometimes what?"

"It happens easier if I touch people or objects."

Sensei reached out toward her with his hands relaxed. Ava stared at them. She had never touched him outside of training. To do so now felt abnormal.

She hesitated, then gently took his hands in her own. At first, she felt nothing at all. Sensei's hands felt strange; she was holding them more like a stranger or a friend than a student. Thousands of times over the years he had touched her: to tweak a technique, to show her how her hand should look during a strike, to shift her closer or farther from the other student she was training with. In all that time, they had never touched in a platonic way other than as teacher and student. Ava was stunned at how bizarre she felt when the touch had a different intent behind it.

She was starting to worry that her racing thoughts were going to impede her ability to read anything from him.

Then it hit her.

Her entire body jerked. Her hands clasped his, hard. As they had during training a few days ago, her pupils flared.

"Ava?" He spoke calmly. If he didn't condition his hands daily, her grip would have been strong enough to hurt. "What's happening? What do you see?"

"A little boy."

Sensei felt a chill spike down his spine but forced himself not to react. He swallowed audibly.

"The boy with the blonde hair." Ava loosened her grip on his hands. She let go of one hand and cupped his other hand with both of hers. "He's playing in the yard. The sun is shining. It's chilly. I feel chilly." She shivered. "'Our son looks so beautiful in his new jacket.'"

"Ava." Sensei tensed, his heart ramming painfully into his ribcage. He couldn't seem to find his voice.

"'Dan, get my phone, I want to take a picture of him playing in the leaves.'" Her voice was higher than usual, more feminine that her usual slightly husky tone. Daniel knew that voice like he knew his own. To hear it coming from Ava was unimaginable.

He held his breath, watching her. Her face was completely lax. She held his hand in both of hers and spoke words he hadn't heard in seventeen years.

"'My God, he's beautiful. I want to get the rake and give him more leaves.'"

"Please don't," Daniel said softly, knowing it would do no good but unable to stop himself. "Stay with him. Keep him safe." His hand closed around hers. He didn't realize he did it.

Ava's grip tightened. Her voice turned raspy. "She looked away. She left him and she looked away. He saw the dog across the street, and he wanted to pet it. It only took a second. He ran over to pet the dog and the car-"

Daniel yanked his hand back. With the connection abruptly broken, Ava flinched. She had leaned forward somewhat during the vision and now she straightened. She took a few breaths to clear her head. The agony was immense; it lingered. It felt as if her body had been hollowed out and left empty. A pain in her chest, both physical and psychological, made her double over, holding a hand to her heart. Tears that were not hers rolled down her face.

"Are you okay?" Daniel asked, his voice unsteady. He hadn't meant to recoil so violently.

She exhaled. It felt as if large needles were being pushed through her throat each time she inhaled.

"It hurts." The physical pain in her chest had subsided, but the emotional pain was still there, aching like an infected tooth. She rubbed her fist over her heart.

"I suppose it does," Daniel said carefully. "Do you need anything? Some water?"

She nodded. Her breath was coming out in harsh exhalations. As he left the room to get water, Ava continued to cry the tears of someone else and feel the grief that belonged to another woman. A mother. She did not want to feel this pain, this hollowness inside her that felt like a part of her was missing and yet set every nerve on fire.

Her body had coiled tightly during the vision. She slowly unwound her legs from the lotus pose, grimacing at the pain of having clenched her muscles while sitting in the position. She rolled to the side and leaned over, holding herself up with one hand while she waited for the sobs to stop. The pain was not really in her heart; she knew this logically. Yet her other hand kept rubbing her chest, wishing so desperately for the pain there to go away.

Daniel returned with a bottle of water. He watched her struggle, witnessed a young woman experiencing grief over a child she had never met. The evening had just gotten significantly stranger.

It was one thing to believe in the paranormal; it was quite another to witness it.

Ava sat back on her heels. She crossed her arms over her stomach and leaned over until her face was inches from the floor. Daniel thought she was going to vomit, but she only posed there, breathing heavily.

Finally, slowly, she straightened. Ran her sleeve across her eyes to wipe the tears. Sensei handed her a tissue, and she blew her nose. He opened the bottle of water and held it out to her. Gratefully, she chugged half of it.

"Take it easy," he soothed. "Do you understand what you just saw?"

Exhausted, she sat, stretching her legs out at an angle from Sensei so they were still facing each other somewhat.

She did not want to look at him, but she had to. His eyes were neutral. No emotion showed on his face. Discipline had enabled him to keep this information from her all these years – until she sought it out. Why had she gone looking? She did not want this.

"You had a son," she said. When he didn't say anything, she took it to mean he wanted her to continue. "He was playing in the leaves. Your wife told you to go get her camera so she could take pictures. Before you came back, she went to the shed to get the rake to get more leaves for him. It was not far from where your son was playing, but by the time she came back, it was too late. He was running into the street to get to the dog in the neighbor's yard. A car hit him, killing him instantly. You came out of the house to the sound of your wife sobbing."

Sensei was quiet. He had lowered his head and seemed to be thinking.

"I went too deep. You did not want me to have that information."

He lifted his head. "You did fine. I should have been more specific about what you were to look for."

The music was too loud. It was no longer calming, luring her to a deep meditation. Ava felt as if it was drilling into her head.

"I am sorry," she said. "I invaded your privacy."

Daniel leaned forward and brushed the tears from her cheeks. "You did exactly what I asked you to do, Ava. I wasn't expecting you to be able to get so much information from a place I keep hidden so deep. I wasn't prepared. You get all the information, don't you? You empathize, feeling the emotions in the vision as well as seeing what happened."

She nodded.

"It wears off?"

She nodded again. "The memories of the emotions remain. The emotions themselves fade."

"Good. I don't imagine you want to hold onto everyone else's feelings as well as your own. Can you do any more tonight? Something simpler?"

Of course, she nodded. Daniel knew she would accept any challenge and try anything he asked. He had to be careful not to overload her.

"I think asking you to pick anything was too broad, too random. This time, try to find out what my first car was as a teenager. Search only for that information."

Her palms were sweaty. Ava rubbed them on her jeans. She took deep breaths, trying to relax. When she had as much control as she felt she was going to get, she reached out and took one of Sensei's hands.

"Oh," she said. Jumbled images whipped through her head. She saw them like she was watching parts of a movie with the volume turned high, flashing in between the images of the room she was currently in. A bolt of pain spiked into her head. As the images began to slow, a sense of dread seeped into her. Her entire body felt cold.

"What do you see, Ava? Do you know what car I drove to prom?"

"She thinks you blame her."

"What?"

"For Danny. She thinks you blame her for his death."

"Back it off, Ava. Concentrate on a vehicle, of my life as a teenager."

She closed her eyes for a moment. One hand shot to her temple, the heel pressing against her head. When she opened her eyes, her pupils were the size of pencil erasers.

"'I deserve this. He shouldn't have to look at me every day. He doesn't have to be reminded of what I did.'" Her voice had become more feminine again, the voice of his wife.

Ava's head felt suddenly full of lead. Her eyes drooped, and she wanted nothing more than to lay in bed and disappear under the blankets. She started falling back. The action seemed to take a long time. Daniel leaned forward and caught her so she wouldn't hit her head on the floor.

"What's going on, Ava?" he asked as he gently lowered her until she was lying down. There was nothing in the room to put under her head, so he left his hand under it.

Ava felt groggy. Her head rolled to one side. She saw Sensei enter the room as her husband, saw him run toward the bed she was lying on. He picked up the bottle that had held her prescription sleeping pills. She saw him pick up the phone to dial 9-1-1.

"'Please... don't call,'" she said. Her words were starting to slur. "'Lemme go. I wanna be with our son. I wanna be with Danny.'"

Daniel understood. "Ava, this isn't the information we need. Can you listen to my voice? Stop where you are. Breathe. Leave this memory of my wife. Close your eyes and concentrate on a car. Listen to the memory my mind is telling you about."

Ava inhaled and opened her eyes wider. "'That piece of shit won't make it through the first winter,'" she sneered in a gruff, male voice. Her face went blank. "'A nineteen ninety-four Chevrolet Caprice.'"

Sensei smiled. "Ava, come back to me. Can you do that? Leave The Interval and come back to the Meditation Room."

She blinked, closed her eyes. Opened them. "'You care for it, clean it, pay for the gas. I'll pay for the insurance unless you fuck up and get in an accident. Then it's your problem.'"

With his other hand, he touched her shoulder. "Ava, listen to my voice. Come back to me."

Exhaling, she shook her head. "I cannot."

"I want you to picture a door. Any door."

"A d-door?"

"Think of a door from your house, or your childhood. Concentrate on what it looks like. Can you see it?"

After a pause, she nodded.

"Describe it to me."

"It is made of iron. Green ivy hangs on it. It is the door I always imagined when I read The Secret Garden."

"Good. You are the only one with the key. Say it back to me."

"I am the only one with the key. Like Mary in the book."

"When you unlock the door and open it, you'll be back in the Meditation Room. Do you understand me? That's how you'll get back here. You only have to go through the door."

She nodded as if drugged, slow, wobbly.

"Repeat back to me what I want you to do."

"Unlock the door. Open it. Walk through the door into the Meditation Room."

"Good. Now do it. I'm right here."

Ava rose into a sitting position. She lifted a hand, her palm facing Sensei. She made a pushing motion. "It is heavy." Her hair lifted off her shoulders, settled. Sensei felt as if a breeze had blown past him. When she turned her head slightly and looked at Daniel, her eyes were clear.

"Are you back?" he asked.

"Hai, Sensei. I found the car."

He smiled. "Not exactly. You found my best friend's car that we took mud running. But you found a car, and you controlled the end of the vision. That's a start."

Ava looked down at her hands. She was still holding Sensei's hand. She had been able to break the mental connection without breaking the physical one. She had touched someone, been overwhelmed by images, and been able to control them into something she could use. At least partially.

"I know that look," Sensei said, standing and pulling Ava to her feet. "You should wait to try this until we meet again. I know you won't, so just be careful. Don't push yourself too hard. That's enough for today."

· · · · ·

Isabel met Griffin in a strip mall in front of a rundown brick building with a large sign that read "Jay's Kickboxing Studio". He turned Rover off and was walking around to her door before she had even shut off her car.

He wasn't actually suggesting kickboxing, was he?

She stared at the sign. It didn't look like anyone was in the building; it was dark and there was no "Open" sign that she could see. Maybe they had just parked there but they weren't going to this building.

Getting out of the car, Iz was struck again by how good-looking he was, with a black jacket, lighter than the one he had been wearing, open over a gray Henley shirt. God, she loved seeing him in Henley shirts. He must have women lining up to give him their numbers. Why the hell was he with her?

"It's good to see you," he said, by way of greeting. He leaned in and gave her a light kiss, then a hug where he inhaled deeply. "You smell fabulous. Like spring."

"Thank you." It took an effort to keep her voice even. Every time he touched her, her heart stuttered, and her voice seemed to go up an octave. Her mouth would be on fire now for several minutes.

"It's this nice weather," she added, nervous.

The days were already starting to get longer, and today had almost reached fifty degrees. Isabel had gone for a walk during her lunch and both breaks, enjoying the tease of spring. Though the evening was already chilly, the warmer weather had lifted her spirits. The walks in fresh air made her feel invigorated.

"What do you think?" he asked, looking over at her.

Isabel looked at the building. She turned back to him. "Are you joking?"

"Nope."

"Griffin, I've never done anything like this before."

"That's the point. Jay will let us watch a little and try it out if we want."

"I..."

"Come on," he grinned. "No charge for the trial class. There are times when it's not busy, so you won't be overwhelmed. What you're wearing is fine."

"You want me to try kicking someone in jeans?"

"It's not just kicking, you know. You also punch. Besides, if you ever get attacked, do you think the guy's going to wait until you change into a pair of sweatpants?" She giggled. He poked her in the shoulder. "Give it a shot. You can always say no if you don't like it."

What the hell.

They walked into the building. The small reception area was empty. Griffin casually took Isabel's hand and started leading her around the receptionist desk.

"Wait," Isabel said. "What are you doing? It looks like it's closed."

"Jay's an old friend."

There was a hall on each side of the reception area. Griffin pointed to the left side. "Those are the locker rooms. Women to the right, guys to the left. This side has the workout area."

"Have you done this before?"

Isabel followed him down a long, dimly lit hallway. He was still holding her hand.

"I've stopped by before. I've never tried kickboxing."

They entered a large room with a boxing ring and stations all around it with punching bags and weight sets. A large man wearing a sleeveless shirt and shorts was punching one of the bags. He kept his hair high and tight, military style.

"Jay!" Griffin called, leading Isabel toward him.

Isabel watched the guy's muscles bulge as he punched, the tattoos covering both arms shifting as he worked. His hands were wrapped in white material. He was all muscle, his chest tight, hard as steel. This was Griffin's idea? One hit from him and Isabel would fly across the room.

"Jay!" Griffin called louder.

The man looked around, stopping the bag from swinging. His eyes, a hardened steel gray, instantly softened when he saw Griffin.

"Griffin! You finally decided to check out the gym!" Picking up a towel off the floor nearby, he began wiping sweat off his hands and face as he walked toward them.

As they neared, Griffin, though he towered over Isabel, looked tiny compared to Jay. He was tall and lean compared to Jay's muscular build. Jay wrapped his arms around Griffin and swallowed him in a hug, pulling him away from Isabel. She noticed a Marine tattoo on his shoulder: Semper Fi was written in red, white, and blue with a bald eagle hovering over it.

"Good to see you, man," he said softly into Griffin's ear.

There's a story there, Isabel thought. Something strong connects the two men.

"You, too. It's been too long." Griffin stepped to the side and put his hand on Isabel's shoulder. "This is Isabel. We thought we'd give kickboxing a try."

"Nice to meet you," Jay said, extending his hand. "Pardon the wraps."

Isabel stepped forward and shook his hand firmly, but her insides were tumbling.

"You have any experience with kickboxing?" Jay asked her.

"I had a crush on Jean-Claude van Damme when I was in eighth grade."

Jay burst out laughing. "Wanna give it a shot?"

Isabel raised an eyebrow. She didn't know what to say.

"How about you try on a pair of gloves and throw a few punches? See how it feels?"

His eyes were kind. She didn't feel threatened by him, despite his size and the stigma that usually came with so much body art. She was more threatened by the situation because she had no idea what to expect. Her experience with punching consisted of thumping Gabriel on the shoulder affectionately. Gabriel always laughed.

"Okay."

"Alright! Set your coat and purse right over there." Jay put his hand on her shoulder and pointed. "We're the only ones here, so you don't have to worry about them getting stolen."

Griffin walked with her to the bench and took his coat off. As they walked back toward Jay, he unbuttoned his shirt and began rolling up his sleeves.

"You're first," he said, giving her a grin. "If you survive, I'll give it a try."

"Wow. Thanks."

Jay helped her put a pair of boxing gloves on. He rested his hand on top of the punching bag. Relief flooded through her. At least she didn't have to try to hit him.

"Just give it a good punch," Jay suggested. "I'm sure you have someone you'd love to slug. Pretend the punching bag is that person."

Isabel thought for a moment and struck the bag the way she had seen people hit in movies. In her mind, Jeff Watson's head exploded. She smiled. That felt exhilarating, even if the bag barely moved.

"Good," Jay said. "This time plant your feet, like this." He demonstrated. Isabel followed his instruction. Jay adjusted her right hand as he spoke. "Your fist, wrist, and arm should always line up. When you punch, put your hips into it to give you more power." He demonstrated by moving his right hip forward as his right hand struck the bag, using his entire body for strength instead of just his hand. "Don't hold your breath."

He stopped the bag from moving.

This time when Isabel hit it, it moved a little and she felt like she had given it a solid punch. Jeff was going to go home bleeding.

"There you go! Feels good to let it out, right?" Jay smiled at her.

"How much time do I have?" Isabel asked, ready to go again. She motioned to the punching bag. "That guy's a real asshole."

• • • • •

Something was binding her wrists. Panic instantly leaped into her, consuming her. She struggled against the rope, twisting her hands, and her dislocated shoulder screamed in pain. She stopped struggling. Tears bit at the backs of her eyes. Wherever she was, there was no light source. She was in complete blackness. She couldn't see if she was in a room, in a building, on the ground. No sounds. No smells. When she tried to lick her lips, she found they were bound with thick tape.

Raising her hands slowly, mindful of her shoulder, she found the edge of the tape on her face and slowly started peeling it off. A muffled cry escaped her as it pulled and tore.

When you take off a Band-Aid, tear it quickly. It'll hurt more if you do it slowly.

Someone in the foster system had told her that. One of the older women taking care of her briefly before she had been moved to another house. Once, when Ava had scraped her leg, the woman had put a Band-Aid on the scrape, and a couple days later, she had ripped it off quickly. Ava barely felt anything.

Now she took the edge of the tape in her fingers, making sure she had a firm grip, took a deep breath, and yanked.

The pain in her shoulder was excruciating. The scream started muffled and erupted as the tape was ripped off. Ava fell backward onto the floor, which sent another shock of pain up her arm and through her shoulder. She screamed again.

Realizing her feet were free, she rolled onto her good shoulder and leaned up, fighting to stand. She held her bound hands in front of her, walking slowly, until she felt something stop her. Feeling along it, first one way, then another, she realized it was a wall. She set her jaw, leaned her dislocated shoulder gently against the wall, and planted her feet. Taking a deep breath, Ava reared back and slammed her shoulder into the wall.

The pain as it was forced back into place was exquisite.

She was five years old.

• • • • •

"Oh my God," Isabel purred. She slowly chewed the bite of steak with her eyes closed. One hand rested on her chest. Her moan caused glances from nearby patrons.

Griffin chuckled, cutting into his own steak. "You're enjoying it, I gather?"

She had already stuffed another bite into her mouth. "Mmm hmmm," she said, covering her mouth with her hand as she chewed. She laughed, swallowed. "I'm starving."

"You burned a lot of calories tonight. Jay said you're a natural at kickboxing. Did it help work out some frustrations?"

Isabel took a drink of wine, nodding vigorously. Her hair was still damp from the shower she'd taken afterwards. Jay loaned her a shirt and pants with strings on them so she could keep her regular clothes from getting sweaty, and she had pounded the piss out of that damn bag.

"Why aren't you a certified therapist? You're so good at it."

He grinned. "Missed opportunity. Look at you, enjoying your meal. You've eaten almost all of your food."

Isabel glanced down and was stunned to see he was right. Only a small sliver of steak and a couple mushrooms were left. During their conversation, she had enjoyed both the chatting and the meal.

"I did, didn't I?" She was quite proud of herself.

The restaurant they were in was a place Griffin had suggested. Isabel never would have come here on her own; it was too upper class and out of her budget. But he promised her a steak and a semi-private seat. Not many people would be eating this time of night, he said. He knew the owner, Will, and could get them a table away from everyone else.

Iz wondered if there was anyone in Madison Griffin didn't know.

Now he grinned at her. God, his teeth were absolutely perfect. He could be in a toothpaste commercial. "You're going to need a moist towelette, the way you're going at that thing."

Isabel snorted, laughed, snorted again. She covered her mouth with her hand again. "I feel like I can run a marathon. Kickboxing. Who knew? Man, this steak is delicious. I feel like I'm on drugs. Sorry. I'm rambling."

"I like listening to you ramble. You have a workout high."

"I haven't felt this good in years," Isabel said, stuffing her mouth with more meat. "I feel thirty pounds lighter."

"I'm glad it's working for you. Though you can't afford to lose any weight."

She stabbed a sauteed mushroom and popped it into her mouth. As pleasure coursed through her, she closed her eyes and savored the flavor.

Griffin watched her, amused.

"I can't keep eating out with you all the time," she said, finally starting to slow down. "If you ever let me pay, it's going to drain my pathetic budget."

Over the past week, he had taken her to dinner four times. The leftover boxes in her refrigerator were starting to pile up.

Finished with his own meal, Griffin pushed it to the side. "Don't worry about it. It's on me."

Her eyes darkened. Griffin caught tenacity and pride in her gaze. "You don't have to do that."

"I know." He sipped his wine. "You're not an obligation to me, Izzie. You're my girlfriend."

A silky ribbon of warmth wound its way around her, heating her skin. "That's going to take some getting used to."

"Exactly how long has it been since you've had a boyfriend?" Griffin asked.

Isabel squinted, thought about it, did some math. "Almost four years."

"Wow."

"And I've only dated a couple guys. Like, ever. That's all I've ever dated. I've only had sex a couple times, so I should probably tell you I don't have a lot of experience. When I suck at being a girlfriend, that's why."

Griffin paused a moment to collect his thoughts. He was a little startled by the admission, but it was nothing serious. He had to ease into the relationship, no diving in like a rutting stallion, that's all.

"'When you suck'? You automatically assume you won't be good at it?"

Isabel finished her wine. "I don't jump into bed with just anyone. Apparently, being a girlfriend comes with certain duties I wasn't willing to perform without getting to know the guy first. I told myself I loved my first boyfriend, and I tried to sex thing. Big disappointment, and I hated myself for letting him talk me into doing it in the first place. So, I told him I wasn't ready.

He wasn't willing to wait. Neither was boyfriend number two, when I was upfront with him. Therefore, I don't have a lot of experience."

No wonder she didn't trust anyone, Griffin thought. No one had given her a reason to.

A thought occurred to him, made his stomach plunge. "I was too forward when I kissed you." When she looked confused, he added, "The morning after you got plowed at The Raz."

"I don't pick up on flirtation. I was caught off guard. But kissing was fine. It was... very... fine."

Scarlet rose from her neck to the tips of her ears as she remembered. Griffin watched her raise a hand to fuss with her ear lobe. He thought it was absolutely adorable that she blushed so easily.

"Also, my attitude sucks. I know people are generally using others for their own gain and I'm not shy discussing it. Guys don't like that, either. A brooding woman is a lousy girlfriend. The odds are stacked against me, and it's my own fault."

"Or your decision."

She shrugged. "Maybe. Anyway, that's why I sucked when you kissed me," she said, stacking her dishes at the edge of the table for whomever was going to buss the table.

So considerate, he thought, watching her gather the dishes. Making the next person's job easier, because why not? It was a simple act, but a kind one.

"You didn't." He leaned back in his chair.

"I didn't what?"

The waiter brought the check over and handed it to Griffin. Griffin waited until they were alone before he said, "You didn't suck. Your instincts are just fine."

He didn't have to look at her to know she was blushing again.

As they walked out to his Rover, Isabel almost yanked her hand away when he reached over and took it. Then she almost giggled. Had it really been so long since she'd dated? She tried to think back to either boyfriend and remember if she had even let them hold her hand or touch her in public. Usually she hated that, but with Griffin it felt natural.

"So how often can we go to Jay's?" she asked as he opened the door for her. Another thing she would have to get used to. She climbed into the car and turned in the seat to face him.

"As often as you want," Griffin said. He rested his hands on her knees. "I work for clients with volatile moods. I have no shortage of frustration to work out."

The kiss still caught her off guard. The soft press of lips, the warmth, the unexpected giddiness that had her gripping his wrists to steady herself. Her legs were warm under his hands. Little flutters seemed to ripple from her stomach.

As surprising as it was, her body craved more the moment he pulled back.

"You'll let me know if I go too far?" he asked, his eyes roaming her face as if he found abundant beauty there.

Mischief filled her eyes. "If you'd gone too far, your balls would already be hanging from your rear-view mirror."

"One kickboxing lesson and you think you're van Damme." He put his fists up and gently brushed one against her chin. "I've created a monster."

Isabel grinned. "That's delicious."

· · · · ·

CHAPTER FIVE

Tuesdays were generally slow at the grocery store. Ava shopped for groceries when most people were at work, but her schedule was off today. She woke up late, after a particularly vivid dream about being tasered by her foster father. She started her workout late and had to shorten it to be able to start work on time. The shortened workout left her feeling lethargic, effecting her work. What usually took her a few hours to complete took longer. She ended up going to the grocery store later than usual.

She had to focus. Remembering childhood torture was pointless. What had happened to her was in the past and changing that was not an option.

Tomorrow was a new day; one she could start right by waking up on time and getting enough exercise. Today was lost, and she simply had to accept it.

Focus.

She practiced breathing exercises as she placed fresh fruits and vegetables in her cart. She would get back on track. A little extra discipline would be just what she needed. More training. More work.

"Ava?"

She jolted. Gabriel was standing a few feet away.

She had been so absorbed in her thoughts that she had not noticed him standing there. Her lack of awareness of her surroundings infuriated her. Since early childhood, she had been able to recall every person in any space she occupied. At this point she could not remember what clothes she had put on this morning without looking down.

Focus.

"Hi," Gabriel said, walking over to her. He carried a small basket. Ava felt her throat closing.

"Hello," she managed. When he did not say anything more, she blurted, "Why are you here?"

He gave her that slow, lazy smile. "My fridge is empty."

If she could just stop staring at those mesmerizing blue eyes for a moment, she could break the connection and resume her duties.

Moving the basket handle up so it sat in the crook of his arm, he picked up a Granny Smith apple and rolled it from one hand to the other. Ava liked his hands. They were rough from wood working, with little cuts here and there. Some were mostly healed, some fresh. Obviously, he was not afraid to use his hands and did not mind a little pain.

She exhaled harshly. "You are everywhere I go."

"That's one of the joys of a small town." He set the apple down, glanced over the produce to see if there was anything he wanted.

"No, it is not," Ava said, annoyed at how casual he was behaving. Meeting here in the grocery store might be normal for him, but it was a disaster for her. It interrupted her schedule, flustered her. "I cannot focus when I am thinking about you."

He raised the one eyebrow in that odd way he did. She hated how much that captivated her. Forcing herself to break her gaze, she began rooting through apples, checking for bruises.

"You've been thinking about me?" His tone indicated he was surprised by that. He kept perusing the fruits.

Ava made a disgusted sound. "It is interfering with my work and my training."

As if anything he could say would allow her to go back to the way things were. As if he could flip a switch and she would stop thinking about him.

"I've been thinking about you, too." He studied the red seedless grapes. Setting his basket on the floor, he lifted a bag of grapes and inhaled deeply.

"Stop it," she snapped. One hand gripped the handle of her cart until the blood drained from her knuckles. "Do not think about me and do not bother me. I do not need you confusing my routines with your attractive smile and your fascinating raised eyebrow."

Her tone made it clear she was furious, but the way she spoke tickled him to no end.

"You're allowed to have fun once in a while. It wouldn't hurt you to relax a little."

He was amused, she could tell. That made her even more livid.

"You," she said through gritted teeth, "do not know what does or does not hurt me."

That he could make her lose control of her emotions, especially anger, was the biggest insult. She began throwing random apples into a bag without checking them for bruises or freshness.

"Why don't you tell me? Invite me over to your house."

"What? No!" The very thought appalled her. Her house was her sanctuary. The power of deciding who was allowed inside and when was entirely up to her.

The eyebrow raised again. Damn him. How was it that she could be furious with him one moment and so distracted and fascinated with him the next with such a simple movement of muscles?

"Why not?"

"I do not want you in my house." She set the bag of apples in her cart. Her insides felt like they were shaking.

"Why not?" he repeated. "I'm not a serial killer."

"Because it is mine," she said, turning away from him. He thought he heard panic in her voice.

Reaching into the plastic bag of grapes, he plucked a large one off the bunch and set the bag back in the bin. "Hey, Ava, give this a try."

"What-" She turned her head to see what he was talking about, and he popped the grape into her mouth. Before she could get defensive, he cradled her chin with his thumb, her jaw with his fingertips, framing her face but not so much it made her feel attacked. Her eyes widened.

"Just taste it," he said, before she could spit it in his face. "Don't think so much."

She chewed it slowly, her eyes never leaving his. He saw shock in those gray eyes that he would come so close to her, would touch her, knowing what she could do to him. Then a different kind of surprise when the natural flavor of the grape burst open in her mouth.

The weight on her chest was making it hard to breathe. Her pulse had quickened, yet she had trouble inhaling. How was it possible that his proximity was making her feel helpless, yet her body was not responding with instinct? She could not raise a hand to him right now if she tried.

"Why don't you come over to my house?" he asked, lingering a moment longer before he stepped back. He wanted to kiss her. He wanted to taste the sweetness of the grape on her tongue but knew he would be seriously injured if he tried. "I'll cook dinner for you Saturday night."

His voice was gentle, easing some of the panic she felt at the thought of him being in her house. He already knew where she lived; everyone in town knew the Farley house. Her trepidation was not that a stranger knew her address, which was public knowledge. Still, allowing him inside her house felt too personal... too much like giving in. She was not ready to do that.

The alternative was rearranging her entire schedule to go to his house instead. She could admit it was a nice house, with old charm restored and updates added for convenience and comfort. He had a large plot, which allowed privacy. Sitting on his back deck and on the roof had been... curiously pleasant.

"If it will get you to leave me alone, I will come over." She still felt his fingertips on her face. Part of her, buried very deep, was disappointed he had stopped touching her. Feeling unsteady, she reached up and touched her jaw where his hand had lingered.

"Outstanding," Gabriel said, looking pleased with himself. "I'll see you at six."

Ava blinked and collected herself. She walked briskly away from him to finish her shopping.

•　　•　　•　　•　　•

Izzie-

Come in and have a drink. I bought you something. It's sitting on the counter.

-Griff

Isabel read the note and plucked if off the door to Griffin's apartment. He had very elegant writing.

She could hear water running as she opened the door and stepped in; he was taking a shower. Tucking the note in her purse, she smiled. Of course, it was silly, but she didn't care. Had a guy ever actually handwritten her anything? Not since Kindergarten, when they were assigned to.

Griffin had to work late again and wasn't able to meet her at Jay's. She had taken her frustrations out anyway, happily envisioning Jeffrey's body every time her hand made a connection with the body bag and then her partner's punch pads. She even felt strong when she had the pads on and was getting punched and kicked; she wasn't the weak little flake she had been only a week earlier. After every shower at the gym, she felt she'd earned each drop of sweat and each sore muscle. Getting beat up was oddly liberating.

A medium-sized box sat on the island. Setting her purse on one of the stools, Isabel smiled again at the shiny purple wrapping paper and the huge white bow. A card was tucked beneath the bow, so she opened that first.

I think these will help.

-G

Curious, she opened the box carefully after tucking the card into her purse.

A pair of brand-new boxing gloves lay inside. They were smaller than the ones she usually wore at the gym, so they would fit her hands better. She wouldn't have to waste so much time searching for the few smaller pairs anymore.

In the bathroom, the water shut off. She barely registered the sound.

A lump built in her throat, threatening tears. She swallowed hard. The gloves were shiny, pristine. Sliding one on, she found it fit perfectly. She hugged it to her chest. She pulled it off again and ran her index finger over it, marveling at the smooth material. Speechless at how simple yet thoughtful the gift was, she was completely lost in her thoughts when the bathroom door opened.

"Do you like them, then?"

Isabel let out a squeak and spun around.

Griffin was standing in the bathroom doorway in a pair of jeans and socks and nothing else. His hair was tousled, as usual, even after the shower. He was unfolding a tee shirt. He wasn't as lanky as she had originally thought; there was a definition of muscle in his trim figure.

"Not Ichabod," she mumbled.

"How's that?"

Isabel averted her eyes. "Nothing. I love them," she said, squeezing them tighter against her chest. "Thank you."

"It seemed like the ones at the gym were a little too heavy. Jay helps out veterans a lot, mostly guys, so he doesn't keep many of the smaller weights on hand."

She blinked and turned away from him, hoping he didn't notice her eyes misting. She set them back in the box. "These are perfect."

On impulse, she walked over to him.

"I'm glad you like - oh, hello."

He was momentarily thrown off balance when she threw her arms around his waist. She pressed her cheek to his chest, hoping he didn't feel her hot tears against his bare skin. When his arms came around her, she thought she would melt into him.

The combination of the random act of kindness and how easily he touched her had her fighting back tears.

When was the last time she had hugged anyone but Gabriel? Really, truly hugged someone. When was the last time a guy dared hug her back?

"Thank you," she said into his shoulder. When her urge to cry eased up, she stepped back and turned away to give herself time to wipe the tears.

"You're very welcome. I didn't realize you'd like them so much."

"I love them," she repeated, slipping them on. They fit perfectly. She executed a couple jabs she had learned last week. The gloves felt right on her hands, as if they had been made especially for her.

"I'm going to finish getting dressed," Griffin said. "Pour me a glass of wine? There's some sangria on the counter."

Isabel put her gloves back in the box and wrapped her arms around the cardboard. What a thoughtful man, she thought, her lips curving. The gift was unexpected and simply perfect.

She poured them each a glass of wine and carried the glasses to the sliding glass door in the living room. The view was gorgeous. Too bad it was still too chilly to sit out on the balcony tonight. The next couple of days were supposed to be warmer, but who knew in Wisconsin?

When Griffin came up behind her and stood a little too close, her pulse quickened. She turned around and held out his drink.

"Your wine," she said, unable to stop the slight waver in her voice.

"Many thanks," he said, taking a drink. "Ahh... sangria. Always makes me feel amorous."

Isabel swallowed.

Griffin took a step closer. Now she was backed against the door. His mouth was slow, tender. Always so tender. She loved his lips. They expertly coaxed hers, they roamed down her neck and along her collar bone as if he had all the time in the world to spend on her. Just as slowly, he moved back up until his mouth fastened once again on hers. She was afraid her shaking hand was going to drop her glass of wine. His fingertips drifted down her arm, causing goosebumps to rise along her skin. When he pulled back, her body screamed for more. Either he or the wine was leaving her reeling; she wasn't sure which.

"Sangria tastes good on you," he said, licking his lips. He smiled.

Holy fuck, she thought, trying to stop her head from spinning. Her nerves were in overdrive. Kiss me again.

"I thought we could try Italian tonight," Griffin said, lifting her hand and tangling his fingers with hers. He watched their entwined hands, fascinated. His seemed to swallow hers up.

Why the fuck are you waiting for him? You don't need permission.

"You look like you don't like that idea," Griffin said, frowning. He set his wine glass next to hers. "Maybe we could -"

Damn right I don't.

"Sweet Jesus, stop talking," she ordered. She pulled his face down to hers and took what she wanted this time. He let out a startled grunt when her mouth met his. This time, she focused on everything: the taste of the wine on his lips, the seconds it took him to recover from her brazen move, the fresh smell of soap from his recent shower. His skin was soft, his damp hair curly at the edges. She combed her fingers through it and pressed her body to his. Griffin ran his hands down her sides and around her hips to grip her bottom, squeezing indulgently before he lifted her. She wrapped her legs around his waist.

I've always wanted to do that, she thought.

Hot. Her skin was so hot. His body as firm as bronze. Isabel dug her fingers into his shoulder blades, thankful he was wearing a shirt. She was afraid she would have shredded him if he hadn't been.

Encircling his arms around her, he squeezed their bodies together, nipping at the long curve of her throat. She leaned her head back to give him full access.

And smacked it on the patio door, hard.

"Fuck me!" she yelled, pressing her hand to the back of her head.

Griffin's eyes were amused as he studied her. "I'm all for it, Love, but we better look at your head, first."

He set her down and gently leaned her head forward so he could see if she broke the skin. His fingers tenderly parted her hair.

"Fucking ow!" she growled, wincing.

"Sorry about that." He verified her skin was intact before kissing the top of her head gently and releasing her. "You may have a bump, but you're not bleeding."

Hesitantly running her fingertips over the spot, she scowled at him. "That's what I get for trying to be proactive."

He picked up both their wine glasses, handed hers over. "I certainly hope one little mishap doesn't dissuade you from doing it again. That was..." He exhaled, shaking his head. "Amazing."

"Well, you can't kiss me like that and expect me to just sit down and eat dinner. I wasn't done with you yet."

He grinned. She could fall in love with that perfect smile.

Oh, stop it. You just started dating.

"Just for the record, you have nothing to worry about in the experience department." He slid his free hand around her waist, kissing the top of her head again. Gently. "Your mouth knows exactly what it's doing."

She blushed furiously. Her head was throbbing, and she felt like a klutz, but she couldn't stop smiling. Leaning her head against his chest, she felt her body light up again when the hand around her waist squeezed with obvious affection.

"So..." he said, sipping his wine. "Was that a yes to Italian?"

•   •   •   •   •

The days were getting longer, with the sun hanging on until just after seven, but the cold still had a snap to it during the mornings and evenings. Ava walked to her mailbox with the last drizzle of sun almost gone from the horizon. After a fairly mild day, she had her heavy coat and gloves on again. She was usually unaffected by the weather, but as she saw her breath waft in front of her and made the mile-long trudge to check her mail, she yearned for spring.

Everything seemed to be taking a toll on her body lately. The simple act of putting on her coat to come outside just now had been momentous, almost not worth doing. Not much more than junk came through regular mail anyway. But her purpose for her daily walk to the end of her driveway in spite of whether she knew mail was waiting or not was because of the exercise, not the payoff of what was inside. Once she started giving herself a break on the little things, she could continue to indulge until she lost all her discipline. What then?

At the mailbox, she pulled out the meager contents and began the walk back to the house.

The wind was at her back now, not as cold as when it was blowing directly into her face. Ava walked slower than she usually did. Her head was throbbing. In addition to a body that felt like it was letting her down, extra training with Sensei that made her mind feel like it was being stretched repeatedly like a rubber band, she now had to try to be social with Gabriel on Saturday. Why did he have to insist on being friends now, when she had so much going on? Why couldn't he just leave her alone?

She thought of his blue eyes, full of so much sorrow even as he continued being kind to her, to others. He must know each day would be just like the last; waking to know his sister was still as dead as yesterday, knowing he still did not know who killed her, he still could not give his other sister any comfort even as he saw her struggle with each breath.

Mounting the front steps, Ava stood on the welcome mat a moment, letting the cold envelope her. Empathizing with Gabriel would only bring her trouble. Emotions were a luxury she could not afford.

She closed her eyes and inhaled through her nose, holding her breath. The silence around her was uncanny, welcoming. Ava was amazed by nature's ability to stay beautiful even during its cycle of death. She exhaled.

Inside, she took off her boots, coat, and gloves. As she had thought, the mail was junk. She dropped it in the garbage under the kitchen sink and filled a glass with water.

A few minutes of yoga would clear her head of Gabriel and allow her to relax. Tonight, she had free time – something she rarely had – and she did not want to spend it thinking about a man she knew little about, who's proximity would only cause her grief. She certainly did not want to worry about keeping up with conversations and answering questions.

Five minutes later she walked downstairs in yoga pants and a long-sleeved tee shirt. Refilling her glass of water, she set the glass on the coffee table and prepared for yoga.

Her living room had a large open space for just this purpose. Kneeling in front of a wooden chest under the large north window, Ava pulled out her yoga mat.

But after fifteen minutes, when she could not keep her balance enough to ease into the firefly pose and almost knocked herself out getting into the crow pose, she rolled her mat up and put it back in the trunk. She sat on the sofa and stretched her legs out.

She huffed out a breath, frustrated. Why were her thoughts so scattered? After years of practicing meditation, she could eliminate absolutely every distraction from her mind and sit in silence at any given time. She had been able to do this as young as nine years old. Until now. What was happening to her?

A sound had her eyes open and her sitting up instantly, her hands up in a defensive posture and her legs curled under her, ready to spring into action if needed.

The girl with the braid was standing in her living room.

Ava relaxed her hands, knowing she could do nothing physically to the specter.

"Hayden." Saying the name out loud somehow made the semitransparent being more daunting.

The girl was standing near the front door wearing a nightgown. Her mouth was moving, but she wasn't making any sound. Her eyes were staring blankly across the room.

"Leave my house," Ava said. She did not want to deal with this now; she could not. She was too exhausted.

The girl's empty eyes seemed to stare through Ava. Her lips seemed blue in the lamplight. They continued to move, as if she were talking.

Feeling anger churning inside her, Ava opened the little drawer in the coffee table and pulled out one of many throwing knives. She whipped it at the girl, knowing it couldn't injure her but needing to vent her anger. She was tired of the intrusions. The knife sailed through the girl's neck and lodged into the door casing behind her. The girl continued moving her lips, undeterred.

Ava grabbed another knife and hurled it. This one passed through the girl's eye and stuck in the casing a few inches from the first one.

"Leave, now," Ava said. She leaned back on the arm of the couch and draped her arm over her eyes.

She considered the conversation over.

• • • • •

In all her years in the kitchen, Isabel had never considered cooking an arousing experience. Until now.

She and Griffin easily moved around his large kitchen, gathering ingredients for the recipe they had picked out as if they had been doing it for years. Griffin told her where the skillets and measuring spoons and cups were as he started dicing chicken. She began measuring the rest of the ingredients. They chatted about work and kickboxing as they created their dish. For once, Iz moved gracefully, not bumping into Griffin or counters. They felt right working in the kitchen together.

Standing at the stove frying bacon, she'd set a package of frozen corn on top of her head to ease the swelling. She stood at an angle so she could talk to Griffin while he was at the island using the cutting board.

"Jay gave me a schedule of programs at the gym so I would know when it wasn't busy," she said, sipping her wine. "He also wrote down the hours that were the busiest so I can avoid them. How sweet is that?"

"Wonderful. Just let me know when you want to meet there. If it's after hours, I have a key."

She smiled. "That's delicious."

Griffin cupped a pile of diced chicken in his hands and dropped it into a bowl.

"Oh, you butt bastard!" Isabel growled.

He looked up, startled, to see her poking at the bacon with tongs. "You're going to fry, you little jack wagon."

He watched her, enjoying the concentrated scowl on her face, the way she posed with one socked foot propped up on its toes. Her long hair was pulled back into a loose ponytail. Suddenly she jerked as the bacon splattered. The bag of frozen corn slid toward the side of her head.

"You little fuck nugget!" she barked. "You're going to stay in the pan the longest, you vindictive shit-stick!"

Despite his efforts to remain quiet as he observed her, Griffin burst out laughing.

Isabel glanced over at him. The bag of corn inched dangerously close toward her ear. "What are you laughing at?"

"Are you trash-talking your food while you're cooking it?"

Color rushed into her cheeks. "I guess I am. Sometimes I... sing to it. If it behaves well."

Griffin carried the bowl of chicken over to the stove and set it on the counter. Keeping his slimy hands far from both his body and hers, he leaned over and planted a kiss on her mouth.

"What was that for?" she asked as he walked to the sink to wash his hands.

"For you being you."

Smiling, Isabel jerked as another drop of grease splattered against her arm. "Butt pirate!" The bag of corn hit the floor. "Ass hat!"

"Why didn't you just bake it in the oven?" Griffin dried his hands on a towel as he walked toward her.

"I need the bacon grease and it has to be extra crispy. That's easier when it's pan fried."

"Look at you, Martha Stewart." He picked up the bag of corn.

Isabel snorted, then jerked again, glowering at the bacon. "Son of a -"

Griffin gripped the wrist with the tongs and swept her into a low dip, devouring her next curse in a kiss.

$$\bullet \quad \bullet \quad \bullet \quad \bullet \quad \bullet$$

"My compliments to the chef."

Griffin raised his glass of wine and smiled at Isabel across the island.

"All I did was verbally abuse the ingredients." She raised her glass, tapping it gently to his. Sipping it, she smiled. The wine paired well with the recipe they had made together, which had turned out very well. She would definitely be adding it to her rotation of monthly meals.

Griffin grinned. "You provided entertainment as well as helping prepare the feast. It was delicious."

"We rocked that pasta dish. It had bacon in it, though. We were bound to succeed."

Standing, Griffin held his hand out to Isabel. When she took it, her breath caught as he pulled her close. He swayed as if music was playing, moving in a small circle in between the kitchen and living room.

"Stay the night with me," he murmured.

Isabel's foot stuck on the floor, making her stumble. "What?"

Griffin steadied her while she regained her footing. "Stay with me. I don't want you to leave."

"I have to go to work tomorrow. All my work clothes are at my apartment."

"Let's go get them and bring them here." He dipped her slowly, brought her back up. "We can make out."

She snorted.

"Stay with me." His eyes were serious now, the laughter gone from them.

Had anyone ever made her feel so needed?

"Okay."

He leaned down and pressed his lips to hers. They were warm, his lips, and she liked that she could still taste the wine on them. The pants he was wearing were a wool blend that made his ass look especially delicious. She had been trying not to stare at it all night. Now she wanted to grab it unceremoniously and give it a good squeeze.

Letting the kiss gradually intensify, Griffin cupped his hand behind her head. Isabel felt so small when he did that. He could palm her head like a basketball with those large hands. He brushed the backs of his fingers down her throat with his other hand and released a moan from her. The room was spinning around her. Her breath was coming in little gasps that sent spears of desire pulsing through Griffin's blood.

Isabel could take no more waiting. She grabbed his butt with both hands, enjoying the feel of it through his dress pants.

Griffin pulled back. "You saucy rascal." He grinned.

Giggling, she gave a couple quick squeezes. "You have a nice butt."

"You have a nice everything."

His mouth returned to hers. They continued swaying as they explored, moving back toward the living room. Griffin turned so his back was to the couch and sat, pulling her down to straddle him. Hands caressed and navigated. Tongues tangled. Isabel began unbuttoning his shirt, her heart beating so hard she thought she was going to pass out. Her fingers weren't working. She kept fumbling with the fabric. Griffin placed his hands on top of hers.

"Relax," he murmured. "We're not in a hurry."

He sat back against the couch and watched her, rubbing his hands up and down her thighs. Isabel kept glancing at his face, then away, clearly uncomfortable, but she kept her hands busy with his shirt.

"How many damn buttons does the fucking thing have?" She freed it from his pants to get the bottom buttons. "Stop watching me." Her tone was sullen.

"I like watching you." He slid his hands up her thighs, under her sweater, along her sides. Her sharp intake of breath made him smile. "I would like to do all kinds of things to you."

Unable to control it, she shivered. The animal part of her wanted to rip his shirt off and dig her claws into him. The modest side wanted to curl into herself until he stopped watching her.

Finally free of buttons, she parted his shirt. She ran her fingers down his chest and watched the muscles twitch at her touch.

I'm doing that.

Her mind wanted to argue. It wanted to tell her she was not worth him, that he felt nothing for her. But his body was reacting to her, showing her that her mind was lying. That it was trying to betray her.

Griffin pulled her sweater over her head. For a moment he could only stare at her, speechless. She had a long torso, golden skin he wanted to explore with his hands and mouth as he made his way up – and down - her body. The bra she was wearing was a blue-gray semi-lacy number that left the tops of her breasts exposed.

Wondering why he was staring so long, Isabel crossed her arm over her chest.

"No, don't do that," he said softly. His tone was full of awe. He took her hand and pulled her arm away. "You're beautiful."

Leaning up, he pressed his chest against hers, wrapping his arms around her to seal their bodies together. He moved his mouth against hers.

"You're so beautiful."

"I don't feel beautiful," Isabel said. She ran her hands through his hair. That hair that always seemed to look like it had just missed being combed.

"We'll have to change that." Griffin gazed into her eyes, brushing a strand of hair from her face.

His tongue was magnificent.

Shifting forward to relieve a cramp in one of her calves, Isabel's pelvis ground against his and sent a flash of heat coursing through her that was almost painful. She gritted her teeth against the sensation instead of acting on her impulse – which was to grind against him until this aching need was satisfied. She straightened her leg slightly until the muscle loosened.

Griffin dug his fingers into her hips, exhaling slowly.

"Sorry," Isabel said when she saw the intense look on his face. She put her palm on his chest.

"Not your fault," he groaned. "I'm just... very turned on right now."

Her face turned scarlet.

Griffin ran his index finger along the skin above the top of the right bra cup, making goosebumps rise over Isabel's entire body. He tucked his finger just inside the cup, pulling forward slightly and running it in the opposite direction. Isabel leaned back and rested her hands on his knees. She let her head fall back so her hair brushed his legs, her neck exposed. Her body was presented before him like a gift. Griffin allowed himself a long, indulgent look at her subtle curves as he slowly moved his hands up and down her stomach, watching her skin quiver.

When he put his fingers on the button of her jeans, she leaned up instantly and covered them with her own. She yanked her hands back as if she had touched a hot surface.

"Sorry."

Raising his eyebrows, he moved his hands casually to her hips. "Too much?"

"No, I-"

"Isabel." Griffin ran his tongue along her collarbone, grinning against her skin as she shivered. "Don't fib."

"It's just been a while. It's fine, really. Go ahead."

Leaning back, he studied her face. "You realize you're incapable of lying, right? You have this sign on your forehead that lights up in neon every time you try, that reads, 'BULLSHIT'." He motioned across his own forehead, miming a marquee sign.

"I don't-" she sighed.

"And that's fine. You don't have to."

"That's not-"

"It doesn't have to be." He smiled.

"You aren't-"

"And I'm not going to."

"Griffin-"

"Isabel."

"Suck my lady-dick!" She barked, but her eyes were laughing. She set her hands on his chest and shoved herself off his lap. She picked up her glass of wine and carried it to the kitchen to refill it.

Griffin tried to suppress his laughter. "Before you get yourself a refill, why don't we go get whatever you need to stay the night?"

"Eat my ass!" she fired back.

He burst out laughing.

• • • • •

Ava was pinned. Vincent had settled just enough of his weight over her to let her know she was going nowhere. He placed his right arm under her neck and his left arm across her throat in a firm but painless choke hold. Ava waited for him to apply slight pressure to let her know he was in position, so she could begin her counter move.

She had raised her arms around his, crossing them at the wrists, using one hand to grip his jaw and the other to support it. She made sure she had her hands positioned correctly. All she had to do was force his head up and she would shift the energy in her favor.

Instead, she froze.

Suddenly the pressure on her neck seemed too constricting. His body was too heavy, pinning her, choking off her air. She could not breathe. Why was she unable to breathe? He was not applying full pressure. One of his legs was angled so he was not putting his full body weight on her. She should not have felt trapped.

You like that, don't you?

The voice filled her head as Vincent's face faded and another man loomed over her. The large shadow above her blew hot breath into her face, making her gag.

Coughing, she bucked under him, trying to shove his body off hers. Of course, he was heavier than her and he did not move. She took a deep breath, closed her eyes. Tried to convince herself she was safe.

Vincent patiently waited a moment, confused by her reaction. When she stilled beneath him and closed her eyes, he prompted her on her technique. "Push up on my chin to throw me off balance."

Panic, a feeling she was familiar with, shot through her body, spreading to her limbs. Her heart was thudding so loud every other sound seemed muffled. She put her hands on Vincent's arm, pushed.

Get off get off me.

"Am I pressing too hard?" Vincent asked, his voice seeming to come from the other end of a long hallway.

It is not real, she tried to tell herself. Your fear is not logical.

But she could not breathe. Short gasps of air were all she could draw into her lungs. She was starting to feel dizzy.

And she felt his fingers wrap around her throat, squeezing as he shoved her nightgown up around her chest with his other hand.

You're practically begging for it, you little tease.

She was no longer in the dojo. She was not a grown woman practicing with a trusted partner. She was five years old again, locked under a man she barely knew.

She clawed at his hands, at his arms, trying to pry his thick fingers off her throat. He laughed. With a painful yank he ripped her underwear off her, leaving red marks on her hips where the fabric raked across her skin.

No.

Ava… The Monster cooed in her ear. You know what to do. You don't have to go through this.

"Sensei?" Vincent said. His voice was so far away.

Daniel had been practicing with a hanbo. He could see, even from a distance, that something was wrong with Ava. He set the staff down and crossed the mat.

She started batting helplessly at Vincent's arms, trying to get him to release her. She brought her knee up to drive it into his groin, but the technique had no power because of the angle he was at to her leg. Her knee struck him weakly on his inner thigh. The error should have been obvious to her.

No please no

I will take the pain away, The Monster soothed.

"No," she panted, her hands slapping at Vincent uselessly.

"Yame," Sensei said, the Japanese order to stop training.

Vincent relaxed his hold but kept the position. He wanted to get up, but he risked either a successful knee to the groin or opening his face up to Ava's hands once his arms were fully out of the way. He looked at Sensei, his expression questioning.

Sensei held up a finger for him to wait. Ava hadn't stopped when he gave the command. She had not disobeyed him since she was a young child.

"Ava," Sensei said calmly, "stop struggling. Vincent is not applying pressure."

I don't want this make him stop make The Bad People go away

Daniel frowned. The thoughts seemed to rush at him, blasting through his head in a young child's voice. Had Ava just sent a telepathic message? Or had he simply picked up on her thoughts because of his proximity to her?

He could tell by the sharpened look in Vincent's eyes and the slight jerk of his head that the young man had also caught the message.

Ava continued to struggle like a wild animal. Her hands were scratching against Vincent's uniform. Her body was writhing beneath his. Tears were running down her temples.

Beneath him, Ava had closed her eyes against the horror of what she knew was coming. She felt insignificant, tiny compared to Mack's bulk.

The shadow leaned down and pressed his mouth to hers. She gagged at the smell, the feel of his lips against hers sickening. She smelled alcohol on his breath, cigarette smoke on his skin and on his clothing.

"No no no no no no-" Ava panted the word as she fought to get free, terrified of an assailant Vincent and Daniel couldn't see.

Cannot breathe

She gasped, fighting for air. Her throat was convulsing. She shook her head, opened her eyes. They were blind with fear. The pupils had expanded until her eyes looked freakishly unreal.

"Should I get up, Sensei?" Vincent asked quietly.

"You're keeping her from hurting herself or you. Hang tight. Ava, you're not in danger."

Every part of her knew what was about to happen. She twisted like a cat, trying to free herself from Mack's grip. With a viscous thrust he was inside her, spreading excruciating pain and shame and hatred and fear.

Ava squeezed her eyes shut again, threw her head back, and screamed; a high-pitched sound filled with agony. Vincent recoiled. Daniel barked an order for him to stay put and he leaned forward again, holding Ava in place. Her struggles became more fervent. She bucked almost hard enough to throw Vincent off her. Daniel steadied him with a hand on his shoulder.

Give it to me, The Monster said, its lips brushing against her ear. Give the pain to me.

"No," she cried, a heartbreaking sound like the keening of a wounded animal. "Do not let The Monster in."

She had gripped her partner so hard her fingernails pierced the sleeves of his uniform and dug into his flesh. Sweat gathered in her hair and flattened it to her head. Her terror was all-encompassing; she should have known Vincent's arm was hovering half an inch above her throat, and she would have realized he was not putting any pressure on her neck. No part of his body was holding her down anymore. Yet she continued to struggle as if she were being held captive when she could have easily slipped out of Vincent's hold.

Stop please stop it hurts stop-

Stop fighting it, The Monster purred. Give it to me and I will take it away.

Fire ripped through the length of her. Nausea twisted her stomach. She felt the blood oozing down her legs and the suffocating weight of him.

When she felt her grip on reality began to slip, she welcomed it. The loss of control was like letting go of a tether in the middle of a raging sea.

The Monster took over.

And then, nothing. Her mind went to a place where she felt no pain.

As the heavy body grunted and jerked above her, she stopped fighting. Her eyes glazed, her hands stopped shoving against her attacker, and her body relaxed. She felt nothing.

Ava's body shuddered suddenly, then stilled beneath Vincent's. When she opened her eyes, both Vincent and Daniel saw her sockets were black. Her head drifted to the side in complete submission. Her grip on Vincent's arms relaxed. Her face was red and sweaty, her chest hitching with every breath.

Daniel leaned over and began to murmur softly in her ear. Taking one of her hands, he pried if off Vincent's arm, loosening her nails from his skin. Vincent winced. Daniel pulled her other hand away, holding it loosely, hating how cold it felt.

After a moment, he looked at Vincent and nodded. Vincent slowly moved off her.

Ava lay motionless on the mat, her face impassive. She blinked slowly and her eyes were gray again, the whites bright under the fluorescent lights. Her nails were darkened with Vincent's blood. Still breathless, she was wheezing, her chest moving up and down in quick jerks.

Daniel continued to hold her hand, watching her carefully. He brushed her clinging hair back from her face. "Vincent, are you injured?"

"I'm okay, Sensei."

"Bow out and get changed," he said, keeping his voice steady. "Tend to your wounds if you need to."

"Hai, Sensei. Arrigato, gozaimashita."

Vincent stood shakily and walked to the center of the mat, in front of the kamidana, to end his training session.

"Ava?" Daniel said.

He was unnerved by the emptiness he saw in her eyes. The blackness had been bad enough, but now her gaze was as dead as a trophy mount's. After all the fighting she'd done when David first brought her to him, she had never been despondent. Even as she had stopped fighting and accepted his authority as guidance, not abuse, that fire had remained inside her. What had to happen to make the light leave the eyes of the strongest person he had ever met?

"Can you hear me?" After a moment, he snapped his fingers in front of her eyes. The crack echoed in the dojo. She didn't blink. "Let's sit you up. Slowly."

Placing one hand behind her head for support and holding her hand with the other, he eased her into a sitting position. Her body responded but her eyes continued their empty gaze at nothing. The flush on her cheeks and the clammy feel of her forehead was not reassuring. He rested a hand on her shoulder.

Vincent came out of the changing room with his bag. He had left the tee shirt on but taken off his uniform top, revealing the cuts in his arms from Ava's nails. They were deep. He had washed the blood away, but a couple were seeping again.

"Is there something I can do to help, Sensei?" He set his bag against the wall.

"You two are intimate, correct?" Daniel glanced at his student.

Vincent dropped his eyes immediately. Crimson lit the tips of his ears.

"I'm not judging. I need an honest answer. Are you intimately involved with her or not?"

"Hai, Sensei."

"She shouldn't be alone tonight. Is her staying with you a problem?" Daniel checked her pulse. She was still unaware of her surroundings.

"She can stay at my apartment."

"Good. Get a bottle of water from The Meditation Room." When Vincent was out of the dojo, Daniel squeezed Ava's hand. "Ava, can you hear me?"

She didn't speak, but her hand just barely tightened on his. There was hardly any strength to it.

"Is this related to what we've been working on after class?"

This time she didn't respond. He decided to try to communicate with her mentally. Since he had no idea how to do that, he concentrated on short sentences and focused all his energy on transmitting calm energy to her.

Can you hear me? I want to help.

Daniel felt something nudging, a prodding sensation, as if someone had walked up behind him and was poking him in the back of his neck. He reached up and had almost touched his nape when he realized it might be Ava. He lowered his hand.

Is that you?

Vincent returned with a bottle of water, opening it before he handed it over. For now, Daniel would have to be satisfied with the present. He would discuss other methods of communicating with her at another time.

He lifted the bottle to Ava's mouth, tilting it slightly to see if she would respond. Her lips parted and she accepted a small drink.

A tear slid down her ashen cheek.

Hurt me he hurt me

Not used to hearing her voice in his head, Daniel took a moment to think about the words she was projecting. He was sure the thought was about someone from her past, not Vincent. The two did not have any issues; Vincent was a good partner, and Ava held no animosity toward him. Their compatibility and Ava's absolute trust in him convinced Daniel to put them together for training all these years. But mostly, something inside told him Ava did not mean Vincent when the thought flashed through his mind.

"She's not leaving here until I see improvement." Daniel addressed Vincent. "If she improves, you'll need to take her to your place and keep an eye on her at all times. Understand?"

"Hai, Sensei."

Pausing, he decided they had to discuss the obvious while Ava wasn't mentally with them.

"Did you hear her in your head?" he asked, studying Vincent's expression.

"I heard her." He seemed disturbed by what had happened, but not particularly surprised.

"Have you heard her before tonight?"

Vincent considered this. "I think so."

"What was she doing when it happened? Was she under stress?"

Vincent gazed at Ava with absolute devotion. "We were having sex." He took her free hand. "She asks me to make The Monster go away when she needs sex."

When she needs sex, Vincent said, not when she wants it. Daniel wondered about that but left it alone for the time being.

"'Don't let The Monster in,'" he said thoughtfully, remembering her outcry earlier.

"I thought it was figurative," Vincent said.

"What do you think now?" Daniel checked Ava's blood pressure again.

"I think she's haunted in more ways than one."

Daniel studied him, wondering how much he knew about Ava's ability. He decided it was a discussion for another time.

"I'll call tomorrow to check in. If anything changes or you need anything, call me immediately."

"Hai, Sensei. Arrigato, gozaimashita."

"Ava?" Daniel leaned toward her, checking one last time to see if she was recovering.

Her eyelashes fluttered. "H-hai, S-Sensei?" Her voice was barely above a whisper. It sounded raw.

"How are you doing?"

She apologized in Japanese. Her voice broke as she tried to choke back a sob. She swallowed, the air seeming as hard and sharp as razor blades. "I... I am fine, Sensei."

"Not even close. Does this have anything to do with what we've been working on after training?"

She closed her eyes, shook her head. Her voice was soft and disconnected. "N-no, Sensei."

"Was it something Vincent did?"

She shook her head again. Touching her temple, she tried to think past the throbbing in her head. "I p-panicked."

Daniel studied her. She didn't lie. If she said it was unrelated, there was more going on regarding her ability or she honestly didn't think the two were connected. Daniel would have to think about that more. Now wasn't the time to press the issue.

With shaking hands, she used the sleeves of her uniform to wipe the tears off her face. Absently, her hand drifted to the base of her neck, resting there. Though Vincent's hold had been with his arm, Daniel could see faint red finger marks on Ava's throat. Physical choking marks when Vincent never touched her with his hands.

Her eyes wandered the room. Daniel could tell she wasn't entirely aware of what was going on around her.

"It's been a while since you've had to be held down," Daniel said. "You would have hurt yourself if Vincent let go."

"Hai, Sensei. I understand." She apologized again. Her body was exhausted, her pride bruised. Just saying the word panic made her want to cringe.

"Are you better now?"

"Hai. Sensei." She could barely catch her breath enough to form the words.

"You're going to stay with Vincent tonight."

Ava's eyes jumped to Vincent, back to Sensei. "I do not-"

"This is not a negotiation," Daniel said, his tone like steel. "Go home with Vincent, or you'll be taken to the emergency room."

She swallowed. "Hai, Sensei."

He stood, helping her to her feet as he did. "Let's bow out and you can go change."

Several minutes later, Ava followed Vincent out of the dojo with her duffle bag and backpack. The evening was chilly, but she did not feel it. Her mind and body were numb. She wanted nothing more than a long, hot shower and to lay down.

They were parked close to each other. Ava stopped when she reached her Equinox and used the fob to unlock the door. Vincent kept walking until he heard the thunk of her locks disengaging. He turned back.

"What are you doing?"

"I am going home." Ava glanced at the dojo to make sure Sensei was not visible in the window or door. "I am tired."

"I'm taking you to my apartment, like Sensei said." Vincent took a step toward her. Ava could tell by his posture and his tone that he was going to make it happen whether she liked it or not.

"I am fine, Vincent," she said. Had she not been so exhausted, she would have instantly changed her stance to let him know he was not going to force her to do anything. Instead, she dropped her head in exhaustion. Knowing she was beyond the ability to defend herself made her suddenly feel like crying.

He took another step toward her, so he was within reach. "Get your overnight bag. I'll drive."

Ava tossed her workout bag onto the passenger seat. When she turned back, Vincent was on the other side of her door. She jerked in surprise. Another indication of how bad off she was; she had not sensed Vincent moving in on her.

"I will text you when I get home, so you know I am safe." She could barely get her voice above a whisper.

"You'll get in my vehicle, or I'll drag you to the ER," Vincent said, resting his hands on the top of her car door. His voice was firm but patient. That he was so calm and unyielding infuriated her, and the fact that she was so easily annoyed by his patience made her even more angry.

"I want to be alone." Puffs of vapor burst into the cold air with every word. Her nails were digging into her palms.

"Sensei doesn't think you're well enough to drive or be alone. You might not have a problem lying to him, but I do."

Ava bristled. He was right, of course; she had never lied to Sensei and never would. She was outraged that Vincent used that against her. She hated that they both thought they could force her into doing anything. She stepped away from her car and slammed the door. Opening the back door, she pulled out her overnight bag.

She didn't speak during the drive and Vincent didn't try to engage her. At his apartment, he didn't join her in the shower. He waited in the living room, giving her privacy and space. Sensei called to ask how much trouble she had given Vincent outside the dojo. Even after knowing Sensei for twenty years, little things like this still surprised him. Sensei didn't have to look out the window at the dojo to know Ava had balked at the idea of staying with Vincent, just like he didn't need someone to tell him they were sleeping together.

Vincent let Sensei know Ava hadn't spoken to him since he made it clear she was staying the night at his place. They spoke a few minutes more before hanging up.

The water ran for almost thirty minutes before Vincent heard Ava shut it off. He knew she wasn't being vindictive and purposely running him out of hot water. She wasn't built that way. It had taken her that long to decompress.

Keeping himself busy in the living room while she dressed, Vincent waited until he heard the bathroom door open, and he saw Ava walk into the bedroom. He showered, not surprised to find she hadn't used all the hot water. Knowing her, she had probably taken a cool shower for his sake as well as to get rid of the sweat. He wondered briefly if she would be gone when he came out, having walked back to her vehicle so she could drive home. But that wasn't her way. If she was going to put up a fight about staying here tonight, she would have done it to his face.

His arms stung under the pressure of the water. He gently rubbed the dried blood away from the cuts Ava's nails had put in him.

After he dressed, he entered the bedroom to see if she wanted dinner and found her lying in his bed. She was trembling while she slept, clutching the bedding to her chest. Vincent was shocked to see tears on her cheeks.

The plan had been for him to sleep on the couch so she could have privacy. Now he dismissed the idea. He walked to the other side of the bed and carefully climbed in, staying on top of the blankets. Her body twitched and she cried out.

"You're okay now." Vincent pressed his body against her back, moving slowly so he wouldn't get an elbow in his solar plexus. She was rigid.

He touched her shoulder lightly before applying a little more pressure. When he wrapped his arm loosely around her, she stopped trembling and relaxed against him.

•   •   •   •   •

When he woke in the morning, Ava was gone.

•   •   •   •   •

Sharing a bed with someone, after sleeping alone for twenty-six years, was strange. The sense that a presence was next to Isabel as she lay in a foreign bed made her feel out of place. Hearing the soft sounds of Griffin's breathing was oddly comforting and feeling the warmth emanating from him was a gift.

She shifted, lying on her back, staring at the ceiling she could barely see.

Griffin had asked her to stay the night. She'd agreed, unsure what to expect.

But changing into her pajamas, knowing he was waiting for her in his huge bed… she couldn't put into words how right it felt, how much like home.

Griffin rolled over and snuggled against her. The simple act warmed her from head to toes. He tossed an arm across her chest, draped his leg over hers. As he settled to get comfortable, his breathing evened out again.

Relaxed, content, Isabel slept.

•   •   •   •   •

CHAPTER SIX

I'm sorry. I'm so sorry.

Ava raised her head from the book she was skimming, glaring at the intrusion. The bookstore was supposed to be quiet. At this time of night, only a few other people were in the store. None of them looked like they had just spoken.

She had finished her work early and decided to treat herself to a used bookstore she had never visited. That New Book Smell was in a strip mall that included a Pier 1, a Dollar Tree, a workout facility, a couple restaurants, and a myriad of other useless stores people insisted they needed. The location wasn't very far into the city, providing a little change but nothing overwhelming. It was quaint, and had several oversize recliners to sit and read in.

People being loud in a bookstore, however, was unacceptable.

She glanced down at the book in her hands again, trying to decide if she wanted to buy it or just get a copy from the library. She could usually tell within the first couple paragraphs whether it was a keeper or just a good read.

Don't let him find me. The voice was quiet, laced with agony, yet Ava still found it annoying. This was supposed to be a place of stillness for her, if not quite a place of peace.

Ava smelled and tasted alcohol and wiped her hand across her mouth. A cold breeze stirred her hair. The voice she was hearing, male, young adult, had a slight echo to it... the sound of a memory.

"No," Ava said, closing her eyes. "Go away."

It was Friday night. She was indoors, at a bookstore. She couldn't be smelling fresh snow or tasting an alcoholic beverage she had never drank. There had not been snow for weeks. She tried to concentrate on breathing.

Where is he? An older female this time, her voice filled with irritation. The sound echoed through the tall stacks of books.

Ava looked at the words on the page in front of her, trying to focus. The smell of alcohol was strong. Her head felt light and heavy all at the same time. She was having trouble lifting it as she felt the room spinning around her. She turned the page of the book, started the next paragraph.

It is not winter. I am not in an attic. The sun is not shining.

Please don't let him find me. The male voice again. She noticed now that it had a slight accent to it. The woman's voice had an accent, too.

"Shut up!" Ava said loudly, slamming the book down on the table in front of her. A young man in a suit perusing the nonfiction section jumped at the loud sound and stared at her. At the next table, a woman in her mid-thirties with thick, dark glasses blinked at her.

"Excuse me," Ava said. She gently set the book back in the stack she had taken it from and began making her way toward the front of the store. She passed aisles of books stacked above her head, people standing and reading, people in corners sitting in chairs and lounging on couches, unaware of what was going on around them. Feeling as if her simple enjoyment had been spoiled, Ava hurried outside angrily, pausing in the coolness of the evening to gulp in the fresh air. Doing so helped clear her head.

Stop, she thought. Just leave me alone.

She felt as if an ice pick was being ground into her temple.

Pressing her hands to her ears, all she heard was the sobbing of the man and all she smelled was alcohol and she couldn't shut it out even when she closed her eyes -

"Ava?"

It took several moments for the voice to cut through. Someone was standing in front of her and that finally made her open her eyes. Isabel, the woman from the restaurant the other day, was staring at her worriedly.

Sister she's Gabriel's sister

"Are you okay?" When Ava didn't answer, she added, "I'm Isabel. We met at the diner in Langdon a couple weeks ago."

Her expression was so worried, so full of compassion. Ava was instantly suspicious. What did this woman care if she was okay or not? It was not her business.

She rubbed her fingers across her forehead. "I know who you are. Why are you here?"

Isabel gave her an odd look. "I picked up dinner at the Chinese place a couple doors down. I came over because it looked like you were in trouble."

"I can take care of myself," Ava said, taking a step toward her car, and found she was not fine at all. Her legs almost buckled when a wave of dizziness shot through her.

Isabel reached out to steady her, but Ava stepped away, raising an arm to block. She leaned against the railing for the set of four stairs leading down to the parking lot.

"I've never seen someone so pale. Maybe you should go to the emergency room-"

"That is not going to happen." Ava took several deep breaths. An anvil was sitting on her chest, trying to drive her to her knees. "I can make it home. I will be fine."

"Are you sure you'll be able to drive?"

Ava nodded. She was going to hyperventilate. If she could get to her vehicle, she could wait it out.

Isabel was quiet for a moment, contemplating. "Do you want to hang out at my place for a little while? It's only a few minutes from here. You can catch your breath."

"I need to get home."

Her whole body was trembling. The headache was getting worse. Her stomach-

Ava leaned over the railing and vomited over the side. Bile and partially digested food from this afternoon hit the concrete below and splattered. Someone using the stairs into the guitar shop below was going to get a surprise.

Worse, it's getting worse. She was reacting more strongly to each vision.

"Oh, my God," Isabel said. She took another step, hesitated. "Ava, I can't let you drive like this."

"There is nothing you can do to stop me."

Despite her legs wanting to buckle, she leveled her gaze at this stranger who insisted on invading her space.

The resolve in Ava's eyes told Isabel that if she tried to manhandle the younger woman into her vehicle, she would end up bleeding.

"Let me drive you back to my place for a little while to have a few bites to eat and something cold to drink. Or to put a cold rag on your forehead. I'm not leaving you alone. You'll hurt yourself or someone else on the road if you try to drive."

Ava considered this. It was not responsible to try driving while she was so ill. She needed only a few minutes to calm down and let her body relax. Isabel was right; she needed to consider the safety of everyone potentially effected by her actions. It occurred to Ava that Isabel was just as annoyingly patient as her brother.

She nodded briefly at Isabel.

Her legs were not quite steady as she followed Isabel across the parking lot. Both hands were tingling as if they had lost blood flow. Her feet scuffled across the pavement, seemingly unable to get a clear signal from her brain to lift as she walked.

Isabel's car had been running while she ran in to get her order. She moved the food bag to the back seat before Ava got in.

In the car, suddenly frigid though the car was warm, Ava's teeth began to chatter. The smell of food nauseated her all over again. Sweat broke out on her forehead. She pulled the door shut and wiped her mouth with the back of her gloved hand. Leaning the seat back so she could rest a few minutes during the drive, she closed her eyes, took deep breaths. She did not feel as dizzy lying down.

On an intellectual level, she knew stress took many forms, and buying a new house was stressful. The fact that she had lived in her new house for six months now made her think her stress should have been lessening, not growing. New towns had never bothered her before, but she was farther from David than she had ever been. Maybe some part of her felt stressed over that, but she did not know why. She did not need him. She was an adult. She had taken care of herself for years. She was financially, physically, and mentally capable of taking care of herself and her new home. Her physical proximity to her previous foster parent should have no bearing on her current stress levels. She had what she needed and had privacy, which she demanded. She preferred being by herself.

The ride was short. In just six or seven minutes, Isabel was maneuvering the car through a parking lot. Ava sat up slowly. She was still weak, but she would be able to take care of her body. The smell of food wasn't making her nauseous anymore, and she was not shaking as bad.

"How are you doing?" Isabel asked as she parked the car. She was frowning. On impulse, she reached out to touch Ava's arm. Ava used all her willpower to keep herself from smacking the hand aside.

She swallowed. "Better." She remembered her manners and added, "Thank you."

Her color is coming back, Isabel thought. She was comforted to see Ava wasn't as pale as she had been leaning outside the bookstore. For a moment Iz had thought she was going to have to carry her to her car and make a trip to the nearest emergency room.

Inside the apartment, Isabel turned lights on as she moved through her living space, setting her keys and the food down on the kitchen counter. She filled a glass of water for Ava, who stood just inside the door with her back against the wall.

"You can sit down." Isabel set the glass of water on the coffee table in the living room and motioned toward it before returning to the kitchen.

She's more nervous about being in my apartment than I am having her. Doesn't she have any friends?

Ava walked silently to the couch and sat. She took a sip of water, then gulped half of it down. She hadn't realized how thirsty she was. She took a shaky breath.

Something dark was standing in the corner with its back to her.

Isabel returned with a bowl of Saltine crackers. Her manner was cool, controlled. "These should help your stomach."

While Ava nibbled on a cracker, Isabel refilled her water.

The thing in the corner turned and looked at her. It was a young man, older than her but not yet thirty. He had light brown hair and eyes the color of honey. He was very tall. He took a shaky step toward Ava.

"I have ruined your dinner," Ava said when Isabel sat down on the opposite end of the couch. She carefully turned to look at her host and ignored the man in the corner.

"It's good reheated." She watched Ava for several seconds. "It's good to see you again."

I have a visitor in my apartment. I never have visitors.

Ava was confused at the awe pouring off Isabel. She seemed genuinely surprised that Ava was here. Ava did not like visitors at her house, but this odd woman did not get many and seemed to view that negatively.

The man took another step toward her.

"I wish you were feeling better. But I'm glad I ran into you," Isabel continued.

"Why?"

Out of the corner of her eye, she could see the dark figure, dressed entirely in black, inching forward.

Please don't let him find me.

Isabel smiled. "Because I like you."

Because I don't have friends and I think you're incapable of lying to me.

"You do not know me."

"Not yet."

"I do not make friends. I am not good with people."

Rejected already. That must be a world record.

Isabel laughed. Her pain and insecurity were hidden deeper than anyone Ava had ever encountered. Maybe even so deep Isabel did not realize it. "I intentionally push people away, so we should get along just fine."

Ava nibbled on a cracker, wishing her stomach would stop turning. It was getting worse as the thing came closer to her, teetering as if on stilts, reaching a long-fingered hand out toward her.

Focus.

She was not sure how she felt about having another friend. She would have to keep more appointments and allow time for activities to do with this friend as well as her brother. She did not like being obligated to anyone. She was already annoyed at the addition of Gabriel to her life. She had not even had time to adjust to that yet. Things were moving too quickly.

"You are very kind," she said carefully. She looked at the dark thing coming toward her pointedly. "I do not think I would be a very good friend."

The man's eyes were a mesmerizing color surrounded by all the darkness. Ava thought they were beautiful but that was no reason to be distracted. The more she catered to him, the more he would pester her.

Isabel studied her. "If you don't want to put the time and effort into being my friend, just say so. I need honesty more than fake friends. I just thought you could use someone on your side. I like you. You're brutally honest. I don't see that anymore."

I need someone on my side, too. The thought was a plea.

Ava thought about it. Would it be such an inconvenience to try? In reading Isabel, Ava knew she was an honest person with enormous guilt on her shoulders. She had no self-esteem but wanted to help everyone she encountered. There was nothing threatening or deceitful about her. As with Gabriel, Ava found herself wanting to help this lonely woman. She could always say no if invited somewhere she did not want to go. No one was forcing her to reciprocate. If putting effort into the friendship became too much and she stopped, Isabel would eventually go away.

A thought slashed through, strong and full of remorse: I'm not contributing to this world anyway. If I died, would anyone notice?

Ava glanced at her sharply. From the corner of her eye, she saw the man's head lift and whip to the side to gaze at Isabel. His head tilted as he studied her curiously. After a moment, he faded away.

Isabel was looking at her glass of water, lost in thought. She was thinking about Gabriel, how much she loved him, and the thought of killing herself was buried so deep she didn't even realize it had flickered through her mind.

"I will be your friend." Ava shifted on the couch.

Isabel let out a bark of laughter. "I love the way you talk. I feel like we should shake hands or swap spit. How are you feeling?"

"Fine."

She cocked her head. "Don't give me that bullshit. You're still flushed, and your hands are shaking."

Ava took a moment to think about what she was feeling. It took her another moment to force herself to share the status of her health with another person. "My stomach is not as nauseous. The crackers helped. I do not feel as dizzy. I still have a headache."

"Do you want something for the headache? I have aspirin, Tylenol, Pamprin..."

Ava shook her head. "I do not take pills. But thank you," she added, thinking that was what a friend would say. She would have to study what friends did for each other, so she knew how to be one.

"So, what do you think of my brother?" Isabel asked casually. "He said he sees you around Langdon."

"It is a small tow. The probability of our interaction is high." Ava said. After a moment, she added, "He is going to cook me dinner Saturday night."

"Reeeaaally?" Isabel dragged out the word, excited to hear the news. Wouldn't that be something if her brother and her new friend began dating? Iz had told Ava the truth; she did like her, and she wanted to be her friend. For some reason, she felt certain Ava would never hurt her, and would always be loyal. She trusted the younger woman even though she'd only met her twice now.

"He will not go away," Ava stated.

Isabel snorted. "What do you mean?"

Ava nibbled on another cracker, considering. Without the man advancing toward her, her stomach was finally settling.

"I see him when I go to the store, or when I am purchasing fuel. Which is statistically normal, given the population of the town and the limit of business choices."

Isabel felt she had more to say. She was fussing with the rim of the bowl, and her posture had become rigid when she talked about Gabriel. Sitting on the far end of the couch, she kept her head down, her hair blocking her face from Isabel so she couldn't see her expression.

"He always approaches me." Finally, she lifted her head. Her eyes shifted around the room before settling on Isabel's. "Even if I do not see him, I am thinking about him. He is distracting me."

Isabel felt a little flutter in her stomach. "That's so sweet."

"No, it is not. I have work to do and training. I need to focus. I do not have time for... people." She set the bowl of crackers on the coffee table slowly, deliberately. Her voice was clipped. "I do not know how to be part of society and I do not want to know."

Shocked, Isabel couldn't stop gaping. "Have you ever been in a romantic relationship before, Ava?"

Ava shook her head. "I do not do romantic relationships. Gabriel is willing to be my friend. But I do not want friends, either."

So, it's not just me. She doesn't want to be around anyone.

"But what you're describing for Gabriel," Isabel objected, "the distraction you're feeling... that's usually the feeling a person has for someone she's attracted to, Ava, not a friend."

How did someone as gorgeous as Ava not understand attraction? She could have her choice of any man in the world.

"I just want to be left alone," Ava said, sounding tired. "It is hard for me to be around people."

"Why?"

"You all get in my way. You take up my time. You do not say what you think and then get upset when I do not understand your intent. You hurt each other for no reason and beg for forgiveness when you are caught in the act."

Isabel nodded slowly. "That is depressingly accurate."

And it's why I don't see the point sometimes, she thought.

Ava looked at her, her focus intense.

Iz cleared her throat. "I don't know how we've survived this long. We should have moron-ed ourselves to death thousands of years ago."

"But some of you are... interesting. Like you." After a moment Ava added, "Does this mean you are my Bee-eff-eff?"

Iz snorted and covered her mouth. "I'm sorry, I'm not laughing at you. Since you're the only friend I have who's a girl, I guess that makes you my BFF, yes. Although I'll never use that ridiculous term."

"The only way I know how to be a friend is by studying the behavior of other people. I have researched popular television shows and watched YouTube videos to gain insight on human interaction."

Isabel withheld another giggle. "You don't have to research how to be my friend, Ava. Just be yourself; that's what drew me to you in the first place. I can't tell you how refreshing it is to meet someone who doesn't follow the script of what they think others want them to be."

Her eyes held a certain affection that gave Ava's stomach a strange feeling. Suddenly, she had the urge to hug the older woman. The feeling startled her. She never had an impulse to touch anyone except David, and then, only rarely. The sensation was so foreign it made her skin itch.

"So, what do you do for a living?" Isabel asked. She seemed genuinely interested, Ava thought, eager to discuss it.

"I am a freelance editor."

"Do you work from home?"

Ava shook her head. "Yes. I started my business two years and three months ago."

Isabel's eyes lit up. "I would love to work from home. No office politics, no idiots to work with, no asshole boss breathing down my neck. Gabriel has his own business, too. He's a genius at carpentry and woodworking. He builds furniture mostly. He built that blue table just inside my front door and that accent cabinet that my TV sits on."

Ava glanced at the cabinet across the room. It was extraordinary work, and it seemed Gabriel had made it especially for his sister. No veneer or wood composite made up that solid piece; it was all wood. It had two glass doors with shelves in between. The blue it had been painted, darker than the hue of the table Ava had noticed in the entryway, was like the color of clouds when a storm is building. To make it unique to Isabel, Gabriel had used a cream inlay for a lotus design. It was beautiful.

Ava had a sudden vision of Gabriel drawing the design on the wood, thinking of Isabel.

The lotus flower grows in mud but still produces a beautiful flower. Isabel has had a rough time since Hayden died but she grew up beautiful anyway.

"You say his name a lot," Ava said. "Are you close with him?"

"We're really close. I just wish his last girlfriend hadn't been a cheating whore. Sorry," she said instantly. "I rarely think before I speak."

If I knew where that bitch lived, I would make her pay for what she did to him.

"I prefer honesty." Ava studied Isabel, curious about what had caused this stranger to become so enraged at the thought of her brother's mate. A sudden emotion flooded her, making her feel extremely feverish and angry at the woman Isabel was thinking of.

"If she cheats on him, why does he stay in the relationship?" She tried to remain calm. Rarely did other people's emotions overtake her, but Isabel's were extremely passionate, and she had almost no control over them.

"Oh, he dumped her ass like yesterday's dirty underwear as soon as he found out," Isabel said, and Ava sensed pride in her tone. She did not understand the dirty underwear reference, but she understood what "dumped" meant. The strange feeling slowly drained out of her.

"She is no longer part of his life, yet you are still angry with her."

"You're damn right," Isabel said, her body rigid. She had to try to relax her clenched teeth. "I wouldn't piss on her teeth if her gums were on fire."

Ava tilted her head. "Why would her gums be on fire?"

Frowning, Isabel looked over at her and burst out laughing. "It's just a saying. Like, if she were drowning, I wouldn't throw her a line. She almost ruined my brother's life. She can go fuck herself. Sorry! God, I'm a horrible host. My manners are ridiculously rusty."

"Your inability to avoid sensitive subjects is entertaining. I would like to understand more about why this cheating whore makes you so angry."

Iz snorted. "You're so unique, Ava. I think we're going to get along fine."

She sobered as she began talking about her brother. "They dated for three years. There was talk of her moving in with him, she came to a few of our Sunday dinners... things were heading in the marriage direction, I think. Then she goes and cheats on him. He was going to take her back, the stupid SOB, but I told him if he did, I would kick his ass. So, he was out on Friday night with the guys, trying to deal with it – they usually go to Spencer's Bar on Fridays. Knowing that's his usual spot, she shows up with him, Stuart, for God's sake. His parents must have hated him to give him that name."

She rolled her eyes as if the fact of his name was more of an offense than the adultery. "That bitch cheated on my brother for someone named Stuart. Anyway, I digress. They show up and Gabe's friends were helping to keep his mind off it. They arranged it so he was sitting with his back to her, they played Darts, they did everything they could to ignore her. She got so pissed she started arguing with Stuart, and he popped her on the mouth."

Isabel made a fist and brushed it across her own chin.

"Gabriel wasn't going to stand by while a guy hit a woman, so he popped him right back. The problem was that Stuart was too stupid to let it go. And once Gabriel started, he didn't stop."

Ava understood. It was why The Monster had caused her a broken her wrist while she was chained in the barn, why it had continued to fight when the chain cut down to her bone. It was why, even after she was free and there were no restraints, it refused to stop fighting. Because once The Monster was out, it didn't want to stop. It couldn't stop. It had to be stopped.

"I don't know why he did it," Isabel said softly, but she clearly admired her brother for it. "I wouldn't have defended her. He really doesn't like men who hit women. But it took all three of his friends and the cook from the bar to drag him off Stuart. The asshole pressed charges, of course. Gabriel was arrested and charged with assault, which would have been a Class A Misdemeanor."

"A sentence of possible jail time in Wisconsin," Ava said.

Isabel nodded. "Rachel stepped in and said he was defending her from Stuart. She was prepared to add a history of violence with Stuart and press counter charges. Stuart dropped the charges, and Gabriel got a lucky break."

"But you are still unsatisfied."

Isabel's eyes were cold. "None of it would have happened if she didn't show up and try to make him jealous. I wouldn't have done anything about Stuart smacking her, personally, except give him a medal, but I'm in the minority. She used him and then acted like a hero when she helped keep him out of jail. Fucking bitch."

Ava watched the emotion build inside Isabel as she relived it. It was still overflowing, though Ava knew that the incident happened months ago. Isabel was just as angry as she had been when it happened. She would, if she saw this woman again, go after her with everything she had.

Though she knew it was not appropriate, she found herself wanting to see Isabel confront this Rachel woman. Watching Isabel show her love for her brother, while simultaneously punishing a woman without morals, would be extremely satisfying. Sensei would not approve.

Is this what friendship did? Was it normal to feel such fierce loyalty? Ava did not know Isabel well, but she was beginning to know Gabriel, and perhaps the combination of their emotional impact on her was triggering her feelings of distaste for Rachel.

"How are you feeling?"

It took Ava a moment to answer. Isabel's quick change of conversations was exhausting.

"Casual conversation has distracted me from my symptoms. I am feeling better now."

Isabel brightened at the thought of being able to help. "Are you feeling well enough to try some mei fun? I bought extra."

Ava wasn't sure if she could eat, but it had been several hours since her last meal.

"Okay."

Isabel stood and walked to the kitchen, pulling the food out of the bag, and putting it into a container to heat it up.

Ava folded her hands and gave thanks as she waited for Isabel to return. She lifted her head in time to catch a stray thought from Isabel.

Someone's in my house and I'm actually serving them food.

Ava did not understand why this would excite anyone, but she was fascinated at Isabel's enthusiasm.

Please let her be interested in Gabriel. He deserves to be happy.

Ava stared straight ahead, glaring, and wishing she could stop the noise.

Everyone seemed determined to make their coupling an issue. Perhaps if she had sex with him, she would release the tension and he would move on, so everyone else would stop thinking about it. She would get rid of whatever silly emotions were plaguing her, and he would get rid of his masculine drive to lay with every member of the opposite species.

Her anger was clouding her judgment. She knew Gabriel was not like the man she met in the grocery store that hit on her. Lumping every male into one category was irresponsible and unfair. However, it was natural for any male attracted to a female to want to mate, and she could not fault him for following his nature.

Especially when she shared his impulses.

Besides, maybe if she rid herself of these aggravating physical urges, she would be able to focus better. If the manifestation of Hayden was directly related to Gabriel's buildup of emotional and sexual tension, the spirit might leave once that tension was released.

Isabel returned with two plates, forks, and napkins. She was acting casual, but her eyes were sparkling. Ava had to force herself to stop scowling.

"Thank you," she said, twirling noodles onto her fork. "You do not get many visitors."

Isabel looked deflated. "Is it that obvious?"

I fucked it up already. There goes any chance of another visit.

Ava realized her observation had been too blunt. "Sometimes I use the wrong words. I meant... you made the food look pretty. I always eat take out from the container it comes in."

Isabel relaxed, and Ava was relieved she did not have to lie. She had told the truth and still managed to make Isabel feel better.

It was what a friend would do, she was sure.

• • • • •

"Has anyone seen Greg?" Tom asked, shoving fries into his mouth. He wiped grease off his lips with the back of his hand, something Abby would have scolded him for.

They were at Spencer's again. While the mood was lighter than last week, they were still down a man. The loss was felt.

Jeremy took a sip of beer. "I texted him a couple times this week. Haven't heard back."

"How about you, Gabriel?" Tom asked.

Gabriel was staring at his bottle of beer. He hadn't said much since arriving. Tom noticed his friend gazing into the distance on more than one occasion.

He ate another French fry. "Gabe, have you heard from Greg since last week?"

Gabriel slowly rotated his beer bottle in his hands, his eyes out of focus. He was frowning. Both his friends noticed he hadn't shaved in a couple days.

Jeremy grinned at Tom. He cleared his throat and said casually, "So, Isabel and I started fucking."

Gabriel's head snapped up. "What did you say?"

Jeremy and Tom started laughing.

"What, I'm not good enough for Isabel?" Jeremy asked. "We're two consenting adults. She's hot..."

"That's not funny," Gabriel said, almost knocking his beer over.

"I'm not having sex with your sister," Jeremy said. "Relax."

Gabriel loosened the grip on his drink.

"Where were you?" Tom asked. "We were asking if you've heard from Greg."

"No."

"We probably won't until he's done having his period," Jeremy said.

"Cut him some slack," Tom said around another mouthful of fries. "We were pretty hard on him last week about Charity."

"It's about damn time, too." Jeremy stole a French fry off Tom's plate. "He wasn't taking our not-so-subtle hints."

Gabriel finished his beer and set it at the edge of the table. "Did we treat Abby that way when you were dating her, Tom?"

"Of course not. She isn't a manipulative bitch."

"True. You struck gold with her."

Tom smiled, his eyes softening as he thought of his wife. Gabriel saw the obvious affection in his friend's eyes and thought of Abby's quick laugh. They had seemed to be made for each other from the start. What was more important, to Gabriel, was how quickly Abby had accepted Tom's friends as if they were family. She was the type of woman who loved easily and always had to be touching, reassuring, making sure no one felt left out.

Ava was nothing like her, yet he found her so appealing.

Karen came by and dropped off a second round for everyone. Jeremy flirted with her, but he didn't seem to be making much of an effort.

"When is he going to pull his head out of his ass?" Jeremy asked, getting back to Greg once Karen wandered off.

"He'll come around," Tom said. "Women like that wear out their welcome eventually. He'll get sick of her bullshit and realize we were only trying to look out for him. Or..."

"Or what?" Jeremy asked.

"Or he'll have stars in his eyes until he's stupid enough to marry her, and then he'll be stuck until he gets a divorce. She'll fight him every step of the way and make his life miserable."

"Wow. That's optimistic."

Gabriel was staring at his new beer bottle, lost in thought again.

"You're not thinking about Greg, are you?" Tom asked. "From the look on your face, I'd say your head is wrapped around a woman."

Gabriel nodded. There was no point in denying it. Ava had been on his mind since she had chosen to stand by him at Hayden's grave. Every thought seemed to somehow lead back to an analysis of her. This morning he had been thinking about fixing the brakes on his truck and ended up thinking about taking Ava camping.

Her eyes were so haunted yet rimmed with an underlying fuck you that never quite went away. And then she had unleashed that fuck you on a man twice her size without a hitch in her breath. Now she would be coming to his house for dinner. Wasn't that a kick in the ass?

"What's her name?" Tom asked gently.

Gabriel jumped. "Ava."

"Sounds sexy. When do we get to meet her?" Jeremy asked.

"We're not dating. She's a friend. She... she stayed with me when I visited Hayden's grave."

"How do you two know each other?" Tom asked.

"We don't, not really."

"Did she know Hayden?" Jeremy asked.

Gabriel shook his head. He thought of her silently standing there, her gray eyes downcast, her very presence comforting him.

"A stranger stood with you at Hayden's grave?" Jeremy raised his eyebrows.

Tom thought about that for a few seconds. "That's either extremely weird, or extraordinary."

• • • • •

Gabriel set a pan of chicken surrounded by vegetables in the oven and punched numbers into the digital timer next to the stove. Taking a drink of his iced tea, he moseyed toward the patio doors in the great room. Dark clouds were rolling in, and the view from the glass doors was breathtaking. This would be the first time it was warm enough for rain, not snow, and Gabriel was looking forward to it.

Ava was coming to his house. He hadn't quite believed she would accept when he asked her.

Something in her eyes tugged at him. Not in a sexual way – although he would have to be dead not to be attracted to her. Those infinite gray eyes, always watching, always studying, waiting for an attack. He wanted to make her feel safe.

Doubt was creeping in like a stalker. What the hell was he doing? Who was he to make anyone feel safe? She had no more reason to trust him than a random stranger in a gas station. As far as feeling safe – what could he offer that she couldn't already provide herself? Obviously, she was able to physically take care of herself.

Then there were the walls she had built. She was practically surrounded by a fortress, refusing to let anyone close. Why was he trying so hard to be a friend, give her someone to talk to? What was it about her that made him want to convince her that everything was going to be all right?

Yet here he was, making dinner, his heartbeat quickening in anticipation of her coming over. He wanted to get to know her. He was intrigued. If that turned into something more, so be it.

He began cleaning up the dishes he'd used for the recipe. Ava was always early so she could arrive at any minute.

Just as the thought struck him, the dogs started barking from the back yard. They raced around to the front of the house. Gabriel heard a vehicle pull into his driveway and smiled. She was fifteen minutes early.

Refilling his tea, he fixed an ice water for Ava. When he stepped out onto the front porch, she was still petting Ozzie beside her Chevy. It looked like the dog had assaulted her as soon as she stepped out of the vehicle. Maya was watching from the bottom of the porch steps.

"Why don't you go say hi?" Gabriel said to Maya. Overhead, the ominous clouds loomed. The wind was picking up. They were in for a hell of a storm.

Ava straightened at the sound of his voice. She walked toward him with her thick hair hanging loosely around her shoulders. "She did."

"Really?" He glanced sideways at Maya. "She came up to you?"

Ava glanced at Maya with something that could have been respect or understanding. "She says hello in her own way."

Gabriel watched her ascended the steps. The evening was warm enough for her to wear a jacket made from a thin hunter green material. Instead of the ass-kicking boots he was getting used to seeing her in, she was wearing sneakers.

"I have chicken in the oven," he said, opening the door for her. "I hope you're hungry."

"I am capable of feeding myself," she said, staying where she was. Gabriel remembered she didn't like people behind her and stepped inside. The dogs wandered in, a chorus of toenails clicking on the hardwood floor. Ava followed them.

"I didn't invite you to dinner because I don't think you can feed yourself." Gabriel motioned to the pegs on the wall and gave her room.

Ava maneuvered out of her coat and hung it on the wall.

Gabriel had to take a moment to catch his breath.

She was wearing a dark short sleeved purple sweater and faded blue jeans. The clothing fit her body without revealing any part of her; the neckline didn't show cleavage, the jeans weren't too tight and didn't sit too low. Gabriel wondered just how she managed to look so damn appealing even when she wasn't trying to.

"Come on into the kitchen," he said to keep from drooling. "I have drinks ready."

It unnerved him that he couldn't hear her behind him, that she walked so silently she didn't set off a creak in the floorboards. He didn't expect her to attack, but she didn't talk. It was like the feeling that someone was watching him but not being able to see anyone in the room.

Is that how Ava felt when someone was behind her?

Lifting a glass up from the counter, he offered her the water.

They stood next to the sink, watching each other as if waiting for the other to yell "Gotcha!" She had been surprised when he handed her the water without her asking, though her facial expression had not changed.

Finally, he said, "My invitations are never, and will never be, because I think you're incapable of anything."

"Then why are you making dinner?"

He set his tea back down. "Because you don't like going to movies, or eating in public, or going to bars. Or anything else most people do. I thought we could stay in, where you're a little more comfortable. We can hang out with the dogs, maybe listen to the storm."

She stared at him for a long time, so long he began to wonder what the hell she was thinking. Her gray eyes seem lighter than usual, almost a shade of silver.

They were standing close together, as if in a face-off. Ava became aware of it at the same time he did. He saw the awareness come into her eyes. Gabriel expected her to step back immediately, put some distance between them, but she stayed where she was. She lifted her face, gazed at him with an expression he couldn't quite read.

I need to shave, he thought, right before she kissed him.

At first, her lips brushed his while her hands remained at her sides. It was nothing more than a curiosity, an exploration. Her eyes remained open, thoughtful. The kiss was soft. She pulled back and studied his face, her head tilting in that curious way.

What the hell was that? he thought. Up to this point, she hadn't given him any indication that she was interested in him that way. That she was interested in anyone that way. In fact, she had expressly told him she wasn't interested in touching, in dating. After Rachel he was in no hurry to jump back into anything.

Before he had time to give it more thought, she moved in again.

Raising her arms, her hands took the sides of his face firmly. She drew him down to her and plundered. The curiosity was gone. Her mouth was demanding and possessive, making his own respond with just as much hunger. Her tongue introduced itself, toyed with his. She closed her eyes and consumed him.

Holy shit, he thought, and then thought ceased to be an option.

He felt the blood draining from his head. Moving of their own volition, his hands came up and took her hips. He slipped his thumbs through the belt loops of her jeans and pulled her body roughly against his. A little moan escaped her and fed his desire like an accelerant. One hand circled around to the back of his neck, drew him closer to her as she deepened the kiss.

Careful, his mind warned as his hands moved up her back, exploring those tight muscles. She's been through enough without you acting like a randy teenager.

Lust ripped through him anyway. Running his hands down her back, he gripped her backside and lifted her onto the counter. He gradually became aware of a sound so soft it was almost inaudible. A murmur somewhere between a growl and a purr. The hairs on his arms and the back of his neck rose.

Ava nipped his lower lip and ran her hands through his hair. She wrapped one slender leg around his backside and yanked him tighter against her. When she tilted her head to one side to expose her neck, Gabriel realized the sound was coming from her. Her throat vibrated under his mouth.

One hand was on her hip, the other cupped around the back of her neck. She was emitting that odd growling-purring sound, and he wasn't sure if it was a warning or a sign of contentment. He couldn't help noticing the way her strong body felt under his hands.

Sliding one hand under the hem of her shirt, Gabriel's fingers explored her flesh. They came to a thin ridge of raised skin on the left side of her back, just above her hip. He paused only a moment before continuing to run his fingers along the extensive line of scar tissue. It ended just below her shoulder blade.

Show some control. Someone beat the fuck out of her. Someone took her body and used it and now you want to do the same damn thing for your own pleasure.

Fuck.

Gabriel took her by her well-toned arms and pulled her back slowly, even as he took a half step back. As their lips parted, a small snarl escaped her mouth.

"Ava," he wheezed. "We should... if we're going to..." Christ. "I didn't realize you were interested in me... like this."

He noticed her chest was heaving. Her eyes studied his mouth hungrily. Her long, dark hair was tangled from him running his hands through it. Seeing her a little out of control surprised him.

She said nothing.

On an impulse, he lifted his hand and brushed a strand of her hair back from her face.

"What's going on here?" he asked quietly.

"We were kissing," she said. "You stopped." Her tone accusatory.

"W-why did you kiss me? Any other time I've tried to touch you, you've almost decked me. Now you're kissing me like you want me to..."

Fuck you right here on the kitchen counter, he almost said. He took another step back to make sure he wasn't going to go after her.

"I..." She slid off the counter, her eyes never leaving his. The intensity was slowly draining from them. "I am curious about... you."

He wasn't sure how to feel about that. He wasn't sure he believed it; that had been more than curiosity.

"Are you curious about me?" she asked.

Gabriel was stunned to see she was anxious.

"Well, hell yeah," he said, his lips quirking. "We should just... slow things down a little. I was caught off guard."

You dumbass, why don't you accept what she's offering you?

The right side of her mouth twitched.

Gabriel felt another shock that he could almost make her smile. The emotion was followed by another wave of lust which, if he didn't get control over, would propel him into big trouble.

She had said she didn't like physical contact and balked at relationships, yet he had felt something between them instantly at the grocery store. The air left his lungs every time he saw her. His stomach clenched at the sound of her voice or with one look at those beautiful eyes.

Gabriel had known she felt something, too, but if she wasn't willing to act on it, he wouldn't press the issue. Now this. Why couldn't women make up their damn minds, and then let men know what was going on when they did?

They seemed to be at an impasse. Gabriel wasn't sure what to do now.

A crack of thunder, so loud it rattled the windows, made him jump. Ava didn't respond.

Food. The food was cooking. That gave him an excuse to break away. He turned from her and checked the timer. They had plenty of time to kill. He picked up his tea for something to do.

"Do you like storms?" he asked.

"Yes." The anxiety was gone. She was regarding him with an expression he couldn't read, her gray eyes direct and unflinching.

"I don't know why, but they calm me," he continued. And I need a lot of calm right now. To keep his hands busy, he pulled out two plates and cutlery and set them on the counter. "The more rain, the better."

"I sleep better during storms." She lifted herself easily onto the counter, watching him work.

"Does that mean you don't sleep well otherwise?"

"I have insomnia and somnambulism."

"Run that by me again?" Gabriel watched her as she watched him.

"Insomnia. Inability to sleep."

"That part I understand."

"Somnambulism. Sleepwalking."

"That sounds like a bad combination. Do you have to take something that knocks you out completely to get a good night's sleep?" Yes, analyze. Nothing eased sexual tension like clinical talk.

"I do not take drugs."

He admired that. "Do you know what causes the nightmares?"

"I know."

He turned toward her, took a drink of his tea.

"Knowing doesn't help? I mean, you know, psychologically?"

"No. What happened cannot be changed."

Now, wasn't that interesting? he thought, getting a small serving platter and bowl out. He was fascinated by her, not just physically but by her story as well. He was only getting small pieces at a time, but every glimpse into her world made him even more curious to know more.

The discussion didn't seem to be bothering her, and he was curious, so he continued to talk while he prepared for the meal. He moved around the kitchen comfortably and was surprised at how pleasant it felt to have her present while he worked.

Opening a drawer, he pulled out a pair of oven mitts and tossed them on the counter next to the stove. He glanced around the kitchen to make sure he had everything ready for when the food came out.

"Do you want something to drink with your meal?"

"Water is fine."

Finished, Gabriel went to the sink to wash his hands off. Ava was next to him on the counter.

He glanced up at her. "Do you drink anything besides water?"

"I allow myself coffee in the mornings."

"Coffee and water. Anything else?"

"No."

"Why is that?"

"Water has everything I need."

When he glanced at her, she was staring at him. He flicked water at her. Jerking, her eyes widened. He smiled to let her know it was a prank before flicking more droplets her way. After a moment, she leaned over, stuck her hand in the water, and flicked some back at him.

His grin was quick and easy and stretched just a little more than the half smile he usually offered. Ava felt a wave of emotion for him that made her uncomfortable even though she could not identify it.

Gabriel handed her a towel to dry her hand off as he dried his own. Glancing out at the sky, he wondered how bad the storm was going to get.

Thunder rumbled in the distance. The sky was so dark now that it didn't appear to be daylight anymore. He should have checked the weather before expecting Ava to be out in it. Storms here could be bad enough to spend a few hours on alert making sure you weren't affected by a flash flood or a power outage.

As the food still had cooking time left, he took his tea and motioned for her to follow him. The dogs trotted ahead to the living room. Maya instantly settled in front of the fireplace. Ozzie sprawled on the dog bed to the side of the hearth.

"Isabel said your last girlfriend was a cheating whore."

Gabriel choked on the ice cube he had been sucking on and almost dropped his glass. He began coughing, sitting on the couch, and using both hands to try to steady the glass enough to set it on the end table.

"What?"

Ava sat at the other end, perched on her ankles. "Isabel said your-"

"I heard you. I meant, when did you talk to Isabel, and why would you be talking about my ex-girlfriend?"

"Isabel is still angry at her. She told me about Stuart and the threat of a lawsuit. She is proud of you for assaulting him."

For God's sake, Isabel.

"I didn't realize you two were friends." The piece of ice lodged in his esophagus had finally melted enough to fall all the way down, leaving a freezing trail that somehow burned.

"I had mei fun at her apartment. I am her bee eff eff now."

Gabriel took a drink to hide his smile. "I bet she's thrilled."

"She also thinks my mating with you would be good."

"I'll make sure to tell her to mind her own fucking business," he said, his temper simmering.

"She did not actually say-" Ava broke off and glanced around. "Please do not tell her that I told you."

"Did she have any other wise insights about us?" he asked wryly.

The timer went off in the kitchen.

"Time to eat," he said, standing. He was thankful for the distraction.

In the kitchen, he began pulling everything together. He shut off the oven, set the pan on a trivet, and transferred the food from the baking dish to the serving plate. He pulled serving utensils out of a drawer and plated the food. Ava watched all this intently, as if she wanted to memorize every detail.

Picking up both plates, he motioned to his tea.

"Do you want to carry the drinks?" He waited until she had picked them up. "Where do you want to eat? I have a formal dining table, but the view of the storm will be best from the breakfast room."

"The breakfast room is adequate."

She followed him to the table, which was smaller and more intimate than the formal dining table she could see from the kitchen. Gabriel set the plates and eating utensils down and pulled a chair out, standing behind it. He seemed to be waiting for her.

She set his tea down and stared at him. His hands were resting on the back of the chair he had pulled out.

"Hasn't anyone ever pulled out your chair for you?" he asked, his eyes twinkling with amusement.

"I am capable-"

"-of pulling out your own chair," he finished. He motioned to the chair. "Sit down, Ava. It's a courtesy, not an insult."

She sat leaning slightly forward, placing her palms flat on the table as if she planned to launch herself up onto the tabletop. Her body was tense. Her head tilted so she could see him over her shoulder.

"Everything okay?"

Breathing deliberately, Ava said, "I do not like people behind me."

"Shit. I forgot." Gabriel instantly stepped forward and to her side as far away from her as his stride would take him, so he was within her line of sight. "My mistake. I won't do that again."

Lightning flashed, reflecting off the windows. Gabriel flinched, not expecting the sudden brightness. Ava stiffly moved her hands to her lap.

"You already told me that. It was careless on my part." He watched her slowly settle, her arms resting, her shoulders dropping. Seeing how much effort it took filled him with guilt.

Damn fool she already told you that-

She felt his mind start to tell his arm to reach for her, to apologize, but before his hand lifted, he shut it down.

You can't give her a hug you can't touch her-

She looked up at him. His eyes were dark with worry, his mind a jumble of stress, his instincts raging at him to reach out to her. The impulse to use physical contact for comfort was strong in him. Holding himself back was stressful to him.

Ava slowly lifted her arm and leaned forward, setting her palm on the table near him. She did not want him warring against his instinct to be polite.

Yet she could not abruptly change her behavior, either. She was unsure how to make her intention clear. He understood somehow anyway and briefly rested his hand over hers. Before sitting on his side of the table, he gave her hand a squeeze.

Picking up his fork, he was halfway to stabbing a carrot when he saw Ava sitting statue-still, her head bowed, and her eyes closed. Her hands were folded in prayer. He slowly set his fork down and followed suit, waiting for her to speak. After a moment, he opened his eyes. She remained in the same position, but she seemed to be praying silently. Gabriel lowered his head again, folding his hands in his lap, and kept his eyes downcast until she raised her head. She opened her eyes and picked up her fork.

"I did not mean to interrupt you," she said. "It is kind of you to wait, but unnecessary."

"It's all good. I didn't figure you for the type."

"What type is that?" she asked, her tone icy. When he glanced at her, her expression was carefully neutral.

Hit another nerve, he thought. "I just meant I wasn't expecting it. I started to dig in without realizing you weren't ready. Next time I'll know better."

She relaxed slightly at that and began eating.

He was amazed at how much she could eat. Ava's eyes were focused completely on the meal as she shoveled in two plates without hesitation, glancing outside when lightning burst across the sky or thunder rolled. The coming storm seemed to serve as entertainment for her.

He ate his meal and studied her, amused. They didn't speak, yet the silence was not awkward. He refilled her plate and her glass of water and sat back with his beer to watch her finish her second helping with as much vigor as she had shown the first. She didn't seem bothered that he was watching. He was tickled that she ate with such abandon and encouraged by her obvious enjoyment of the food. She finally set down her fork.

"Do you want more?" he asked, ready to fix her another plate if she wanted it.

She finished the second glass of water and wiped her mouth on her napkin. "Just water, please."

Gabriel thought she had to drink about a gallon of water every day as he refilled her glass. When he glanced up, he found her gathering their dishes. He hurried around the counter to stop her.

"You don't have to do that," he said, setting her glass down to take the dishes from her. He noticed her brief pause when he stepped close. He could imagine her picking up a dirty fork off the top plate and sticking it in his eye.

"Let me get those," he said, gently touching her shoulder with one hand before reaching for the dishes. She didn't exactly relax but she turned toward him and held out her hands in an offering. As they carefully shifted the plates from her hands to his, their fingers brushed together.

Gabriel had never been so aware of every act of physical contact until he was forced to avoid it.

Another rumble of thunder sounded, louder and closer. Gabriel carried the dishes to the dish washer and began loading it.

"Excuse me," she said, disappearing around the corner to the restroom.

Dinner was a success, he thought. She obviously liked to eat. They hadn't spoken during the meal, but before dinner he found out she loved storms, had insomnia, and was prone to sleepwalking. Not the greatest information, but he was slowly learning more about her.

And even though she stilled when he came close to her, she no longer put her hands up in defense. She was slowly getting used to him being close to her, giving her an occasional platonic touch. For the first time since he'd met her, she didn't look like she was waiting for the quickest opportunity to bolt.

He closed the dish washer and walked into the great room. The room had little furniture except for the piano. Large windows on the east and south walls would allow magnificent views of the storm. Gabriel watched the wind bend and sway the branches on the trees.

He sat at the piano and lifted the lid to the keyboard. Storms always inspired him to play. He began the first movement of Beethoven's Moonlight Sonata. The song always reminded him of inner turmoil, as did thunderstorms. As his hands flowed over the keys, he lost himself in the music, the rhythm and meditation of performing. Music is therapy, his mother always said. When he was younger, he thought it was torture. Now he was glad for the outlet. Every Sunday, when he and Isabel played after dinner, and sometimes Beth joined in, it was therapeutic. It brought them all together in a way nothing else did. Through their different lives and busy schedules, no matter what silly arguments they had gotten into, music brought them together at least once a week.

Movement made him look up. Ava was standing across the room, fixated on him. She watched him play as if mesmerized, though when he had shown her into the kitchen earlier, she had barely glanced at the piano. She walked toward him. He continued playing as he watched her approach like a wild cat stalking prey, wondering what was going on in that unique mind.

She stopped at the edge of the piano, watching his hands move over the keys with utter, childlike fascination. Her innocence made him smile.

"Do you play?" he asked, resting his hands in his lap.

She seemed distressed that he had stopped. After a moment, her head twitched slightly, as if she was waking from a trance. Shaking her head, she did not realize her breath was coming in short gasps.

"Have you ever heard someone play live?"

She shook her head again. Gabriel watched her eyes scan the keys, his hands, back to the keys.

"My sister and I play something every Sunday after dinner at my parent's place," he said. "Their piano isn't quite as nice as this, but it sounds good. Maybe you can come with me and hear us play together sometime."

Did he just invite her to meet his parents? Gabriel stopped that line of thinking. She was a friend. Sometimes he brought Tom with him if the wife and kids were out of town. This would be no different.

He moved over on the bench and motioned to it. "Have a seat."

Hesitating only a second, she walked around the edge of the piano and sat next to him. Gabriel was surprised; the bench wasn't long, and their bodies had to touch for both to fit on it. She reached out and stroked the smooth keys with reverence, not pressing hard enough to make sound.

"My ex loved Game of Thrones. Did you ever watch the show?"

She shook her head. "I read the books."

"Rachel always wanted me to play the music from the show." He began to move his hands, playing the main theme. "I don't watch a lot of television, but I learned some of the soundtrack because it's so beautiful."

She nodded, her eyes wide, watching his hands move flawlessly. When he had to lean in front of her to reach farther down the keyboard, she didn't move. Her body was stiff beside him, canted slightly forward, her eyes following his hands as they moved up and down the keys. As the song began to build momentum, he felt her muscles tightening, tightening. All the while her eyes were wide and watchful. When the music stopped suddenly, she gripped his thigh, and he heard her sharp intake of breath when softer music continued quietly for a few more seconds until it faded away. He left his hands resting lightly above the keys.

Gabriel observed her reaction to the music with fascination and amusement. She was completely caught up. How long had it been since he had experienced something so engulfing that the rest of the world disappeared? Since he was a young child, he thought.

She suddenly realized he was no longer playing. The expression on her face was one of profound regret. At the same time, she realized she was touching his leg. Instead of snatching her hand back, she withdrew it slowly.

"Do you want me to play something else?" he asked.

She looked up at him hopefully, and he would have played until his fingers bled if she asked it of him. She nodded.

"Any requests?"

Wrinkles appeared between her eyebrows, then vanished. "I do not know the names of any songs."

Gabriel thought for a moment. "Just tell me if you don't like what I'm playing, and I'll try something else."

He began with the theme song from "Phantom of the Opera."

As it turned out, there was no end to the music Ava liked.

• • • • •

Isabel jerked awake. Someone was restraining her. Panic rose as she began thrashing wildly. Just as she realized that was the wrong reaction and was figuring out how to plant a punch, she heard Griffin's drowsy voice.

"Calm down, Ali. You're not in the ring."

"Did I fall asleep?" she asked groggily, looking around. Griffin hadn't been restraining her; she had wrapped her arms around him and gotten them snagged under his button-down shirt. She was splayed over him as he sat on the couch with his feet on the coffee table.

"I'd say that's a hard yes. We both did."

"Well, fuck me."

"Bend over, I'll drive."

Snorting, Isabel disengaged her arms from him and used his chest to push herself up. The television was on, the sound low. She'd fallen asleep during whatever they'd been watching.

"What is it, nine o'clock? I'm becoming my grandparents."

Griffin looked amused. His hair, unruly as always, stuck up in little wavy spikes. "Just past eight."

"Great. I'm worse than my grandparents."

"I've been enjoying it." He nuzzled her neck.

Isabel stiffened, jerked in his arms. "Fuck!" She scrambled to her feet, had to fight the wave of dizziness that swept through her. "I have to go." She headed for the kitchen.

Griffin stood, picked up the wine glasses, which they had barely touched, and followed her. She stood at the kitchen sink, downing a glass of water.

"Where?" he asked.

"I have to sing tonight. Shit. I can't believe I forgot. I have to go home, grab my guitar, and get to The Raz before nine. Fuck!"

She was searching for something frantically, checking each of the stools at the island, the nook by the door, then moving to the living room. She looked under the coffee table, checked behind the wingback chair.

"What are you looking for?" Griffin asked, trying to keep up with her flitting around the flat like a dragonfly.

"My damn purse."

"Would that be the one slung over your shoulder?"

Isabel had gone to the patio door to see if she had carried it outside. Now she looked down and saw it hanging by her hip. "Are you kidding me?!"

Griffin laughed. "I'll drive. We have plenty of time."

She dug in her purse for her keys as she walked back into the kitchen. "You don't have to pretend to like my music just because we're dating."

Griffin walked up beside her and lifted her keys from the island. She closed her eyes, her face turning scarlet.

"I'm not pretending," Griffin said. "But if you don't want me there, just say so."

Closing her hand over the keys, she felt a thrill when he held onto the ring a beat longer. He leaned down and kissed her. "If you want to be there, I would like that."

"Don't throw up in my car this time."

She punched him in the shoulder.

•　　•　　•　　•　　•

He was dreaming of camping. Of a sizzling summer morning when he was still groggy after waking and could smell sausage cooking. Could hear the sizzle of eggs frying. And then heard the screaming.

The sound launched him from sleep like a stone from a trebuchet. Gabriel sat up in bed, his heart hammering against his rib cage. He opened his eyes to pure darkness, which lasted only a moment before the room flared with lightning, blinding him. Bright splashes pulsed around his face for several moments even though he'd closed his eyes against the assault. As they adjusted, he thought he heard a thump from another room.

Ava.

Ava was in his house.

She hadn't tired of the piano for three hours. Gabriel played everything from Mozart's "Lacrymosa" to the Mos Eisley Cantina song from Star Wars before she was finally contented to step away from the piano. Then it had taken another twenty minutes to convince her to stay the night because of the storm. Rain had been pounding and lightning had flashed not twenty yards from the front porch, and she had still tried to argue with him.

Gabriel had loaned her a pair of shorts with drawstrings and the smallest tee shirt he owned before showing her to the guest bedroom that wasn't currently being used as a catch-all. When she walked into the room, she had winced as one does when someone is blaring music too loud.

Thud.

The guest room was across the house from the master bedroom. What the hell was she doing that he could hear it all the way across the house during a severe thunderstorm?

Thud.

He leaned over and fumbled with the table lamp. The blast of light was only partly dimmed by his hand as he waited for his eyes to adjust.

Thud.

Blinking at another flash of lightning, he pulled on the tee shirt he'd tossed to the floor last night before lights out. The lightning was blinding him every damn second, and thunder was filling the house, distracting him.

One of the dogs whined. Ozzie was lying near the fireplace, watching him. Gabriel didn't see Maya.

Thud.

"For Christ's sake."

He shuffled into the hallway and walked toward the guest bedroom, brushing his hand along the wall as a guide. Ozzie trotted out curiously at his side. With no windows in the hallway, he was shielded from the worst of the lightning. His eyes began to adjust better. Maya was standing in the doorway of the guest bedroom, her head lowered. The door was wide open even though he had closed it on his way out hours ago.

Thunder grumbled low, then grew until it made the windows rattle all over the house.

Thud.

The room was frigid, the cold seeping out enough that he could feel it before he reached the door. Gabriel stood in the doorway and waited for a flash of lightning so he could see.

"Stay," he commanded Ozzie and Maya. He kept his voice low. Both dogs sat. "Ava?"

Lightning lit up the room. In the seconds he had to view it, he saw the bed was empty. The blankets looked as if a large dog had gotten a hold of them and shook them viciously. He felt along the wall and hit the light switch, squinting against the sudden onslaught of luminescence. What he saw made his jaw drop.

The curtains at the south-facing window had been yanked apart. The cloth was torn on one side, some hooks hanging empty. The window was wide open. Lightning burst across the rain-splattered glass. The floor below the window was wet.

Ava was standing next to the window, naked. Her long, thick hair tumbled three quarters of the way down her back. Her bottom looked absolutely mouthwatering. Her left hand was pressed against the upper glass, her fingers splayed. The right hand was fisted on the wall. She drew it back and slammed it into the wall, causing the banging sound he'd heard.

My God, she's the perfect specimen of a woman, Gabriel thought, and then all coherent thought left his mind when she turned around.

Holy fuck, she has perfect breasts. He stared. The part of him capable of thinking didn't kick in for at least thirty seconds, and by then he had a good eye full. Breasts. Curves. Legs. Scars. Holy shit... Rain was coming in the window and had given her skin a glistening sheen.

"This is not my house," she stated, her tone accusatory.

"Ava," he blurted. He forced his head down, his eyes onto the floor. The clothes he'd lent her were lying next to the bed. "What are you doing?"

Suddenly, Ava threw her head back and began to scream. Gabriel jumped at the suddenness and volume of the noise. Ozzie stood and started toward him. Maya stood and started to howl.

"Quiet!" Gabriel said to the dogs. "Stay!"

In three strides he was across the room. When he touched Ava's shoulder, he received a fist to the mouth for his efforts. It felt like an explosion went off in his jaw. Gabriel pressed his hand to his mouth, letting out a string of curse words his mother would have slapped him for.

To keep from staring at her body, he walked to the other side of the bed for the shirt and shorts. Deep breaths, he thought. Just get the damn clothes on her.

Ava continued to shriek, the sound high, like that of a child who has been terrified by a nightmare.

"Ava!" he said sharply over his shoulder. "Wake up!"

She stopped screaming. In the quiet that followed, Gabriel was able to think better. He steadied himself, turned, and that's when he noticed the knuckles of her right hand were bleeding profusely. A thick drop of crimson lazily slid down the back of her hand. And he had a hole in his wall.

"Fuck me."

Running his hand through his hair, he held the shirt and shorts out to her at chest level to block his view of her body. His imagination filled in plenty of detail.

Breasts. Breasts. Breasts.

Jesus, think about something else.

Sunday dinner with the family. Playing the piano. Aaron Rodgers and the Green Bay Packers.

Ava didn't look at him. She stared straight ahead, her eyes blank. Her wounded hand needed tending to, and he couldn't do that while she was naked.

She'd told him she had a problem with sleep walking, called it some big damn word. His sleep-fuzzy brain hadn't remembered before now. He hadn't understood the extent of it.

"Why are you naked?" He reached out and took her hand, meaning to put it through the sleeve of the shirt.

Ava slapped him across the face with her other hand, hard. The intent behind the slap seemed more calculated, less instinctive. As if she enjoyed it.

"Christ, Ava. You can't walk around my house naked." Irritated, he tried again.

This time she sidestepped before he could get a grip on her and shoved him passed her. Because she used his own momentum against him, he almost slammed into the wall. If he didn't know any better, he would have sworn she was laughing at him.

"Stop it! I'm trying to help you." Gabriel pushed the shirt toward her, careful not to touch her this time. "Put this on."

She reached out. The movement was mechanical; she stiffly held her arms out, waiting. Her eyes looked so eerie anyway, and when they were open and saw nothing, like now, they were downright spine-chilling.

"Lift your arms over your head," he said softly. When she did, he was surprised. He smirked. "I didn't think that would actually work."

Avoiding direct contact as much as he could, Gabriel stretched an arm hole open and maneuvered it around her left hand. The right hand was still bleeding, and he had to be more careful. He took the hem and pulled it down, unsure how to get it around her head. He couldn't stretch it out enough and avoid touching her. But when the neck touched the crown of her head, she lowered her arms and covered his hands with hers to pull the shirt down. Despite the frigid wind and rain coming in the window behind her, her hands were warm against his.

The shirt covered just below her butt.

"Here are some shorts," he said, picking up the shorts off the bed and pressing the fabric against her hand.

Moving slowly, Ava leaned over and put one foot in a leg hole, then the other. Since she seemed capable enough, Gabriel turned his head as she pulled them up. Thank God she didn't need help with that.

He moved around her and closed the window, locking it securely. Why the hell had she opened the window when the temperature was barely forty degrees outside?

"Did the storm wake you?" he asked, studying the hole in the wall. His voice was suddenly hoarse. His mouth felt like sandpaper. He would have to call someone to fix the hole.

When Ava didn't answer, he said, "Ava, did the storm wake you?"

Figuring she was completely covered by now, he turned back.

She was gone.

"Shit."

Sneaky as a ninja, she had slipped from the room without making a sound. Apparently, the dogs had followed her because they were nowhere to be found. A thorough search upstairs revealed nothing. He descended the steps with his heart racing.

Ozzie was standing at the bottom of the steps. Since Ava had liked watching him play piano, Gabriel decided to start in the great room and circled around the first floor. He was a minimalist decorator, so there weren't many places to hide. Ozzie trotted after him, his tail twitching uncertainly.

Maya was standing in the center of the great room and Gabriel instantly knew he had chosen correctly. He flipped on the overhead light. It wasn't the piano Ava was standing near; it was the large windows on the west side of the room. She stood close to the glass with her palms pressed against it on either side of her head. Her forehead rested against the glass as if she had suddenly become tired and needed a moment's rest.

Lightning filled the room, making Gabriel wince. The storm was still going strong. Rain beat against the glass and the wind was strong enough to sing. Ava stood amid all of it, unflinching even as another cacophony of thunder shook the house.

Gabriel felt like he was in a Vincent Price movie.

"Ava-"

Another burst of thunder. Trying to talk across the room was pointless.

He walked over to her. The urge to touch her shoulder was strong, but he kept his hands fisted at his sides. "Come to the kitchen with me. I need to clean your hand."

When she turned to him, her eyes out of focus. Her head tilted to the side as if she couldn't quite understand what he was saying.

"Let me clean your hand."

Lightning lit the room as it struck close to the house, causing Gabriel to jump. He let out a curse. Thunder instantly followed, a furious crack, followed by a quieter set of rumbles. The constant pulsing electrical discharge was giving him a raging headache.

Ava took a step toward him and was so close he could smell the rain on her skin. Gabriel touched her elbow, didn't get assaulted, and led her toward the kitchen. He had never communicated so much with someone using so few words.

The dogs followed warily behind him, laying in their usual spot in the breakfast room when Gabriel led Ava into the kitchen.

He turned on the overhead light. The extent of Ava's injuries was startling; dried blood covered her hand and fresh blood ran down her wrist. The skin on the first two knuckles was torn several layers deep, sticking up in rags and hardened by the blood. The other knuckles were battered to a lesser extent. The hand had already started to swell.

Positioning her in front of the sink, Gabriel pulled white dish towels out of a drawer and set them on the counter.

"I have to get supplies from the medicine cabinet in the bathroom," he said firmly, moving his hand from her shoulder to her elbow. "Don't go anywhere."

When he came back, he expected her to have wandered off again. Not much would surprise him at this hour. Oddly, she was still standing at the sink. Her battered hand was resting on the edge, twitching. She must have hit a stud to do that kind of damage.

Gabriel set the supplies on the counter, hoping he wasn't going to get his ass kicked for cleaning up this mess.

"This will probably sting."

Carefully taking her hand, he ran it under a gentle stream of warm water. Ava didn't react. Her eyes remained open but unfocused. She allowed him to move her arm around as he needed without resistance. He watched closely but her impassive expression didn't change. Even after he'd patted her hand dry, when he poured hydrogen peroxide on it for a more sterile cleansing, she didn't react at all.

He chatted while he worked to soothe her if she needed it, but also to let her know what he was doing.

"We'll let that disinfect for a few seconds," he said, holding her hand up and blowing gently on her knuckles.

A sudden memory of his mother doing the same for Hayden when she had scraped her knee trying to learn to skateboard hurled through his head. She'd begged Gabriel to teach her, so he finally gave in. When she fell, she told their mother she had taken the skateboard without his knowledge. She'd been afraid he would get in trouble if he were the one giving the lesson.

Ava's head whipped up. "Hayden."

Gabriel stared at her. "What did you say?"

Using her other hand, Ava raised her twitching index finger and touched it to Gabriel's forehead. "I f-feel her. Here."

She's asleep, he reminded himself, talking nonsense. It's nothing more than that.

He used a clean towel to dab the excess peroxide off the wounds. She had really beat the hell out of her knuckles, peeling the skin away. The bruising had already started in a rainbow of colors. What had she been dreaming about to cause her to do such a thing?

Five minutes later, with triple antibiotic applied to ward off infection and a bandage wrapped around her knuckles, Ava looked like a prize fighter in an MMA tournament.

As he turned her right hand to make sure the bandage was secure all around, he noticed little pale slashes, barely visible against her already pale complexion, on her inner forearm. Down at her wrist, thicker, slightly darker scars were embedded on the tissue. Something had been wrapped around her wrist so tight it had scarred her, he thought. He lifted her hand, squinting to get a better look. Was that a faint imprint of an oval shape? It took a moment for Gabriel to conclude the only thing that made that kind of an imprint was a chain. A tether for medium sized dogs maybe. He set that hand down gently and lifted the left hand.

The inside of the left arm had more of the smaller, barely visible scars. Her palm had a long, thick scar on it where something had cut deep into her. Gabriel noticed her wrist didn't look quite right. The ulna jutted out at an angle just a little more than it should. She had broken a bone in her wrist, and it hadn't healed properly.

Yet somehow, even with all these scars, she was beautiful.

"What the hell have you been through?" he asked softly.

Glancing up, he found her staring at him, through him. Without thinking, he ran his thumb along the scar on her palm.

She slapped him across the face. The sound was a sharp crack against his skin.

Holding his jaw in one hand and her scarred hand in the other, he glared at her. "Stop slapping me."

If she heard him, she didn't acknowledge it. Her eyes were hollow and drilling through him, unwavering. Her breath was steady. To her, not a thing had changed.

They were going to have a conversation in the morning.

Letting go of her hand, Gabriel turned away from her to get them each a glass of water. The lightning was finally moving away so he wasn't getting blinded every few seconds. As he took ice from the freezer, he glanced back at Ava. She was standing where he'd left her, like a robot waiting for a command.

"It seems your battery's dead." He walked around her, leaned over to fill the glasses with water.

Ava sighed heavily. Gabriel straightened, set one glass down on the counter. He held the other out to her.

"Here's some water. Battery's totally dead," he added when she didn't budge. "Well, I'm dying."

He chugged the entire contents of the glass. Thank God, he thought. His throat no longer felt like gravel during a drought.

"Let's get you back to bed."

He moved his hand to her shoulder to steer her. Turning her toward the stairs, he walked slowly, navigating her around the counter and through the hallway.

"How did you get those scars?" he asked, more to himself. He flipped the light switches off as they left each room, turned the one on for the stairway. "Maybe someday you'll tell me your story."

Glancing back at the dogs, he gave the command to come with him.

Helping Ava up the stairs, he thought this was the oddest date he had ever been on. She said she had trouble with sleepwalking, but this was off the charts. And she never said anything about taking off her damn clothes.

As they walked toward the guest bedroom, her head snapped up. Slapping her hands over her ears, she stopped just short of the doorway.

"Too loud," she said. She shook her head. "I will never get to sleep."

Gabriel looked around the empty room. "What's wrong with this room?"

"It is too loud."

Her hands were no longer pressed against her ears but hovering near them.

"It's quiet in there except for the storm." He stepped into the room and looked around, checking to make sure the television and the little stereo was off. "All clear."

Those uncanny gray eyes gazed into nothing. "You cannot hear them?"

Irritation was forcing its way under his skin. The emotion showed in his tone. "Who?"

When she didn't answer, he sighed. "The hole in the wall does make it chilly in here. The other bedroom is full of shit right now. I can sleep in here. You take my bed."

Dammit, he liked his bed. Especially now that he had been disturbed in the middle of the night. The one in the guest room wasn't as firm, and the room was getting even colder with the hole gaping. He'd have to take the couch. He closed the bedroom door to contain as much of the chill as he could. As an afterthought, he found a thick blanket from the catch all bedroom and tucked it against the bottom of the door to seal the guest bedroom even more. He'd put plastic over it when he was more awake. He was just too damn tired after wrestling with Ava.

She had lowered her hands. Her eye lids were starting to droop.

Gabriel held his hand out to her. Blinking slowly, she put her hand in his. He tugged on her to get her moving in the opposite direction. She looked back at the guest bedroom and shivered.

As he entered the master bedroom, he heard thunder again, farther away.

"This house is old," Ava said softly, her fingers fidgeting with the hem of the shirt she was wearing. She stood beside him, still holding his hand, as if she was embarrassed to be in his bedroom.

"It was built in 1860." Gabriel folded the blankets back. When she made no move to lie down, he took a step back, pulling on her hand so she could step forward and sit down. Her eyes regarded him solemnly. When she looked at him like that, with her eyes a little wide and lost, he saw just how naive she was. She was not only young but socially stunted. A combination like that could be dangerous if someone were looking to take advantage.

Placing his hands on her shoulders, he gently pressed until she sat on the bed. He lifted her legs and tucked them under the blankets. After a moment, he took her hand again and sat on the edge of the bed.

"They are all still here." Her voice was drifting in and out. Her eye lids were almost closed now.

"Who is still here?"

"The judge with the burnt face is angry." She closed her eyes.

"Try to sleep," he soothed, stroking her hair. "I'm right here."

Keeping her hand in his, he brushed her hair from her face with the other. He had already made the decision to stay with her. He would lay on top of the bedding and hold her hand until he was confident that she was fully asleep.

The dogs were watching him from the doorway.

"Go lay down," he whispered to them. They took their place on the large bed by the fireplace.

Hoping she was far enough under not to notice, he rested their hands on her stomach and slid his from under hers. Easing off the bed, he turned the lamp off and slowly walked around to the other side. He climbed on top of the bedding slowly, trying not to disturb her, settling in before he rested his hand over hers.

"I'm right here," he repeated.

$$\bullet \quad \bullet \quad \bullet \quad \bullet \quad \bullet$$

"We're going to die."

Isabel was gripping the arm rest and the center console as Griffin navigated through Madison in rain-soaked streets. Waves of water splashed as high as the window when he drove through them. The rain was still coming hard, making it difficult to see even though he had the wipers on full force.

"Try to relax."

Griffin was driving the way one would to church on Sunday if one were ninety-five years old.

"What good has relaxing done for you?" She exhaled audibly as he slowed to make sure they didn't hydroplane crossing a viaduct.

"What good has freaking out done for you?" he asked, grinning. "At least relaxing is beneficial. Stress has a negative impact on your body."

"I'll give you a negative impact on your face," she said, but her tone was full of strained amusement. "I wish I had your secret to peace." She braced her arm on the dashboard as a car with its lights off drifted into their lane several inches before whipping back into their own. "Pick a lane, you inconsiderate a-hole!"

Griffin gave his horn a quick beep. The car sped up and disappeared into the wall of heavy rain.

"Somebody left the gate open," Izzie muttered. She dropped the hand she had braced on the dashboard but kept the other one locked on the arm rest. "Sorry. I'm a horrible passenger-seat driver."

"Is that like a back seat driver?"

"Exactly. I'm even worse when I drive. I bitch during the entire ride."

"We're almost to my place. You're not going to try to make it home in this, are you?"

"Fuck. I wasn't even thinking about that."

He pulled into the car park. When Isabel realized he was turning into the underground parking lot instead of going to her car, she frowned.

"You're going to make me carry my guitar in this?"

"Of course not." He parked, shut off the engine.

"My car is back there." She pointed in the general direction of the parking lot. She wasn't exactly sure which direction they were facing.

"I'm aware of that."

Isabel could only follow him as he exited the Rover and took her guitar out of the back seat. She had trouble keeping up with his long strides as he walked to the elevator.

"Griffin, there's no point taking that upstairs. It's late. I need to go home."

He stepped into the elevator and turned to face her, hitting the button. "It's half an hour to your place. Probably more in this rain. You could barely handle the drive here."

"I wasn't driving."

The doors started to close, and she turned sideways and scooted in with him.

"It's different when I'm the one in control."

But she trusted his ability to handle his car more than hers. She hated driving; the responsibility of the lives that were in her hands when she was behind the wheel – not only the passengers in the vehicle with her, but the other drivers on the road that she effected. The constant stimuli coming at her was maddening. If she were rich, she would hire a driver for herself immediately.

They reached the floor, and he held his hand out for her to go first. When she stood her ground, he stepped out. Making a disgusted sound, she followed him.

"Griffin."

He unlocked the door, turning on lights as he entered his flat. He set her guitar carefully to the left just inside the door.

"What was that number you did about leaving?" he asked, going to the kitchen. He pulled out a couple wine glasses. "The third one, I think."

"Griffin, don't pour me a glass. I'm not staying."

"Why not?"

Thunder bellowed and the lights flashed off, then back on.

"I'm tired. I'm usually tired after I sing."

"So go to sleep." He poured the wine, something red.

"I will, as soon as I get home." She dug in her purse for her keys, sighing. Tonight, she seemed exceptionally tired. "I think I'll be dead as soon as my head hits the pillow."

"Why do you fight so hard to be independent even when you know it makes more sense to ask for help?"

Lifting her head, she gazed at him. "What do you mean?"

"It is late," he said, bringing her the wine. "There are flash flood warnings in three counties and you're dead on your feet. Just stay. You would rather risk getting into an accident than ask for my help?"

For a long time, she stared at him. He thought she might make excuses to make her choice sound more convincing, but in the end, she decided to be blatantly honest.

"Yes."

Lightning flashed, coming through the patio door, and nearly blinding her.

"Is it just me helping you that upsets you, or do you do this with everyone?"

"Everyone. I don't like asking for help."

"Why not?"

Seeing her realize it was true, watching the shame wash over her, made his stomach twist. "I don't know."

"Then stay. You've stayed here before. Don't be such a..."

Her eyes narrowed. "Such a what?"

"Fire crotch."

She had snatched the wine from his hand and taken a drink, and now she sprayed it all over his shirt. Coughing hard, she leaned over and covered her mouth, holding the glass out so she didn't break it.

Griffin patted her on the back, too gently to do any good even if an object had been lodged in her throat instead of liquid going down the wrong pipe.

It took her several seconds to recover. The coughs fizzled out and finally stopped. She slowly straightened, staring at him.

"Well played," she croaked.

He shrugged. "It's all I could come up with on short notice."

"Somehow you managed to insult me and make me laugh about it." Then she saw she had spilled the remainder of the wine on the floor. "Shit. I ruined your shirt, and I made a mess on your floor. Dammit."

"I guess you'll have to make it up to me by staying the night," he said, walking past her toward the bedroom. "Cleaning supplies are under the sink."

Isabel glared after him. He pulled his shirt off just before he disappeared into his room, making her blush.

"What are you, twelve?" she muttered to herself. She opened the cupboard under the sink and found what she needed to clean up her mess.

Why did she refuse help? She never asked for it, and she never accepted it. She had no problem helping others; didn't see it as a weakness of their character if they needed help. Yet here she was, willing to risk her safety instead of just accepting Griffin's offer.

She tossed the soggy paper towels in the trash and put the cleaning supplies away. Holding her wine glass, she tapped her index finger on the rim thoughtfully. No one had ever made her think, really think about herself and her actions before.

"Those cogs in your head are turning."

Isabel jumped as Griffin entered the kitchen. He was wearing a fresh tee shirt.

How the hell can a tee shirt look so sexy? Isabel thought. I want to undress you with my teeth.

"You're making me blush."

"What?" She jumped again. The wine was already making her feel heady. Apparently, she'd consumed more than she thought.

Griffin wiggled his eyebrows. "I admire your ambition, but I don't think you can work my zipper with your teeth."

Instantly her face turned scarlet. "Did I say that out loud?!"

He laughed, draping his arm around her shoulders. "You're a spunky little thing, aren't you?"

Isabel pressed her fingers to her eyes. "I'm leaving. I'd rather risk dying in a car accident than continue to humiliate myself."

"Knowing you want me is flattering, Izzie."

All the humor had left his voice. Iz raised her head and looked into his golden eyes. She was so close she could see the different shades of color and watch as his pupils dilated just before he leaned down.

How did such a simple act convey so much? she wondered. Firm but gentle, his kiss warmed first her lips, then her whole body. Everything inside her went soft. Her stomach fluttered, plunged. She felt drugged, the way she did as she lay in bed and was floating in between sleep and alertness. Griffin turned toward her so he could deepen the kiss and cup his hand behind her head.

This wasn't the hungry need of the other night that had all but possessed her and had her taking what she wanted. This was a gentle wonder of two people investigating each other. Isabel shivered when he ran the tips of his fingers up her spine slowly, back down again.

They parted. She took a few seconds to catch her breath. She couldn't quite get her eyes to focus.

"So, what was that number?" Griffin asked softly, touching her hair.

"What number?" She was still dazed. Numbers were the farthest things from her mind.

He grinned. "The third song you sang at The Raz. The one that talks about leaving. I haven't heard that one."

Isabel took a step back, sliding her hand down his arm until they were no longer touching. Separated, Griffin thought. She's put distance between us. Her eyes became carefully emotionless.

"That's because I wrote it." She picked up her wine and took a gulp.

"Really? It's beautiful."

Busying herself getting the wine out, Iz didn't say anything. She jumped when another loud clap of thunder filled the apartment.

"Compliments bother you."

"Refill?" She finished topping off her glass and held the bottle up.

"Please."

The apartment was silent as she poured his wine and returned the bottle to the refrigerator.

"Thank you."

Griffin thought of the passion in her eyes when she sang, of the specific lyrics of the song. How the crowd at The Raz went quiet when she began to sing.

Where did you go?

Child of sorrow

Moments of fear and pain and loneliness

Are the last you ever felt

"Is it about your sister?"

Isabel leveled her gaze at him. "You're not very good at taking hints, are you? Do you have any whiskey?"

"I forgot to pick some up for you. I'll remedy that the next time I'm at the grocery store." He took a step toward her, watched her take a step back. "I pick up on body language more than you know. I'd rather you talk to me instead of going silent."

"I'd rather stay silent than say something I'll regret."

Griffin took another step toward her. Her eyes were the color of wet moss. At first, she seemed to stand her ground; then she took a step back. Thunder grumbled; lightning sent a crazy pattern across the living room wall.

"Why does talking about her upset you now? We discussed it when we first met, and when I first heard you sing at The Raz."

Isabel had already finished her second glass of wine. God, she wished for whiskey. It made her agitated, which she preferred to the sad, caged feeling she had right now. The feeling of a million spiders crawling under her skin. She turned to pour herself another glass.

"I was drunk. I said a lot of things."

"You weren't drunk at the grocery store."

"I was having a meltdown. I didn't mean to blurt it out." She swung around and held up the bottle. "Refill?"

"No, thanks. Why did you play the song tonight in public if you don't want to talk about it?"

"I wanted to see what other people..." She exhaled, set the bottle on the counter. Resting her hands flat on the marble, she closed her eyes and took a deep breath. "As an artist and a writer, I wanted feedback on a project I've been working on."

This time when Griffin took a step toward her, she stayed where she was. He rested a hand on her back. "And as a sister?"

"As a sister, I'm not ready to discuss it."

Only the sounds of the storm could be heard for several seconds. Isabel wouldn't look at him. He saw a clear drop hit the counter behind the curtain of her long, blonde hair.

"Izzie-"

She wrenched away when he tried to rub her back. "Don't. God damn it." Picking up the bottle of wine, she shoved past him and walked into the bathroom, slamming the door.

•　•　•　•　•

A moan brought him slowly out of sleep. Something thudded against his leg. Gabriel opened his eyes to pure darkness. Rain was pounding on the windows again. Beside him, he heard strained breathing.

Ava.

Was this a dream? Hadn't he had it already?

He'd fallen asleep waiting to make sure she was okay.

She moaned again, kicked. Gabriel blinked as he sat up, wondering what the hell she was doing now. Damn, but she was a restless sleeper.

The alarm clock on his bedside table showed it was just past four in the morning. He leaned over to his table as she kicked him again, fumbling with the lamp until he found the switch. Turned it on.

"I want to brand her."

"What?" Gabriel turned back toward her, surprised at the mechanical tone of her voice, and confused by the words. He wasn't fully awake yet. Soft light showed she had twisted herself in the blankets. He caught a flash of bare shoulder and sighed.

"She should know she's a dog."

He didn't recognize the feminine voice coming her.

"What are you talking about?" Gabriel rubbed a hand down his face, tried to make sense of what was going on. He wished he had coffee. Slowly, his eyes adjusted to the light.

Ava was sitting up now, her knees up to her chest, staring straight ahead. The blankets covered most of her, but he could see her shoulder, her side, the curve of her butt before the blanket interrupted his view. Once again, she was naked. How the hell did she manage to take off her clothes in bed without him knowing it?

She let out a low growl. The sound was feral. The side of her upper lip curled slightly.

"Ava?"

"Let's do it in Hebrew. Nobody will understand what it means. It'll be our secret."

Her voice changed, became somewhat masculine, but maintained that mechanical, lifeless tone. "I don't know fucking Hebrew."

Gabriel winced at the hatred in that tone.

Her voice returned to that first imitation; feminine, with a slight southern accent. "We'll go to a tattoo artist who does. It's pretty when you write it."

She remained sitting, staring straight ahead, her eyes unfocused. Gabriel didn't think she could see the room around her. Her eyes filled and she began rocking back and forth.

"Can you hear me, Ava?"

"I can hear you." Her voice was soft, immature. If Gabriel hadn't watched her mouth move, he would have thought he was listening to a child.

He shifted on the bed, so he was sitting at an angle in front of her. If she moved her legs away from her chest, the bedding would fall and expose her. But he wanted to watch her face while they spoke.

The higher pitch of her voice and her choice of words made him realize she wasn't fully awake. "What are you dreaming about?"

She frowned. Tears were streaming down her face. "I do not understand."

"Where are you?" Gabriel reached out to take her hand, stopped himself just before he touched her.

"I am at the trailer."

What trailer? "Where are your clothes?"

Her lower lip trembled. "I am not supposed to talk about it." She wrapped her arms around her legs and pulled herself into a tighter ball. Her thick hair flowed over her torso like a protective blanket. He couldn't believe how leaky her eyes were; the tears just kept coming without effort. Her face remained completely without expression, yet salty lines ran down her cheeks as if they would never stop.

"Ava, how old are you right now?" Gabriel asked. Her movements, word choices, and pitch of her voice were like listening to and watching a completely different person.

"Six."

"Jesus." Gabriel ran a hand through his hair. He felt like he had fallen down the rabbit hole. What the fuck was he supposed to do with a woman who was dreaming she was a six-year-old child?

"They can get me when I'm not in The Interval."

He didn't know what that meant. "Can I talk to adult Ava? Can you wake up for me?"

"They branded me."

"Who did?" Gabriel reached out instinctively to touch her shoulder, pulled his hand back. She was no longer writhing but that didn't guarantee his safety.

"The Bad People," Ava whispered, shuddering.

Gabriel leaned forward, reaching for her again, the reflex to comfort automatic. He had almost touched her pale skin before he stopped himself. "Ava, can I touch you?"

"I do not like to be touched."

"I won't hurt you like the Bad People did."

"Promise?"

His heart ached at the wariness he heard in her voice. "I will not hurt you, Ava. I promise."

After a moment, Ava said, "Okay."

Gabriel reached out and put his hand on her cheek, feeling the hot tears on his palm. Her eyes slipped closed. She let out a long sigh, her breath shuddering. She turned her head into his hand and her head suddenly became very heavy. Gabriel realized it was dead weight; she was completely asleep again. Her arms fell to her sides and her legs relaxed. She slumped toward him.

Catching her before she plunged into him, he eased her onto her back. She was tangled in the blanket from kicking in her sleep earlier. He leaned over her, trying to pull the bedding from under her body enough to cover her completely without waking her. The bare skin along her shoulders rose with goose flesh.

"Ava," he said softly, rubbing his thumb across her cheek. "What did they do to you?"

He brushed a strand of hair from her face.

Her gray eyes flew open. She stared at him, and he thought, I'm dead. The clarity in her eyes told him she was fully awake and alert. He could feel the raging energy from her building to strike out because of his proximity. He was surprised she hadn't already. Beneath him, he felt her body coil.

"You were dreaming," he said, keeping his voice even. "You fought in your sleep."

Her stormy eyes shifted, and she saw his swollen jaw. "You are injured."

"I tried to comfort you earlier. You didn't like it."

The fury began to drain away. He felt it go, felt the surrender, the easing of it from her body like blood flowing from a wound. The muscles remained tense. Her eyes remained on his.

She shifted to sit up, but he was leaning over her. "Release me."

He sat up, keeping his movements slow and easy, so he didn't startle her. Like she was a wild animal.

"I injured you." She fought to free herself of the blankets and stood.

Gabriel's eyes shot to the headboard, the doorway, his hands. The effort to look away took every ounce of his willpower. God, she was beautiful.

"You thought I was someone else. People were hurting you in your dream."

"You should not touch me. You should never touch me."

"I wanted to make you feel safe."

He ran his hand down the back of his neck. How the hell was he supposed to think with her looking like that?

"You cannot make me feel safe. You should not have tried."

He was confusing now with what had happened earlier when she'd been sleepwalking. To have his sleep disrupted so abruptly was disorienting. He tried to gather his thoughts.

She began to pace back and forth along the side of the bed as if it were perfectly normal to walk around naked in front of him. She folded her arms across her chest, more out of anger than to cover herself.

"Ava, you're not wearing any clothes." Stating the obvious was all he could manage at the moment.

"I sleep naked." The flippant way she delivered the comment made him want to bang his head against the wall.

Gabriel shifted on the bed again, trying like hell to avoid staring at her body. She was perfect in every way, and her rigorous workouts toned every single muscle. It was like watching a piece of art stand up and walk around a museum.

"Please put some clothes on."

As if he hadn't spoken, she said, "I told you I do not sleep well. I told you I do not want friends. Now I have struck you."

He could feel the swelling in his jaw, and his cheek still stung from her earlier smacks, but he said, "It was a slap. I'm fine."

She stopped, glared at him. Contempt filled her voice. "I do not slap."

"For God's sake put some clothes on. You're driving me insane."

"No one has ever had a problem with my body before." She dropped her arms from her chest. Staring down at herself, she tried to find the flaws he was seeing that made her unworthy of looking at. Maybe it was her scars. People, she had learned, could not handle the stories her body told.

"I don't have a problem with it. That's kind of the problem."

She lifted her head, found his eyes. "Why?"

"Seriously?"

"I do not know what that means." Her eyes were full of confusion, trying so hard to understand. Her innocence almost made him laugh.

"You're unbelievably gorgeous, Ava, and you're walking around naked in front of me like it's just a normal Sunday. I'm having a little trouble focusing on the conversation."

Ava frowned down at herself again, glanced around the floor, and picked up the tee shirt she had discarded sometime during the early morning. She slipped it on, obviously still not understanding the problem.

Gabriel sighed. Now that he had a few moments to think, the fog was clearing, and he was able to remember this was the second time Ava had startled him awake.

"My jaw will heal," he said. "This is the second time you've woken me up."

"I have nightmares every night," she said dismissively. She found her panties, snatched them off the floor. "I told you that."

"Are you okay? They sounded painful." He remembered her childlike voice during this latest one, the mannerisms as she spoke. "I don't like seeing you cry," he added.

Then turned his head as she pulled her underwear up without shame.

"I cried?"

"Like your heart was breaking. You said the Bad People branded you."

When she didn't answer immediately, he turned back to her. She was looking at him with curiosity again, the anger tempered. She sat on the bed, extending her left leg toward him. Sometime, when he wasn't looking, she had put on the shorts he'd loaned her. As she pulled the material of the shorts up, he saw a series of symbols high up on her inner thigh in black ink:

"You have a tattoo," he said. How had he missed that earlier when he had seen her naked in the kitchen? Oh, yeah. Her amazing chest. That, and the tattoo was positioned so that when she stood, it was hidden between her thighs.

"My foster parents made me get it when I was six."

Though he didn't approve of disfiguring young children, he was struck by its simple beauty.

"It means 'dog,'" she said bluntly.

He remembered what she said in her sleep and his stomach clenched. "What the hell kind of tattoo artist would do that to a child?"

"It was not the worst thing he did to me."

The acid in his stomach suddenly felt like an ocean ebbing and flowing inside him.

"Why would anyone want 'dog' printed on a child?"

"They wanted me to always remember I am worthless." She stated this directly.

Gabriel clenched his jaws, then immediately let up when the pain from Ava's punch shot from his mandible up into his temple. He rubbed his jaw absently. "Is it written in Hebrew?"

She looked at him sharply.

"When you were dreaming, you were talking in your sleep. You said, 'Let's do it in Hebrew.' Something like that."

Ava's expression chilled. "It is Hebrew," she confirmed. "My foster parents held me down while another man gave me the tattoo. It is in a sensitive area. Sometimes I... still feel the needle going in."

"My God, Ava."

"I told you they liked the sound of my screams."

Hearing her say it is one thing, he thought. Hearing what they did to get her to scream was something altogether different. The muscles in his shoulders were tightening with anger. He couldn't seem to keep his hands from balling into fists.

"You're not a dog."

"Obviously."

Gabriel felt his fury boiling just below the surface, ready to blow. He wanted to kill those people. The desire to wrap his hands around another person's throat had never been so strong. What the hell had a six-year-old done to warrant that kind of torture?

Impatient, Gabriel leaned forward. He kept his eyes on hers, waiting until she acknowledged his closeness, then rested his hand gently on her knee. "You're not a dog," he repeated. "You're not worthless."

She stared at him with those fascinating gray eyes for several moments. "I need water."

When she left the room, Gabriel sighed, leaning back against the headboard. What kind of people were the government letting care for children? He wanted to punch something. He wanted to find everyone in Ava's life that had ever hurt her and pound on them until they were unrecognizable. Why didn't she feel the same way? She seemed indifferent to what had happened to her even though she had nightmares about it still. Gabriel had a feeling he only knew a fraction of what she had gone through, and it was making the bile rise inside him like lava.

She returned with two glasses of ice water and stiffly handed one to him.

"Thank you," he said, feeling no better after a gulp that went down like liquid fire. "Do you remember earlier? Do you remember walking around the house?"

She avoided his gaze. "I sleepwalk."

As if that explained anything. He decided not to push the issue for now, since it seemed to be a sore subject. He was too damn tired.

"I'll sleep on the couch now that you're feeling better," he said, standing with his water. He pulled his side of the bedding up toward the pillow. "I was going to earlier, but you were upset -"

"I am safe here." She looked anxious at his intent to leave.

Safe?

"What do you mean, safe?"

"I know you will not hurt me." She looked down at the clothing she was wearing, fidgeting with the hem of the shirt. "I will not hurt you."

Frowning, Gabriel felt she was trying to make a point, but he just wasn't catching on. "Okay."

"This bed is more comfortable for you than the couch. I did not mean to kick you out of your own bed." She tucked her legs up underneath her and watched him, her gray eyes dark in the soft light of the little table lamp. Around her face, her thick hair was slightly mussed from tossing in her sleep.

"You want me to stay here with you?" he asked, surprised.

"I am safe here," she repeated. She chugged half of her water before setting the glass on the table. Tugging at the neck of the tee shirt, she rolled her shoulders uncomfortably.

Gabriel ran a hand down the back of his neck. "I'll turn around so you can get undressed, if you're more comfortable that way."

"You do not mind?" Ava asked, watching him turn around.

"No. I just hope I don't embarrass myself in my sleep."

Wondering what the hell he had gotten himself into with this young woman, Gabriel heard shuffling as she took off the borrowed clothing and climbed into bed.

"Are you covered?"

"Yes. I left my underwear on. Does that help you to be more comfortable?"

Gabriel turned, almost laughed. "I'll manage."

He turned off the lamp and slid under the blankets, lying on his back. The throbbing in his jaw had settled to a dull ache. How the hell was he going to explain the swelling at the family dinner Sunday? How did anyone explain any of this? He didn't understand her. She didn't like physical contact, yet she was

288

lying almost naked next to him in bed when he had a guest bedroom and a roomy couch either of them could have used. She talked in her sleep and had punched a hole in his damn wall. Her foster parents abused her and had her tattooed at six years old. Christ, she had been abused at such an early age. Who the fuck did that to a child?

"Do not be angry."

Her voice startled him. He realized he was shaking with rage at the thought of people taking a needle to a child's body for the purpose of degradation.

"I'm not angry with you," he said, trying to calm down. His mind was galloping; he couldn't seem to slow it down. He couldn't get his muscles to relax.

"I know."

He heard her shift, and a moment later, her hand brushed against his arm. The contact surprised him. She ran her fingertips down his arm until she found his hand, held it loosely.

"Do not be angry," she repeated, her voice a whisper. "It is done."

If only it was that simple, he thought. If only his anger didn't return each time he thought about a grown man taking a needle to a child's skin as he watched her writhe and cry and scream. People who were supposed to protect her had held her still while another mutilated her body. How could he not be furious?

"I want to take you to David," she suddenly said.

"Who's David?"

"My foster father. The man who raised me."

"You're still in contact with him?" Immediately his muscles bunched so hard they ached. He imagined getting the man alone at some point during the visit, "accidentally" ramming his fist into the abusive bastard's face. Repeatedly.

"He is my family." Ava's tone was nonchalant. That infuriated Gabriel even more. The warrior, the woman who didn't take shit off anyone, still chatted with her abuser.

Gabriel rolled toward her. In the darkness, he could only see the moonlight reflecting off her eyes. "You visit the man who thought it was okay to give a six-year-old a tattoo? The man who covered your body in scars. Do you really think I'll just shake his hand and have a polite conversation with him?"

Her tone was disgusted. "David would never hurt me."

"You said your foster parents-"

As if he were an incredibly naive child, she shook her head and said, "I had many foster parents until I was seven. David was the last. He legally adopted me."

Gabriel could hear admiration and possibly even love for the man in her voice. "The tattoo, the abuse, was done by someone else?"

She nodded. "David would never hurt me. He raised me as his own."

Relaxing slightly, Gabriel exhaled. "Okay."

"We will go tomorrow."

"Oh." He hadn't realized she meant so soon. "Okay."

She shifted a little more, and a moment later her breathing became heavier, slower. Just like that, she had fallen asleep.

Gabriel held her hand and listened to the sound of her breathing. He tried to force himself to relax, to allow the peaceful sound of her sleeping to calm him. It would be a while before his mind shut off.

• • • • •

Her own tears woke her.

Isabel couldn't remember the dream, but she rose from it crying, with something like a moan on her lips as she became lucid. She sniffed, waiting, trying to remember where she was and what was going on. Tears were running steadily down her cheeks. She choked back a sob. When she heard Griffin breathing beside her, guilt filled her.

The wine headache was certainly not helping. As she rose quietly, trying not to wake Griffin, she felt a thundering pulse in her temples. Crying was not helping her sinuses, which made the headache worse. Delicious. She'd made an ass out of herself. Again. And now she had a massive headache. Griffin was going to go into Witness Protection after last night just to get away from her.

On top of all that, she'd had a nightmare. Maybe.

What the hell had she dreamed about?

She slipped out of the bedroom, walking through the closet to get to the bathroom. Pulling the door around, she used the sink to splash icy water on her face until she was gasping. The shock temporarily took away the urge to cry. After a short break, she splashed herself again. The frigid water sent shards of glass into her temples, adding to her headache, but at least she was finally able to stop crying. Damn tears and all they did to the human body. They did everything except make things better.

Burying her face in a towel felt equally satisfying, and she gave herself a ten count before she finished patting her face dry.

Using the light over the sink in the kitchen to avoid hitting into living room furniture, Iz found the couch. She curled up on the end and wrapped her arms around her legs. Sometimes she was just so damn tired she couldn't sleep.

But she must have dozed. She was endlessly falling. Her stomach was churning, spinning as she twisted through blackness. Images of water rushing and a shadow chasing her flashed through her mind. When she felt something brush against her arm, she cried out without opening her eyes. She didn't want to see the shadows around her.

"Take it easy." Griffin wrapped a small blanket around her and rubbed her arms. "You're freezing."

A small moan escaped her. She shivered. "I didn't mean to wake you."

"I woke to your absence," he murmured in her ear. "Come back to bed."

"Don't deserve it."

"I want you next to me." Griffin lifted her off the couch as if she weighed nothing and carried her toward the bedroom. Iz rested her head on his shoulder. She felt a bone chilling cold so deep she didn't think she would ever get warm.

He'd turned on the lamp in the bedroom, spilling soft light from his side of the bed.

"It hurts," Isabel whispered, looking into his eyes as he set her gently on the bed. Her eyes were glassy. Her lower lip trembled. Climbing into bed beside her, he pulled the blankets up around them.

"What hurts?" He touched her hair, her face. Using his thumb, he brushed a tear from her cheek.

"It's been so long. It shouldn't still hurt so bad." She curled into him. Her body wouldn't stop shaking.

"It doesn't ever go away, Love. It only becomes a little more manageable."

The sound of his heartbeat, steady against her hand, began to calm her.

Her breath stopped hitching. Finally, she could take a real breath. She filled her lungs.

"I'm sorry. I should have gone home."

"I'm glad you're here." He tucked her head under his chin, pulled her legs up over his and wrapped his arms around her until they were tightly tangled together. Skimming his fingertips down her leg, he kissed the top of her head. "Were you close with Hayden?"

He felt her stiffen in his arms. "Shh." The tremors that had finally ceased started again. Isabel pulled back, tried to twist out of his embrace. His fingers grazed back up her leg, bringing gooseflesh to the surface. He brushed his lips against her temple. Lifting her hand, he rubbed the back of it across his cheek. With a nuzzle to her neck, he laced his fingers with hers.

"Don't be sad, Izzie."

"I don't mean to hurt people. It's the only thing I'm good at."

He gazed at her troubled eyes. "That's not true. Why don't you want to talk about her? What are you afraid of?"

Isabel took a breath, closed her eyes. When she exhaled, she opened her eyes with a deadened expression in them. "I'm afraid if I talk about her, I'll start crying. And once I start, I won't ever be able to stop."

CHAPTER SIX

Gabriel did sleep, finally, and woke alone. Through the thin crack between the curtains, he could see sunlight. He squinted as his eyes adjusted. Lifting his head, he glanced around the room. Ava was gone. The dogs must have gone with her; the large bed by the fireplace was empty. Letting his head flop back on the pillow, he waited several seconds to see if he was going to slip back into sleep.

The room was too bright with the early morning sun. He rolled onto his back and sat up. Pulling on a pair of jeans and a tee shirt, he used the bathroom and brushed his teeth before making his way downstairs.

A quick glance out the front door told him Ava was still here; her car was parked in his driveway. But when he entered the kitchen to make coffee, she wasn't there. He glanced toward the breakfast room and jolted.

Ava was perched on the railing of the deck. There was no other word to describe it. She was crouched on the thin edge of the deck like a damn bird, her feet planted on the railing, her butt settled on her heels. She was several feet off the ground, watching the dogs run around in the back yard. One wrong move could send her over the edge and injure her badly even if it didn't break her neck. He had two chairs on the deck, yet she had chosen to sit up there like fucking Big Bird.

"Why not?" he said to the empty kitchen.

He started a pot of coffee and walked through the breakfast room to the patio doors. Hoping he wouldn't startle her, he slid open the door. She tilted her head, making her look even more bird-like.

"Good morning." He walked over to where she roosted and looked out at the dogs.

"Good morning."

The sun was a warm contrast to the cool air. The dogs were sniffing around the yard lazily. Occasionally, Ozzie lifted his leg to mark his territory for the millionth time.

"I have chairs to sit on." Seeing her balanced on the edge made him nervous.

Her ashen eyes studied him. A thermal plaid hoodie covered her, and she had her arms wrapped tightly around each other and tucked between her chest and knees. "I like this view."

He couldn't argue with that.

"I'm making coffee, if you're interested."

She closed her eyes, breathed deeply. "Coffee is good."

Without adjusting her height, she pivoted on the ledge, making his stomach drop into his bowels. Then she set her hands on his shoulders, surprising him, and hopped down lithely. He put his hands on her arms to steady her, but of course she didn't need them. It was then he noticed she wasn't wearing her shoes. Weren't her feet cold in just her socks?

The dogs ran onto the deck just as he opened the door. They waited patiently for the command to come in.

Walking with her into the kitchen, Gabriel reached into the cupboard to find her a coffee mug. "Do you take sugar or creamer? I have flavored creamers. Hazelnut, Biscotti, and French Vanilla. My sister likes variety. Or I have milk if you prefer."

"French Vanilla creamer, please."

He pulled the jug out of the refrigerator and set it on the counter in front of her. She sat at the breakfast bar, listening to the coffee pot, resting a hand on her palm. She looked comfortable there, he thought, getting her a glass of water, and setting it in front of her. She smiled slightly, just the barest curl of the edges of her lips. He paused to watch her.

"Why are you looking at me like that?" Those smokey eyes were suddenly focused on him.

"You almost smiled. I haven't seen you smile before."

As she took a drink of water, her eyes seemed to dance over the glass at him.

"You should do it more often," he said. "Your face lights up."

He wasn't sure how to bring up her wandering around naked. Ignoring the matter didn't seem mature, but neither did talking about it like some prepubescent kid. She didn't seem embarrassed by it. Maybe she didn't remember waking after her second episode. Was she upset to have found him next to her when she woke up? She didn't seem upset, but with her, it was so hard to tell.

He decided to tread carefully.

"Did you sleep well?"

She shrugged. "I did not have nightmares the second time I fell asleep."

So, she did remember, at least one of the disturbances.

The coffee was finished. He lifted the carafe and poured her a cup, then one for himself. Taking a spoon out of a drawer, he set it and the mug on the counter in front of her.

"How did you sleep?" she asked, adding the slightest bit of creamer, and stirring. The question came out sounding awkward. Gabriel had a feeling she didn't really care but had been taught that feigning interest was part of social etiquette.

"I was up for a while after you told me about your tattoo," he admitted. "It's hard to sleep after a discussion like that."

Having someone as beautiful as her lying next to him certainly hadn't helped.

"I should have driven home last night, like I told you. Your sleep would not have been interrupted."

He gave her a lopsided grin. "You're stubborn as hell, Ava Reid."

The sudden change in mood confused her. Gabriel watched her study him, trying to figure out what the change meant.

He took a sip of his coffee. "Do you eat breakfast?"

She nodded.

"Of course, you do. Do you want me to make you something?"

Despite not being fully awake, he noticed that slightest curve of the lips again, what he was beginning to think of as her version of a smile.

"I have eaten."

Gabriel glanced around the kitchen, which was as neat and tidy as he had left it last night after dinner. "Here?"

She nodded.

"How long have you been awake?"

"Three hours and seventeen minutes." As an afterthought, she added, "I borrowed some clothes for my workout."

Gabriel closed his eyes and sighed. He was still getting used to the idea of being awake.

The dogs were lying on the floor near the breakfast nook, soaking up sun.

"I need to walk the dogs-"

"They went with me on a run. They are exerted."

The way she spoke amused him to no end.

"I can see that." They hadn't even opened their eyes when he said "walk".

"I also used the shower next to the spare bedroom."

He shook his head, amused. "Do you mind if I take a few minutes to shower?"

"I will keep myself occupied."

He left her in the kitchen while he took his coffee and shuffled upstairs.

•　　•　　•　　•　　•

Griffin woke wrapped around Isabel with his face buried in her hair. For several moments, he basked in the glorious feel of it, how the smell of her was more invigorating than a cup of coffee. She had long arms and legs that rested perfectly against his. Her bottom snuggled against his groin as if it had been created for that very purpose. The soft curve of her neck as it merged into her shoulder was the best spot for him to rest his chin. He could surround himself with her and feel her pressed against him. Was there anything better on a Sunday morning?

When his body began to respond to hers, he slipped quietly from bed and started water for a shower – a cold one. Isabel probably wouldn't be awake for another hour at least. He would have to find something to do until then.

The water shocked his system into behaving. As he flew through his cleaning ritual at hyper speed, he wondered if he and Isabel would be spending time together today. She would need coffee first thing after she woke up, and maybe she would play her guitar for him, or they could watch Netflix all day. Griffin didn't really care what they did, as long as they did it together.

He exhaled as he shut off the frigid water, grabbing a towel and draping it over his shoulders. Shaking his head so his mouth made silly slapping noises, he rubbed his arms to get the blood flowing. He scrubbed the towel through his hair a few times before wrapping it around his waist.

The film of fog on the mirror caught him off guard as he reached for the mouth wash. Just like that, without warning, it hit him. He exhaled again, this time his breath shaking, and slowly reached up to wipe away the mist.

Four years, and his reflection still sent a stab of agony into his heart every once in a while. He gazed into his own eyes but didn't see his face in the mirror. He saw the face of someone terribly similar to him, with the same honey-colored eyes, only a little darker. The face in the mirror was missing the scar on the bottom right side of his chin from where a piece of metal sliced him open when he was seven and getting into trouble with his brother.

Four years, and sometimes the reflection Griffin saw in the mirror wasn't his own.

• • • • •

Twenty minutes later Gabriel returned to the kitchen expecting Ava to have disappeared. She was still sitting at the breakfast counter. The dogs had moved, now lying on the floor by the patio doors. Gabriel refilled his coffee mug, feeling more awake.

He reached for Ava's almost empty water glass, meaning to refill it for her, just as she reached for it to finish it off. His hand settled over hers. For a moment, everything seemed to stop. Ava, watching the dogs, turned toward him at the physical contact. Gabriel heard a noise like all the air being sucked out of the room, then absolute silence.

Ava's eyes rounded and her pupils exploded. They were focused on a point somewhere past Gabriel's shoulder.

"It was so hot that night," she said, pulling at the neck of her sweater with her free hand. "We swam three times during the day just to cool off. Beth kept complaining about wanting air conditioning."

"What...? Oh... Is there anything I can do for you?"

"I wish she hadn't come. She always complained when we went camping. All she cared about were makeup and gross boys."

Gabriel lifted the hand not holding hers, feeling Ava's forehead before he realized his mistake. Oddly, she didn't strike out at him. He paused, waiting for her to get defensive. When she didn't, he felt her skin, found it slightly feverish.

He would have to talk to her about this, so he knew what to do for her. Currently, he was at a loss.

Brushing his fingers down her temple, he kept the hair out of her face. "What are you talking about, Ava? What's happening right now?"

On a sigh, she lifted her hand and pressed it against his. "Oh, Gabriel. I miss you."

"I'm right here."

She closed her eyes, pressed her face against his hand. The gesture was so innocent, yet he felt such deep emotion pouring off her. What the hell was happening?

"I don't want to go. Please don't make me go. Just a little longer, please."

The agony in her voice was heart wrenching. Gabriel wanted to help her, wanted to do whatever it took to take that sorrow away.

"Stay," he said. "Don't go. Stay with me."

"I miss your smell. You always had a special smell."

Ava let out a sudden exhalation, followed by gasping as if she had been choked almost to the point of passing out. At the patio door, both dogs sprang to their feet in surprise. Maya let out a whine. Ozzie barked twice. Ava straightened on the stool, putting distance between her and Gabriel. He let go of her hand.

"Breathe," he said.

She was coughing now. With a hand pressed to her chest, she stumbled off the stool and stood a few feet from the breakfast counter, bent over.

"What do you need?" Gabriel asked, walking around the counter. Ozzie was creeping closer. "Get back." The dog slunk back toward Maya.

As he neared Ava, her head shot up and she snarled at him.

"Settle down," he said nonchalantly, though his heart was thudding so hard he could barely hear anything else. He reached out and took the hand that was flailing. Settling his other hand on her shoulder, he guided her to the breakfast room table, where the chairs were more comfortable than stools. He left her to refill her glass of water.

When he returned to her side, he asked, "Do you take medication for this? Should I get your purse?"

"I do n-not take pills." Her voice was raspy. She sounded exhausted. She took a long drink of water.

"What is it? Epilepsy?" he asked, watching her. The pupils were back to normal. Some of her color was coming back. "Seizures?"

She tensed.

"I don't need to know details, but I need to know what to do for you when this happens."

She closed her eyes, took three deep breaths. "I will not burden you with this anymore. I never should have agreed to coming here."

Standing, she paused as a wave of dizziness hit her. She placed her hand on the table to steady herself.

"Don't do that," he said. "Don't run away because it's easier."

"I told you I do not run." She yanked her arm away from him.

"Yeah, that's what you said," he said wryly. "Telling yourself that may give you eight hours of sleep at night, but it's still bullshit."

Ava took a step away from the table, steadied herself, and walked toward the foyer to get her jacket and boots. Gabriel stood and followed her.

"You're not burdening me with anything. I just want to know what I can do to help you through it. Why do you quit every time you can't control every aspect of our friendship?"

She put her jacket on, zipping it angrily.

"God damn it, Ava, talk to me!"

Gabriel reached out and clamped his hand on her shoulder, deliberately tight. She reared up, her left arm twisting and drawing back against her body as she pulled it to her side, curling her hand into a fist. Gabriel had been ready when he reached for her, and he was prepared to get knocked on his ass. She struck out. He closed his eyes. It was going to be bad.

A puff of air rushed at his nose. Then nothing.

He opened his eyes. Ava's fist was less than one inch from his face. Her eyes were wild, as if she had barely been able to restrain herself.

"Go ahead," he said softly. His stomach pitched. His heart pounded against his rib cage. He kept his voice level and his eyes on hers. "Do it. You want to clock me because I'm trying to help you, go ahead. I'm still going to help."

She lowered her arm. "Why?"

"Because you're my friend, Ava. Friends are there for each other."

Her eyes, appearing ashen in the early morning sunlight, studied him for several moments. Gabriel knew she was trying to figure him out, trying to logically categorize his actions. When she was unable to, her shoulders slumped slightly.

"I do not want to talk about it. Ever."

"Fine," he said. "But I need to know what I can do when it happens."

"I cannot guarantee your safety."

"I'm not asking you to."

Her brows furrowed, then relaxed instantly. She didn't understand. But she said, "Try to get me as low to the floor as you can so I do not injure myself."

"Okay."

"If you speak, do so calmly. It does not matter what you say. If I can practice breathing exercises, I come out of it quicker. Maybe... encourage me to breathe."

"I can do that. Anything else?"

She thought for a moment, then shook her head.

"Outstanding." He cleared his throat. "You said something about wanting me to meet David?"

•   •   •   •   •

The sound made Griffin pause in the middle of the design he was working on. He was sitting on the couch with his laptop, trying to put in some extra time so his work week wouldn't be so long, and he thought he heard a cough. He glanced toward the bedroom door.

There it was again.

Setting his computer aside, he checked the clock on the cable box and figured Isabel wouldn't be too mad at him if he woke her up now. It was just past eight thirty. He could make coffee while she was getting dressed-

"No, don't!"

The sound of her voice, terrified, choked with tears, had him moving to the bedroom door. She was struggling in the bedding, having twisted herself so tightly her hands were bound in the fabric. Tears streaked down her cheeks even though her eyes were shut.

"Isabel," he said, walking around the bed.

"Don't go into the dark!" Another sob escaped her as she bucked, her midsection rising so high in the air she looked possessed. She slammed back onto the bed and kicked. Tied up in the bedding, she struggled as Griffin sat beside her and tried to get her untangled. She was thrashing her arms and legs and a quiet sound somewhere between a snarl and a scream was building until she jerked into a sitting position and let it out at top volume. It turned into a scream of pure terror.

"Isabel!" He took her shoulders, gave her a brusque shake.

Her eyes flew open, but she continued to struggle a few seconds more until her body caught up to what her mind was seeing.

"Griffin."

"That didn't look pleasant." He rubbed his hands up and down her arms. Her dull tone bothered him. In the silence that followed, he regarded her bleary eyes and tussled hair. She touched his arms as if she needed to verify he was really there.

"Do you want to talk about it?" he asked, already knowing the answer.

"No."

"I'll make some coffee." He shifted to stand, but her hands clamped down on his arms.

"Could you just-"

Griffin watched her let go of him, hug herself as if that's all she thought she would get. As if that's all she thought she deserved.

"What?" he asked gently. Trying to encourage her, he cupped her jaw, rubbed his thumb over her cheek.

"Could you maybe sit with me for a minute? Just a minute."

"All you ever have to do is ask."

He climbed over her to his side of the bed and leaned against the headboard. Pulling her against him, he felt her heart thudding madly and wrapped his arms around her. He would have wagered a year's salary she had been dreaming about her sister.

To ease her rigid posture, he ran his fingertips along her spine. After a few passes, she settled against him more firmly. He thought she was just about to relax when she put up that wall again.

"Sorry." She sat up. "I just needed to catch my breath."

"It's okay to ask for help, Isabel."

"Can we not do this today?" She slid to the edge of the bed and rubbed her eyes. "I don't have the energy to listen to you impart one of your wise life lessons. It's too early in the morning."

Standing took more effort than she cared to admit.

"You're still shaking. Come back. You weren't done."

"I have it under control." She'd placed a hand on the bedside table for support.

Because it embarrasses you if you don't, he thought.

"I know," he said aloud, keeping his tone casual. "I want to make out."

He wiggled his eyebrows, making her snort laughter.

Reaching up to her, he took her hand. "Sit with me."

She looked uncertain, but she sat down again and dropped her head on his shoulder. Her body was relaxed now even though she was still trembling; she sank into him with a sigh. Raising her right hand, she rested the palm against his chest so she could feel his heartbeat.

"I know I'm cranky when I get up anyway, but it's worse when I have a nightmare. Sorry."

"Thanks for saying that," he said, kissing the top of her head. "All is forgiven if you spend some time with me today."

"Aren't you sick of my crabby ass yet?" She gazed up into his eyes.

"Of course not." He tugged on the end of her hair. "What was the dream about?"

"I don't know. It was gone as soon as I woke up."

Sighing, she draped her long leg over his. He could tell she was being honest; her body had remained relaxed when she told him, and she hadn't hesitated before she spoke. It was probably better that she didn't remember.

"Have you been up long?" she asked, toying with his hair.

He glanced at his watch. "Almost an hour and a half."

Nudging him in the side, she started to sit up. "Why didn't you wake me up?"

He pulled her back down. "You don't like getting up early."

"I'm imposing on you in your apartment. I would get up at four AM to be out of your hair if that's what you wanted."

Wiggling against him, she laughed when he wouldn't let go of her.

"You're not imposing on me, Izzie. I like waking up next to you."

Surprise flashed through her when he tilted her face up and kissed her. The warmth of his hands drew goosebumps along her body where he touched: her shoulder, her back, her bottom. Isabel didn't think she would ever get used this. Someone willing to spend time with her without getting sex in return. Without asking for anything from her.

Her breath caught when Griffin captured her earlobe in his teeth and gently bit. The shudder that ran through her nearly pushed her over the edge. He trailed kisses along her jaw, back to her mouth, before he pulled back and gazed into her drowsy eyes.

"Shall I make some fresh coffee?" he asked, grinning.

"Coffee," she repeated, dazed.

"You're awake, then?"

"Every part of me is awake now," she muttered.

He kissed her again, and it warmed him to see her smile. "I'll go make that coffee."

She watched him leave the room, getting a beautiful view of his butt. When he returned a few minutes later, he had a tray with two mugs of coffee and a small bottle of French vanilla creamer that he set on the bed.

Isabel leaned up, tucking one leg under her. "You're so sweet."

Griffin poured some creamer into a mug and stirred, glancing at her to see if it was enough. She nodded. He handed it to her with another kiss. Isabel put her hand on his cheek when he pulled back

Closing her eyes, she breathed deep with the mug held under her nose. "This is my version of breakfast in bed."

"Are you glad you stayed?"

The smile she gave him was amused. "Absolutely. Your expensive coffee is way better than mine."

He feigned dejection. "That cut deep."

"I'm glad I stayed," she said soberly.

A little too glad, she thought. She didn't want to make it a habit. Waking up and having him there, especially after the residual feelings of the nightmare, had meant more than she could explain. She needed to be able to handle it herself.

Griffin kissed her in response, paused a moment. "Why don't you kiss me?"

"What? I always kiss you."

"You always return my kisses." He tugged on a lock of her hair.

"Isn't that the same thing?"

Not even close, he thought. If he never instigated another kiss, never held his hand out to her again, she would leave it at that. She would never reach out, because too many times she had, and her hand had been slapped away.

"Are you having dinner with your family later?" He nuzzled her affectionately.

Closing her eyes, she let her head fall heavily against his chest. "Ugh. Yes. I shouldn't be that way. I love my family. We actually had a good weekend last Sunday. My sister joined in when we played a song. She hardly ever does that."

"The violinist?"

She was surprised he remembered.

She nodded. "Beth. She's so good at it. You should see her face when she plays. She just... goes somewhere else. It's magical."

"That's how you get when you play your guitar."

Griffin wished she could see herself the way he did, all the wonder and beauty he saw every time he looked at her face. Even for just one moment, so she could have an idea.

He kissed the top of her head. "I have to meet my parents today, too. They're in Madison for a few days."

"That's good," Isabel said. Something she felt from his body told her he was not liking the idea. "Isn't it?"

She pivoted in his arms. His expression was guarded.

"What's wrong?"

Resting his forehead against hers, he sighed. "My parents and I had an argument on the phone a couple days ago and I don't want to see them."

Iz frowned. "That blows."

"I think we should fix things between us, but I'm too annoyed to deal with it right now. I'd rather spend the time with you."

Fluttering filled her stomach.

She took his face in her hands and smiled. The smile was sad. "That's sweet. But you're right; you should fix things. You might never get another chance."

An hour and a half later, Ava parked the Equinox beside an old farmhouse that had been well taken care of. It was almost due for a new coat of paint, but otherwise looked tended and clean. Gabriel and Ava got out of the SUV and Gabriel had time to glance around at the spacious yard, surrounded by plenty of fields and woods. Knowing Ava had been able to spend at least part of her childhood in this wide-open bliss made Gabriel feel a little calmer about her previous foster parents. He was having trouble letting that go.

A somewhat short man with salt and pepper hair – mostly salt – opened the front door and stepped out onto a low front porch. He was drying his hands on a towel. From the look he gave Ava, Gabriel was sure she hadn't mentioned them visiting.

"David," she said simply.

She walked up the two porch steps and gave him a hug. She was an inch taller, her long arms wrapping loosely around his shoulders.

Gabriel was astonished at how much emotion was conveyed in that simple gesture. This was a man she cared for deeply.

"Ava," David said. "I didn't realize you were coming."

"I brought a… friend." She motioned back toward Gabriel.

"Gabriel Harris," he said, standing on the bottom step and extending his hand. "It's a pleasure to meet you."

They exchanged a firm handshake.

"David Reid. Pleasure's mine. You must be somewhat tolerable if Ava brought you to meet me." There was amusement in his tone.

Gabriel returned the smile. "That's a compliment."

"It sure is."

"It is not a big deal," Ava said, walking pointedly past them both. "Where is Buck?"

"He's around here somewhere. Probably running in the woods."

"Who's Buck?" Gabriel asked, as Ava walked around the side of the house.

"My lab-mix. Ava gets along better with animals than with people."

He moseyed down the steps.

"I've noticed," Gabriel said. "So, you're her foster dad?"

"I'm her father," David said firmly.

Gabriel sensed this was a point of pride with him.

"I didn't mean to insult you," he said. "Ava calls you her foster father."

Surprisingly, that fact didn't seem to bother David. "Ava is absolutely honest. She doesn't call me her father because the definition of the word doesn't include a man not biologically related."

His explanation sounded so similar to the way Ava spoke that Gabriel smiled.

They walked in a lazy arc toward the back yard. "My wife and I started the adoption process after three months of fostering her. We wanted her to know stability, and she couldn't do that if she kept bouncing around in the system. She was the last child we fostered."

"I didn't realize you're married. Ava didn't-"

"Ruth died seven years ago. It's just me now. Ava was always closer to me, anyway. Well, as close as she can get to people. She loved Ruth in her own way, I think."

"I'm sorry."

David shrugged. "She had a good life. We had a good marriage, helped a lot of kids. She went peacefully. That's better than most get."

They were standing in the back yard now. Beyond a neatly clipped lawn was a field of tall grass. Ava was standing in the field. She let out a piercing whistle. A moment later a large black dog bounded out of the woods and ran toward her, barking happily.

"How much do you know about her?" David's voice was somber.

Gabriel thought of how comfortable he was getting with Ava, how he was starting to pick up on her moods and her wants by reading her body language instead of verbal communication. He thought of long spans of time when he didn't hear the sound of her voice, and how she never offered information about herself willingly. In many ways, their friendship was deeper than most because of the lack of verbal fumbling. In other ways, it lacked.

"Not much," he admitted. "She doesn't like to be touched. She has trouble sleeping. I wouldn't pick a fight with her."

David chuckled. "When she was ten, she beat the crap out of five high school guys for picking on a smaller kid one summer. The older boys were so embarrassed they didn't tell anyone. Ruth was terrified they'd come after her. I bet her twenty bucks Ava would win round two if they tried."

"Did they ever?"

"I seem to recall they crossed the street if they saw her after that. Never picked on the smaller kid again, either." He shook his head. "Ava didn't even know the kid she defended."

"She has more empathy and compassion for people than she'll ever admit."

David gave him a long, thoughtful look. "That's pretty insightful."

Gabriel didn't say anything, unsure how to answer. He watched Ava heave a stick for Buck to fetch.

David took a step forward and turned so he was looking directly at Gabriel. He was shorter by almost half a foot, but David's presence was abruptly ominous. "What, exactly, do you want from her?"

"I enjoy her company."

"Is that all you enjoy?"

"Jesus." Gabriel ran a hand through his hair. "I'm not having this conversation."

"Ava is perfectly capable of taking care of herself. If you're using her, you'll be sorry you thought you could get away with it."

"I know that."

"Do you?"

"She made that clear when she kicked some guy's ass in a restaurant. He was twice her size and outweighed her by at least a hundred pounds. She did it as easily as if she were pushing in a chair or sweeping a floor. I have no doubt that if I cross the line, she'll throw my ass back over it with more than broken bones."

David smiled, but he still looked weary. "You think I'm an asshole."

Gabriel looked over his head at Ava. She was standing with her arms folded across her chest, watching Buck run in the field. He returned his attention back to David. "I think you're a father."

They were silent for several moments.

"I'd be a damn liar if I said I didn't want more than friendship," Gabriel said. "I'm not blind. She's beautiful. She's intriguing. But there's something…"

David nodded. He understood.

"There's something," Gabriel repeated. He shrugged. "I'm not sure what she wants. I don't know if she knows."

David turned back so he was watching Ava and Buck, no longer challenging Gabriel. Relief settled over him. "And if she only wants to be friends?"

"I'm lucky she accepted me into her life at all. She's had a hell of a life for someone so young."

David shifted, seemed to consider something. He turned toward Gabriel again – not in confrontation this time, but to keep Ava from seeing his face. "I'm going to tell you something because I think you mean well, and I want you to understand Ava. I'm a good judge of people, and I get the sense you're a decent person. So, I want to explain to you why, if she can't be in a relationship with you... I want you to understand why that is."

Gabriel shoved his hands in his pockets. Despite being outside on a mild spring day, he suddenly felt suffocated in the tension. He instinctively knew he was about to hear something he didn't want to hear. Something probably related to the people who had given her the tattoo.

Ava was wrestling with Buck now, oblivious to the men and their conversation. Both woman and dog were lost and satisfied tackling and rolling in the tall grass. Gabriel thought he was seeing Ava as she may have been as a child before the abuse.

"Ruth and I are friends with a police officer in Verona. Sue Elliot. Good woman, great cop. In 2002, Sue and her partner took a call at what was believed to be an abandoned barn at the edge of the county. An anonymous call came in, someone heard screaming. Sue had trouble finding the place. It was an old building, roof caving in, mold, manure everywhere. She and her partner went in and secured the building. Sue found her."

Gabriel waited, feeling a chill deep inside him. The hairs at the back of his neck were stirring.

"We didn't find all this out until later, of course. Ava had just turned seven. She had been in the foster system since she was born. They kept having to move her from home to home because she had behavioral problems. The last legal foster family, the one before we took her in..." David wiped a hand down his face. "Ava was their last ward. They were having a lot of trouble with her, so they went online for help. There are people out there that offer to take troubled kids. Parents actually believe they're honest people with experience in dealing with kids with behavioral issues. They give their own kids away if you can believe it. They call it 're-homing' for God's sake, like a damn dog."

"That can't be legal." Gabriel was unable to accept parents would give their children away to a stranger. Especially to a couple that would mistreat that child.

"Of course not. Usually, the parents are at their wits' end, so they're easy marks. The people that take the kids are manipulative and know all the right things to say about whatever problem the parents are having with the kids. Anyway. I'm not excusing throwing your child away when things get tough. The foster family couldn't handle Ava and they 're-homed' her to a couple they found on the Internet."

Gabriel felt his stomach turn.

Ava and Buck were sitting on the edge of the lawn now, relaxing after their play. Ava had one hand on the dog's back. Her eyes were closed, her face lifted to the sun.

David shifted his weight. "The couple that took her were sadists. They had her for two years. When they were done with her, they left her in an abandoned barn. Sue brought us pictures. It was against procedure and everything she believed in, but she wanted us to see what had been done to that little girl. She wanted to make sure we wouldn't turn our backs on her like everyone else had."

"What was in the pictures?" Gabriel didn't want to know.

"Ava was chained to a wooden post. She was malnourished, dehydrated. Her ribs and spine were visible through the thin nightgown they'd put on her. She was so filthy..." David sucked in his breath.

Gabriel watched as Ava's eyes suddenly shot open and she stood, startling Buck. She turned and frowned at David. As if he sensed her looking at him, he turned toward her. He tried to smile, gave her a wave to let her know he was okay. After a moment of hesitation, she relaxed slightly. She leaned down to pet Buck.

"I swear that girl's got radar." David let out a shaky laugh, facing Gabriel again. "Anyway. We could see in the pictures that her wrists and ankles were raw from chains. Sue said Ava must have fought the entire time they had her in the barn. Hours, maybe days, she said. The chain cut down to the bone at one point on her wrist, but she was still fighting hours later... ah, shit."

David took a handkerchief from his pocket and wiped his eyes.

"Jesus Christ," Gabriel said. He wanted to punch something. Repeatedly.

David cleared his throat. "That little girl fought so hard; she broke her own wrist trying to get free. And that was just at the barn. She had two years of severe abuse before that. Those assholes took knives to her just to watch her bleed. Stun guns. I guess they got bored with her at some point and left her in the barn."

"They had "dog" tattooed on her inner thigh in Hebrew," Gabriel said softly. David looked at him sharply. "We're not having sex," he said quickly. He suddenly felt it crucial that this man know Gabriel wasn't taking advantage of Ava. "She showed me after she woke up screaming from a nightmare."

"It's a horrible sound, isn't it?" David asked. He ran a hand down his face again. "Every night, even years after we had adopted her, and she was adjusting better. I think sometimes she stayed up all night for our sake, so she wouldn't scream."

"What happened to the people who abused her?"

"They were arrested and put in prison. The woman committed suicide a few months later. The man was stabbed to death in his cell, I think. I thought it would make me feel better knowing that, but it didn't. It still doesn't."

Gabriel didn't feel better, either. It seemed unfair that nothing more could be done. Ava still had scars from what these people did to her, and they were just dead. What could anyone do with that?

"How did she learn to fight?" he asked.

"After she was released from the hospital, Sue put us in touch with the social worker assigned to her. For weeks she was like a zombie. Then one day... she snapped. I've never seen so much rage in such a tiny person. She attacked Ruth, damn near clawed her eyes out. I managed to get her arms pinned and told Ruth to drive. We took her to a young man I had known since he was a boy. Daniel Ward, a man who has been teaching martial arts since he was eighteen. He owns his own school now. Daniel took Ava from me and held onto her for three hours. She fought against him the entire time with everything she had. Tore some of the stitches out, although he did his best to keep that from happening. Finally tired herself out. Daniel told me to bring her to him every day for two hours a day and her training began. She never quit."

"Didn't he think it was dangerous to teach a kid with that much anger how to hurt others more efficiently?"

David laughed. "You've obviously never studied martial arts. The first thing taught in a traditional Japanese dojo is manners. Before a student ever learns a strike or a kick, she learns to show respect."

"Why the hell would Ava have any reason to respect anyone, especially a male, after what she had gone through?" Gabriel couldn't keep the bitterness from his tone.

"It had to be earned. For the first few weeks, every class I brought her in, Daniel held her down for two hours while she fought against him. He kept her from hurting herself, and he didn't have to beat her or torture her to do it."

David scratched his chin thoughtfully.

"Ruth had her doubts, too, but someone as smart as Daniel doesn't teach deadly techniques until the person is mature enough to know they're only used as a last resort."

Ava was kneeling beside Buck, stroking his coat slowly. She watched him with an expression Gabriel couldn't read.

"What those people did to her, all the things they did," David said, taking Gabriel's arm, "I haven't even scratched the surface. It's up to her to tell you the rest. Or not."

Gabriel nodded.

Ava was walking back toward them. Her face was flushed, her eyes clear. Buck trotted happily beside her. Gabriel watched her approach and thought of how disengaged she had been when she grabbed the woman at the restaurant and yanked her forward. How she had punched the woman's boyfriend in the throat without emotion. Could she be reached? He had felt her passion – had been a part of it – but could she truly be reached on an emotional level?

They walked toward the back door. A small ground level patio had three large plants on it with large, plastic-looking leaves. Ava brushed her fingers over the leaves as she walked past them.

They entered a dining room, which had a simple table for two. Buck immediately went to his water dish next to the door. Continuing to the kitchen, Gabriel saw remnants of David's wife in the pocket valance over the window and the old back splash, both in a country theme.

"Gabriel, would you like a root beer or something else to drink?" David asked.

"Sure."

David busied himself getting both he and Gabriel a bottle. "Do you need a glass?" When Gabriel shook his head, he grinned. "Good man." He handed Gabriel the bottle.

Meanwhile, Ava had gotten herself a mason jar out of the cupboard and turned on the faucet.

Not filtered water? Gabriel thought, just as David touched her shoulder and shut the water off. He walked to the refrigerator and took out a filtered water pitcher. The look Ava gave him was one full of such adoration that Gabriel could almost feel it across the room.

"You bought a pitcher just for me?" she asked, holding her mason jar while David filled it.

"It took me long enough." He glanced at her bandaged right hand. "What happened there?"

"I punched a hole in Gabriel's wall."

David seemed to accept this as easily as he would have accepted her telling him she didn't like peas.

Buck, having had his fill of water, walked over to Gabriel, and began sniffing his shins. Gabriel let him sniff, ignoring the dog while it familiarized itself with his scent. After several moments of sniffing and snorting, Buck wagged his tail and bumped his nose against Gabriel's hand. He leaned down and began scratching the dog's chest.

"Let's sit in the living room," David said. "There's more room in there."

He led the way through a double doorway into a large room with natural light streaming from a south-facing bay window. Gabriel sat on one end of an old, gray couch with a quilt draped over the back of it. Despite its age, it was surprisingly comfortable. Ava brushed her hand over the quilt and sat on the far end.

David sat in a recliner that looked like it was brand new when the house was built. It had been lovingly taken care of, but the cloth was worn smooth with indents where David sat. A cigarette burn was in one arm.

"I used to smoke," David said, following Gabriel's gaze. "I stopped as soon as we-" He glanced at Ava, who was petting Buck.

Ava raised her head to see why David had stopped talking and caught him watching her. She turned her attention to Gabriel. "The first time Ruth gave me a bath, she saw the cigarette burns on my back. David stopped smoking after that."

Though Gabriel felt as if his coffee was going to make a guest appearance, he said, "Just like that, you stopped? That's impressive."

David gazed at Ava with tenderness. "I wasn't going to have that reminder around her," he said simply. "After what those fu... after Ruth told me about the damage... it was easy to throw them away and never look back."

Gabriel was not surprised to hear the contempt in the older man's voice regarding her abusers.

Buck shifted over to Gabriel to get attention. His fur was slightly wiry, his muzzle mostly white. Everything on the farm was old, Gabriel thought as he petted the dog. Old and well used and loved. Gabriel was sure that if he hung around this man, he would hear some interesting stories.

They chatted for over two hours. Gabriel liked David's easy manner and gift of storytelling. His eyes sparkled when he talked about Ava. Gabriel thought Ava might reveal more around the person she seemed the most comfortable with, but she was just as introverted as she was in Langdon. She spoke little, listened intently, and only commented when spoken to. During the entire time they were there, Ava barely spoke at all.

Still, Gabriel enjoyed the visit. As Ava drove them back to Langdon, he replayed the conversation he and David had while Ava was wrestling with Buck. He was suddenly sure Ava had purposely given them the time to talk while she out of earshot.

• • • • •

During the drive home, the silence began to get to Gabriel. Ava didn't speak or turn on the radio. She had meant it when she said she didn't listen to any music.

He was beginning to get edgy.

"Will you come with me to dinner at my parent's house?"

His voice filled the vehicle and seemed extremely loud. He cleared his throat.

"It's... ah... nothing special. My family has dinner together every Sunday. It's my parents and my two sisters. We hang out for a few hours."

Ava was silent for several seconds. Gabriel wondered if he should explain again that it was just a friendly dinner, nothing to feel intimidated about.

"The house they live in," she said, "how long have they lived there?"

That was the last thing he'd expected from her. "We grew up there."

"You lived there when Hayden went missing?"

Strange, he thought. She was so damn strange. Why would she ask that? "Yes."

She exhaled heavily, as if to mentally prepare herself for something, then nodded. "I will go with you."

"Really?"

He hadn't expected her to agree, especially without some cajoling. If he were to be honest with himself, he didn't really know why he'd asked her.

"My parents have a huge house, but it will be both sisters, my sister's husband, and my mom and dad. Is that going to be too crowded?"

Ava gave him a sideways glance. "It is too crowded when you are around. But I tolerate you."

•　　•　　•　　•　　•

The smell of new growth greeted Gabriel as Ava turned her Equinox into his parent's driveway. They had taken her SUV because there was more room for her and the dogs. When he offered to drive so he didn't have to give her instructions to the house, she told him she "did not ride with people". Whatever that meant. She was familiar with the town, so a few miles to his parent's house wasn't a big deal. During the drive, she had seemed to anticipate which direction he was going to tell her to go and usually turned on the signal before he got a word out.

After all the rain from the night before, the day was shaping up to be sunny and warm. Patches of green were starting to poke through the dead grass. The trees had lost the brown, withered look they had during the winter and were now preparing for buds. There was a hint of chill in the shade, but in the direct sun, it was easy to be optimistic for a beautiful spring day.

Already his mother's pansies and violas were a bright splash of multiple colors around the front porch. March was almost over, and the early blooms had arrived. Finally, winter was making its retreat. By late-April, his mother's lawn would be perfectly landscaped and look like something out of Better Homes and Gardens.

The dogs began whining from the back seat as the scents became familiar.

It occurred to him that Ava might be intimidated by his family's wealth; Rachel, who was middle-class, had been nervous around his parents because of it. She was never quite comfortable in the big house.

At Gabriel's instruction, Ava eased the truck toward the back of the house. She seemed uninterested at the size of the property or the gorgeous early landscaping both his parents took such pride in. Her face was expressionless.

Gabriel had her park in front of the garage next to Jack and Beth's car.

"Beth is always here first," he said conversationally. "She's married to Jack. No kids yet."

Ava seemed to consider this intently, her brow furrowing. "It is hard for her."

"What is?"

But she had already opened the door and stepped out.

Gabriel let the dogs out and they barked happily, running toward the grass. He walked toward the house, watching Ava. If she was nervous, she gave no indication. Her lack of nerves made him slightly uncomfortable. What was his family going to think of her? Would they get along? Did Ava really get along with anyone? And why wasn't she fidgeting, like any other woman would be in her situation? He had been nervous to meet David. Whether a man was dating a woman or not, he was still usually a little unnerved if he met her father. Just as the father sized up any man his daughter was in contact with, whether they were sleeping together or not.

He opened the side door and let out a whistle to the dogs. Ava waited patiently while they ran to the door in a flurry of wagging tails and clicking toenails. They sprinted ahead through the rooms.

Stepping inside, Ava felt waves of emotion wash over her. She paused just inside the door, bracing her hand on the wall. Shadows of memories sped past her: children running in and out of the house, someone singing from the screened porch, Gabriel and his father cursing under the hood of a vehicle on a sweltering summer day in the garage. And darker shadows - a frail woman taking laundry out of the dryer and seeing a small shirt that had been tossed in accidentally, even though the child who wore it was no longer there. The woman wailing, plunging her face into the shirt, and sagging to the floor until her husband ran in and tried to comfort her. A young blonde girl hiding in this space, by the closet, because it was the quietest and no one knew she was missing anyway. She would sit and cry and rock until she had no more tears left.

Voices bombarded her, full of sorrow and guilt, rushing at her with the force of years of pain.

I wish I could help my family heal -

How can I reach my wife -

Baby where's my baby -

I miss her so much -

I couldn't protect my child -

Ava inhaled sharply. It was so hard, so consuming to be suddenly filled with emotions she was incapable of dealing with. They hit harder than any strike.

"Ava?" Gabriel realized she wasn't following him and turned back.

She thought about training in the dojo, how she was able to take whatever was happening in her life and completely shut it out once she began the class. When she was in her uniform and her foot hit that mat, the outside world disappeared. What made that happen? Her uniform? The building the dojo was in? The mat she trained on? The traditional Japanese routine her and Sensei performed before and after each training session?

Of course not.

It was all her frame of mind. Nothing physically kept her thoughts or her life outside the dojo walls. She simply shut off that part of herself and focused on the part that was survival, training.

Gabriel was watching her, concerned. "Are you coming?"

She nodded, took another deep breath. Exhaled. As she walked toward him, she imagined her clothes dropping away and her uniform sliding onto her body. She thought of the routine she performed across from Sensei: kneeling on the mat, bowing, speaking the words she spoke in Japanese, bowing again.

She was not in the dojo, and she could not change her clothes now.

Instead, she pulled herself back from the house, imagining it growing smaller below her, unable to affect her.

The voices, emotion, and shadows abruptly stopped.

Gabriel led Ava to the kitchen, where he knew everyone would be congregated as they waited to meet his friend. He had given them short notice, texting on the way over.

His mother and Beth were fussing over whatever they were cooking, their voices low. Jack was sitting at the island table, checking something on his phone. His dad was standing at the island holding a beer when they entered the room. He grinned when Gabriel and Ava entered.

"Gabe!" His voice boomed, delighted. He gave his son a strong hug. When he pulled back, he studied his son's mouth. "Hell of a shiner you got there."

"It's a long story," Gabriel said, not ready to admit to his father that he and Ava had spent the night together.

"Wanna beer?"

"Sure."

Gabriel's father had some gray in his thick hair, but most of it was the dark brown he'd passed onto his son. He also had the denim blue eyes, which were filled with affection when he pounded Gabriel on the shoulder.

"Jack, make yourself useful and get Gabe a beer," Josh Harris said cheerfully, turning toward Ava with his arms out. "Welcome-"

Too late, Gabriel realized he had forgotten to mention to Ava that his family was very affectionate. "Dad, she-"

Ava pivoted on her left foot and raised her right, so the edge of her boot was half an inch from Josh's throat. Her hands instantly became fists at her chest. "Do not touch me."

The room fell silent. Josh loomed over Ava and was built like a linebacker. Even in her boots, she barely came up to his chest. Still, her foot reached his throat and she held herself perfectly still, ready to strike. Josh froze with his arms out, ready for a bear hug. Everyone was staring at Ava. Ozzie and Maya slunk into the kitchen, sniffing at a safe distance.

"Dad," Gabriel finally managed, feeling as if time had stopped. "Ah...she's not used to hugs. I forgot to tell everyone."

He came to Ava's side, put his hand up so it hovered just above her shoulder. "Ava, he won't hurt you. We hug when we get together. It's a family tradition."

Isabel glided into the kitchen, almost dropping her guitar. "Sorry I'm late. My stupid car-" She noticed her mother's and sister's frozen postures, Jack's eyes the size of ostrich eggs, her father poised with the sharp edge of a black boot at his throat, and Ava's impressive defensive stance. She looked like she was doing the splits standing up. "What'd I miss?"

"Ava has trouble with physical affection. I was just explaining to her that we're a very affectionate family," Gabriel said, resting his hand on Ava's shoulder. His touch was feather light and he made sure not to grip her with his fingers.

Ava's eyes rotated in their sockets, so she was looking at him, but she kept her foot where it was. "Why?"

"Well, ah... I don't know. I guess that's just how we are."

Isabel cleared her throat. "Ava, this family knows all too well that life is short. We hug each other because each time could be the last time."

Ava had jerked her head slightly at the sound of Isabel's voice. Now she slowly lowered her foot. After a moment, she loosened her hands and placed them stiffly at her sides.

"We have no biological or emotional relationship, but embracing is a socially acceptable practice," she said to Josh. "I understand if you are driven to follow cultural habits."

Isabel snorted laughter.

"Does that mean I can give her a hug?" Josh asked, glancing at Gabriel.

"Yeah, Dad," Gabriel said, grinning. "You can give her a hug."

Ava accepted the hug stiffly, keeping her arms at her sides, and was relieved when he pulled back. She stepped back so she could see every entrance in the room and seemed to take inventory of everyone in it.

"I won't hug you," Isabel promised. "Excuse me."

Ava watched the dark figure from her apartment materialize behind her. She moved past Ava to set her guitar in the library. The dark figure followed her out of the room.

Beth cautiously came over to Ava. "Can I give you a hug?"

Ava looked bewildered and slightly irritated. She took a deep breath, let it out slowly. "Okay."

She remained rigid as Beth embraced her. Gabriel almost laughed at how uncomfortable she looked.

"I'm Beth, Gabe's older sister. This is my husband, Jack."

"I know."

Beth gave her a curious look, then shook it off as her being eccentric. The woman didn't look edgy, but she was trying to put as much distance between herself and everyone in the room as she could. Her brother had an odd taste in women.

"Do you like to cook?" she asked, trying to engage the stranger in conversation. "We're making honey glazed ham this weekend."

"I am capable of preparing my own meals," Ava said.

Beth glanced at Gabriel to see if she was joking.

Allie walked up behind Beth. "I'm Gabriel's mother. You can call me Allie. Can I give you a hug?"

"You, too?!" Ava was astounded.

Isabel snickered as she came back into the room. The semitransparent man followed her.

Ava accepted a quick hug from Allie. Taking a step back, she regarded them with suspicious eyes.

"You perform this ritual at the beginning of every visit with every person in the family?"

"Yes," Allie told her.

"How do you get anything else done?"

Isabel let out a cackle. "Oh, my God, Ava, you slay me."

Instead of hugging, Jack reached out and took Ava's right hand to shake it. "Nice to -"

Ava's legs parted and she gracefully slid to the floor into the splits position, retrieving her right hand from Jack and punching him in the groin with her left. The movements were sudden. Jack didn't realize what had happened for several moments. His body absorbed the shock first, and he took a step back before his legs gave out underneath him. He hit the floor hard, toppling over onto his side. Cupping his groin, he let out a low, breathless moan.

Ava lifted herself until she was standing over him. "Do not put your hands on me."

"Jack!" Beth shrieked. She ran to his side, kneeling and fussing over him.

"He was trying to shake your hand," Allie said, her eyes bulging. She knelt to help her son-in-law.

"You said you give hugs," Ava said evenly. She glanced at Gabriel. "What is wrong with your family?"

Gabriel was trying to not to laugh even though his balls ached in sympathy for Jack's. Isabel was leaning on the counter, almost in tears.

"This is not funny!" Beth yelled. "Now I'll never get pregnant!"

Ava narrowed her eyes and turned her head in a way that made Beth feel ridiculously inadequate. "The brief strike was not enough to cause permanent damage. He is not the problem anyway."

Beth glared at Gabriel. "What did you do, post our problems on social media?"

For a moment, he lost his sense of humor. "What? No, of course not. I haven't told her anything."

"What is she talking about, then?"

"You just announced it when you said you'd never get pregnant," he snapped.

"Why the hell did she punch him for trying to shake her hand? Who does that?" Beth turned back to Jack, who was trying to sit up.

"She was defending herself."

Trying to reign in his irritation now, Gabriel took a step toward Ava before he remembered she didn't need his protection.

"From a handshake?" Beth asked, helping Jack into a chair. "How stupid do you have to be to feel threatened by a handshake?"

"He put his hands on her without her permission." His own hands wanted to curl into fists. She was being ridiculous, lashing out when she didn't have the whole story.

Ava's eyes shifted to his and she tilted her head, studying him thoughtfully. The need to protect her blasted out from him in waves. Equally fascinating, she thought, was his anger toward his sister for talking to her that way. Ava felt a stirring in her chest at his compassion.

"I'm fine," Jack rasped. Taking Beth's hand, he squeezed it reassuringly. "Less stress, remember? Try to relax, honey."

"Let's all just settle down," Josh said, raising his hands.

"This was a bad idea," Gabriel said, turning to Ava. She looked almost bored. "I should never have brought you here."

"Hold on," Allie said. "We got off to a bad start. Let's just all take deep breaths and calm down. Ava, would you like something to drink?"

"Did everyone forget my husband's groin was just assaulted?" Beth wailed. Her cheeks were bright red, her eyes threatening tears even as the anger filled them.

"Beth, quit hovering," Jack wheezed. "Just give me a damn minute."

"Yeah, fine," she snapped. She stalked to the island and picked up her glass of wine. "I'm the crazy one."

Allie exhaled and turned her attention back to Ava. "Ava, would you like a beer or a glass of wine?"

"I do not drink alcohol."

She stood apart from everyone, her eyes roaming the room, taking in everyone's position. Beth was glaring at her, but Ava had no interest in her. She was studying the dark man hovering near Isabel, his sad eyes watching her intently.

"Recovering alcoholic?" Beth sneered. She brushed her light brown hair back from her flushed face.

"Stuff it, Beth," Isabel shot at her.

"I do not use mind-altering substances," Ava answered simply.

"How about an iced coffee, tea, or a soda?" Allie opened the refrigerator in anticipation.

"Water, please."

"Well, la-di-dah," Beth said.

Ava felt Gabriel's anger beside her and gazed at him again. He was glaring at his sister, his contempt for her vibrating off him. She suddenly felt the urge to comfort him, to let him know she was not bothered by this stranger's illogical emotions.

She turned her attention back to Beth. "Your attempts at insulting me are only valid if your opinion matters to me. It does not."

Iz snorted.

Ava brushed her hand against Gabriel's, surprising him. He glanced down as she curled her hand into his palm, resting it there.

"Honey, cool it," Josh said, patting Beth's arm. "Just calm down. It was a misunderstanding."

"We're having enough trouble," Beth hissed. "This could set us back or even end things permanently."

"For fuck's sake, Beth, you were having trouble before Ava punched him in the nuts," Isabel said. She walked to the wine fridge. "Who knows? It might just be an improvement."

Gabriel barked out laughter. Jack, still somewhat wheezy, joined him.

"Well, I'm glad this is all so goddamn hilarious to all of you," Beth said, her voice breaking. She stormed out of the kitchen.

"Isabel, you know she's sensitive about the subject," Allie scolded. "And really? Do you have to be so crude with the way you talk?"

Next to Gabriel, Isabel's body began to tense.

"I'm sorry," Jack said to Ava. "She shouldn't have spoken to you like that."

Ava leveled her gaze at him. "She is being irrational. Her misdirected anger has nothing to do with me."

Jack was still squirming in the chair, but color had returned to his face, and he was able to talk a little easier. "Well, that's... a very logical way to think of it."

"I am a logical person."

Isabel giggled.

"I didn't mean to startle you," he said, slowly holding out his hand this time. "I didn't think you would appreciate another hug."

She gripped his hand firmly after only a slight hesitation. "Hello."

"Oh, sorry." He let go quickly. "I didn't realize you'd injured your hand. What happened?"

"I punched a hole in Gabriel's wall."

"She did?" Isabel asked, turning to her brother.

"It was outstanding." He grinned at her. "Probably would have gone through to the joists if I hadn't stopped her."

"Is that what happened to your jaw, too?" Iz asked, tilting her head as she studied the bruise.

Gabriel nodded. "I touched her without her permission."

When it happened, he'd been surprised, even angry, but as he looked back on it, he felt a surge of pride that she could defend herself.

His parents and Iz were dying to hear more, but no one pressed the issue.

Jack continued talking to Ava. "We're trying to have a baby and we're running into some issues. It's been a difficult year. I hope you don't hold my wife's emotions against her."

"It appears you do not hold my striking you in the testicles against me."

322

Isabel and Gabriel looked at each other and snorted like ten-year-old children.

"Being thrown into the family can be pretty overwhelming."

Allie held out a glass of water for Ava. Gabriel watched Ava carefully avoid his mother's hand as she took the glass.

"Thank you." She turned to Jack. "I do not understand mankind's obsession to fondle each other."

"People are social." Jack motioned around the room with his can of beer. "Look at us. We gather often. We like to touch, to reassure."

Unable to keep from grinning once he saw Iz was doing the same, Gabriel pulled out a stool from the island table for Ava. She didn't tense when he laid his hand on her shoulder, he noticed. When he sat on the stool next to her, she scooted closer to him, so she was sitting between his knees, turned slightly toward him. He rested a hand on her leg.

"People incessantly speak of how social humans are," Ava said, continuing to scan the room.

"I must be defective," Isabel said, plucking a grape out of the tray set in the middle of the table.

The shadow next to her was growing stronger from the sorrow that filled the room. There was so much of it, his body was pale but visible from head to foot. He studied Isabel with fascination. Twice he reached out toward her. Both times he withdrew before his hand passed through her.

Ava was having trouble blocking him out. She turned her attention to Isabel to try to ignore the form.

Isabel sat next to Jack. That was the only available spot left since Josh sat at the head of the small table. Even though it was the only place left to sit, she lowered her eyes, her shoulders slumping, as if she was apologizing to Jack tolerating her. Jack squeezed her shoulders affectionately and Ava watched Isabel's face light up even as she flushed.

The dark man gave her one last, wistful glance at Isabel and vanished.

"Our family gathers here every Sunday," Josh said, plucking a cube of cheese off the tray, and popping it into his mouth. "It's something Allie and I have maintained over the years, even after the kids all grew up. Our family stays close."

Beth came back into the kitchen, watching them sullenly. Allie motioned to her own glass of wine. Beth nodded. As Allie began refilling both their glasses, Jack leaned forward.

"What about your family, Ava? Do you get together often?"

Gabriel felt Ava tense. Underneath his hands, she was statuesque. "I visit my foster father."

"We were just there earlier today," Gabriel said, lightly rubbing his thumb back and forth across Ava's knee. "He's great."

Beth leaned against the counter, watching Ava. She noticed the change in Ava's posture and, feeling vindictive, wanted to pay Ava back for humiliating Jack. Now she had a chance.

"What about siblings?" she asked, sipping her wine casually.

"I have none."

As the voices grew in volume, in her mind, she slipped just a little, sinking closer to the image of the house she was hovering above. The closer she came to the house, the louder the echoes of the voices became. She imagined kicking back up as if she were swimming until she could not hear them.

"No foster kids you became close with? No one you liked more than the others?"

Ava said nothing, as she felt she had already answered.

Beth added more wine to her glass. "That's unusual for the state to let a man take in a female foster kid, isn't it? Against the rules, or something?"

"I am not familiar with the regulations of Wisconsin's adoption policies." There was an edge to her voice now.

Her muscles were tightening under Gabriel's palm. He had to find a way to steer the subject from her childhood. Beth was obviously picking a fight; he could see it in her eyes and hear it in her tone. If he knew it, he was sure Ava did, too.

Ava gazed at Beth, her gray eyes dark, her face impassive. She waited for Beth to look away before turning to Gabriel.

"Where is your bathroom?"

"I'll show you." He stood.

"The ham has quite a bit longer to cook," Allie said as Gabriel and Ava were leaving. "Let's move to the living room while we wait to eat."

Gabriel led Ava into the long addition connecting the house to the garage, where they had come in when they first arrived.

"Sorry about Beth. She's been a real bitch lately."

The restroom was across from the exit leading onto a screened porch. He flipped on the light for her and turned to step out, surprised to find her standing right in front of him just outside the doorway.

"Whoa."

Her eyes, so odd, studied him so intently, roamed his face. His heartbeat kicked into high gear.

"What are you looking at?" he breathed.

Seizing his shirt, she pushed him into the bathroom and kicked the door shut, spinning him around, and slamming him back against it. Before he could catch his breath, she was pressed against him, assaulting his mouth. He tasted greed and hunger on her tongue as well as the sweet, crisp blast from the grapes she had eaten earlier. Her hands raked through his hair.

Gripping her hips, he pulled her against him, hardly able to think as his hands formed around her, claimed her as his. His mouth found her pulse raging in her neck and skimmed the surface from ear to collarbone, hearing her quick gasps as she ran her hands under his shirt to find flesh. The rough texture of her bandaged hand scraped against his chest. His pulse was pounding. He couldn't hear anything but that growling-purring sound she was making again. Her mouth found his again, briefly, aggressively.

And suddenly, she placed her hands on his chest and shoved herself away from him. She stood staring at him, breathless, her shoulders heaving. After a moment, she grabbed his shirt again, pulled him forward as she simultaneously opened the bathroom door, and shoved him outside. Before he realized what was happening, she had slammed the door in his face.

Gabriel stood staring at the door, stunned. His heart was racing. The sound of his own breath tearing through his lungs amazed him.

Shaking his head, he started toward the living room to join his family, smiling.

"Well, fuck."

What else was there to say?

• • • • •

Things settled down, Gabriel thought, when conversation started in the living room before the meal. They had left the couch open for him and Ava. He sat on one end, making sure she had enough room and didn't feel he was crowding her. The room was a straight shot from the kitchen through two rooms, so Ava would easily see and hear them once she was finished in the restroom.

At first, standing in the doorway, no one noticed her. Gabriel didn't know how long she stood there, but Isabel finally said her name, startled. Everyone turned to look at her. Iz invited her in.

Gabriel felt every drop of liquid in his mouth dry up. She had such a presence about her. That thick, dark hair flowed down her back and shoulders; those intense eyes captured every detail in the room. Knowing how she felt in his hands, Gabriel felt a flush of heat as he watched her cross the room toward him.

She set her glass of water on the coffee table and sat on the couch. Gabriel was surprised at how close she sat; they weren't touching, but she was only six inches away from him. Usually, she sat as far from him as possible.

As conversations started again, she sat silently, watching everyone else talk. Gabriel was trying to follow Isabel's conversation, but he was distracted. Beth and Jack were talking with her parents about their first appointment with a doctor to see if the problem was with her or with him. Then Isabel heard what they were talking about and started listening in.

Allie checked her watch. "Come into the kitchen with me, honey. I have to check the meal."

Jack stayed behind while his wife and mother-in-law disappeared to the kitchen to work their magic.

"You finally made an appointment," Isabel said.

Jack nodded. "I think that's why she's extra..." he glanced at Josh, "... frustrated. She's afraid she's defective."

"She thinks being unable to bear children makes her less of a woman."

He glanced at Ava, thoughtful. "Yes. It doesn't, and it doesn't make her any less of a person, or any less beautiful, to me. But she won't see it that way."

"You are a compassionate person." Ava found herself feeling something awkward about this man she had just met. It made her chest feel like it was filling to the point of bursting, and her eyes wanted to water.

"What about adoption?" Isabel asked. "Have you considered that?"

"As a last resort, yes." He rubbed a hand down his face. "She wants to carry one and give birth, if she can."

"I hate that this is happening to you, Jack. You're such a sweetheart." Isabel rubbed her hands up and down her arms.

"Unfortunate events happen to everyone," Ava said. "Your opinion of his character does not make him immune to negativity."

Iz studied her. "I know. But people all over the world pop out kids like Pez dispensers and they don't even want them. They treat them like burdens. People should be able to have children when they want them and will actually raise them."

Ava gazed at her. Her gray eyes were unreadable.

Allie and Beth came back into the room. "We have about ten minutes left."

"What about you, Ava?" Jack asked. "Do you want children?"

Isabel was relieved when Ava's eyes shifted to Jack's. She didn't know why, but Ava's eyes had spooked her for a moment. They were so direct, so probing.

"I guess I should ask if you have any, first," Jack said. "I didn't mean to presume anything."

He was waiting, his arm around Beth's waist. Ava noticed everyone in the room was looking at her expectantly. They were so odd, she thought. They asked so many questions. They were so interested in her, a stranger. Gabriel barely knew her, yet his family so willingly accepted her into their circle.

"I cannot have children," she said. Beside her, Gabriel jolted.

Isabel suddenly wished for whiskey. Her mother had some on hand for her, but she didn't want to leave the room. Ava must be devastated. And what did Gabriel think? Seeing the shock on his face, she guessed this was the first he was hearing of it.

"I'm so sorry." Jack's hand rubbed his wife's side.

Beth's face had gone pale.

"Your sorrow is unnecessary. It was never a choice for me." She leaned over, brushed at the leg of her jeans absently. When she sat up, everyone was staring at her. Not with curiosity now. With pity. The sadness pressed down on her, so heavy she felt she would buckle under it.

Think of training. Think of rising above the emotion.

In her mind, she kicked her way up, up, away from the house below her until the emotions and voices fell away.

"Why... why can't you have children?" Beth asked. Her voice was barely above a whisper.

Ava leaned forward to retrieve her water. As she sat back, she crossed her legs casually. "There has been too much trauma to my reproductive organs to support conception and incubation."

Josh choked on his drink and started coughing.

"Oh, my God," Allie said.

"Holy fuck." Isabel felt like she was going to throw up.

Jack sat up in his chair so fast he almost knocked Beth off the arm, where she sat, crying silently.

Gabriel said nothing, only reached toward her with his palm up. Ava surprised him by resting her hand in his, her eyes widening slightly in surprise. The warmth radiating off her was fascinating to him.

Suddenly, her eyes darkened. She winced, put a palm to her temple. "Stop."

"What's wrong?" He moved his thumb back and forth across her fingers.

"Stop feeling sorry for me." She raised her other palm to her temple and pressed. "It is too loud. You are all too much at once."

Gabriel touched her elbow. "Are you okay?" He kept his voice low.

Ava stood suddenly. "I need water." She closed her eyes, shook her head slowly, as if she heard something high in pitch. "Does anyone else need their drink refilled?"

"Ava," Isabel said. "Forget about the w-"

"I need to leave the room," she said shortly. "Your sorrow is suffocating."

She slipped quietly away. After a moment, Gabriel followed her.

In the kitchen, she was chugging her water at the sink. She stiffened when he entered the room.

"Hey." He walked toward her but stopped several feet away. "I'm sorry. I didn't realize you can't have children."

Reaching into the refrigerator, she pulled out a cold bottle of water this time. She set her glass to the side.

"I cannot regret a choice I never had." She shook her head again, tried to get rid of the lingering emotions. It was too hard to imagine herself pulling back, of rising above the house. She had lost the control and could not seem to get it back.

"It upsets you."

"You are mistaken." Ava took a step toward him. "Your pity is upsetting. It is... heavy."

She opened the bottle of water without taking her eyes off him. "I told you I am not a good mate. I am unable to carry on your lineage."

His first thought was how normal her unique speech patterns were becoming to him. He was getting used to the way she voiced her thoughts, the way her mind worked. His second was that he should have run in the opposite direction at her mention of them having children together, but he wasn't even startled at the thought. She was a direct person. Being blatantly honest, no matter how abruptly the message was received, was the only way she knew how to be.

"There are other options," Gabriel said. "It's a little early in the friendship to be discussing children."

"You want to know what caused the damage."

He flinched. "I would never ask you that."

"But you want to know." She took another step toward him. "Your family is curious. They ask questions, always asking." She pressed her fingertips to her temple, wincing. "Now they are sad because they do not like the answers. You will not like the answer to your question. Do you still want to know?"

Mesmerized, he nodded.

"My foster father sexually abused me. He was violent."

She felt the rage and horror slice through him; he had been suspicious, she could see, but to have that suspicion confirmed somehow made the knowledge worse. His mind was recoiling from the truth, struggling to understand it. Ava felt a shudder, and the emotions inside him settled to a simmer of furious sorrow.

"I'm sorry to interrupt," Allie said from the doorway, trying not to let on that she had heard Ava. "I need to take the ham out."

"Excuse me." Ava moved away from the island table to get out of her way. "May I assist?"

"I've got it covered." Allie glanced at Ava, reconsidered. "You know what? You can set the table. Plates are-"

She watched, surprised, as Ava walked to the cupboard and pulled out a stack of plates. As she took the ham out of the oven and was getting the side dishes ready, she noticed Ava went to the cutlery drawer as if she already knew where the spoons and forks were kept.

Odd, Allie thought, moving around the young girl easily. Odd but polite. A little jumpy, but Allie knew why now. Who wouldn't be after being raped?

"Gabe," she said over Ava's head, "Let everyone know it's time to eat."

329

• • • • •

By the time Isabel was getting ready to leave her family's house several hours later, she was exhausted. It had been the weirdest Sunday dinner ever. After the meal, they had played their instruments. Beth had played a mournful solo by Ji Pyeong Kwon that had Ava sitting at her feet, listening intently. Iz and Gabriel played a few songs that equally delighted Ava, and Beth joined in. After the initial awkwardness, the evening had gone quite well.

Before Isabel left their driveway, she checked her phone and saw Griffin had left several messages.

"Shit," she muttered. She texted him a quick note to let him know she would be at his apartment in forty minutes and started driving.

She had completely forgot to let him know she would be late coming over tonight. The last thing she anticipated was staying late at her parent's house, but having Ava there made it much more interesting. The more she learned about Ava, the more she liked her.

"Fuck," she said to the empty car. "I totally suck at this girlfriend shit."

When she reached Griffin's apartment, she checked her phone again. He hadn't texted her back. That couldn't be good. Did he even want her here now? Several scenarios ran through her head as she walked up the stairs to his apartment, all of them ending with him telling her some version of her being a selfish bitch that he never wanted to see again. She knocked on his door with unsteady hands.

It took several moments for Griffin to answer the door, and when he did, he had his phone up to his ear. He stepped back so she could come in and shut the door behind her a little too hard. Isabel jumped.

"I understand that," he said. His tone was oddly formal, nothing like how she was used to hearing him talk. "No."

Isabel set her purse on the island and sat down on a stool, wincing when Griffin pulled a glass out of the cupboard and set it on the counter without looking at her. He pulled out a bottle of wine absently and poured some in the glass, then slid the glass over to Isabel with barely a glance.

Fuck, she thought. This is bad.

"No, that's what you decided. I listened while you talked at me." Griffin lifted his own wine glass and downed the rest of it. He finally looked at Isabel.

She mouthed, Do you want me to go? and motioned toward the door. With that same absent look, he shook his head.

"This may come as a surprise to you," he said into the phone, "but I'm twenty-seven years old and perfectly capable of making my own decisions." After a beat: "I said no."

His fingers were tightening on the cell phone. Isabel was stunned to see his other hand curled into a fist on the counter. He was quiet for a long time, then suddenly barked, "Yeah, and look where that got him!"

He hung up his phone, stared at the screen for a moment, and then winged it across the room. It crashed into the wall and fell to the floor. Isabel jumped. She watched him silently as he turned away from her and stood with his hands on the counter, his muscles flexing. She didn't know what to do. Should she try to comfort him, or had she messed up beyond repair by ignoring him most of the day?

He exhaled loudly and turned toward her. His eyes had returned to that warm, honey color she was used to, and his easy smile was back in place.

"How was dinner? Was it as bad as you thought it would be?"

Iz had to take a moment for her head to catch up to the sudden change in attitude. "I'm so sorry I ghosted you." The words tumbled out rapidly. "I got so caught up, and Gabriel invited a mutual friend who doesn't... understand social behavior. I didn't mean to ignore you."

Griffin blinked. "You don't have to apologize. So, it went well?"

She nodded. "It was highly entertaining."

He wrapped his arms around her, burying his face in her hair. "See? You had nothing to worry about."

"Are you okay?" Isabel asked. She felt a power shift, as if he needed reassurance from her.

"Hmm?" He poured himself another glass of wine.

"I think you broke your phone against the wall."

Glancing over at it, he waved a hand dismissively. "I'll buy a new one. Have you eaten?"

"I just had dinner with my family."

"Right. I knew that." He ran a hand through his already messy hair.

"Griffin, who were you talking to? I've never seen you so upset."

"I'm sorry I didn't handle that better. My parents sometimes think they can run my life. Or at least my mother does."

Because she felt the impulse, Isabel stood and gave him a strong hug. Griffin was at first surprised, then held on as if she were the last life jacket on the Titanic. Iz could feel the tension start to drain from him. His shoulders, tight and pulled inward, slowly eased down. What the hell were his parents trying to control that had upset him so much?

"I'm really glad you're here."

The words lit her up from the inside.

"Me, too," she said.

Inhaling deeply, Griffin gave her a final squeeze before releasing her.

"Your visit didn't go well?" she asked, watching him refill his glass. The wine was heavy tonight, and dry, she realized, as she finally took her first sip. He must have really been having a bad night.

"It made me thankful I only see them three or four times a year."

Iz winced. She knew what that darkness felt like.

Agitation stirred inside her. It was too easy for her to empathize with the emotions of others, especially the negative ones. She felt the darkness begin to pull her down.

"It's not for you to worry about," Griffin said, kissing her forehead. "I shouldn't have said anything."

"Of course, you should. Everyone needs to blow off steam to someone."

"I'm better now that you're here. Just being near you helps." He draped his arm around her shoulders in that way he did, making her feel both adored and like a sports buddy. "Do you have to leave, or can you stay a bit?"

"I should get ready for the work week," Isabel said, looking up at him. His eyes darkened. He looked disappointed. "But... I can come back if you want."

"Yeah?" He grinned. The amber in his eyes cleared, and for the first time since entering the apartment, Isabel saw that perpetual hope he always carried in them return.

"Sure. If you want."

He grabbed her arms and pulled her up on her toes, covering her mouth with his. It was meant to be a quick, reassuring move, but he slid an arm around her and banded them together, deepening the kiss until she was drunk with it.

"I want," he murmured against her lips. He set her back on her feet. "Do you want me to go with?"

"You don't have to."

"I know I don't have to. Do you want me to?"

This time she shook her head. "I'll be faster if you're not there to distract me."

He wiggled his eyebrows, making her laugh.

"Hey," he called, as she was heading for the door. She turned back. "Maybe you can bring some extra clothes and stay the night."

"Maybe."

•   •   •   •   •

"What do you think?" Gabriel asked as Ava parked her vehicle in his driveway. "That wasn't too terrible, was it?"

The sun was almost below the horizon behind Ava, spilling shadows over her. She was turned slightly in the seat, so she was facing him, but her expression was hidden.

"May I have a glass of water?"

Her voice was low.

"Of course. Come on in."

Despite the coming darkness, the temperature was still in the forties. Gabriel crossed to the front porch thinking the light jacket he was wearing felt much less constricting than the heavy winter coat he'd had to wear just a few days ago. It wouldn't be long before he would have to start mowing the lawn and trimming trees. He loved this time of year. Would Ava visit more often this summer? He hoped he would have won her trust by then, that she would sit with him on the back deck during sunsets and join him when he and Isabel hung out.

She walked with him, frowning when he entered his house without unlocking his door. His unwillingness to protect his belongings and – more importantly – his privacy was infuriating.

When she hung her jacket next to his, he was somewhat surprised. Did she want to stay longer than it took to drink the water? He loved her company, but figured she'd had enough of him for one day.

While he prepared her ice water, she walked around the counter between the kitchen and the breakfast room, leaning back against it on her elbows. She looked out the large windows of the breakfast room at the back yard. It was almost completely dark now.

"Why do you leave your door unlocked?"

The edge in her voice surprised him. The tension had been building over the past hour; she had been a bundle of nerves after he and Isabel had played their last song after dinner.

He walked around the counter with both their waters. She didn't move to take hers, only looked up at him, so he set the glasses on the counter.

"Langdon has thirteen hundred people in it," he said, hooking his thumbs into his belt loops. "I live in the country, outside of town. Sometimes I forget."

The energy coming off her was almost tangible. He could practically feel her humming from it. There was a challenge in her eyes that hadn't been there before.

"Your doors were unlocked when I slept here?"

"I locked them because you were here."

Unsure what had her so upset, Gabriel waited for her to explain herself. She was flushed, though she leaned against the counter in a relaxed position. Her eyes were scanning her surroundings restlessly. What the hell had set her off? Locking his door couldn't be the real reason; she had started fidgeting at his parent's house.

"Seeing you with your family... I felt..." She searched for the words, frowned. "...kindred."

"That irritates you?"

"Yes." She practically spat the word. "I have taken precautions to keep from forming relationships with people. My attraction to you is illogical."

With that lazy smile she found so appealing, he leaned against the wall near her. He could feel the heat between them. And was impressed when she didn't pull away or raise her hands in defense.

"Logic has nothing to do with attraction." He bumped her foot with his.

She frowned, trying to figure out why he did it. It served no purpose. It was not done hard enough to move her out of his way. He had not injured her to make a statement, or to defend himself. He had touched her simply to make contact.

She kicked him back, a little too hard. The feeling in her stomach was one of comfort. The flutter in her chest... she did not know. So many new emotions were swirling inside her.

Gabriel shifted so he was standing in front of her, giving her plenty of space, but wanting to see her face. The way the expressions quickly appeared and disappeared as she contemplated was fascinating. He watched her try to work out his silly gesture in her head. He could see her trying to rationalize it, concentrating so hard, he almost laughed.

She lifted her eyes and studied him intensely, still a little pissed. Reaching up with her bandaged hand, she gripped his shirt, pulling him slowly but deliberately down to her. Her mouth was on fire and lit his as she explored it. Head spinning, his hands came up automatically to cup her elbows as he eased forward to press his body against hers.

She seemed to be feeding off him, her movements measured yet despairing. The hand not grasping his shirt slid from his shoulder to the back of his neck, clutching his hair possessively. I want, that grip said, and it was as much a stimulant as her tongue teasing his. If he didn't watch it, he would lose himself in the madness of taking her. He pulled back while he was still able.

"Wait," he panted. Disappointment flickered across her face. "Slow down."

Their faces were inches apart, worlds apart.

"I don't want to hurt you."

"You cannot hurt me." She stood slowly but stayed against the counter. Letting go of his shirt, she kept her hand on his chest, resting flat against the thudding of his heart.

He leaned his forehead against hers. "I want to rip your clothes off and fuck you right here on the counter. Just give me a minute to settle down."

She moved her other hand so both palms were on his chest now. She shoved with just enough attitude to put a little space between them but not enough to send him flying across the room, which she was perfectly capable of doing. "So, rip my clothes off."

"Ava, your first time shouldn't be like that."

She tilted her head just slightly, looking at him like she was studying a bug under a microscope. "Why would you think it is my first time?"

Caught off guard, he stepped back. Of all the responses he had anticipated that one hadn't made the list. "I mean... I know it's not technically you're first time... You told me you were... abused..." Dammit, he was fucking this up.

Her lack of expression was maddening. "So?"

"The first time you make love by choice should be special and... gentle." His hand ran down the back of his neck. "It should be in a bed, taking it slow, not on a kitchen counter like an animal."

"You are under the impression I have not had consensual intercourse as an adult."

It wasn't a question.

For a moment, he was speechless. When he could find his voice, he couldn't find the right words. "You don't like to be touched. After what you told me about your abusive foster parents, I assumed..."

"You assumed wrong."

"Jesus Christ, Ava."

Again, she had rendered him silent. She could do that to him; say something so simple that stopped his train of thought cold.

How could she be so nonchalant about this? When he first met her, she couldn't even stand for him to be close. She had done everything she could to keep him at a distance. As she began to get used to him – he wouldn't go so far as to say she warmed up to him - she softened, so very slowly. She stiffened if he brushed against her and still reacted as if he was attacking her. The way he gradually touched her, working from an accidental brush of fingers to deliberate caress, was a result of him thinking she had no positive experience in that area. He had been so careful. The last thing he wanted to do was anything that would remind her of the abuse.

"You are angry at me for having sex before I met you." Her tone was emotionless, her eyes guarded.

"No. It's your life. I feel like an ass for misunderstanding this whole time." He didn't know what to feel. He was embarrassed, but mostly stunned. She had changed directions on him yet again.

"I control the few urges I have," she said. "Sometimes, the most primal of them need satisfied. A few years ago, I chose a partner who understands that physical release is all it will ever be. I never wanted it to be more than that."

Gabriel wasn't sure what to think about that, either. "Is that a warning? 'Don't bother pursuing you; I'll never be more than a fuck buddy?'"

"It is a fact. I have never-" She was staring at him, her eyes intent. "I have never felt attracted to another human being before. David and Isabel explained to me that is what I feel when I am near you."

He straightened, raised an eyebrow. "You talked to Isabel? About sex?"

Though the house was spacious and open, Ava suddenly did not have enough room to breathe. She stepped away from him.

"I do not have anyone," she said. She lifted her head. "I did not have anyone to ask... what the feelings are inside me. I do not process emotions well. She was kind to me."

The purely Neanderthal, egocentric part of him wanted to beat his chest in triumph that she was attracted to him. Especially if she had never been attracted to men before. Was that possible? Never? Was that because of the abuse?

She walked toward the breakfast room with her arms folded across her chest.

"I do not want to... crave you."

He couldn't help but feel satisfied that she returned his attraction. It was so hard to tell with her. One minute she was looking at him like he was a juicy prime rib and the next she was literally slamming the door in his face. Hearing her say it out loud gave him a stab of pure testosterone-filled pride.

Sometime while he was lost in thought, Ava had walked across the room and was now standing in front of him. She leaned up and touched her lips to his, just a light dance. Gabriel brushed his knuckles gently down her neck, feeling her pulse quicken, her breath catch. He slid his hand around to cup the back of her head and took the kiss deeper, drawing her against him. Firm body, soft skin, eager mouth. He felt her surrender a little of her careful control.

Grasping his sides, Ava held on and let herself get lost in him. Their bodies were pressed close together and the air seemed to crackle with energy. As heat coursed through her, as she raked her hands through his hair, she didn't see images this time. The vision came not in flashes but as if she were living the experience.

Gabriel was above her in the vision, moving with her. Her legs were wrapped around him, and her hands clutched his forearms. She smelled his unique scent, felt every thrust. They were moving as if in slow motion, but her heart was racing. They were on a bed she didn't recognize, one with a headboard that had decorative spindles. Each thrust sent dizzying sparks of sensation the entire length of her body.

In the kitchen, Ava let out a rather enthusiastic moan against Gabriel's lips that startled him even as it sent a rush of lust through him. They were kissing – great, phenomenal kissing - but it was only kissing. His hands remained framing her face and he felt as if he couldn't move them.

In the vision, Ava felt Gabriel's mouth along her neck. She reached up and gripped the spindles. When his mouth found her breast, she went wild.

Standing next to the breakfast bar, Gabriel felt Ava's body coiling against his. The energy she was generating was insane. Her pupils were dilated now. Her body was feverish, her mouth ravenous. She was pressing against him, the sounds she made against his mouth incredibly arousing, her hands tightening like claws on his sides. Something odd was happening to them, with them, around them.

On the bed, they moved as if their lives depended on their coupling. It was feral. Their bodies were slick with sweat. Her hair was damp, clinging to her neck and shoulders as she raced toward release. Gabriel's hands gripped hers over the spindles of the headboard as he plunged again, again, again. She arched her back, her breath coming in short gasps-

In the kitchen, Ava suddenly stiffened and let out a low, guttural moan. Her grip on Gabriel's sides was almost painful, but exquisitely so. Her body was unyielding as it pressed against his. Staring into her sightless eyes, he saw the gray in them was crystalline, as if they had suddenly turned to diamonds. Then she exhaled, her body relaxed, and she all but fell into him.

He took her shoulders. "Are you okay?"

She raised her head sleepily. Her body was trembling, her breath labored. "Y-yes."

Gabriel remembered what she said about getting her as close to the floor as possible and helping her with breathing exercises. "How's your breathing? Do you need to sit d-"

Almost instantly, her pupils shrank, and she blinked to clear her head.

Crimson rose from her neck to her forehead. The tips of her ears burned. "I h-have to leave."

"Ava, what-"

She took a deliberate step back, wobbled, but shrank away when he instinctively reached out for her arm. Her hand fluttered around her chest, her cheek, down by her lower abdomen, not quite touching any of those areas.

He had never seen her flustered before. Gabriel ran through what they had just been doing and her body's response again – and was stupefied. He was a good kisser, but he'd never had that explosive of a reaction just by kissing a woman.

"Did you just have a-" he started. "Was that an or-"

"I need to g-go." She flushed even harder, took a step back. She could not get her heart to stop dancing in her chest like a butterfly. Her skin was feverish – had the room gotten hotter in the past few minutes?

"Ava, that's nothing to be ashamed of." Although he was pretty pleased with himself.

"What do you know of shame?" she snapped. She turned from him. A noise like thousands of people screaming was filling her ears, distracting her. "This was a mistake."

The rage that had consumed her when David had first taken her in was boiling just under the service. Control. She had to regain control, or everything would fall apart. Allowing herself to feel pleasure had opened the door to the rage.

Suddenly she whirled on him. "Why did you have to interfere with me? I was fine on my own."

"Were you?" His eyebrow arched.

"My life was disciplined. I could handle it."

Gabriel was startled to see her eyes had a wild look to them. The sound of her breath was audible; short, shaky gasps that seemed to fight their way in and out of her body. At her sides, her hands were open like claws, shaking.

"That's no way to live, Ava."

"It is my way to live! Now you are… interrupting my routines. You put so many impressions inside my head..." She raised one hand and smacked her palm against her temple. "You have no concept of what they do to me. Do not touch me!"

Her body instantly went into defense mode when he reached out to comfort her. Taking a step back into a stance, she raised her hands. He could see the pulse jumping in her throat.

"Running again?"

The challenging tone of his voice made her bristle.

"I cannot handle all of you inside my head. I do not want to form relationships with you and your family. I want to be left alone."

Embarrassed and furious, Ava turned and strode toward the door. She was shocked to feel tears threatening at the corners of her eyes.

Keep going, the voice in her head purred, the voice of The Monster, the only one who had ever been there for her without fail.

She yanked her jacket off the peg and threw the door open, walking out onto the porch on unsteady legs. Whether or not he was behind her, she did not know. The sounds in her head were too loud to hear him and she could not focus enough to sense him.

Leave him, The Monster growled. He doesn't matter. No one matters. Only your life, only your survival is important.

The cool air did nothing to clear her head.

Keep moving, keep going until there is only you, until everyone is gone and you're the only one left.

She climbed into her car and drove without looking back.

·   ·   ·   ·   ·

Griffin opened the door and was initially disappointed when he didn't see an overnight bag in Isabel's hand. His gaze ran the length of her body – it was hard not to – and he saw a black strap over one shoulder. A spark of hope lit inside him.

"You don't have to knock, you know," he said, taking her hand and pulling her in for a kiss. "You can just come in."

"I could be a burglar," she laughed.

"You're the sexiest burglar I've ever met. What's this?" He tapped the strap slung over her shoulder.

She slid her thumb under it and lifted it, bringing the bag around for him to see. "An overnight bag."

"Yeah?"

She nodded. "If that's still an option."

Sliding his hand around her waist, he pulled her close, causing her to drop the duffel. "In that case, you can take anything in my apartment, burglar."

His mouth took hers in a long, slow kiss. Isabel felt weightlessness settle over her and realized, abruptly, that she trusted him completely. He had seen her at her worst and remained loyal to her. He was the only person she trusted except Gabriel. And for the first time, it didn't scare her.

Her brief past relationships were not determining her future with Griffin. She was in the presence of a man and didn't fear he would treat her as others before him had. She smiled against his mouth.

"What are you smiling for?"

Blinking slowly, her dazed green eyes regarded him with amusement. "Nothing. Everything. What are you drinking?"

Griffin turned toward the kitchen. "Peach Moscato. Do you want me to pour you a glass?"

"Sure."

Her hands began to shake, and she felt the empty fluttering in her stomach again. Walking to the living room, she stood at the patio door and looked down at the park below.

The view was amazing during the day. A jogging path and playground to watch people from a distance. Trees that would be lush in the summer, a pond close enough to walk to.

Tonight, she only saw benches under sidewalk lights. The rest was hidden in shadows.

Her body felt like a wire stretched so tight, it was ready to snap.

Griffin came up behind her and reached around to give her the wine. "Are you okay? You're trembling."

"Fine." Knee-jerk response: they both knew it. She turned around and looked up at him.

"Holy buckets, how tall are you?" she suddenly asked. Because it was so light and she loved the taste, she took a long drink of her wine.

"Six three. What does that have to do with anything?"

She chugged the rest of her wine and pressed her hand to her mouth, embarrassed. Her nerves were all over the place. Her eyes felt too big, her skin too sensitive. Had the room gotten brighter, or had her eyesight improved?

"My mind is racing. Sorry."

Setting both glasses on the entertainment center, he framed her face with his hands. "What thoughts are whizzing through it now?"

She loved when he touched her. How he touched her. Still, her eyes darted everywhere but to his face.

"I'm wondering why some animals like pandas are always black and white, when others, like dogs, have assorted colors. I'm wondering why the hell extreme sitting is a sport."

"You really let that thing go wherever it wants, don't you?" He trailed a finger down the long column of her neck. Her pulse raced.

The room was suddenly too warm. How had she become so warm?

The feel of his thumb as he brushed it across her cheek made her skin flush.

"I'm wondering why I'm so relieved when I see a text from you or hear your voice. It's like my..." Her hand hovered at her chest a moment. "...chest is finally free from this unbearable weight. And can people really get vanilla flavoring from the anal glands of beavers? Who was the first person to figure that ou-"

"Good God, woman." Griffin laughed, leaning down, pressing his lips to hers.

She felt like sparklers had been lit inches from her face. White lights popped and fizzled behind her closed eyes. Hungrily, she reached up and gripped his hair in her fists, pulling him closer. His startled grunt was like adrenaline being pumped directly into her bloodstream.

Need washed through her, filled her, drove her to take. Her body was on fire. He was the key to releasing the ache that was building inside, saturating her, drowning her.

Everywhere his hands touched, her body sang. She longed to taste every inch of his skin. When he slid his hand down the small of her back, over her rear, he pulled her against him with possessive demand.

She wanted him to touch her flesh, all her flesh. Moving so slow was torturing her. She wanted more, now. Instead, he teased longer, holding his body against hers with too many clothes between them.

Her fingers were numb when she found the first button of his shirt, started to open it while her mouth was still busy. He was patient as she fumbled through the rest of the buttons. Unable to believe this was happening, that he wanted her as much as she wanted him, her fingers kept sliding off the material.

At last, she could feel skin. He slid the shirt the rest of the way off, throwing it over his shoulder.

Her shirt lasted less than a minute longer. He pulled it over her head and tossed it somewhere. The urge to cover her chest was strong, but his mouth pressed soft, wet kisses along her shoulder, up her neck. Other urges became stronger.

Noting her bra had the clasps on the front, he unhooked them slowly, brushing his knuckles against her skin as he did so. He slid his fingers under the straps and over her shoulders, so it dropped to the floor. For a moment he could only stare.

Her flesh was pale, her flat belly quivering. As his hands captured her small, firm breasts, she arched her back, so they pressed against his palms avidly. Pure animal instinct had him wanting to devour. He made himself slow down, nipping at the pulse in her throat until the need to drag her to the floor and drive into her was under control.

She wrapped herself around him and felt something building, a scream or a sob, unable to contain the lightning coursing through her. She was fascinated with his body; the long lean torso, the muscles along his shoulders and down his back bunching as he fought for control.

Everywhere his hands touched made her stomach flutter and her skin tingle. Each time his tongue sent a new thrill through her, her hands, gently exploring his skin, suddenly gripped, and her fingers dug into him as she rode the feeling.

Realizing she probably wasn't clearly conveying her wishes to go farther, she wrapped her arms around his waist and slid her hands down to grope his bottom.

Very nice, she thought. Firm, she thought.

She brought her hands back to the front of his jeans. Flushing from head to toe, drawing her hands back, she reached again. Somehow, she managed to undo the button. As she pulled the zipper down, her breath caught. She realized she had never undressed a man before.

Plunging his hands into her hair, Griffin took a deep breath to steady himself. His body wanted to ravage her; his mind wanted to savor every bit of her. The hesitant touch of her hands was shredding his control. He wanted to make sure he could draw back if she wanted to stop, was afraid he wouldn't be able to.

She suddenly didn't know where to look. Too shy to look at his face, she kept her eyes trained on her hands and where they touched him. Watching his skin jump where her fingers caressed thrilled her. Did she really have such an effect on him? She couldn't quite believe she did. She was nobody.

Griffin slid his hand along her jaw, cupping her face.

"Look at me, Isabel."

Her stomach pitched. She glanced up quickly, then away.

"That's cheating, Love," he chuckled. His free hand skimmed down her belly, over her jeans, down the front. He pressed his hand between her legs. A rush of heat moved through her. She let her head fall back against the cool glass of the patio door. To steady herself, she braced her hands on his arms.

Griffin used the opportunity to step closer so she couldn't lower her head.

She moaned low in her throat. The sound spoke of need and pleasure so close to pain.

"That's the way," he murmured. He eased the zipper down on her jeans. "You deserve the right to hold your head high." Slipping his hand under the denim, below the fabric of her panties, he kept his amber gaze on her.

"You deserve the right to ask-" he brushed his palm lightly over her. "-no, to demand what you want. What do you want, Isabel?"

His eyes held hers. He kept his hand moving, teasing.

Her breath caught.

"Tell me what you want."

"You," she exhaled. "I want you."

He slid his fingers into her. A startled cry burst from her. Pleasure flickered across her face, and she felt her legs weaken. Her hips thrust forward, pumping against his hand. A thin layer of sweat coated her skin. He ran his lips along the length of her neck, feeling her pulse raging. Massaging her breast with his other hand, he brushed the swollen nipple with his thumb. Then he leaned down and skimmed his teeth over the already sensitive skin.

Shocked at the explosion of stimuli, Isabel's knee came up and her leg shot back, her boot slamming into the glass patio door.

"Holy shit!" The words rushed from her mouth on an exhale before she could stop herself. Her body vibrated against the glass. Her legs wanted to buckle.

"It's a thick door," he said, grinning. "But the next time you could break it."

Before she could respond, he scooped her up, taking her breath away. He carried her through the living room.

I give myself ten seconds more to screw this up, she thought as he drowned her in another kiss, and that's being generous.

Laying her gently on the bed, he remained sitting, looking down at her. Absently, he turned on the table lamp, keeping his eyes on her.

"I can see those wheels turning again," he said, untying her boots one by one, slowly. "You're thinking too much, Miss Harris."

How could he make such a simple task so sensual? Sliding each boot off, he gazed at her with a hunger that made her feel incredibly sexy.

He began sliding her jeans off.

"It's been a while," she admitted. Was she wheezing? It felt absolutely wonderful. It terrified her.

With a tenderness she found endearing, he slid her panties slowly down her legs. He lifted one foot and kissed along the inside of her leg, starting with her ankle.

"I tend to ruin things long before they get this far." She shivered. How had she lived without this ache? Her body was molten lava.

"We'll go as slow as you like," he said, amused.

She gasped as he kissed his way up her calf. Her chest tightened.

"Don't..." she moaned. "Don't stop."

His laughter was charming. His eyes had a sparkle to them, and deeper down, that rudimentary hunger that was a little dangerous.

"So, we've cleared that up. What else are you worrying about?"

Isabel tried to shove the darkness out. It hovered anyway.

"Please don't hurt me."

Griffin had been kissing just below the inside of her knee and now he paused, looking at her from under his long lashes.

Isabel took a deep breath. She raised her eyes to the ceiling, so she didn't have to look at him. She felt foolish and weak.

Moving like a panther, he crawled up her body until his face was close to hers. He rested his weight on his forearms, gazing down at her. As he pressed his body to hers, she felt how ready he was. But still, he didn't rush.

"I'm crazy about you," he said softly.

His eyes were warm pools of honey, mesmerizing. Whatever happened between them, he wouldn't intentionally hurt her. She trusted him. She wouldn't be here, like this, if she didn't.

She nodded, the need for him returning twice as strong, coursing through her.

Doubts catapulted out of her head when he lowered his mouth to hers. The urgency in his kiss spun a pleasant dizziness through her. Clasping her hands, he laced his fingers with hers and drew her arms above her head.

The more he pleased her, the harder it became to take things slow and easy. The way her hands flexed in his as his mouth explored her body was maddening, showing him what she liked, what drove her wild. Her body fought with his, trying to touch more, to ring every ounce of pleasure from each point of contact. She was as delirious as he to give.

She let out a moan, the kind that begged for release. Freeing his hands from hers, he trailed his fingers down her side, across her thigh, finding the hot and the wet, cupping, pressing. He guided her up until she peaked again. A pulse shot from her lower belly to her head, leaving her feeling drunk and giddy. Her hands dug into the bedding, gripping as her rigid body strained against his hand. Then relaxed as her body sagged, loose and quivering.

Whoa, she thought. Whoa.

Griffin leaned over and opened the drawer of the bedside table to get a condom.

Breathless, Isabel lay silently with her eyes closed. An overwhelming urge to cry hit her, a rush of emotion so powerful she wasn't sure what to make of it.

Her legs were still trembling. She was starting to wonder if she would ever catch her breath when she felt his mouth on her belly as he kissed his way up toward her chest. Opening her eyes, she watched him move toward her, trailing kisses up her torso.

Now just a breath away, his lion's eyes gazed into hers. With a hand that wasn't quite steady, she brushed the hair from his forehead in a gesture he found deeply moving.

He slipped inside her. Watched those mossy green eyes grow large as marbles. As he immersed himself in her body, her scent, he saw fervor leap into her eyes, arousal flare. She moved with him, her fingers digging into his shoulders. Her body matched him, thrust for long, slow thrust. When his mouth found that sensitive place just behind her ear lobe, she bucked under him.

It was as if her body had been waiting for his to fit against it. Even through the haze of elation, Isabel noticed how perfectly their bodies joined, his hands molded to hers, her forehead pressed just so to his shoulder.

The need to cry intensified. Beautiful, she thought. It's so beautiful.

She bit her lip, moaned as Griffin lifted her hips and went deeper. Every part she had purposely closed off for years was tender. Every nerve was lit with pleasure so deep it was just shy of pain.

Their movements became more urgent, their breath quickening. Her head was spinning, high on every impression careening through her body. She was on the edge of something. Of what, she didn't know, but she was weightless, just about to plummet. For once she didn't care where she was going to end up. For just this moment she didn't give a damn about anything but the frayed ends of every nerve screaming-

The sound of astonished pleasure that burst from her lips as she crested again was extremely loud. She felt his grin against her shoulder and a moment later, his release mixed deliciously with hers.

They stayed joined, both breathless. Griffin settled comfortably on top of her. His heart was thudding against her chest, his face buried in her hair. He turned his head so she could feel his short bursts of breath against her neck. The weight of him was deeply satisfying in a way she didn't understand.

Her legs were twitching around his hips. She was embarrassed by how loud she'd been; usually she was too shy to make any noise at all. Vaguely, she wondered if the neighbors in the other apartments had heard her.

Lifting himself off her, Griffin pulled off the condom and tossed it in the trash can beside the bed. He turned back to see her entire body was beautifully flushed.

Isabel's heart was still thudding. Would she ever be able to catch her breath? She felt like she was soaring. The thrill of his touch kept coming back in waves. She could feel every muscle clench and release. Her body was sore with a pleasure and exertion she had never experienced. When he shifted so he was lying beside her, he tucked her neatly against him. The feel of his skin against hers made her body start buzzing all over again.

Holy shit. Her head was spinning. It was literally spinning, making her giddy and happy and a little afraid. She pressed her hand, palm flat, onto the bed to try to ease back into reality. Suddenly all the hype about sex seemed legitimate instead of one big letdown.

She turned her head to the side, trying to catch her breath, resting a hand on her chest. Ragged pulses jumped at her fingertips as her heart continued to pound against her rib cage. Her body's overjoyed reaction to his fascinated her.

Doubt began to creep in. She was afraid to look at Griffin for fear of what she would find on his face.

You've just had the best sex of your life, she thought to herself. But for him, it was just sex. Don't get too attached.

The thought made her want to cry. She liked Griffin. He made her laugh; told her she was important. He was so much more than what they had just done. Not that that wasn't phenomenal. But if he didn't think so, if she had only been mediocre for him, or even worse, not good at all...

"Hey," he said softly, brushing her hair away from her temple. "What's going on in that sexy head of yours?"

She gathered herself, turned her head to look at him.

Those eyes she adored watched her as he caressed her temple. Isabel couldn't see anything but concern in his expression. His other hand rested on her stomach.

"I'm just stuck inside my head," she said lightly. "Worrying too much."

The hand resting on her stomach moved up toward her breast, his fingertips grazing across her skin. Goose bumps rose where he touched. A shiver ran the length of her body.

"How can you worry about anything at a time like this? We just had mind-blowing sex."

"Yeah?" she asked cautiously, afraid to believe he had enjoyed it as much as she had. And boy, had she enjoyed it. No one in her past had ever pleased her as thoroughly. None had ever taken the time.

"Don't you think so? I haven't had that much fun since I spun donuts in my first muscle car."

Leave it to a man to equate sex and cars, she thought, amused.

She exhaled, relaxing against his body. She still felt shaky. Was that normal? His breath was still ragged, she noticed. "I was afraid I was the only one who thought so."

Griffin studied her for several seconds, his golden eyes intense. "We're going to have to work on that self-esteem problem, you and I."

"Good luck with that." Her tone was sarcastic, but deep down, she knew it was going to be a full-time job.

Leaning down, he brushed his lips against hers. Her stomach flip flopped.

"What could you have possibly done that makes you think you don't deserve to be happy?" he asked.

You have no idea.

She swallowed. It was painful to do so. Her heart was jackknifing again, this time not in a pleasant way.

"That's a discussion for another time." He propped his pillow up and shifted so he was leaning back against it. "Sit with me."

Isabel rolled onto her side and scooted up, so she was sitting next to him, trying not to be too clingy. Surprising her, he pulled her to him, so she was sprawled across his chest. Leaning over her, he pulled the bedding up around them.

She pressed her palm to the place over his heart. Was there anything more beautiful than a beating heart? A tear formed at the corner of her eye, large and impossibly warm.

"Are you okay?" Griffin asked softly, toying with her hair.

She nodded silently, but the gesture made the tear roll from her eye, and he felt it against his chest.

"Are you sorry?"

"No." He could hear the shock in her voice. She tilted her head up to look at him. "No. Fuck."

She sat up, her back to him, and dragged the heel of her hand across her left cheek. Wrapping her arms around her legs, she hunched over, pulling away from him.

"What's wrong?"

"Nothing."

"Then why are you crying?" He put his hand on her back.

"I'm not crying!" She used the back of her hand to swipe across her eyes.

The long, slender line of her back was sultry, yet vulnerable. Griffin patiently waited, but she didn't say anything else.

"Did I hurt you?"

"Of course not. It wasn't you. I mean, it was, but not the way... it was just so..."

"I'm going to hit you with a pillow."

"What?"

"Take a breath, or it's pillow therapy for you."

She closed her eyes, inhaled. Waited a beat. Exhaled. Concentrated on the air filling her lungs.

"It was amazing," she said softly. "Overwhelming... in the most beautiful way."

Griffin pulled her back down to him. "Glad to hear it." He kissed the top of her head.

"I'm not very-"

"Stop it."

"What?"

Picking up a remote from the bedside table, he turned on the television. "Whatever you were going to say that berates yourself."

She frowned, tilting her head up at him. "How do you know-"

A spark of irritation flared in his eyes. "Because that's the only way you know how to talk about yourself. I'm hoping to change that."

He turned down the volume on the TV, changed the channel to something that played soft music.

"Do you want your wine?" he asked, nudging her aside and tossing back the blanket. He picked up his boxers. At the following silence, he glanced over his shoulder at her.

"Okay."

How quickly the air changes when anger enters the room, she thought.

Watching him walk away, she slid down on the bed and rested her cheek on the back of her hand. She was not surprised to have ruined everything, especially after phenomenal sex. Anytime something good happened in her life, she ruined it somehow, usually with her mouth. Somewhere along the line – she was sure it was after Hayden's disappearance – she had become a smart ass, and it had gotten her into trouble ever since.

Griffin laughed at her sarcasm. He seemed to be the only one who understood her. Her mother acted like she used it to purposely hurt everyone around her. Who knew? Maybe she did.

"Do you ever oil that thing?"

Isabel almost managed to avoid jumping at the sound of Griffin's voice. Almost.

"What?" She leaned over the bed, looking for her shirt.

"The machine in your head that's always pumping out your endless thoughts."

"Ha-ha."

He set the wine on the bedside table and disappeared into the closet. Isabel heard him digging around while she crawled to the end of the bed, trying to remember where her shirt had gone. She sat up, blowing her hair out of her face. Griffin walked out of the closet with a tee shirt and tossed it to her. She covered herself as quickly as possible. The shirt would hang almost to her knees when she stood, and she was glad. She suddenly wanted her body to be hidden.

Leaning down, he picked up her underwear and held them out to her.

She snatched them from him, lying flat on her back to pull them on. She felt less exposed, emotionally as well as physically now that she had most of her body covered. She crawled to the head of the bed as Griffin sat and held out her wine. As her fingers touched the glass, he hesitated, held onto it.

"What's going on up there?" he asked softly, glancing up at her forehead.

She tried to pull the glass toward her so she could chug it, but he wouldn't let go.

Wanting the wine, she said stiffly, "You're pissed off because you don't like hearing the truth when it doesn't suit you."

"Is that what I am?"

"Give me my wine." Her body was suddenly cold.

He released the glass.

Iz felt the sting of tears in the back of her throat. She upended the glass, downing the liquid as quickly as she could. Then scooted to the edge of the bed.

Without looking at Griffin, she asked, "Did you get any whiskey?"

"Bottom cupboard to the right of the refrigerator."

The silence spread between them as she left the room.

Isabel pulled the bottle of whiskey – her go-to, Jack Daniels No. 7 - out of the cupboard and began searching for a glass to put it in. She checked a couple cupboards over the counter before moving across the sink. She found a juice glass and used that, being entirely too generous when she poured it.

Two fingers, my ass, she thought. That's for pussies.

To settle her nerves, she took a gulp of liquid courage straight from the bottle. She preferred the shield of rage the alcohol wrapped around her to the weepy weakling that twitched after intimacy.

Griffin seemed to be waiting for her when she returned to the bedroom. He was sitting against the headboard again, and though she was too nervous to look at his face, she knew he watched her walk around the bed and sit, pulling the bedding around herself protectively.

She gulped whiskey. If she was going to get dumped or kicked out, she was going to be plastered when it happened. What an idiot she had been to think she had balanced the scales for her past sins.

"What's this about me not wanting to hear the truth?"

"You don't mind me be being brutally honest unless it has to do with me." The weariness in her voice overrode the edge of annoyance. "Truth is truth, whether you want to hear it or not."

Griffin ran his index finger down the side of her face. "It's interesting you equate belittling yourself with the truth."

Shrugging, she set her glass on the table. The whiskey wasn't mixing well with the wine. Her stomach was sour.

"First, I'm not pissed. I'm frustrated because I don't like when you talk about yourself like that. I think you're wonderful."

He lifted her hand and kissed the palm. The gesture was kind, and his kindness made her feel weepy again. She preferred being pissed to crying in front of him. She snatched her hand back. Still glaring at him, she tried to find her glass with her other hand, waving it around near the bedside table.

"Second, whatever you were going to say, I can guarantee I don't agree with it."

"That doesn't make it false." Her fingertips bumped the juice glass and she picked it up, bringing it around. She wanted an intravenous line hooked up so she wouldn't be able to stay sober. She should have known bringing sex into the relationship was going to ruin it. She should have backed off. Griffin was willing to give her time. Why hadn't she taken it?

"No," he said, "but facts can prove or disprove your statement, so let's have it. What were you going to say?"

Iz took a long sip of her whiskey again. "I was going to say I'm not good at having sex. I don't have much experience. The proof is I've only had two partners, and neither partner lasted long. I think that's pretty definitive evidence."

"That's what I thought you were going to say, and I was right. I don't agree with it."

She brought her knees up to her chest. "Tough shit. That doesn't negate the fact."

He grinned with just enough conceit to piss her off.

"You said yourself facts prove or disprove the statement. You not agreeing with it isn't proof or fact. It's an opinion. It's anecdotal."

Her prissy tone was entertaining, but the thought of her believing everything she thought about herself wasn't.

Griffin took a slow sip of his wine. When he spoke, his voice was quiet. "You're so convinced of your insignificance that you can't see what's right in front of you."

He set his wine on the table.

"Which is?"

"Me."

"What's that supposed to mean?" Isabel's hand twitched. She wanted to reach for her drink again, but she was curious now as well as pissed.

"You're forgetting you have a third partner now. I happen to enjoy making love with you very much. Fact number one."

Her face instantly flushed. "That... well..."

He raised his eyebrows. "Do you disagree? Don't you think I enjoyed having sex with you?"

How the hell did she get herself into this situation? Isabel had no trouble openly discussing sex in general... but she had never discussed her performance so openly before. She was already self-conscious and inexperienced, and having a post-game analysis of her failures wasn't high on her agenda. She reached over and picked up her drink. At least if she finished her whiskey, she might not remember shoving her foot in her mouth as clearly.

"It appeared that you did." Trying to sound objective wasn't working. The tips of her ears were so hot they were practically scalding, and her cheeks must have been the color of a fire hydrant.

"And you have evidence to back up your theory that I enjoyed it?" He wiggled his eyebrows.

She glowered at him. "You're enjoying this, aren't you?"

"Immensely. What makes you think I enjoyed the sex?"

"Oh, for fuck's sake."

"You want facts, truth, so let's hear it."

"You're being an ass. You know whether or not you enjoyed it." Isabel tried to get off the bed for a refill, but Griffin grabbed her wrist and tugged, causing her to fall onto her back.

"I'm trying to show you that whatever your mind is telling you to make you doubt yourself, it's lying. My body reacted to you; that's a fact. Fact two." He leaned down and captured her mouth, stealing her breath in a kiss so hot and possessive she could do nothing but enjoy the ride. It was brief but almost aggressive, leaving her lips burning and her head spinning.

When he raised his head, his eyes had that fierce longing she had seen when he was inside her. The need for her. She could only blink at him.

"Fact two," he repeated. "I don't kiss a woman like that unless I enjoy it. I very much enjoyed making love with you. I'm looking forward to doing it again. Soon."

Isabel's head was still reeling. She couldn't quite get her breath back.

"And did you enjoy it?" Griffin continued.

"Well, I... yes-"

"I'd say you enjoyed it at least three times. Especially that last time, from the sound you made. We'll call those facts three, four, and five." He flashed another grin when she turned an even darker shade of red.

"Jesus, can we talk about something else?" Iz began fidgeting with the hem of her borrowed shirt. "Anything else?"

"We've established we both enjoyed it. So, what part of all the evidence presented convinces you that you're no good at it?" He ran his fingertips lightly up her calf. "Where is your proof?"

"I'm going to refill my drink."

Isabel leaned forward but he wrapped his arm around her waist and pulled her back, tossing her onto the bed. He smoothly rolled on top of her.

"Come now, you wanted the truth, did you not?" His eyes were laughing at her.

"You idiot." But she was having trouble keeping a straight face when he nuzzled her neck.

"I think you're still unsure. Perhaps we need to gather more facts."

"You're such a – oh." Isabel's breath caught as his hand slid up her inner thigh. Griffin leaned down and covered her mouth with his. The kiss was spirited and had her melting under him. When he raised his head, she wasn't sure she could remember her name.

"I believe there are a few body parts I neglected to sample. I wouldn't want them to feel left out."

He beamed at her.

Isabel returned the smile, feeling the remainder of the tension drain out of her. "I disagree, but feel free to prove me wrong."

· · · ·

She ran.

Fallen branches and soggy leaves gave way under her feet soundlessly, sinking into the mud. Trees rushed past. She jumped over a large maple that had been cut down and left to rot years ago. Climbed the incline toward the lookout. No moonlight made it through the woods; she was running in complete darkness.

After two hours in the woods, she still had not been able to get rid of all the energy inside her. Her calves were quivering. Her throat and lungs burned from exertion. Sweat soaked her outfit and ran down her face, stinging her eyes. Still, she ran.

The cool air brought color to her cheeks. Too distracted to appreciate the pleasant weather, Ava reached the top of the lookout and hoisted herself over the short stone wall that served as a railing for visitors. Her muscles were screaming, her heart knocking.

The park had a long, wide strip of worn earth – not quite a path – that lead from the lookout to a parking lot. Trees had been cleared and grills installed to make it a place for picnics. Ava walked this cleared area for a few feet before turning off it to start back down the hill through the woods instead. She began running again.

Halfway down, her boot hit a thick branch that didn't give. She went sprawling. She tucked her head and shifted into a shoulder roll to minimize the damage, but her momentum on the decline carried her another twenty feet before she was able to gain control. She ended in a crouch that had her skidding on one knee and one foot, dragging her palms along the ground another few feet, before her speed was finally expended.

A smaller branch had lodged itself into her left palm. She may have sprained her left ankle. The pain in her right shoulder was torturous. Her left knee was shredded and bleeding. Breathing heavy, growling, she gripped the branch and yanked it out of her palm. Her right shoulder erupted in fire from the movement. Ava yelled in furious agony. Reaching up with her bloody left hand, she ran her fingers over her right shoulder. The shape was normal, with no bulges or deformities. That was good. She hadn't dislocated it again. Something had cut her above the left eye and blood was dripping down her face. Using her sleeve, she wiped it angrily away.

Irritated with herself for her clumsiness, Ava stood with some effort, feeling blood dripping from her left palm. She was able to put weight on her ankle even though it was incredibly painful. No sprain. Had she sprained it, she wouldn't have been able to walk on it unless it was a life-or-death situation. Grumpy and full of various aches all over her body, she continued down through the trees at a hobbling walk.

Twenty minutes later, she drove her SUV toward home. Running had done nothing to rid her of the itchy feeling just under her skin. She had planned to work out in her basement, but now she would have to patch herself up. To be able to participate in class tomorrow, she would be better off tending to her injuries, icing them. Later, before bed, she would take an Epsom salt bath to help with the ache and hopefully relieve some of the stress in her body.

As soon as she entered her house and dropped her keys in the bowl, she began peeling her clothing off. The cuff of her jacket and shirt were soaked with blood. She dropped both in the entryway. Taking a moment, she leaned down and untied her shoes, eased them off with a harsh exhale. She was limping slightly as she crossed the dining room.

At the bottom of the stairs, she pulled her yoga pants down. Holding a steadying hand on the doorway, she peeled the pants off and left them there as she hobbled upstairs. That she needed to hold onto anything infuriated her.

On her way to the master bath, she pulled off her bra and dropped it on the floor. It was soaked in sweat. She would have to gather all her clothes tonight and do a load of laundry to keep the house from smelling. Something sticky, probably blood, was in her hair and on the left side of her face. Nude, Ava turned on the shower and waited for the water to warm up.

Usually, she was in and out in seven minutes. Her hair took the bulk of her time. Tonight, she gently worked around the aches, massaged the dried blood out of her hair, let the hot water beat down on her sore muscles. She allowed herself to waste time. She just didn't have the energy to move more efficiently.

She considered calling Vincent. No matter what he was doing, he would answer her call. It wasn't sex she was seeking, but solace from someone she knew she could trust. Knowing he wouldn't speak. His mind would be still. She could press her back against him and know he wouldn't attack her.

She didn't call. She bandaged her knee and wrapped her ankle, cleaned the various cuts she'd suffered tumbling down the incline. Then she was ready to start on the stitching.

The coffee table in the living room looked like a nurse's station by the time she began stitching the hole in her palm. The activity took concentration, which allowed her mind to focus on something other than Gabriel.

Until the shimmer appeared before her.

It was the tall, darkly dressed man that had hovered near Isabel. He appeared across the coffee table from Ava, watching her pull the needle through her skin slowly. Ava glanced up at him. She thought his golden eyes were quite beautiful, and they watched her, curious, as she finished closing the wound on her left palm.

"What is your name?" Ava asked. She tied off the thread and snipped the excess. There was enough thread left for the cut above her left eye, so she tied another knot in the end. She needed a mirror to stitch this wound.

Pulling out the stand on the mirror to prop it up, she adjusted it so could see her forehead when she sat on the couch. She began. She kept her face still and moved only her eyes, glancing at the tall man.

"Why are you here?"

The eyes grabbed her. Not just the color, but the sorrow in them. Ava recognized that look in others. The blackness that surrounded him was not only the dark clothes he wore. A shifting fog of black mist had followed him at Isabel's parent's house. The energy surrounding him was volatile, but Ava instinctively felt the spirit itself was not dangerous. He looked confused as well as miserable.

She tied off the last stitch and snipped the thread. Setting her tools down, she studied the quiet man in front of her. Ignoring these visitors had been a lifelong practice. What would it hurt to try something else?

Because her left hand now had stitches, Ava reached carefully out with her less injured right arm and sank it into damp blackness. The man watched her. His image did not change. Her hand was still visible to her; it hadn't disappeared into some other dimension. The feeling was like holding her pot of boiling water and feeling the steam flow over it. But this steam wasn't hot.

Help me.

She yanked her hand back, letting out a groan when her shoulder protested. The voice had not come to her as a sound but as a thought.

"I do not know how to help you."

The tall man shimmered again, the darkness around him swirling. The blackness became transparent, fading until he disappeared completely.

• • • • •

CHAPTER SEVEN

Blackness engulfed her. She listened for the sound of something familiar but heard nothing. Had something woken her up? A sound, a dream? A feeling of uneasiness engulfed her. She sat up, felt a chill against her naked body, and pressed a hand to her chest. Normally, she didn't sleep nude.

Gradually, she became aware of steady breathing beside her. She relaxed. Griffin's apartment. She stood and walked carefully around the bed, ran her hand along the entertainment center as she passed it so she wouldn't crash into it.

The light above the kitchen sink cast enough of a glow to see vague shapes as she stepped into the living room. She saw the work shirt Griffin had shed when they were standing at the patio door earlier that evening. He had tossed it halfway across the room in his enthusiasm. Blushing, she thought about how quickly she had succumbed to that heat. She picked the shirt up and slipped into it, closing the middle five buttons to keep her body mostly covered. The cuffs stretched far past her hands, and the bottom hem hung halfway down her thighs. His scent drifted up from the fabric. Wrapping her arms around herself, she raised her hands to her nose and inhaled the fabric deeply. Was there any better smell?

Isabel exhaled, remembering how his mouth had grazed her skin, bit gently, then not so gently. Her body tingled at the memory.

She walked to the refrigerator and took inventory of what he had to drink. A bottle of water sounded good for now while she decided if she wanted orange juice or not. Her body was completely relaxed and sated, her mind not rambling to itself, her emotions not overwhelming her. She gulped down water and let it send cold blasts down her throat, making her feel like she was taking deep breaths on a frigid winter day. She raised a shirt cuff and inhaled again, loving the way Griffin's scent was all over the material. A small mewl of pleasure escaped her.

"Do you mind sharing that?"

Isabel spun around. Griffin was standing at the edge of the island in a tee shirt and boxers, his hair sticking up. Behind him, lamplight from the bedroom glowed, giving him an ethereal look.

"Well, look at you," he said, amused. When she frowned, he motioned.

The hand not holding the water bottle was up by her chest, curled into a fist. She instantly relaxed it. "Sorry."

"I told you your instincts are improving. I'll get my own bottle. I don't want you to beat me up."

"Shut up." She punched him playfully on the shoulder as he walked past her to get into the refrigerator.

Twisting the cap off, he chugged half of it down. "You drained all my fluids, you animal."

She snickered.

"Were you sniffing my shirt?" He rested his hand on her hip.

Feeling like a freak, Iz averted her eyes.

"Don't be embarrassed. You were smelling me on my shirt?" Something in his tone made her glance up. He wasn't making fun of her; he seemed genuinely intrigued by her actions.

Hesitant, she nodded.

Tilting his head to the side, he studied her. "That's sweet."

Circling his arm around her waist, he pulled her roughly against his body. Isabel's breath caught and water splashed out of her bottle.

"You look damn sexy in my shirt." His lips grazed her neck. His water bottle forgotten, he shifted so he was standing in front of her with both hands on her hips now.

Instantly her stomach felt like it had plummeted eighty stories in an elevator. She set her water on the island so she wouldn't drop it. Heat began churning in her belly.

"I've thought about you many times," he murmured. And lifted her easily onto the island. The marble was freezing on her butt. She let out a hoot. "I've thought about getting you on this counter since I first saw you."

"You didn't think to warm it up a little first?" she laughed.

He stepped forward so he was standing between her knees. Instead of instigating sex, he slid his hands along the outsides of her legs and rested them against her hips. The movement brought their faces close, so she could see the different shades that made his eyes golden. Isabel was surprised at how reassuring the gesture was. It was sensual as well as comforting, intimate and sincere.

"I'm glad you stayed the night."

The sound of his voice filled her with warmth. A tightness filled her chest when he rested his forehead against hers. The pose created such a connection, she thought, that offered so much communication without words. She wondered if he meant it that way or if she was projecting her own emotions onto his intent.

"I'm glad you invited me to." Closing her eyes, she let herself think for a moment that she deserved him.

"You can stay any night you want."

A less observant man would have missed the slight tensing of her muscles. Griffin was very observant. Apparently, Isabel was a little nervous when it came to anything hinting at a commitment.

"Or we can stay your place."

Isabel snorted. "Yeah, why sleep in the Penthouse when you have the choice of the luxurious White Trash Hotel? No, thanks. Here is just fine."

Griffin slid her toward him, settling her firmly against him before lifting her and walking toward the bedroom. On instinct, her legs wrapped around his waist so she wouldn't slip. She wrapped her arms around his neck.

"You could warn a person," she said breathlessly.

"Only if you warn me when you're going to be self-deprecating." His tone was cheerful enough, but she heard the underlying irritation. "I told you we're going to work on that."

He stopped just outside the bedroom, pressing her back against the wall. She let out a little gasp before he captured her mouth with his. He kissed her senseless, then continued into the room and lowered them both to the bed.

Much later, when her heart had settled enough and she had her breath back, Isabel propped herself up on her elbows and looked at him, a comfortably exhausted smile dancing on her lips. "You distracted me."

"You distracted me. I went to the kitchen to rehydrate, and found you in my shirt, looking sexy."

"Whoever was the distractor, our waters are still in the kitchen." She started to move but he set his hand on her shoulder.

"I'll get them." He brushed his fingertips along her cheek. As he slipped into his boxers, he took a moment to watch her.

Lying back on the bed, momentarily forgetting about modesty, Iz drew her arms over her head and stretched. Her arms and legs elongated until she was a narrow line of naked perfection. A jolt of lust sliced through him.

He walked into his kitchen for the water.

Fuck a duck, he thought. Isabel was on his mind all the time, racing through his thoughts nonstop from the time he woke until the time his overworked mind passed out late at night. That had been before the sex. Now... bloody hell. He would be lucky if he could concentrate on anything else.

That she had been willing to have sex had surprised him. He'd thought she would take longer, need more time to bare herself physically to him. Sex, for Isabel, was deeply personal and meant more than a physical act of release or pleasure. For her to share that part of herself, she had to trust him explicitly. Griffin was humbled.

On his way back to the bedroom, he stopped in the doorway.

She was lying on her side, her right leg drawn up at an angle to her body and her cheek resting on the back of her hand. Her lips were curved in a slight smile. She looked like the painting of an angel. It was suddenly hard for him to breathe watching her there, her body taking on the beauty of classical art.

She lifted her eyes and saw him standing there. "What are you looking at?" Her tone was playful.

Griffin cleared his throat. Her skin glowed in the lamp light. Her eyes were soft, free from the sorrow that usually hovered in the background of every stare. The tranquility on her face removed the little lines of distress he usually saw. He walked to the bed and sat down, gazing at her. The hand that set a bottle of water on the bedside table was not quite steady.

"I'm looking at you."

Tucking a strand of hair behind her ear, he brushed his knuckles against her cheek. A shudder coursed through her that made him smile. Isabel sat up as he handed her the other bottle of water.

"You're one of a kind, Isabel."

A little unnerved by his serious tone of voice, Iz kept the bottle to her mouth and took another swig to make sure she was steady. "I don't think the world could handle two of me."

For a moment, his smile seemed to falter just a bit. Something changed in his eyes briefly before they returned to warm, charming chestnut. The look was there and gone so quickly Isabel wasn't sure if she had seen anything at all.

Plucking the bottle from her, he took a drink. When he returned it to her, he poked her stomach, grinning.

He shifted so he was sitting on his side of the bed, settling under the blankets. He glanced at his alarm clock.

"Looks like tomorrow's going to be a no-underwear day to help me stay awake. It's almost two." The way he rubbed her leg almost absently but with obvious affection ignited her pulse. Did he really see it as such a casual gesture? To her, it meant the world.

She took a final gulp of water and set the bottle on the bedside table. "All I wanted was a drink of water." Her tone was accusing. She narrowed her eyes at him. "You're the one who's kept me awake for over an hour."

Griffin leaned forward and kissed her, slow and warm. "You were irresistible in my shirt."

Isabel framed his face with her hands. Her eyes were clear. She didn't have that faraway look on her face she often had when she couldn't concentrate.

"Something in your eyes," she said softly. "They're so forgiving. You look at me without judgment and I almost feel like I'm not -"

The shield came up and the cloud returned, so quickly Isabel twitched. Her eyes darkened, and Griffin saw the consummate happiness that had been there moments before replaced with caution and an underlying sorrow.

"We should get to sleep." She sat up, dropping her hands from his face. "It's late."

"You're not what?" he asked, taking her hand. He kissed the underside of her wrist. "What were you going to say?"

But she was already scooting down, arranging the pillow, pulling the bedding up. "Nothing. I'm going to be dead tomorrow during work. I guess I'll have to try the Griffin Method and go without underwear."

Bollocks, he thought. He'd lost her. But he'd had her for a moment. One beautiful moment that she hadn't shown him before.

"Let's call in sick." He tugged on a lock of her hair.

"What?"

"When was the last time you took a day off?"

"Over a year ago. But I wasn't exaggerating when I said I make sure the lives of my boss and his team run smoothly. They'll freak the fuck out if I call in."

Griffin picked up one of her hands again and nibbled on her knuckles. "They'll get over it. Spend the day with me tomorrow."

"Doing what?"

He wiggled his eyebrows. When she snorted, he kissed the back of her hand. "We'll think of something. Come on. You can use a break."

"I might hear the explosion of Jeffrey's head from here," she said thoughtfully. "That alone would be worth it. Okay. I'll call in if you do."

"In that case," he said, drawing her into a deep, slow kiss that made her tingle in every part of her body, "do we really need to sleep just yet?"

•　•　•　•　•

The pain was excruciating. Fire started in her groin and shot straight up into her chest, spreading to her hands and feet. Large bruises were forming on her tiny wrists, painting them in shades of purple and red. The bite in her shoulder was throbbing. Her legs were numb. Mack had smacked her across the face and her lips were bleeding. Every part of her was in pain. She felt like she had been ripped apart.

Ava lay on her stomach on the dirty, threadbare carpet staring under the bed. A beer can lay on its side at the far end. Some piece of food was covered in mold in one corner. A slice of pizza, she thought. Used condoms were scattered across the filthy floor under there, a sock, a book, several dust bunnies. Her stomach clenched from the smell.

She could feel the blood oozing out of her, hot and thick. Just after Mack had climbed off her, she had gotten sick on the floor closer to the bed. The smell of it was making her feel queasy. But her body was frozen. They had left the trailer several minutes ago, laughing, and still she was unable to move from the place he had dumped her on the floor when he was finished with her.

Get up, Ava.

The voice came from within yet was not a part of her. Ava was used to hearing them by now. For as long as she could remember, they had been part of her life, sometimes accompanying a figure, sometimes appearing out of nowhere without any indication of who was speaking. They were why she had been laughed at in the other foster homes, the reason she did not stay at any house for long.

But this voice was different. It was not coming from somewhere in the trailer.

It was coming from somewhere inside her.

Just now, she was so battered she could not even raise her head.

Get. Up.

It was deep, that voice. Strong. It made her stir on the floor, raise her eyes. She was alone in the trailer; for how long, she did not know. The old pickup truck had driven away but she had no way of knowing if they would be out all night or if they had just run to the store to get more beer.

So, you're in pain, the voice said. Pull it together and stand up anyway. It's going to get worse.

Ava felt tears burning and felt like she was dying. Her body, her voice. Everything she was felt broken. And some mean, horrible thing inside was making things worse, not comforting her.

What good would it do to comfort you? Your body will still be crushed. Your tears will still burn on your cheeks. Comfort will only make you a victim. You are not a victim, Ava.

She sniffed. It hurt to breathe.

You listen to me, the voice said. Are you listening?

She nodded, tears spilling over and dripping onto the ugly brown carpet.

What he did to you tore your body open. He will do it again and again. But he's not going to break you. He can take all the blood he wants, but don't give him the satisfaction of your tears, or your pain, or your shame. He can't have you. You will shred his soul and he will beg for your mercy.

Ava nodded. Her five-year-old hands curled into small, weak fists against the carpet.

Now get up. Don't lie on the floor like a dog.

Uncurling her hands, she tried to lift herself up.

With a scream, she fell back to the floor. The bones in her wrists felt like toothpicks ready to snap. Every breath sent spikes of pain into her throat and chest. A sharp cramp knotted in her belly.

Get up. You think this is pain? You haven't begun to feel pain.

Gritting her teeth, Ava planted her hands flat on the floor and pushed herself up. Agony shot through her arms, humming through her body like an electric charge, until she thought she would die from it.

Don't you dare. Give it to me. Give the pain to me and keep fighting.

"I do not know how."

The sound of her voice in the silent trailer was too loud, too hysterical.

Fight it.

Ava exhaled and moved her knee forward to support her arms. The pain relented a little more, now a throbbing she could handle if she didn't think about it too much. She shifted into a sitting position.

The sound of a vehicle coming down the road had her heart racing in her chest.

Stop it. You are not afraid. You can only be afraid if he controls you, and he doesn't control you.

"I am not afraid," she whispered.

You're going to have to do better than that.

The truck was coming up the driveway.

"I am not afraid." Her voice was barely audible in the small trailer. Bracing herself, she set her feet on the floor and shoved herself up until she was standing. Blood dripped into her eye and down her legs. Dizziness swept over her, but she bit her lower lip until the controlled pain forced her to focus.

Your body is just a vessel. Separate yourself from the vessel and you won't feel the pain.

"I am not afraid."

The truck pulled up to the trailer and parked.

Take my hand.

Ava felt something take her hand - not just her physical one, but a piece of her inside that seemed to separate from her body and move away.

Come with me. Deep inside. He can't get you here. No one can hurt you here.

"I am not afraid."

Her own voice seemed to be coming from somewhere far away. She was disappearing inside herself, to a place where he couldn't get her. The body she was in felt like a suit she was wearing; she could feel the pain only as a sensation against her skin. It no longer registered as pain. It was like being in a dream.

Wait here. I will come get you when it's over.

Her physical body was numb. It balled her hands into fists and waited.

I'll stand up and fight and I won't stop fighting until I am unconscious or dead.

In the present, Ava became aware of her surroundings slowly. Tall bookcases were on either side of her; she was standing in the reading nook, naked, staring out the large window. Her hands were curled into fists at her sides.

The dream was fading but the way it felt on her skin was slow to dissolve. Her body felt like it was coated in a layer of grime. A headache was in full swing. The morning sunlight felt too bright against her sore eyes.

Years had passed since she had dreamed of the first time The Monster had come to her. She wondered what had preempted the dream; was working with Sensei on her ability stirring up her past? Was it an overload of stimulation at Gabriel's parent's house? At this point, there were too many possibilities and no way to narrow them down.

None of it mattered anyway. The dream had recurred, regardless of the cause.

Her body reminded her of the tumble she had taken yesterday. Her knee was throbbing. It gave out for just a moment before snapping back into place. Ava stumbled into the bookcase and slammed her good shoulder against it. Leaning against the shelves for a moment, unable to take her weight off her left leg because of the injury to her right ankle, she turned to sit on the bench seat of the reading nook.

She had barely started to bend her legs when she tensed and reversed her position, standing with her hands ready to fight.

Hayden was standing a few feet in front of her. Ava limped a step toward her, then another. What was she supposed to do with a spirit that refused to speak? That refused to make clear what she wanted?

The young girl smiled slowly, a slight lifting of the corners of her mouth, and Ava suddenly saw the full version of Gabriel's half smile. Ava took another step toward her, reaching out. She wanted to ask so many questions.

But Hayden was already gone.

● ● ● ● ●

Far away. The voice was so far away, it barely registered in Isabel's subconscious. But the distress in the voice had her stumbling awkwardly up from sleep, trying to clear the confusion even before her eyes opened to the unfamiliar room. For a moment she listened, unsure if she had been dreaming and the voice was from her dream.

Beside her, Griffin grunted, and Iz heard his rapid breathing pattern. A moment later she felt him jerk. Panic gripped her for an instant as she realized something was wrong with him, terribly wrong, then went cold and dormant as instinct took over. Leaning over, she turned on her lamp so she could see him. She kept her eyes closed for several seconds until they adjusted to the light. When she opened them, she saw Griffin was lying on his back, his chest heaving with every strained breath. Both hands were curled into fists, gripping the bedding tight enough to drain the blood from his knuckles.

"No. Don't listen to them."

Messy as always, his hair was sticking up more than usual. He had been moving in his sleep for a while before his voice finally woke her up. Isabel reached for him, hesitant. What was he dreaming about?

"Don't leave me. We're the same." The plea in his tone made Isabel shiver.

A tear slid down his temple. Isabel touched it gently, fascinated by the liquid on her fingertip.

"Griffin." She kept her voice soft, surprised to see him so distressed. He was usually so calm. Unsure of what to do for him, she shook his shoulder.

"We're the same."

His movements were becoming more agitated, his breathing more erratic. Beneath her hand, his skin was cold even though he was sweating profusely. Isabel watched as he writhed on the bed in an attempt to get away from whatever was in his dream.

"Help him."

"Griffin," she said, more firmly now, and this time when she shook his shoulder, she wasn't gentle.

He sat bolt upright with a loud, stuttering exhale, making Iz rear back in surprise. For a moment he stared straight ahead, panting, unaware of his surroundings. His hands were still grasping the bedding. As if suddenly realizing he wasn't alone, he turned his head toward her. Iz didn't think he was fully aware of what he was looking at. When she reached up to touch his face, make sure he was fully awake, he caught her wrist in his hand.

"Did I hurt you?"

"No." But she wanted to pull away from him. Seeing him this out of control made her stomach clench and her pulse quicken. She didn't understand why it upset her so much to see him having a nightmare. Didn't everyone have them?

She noted his shaking hand as he ran it through his hair. Just as she saw the moment he realized he was gripping her wrist and released it.

"You woke up," he said, his voice thick with emotion. "Was I talking or moving? I had to be doing one or the other to wake you up."

"Both," she said. She wasn't sure if she should touch him. She wasn't sure if he wanted her to. She didn't know what to do for him to make it better. And suddenly she felt like crying. Someone like Griffin didn't deserve nightmares. Someone who was always trying to help others deserved nothing but pleasant dreams and waking peacefully. Isabel deserved nightmares and much, much worse.

"Are you okay?" she asked. Instinct had her lifting her hand to reach for him again, but she was too unsure. She pulled it back. Someone like her couldn't comfort anyone.

"Yeah." His voice was still shaky, but he wasn't as pale. He raked his palm across his cheek and seemed surprised to feel tears.

Feeling useless, Isabel's hand moved this time before her mind had a chance to think about it. She took his hand and gave him a reassuring squeeze. To her relief, he squeezed back. Iz lowered her head to his shoulder and draped her arm around his back.

"You don't have to talk about it."

"I'm okay," he said. "I lost a close friend a few years ago."

She squeezed his hand again because there were no words.

"Every once in a while, it creeps up on me."

Isabel knew the feeling. Even after sixteen years, the loss of Hayden could crash down on her on a whim, with no provocation. She wondered how long it had been since Griffin had lost his friend, and how close they had been.

"He killed himself."

She jolted. That was an odd thing to blurt out. "Why did you tell me that?"

Griffin rested his chin on the top of her head, letting out a long sigh. "Because talking about it helps me move on."

A ball of acid seemed to be growing in the pit of her stomach. The way you think I should, she thought, bitter.

"I don't think you ever really move on from something like that," she said, sitting up. Leaning over, she reached for her glass of water with a quivering hand.

Why would anyone take his own life? She didn't understand it. She never would. Hayden had probably been slaughtered like a common farm animal because it pleased some sick-minded bastard and yet someone out there chose to end his life because he didn't want it anymore. Why couldn't Griffin's friend take Hayden's place? The person who wanted to live was able to, and the one who wanted to waste his life could be dead. One for the other, instead of two people dying so needlessly none of it mattered because whether you died because you took your life or whether you died because some asshole killed you, the end was still the same. You were fucking dead.

"I choose to move on," Griffin said. He brushed his fingertips over Isabel's inner thigh. "I chose to accept the choice my friend made for himself."

"Aren't you the enlightened one?" Iz said, her tone dripping sarcasm.

"Not enlightened. Stubborn. I can only move forward."

"My sister didn't choose to get kidnapped, raped, and murdered. Someone made that choice for her. And I sure as hell can't just flip a switch and get over her death."

She set the glass of water back on the table. Her hand was shaking so bad she almost sent the glass crashing to the floor.

"Isabel."

"I'm sorry." Hot tears oozed down her cheeks. They seemed to scorch her skin. She tried to catch her breath. "I'm so sorry. That... I didn't..."

Griffin took her face in his hands and gazed into her eyes. Her breath was coming in short gasps, her eyes large and round as she stared into his. The green in them had turned to dark emeralds as the tears reflected the light in them.

"What a horrible thing for me to say." She squeezed her eyes shut tight, hoping she could erase the past few seconds. "I didn't mean to make this about me. Fuck."

She ran her hand through her hair. Sighed heavily.

"I don't know how to comfort you. I don't think it's fair to try, when I'm not comforted by anything anyone says about my dead sister. I don't want to lie to you and tell you it will be okay."

"You miss her."

"Y-yes."

"That's okay. I miss him, too."

"It's not about me. It was your nightmare. I'm sorry." If she could only breathe, dammit, she could try to explain what she meant, that she understood but she just didn't know how to put into words what her heart was trying to say. That she felt the ache of someone being gone and knew what it was like to know nothing would ever fill that void.

"It's about both of us." This time he combed his hand through her hair. "We're the ones who are left."

"They left us," she breathed. God, it hurt so bad just to breathe sometimes.

"Yes. Whether by their decisions or not, they left us. I can forgive my friend for leaving me. One day, you're going to have to forgive Hayden for leaving you."

• • • • •

Sitting at the desk in her office, Ava finished typing an e-mail to a client and attached the finished document. She sent the encrypted e-mail and entered the date and time in the spreadsheet she kept that logged the progress of every document she processed.

At two thirty this morning, she realized she would not be able to return to sleep. So, she had completed an early morning workout and began work much earlier than usual. Already three projects had been completed. Though she enjoyed using her work to keep her busy, she was not enjoying the nagging at the back of her conscience that kept moping about what she had said to Gabriel. Her behavior had been so embarrassing, especially when they had been kissing. She had opened herself to receiving anything and everything by simply letting go of discipline. She had let everything that came through carry her away. She was disgusted with herself.

The taste of him was still on her tongue.

Ava shoved back from her desk and stood, unable to drag her thoughts back to work now that she had let a sliver of distraction in. She ran a hand through her long hair. On the edge of her desk, her cell phone sat silently, waiting to be of assistance. All she had to do was pick it up and bring up Gabriel's contact information...

Snarling, upset with herself for feeling the need to contact anyone, she turned from the desk and slammed her palm into the wall. For a moment, she kept her eyes closed and her hand pressed against the small crack she had made in the paint. The throb of her recent injury grew as the adrenaline rush was replaced with the realization that she had reopened the hole in her palm.

When she removed her hand from the wall, she left a thick smear of blood.

Once again, she cleaned and disinfected the wound.

As she wrapped her hand at the breakfast bar, she wondered what she should do. In all her life, she had not encountered an infatuation or even a crush. Her focus, even throughout her teen years, had been martial arts. Perhaps because of the abuse she endured as a child, her thoughts and urges had not drifted toward sex until she was seventeen. Even then, she waited another two years, carefully considering and analyzing her options before she approached Vincent.

When she began a sexual relationship with Vincent, he knew not to hope for an emotional one. That point had been clear at the very beginning. Of course, she found him physically attractive. Besides being pleasant to look at, with short, dark hair and even darker eyes, his body was in peak physical condition. He had an intensity in his eyes that matched no one else's, except for Sensei's. Discipline was vital to him, another quality Ava found incredibly appealing. Most importantly, she trusted Vincent enough to allow herself complete vulnerability around him. In that alone, he was the only logical choice for a sexual partner.

She never had to deal with repetitive thoughts of him, or overwhelming physical reactions to him. When that clawing, hungry sensation hit her, Vincent seemed to know, and he was there to keep The Monster at bay. He did not ask her questions. He did not whine about her use of his best attributes to her advantage. And somehow, he managed to be a comfort to her after without being clingy or demanding. He was everything she needed and nothing she did not. He was perfection, as a friend, a lover, a sparring partner.

But her pulse did not buck every time she was near Vincent. When she thought of him, her stomach did not feel empty and shaky. In the proximity of him, the hairs on the back of her neck would not rise, her skin would not itch for a touch, just some slight brush against him to calm the restlessness she felt when they were in the same room. The sight of Vincent did not make her heart feel as if it was lunging to break out of her chest to get to him.

Ava felt all these things when she was near Gabriel, and more. So much more. Such as now, her lips were feverishly hot, as they had been after he had kissed her. Raising her hand, she touched her fingertips to her mouth, intrigued.

Gabriel did not study martial arts. Martial arts required strict discipline, a particularly intense mindset during training. The common person did not know martial arts of any kind and avoided confrontation at all costs. Ava had studied moves for every possible scenario an attacker might try, had trained her body to accept assaults without going into shock, and kept her body in peak physical condition to be able to stand more abuse than an average body. She knew, because of her years of training, that she would survive most confrontations.

Gabriel was... spontaneous. According to Isabel, he could handle himself in a confrontation, as he had with the abusive man that assaulted his previous mate. But the way he fought was strictly by instinct. There were so many ways a confrontation could tip against his favor. He had no formal training, no muscle memory instilled. He had only strength and determination and the sense that he was doing the right thing.

She was finishing up with the bandage without realizing it. So deep were her thoughts that she did not feel a difference until she turned her head, and her hair did not fall forward into her face. Raising both hands, she pressed them to her head and found her hair had been manipulated into a braid again. As she ran her fingers over it, she felt the same pattern as before; one long braid wrapped around the crown of her head, with a few strands left loose at her temples.

She pivoted in the chair. Hayden was standing behind her, her light brown hair pinned up in the same pattern as Ava's. She reached out toward Ava, smiling.

As always, she wore the blue nightgown and stood – or hovered – barefoot on Ava's kitchen floor. Ava reached out and ran her index finger along Hayden's palm. The feeling was misty, like walking through fog.

He likes you.

Ava jerked her hand back as the thought came to her in a conversational tone. Hayden was smiling at her, waiting with her hand extended.

He's liked you since he first saw you.

Ava stood slowly. Taking the little girl's hand, which somehow had no solid form but lightly gripped back, she let Hayden lead her to the half bathroom.

Ava looked at what had been done to her hair in the mirror above the sink. It was beautiful. Ava never put it that way, but she liked it. It was practical as well as pretty; while she was working out, it would keep her hair out of her face and off her body, so she would sweat less. She glanced down to say she found it pleasing, but Hayden was no longer in the doorway.

The only evidence she had been there was a faint, cool dampness lingering on Ava's palm.

$\bullet \quad \bullet \quad \bullet \quad \bullet \quad \bullet$

In the mornings, when everything was quiet, darkness had a way of invading his thoughts. He could usually get more work done at home in the mornings and evenings, when he didn't have people constantly interrupting him. But some mornings, everything was just too quiet, and his imagination took the drawing pad and pencil and ran with it.

Griffin always felt as if something heavy had slammed into his chest when he felt depressed. He literally felt like it hit him. It didn't come around often, but he hadn't been able to get rid of it completely. Not yet. Not even after four years.

He put work away – what was the point in taking a sick day if he was working anyway? - and began to put what was in his head down on paper. As it always did when he was caught inside his art, his hand took over, removing thought, opinion, emotion. All that was left was muscle memory and instinct.

At first, the lines were incoherent. A trapezoidal shape, a lumpy circle at one side, a few splotches outlined beneath the trapezoid. As he filled in shadow and manipulated the lines to form what he saw in his mind, the objects became clearer. A bathtub. Someone slumped over in it, facing away, only the hair visible. Blood dripping down the side of the tub and pooling on the tile floor.

His breath was coming in short, harsh gasps. His hands were sweating, making it difficult to hold the pencil. Griffin dropped the sketch pad and pencil onto the table and looked at what he had created. What he had recreated, from memory. Rubbing his slick hands down his thighs, he flipped the page over, so he didn't have to look at it. Now all he saw was a clean, white page, ready to hold his creation.

He stood abruptly and walked to the kitchen sink, running his hands under icy water. He lathered them with soap, rinsed them, then stood with them under the water to keep them from sweating.

Usually once he was able to get the image out of his head and onto paper, it was easier to move on. Today it seemed to be holding on, more stubborn than usual. He would channel his energy into drawing Isabel instead.

She was currently sleeping. There was no way she was going to get out of bed just before seven this morning when he'd woken her with his nightmare. Once he assured her he was okay, and she'd left a message for her boss, she dropped back into sleep like the dead. He'd watched her for a while, content to run his fingers through her hair, until he decided to get up and try to be productive.

Now coffee was ready for when she woke. As he shut off the water and dried his hands, he thought of her wry smile, the corners of her lips turning up just a little.

The familiar hammer to the chest made him jerk as if struck. Rubbing his breastbone, he shook his head. He didn't want to be depressed today, not around Izzie. The nightmare had been a precursor so he knew it was coming, but he'd hoped he would have more time with her before it fell over him.

Four years, he thought. Why the hell did you have to give up?

A headache was already pulsing, the kind that starts in the temples and behind the ears and stays steady all day, no matter what pills he took or how many of them. He reached into the cupboard over the sink and took out a bottle of aspirin anyway, sticking his head under the faucet to wash them down. Maybe he could get a head of it, and it wouldn't be so bad.

Back in the living room, he began a sketch of Isabel from memory. He thought of her dark green eyes, of watching her in a particular pose when she wasn't looking, and his hand activated.

As he filled in shadow around her ear on paper, he noticed the headache less. That soft spot just behind her ears, where she loved to be kissed. That thought made him smile. Drawing her ear made him want to touch it with his hands, nuzzle it.

He set the design on the coffee table and stared at it.

There was only the line of her jaw, her ear, one eye, and her nose from a profile point of view, but already he saw her in it. Later, when he could look at her, he could fill in more details. He tossed the pencil down and walked into the bedroom.

Isabel was lying on her side facing the patio door. Griffin climbed into bed and spooned her. Instantly, she snuggled back against him. He trailed a finger down her shoulder, leaning over so he could watch her face. It was a wonder to see her face so pure in her sleep, he thought, when she didn't take the weight of the world on herself.

He leaned down and kissed her shoulder. A little moan slipped out, and her hand twitched.

"Izzie," he said softly, grinning, "it's almost nine. Are you ready to get up?"

She let out a little puff of air that almost sounded like a pout. Griffin kissed her shoulder again, this time trailing his tongue along her skin. He could run his hands along her flesh all day, marveling at how smooth and soft it was.

"Isabel...."

This time she shifted, and her mouth moved as if she was chewing gum. Griffin chuckled. If he dragged it out any longer, she would see it as him teasing her and she would be pissed when she woke up. Well, more pissed than usual.

Sighing, he gave her a firm shake.

"Isabel, wake up."

"Fuck."

"I know. Coffee's ready to make you human again."

Groaning, she rolled onto her back, kicking the bedding off before settling again. The woman could sleep through a hurricane.

"Izzie, why don't I go get you a cup of coffee? Maybe the smell will help wake you up."

In a perfect Australian accent, without opening her eyes, Isabel said, "Why don't you roll over and lick yourself like a good dog?"

As if to illustrate, she rolled back over so she was facing away from him and sprawled out.

Griffin cracked up. Her hair was tousled, and she was in a very unladylike position with her legs spread wide open. She looked ridiculous and she had just cussed him out using an accent she didn't naturally have. He gave her a firmer shake.

"Isabel, wake up."

Swinging her arm in a 'fuck off' gesture, she slowly rolled over and squinted balefully at him.

"What?" she croaked.

"Good morning, Sunshine." He grinned.

"Eat me." She rubbed her eyes with her fists.

"Gladly." He wiggled his eyebrows. Then had to bite back a groan of lust as she raised her arms above her head and stretched, long and hard. Her back cracked in three places.

"Ugh. Fuck mornings. Fuck them and all they fucking stand for." The thick grogginess of just waking up was still in her voice.

"You are a ray of sunshine in my dreary, boring life." Griffin picked up her arm and started noisily kissing from her wrist up toward her elbow, Pepe Le Pew style.

Giggling, Isabel yanked her hand back. "You idiot."

"Bollocks," he said, looking at his alarm clock. "Laughter before nine AM. It's a miracle."

She couldn't help it; she gave him a sleepy smiled. He was so goofy.

"And a smile! Thank you, Jesus!"

Iz kicked at him.

Turning serious, he lightly rubbed behind her knee. "Want me to get you a cup of coffee while you get dressed?"

She took a deep breath, let it out. Nodded.

Forty minutes and two cups of coffee later, she was human enough to agree to go to breakfast. In the passenger seat of Rover, Iz turned in her seat and looked behind her at all the space in the back.

"This vehicle is ridiculous."

Griffin turned the key. "What do you mean?" He turned to see what she was looking at.

"You're one person. What do you need all this room for? You're not the kind of guy who overcompensates for what he lacks physically with large material items – and you aren't lacking. So why do you have this thing?"

He gave her a quick glance before straightening in the seat. "The timing worked out on it. Why don't you find some music to listen to?"

Isabel's attention wasn't so easily diverted. As Griffin drove toward a cafe he had taken her to during the past few weeks, she was staring at the back seat. "You keep this beast meticulously clean for a guy. You must have some kind of personal reason for keeping it."

Even though he had the heat on, he felt a cool chill run up his spine. He reached out and tapped the touch screen to turn the radio on.

"What kind of music do you like? Alternative? Rock? Find a station you like."

Iz finally turned around in her seat. "Are you serious?" She ogled at the screen. "My car still has dials. I don't know how to use this thing."

"Play around with it."

She began tapping the screen, running through the menu slowly, trying to figure out how to use it.

"What is it with guys and their expensive toys?" she grumbled. "I need a goddamn PhD to figure this thing out."

"Jesus, Isabel. Who cares what car I drive?" He turned into the restaurant parking lot.

The sudden fury in his tone startled her. Sitting straight up in her seat, she clasped her hands in her lap and stared out the window. Griffin parked the car. For a moment, the only sound was his fingers thumping on the screen as he brought up the audio app and adjusted the volume to low. Metallica was singing about how nothing else mattered, and Isabel thought that about summed it up perfectly.

He rubbed a hand through his hair. "Shit."

"I'm... sorry," Isabel said uncertainly.

"For what?" His voice had deepened with the anger. He pressed his fingers to the bridge of his nose.

"Whatever I fucked up. I'll call an Uber."

Griffin's hand shot out and grabbed her forearm as she opened the door and was leaning out. He gently pulled her back inside. With her other hand still holding the door, it swung shut, filling Rover with a bang that seemed extraordinarily loud.

"Why would you call an Uber? We're going to have breakfast."

"It didn't sound like you wanted to spend time with me."

You can't even look at me, she thought, cringing inside. Why would you sit across a table and eat with me?

He was still holding her arm, fairly certain if he let go, she would split. Rubbing his thumb across her skin, he tried to settle his heart down.

"Of course, I want to spend time with you. I took the day off to be with you." His voice was softer.

Now he stared at his hand where he held her arm. Under his fingers, he felt her pulse was still throbbing. She was still in fight or flight mode, and Isabel was a flight risk. After a moment, he slid his hand down to grasp hers.

Deep breaths. Think before you speak.

"The friend I told you about, the one that killed himself, left Rover to me when he died. He said I could keep it or sell it and I... can't sell it just yet."

Isabel's insides were twisting into heavy knots, making them feel like molten lava, while her skin seemed to be frozen.

"Why did you assume this is your fault?" Griffin asked. He hated that he'd put that wounded look in her eyes.

She focused on the vent closest to her that was gently blowing heat. She refused to look at him. The sheen of tears was on her eyes, but they didn't spill over.

"Of course, it is."

"You didn't answer my question. Why do you think that?"

That relentless patience was back in his voice again.

"I fuck things up. It's what I do." A tear spilled over on the right cheek, and she thanked God, he couldn't see it. Damn her tears. Why couldn't she be strong, like Ava? A wall of stone, impassive, taking her punishment and waiting until she was alone in her apartment to bawl her eyes out. Instead, she had to be a blubbering mess, humiliating herself in front of him.

"Not this time." Griffin shifted in his seat, so he was turned toward her. He scrubbed his hands down his face. "I owe you an apology."

Isabel shifted uncomfortably. "That's not necessary. Let's just go in."

She didn't think she would be able to swallow anything more than coffee.

"I'm sorry I snapped at you. I'm a little raw this morning after that dream. That's not an excuse."

"You're having a bad day and you don't want me around. I get it."

She started to pull away, to reach for the door, but Griffin tightened his grip on her hand. "No, you don't get it. I'm apologizing. I didn't say anything about not wanting to be with you."

"I'm the one you snapped at, so it's pretty obvious I'm the one you're pissed at. You don't have to pretend to want to spend time with me just because-"

Griffin slammed his fist onto the center of the steering wheel. The horn barked out a quick, sharp squawk. He turned back to Isabel with a layer of steel in his eyes she hadn't seen before.

Taking a deep breath, he exhaled loudly, fighting not to take out his frustration on her. "I'm going to say this once, and then I'm going to keep my mouth shut because it's your family and none of my business."

Shocked, Isabel frowned. She had no idea what the hell he was talking about. She was gripping the inner seam of her jeans with extreme intensity.

"Everything bad that happens isn't your fault. I don't know why your mother got it into her head that you're to blame for everything, but she's wrong. And shame on your dad for not stopping her from doing it and for not telling you she was wrong."

He paused, reminded himself not to crush her tiny hand as he held it.

Isabel felt that if her eyes grew any bigger, they would pop out of their sockets like a character in a cartoon. There was fury in his eyes, but not at her; he was livid at her mother, a woman he had never met, because of the way she treated her daughter.

"Do you understand me?" he asked. His hands gripped her arms now with a desperation that conveyed he needed her to believe what he was telling her. "Do you hear me? I was being an asshole just now, not you."

Dazed, she nodded.

"You," he said, giving her a little shake so she would look at his eyes. "You're not something that passes my time until someone better comes along. Stop treating yourself that way. You're important to me."

380

Though her shocked expression never changed, her eyes welled and spilled over.

He let go of her arms and took her face in his hands. When he spoke, his voice had softened. "Oh, Izzie. Don't cry."

He rested his chin on the top of her head. As he moved his hand up and down her back, she curled against him. Her body felt fragile, vulnerable enough to break with a harsh word. Yet it molded to his so naturally, filling in everything he felt he was missing.

He pulled away and brushed hair from her face. Reaching into his jacket, he pulled out a handkerchief.

"This isn't the same one from the night we met, is it?" she asked, raising her eyebrow.

They both laughed.

Isabel cleaned herself up while Fog Hat was taking it easy in a slow ride on the radio.

"I just realized I know what kind of music you play but not what you listen to." His voice had lightened, leaving none of the fury she'd heard moments before.

"I can listen to anything." She gripped the handkerchief in both hands and fidgeted with it. "Thank you for saying that about my family."

"You needed to hear it. I hope someday you believe it." Letting his temper run rampant hadn't been one of his finer moments. "I won't say anything more on it; it's not my place to come between you and your family."

She felt she was on more solid ground again. Her pulse was leveling. Christ, he was so easy to like. Around him, she felt okay if she relaxed instead of feeling guilty. With him, she could laugh and the sound of it didn't make her own skin crawl.

He pressed his mouth to hers. The kiss was driven, wanting, yet remained gentle and thorough. His hand rose slowly to cup her chin. He had such warm, strong hands.

Outside, other people were coming and going, getting into their cars, or getting out of them, slamming their doors shut, but Griffin heard none of it. He only heard Isabel's soft noises as he kissed her. He pulled back to lean his forehead against hers again. Something strong passed between them when they did this; he couldn't explain it, but he enjoyed the feeling.

"We should probably eat breakfast while it's still morning." He straightened in the seat. "You need your second round of caffeine."

• • • • •

The man stood leaning against the sink, his hands braced on the counter on either side of him. He wore only a pair of dark blue boxers. The bare flesh of his chest was pale and pebbled with goosebumps. His short, light brown hair was spiked as if he had just tumbled out of bed.

Pushing himself off the counter, he stepped into the tub, careful not to bump the item he had set on the rim.

In spite of the warm bath water, he was drenched in a cold sweat. He wrapped his arms around his knees, rocking back and forth. His skin was slick and rubbery. Tears filled his eyes as he thought of the misguided pain some would go through. That couldn't be helped. With shaking hands, he covered his mouth. Disappointment was the worst part. He was disappointing people, and that was enough to make him feel like he was drowning.

The polished silver gleamed on the side of the bathtub. He had taken diligent care of the gun, went to target practice with it once a week, cleaned it after every use. He was as familiar with it as he was with his own hand. Now, when he picked it up, it seemed to weigh so much more than it ever had.

Carefully handling it, he practiced how he would hold it. He turned it so it faced him, placing the barrel in his mouth. His left hand took the grip of the gun. With his right, he steadied it, with his thumb on the trigger guard. He angled the barrel down, pointing it at the spot approximately where the base of his skull met his spinal column. He didn't want any mistakes and pointing it at his spinal cord was the quickest, most reliably fatal way to ensure no errors.

He pulled the barrel out of his mouth. Shutting his eyes tight, tears streamed down his face.

"I'm sorry," he whispered.

He put the barrel back in his mouth and pulled the trigger.

Ava rocketed out of the vision with a guttural scream and lurched forward. Her hand immediately flew to her mouth to verify she still had one. Her fingers moved over her jaw, down her neck. She made a retching sound that echoed off the bathroom walls.

Beneath her, the empty bathtub numbed her butt and stiffened her limbs. The lights were blinding her, making her head throb. Her breath was coming in gasping-wheezing sounds that made her sound possessed. She gripped the rim of the tub to steady herself.

She did not remember coming into the bathroom or stepping into the tub. Her last memory was thinking of Gabriel and trying to finish editing a client's rather large document.

Shaking. She hated the shaking, the lack of control over her own body that seemed to be more frequent lately. She was a well-disciplined person, with strict routines and precise boundaries, with no room for error. Why had her body been betraying her?

A sigh filled the room, echoing off the walls. Ava glanced around, searching for the source, and found Hayden standing in the doorway. Her head was tilted, like she expected Ava to do something. Like she was waiting for her.

Waiting for what?

• • • • •

Gabriel took his iced tea and walked back into his office. Spinning around in his chair to face his desk, he looked at the series of sketches he had started and wondered if he would ever get a look inside Ava's house.

After her abrupt exit recently, he doubted it.

He wanted to create a piece of furniture for her that was unique to her personality and her house, but that was hard to do when he didn't know the house. For now, he was starting simple using the little he knew about her. He was designing a pair of wooden nun chucks. He had no idea if Ava used nunchucks, and he had never designed a weapon before. This project was completely unfamiliar territory for him. The length and weight of the wood had to be precise, and any details he carved into the wood ran the risk of compromising the efficiency of their use as a weapon.

Not that Ava needed a weapon to defend herself, but Gabriel thought she might appreciate a gift that could be useful as well as beautiful.

On the side of one of the batons, he was considering different images: the yin/yang symbol, a dragon, a tiger, writing a phrase in the style of whatever language her main style was. So far, he had tried phrases in Chinese and Japanese.

Ava reminded him of a tiger. It was a large cat no one seemed to think much of that lived in the shadow of the lion but could just as efficiently maim with its plate-sized paws and teeth larger than a man's finger. People underestimate the tiger, and they seemed to underestimate Ava, too. If he chose the tiger, he would draw it at such an angle that one front paw extended forward disproportionately, with large claws.

Making anything for her was probably a waste of time anyway. She would see it as manipulation if he could get her to speak to him again. After her last outburst, he doubted there was any point reaching out. She needed a friend; that fact was obvious. But if she refused the gesture, he could nothing about it.

However, when he had a creative spark, he couldn't get rid of it until it was sated. He would make the nunchucks and leave them on her porch letting her know he expected nothing. That would be that.

Taking a sip of his tea, he returned to his sketches.

His cell phone rang. Glancing over at it, he saw his mother's smiling image filling the screen and debating whether to answer it. In the end, he picked up the phone.

"Hi, ma."

"Gabriel. Your father and I were discussing Easter dinner next Sunday."

That meant his mom and Beth had been discussing it, and his dad had left the room as soon as he could get away.

"Outstanding." His tone listless, Gabriel added a few marks to one of his sketches to deepen the shadow. He was leaning toward the tiger.

"We thought maybe... you could bring your little friend over again, unless she's spending it with her family."

"My little friend? I'm not eight years old, mom."

"Of course not. We just thought, if her family didn't live around here or something, she's more than welcome to spend Easter with us."

"You mean you and Beth want to grill her." Gabriel began outlining the head of a tiger.

"We didn't find out much about her," Allie said. "It would be nice to get her know her better, and it's a time for family. Will you ask her?"

"I don't know if she wants to talk to me, mom, but if she does, I'll give it a shot."

"What did you do?"

"You know, women are not as perfect and innocent as you claim to be." Gabriel's fist clamped down hard on the mechanical pencil. "I didn't do shit except try to be her friend. She's not a social person. If she doesn't want to be there, she won't be pressured into it."

After a long pause, his mother said, "Well, extend the invitation, and see what she says."

Dropping the pencil angrily onto his desk, he exhaled. "I'm sorry, mom. I didn't mean to snap at you."

"I know, honey. It's obvious you have feelings for her."

"Don't get all sentimental," he warned. "I'm trying to be her friend, not propose marriage."

"Of course." On the other end of the line, Allie smiled. "She just needs time and patience. With what she went through... I'm surprised she finds the energy to get out of bed every morning."

"I know. I'm just... frustrated."

In more ways than one, Allie thought, but kept that to herself.

"It will be wonderful to see you Sunday," she said. "We won't count on Ava, so if she shows up, we'll be pleasantly surprised."

●　●　●　●　●

As soon as she entered the dojo, Ava felt a wave of nausea strong enough to force her forward, dropping her gym bag and holding a hand to her mouth. She braced her other hand on her knee for over a minute until the nausea passed. Sensei never came out of the back room until class started, and Ava was grateful he hadn't witnessed her almost being sick.

Once he did come onto the mat, however, he began asking questions. Ava was easing into stretches when he stepped onto the mat, bowed, and took his place in front of her. His eyes narrowed as he took in the bruising and stitching around her eye and her wrapped hands.

"It looks like you had an interesting weekend."

"Hai, Sensei." A sharp pain slashed through her temple, making her wince.

Daniel, help him blow out the candles. He's too young.

Ava carefully eased into a kneeling position, her left ankle screaming in pain. They bowed in and Ava thought Sensei was going to let it go. Her nerves were just beginning to settle when he returned to the conversation.

"Tell me about it."

She was ready to work out. Her body wanted physical exertion. "There is nothing to tell, Sensei. None of my injuries will affect my training."

Danny, look at Daddy. Smile at Daddy so he can take a picture.

Ava closed her eyes, swallowed, tried to breathe. Her pulse was already too fast because of the pain.

"You're favoring several body parts. Explain your injuries or we don't train."

A flash of rage almost had Ava jumping to her feet. She had a right to train. Money transfers each month from her financial institution to her teacher's guaranteed her a right to train every Monday, Wednesday, and Thursday for two and a half hours each day without wasting time on other insignificant matters. Discipline must be absolute. When it stopped being absolute, the entire structure crumbled.

Curling her hands into fists, she struggled for control. "My right hand has superficial cuts and bruises on the knuckles. My left hand has a hole in the palm that needed stitches. I had to put stitches in a laceration above my right eye. My left knee was draining blood and pus, so I had to bandage and wrap it. My left ankle is not sprained, but it is close to being so. My right shoulder was almost dislocated again. I have tended to all these injuries properly. None of them will affect my training."

"They're already effecting your training. You're limping, your hand is bleeding, and you're distracted. What caused the injuries?"

Hard, lovely laughter rang through Ava's head, making her flinch.

Daniel, what are you doing?

She saw an image of a man and a woman, the man holding the woman briefly on a sandy beach before tossing her into an ocean.

She shook her head. The woman had long, brown hair, was wearing a ridiculously large hat, and sunglasses. When she surfaced in the water, she was laughing and coughing.

"You think that's funny?" she yelled. She dove for the man, tackling him into the water.

The man was Sensei.

Go away, Ava thought. Please go away.

Everything was happening too fast. Too many emotions were flooding into her, making her feel trapped. Amusement, sorrow, something so strong it washed over her and enveloped her, made her feel weak and strong and dizzy and weepy all at once. She did not know what that last emotion was.

Ava positioned herself for pushups, ready to work. Keeping her muscles active while they engaged in idle talk would help to keep her body distracted and lessen the pain.

"Ava, what happened?" Sensei asked, his tone firm now. "Let's start with your right hand."

"I punched a wall, Sensei."

"Why did you punch a wall?"

She dropped her head, inhaled. "I do not know. I was not aware I was doing it."

Daniel frowned. "Explain."

Massaging her forehead, careful to avoid the space over her right eye, Ava listened for the other voices and was relieved when she heard none.

"I have somnambulism. I walked over to a wall and was punching it in my sleep."

"I see." He didn't, not really, but what else could he say? "What about your right shoulder?"

"I fell down an embankment in the woods while training. The shoulder, knee, ankle, left hand, and cut above my eye are from the fall."

She hovered inches from the ground, her legs straight, arms slightly bent, waiting for him to start counting the pushups. He still did not start class.

"Did the doctor release you for training?"

"I did not consult a doctor." Her arms were shaking. The injury in her left hand and her stressed shoulder were weakening her ability to stay posed for pushups for an extended period. With a growl of resentment, she relaxed into a kneeling position.

"You said you have stitches above your eye and in your hand."

"I kept the stitches small. I packed the wounds efficiently, so I should not reinjure myself during training."

Daniel stared at her. "You administered your own stitches?"

Ava was unable to keep from sighing. What had Gabriel and his family done to her, that she had to work so hard to be polite to her teacher now?

"I know basic first aid and triage. I made sure there was no debris in or around the wounds. I have been regularly cleaning and dressing them. I have had no fever or red streaks on the skin. I will remove the stitches after two weeks, as recommended."

He regarded her thoughtfully, trying to decide if he should examine the wounds himself to see if she was cleared for training. Ava could be stubborn as hell, and she would push herself beyond her limits if he didn't keep an eye on her. Then again, wasn't that what life was about?

"Let's begin." They set up for pushups and he began counting them off in Japanese, watching her closely. "Ichi, ni, san, shi..."

The rhythm and structure began to put her at ease.

Until the wave of nausea hit her again. They had just finished a set of pushups on their fists and Ava had all she could do to keep from vomiting on the mat.

"Do you need a few minutes?" Sensei asked. She had gone pale, and her eyes were barely open, as if to shield against the light.

She shook her head very slowly. Dizziness was now added to the nausea.

They began another set of pushups. Images, like pieces of pictures, flickered through her head, too fast for her to process. She winced. A trickle of blood slid from her ear, down her jaw.

Despite sharing Sensei's detachment for his wife during a previous vision of her suicide, Ava realized that indifference as she watched him stand over her body had been fleeting. What he truly felt for her, before the death of their son, he identified as love. He had cared deeply for this woman whose image flashed in Ava's mind with bright smiles and embraces full of passion.

"How are you doing, Ava?" Daniel asked, watching her struggle. She was trying not to, but she kept wincing. Her balance and concentration were off.

"Fine, Sensei. Arrigato, gozaimashita."

Her voice was strained, and she was only repeating a trained response. Daniel could tell when his students were truly thankful and when they were being respectful to him and the Japanese tradition.

In between sets of pushups, she pressed her palm to her right eye.

Daniel counted off the next set in Japanese, watching her as he did to see how she reacted.

Daddy.

"Ugh." Ava turned her head to the side, closing her eyes and pressing her right palm to her temple. She shook her head, resumed the position for the next set of pushups. Something seemed to be sitting on her chest, constricting her lungs.

Love, she thought. Such an intangible concept. How could something invisible weigh so much?

Another image of his wife, this time holding a tiny, silent baby to her chest as she stared down at it with amazed gratitude. Sensei leaned over her, watching their baby son sleep against her, his heart filled with adoration.

The images sped up again, shuffling like slides on a film projector. She feared she would vomit on the mats.

They were halfway through another set of pushups when his wife's face, clearer than the everything else, appeared suddenly in her mind, and she heard a woman's voice. Ava's right wrist buckled, and she almost collapsed to the floor.

Daniel.

She let out a strangled cry. Sitting back on her calves, she pressed her left palm to her temple now, turning her head and moaning softly. Small gasps of air were all she could pull into her lungs.

"Ava," Daniel said. "Can you tell me what's happening?"

Dandy, tell me the story about Hungry Hungry Caterpillar.

"Dandy." Ava spat the word, trying to get rid of it. She pressed her palm to her aching chest. She couldn't breathe.

"What?" Daniel leaned forward slightly. "Why did you say that?"

"Dandy, read me a story." The voice of a young child came from Ava's lips. She closed her eyes. Her voice lost the childish lilt when she said, "He called you Dandy. 'Daniel' and 'Daddy' put together. Your wife thought it was funny that he fused the two words together."

She ground her palm into her eye. "Stop it."

"Ava, work on your breathing, like we practiced. You need to get control of this."

"You need to get control of it," she barked, pressing her fingers to her forehead. "They are your memories. You are not even trying to block them from me anymore."

A moment later she realized she had been disrespectful and apologized in Japanese. "They are distracting. They hurt my head."

"You're picking up on my memories?"

Hesitantly, she nodded. She apologized again in Japanese. "They are... very loud today."

"We need to focus harder on how you can control it, so you can make it stop."

"Hai, Sensei."

"Your ear is bleeding. Let's get that cleaned up and I'll shut down the extra noise in my head."

•　　•　　•　　•　　•

"So," Griffin said, as he held open his apartment door for Isabel, "how did it feel reading Chuck Palahniuk to an elderly boxer-lab-mix?"

"Dundee enjoyed it," Isabel said, referring to the dog, who had crawled as much as he could into her lap and immediately fell asleep. "I don't know that 'Choke' is an appropriate book to read to an elderly dog, but it's quite entertaining to me. What did you read to your charge?"

"Rodgers has very specific taste." Griffin draped his jacket over an island stool. "He's into sports biographies, which is why I read him a bio about Vince Lombardi."

"Why the hell would someone name a dog Roger?" Isabel took a bottle of water out of his refrigerator and twisted the cap.

"Not Roger, Rodgers. As in Aaron Rodgers."

"For fuck's sake. Someone named a dog after the quarterback of the Green Bay Packers? How pathetic are sports fans?" She took a deep drink of water. Reading aloud, something she hadn't done since her senior year in high school, had given her cotton mouth.

"Not pathetic. Dedicated. Rodgers likes hearing about previous managers." Griffin took the bottle from her and stole a sip of water.

"You could read the ingredients off a box of flea treatment and Rodgers would be thrilled," Isabel said. "I would, too. It's not what you read, it's the sound of your sexy voice."

"Reeeeaaaally?" he dragged the word out, raising his eyebrows. Grabbing her around the waist, he yanked her against him.

"I thought that the first time I met you." She brushed the hair back from his forehead. "If you read the procedure on small bowel resection surgery, I'd still fall at your feet."

Laughing, he gave her a long, slow kiss. "I like it when you flatter me."

"The rest of my flattery will have to wait," she said, sighing. "I want to take a nap in the middle of the day, just because I can."

"I told you reading to dogs in shelters was therapeutic. You can take a nap in a minute," Griffin said, tugging on her hand. "I bought something for you the other day."

He left her at the island and walked to a cupboard near the refrigerator.

"Why did you buy me something?" she asked.

"I came across it and it made me think of you." Kneeling in front of the cupboard, he pulled out a long black box. He stood and pivoted, handing the box to her.

Frowning, she read Bushmills Single Malt Irish Whiskey. Aged 21 Years.

"Holy shit," she said. "It came in a box."

"When whiskey comes in a box, it's classy. When wine does, it's trashy. I don't get it, but that's how it is."

Isabel wasn't a connoisseur of whiskey. Once she found out it had a bite to it that fought back and made her feel agitated instead of weepy, she had picked the first brand off the shelf that she could afford. Her brand didn't come in a box. She knew enough to understand whiskey that came in a box cost a small fortune.

"I also bought some whiskey tumblers to keep around here so you have something more suited to your drink of choice," Griffin said. "Whiskey out of a wine or juice glass is just wrong."

Iz found her hands were unsteady as she opened the box. Gifts made her uncomfortable from people she had known all her life. Griffin had known her less than a month. She hadn't gotten anything for him.

The amber liquid inside looked delicious and smooth. At that moment, she wanted to pour it on Griffin's body and lick it off. She blinked the image away.

Griffin couldn't quite tell if she was just in shock or if she was angry that he had bought it for her. Her eyes were wide and unblinking, focused intently on the bottle.

"H-how much did this cost, Griffin?"

"What does that matter?"

"It looks really expensive. You didn't have to buy me anything this expensive." She reached out and gingerly touched the bottle, then yanked her hand back as if it was hot. "Mine costs, like, twenty bucks."

"I would spend every last dime on you without thinking twice about it," Griffin said absently. "Have you ever tried it?"

"No. I've never even heard of it."

"Well, let's try a drink before your nap, and see how good three-hundred-dollar whiskey is."

"Three hundred dollars?!" Isabel almost dropped the bottle.

"Shit," he muttered. He snagged the bottle from her. "I didn't mean to blurt that out. Enjoy it. It's a gift."

"I could pay two bills with that money!"

Griffin reached into a cupboard and brought out two expensive looking tumblers. "If you want help paying your bills, I'll help you. For now, enjoy some whiskey."

"Griffin-"

He leaned over and stopped her protests with a kiss. Isabel couldn't help it; she softened, leaning back against the island as her legs threatened to buckle. What a sweet gesture, she thought, framing his face with her hands as her lips warmed to his. It was the sweetest thing anyone had done for her in a long time. Not because of how much it cost, but because he saw it and it made him think of her. Because without thinking, he offered to pay her bills if she needed help. Her pride would never allow her to accept that, of course, but he had offered without her asking. How many times, in the brief time they had known each other, had he caught her before she started to fall?

She slid her arms up around his neck and pressed her body against his.

"Mmm." Griffin broke the kiss and gazed at her. "I see my powers of seduction are working."

"You're the sweetest person I know."

His arms were wrapped around her, his hands still holding the bottle and the two tumblers. When she shifted, the glass rubbed together and made a grinding noise. Isabel let go of him instantly.

"Sorry!" She started to push away from him, but he flexed his arms to hold her tight against him.

"Slowly," he said, grinning. "I don't want to drop these. Let me step away from you."

He set the glasses on the island and poured whiskey in each. Handing her one, he tapped his glass to hers.

"To..."

"The good things in life," Isabel said softly. "Even if they're hard to find sometimes."

"To the good things in life."

They sipped.

Isabel closed her eyes. "Oh. This is good."

"The description sounded like something you would like. I don't know anything about whiskey, but I remember reading something about honey and dark mocha."

"It's really good." Iz set her glass down and slipped her arms around his waist. "Thank you."

"You are most wel-"

Isabel's cell phone suddenly rang. She continued nuzzling into his chest, ignoring the call, but he glanced over her head to see her screen.

"It's your mum." He felt her muscles bunch against him. "Don't you want to talk to her?"

Pulling away from him with a sigh, she turned away and snatched up her phone. "Hello. I know it's Easter next Sunday."

Closing her eyes, Isabel reached for her drink and took a healthy swig. She leaned her head back and rotated it, cracking her neck.

"I'm not sure if I'll be busy next Sunday. I might... have plans."

Isabel took another drink and slid the tumbler to the side. Turning so her butt was against the island, she angled her head toward her shoulder and propped her phone there while she hoisted herself up onto the granite.

"I know we always have Sunday dinners together," she said, absently rubbing her temples. Griffin walked over to her and stood in front of her, keeping a few inches from her so she didn't feel crowded. He rested his hands on her thighs.

"I know, but..." Raising her free hand, Isabel held it up like a claw and clenched her teeth.

Griffin grinned, moving his hands up and down her legs.

"I understand that-"

The grip on her phone was tightening.

"I don't know if Griffin and I have plans." Her eyes widened and her jaw dropped. "Oh, shit."

Confused, he tilted his head.

"Fuck." Isabel ran a hand through her hair. "No, I-" She closed her eyes again. Listened. "No. Mom... Mom... Will you listen? He's my boyfriend!"

Griffin watched her put her hand to her mouth, close her eyes again, rub her forehead. "I'll find out."

When she opened her eyes again, she looked tired. "I said I'll find out. I have to go. Bye."

Dropping the phone on the counter, Isabel put her fingertips to her temples.

"What was that all about?" Griffin gripped her hips, pulling her against him.

"I did not mean to blurt that out." She held up her empty tumbler. "More."

"It's more to be enjoyed slowly..."

"Please."

He poured a second glass. "Do you not want your family to know about me?"

Trying to sip slowly, to hold onto the thought behind the gift of the drink, Isabel took a deep breath, let it out.

"You're mine," she stated, gazing at him. "I like having someone I don't have to share with my family. I like not feeling like I have to compete with my feelings for you. You're all mine."

Dropping her head, she frowned. "I want you for myself. It's selfish, and childish. I -"

Griffin gripped her shirt and yanked her toward him, giving her a rough, searing kiss. "You had me at 'You're mine.'" He beamed.

She smiled. "I may have inadvertently volunteered you to eat dinner at my parent's house on Sunday."

"Is your mum a good cook?"

"Ha. Mum. She's an excellent cook. My whole family will be there. Brother, sister, brother-in-law."

"I love food."

"My parents will be there. You'll be meeting my parents."

"Yeah, I got that part. What time?" He took a sip of her drink as she ogled at him.

"That doesn't bother you? We've only been dating a few weeks."

"Just let me know what we're eating so I bring the right wine."

• • • • •

Two hours later, Ava was anxious to start working on control.

Training, though more exhausting than usual because of her injuries, had allowed her to clear her mind of all distractions. It was a reprieve. The pain reset the focus she had been losing over the past couple weeks. Her body responded willingly to her commands. Her head cleared of personal matters that should not have been bothering her to begin with. For the first time in several days, Ava felt less like a puppet being used by some other force.

But it was also grueling, and as her body tired, her mind dulled.

They were almost finished with training. Ava was having trouble doing her part so Sensei could practice his full technique. For some reason, she was not blocking his kick correctly to allow him to continue to the second part of the move. She was frustrated with herself. He had told her to take a break and now she was anxiously waiting for him to return to the mat so she could be a good partner.

"I'm going too easy on you," he said from the back hallway as he walked toward the mat. "I felt sorry for you because of your injuries. I've been giving you a break, decreasing the speed and power of my techniques."

He bowed to the kamidana, they bowed to each other. "You don't get any more breaks."

"Hai, Sensei. Arrigato, gozaimashita."

They took their stances, facing off. This time, he came at her full speed and almost full power. Ava moved too late, and the kick hit her square in the abdomen. She was knocked across the mat before falling on her stomach.

"You're still trying to stop it head-on," Sensei said sternly. "If I hadn't held back, that kick would have broken bones. You have to deflect it."

"Hai, Sensei."

Using more effort than usual to stand, Ava took a moment before she raised her head. Daniel could see the fury in her eyes. She was able to keep it from effecting the cadence of her voice or her expression, but she couldn't keep it from showing in her eyes.

"Again. We're staying here until you get this."

"Hai, Sensei."

They took their stances. Daniel saw Ava twitch and blink. Her eyes became distant.

"You're already zoning out," he said, exasperated. "Where are you today?"

He started toward her.

"He is waiting for me."

Realizing too late that Ava wasn't herself, he tried to shift and move his kick past her.

Ava blocked the kick using a technique from a style and level she wasn't currently training on. Instead of allowing him to move onto his next technique, she struck back. Daniel blocked her, pivoting his hand so he could lock her wrist. He was able to get a good look at her face. Her pupils were dilated, making her eyes look as predatory and emotionless as a shark's. Then her eye sockets turned black.

"Ava-"

Before he could say more, Ava threw another punch, still in defense mode. She began striking and kicking using every style and level she had been studying for years, using full power and speed. Daniel could see she was not practicing; she was convinced her life was in danger. He moved around the dojo as he countered her assaults, trying not to hurt her even as he defended himself.

"Ava, listen to my voice," he said as she swung. He deflected a blow and caught her wrist in another lock, hoping to buy time to get through to her. "I'm not your enemy."

She twisted out of his grip and kicked at his stomach. He blocked, held her leg.

Ava snarled; her eyes glazed.

"You're in the dojo. Can you hear me?"

She lifted into the air and spun around, kicking at his head. Daniel let go of her leg and ducked, moving away from her. She did a forward role and struck with a tiger claw.

Around the dojo they went; punching, kicking, blocking, using wrist locks and arm locks, gaining speed as her adrenaline spiked.

Daniel could no longer justify keeping her busy while he waited for her to regain control. One of them was going to get seriously hurt if they continued like this; she was his fastest and most dedicated student. He blocked her next strike and gave her a solid punch in the solar plexus to slow her down. Leaning over slightly, she wheezed to try to catch her breath. Shifting his stance so they were side by side, Daniel put his palm on the back of her head and drove it forward as he planted his leg in front of both of hers. She was driven unceremoniously to the floor. As soon as she hit the mat, he had her wrist locked, his palm on her elbow, and his knee in her back. She was pinned.

She struggled violently against him.

"Ava, stop," he repeated firmly. "You're going to dislocate your shoulder."

"Take your fucking hands off her."

The voice was deep and full of rage. Her entire body was vibrating with hatred. Her ear had begun to bleed again. The cut above her eye was freely flowing, trickling down her forehead. Dried blood was smeared down her temple. In his hand, the bandage on her left palm was soaked with blood. More of it was slicked all over the mats.

"Yame." Daniel said firmly. He used his body weight to hold her in place, knowing if he shifted at all, she would find a weak point and use it to shove him off her.

She put her free hand on the mat and pushed up even though it put immediate pressure on her right arm and shoulder. Daniel was worried she would pop it out of joint again. He thought he might have to knock her unconscious before she injured herself more.

"Listen to my voice." He kept his voice calm, his breath steady. "Come back to me."

"You couldn't hold onto your son," she growled. "What makes you think you can hold onto her?"

"Come back to me, Ava," Daniel repeated patiently. "You're safe now."

She snarled at him, but her body was finally wearing out. Daniel knew better than to ease up.

Her struggles became less structured, more panicked. A half-sob, half-growl of fury escaped her. Part of her hair had come out of her ponytail and little pieces were sticking up like lightning bolts. More blood was smeared across her cheek. Sweating, her face flushed from exertion, tears running every which way down her face, she let out a resigned sigh.

He felt her body deflate as if something had left it. She stopped struggling. She was only drawing in shorts gasps, her throat choked with tears. After a moment, she was able to draw in a little more air with each inhale. He could hear her straining to control her breathing. Her free hand was splayed on the mat, her fingers sinking into the material as she fought to regain control.

Gradually, the pauses between her inhales and exhales lengthened as her breathing slowed. Her hand remained rigid, but she was no longer imprinting her fingertips into the mat. Her body slowly relaxed underneath Daniel's hands.

After a moment, her voice drifted up. "Sensei?"

She sounded confused.

"Are you back?"

"Hai, Sensei." She apologized in Japanese.

Daniel gently released her.

She rolled into a kneeling position and bowed, repeating her apology. He could see she was trembling even from a few feet away. Still, her brow was furrowed, and her eyes were shifting. She was trying to work something out in her head.

"That could have turned out a lot worse," he said.

Ava apologized a third time in Japanese. The trembling increased.

Daniel chose his next words carefully. "Let's talk about it."

From her expression, she clearly didn't want to discuss it. But the episode had disturbed training and directly involved Daniel. They would take care of it now.

"I do not know what to say, Sensei," Ava said quietly. Running her fingertips over her cheek, she blinked in surprise when they came away wet with blood.

"Let's bow out first, then we need to tend to your wounds. We'll discuss it then."

"Hai, Sensei."

Several minutes later, Ava stepped out of the tiny bathroom holding a towel to her left palm. The cut above her eye was red from her cleaning it but had finally stopped bleeding. She had washed all the excess blood off the visible parts of her body. She was sore, but her left ankle, knee, and right shoulder were in agony. She had kept the wraps on them, even though they were disgusting sweaty bands, to give those parts as much support as she could until she could shower and change them at home. What the hell had she done?

"The lighting is better in my office," Sensei said, motioning for her to follow him.

He had set two first aid kits on a wooden desk set up in one corner. The room was too bright, but Daniel needed the light to see how she was healing. He began checking her over, starting with the cut over her eye.

"Nice stitches."

He gently touched the skin around the wound to make sure it wasn't feverish.

"You were in an altered state right before I kicked?" he asked, turning her head to catch the light better.

Ava winced as he checked the stitches and made sure none of them had been knocked loose or split open.

"Now's not the time to be shy, Ava." He put ointment on the cut and began opening a large bandage.

"It is not that, Sensei."

The expression on her face was one of profound loss and confusion. Daniel found himself wanting to embrace her, as he had embraced his wife when she lost her mother.

"What, then?" he asked.

"I do not know what you are talking about."

Pausing, Daniel glanced at her. "We were practicing my technique. I kicked, and you attacked me."

Her body jerked at the absurd suggestion. "I would never attack you, Sensei."

"Why did you apologize to me when I had you on the floor?"

"I was not being a good partner, handling your technique properly. I thought I made another mistake, and you used a different technique to teach me a lesson."

Something had taken her over. Daniel didn't like the idea. What was the alternative? Selective memory loss to cover the fact that she had attacked her own teacher? She would consider it a horrible breach of trust, but she had survived far worse without blocking it out.

Holding the large bandage up, he said, "I'm just covering the wound so sweat doesn't run into it. You can do something more permanent once you get home."

"Hai, Sensei."

Daniel gently pressed the bandage to the cut above her eye. As he smoothed it down and made sure it was firmly attached, he turned his attention back to Ava.

"What's the last thing you remember?"

"You said we were going to train until I understood the technique."

"And then you were on the floor, and I had you in a lock?"

"H-hai, Sensei."

He thought about that for several moments. "It appears you have a heightened sense of danger while in an altered state. That makes sense. I apologize for not realizing what was going on sooner."

Though she did not believe he owed her an apology, she thanked him for it. "Arrigato, gozaimashita."

He could barely hear her; she was talking so quiet. As if all her energy had drained.

"I'll have to think about this. You don't remember fighting me at all? Or anything you said after I pinned you?"

"No, Sensei. What did I say?"

"We're going to bench this issue until I have a chance to think about it more. What about last Thursday? With Vincent? You remember that."

Several moments passed before she said, "Hai, Sensei."

"Tell me about it."

"It is a personal problem, Sensei."

"It became my problem when you attacked me in my own dojo," Sensei stated. "Talk."

Ava took a deep breath, released it. "It was a memory."

"A memory?"

When she didn't continue, he gave her a pointed look.

"You are aware that the senses stimulate memories for people: a smell or a sound can prompt a recollection of an earlier time in a person's life. The emotions associated with those memories are also stirred by those same stimuli."

Trying not to smile at the clinical way she described it, he said, "I think of my grandma and the joy of childhood when I smell homemade apple pie. Is that what you're referring to?"

She nodded. "Memories are different for me than they are for most."

"How so?"

The quaking had ceased, but she looked unnerved. Thick bands of gray under her bloodshot eyes made her look like an extra out of an old black and white monster movie. Her skin was pasty.

"Stimuli can prompt a memory, but... I recall every sense. A memory for me is like a post-traumatic stress disorder flashback."

"You relive the experience."

Her eyes were smokey. She closed them a moment, inhaled, nodded. When she opened them, there was no light. Just a dull acceptance, similar to what had been there when he began training her, after the rage had passed. That had been before she began to trust her new life with David and Ruth.

"I do not know how to stop the memory once it starts."

"What..." Daniel cleared his throat, considered what he wanted to ask her. He wanted to know what the memory on Thursday was about, but her past was a deeply personal matter. "That's never effected your training before. You've had three instances in less than a month. Do you know why?"

"Vomiting the w-water was... part of a... vision. Last Thursday's incident was a memory. I do not know what tonight's was. I do not remember the event you speak of."

Ava felt as if she was going to pass out from exhaustion. If she could only close her eyes for a moment...

"What was the memory about on Thursday?"

She brought her fingers to the bridge of her nose. "My f-foster father."

"David?"

She shook her head. "The one before. M-Mack."

Daniel mulled that over.

"Usually-"

She lowered her hand, opened her eyes slowly. Uncomfortable in her own skin now, she wished Sensei would stop talking. A hot shower and a warm bed were all she wanted now.

"Usually what?" Daniel hated to keep pushing her. She was half out of it from exhaustion. But he needed all the pieces to make an informed opinion.

Ava was starting to lose her ability to conceal her emotions. "I have nightmares," she said tightly. "My memories usually come as nightmares that wake me throughout the night."

"And these memories are usually of Mack, the foster father before David and Ruth adopted you."

Nodding, her eyes closed, Ava's head started to dip.

"He abused you."

Her head jerked up; her eyes flew open.

"You relive his abuse through nightmares."

He was running it all through his head, putting the pieces together, trying to be quick because she was about to drop. She had leveled her gaze on him but was no longer speaking.

"But lately you've relived memories during the day... as well as through the nightmares?"

She nodded.

"I need to think about this, and you need to get some sleep. Do you need me to drop you off at Vincent's? You shouldn't drive."

Once again, she nodded.

Later, he walked her to Vincent's door. In the hallway, she stumbled on the carpet, and he caught her by the arm. Instantly her muscles stiffened in his hand. She twisted her shoulders and her head in a way that made it obvious his touch revolted her. He ignored her reaction and lifted his hand to knock.

Ava tilted her head to the side, digging in her purse. "He is not home."

Daniel watched as she pulled her keys out and used both hands to isolate the correct one.

"Maybe you should take tomorrow off from training."

She lifted her head. Insult filled her eyes. "I am capable of training."

Opening the door with a little too much enthusiasm, she stalked in, dropping her bag just inside the apartment. She put her hand to her forehead. Though her ear had stopped bleeding, a hint of dark crimson stained her jawline.

He'd hurt her feelings. He saw that as well as the insult in her eyes. In sixteen years of training with him, she had only missed a partial hour a few weeks ago because he demanded she go home. Otherwise, she'd had a perfect attendance record. Her attendance was important to her.

"Ava, I know you're capable. I think you should give yourself a break. You're pushing yourself too hard, physically and mentally."

She fumbled out of her jacket, took the belt of her dojo uniform off. "Thank you for the ride, Sensei."

Now fuck off, was what she wanted to say, Daniel knew, even though she would never tell him that. He almost grinned despite himself.

After he left, Ava stripped down and showered. The hot water felt great, but she couldn't stand up for long. She hurriedly washed her hair and scrubbed her body and had to sit on the edge of the tub to dry off. Sitting with her hair wrapped up in one towel and the other towel around her shoulders was the last thing she remembered.

Vincent realized his apartment was unlocked as soon as he started to turn the key. His body was immediately on alert until he caught Ava's scent. All his senses tuned into her: the feeling of her presence in the apartment, the smell of his soap in her hair and on her body, a soft sound she was making in another room.

He locked the door behind him. It was not unusual for her to visit any day of the week, but the energy in his apartment was off. Hanging his jacket in the closet, he listened for any sounds that would explain what was going on. Ava didn't play games. She let him know instantly where she was when she visited.

He was quiet as he walked to the end of the hallway, ready for anything.

Or so he thought.

Ava was in his bedroom. She stood, nude, in front of the sliding glass door leading onto the balcony. Her left hand hung at her side wrapped in white gauze. Her left knee was also wrapped, and one of his ice packs was strapped around it. Even more gauze supported her ankle, and another ice pack was strapped to that. When she lifted her hand to the glass door, Vincent saw her knuckles were bandaged, though not as heavily as the left.

"Ava," he said softly.

Something was in her right hand.

Vincent didn't realize it was a marker until she began writing on the glass patio door.

As he neared her, walking slowly, he saw she had been writing on his door for quite some time. Half of one panel of glass was covered in black sentences.

She had written "I'll tell you a secret" repeatedly on the glass and raised her hand to start again.

"Ava." Deliberately sharpening his tone, he made sure to do so while he was still ten feet from her.

The hand with the marker paused. Ava turned her head to the side but didn't look at him. Her long hair fell forward too far for him to see her face. Her right hand twitched as it hovered just above the glass.

"What are you doing?"

Dropping her hand, Ava slowly turned her body toward him, pivoting her feet awkwardly as if she had just learned how to use them. Vincent saw bruising above her left eye surrounding yet another bandage. Her eyes were milky and blind.

"'I'll tell you a secret.'"

The voice was feminine, but not Ava's. Young, childlike. Even when they had first began training together, her voice hadn't sounded like that.

Vincent took a step closer. She instantly dropped the marker and stepped back into a stance, raising her hands to defend herself.

"Back away."

The voice was deep, rumbling from Ava's throat in a menacing growl.

Vincent retreated two steps, but Ava stayed as she was. Her thick, damp hair hung past her breasts and down her back. Her body was beaded with sweat from the exertion of holding the stance while it was so weak.

"Ava, it's Vincent."

How long had her eyes been like that? He wanted to talk to Sensei about her eyes changing, and the writing. Was his teacher fully aware of what was going on? He pulled his phone out of his back pocket and accessed the camera. Zooming in on her face, he held the button down to take several pictures, hoping one or two would turn out. The flash caused Ava to squint and turn her head away. She broke her stance and pivoted back to the glass door, laying her palm against it. Vincent pointed the phone at his patio door and took pictures of the writing in marker, avoiding getting Ava in the shot. He would send them to Sensei first thing in the morning.

Moving slowly, Vincent stepped toward Ava again. Her head whipped around at that, but her eyes were no longer milky. They had returned to their natural gray shade, staring at him with suspicion.

"Ava?"

"I will wash the writing off your door."

"I don't care about my door. Are you okay?"

"Vincent," she said, sighing tiredly, "I believe this is going to kill me."

•   •   •   •   •

CHAPTER EIGHT

All the flowers were dead. Shriveled and discolored, they lay around the grave, scattered from a previous day's wind. With dark gray clouds overhead and dead flowers on the ground, Isabel felt like she was standing in a scene from one of Edgar Allen Poe's works. She looked down at Hayden's marker. It was the same marker she had seen thousands of times before and would probably look at thousands of times more. If the sky opened right now and the wrath of the storm crashed down on her, if the ground opened and swallowed her up, would anyone raise an eyebrow?

"I failed you," she whispered. "I didn't know."

The day was warm. When the tears came, they were hot as they slid down her cheeks. Isabel knelt and gathered the dead flowers thoughtfully left by family members.

It was a silly tradition, really. I love you, have a symbol of my love by accepting something pretty I severed from its body so it would die in a few days. Our love is like this flower – a decapitated, dying, once beautiful thing.

Carrying the old flowers back toward her car, she tossed them in the nearest garbage bin as she passed it. Her hands were shaking again.

"I deserve Griffin," she said softly. She brushed the back of her hand over her cheek, trying to be grateful. An attitude of gratitude, isn't that what the experts said? I have Griffin, a boyfriend that stands up for me. The temperatures almost reached sixty degrees today. There is so much to be grateful for.

Yet each step made her feel as if her shoes were filled with lead. She wished her depression were a physical thing standing in front of her so she could kick its ungrateful ass.

"You're an asshole, depression." She yanked open her car door. "Eat a bag of dicks."

•　　•　　•　　•　　•

A storm was coming. Ava could sense it. Was that part of her ability, or did she simply smell it, as animals could? How close did a storm have to be before a person could smell it?

Because storms this early in the season could still be chilly, she shut all the windows in her house before she left for class. She wasn't sure when the storm would start or if rain would come in the windows. Having the windows open during the day had helped lift her feelings of claustrophobia, which always surfaced at the end of winter. Months of closed up buildings was wearing on her, especially with her life seeming to spiral out of control. She was reluctant now to lock herself in.

In the Equinox, she rolled her windows down a little. She had been enjoying the cool but fresh air, the feeling of being released. Even today, when the temperature had reached the mid-fifties, she was grateful to be able to open her windows and air out the house and car. She hated being caged for so long in the winter.

The air washed over her as she drove, helping to clear her head.

During her last class, she had attacked Sensei. She did not remember it, but he said she had, so she believed it. The embarrassment was almost too much to bear, even more so than describing her injuries from her careless training the night before. If she had been the type of person to avoid confrontation, she would have skipped tonight's class. But she was not that type of person. She had to face him. She had to face herself.

Pulling into the parking lot several minutes later, Ava closed her eyes and took deep breaths, readying herself for training. Total concentration was needed. No more distraction, no more allowing herself to get taken over by everything else. She would focus and complete training to the best of her ability instead of succumbing to whatever whim the spirit realm had. Letting it control her was causing almost as much stress as the invasion into her life of other entities.

Ava did not do stress.

During training, she practiced each technique slowly, methodically, making sure her stances, strikes, and kicks were lined up and she followed through. She focused her gaze on Sensei's eyes so she could draw energy from him, and flawlessly executed every move and countermove. At the end of two and a half hours, when he called out in Japanese to end their class and bow out, she looked around, surprised the session was over so quickly.

Showering and changing as quickly as she could, she wrapped her left hand and knee. The hand was routinely agitated because of the physical strain she put on it. She had to bandage it and then wrap it in several layers of thick gauze to keep it protected from impact. The twisted knee was taking longer to heal because it was also abraded, but the cuts and bruises were coming along well.

Her ankle, finally starting to feel better during the day, trembled with exhaustion after class. Kneeling on the floor to bow in and out exacerbated the sprain. Still, she only had to wrap it after classes now instead of every day. The limp was almost completely gone except for an hour or two after class.

Her shoulder was down to a pulsing ache that increased to an almost intolerable pounding after several rounds of pushups. There was nothing she could do for that except soak in Epsom salt baths at night and ice it regularly.

She had mostly forgotten about the cut above her eye, except that after any sort of exercise, even her daily running regimen, made her head throb. The redness in the skin was gone, and tonight she did not bother putting a bandage on it. The fresh air would keep it from being in a constant moist state.

She met Sensei in The Meditation Room. Setting her bag and mini backpack in one corner, she limped over to where they sat to meditate. He was standing near his desk, just finishing up an apple as he frowned over something he was reading.

"Are you hungry?" he asked, motioning with the apple. "I have extra."

"No, Sensei. Arrigato, gozaimashita."

Tossing the core into the trash, he brought the paperwork he was reading and a mini recorder over and sat across from her, cross-legged. He studied her until she became self-conscious and wanted to squirm.

"You did well in class today."

"Arrigato, gozaimashita."

"How are your injuries healing?"

"Well, Sensei. Arrigato, gozaimashita."

"Your head looks better. Monday it was pretty raw. Today it looks like it's starting to heal."

She thanked him again in Japanese.

"Do you remember anything about Monday's confrontation with me?" Daniel watched her eyes closely for any signs that she was embarrassed or holding back information. She wasn't. Her eyes were blank.

"No, Sensei."

"Did you have any feelings of loss of control or of... being taken over?" Daniel set the activated recorder and paperwork to the side, out of the way.

"No, Sensei."

Though her voice was calm, her face expressionless, he noticed her breathing was becoming labored. Her chest rose and fell in short, steadily increasing hitches.

"Does talking about our altercation Monday upset you?"

"No, Sensei. I do not know how to help you."

Something in her expression wavered. Barely there, Daniel wasn't sure if it was a twitch, a ripple, or a figment of his imagination. He couldn't even explain what he saw, just that Ava's face had momentarily changed as he looked at it.

"You said something strange on Monday," he said, watching her carefully. Her left hand twitched.

"You said, 'You couldn't hold onto your son, what makes you think you can hold onto her?' Do you know what that means, Ava?"

"Let's stop pretending," the thing inside Ava said. "What do you really want to ask me?"

Daniel felt ice along his spine at the inhuman voice coming from his most beloved student.

"Who are you?" he asked.

"Ava calls me The Monster."

"What do you call yourself?"

Ava's eyes slipped closed, and her body tipped sideways. She righted herself, leveling her gaze at Daniel.

"My name is not important. Leave her alone. I won't let you hurt her."

"I would never hurt her," Daniel said. "She doesn't need you anymore. She can take care of herself."

Ava blinked several times. When she raised her head, her eyes were full of confusion.

"I am sorry, Sensei. What did you say?"

Daniel watched her eyes move around the room as if she were trying to remember why she was there. Her hand came up and absently rubbed the back of her neck.

"I was just saying I've been doing some research in between our meditation sessions," he said, deciding to think further on the other subject before discussing it with her. "I know you're anxious to get past meditating, but your focus has been off, and you haven't been able to go into a deeper state consistently. It takes practice."

"Hai, Sensei."

"You've been able to get there; now you just need to keep going until you can do it at any time, no matter what the conditions around you."

"Hai, Sensei."

"However, we need to keep you safe while you're working your way up to that higher level of meditation. Have you ever read anything about spirit guides?"

"No, Sensei."

"Do you remember seeing someone throughout your life? The same spirit over and over again?"

Ava frowned. "No, Sensei."

"Think back. Was there ever a figure, in your dreams or during stressful times, that you recognized? Maybe you weren't sure why you recognized the person?"

Stressful times. Like when Mack would wake her up in the middle of the night with a hard smack across her face. Or when ice water hit her skin early in the morning, followed by laughter from Mack and Janine just because they thought it was funny to see her reaction. Stressful, like when Mack was on top of her, and she felt like her body was being torn in half.

Ava tried to think of everything her senses had taken in when those things happened. There were so many holes in her memories... she remembered the beginnings of so many punishments, so many humiliations, but she could not always remember how they ended. How could that be?

"The Monster."

She wasn't aware she had spoken. Daniel watched her frown and shake her head slightly, as if something just happened that she didn't understand. Then she began to mentally scan through her childhood to see if she had missed anything. He watched her eyes glaze as she recalled moments in her life she would rather forget. She blinked, clearing her gaze, and looked at him warily.

"I do not remember any person or figure like you describe."

"From what I've been reading," he said cautiously, "spirit guides are here to help people, not harm them."

"How do they present themselves?"

"They can be a loved one, a ball of light, relatives, plants -"

She glared at him. "I have not been aided by a plant."

He grinned. "That does seem like a stretch, even after everything I've seen. But the more I dig into it, the more it sounds like spirit guides help guard mediums against negative spirits. That's one of the things they do, anyway."

Ava thought about this.

"Are you sure you haven't had a recurring dream, or an image?"

"Light," she murmured. "A ball of light."

"That seems to be a common theme, according to what I've read. Tell me about the light."

"I..." Ava searched, rubbing her forehead. "I do not remember much. It led me to the woods."

Daniel waited, watching her. Her voice was fading in and out as she only now started remembering certain parts of her childhood. She raised her head and looked at him.

"I followed the light into the woods to hide from Mack sometimes."

"Do you remember the first time you saw it?"

She had begun to shiver, her body quaking almost imperceptibly. Her right hand, resting on her knee, was twitching. Ava appeared not to notice.

"I think I first saw it when I was five." She sounded surprised.

"I e-mailed you some links for research," Daniel said. "I want you to read through the information on the sites I sent and see if you can identify anyone in your life that may be a spirit guide. According to what I've been reading, all you have to do is ask to get one. If you create relationships with spirits, maybe they can help you with the negative energy, the nightmares."

And maybe The Monster, he thought.

"Hai, Sensei."

"Okay, let's see if you can call Hayden tonight."

Ava spent the next several minutes lowering herself into deep meditation. Around her, the walls of The Meditation Room disappeared. Sensei faded so far into the background that she could no longer hear his heartbeat or each inhale. The lights had been dimmed, allowing her to eyes to rest. She breathed deep and slow.

Entering The Interval was different than searching for someone's memory. When she concentrated on searching for a specific spirit, she found she was taken to The Interval. When she touched someone, like Sensei, and he had a specific memory in mind, she seemed to become part of the memory. Of course, so far, she had only done that once, and they had been the wrong memories.

She shook her head. Her mind was in overdrive. If she could not calm it and concentrate, she had no chance of controlling other outside influences that bombarded her. She took deep breaths, letting her lungs fill completely, imagining the ocean's tide ebbing and flowing to give her one image to concentrate on.

Breathe in, hold it. Let it out.

Soon she heard the waves. She felt the sand beneath her feet.

Breathe in, hold it. Let it out.

The sun was warm against her skin, the smell of salty water filling her nose.

Breathe in, hold it. Let it out.

The cries of seagulls filled her ears. The sand pushed between her toes, grainy and hot against her skin.

A fog was rolling in from the ocean. It came in off the water and blotted out the sun. Ava felt the dampness surround her, clinging to her flesh. It glided around her ankles, whirled up around her thighs and waist. The fog spun around her chest and head until she was surrounded by it. The sound of the ocean faded, and then it was gone.

"The Interval," she whispered.

In The Meditation room, Daniel leaned forward slightly. "Ava, can you hear me?"

She could hear Sensei's voice as if from a distance, echoing and muffled. When she opened her eyes, she was surrounded by dark fog. The murk pooled at her feet and hovered above her. A whisper floated toward her. She could not discern the word, only heard a voice. Awareness filled her.

I am here, she thought. I brought myself here.

"Hai, Sensei."

"Where are you?"

"The Interval." She said the phrase with reverence.

"Can you explain that to me?"

"It is the place between where we are and where they are."

"Who are they?"

"The dead."

Ava's eyes were opaque. They looked like someone had replaced them with onyx stones, white and polished to perfection. "It is quiet. There is so much fog."

"Ava, try to call the girl you keep seeing. Try to find Hayden."

Her body began to tighten, the muscles bunching from her toes to her neck. Sensei watched the relaxed posture stiffen until it looked uncomfortably rigid.

"Feel the muscles in your body relaxing," Daniel said. "Listen to each breath you take in and let out. Listen to my voice. Remember, you have to practice if you want to be able to control this."

"H-hai, Sensei." She fought to settle her nerves. Sensei would not let her get hurt. She was safe.

"Call to her."

Ava took a deep breath, let it out slowly. "Is anyone there? Hayden?"

She took a step forward, stretching her hands out so she would not run into anything. The fog began to recede, still thick, but fading back so she could see farther in front of her. She lowered her arms and turned slowly in a circle, trying to find anything familiar.

"Hayden?" she called.

A figure formed out of the fog and stepped toward her. Ava recognized the long braid and the Harry Potter nightgown. Her breath caught. The young girl with the denim blue eyes separated from the fog and stopped three feet in front of her.

Talk to her, Sensei had said, but he had not told her what to say. Ava was not social; she did not seek the company of others. She had forgotten to ask Sensei what to say once she found Hayden.

"My name is Ava."

Being here was like breathing through a wet rag. Ava felt panic trying to rise inside her and shoved it down. She forced herself to meet Hayden's eyes.

"You are Gabriel's sister," she said. "And Isabel's."

She was out of things to say. Hayden had not spoken at all to her. The girl had only stared with those odd eyes. Looking at them was like looking into Gabriel's eyes.

"Hello."

The sound of her voice, although quiet, startled Ava. She stepped toward Hayden, curious.

"Do you know who I am?" she asked. She reached her index finger out. Hayden watched her try to touch the image of her body, her finger passing through like smoke. The gesture seemed to amuse the young girl.

In The Meditation Room, Sensei watched Ava's hand reached toward him. Her milky white eyes stared straight ahead, not moving, not blinking.

"Why do you come to me?" she asked the girl in front of her. She drew her hand back, rubbing her index finger and thumb together.

Hayden took a step forward. Ava felt a coldness sweep over her.

"No," she said automatically, flinching.

"Ava," Daniel said, "what's happening?"

Hayden reached her hand out, beckoning.

Hesitant, Ava reached toward her. Around them, a hum began to rise steadily. At first it was low, almost inaudible. As it grew, Ava realized it wasn't a hum but the sound of voices speaking all at once. More forms separated from the fog, silhouettes that moved in toward Ava in a circle. The voices grew until Ava could not hear anything else.

Can you help me? An old woman asked, her eyes barely visible behind the many wrinkles on her face.

Get your ass back here, you little shit! This came from a middle-aged man with dark hair and blazing eyes.

I need to see my son. A young woman reached for her, her eyes haunted and hollow.

Please help me. I can't find my sister. She was in – A teenage girl pushed between the others, fighting to see Ava.

God. Oh God. It hurts. Ava did not know which shape the man's voice came from.

Mommy! A little boy called out.

I'm going to kill you, you little son of a bitch. Nobody steals from me. Ava drew back from the heavy-set man with white streaks in his hair.

"Hayden!" Ava called. She stretched her hand out, reaching, grasping, but Hayden's hand remained just out of reach. Other hands were reaching toward her, trying to grab her.

"I've watched you," Hayden said.

"Why? Why are you coming to me?" Ava drew her hand back.

"You see me."

Shadows were closing in around her. Shadows of the dead. Ava backed away from Hayden and looked for a break in the bodies. They were swarming, tightening the circle, swallowing Hayden, and coming for Ava. They were begging her to help them. They were all talking at once so she could not see who was speaking anymore.

Please help me. My grandma -

Can you help me?

I lost my son in the war. Can you tell me if -

Ava looked around, frowning. The voices were all running together in their fight to be heard.

"You see all of us." Hayden was smiling.

Ava's eyes widened as more figures stepped forward out of the fog, encircling her. There were so many faces, different ages, various stages of death. Ava stepped back only to find more were standing behind her.

"Stop," she said, as the panic began to rise again. "I do not want to talk to all of you."

She tried to back up but there was nowhere to go. Her hands came up to defend herself and she realized she had no defense against beings with no physical bodies. "They have no bodies. I cannot fight them without bodies." Her voice was riddled with panic.

"Ava, you are safe. Listen to my voice. You are not in danger there." Sensei's voice came from far away, almost drowned out by the beckoning voices of the shadows.

In The Meditation Room, he gripped her outstretched hands.

I have a child out there, somewhere. Please help -

My sister hasn't e-mailed me in two weeks. I think she's –

Help me tell my wife where to find my –

Please help my family move on –

Please help Please help Please help-

"Breathe. Take a breath. You have the ability to control this."

Sensei's voice calmed her only slightly. The fog seemed to be getting thicker, making it harder to breathe. Still, she could see those haunted figures merging from the mist.

"They are coming." Everywhere she turned, Ava saw shadows. "There are so many."

"Don't panic. You can control this. That's why we're here."

"They keep touching me. I hear all their pain. I feel it on my skin."

She gripped Daniel's hands with such force he grimaced.

"Block it out. Block them out. You are in control here."

"No, I am not." Her breath was coming in fast, hitching gasps, and she leaned back onto her palms. "I do not know what I am doing."

Faces. Nameless faces swam in her head. Bodies like vapor. No way to fight vapor. None of her training could protect her from unsubstantial matter.

She dragged herself backward, cringing, shutting her eyes against an invisible attack. "Too many."

"Get to the door." Sensei's voice was steadier now, louder. She could hear him more easily over the other voices.

"They are all around me."

"The door is right in front of you," Daniel said. "All you have to do is know it's there. Open the door and come back to me."

Ava lurched forward as if shoved, sucking in air in loud gulps. Her eyes flickered around the Meditation room, not seeing anything in it. Her hands reached out, searching for something to grip, to convince her she was in this world. Daniel put his hands out so she could find them again. When she did, she held them in a vise-like grip. She tried to take deep breaths, but she couldn't get enough air.

"Take it easy," Daniel soothed. "You're in the Meditation Room. You're safe."

He gave her time to settle down. He wasn't happy with her breathing; she was having trouble getting control of it. Her body was trembling.

"Breathe. You're doing fine," he said, keeping the cadence of his voice soft and reassuring. He pressed a bottle of water into her hand. Ava unscrewed the cap and downed the entire bottle. She was panting by the time she was finished.

Hard, sharp pain sliced into her chest. She leaned over, one hand clutching her heart. She needed to get control. With her pulse racing, panic wanted to set in again. Tears were streaming down her face, and she hated herself for them. When her hands reached out again, Daniel gripped them to steady her.

"Easy." Daniel pressed his fingers to her wrist, checking her pulse. It was skyrocketing. If she couldn't get her breathing back to normal, she wouldn't be able to relax.

"Ava, look at me."

Her eyes rolled, searching the room for danger, waiting for the next assault.

"Look at me."

Those gray eyes found his hazel ones, blinked hard.

"That's right, just look at my eyes. Keep looking. Nothing else matters."

They started to drift to the side, and he clamped his hands down on her wrists.

"Keep your eyes on mine."

They locked onto his, and he matched his breathing pattern to hers. After only a few seconds, his lungs were burning, and his fight or flight response tried to kick in. He fought it, forcing himself to gradually slow his breathing. He kept his eyes on Ava's, his hands on her wrists. As he slowed his breathing, he lessened the pressure on her wrists until he was comforting her rather than restraining her.

"Good. Deep breaths." He checked her pulse. Better. "What did you see?"

Beneath his fingers, her pulse bucked. She forced herself to take steadying breaths and told him everything. Each time she found herself talking faster, breathless, she took a moment to breathe and calm herself down. By the end, she was stronger for getting through it but also had a better understanding of what had happened.

For the first time, she had summoned the spirit she wanted. Though she didn't get any answers, she had more information than before. She had willed the door into existence, stepped through it, and controlled the end of the vision. These steps were good. They all showed progression. She was pleased that she had made so much progress.

This time she was able to summon Hayden; next time, maybe she would be able to shut the others out.

"That's enough for tonight," Sensei said, still holding her wrists. "Think about your childhood. Try to remember if there was anything comforting when you were stressed out, someone you saw repeatedly in your dreams. Read the links I sent you. We need to find out if you have a spirit guide. You're exhausting your body. Back off on your training at home."

"Hai, Sensei."

She had shut down. She answered because it was good manners, not because she agreed with him.

Helping her to her feet, he watched her put her jacket on to make sure she wasn't lightheaded or otherwise impaired. He didn't see any signs that she was incapable of driving herself home, or to Vincent's apartment if she chose.

"It was an interesting night."

"Hai, Sensei." This was said thoughtfully.

"Have a good night, Ava. I'll see you tomorrow."

"Hai, Sensei. Good night."

●　　●　　●　　●　　●

Griffin was surprised when he entered an empty apartment.

He set his laptop case on the island and began unbuttoning his shirt, looking for signs that Isabel had stopped by. On his way to the bedroom, he thought about how different the apartment felt when she wasn't in it, how quiet and unsettling it felt. He tossed his shirt into the basket on the floor and realized the basket wasn't where it usually sat. Picking up his shirt, he glanced around the room, baffled.

Carrying the shirt to the closet to drop off in the laundry cove on the way to the kitchen, he grabbed a tee shirt. He saw the laundry basket was sitting on the floor under one of the counters.

"What the bloody hell is that doing in here?" he asked himself. He tossed his dirty shirt in and pulled the clean one over his head.

He carried the laundry basket as far as the doorway before he realized it made more sense to keep it in the walk-in closet than to have it in his bedroom. After all, he dressed himself in the spacious closet. Why the hell hadn't he thought of that sooner?

Isabel must have figured it out and moved it.

Grinning, Griffin set the basket back in the closet and moved through the bathroom toward the kitchen. He wondered if she had decided not to come over.

She doesn't have to come over every night, he reminded himself. Don't get all clingy on her.

But he wanted to be with her. Already he missed her, and he had only just seen her this morning before work. Her hair had been tangled and her eyes had barely been open, and he had kissed her until it drove him mad with lust. While she was still half asleep, he had made her tremble and whimper until she sobbed out his name.

He had never been late for work because of a woman before Isabel.

The knock at the door came as he was pouring himself a glass of wine. He walked toward the door sipping. It was light and semi-sweet, reminding him of spring. And of Isabel.

"What's wrong?" he asked as soon as he saw her face.

"Hi." Her voice was soft, as if the effort of pushing enough air out to make words was almost too much for her. "I didn't know if you wanted me to come over tonight."

"Of course, I do." He stepped back, watching her eyes fix on the ground directly in front of her as she stepped inside. "You don't have to knock, Izzie. You can just come in."

Standing stiffly, she shrugged out of her jacket. Griffin took it and hung it for her in the closet.

"Oh," she said, surprised. "Thank you."

She walked to the kitchen and set her purse on an island chair. "Can I have some wine?"

Her voice was so small, he thought. So... vulnerable. To look at her, one might think she was acting aloof. Her expression was carefully neutral, her stance just rigid enough to let everyone know she wanted to be left alone. But her voice, on the verge of cracking, told an entirely different story.

"What are you in the mood for?" he asked, setting his glass on the island so he could pour her wine. Her back was to him, her head down as she stared at the wine fridge. Griffin found it strange that she asked if she could have wine. Since when did she feel the need to ask for a drink? And why did it surprise her that he would show her kindness by taking her coat?

"I should go."

She was standing with one hand across her belly, holding the elbow of the other, the hand of which was fidgeting with her collar. As he took a step toward her, she turned with her head down, making it easy to slip his arms around her. Her head rested against his shoulder. They fit together as snug as puzzle pieces.

"Izzie, what's wrong?" he murmured. He stroked her hair.

"I'm not good company tonight. I didn't mean to come here. I just... it's habit."

She tried to back away, but he held onto her.

"Did you have a bad day at work? Talk to me." He rubbed his other hand up and down her back.

"I don't want to talk."

"Then don't. But stay."

Without realizing it, he had led her into a slow dance, rocking from one foot to the other, turning slowly. The steady rhythm soothed her. Mindless motion. Griffin's arms around her.

"I went to Hayden's grave."

The tears came, hot and slow, burning her skin as they slid down her cheeks. How could she explain that she went there sometimes because she felt it was the only place she could be sad without being judged? She didn't second guess herself or ask herself why, after over a decade, she still couldn't move on.

She sniffed.

Griffin lifted her and carried her to the sofa, cradling her as she silently cried. Sitting on his lap made her feel childlike but she didn't care. Her feelings were childlike; she missed her sister and the emotions that loss was bringing up today were as they had been the year Hayden disappeared. Raw terror, confusion, a sense of dread that nothing would ever be the same.

Nothing had been the same.

He continued to rock her, stroking her hair, and kissing her temple or forehead. Sometime along the way, she drifted off to sleep.

•   •   •   •   •

Scattered papers littered the top of the desk and the floor around it. Gabriel finished yet another drawing, studied it, and tossed it to the left. The paper whipped into the air, paused, then drifted to the floor to join the others.

He leaned back in his chair, linking his fingers, and pressing his hands against his eyes. The right design wasn't coming to him. He was close; he could feel it. Something was off that he couldn't put his finger on; the position of the tiger, the shape of its mouth, the way the paw appeared to be reaching forward. He still had to play with it. For now, he had to let it rest a while. Creating something specifically for someone didn't come with a timeline. The inspiration would be there when it needed to be.

Digging through the mess on his desk, he found a notepad and pulled it out from under loose papers. He opened the lap drawer and took out a pen, writing "Tiger – images". After he had stepped away from it for a while, he would look up images of the animal on-line and see what kind of inspiration they stirred.

A knock at the door made him jerk. Snorting at his silliness, he pushed his chair back and stepped out of his office. He had no idea what time it was, but from the ache in his back, he guessed he had been sitting at his desk far too long.

His idea that Isabel had stopped by for another weeknight visit drained out of his head when he saw Ava standing on his porch. Her hands were in the pockets of a jacket that seemed too heavy for such a mild night. Keeping her head slightly forward made her hair partially curtain her face, and with the shadows from the porch light, he couldn't see her expression.

"Hi." How did she manage to make him feel inadequate so much of the time?

"Hello."

"Ah, come in," he finally said, stepping aside.

He thought he noticed a slight limp as she slid past him.

They went through their normal routine: he prepared a water with ice and set it on the counter for her, opened a beer for himself. He suggested they sit in the living room even though it was too warm for a fire. Even with a limp, she didn't make a sound as she followed him through the house.

As he sat at one end of the couch and she the other, he watched her, waiting for her to explain why she had come. Her left hand was bandaged. Gabriel was certain she'd punched his wall with her right hand, had bandaged it himself. More than once, she winced as she tried to get comfortable. She sat with her back against the arm of the sofa, one leg up to her chest, the other stretched out in front of her, with her water in both hands. She remained silent. What was he supposed to do with that?

"Is everything okay?" he finally asked. "Has something happened to David?"

Her head jerked up, twitched. "David is fine."

It was then, when she raised her head, that he saw the cut above her eye, the stitches.

"What happened? Are you okay?" He started to move toward her, but she shook her head and pulled back, irritation flickering across her face.

"I am fine."

When she didn't say anything more, Gabriel cleared his throat. "Why are you here, Ava?"

She leaned forward and set her glass on the coffee table. "I lost control."

Returning to her spot against the arm of the sofa, several emotions flashed across her face: confusion, sorrow, agony, guilt, embarrassment. Her eyes shifted as she considered what to say.

"During our last conversation, I raised my voice."

Gabriel almost smiled. He forced himself to remain expressionless and keep quiet.

"I am sorry for losing control," Ava finally said. "I do not know why it is so easy to lose my temper with you."

Damn, he thought she'd never get around to it. Losing control, for Ava, was the most humiliating act she could commit. It must be seriously eating away at her that she had yelled at him. Not because she thought she was wrong, but because she had stooped to the level of common human behavior and let emotion rule her conversation. God forbid.

"You came here to apologize?"

"No."

Agitated, Ava stood and walked to the large window looking out over the front lawn. His suspicions that she was limping were confirmed as he watched her gait. Very slight, but the limp was there.

"Maybe. Everything is falling apart. Nothing in my life is as it was. I have no control over what is happening to my body or my... emotions..."

She had pressed her hands to the glass window and now she leaned her forehead against it as well. The cool glass against her body did nothing to ease her feverish skin. Closing her eyes, she tried to collect her thoughts. She was a stumbling fool when she was around him, always messing up her words.

"I'm glad you stopped by. I missed you."

Turning, she studied him. In the lamplight, her eyes looked black.

"Why?" Her head was turned slightly, trying so hard to understand. The innocent curiosity on her face tugged at him.

Gabriel set his water on the end table next to the couch. "Why don't you come over here and find out?"

The suggestion bewildered her. She straightened. Her body stayed still as a deer listening for a predator.

"You're not afraid of anything, right? So, you have nothing to worry about."

Taking a daring tone was rather juvenile, but Gabriel was tired of waiting around and being cautious. If he didn't push her a little, neither of them would ever know her boundaries. Treating her with kid gloves had gotten him nowhere.

Ava walked toward him, stopping several feet away.

"Is that the best you can do?" He took a drink of his water, keeping his eyes on hers.

She took another small step. Another. Another, until she was standing directly in front of him.

Gabriel lifted his hands without worrying if she felt threatened. She instantly slapped her palms down on them, pressing so he couldn't raise them any higher to touch her. Her right hand wasn't completely healed from its assault on his wall. The knuckles were bruised, but the torn skin was healing.

Lifting one eyebrow, he gazed at her. Seconds passed.

"We're back to this?"

"I do not like to be touched," she said automatically. She could have inspired him to move his hands away from her with a simple strike to the throat, but she did not.

"Then why are you here, Ava? If nothing's changed, if you're not here to apologize, why did you come here tonight?"

Ava's brow furrowed slightly and smoothed again as thoughts flickered through her head. They were staring at each other, both too stubborn to look away. Finally, she slowly slid her hands off his.

"Why wouldn't I miss you?" he said, setting his hands on her hips. He tugged slightly until she stepped forward, standing between his knees, looking down at him. Tucking his fingers into her front pockets, he gazed at her. The stutter of her breath made him smile.

"I..." She faltered, struggled so hard to find the right words. "I continued to think about you after our disagreement. I was – I am unable to stop thinking about you."

His lips curved. "I didn't like how we left things, either. I didn't mean to upset you, Ava."

He took his hands from her pockets, making the skin beneath feel cold in their absence. Sliding them up her hips, he eased them under her shirt, but only an inch. He moved his thumbs on her bare skin in tiny circles.

Her breath seemed to catch in the back of her throat, making it hard to breathe.

"I will refill your water," she said abruptly. She dragged her eyes away from his steady analysis and searched for his glass as if she had been mesmerized.

"Don't bother."

"Your glass is -"

"Everything I'm interested in is right here." Those blue eyes stayed focused on hers. "Why are you here?"

Her eyelids fluttered.

"You're not here to apologize, and you don't want a relationship. What do you want?" His voice was low, hypnotic, making her want to answer more readily than if he would have demanded it.

"I..." She swallowed. Driving here after she'd showered off the sweat from class, she had wondered what she would say to him. An apology was necessary;

she had not meant to yell at him. To deny his friendship out of selfishness was both unhealthy for her and cruel to him. He had not done anything to upset her or make him not worthy of her friendship. She was willing to be his friend, nothing more. But standing here, trying to put into words what she had practiced saying had left her. She could not remember a single sentence. She had not expected the heat to be so overwhelming. For the first time in her memory, her palms were damp. Guilt, an emotion she generally did not feel, hovered over her, suffocating her. It was making her want to run off the extra energy swirling in her body.

"You have shown me nothing but kindness. I lack experience in social situations and mishandle interpersonal interactions that are common for most people."

Which was a fancy way of saying she fucked up, Gabriel thought, clenching his teeth to keep from grinning.

"I am sorry I overreacted to your… hospitality."

Her idiosyncrasies made it difficult to keep a straight face.

"I won't hurt you, Ava."

"You will. You are human, and that is what humans do. But I know you will not do so out of malice."

Gabriel wasn't sure what to say to that. He had hoped she was going to clarify things when he saw her on his porch, but he was more confused now than ever.

Ava combed her hand through his hair thoughtfully, focusing on how it felt brushing against her palm, the back of her hand. It was soft, whispering against her fingertips.

Touching him was a distraction, but she could not help but reach for him. Touching him gave her pleasure, and that was fascinating.

She felt her insides quivering rapidly. Confused, she wondered why she had not felt this way with Vincent. He did not make her head feel like it was spinning, or make her extremities feel like they were tied to balloons, floating off while her body remained on the ground.

Sexually, he pleased her. There was no doubt about that; her body was sated each time she left his apartment. But this warring feeling inside her body, this uncontrollable need to consume even as she tried to back away, was missing with Vincent.

She wanted Gabriel. She wanted to touch his skin, feel it react under her fingers, explore the muscle. Just now she felt her body would catch fire if she did not feel his mouth on her. Being this close to him was making her breath back up in her throat and they were not even behaving in a sexual manner.

But dating meant being accountable to another person, explaining herself.

"I do not want to be obligated to anyone." She was short of breath. Knowing his proximity was affecting her embarrassed her. But she could not seem to stop the way her pulse quickened when she was around him.

"Is that what I am?" Gabriel asked. "An obligation?"

Shaking her head, she let out a defeated sigh. She shifted forward so when he turned his head, his temple lay against her stomach, her body fitting snug against him. When his arms wrapped around her and bound their bodies even closer, she closed her eyes. Their breathing was the only sound.

A kind of peace settled over her. She was as relaxed as she could be outside of her home. She felt inhales and exhales from Gabriel against her stomach, but he was so still she nearly forgot he was there.

He rested his hands on her hips and slowly stood, the length of his body gliding up hers just short of making contact.

"Ava," Gabriel said softly, resting his hands lightly on her shoulders as he looked into her eyes. His voice was urgent. "I want you."

He could have her, she realized. That she was willing fascinated her.

He kept looking at her, searching her eyes.

"I want you," he repeated. "Only you. I don't just want to be your friend."

She had thought he wanted sex, but he was speaking of a relationship, of commitment, of a pledge to be with her and only her.

"You are asking if I will be your mate."

What an odd way to put it, he thought. He nodded.

Panic rose in her, sharp and paralyzing.

"I do not like dating," she said.

"Have you ever done it before?"

Hesitant, she shook her head.

"Then how do you know you don't like it?"

She considered this. He tried not to take his impatience out on her by gripping her shoulders too hard. Having already seen her naked had his blood

427

boiling and his heartbeat jacked up. He knew what was under that thin top, what promised to be there when he peeled away the jeans.

"I have never been anyone's mate." Her voice rose as terror tried to find its way inside her. "I do not know the rules."

Gabriel gave her shoulders a soft squeeze. "Forget about rules. Do you like being around me?"

She twitched. When she felt like bolting, Gabriel brushed his palm down her cheek. A shiver ran through her.

"You are more tolerable than most people," she said, unsure why her voice sounded funny. Her tone was higher than normal. Why was her body betraying her?

Gabriel gave her that half-smile she liked, and the one eyebrow rose.

He tucked a strand of hair behind her ear. The flash of longing in her eyes, not for sex or passion but just to be touched, was so strong he felt his chest tighten. Yes, he wanted her, with a primal lust that made his entire body ache. But she didn't need mindless sex. She didn't need another person treating her like she was a toy to be played with and used up. Gabriel found himself wanting, above his own wishes, to give her what she so desperately yearned for. How had he missed it before? That loneliness in her eyes, the deep sorrow clawing just below the surface of her emotionless mask.

"Is that all? Tolerable?" He slid his fingers down her arm, lifting her hand. When he covered her hand with both of his, she blinked slowly. "Do you enjoy how this feels?"

"My sexual needs-"

"I'm not talking about sex," he said. "Does the person you chose to satisfy you in bed ever give you a hug? Does he hold your hand, sit next to you, rub your shoulders after a hard day?"

She took a step back, breaking contact with him. "I do not want those things."

"If he believed you when you told him that, he's a fucking idiot."

"He is not an idiot," she said, fury lighting her eyes. "He gives me what I ask for and leaves when we have taken what we need from each other. I trust him with my life."

"Obviously, he doesn't look beyond what you tell him you want, or he'd see the person trapped inside that perfectly disciplined body, screaming to be let out. He would comfort you even when you told him you didn't want him to and be there for you even when you told him to go. Because he would know it was a lie, just like I do."

"That is not his function."

"Christ, Ava, he's not a machine. Neither are you."

"He understands this body has physical needs and is willing to fulfill those needs, nothing more."

"Your body is not some… thing interfering with your life," Gabriel said, taking a step toward her. She stepped back with one foot, putting her in a stance, bracing herself. She didn't raise her hands, but her fingers flexed at her sides.

"It is a vessel." Something slipped from her carefully controlled expression. He wasn't sure what, but for half a second, he saw a vulnerability in her eyes that she covered quickly with indifference. "It is a covering, packaging that was destroyed years ago. I have seen the lust in the eyes of a hundred men a thousand times before. It means nothing to me."

"You are a beautiful person. Not only because of your body," he added when she gave him a knowing glare. "That's a bonus. You take such care of yourself. You manually form your body into perfect shape, the way I work with wood. I cut away the excess, sand down the layers until it becomes the perfect image I saw in my head when it was just a piece from a dead tree. Until it is the best it can be. I admire that. But it's not just about your body. You've intrigued me since I first saw you."

The self-righteous gaze of disgust faltered. "Why? I am no one."

"You're someone to me." He held his hand out to her. "Be my… mate," he said softly. The corner of his mouth curved at the use of her word.

"I do not want to give up my time."

"Then don't."

Ava reached for his hand but did not quite touch it. "There are things about me you may never know. Parts of me I will always keep to myself."

"They're yours to keep."

She finally took his hand. He pulled her closer, slipping his arm around her back. She smelled the soap he used in the shower, the faint hint of beer, and sawdust.

"What am I supposed to do as your mate?" She was not sure what to do with her hands. They were standing close, but he was not instigating sex.

Feeling awkward, she rested her hand on his chest because his heartbeat comforted her.

"You don't have to do anything you don't want to do. Be Ava. Who you are is who I want."

Her eyes were full of wariness. "Alright."

•　　•　　•　　•　　•

Isabel rose groggily from her nap with no clear recollection of the past few hours. As she tried to open her eyes, they rolled and squinted and fought against the soft light of the lamp on the bedside table. A sigh escaped as she tried to figure out if it was morning or afternoon, a workday or weekend. The brain fog was heavy; she couldn't fight through it.

When she opened her eyes, Griffin was laying across from her, gazing at her. They were lying on their sides on the bed, on top of the blankets, facing each other. His palm was resting on her cheek.

"Hello, beautiful."

"I fell asleep?"

"Only for a bit. Half an hour."

The apartment was silent. They watched each other without speaking for almost a minute. Iz studied his honey-colored eyes and found they were more varied than she originally thought. She had thought they were solid amber, but this close view allowed her to see the different shades throughout the irises.

Griffin moved his hand from her cheek and took her hand.

"I don't remember much about her before the summer she disappeared," Isabel said. "Is that normal?"

Holding back the urge to pump his fist in the air now that she was finally talking, Griffin rubbed his thumb over her hand.

"'Normal' doesn't have a place in grieving. You were young, and it happened during your formative years. Traumatic events during that period in anyone's life are going to make an impact that lasts."

"We used to sit around the dining room table during thunderstorms and tell ghost stories." Isabel shifted to get comfortable. "Beth made hot cocoa, the kind on the stove that you make with baking cocoa, milk, and vanilla extract."

He rolled onto his back and tugged her over, so her head was resting on his chest. She snuggled in, draping her leg over his. When she tucked her hand up under her chin, a gesture he recognized as one she did when she was hiding inside herself, he placed his hand over hers.

"She would pour it into these fancy clear glasses and add whip cream. Mom would light kerosene lamps and turn off the lights. Everyone would sit at the table and tell ghost stories. I guess I remember more about her than I thought I did."

"Did you have a favorite story?"

"Sometimes we read from books. Scary Stories to Tell in the Dark was a book we used so often we wore it out. But my favorite has always been The Legend of Sleepy Hollow."

"Ah, the classics." He toyed with a lock of her hair.

"I read that every year around Halloween and sometimes a couple times before. For around the table, though, we picked a shorter kid's version. Gabriel always tried to scare me afterward, but Hayden and I ganged up on him and beat him up."

Griffin chuckled. "That sounds like a great family tradition."

"We stopped doing it when Hayden went missing."

Her body was beginning to tense. Rubbing her back, he leaned down and kissed the top of her head. Her hand flexed under his before gripping it, holding on.

"I remember the first storm after her disappearance."

Feeling her breath constrict, Isabel closed her eyes and felt them fill. When she opened her eyes again, her vision blurred, and she saw the room through a prism of tears that would not fall.

"I felt it coming. It felt like my body was full of electricity. The hair on the back of my neck and on my arms stood up."

Her chest was hitching. Griffin drew her closer to him.

"I was so scared. I didn't understand how we were going to go on without her. I came downstairs and all the lights were off. Beth wasn't making cocoa. Dad wasn't with Gabriel and Mom around the table, lighting kerosene lamps. It was dark, and so quiet. I heard the storm coming and I thought... at first I thought..."

"Maybe the tradition would put everything back to normal."

She nodded. "If we had kept doing it, at least I would have known it was okay to go on without her."

"It is okay, Izzie."

"I would have known I wasn't crazy when I wanted to laugh."

"You aren't crazy. It's okay to laugh." Griffin rubbed his hand up and down her arm. Her skin was cold again. "The way you wanted to deal with your sister's death was healthy. The way you watched it dealt with was not."

Her chest ached, the pressure on it unbearable. How was she supposed to stand it? Her hand gripped his shirt, loosened, gripped it again as she tried to catch her breath.

"I shouldn't..." She let out a shuddering breath. "I shouldn't have started talking about this. I can't talk about this. I can't breathe."

She tried to push away from him, but he held onto her, drawing her close.

"You are breathing. You're doing it, Isabel. Tell me about how you told stories around the table. Did everyone tell a story, or just you kids?"

"We... we went around the table. Anyone could pass if they didn't want to talk."

She still had his shirt in her hand and was bunching it in her fist, tugging it toward her, releasing it, then doing it all over again. She gulped in air and felt dizzy.

"That's enough now," Griffin said. He kissed her temple. "Tell me about your music."

"What?" She couldn't switch topics so quickly, didn't understand his sudden interest in her hobby. "My-"

"What artists inspire you?"

He leaned up, raising his pillows, and adding hers so he could hold her comfortably. Isabel tried to use the opportunity to put distance between them, but he took her hand and pulled her against him. He almost laughed at how determined she was to pull away.

Still huffing but more in control of her breathing, she nestled against him again. "Bishop Briggs, ZZ Ward-"

"So, I was right to compare your voice to theirs the night I first heard you sing."

"I only wish I were as good as they are. They have good, strong voices. I also like Evanescence, Halestorm, Within Temptation, Lacuna Coil."

She blew out a breath, thinking. "I'm all over the place musically. I like Seether, Creedence Clearwater Revival, Johnny Cash... sometimes I get so sick of all the excess bullshit in today's music, and I put on Johnny Cash just to hear the good, clean sound. Just music. Nothing fancy. Just a man and his guitar. His voice was so amazing. When I listen to a song by him, it's like he's talking directly to me through his passion. All those other special effects and auto tune make the conversation between the musician and the audience impersonal."

Grinning, Griffin leaned down and kissed the top of her head. The hand that had been so desperately groping his shirt was now relaxed against his chest. The tears had dried up. Isabel's breathing was back to normal.

"Are you hungry?" he asked, toying with her fingers.

She sighed heavily. "I could eat."

"Why don't I order a pizza? We can eat in bed and fall asleep to whatever we decide to watch."

She smiled. "Perfect."

• • • • •

Gabriel woke suddenly, as if startled, but he didn't know why. He heard nothing in the darkness. He felt Ava next to him, but she wasn't talking in her sleep. She was, however, extremely rigid, as if every muscle in her body had an electric current pulsing through it.

"Ava," he whispered, not sure if she was awake or not. "What's wrong?"

"You are touching me."

He became more aware of his position. He was lying on his side. To say he was touching her was an understatement – he was spooning her, his arms and legs wrapped around her intimately. Their bodies were pressed tightly together. His face was nuzzled against her neck, for God's sake.

"Shit," he breathed. "I must have done it in my sleep. I'm going to move back now."

His testicles had shrunk into his abdomen at the thought of her wrath. He waited to make sure she was ready for him to move without giving him an elbow to the ribs or head butting him. Just as he started to shift cautiously, her voice, so quiet he barely heard her, stopped him.

"You do not have to move."

He paused. "Are you sure?"

Her muscles began to relax. He felt her breathing deliberately, working through getting used to his touch. It was then he noticed her arm was lined up with his above the blankets, and their fingers were entwined. She was leaned inward slightly – sometime during the night, she'd pulled him tight against her. Obviously, he wasn't the only one subconsciously seeking companionship during sleep. She may have conditioned herself not to want to be touched, she may have been abused to the point that her natural reaction was to avoid and fight, but somewhere inside her was the primal instinct to reach out, to connect with another human being.

"It feels... weird." Ava shifted just enough to let Gabriel feel every part of her body that was touching his.

"Weird?" he squeaked.

"Not bad... Different. You are the first person I have ever shared a bed with overnight." After a long pause: "How does it feel for you?"

He cleared his throat, trying to instruct himself not to get aroused. "It feels pretty great."

"It is what mates do, right?"

Amused, Gabriel shifted his legs to stimulate blood flow. "People dating often sleep close together, yes. Haven't you ever snuggled after sex?"

"That was not Vincent's function."

"Does he know you talk about him like that?"

"Like what?"

"Like he's a robot or your man servant."

"I do not understand the value of that question. His purpose was sexual release. Once an orgasm was reached, intimate contact like what we are doing now served no purpose."

He snorted laughter in her ear. Turning away, he continued laughing.

"What is so funny?"

"Sorry. I didn't mean to blow out your ear drum. I love the way you talk."

Her hair was swept away from her neck, so his cheek could rest directly against her skin. He snuggled close to her again and brushed his lips against the back of her neck.

The way she moved her head forward and her shoulders up made him think of E.T.

"Was that bad?" he asked.

"It tickles. I... enjoy it," she said softly, her voice full of awe. "Vincent never did that."

Snorting again, Gabriel said, "It's generally frowned upon to talk about what your previous boyfriends did or didn't do in the sack." He brushed his chin against her neck this time, watching her squirm as it tickled.

"We never had intercourse in a sack, but I will refrain from discussing my sexual history if you prefer."

He chuckled.

He could feel her warmth. He was very aware of the length of her body, which fit snugly against his.

"Gabriel?"

"Yeah." He couldn't stop his heart from thudding. Could she feel it against her back?

"Am I your friend?"

What an odd question. He shouldn't have been surprised; everything about Ava was odd. Yet she still managed to catch him off guard. "Yes."

After a beat: "How do you know?" He had said it so easily, with such conviction, as if it was simply a fact.

"I just know."

"That is not an answer." Disappointed, she shuffled, bumping her rear end into his groin. Though the movement was innocent, Gabriel's body immediately reacted with a burst of lust. His pulse throbbed in his temples. He bit down on a groan.

"Jesus, Ava." Embarrassed, he shoved himself backward, separating their bodies. His heart was pounding so loud at the sudden adrenaline rush he was sure she could hear it. Startled at his sudden reaction, Ava sat up and pivoted toward him, her hands ready to defend herself.

He leaned up and turned on the light. Making sure his lower half was covered, he tried to collect himself both mentally and physically. Embarrassed that his body had so easily become stimulated, he bunched the blanket in his lap to be less conspicuous.

"You are angry with me," she stated.

"I'm angry with myself." He let out a shaky breath and glanced at her. She still had her hands up, and the bedding had slipped, almost revealing one breast. She was killing him. He was going to die of longing. "You're about to flash me."

"Flash...?"

He motioned to her chest. She looked down, pulled the blankets up. Suddenly she looked incredibly sad. He would have given anything to rid her of that lost, agonized look of defeat. The look he had put there.

"I'm sorry," he said, running his hand along the back of his neck. "I'm not mad at you. I'm..."

Sweet Jesus.

She gazed at him with those consuming gray eyes, trying to understand. They looked black in the soft lamp light.

"My body was reacting to yours in a way that was... not friendly." He cleared his throat. "More intimate. I don't want you to think I'm just another asshole trying to get into your pants."

Damn it, he hated being flustered.

Ava frowned. "I am not wearing pants." She pulled the blanket away from her chest and looked under it as if to make sure. Gabriel couldn't help but get a quick peek of her chest before he realized what she was doing.

"It's an expression, Ava. I don't want you to think I'm dating you just to have sex with you. I get the feeling you've had enough of men using you."

For a moment, she was speechless. She stared at him with unblinking eyes.

"I need water." She stood so abruptly she yanked the covers off him. Gabriel was too busy trying to cover himself to worry about her. When he looked up, she was gone, striding out the door completely naked.

Exhaling, Gabriel straightened the bedding to keep his hands busy. "I fucked that up," he muttered. He didn't know how to talk to her. If he tried to be gentle, she seemed to take offense. If he spoke to her like a normal person, he was likely to get his balls handed to him. She could do that literally.

She returned minutes later with one of his towels wrapped around her and holding two glasses of water. She thrust one at him, avoiding eye contact. Sitting on the bed, she held her glass close to her chest for several moments before setting it deliberately on the bedside table. Fidgeting with the hem on the towel, she said nothing. Though her expression was carefully neutral, Gabriel was picking up on her emotions more easily now. Her eyes had lost the curiosity he had become used to seeing in them during their conversations.

She only fidgeted when she was upset or uncomfortable. Her shoulders were hunched ever so slightly forward, pulling her in toward herself protectively.

Gabriel set his glass down and shifted so he was facing her. "I'm sorry. My damn body reacted to being so close to you."

She stared at him with those eyes that seemed to have already lived a thousand lives. How much sorrow had those eyes witnessed? He couldn't even imagine. And she wouldn't tell him.

Leaning toward him, Ava brushed her lips lightly over his. Though he felt the platonic intention behind the act, his pulse quickened. She kept her hands to herself, didn't deepen the kiss. When she pulled back, he couldn't read her expression. She watched him, ever vigilant.

"You don't have to do that," he said, finding his voice shaky.

"I do not do anything unless I choose to."

She watched him a moment longer, her head tilted just slightly, her eyes, now soft as ash, studying him. It occurred to him that when she was curious about something, she didn't blink, giving her an odd, feral look. Turning away from him, she took another drink of her water. She unwrapped the towel and lay it on the floor beside the bed before he had a chance to look away. Sliding under the blankets, she turned back to him.

What now? he thought, watching her. Did she expect something from him? Did she think he expected something from her? He shut off the light and lay next to her on his side, wondering why she had kissed him a moment ago. The moon let in just enough light to reflect off her eyes.

"You are kind to me," she said softly.

"I don't under-"

She reached out and put her palm against his mouth. "Thank you for being kind to me."

She let her hand drop, shut her eyes. Baffled, Gabriel placed his hand over hers and gave it a squeeze. Ever so gently, she squeezed back.

• • • • •

Sweat and alcohol. Lipstick and urine.

The little girl fought against the hands holding her down. Such big hands, pressing on her wrists and ankles. But they were drunk, and stoned, and she slipped away when the woman freed one leg to push her stringy hair out of her eyes. The little girl kicked as hard as she could, and the woman toppled over backward.

She ran. First outside, into the muggy summer afternoon. Hiding under the trailer, she heard them stumble down the stairs to look for her. When they were checking the truck, she sneaked back inside the trailer and hid under the sink.

Her chest hurt from sobbing. The skin on her wrists and ankles was raw. Four fingernails were torn to the quick as she struggled to get away. A large purple welt was growing on her cheek where the man had smacked her. She was still dizzy from a blow. Under the sink, her knees up to her chest and her arms around her legs, she waited for the inevitable beating.

Light shown through the cracks on the door. Ava closed her eyes, sure he had found her, sure he was pointing a flashlight at the cupboard and any moment he would throw it open. The light was so bright it pierced her eye lids. Because there was no sound with it, she leaned forward and slowly opened the cupboard door.

The light dimmed so it didn't hurt her eyes. It was a small round ball the size of a grapefruit, the luster emanating from it muted and tinted blue. It hovered just outside the cupboard. As Ava watched, it retreated two feet, came back, then retreated again. Something inside her told her to follow it. She didn't know what, and she didn't question it. She uncurled herself and climbed out of the cupboard, never taking her eyes off the ball of light.

As she stood, it swirled around her. Then it floated to the door. Ava hesitated.

Outside, she heard Mack and Janine grumbling. They were coming back inside.

Grabbing a blanket off the back of the couch, Ava followed the light and pushed the door open.

It led her to the woods half a mile from the trailer. She kept expecting Mack and Janine to come after her, but they didn't. Barefoot, she walked through tall weeds into the cover of the trees. The ball of light hovered in front of her, chest height, changing colors and spinning slowly. Fascinated, Ava reached out to it and felt warmth as her hand neared it. She wondered what it was.

Abruptly, it stopped. Ava looked around and saw she was standing in a space roughly the shape of an oval where the weeds and grass had been flattened. Although she didn't know it then, it was where deer had slept.

The ball of light slowly sank toward the ground, stopping a few inches above the leaves and dirt. Ava lowered herself, looking around at the trees and thick brush surrounding her. It was a good place, she thought. When she sat down, she couldn't see above the weeds. No one could see her.

Tired from fighting, she bunched the blanket up and used it as a pillow as she curled up on her side. Her hand was resting palm up on the ground near her face. The ball of light dimmed until it was merely a soft hint of blue and settled in her palm.

It was still there when Ava's eyes slipped closed minutes later.

Moaning, Ava teetered. As she reached for the light, trying to hold on to the feeling of comfort it had brought her, her hand bumped a picture off the wall. It fell down the stairs, the glass shattering below.

Gabriel shot up from sleep even as he sprinted from the bed and followed the sound of breaking glass. His pulse rocketed when he saw Ava at the top of the stairs, off balance. Her arm was extended as if she was reaching for something. Rushing over to her, he slipped his arm around her waist, her back against his side, and hauled her off her feet, swinging her around and away from the stairs. He was prepared for the fury of blows.

They never came. Ava allowed him to carry her into the hallway.

He didn't set her down until they were a comfortable distance from the stairs. Her eyes were wide with shock. Tears were drying on her cheeks. He held her by the arms and tried to shove the image of her almost plummeting down the stairs out of his head.

"Ava? Are you awake?"

"The light," she whispered.

"That doesn't help much."

He brushed his thumb across her cheek.

The crack of her palm against his cheek echoed in the hallway.

"I'm getting damn sick of that. Wake your ass up."

"I followed the light."

"Why don't you follow me back to bed? Take my hand."

He held his hand out to her and was surprised when she took it.

"Holy shit, it worked," he muttered to himself. "Come on. Let's get you back in bed."

He turned the lamp on as she was crawling into bed. After making sure she was secure under the blankets, he waved a hand in front of her face to make sure she was still asleep. It was unsettling that her eyes were open while she slept.

Despite her not being awake, he thought some part of her subconscious would hear him.

"I'll be right back," he said softly. He brought the blankets up around her shoulders.

He cleaned up the broken wood and glass on the stairs. The picture was of the family. His mother had given it to him as a housewarming gift years ago. It hadn't been ruined in the tumble down the stairs, so he could build a new frame for it. Taken over a year before Hayden disappeared, it showed the family when it was still complete, when it was still whole.

Just in case her glass was empty, Gabriel fixed Ava another water and headed upstairs. When he returned to the bedroom, he found her sitting up, her posture stiff, her hands gripping the bedding at her chest in a childlike pose. He set her water on the nightstand and walked around to his side of the bed.

"What's wrong?"

He slid into bed next to her. When she blinked and turned to look at him, he jumped.

"You're awake."

"You were gone. I waited... for a long time."

"I had to clean up a mess." He touched her shoulder. "Everything okay?"

"I waited for you."

Her gray eyes were iridescent, liquid ash against her pale face. The way she held her hands against her chest was not out of embarrassment of her nudity, but out of a subconscious need to protect herself.

"I'm here." He moved closer to her.

Frowning, she considered. "I followed the light. I was afraid."

Gabriel lifted his hand from her arm and slid it around her shoulders, pulling her against his chest. To his surprise, she leaned against him. Her body was stiff and awkward; she didn't know how to snuggle. But she was trying.

"It's okay. You're okay."

Overwhelming affection bubbled up inside him unexpectedly, cutting off his breath. How hard it must be for her to trust anyone, he thought. He remembered what David had told him about what had been done to her as a child, and he felt ashamed that he hadn't been more understanding about her hesitation. Her unbreakable shell of confidence sometimes made him forget she had feelings, too, and needed patience, compassion.

Shifting, he adjusted his pillow so he could lean back against the headboard. Ava watched him move the pillow and place it just right, then spend several more seconds finding the right position to sit in. Finally, he took her hand and pulled her down to him. She nestled in the crook of his arm, her hand resting on his chest. Bending her leg, she rested it across his belly, just below his navel.

"Comfortable?" he murmured, resting his hand on her bent leg.

She nodded against his chest.

"My mom invited you to Easter dinner on Sunday." Lazily, his fingers grazed across her shoulder.

Ava thought about that. A warm feeling spread through her. "I have never been invited to dinner."

He let her think about it, brushing his fingers against the back of her arm.

"Do you want me there?"

"Absolutely. But I don't want you to feel obligated. If you don't want to give up your time, I understand."

"I find your family entertaining. I will come."

Gabriel gazed down at her just as she raised her head to look at him. Her eye lids were beginning to droop. Brushing his palm over her cheek, he leaned down and kissed her. It wasn't the fierce passion he had shown before. His mouth was soft against hers, taking its time, exploring texture and taste. Endlessly long and intoxicating, the kiss was steady, with no intent to go further.

Ava had never been kissed unless the result was sex. Seduction was unnecessary; when the fever took her body, she wanted only to drive it out. This slow caress of lips stirred something deep inside her. It left her head spinning with passion but also with confusion. The emotions inside her were muddled and tangled together. She could not understand what she was feeling, let alone figure out why she was feeling that way.

He kissed her forehead and rested his cheek on the top of her head. His arm was strong around her, his other hand resting on top of hers on his chest.

She was still trying to decipher her emotions when she drifted into sleep.

• • • • •

Griffin's shower was incredible. It was the walk-in kind that didn't have a tub. Frameless glass panels on either side of the door gave it an open feeling, making Isabel feel as if she had endless space to work in. The shower head, high above to accommodate Griffin's six-foot-three frame, and the rest of the hardware, had a brushed nickel finish. There was also a detached sprayer. She had never used one of those.

The entire enclosure was designed to prevent one from feeling claustrophobic; Isabel felt like she was on display.

The door is closed. Griffin is asleep. No one is watching you, judging you.

This wasn't the first time she had showered at his apartment. But each time was surprising, making her feel tiny in such a large space. She supposed the glass was meant to give the impression of endless room, and it worked.

Her aching muscles began to relax. After finishing with her hair, she simply stood, letting the water run over her body. She relished the strong water pressure; the pressure in hers was horrible. Washing her hair took forever unless she used the kitchen sink, where the force was only slightly better. She wanted this shower. It was bigger than the kitchen in her apartment. The only thing she would change was using frosted glass, so she didn't feel so exposed.

When she heard a noise, she wiped water from her eyes and opened them to see Griffin standing naked outside the glass. "Mind if I join you?"

Instinctively, she brought an arm across her chest, her hand held in a loose fist. Nodding, she stood back from the door to give him room.

He stepped in. Isabel avoided looking at his body as if she were in middle school and had just found a dirty magazine. Ridiculous; how many times had they made love? Seeing him naked in the shower for the first time shouldn't have been a big deal.

Trying to be casual, she set the soap down with one hand while leaving the other over her chest.

"You steamed it up in here," Griffin said, stepping close.

"I like it really hot. I can't get used to the size of this shower. I would never leave my bathroom if I had this in it."

He grinned. "There's a delicious visual."

His fingers gripped her wrist gently and pulled her arm away from her chest. He slid his other hand around to her lower back. Uncurling her hand, he wrapped his fingers around it and began to move. Her body automatically moved with him.

"I think we should go to dinner tonight," he said. They turned in a little circle as their feet moved and their bodies swayed.

"O-okay." Isabel inwardly cringed. Dinner meant public. Public meant people. "Are you slow dancing with me in the shower?"

"Who doesn't slow dance in the shower?"

"Who does?" she laughed. She liked the feel of his hand wrapped around hers, so large and protective, covering her small one easily. His body was close to hers, heat pouring off it and mixing with her own. Water pelted them in a hot spray, sending droplets across his chest.

"I know this place that's sparsely populated," he said. He felt her hand relax slightly in his. "The food is excellent."

He stopped and ran his hand over her wet hair.

"What time do you have to leave for work?"

"Seven-twenty. For some reason, I wake up earlier when I stay here. I have over an hour before I have to leave."

"I'm sure we can figure out something to pass the time."

"Oh, really?" Her eyebrow shot up.

Grinning, he gazed down at her. "I have a few ideas."

"Lucky me."

His hand moved from her lower back up to her neck, cupping the back of her head and pulling her in for a kiss. It was such a natural move that Isabel's body was responding to him before her head realized what he had done. She had no time to feel self-conscious. They stood underneath the spray of water, tasting, for endless seconds.

She felt drugged. His mouth was like magic. From its teasing alone, Isabel could feel her heart raging against her chest. As their tongues danced, their bodies close, he kept his hand at the back of her head while the other held her hand as if they were still dancing. Her body was hot, so hot in the already steamy shower she wondered how her skin wasn't bursting into flames.

He trailed kisses down her neck, biting a little around her shoulder before soothing the sting with his lips. As he continued to touch, he shuffled them out of the direct spray, toward the back of the shower.

Isabel felt her heart slipping slowly over a precipice she had promised herself never to approach. The way he was caressing her was undoing her, making panic rise in her throat. She felt the difference in the touches, the kisses. Their relationship had never been just about sex, but this was deeper than before. Every nerve in her body was responding to him in a way that felt magnetized. How could that be? How could everything feel different just because she suddenly thought she was in lo-

"Miss Harris, those cogs are going to rust in this humidity."

His mouth returned to hers as he gently backed her against the shower wall. Lacing his hands with hers, he brought them slowly up over her head. He moved his body against her once, twice. An ache, deep in her belly, built until she let out a choked sob.

I shouldn't, she thought. I shouldn't do this when I don't know what it will cost me.

Pinning both wrists with one of his hands, he lifted her leg around his hip as he slipped inside her, locking them together. Tears stung at the backs of her eyes. Sensations flooded her, not just physical but emotional, as he moved inside her in long, slow strokes. His golden eyes studied her and for once she was unable to look away from him.

With her back pressed to the wall, her wrists bound above her, she could only feel. It was too much. Not enough. Her body was trembling as it climbed, her breath tearing as she tried to fill her lungs with air. The first wave struck her, and she tightened her leg around him, pulling him tighter to her as her vision blurred. Her back arched, stirring his blood when a long, low moan vibrated against his lips as he fastened them to her neck. Turning her head to the side, she clenched her fists.

Griffin released her hands and braced his palm on the wall beside her head. Isabel's arms, exhausted from the first orgasm, weakly slid down the wall. She managed to move them to his shoulders to steady herself. His eyes were so intense, his movements becoming more urgent even as he maintained those long, soul-sating thrusts. Her fingers flexed as the pressure began to build again.

He drove into her so deep she was lifted to her toes. Arching her back again, she reached for something to contain the sensations coursing through her. Her palm slapped against the side wall. Another stroke had her other hand slamming onto the tile next to her hip. Griffin saw her eyes were blind with pleasure and could hold back no longer.

"Jesus, Izzie." He forced the words out, raw with desperation.

She tried to call out to him. His name was barely a whisper on her tongue.

The world around them seemed to detonate. Isabel thought of falling, endlessly falling, as her pelvis vibrated against him. Griffin gathered her close, so close, pressing her against the wall with his body as he exhaled a shuddering breath. Her forehead dropped to his shoulder. She felt as if her feet were leaving the ground.

The moment spun out endlessly. She was afraid to let go for fear her entire body would unravel and spill everything she was feeling out at his feet.

He released her leg and it slid, boneless, from his hip down his leg. They were both winded. She might have slid to the shower floor if his body was not pressing her against the wall. Her legs were shaking so bad they couldn't hold her full weight. The water pounded like rain. Isabel could hear nothing but the falling water, the drumming of their hearts.

Slowly, Griffin eased back. For a moment he rested his forehead against hers as he caught his breath. He ran his hand over her hair, letting it rest at the side of her neck.

He reached over to pluck a loofah off one of the hooks and liberally soaped it before turning to Isabel. Nudging her around until her back was to him, he swept her hair over one shoulder. A shiver ran through her when he leaned down and kissed the place where her neck and her collar bone met. He began moving the loofah slowly, gently, over her body, until she thought her heart would simply give out. All tension drained away on a sigh as she leaned her head back against his chest.

• • • • •

Seconds passed. Minutes. Hours. Griffin gently ran the loofah over Isabel's body, then gave it to her so she could do the same. Taking it back to hang it up, he ran his hands over her as they stood beneath the water to rinse the soap off. Dizziness swirled around her in the steamy shower, making her feel half asleep. She was completely relaxed, and exhausted.

Her legs buckled. Griffin scooped her up and stepped out of the shower. He used a couple fingers to hook a bath towel off the rack and drop it on the floor. Nudging it with his foot, he spread it out as much as possible. The tenderness in his eyes as he set Iz down made her throat close. Something in her chest was clamping down. Still dazed, she sat with her knees pulled up to her chest.

Griffin turned to shut off the water. Walking to the linen closet, he pulled out more towels and brought them over to Isabel. He knelt in front of her and draped a towel around her shivering shoulders, rubbing his hands up and down her arms. She pulled the towel tight around her.

A moment to think, that's all she needed. She couldn't do that when he was touching her, making her body light up. He went about drying himself off as she sat on the floor silently.

When he was done and had pulled on a pair of boxers, he took her by the shoulders and helped her stand. He rubbed a towel through her hair to soak up the excess water. Then he took a fresh towel and wrapped it around her, rubbing his hands up and down it to dry her body. His touches were light, tender. A little frown was on his face as he concentrated, making sure she was fully dry. Occasionally, when he leaned over her to reach somewhere lower, he would kiss her shoulder with such unbridled affection that Isabel felt like her insides were vibrating.

Any moment she would shatter. Tears were fighting to escape. Her chest was burning. When he was done, he lifted her and carried her to the bedroom.

Setting her on the bed, he turned a lamp on before he stretched out beside her, holding her close.

"Why are you so quiet?" The sound of his voice made her jump. "What are you thinking?"

"Nothing you want to hear," she mumbled. He was startled to see her wipe away a tear.

"Was I too rough?"

"N-no." She refused to look at him. Her body was trembling. Griffin pulled the blankets up around them knowing she wasn't cold. Iz clutched them to her chest protectively.

Propped up on his elbow, looking down at her, worry creased his face. "What's wrong, Izzie?"

"I..." She swallowed. "I love you."

The shock on his face was obvious. Isabel felt a tear slide down the side of her face and hated herself for it.

"I'm sorry," she whispered. "I didn't mean to."

He said nothing. His amber eyes stared at her.

Isabel felt as if her heart was shattering into a million tiny pieces, and each piece had shot into her blood stream, driving shards of pain throughout her entire body.

"Okay." She sat up and turned her back to him.

"Isabel-"

"I'll just get my things."

She started to stand. Griffin grabbed her arm and pulled her back down on the bed. Surprised, Isabel fell onto her back. Before she could move, he rolled on top of her.

"You're not going anywhere," he scolded.

Was that amusement on his face? He was laughing at her.

He could see her face, could see all of her. She was exposed, vulnerable. Did he want to humiliate her? Feeling the tears pushing against her eyes, Isabel turned her head away from him.

"Let me up."

"Why? So you can run away?"

"As opposed to what?" she snapped, glaring at him. She preferred the rage to humiliation. "You holding me down and humiliating me?"

"Humiliate..." Griffin's eyes softened. "Why would you think that?" He rubbed his thumb along the salty stain the tear had left as it traveled down her face.

Jesus. She had really fucked everything up. It had been going so well.

"Just let me up. I need to be alone for a while, and then we'll get back to casual fucking. I won't make that mistake again."

"Isabel, we're in the middle of a conversation. What mistake?" He was not letting her up. It infuriated her.

"Bringing emotion into it. Telling you I love you. That's the last you'll hear of it from me." She squirmed underneath him. "I just need a little time to... deal... Christ, Griffin, let me up!"

At the desperation in her voice, he shifted off her. Isabel stood shakily and walked to the chair to get her clothes.

"Isabel." His voice was quiet. The underlying amusement she usually heard in it was gone.

She slipped into her bra and panties with trembling fingers. She searched the floor frantically for her socks. One of them was missing, of course. "Where the fuck is my other sock?"

Anger was good. It helped stop the heartache she knew was coming, or at least put it off until she was alone and could deal with it without an audience. She flexed her fingers a couple times, curling them into fists and releasing them to try to get rid of some of the excess energy coursing through her.

"Isabel!" His voice was sharper now, authoritative.

"What?" She slid her jeans on. Her shirt was tossed over the back of the chair. Good. Do one thing, then the next. Keep moving, so the pain of knowing he didn't love her wouldn't catch up.

"For God's sake, look at me. If you're going to accuse me of an entire conversation, complete with emotions you assume I have, have the decency to face me while you do it."

Because it gave her a moment to compose herself while keeping her dignity, Isabel pulled her shirt over her head as she turned back to him. She was slow to fit her head through the collar.

"What?" she asked again. "I'm facing you."

She needed to keep her hands busy. She reached back and began braiding her hair.

"What the hell just happened? Leave it," he said absently when she glanced down to look for her sock.

"I made a mistake." Her fingers flew through the motions of weaving her hair, helping to divert her attention even though she was looking at him. She kept her eyes on his chest. so she didn't have to see the disgust she was sure was in his eyes.

"By saying you love me?"

"Obviously, you don't return the sentiment." She dug a hair band out of her pocket and twisted it onto the end of her braid. "I probably don't, either. It was just a post-coital utterance. A hazard of amazing sex. Let's just forget it ever happened." She spotted the sock under the bed.

"Why don't you let me decide what I feel? I said leave it!" he barked when she started to kneel and get the sock.

She straightened slowly. Griffin was sitting on the side of the bed, his eyes a darker shade of gold than usual, his bare chest rising and falling visibly. Gazing at her calmly, he didn't speak for several moments. He was retracting his anger, but he was obviously furious. A few weeks ago, Isabel would have thought it impossible to piss him off. Of course, she had a knack for being able to infuriate anyone. Mother Theresa would have probably folded within ten minutes of meeting Isabel.

Griffin opened his mouth to speak, closed it. Tried again. "Why would you... You assume this is casual for me?"

He could see she was hardening herself, building a protective shell around her emotions. Her expression shifted into a carefully neutral expression, and her shoulders were hunched forward. She gripped her elbows with her hands.

"You're a guy, aren't you?"

"That's not an answer."

She shifted uncomfortably. "I don't expect anything from you."

"Jesus Christ, Isabel. Stop talking to me like I'm a one-night stand."

"What do you want me to say?"

"Anything that isn't bullshit. You don't have to protect yourself from me. You did nothing wrong, expressing your feelings honestly."

Without the warning of an urge or a tickle, tears slipped down her cheeks. "Obviously, I did, since you don't feel the same." She swiped at her cheeks angrily.

"Who says I don't?"

"Your silence laid it out pretty effectively." Her tone was sarcastic, but he heard the pain underneath. How could she be so intelligent, yet so clueless?

"Isabel, I've loved you from the moment you told me you almost ran a cart up my ass in that grocery store. I was surprised to hear you say it first, that's all."

She forgot how to breathe. The knowledge, the instinct, the self-preservation was just gone. She stared at him, her eyes wide, her body locked in a rigid pose of disbelief. All the air seemed to have left the room.

"Breathe."

She exhaled loudly, her shoulders heaving. Had she heard him right? She couldn't catch her breath. A hundred thoughts were racing through her head, none of them coherent or complete. The floor seemed to be tilting under her feet. She hadn't imagined all of it. When she told him she loved him, he had frozen. Hadn't he?

"I'm not crazy," she said.

"Who said you were?" He patted the bed beside him. "Come here."

Hesitating, Isabel looked at the floor, trying to decide if she would be weak for giving up so easily. Or if she was crazy for making too much out of -

She was knocked back a step by something hitting her in the chest. Instinctively, she caught whatever it was and stood staring at it. A pillow. He threw a God damn pillow at her. She raised her head.

"What the fuck?" she spat.

"It's the only thing I could think of to stop that mind of yours from racing around like a gerbil on crack. Good God, you just let that thing run loose, woman."

He had a half smile on his face. "Come sit with me."

Iz walked slowly around the bed and sat down, propping the pillow up behind her. Griffin tugged her so she was lying on his chest. His heartbeat began to lull her racing thoughts.

"Someday," he said mildly, "you're going to tell me why you feel the need to punish yourself so harshly."

He felt her stiffen in his embrace and began rubbing his hand up and down her back.

"Not today. Someday." Griffin rested his chin on the top of her head. "Relax. I just told you I love you, not that you have a life-threatening illness."

"I don't..." Isabel curled the hand on his chest into a fist. "I don't know what to do with that."

"Just let it happen." Griffin uncurled her hand and rested it flat on his chest. He pressed his hand on top of it.

She nodded against him. "Okay. Okay."

"We'll get some therapy later by reading to some shelter dogs. You'll be fine. Just take it as it comes."

Exhaling, she nodded again. "I didn't mean to blurt that out."

"I'm so very glad you did." He lifted her chin and kissed her slow, deep. Her insides felt wobbly, like Jell-o. "I like those rare moments when you open up to me. You're very direct, Isabel, except when it comes to your emotions. I want to see more of them."

Iz turned her head toward his chest more, breathed him in. He was so open with his emotions. He gave them freely, without worrying about how people would use them against him. How could she not love that?

Griffin wrapped his arms more tightly around Isabel and felt her surrender a little more to him. She was still holding something back, something that she felt was too terrible to talk about. He wanted to know why she felt the need to protect herself. But she had opened to him, taken a big step. He knew how hard it was for her to admit to having any emotion, which she considered a weakness. He still had a long way to go to gaining her full trust.

Luckily, he was up to the challenge.

●   ●   ●   ●   ●

Vincent studied Ava across the table at the coffee shop. She was staring out the window, expressionless, her eyes distant. She hadn't wanted to meet at his apartment tonight after class. Instead, she asked if they could meet at a random coffee shop near the dojo. Something was on her mind, but she hadn't said much since they'd ordered their drinks and taken their seats.

"Are you making progress with Sensei regarding your ability?" Vincent asked, taking a drink of his tea.

"Hai, Senpai," Ava said thoughtlessly, addressing him as she would in the dojo, as a higher ranked student with more experience. He smiled at her automatic response.

"I can only..." She struggled to find the correct way to describe what had happened Wednesday night. How did one use normal terms to describe the paranormal?

"I can access the other side but not the information I wish to receive, not exactly. I have no control over who comes through or when. I still do not know how to block them out when I want to."

"Didn't you just start learning how to work with it?"

She sighed. "It is frustrating." Running a hand through her hair, her eyes were listless. "I should have started years ago. I should already have this under control."

"That kind of thinking will get you nowhere. You can only move forward."

"Knowing the logic of that statement does not make me any less frustrated."

That wasn't it, he thought watching her. She was annoyed with herself for not picking it up more easily, but she was pleased with her progress. He could tell in the way her shoulders squared and the cadence of her voice when she talked about it. When she leaned forward under the hanging light above their table, her eyes were alive with excitement.

"What else is on your mind tonight?" Vincent reached over to take her hand.

Ava jerked away from the contact. Embarrassed, she cupped her hands around her mug and avoided looking at him.

"Tell me."

Ava forced herself to meet his gaze. "I am confused. I do not know what to do."

"Is this regarding why you didn't want to come to my apartment tonight?"

Now lines appeared between her eyebrows and her eyes were troubled. She nodded.

"I have a... friend," she said. She began to fidget with the used tea bag sitting on the table. "I told him I am not interested in an intimate relationship, and I do not need friends."

Struggling to correctly present the facts, Ava found she was not exactly sure just what the facts were. If she could not figure out how to explain herself to Vincent, how did she expect him to understand her?

"He persisted?" Vincent coaxed when she didn't continue.

She nodded.

He realized that while he had given her what she needed physically, he hadn't prepared her for an actual relationship. The thought never occurred to him that she would not know how to handle one when it came along. She was a beautiful, gifted woman; it was going to happen sooner or later even if she didn't pursue it.

Vincent refrained from showing his amusement. "And you let him?"

Her head whipped around at that. "I cannot control the actions of other people."

"Ava, if you had no interest in this person, you would have shut him down in a way that would make it clear he needs to end his pursuit."

Despair rose inside her, starting deep in her stomach and surging into her throat. Vincent was telling her what she already knew. She abhorred men who refused to get the message and continued to pursue her. Knowing she had unconsciously gone easy on Gabriel, that she should have been able to stop him immediately, infuriated her. Ava did not play games; she believed she had done everything she could to stop Gabriel from wanting to be with her.

"What's his name?" Vincent asked, sipping his tea.

"Gabriel."

Vincent heard the way her voice changed just slightly when she said the name, saw her eyes go from dull to hopeful.

She doesn't even realize it, he thought. She has no idea how her body reacts to him.

"We talk, like you and I," she said. "Or we are silent."

"Like you and I," he said.

"Yes."

"There's nothing wrong with wanting a relationship, Ava."

The lines between her eyebrows appeared.

"I do not want a relationship," she repeated. "They are messy, time consuming, pointless. But when we are near each other, I feel..."

She put her fist against her chest and rubbed, trying to find the words.

He nodded.

"I agreed to be his mate."

"So you wanted to tell me you've found someone, and you and I need to stop the sexual aspect of our relationship."

Ava's tone was full of confusion and remorse. "I do not want to hurt you."

"You won't hurt me. Your happiness has always been my priority."

"Your feelings should not matter to me. We take what we need from each other. You no longer have what I... think I want."

"Not sexually," he said. "But you're still my best friend."

Her breath hitched, but she said stubbornly, "I do not need friends."

"Remember who you're talking to, Ava."

A single tear slowly made its way down her cheek. Vincent reached out and brushed it away with his thumb.

"I trust you with my life. I would die for you."

"And I for you. That will remain the same no matter who comes into your life."

"I do not know what is expected of me." Ava sipped her drink. It had gone cold. She slid it to the edge of the table. "I do not understand how everything works."

He gave her a wry smile. "Nobody does. Most people won't admit it."

"I am confused by his behavior." Ava shifted in the seat. "I kissed him before...before I agreed to be his mate. He is obviously attracted to me physically. But since I agreed to join with him, he has not instigated sex."

A middle-aged man and woman sitting in the booth behind her glanced up. The barista wiping a table a few feet away whipped his head around and gave her a baffled look. Unaware she had drawn attention in the quiet café, Ava stared at her hands while she fidgeted with them. Vincent sipped his tea to keep from smiling.

"Do you want him to?"

It took her a moment to answer. Several emotions passed across her face: confusion, embarrassment, helplessness, misery.

"I know it is inappropriate to speak to you about this. I do not have anyone else –"

"You can ask me anything," he assured her. "That hasn't changed, either."

Sliding her glass of water across the table toward her, she took a sip as she tried to convey her uncertainty. Vincent spoke first.

"Does he know about your childhood?"

"Yes."

Vincent thought about that. "Did he know before you were a couple? Before you agreed to it?"

"Yes. He returned my kiss like a mate would. But he-"

She dropped her eyes to her hands again. The barista appeared with a tray.

"I brought you more tea," she said, smiling as she set it on the table. "I hope that's okay."

"That's very thoughtful of you," Vincent said smoothly, leaning back so he was out of her way. She set a fresh mug down for each of them with a tea bag and lemon on the saucer.

"Milk for you, right?" she asked Ava, lifting a small pitcher, and setting it on the table.

"Thank you, Heather," Ava said.

The woman blinked. "How do you know my name?"

Ava stilled, swallowed. "Your name tag."

Automatically glancing down, Heather patted her chest where the pin usually sat on her smock. "I lost it earlier this week. My boss has been hounding me about getting it replaced."

"I have been in here before."

Smiling, Heather lifted the tray and tucked it under her arm. "Of course." She brushed her hair back from her face. "It's been a long week. I've seen so many faces; I just don't recognize yours. Enjoy your tea."

Vincent waited until she had walked away before he said, "I didn't realize you came here enough to know the staff."

Ava's gaze was weary. "This is my first visit."

"You read her?"

"I only received her name."

They prepared their tea. Ava wished for coffee, but she already had trouble sleeping and coffee would compound the issue.

"What were you going to say before Heather came over?" Vincent asked. "Something about Gabriel knowing about your abuse."

"He thought I had not had consensual sex because of the abuse and because I do not like to be touched."

"That's probably why he doesn't want to rush things. He thinks you don't have experience, and he wants you to be sure before you take that step."

"I told him I had already chosen a partner to satisfy me sexually and I needed nothing else."

The couple behind them glanced over again. The man had a hint of a grin on his face.

Vincent had been taking a drink of tea and he almost choked on it. He coughed. "You told him that?"

"Yes."

"What did he say?"

"He thinks I am wrong, that I need more than just sex even if I will not admit it. And now he will not have sex with me. I do not understand why people are so complicated. Why are they so difficult?"

Swallowing forcefully, he watched her irritation grow. Keeping his voice low, he said, "I think he was asking if I was more than a fuck buddy, if you'll excuse the phrase. He didn't want to get in the middle of something between you and I."

Ava frowned deeply as she considered this.

"Once he found out you were unattached, as it were, he felt comfortable pursuing you. If I'm not mistaken, the reason he isn't having sex with you as your boyfriend is because he wants there to be more between you than sex. Does he offer more? Does he hug you and hold your hand?"

"Yes, and it is very strange." She said this in the same tone as she would have explained witnessing a UFO landing in front of her, full of awe and bewilderment.

Vincent almost choked on his tea again. He put a hand to his mouth to cover his smile.

"This is good, Ava. He wants to be with you. Not just physically, but in every way."

The couple behind her stood and put their jackets on. The man glanced at Ava once more before resting his hand on the lower back of the woman as they left the café.

"I see his dead sister."

Vincent sat up straight. "Does he know you're sensitive?"

"No. What I am feeling may be a subconscious reaction to seeing his sister," she added.

Her tone was hopeful. She would rather her connection to Gabriel be anything but attraction, Vincent realized. He chose his words carefully. "What you're describing is attraction, Ava."

She sighed. Having to admit the obvious, that she had sensed the truth all along and had not wanted to face it, made her feel ridiculous and inept.

"It is simpler my way," she insisted. "I have a schedule. I can depend on myself. I answer to no one."

Because she was looking down and couldn't see it, he smiled. "You've never settled for simple. Do you like being with him?"

Ava closed her eyes, thought of Gabriel's easy smile, the way he raised one eyebrow. The way he could be in a room with her and somehow make the experience better than if she were in the room by herself, even if they were not speaking. Although her natural reaction to people was to be on guard, in his company, she felt... comfortable. As she did when she was in the dojo, or around David. When Gabriel was near, she felt a connection to rest of the world that she was normally lacking. She felt she could be a part of it as long as he was with her to connect the two worlds. Yet he never made her feel inferior to people for being so far separated from society.

All those things were hard to explain, so she said, "Being with him is... pleasant."

It was all she was willing to admit.

Vincent nodded. "Then I think you have your answer."

. . . . .

"I have to say, seeing you all sweaty and worked up really does it for me," Griffin said, grinning as he took Isabel's jacket. She picked up her gym bag and set it in front of the little laundry closet next to the restroom.

"Ugh. I sweat so bad. I'm so glad they have showers. But I kicked major ass."

"Yeah, you did."

He held up his fist and she bumped it, grinning.

"Can we celebrate with high dollar whiskey?" She started toward the cupboard where the whiskey he bought her was kept.

Pulling her back against him, he nibbled on her neck. "Why don't we celebrate with each other?"

Snickering, she snaked her arm back above her head and ran her hand through his hair. She luxuriated in the feel of him against her, the way his hands possessively held her arms. In a purely self-serving move, she reached around with her other hand and grabbed his bottom.

"Oh my," he said, his breath tickling her ear. "Feeling randy, are we?"

"I'm getting mine," she said, squeezing a few times.

Slipping his hands under her shirt, he molded them to her breasts. "These are mine."

She let her head fall back against his chest as his hands began to move. Closing her eyes, she felt herself begin to drift. She wanted to wrap herself around him, become part of him. His heart was thundering against her back and hers was drumming so loud that at first, she didn't hear the knock at the door.

Griffin paused. "Bloody buggering hell." He squeezed her shoulder as he stepped away from her. "Who the bloody hell is that?"

"You're not expecting anyone?" Isabel put a hand to her forehead, fighting the wave of dizziness that rushed over her. She couldn't imagine a time when she would be used to Griffin's touch. It overwhelmed her in all the right ways.

Watching him walk over to answer the door, she straightened her shirt and ran a hand through her hair. He gave her a quick grin.

"No-" The way he broke off and the sudden severity of his pose made Isabel wish for a drink. "What are you doing here?"

"Are you going to invite us in?" a brisk voice asked.

Feminine, Iz thought. The accent was unmistakable.

She didn't like seeing Griffin upset. Instantly, her guard was up.

"Come in," he said. He stepped back stiffly and gestured. A woman, dressed in clothing that seemed too elegant for the apartment, stepped inside, followed by a man. The woman looked aloof, with perfectly styled, glossy brown hair and expensive earrings.

"It's good to see you, Griffin," the man said quietly. He looked to be in his mid-fifties, his hair deep brown with slashes of silver.

"You, too."

Griffin walked stiffly into the kitchen, mouthing I'm sorry to Isabel as he walked toward her. "Mum, Dad, this is Isabel Harris, my girlfriend. Isabel, these are my parents, Nathan and Eve Turner."

A short-lived thrill shot through Isabel at the word girlfriend. She reached out to shake his mother's hand. The woman looked at her hand as if she preferred it to be sterilized first, then reached out and briefly, limply, took Isabel's hand. Isabel hated flaccid handshakes. They spoke volumes to the character of the people giving them.

"Hello," Isabel said, because she wasn't going to lie and say it was nice to meet her. Jesus, what a joke. She shook hands with Griffin's father, whose grip was firmer and whose eyes were kind.

"Nice to meet you, Isabel."

"Would you like something to drink?" Griffin asked, pouring himself a glass of wine.

"Your father is driving," Eve Turner said with authority.

"I have beverages besides alcohol."

"I'm fine," his father said. "Thank you."

"I'll take freshly squeezed orange juice," his mother said, turning her head back to her husband and lifting her coat from her shoulders. He dutifully took it and draped it over the back of a stool.

"This isn't a fancy restaurant," Isabel said. She walked to the counter where the whiskey Griffin had given her was stored and proceeded to pour herself a glass. "He doesn't have oranges lying around or a juice press."

"I have water, wine, orange juice or cranberry juice from the store, milk, and soda. And whiskey if Isabel feels like sharing."

"I don't." Isabel looked up at his mother and took a slow sip.

"Water." His mother stared back with obvious disdain. "I don't suppose you have a lemon slice to put in it, either."

"I forgot to tell Giancarlo, our man servant, to stop by the orchard and pick one this morning," Isabel said. Griffin smirked. She glanced at him and lowered her voice. "Do you want me to leave?" She searched for his hand, gave it a squeeze.

Griffin's mother was staring at her icily.

"No," Griffin said instantly. Please don't, his expression pleaded. He squeezed her hand back. The look on his face was a little desperate.

He handed a bottle of water to his mother, who looked at it as if it was a snake. "What are you doing here?" he repeated, wrapping his arm around Isabel's shoulders, and holding her close. She could hear him clenching his teeth so hard they squeaked. Iz put her arm around his waist, wishing she could comfort him.

"We're in Madison for a couple weeks." Nathan Turner said. "We wanted to spend some time with you, Griffin." He glanced at Isabel. "Maybe talk some things over."

"I take it she's the reason you refuse to take your father's offer at the business," his mother said stiffly, still looking at Isabel. His father gave Griffin an apologetic glance.

"She is Isabel," Griffin said, giving her a squeeze. His hand moved from her shoulder to her lower back. "Yes, she's a big part of my choice to stay in Wisconsin."

"I am?" She flushed. She had no idea he had made such a big choice based on his relationship with her.

His hand slid around her side and pressed her closer against him. She could feel his muscles, tense and quivering slightly.

"I'm not moving to New England," Griffin continued. "Also, I have a job doing what I love. I'm not an investment banker. I'm a graphic designer."

Isabel slid her thumb just under Griffin's shirt and rubbed it against his side. His body lost some of its rigidity.

"Drawing cartoons is hardly a career." His mother's voice lacked emotion. Iz found herself loathing the woman. How could anyone speak to Griffin like that? He was the warmest, most caring person she'd ever met. He believed in her even when she continually showed him she wasn't worthy of his faith. Who did this woman think she was?

Griffin slammed his wine glass down on the counter. "Drawing cartoons?"

"I think what your mother is trying to say," Nathan said, clearing his throat, "is she loves you very much. She wants to make sure you're taken care of. The position at my company is to get you ready to take over the business when I retire."

"I don't want your business." Griffin tried to keep his voice neutral, but the rage was making it shake. "I'm sorry, but I don't. I have dreams of my own, here in Wisconsin. Now, I have plans with Isabel tonight and -"

"You're young," Eve Turner interrupted. "You have no idea what you want. You'll grow out of this silly infatuation with drawing and understand-"

"This infatuation has been my passion since I was four years old." His voice had become dangerously calm. "You might have understood that if you'd raised me, instead of the pawning me off on the nanny."

A steel curtain fell over Eve's eyes. "Don't be trite. You don't listen to the people who have more experience than you, who can guide you to make the right decisions. Neither did Connor."

"We're leaving," Nathan said. He picked up his wife's coat.

"Who's Connor?" Isabel asked in the sudden silence.

She felt as if the air had suddenly been removed from the room. Taking a breath was a struggle with the tension. Beside her, Griffin rested his hands on the counter, pressing hard enough to make his knuckles lose their color. He was shaking.

"Connor," he said slowly as he looked at his mother, his voice soft, "knew exactly what he wanted. When you continued to get in the way of his dreams, he blew his fucking head off."

Isabel's body jerked against Griffin's.

The friend, she thought, the one who's vehicle Griffin now drove, the one who killed himself. That must be Connor.

What the hell was going on?

Eve Turner glared at her son. "How dare you speak to me about my own son that way."

460

Isabel felt like someone had swung a baseball bat against her chest. Not a friend. His brother. His own brother had committed suicide.

Beside her, Griffin was still leaning on the counter, his entire body shivering. He had dropped his head, so he was no longer looking at his mother, at anything but the counter.

"Eve, we need to go right now." Nathan set his hand on her arm, but she jerked away from him.

"How dare you blame your brother's death on me!" she hissed at Griffin. "He was obviously deeply troubled-"

"Get out."

Isabel stood frozen, staring at Eve and Nathan, her fists at her sides, unaware she had stepped between them and Griffin.

"Excuse me?"

"There's no excuse for people like you."

Eve had never been spoken to this way. She didn't care for it. "What did you say to me, you little-"

"Get out, or I'll kick your uptight ass out," Isabel said. She took another step toward them. "You will not talk to him like that in his own home."

"You are nobody, a current flirtation. An itch to be scratched." Eve eyed her dismissively. "Just who the hell do you think you are?"

Isabel took another step toward the hateful woman. She couldn't believe she had talked to Griffin's parents that way. The words hadn't seemed to come from her mouth. Yet she couldn't stop.

"If you don't leave right now, you're going to find out."

"She's threatening me!" Eve couldn't hide the shock in her voice. She turned to Nathan, staring at him with wide eyes, her mascara making her eye lashes look like spider legs.

He grabbed his wife by the shoulders and shoved her toward the doors. "Go to the car now. I'm not losing another son."

When she was gone, he looked at Griffin, who was still hunched over the counter, then at Isabel.

"I apologize for her behavior," he said. "She went too far. Thank you, young lady, for caring so much about my son. You seem like a lovely person. Griffin... I'm so sorry. I want to... I need to fix this with you, even if it can't be fixed with her. I'll give you a call."

Stunned, Isabel watched him leave. She was afraid of what she would see when she turned to Griffin. Holy shit, she had just threatened his mother. What had she been thinking? Where had that fire come from?

She turned. Now that the threat was gone, her hands began to shake. "Griffin."

He didn't answer. His tall body was still quivering, his face pale. The silence in the apartment stretched out for several seconds.

"I thought you said you don't have siblings." She didn't know what else to say. Griffin flinched.

He looked exhausted. "I don't. Connor's dead. Fuck."

He straightened, picked up her whiskey, and downed it in one gulp. Grimacing, he coughed as his eyes began to water. She had poured herself a generous amount.

Griffin walked around the side of the island and sat heavily on a stool. "Thank you."

"For what?" Isabel couldn't think of a single reason he was thanking her. She had spoken to his parents in a way that would have gotten her smacked if she were talking to her own, threatened his mother, and kicked them out of his apartment. What part of that deserved a thank you?

"For standing up for me. I lied to you." He scrubbed a hand down his face.

"You've never lied to me," Isabel said, taking a cautious step closer.

"I told you my friend committed suicide, gave me the Range Rover." He ran a hand through his hair. Iz walked quietly, hesitantly to him. "I never... explained to you that it was my brother."

"But he was your friend, wasn't he?" Isabel lay her hand on his arm. "He wasn't just your brother."

Griffin looked at her, his eyes glassy. "We were twins. He was my best friend."

She felt as if her heart was breaking, as if a piece of her was being ripped away. Not just his brother, but his twin. A deep bond that one couldn't understand unless one had that connection.

He blew his fucking head off, Griffin had said. Was he the one to find his brother? God, how did anyone move on from that?

"When did it happen?" She had to distract her mind from consuming his grief. Her empathy was greedy; she didn't only feel what others felt but took it upon herself to feel it as well. As if by doing so, she could lessen their pain. But she couldn't lessen anyone's pain, and it wasn't hers to take on.

"Four years ago."

Isabel stepped forward and put her arms around him. When he buried his face in her hair, she felt the weight of his loss. Did he have anyone else to share this burden? Obviously, his parents were no help to him. His mother was a horrible woman, Isabel thought, to throw his brother's death in his face. He seemed to have no other family to talk to. Despite being in an intimate relationship with him, one where she felt he was open with her about his life, he hadn't told her all the details, either. How did he hold that inside for so long?

He clung to her as he trembled.

She didn't speak. Nothing could be said to take away the ache of a lost sibling.

Isabel knew that better than anyone.

· · · · ·

CHAPTER NINE

The phone rang just after six o'clock on Friday evening.

Ava had finished with her work for the day and put in an extra-long three-hour work out. She was getting ready to shower when the phone interrupted her. Frowning, she checked the screen.

Ava preferred to communicate through e-mail and text, but since the number on the screen was Isabel, she answered. She put it on speaker so she could undress while she talked.

"Hello."

"Ava? It's Iz. I was wondering if you're busy tonight?"

Ava removed her shirt. "I do not have any plans until later."

"Do you want to hang out?"

Hang out. Isabel was forever using that term. Apparently, it meant sitting around talking.

"I am available to... hang out. What time?" she asked, thinking of Gabriel stopping by after Guys Night Out. She had at least a couple hours.

"What time are you free?"

"I have to shower." She removed her yoga pants, dropping them in the sweaty pile of clothes next to the door.

"It'll take me some time to get to your place. You should be done before I get there. Does that work?"

"Okay."

Fifty minutes later she heard the knock at the door. She answered and was pleased to see Isabel had brought her guitar.

"Are you sure you don't mind my company?" Iz hesitated on the porch.

"You didn't sound very enthused on the phone."

Behind her, the sun was softening. The day had been mild enough for Ava to do all her training outside.

"I never sound enthused."

She stepped back to give Isabel room to enter. As Isabel walked past her, Ava felt a strong pull of longing and fought a wave of dizziness. It weakened as Isabel put distance between them.

She seemed nervous as she set her guitar under the front window.

"I love your house," Isabel said, unzipping her hoodie.

"I did not build it."

Snickering, Iz glanced out the window. "I was thinking maybe we could make this a regular Friday night thing if you're interested. An hour or two of us getting together. Or, maybe once a month or something, if every week is too much."

Isabel couldn't stop moving. She wandered around the room, putting her hands in her pockets, taking them out, resting them on a bookshelf as she read the titles, running a finger along the spines. Ava felt like she was going to vomit.

"Or maybe you're too busy. Or just don't like me. Never mind. It's probably a stupid idea."

"I would like that." Ava found herself appreciating Isabel's company – when she was not being made nauseous.

"Really?" Stunned, Iz paused in the middle of pacing.

Ava nodded. She had to look away when Isabel started pacing again.

"I was going to make myself dinner," she said, walking toward the kitchen. "Are you hungry?"

"Sure."

Isabel followed her and sat on an island stool. In spite of sitting, she kept fidgeting, picking up the salt and pepper shakers, straightening the cooking magazines Ava had stacked on the counter, tapping her fingers.

Ava finally turned around and slammed her palms on the counter. "Stop. Moving."

Startled, Isabel stared at her. Ava's eyes seemed to be pulsing, making it impossible to look away from them.

"He will come back to you."

Isabel froze. "What?"

She slid her hand across the counter until she was gripping Isabel's. Her hand was warm and dry against Isabel's cold and damp skin. Comforting. Strong.

"Some people go away and never come back," Ava said. "But he is not one of them."

"How did you... what..."

Letting go of her hand, Ava turned and began gathering ingredients.

"I'm kind of seeing this guy," Isabel said after several seconds, her face turning red.

"I know."

She pulled out a skillet and saucepan.

"I'm not here just because he's not available, you know. I don't want you to think-"

Ava turned to look at her. "You would have asked me to... hang out... sooner but you think I do not like you. Tonight your fear of losing him was stronger than your belief I do not like you, so you asked. Sometimes the best decisions are made out of desperation."

"Uh... okay."

Ava filled the pan with water and set it to boil. Pulling out a variety of vegetables from the refrigerator, she set them on the counter in front of Isabel. She grabbed two cutting boards and two knives. Isabel began slicing a red onion, while Ava started with mushrooms.

"You are mistaken," Ava continued. "I find you entertaining and loyal. I would like to set aside time for us to get together each week. I would like to see more of my bee eff eff."

Isabel let out a long snort and almost cut into her palm. "You crack me up, Ava."

"A bee eff eff would want to know all about her friend's boyfriend, right?"

"I suppose," Iz said, feeling her face warm. "I don't usually talk about that kind of thing..."

"Thin slices," Ava said. She pointed to one of the slices with the tip of her knife. "That size."

Isabel nodded. "He's having some issues with his parents, mostly his mother. He's trying to work some of them out tonight. I've seen her with him and I'm a little worried."

Ava listened, finishing with the mushrooms, and moving on to a tomato. The water began to boil, and she turned it down.

"I thought I had issues with my parents." Isabel slid the onion to the side and prepared to cut more.

"That is enough," Ava said. "Break the stems off these." She handed her baby spinach.

They stayed silent, working. Iz found herself relaxing, enjoying the meal prep. Her mother had never done this with her. This activity was reserved for Beth. Isabel had taught herself how to cook, and it was a means to feed the machine, not anything special or to be enjoyed. Sitting here with Ava, she found herself getting caught up with the companionship and being part of creating something from raw ingredients.

"Your mother is a fool." Ava snapped her mouth shut as soon as the words were out.

"What?" Isabel paused, pausing in her work.

"What is his name?"

Iz frowned. "Who?"

"Your mate. What is his name?"

"My mate?" Her eyes cleared when she realized Ava was talking about her boyfriend. "Griffin. And if his parents aren't bad enough, he'll have to meet my parents for Easter dinner on Sunday. I let it slip I was seeing someone, and my mom made me invite him."

"Gabriel said she invited me as well."

"You'll get to meet him, then."

"He makes you happy."

"We'll see how long he lasts until I push him away. He's stubborn. I give him a few more weeks."

Ava finished with the tomatoes and set the knife down. She cocked her head at Isabel. "Why do you do that?"

"What?" She slid the pile of stems to the side and brushed her hands together.

"Purposely push him away when he makes you happy?"

"Everyone leaves. It's just a matter of time. Better to disconnect early on in the relationship when it hurts less. Where do you want these?" She held up a handful of baby spinach.

"They can stay there." She was frowning. "If you believe that, why not enjoy what time you have together?"

"I might start liking the relationship. Then I'll be dumb enough to think it will last."

I already love him. It will kill me when he leaves.

Ava winced at the sharp, strong emotion that flooded over her. Isabel was already in too deep, she thought. She was trying to solidify her heart and act flippant, but her emotions were swirling around and pouring off her like sweat.

She poured olive oil into the skillet and tossed in the veggies, adding balsamic vinaigrette. Turning up the heat on the water, she made sure the dry pasta and colander were ready.

"What about you?" Isabel asked, gathering the parts of the vegetables that needed to be discarded. "Does my brother make you happy?"

Ava raised her eyes to meet Isabel's. Her gaze was so intent, and she stared so long that Isabel looked away.

"Don't tell me you believe in all that happily ever after shit?"

Shaking the skillet back and forth to stir the vegetables, Ava added a little more vinaigrette. She did all this without taking her eyes off Isabel.

"Where's your damn garbage?" Isabel stood and gathered the discarded pieces of vegetables.

"Under the sink."

Isabel tossed the waste and began washing her hands. "Why are you staring at me like that?"

"I do not like being lied to."

She added noodles to the boiling water, ignoring the shocked expression on Isabel's face. Continuing to prepare dinner, she felt heavy waves of emotion vibrating off the older women's body as she stood at the sink. Ava moved around her easily, trying to block out the strong sensations pummeling her. She had avoided people for so long, she had forgotten how to defend herself against this constant onslaught of feelings.

"What makes you think I'm lying?" Isabel picked up the knives and cutting boards and set them in the sink. She picked up one of the knives again and an image flickered through her head quickly of her dragging a blade across her skin, making little beads of red rise as the skin split.

Ava looked at her sharply and saw she was staring at the blade curiously. "You are already in love with him."

Her statement had the desired effect and Isabel dropped the knife. It clanged in the sink.

"Huh?"

"Just because you are afraid to lose him does not make it any less true. You did not lie about pushing him away," she added. "You push everyone away."

She turned down the vegetables and stirred them, then stirred the noodles.

"Pasta bowls are in that cupboard," she said, pointing. "Flatware in that drawer."

Isabel took out the dinnerware without speaking. She pulled open the drawer Ava had pointed to and stared into it, feeling tears build at the corners of her eyes.

"I'm not really hungry," she said softly, pulling forks out. She closed the drawer. "This was a bad idea. I shouldn't have tried to do something I'm not good at. I'm sorry I bothered you."

She used the back of her wrist to wipe under her eyes and started around the island. She had just stepped out of the kitchen when something pierced the wood between her feet. Looking down, she was filled with fury, and she spun around.

"Did you just throw a fucking knife at me?"

"It is a paring knife. It is not the appropriate use of the knife, and it is damaging to the hardwood floor. Had you made it to the front door I would have had to use my shuriken." Ava stood holding objects in her hand that Isabel couldn't quite see. She shifted them slightly and they made a sound like metal clanging.

"You threw a fucking knife at me."

"I needed to snap you out of your current train of thought. Did you know I can pin you to my door casing using shuriken?" Her tone was full of curiosity, with no hint of arrogance as she held up a black palm-sized piece of metal in the general shape of a star with a hole in the center. "You wear your clothing slightly baggy because you are self-conscious about your body. That leaves just enough room for the sharp edges to catch the fabric without touching your skin."

"Are you threatening me?" Isabel leaned down and gripped the knife, yanking. It was embedded into the wood deeper than she thought. Jesus, Ava had thrown it so hard it stuck into the floor at least an inch. She pulled it out with major effort, managing to cut the sensitive skin in between her thumb and index finger. Ava kept her kitchen knives incredibly sharp.

"I do not make threats." Ava's expression hadn't changed. Her breathing was normal. She set the throwing stars back in the drawer she had taken them from and took the noodles off the stove, pouring them into the colander.

"What the fuck do you call throwing a knife at me?!" Isabel's voice had gone up an octave, her face was scarlet, and her chest was heaving as her blood pressure skyrocketed. How the hell was Ava acting as if this was just another Friday evening?

"I did not throw it at you. If I had, it would be in you. I threw it at the floor to stop your progression out of the room."

"How about saying 'hey' or 'wait'? like a normal person?"

"You stopped listening the moment you started lying. An extreme approach was needed."

Ava poured the noodles into the skillet and began shaking it, mixing the vegetables, noodles, and balsamic vinaigrette together. She glanced over at Isabel.

"Put pressure on your hand or you will continue to bleed on my floor."

Isabel looked down and saw her hand was bleeding more than she thought it should be. Should she be losing that much blood? She set the knife on the counter and pressed her left index finger and thumb on the wound. It was like trying to stop the bleeding on a bat wing; there was nothing to grab onto.

Ava shut off the stove and set the pan on a different burner. She took Isabel's wrist and walked her to the sink. Turning on the faucet to cold, she held Isabel's hand under the frigid streaming water.

"Why does it embarrass you to love him?" Ava asked softly. "It is a pure emotion; I feel it from you."

Isabel's eyes welled. She stared down at the cut because it could be fixed. The skin would heal, and no more blood would escape. Her heart wasn't the same way. She had already let too much of what made it survive out. It couldn't survive on what was left.

"He'll leave me. Everyone leaves."

Ava grabbed a paper towel and pressed it to the wound, holding Isabel's hand up above her heart.

"I will not talk about him anymore since it hurts you. A bee eff eff should not upset her... eff."

Isabel snorted in spite of herself. "I'm an asshole. I'm sorry I lied. I want to believe it's just casual, but... I love him. I don't want to. It makes everything so..."

"I understand." Ava walked to her first aid kit on the counter and pulled out a Band-Aid and some gauze. "It is much easier to stay away from humans."

She put the Band-Aid on, then wrapped it in gauze to make sure it would stay.

"You're a really good friend, Ava." Isabel flexed her hand a little.

"I do not know you well enough to know if you are a good friend, but I enjoy your company."

Iz laughed. "I'll take it." She inhaled. "That smells really good."

What they had concocted was waiting to be consumed. Isabel suddenly had an appetite.

"We can watch a movie while we eat. Or talk."

"Let's talk," Iz said, picking up a pasta bowl and handing it to Ava. "I need the practice."

· · · · ·

The temperature was in the mid-forties when Gabriel walked out of the bar just past one and took a piss behind his truck. He pulled out his phone and grimaced at the time. For a couple moments (while he was pissing), he contemplated whether or not to call Ava. He hadn't meant to stay out so late; usually the guys were done before eleven. Ava had insomnia, but that didn't mean she wanted to be disturbed at one in the morning.

He finished his business and zipped his pants. Walking to his truck, he got in and started it before he punched her Contact.

She answered on the second ring. "Hello."

"Hey," he said, keeping his voice low. "Did I wake you?"

"No."

"Is it too late to come over?"

472

"No."

He didn't ask if she was sure. Ava didn't speak unless she was sure about what she was saying. "I'm sorry to call so late." He knew he was rambling. "The guys and I don't usually stay out past eleven."

Gabriel put the truck in gear and backed out of the parking lot.

"You do not owe me an explanation."

"I know, I just... want you to know this doesn't happen very often. I'll be there in ten minutes."

"Okay."

The air felt good on his face as he drove. The past couple hours, he only drank water and a soda, but the alcohol before that had made him feel thick and lethargic. The fresh air was invigorating. Gabriel breathed deep and wanted nothing more than to see Ava's face.

Pulling into her driveway a few minutes later, he realized she had not put up a fight about him coming to her house. When he asked if he could come over, she hadn't hesitated. She'd simply said yes.

And she had turned the porch light on for him, he saw as he parked next to her vehicle.

She opened the door before he had the chance to knock. Standing there, looking up at him with eyes the color of a storm, Gabriel momentarily forgot about everything else. She was wearing worn yoga pants and a tee shirt, her hair pulled back into a loose ponytail. Her beauty was natural and didn't come from bottles and brushes.

"Hi." He couldn't stop staring at her.

"Hello." She stepped to the side. As he walked past her, he caught the unique scent of her: a forest after a hard rain, fresh foliage just starting to bud. He wanted to surround himself in that scent.

She walked toward the kitchen. "Do you want something to drink?"

"Just water. Thanks."

He sat at the breakfast bar and watched her put ice in two glasses. "What were you doing when I called?"

"Reading." She set a glass in front of him. "I have the windows open, and it is nice to smell the outdoors while I read."

"Sounds peaceful." Gabriel took a drink. Her filtered ice water tasted much better than the alcohol he'd had earlier in the evening, even better than the shitty tap water at the bar. He had a feeling he had overdone the booze a little and would feel it tomorrow morning.

Ava set her glass down carefully and rested her palms on the counter. Her eyes were trained on something past him, in the living room. Gabriel turned to look but saw nothing out of the ordinary. Her gaze was so intent he felt a chill.

"Are you okay?" he asked, touching her hand.

Her other hand slammed down on his, pressing her thumb between the hand bones of his index and second finger and flipping his hand over so it was pointing toward the ceiling. Then twisting it further, so a jagged pain shot through his arm while simultaneously feeling as if a jolt of electricity was coursing through it.

"Ow! Jesus, Ava-"

"Leave. I don't want you here for this."

Gabriel tried to move but she adjusted, keeping his hand trapped. "Fuck."

"I will never leave you."

Through the haze of pain, Gabriel realized what was happening and forced himself to stay calm. He drew in a deep breath. "Ava, will you let go of my hand?"

"Don't go blaming yourself, do you understand me?" She was still staring over his shoulder, her eyes out of focus. "This is on them."

It was only now, as he accepted the pain, that he realized she was speaking with an accent.

"Why don't you tell me who you're talking about?"

Ava's eyes had glazed over, her pupils large and pulsing. Gabriel could only wait until she came out of whatever seizure she was in. She wasn't going to let his hand go until she didn't feel threatened or whatever was happening ended.

"Do you hear me?"

Though she wasn't looking at him, she seemed to expect an answer.

"I hear you." He didn't know if he was helping her or not. He didn't know what answer she needed.

"You didn't do this."

Abruptly, her arm convulsed, her hand clamping harder on his before shoving away from him. The pain was unbelievable. In her socks, Ava skid across the linoleum a couple feet. Gabriel swore and rubbed his wrist.

When he looked up at her, she was standing in the center of her kitchen looking exhausted, her head tilted to the side slightly as if she was too tired to hold it up.

"Ava?" Gabriel said cautiously.

"Yes," she sighed.

"That was particularly strange. You okay?"

"Fine. D-did I injure you?"

"I'll get over it."

Ava stepped forward and took his wrist. She began kneading the muscles firmly. "I told you not to touch me."

"I didn't realize what was happening until it was too late." A stab of pain made him grimace. Ava slowly turned his wrist in the opposite direction from the way she had twisted it when she was having the episode, countering the stretch.

"Isabel came over tonight."

Gabriel raised his eyebrow. "Yeah?"

"We made dinner."

"Did you have fun?"

Ava nodded. "We are going to 'hang out' every Friday for a couple of hours. I think I am getting better at being a friend."

She hid a yawn behind her hand.

"I should go; you're tired." Gabriel squeezed her hand. "Thanks for letting me come over so late."

She wanted to run her fingers over the stubble on his face. It looked soft, like kitten's fur.

"You may stay here."

He raised an eyebrow. "That would be outstanding."

Watching her refill her glass of water, Gabriel rounded the breakfast bar. "Right behind you," he said easily, slipping his arms around her waist.

Her body tensed but she didn't raise her hands in defense. Gabriel liked that. She was getting used to him touching her, so he didn't have to be so careful around her. Apparently announcing his arrival was key to keeping all his body parts intact. She relaxed almost as soon as she had stiffened.

He leaned down and brushed his lips against the bare skin on her shoulder, just past the collar of her shirt. "Tonight was the first time I wanted to ditch Guy's Night and spend it with my girl instead."

Lithe as a snake, she looped her arm around the back of his neck. She set the pitcher on the counter. Gabriel closed his eyes and concentrated on how her body felt against his, the way her scent surrounded him.

"I like the way you smell."

"I use unscented body soap-"

Chuckling, he ran his fingertips up her side. "Not your soap, or your shampoo. Your smell. Your hair smells like the woods after a thunderstorm."

"You smell like sawdust."

"I work around wood all day."

"I like your smell, too. There is a smell of something else sometimes... wet leaves and water..."

Gabriel stilled against her, an image flashing through his mind of walking through the woods after a night of rain. His father was on one side of him, a few feet away, a uniformed officer on the other side of him. His shoes kept sinking into the mud and leaves clung to his shoes and pant legs.

He was remembering the morning Hayden had disappeared. He had searched the woods for her with his father, then they had searched again later, with the police. Sometimes late in the summer, when it was unbearably hot and muggy and he was jogging in the woods, he thought of that day.

The image now was like a punch in the gut.

Ava turned and gazed at him. Her eyes were dark. Picking up her glass of water, she took his hand and gave it a little tug.

At the bottom of the stairs, she stepped aside so he could go first. He kept her hand in his as he walked up. The sounds of his boots on the stairs were satisfying to her. She did not understand why. It should have annoyed her; he did not need to make so much noise. But she was not annoyed.

Turning on the lamp beside the bed, she set her water down and sat on the edge to take off her boots. Gabriel walked to the other side.

She pulled off her jeans and shirt and dropped them on the floor. A pleasant shiver ran through her as the breeze from the open window whispered across her flesh. She slid out of her bra and panties and crawled into bed. The scrunchy was still damp when she pulled it out and ran her fingers through her hair.

Gabriel was sitting with his back to her. He had pulled off his boots, socks, and jeans. Ava knelt behind him, hesitantly pulling up his shirt. He lifted his

476

arms so she could take it off. The feel of her breasts against his back was a shock; she felt him tense and draw in a shaky breath.

Backing away, she slid under the bedding and lay on her side. She touched his back.

"Are you covered?" he asked. His voice was hoarse.

"Yes," she said, still confused as to why he avoided her when she was naked. No man had ever turned from her figure. Most were drawn to her body like starving wolves, slobbering with glittering, hungry eyes. Like the man in the grocery store had been.

He lay back and turned toward her. She was staring at him with her strange gray eyes, her hands tucked under her chin.

"You're so beautiful," he said softly. He reached over and brushed her hair back behind her ear.

A warm, pleasant sensation slid through her entire body.

"If you think I am beautiful, why do you refuse to touch me?" she asked.

"I just did."

"Not like before."

She touched her fingertips to his lips, then to hers, remembering the heat that had consumed them both before.

"Touch isn't the only way to appreciate beauty."

Her eye lids were starting to feel heavy. With half closed eyes, she reached toward him, forgetting what she meant to do once her hand touched his face. He took her hand and kissed the back of it.

Rolling over, she put her back to him and nestled against his body. Taking his hand, she pulled it around her and clasped it between her hands. His arm lay naturally between her breasts, fitting perfectly. His heartbeat kicked up a notch, both from yearning and from her trust. She didn't like anyone behind her.

He rested his chin on her shoulder and let out a sigh of pure contentment. That she had made him content fulfilled her in ways that baffled her. Yet she was also deeply satisfied that she had that effect on him. She had never been concerned with a man's feelings before.

Her body felt comfortable against his, and his steady breathing near her ear was like the hypnotic ebb and flow of the sea, and before she could contemplate further, she was asleep.

• • • • •

The sound of birds chirping woke Gabriel too early in the morning to be appreciated. Fucking birds. The tradeoff of nicer weather was the symphony nature felt it needed to perform at top volume every damn morning. Ava had left a window open, so the symphony was drilling into his ears at top volume right now.

He knew before he turned his head that she wasn't beside him. Morning light was sneaking through a tiny crack in the light-canceling curtains; she wouldn't have slept late enough for the sun to be up. He raised his head and listened. A steady thumping noise was coming from somewhere downstairs to accompany the sharp, piercing birdsong.

"Get laid already," he snarled at the birds, one of which was right outside the window, on a branch, singing its heart out. "I need to sleep."

Curious about the noise downstairs, Gabriel rose and pulled on his jeans. Ava had tossed his tee shirt toward the end of the bed last night. He found it and put it on. The noise was quick but constant, consistent. The baseline of a song? Ava said she didn't listen to music unless it was live. He put his socks and boots on.

In the kitchen, he found she had set out a coffee cup and made a pot. This simple consideration touched him, and he stared at it for several seconds before he picked up the mug and poured himself a cup.

Ava was not on the first floor. The sound was coming from the basement, apparently, so Gabriel opened the door and found the lights were on. He walked down the steps to a large, open room with an area for laundry. A small room next to the stairs housed the essentials - water heater, furnace, water softener. To his left was a doorway, and that's where the noise was coming from.

Gabriel entered a huge, open space with floor mats lined up from just inside the door to the far end of the room, spanning approximately seventeen feet by fourteen feet. To the right, hanging on the wall in what looked like a bamboo rack, were several swords. The bottom two looked real; the ones above made of wood. A glass case sat below it, filled with nunchucks and throwing stars.

To the left, where Ava currently was, stood a full torso dummy. A few feet away, suspended from the ceiling, was a one-hundred-fifty-pound punching bag. Ava was kicking it repeatedly, causing the thumping Gabriel had heard. She did several with her left foot and then switched to her right.

Her damp hair was braided. She wore a black uniform of some kind with a belt around the waist and funny little slippers. Gabriel lifted his foot to walk toward her.

"Do not walk on the mats with footwear on." Her voice, though she was working out rigorously, was firm, with no room for bargaining. She continued kicking.

Gabriel set his foot back down and leaned against the wall, unsure what to do. He noticed a little shelf on the wall, centered above the mats. The shelf looked like it was just over his head, maybe slightly lower. Odd things were placed on it: a mirror, two candles, what looked like a sprig of some kind of plant, two little white bowls with something he couldn't see in them, a piece of braided rope, and a small, round doll-like object. A scroll with Asian writing on it hung just below the shelf.

Ava had finished kicking and walked to an odd upright column standing a few feet away from the body bag. The contraption was mounted to the wall, with vertical supports on each side of it. Two wooden stick-like rods protruded from it from the top of the center vertical piece. A longer piece, bent at an angle, protruded from the bottom. Ava began moving her hands between the upper rods, so her wrists and arms struck the wood. Her movements started slow and gradually sped up until she was moving so quickly, Gabriel couldn't follow exactly what she was doing.

He didn't know how long she practiced. Watching her was timeless, hypnotic. After a while, Gabriel could imagine a person standing in front of her, and the moves she was doing mimicked blocking punches. So that's how she practiced when she didn't have a partner.

She switched to kicks, using the central column to attack at various heights with her knee and various points of her feet. After a few minutes, she started moving her legs against the lower downward limb. Was she practicing blocking with her legs?

Gabriel watched in amazement. Her body was fluid yet deadly. Several times the power behind a move rattled the contraption against the supports, which were mounted to the wall. Gabriel thought he could watch her move like this all day and not get bored.

Ava was walking toward him. When she stepped on the mat, she faced the little shelf and bowed, arms at her sides, then continued until she was across from it, kneeling directly in the center of it.

Unsure what to do, Gabriel stayed where he was. "What-"

"Do not speak," Ava ordered. Her tone was authoritative but not condescending.

She pressed her hands together in front of her chest. Closing her eyes, she bowed low to the floor, sat up, and clapped twice. Then she repeated this odd ritual, clapping only once the second time. She sat absolutely still, her hands resting on her knees in a position not quite a full fist, for several seconds. Her eyes were closed.

Gabriel wondered if this was why she prayed before her meals. Was it related to her ability to fight? How did the two connect?

She opened her eyes and stood. Turning to face him, she said, "Never set foot on the mats with outdoor footwear of any kind. Only socks or bare feet." She paused. "I do not like feet, so only socks."

He was silent. After a moment, he said, "Can I talk now?"

She nodded, the hint of a smile on her lips.

"What's that thing against the wall?" He pointed to the contraption she had been pummeling earlier. "The wooden thing."

"It is called a mook yan jong. I practice punches, kicks, and blocks on it."

"It's wooden," he reiterated.

She only stared at him, rolling tension out of her shoulders.

"You were smacking your arms and shins against that thing really hard. What do your arms look like?"

Ava had walked to the edge of the mat to a shelf and picked up water. Now she set it down and pulled up her sleeves.

"They look like arms," she stated obviously.

They looked fine. There was no bruising or broken skin, only redness from the workout. Still, he didn't want to see her get hurt. She had been hurt enough, he thought, for ten lifetimes.

"You're not bruised."

"My body is used to the impact. I condition it so it does not go into shock if I am struck."

"Why doesn't your wooden dummy thing come with protective pads?" he grumbled.

"The way an attacker's fists would?" She took another drink of her water.

"They could at least - Christ, Ava, did you just make a joke?"

Her mouth twitched.

The concern left him, and he gave her his lopsided smile.

"What are those things on your feet?"

"They are called tabi or tabi socks. They are part of this traditional Japanese uniform."

She turned to the shelf with all the decorations on it, bowed, and stepped off the mat beside him. "I need a shower."

Before she left the large room, she stood in the doorway and bowed again.

Gabriel followed her out of the room, glancing over his shoulder at the shelf. "What's that shelf thing?"

"A kamidana."

She motioned for him to go first up the stairs. They walked up to the kitchen.

"What is the karma-chameleon-thing for?"

"Kamidana means 'God- or spirit- shelf'. They are used in traditional Japanese homes and dojos. In dojos, they are used to show respect and help focus during training. In homes, they are like altars. If you are in my dojo, do not walk directly under the kamidana, ever."

"Which part of the basement is your dojo?"

"The doorway you stepped through marks the entrance to the dojo. You should bow anytime you enter or exit."

"I don't really know how."

"I will teach you."

In the kitchen, she drank from a glass of water already sitting on the counter. Gabriel watched her, sipping his coffee. She was more relaxed when she was talking about something other than herself.

He was baffled by all the information and felt he had reached the limit of his understanding for this early in the morning. Then he remembered one thing he wanted to ask her. "I have one more question. Is that why you pray before a meal? You seemed to do the same thing to the karma chameleon-"

"Kamidana. You may call it a shelf." The right side of her lips twitched again. She was amused with him. "One has nothing to do with the other."

"That's a lot to remember," he said. "On top of learning a totally different culture, you have to learn every technique."

"It is not all taught at once. Otherwise, no one would learn it and it would not have survived thousands of years. In traditional martial arts training, a student is always learning, even when he does not realize it." She leaned down and took off one tabi, then the other. "Do you need a shower?"

"Uh... yeah, I'll wait until you're done..."

Ava set her glass on the counter and walked toward the stairs. She unhooked her belt as she walked, folded it and set it on an island bar stool. She took off the black robe-looking top and dropped it and the slippers by the basement stairs to wash.

"Separate showers will waste time and water," she said mildly. The tee shirt underneath the uniform top was damp with sweat. "We should shower together."

She pulled her tee shirt off and dropped it at the basement steps. Gabriel's eyes instantly jerked away from her. He almost spilled his coffee. She pulled off the uniform pants and started upstairs as she unwound the braid from her hair.

"Jesus Christ," Gabriel whispered, running a hand down his face. "That is not normal."

He trudged after her, only once looking up at her. His restraint was fairly remarkable, he thought, since he was having trouble looking at anything else. With a thin sheen of sweat glistening on her body, she looked like a supermodel at a swimsuit photo shoot. His mouth watered at the thought.

By the time he reached the second floor, her bra was on the floor at the top of the stairs and her underwear was just inside the bedroom door. He could hear water running in the bathroom.

Thank God, he thought. Now I can take a minute to get my shit together.

"You smell like alcohol," she said, making him jump. He put a hand to his chest, laughed silently at his own uneasiness. The shower engaged and he heard the curtain rustle. He thanked Christ he hadn't walked toward the bathroom yet or he'd have gotten another eyeful.

"Yeah," he said absently, untying his boots.

He entered the bathroom. He felt like some lovesick teenage idiot, fumbling his words and unable to make conversation. Pulling off his shirt, he tossed it out onto the bedroom floor.

He needed to brush his teeth. For now, he used some of her mouth rinse and swished it while he took his jeans and boxers off. Breathed deeply. Ava had brought in a towel for him and set it on the closed toilet seat. He spit mouth rinse into the sink.

"Will you have the dogs today?"

She so rarely asked him questions that he had to take a second to respond. "I pick them up around noon."

He stood uncertainly, trying to settle his nerves. How was she so comfortable being naked around someone she hardly knew? And why wasn't he tripping all over himself to get in the shower and see her naked? What the hell was she doing to him, that he was hesitating on the other side of the curtain of a beautiful, naked woman that was his girlfriend?

Mate, he reminded himself. She calls me her mate.

"Gabriel."

"Yeah?"

"The water is going to get cold."

He took a deep breath. "Yeah."

Pulling the curtain back, he tried to focus on the floor of the tub. He stepped in and it instantly felt too small for the two of them. She had soaked her hair already and was massaging the shampoo in. Despite his best intentions, Gabriel's eyes kept pulling upward as if heavy magnets were forcing them. He closed his eyes and swallowed with difficulty. Raising his head, he didn't open his eyes until they were aimed at what he hoped was about head height.

With her hands still in her hair, rubbing shampoo through it, she turned sideways and started to scoot by him so he could use the water. He couldn't stop their bodies from brushing against each other; the shower was too narrow. His body reacted. He noticed, as her breasts grazed his chest, that her nipples reacted as well.

He forced himself to get busy making sure he was wet before she kicked the shit out of him for looking at her or taking too long. Or both. When he was fully soaked, they switched positions again. She handed him the loofah and pointed to a bottle of body soap on a shelf behind him. She began rinsing the shampoo from her hair.

Like poetry, he thought, watching her run her hands through her hair. Every move is like poetry brought to life.

Her eyes were closed against the spray of water. Her upturned face looked at peace, even if only briefly.

Since he kept his hair short, he used the unscented body soap on his hair as well as his body. He watched Ava pour conditioner in her palm and rub it all over her hands. She lifted her arms over her head as she ran her fingers through her hair, making her breasts lift and shift in an optimum way to entice and arouse. Gabriel wanted to scream.

He looked down at the floor of the bathtub as he let the water run down his body. How the hell was he supposed to casually shower with her? She even made applying conditioner look sexy as hell. He wouldn't be so confused if they just had sex and got it over with. But seeing her naked and not having had sex was backwards to how he normally did things.

They switched places again and he handed her the sponge.

Don't look Don't look Don't look

He looked at Ava's face to see her lips were barely curved.

"What are you smiling at?" he rasped.

"Your modesty amuses me," she said, running the loofah over her skin.

"I'm so glad you find this funny." He stood waiting for a final rinse off, wishing he could have avoided brushing against Ava's soapy body so he could get out of this tiny bathtub and be done with it. He fought not to let his gaze slip below her neckline.

"There is no reason to be embarrassed. Our bodies are responding naturally to each other. When I see an attractive woman, I do not look away."

"How many times have you seen one naked?" he murmured.

They switched positions again. She began separating locks of her hair and squeezing them slowly to get as much water out as she could.

"Twice. Although the first time, I felt no attraction."

That made him pause with his hands in his hair. "Really? How does a woman who doesn't socialize at all get into a situation where she sees a naked woman?"

When he opened his eyes, he found her looking at him without emotion. He let the water rinse the soap off, rubbing his hair absently.

"I identified the body of one of my foster mothers. I had not seen her in years, since I was very young. One of the distinguishing marks on her body was a tattoo below her right breast."

He forgot about being modest. They stood, both dripping water, looking at each other in the small shower, not speaking. Although she was done with her shower and could have stepped out, she continued standing there.

Gabriel didn't know what to say. Ava had revealed this information as if she were telling him about a new recipe she had tried. Her eyes were direct, her face relaxed.

"I'm sorry, Ava."

"Why?"

"Because you had to do that."

"No one else would. She did not have family or friends. Her husband was dead."

"Were you still a child?"

He turned off the water. Still, they stood staring at each other.

She shook her head. "I was nineteen."

"It still sounds awful."

Gabriel was silent, thinking about how he would feel if he had to identify his mother's body. That would traumatize him as an adult, let alone a child. He didn't have the closest relationship with his mother, but she was still his mother. The thought of having to identify a birthmark or a tattoo on her naked body made him shudder.

"What happened to her?" he asked.

"My foster mother?" When he nodded, she said, "She overdosed on heroine."

She pulled the curtain open and picked up a large towel, handing it to him. Picking up another one, she moved it through her hair roughly.

Drying off, Gabriel wondered how a person could be so unemotional about the death of someone she knew. Parent-child relationships were complex, even abusive ones. Was that true even in foster situations?

Bending forward, she twisted her hair up the way women do so easily, turban-style.

Wanting to change the subject to anything, hoping for a lighter tone, Gabriel said, "You said there was another time?"

She stepped out of the tub, wrapping a third towel around her body. Feeling like he could finally relax, Gabriel exhaled silently.

She picked up her toothbrush and toothpaste. Water droplets glistened on her shoulders.

"A friend took me to a strip club once and paid for a private dance for me. He knew the dancer. She took everything off. There was not much to take off," she added, as if that aspect of the incident fascinated her more than seeing the stripper.

Gabriel wrapped his towel around his waist, thankful to be partially covered again.

"A guy friend took you to a female strip club?" He rubbed his head again without thinking about it.

"I was curious." Her speech was slightly impaired as she spoke around a mouthful of paste.

"That must be a hell of a friend."

"Vincent is one of three – four - people I trust."

Gabriel wasn't sure what to say to that, so he didn't say anything.

Leaning forward, she spit and rinsed her mouth with water.

He picked his folded jeans and boxers from the floor but paused when she spoke again.

"I asked him to," she continued. "My experience with people is limited. I had not seen a naked female except Ruth, briefly, when she changed. And my foster mother, who was dead."

Leaning forward again, she took the towel off her head and hung it.

"Didn't you change in the locker room after gym in school?" Gabriel slipped into his boxers and jeans. He was intrigued by her sharing this information with him. It was the longest conversation they'd had where she had participated equally.

Ava unwrapped the towel around her body, drying herself the rest of the way off. Gabriel kept his eyes focused on her face. She shook her head.

"I was home schooled. Given my abusive history, David and Ruth thought it best to minimize exposure to my peers to prevent injury."

"They thought you would get hurt at school?"

"I was not the one getting hurt."

Ava walked out into the bedroom. Gabriel followed, picking his tee shirt off the floor.

"What happened?"

"I started school late because my abusive foster parents did not enroll me when I came of age. By the time David and Ruth took me in, I was seven. They had to wait until my body was healed and by then I... I was... angry..."

486

Gabriel nodded, sniffing his shirt. He didn't want to put it on right away; it smelled like a bar.

"David told me your martial arts teacher had to hold you down for several weeks before he could start training you."

"Yes. When I could go to Sensei without him needing to restrain me, they put me in school. They thought I was calmed down enough to sit in a classroom."

"And?"

"I was not calmed down enough."

He dropped his shirt to the floor again. Sitting on the side of the bed, he began to put his socks on.

"The first day a boy twice my size pushed me in the playground. I broke his nose."

Gabriel felt a twinge of pride for the little girl who had the guts to stand up for herself, followed by instant guilt. A broken nose? That was overkill. Especially as punishment for another seven-year-old.

He pulled on his boots.

"I was small for my age, malnourished. I was the new kid, and I did not speak to anyone. The boys thought I was an easy target."

Standing, he turned to face her as he put his shirt back on. He winced at the smell of alcohol on it, but he didn't have another shirt with him.

"They were wrong." Flinching, Ava rubbed her forehead. Her voice had dropped suddenly on the last word, deepening dramatically. She had slipped into her panties and pulled the straps of her bra over her shoulders. Sunlight played across her skin, giving it a golden hue. When she turned away from him, all he saw now were endless legs, a fantastic, tight ass, and a long, lean back that had been scarred by sadistic assholes years ago.

"I did not know martial arts back then, but I had fought against Mack for so long, the boys were like dolls. Their bones snapped so easily. I broke two boy's arms and cracked another boy's ribs before the teacher pulled me off them, and I gave her a black eye."

She applied deodorant and slipped on a shirt. Pulling jeans over her narrow hips, she turned back to him as she buttoned them.

"The girls watching were crying. I remember thinking, 'They are so weak. How will they make it in this world if such a simple thing as this makes them cry?' Even some of the boys were crying."

"Christ, Ava."

Raising her head, she reached behind her and pulled socks out her top drawer as she looked at him.

"Was I to let them do as they wanted?"

Gabriel stared at her. Her tone had become something mechanical during the last three words. This was not the Ava he was used speaking to; this was some heartless thing he had never met before, with no concept of compassion or empathy.

"No, but... that doesn't mean you had to... go so far."

A quick shake of her head almost made her stumble. She leaned against the dresser to steady herself. Her eyes were slightly out of focus. They cleared and she blinked rapidly.

"The Monster," she mumbled. Unease flickered across her face.

Thinking he misunderstood her, Gabriel shoved his hands in his pockets, trying to rationalize what he was hearing. Was the change in her voice another part of the seizures?

"After you punched the teacher, what happened?" he asked, hoping she would calm down if he kept her talking.

She squeezed her eyes shut. "Lawsuits. The parents of the injured... children..."

Inhaling raggedly, she pressed her palm to her forehead. The socks dropped from her limp hand.

"It would all go away if David and Ruth paid the doctor's bills. It was firmly suggested I was taken out of school. A psychological evaluation was demanded."

"Ava, are you okay? This looks worse than -"

"You need to leave."

She exhaled a noise that sounded like a growl.

"What? I'm not leaving you like this."

He stepped toward her. Her head snapped up, her eyes flashing. For a moment, they were completely black. Not just the irises. The sockets were like oil pits.

"You will not touch her."

The voice, full of rage, stopped him instantly. It was not Ava's voice.

Standing across the room from him, Ava closed her eyes again and stepped toward the bed. She staggered. Gabriel watched her warily. This looked nothing like what he had experienced before. This was new level shit and she had not warned him of it, let alone told him what to do if it happened.

Opening her eyes, Ava looked at him intently. Her eyes were gray again, but her expression was predatory.

"Ava..."

"Make The Monster go away."

She took a step toward him.

"What?"

Taking another step, her eyes glazed for a moment before returning to their clear, sharp intensity. Every exhale seemed to wrench from her throat, something between a sob and a snarl.

"I need..."

He was surprised to hear the panic in her voice. "What? What do you need?"

Clamping her hands on his shoulders, she clung to him desperately. "Make The Monster go away."

"I don't know what that means."

The last thing he expected was her mouth on his. It was hot and hard, demanding. Gabriel's hands moved to her waist and dug in. Her moan was a sound of desperation. Her mouth consumed, ravaged. Backing him against the bedroom wall hard enough to rip the breath from him, she pressed her body against his.

Too fast, he thought, when he could form coherent thoughts in his head. This is happening too fast.

She was trying to use sex to deal with incredible stress, probably because of her medical condition. That didn't sit right with him. Especially because she didn't avoid her problems; she confronted them and kicked their asses until she could walk through the wreckage of them.

He pushed her gently back. "Ava, stop." Knowing she would take it as rejection, an insult, he cupped her face in his palms. "You're upset."

Her breath was ragged, hitching as she fought for control. Control of what? he wondered. What was doing this to her?

She gripped his wrists and closed her eyes, letting out a long exhale that was almost a moan.

"I don't want sex between us to be a solution to a problem," he said softly, stroking her hair. He moved his hands to her shoulders, then rubbed them down the length of her arms to gently take her hands.

Her breathing was slowing. Each inhale didn't seem as painful as it had been seconds before.

Looking into his eyes as if seeing him for the first time, she backed away. Gabriel didn't see insult or pain in her eyes. He saw clarity. He saw the old Ava.

Looking down, she saw she still needed socks. She glanced around and walked over to where she had dropped them.

"Ava."

"You will not have sex with me."

Because his head was still spinning, he missed the curiosity in her tone. He took what she said as an accusation.

"It's not that simple-"

"Sex is not what stops it," she said softly, her eyes distant, her head tilted. She sat on the bed and put her socks on.

"What are you talking about? What just happened?"

"I need to go."

"What?" Gabriel felt like he was ten steps behind in a race he hadn't practiced for and didn't know the course.

She stood, not comfortable leaving him in her house but not having a choice. "I need to leave. Coffee is in the freezer if you would like to stay. I do not know how long I will be."

"Where are you going?" Gabriel watched her, bewildered. "What the fuck just happened?"

Ava started around the bed. "I have to go. There are clean men's shirts in the walk-in closet in the spare bedroom. Vincent's shoulders are not as broad as yours, but he wears his clothing baggy."

"Who the hell is Vincent?"

"He is – was – my... p-partner. I train with him at the dojo."

She had stuttered just enough to let Gabriel know exactly what kind of partner Vincent had been, and a jab of anger stung him.

"You want me to wear your ex-fuck-buddy's clothing?"

Ava stopped several feet from the doorway and turned back to him. The miserable expression on her face tamped down some of his fury. Guilt washed over him at his juvenile insult.

"Sorry." He rubbed a hand down the back of his neck. "I shouldn't have said that, even though your offer is inappropriate. I know you don't see it that way."

"Your shirt smells like alcohol."

"I know why you offered." He pulled his shirt off and tossed it in the laundry sorter on the floor by the dresser. "I'll see if anything fits. Thanks."

"I have to go."

"You won't trust me with whatever this is?"

"I told you there are some things you will never know about me."

"Yeah, that's what you told me." He scrubbed his hand down his face. And he had promised to accept not knowing. "Will I see you tonight?"

Surprise flickered across her face. "If you want to."

"I do. Do you want to stop by my house?"

She nodded.

He closed the distance between them. Watching her go doe-still as he approached, he slowed his pace. He liked her primal response to his closeness: her sharpened gaze, the primed posture, the barely audible intake of her breath. As soon as his hand slid under her hair to massage her neck, she relaxed, just a little.

"If you want, you can bring an overnight bag," he said casually.

"I do not know if I will be staying the night."

"It will have what you need if you do."

Under his massaging fingers, he felt the muscles in her neck begin to stiffen and pressed harder to ease the tension. The muscles were like bars of steel.

"If you don't need it, you can go home and empty it out."

For a moment she stayed rigid. Her head was tilted up, her eyes watching his. When her lids began to grow heavy and her body began to relax, he gave her a lazy smile.

"You said you had to go."

She blinked. "Yes." She took his hand off her neck and held it in both of hers. "I need... I need to go."

After she had gone, Gabriel wondered what she was suddenly so interested in as he looked through the closet in the spare bedroom that had been converted into an office. Something had occurred to her; he could see it in her expression. He wished she would let him in on that part of her.

Vincent, he thought, flipping through a few shirts and slacks hanging in the closet, is not one for diversity. The man liked black. Every article of clothing was black. He also dressed nicer than Gabriel, wearing button up shirts and slacks. A couple ties were looped over hangers as well.

Gabriel was more of a casual dresser; he avoided wearing any type of clothing that needed to be hung up or ironed. He wore jeans and tee shirts – decent, clean tee shirts, without holes – unless he was working in the garage. The dress pants in his wardrobe were for occasions where he was forced to wear them – a funeral, certain family pictures, when he was meeting with potential clients. Otherwise, they hung uselessly in a corner of his closet.

A small cabinet was set up under the few hanged items, so he took a peek in it and saw socks and underwear, as well as tee shirts, both short- and long-sleeved. Grateful, he took out a tee shirt. Wearing another guy's underwear was beyond his comfort zone.

Standing at the kitchen counter as he waited for the coffee to finish brewing, Gabriel began searching drawers for flatware to find a spoon. The third drawer he opened had sharp objects in it. Gabriel studied the drawer and saw it was neatly lined with throwing knives and ninja stars. Pursing his lips, he shook his head.

Only Ava, he thought. Outstanding.

• • • • •

Are you busy today? Wanna stop by?

Isabel stared at the text from Griffin until the words blurred on her phone. Her first instinct was to pretend she had not read it. She set her phone beside her on the couch and took her guitar pick out of her mouth, placing her fingers on the strings to form the "G" chord. Her right hand hovered above the strings across the sound hole, ready to strum.

What was the matter with her? Griffin had done nothing wrong, yet she was acting like a spurned ex. Why the hell had she opened her big mouth and told him she loved him?

Her hand jerked slightly and glanced off some of the strings, causing a variety of sounds – none of them pleasant. Letting out a string of curses, she tossed her pick onto the table. Instead, she began picking with her fingertips instead of strumming. It was therapeutic, her fingers randomly plucking the strings, soft sounds coming from the instrument, as if it were whispering a secret conversation to her. This song came to her sometimes like a lullaby, soothing her.

His brother committed suicide, Isabel thought, and all I can think about is me telling him I love him and how I can avoid him for the rest of my life.

She was the biggest asshole in the world. Friday he'd texted her that he was going to dinner with his parents and would be home late. "Good luck" she had replied, feeling awkward and humiliated about her behavior. She had worried about him for hours. Had his mother made him feel like shit again? Had she berated him for not wanting what she felt he should? She didn't know because she couldn't face him and ask.

Later, when he'd texted that he had survived dinner and wanted to see her, she hadn't known how to respond. It was later in the evening, so she made up an excuse about being exhausted and going to bed. When he told her goodnight and that he loved her, she cried into her pillow. She should have gone to him, let him tell her about the dinner. He needed her and she had failed.

Now she felt like screaming.

Her phone indicated a new text had come in.

Or I can come over there?

Damn it. She was a coward. Instead of hiding in her apartment, moping about her inadequacies, she should be comforting her boyfriend. She should be listening to and holding him, not being embarrassed that she had fallen in love like some sappy idiot.

Her fingers flew over the screen as she typed:

Not feeling well. I'll call you tomorrow.

Sending the message before she could chicken out, Isabel nearly threw her phone on the coffee table and rested her chin on the side of her guitar. She placed her fingers back on the strings. Hot tears slipped down her cheeks, scalding her skin. After a sigh, she continued moving her fingers, feeling the vibrations against the side of her face as she played.

How long she sat there, she didn't know. Her eyes blurred through the tears, and she zoned out until she heard the knock at her door. Blinking rapidly, it took her a minute to register what the sound was. She set her guitar aside and stood shakily. Dizziness swept over her.

She always felt drained after she played that song that had no beginning and no end. She called it Hayden's Song, because she didn't know where it came from, only that she had started playing it after her sister disappeared.

Griffin stood outside her door, wearing a light jacket that was unzipped just enough to show a black shirt that made his eyes seem inordinately dazzling. His hair, as always, looked like someone had just hit him with a blast from an air compressor.

"What are you doing here?" she asked, her throat feeling thick. How long had she been playing that intoxicating song?

"Why are you crying, Isabel?"

"What?"

She raised her hands to her cheeks. They were hot with moisture. For some reason that realization sent an arrow of panic shooting through her bloodstream. Wiping her face furiously with her palms, she ducked her head and stepped back so he could come in.

Gradually, she became aware of her surroundings. Curtains covered all the windows in her apartment, making it gloomy. She only had a couple lamps on. When she glanced at the coffee table to refill her mug, she realized she hadn't made herself any coffee yet. And apparently, between Thursday and Friday night, she had gone through a bottle and a half of whiskey. The evidence was strewn across the table.

Jesus. No wonder her head was up her ass.

"Do you want some coffee?" she muttered, walking toward the kitchen. "I haven't been up long. I was just going to make a pot."

"Sure."

She began fumbling in the kitchen, trying to muddle through the mechanics of filling a carafe with water and dumping coffee grounds into a paper-thin basket.

Griffin walked toward the living room. It had taken a few moments for his eyes to adjust to the dim lighting. He noted the bottles of whiskey tipped over on the coffee table, the half empty bottle of wine open on one end of the table, the glass with remnants of red wine in the bottom on the floor by the sofa, the second wine glass broken on the table.

"Is it laundry day?" He shed his jacket and draped it over the back of the sofa.

"What?"

Isabel walked toward him. He turned around, pointed at her outfit. She was wearing a gray tee shirt with a snarling Baby Groot from Guardians of the Galaxy on it. The pajama bottoms had "I Am Groot" written vertically down her left legs.

"I haven't gotten dressed yet. I just woke up." She stopped several feet from him.

"It's one in the afternoon, Izzie."

She raised her head, looked around. "It is?" Glancing at the clock on her cable box, she ogled the readout. "Fuck."

"What was the song you were playing before you answered the door?" He leaned against the back of the sofa, crossing his legs at the ankles.

Isabel rubbed a knuckle in her eye like a child just waking up. "Why are you here, Griffin? I told you I wasn't feeling well."

"I want to know why you're avoiding me."

He held out his hand to her. Automatically, she stepped back.

"I'm not-" she started, but she couldn't lie to his face. "I'm..."

Taking a hesitant step toward him, she jumped when her coffee pot began to sputter. "Coffee's done."

She turned and walked back toward the kitchen, her legs shaky and her knees loose. The feeling of being underwater, not quite awake and part of what was going on in the real world, lingered as she poured two mugs of coffee. She added creamer to hers and left it on the counter while she carried his mug and the bowl of sugar to him.

I should have been there, she thought. I'm never there when I'm really needed, and someone gets hurt because of it. I shouldn't leave him alone.

"I shouldn't have left you alone in the dark."

Griffin studied Izzie as she stood before him, holding his coffee mug in one hand and a bowl in the other.

"I'm not sure-"

"Sugar, right?"

Spooning sugar into his cup, he stirred slowly, watching her return the bowl to the kitchen and pick up her own coffee. When she returned, he noticed how pale she was, how dark the smudges under her eyes were. He followed her around the sofa and sat with her, continuing to watch her odd behavior.

"I should have been there. I shouldn't have left you alone in the dark." She sipped her coffee thoughtfully. Unable to look directly at him, she stared straight ahead at a place on the floor. "How did dinner go with your parents?"

"About as well as can be expected. My dad's trying, at least."

"That's good." Frowning into her coffee mug, she traced the lip of it with her index finger. "I should have been there for you, after, to listen if you needed to talk. I was worried. The last time you talked with your mom, you were so upset. I should have been there, but I left you alone in the dark."

"It turned out alright." Griffin set his coffee on the table.

I left you alone in the dark. Why did she keep saying that? There was something there she wouldn't quite reveal to him but couldn't quite let go of.

"What's in the dark, Izzie?" he asked, resting his hand on her knee.

She flinched. Unable to take her eyes off his hand, her left hand, the one holding her coffee, began to tremble. She reached up and pressed her right hand against the mug to steady it. Her instinct was to pull away, but she didn't want to. Not anymore.

"I'm sorry about your brother. I'm sorry you don't have anyone to talk to about him."

"I have you," he said softly. "What's in the dark? What are you so afraid of in the dark?"

A tear traced the shape of her cheek and fell to the leg of her pants. The look of sorrow in her eyes was so consuming, so overwhelming, that Griffin couldn't take his eyes off her. He wanted to take the pain away.

"You were there when he killed himself, weren't you?"

The color drained from his face. "What makes you think that?"

A headache was boring its way into her temples. She raised her head and looked at him, her stomach suddenly turning sour and her legs feeling boneless. Thankful she was sitting down, she couldn't imagine what he had seen, how horrible it had been.

"When you had the nightmare, you were talking in your sleep. You said, 'Don't leave me. We're the same.'"

Griffin's eyes had lost the light that usually gave the irises their shine. They were listless, weary.

"You tried to talk him out of it."

"I was there."

Isabel nodded and more tears spilled over her cheeks. "I'm so sorry."

They were meaningless words, inadequate words. Isabel felt hollowed out. She wished he had never told her about his brother.

Running on instinct, he took her hand gently and was relieved when her fingers curled around his. They were cold and trembling.

"I missed you." Griffin hooked his arm around her shoulders and pulled her to him, kissing her forehead.

He felt her body relax against him, felt the tension drain out of her. "I didn't think you would want to be around me."

"Why would you think that?"

A shudder ran through her, making her teeth chatter. Covering her hand in both of his, he tried to warm it with his body heat. Her skin was so cold.

"Because I'm weak. I can't handle your brother's death and I can barely think about anything else since I told you I love you."

Griffin lifted her hand and kissed the back of it. "My brother's death is not for you to handle, Izzie."

"It shouldn't be. But it is, because it's painful for you, so I steal it and twist it until it becomes my pain. I'm so selfish, but I don't know how to stop empathizing until other people's tragedies become my own."

"You don't steal the pain; you try to take it onto yourself to spare the people you love. It's why you never defend yourself against your mother or Beth. But you can't stop all the pain in the world, Izzie. You can't feel other people's pain for them. They have to go through it. And you can't take it all on yourself because it's killing you."

"I deserve it," she whispered.

"Why?"

"Because I -"

Eyes wide, she stared at him, tears just on the verge of overflowing. Her lower lip was trembling. Her body was stiff against his and he could see the pulse in her throat jerking rapidly.

"What's in the dark, Izzie?" He framed her face with his hands, brushing tears from her cheeks. She looked so vulnerable at that moment. He wanted to lift her in his arms and protect her from the world.

Closing her eyes and taking a deep breath, she opened them and exhaled slowly. "I love the way you smell. I would know your smell anywhere."

Damn it, she was so stubborn. Griffin pressed her close to his chest and wondered if she would ever trust him.

• • • • •

A man in a sweatshirt and jogging pants finished locking his apartment and turned toward Ava. He walked toward her as she made her way down the hall to Vincent's apartment. Ear buds were blasting something loud and distracting. His eyes scanned her up and down as they continued toward each other, giving her an appreciative smile. His thoughts, lewder and more aggressive than some of those she had picked up on from other men, made her nauseous.

…fuck her right up against the wall of my apartment, give her something to smile about. Bend her over and -

To keep from continuing the connection and taking her fury out on the man's face, Ava brought an image of Gabriel in her head. The noise stopped. Only Gabriel filled her vision now, his reluctant smile, his kind eyes.

She kept her expression neutral as she stared at the man in the hallway, maintaining eye contact until he shifted his gaze away, uncomfortable. He stepped closer to the wall and continued past her. It was all over in a matter of seconds.

As she reached the door and touched the knob, the knowledge that Vincent was home came to her. She opened the door and entered, as she always did. Walking through the hallway between the closet and the bathroom, the soft sound of Vincent's voice drifted to her from the kitchen. She rounded the corner and froze.

Vincent was sitting at his little kitchen table by the window with a cup of tea. A woman with fiery red hair was sitting across from him, her hands wrapped around a mug of coffee. Both raised their heads when she suddenly appeared.

"Ava."

Vincent's expression didn't change. His voice remained calm and quiet as he regarded her.

"Excuse me. I did not know you have company." Ava felt a stab of jealousy toward the woman. The woman was taking up Vincent's time, and she needed to talk to him.

"This is Mattie. She's a friend of mine. Mattie, this is Ava." He stood and offered her the third chair.

"Sumi maisen." Ava took a step back. "I did not mean to intrude."

"Do you train, too?" Mattie asked, standing. As she walked toward Ava, she extended her hand. "With Ward Sensei? We use that phrase in class."

Only dropping her guard slightly, Ava nodded. She shook the woman's hand and pulled hers back instantly.

"Which style?"

Taking a step back to put more distance between herself and the genial woman, Ava kept an eye on her in her peripheral vision as she glanced at Vincent.

"I need to talk to you, when you have a moment." She looked at Mattie again and bowed her head slightly. "Sorry to interrupt."

Vincent watched her turn to leave, curious.

"Actually, I have to get going," Mattie said, walking back to Vincent. "Thank you for the coffee. Hopefully one of these days I'll get that technique down."

She leaned in and kissed him on the cheek. "I'll see myself out. Nice to meet you, Ava," she said as she passed her walking toward the door.

After she was gone, Ava turned back to Vincent. His face had a look of amusement on it.

"You could be polite and tell her it's nice to meet her." He picked up his tea and set the cup in the sink.

"I do not lie." She glanced at the door again. "However, I did not mean to send her away and interrupt your visit."

"You didn't. We were almost done. You don't like her."

"My opinion is irrelevant."

"I'm curious."

"I do not like anyone."

"Will you sit with me?"

He sat at the table. Hesitant, she sat across from him and set her backpack next to her feet.

"Do you want coffee? There's some left. It's still warm."

She shook her head. Vincent saw she was restless, and it wasn't because of Mattie.

"What's bothering you?"

"Do I ever lose time with you?"

Now that she had said it, she felt the tightness in her chest loosen a bit. Just asking the question, getting it out there in the open, was a relief. Vincent would tell her the truth. He never lied to her.

He was studying her, his shark's eyes intent on her face. "You mean, during visions?"

"I do not... I do not think so. Do I ever lose time... that I do not seem to remember afterward? Do you ever see me act in a way I normally would not, and not remember it?"

"No. The only time you act strange is during your visions, and you remember those."

"Not even when I sleepwalk?"

Shaking his head, he took her hand. "What are you getting at, Ava? What are you trying to find out?"

"I am sorry I interrupted your visit with Mattie. I need to leave."

She stood and picked up her backpack.

"Ava, be careful," Vincent said, touching her shoulder. "You look tired."

Emotions flashed through eyes, but she only nodded before briskly walking out the door.

•   •   •   •   •

Guilt grew the closer she came to David's house. Since moving out at eighteen, she felt she had not contacted him unless she needed something. Because she was self-sufficient, her needs were limited to information from her childhood, so her contact with him had been limited. Even her visit with Gabriel had not been a social visit, not really.

Now she was visiting him, again because she needed information. Her own selfishness infuriated her.

The front door opened as she parked her vehicle. Buck rushed out and barked once, heading toward the car. David walked across the porch and started down the steps. Suddenly, as she walked toward him, her body felt unsteady, as it sometimes did when she had the flu and had not eaten in two or three days.

"This is a welcomed surprise," he said, smiling.

The embrace he gave her calmed her nerves, and she held onto him a beat longer than a normal hug. Feeling her hesitation, David didn't speak. He held onto his daughter as she clung to him and waited for her to be able to tell him what was wrong.

When she finally pulled back, some of the distress had left her eyes.

"Come on in," he said, touching her shoulder. "I'll get you some water."

"Thank you."

"Is that from training?" he asked, pointing to the bandage on her left hand.

"Not in the dojo."

They entered the kitchen. David poured her a glass of cold water and took a root beer out of the fridge for himself. For a moment they stood next to the sink, looking at each other.

"And the one above your eye?"

"They are both from falling in the woods. I was training and I lost my footing."

His eyes widened. "You lost your footing? That's never happened before."

Embarrassed all over again, Ava avoided his gaze. "I was upset. I had a confrontation with Gabriel and I-"

"Did he hurt you?" David's hackles were up immediately.

"No-"

"Are you okay?" He touched her shoulder again, running his eyes over her to see if any other part of her was injured.

"I am fine."

"What did he do to you? Why were you upset?"

"He did not do anything. I... I was upset because I met his family." His questions were starting to wear her out.

"He took you to meet his family?" David took a step back.

"Yes. After we left here, he asked if I would have dinner at his parent's house. It is a Sunday tradition, with his sisters and his parents. I know one of his sisters. I am her bee eff eff."

David grinned. Then he remembered why he was so shocked. "And you agreed to meet them? That sounds like quite a crowd."

"I..."

"Let's move to the living room."

As they walked, Buck leading with a lazy gait that spoke of age, David thought about Ava willingly accepting an invitation to be enclosed in a house with several other people she didn't know. That was a first for her.

"So you lost your footing while training in the woods and you cut your hand and your head." David sat in his twenty-year-old recliner with the cigarette burn. "That must have been one hell of a Sunday dinner."

Ava sat on the couch, where she had sat days before with Gabriel. "Those were not my only injuries. I had a minor sprain in my left ankle, twisted my left knee, and almost dislocated my right shoulder again."

"My God, Ava. What was in his mother's mashed potatoes?"

She didn't smile.

David set his root beer down and watched her, curious. Emotions had always been easy for her to mask, but she was having trouble now. They were flashing across her face and there were too many, too fast, to keep up with.

"Why were you upset after meeting them, Ava?" he asked. "Did something happen?"

She raised her head to look at him. "It went well. I wanted to please him, even at the risk of overstimulation. He grew up in the house. I expected the psychic chatter. But I felt..."

Absently, she raised her hand to her chest and rubbed her fingertips back and forth slowly.

"Connected," she finally said. "I do not want to feel connected. That is why I was upset."

She stood, pacing the room. "That is not why I am here."

As she wandered the room, she spotted the purple cow lying down on the bookcase that Ruth used to have on her desk. It had a rose in its mouth, and if you touched its head, it would weave and bob like it was drunk. Ava remembered wandering around in her office on rare occasions, running her hands over the bindings of her books and poking that purple cow's head to watch it bob. Ruth had always allowed her into her office, always let her explore, always stopped what she was doing to spend time with her.

"I wanted to ask you something about my childhood," she finally said.

"Oh?" Surprised, he sipped his root beer. Revisiting her past was not something Ava did. Though her life with David and Ruth had improved, memories of the trauma she sustained before them continued to haunt her. She associated her past with pain.

He was also surprised because as a child, she had never asked questions about anything. She was more of an observer, learning by watching or reading about subjects.

"Did I have blackouts when I was younger?"

She saw the shift in his eyes and knew the answer.

"Not blackouts exactly. There were periods of time when you... went away."

"What does that mean?"

David leaned forward and rested his elbows on his knees. The old chair creaked under him.

As far back as she could remember that chair had been part of Ava's life. She wondered if he would ever get rid of it.

"After Daniel – Sensei – first met you and restrained you, you stopped being a threat to Ruth or I. Martial arts gave you an outlet for your rage. Unless you were provoked, like at school. He was working with you, and we started home schooling you. You were... obedient, polite. Not quite trusting, not yet. But we were able to control your environments, and that calmed you down. Your life was structured, as close to normal as it had ever been."

Buck walked over and settled at David's feet with a groan. David absently reached down and scratched the top of his head.

"But sometimes... We noticed that when you were scared, or hurt, you... went away. I don't know how else to explain it. You were here, your body could function, but..."

"But what?" Ava prodded. She sat back on the sofa.

"Sometimes there was nothing in your eyes. And sometimes there was something else in them."

The Monster, she thought.

"Nightmares were especially hard. We would hear you screaming during a nightmare and go to you, and you usually weren't there."

"When I... went away... did I remember what happened after?"

"Sometimes. Sometimes you didn't."

"What did you do when it happened?" She had leaned forward without realizing it.

"We stayed with you until you came out of it. We never left you alone. My voice seemed to help, so I would talk to you. We never touched you."

"How did you know not to touch me?"

"Ruth tried to hug you the first time. You nearly strangled her."

At the look of horror on Ava's face, David stood and crossed the room to the sofa. He sat beside her and patted her knee. "You have to remember she was a teacher, and a foster mother. She was used to nurturing. You were the only child in our house that didn't need her the way the others had. None of it was your fault."

Ava nodded. She looked so sad sitting there. David wanted to embrace her, but he wasn't sure if she'd be receptive to physical contact right now.

"It took a couple years of being with us, even though the nightmares continued, for the other thing to stop being there when we came to you during your nightmares. But you never hurt Ruth after that first time because we knew not to touch you. You were extremely combative when you had that look in your eyes, and I knew you weren't in control when that happened."

Ava ducked her head, feeling numb. How many times had Ruth wished Ava needed her over the years? How many times had Ava made her feel useless because she never asked for or accepted anything from her? Had she inadvertently made her feel like less of a mother, less of a person, when she pulled away from Ruth's naturally helpful, caring hands? She had not meant Ruth any harm by being self-sufficient. She simply had not needed the woman.

"Did she like me?"

David was shocked at how small and vulnerable Ava's voice sounded. For a moment, he saw the little seven-year-old girl before him whose body had come to him broken and whose spirit had, for a while, hidden inside that body, refusing to speak.

"She loved you," he said, clearing his throat against the emotion that momentarily blocked it. "You were her daughter."

"How do you know?"

"Because I love her."

He knew the answer would not satisfy her. Explaining emotions of any kind to Ava had always been difficult. But there was no other answer.

She seemed to be considering all this. "But you made the decision to adopt me. You chose to stop fostering other children."

"We made the choice together. She was already considering getting out of fostering." David touched her shoulder and waited until her eyes met his. "Ruth lost a baby before you came to live with us."

Ava frowned. "You told me she was unable to have children."

"She was, after the miscarriage. She wasn't even supposed to be able to get pregnant. It was a miracle she did. She was so happy, Ava. You should have seen her."

David smiled at the memories. He was still touching Ava, and she felt the vast love flowing through him. Images flashed through her head as she experienced what he had gone through: Staring at a pregnancy test for several moments, until it slipped from his wife's numb fingers and fell to the bathroom floor. Tears blurring his vision. Seeing his wife in a new way, her body a wonderful mystery to him as he thought of life growing inside her. Pressing the side of his head to her belly as he wrapped his arms around her abdomen, feeling closer to her than he ever had before. Then suddenly, her stumbling into his library with dark blood staining her jeans, bent over with her hands on her belly as cramps racked her body, unable to find words as terror flashed across her face.

Ava's strangled gasp reminded David that he was touching her. He quickly pulled his hand back, but not before she saw the tiny coffin and the marble marker waiting to be set above the dead.

"Aaron." Ava closed her eyes and tried to think of anything else but the engulfing grief flooding through her system. "Aaron Michael Reid."

Swearing under his breath, David scooted over on the sofa to put space between them. The only way to alleviate the effects of the vision was to break the connection. When that wasn't enough, he stood and walked a few steps away, rubbing a hand down his face.

Ava was hunched over on the sofa, holding her lower abdomen.

"I'm sorry," David said. "It's been years since I had to block my emotions from you. I'm out of practice."

Ava wiped her mouth with the back of her hand. Her other hand was still on her abdomen, David noticed. She was trembling.

Feeling the need to finish what he started, knowing he owed Ava the truth, he took a moment to make sure his voice was steady.

"The baby was long gone by the time you came around. We made sure to keep our distance from you any time we thought of him so this wouldn't happen."

"She never finished."

Tears slipped down her cheeks. The sight of them made his stomach clench but he didn't want to fuel any more pain, so he kept his distance.

"She never finished grieving for him," Ava continued. "You asked her to take me in. She was not done grieving for Aaron, and she took me in anyway."

The swirl of emotions in her eyes broke his heart. David went to the sofa and sat beside her, taking her hand. "She loved you. She saw a child in need, and she did the right thing. You helped to... heal that part of her that was broken. When you came to live with us, you gave me back my wife and gave us a child."

Ava let him hug her. This time it felt different than it ever had before. Instead of tolerating the contact, the sensation of his arms around her was comforting, like taking deep breaths or being out in nature. She hesitantly pressed her hands against his back and squeezed.

It was the first time she had ever given him a hug.

• • • • •

"Close your eyes."

Isabel frowned at Griffin, skeptical. No amount of coffee could convince her this exercise was going to work. A person couldn't choose not to be sad, or pissed, or grumpy. Sometimes shit just happened and you had to wait for sleep and a new day to hit the reset button.

"Just do it." Griffin flashed his award-winning grin. "Part of changing your mood is making the attempt."

"You're hopeless."

But she closed her eyes.

"Think of a time you and I did something together."

She raised an eyebrow. "There was that time in the shower..."

"Not that," he said, poking her in the ribs.

Snorting, she squirmed, and her knees bumped his. They were sitting cross legged across from each other on the couch.

"Well, there was that other time, on the island in the kitchen..."

"Jesus, Izzie, stop thinking about sex for two seconds!"

Sneaking a glance out of a partially open eye, she saw him trying to keep a straight face. He caught her peeking and tackled her onto her back. She let out a yelp that lost all sound when his weight forced the air out of her lungs.

"You're cheating," he said, swallowing her protests in a kiss.

"You're right," she said, when he raised his head and looked down at her, "my attitude has definitely changed."

"Sex doesn't count. You have to be able to do this on your own." He leaned up and returned to his sitting position. "What would you do if you were at work or shopping at the mall and having a really difficult day?"

"I'd find the nearest bathroom and rub one out." She started giggling.

Shaking his head, he took her hand and pulled her up into a sitting position.

"Think about the time I took you to the little restaurant in Waverly. When you first told me you sang at The Raz. Close your eyes."

Iz obeyed and thought about the long drive, how she had been so excited that he asked her to dinner even though she knew it wasn't a date. When she got there, he'd kissed her in the parking lot by way of greeting, she remembered, confusing her.

"Why are you smiling?" he asked. "What are you remembering?"

"You kissed me when you greeted me." She thought of his mouth on hers. "Right on the lips. I didn't know what to think."

"Good. Keep going. What else do you remember? What did you smell? What did you hear?"

"Glass clinking together. Sizzling from the grill. Kitchen sounds. But then we walked past the kitchen and sat down, and it was quiet. Only a few customers. You started to draw me."

"You look good in different mediums."

Scoffing, Isabel replayed the evening, smiling at snippets of conversations she remembered. Griffin telling her about previous girlfriends arguing about where to eat, her telling him to leave them in the car. She remembered enjoying his company, wondering why he wasn't out with his girlfriend. He said he liked to hear her voice, and she let it slip that she sang at The Raz on Saturdays.

Her smile turned to a frown. The Raz. Where she had drank too much and made an ass of herself.

"What was that?" Griffin asked. "What just happened?"

She opened her eyes. "I was thinking about you saying you like my voice, and me telling you I sang on Saturdays. Then I remembered the first time you heard me sing at The Raz, where I got drunk and acted like an idiot."

"You're thinking too much. Just think about the one evening, only you and I at the diner. Think about how you felt when we were talking. Forget about getting drunk at The Raz. That was a different memory."

"But-"

"No buts. The Raz hadn't happened yet. We're sitting in a restaurant, talking, and enjoying ourselves. Close your eyes."

"We talked about weird things we've eaten," Isabel said, letting her eyes slip closed. "Small talk. I like the sound of your voice. I kept waiting for you to tell me it was a joke."

"What was a joke?" Griffin watched her begin to relax again. Her shoulders became less rigid, the lines between her eyebrows disappeared.

"That you wanted to be my friend."

He had wanted more than that but hadn't wanted to push too hard so soon after meeting her.

"We talked for hours. I was too tired to drive home so you gave me a lift and walked me to my door. You smelled really good."

Grinning, Griffin snapped a picture of her with his phone. As soon as the light flashed and she heard the minute click, her eyes flew open.

"What the fuck was that? I don't like having my picture taken. You had no right-"

"Take it easy." He reached out and took her hand, giving it a squeeze. "I just didn't have a mirror. Look."

Turning the picture around so she could see it, he pointed. "See that odd little curvature right there? Right under your nose? That's what we call a smile here in the Midwest."

Isabel punched him in the shoulder. "Very funny."

Keeping the camera turned toward her, he touched the screen of his phone to bring up menu options, pushed the delete button, and verified he wanted to delete it. The picture disappeared.

"There. Now it's gone."

Relief rammed into Iz like a punch to the stomach. She visibly relaxed. "Thank you."

Griffin took her hand and kissed the back of it, pulling her toward him. "How are you feeling?"

Thinking about it, thinking past the relief of not having her picture on his phone where anyone could see it at any time, she found herself more relaxed. The sadness was mostly gone. The hope she'd felt on that night in the diner lingered. The excitement of a new friendship, the admiration of his gift of art, the genuine enjoyment of the moment. By conjuring up a good memory, she had changed her mood.

"Better," she admitted, smiling again against his chest. "Shit. It worked."

Griffin was running his hands slowly up and down her back. He could feel how relaxed she was. The tone of her voice had lost that lifelessness. He hated the sound of that. The last time he heard it, his brother had killed himself.

Isabel leaned up, looking at him. "Thank you."

"For what?"

His pulse picked up. She was splayed over him, holding herself up by her forearms, gazing at him with her beautiful forest green eyes without a hint of sadness now.

"For helping me claw my way out. Sometimes it lasts months. If I start to go there again, I'll try to think of a good memory and see if it works."

Leaning down, she kissed him, and his heart thudded against his rib cage. He molded his hands to her bottom and tugged so they were pressed center to center, instantly arousing him. But his body's response wasn't what he was thinking about.

"Hey," he said softly, tugging on a lock of her hair. "You kissed me."

He could tell by the look on her face that she still didn't understand the difference between returning his kisses and instigating them, but that was okay.

She had kissed him.

• • • • •

CHAPTER TEN

G abriel woke to absolutely no sound, and it made him instantly suspicious. He shoved himself up, looking around the room even though he already knew Ava wasn't in it. But it was dark. Too dark. He glanced at the alarm clock. It was too early for her to be awake and working out, he thought. Just past one.

Rolling over, he sat up and turned on the lamp. He pulled on the jeans he'd discarded not long ago. Rubbed a hand down his face. Still, he heard nothing. When a figure passed the doorway of the master suite as he was turning to start a search, he startled. He recognized the shape of Ava's body and stood where he was, thinking she had only awakened to use the toilet. She came out of the bathroom, but instead of returning to bed, she left the room. Hoping to convince her to get dressed, he snagged her tee shirt and shorts off the floor as he followed her.

What was she doing now? he thought as he moseyed out of the room, rubbing his eyes. The hallway was empty. He glanced over the balcony but didn't see her on the stairs.

She exited the spare bedroom, heading toward the third. Completely nude, not making any sound, she slipped into the room. Gabriel walked to the doorway and watched her wander to the west double window, checking the locks. Her long fingers ran over the mechanisms, made sure they were engaged, then pushed up on them to make sure the windows wouldn't open. She did the same on the south window.

"Ava?"

Ignoring him, she finished what she was doing and walked toward him. As she neared, he saw her eye lids were heavy but not closed, her face slack.

And, he saw, she was going to walk right through him if he didn't get the hell out of her way.

He scooted to the side and watched her move toward the stairs. "Ava."

As he suspected, she ignored him again. Gabriel followed her to the first floor. At the base of the stairway, he bumped a switch, flooding the entrance hall with indirect light that had his eyes protesting. Ava didn't seem to notice. She checked the locks on the front door, then pulled the door a couple times before she stepped back.

"Will you put on some clothes?" he asked. His eyes were finally adjusting. Using all his willpower, he kept them focused above her neck.

Turning, Ava hesitated, though she didn't look at him. His heart was hammering, filling his ears with a pulsating beat that seemed to echo his desire to feast on her. To help keep his eyes from drifting down, he held her clothes at just the right level to block his line of sight to everything below her shoulders. They were beautiful, sleek shoulders, smooth and pale against her dark hair. He wanted to explore them with his hands, his mouth.

Clearing his throat, he raised his eyes to her face. "Please put on your clothes."

Ava turned her head to her left. "There."

Gabriel looked to see what had caught her attention and sighed when she walked past him to check the large window in the living room. She was killing him. He followed her, watching her run her hands over the locks on the windows in that room before moving on to the sunroom. The windows were floor to ceiling and didn't open, but that didn't stop her from skimming her hands along the glass edges.

"I'm going to touch you, Ava." He walked up beside her, giving her a moment to prepare. She gave no indication that she had heard him. "I hope that's okay."

Preparing for an assault, Gabriel placed his palm lightly on her shoulder, making sure his fingers were raised so she didn't feel like he was grabbing her. She stilled, her right arm lifted with her hand as far up as she could reach on one of the windows and her left resting lower on the glass. Gabriel pressed the clothing against her lower arm.

"Put these on."

Ava turned to him, laying her right hand on top of the clothing. "I have to check the locks."

"I know. Put these on first."

The shorts dropped to the floor as she took the shirt and slipped into it. Gabriel felt less perverted now; not much of the light from the foyer reached into the sunroom and it was a cloudy night. He could see Ava's outline and feel the proximity of her body, but he couldn't see any detail. He picked up the shorts with his head turned, knowing he wouldn't have the discipline to look away from her. His imagination filled in plenty of blanks.

"Take these," he said softly, brushing the shorts against her hands.

Ava took them and leaned down to put her feet through the legs. Even in baggy shorts and a loose-fitting tee shirt, she was stunning. She continued to check the windows.

Gabriel watched her move around the perimeter of the room, running her fingers along the edges of the windows. This room took a while; three walls were mostly glass.

After a moment, he walked back into the living room and turned on a lamp, then went to each room Ava hadn't been to yet and flipped a light switch in each so he could follow her without smashing into furniture. Did she do this every night she stayed here, and this was just the first time he had found her doing it? Was it some leftover result from her abusive childhood?

Finally, fifteen minutes later, she checked the lock on the final window in his office at the front of the house next to the foyer. Turning away from it, she walked to the center of the room and stood. Gabriel had been leaning against the door casing and now he straightened, yawning.

"All locked up?" He walked toward her.

"All locked up now." Her voice was groggy.

Her eyes were almost closed now. How she was able to walk around like that, he didn't know. She was facing him, but Gabriel didn't know if she was aware of him.

"Ready to go back to bed?"

"Bed."

"Can I touch you?"

"Touch you."

He took that as a yes but kept his guard up when he took her hand. He maintained a light grip, leading her up the stairs slowly, hoping she wouldn't stumble and break her neck.

In the bedroom, he nudged her close to her side and tugged her until she sat on the bed. Unsure if he should undress her, he decided that was up to her and walked to his side of the bed. His mouth was like cotton. He took a drink of water and almost choked on it when he glanced over at Ava.

She was standing, naked again, in the doorway, her right arm lifted.

"Oh, for shit's sake," he said, standing.

Behind her, looking over her shoulder, he saw nothing in the hallway. Her right arm was lifted, and she was pointing toward the spare bedroom that had become a catch-all, but Gabriel saw nothing out of the ordinary.

"There," she said.

"I'm going to touch you." His voice was barely above a whisper. He set his hands on her shoulders, lowering his head until it was beside hers to get her point of view. Still, he saw nothing but a closed office door and the stairway.

"What do you see, Ava?"

"The judge with the burnt face."

Keeping his hands on her but raising his head, Gabriel said, "Hey, Judge Wapner, we're trying to get some sleep here! Beat it!"

Ava's head twitched. "He is gone."

"God bless America."

She turned into him, tilting her head down so she was nestled against his shoulder. Surprised, Gabriel cautiously put his arms around her. Despite being naked, her skin was warm. He let his fingers skim down the line of her back, just a little.

"Come on, let's go to bed."

This time she lay quietly while he pulled his jeans off. When he settled next to her, she rolled over as she had before, backing against his stomach.

She's beginning to trust me, he thought, resting his hand on her shoulder. That realization meant more to him than he thought it would.

He watched her with his arm propped on his hand for a while. At one point, her mouth dropped open, and she inhaled deeply – not quite a gasp. He waited, but she closed her mouth on a sigh and continued sleeping. He fell asleep watching her, forgetting to turn off the lamp, and that was how he managed to wake up in time to see her explode out of her next nightmare.

• • • • •

Electricity felt like millions of teeth biting and ripping from the inside out. She couldn't move. Her heartbeat stuttered. With her body so stiff her joints hurt, Ava's fingers curled into claws as Mack pressed the taser against her skin. Tears ran down her temples. From somewhere far away, Janine's raspy laugh echoed in her head.

"She looks like a fish!" Janine hooted. She crowed again, dropping ashes from her cigarette all over the kitchen floor.

Mack finally released the button and the current stopped. Ava gasped in oxygen hungrily, her entire body collapsing. Her muscles erupted into spams. She stared up at the dingy ceiling with the nicotine stains as the blood pounded in her head and her eyes watered.

They were not done with her yet.

Mack dropped the taser carelessly to the floor. The reverberation of it hitting the tile sent knives into Ava's temples, blinding her with pain. He grabbed her by the hair and dragged her toward the bathroom. She squealed in agony.

"Lord, what are you doing to her now? I'm hungry." Janine picked at the already chipped nail polish on her thumb nail.

"It'll just take a minute."

His voice was gruff. Ava would never forget that voice, or the way it laughed when he made her bleed.

As he filled the bathtub with water, she panicked. She tried to crawl away, but Janine put her cigarette out on her back before kicking her in the side. Ava curled into the fetal position, her stomach clenching violently. The pain in her side was bone deep. She felt like passing out.

My turn, The Monster said. Give the pain to me.

She fought to hang on as Mack lifted her by an arm and dropped her into the tub. Her elbow rapped against the side hard enough to render her arm numb from her wrist to her shoulder. Shock had her gasping, taking in a mouthful of the dirty lime-filled water. Coughing, she flailed the arm she could still feel, trying to crawl out. The water was frigid.

Don't fight me, The Monster insisted. It will only hurt more. Separate yourself from the vessel and let me handle this.

Ava felt it nudging her, trying to take over. A sensation of prodding against the back of her neck had her thrashing even harder in terror.

Mack stuck his meaty hand on her chest and pressed her under the water. His face was a watery blur as she struck out, trying to free herself. Her tiny hands glanced off his arms uselessly. Lungs burning, head pounding, she tried to hold her breath as long as she could and keep The Monster away at the same time.

Something appeared behind Mack.

A small ball of light. First it was not there, then it was. Small, then growing larger, until it was the size of a softball. It zoomed down toward the water, hovering just above it. Its light spread over the surface of the water, but Mack did not see it.

Hold on, Ava heard in her head. It will be over soon. The voice was soft and reassuring, like being curled up in a warm blanket. The invading sensation was not there like it was with The Monster.

Don't listen to it, The Monster growled. Listen to me. I'm the one who takes the pain away. Give me your pain and I can make this all go away.

Mack brought her up, gasping and choking. Her body was starving for oxygen, her lips shivering. Vaguely, she heard them both laughing above her.

She thought, I will die now.

Mack pushed her back under the water.

I know it hurts. Don't give up.

Lies, The Monster snarled. It lies to you. Haven't I helped you before?

The light was changing colors, then fading to gray as she began to drift into the darkness. She wanted it to be over, even if that meant forever. She knew what death was. It seemed peaceful compared to this.

Gabriel woke to the sound of Ava mewling and kicking in her sleep. The sounds were those of a trapped animal, something he had never heard from her before.

Because the light was on, he could see she was twisting in the blankets. She was fighting so hard that she had mostly pulled them off him. Her hands were raised toward the ceiling, reaching. Eyes open, her pupils were dilated and staring blindly at the ceiling. Her mouth was open wide. She wasn't breathing.

"Wake up," he said sharply, sitting up. Seeing her not breathing kicked his pulse up, made a fist squeeze around his heart.

In her dream, Ava's lungs were screaming for air, just a small taste to take away this searing ache-

Ava reared up in bed, gasping and clawing at her throat. She dug her heels into the mattress until she was backed against the headboard and kept kicking.

"Jesus." Gabriel tried to peel her hands away from her skin. A fist struck him in the mouth, followed by an elbow to the jaw and another fist to the mouth that sent him tumbling off the bed. He swore all the way to the floor.

Ava was scoring red slashes into her neck. The sound she was making was somewhere between a gasp and a wheeze. The headboard slammed against the wall repeatedly as she flailed her legs, sending echoing thuds around the room.

Shaking his head, Gabriel sat up and pressed a palm to his temple to ease the ringing in his ears.

"Son of a bitch."

Instinct had everything inside him fighting to raise his voice and try to pry her hands away from her throat again as he stood beside the bed. He had to force himself not to. His mouth was already bleeding, and he had fallen on his shoulder wrong. Instead, he stayed where he was.

"Ava, stop." He kept his voice calm, quiet.

She froze with her nails pressed into her throat and her eyes wide and blind. Her long legs were curled up close to her chest.

"Take it easy," Gabriel said. "You were dreaming."

Finally, she inhaled, a long, gasping-sobbing sound that made Gabriel's legs want to buckle.

He walked around the end of the bed, wiping blood off his mouth with the back of his hand. With his eyes on her hands, he lowered himself slowly onto her side of the bed.

"I'm going to touch you, Ava."

Surprise rocked him as her hands flashed out. Eyes still sightless, she reached for him. He took her hands and brought them to his chest, slipping his arm around her when she pushed her body against him. She curled into the fetal position in his lap, long limbs tucked in. Compliance was the last thing he expected. Her body was trembling so hard her teeth chattered. Her skin was cold, yet slick with sweat. Each ragged breath wracked her body with shudders.

He wished he could do something for her besides be there after the fact. He felt ineffective and guilty, ashamed of his entire gender.

"I'm so sorry," he whispered. He rested his chin on the top of her head. "I'm so sorry for what those bastards did to you."

Reaching over her, he propped his and her pillows up against the headboard. He wrapped his arms around her – she was a ball of limbs – and pivoted so he was leaning against the headboard with her on his lap. Her head rested on his chest, her knees up by her chin, her arms tucked against her body.

They sat that way for several minutes. Gabriel didn't say anything more – what could he say? No words would take back what had been done to her. Nothing he did or said would stop the nightmares from coming. Every damn day she had to live this, and every night, too.

Gradually, the tremors lessened. Rubbing his hand up and down her arm, he tried to get heat back into her. He pulled the blanket up around her legs without letting go of her. Figuring she was probably dehydrated after all that gasping and sweating, he leaned over and picked up her glass of water off the bedside table.

"Drink," he coaxed, touching the glass to her shoulder so she knew where it was.

Without opening her eyes, she reached out, hesitant. Gabriel pressed the glass into her palm, watched her take a long swallow. Her lashes were damp with tears.

"Okay?" he asked, setting the glass back down.

Instead of answering, she settled against him once more. She shifted slightly so her hand rested above his heart.

Gabriel held her, stroking her hair until she relaxed against him. It occurred to him as he was drifting off that during the entire encounter, he hadn't once noticed she was naked.

●　　●　　●　　●　　●

"I don't know what I was thinking."

Isabel paced from the coffee pot to the sink and back again. She was wearing a cute multicolored striped sweater that accented her chest. Currently, she was using the sleeves of the shirt as rubber bands, pulling on them while she fidgeted with her hands. If she wasn't careful, she was going to make the fabric lose its shape.

"Do you want creamer?" Griffin asked, already knowing the answer. He poured coffee into her tumbler and rested his hand on the refrigerator handle as he waited for her answer.

"We've only been dating for a few weeks." She was still stretching the sweater hard enough to ruin it. "That's too soon to meet my parents, right? You're probably freaked out. I shouldn't have mentioned it so soon. I let it slip to my mom and she technically invited you..."

She was talking too fast but couldn't seem to stop.

Griffin liked that sweater. He didn't want it ruined.

"Should've made decaf," he murmured, amused. He tended to her coffee, adding creamer, and stirring it as he listened to her. "Do you have another tumbler so I can take some coffee with me?"

"You're probably thinking you shouldn't have said yes to be polite. You agreed too fast and now you can't get out of it without being an asshole." She walked toward him, not looking up. "But you're not an asshole, it's perfectly okay if you don't want to-"

"Isabel."

He took her shoulders gently. The flinch when he touched her irritated him, even though he knew she did it because she was startled and not because she expected him to smack her. That she focused on his chest and not his face made him even more frustrated.

"I didn't agree to be polite. I agreed because I want to spend as much time with you as possible."

"That's a sweet thing to say-"

"No." He gave her a firm shake this time. When her eyes widened, he clearly saw the heavy green surrounding her pupils. "It's not a thing to say at all. If you're going to question everything I say, do it on your own time. When you're with me, be with me. Stop wasting all our time together wondering why I choose you."

Isabel sucked in a breath as he lowered his head, and he lifted her chin. He kissed her in a way that made her head spin. Pins and needles shot from her head to her toes. The kiss wasn't gentle.

"I choose you. Now stop ruining your sweater and breathe."

His tone was direct, firm. He stated wanting to be with her and meeting her family like facts with no alternatives.

She froze with her hands up by her chest, no longer tugging at her sleeves. They still covered her hands, hooked on her thumbs, and her eyes were unbelievably large, but she was breathing steadily and looking into his eyes instead of avoiding them.

"Say something funny," she said.

"Something funny."

Smirking, she shoved his chest. He slid his arms around her but kept the hug light, friendly.

"Do you have anything else for me to put coffee in?"

She frowned. "You can use the tumbler. I'll wait until we get to the house."

"I already put creamer in it for you. I can wait until we get there. Are you ready?"

Before she could start searching, he held her keys out to her.

"You want me to drive?" Alarm flashed through her as she slid her jacket on. "This is going to be interesting."

"They're not my parents." He watched her take a quick inventory of her purse. "Do you prefer not to?"

"It's fine," she said, frowning again as she pulled a stained, barely legible receipt from her purse. She tried to decipher it, shrugged, and tossed it onto the table. "You might want to turn up the stereo to drown me out."

Griffin found out what she meant soon after they left the parking lot. At a four way stop sign, the vehicle in front of her sat for several seconds even though they were the only vehicles in sight.

Finally, Isabel laid on the horn and yelled, "It's not going to turn green, Sargent Shithead!"

A few miles later, when someone in a Toyota cut her off and then poked along below the speed limit, she laid on the horn again and yelled, "Move it, you fuck nugget!" Then she glanced over at Griffin and said, "My car has its invisible paint on today."

He grinned, leaning back in the seat at a slight angle so he could watch her.

It wasn't just idiots driving recklessly that she commented on. At one point, they stopped at a light and she glanced over at a strip mall. A young woman was carrying several shopping bags, wearing expensive boots that went up past her knees.

Isabel stared at her and said, "Holy buckets, those are some hooker heels."

Talking constantly seemed to keep her attention off how nervous she was.

"Hey, Colonel Crack Whore! Stay in your own lane!"

A young woman, probably used to getting her way because of her looks, flipped Isabel the bird as she passed, barely in the opposite lane.

"Gutter slut!" Isabel shouted.

"Why are you so nervous driving?" Griffin finally asked when they reached the outskirts of Madison and had some peace on the highway.

"I'm not nervous driving," Isabel said. Her grip on the steering wheel told a different story. "I don't like driving with passengers."

"Why not?"

When she finally answered, her voice was strained. "I don't like being responsible for other people's lives."

Some of her nerves settled once they reached Langdon, a tiny town Griffin hadn't really known existed before he met Isabel. She was familiar with every business, every road, every stop sign. Instead of barking out insults now, she grumbled. Griffin couldn't hear everything she was saying because she was mumbling, but an occasional word came through.

"...douche canoe... fuckhead...."

He turned toward the window so she wouldn't see him laughing. Her choice of words was endlessly entertaining. However, her statement about not liking the responsibility of other people's lives was interesting. He was still mulling that over when she pulled into the driveway of an impressive property.

The house was huge. He could tell by the perfectly cared for flowers and recently spread mulch that landscaping was important to one or both of Isabel's parents. Did they do it themselves, he wondered, or pay to have it done? His mother would never get her perfectly manicured nails dirty.

Isabel was rubbing her thumb and forefinger along the outside hem on her jeans. Because he was used to dressing in trousers and a button-down shirt or sweater when meeting with his own parents, Griffin had automatically done the same today. A thin sweater seemed appropriate enough for a family dinner, since the temperature was supposed to remain cool. Isabel wore jeans and sneakers, and Griffin wondered if he had overdressed. His trousers were dark, at least; maybe they could pass as dark jeans.

Isabel parked her Malibu. She was taking deliberate breaths in, holding them, letting them out.

"Do you have to do calming breathing exercises every Sunday or is it just because I'm here?" he asked, half-joking.

"Every Sunday."

He was saddened that she didn't feel comfortable around her own family. Yet she came back, every Sunday, to be tortured again and again. Why?

"Don't worry," she said, trying to smile. "They hide the whiskey when I'm here."

He tugged on her hair. "This won't be a repeat of The Raz?"

Shaking her head, she suddenly looked exhausted. Yet she smiled. "I grew up in this house. I know where to hide if I need to."

"You don't have to hide, Izzie. I'm here."

Suddenly something shifted in her expression, and she sat up straight, excited. "You're going to love Ava. If we're lucky, she'll punch Jack in the nuts again."

•　•　•　•　•

The aroma of baked ham hit Isabel as soon as she opened the side door. She didn't realize her hand slowly curled into a fist, but Griffin, who's hand was wrapped around hers, noticed instantly and squeezed reassuringly. He watched her as they stepped into an entryway-like hall and she led him passed a laundry room, half bath, and pantry on one side, and a screened porch on the other side. Already her muscles were tightening, her shoulders curving forward slightly, her neck dipped down just a little. She took a deep breath before stepping into the kitchen, where two women were with their backs to the door were enthusiastically discussing recipes.

Griffin reminded himself that he only had one side of the story, and he owed it to these two people to give them a chance.

"Smells good," Isabel said, setting her purse on the island table.

Both women turned, their eyes warm and bright. The older, her mom, Griffin presumed, had light brown hair and green eyes a couple shades lighter than Isabel's. She was short and athletically built, the opposite of Izzie, but the similarity to the woman standing next to her was undeniably. Beth had brown hair and brown eyes and her build mirrored her mother's. Griffin wondered if Isabel's father had passed the tall, willowy look to her, because her mother certainly didn't. Both women's eyes lit cheerfully when they turned.

"Iz," Beth said, giving her a hug. "Happy Easter."

She looked exhausted, Griffin thought. Stressed out and exhausted.

"Happy Easter," Isabel said. "This is Griffin."

She turned stiffly to hug her mother.

"Nice to meet you," Beth said, leaning over and hugging Griffin. "I'm Beth, Isabel's sister."

"Oh. Hello." Isabel hadn't mentioned they were a hugging family, which meant she probably thought the behavior was normal in every household. "Pleasure's mine."

"Oh, I love your accent!" Beth pulled back and looked at him. "Australian?"

He nodded.

"Mom, he's Australian!" she said loudly.

"Jesus, Beth, he's not a rare collectible stamp," Isabel said, snorting.

"Allie Harris," her mother said, laughing. "It's so nice to meet you. Please pardon my oldest daughter's manners."

"We're not very cultured," Iz said, picking up a black olive and tossing it up in the air. She caught it in her mouth. "The closest we've come to Australian culture is watching reruns of 'The Crocodile Hunter'."

Griffin grinned. "Nice to meet you, Mrs. Harris. Griffin Turner."

"Allie, please. Isabel didn't tell me anything about you. I didn't even know she had a boyfriend until a few days ago."

"For Christ's sake." Isabel rolled her eyes.

"Watch your mouth, Isabel, it's Easter Sunday. Let's join the guys in the living room and get to know each other." Allie started tugging Griffin's coat off. "Let me take your coat. Isabel, why don't you hang coats in the foyer?"

Isabel took Griffin's jacket from her mother and walked through the library to the foyer slowly, taking deep breaths. She took her time, trying not to shiver as she hung first his jacket, then hers.

Was this a good idea? Griffin said it was fine, he wanted to be here. So far, he hadn't lied to her, not even a little one to spare hurting her. She trusted him. Yet how could all this commotion be a good thing for anyone? If the situation were reversed, and she were meeting this many people at once, she would be having a meltdown in the nearest bathroom right now.

"Isabel?"

The sound of her mother's voice sometimes made her skin crawl.

She made her way to the living room. Jack and her father were discussing racing in the two adjoining recliners. Her mother and Beth here sitting in the love seat, at the very edge, staring at Griffin. Griffin was sitting on the couch.

"There you are," her mother said. "I forgot to ask Griffin if he wanted anything to drink. Can you get drinks for you two? He's in the middle of describing his job."

"Sure."

Griffin gave her an amused grin. "If you want to open that wine we brought..."

"We should save that for the ham. I'll see if we have something for before dinner. Did he meet Dad and Jack?"

Her mother nodded.

He seemed relaxed, comfortable. Unlike her, he fit right in with her family and was at ease socializing.

While she was in the kitchen, she heard the side door open and the dogs charge in. Gabriel was here. Instantly her stress level decreased, and she smiled while she poured two glasses of a light white wine.

Ozzie bumped into her legs, wagging his tail so it thumped loudly against the island cupboards.

"Hey, Oz." She indulged him in a rough scrub around his ears and smiled as he moaned dramatically.

As she straightened, continuing with the wine, Maya walked in, her toenails on the tile the only sound she made. A moment later Gabriel joined her.

"Hey, sis."

"I'm seeing someone," she blurted, then slapped a hand over her mouth.

"Good for you," he said instantly. Isabel's eyes were huge and glassy. Her left hand was braced on the counter as if she was preparing herself for bad news. She slowly lowered her right hand from her mouth.

"I have been for a few weeks now." As she spoke, her hands became animated, and her face lit up. "I didn't say anything because... well, it's been a while and I didn't think it would last much longer than a day or two. I don't have the best track record."

"You have the right to a private life, Iz." Gabriel glanced behind him as Ava entered the kitchen, standing just inside the doorway at an angle to avoid exposing her back to anyone.

Isabel sighed, covered her face with her hands. "I'm such a moron."

"Why? Because you're excited about a guy? There's nothing idiotic about that. How long has it been since you dated Dick?"

Iz pursed her lips, but she was smiling. "His name was Tony."

"That's what I said."

Snorting, Iz brought her hands down and set the wine aside. "Four years and some change."

"Damn," Gabriel said slowly, drawing the word out. "Dick never put that look on your face or gave you that glow."

Isabel looked at him pointedly, trying not to laugh. "His name is Tony."

"Whatever. I've never seen you this happy before. Good for you. What's his name? The new guy, not Dick."

Iz snickered again. "Griffin. He makes me laugh."

Keeping his eyes on his sister, Gabriel reached back for Ava. After a moment, he felt her hand in his, cool and firm as she stepped up just behind him.

"It's about time. You look really great, Iz."

"I've had so much sex." Isabel blurted the confession before she knew she was going to speak.

"Jesus, Iz, you could have kept that one to yourself." Gabriel picked up a piece of cheese from the relish tray. "Is that why you didn't invite him today? You fucked him to death?"

Isabel started giggling. "Actually, he's in the living room. I slipped up and mentioned him to Mom. She fell on him like a vulture."

"That's how Ava got dragged into coming."

"I'm sorry," Isabel said, addressing Ava. "Happy Easter, Ava."

"Hello."

Iz was walking around the island toward her even as Ava frowned at the reference to Easter. Holding out her arms, she pulled them back and stopped, remembering Ava's dislike of hugs. She clasped her hands together, uncomfortable.

"Sorry, it's a habit."

"You... can hug me," Ava said, looking dubious. Her arms were stiff at her sides.

Isabel closed the distance and gave her a brief squeeze. "You're never going to get used to that, are you?"

Frowning again, she somberly shook her head, making Isabel laugh again.

Walking back to the glasses of wine, Isabel momentarily forgot to be anxious and enjoyed the company she was in. Without fully understanding why, she had easily become comfortable around Ava. The woman didn't judge and wasn't constantly talking like most people.

"I'm sorry I didn't tell you about Griffin," Iz said softly to her brother, glancing toward the living room. Griffin's laughter made her feel giddy.

Gabriel wrapped his arm around her and yanked her against him. "You're grounded."

She smirked. "I tell you everything. I felt like I was lying."

"You don't owe me an explanation," Gabriel said, kissing the top of her head. "You're a grown-ass woman."

He released her and stole a sip of her wine. Grimacing, he reached in the refrigerator for a couple of waters.

Isabel punched him on the arm, relaxing. They were good.

"We're sitting in the living room. Food's going to be a while." She picked up the two glasses of wine. "I better rescue Griffin from the wolves."

Gabriel handed Ava a bottle of water and followed his sister toward the living room. He was interested in meeting the man responsible for putting color in Isabel's cheeks. She had an enthusiasm in her eyes that he hadn't seen there for years.

The murmur of conversation drifted toward him as they neared the room. Over Isabel's shoulder, Gabriel saw his dad and Jack talking, as comfortable as any close father and son could be. Jack had fit into the family so easily; it was hard to imagine a time when he wasn't part of it.

Isabel walked over to the couch and stepped around a tall man with light brown hair. Griffin, Gabriel assumed. Iz handed him a glass of wine and as he took it from her, his eyes followed her progress in front of him to the other side of the couch, where she sat next to him. He murmured a thank you and turned back to listen to what Allie was saying. Gabriel watched the man's hand slide easily over to Isabel's leg, resting comfortably. He also noticed how Iz calmed down at the touch.

"Gabe!" His father stood, crossing the room to give him a hug. "Keeping busy?"

Gabriel pounded his dad on the back. "Oh, yeah."

"I'm thinking of having a cabinet made for your mother," he murmured into his ear. "Can you squeeze a project like that in?"

"Absolutely."

"Ava, lovely to see you again, dear. May I have a hug?"

Ava stepped forward and stiffly accepted a hug from Josh. Jack stepped up next and held both hands up to show her he meant no harm.

"I don't have to hug you if you don't want me to," he said.

Ava regarded him and resigned herself to endless hugs. They made no sense to her, especially since she had only just met these people. She did not appreciate them invading her personal space. But she lifted her arms and put a tiny amount of pressure around Jack's torso.

"Ava," Isabel stood, motioning to Griffin. "This is Griffin. Griffin, Ava." Griffin stood and offered a hand.

Ava turned toward them. At the sight of Griffin, she recoiled, backing into Gabriel so hard she knocked him into Jack.

"Ava, what the hell-"

Gabriel steadied Jack, making sure he was okay. Ava was plastered against him, trying to back away even more. Her eyes were the size of quarters and she had dropped her water bottle on the floor.

"What's wrong?" Isabel asked, looking from one to the other. "Do you two know each other?"

"No," Griffin said slowly. He lowered his hand when it was obvious Ava wasn't going to shake it. The woman's reaction to him was curious; her face had gone ashen, and she swayed on her feet.

Allie and Beth had stopped talking to watch the encounter. "Everything okay?" Allie asked.

"I don't know," Gabriel said, still looking at Ava.

She was pressed against him and all but crawling up him to stay as far away from Griffin as possible. He was startled to feel her trembling against him. Since she was already touching him, he lightly set his hands on her shoulders.

"How are you doing, Ava?" he murmured.

She could barely force the words out. "I need... I need air."

Everyone watched her quickly leave the room.

Gabriel caught Isabel's dejected look. "She had a rough night," he said. "Bad nightmares. She's been jumpy all morning."

"Does she have nightmares often?" Allie asked. "That poor girl looked terrified."

"Unfortunately, yes. Almost every night."

Feeling less singled out, Isabel took a sip of wine. "Shouldn't you go see if she's okay?"

"I'll give her a few minutes. Sorry to plow into you, Jack."

Jack grinned. "No family gathering is complete without an injury."

Chatter continued, and the tension left the room as quickly as it had entered.

"I'm going to see what your mother has for appetizers," his dad said, giving Gabriel a hearty slap on the back.

"Gabriel," his mother said, standing. She held her arms out. "So good to see you. We were talking with Isabel's boyfriend. Isn't he just so adorable?"

"Fuck me," Isabel muttered. She rolled her eyes.

"Isabel, really," Allie said shortly.

Iz stiffened. Beside her, Griffin slid his hand under her hair and rested it on the nape of her neck, squeezing gently.

"He's not a puppy," Gabriel said to his mother. He held out his hand. "Nice to meet you."

Griffin shook. "Pleasure to meet you, mate. Isabel talks about you often."

Gabriel raised his eyebrow, making Griffin grin.

"Hey, Gabe." Beth moved around Griffin and wrapped her arms around her brother.

"How are you two doing?" Gabe asked softly, not liking how thin and brittle she felt under his hands. He looked down at the top of her head. "Have you heard anything?"

When she kept her arms around him, not speaking, he frowned. "Beth?"

Sniffling, she stepped back. Her eyes were shiny with tears that didn't quite fall.

"Hey," he said, taking a step forward.

"I'm fine." She squeezed his shoulder and walked out of the room. Allie hurried after her.

"What the hell was that?" Isabel asked.

Gabriel shook his head.

"What the fuck, Jack?" Iz glared at her brother-in-law.

Jack walked over to them, shoving his hands in his pockets. "We're waiting for the first round of test results. She's... really stressed out. She isn't sleeping, or eating, and..."

"And what?" Gabriel asked. He hadn't noticed it until then, but Jack's eyes were slightly red, and his cheeks were sunken. He may have lost a few pounds himself. There were shadows under his eyes.

"I hear her crying at night. Every night."

Isabel stood very still. She was aware of Griffin's hand on her neck, caressing, soothing.

"I'm sorry, man." Gabriel's voice sounded like it was coming from far away. "I wish I could do something."

"It just hits her sometimes," Jack said. "It's good to be around family. I'm going to go make sure she's okay."

Gabriel clapped him on the shoulder as he walked by. "Fuck."

"I'll see your fuck and I'll raise you a horseshit," Isabel said bitterly. "This fucking sucks."

Silence weighed heavy in the room several moments, then Gabriel looked at Griffin with a humorless smile and said, "Welcome to a typical Harris Sunday dinner."

Isabel snorted.

Griffin smiled.

"Sorry," Iz said. "Normally it's not this dark. They're trying to figure out why she hasn't gotten pregnant. They've been trying for three years."

Griffin nodded. "That's understandably stressful. Is she going to be upset that you told me?"

"It's kind of in everyone's face right now," Iz said, chugging her wine. "If you spend any time with us on Sundays, you'll hear more about it. Besides, everything I do upsets her, so what's one more thing?"

She turned to Gabriel. "Didn't your girlfriend come with you?"

"I don't know what happened to her. I better go find her."

"Probably a good idea."

When they were alone, Griffin turned Isabel toward him. "How are your stress levels?"

"Hmm? Fine." She glanced toward the library, where Beth had gone. The absent look was in her eyes again, as if she were thinking of everything except where she was and what she was doing.

He skimmed his thumb over her lower lip. "Really? Your heartbeat's elevated and your pupils are dilated."

"I'm worried about my sister."

"Is that why it started before you entered the house?"

He had her full attention now. "What's your point?" Heat sparked in her eyes.

"I'm just worried about you." He leaned down and gave her a kiss, rubbed her shoulders.

"I'm at the bottom of the list of priorities," Isabel said, finishing her wine.

Aren't you always? Griffin thought.

In the kitchen, Gabriel glanced around, looking for signs of Ava. He was baffled. Her water bottle was sitting on the island table. A quick glance into the library told him she wasn't in there; his mom and Jack were comforting Beth.

"Did you lose someone?" his dad asked, crunching on a dill pickle.

"Apparently, my date. Have you seen Ava?"

Josh grinned. "She's right behind you."

Gabriel spun around. Ava was standing in the doorway, one hand on the casing. The pallid shade of her face sent a spark of worry through him as he took a step toward her.

"Are you okay? Where were you?"

"In the restroom."

Her voice was weak.

"Are you sick?" He reached out to touch her shoulder.

"I am fine." She took a deliberate step back. Gabriel tried not to be offended, but it was obvious she didn't want him to touch her. "I need to step outside."

Backing away, she walked quickly out through the entryway, bumping her hip on the corner of a decorative table in an ungraceful move that wasn't like her at all.

"Is she okay?" Josh asked, looking after her.

Gabriel shook his head. "I don't know." He ran a hand down the back of his neck, still staring where Ava had been standing. "I don't know if she wants me to leave her alone or follow her. She's always... closed off."

"It's not about what she wants," his father said. Gabriel turned back and looked at him. "That girl needs a friend."

Nodding, Gabe walked back through the hallway. He could see her leaning on her SUV as he drew closer to the door. As he stepped quietly outside, he was unnerved by the way she braced her hands on the vehicle, leaning forward and gulping up air quietly.

"What's wrong?" He rested his hand on her back. She grimaced and twisted like a cat, as if his touch were corrosive. Immediately he took his hand off her, trying to ignore the pang in his gut that her reaction had caused. Her eyes met his, and he knew she was truly sorry for insulting him. But her body had reacted with complete honesty. He couldn't ignore that.

"Sorry," he said. He was sorry about whatever she was going through and sorry his touch had made her feel that way and sorry that he didn't understand why she suddenly didn't want him to touch her.

"I was not ready," she said, but her voice sounded funny. Like it wasn't used to lying. Turning around, she leaned back against the car with her head back, taking deep breaths.

"You don't have to lie to spare my feelings," he said. "I'll leave you alone."

He turned away from her. When he felt her hand on his, he jumped. She didn't instigate touch. For a moment, his mind and body rejected the idea that she just had. When he gazed at her, her eyes seemed darker than usual. Like little storms, waiting to rage out against whatever was in their way.

"I am... in a place I do not usually allow myself to be," she said. She tugged ever so gently on his hand, so he took a step toward her.

"A bad place?" he asked. Despite the mild day, her hand was cool.

For a moment, she looked away. Then nodded. "I... too much is going on and it is harder to block out negative coping devices I developed as a child to protect myself from people. I was protecting myself when you touched me."

"From The Bad People?"

Her brow furrowed.

"You talk about them in your sleep." Gabriel reached up and brushed her hair back from her face, relieved that she didn't recoil this time. "What made you think you had to protect yourself?"

"I s-saw something..." She glanced toward the house, shook her head. "I let myself get weak."

"You're the strongest person I know."

She wasn't explaining it right. Her head was still in a fog from seeing Griffin in the living room. The tall, dark man she had seen hovering around Isabel at her apartment and again in her own house was sitting next to Isabel, talking with the family. Everyone saw him and heard him speak.

Ava did not understand.

"Is it too much to be here?" Gabriel asked. "Too many people?"

"No." Raising her head, gazing at him, Ava's grasp on his hand tightened. "You want me. You want me?"

He stared, uncertain what she was asking for, only aware that the grip on his hand was brutal and the expression on her face was intense.

"Yes."

"You must be sure. There are things you do not know about me."

"I accept that."

She closed her eyes, shook her head again. "You do not understand."

Gabriel held her hand in both of his, trying to warm that cold, cold flesh. "I want to be with you, Ava. That's all I need to know."

"I must tell you something. You must understand everything, or you cannot know. You cannot know if you really want..."

"Okay." He cupped his hand under her jaw, gazing at her. Everything inside him wanted to wipe the misery off her face. "You can tell me anything."

Taking a deep breath, she said, "I am able to -"

The side door opened, and Isabel stuck her head out. "Dinner's ready. Oh. Sorry to interrupt. Whenever you're ready, the food's done."

"Thanks, Iz." Gabriel kept his focus on Ava. "What is it?"

She shuddered violently.

"Are you cold?"

Shaking her head, Ava took hold of his arms. "We should eat."

Some color had returned to her cheeks, and her eyes didn't look quite as haunted, but Gabriel knew she was holding back whatever she'd wanted to tell him before they were interrupted. Yet he had the feeling, finally, that she was fully committed to being with him instead of backing away at the first sign of trouble.

"Okay. Let's go eat."

Back inside, the kitchen was a cacophony of voices and laughter. Gabriel waited to get in the food line so he and Ava could step in simultaneously, but she stayed at the doorway. He leaned against the wall and watched his family walk around the island table, loading their plates with food. When he felt something bump his hand, he glanced down. Ava was lightly brushing her fingertips over the back of his hand, staring at the crowded table.

"Jump in, kids," Josh said, "before Jack takes it all."

There was general laughter. Even Beth laughed. Gabriel thought she looked better now, a little less rough around the edges.

"We'll wait until it clears out a bit," Gabriel said, placing his other hand on Ava's lower back. He eased it slowly up under her shirt, settling his palm on her bare skin. He felt her long sigh that ended with a tremble and took a step toward her.

Allie was standing back, letting her children go first.

"Go ahead, Mom, we need a minute." Gabriel ran his fingertips up Ava's spine, back down slowly.

She was staring at Griffin, he noticed, following his movement around the table as he teased Isabel, nudging her, and making her laugh. From the look in her eyes, it wasn't attraction, Gabriel thought, but he couldn't quite discern the expression on her face. Familiarity? Curiosity? Maybe it was his accent. His mom and Beth seemed completely infatuated by it. He slid his hand around her side, turning it over so he could brush the backs of his fingers over her flesh. He could feel the goose bumps rise and her grip tightened on his other hand.

His family began filing into the dining room. Beth and Jack, his dad, Isabel, and Griffin. His mom was slowly filling her plate, watching them. He knew she wanted to wait until everyone else had their food and were settled at the table before she relaxed enough to get her own.

"Ready?" Gabriel murmured to Ava.

She tore her eyes away from Griffin, something warring in her eyes. Was that fear? He couldn't believe she was afraid of anything.

Silently, she nodded. Knowing she would prefer it, Gabriel stepped forward to grab a plate. He handed her one before he began scooping food onto his own. She followed him around the table, her eyes growing larger as her attention moved from Griffin to the food. With each new dish, her focus became more and more homed in on her plate. By the time they walked into the dining room, she was gazing at her plate instead of watching where she was walking.

The dogs were following closely, hoping for a dropped bite. Gabriel snapped his fingers and pointed. Ozzie and Maya trotted into the living room to gaze wistfully from afar. Setting his plate on the table, Gabriel pulled a chair next to Isabel out.

"Have a seat," he said to Ava.

Finally, she looked up from her food. She shook her head.

"What's wrong?" he asked.

Isabel glanced up. Having Ava sit next to her would put her between her and Gabriel, the two people she'd known the longest. They thought that would make her feel the most comfortable.

Ava glanced around the table. Everyone was looking at her. "I will not sit with my back to the door."

"Shit," Gabriel said easily. "I knew that. Isabel-"

His sister stood and shifted her plate to the left. She began pointing and moving Gabriel's and her drinks and flatware around. "Griffin can come sit over here, by me. Gabriel, you can sit there, and Ava can sit at the head of the table. Does that work, Ava?"

"Yes, thank you."

As Gabriel and Isabel were moving their settings to make room for Griffin's, Ava took her plate and water and walked to her new seat. Griffin stood to the side, watching Isabel switch everything around and teasing her brother. He didn't notice how close Ava was until she reached out to him.

"Oh. Hello. I'll be out of your way in... just a moment..."

He trailed off as she poked him in the chest with her index finger. Her eyes were wide and curious, her head tilted slightly as she studied him. She pushed against his shoulder.

"Gabriel, why is your girlfriend palpating my boyfriend?" Isabel asked.

Finished with the switch, he looked up. Everyone was watching Ava study Griffin.

"They can see you," she said softly. She reached up past his face, moving her hand in the space just behind his head. "He is not there now."

Gooseflesh rose on Griffin's skin. "Who?"

"The man with the lost face." She placed her hands on his cheeks, staring into his eyes. Hers were out of focus. "You are real, but he is not."

"Can someone explain this to me?" Jack had a fork of mashed potatoes halfway to his mouth but was staring at Ava and Griffin.

Griffin slowly reached up and took Ava's wrists, pulling her hands off his face. "I think my place setting is ready." He gently lowered her hands. Picking up his plate and glass of wine, he walked around Gabriel and Isabel to his seat.

For a moment, Ava stood staring at nothing, her eyes glazed over. She blinked and glanced around, seeming to come back from wherever she had gone.

"Okay?" Gabriel asked.

"Okay," she said as if nothing had happened, her eyes clear. She sat at the head of the table and began adjusting her plate, flatware, and bottle of water to her liking. Conversation began again, tentatively at first, then picking up.

Grateful for the food, Ava bowed her head to pray. Everyone at the table fell silent again. When she lifted her head, they were watching her curiously.

"I didn't realize you're religious," Isabel said. "We would have waited for you."

"I am not." Ava began digging into her ham.

"Didn't you just pray?" Jack asked.

Frowning, she lifted her head. "I gave thanks. One has nothing to do with the other."

"Who were you grateful to, then?" Griffin asked, tilting his head.

Ava studied him the way a lion watches a zebra.

Griffin sipped his wine. "I don't mean to be rude. I'm truly curious."

"I was not thanking someone. I was giving thanks for something. I know what it is like to go hungry for days. My body has been so starved it began to feed off itself. I am grateful for every meal I have."

Silence filled the room until it became awkward.

"Happy Easter!" Isabel said cheerfully.

Gabriel snorted.

Ava continued watching Griffin. He held her gaze, wondering why she had been acting so strange around him.

"Thanks for dinner, Ma," Josh said to Allie, patting her arm. "This is delicious, as always."

"Yes," Jack agreed. "Thank you."

Murmurs of approval went around the table, but Ava didn't hear them. She was still staring at Griffin, wondering about the dark man she had seen before.

The man who looked exactly like him, dressed all in black. Was she seeing Griffin because he was going to die? That had never happened to her before.

"You lost your face," she said, without realizing it.

Griffin tilted his head. "I beg your pardon?"

She was frowning, concentrating on Griffin, yet she was so obviously in awe. Her eyes were boring into his. For several seconds she didn't blink as she studied him.

Isabel glanced from Ava to Griffin and back.

He eased his hand onto Isabel's thigh, unsure why he needed to feel reassured. Trying to ignore the twinge of disquiet surrounding him, he felt marginally better when Isabel took his hand.

"Is this an Australian thing?" Gabriel asked. "Mom and Beth can't seem to get past the accent."

"I do not understand," Ava persisted, her food momentarily forgotten. She was leaning forward, her body rigid as she studied him. "Why does everyone see you?"

Griffin felt sweat trickle down his back. His heartbeat suddenly filled his ears, making it hard to hear anything else.

"Sometimes she says weird things," Isabel said quietly.

"What makes you say that?" Griffin asked Ava. He was unable to break his graze from hers.

Everyone had stopped eating and was watching the two again. Jack reached over to put his hand on Ava's shoulder.

"Don't touch her," Gabriel warned.

"The punch to the balls last week didn't drive it home for you, Jack?" Isabel asked. "She doesn't like to be touched."

"Isabel!" Allie snapped. "I've asked you repeatedly to stop being so vulgar."

Isabel stood and picked up her wine glass. "I've asked for a lot of things. I guess we're both disappointed."

She walked into the kitchen.

"Ava," Gabriel said quietly. She blinked and turned to look at him. "You should eat something."

Glancing at her plate, she frowned and began shoveling food in enthusiastically. Griffin watched her thoughtfully until Isabel returned with a full glass of wine and the bottle.

"Thank you," he said when she refilled his. This was turning out to be one odd Sunday dinner.

Isabel held up the bottle. "Anyone else?"

"I'll have some, Iz," Jack said. "Thanks."

He held his glass across the table so she could pour.

"I saw Rachel in the store the other day, Gabriel," Allie said, cutting her meat.

The glass bottle rattled against the wine glass. Isabel's hand shook visibly, and she had to steady the bottle with her other hand. Griffin reached up and rested his hand on the small of her back.

"I hope you shoved a Molotov cocktail up her ass," she muttered. Before her mother could snipe about her language, she added, "I need a break," and set the bottle down on the table a little too hard. She walked into the library.

"That mouth," Allie sighed, closing her eyes briefly. "Anyway, Gabriel, she told me to give you her best."

"That was big of her," Gabriel said, taking a drink of his water. "I thought she was giving her best to Stuart as often as she could."

"Don't be crude. At least she's trying to make amends," his mother said. "I think she realizes she made a mistake. Ava, have you met Rachel?"

"Isabel said Rachel is a cheating whore." Ava said this in between bites of mashed potatoes and corn.

Allie pursed her lips.

Isabel was walking back in and burst into laughter. When she sat down, Griffin leaned over and murmured in her ear. She nodded.

Gabriel chuckled and glanced at Ava affectionately before turning to his mom. "Why would she? I don't parade my previous girlfriends around my current one."

"She lives in the same small town, that's all," Allie said. "I'm just passing along the message."

"I hope she and Ava do meet," Isabel said, smiling wickedly over her glass of wine. "That will be very entertaining."

Gabriel grinned. "I'd buy tickets to see that."

"So, Griffin," Josh said, happy to change the subject. "How did you and Iz meet?"

"Oh, for God's sake." Isabel muttered.

"She cussed me out in a grocery store." Griffin said, smiling at Izzie with obvious affection. She flushed.

"She didn't!" Allie groaned.

"I deserved it."

"Nobody deserves that mouth," Allie said, reaching out to pick up a dinner roll. "I've been trying to break her of that habit since she was fifteen."

Griffin watched her, his expression hardening slightly. Not enough to be impolite, but enough to show he did not agree with her. "I imagine," he said softly, "if people spent more time listening and less time talking, she might not feel so frustrated as to use profanity."

Isabel paused with her fork halfway to her mouth. Her eyes swept from Griffin's face to her mom's. Griffin's jaw was tight, his eyes like hardened amber. Though he was obviously annoyed with her mother, the hand that clasped hers was gentle, his thumb stroking her palm with endless patience.

Caught off guard at the opposition, Allie avoided eye contact, unsure what to say.

"Or maybe that's just the way she is," Gabriel said. "I love you just how you are, Iz."

Isabel gaped. A sudden urge to burst into tears filled her. No one had ever stood up for her before. Even Gabriel didn't insinuate to their mother that she needed to back off when she scolded Isabel. It wasn't that he was afraid to; he had never given it any thought. The way they were around each other was the way they had always been. Now two people were standing on her side for once. Feeling protected against her mother's scrutiny was refreshing.

"When did you braid your hair, Ava?" Jack suddenly asked.

His voice filled the room, extremely loud after the previous silence. Everyone turned to look at Ava, who was still eating, despite the awkward conversation that had just transpired. She didn't seem to have heard any of it.

Without looking up from her plate, Ava said, "I did not braid it."

"It's beautiful," Beth said. She had barely touched the food on her plate, but her eyes were bright and clear now watching Ava. Her voice was barely above a whisper. "Like a princess."

Isabel gazed at her, trying to pull the rest of some faded memory that was tugging at her as she stared at the long braid wrapped around Ava's head. It brought back bits and pieces of something that made her feel content, amused, and peaceful.

"You didn't come here with it braided," Jack said. "It wasn't braided a minute ago... was it?"

His meal forgotten, Gabriel reached out toward Ava's head, toward the dark braid that looked like a crown. Ava stilled with her fork hovering just above her plate. As Gabriel touched the braid wrapped twice around her head, her eyes rolled until they were settled on him.

"Why does that style look so familiar?" Iz asked. Now she had Griffin's hand, and her nails were digging into his skin. "It's not a common braid."

"I've seen it before," Gabriel murmured, running his hand gently over the silky hair, following the braid for a few inches. A few wisps of hair at her temples had been left out and he let them slip through his fingers almost reverently.

Ava had placed her hands on either side of her plate. Her head was down. She was staring straight ahead at the flower arrangement Allie had bought as a centerpiece for Easter.

"That used to be my favorite braid," Beth said. She didn't notice the tear on her own cheek.

"What's going on?" Jack asked. "Why is Ava's hair suddenly braided and why are you all so fascinated with it?"

Allie had pushed her food away. Her face had drained of color.

"Why did you braid your hair like that?" she asked, her tone accusing. "What did Gabriel tell you?"

Ava did not lift her head or shift her position. "I did not braid it. Gabriel told me nothing."

"Why do I recognize it?" Isabel demanded. "I know that style from somewhere."

"Because," Allie said, dropping her napkin on the table. "Beth used to braid Hayden's hair like that all the time. Excuse me a moment."

She pushed her chair back and left the room.

"Did you braid your hair like that because Gabriel told you about Hayden?" Beth asked, wiping her cheek with her unused napkin.

Ava finally lifted her head to look at Beth. "I did not braid it. I tire of repeating myself."

Gabriel finally seemed coherent enough to join the conversation. "Beth isn't the only one who knows how to braid hair. YouTube can teach anyone in ten minutes. Take a Quaalude, people."

Griffin leaned over and brushed his lips against Isabel's ear. "Are you okay?"

She released her grip on his hand. "Yeah. Sorry. It just took me by surprise. It's not the most popular braid in this decade."

"No, it isn't." Griffin's tone was thoughtful. Interesting, he thought. He found Ava very interesting.

"I'm going to go check on my wife." Josh spoke for the first time, rising. His children watched him leave.

"So," Griffin said, "how about those Packers?"

Gabriel and Isabel burst out laughing. Ava frowned. She picked her fork back up and continued eating as if nothing had happened. Everyone else followed suit as the tension hovered in the room.

"What about you, Ava?" Jack asked.

She glanced up, finished chewing. "I do not watch football."

"Football...?" He glanced at Griffin, then grinned. "No, I mean, tell us about yourself. What do you do for a living?"

Taking a drink of her water, she said, "I work from home as a freelance editor."

"I don't know if I could do that," Beth said. "How do you stay on point, keep working, if you get distracted?"

"Discipline comes naturally to me. But if I get distracted, I go to the basement and practice with my mook yan jong or run in the woods until I expend excess energy. Calm the energy, and the mind is sated."

"You practice with your what?" Isabel asked around a mouthful of ham.

"Mook yan jong. It is a device used to practice Wing Chun for when I do not have a partner."

"That works for you?" Beth asked, carefully sliding her plate away. It was still mostly full of food; she had barely touched it.

"Physical exertion releases endorphins, which interact with the opiate receptors in the brain. The effect is similar to the reaction to morphine or codeine."

"What if your mind isn't the problem?" Beth asked. Jack put a hand on her shoulder. "What if it's your body that's letting you down?"

"If you feed one, the other will automatically respond. Discipline the mind, you will discipline the body. Discipline the body, you will discipline the mind. Until both are in harmony."

"Waking up every morning at the same time and meditating isn't going to give my body the ability to produce more viable eggs," Beth said. "Jogging and yoga aren't going to suddenly make me fertile."

Jack scooted his chair closer to his wife so he could put his arm around her.

Ava set her fork down, done with her first plate. She leveled her gaze at Beth. "Meditation can reduce stress and control anxiety, promote emotional health, and lower blood pressure. Jogging and yoga will stimulate endorphins, increase energy levels, promote a better sex life, and may help you get better sleep. A better sex life would obviously be in your favor. In addition, with your mind and body working together, you will have a greater chance at either conceiving, or accepting that conception is not going to happen."

"My God, Ava," Jack said.

"Have I said anything untruthful?" She turned her focus to Jack. The lack of expression was unnerving.

"Maybe not, but you could be a little more -"

"Regardless of whether or not discipline creates the best conditions necessary for conception," Ava continued, "you will be healthier and more balanced overall. You will not be slowly destroying your body, which is what you are doing now."

The room was silent. Even Jack had nothing to say. He slumped back in his chair with a dull thud, his mouth open. Isabel was staring at Ava with wide eyes, trying not to look too impressed at her ability to fearlessly state facts, regardless of whether the person receiving the information could handle it or not. Gabriel was wondering if he would ever be able to bring his girlfriend back for Sunday dinner. He was sure she would be banned the moment Beth talked to their mother. Griffin was studying Ava. His eyes had roamed between her and Beth as he curiously observed their conversation.

"I am going to have a second plate," Ava said, standing. "The food is very good."

As she walked into the kitchen, Beth whispered, "Take me home, Jack."

He stood instantly, supporting her weight against his body. "Sorry, guys," he looked at Gabriel and Isabel. "This was... not exactly how I planned to spend Easter. Or meeting you," he added, looking at Griffin. "It's been a pleasure, in spite of the..."

He shrugged, unsure how to continue.

They used the side door so they wouldn't run into Ava on the way out.

Ava returned with a plate loaded with more food and sat down.

"Good Lord," Iz said. "Where do you put all that?"

"In my mouth."

Gabriel looked at Isabel and they cracked up.

Griffin finished his meal. "This has been quite interesting."

"Admittedly, more than usual. But things are always interesting around Ava." Isabel nibbled on a piece of dinner roll. She smiled sweetly at Ava and raised her voice as she said, "I love you, Ava."

Ava raised her head, frowned.

Iz snorted. "That makes you so uncomfortable."

Allie and Josh entered the room. Gabriel watched his mom pull away from his dad and press her hand to her stomach, a sure sign she was trying to be a good hostess.

"Where are Beth and Jack?" she asked, sitting slowly.

"They left early," Gabriel said. "Beth isn't feeling very good today."

Ava had already finished her second plate. "She does not like to hear-"

"Ava, can you come with me for a moment?" Isabel asked, standing quickly. She bumped the table with her hip and almost knocked her wine glass over. "Shi-shadoobie," she amended, glancing at her mother.

"Why?" Ava asked.

"I need you in the kitchen." Iz picked up her wine glass and motioned with it, tilting her head, trying to escape.

"I do not think there is anything-"

"It's about my guitar," Isabel said, trying to avoid any more drama. "Let's go get it from my car. I'll play something for you."

Ava's eyes lit up and she immediately stood, picking up her plate.

"I'll get that," Allie said.

"It was very good food," Ava said, glancing toward Allie. "Thank you."

"You're welcome," Allie said. She laughed as Ava seemed to transform into a child before her at the thought of Isabel's guitar. "Go ahead, have fun."

Gabriel watched her hurry into the kitchen and hoped Isabel could find something to talk about to keep his girlfriend occupied.

"I'm sorry about earlier," his mom said. "It took my breath away. I haven't seen anyone wear their hair in that style since your sister. Have you?"

Gabriel thought about it. It was rather old fashioned, he thought; something he imagined seeing in tales of Guinevere and Lancelot. Actually, in those tales, the braid was made of only some of the hair, wrapped once around the head, and the rest of the hair fell long down the woman's back. No, he really hadn't seen a woman wear it wound all the way up, exposing the neck, since his sister.

"I don't think I've ever seen anyone wear it like that except for in medieval movies. I always thought it was unique to Hayden."

"Ava's so beautiful." Allie laughed softly, feeling foolish. "I overreacted. I can't believe it hit me so hard. Oh, my God, Griffin, I'm so sorry. Do you have any idea what we're talking about? How rude."

She reached across the table and took his hand. Griffin smiled. "Isabel told me what happened to Hayden. I'm sorry for you all."

She squeezed his hand. "Thank you. Dinners here aren't usually so... I don't know what. This has been the weirdest one..." She brushed a tear away. Squeezing his hand, she let it go and took Josh's instead. "Gabriel, do you think you and Isabel could play some music and cheer us up a little? I'm really tired of feeling so depressed today."

"Sure. What do you want to hear?"

"Let's go find her and Ava and see if we can figure something out," Josh said, holding Allie's hand as he stood. "A little cheer would do wonders for this family."

• • • • •

Ava pulled into Gabriel's driveway and parked next to his truck. She left the Equinox idling as she waited for him to get out. For a moment, he sat staring out the windshield, silent. Thunder cracked and then hesitantly grumbled for several seconds, as if uncertain about its part in the coming storm. Lightning flashed in the distance.

"Stay with me tonight," he said, still not looking at her.

"We did not discuss sleeping arrangements this morning. I did not pack an overnight bag."

The corner of his mouth twitched. "You live five minutes away."

"I live seven point three minutes away-"

Turning in the seat, he shifted toward her. Ava instinctively pulled back. As she stared at him, she made herself relax and settle in the seat closer to him. He was not trying to hurt her; he was trying to get close to her. She had to remember there was a difference.

Because she did not usually instigate physical contact, she reached out and rested her hand on his. His skin was warm. To find it that way was still a surprise to her. Such heat radiated off him it was a wonder she was not consumed by it.

"Is that a yes?"

Thunder, low and steady, sounded in the west. Ava found herself wanting to be awake for the storm, wanting to watch it with Gabriel. She nodded.

As she followed him up the porch stairs, she noticed he unlocked the door this time. She could not remember if it had been locked when she picked him up earlier in the day. She wondered if he had done it for her sake.

Inside, as he prepared two glasses of water for them, he watched her gazing out the wall of windows in the breakfast room. The lightening was already closer, and soon the rain would arrive.

"Why don't we watch the storm from the bedroom?" he suggested. "The bed faces the patio doors. I'll make us some hot cocoa and we can sit and watch the show."

"Hot cocoa?"

He smiled, handed her the glasses of water. "It's a family tradition. You want to take these, and I'll be up in a minute with the cocoa? I left a shirt and shorts on your side of the bed in case you came over."

Something about him doing that, leaving clothing out for her to walk around in before bed, touched her deeply. It was such a simple gesture, but it made her stomach feel fluttery all the same. Her hands were full of the glasses, so she took a step toward him and met his mouth with hers.

Almost as quickly as it had started, the kiss was over, and she stepped back, slipping quietly out of the room.

Gabriel could still taste her as he heated water.

Thunderstorms reminded him of sitting around the kitchen table with oil lamps lit and hot cocoa, telling ghost stories. Beth made the cocoa from a recipe she had looked up in an old cookbook from their grandmother. It was homemade – the kind you make on the stove with baking chocolate and milk. She then poured it into fancy mugs, complete with whip topping and chocolate shavings. The tradition had stopped the summer Hayden had disappeared, but Gabriel still had a habit of drinking hot cocoa during summer storms. His was a bachelor's version – instant cocoa with Reddi-wip sprayed on top.

Lightning was beginning to flash closer, but the heart of the storm was still a distance away. He bumped the light switch with his elbow and carried the two mugs of cocoa upstairs to his bedroom. Where had the hot cocoa and ghost story tradition come from? He couldn't remember.

Ava was propped up with her pillow behind her back. She had changed out of her clothes and put on the tee shirt and shorts he had left out for her. He felt a stab of lust seeing her there, wearing his too big clothing with her knees pulled up to her chest. How could he deny himself that? he wondered. He glanced down at the bachelor's cocoa and decided next time he would make it the way Beth used to when they were kids. Ava deserved better than instant cocoa and Reddi-wip.

Handing her a mug, he set his own hot cocoa on the night table. "This is a cheap version. I'll use a homemade recipe next time."

He walked to the glass doors and opened the curtains all the way, letting in dazzling flashes of lightning. Ava had turned her lamp on low, so he left his off, leaving a soft glow of light when the lightning settled. He sat on the edge of the bed and untied his boots. Outside, he could hear the wind picking up, the trees swaying as the storm worked its way toward Langdon.

He sat with his back against the headboard and picked up his cocoa.

Hayden loved hot cocoa, especially during the scarier ghost tales. She could come up with some really good stories for being so young. She sometimes dipped her finger into her whip topping and-

Gabriel jerked in surprise when something brushed across his nose. Ava was staring at him, her eyes wide. Her hand was frozen in the air. On the tip of her index finger was a smear of sugary white whip cream.

"Think fast," she said softly.

Gabriel's jaw dropped.

Ava blinked, shook her head. She looked from her hand, still poised with her finger extended, to his nose. "I am sorry," she said. "That was a silly thing to do."

Gabriel stood, walked to the hamper, and pulled out a shirt. Slowly, he wiped his nose off.

"Hayden used to do that when we were kids. That's what she said when she got me. Think fast."

Walking back to the bed, he couldn't stop staring at her. His mind was trying to fit pieces of information together, trying to make sense of everything he had witnessed over the past few weeks.

Ava licked the cream off her finger absently, avoiding his eyes.

"Why did you do that?" Gabriel asked. He could barely find his voice. His mouth was suddenly dry, and the hair at the base of his skull was stirring. Something familiar was pulling at him.

"I do not know."

The pieces seemed to rotate, to slide into place. Blue, the color of denim, she had said when they first met. She had been talking about his eyes. Both his and Hayden's were the same unique shade of blue. So many people told him they loved his eyes. Especially his mother, who used to tell him they were the color of denim when he was a boy.

Your eyes are the same color of blue. That's why it still hurts so much.

Ava said that, too, the day they met, and he'd had no idea what she meant at the time. Now, he thought he did.

Sometimes he caught his mother staring at him, and her eyes were filled with so much pain. Did she see her dead daughter when she looked at him? Did it rip her heart out every time she saw that exact shade of blue staring back at her only to be reminded again and again that her daughter was dead?

Gabriel shook his head, ran a hand down the back of his neck. Every time Ava had what he thought were seizures, she said things that seemed to have nothing to do with what was going on at the time. Her body locked up. Her eyes went out of focus. All the indications had been there if he had only paid attention.

"I am very tired," Ava said, setting her cocoa on the night table. "I am going to-"

"You're psychic."

The statement was so blatant that she froze. Panic flashed in her eyes.

His heart was thudding in his chest. "That's it, isn't it? I did enough research after my sister disappeared. You're the real thing. Son of a bitch."

Ava slid down on her side, pulling the blanket up around her shoulders. She kept her gaze carefully neutral and directed away from him. "Thank you for the cocoa."

He couldn't stand seeing her like that, looking so small and defeated. She was bundled under the blankets like a terrified child. "Ava."

"If you try to touch me, I will injure you."

"I'm not going to-" Another piece clicked into place. "That's why you don't like people touching you? You can't shut it off?"

Ava didn't speak. She was hunched over, her body stiff. Misery swam in her eyes.

"I didn't mean to upset you. Please don't run away from this."

She sat up stiffly and stared at him. Her expression didn't change but the rage pouring off her was palpable.

"I run from nothing."

Gabriel was hesitant to continue; in her current state she could take anything he said wrong or blow it out of proportion. He felt inadequate and foolish for not understanding sooner.

"Why are you angry? You had to know I would find out eventually. This isn't the kind of thing a person can hide."

"What do you want from me?" she spat.

"Nothing." Confused, he reached for her.

She brought her hands up in defense. Instead of the usual fist or open palm he was used to seeing, she had her hands poised in a formation he had never seen her use. He had a moment to think that she had an endless supply of hand positions, all ready to pulverize him the moment he stepped out of line, when she said something that caught him off guard.

"I will not find her for you."

"What?" Understanding dawned on him. "I'm not asking you to."

She looked so utterly, innocently confused by his response that he would have laughed if the circumstances were different. "I came to terms with Hayden's death years ago. Finding her now wouldn't change anything."

She lowered her hands. "Most people need something called closure."

Now he did smile, that lazy curve of one side of his mouth that she found appealing in spite of herself. "I know about closure, Ava. It's a selfish notion for the living, not anything helpful for the dead. There's nothing more I can do for her now."

Tilting her head, she thought about that, her eyes roaming before settling on his again. "You would not want to know what happened, if you could?"

He studied her for a long time. "I've imagined what happened to her a million times. Horrible things I didn't want to think about but couldn't help replaying over in my head. I've exhausted every possibility, dreamed every reunion. I've imagined killing the man who kidnapped her with my bare hands, watching the life leave his eyes."

Ava gazed at him. Her expression was unwavering. She listened with an intensity he was getting used to.

"But... I think some things shouldn't be known. Maybe it's a blessing that I don't know what he did to her before she died."

She said nothing, only looked at him. What went on in her head when she was thinking so much? he wondered.

"So..." he said. "What I thought were seizures... they're... what? Visions?"

Ava nodded. "They are transmissions of information. Sometimes just the information. Sometimes images, sounds, smells, with the information."

"Touching people makes it stronger, doesn't it? You don't like to be touched because you can't control it and the chance of having a vision is stronger."

"Among other reasons."

Gabriel nodded, his stomach turning. "The abuse?"

"Human contact feels like... crushed glass being ground into my skin when my mind goes back to the days of my childhood. I work extremely hard every day to suppress that part of my life so I can tolerate physical contact. Sometimes if I am exhausted or distracted, I am unable to suppress the darkness. That is why I reacted to your touch earlier today."

"I'm sorry."

"I am working with my Sensei on controlling my ability. I believe doing so has opened me up to experiences in both worlds. I should not have allowed myself to dwell in the past."

"I think you get a pass for that, Ava. You've had one hell of a shitty past."

"I do not use that as an excuse to justify deplorable behavior. I want you to know why I have allowed my discipline to slip, and that I am working on amending my behavior immediately."

"I appreciate the explanation, but -"

"I am not a victim. Do not treat me like one."

"I'll do my best not to."

He thought of her standing outside at his parent's house earlier, confused, emotions warring as she tried to tell him something.

"Is this what you were trying to tell me earlier today? When we were at my parent's house?"

She gazed at him, nodded. "It is not fair to hide this part of me from my mate. I thought I could protect you from it, but at dinner today, I realized I cannot. I knew I would have to tell you so you could make a choice."

"Well, I know about it, and my feelings haven't changed." His tone was resolute. "My choice hasn't changed. I choose you."

Gabriel reached for her, paused with his hand raised. "Is it okay to touch you now?"

Ava offered her hand, allowed him to weave his fingers through hers. He ran his thumb up and down hers in slow, soothing strokes. A sudden thought occurred to him as he remembered the night he'd taken her to Sunday dinner at his parent's house.

"After you met my family that first time..." He wasn't sure how to ask without embarrassing her. Hell, he wasn't even sure what exactly he wanted to ask. "You said you were attracted to me. You kissed me."

Her expression remained curious without a hint of awkwardness, so he continued cautiously.

"You seemed," he cleared his throat, "really into it."

"You are referring to my having an orgasm while we were kissing."

Now he was the one to be embarrassed. The flush started at the base of his neck and raced up to his hairline. He cleared his throat again.

"Well, ah, sort of. Something seemed to be happening between us. I felt it. Did it have anything to do with your psychic ability?"

"I was having a vision of us having intercourse."

He ogled her.

"It was very vivid," she added, as if that explained everything.

"So… during the kiss… you saw us having sex?"

"Visions are not like watching movies. They are somewhat like dreams. I did not just see us having sex. I felt it, emotionally and physically. Given more time that night, I could have transferred the physical connection to you."

"Psychic sex?" he pondered.

"I suppose," she said. "I imagine it would be very pleasurable."

"You've never done it?"

Grimacing, she shifted on the bed and pulled the blanket up to her chin protectively. Gabriel didn't think she realized she was doing it, or that her shoulders had automatically drawn forward.

"I have only… connected negatively in that way before. M-Mack… had very dark thoughts when h-he attacked me."

"Hey," he said, scooting closer. "I didn't mean to upset you."

She dropped her head, shook it, swallowed. When she raised her head, her eyes were clear but troubled.

"I could not control the connection with Mack. I could not stop it. But… if the negative experiences were so painful, the positive ones must be very enjoyable. I would like to try it sometime, but I do not know how to instigate it."

"Does talking about your psychic ability bother you?"

Shrugging, she blinked slowly. "I am not accustomed to talking about it. The only people who know about it are David, Sensei, and Vincent. I only recently told Sensei."

He was sure she had just named all the people in her life, except maybe Isabel. What a sad, lonely way to live when she had so much to offer the world.

"Ex-boyfriend Vincent?" he asked, for clarification.

"He was not my boyfriend. He is my uke." At his questioning look, she said, "My training partner in the dojo."

"I thought you two-"

"I had sexual intercourse with Vincent."

Gabriel could almost hear a needle screech over a record. "Excuse me?"

"Vincent was my sexual partner outside the dojo and my training partner inside the dojo. He was not my boyfriend."

"Well," he said, clearing his throat. He turned to pick up his cocoa.

"I told you I chose a partner to satisfy my most primal urges. One who understands the relationship as only a physical necessity."

Gabriel shifted, finding it increasingly hard to make eye contact. "Ah, Ava, that's not something couples usually discuss."

"I am not flaunting our sexual status; I am explaining to you that it was strictly physical. You insist on calling him my boyfriend, and he was not."

Her brow furrowed as she further considered what he said about couples' discussions. "Why not discuss previous relationships? Analyzing past behaviors can be used as teaching tools to avoid repeated errors in the future."

As he thought about how to explain it to her, she picked up her cocoa and used her index finger to swipe more Reddi-wip off the top. Watching her lick it off her fingertip wasn't helping his brain function more clearly.

"Past relationships are taboo," Gabriel explained. "That's just the way it is. Guys don't want to hear about their current girlfriends buffing other guys, and women don't want to hear about their current boyfriends boning other women."

"He was not my boyfriend. Why must I repeat myself with you and your family? Is intellectual disability common in your genealogy?"

When he coughed into the Reddi-wip and it clung to his nose and cheeks, he could tell he wasn't helping to alleviate her doubts of his lineage. He set his mug on the table and pulled his shirt off, wiping his face for the second time.

"It sounds better than fuck buddy, Ava. Christ. What do you call him?"

"I call him Vincent."

Taking a deep breath, somewhere between laughing maniacally and wanting to slam his fist into a wall, Gabriel said, "To answer your question, I guess it's a jealousy thing."

"I do not get jealous," Ava said, taking another sip of her cocoa. "It is a petty emotion."

He chuckled as he tossed his shirt into the laundry basket. "That doesn't stop men and women from feeling it."

"Does it make you jealous?"

"No," he said slowly. "I trust what we have. It just... feels weird to talk to you so openly about a guy you used to have sex with."

Ava set her cocoa down and studied him, frowning again. "You are all so busy with your irrational emotions." She made that wavy motion with her hands at the side of her head again, as if she were hearing something that was too loud. "I do not know how you get anything else done."

"Do you pick up on people's emotions?" he asked. "Is that part of it?"
She nodded.

Isabel, he suddenly thought. He told Isabel everything. Would he have trouble keeping Ava's ability from his sister?

He wanted to ask her so many questions, but he wanted to be respectful. Prodding her about this might push her away. And he had been interrogating her for over an hour. Exhaustion was making him irritable, making his eyes feel gritty.

Instead, he unlaced his fingers from hers and stroked her hand.

"You could have told me. You didn't have to be alone with this."

"Being alone is what I am accustomed to."

"You're with me now."

Her eyes had taken on the intense focus of when she was curious about something. She studied his hand moving over hers. Gabriel felt a wave of affection at how fascinated something like human touch made her.

"If I... find out what happened to Hayden, do you want me to tell you?"

His hand stopped moving instantly. "What do you mean?"

Ava pulled her hand back. It had suddenly gone cold. "I have seen Hayden."

• • • • •

"What do you mean," he repeated slowly, "you've seen her?"

As it always did, discussing her ability was laborious. She leaned back against the pillows, pulling her knees up to her chest. "She started coming to me the night I moved to Langdon."

"How... how did you know it was her?"

Ava hugged her knees tighter. "At first I did not know. The night you found me at her grave, it was because she led me there."

Gabriel felt as if he had been slugged in the gut. He swallowed, remembering how he hadn't wanted to be alone that night. How she had stood next to him while he knelt at Hayden's grave, his mind moving through memories so quickly that even now, he couldn't remember a single one.

"I tried to read you when I took your hand. I thought if I could give you information to comfort you, I would not be so drawn to you. But I felt nothing. I had no control over it at that time. I only have minimal control over it now."

Stunned, he didn't know what to say. In theory, he was fully willing to support her. Thinking of his sister wandering around him, trying to communicate with his girlfriend, however, was a little harder to grasp.

Ava continued, "She was eleven or twelve when she died, with long hair tied back into a single braid. Her eyes were denim blue, the same color as yours."

"You could have gotten that information from the news." Gabriel's throat was desperately dry. His tongue seemed glued to the roof of his mouth. Sweat had gathered under his arms and at the small of his back, ice cold against his skin.

She answered in a steely tone, "I do not need to prove my ability to you. I am telling you what I have seen."

"You're right. I'm sorry." He ran a hand through his hair, exhaled. "This is all... really damn new to me."

"She is always wearing a Harry Potter nightgown."

That startled him, she could tell. The picture they showed of Hayden on the news was a school picture with her hair loose around her shoulders, not one taken in her pajamas with her hair braided.

"She loved Harry Potter," he said, taking a drink of cocoa. His hands were not quite steady now. "She read the first book three times and watched the movie in the theater twice. The only one out at the time was the first one."

Scrubbing his hands down his face, he said softly, "That nightgown was the one she was wearing when she went missing. Jesus Christ."

"Do you want to know?" Ava asked evenly, studying him. She was tired of discussing it, tired deep in her soul.

"It would give Mom and Beth closure. I guess it probably would for Isabel and me as well. But don't... ah... go to any trouble looking for the answer."

She nodded, satisfied. She had finished her cocoa. "I am going to sleep."

But as he lay beside her, thinking about what it would mean to find out what actually happened to Hayden so many years ago, he couldn't get to sleep. His mind was tearing through possibilities. What if they actually found his sister's body? What if they could have a real burial, a place to visit that didn't feel hollow because he knew damn well it was empty? To be able to lay her bones to rest after all these years and know with absolution what happened... would that be better? Or worse because he knew without a doubt now that it was over, and she was dead?

"Shut up."

Ava's voice startled him out of his contemplation. "What?" he asked gruffly.

"You are thinking too loud. Shut up and go to sleep."

•　•　•　•　•

The sound of a guitar greeted Griffin as he reached the door of his flat. Smiling, relieved, he quietly walked in, hoping not to disturb Isabel as she played.

She was sitting in a wingback chair in the living room with her back to him, unaware he'd come home, singing unabashedly. It was the first time he had heard her sing while totally relaxed. For a moment he stood in the kitchen, holding the briefcase with his laptop, watching her.

Her hair was pulled back into a loose ponytail, which was draped over her shoulder. From where he was standing, he couldn't see much more than her shoulders and the exposed back of her neck, but that was enough to eliminate all the moisture from his mouth and make his pulse do a violent hiccup. He lowered his bag to the floor and walked as quietly as he could toward her.

Afraid of startling her, he stepped around the chair, only to find her eyes were closed as she sang and strummed the guitar. For the first time since he had met her, her face was relaxed while she was awake. Her body rocked gently to the beat of the song, something slow and beautiful that he didn't recognize.

Transfixed by her performance, Griffin lowered himself to the coffee table. Her body swayed ever so slightly as her long fingers gracefully moved over the chords. Even as her body was moving, her bare foot was tapping. She continued to sing, unaware he was there.

She did a final strum on the guitar, sat for a moment with her head tilted just a little, then opened her eyes.

Griffin felt a flutter in his stomach. His chest tightened until taking a breath was almost impossible. Something about the way she sang when she was free of self-doubt changed the way she looked, but he couldn't say exactly how. Or maybe it had changed the way he saw her. For just a few seconds, the weight of the world had been lifted from her shoulders, smoothing the lines of worry from her face. She went from being beautiful to being absolutely stunning.

Her eyes were locked on his and he couldn't tell what she was thinking. The moment spun out. Aware that the silence was becoming ridiculously long, he forced himself to speak.

"I'm glad you're here." It was the best he could do while his brain tried to recoup.

Isabel set her guitar aside, leaning it against the end table. "I wasn't sure I should come. We didn't really have plans."

The apartment was oddly quiet without her music. Griffin cleared his throat and the sound seemed extraordinarily loud in the living room.

"You're always welcome here. That's why I gave you a key."

Holding her gaze, he shifted off the coffee table onto his knees in front of her. Moving at an agonizingly slow pace, he slid his arms along her legs so he could cup her hips. His mouth was a breath away from hers.

"What are you doing?" she asked, her voice not quite steady.

"Just looking at you." His tawny eyes roamed her face. Something, he thought, was happening here, something amazing. He was sure she felt it, too. Her voice, for once, didn't have that hard edge to it. Everything inside her was at peace. She accepted everything about herself as she was, and knew whatever was happening between them was real, and nothing to be afraid of.

When he kissed her, it spoke of passion and need, but also of unconditional love. His mouth was firm and hot, and she thought it a wonder hers didn't ignite on contact. It was the mating of lips that songs and poetry were written about. Slow, intense, thorough. The kind that crossed circuits in her brain and left her feeling intoxicated.

He leaned back, just enough to separate their lips. Her eyes were out of focus.

"Have you eaten?" he asked.

"What?" She blinked, trying to shift topics, still feeling the pressure of his mouth on hers.

"I'm meeting my parents for dinner. I want you to come with me."

Isabel was still trying to stop her head from spinning. What the hell had that been? That had been more than simple lust, and now he was talking about food?

"Okay." Never mind that she could barely hold her head up at the moment.

As he rose, he gripped her arms and kissed her again in that same way, making her legs feel as if they couldn't hold her weight. He brought them both up to standing. After a moment, he pulled back. He brushed his thumb across her cheek, still holding her in that profound gaze.

"Okay," she said again.

His mouth twitched.

"Are you ready to go, then?"

Blinking, she swallowed. "I'm going to need a few minutes."

·   ·   ·   ·   ·

"I want to stay on the mats for our discussion this afternoon," Ava's teacher said after class.

"Hai, Sensei."

She agreed without question, he noted, and wondered if that immediate obedience would continue through their discussion.

"Do you need a few minutes before we start?"

Shaking her head, she said, "No, Sensei," and gracefully curled herself into the full lotus position.

"The night you attacked me in the dojo," he said, watching her frown, "something happened that needs to be discussed."

"I do not remember attacking you."

"I know. That's what needs to be discussed."

Daniel watched her closely. She was distracted again tonight. That could work in his favor or make things much worse.

Ava shifted, uncomfortable. "I do not understand how I can discuss something with you that I do not remember."

"It's not you I want to talk to."

Understanding dawned in her eyes. Fear followed close behind.

"I..."

Although she fluidly unwound her legs from the lotus position, her back had gone very rigid. She shifted into a kneeling position, sitting on her lower legs and feet. Clasping her hands in her lap, she refused to look at him.

"I have no control over... that," she said.

"Ava, look at me."

After a pause, she raised her head and locked eyes with his. Inside her gaze, he saw the young child she had been six months into her training; eager to please but so afraid to trust. Her eyes were full of misery. She had such expressive eyes, Daniel thought. He should have known sooner when something else was controlling her just by looking into her eyes.

"There is something that comes to you when you're being attacked."

She flinched. Dropping her gaze slightly, she stared somewhere between his stomach and his chest.

"I think it started coming to you when you were very young, to protect you from the horrible things you endured as a child."

She had gone very still. Daniel was reminded of an animal sniffing for a predator; the unblinking eyes, the frozen posture, the shallow breaths that barely raised her chest with each inhale. Like prey, she was silent, waiting to see if she was in danger or if it was a false alarm.

"I can speak to it, but I have to make you feel threatened to do it."

The only part of her body that moved were her eyes. Ava slowly rolled them until they locked on his again. The fear was gone. He saw understanding and something else that made him falter for just a moment. Betrayal.

"I don't want to hurt you," he said. "Whatever takes over does so only when you feel you're in danger."

"Hai, Sensei."

The total submission in her tone made him break eye contact and turn his head to the side, swearing under his breath. He had given this theory hours of thought, days of thought, trying to find another way. If he had a gentler way to do it, he would have. She would do it because he asked her to, and she trusted him. And he hated himself for it.

"Unless you can give up your control and call it forward," he said, knowing she couldn't. He would have bet ownership of his dojo that she had been at war with the thing she called The Monster since it had shown up when she was a child. Because Ava didn't like not being in control. Even as a child she preferred command over herself, feeling every cut and bruise, to submitting her will to something else and forgetting it all. She had spent too much of her life without any choices about what happened in it.

"I won't do anything without your permission, Ava. But I think you want command over yourself as much as I want to know what is invading you. I need you to trust me."

"I trust you, Sensei."

Her tone indicated that she didn't particularly like him at the moment.

She stood, waiting for him to begin whatever he thought was necessary.

Daniel stood, keeping his distance for the time being. "Sometimes you feel it coming, right? You try to stop it. Other times it happens so fast, you don't even know it's been inside you."

She nodded.

"We need to start slowly to give you a chance to break out of it."

"I cannot-"

"You can," he insisted. He took a step toward her and wasn't offended when she took a step back. "You already have, Ava. You're stronger than you think. It's come over you in the dojo more than you realize and you've come out of it. I believe it's your strength that pushes it away."

From her expression, she looked doubtful, but when he stepped toward her this time, she stood her ground. Her breathing became labored. She held her hands at her sides, as she did when she was at attention in the dojo, listening to instruction.

"I won't hurt you," he soothed, knowing he wasn't the one she was afraid of.

As he circled behind her, her breathing became even more erratic. Her body began to tremble as she fought the urge to follow his progression and prepare to defend herself. She shut her eyes tight and waited for it to be over.

Silently, Daniel continued around Ava, studying her body language, watching her breathing escalate until she was in danger of hyperventilating. He was starting to circle her again when her eyelids sprang open, revealing black pools instead of eyes. She snarled at him. Instantly one leg slid back, and she stood in a stance, her hands ready to defend herself.

"There you are," he said mildly. "What should I call you?"

"You know who I am," it said, pivoting to follow his movements as he continued to circle Ava's body. It maintained a defensive posture as it followed him.

"I know what Ava calls you. I want to know your name."

"Names mean nothing," it snapped. Its eyes roamed around the room, taking in Daniel's distance from it and its own freedom from bondage. "Call me Humpty Dumpty, for all I care. Why am I here?"

"You don't know?" Daniel asked. "You don't know everything Ava knows?"

He paced deliberately around Ava. Her body turned, following him, eyes ever alert.

"I came because I sensed she was afraid. Everything else is static."

"Interesting."

"Why am I here?" it growled. "Obviously, she isn't in danger. I don't enjoy being summoned like a dog."

"Ava doesn't appreciate being used like a puppet."

Daniel kept his voice even and continued circling, switching so he was walking clockwise now. Ava's body adjusted so the thing inside her could keep her eyes on him as he moved.

"You attacked me last week during training. Why can't she remember anything when you take over?"

The thing wearing Ava's face sneered. "Because she is weak. When I first came to her, the man had raped her. She gave herself to me easily. After that, anytime they hurt her, she ran away to hide and let me take over."

"She was five years old."

With a shrug, Ava's head tilted. "Excuses."

"But sometimes she can remember."

"Sometimes she doesn't hide."

Daniel pondered that. "I think you're lying."

It snarled. The pulse in Ava's throat throbbed.

"Ava wasn't afraid when you attacked me last week. You invaded her just before I began my technique. You were looking for an excuse to get her to fight me."

"I don't even know you."

But Ava's head shifted away, avoiding him. The blackness in Ava's eye sockets shimmered.

"Not personally. Maybe someone like me? Maybe you're the spirit of some kid that was bullied at school, so you were all too happy to help Ava when she was being abused. Maybe you have daddy issues you need to work out, and that's why you attacked me last week."

Ava's body lunged at him, her jaw snapping like a rabid dog's. Daniel easily took a step back to elude her.

"Ava, can you hear me?"

He stopped, facing her directly. Her eye sockets seemed to be smoldering, little whisps like black ash floating up from her face. But something else was there... something fighting to break through. Daniel couldn't tell if he actually saw something or if it was just a feeling he had.

"She's run away to her little hiding place," The Monster said with obvious disdain.

"She doesn't need you. Ava? It's Sensei. I know you're in there. I need you to fight."

"What are you doing?"

"Listen to my voice. Listen to yourself. You can do this."

"Stop it," The Monster said. "You fucking selfish idiot human."

"Fight it, Ava."

"I'll give you a fight."

Ava dove into a forward roll that eliminated the distance between her and Daniel, ending it with a crouched stance and shoving her palm into his chin. Having anticipated the attack, he pivoted in time to avoid most of the strike but was hit hard enough to be reminded of how strong Ava was. Even as he countered the next blow, he felt pride at how far she'd come from the scared, furious little girl she'd been at the age of seven.

Whatever had taken over Ava used her muscle memory, confirming Daniel's theory that it did more than sense her emotions. It came at him using everything in Ava's arsenal from every level of style she had studied. Daniel only blocked her techniques to prevent injury. He refused to harm her in any way. This seemed to infuriate whatever was inside her. As it tried to beat Daniel back across the mats and failed, he saw the blackness in the eyes was fading, turning to gray.

"Ava, you're stronger than it is. Fight it."

"Fight me, you chicken shit," The Monster snapped. "Pick on someone your own size."

The last word was in Ava's voice. Her eyes widened as she completed a strike The Monster had started, her pupils dilated but the consuming blackness gone. Daniel blocked the punch and tapped her to the side just enough to throw her off balance.

Turning back to him, she bowed deep. "Sumi-"

Her body snapped into a standing position and her voice deepened. "We don't bow to anyone!"

She let out a final snarl that sounded more confused than angry. Shaking her head, Ava pressed the heel of her hand to her temple, closing her eyes.

Daniel reached out and took her hand. She let out a strangled cry almost too soft to hear. Her breath was coming in short, husky pants. When she raised her head to look at him, he saw The Monster glaring through her. But she was holding it back.

"That's good," he soothed, squeezing her hand. "It only has power if you give it. You are in control."

A shudder wracked her body. She was drenched in sweat. After a few moments, her breath began evening out, erasing any traces of The Monster in her eyes.

Her legs gave out. She dropped to her knees, hard. Daniel followed her down, keeping his hand on her shoulder. Crouching next to her, he waited as she came back to herself.

"That was informative," he said, when she took a deep breath and let it out. She nodded.

Surprised, he squeezed her hand. "You were aware?"

"I saw everything."

"I think it's your choice whether you remember or not," he said, standing to get her a bottle of water. "You decide if you stay close enough to the surface to know what's going on, or go inside so deep, you achieve sensory deprivation. When you don't remember, it's because your consciousness literally wasn't there."

Nodding again, she accepted the water from him and began gulping it down. Sensei pressed down on the end of the bottle to slow her progress.

"Calm down."

Closing her eyes, Ava rested her palm on her forehead and her elbow on her knee. She was unbelievably exhausted. Every muscle in her body ached.

The areas around her stitches were itching, and even her ankle, which had finally stopped aching, was starting to throb. At least her knee and right hand were mostly healed, giving her two less injuries to tend to.

Sensei leaned down and took her hand and arm to help her stand.

"That's enough for now. I'll drive you to Vincent's apartment."

She jerked. "No."

Embarrassed, Ava took a step back and apologized in Japanese. She could feel the blood rushing to her face and that made her even more uncomfortable. She had nothing to be ashamed of, yet her body was betraying her once again with those damned human emotions.

"I do not need to go to Vincent's apartment," she said, taking another wobbly step toward the entrance to the changing room. "I h-have a... I am fine."

He gave her a look that left no room for argument. "You shouldn't drive. You can barely stand up."

"I cannot go to Vincent's." Ava's voice was firm. "I have a m-mate."

It took Daniel a moment to realize what she meant.

"You mean a boyfriend?"

She nodded, leaning back against the door. Suddenly, she looked very shy.

"Oh." He was stunned. He was delighted. He let neither show on his face. Being in a relationship wouldn't be a problem; adults of different genders could be friends, but she was uncompromising about the issue. "Can I drop you off at your boyfriend's house?"

Frowning, Ava resembled a stubborn toddler arguing about bedtime. "Gabriel lives nineteen point two miles away. We both live in Langdon. I am fine."

She finished off the water and glanced around for a recycle bin.

"Ava."

Glancing up at him, she walked toward him when he motioned toward her water bottle.

"I'm not going to be responsible for your-"

As she handed it to him, their fingers brushed together. A vibration like electricity moved through them and Ava suddenly knew she was watching events happen through Sensei's eyes, even though she saw both as him and as if she was watching a movie of him.

The small coffin was being lowered into the ground. The process seemed to take forever, disappearing down a black hallway of dirt and insects that would eventually feed on his son.

Ava's inhale was sharp. Her hand clenched the water bottle, locking Daniel's fingers between hers and the plastic.

He looked over at his wife. She wasn't crying. Her eyes were dull and out of focus from some pills her sister had given her. Someone was standing just behind her, a member of her family that Daniel didn't recognize – an aunt? A cousin? He didn't know. The rustling of fall leaves made him think of Danny playing in them, and the grief seemed so huge it swallowed him whole.

Everything went black.

Now he stood in the bedroom, where his wife had killed herself. She knew that day at the funeral, when she had stared at their son being lowered into the ground. Even as the fog had kept her thoughts from fully forming, she knew she was going to swallow the entire bottle of pills her sister had left, and she would see Danny again. So the funeral wasn't so bad, it wasn't so awfully bad because she would see her son again soon.

He stood over the bed where she had lain and swallowed all those pills and he felt nothing, not a damn thing for her. It was a selfish act, leaving him to grieve alone. Leaving him to pack Danny's and her belongings and take them to Goodwill or Saint Vincent de Paul's. The anger he felt for her paled in comparison to the loss he felt for his son.

Blackness again.

The dojo, his life. Training. Day in, day out. Every day he woke up, trained, trained his students. Visited Danny's grave. Visited his wife's grave because it was next to his son's and he thought Danny would have wanted him to. He slept little. Ate even less. Repeated the next day. And the next.

Winter.

Spring.

Summer.

More blackness.

Twilight. He was sitting in the dojo, stretching. What else was there to do when he didn't have a class? He was thinking of his son's hands, how tiny they were when he curled them into fists during training. The car drove up quickly, the brakes screeching as it skidded to a stop right in front of his business. He stood and started toward the door, intent on telling the driver they couldn't park there. It wasn't that he cared; it was simply a break in his unending routine. It would pass some time.

A middle-aged woman scrambled out, opening the back passenger door of the car. Daniel couldn't see her clearly in the dark and because she was moving so quickly. Someone exited the back seat of car with effort, holding onto what looked like a wild animal that thrashed in his arms.

As they stepped away from the car, the lights from the dojo hit them and Daniel recognized the man. David Reid, a man who had lived in his neighborhood when he was a young child. David had always allowed Daniel to watch him tinker in his garage. He was the one who taught him about using tools, working on vehicles, fixing things around the house. They had kept in contact over the years; the last Daniel knew, David and his wife were fostering children.

The entire entourage headed for the locked door of the dojo.

Daniel unlocked and opened the door as they hurried toward him and saw the hurricane in David's arms was a small girl. She had a cast on one wrist, but she was fighting brutally. David already had cuts on one cheek from where her nails had raked across his skin. His left eye was bruised, his lip cut open, and his shirt torn. His wife, whom Daniel had met only a couple times, had cuts all over her face. Both eyes were bruised, and one was swollen almost shut.

"She needs help," David said calmly when Daniel ushered them into the dojo, locking the door behind him.

Blackness.

She saw herself as a child, thrashing, kicking, biting, screaming as Sensei held her. He sat on the floor of the dojo with her in his lap, pinning her hands and legs, and rocked gently as she took out all her rage. Although his face was neutral, his hands unyielding, empathy and affection were radiating off him strongly. They were so strong that in the Meditation Room, Ava began trembling.

Blackness.

With the next vision came acceptance. A young Ava lay at an angle in Sensei's lap on the floor. Ava remembered the day very well. It was the day she had given up fighting him and resigned herself to whatever he chose to do with her.

Because of his long arms, he had started out pressing her arms against her body just above the elbow to prevent her from continuing to damage her wrist. He then kept her back close to his stomach and looped one leg over her ankles. By the time she'd stopped struggling, her good arm was at an angle to his, her small hand gripping his forearm. Sensei's leg was stretched out along Ava's, but he no longer restrained her ankles. She was winded, her hair plastered to her face, but she wasn't struggling.

Ava remembered sitting on the floor for a long time like that. She remembered waiting for the man to hurt her. She remembered all the strange things she felt from him that did not hurt her body but made her head feel sore and tired. At that point, she had no idea what her ability was, and she had no concept of how dull the psyches of people like Mack and Janine were. She was not used to the steady mental chatter of an educated man like Sensei.

And that was just the intellectual side.

The emotions emanating from him were so overwhelming that in the Meditation Room, Ava felt dizzy. He had been captivated that she had fought so long for so hard these past few weeks, but also proud that she had finally accepted he was not going to let her go. Eagerness to start training her was very loud in his head. And something clanged around in his head like a church bell, something her adult self was surprised to feel from her teacher – love. It was a feeling so pure and compelling, there was no questioning it. It was as absolute as water being wet and fire being hot. Everything he felt for his son was poured into her recovery from the day she arrived in the dojo.

In the Meditation Room, Ava stepped back. Contact was broken.

Her head hurt.

Daniel slowly leaned down to pick up the empty bottle that had fallen to the floor when Ava backed away. He wasn't sure what she had seen, but the feelings stirring inside him were the ones he'd had during the first year after he lost his son and the first few weeks after he'd taken her on as a student. She had so many emotions swimming inside her, and now his were inside her as well.

"You..." She swallowed. "You did not tell David your son was dead when he brought me to you."

"Knowing would have clouded his judgment and he wouldn't have asked for my help," Daniel said. "You needed help, not self-pity."

"You did not treat me like your other students."

Unsure if he was capable of speech at the moment, he shook his head.

"You treated me like a daughter. Your daughter. You still do."

Ava was fascinated by the concept. Sensei had not known her when she was first brought to his dojo sixteen years ago. She should have meant nothing to him. No familial connection tied them. He had no obligation to take on the arduous task of rehabilitating her, an orphan physically and psychologically damaged.

"I lost my son," he said, his voice thick with emotion, "so I took all the energy I was putting into my grief for him and focused it into making sure you didn't stay lost inside yourself. I tried to give you a chance at a life. You deserved a chance."

Words made it sound so simple. Yet what Ava had felt from him moments ago was endless patience when she refused to speak, pride when even a simple obstacle was overcome, and unrelenting strength that had helped her survive on countless occasions. All were priceless gifts that could never be repaid. And he had given them freely when everything had been taken from him.

"You look a little better now," Sensei said gently. "You should be okay to drive when you're ready."

"Hai, Sensei."

Feeling disoriented, Ava left the mats to get her belongings. She had never sensed those things from Sensei, she thought, as she put her jacket on and zipped her duffel bag. All these years working with him, she had never felt anything from him. Having all that information suddenly inside her head and all the emotion slammed into her body made her head disconcerted.

She exited the changing room and crossed the mats to leave. Sensei was sitting under the kamidana, watching her as he stretched.

"Ava."

She stopped at the bench on the other side of the mat to put her shoes on. "Hai, Sensei?"

"Having a boyfriend is a pretty big step for you. Congratulations."

The rise of color in her cheeks almost made him smile. She thanked him, hesitantly, in Japanese, unsure if that was proper etiquette.

"You've made a lot of positive changes this year," he said.

Agreeing in Japanese, she looked doubtful as she tied her laces. Lifting her duffel bag, she bowed to him and told him good night in Japanese. Her hand was on the door when he said her name again.

Turning back, she kept her expression neutral in spite of her wish to go home and wash the sweat off. It was late and she was tired.

Sensei was watching her intently.

"If my son had lived, my feelings for you wouldn't have changed."

Her eyebrows knit together in confusion.

"I would have trained you the same, treated you the same, and loved you the same even if Danny didn't die. You were never a surrogate."

As her gaze bored into him, he saw too many emotions flashing across her face. Unable to control them, she pushed the door open behind her and bowed again.

"Good night, Sensei."

•   •   •   •   •

This was the part Gabriel loved the best – when the wood beneath his hands began to look like what he had envisioned in his head. He blew sawdust off the wood, brushed his gloved hand over it to get any stubborn shavings. It was starting to look like the spindle he'd drawn for his client; elegant, slender. It was one of several hundred he had to make for the client; she wanted each one for her grand staircase to be hand-crafted, so the work was going to last him several weeks. The work was repetitive and somewhat mindless once his hands became used to the pattern.

For now, his day was finished. It was time to crack open a beer and maybe call Ava to see what she was up to.

He left the partially finished spindle in the lathe and covered it with a tarp.

All his tools had a place in his garage, and he set about putting everything away as he thought about Ava. She'd been gone by the time he woke this morning. Although he understood she woke earlier than he did, he felt a pang of regret that she hadn't roused him before leaving. He assumed she went home to get ready for work. Possibly get a few hours of a workout done, too, if the weekend was any indicator of her normal schedule. Still... couldn't she have at least said goodbye?

Maybe that was expecting too much. Hadn't she said she'd never stayed overnight with anyone before him?

He found himself wondering how her day had gone, how training went. Did she enjoy the work she did? Had she chosen it because it gave her the least face to face contact with people? Tonight, he might ask her.

Locking up the garage, his mind wandered as he walked toward the house for a shower. He was surprised to see Ava's SUV in the driveway. And even more surprised to see her still sitting in it. How long had she been here?

As soon as she saw him, she opened the door and slid out of her vehicle. Even from a distance he caught the light scent of whatever shampoo and soap she used and the unique outdoors smell that always lingered on her skin, as if she had just stepped out of nature. All were enhanced by the scent of natural growth that was beginning as spring made its way to south central Wisconsin.

"How long have you been here?" he asked, leaning in to kiss her cheek.

"Not long."

"Did you hear the lathe? Why didn't you come get me?"

Slipping an arm around her waist, he tried not to be offended when she stiffened. They began walking toward the house and Gabriel nonchalantly eased away from her.

"I was not sure I wanted to come in."

"Did you have a difficult day?"

They walked onto his porch. He hadn't been inside since late afternoon, so the light wasn't on. When he reached to open the door, Ava took his hand and pulled him gently back.

"Can we stay out here a little longer?"

"Of course. Just let me turn on the light-" He turned back to open the door again and she didn't let go of his hand.

"I want it dark."

Turning back to her, he tried to figure out what she was thinking. It was too dark to see her expressions, which she kept neutral even if he could see them. He could feel something from her, but he wasn't sure what it was.

"I need to set my chairs out here," he said, unsure what else to do. Her hand was still in his, but he was hesitant to touch her anywhere else after her reaction to his earlier embrace.

Finally, tired of wondering, he said, "You left without saying anything this morning."

"What am I supposed to say?"

That made him smile. So, it had been inexperience. After he confronted her about being psychic, an entire lifetime of possibilities of why she left had gone through his head, none of them pleasant. In the end, it was simple, non-threatening ignorance.

"It's not really... ah... I wasn't sure if you were still upset about me finding out about you being psychic."

That wasn't everything, but at least it was a start.

"We discussed the subject last night."

"I know but, well, sometimes women say they're over something and they're not."

"That is a ridiculous habit. I do not speak unless I mean what I am saying. I am confident we reached an agreeable understanding during our discussion. Do you feel differently?"

His mouth twitched. "No, I think we understand each other just fine."

"Okay, then." She stood at the edge of the porch and crossed her arms over her chest.

"That's not all," he confessed, leaning against one of the posts. "When couples spend the night together, it's customary for the first awake to let the one still sleeping know when he or she leaves the house."

"Why?"

"It's the polite thing to do."

Ava was quiet for a moment. "You humans act civil when it suits you and use excuses like alcohol or emotions when civility confuses you. It is hard to keep up with customs ruled by your moods."

"Fuck manners, then. It unnerved me. You got out of bed and got dressed and I didn't hear any of it."

She could hear the dismay in his voice; he wasn't angry. He was disturbed, as if he woke up to find her missing instead of just having left to go home.

"My survival depends on being silent."

It used to, he thought. It shouldn't anymore. You shouldn't have to defend yourself.

Running a hand through his hair, he turned toward her and leaned his shoulder against the column. "You do it in the middle of the night. When you sleepwalk, I never know until you're already out of bed. It's... eerie."

"I will sleep in my own bed, so I do not disturb you."

"That's not what I'm saying, Ava."

"What are you saying?"

Shoving off the column, Gabriel walked to the other end of the porch and back. "I'm saying I need to get used to your habits. That takes time. I'm saying... I would appreciate it if you let me know you were leaving in the morning."

She opened her mouth to remind him that she had not wanted to be obligated to him, that the very reason she did not engage in relationships was because she refused to be beholden to anyone. A sudden realization made her shut her mouth with a snap.

His sister had disappeared in the night the same way. He went to bed knowing she was there and woke up to find her missing.

Obligation had nothing to do with it. What a shock that must have been. And she had made him feel the same way by being inconsiderate. She wondered if he realized where his uneasiness originated.

In the silence that followed, he felt her staring at him. He could see her head was tilted slightly, as she did when she was studying someone. Not for the first time, he wondered what she was thinking when she stared at him so long.

"Will you come inside with me?"

"Alright."

Gabriel opened the door and stepped in. Everything inside him balked at walking in first, but there was nothing he could do about it. Ava wouldn't budge on this. So, he forced himself to walk to the kitchen, turning on lights as he made his way through the house. As usual, he didn't hear Ava's boots on the floor behind him and had to trust that she was there.

Without asking, he put ice into a glass and filled it with water, letting the silence get comfortable between them. How odd that he had found it so disconcerting when he first met her, and now it was as natural to him as brushing his teeth every morning.

"When do you train with your Sensei?" he suddenly asked, realizing he didn't know much about her normal, daily routines.

The little wrinkles between her eyebrows amused him.

"It's just conversation, Ava." He slid the glass of water across the counter. Turning back to the refrigerator, he pulled out a Leinie's original and grabbed a lighter off the top of the fridge.

"On Monday and Wednesday afternoons, I have private Kung Fu lessons. On Thursday evenings, I train with Vincent on Ninpo."

Gabriel angled the lighter under the bottle cap and sent it flying. Because she seemed anxious and feeling caged in, he asked, "Do you want to sit on the deck? It's nice out tonight."

"Alright."

"I'm going to grab a shower, but I'll meet you out there in ten."

He was done in eight, and when he walked to the dining room patio doors, he saw Ava hadn't turned on the lights. Tired of not being able to see her, he brushed his hand against the switches and joined her on the deck.

She was perched on the railing again, her arms around her knees. Her glass of water sat a few inches away.

Gabriel didn't want to touch her and risk her twisting like she had before, so he kept his distance. He walked casually to the railing a couple feet away and leaned his elbows on it, dangling his beer over the edge.

"Did you have a bad day?"

She didn't look at him. "That is not what you want to ask me."

Cocking his head, he turned so only one elbow rested on the railing. "Is that so?"

"Just ask."

"If you already know what I'm going to ask, why don't you just answer?"

"I do not know what you are going to ask," she said sharply. "I only know you are not asking about what you feel."

He nodded. "This will take some getting used to." After a moment: "Why don't you want me to touch you?"

"I do not want anyone to touch me."

The answer was quick and automatic, and Gabriel had to bite back a sarcastic remark.

Ava took a silent deep breath in, let it out long and slow. "I am not used to explaining myself."

He shifted, ready to defend his curiosity, but she hurriedly continued before he could.

"You are trying to adjust to my idiosyncrasies. I will also try to adjust."

She reached out and squeezed his hand briefly before pulling back.

"I told you I have been working after class with Sensei regarding my psychic ability. He is trying to help me gain control over it."

Gabriel sipped his beer, wondering if this teacher was more to Ava than her martial arts instructor. He could tell she had a high respect for him, but he seemed to be doing more than his duties in the class. Was he a family friend? A distant relative?

"I picked up strong emotions during today's... session... and now my body is agitated." She spoke as if it pained her to do so.

"Agitated how?"

"I am taking everything in, and I cannot shut it off." She shuddered. "Every emotion..."

"Is it painful for you to be here right now?" he asked.

Hesitantly, she nodded.

"Why did you come here?" He set his beer to the side. He had to stop himself from going to her, taking her in his arms. "Why didn't you go home and keep away from people for a while until your body calms down?"

"It is my problem. You did not cause this."

"I'm making it worse for you."

Gabriel took a step back to give her space, but her voice stopped him from further retreat.

"I wanted to see you."

He wanted to high-five himself. Instead, he kept the smug smile from his face and tried to redirect the conversation. "What was going on when you were working with your teacher?"

Ava dropped gently to the deck. He gave her time to deal with her discomfort of the subject. She turned away from him and trailed her fingers along the railing of the deck as she walked a few feet away. She did the same when she walked back.

"I read him."

Her voice was almost too soft to hear.

"You what?"

"I read my Sensei."

"What does that mean?"

Her hair had fallen forward in a protective curtain around her face.

"I touched him and saw our relationship through his eyes. When David brought me to him, my teacher's son had recently died. But he took me on anyway and trained me. He loves me like a daughter."

So, it was a deeper relationship than teacher and student, Gabriel thought. A powerful one. It relieved him to know she had someone like that on her side after the childhood she had.

"Come with me."

Ava watched him walk toward the glass doors. After a moment, she picked up her water and followed him.

He led her to the living room, where he sat on the sofa and set his beer on the table. Confused, she sat stiffly at the other end and set her water aside. She rested her hands flat on her thighs and waited cautiously.

"You don't do very well with emotion or physical affection," Gabriel said, sliding closer. He saw her eyes shift to monitor him.

"I do not see what-"

"I'll get to that. Your childhood was worse than anyone I've ever heard of, and I understand why you shy away from physical affection. I know why you've cut yourself off from feeling anything."

He moved a little closer, resting his arm on the back of the sofa.

Ava glanced at his hand, which was too close to her head to be comfortable. "Add to that, you're psychic, and I think you're an empath as well. The two intertwine, and that really messes you up."

Gabriel reached toward her face, and she blocked him, striking sideways with the back of her hand. They stayed frozen for several seconds, her thumb, index, and middle fingers raised upward, and her remaining fingers curled loosely, the back of her hand pressed firmly against his inner wrist. She raised her eyes to his.

"You know I won't hurt you. You know it. Remind your body."

Carefully, Ava took a deep breath and lowered her hand. Gabriel tucked a strand of hair behind her ear.

"There you go."

Though her body was still stiff, he tugged on her legs until she reluctantly let him pull them up across his thighs. Moving slowly, he untied the laces on her boots and took them off, one by one. They fell to the floor with a solid thunk.

"Do you have cement in those boots?" he asked.

"Of course, n-" she started, then saw the edges of his mouth quivering. "You are joking."

"How are you doing?" he asked, rubbing his hand up and down one thigh. One very sexy, well-muscled thigh.

"My body has released epinephrine, so it is redirecting the blood to my muscles, causing them to shake. My breathing has become shallow. I have a temporary increase in strength and mental clarity."

"Don't hold back on me, now," he said. "Tell me how you really feel."

"I just did."

"I was being sarcastic." He ran his hand along the outside of her leg. It was, indeed, trembling. In his opinion, she hadn't been touched the right way nearly enough in her lifetime. "What does all that mean in English?"

She opened her mouth but before she could tell him she had spoken perfect English, he said, "Tell me in layman's terms."

"It means I am in a state of hypervigilance."

"Why are you so hypervigilant?"

"Because you are too close to me."

Her pupils were dilated, but not so much they made her eyes look black. Just enough to make her look a little wild, like an animal getting ready to bolt.

"Why does that frighten you?"

The withering look she gave him almost made him grin. "I am not afraid of you."

"No, you're afraid of being touched. Am I hurting you?"

"You cannot hurt me." Her voice dripped disdain.

"Then relax."

She was leaning against the arm of the couch. Her legs were at stiff angles over his as he caressed her.

"I do not understand what any of this-"

"Have I hurt you, physically or mentally, since you've known me?"

Gabriel lifted one of her hands, patiently waiting while she resisted allowing him to bring her hand to his lips.

"No," she said.

"No," he agreed. "Yet you still think I will. And you're not hypervigilant because I'm too close to you. You were jacked up before you came here."

He spoke against her wrist, his breath tickling the thin skin there. The sensation made Ava shiver.

"How long have you known Sensei?"

Turning his hand, he linked his fingers with hers. In the soft glow of the lamp light, he could see her gaze begin to shift from agitated to curious.

"S-sixteen years."

"Is he arrogant? Does he use his position to control you?"

"No." She was appalled at the thought; how could anyone think that?

"You trust him."

"With my life."

"Then why does it upset you so much to find out he loves you like family?"

Her hand stiffened in his.

"It's instinct for you to pull away from affection. Even from someone you trust."

"You do not understand... what it costs me to engage in human emotions."

"Explain it to me."

"It is not something I can explain like algebra or biology. Why is this so interesting to you?"

She was pressing back against the arm of the couch. Gabriel instantly felt like an asshole.

"I'm sorry. I didn't mean to bully you."

He separated his fingers from hers and moved back across the sofa, so they were at opposite ends. While trying to get to know her by simply asking questions, he had ended up treating her like her abusive foster parents. He had pushed his methods onto her, thinking he knew what was best. It was as bad as not caring about her and using her to please himself.

"It feels like lapidation," Ava said.

The abrupt sound of her voice in the silence made him jump.

Glancing at her, he saw she had drawn her knees up to her chest and wrapped her arms around them. Despite her solitary posture, her expression was more relaxed. A little distance seemed to calm her down.

"Lapidation?"

"Being stoned to death. Random emotions hitting me from all angles by so many people. Hurting from the inside and outside at the same time."

She shuddered.

"It is not so easy to know what people think. I do not want the constant meaningless chatter that fills my head when I am around people. You are never quiet, any of you. All you do is talk, with your mouths, with your minds. You never shut up. It is too... busy."

She made that motion at the sides of her head again, where she waved her spread fingers beside her ears and closed her eyes.

Gabriel took a gulp of his beer. How painful it must be to interact with people, he thought. No wonder she stayed on her property and only left when it was necessary. Getting to know her wasn't doing her a favor; it was torturing her.

With a sound somewhere between a sigh and groan, she stood, walking to the fireplace. She paced back and forth in front of it.

"I am not explaining it very well."

Gabriel watched her. Clear drops fell from her eyes, hitting the floor as she walked. Ava didn't realize it at first; she kept pacing. As they continued to fall, she raised her hands to her eyes, her fingers fluttering over them.

"What is happening to me?"

She stood, staring at him, as tears rolled down her cheeks, holding her hands up by her face.

"They're just tears, Ava," he said uncertainly, walking to her. He took her arms and held her even when she tried to pull away.

"I do not cry." Astonishment washed over her, making her feel giddy. She held her hands out toward him, showing him her damp fingertips.

"It's okay."

"It is not so bad as before," she said, rubbing her fingertips together and pressing them to her wet cheeks again. "It does not hurt as much as when I first met you."

Gabriel wanted to pick her up and swing her around but was sure she'd lay him out on the floor if he tried.

"You're learning how to deal with emotions."

She rubbed her fingertips onto his cheeks. "Tears!"

"I've never met a woman so happy to be crying."

He used the back of his hand to dry his face off. Watching her walk back to the fireplace, he wondered if she was having a little bit of a breakdown.

Whipping back around toward him, she studied his face. "Why do you cry?"

"I don't, generally."

"People. Why do they cry?"

"I've cracked my elbow against a wall hard enough to bring tears to my eyes," Gabriel said. "But most of the time, it's out of sadness."

He remembered the evening his parents sat everyone down at the kitchen table to tell them the police had declared Hayden's disappearance a cold case. They promised that even though the police had stopped actively searching the woods, they would still follow up on any leads that came in. Gabriel had been drinking a glass of soda at the time, and he stood and threw it at the sink. It shattered, throwing glass everywhere. A shard hit Isabel in the cheek, but she didn't say a word.

"That's bullshit!" he had yelled.

But upstairs, in the privacy of his bedroom, he had lain on his bed and cried. At fourteen, he hadn't known he could feel like his heart was breaking. How had it felt? When they told him the police had given up on Hayden, his body had suddenly felt too small, too full, ready to break at all the emotion raging inside him. And after he began crying? Like the muscles in his chest were being ripped from his body, like his eye lids could no longer hold back what wanted to come pouring out. And when they had finally stopped, he had felt shelled out, empty, weakened.

"I guess," he said carefully, "people cry because we feel an emotion so powerfully, our bodies can't contain it. Crying is the only way to release the pressure."

Ava thought about that. "I am no longer hypervigilant. I believe crying has fulfilled its intended purpose."

Gabriel snorted. "Outstanding. Now that we have that out of the way, what do you want for dinner?"

• • • • •

"How are you doing?" Griffin asked for the fifth time, squeezing Isabel's knee. He glanced over at her, surprised to find her elbow casually propped on the windowsill as she sang along with the radio.

Tilting her head to the side and resting her temple on her hand, she watched him. "Fine. Would you feel better if I had a breakdown?"

She slid her palm over his hand and wound her fingers through his, squeezing just to feel the strength of his muscles.

"No, I'm projecting my own nerves. Sorry. I probably shouldn't have involved you until my family sorts its problems out."

Izzie snorted. "I'd never have met them."

After a moment, he realized what she meant, and grinned. "True. Is Beth doing any better?"

She squeezed his hand. "You're so sweet. I haven't heard anything, so she's at least no worse off than she was before. Mom would have called if she broke a nail."

Griffin thought about the odd Sunday dinner and all the different conversations going on throughout the meal. He remembered Beth asking Ava about working from home, how she stayed focused, and how the conversation had turned into a discussion about discipline, meditation, and taking care of oneself. Griffin had thought at the time that Beth seemed to be looking for any excuse to bring up the subject of personal health. Ava hadn't minced words.

"Ava was pretty hard on your sister at dinner on Sunday."

Isabel leaned forward and turned down the radio. "You think so?"

"Don't you?"

"I think Ava speaks the truth," she said as Griffin pulled into the parking lot of a restaurant. "She can't help it. That's never the wrong thing to do."

Isabel wouldn't normally eat here if she had a bag over her head, her hands bound, and was drugged into submission, judging by the valet parking and the people she saw stepping out of their vehicles. She felt her throat close.

Stopping in front of the building, Griffin leaned across the seat and cupped Izzie's head in his palm. He pulled her to him for a sizzling kiss before releasing her. On legs that weren't quite steady, she slid out of Rover and watched a valet take Griffin's keys and hand him a ticket. He led her inside with a hand on her lower back.

She had never eaten at a restaurant with valet service before.

The next few minutes were a blur. Someone polite but aloof took her jacket. Isabel spaced out and ignored the conversation between Griffin and the maître d'. After a few seconds of small talk, Griffin said they were with the Turner party. She allowed herself to be led to a table near the rear of the restaurant, which was less crowded than the front dining area. Everyone was dressed in expensive clothing, suits and ties and dresses with jewelry that cost more than what Isabel earned in a paycheck. She was wearing jeans and a short-sleeved sweater under a coat she'd been wearing since high school.

Finally, she found herself standing at the table with Griffin's hand in hers, and she began focusing on what was around her just in time to hear his mother's frozen voice cut through her blissful bubble.

"I didn't realize you were bringing a guest."

"Hello, Isabel," Nathan Turner said, standing as Griffin pushed her chair in for her. "What a pleasant surprise."

"Hello, Mr. Turner. It's nice to see you again." Her head was still fuzzy from Griffin's kiss. She set her hands flat on the table to steady herself.

"Nathan, please," he said, touching her hand. He lowered his voice and leaned in close. "I was afraid we had scared you off after our first encounter."

Isabel smirked. "It takes more than family drama to chase me away."

Laughing, Nathan rubbed her shoulder.

Touching came naturally to him, she thought. That's where Griffin got it. It was normal for them to touch whomever they were talking to, to engage with the person on all levels – physically, mentally, emotionally.

Eve, on the other hand, seemed to only want to dominate.

She sat on the other side of the table looking coldly around the room as if she were viewing her subjects.

"Isabel," she said, keeping her tone completely void of emotion.

Iz nodded to acknowledge she had seen the woman and returned her attention to Griffin.

"Griffin," Nathan said, "Good to see you again, son. How are the projects going?"

"I've been coming home late every night," he admitted, thanking the waitress as she set down an ice water for Isabel and him. "Hopefully, it'll slow down soon so I can spend more time with Izzie."

The waitress began taking their orders. While she waited to order, Iz glanced at the woman's shoes. The height of the heels she was wearing would have broken Isabel's ankles. Why would any woman ruin her feet for someone else's opinion? she thought. Or put herself in danger? If she needed to run, or if someone attacked her, the odds of her placing a perfect kick with those spikes were far less probable than a nice thick boot to the groin. Or sneakers. Both covered the foot, were easier to run in, and could pound on someone if they needed to.

Isabel had no idea how to pronounce most of the items on the menu. She asked what ingredients were in three dishes to get an idea what she would be eating. Each time the waitress began telling her what was in them, she grimaced.

"That's nasty," she said, when the waitress gave her an explanation of one particularly disgusting dish. "What about this this one? What's in this?"

Finally, she set her menu aside.

"Do you have romaine lettuce?" she asked the waitress. Under the table, Griffin rested his hand on her thigh.

"I'm sure we can accommodate you, ma'am."

"Praise Jesus. Please put that on a plate with some ranch dressing. Thank you." Under her breath, she muttered, "This isn't a restaurant, it's a torture chamber for animals and poor people."

"Would you like-" the waitress started.

"Just the lettuce and the dressing, please."

"Yes, ma'am. Very good. And for you?" She turned to Griffin and gave him a smile so bright she almost blinded Iz.

Griffin relayed his order before he leaned in close to Izzie. His tone was apologetic. "My mum likes fancy dining."

"I don't understand how she's comfortable sitting through an entire meal with that stick up her ass," Isabel muttered, taking a gulp of her water. "Don't they have cheeseburgers and fries? Who eats this shit? I saw octopus on there, for fuck's sake."

He squeezed her thigh. "I shouldn't have asked you to come. Sorry."

"No, I'm sorry." She took a deep breath. "I'm sure if I was raised with a summoning bell in my hand, I would know how to speak Snob, too."

The waitress left after taking Nathan's orders.

"You've never been to a restaurant like this, I take it?" Eve asked. The icy disdain from her breath practically crackled across the table toward Isabel. She pressed her hand to her neck, where an obviously expensive piece of jewelry hung.

"No. I don't like eating."

Eve gave a haughty laugh. "You don't like to eat?"

Iz mimicked her laugh before removing all emotion from her face and voice. "No."

Griffin smirked.

"How can you not like to eat?" Eve asked, glancing at her husband as if he had the answer.

"It's like loving to eat, only the exact opposite."

Nathan chuckled. "You're funny, Isabel. I can see why Griffin enjoys your company."

Eve didn't appear to agree. Her back remained rigid and her mouth was a constant line of pursed lips.

Conversation continued to be light. Isabel tuned in and out, depending on whether the talk was genuine or polite filler. She didn't feel like drinking for once, so she stuck to her water. She became aware that anything Eve did could turn a person off that activity. She even drank wine pretentiously.

Nathan, however, was as warm and friendly as Griffin. He often touched Isabel's hand as he talked and watched her attentively while he listened. She felt instantly at ease around him. The two looked strikingly similar as well, but Nathan's hair was perfectly tamed. It was strange to see and hear Griffin's behavior without his accent. How had a man so warm and wonderful married such an icy bitch like Eve?

Eve sat beside her husband, but she may as well have been across the room. They never touched, and they never really looked at each other. Eve talked at Nathan, never to him. He was another one of her servants. Where Nathan wanted to know everything about Isabel and Griffin's lives, Eve was only interested in Griffin's job, his status at his job, had he attended any essential functions lately. She actually said functions.

Griffin squeezed her thigh.

She tuned in to find everyone watching her. "Sorry, what?"

"I said, I imagine this is different than the type of place you're used to," Eve said coolly, sipping her wine.

"Oh yeah," Iz snorted. "I wouldn't be caught dead here. Everyone has their nose up everyone else's asshole."

Someone from the next table glanced over. Griffin choked on his wine. Nathan chuckled.

"It's a little too much for me," he agreed. "I prefer to kick back and relax when I'm finally away from work."

"Right?" Isabel said. She really liked him. On any day after work, she could see sitting on a porch, having a drink with him. "And why would anyone want to impress people like this? They wouldn't know fun if it jumped up and bit them in the a-"

"Isabel," Griffin said, somewhere between laughing and still choking, "Tell them about your music."

She smirked. "I doubt anyone here knows anything about my kind of music."

"What about it?" Nathan asked.

"I play guitar." She shrugged. "I like to sing. It's no big deal." She picked up Griffin's wine, had a small sip. It was good. "Ooh, I need a glass of this."

"What style? What genre?" Nathan asked.

"It's not Bach or Mozart or any other classical musical that conceited people have managed to ruin. I prefer music that makes passion flow out of people. If I'm listening to a song, it better inspire me to want to stand on a table and dance, or it's not good music."

"I would pay to see that," Griffin said. He motioned to a waiter and asked for a glass of wine for Izzie.

Isabel blushed to her roots, taking another drink of his wine. "That's not what I meant. I mean, music should evoke powerful feeling, no matter what that feeling is. Sure, Beethoven makes you want to sob uncontrollably, but when Etta James is belting out how her love has finally come along and life is like a song, that gets you in the gut. You can't tell me you don't feel that in your very soul."

She froze, her fist pressed against her stomach. Everyone was staring at her again. Blushing even harder, she gulped the rest of Griffin's wine.

"Anyway, I sing pretty much anything. Rock, alternative, grunge, country. Whatever music expresses the story of the emotion I need to tell in the moment."

"That's brilliant," Nathan said. "I actually agree with you. I hate classical music. I put my headphones on when Eve listens to it."

"I can't stand it."

Everyone's attention turned to Eve. She was sitting with her hands clasped in her lap, staring at Isabel intently. Her body was so rigid, she looked like an arrow ready to be loosed from a bow.

Nathan cleared his throat. "You always listen to-"

"I listen to the music I'm supposed to listen to. I hate it. It reminds me of my parents, all hard edges and sharp sounds."

The table was quiet. Even with the other chatter from nearby tables, the dining area seemed too quiet. Isabel was astonished at the honesty she finally saw in Eve's eyes.

"Then don't listen to it." Finally, she felt like she was talking to a real person.

"Griffin," Eve said, still staring at Isabel, "Is your favorite restaurant still that steakhouse over on John Nolan Drive?"

"Yeah," he said slowly. He was gripping Isabel's thigh firmly without realizing it.

Eve picked up her purse and pulled out her wallet. "What do you say we leave this stuffy little place and go there for dinner instead?"

• • • • •

They ate popcorn instead of dinner.

Sitting in the living room, they watched a nature channel rerun about lions while they ate. Ava rested her socked feet on Gabriel's legs until she finished her bowl. She set it on the coffee table and reversed her position, so her head was resting in his lap instead. He found it oddly touching that she would lay that way, allowing him behind her. Done with his popcorn as well, he set his bowl on the end table.

On the TV, a lioness lay under a tree, patiently allowing her two cubs to crawl all over her and bite her chin and ears.

Gabriel turned the sound down. Ava's hair was still a little damp as he combed his fingers through it. It occurred to him that they'd never had a normal date before this. Meeting for coffee had almost been normal, but she had been so closed off. Later, at his house, she'd had a vision, and that definitely wasn't the way a date usually went.

This was their first regular, uninterrupted date.

Glancing down, he saw his date was dozing off. He squeezed her shoulder gently.

Her eye lids fluttered open. Leaning down so his mouth was close to her ear, he inhaled her scent.

"Do you want to go to bed?" he asked, rubbing her arm. The way he spoke softly against her ear, tickling her, made her stomach flutter.

She nodded.

It was a little early, but he didn't mind lying next to a beautiful woman until sleep came. The moon was bright, too beautiful to block out, so he opened the curtains just enough to let some of the light in. Ava lay with her head cradled on his shoulder, her hand on his chest with her fingers slightly curled. Her leg was draped between his. It was the most comfortable, peaceful coiling of bodies between man and woman. He thought he could stay in bed with her for a month and not have any complaints.

Until she sat up from a dead sleep and yelled, "Molly!"

Gabriel's heart didn't leap into his throat; it catapulted. Because she was naked, and because the moon shown through the open curtains, he was given a spectacular view of her breasts, as they were freed when the blankets flew off her during her outburst.

"Go back to sleep, sweetheart." Despite his raging pulse, he kept his voice calm.

He brushed his hand against her shoulder. Dropping back down against him as if nothing had happened, she sighed. Gabriel pulled the blankets up around them. Since he was already awake, his mind began running through some of the things Ava had previously said during her nightmares or sleep walking.

Something about a little girl in the guest room. Was that Hayden, or a different spirit? And she mentioned a judge with burns on his face more than once.

Is the judge with the burnt face a spirit? he wondered.

"Judge Arthur Franklin died in 1929."

The sound of Ava's voice startled him.

"A prosecutor bribed him to ignore evidence that would have exonerated a man accused of murder."

Unsure what to say, Gabriel said nothing. Did she read my mind? he thought, fascinated.

"The man's brother, Julian, set fire to the house that was originally built here after the judge convicted his brother, Paul Barrett, of murder."

"Who was he accused of murdering?"

"A traveling salesman from Idaho. I do not know his name. It is in the dark. The prosecutor, William Powell, was the real murderer. He was sleeping with Paul's wife."

"Asshole." Gabriel didn't remember hearing this story about the town he had grown up in. Wouldn't something like that be mentioned in school, or at least by the people who lived here as gossip?

"William bribed the judge because he wanted to be with Charlotte, Paul's wife."

Gabriel ran his fingers lightly up and down Ava's arm. "So, William Powell was having an affair with Paul Barrett's wife, Charlotte. William killed some random guy going through town and framed Paul for it so he could be with Charlotte. Then he paid Judge Franklin off to convict an innocent man so he could continue screwing his wife. And somehow Paul's brother found out and killed Franklin."

"Yes."

"And now the judge haunts my house." The information amused him. He hadn't seen any signs of a haunting, but he didn't exactly know what to look for, either. Rattling chains? Sheets with holes poked through where eyes should be?

"The judge haunts himself."

"The real estate agent didn't disclose that information when she was gushing about the natural lighting and the bucolic setting," he mumbled. "I wonder what happened to the prosecutor and the guy's wife?"

Ava shivered. Gabriel pulled her closer.

"William was made to watch while the wife slowly died. Then he was killed very slowly, very painfully."

It was hard to tell if she was awake or asleep. Her voice was dreamlike, but it became that way when she was in the middle of a vision. Realizing he had previously tried not to draw attention to her symptoms for fear of making her feel bad, he made a mental note to watch her more closely from now on. He should know how her body reacted so he could identify when she was having an issue immediately. He couldn't help her if he was too slow to realize what was going on.

"Charlotte was hung. Her neck did not immediately break. The rope was put around her neck and Julian threw it over a tree branch and pulled on it. It took twenty minutes for her to asphyxiate. William was pressed. After he watched his lover die, he had large stones placed on his body until he suffocated."

Fuck me. Gabriel's body itched.

"The pressure from the stones made his eyes pop out of his skull."

"Jesus, Ava." The visual made him want to squirm. "How do you know all this?"

She shivered again. Pulling her against him tighter, he kissed the top of her head.

"Julian used this property to commit all the murders. It is isolated, so no one could stop him. Or hear the screams." Almost as an afterthought, she added, "The prosecutor and wife are buried in the same cemetery as Hayden. I have seen them there."

That gave him an awful feeling in the pit of his stomach. That Hayden shared close quarters with such despicable people made his skin crawl. But he supposed every cemetery was the same. Bad people needed a final resting place, too. The residents of Langdon had been buried in the local cemetery for as long as the town existed, so why wouldn't his sister share the ground with monsters from the past? Besides, Hayden's body wasn't in the coffin.

"What happened to Paul?" he asked. "The guy who was accused of murder?"

"He went mad with grief. They had to move him to a hospital until his death in the forties. He is buried next to his wife. He watches them sometimes."

The hairs on the back of Gabriel's neck stirred again. They were together yet separated even in death.

"And Julian?"

Shifting to get more comfortable, Ava flopped her leg over, so it was nestled in between his again. "Julian hung himself in a tree in your woods after Paul went insane. He avenged his brother, but he still knew murder is wrong. I can take you to the tree if you like."

"No," Gabriel said quickly. "I don't want to know. That's creepy shit, Ava."

"Creepy shit," she said softly.

"I'm sorry you see all those things."

They lay for several moments in silence. Gabriel held her close, aware of the feel of her body against his under the bedding. When he looked down at her, she seemed to be sleeping finally.

How did the information come to her? he wondered. Did she see the spirits? The horribly disfigured judge? The dead, bloated, discolored woman with a rope around her neck and her tongue hanging out between her lips? The bruised man with his eyes dangling on his cheeks?

Could she smell and hear them as well? Singed flesh, blood, decomposition...

Good God, what kind of life could she have, experiencing all these things?

As he was so often since meeting her, Gabriel was impressed with Ava's ability to go on each day, her willingness to keep fighting. Quitting wasn't in her vocabulary. Every morning she woke knowing she would probably see horrible things that no one else saw and no one else understood. Yet she rose from bed and gave each day everything she had.

She was a warrior.

Cupping his hand under her chin, he raised her face to his and kissed her lightly. She made a soft sound against his lips. Her face was pale in the moonlight, untouched by worry or intense thought. He brushed her hair back from her cheek and kissed her again, lingering a little this time.

The way her mouth yielded to his was like a punch in the gut. He hadn't expected it to arouse such a need in him. His only intent had been comfort. Staring down at her, seeing her at peace, he felt his breath catch in his throat. The absence of the carefully neutral expression normally on her face was far different than the serenity that engulfed her now. He could feel it emanating from her. His want to comfort her melted into fierce desire.

"My God, you're so beautiful," he breathed, stroking her cheek.

Her eyelids slid open. His chest tightened as she gazed up at him.

"I didn't mean to wake you," he said softly. He couldn't stop touching her hair. All that thick, dark hair spilling over her shoulders. So silky between his fingers.

Saying nothing, she reached up and traced her index finger over his left eyebrow. When he raised it, her lips curled ever so slightly.

"Look at you, almost smiling."

Leaning down, he brought his lips to hers again. The sound she made this time was somewhere between a moan and a sigh. Every part of his body seemed to reach for her essence; the flow of her hair, the unique smell of her body, the way she surrendered in his arms. Her lips tasted of dark secrets and sacred knowledge. The way she kept looking at him was intoxicating.

More.

"Yes," he breathed, before he realized he had heard the word in his head while Ava's lips were still pressed firmly to his.

The air was thickening with each breath. The room had become humid despite the open window letting in the cool evening air. Letting his fingertips trail down her arm, he ran them toward her elbow and his thumb brushed against her breast.

She arched her back with a sharp inhale.

Sampling the slim line of her neck with his mouth, Gabriel shifted and rolled them until they were lying diagonally across the bed. All that velvet hair spread across the comforter. Beneath him, Ava's body moved against his. He let his hands explore as his mouth returned to hers.

She was so quiet, expressing her pleasure in the quick catches and releases of her breath, fingers digging into his skin, raising her hips eagerly to press heat against heat. The soft, smooth curves of her shoulders shivered as he tasted, caressed. His fingertips skimmed down the line of her narrow back, dipping into scars, intriguing him.

Gabriel....

The sound of his name came to him like a thought in his head or the remnants of some dream. He heard it as if she had whispered it directly into his ear.

He said her name, his voice thick. He was feeling slightly groggy, drunk on her flavor.

As his mouth returned to hers, his hands discovered more places to indulge. The spot on her side just above the curve of her hip, the dip just in front of her collar bone, the inside of her right wrist, where new scars introduced themselves.

Touch me.

Again, he heard the words in his head even as his mouth covered hers.

He skimmed the backs of his fingers over her breast before cupping it, kneading it. Her heartbeat thudded beneath it, the sound seeming to fill his head. Following his hands with lips, tongue, teeth, he began to devour.

Through the thick haze of desire, she let her hands roam over him, skimming, gripping. She touched muscle and made a satisfied little noise in the back of her throat. Pushing his boxers down, she removed the only fabric left between them.

Control faltered; he scrambled to reign it in. Rushing wouldn't do with her; he wanted to savor every inch of her perfect body. As his mouth moved down her belly, exploring smooth skin interrupted by small scars, her muscles quivered.

The strong scent of woman surrounded him. When he gripped her sides, he felt three more scars on the left like an animal had clawed her. Lifting her slightly, he nipped at her abdomen.

She let out a moan.

Get your fucking hands off her.

Gabriel flinched. The voice hadn't been Ava's, yet he had heard it just as clearly as the other in his head moments before. Beneath him, her body was pulsating, her hands thrust into his hair. Thinking he had imagined the other voice, he moved up her body, trailing kisses as he went.

And heard that first voice again, coaxing, then demanding.

Now. Now, now!

Gabriel watched her eyes as they joined.

Her mind shimmered. He felt it the same way he could feel her body trembling beneath him. It was a drugged sensation; the dizzy reaction after spinning around before trying to hit a pinata. Something clicked and settled into place, two puzzle pieces slowly rotating beside each other until the edges lined up and they fit together.

He moved deep inside her, causing a helpless moan to escape her.

Get him off you.

Gazing down at her, Gabriel saw a flash of panic flicker across Ava's face. Something nudged in his mind to let him know the panic wasn't meant for him. He could feel Ava reaching for him with her mind, feel her hands pulling his body against hers. Panic was replaced with fascination, need.

Ava felt The Monster raging, trying to keep her from submitting, but she was lost in sensation. She could not get close enough to Gabriel, to his body, his mind. He laced his fingers with hers and she felt each thrust move through her in waves of staggering sensations.

The pace changed; the energy became more intense. The room around them disappeared and she saw only him. Every sense amplified with startling clarity. His ragged breath echoed in her ears. Her mouth was full of the taste of him. His scent surrounded her. And her sense of touch – so exquisite it was just short of painful. Every nerve inside her was on fire, erupting as his body moved with hers.

On a strangled gasp, Ava arched her back and sank her nails into his hips. Her muscles clamped around him as she let go. Her gray eyes looked silver in the moonlight, glassy and blind with her release. Gabriel lost himself in her, burying his face in her hair.

The air left him as his muscles lost all strength.

In the silence that followed, he felt a dull pulsing in the back of his neck, followed by a pulling sensation in his head. He felt his connection to Ava slip away. Instinct made him want to reach for her, reach out to her, but he focused on getting his breath back. Had she felt it?

Get off me.

Gradually, he became aware of the room around him. It took him a few moments to realize he had collapsed on her. With a grunt, he raised up on his elbows, so he didn't crush her. He gazed down at her, feeling like a teenager in the back of a pickup truck. He still didn't have his breath back.

Get off.

Again, he was astonished that her mouth hadn't moved, but he heard the voice as clearly as if she had said it urgently next to his ear. That second voice, the one filled with rage.

"Are you okay?" he asked, brushing a strand of hair from her face.

"I am fine."

She was winded, he noticed. Knowing her strenuous workout habits, and how hard it was to take her breath away, he allowed himself a certain amount of self-satisfaction.

Get off Get OFF GET OFF.

He felt she was a live grenade beneath him, ready to explode at any moment. The hair on the back of his neck and on his arms was at attention. Every part of his body was suddenly telling him he was in danger. "What's wrong?"

"I need water."

Staying where he was, wanting to stay connected to her, he reached over to grab the glass from the night table.

"You need to release me right now."

Her voice was calm, but there was no doubt that it wasn't a suggestion. He eased off her.

Her chest was heaving slightly as she leaned up. It was obvious she was having trouble catching her breath. He realized it was no longer from passion.

"Ava-"

She stood and walked to the bathroom, closing the door behind her.

Confused, Gabriel searched for his boxer shorts and pulled them on. The sudden feeling that he had acted too soon, despite her willingness, nagged at him. He put a pillow behind his back.

This wasn't his first time with a woman. He understood body language. Not to mention that odd mental connection he had felt, even if he wasn't entirely certain of its possibility. Something strange and very intimate had happened there.

Had he hurt her? She was hard to read, but her reaction had been defensive and a little off balance. If he had hurt her physically, he was sure she would have let him know physically. Mentally... he wasn't sure. But she had given no indication that there was a problem until -

The door to the bathroom opened. Gabriel watched Ava as she walked to the bed, picked up her panties and slipped them on. She sat on the edge of the bed and picked up her glass of water. The hand holding the glass was steady, but she brought her other arm across her chest protectively. He waited while she drank half of it down before speaking.

"Did I hurt you?"

"No." She swallowed. "I..."

She looked so lost sitting there, trying to find the right words, trying to calm her breathing. Gabriel wanted to reach for her but didn't think that would help. The fact that she was still having trouble breathing unnerved him.

"I do not like being held down," she said. Her voice wasn't quite steady. "I was not expecting it."

He hadn't just held her down, he thought, feeling his stomach tighten. He'd pinned her, and when he rose, he'd still held her down with a good portion of his weight. For any other couple, this would have been a normal post-coital position, but for Ava, it was a cage.

"I am sorry." Her voice was barely audible.

"Ava." Gabriel ran a hand through his hair. He was a damn idiot. He swore. "Don't apologize." He reached for her, paused. "Can I touch you?"

Her body began shaking. "I need to get control."

"You need to let me help you." He turned so he was at an angle to her. She stiffened, but she didn't raise her hands in defense. "God damn it, Ava, let me give you a fucking hug."

His choice of words was contradictory to his intent, and he would have laughed if he hadn't felt so furious toward the people who had created this inside her. And at himself for bringing her fears to the surface.

He softened his tone. "Come to me."

She hesitated, inched closer. Careful not to hold too tight, he let out a relieved breath when she climbed onto his lap with her legs curled up to her chest. He gathered her gently in his arms and rested his chin on the top of her head.

"You took my breath away. I'm sorry."

"Do not feel sorry for me." Her voice was a little stronger.

"I don't. I'm apologizing because I made you panic. I should have known better."

"I do not want you to think I use my past to manipulate you."

"I don't think that."

He ran his hand over her hair. After a moment, Ava slowly turned so her back was to him and pulled his arm around her shoulder, so he was hugging her loosely. She stretched her long legs out along the length of his. She felt right leaning against him, though she was still not fully relaxed. He began running his fingertips along her arm lightly, sending tingling sensations up and down her spine. The sensations were odd but pleasant.

"Relax," he murmured. "You're safe with me."

With deliberate care, she rested her head back on his shoulder. Inhaling through her nose, she held her breath a moment, exhaled through her mouth. She repeated the exercise, her body slowly relaxing against him with each breath. The tremors slowed, then stopped. Gabriel smiled against her hair, grateful that she'd accepted his embrace.

"You have the most beautiful body." He continued caressing her arm, marveling at the smooth skin.

"I have many scars."

"They don't make you any less beautiful." His tone was so easy, so matter of fact, as if her beauty was not negotiable.

She relaxed a little more, settled more firmly against him. He thought she was as relaxed as she could be around people. For now. He wanted to work on that. He was willing to work on that.

"How are you feeling?"

"I am all right."

She's on autopilot, he thought. Hers was an automatic response, probably one she had told herself thousands, if not millions of times to get her through her worst days. From the very core of his being, he wanted to fix that impulsive answer.

"Let's try that again. Try to mean it this time. How are you feeling?"

"I-"

He ran his hands up her arms, brushed her hair to the side, and began kneading the muscles around her shoulders. To make sure she didn't feel like he was trying to throttle her, he used his knuckles to work the knots. She let out an involuntary purr.

"It is not fair to bribe me with physical relief. My body's natural reaction gives you an unfair advantage."

"You've been carrying today's tension in your shoulders for hours. Just let it go."

His voice is like Sensei's, she thought. Calm and rhythmic, hypnotic.

He knew just how to settle her nerves. He applied just enough pressure; strong enough to be physically helpful but not too much to make her feel threatened. Soon her head lowered so her chin was almost resting on her chest.

"Better?" he asked, his hands never stopping.

"Yes."

She answered without thought but with a stronger voice. Good.

"It's okay to feel." His voice was like syrup, coating her raw nerves. "Your Sensei doesn't mean to hurt you by loving you. Neither do I."

She tensed at the mention of the emotion.

"Settle down." Those hands moved, caressed, compelled the tension away. He brushed her hair back again and nuzzled her neck. The movement was so natural, so smooth, that she had no time to tense up or worry that he was attacking. She simply reacted by pressing her body against his.

"I can't get enough of you."

"I enjoy sex with you," she said. "You are very thorough. Besides being physically gratifying, I had a proper cardiovascular workout, so it was not a wasted effort."

He burst out laughing.

"Why is that funny?" She leaned to the side and craned her neck to stare up at him with an amusing furrow between her brows.

"You make it sound like a business transaction." He set his mouth to work on the side of her face.

"It was mutually beneficial."

He smirked, his breath tickling her ear. "Mutually beneficial, you say. Let's benefit each other some more."

He lazily ran his fingertips up and down her sides, stirring her. Using his teeth, he moved from her ear down her neck. She drew in a shuddering breath. Her body came alive, pressing against him, undulating, her arm reaching up over her head to run her hand through his hair and tug.

Gabriel wanted to please her more, take his time, let his hands become familiar with her body.

He wanted to remember everything.

· · · · ·

"What the bloody fuck was that?"

"That was weird, right?" Isabel asked, fastening her seat belt. She half-turned in the seat so she didn't have to twist her neck while she spoke. "I mean, I've only met them a couple times, but that seemed really fucking strange."

They watched the Audi with Griffin's parents leave the parking lot. Griffin sat for a moment after he started Rover, watching the Audi disappear down the street. His hands were on the steering wheel, gripping it tight, his head turned away. Isabel watched him warily, wondering if he was upset.

"You broke my mum." He turned his head, but now he stared at the steering wheel. "She's never liked this steakhouse."

Unsure what to say, Isabel said nothing.

The dinner had almost been pleasant. After her odd behavior at the first restaurant (Isabel couldn't even begin to pronounce the name of it), Griffin's mother seemed to have resumed her typical snooty attitude once they sat down at Terrace Steakhouse. She hadn't spoken much, and when she did, it was with her normal air of arrogance. But she seemed to be trying.

Her behavior had freaked Isabel out. A lot.

Apparently, it had also confounded Griffin, who was still staring at the center of his steering wheel.

"Griffin?"

He looked over at her as if he had forgotten she was there.

"Can you wait to yell at me until we get to your apartment? Or are we going to sit in the parking lot all night?"

Glancing around, he put Rover in reverse. Something about watching a man's hand shift gears was so appealing, Isabel thought. So sexy. Why was such a simple act so enticing?

"Right. Here we go, then. Why would I yell at you?"

"Because I broke your mum."

She still wanted to giggle every time she heard that word.

His hand had been resting on the gear stick and now he rested it on her leg.

"I should have said you fixed her. Or you let her see she could use improvement, at least."

"Glad I could help."

Isabel wondered if Eve's sudden attitude shift really had to do with her. She didn't understand how it could; they'd barely met, why would Eve care about Isabel's opinion? But Griffin was good at reading people, much better at it than she was. She trusted his instincts.

It would be interesting to see how things played out.

● ● ● ● ●

CHAPTER ELEVEN

Ava began slowly adjusting and settling into a new routine as April came and went. The new routine included Gabriel, sometimes Isabel, and often a plethora of emotions. The emotions took a long time to get used to, but she did not mind Gabriel or his sister.

The very next time she stayed over at his place, Gabriel woke to being jarred by a strong shaking of his arm. He sprang out of sleep, sitting up to find her staring at him blandly from her side of the bed.

"What? What's wrong? Is it a dream? Did you have a nightmare? Are you seeing a spirit?"

His eyes darted around the room even though he couldn't see much. When they returned to Ava's, she was giving him a look like he was a little crazy.

She was already dressed, her hair damp from a shower. Had she already worked out?

"I am leaving to go to work."

"Jesus." He ran a hand down his face. The alarm clock showed it was barely seven o'clock in the morning.

Without another word, she stood abruptly and headed for the door.

Gabriel tried to clear the fog from his brain enough for conscious thought. He almost laughed at her professional manner.

"Wait."

When she turned, he held out his hand. The frown on her face as she hesitantly walked back made the corners of his mouth twitch.

His eyes were barely open, and he was rubbing his other hand down his face. He could hardly be called even a little threat. She took his hand. Pulling her down until she was sitting on the bed, he leaned up and kissed her long and slow.

"Good morning."

"Good morning. I have notified you that I am leaving, as you requested."

He smiled drowsily.

She turned to stand.

"Ava."

Turning back, she sighed. "I have given you proper notification. I do not understand why there are so many customs for sharing a bed. What more do you want from me?"

Reaching out, he rested his hand on her chest, just above her breasts, and slowly curled his fingers. As they tightened just enough to begin capturing the fabric, she automatically reached up to stop him. Gabriel kept his eyes on hers. For a moment, she clutched his hand, ready to continue to twist it so he would release her. Yet his eyes were not showing aggression or ill will. They were showing desire. And he had raised his eyebrow in that way that seemed to say, Really? We've been over this.

She relaxed her hold and allowed him to pull her down for a kiss.

"This is the morning-sex-before-work custom," he said, toying with her mouth.

"I am already dressed."

"Not for long."

Later, Ava had to admit morning sex before work was a nice tradition, even if it threw her schedule off.

After that, it became an easier habit to let him know when she was leaving if she stayed at his house. She found that if she gently ran her hand through his hair, he would rouse enough to tell him she was going to work. That seemed like less of a jolt to him, so she continued doing it that way. It also usually led to sex before work.

Intercourse was no longer used as an unwanted but necessary release. Gabriel filled her with overwhelming sensations, emotionally and physically. After morning sex, her day was more productive, her focus razor sharp. She flew through projects and trained harder than she ever had. Her body seemed unstoppable, tireless. Her emotions were equally baffling, but instead of fighting them, she chose to accept them and see where they led. She was physically and mentally improving. How could that be wrong? If she was incapable of understanding the emotional part of it, that was only because emotions were her weakness.

On the afternoons that Ava trained, Gabriel usually stopped by her house. It was easier for her to be at home after her training and sessions with Sensei regarding psychic phenomena. She was often exhausted.

On her off nights, she went to Gabriel's house. She took a change of clothes, two sets of workout clothes, and toiletries. In addition to her morning workouts, she worked out in the evenings. He found she enjoyed anything physical, anything using hand-eye coordination and involving exercise.

Sometimes they took walks in the woods on Gabriel's property, reminding him of when she told him Julian Barrett hung himself from one of the trees. More often, they jogged in the dog park where he had asked her to coffee that first time. He would stick to the trails and follow them throughout the park while Ava stayed in the woods. No matter how fast he ran, she always came out several yards ahead of him on the trail. And no matter how long he worked out, she always continued long after he'd quit. Her endurance was captivating.

As the days warmed and they were able to be outside more, he was starting to see just how fast she really was. And dedicated. When it rained, even when it stormed, she used the woods for exercise.

They cooked meals together or ordered in – Ava didn't like restaurants. Gabriel didn't mind. He could be social on his own time if he needed to be around people. He loved to watch her enjoy her food, concentrating on each bite she took, not speaking until her plate was clean. Although she chose a variety of healthy foods to make a balanced diet, she didn't shy away from the occasional skin on chicken or mashed potatoes and gravy. She burned an obscene number of calories daily and needed the fuel to compensate.

In the late evenings, they sat on a porch, his or hers, and listened to the natural sounds around them. They hardly ever spoke during these times. Ava took the first few minutes to pose in odd positions with her arms and legs all twisted around herself or simply sit cross legged, eyes closed, breathing deep. Always after, she joined him in the chair next to his or on the bench next to him. Gabriel had never experienced peace quite like he did on those nights with Ava.

Sometimes they sat on his roof and watched the stars. Ava loved it up there, as he had guessed, and sitting up there with a blanket was one of her favorite pastimes. They often lay down, and he found himself dozing on more than one occasion.

But some evenings when she was done with training and that extra session with her teacher, she came home looking like she had been working in a factory for sixteen hours. Sweating profusely, her clothes clung to her body, so she had to peel them off. Her eyes were sunken, with dark crescents under them. Her skin was pale. Often her hands shook so hard she had trouble gripping objects like the loofah or the bottle of body soap when she showered.

Touching her, at least initially, was forbidden. She stayed in the shower sometimes as long as forty-five minutes. When she emerged, she didn't seem any better. Her body looked drained of all energy.

On these nights, Gabriel felt like he was about to walk into an ambush at any minute. He hated seeing her that way when there was nothing he could do for her. One night, when Isabel was over, she told him she thought it was sweet that Ava came over even when she was so exhausted.

"She wants to spend time with you," Iz said, punching him in the shoulder. "Even when she feels like shit, she would rather feel like shit with you."

After that, his perspective changed. When Ava came home looking like hell, Gabriel gave her space and didn't force conversation. He showered with her so he could wash her when she couldn't hold onto anything. Doing so added an intense intimacy to their relationship that he'd never known. It cost her to admit she was unable to do something. That she let him bathe her gently and wash her hair spoke volumes of the trust she had in him.

He talked to himself, keeping his voice calm, talking about his day, until she was able to respond. If she didn't respond, he didn't take it personally. The sound of his voice seemed to make her feel better, settle her.

He was also relieved to learn Isabel and Ava spent a couple hours together every Friday night. Gabriel knew Iz needed a friend, a close, loyal friend so she wasn't stuck in her head so much. And Ava needed the same, as well as a little practice socializing. Knowing they were looking out for each other was a bonus.

Certain aspects of her ability were surprisingly easy to get used to. A couple times, he heard her talking in another room. When he entered the room, she was alone. She immediately stopped talking. From her neutral expression, it was hard to tell if she was annoyed with him for interrupting or uneasy that he had walked in on her communicating with someone he couldn't see. She'd stopped avoiding conversations about her ability now that he knew, but she didn't seem to embrace it, either. Anytime he had a question he felt guilty asking her about it.

One night, when they prepared to shower together, he found her bathtub full of water. Ava walked in, noticed the water, and pulled the trip lever up to let the water drain. Gabriel asked why she'd filled the bathtub when she knew they were taking a shower.

"I did not fill the tub with water," she said, walking back into the bedroom to undress. He followed her. "Anton did."

"Okay, I'll bite," he said, earning an amusing scrunch of her brow. "Who is Anton?"

"He is the previous owner of the house," Ava said, peeling articles of clothing off and tossing them into her laundry sorter. "Sometimes his sorrow over the loss of his wife replays in the house."

"This has happened before?"

"Yes." Totally nude now, she walked toward the bathroom. "Not often. He is at peace, but sometimes the emotions hit without warning."

"This could happen again?"

As Ava leaned over to start the water, the bathroom door slowly closed. Gabriel turned to stare at it.

"Yes." She straightened, glanced at the door, then at him. "That will happen again, too."

"He likes to close doors?"

"Sometimes."

So far, that was the only time either incident had happened while he was there. Gabriel was left feeling strange about the encounter as well as Ava's candor about it.

Other times, evidence of her ability was less subtle.

Without warning, she would say something in passing or do something that would remind him she received information from sources he couldn't understand. As she was making dinner one night, she told him she had made vegetables as a side since he didn't like rice. Brushing it off, it occurred to him halfway through the meal that he never told her he didn't like rice. When he asked her if Iz had told him that, she shook her head and said nothing more.

One morning she left Peanut Butter Crunch and Kix cereal boxes on the counter, along with a bowl and spoon. When he asked her about it later that evening, she said she bought the cereal for him so he could mix them for breakfast. He'd never told her he used to mix the two as a child, or that he had been thinking of trying it again.

The interruptions to his sleep occurred every night or early morning, waking him either to her vocalizations or to an empty bed. He was getting used to being roused during each sleep cycle. Because he worked from home, that wasn't a problem. If she was still in bed, screaming or talking, he spoke to her until she went back to sleep. If she was wandering around the house, he followed her and tried to coax her back to bed. He found he could gently guide her if he put his hand up by her shoulder or arm, an inch or so away, to spare himself getting smacked.

Gabriel realized that the intensity of the nightmares seemed to be decreasing. The nightly interruptions weren't always thrashing or screaming now. Often, she simply wandered the rooms, checking the locks. He considered this change a minor improvement.

No matter how hard Ava pushed herself, she could not seem to make much progress with controlling her ability. She worked with Sensei for two hours every Monday and Wednesday afternoon, and she worked on her own at home every day. So far, the best she could do was control her visits to and from The Interval. Summoning a spirit at will was beyond her grasp. Hayden came to her when she was not expecting it. Ava might get her to answer a question or two, but they had no value. The information she received was a favorite song or a game she and her siblings used to play. She never answered the most important one Ava always asked – why was she seeing Hayden's spirit?

Ava constantly searched for other ways to increase her ability. She added another meditation session to her day – a deeper, longer session. She tried lucid dreaming. Briefly, she added an extra hour of exercise to her regimen, but that threw her balance off, so she had to return to her previous schedule.

She had to find something to move things along.

She was getting impatient.

· · · · ·

A large, calloused hand gripped Ava's chin and lifted until her gray eyes were forced to stare into his dark ones. His breath reeked of beer and cigarettes. She started to gag but he was holding her chin so tight she could not open her mouth.

"My little doll." He exhaled stale, smothering breath into her face. "I want to see what your insides look like."

He let go of her chin and her head dropped heavily to the floor. She bit her lip hard enough to taste blood. Before she had a moment to catch her breath, the searing pain ripped through the right side of her back, from under her shoulder blade to her hip.

Ava screamed.

"Ava, Ava, Ava, Ava."

Gabriel sat up the instant he heard the piercing shriek. His hands reached out even before his eyes opened, bumping cold skin just before she hurled herself toward the door.

"Fuck."

Stumbling out of bed, he almost tripped on his shoes. He paused a moment to get his bearings, let the dizziness pass, and turn on the lamp. After taking a deep breath, he went after her.

The sound of glass shattering downstairs told him where to start looking. He started toward the stairs.

Christ, she hadn't had one this bad for a while now. Things had been settling down.

At the bottom of the stairs, he saw the curtain covering the tall window next to the door was mangled. The rod had been snapped in two and was barely holding the fabric up.

"Ava?"

He turned on lights as he walked to help wake him up. Through the foyer, he saw the jackets along the wall were strewn all over the floor by the front door. Boots and shoes were knocked to hell and gone. Was she bouncing off the walls like a pinball as she ran?

In the great room, he found her, up against one of the floor-to-ceiling windows. She was naked, of course, her fingers curled like claws and making clacking sounds on the glass. Gabriel heard a low moan coming from her.

Calm, he thought. She was jacked up tonight. Or this morning. He had no idea what time it was.

"Ava, it's Gabriel. You had a nightmare."

Whipping around toward the north side of the room, she scrambled over the piano bench, knocking it over when she launched off it and struck the double-paned glass. She clawed at the window, then banged her palms against it. The whimper she let out broke Gabriel's heart.

"Come back to bed, Ava. You're safe now."

Spinning around, Ava bolted toward the kitchen. He tried to keep up. Even nude, she was abnormally fast. Before he could stop her, she picked up a thick cookbook from the breakfast bar and hurled it at one of the windows in the breakfast room.

"Whoa!" Gabriel yelled without thinking. "What the fuck?"

Running at the window, she slammed into it, pounding her palms on the glass.

The glass held up; it was double pane, like in the great room, and he thanked whoever could hear him for that. Until Ava turned around, facing him.

She was terrified. Her eyes were large inky pools that made her look a little insane. Tears streamed down her cheeks. She was breathing heavily, her eyes flitting left and right, but Gabriel didn't think it was his house she was seeing.

She vaulted onto the breakfast bar. Skidding cross the counter, she smacked into the ceramic crock holding his cooking utensils and sent it spinning toward the stove. The spatula, ladle, and various spoons clattered across the counter and hit the floor. Ava jumped down and ran toward the formal dining room.

Gabriel reached the room just as she lifted a chair and slammed it against the south window.

The window shattered, sending shards out into the night and bits inside across the hardwood floor. Trying not to cut his feet, Gabriel ran to Ava just as she put her hands on the windowsill and attempted to hoist herself up. He grabbed her around the waist and swung her back into the room.

Ava began thrashing as soon as he touched her. Carrying her on his hip like a parent carrying a toddler throwing a fit, he walked-hobbled through the living room toward the stairs, trying to avoid her battering limbs. On his way passed the fireplace, he saw the broken candle holder on the coffee table. That must have been the glass he's heard shatter when he wasn't quite awake.

Getting her upstairs was a nightmare. She flailed, panicked, and though her back was to him, rendering her fists useless, her heels were not. Several times he thought she was going to send them over the railing to their deaths.

In the bedroom, he finally made it to the nightstand on her side of the bed. He picked up her cell phone. She swatted it out of his hand. He picked it up again.

"Knock it off!"

Please don't be locked, he thought, and swiped his finger across the screen. Her home screen came up.

Staring skyward, Gabriel let out a breath. "Thank you, Jesus."

He went to her Contacts, trying to ignore the blows to shins and ankles. Scrolling, scrolling, hoping she kept the number he needed under something he would recognize... there it was. Hopefully, the voice on the other end of the line wouldn't hunt him down for waking him up at ... what the fuck time was it?

A voice answered on the second ring.

"Ava, what's wrong?"

Hearing her teacher's soothing voice made the entire situation seem even more dreamlike.

"Ah..." Gabriel wet his lips. "This is Gabriel Harris. I'm Ava's boyfriend. She had a nightmare and – dammit, Ava, calm down!"

She reared back, almost knocking the phone out of his hand again and cracking his skull open in the process. He couldn't talk on the phone and hold her at the same time. He shoved her away from him and shut the bedroom door behind him, leaning against it to keep them contained to one room.

Ava scrambled to the glass door leading to the balcony and pressed her hands against it. It was only when her palms left wide smears of crimson that Gabriel noticed they were bleeding from trying to crawl out the broken window downstairs.

"God damn it. She threw a chair through a window and she's bleeding," he panted into the phone. "I can't snap her out of it this time."

"Put me on speaker phone and turn the volume all the way up."

Gabriel did as he was told, setting the phone on the bedside table in case he needed to restrain her again.

"Ava."

The man on the other end of the line began speaking in Japanese, keeping his voice steady and calm. At first, his words seemed to have no effect. Ava pounded her palms on the glass door. She stumbled to the fireplace, almost smacking her head on the brick corner. With her fingers splayed, she ran her hands over the top of the mantle and shoved its contents over the edge. The folded American flag and the ashes of his grandfather tumbled onto the hardwood floor. The first wooden box he had ever made tumbled onto the dog bed lying next to the hearth, popping open and spilling out the few items he'd kept from Hayden's childhood.

As if this was all perfectly normal behavior, the man on the phone continued to speak almost conversationally. Gabriel had no idea what he was saying. He only knew that after several seconds, Ava's frantic struggle to get out of the house slowed. Moments later, she froze at the west window and tilted her head, listening to the voice.

Gabriel picked up the water glass on Ava's night table and downed the contents in two gulps. His arm was shaking from hauling Ava up the stairs at an odd angle. Making the decision to clean up the mess in the morning – or whenever he happened to wake up – he watched Ava's body slowly relax. Her chest was heaving, but she'd stopped struggling.

"How is she doing?"

The voice flowed from directing a conversation in Japanese to Ava to talking to Gabriel in English so smoothly that at first, he didn't realize he was being addressed.

"She stopped."

"What is she doing now?"

"She's standing at the window. I need to bandage her hands."

"Keep me on the line until you're sure you can do it without her injuring you."

Gabriel walked over to Ava. Her head was still tilted as if she was listening. Her eyes stared straight ahead, as sightless as a doll's. Sensei's voice had calmed her as she tried to break through the glass, so her hands were flat against the door, just above her head.

"Ava, I'm going to put my hands on you," he said softly.

He reached out and brushed his fingers against hers, then picked up her hand. She allowed him to. Her hands were too bloody to tell how badly she was cut.

To Gabriel, she looked like she was sleeping standing up with her eyes open. It was uncanny.

"I'll be right back to clean your hands."

He kissed her forehead gently, walked back to the phone.

"She'll let me touch her," he said, picking up the phone and taking it off speaker. "She's okay now. Thank you."

"You're welcome. Nice to meet you," the man added.

Gabriel didn't know whether to laugh or scream. "I don't know what to call you. You're in her phone as Sensei. She never calls you anything else."

"You can call me Daniel."

"Nice to meet you, Daniel. Sorry I woke you up at... I don't know what time it is. I didn't know what else to do."

The man on the other end of the line was quiet for a moment.

Finally, he said, "We should talk."

• • • • •

"I'm sorry."

"Hmmm? For what?"

Griffin shifted, pulling Isabel closer to him. He was barely aware that she had spoken or that he had responded. As soon as he settled, he was asleep again.

The sound of her whimpers woke him. He didn't know how long he'd been sleeping. Instead of being wrapped around her, he was now in the middle of the bed and she was huddled at the edge on her side, shivering.

"Noooo." The word ended on a low moan.

Rubbing his palm over his eye, he sat up. A quick glance at his cell phone showed it was almost seven. Going back to bed wasn't an option. Snuggling a little longer was, however.

"It should have been me."

"How's that?"

Griffin leaned over and touched her on the shoulder. She jerked violently, startling him. Trying not to scare her, he inched a little closer and eased his hand onto her this time.

"Take it easy, now."

She was making those pitiful whimpering sounds again. Under the blankets, her feet moved restlessly. Tears were smeared across her cheeks. Her face was pale.

Griffin gently rolled her toward him until she was tucked against his body. "You're okay, Izzie."

"It should have been me." She let out a choked sob. "I'm sorry."

"Oh, Izzie." Gathering her close, he kissed her forehead, brushed her hair away from her face. "When are you going to let go of that guilt?"

Another cry, this one softer. Her lower lip was trembling, and tears beaded in her eye lashes. Her heart was racing, her legs still moving sporadically. Griffin tried to get heat back into her by rubbing his hand up and down her exposed arm.

"Don't go into the dark. I'm s-sorry."

Her hand shot out and clasped his tee shirt, pulling him closer to her. Another sob wrenched out of her, and she pressed her forehead against his chest, shuddering.

There is a fine line between helping someone in need and manipulation. Griffin knew this. He knew the subconscious was more malleable, more willing to give, to learn, and to accept, than the conscious mind. He knew Isabel was tearing herself apart keeping her secrets.

"What are you so afraid of, Izzie?" he whispered, wishing desperately to relieve her of the pain she felt. He stroked her hair. "What happened when your sister disappeared?"

"Don't go into the dark. It's not safe."

"Tell me what's in the dark." He kissed her forehead again. "What do you see?"

"He's out there," she sobbed. "The man. The man in the blue hoodie."

"Who is the -" Griffin swore under his breath. He couldn't abuse her trust. "Bloody hell. Wake up, Isabel."

He gave her a gentle shake. She clung harder to him, squeezing her eyes shut tight. Tears spilled over like liquid diamonds. With another, firmer shake, he repeated her name.

She woke on a sob that turned into a moan. Pushing up from the bed, her head snapped forward. A wave of dizziness had her pressing her fingers to her forehead.

"Easy." He touched her arm to let her know he was there.

"Hayden?"

Looking around, Griffin saw confusion in her eyes fade slowly to disappointment as she became aware of her surroundings. Her shoulders sagged. A deep sigh made her body shudder.

"Good morning, Love." He rubbed her thigh.

"Morning."

Trying to shake off the remnants of the dream, Iz slid down and twisted so she was lying on her stomach with her head turned away from Griffin. She didn't want him to see she'd been crying. She thought she had called Hayden's name as she woke, but she wasn't sure. For a moment, just a moment, she had believed Hayden was still alive.

A warm hand settled on her back. "I like waking up with you beside me."

"Yeah." She didn't want him to hear the tears in her voice. Swallowing, she hoped she had masked them and was getting herself together.

He pulled the blankets down, exposing her back. Running his fingers along the hem of her shirt, he slid his hand under the material, touching the bare flesh beneath. The resulting sigh his touch coaxed out of her made him smile.

"You have the softest skin," he said conversationally. He slid his hand up higher, letting his fingers explore, examine. The line of her back, long and lean. Silky skin. Firm muscle underneath.

"I like your hands." The way he was massaging was relaxing her. She turned her head toward him, feeling a little steadier.

"How are you doing, Izzie?"

"I'm okay."

"Bad dream?" He felt her stiffen under his hand and continued caressing as if he hadn't. "Who's the man in the blue hoodie?"

"What?" She raised up and twisted toward him, her eyes filled with fear. The color that was just starting to appear left her face.

"You said the man in the blue hoodie is in the dark."

Isabel slowly lowered herself back to the bed, her pulse thudding painfully in her temples. "I was talking in my sleep?"

"Who is he, Isabel?"

"It was just a nightmare."

But she felt like an anvil was sitting on her chest, preventing her from taking a breath. She rolled onto her back to try to get more air.

"What's in the dark?" Griffin asked gently. He rested his hand under her shirt, on her stomach. His thumb moved in a lazy circle around her navel. "You say it in your sleep when you're upset."

Hands were closing around her throat. She couldn't breathe.

"I need to get ready for work."

She sat up too fast and all the blood drained from her head. Blinking, she pressed the back of her hand to her forehead. She could feel tears coming again, making it even harder to breathe.

"Hey," Griffin said. She moved too fast, and he missed her arm as she clambered off the bed. "You have plenty of time. Talk with me a bit."

"No."

She stood in the walk-in closet, pulling off her tee shirt and shorts.

"Isabel, this is killing you. You need to talk about it with someone."

Isabel stepped into the doorway and glared at him as she pulled the straps of her bra over her shoulders. "Are you sure you're not a shrink?"

He gave her a patient look. "My mum is a retired psychologist. I may have picked up a few things here and there."

She stiffened. "How the hell did anyone ever open up to that icebox?"

Looking a little sad, he said quietly, "She's changed quite a bit since Connor died."

Anger overrode the sympathy she felt for snapping at him. "Do you often feel the need to fix broken people? Or is it just me?"

Griffin shook his head. "Izzie, I'm not with you because I want to fix you. You're not broken."

If you only knew, she thought. The shaking in her hands started as she pulled her jeans on. She carried her socks into the bedroom and sat on the end of the bed.

"Talk to me."

"We'll have to talk later. I need to stop at my apartment before I head to work."

Standing, she started toward the door.

"Can you at least talk to Ava about it, if not me?"

Iz spun around. "She doesn't need to hear about my first-world problems, Griffin. She spent over two years with a foster family that tortured and abused her in every way a person can be abused. My panic attacks are trivial next to that."

A headache had abruptly spiked through her temples without warning and was rotting there. It blurred her vision, made her anger reach fury level with little to no provocation. Work was going to be a challenge.

"Thank you," she suddenly spat.

He was confused.

"You just made an already shitty morning even worse. Now I get to deal with this and the assholes I hate all day."

"Isabel-"

But she had already gone. He didn't hear the door slam, which he was expecting. Assuming she had left it open, he forced himself out of bed and walked into the living room.

She hadn't left the door open. She had closed it quietly. Somehow that was worse than if she had just slammed it. He knew she wanted to.

Exhaling, he walked to the island and leaned his elbows on it, resting his head in his hands. Personal relationships were always off limits when it came to helping people. It was his hard and fast rule, one he had broken since day one with Izzie. After all, he was applying what he knew from his mum's practice, and a psychologist never treated his own family members or friends. Sometimes he just couldn't seem to shut it off. Not that he was a psychologist, but the principle was the same. It was just a bad idea because he was too close to her.

A half empty water bottle was sitting on the marble top. Griffin slapped it across the room, where it hit into the wall and fell to the floor, spinning.

He pushed too hard.

Now both their days would be shitty.

•   •   •   •   •

When Gabriel woke several hours later, he reached for Ava. He jerked into a sitting position when he found her side of the bed empty. Shoving his hand through his hair, he looked around the room.

Sunlight was coming in through the deck doors. The glass had two thick smears of maroon slashed across them from Ava's hands. The mess on the floor by the fireplace would need to be cleaned up today.

Listening, he didn't hear the shower. It was late enough that she was probably gone, working at home already while he slept the morning away. And she had left without letting him know. Again.

Throwing the covers off, he paused at the sight of blood on the sheet. The cuts had opened up sometime during the night – or morning – and she'd bled as she slept. She had also touched him; he had red smudges on his chest and stomach.

"Great."

He yanked on his jeans, already making his way toward the door. After quickly brushing his teeth, and wiping the blood off, he stalked down the stairs, intent on using his irritation to bust quickly through the cleanup of the mess Ava had made all over the house.

So, she had left without letting him know, and he had no idea what condition her hands were in. He would spend all day worrying about it if he didn't text her, which made him feel needy. If she just used a little common courtesy before she left...

The smell of coffee hit him at the base of the stairs. Being irritated at her grew harder as he made his way toward the pot of coffee she had obviously made for him. When he rounded the corner and saw her sitting at the breakfast bar, he stopped.

She was perched on one of the stools, one knee drawn up to her chest, a coffee mug on the counter in front of her with her bandaged hand wrapped around it. Her head was turned away from him as she stared out the breakfast room windows.

"What are you still doing here?" he asked, coming into the kitchen. He glanced at the clock on the stove. "Shouldn't you be at home, working?"

She had a notebook on the counter. Three columns were filled with her careful handwriting. Turning when he walked into the kitchen, her eyes scanned him up and down.

"I have two appointments set up to meet with installation professionals."

"Appointments... Here?" His brain was too foggy. He picked up the mug she had left on the counter for him and poured himself some morning fuel, adding sugar.

"I have called three companies to get estimates on replacing the window in the dining room," she said, setting the notebook aside. She sipped her coffee. "Two are coming today. The third cannot come until tomorrow. I will be here during all appointments, so it is not an inconvenience for you."

"You set up three appointments?"

When she brought her other hand up to brush her hair back from her face, he saw a fresh bandage on that hand as well. She must have had one hell of a time trying to get them wrapped by herself.

"For the broken window," she repeated. "Let me know which company you chose to do the work, and I will pay for it. I will be here when the work is done so it does not affect your schedule. I will try to find a chair that matches your dining set."

"You won't find one. I made it."

Misery flashed in her eyes.

"I'll take a look at it, see if I can repair it."

Gabriel looked around the kitchen. Everything she had knocked off the counters last night had been picked up. The windows, counters, and floor had been cleaned. The cookbook was sitting exactly where it had been before she hurled it at the patio door. Everything was back in its place.

"Did you clean up this morning?" He poked the ladle with his index finger, and it spun around in the ceramic crock it was sitting in.

"Of course. I made the mess. I waited to wash the glass on the door in your bedroom and pick up the things off the mantel. I did not want to wake you."

She was bothered, he could tell. The gray in her eyes seemed to be swirling. "I hope I did not ruin anything."

"You could have waited until I woke up. I would have helped clean up."

Frowning, Ava twitched. "I made the mess," she repeated.

Walking around the counter, he came toward her. He noted the automatic stiffening of her muscles and chose to ignore it. Slipping his hand around the back of her neck, he pulled her to him for a long, slow kiss. Though she reciprocated, she was slightly pushing back against the hand cupping her neck. Automatically pulling away from him. He brought his other hand up and used both to cup her face lightly so she wouldn't feel like he was dragging her toward him. Deepening the kiss, he brushed his thumb over her cheek as his mouth coaxed hers. Finally, she relaxed against him. Then relaxed a little more.

That's right, he thought. I won't hurt you.

He pulled back, studied her face. "Good morning."

"Good morning." She blinked slowly.

"Are you okay? Last night was a bad one. This morning. Whenever."

He leaned over the counter and retrieved his coffee.

"You took excellent care of my hands. Thank you."

"That's not what I asked. Are you okay?"

Those strange gray eyes regarded him with an expression he couldn't quite read. "You are not upset that I damaged your property?"

"I'm more concerned about the damage to your body." He picked up a wrapped hand, kissed the top of it. "I care about you, not objects."

"My body will heal."

She seemed to be contemplating as she sipped her coffee. Gabriel liked watching her do ordinary things. They were somehow more exotic after all the outrageously impressive things he had seen her do.

"I had to call Daniel to get you to come out of your nightmare last night. This morning. For the sake of argument, I'm just going to say this morning."

Turning toward him, she looked only slightly interested. "Who?"

"Daniel. Your Sensei. You don't know his name?"

Realization broke out on her face. "I am to call him Sensei, inside or outside the dojo. All his students are."

"He told me to call him Daniel."

She shrugged. "I will adjust to hearing it. Why did you call him?"

"Because you put a chair through my window, Ava. You were bleeding, and I couldn't stop the blood if you wouldn't let me near you. Luckily, he's in your phone as 'Sensei', so I didn't have to waste time trying to figure out what his real name is."

He had also added Daniel's number to his own Contacts for future incidents, but he didn't think now was the right time to tell her that. She was radiating unease.

Having finished her coffee, she stood and rounded the counter to refill her mug. "I am sorry I am an inconvenience to you."

"You aren't. I'm telling you because he wants me to come with you to class this afternoon so I can drive you home after. I don't want you to think we ganged up on you or talked behind your back."

The shame was evident on her face, with an underlying irritation. "He does not think I am capable of taking care of myself."

"He thinks it's getting dangerous for you to drive after the psychic sessions. Apparently, you refused to let him drive you to Vincent's to rest up... because of me."

Gabriel had found this endearing when Daniel mentioned it on the phone this morning, but he also found it a little amusing.

Ava had taken creamer out of the refrigerator and now she poured it into her cup.

"Speaking of Vincent," Gabriel added, clearing his throat, "I noticed something about your closet the last time I stayed over."

Stirring her coffee, she gazed at him uneasily. Faint color rose in her cheeks.

"I didn't see Vincent's clothes in your closet."

"I..." She lowered her eyes, her fingers raising to fidget with the neckline of her shirt. "I removed them. I returned them to Vincent."

The right side of his mouth twitched.

"You are making fun of me."

"Never. I'm touched." He watched her try to work out what she was feeling, to understand.

"I purchased tee shirts and socks in your size," she said, her tone cautious. "They are in the small dresser."

"I saw that, too," he said. He'd initially been looking in her closet to borrow one of Vincent's tee shirts on a morning he spilled coffee on the extra shirt he brought from home, knowing he was staying over. He planned to mention it once they met up after work. He opened the closet, surprised to see Vincent's clothes were no longer hanging up. When he opened the drawer, he spent a full minute staring in the drawer that had multiple colors of tee shirts folded neatly in it instead of Vincent's black wardrobe.

"Thank you," he said, brushing his lips over hers. "You're welcome to leave some things at my place if it makes things easier."

"I will have to think about what to bring."

"It might be easier if you didn't have to lug around so many sets of workout clothes."

She nodded.

"Let me know when you have to leave for training," he said, rounding the counter to refill his coffee mug.

Instantly, her voice chilled.

"I do not need a babysitter."

Her eyes were little tornadoes of fury as she glared over her mug out the breakfast room windows.

"That's not the only reason he wants me there. He thinks I should be involved when you two work on the extra thing after the training. The… you know, psychic stuff. It'll give me a better idea what's going on, how to handle it."

Still angry, she said nothing. Gabriel sat next to her again. He could feel her fury.

"And maybe he just wants to meet the guy dating the girl he considers his daughter."

She set her mug down. "Why?"

"To make sure I'm good enough, or at least passable. Nobody's ever good enough for a dad. Ask David. I'm sure he feels the same."

"I do not require their permission to engage in sexual activity." Her tone was damn near dripping with condescension, and Gabriel almost snorted. "And I hardly need their approval for a mate. I have carefully scrutinized the pros and cons of having a relationship with you. You are a good provider, physically fit, with a mild demeanor. Your attributes offset my imperfections, as mine do yours, making our relationship well-rounded. We have many things in common, but not so many that we bore each other. I have made a suitable decision, beyond reproach from David or Sensei."

Now Gabriel did laugh, his stomach muscles aching at the confused frown she gave him. "Sorry. I just love when you sweet talk me, honey."

He would have been offended by her itemization of their relationship if he hadn't felt the electricity that pounded between them every time they were in the same room. Suitable decision, his ass.

She sent him a scathing look and began unloading his dishwasher. Raising his eyebrow, he watched her start putting dishes away as if she had lived with him for years. She knew where every item belonged.

"Their approval has nothing to do with your choice in men and everything to do with protecting their daughter," he continued. "Anyway, my point is, I think he's right. I should have a better grip on your psychic ability. He also might be able to help me where your nightmares are concerned, so you don't keep hurting yourself."

Sighing, she walked around the counter again and sat next to him. The lines between her eyebrows appeared again. "I can concede the logic in that. I have never done so much damage as I did this morning."

"What was the nightmare about? You never talk about them."

Leaning back against the counter, he watched her to see if she would shut down, unwilling to discuss the subject. Her expression remained neutral, the gray in her eyes darker than usual. Turning her left hand over, she looked down at it and lightly ran her right thumb against the gauze covering the deep gash.

"No one has ever asked me that."

Patience was the best tool with Ava, he was finding. She was a thinker. He let her think. He sipped his coffee and stared out the sunroom windows.

"'I want to see what your insides look like.'"

Something cold and slimy ran the length of Gabriel's spine. He turned to look at Ava.

"That is what he said to me. 'I want to see what your insides look like.' I do not know what he used. He started in my back, here. That is what my dream was about."

She reached her left hand over her right shoulder and used her finger to touch where the large, deep cut was that he had felt the first time they'd made love. Over the past month, on the rare occasion when he was awake and Ava was asleep, turned away from him, he had looked closely at that scar. It was half a centimeter wide, maybe, and though it was fully healed, he imagined the wound being inflicted on a five- to seven-year-old child. How she must have screamed.

The scream that woke him when she shot out of bed this morning echoed in his head.

Gabriel lifted his eyes toward the ceiling and took a deep breath, trying to combat the nausea he felt churning in his stomach.

"How..." He had to clear his raspy throat to make sure he could speak. "How the hell did you survive what they did to you for so long?"

"Janine was a nurse. She put me back together. I learned how to treat wounds by watching her."

He felt as if someone had driven a train through his chest.

"Sometimes she would put me back together and Mack would cut me open again in the same place to see how I was healing."

"My God."

"That is why that scar did not heal well. He cut me open again before it had time to fully close. Janine put me back together so I would be whole, and he could play with me all over again."

Gabriel felt a wave of affection so strong he was nearly staggered by it. There was sorrow, yes, for the torture she had endured. Two years must have felt like two lifetimes for such a tiny child. And fury for the people who had done this to her. But mostly he was so proud that she had held on, never giving up. Even when the pain had been unbearable, when no end had been in sight, she'd never given up.

Where had her strength come from? he wondered. What was it inside her that said fuck you to the world, even though the world had only ever beaten her down? Why hadn't she grown up learning to submit instead of fighting it the entire time? Children did as they were told; they didn't know any better. Yet Ava had fought the entire time, going against everything she was being told to do, until she was free.

How could he not admire a woman with such strength?

Ava abruptly slid off the stool, backing away from him. "Do not do that."

She'd startled him. His hand bumped his mug, knocking coffee over the lip.

"Do what?"

She took another step back. "What you were just feeling... it is illogical and unwarranted."

Frowning, her eyes darted around as if she was trying to figure out a complex math equation. Ava, who could kill an attacker with one perfectly placed strike, was uncomfortable with compliments.

Gabriel plucked a rag from the sink and wiped coffee off his hand. He watched her watching him warily.

"Relax." He gave her a wry smile. "Don't panic over a passing thought. When are you going to get those estimates?"

Ava stood staring at him, gauging his sincerity.

"The first appointment is at eight thirty," she said, briskly stepping forward to pick up her coffee. "He or she will be here any moment."

Gabriel reached out and caught her wrist, sliding his fingers down to take her hand.

"Hey," he murmured, stepping in close. "Thank you for telling me about the dream."

Already her pulse had quickened. The proximity to him snapped her nerves to attention, made the hairs on the back of her neck and on her arms rise.

Kissing her forehead, he slid his hand up to her hip. "You don't have to pay for a new window."

"I caused the damage. I need to do this."

"It could just as easily have happened at your own house."

"I need to do this," she repeated. Her eyes remained steady on his.

"Okay. I'm going to get started in the garage."

Five minutes after he stepped out the back door, the knock at the front door came. Ava walked through the great room and foyer to answer it.

"Good morning," the man at the door said, grinning at Ava as he offered her his hand. He was wearing a tool belt with various gadgets on it.

First call of the day and I get this beauty.

Ava tried not to show her disgust as she reached out to shake the man's hand. He saw the gauze on her palm and gently took her fingers only so he wouldn't hurt her.

"I'm Calvin. You can call me Cal. I'll be getting some measurements today."

I'd love to get more than an estimate. Wow.

Relax, Gabriel had said. *Don't panic over a passing thought.*

He was right. The carnal thoughts of a middle aged, overweight man this morning were a minuscule portion of his life. How many millions of other seconds had he spent helping people through his various jobs, caring for his three children, nursing his wife back to health when she was sick with multiple sclerosis, helping his mother after his father died? A few seconds of less than perfect thinking should not make him a bad person.

Taking a step back, Ava allowed him to come inside, making sure her expression did not show her dismay. If only she could genuinely believe the good in people outweighed the bad. She needed an excuse to get away from this man as soon as possible.

"The dining room is through there," Ava said shortly, pointing with her left hand. She used the fingernails of her right hand to dig into the gash on her palm. The pain was bright and refreshing.

Following Cal through the living room and into the dining room, leaving plenty of space between them, Ava walked around the table, so it was between her and the man. She wanted as much room between them as possible. People made her itchy. She hated having to deal with them. When she was done here, she was going to talk to Gabriel about locking them in the bedroom at night to minimize the damage she did during nightmares.

Calvin was looking at the wrecked wood around the window, the shards of glass. Ava had cleaned the rest of the mess up and set the chair aside. He turned toward her and raised his eyebrows. "What happened here?"

"I am having a bad morning." She raised her hands and began peeling the bloody gauze off her right hand. "Do you need me for this? I need to change my gauze."

"My goodness, ma'am, do you need help?" He asked, moving toward her.

Ava brought her left fist back to her side, ready to strike. "I need you to do your job so you can leave."

He held up his hands. "Okay, okay. It looks deep, young lady. I don't want you passing out on me."

"I will be in the kitchen, if you need me."

•   •   •   •   •

Isabel looked at the stack of invoice in front of her, drumming her fingers on the top of her desk. The headache was pushing against her eyes now as well as out at her temples. She opened her bottom desk drawer and dug in her purse for pain medication. The damn purse had so many pockets in it, and she couldn't remember which one had her Tylenol... ah, there it was. She closed the drawer and leaned up.

Jeff was standing over her desk. He never stood by her desk. He always stood over her desk and stood over her.

"Checking your Facebook status?" he sneered.

Isabel bit the inside of her cheek to keep herself from snarling a response.

She spoke slowly and kept her tone even. "I need headache medicine."

She popped four pills in her mouth, chased it with water. She could have ground cement with how hard she was clenching her teeth.

Jeff looked at the invoices. "That's quite a stack of invoices."

My head's fine, thanks for asking, you fuckshit.

"My vision's 20/20, Jeffrey."

As intended, his face scrunched at the way she said his name with distaste. She had a moment of satisfaction before the pain in her head sent daggers into her eyes.

Isabel lifted the top few invoices from the stack and set them on the document holder to the left of her monitor. She opened the program she used to enter the invoices. Jeff was still standing over her. She continued clicking into the program to get to the right screen.

"Anything else I can do for you, Jeffrey?" She said his name crisply and with a little high-pitched lilt at the end because she knew he hated it.

Jeff inhaled loudly. "Make sure those invoices are entered by the end of the day."

Isabel didn't bother answering. She always finished invoices. However, how easy the work she completed was dependent on how many interruptions she had, most of them coming from her obnoxious leader, Jeffrey. If he wanted her to finish the work, he'd have to leave her alone.

As she processed the paperwork, she fought to keep her eyes clear of tears, which meant not thinking about this morning. She had already wasted too much time on it, and too many tears. Why hadn't Griffin just held her until she felt better? Who the hell was he to decide how she worked through her issues?

Immediately stopping that kind of thought, she berated herself for bringing it up. It would only start that circular thinking again, where she went round and round with ideas that led nowhere and only distracted her from work.

The invoices were complete less than two hours later. Iz scanned them in and listed the information into a balancing spreadsheet before she started sorting and opening the mail. She had procedures to update, which would keep her mind numb for the rest of the day. All the pertinent tasks were done for the day; she could slow down a bit and try to relax.

Griffin sent a text, but she ignored it. She was afraid she would start to cry. Anytime she thought of reading it, she started replaying the conversation they had that morning, and her concentration was blown.

A few minutes into reviewing procedures, she realized proofing on the computer screen was turning her headache into a migraine. It was making her nauseous. Sweat broke out all over her face even as her body suddenly chilled.

Jeff walked over to her desk with a sheet of paper. He made a show of shaking the paper before setting it on her desk. "I need you to enter my expenses from last-"

"I'm leaving," Isabel said, and began closing the windows on her computer.

"Excuse me?"

Nausea rolled through her again, and she leaned over, covering her mouth, even though she knew Jeff was too selfish to care. Taking deep breaths didn't help to alleviate the nausea.

"I'm sick. I'm leaving." She felt bile rise into her throat.

"Did you finish the invoices?"

"Over an..." She let out a sound that was part burp, part dry heave. "...hour ago."

Slowly sitting back up, she closed the last programs on her computer and shut it down. She made sure nothing on her desktop had client information on it. With an impatient glare, she snatched Jeff's scribbles, which she was supposed to somehow translate into his expenses, locking them in one of her drawers. She pulled out her purse.

"You can't leave," Jeff said. "I need you here."

"This isn't a vacation," Isabel said. "I'm sick."

"You took time just a few days ago."

"One damn day."

The pressure on her eyes was explosive.

She stood, rested her hand on the desk until the feeling of vomiting settled slightly. In reflex she'd covered her mouth again, but what she really wanted to do was vomit all over Jeff, so he understood she wasn't making this up. Sweat was standing out on every inch of exposed skin, even though she was shivering. It had to be obvious to Jeff that she was sick.

"Isabel, I'm sure you can understand that short of a death in the family, for which I'll need a death certificate-"

"I'm done talking about this," she snarled, standing, and taking a step toward him. She dry-heaved again. He backed away, his eyes widening. "The rest of my duties can wait until tomorrow."

She didn't wait to hear if he replied. She pulled her jacket off the back of her chair and walked past him.

Several employees saw them speaking before she left, and several saw her tears and the wobbly way she was walking. She had kept her voice low, where his was loud so everyone could hear. Isabel was glad. Let him try to reprimand her for this. She would go to Human Resources and tell them he acted inappropriately when she was damn near vomiting at her desk. Half a day wouldn't kill the company.

As soon as the fresh air hit her, her stomach settled slightly. She breathed deep, feeling less lightheaded. The air in that building was so stale, making her feel like she was choking on it. Walking to her car, she stood a moment, allowing herself to breathe. She had to brace herself on her car to make sure her legs didn't buckle.

Okay, she thought. Okay. Fuck this. Go let this out of your system before you poison your body more.

She drove to Jay's, glad she kept a gym bag with a change of clothes in her back seat for this very occasion. She slowly ate two breakfast bars she kept in her purse to see if lack of food was part of the problem. Had she eaten anything since last night? She couldn't remember. She would either throw up and never make it to Jay's or feel good enough to try practicing. At first, she'd have to take it easy. That was fine. She could do that.

As she signed in at the gym, her stomach already beginning to settle, her mind began to focus on the workout instead of this morning's argument. Her body started to rev up as she changed her clothes. Each piece of clothing brought another layer of determination. By the time she stepped into the gym, she was ready to kick ass and chew bubble gum.

A quick warm up followed by thirty minutes of strength and weight training didn't tire her out like she expected it to. She was no longer weak and shaky. Instead, her adrenaline was spiking, pushing her to do more, more, take this raw edge of power and force it to do her bidding. Right now, her bidding was beating the shit out of the punching pads the guy in front of her had strapped on his arms. He was four inches taller and outweighed her by eighty pounds, but at that moment, Iz felt she could take him.

"Jab and cross, that's it! Jab and cross! Keep your elbows close to your body, Isabel!"

Isabel blew hair out of her eyes as she swung with everything she had.

"Back straight! Protect your face!" Jay yelled.

Thud-thud. Thud-thud. The sound of her fists on the pads was satisfying. Thud-thud-thud-thud.

Isabel imagined Jeff looming over her desk with that stupid look on his face. She pictured his face under her fists as she whaled on the pads.

Get my expense reports entered, Isabel.

Thud.

Enter these applications into the system, Isabel.

Thud, thud, thud.

Answer my phone for me, Isabel.

Thud-smack-THUD-THUD-SMACK.

"Okay, Isabel, that's good! Let's call it a day!"

Get over you sister's death, Isabel.

Fucking people and their bullshit. Thud-thud. Why the hell did they have to take it out on her? Thud-thud.

"Harris, give it a rest! You've had enough for today."

Stop swearing so much, Isabel.

WHAM! Grunt.

"Whoa!"

Everyone thought they could walk all over her, step on her, kick her around because they were all used to her being polite and not standing up for hersel-

A bump on her shoulder had her spinning around and striking.

Jay put a hand up to block his face and batted her hand away as if she was an annoying fly. As soon as she realized what she had done, Isabel dropped her hands.

"Fuck me! I'm so sorry, Jay!" Her face burned.

Jay gave her a smile. "It's all good, Harris." He nodded to Izzie's partner. "Hit the showers, Kyle. You took it like a man."

Kyle, looking winded, bumped gloves with Iz and walked toward the locker rooms.

"Your jabs are getting really good, Isabel. Your punches are a lot stronger than when you first came here."

"Really?" Sweat poured down the middle of her back, soaked under her arms. She wanted nothing more than to shower off all this funk.

"You almost knocked Kyle on his ass. I think you scared him a little."

"Oh... I must have zoned out."

"You need to protect your face a little more."

Iz wiped sweat off her forehead with the back of her wrist. "Thanks. I'm really sorry for trying to hit you."

"Stop apologizing." Jay put his hand on her shoulder. "You have a God given right to protect yourself. Anytime you feel threatened, and your body reacts to that, you are in the right."

"For all the good it did," Iz said. "You swatted me like a gnat."

"Don't compare yourself to any of the guys here. You'll be disappointed. Instead, think of the progress you're making every time you come in here. Every hour you spend here is building muscle, toughening your body. Progress, not perfection."

Isabel smiled. "Progress, not perfection. I like that."

"Remember it. It's one of the most important lessons in life. Hit the showers."

"Thanks, Jay."

They bumped gloves.

Isabel walked to the locker room, pulling off her gloves.

In the shower, she ran her hands through her already damp hair, letting the cool water pulse over her body. She was sore, she had a few bruises, and she wasn't strong enough yet, but she was enjoying the physical exertion kickboxing took and how powerful it made her feel. It felt amazing to let out her frustrations after a rough day. It felt good to work out to the point of dripping smelly sweat, then shower it all away and feel clean again. It felt absolutely fabulous to intimidate a man much bigger than her.

Without warning, she burst into tears. She covered her eyes with her hand, sobbing soundlessly. Afraid others in the locker room would hear her, she put both hands over her mouth and shook as the water cascaded over her. The tears were hard, hot, brief. As quickly as they started, they stopped. They left her feeling shocked and confused.

Isabel finished her shower, staying in a little longer than was necessary to make sure her face was clear of any signs of crying. Her body was drained, and she was emotionally exhausted. She dressed quickly in clean clothes and walked to her car.

Sitting for a moment, she checked her phone. Griffin had left a couple more messages. She wished she were strong enough to read his texts. That wasn't something she could build muscle for in the gym.

"Fuck it."

She started driving toward her apartment, telling herself she wasn't avoiding Griffin. She just didn't have the energy to deal with him at the moment.

•   •   •   •   •

Gabriel wasn't sure what he expected Ava's teacher to look like, but it wasn't a normal guy with a lean build. Daniel kept his dark blond hair cut close to his head and the uniform he wore (it is called a gi, he heard Ava's voice in his head) looked as natural on him as jeans did on Gabriel.

Gabriel supposed he'd expected an intimidating, overly masculine jock with exaggerated muscles and an ego to go with it.

Instead, Ava introduced him to a rather conversational person with a firm handshake. While Ava went to a back room to change, Daniel invited Gabriel to sit on a bench along the front window as they talked. Daniel asked Gabriel several questions about his job, where he worked, what he liked to do for fun. Gabriel found himself instantly at ease.

When Ava came out of the dressing room, she was dressed in her uniform (a gi, he reminded himself) with a tee shirt underneath. Her hair was braided the same way it had been when she came to dinner with his family in March. She sat in front of the kamidana, her legs tucked under her, so her butt rested on her ankles.

"What are your injuries this time?" Sensei asked, walking onto the mat, and kneeling the same way Ava was, across the mat from her.

She glanced down at her hands, still covered in gauze from the broken window. "I cut them, Sensei."

"How deep? Did they require stitches?"

She shook her head.

Unconvinced, he motioned for her to come over. "Let's see them."

Ava crawled across the mat and sat once again. She began unwrapping the gauze.

"What happened?" Sensei asked.

"I broke a window and tried to climb out, Sensei. I cut them on the glass."

"During the nightmare this morning?" He glanced at Gabriel, who nodded.

Gabriel was somewhat surprised at the candor with which they spoke about physical injuries and damage to a house. They appeared to be as comfortable as two people discussing the weather. He was just starting to get used to Ava sleeping naked.

Ava held out her bare palm to Daniel and he examined it closely. The skin was torn and ragged, a large cut through the center of her palm. Smaller cuts surrounded the larger one.

"They are feeling better today," she said. "I am capable of training."

"Show me the other one."

She unwrapped the other one. From the bench, Gabriel watched her expressions as she moved. Irritation, impatience, finally acceptance all showed on her face as she did as she was told. Finally, she held out her hand to Daniel.

He cupped his palm under the top of her hand, barely pressed on the deep gash in the meat of her thumb with his other hand. Blood beaded on her skin. Her expression remained impassive but her back stiffened as pain sliced through her.

"Uh huh. I thought so." He was gentler as he examined the injuries. Letting go of her, he sat back. "We'll focus on paranormal work today. You'll open those up the minute you start training."

"I can train, Sensei."

Gabriel recognized the stubborn tone of her voice and smiled.

"It wasn't a suggestion."

"Hai, Sensei." Ava lowered her head just a little. She wouldn't argue with him out of respect, but she very clearly did not agree with him.

"Take care of your hands."

As she wound the bandage around her left hand, Daniel picked up a recorder sitting against one wall and activated it. "Let's move to the middle of the floor in case you become... mobile. Do you want to work on calling a spirit or blocking negativity first?"

Resigned, Ava finished wrapping her right hand. "Calling, Sensei."

They moved to the middle of the floor and sat facing each other. Both sat in a half lotus position.

Gabriel wondered what Daniel meant when he said Ava might become "mobile", but he kept quiet. He was here to observe and drive Ava home afterward. Any insight he gained that might be of help later was a bonus.

Watching them work together was fascinating. The way they communicated, both verbally and with body language, was like no other duo he had ever witnessed. For that experience alone, he appreciated the invitation.

"Gabriel, you might want to take your shoes off," Daniel said suddenly. "Just in case you need to come onto the mat for any reason."

He untied his boots while he watched Ava take several long, deep breaths. She closed her eyes, relaxed her shoulders. Resting her wrists on her knees allowed her hands to dangle limply. She remained in this pose for a few minutes.

Nothing happened.

Then Gabriel saw subtle changes: she exhaled on a sigh that seemed to echo around the room. She continued to take deep breaths, but her eyelids were fluttering rapidly. A thin trickle of blood seeped out of her ear.

When she opened her eyes, they had turned opaque.

In the Interval, Ava was enveloped in gray. Not mist... gray that limited her ability to see more than two feet around her.

"I am here, Sensei."

"You can hear me?" he asked.

She nodded. "There is no one here."

"What do you see?" he encouraged.

"Fog." She raised her hand, pushed at what surrounded her. "Not fog. Gray."

Daniel glanced at Gabriel. "Call to her, Ava."

"Hayden?"

Gabriel frowned. They were trying to reach Hayden? Ava hadn't mentioned trying to reach his sister when she told him about these sessions with her teacher.

"Yes," Daniel said, watching Gabriel from his periphery. "Call to her."

"She is here."

Gabriel felt giddy.

"You know what to do." Daniel leaned forward.

"What do you want, Hayden?"

On the bench, Gabriel tried to get more comfortable without making noise. This was all just a little too surreal.

Ava jerked, leaning back. She gulped in air. "The others are here."

Gabriel thought, Others?

"Stay calm." Daniel reached out and rested his hand on hers. "They always are. Focus on Hayden. Breathe."

He breathed with her so she could mimic him. Gradually, she calmed down and sat up straight again. Sensei kept his hand on hers. After a moment, she turned her hand up and gripped his, tight.

"I want you to leave me alone."

Both Daniel and Gabriel stared at her, surprised at the anger in her voice.

"If you are not going to tell me why you appear to me, go away."

In the Interval, Hayden gazed at her, her blue eyes like beacons in the dreary atmosphere. She stepped forward, cupped her hand to her mouth. Ava leaned down so the girl could reach her ear.

In the dojo, Ava leaned over and moved her head to the side, listening. After a moment, she leaned forward, bracing herself on one hand, and cupped her other hand as she stretched toward Sensei. He leaned toward her and turned his head. She whispered in his ear.

When she leaned back, he stayed as he was for a moment.

"Can he hear me?" he finally asked, his voice not quite steady.

Ava nodded. Her movements were slow, dreamlike. Her unfocused eyes were directed at a point somewhere between Daniel's chest and neck.

"Does he... understand...what happened to him?"

She nodded again.

Daniel cleared his throat, pulled himself together. "Ava, is Hayden giving you this information?"

She nodded a third time.

He glanced at Gabriel, who was transfixed, then back at Ava.

"Why is she giving you this message to give to me?"

She held very still, her breath slow and deep as if she were sleeping. "Because he loves you. Because you are trying to help her."

"What about Gabriel? Does she have something for him?"

Her crystalline eyes turned to Gabriel, making a chill run down his spine. If that wasn't a creepy expression, he didn't know what was. Jesus.

"I-it's c-c-cold." Her teeth chattered. "But it's better than - augh-"

Water gushed out of her mouth. Gabriel sprang to his feet, but Daniel held his hand up again. He moved to Ava's side and took her arm, helping her rise up to her knees. The top of her uniform and her pants were soaked.

"She's okay." Daniel spoke to Gabriel over Ava's head. "She's done this before. Come over to her other side here and keep her leaning forward so she can get rid of all the water. I'm going to get towels."

He waited until Gabriel rushed over to Ava, kneeling beside her, before he left them. Gabriel barely noticed. Sweat stood out on Ava's forehead. She was shivering, her teeth chattering loudly. Her lips were turning blue.

"Ava," he said softly, rubbing her back. "How can I help you?"

She turned her head to look at him, and her eyes were blue.

"The color of denim," he whispered.

"Gabe," she said in a small voice. Her hand tightened on his. "Think fast."

Daniel came back with an armload of towels. He dropped them on the mats and knelt to start cleaning up the water. Seeing the astonished look in Gabriel's eyes, he paused.

"What happened?"

Gabriel didn't seem to hear him.

"Hayden?" he said, leaning toward Ava. He was gripping her hand tighter than he meant to.

"Gabriel, tell me what happened." Daniel didn't like the half-crazed look in the younger man's eyes.

"Her eyes are blue," Gabriel said, his gaze never wandering from Ava's. "Just like mine, they're the same color as mine."

"Ava, can you look at me?"

She paid no attention to her teacher. Raising her hand, she touched Gabriel's cheek.

"You're so old," she said in that same small voice.

"Hayden." Gabriel pressed his hand on top of Ava's, closed his eyes.

"Be careful, Gabriel," Daniel said softly.

"The river," Ava said. "I- augh-"

More water poured from her mouth. This time it hit the mats and spread outward. The smell of fish, wet grass, and moss filled the dojo. Daniel tossed towels down to keep it contained, his eyes trained on Ava.

Gabriel took Ava's face in his hands. "Hayden, you shouldn't use her like this. It's not right."

"I miss you, Gabe."

"I know. I miss you, too." He gave her a fierce hug, then pulled back. "Leave Ava alone."

"It was the river, Gabe. It was the -"

Ava's eyes turned from blue to gray and rolled upward. When she began to topple over, Gabriel caught her. He eased her down until she was lying on her back, away from the pool of water. With shaking hands, he untied her belt and opened the top of her wet uniform. He tugged her arms loose, lifted her body gently, and eased the top out from under her.

"No wonder she's a damn zombie when she gets home," he snarled. "Does she do this every time you have one of these little paranormal meetings?"

Daniel handed him a couple towels. When he spoke, his voice was calm.

"She's been able to visit The Interval for several weeks now. She isn't always this exhausted. Only when-"

Gabriel raised his head. "When what?"

"Communication with them doesn't drain her as much." Daniel finished wiping up the water and pushed the towels into a pile. "When they use her body... that's a different story."

"How often does that happen?"

"Rarely. That's why we're working on this. So she can control what comes in and how she handles it."

"You're not doing a very good fucking job."

Pressing his fingers to his eyes, Gabriel took a moment to calm his nerves before he wiped Ava's mouth. She stirred, her eyes fluttering.

Daniel wondered just how hard it had to be for Gabriel, torn between being able to talk with his dead sister and keeping his girlfriend safe. To have one, he had to hurt the other. He'd just chosen Ava, and now he would have to live with that.

"Do you believe my dead sister was just communicating through her?"

"Don't you?"

Gabriel brushed his thumb across her forehead. What the hell had he gotten himself into?

"Ava's eyes are gray," he said. "She just looked at me with blue eyes. Hayden had blue eyes, the same shade as mine. The things she said..."

He gathered the wet towels and added them to the pile. Lifting her head, he rested it on his lap.

"Christ. How can I not believe her? She doesn't lie."

"No. She doesn't."

"What now?" Gabriel touched her pale face.

Daniel picked up the wet towels to take to the back. "Now we wait until she comes around. She'll be wanting to go another round."

•   •   •   •   •

The phone was ringing. It took several seconds for Isabel to become aware of it, as she was playing her guitar with her eyes closed. The old-fashioned telephone trill finally broke through her strumming. Leaning over her guitar, she saw Griffin smiling up at her from the screen.

She turned the phone face down.

Returning to her instrument, she continued strumming. The image in her head of Griffin on her phone kept distracting her, making her fingertips bump wrong strings, making her palm drop and flatten the chords.

"Dammit."

Setting her guitar aside, she stood and walked to her pitiful balcony. It was far too small for even a lounge chair, but it was hers. She stood looking out at nothing, thankful for the warmth of the day, so she wasn't caged inside. Leaning her elbows on the railing, she closed her eyes and turned her face up to the sun.

There was only one place she could go and not feel the need to think everything to death. She shoved her wallet into her back pocket, grabbed her keys, and headed for the cemetery in Langdon.

Even driving made her feel like she was doing something, keeping busy, instead of trying to find logic in emotion, where there was no logic. The only way to fix things between her and Griffin was to talk to him. She knew this. It was no big secret, no puzzle she had to work out. She also knew she was exhausted and not yet ready to face that particular discussion. That was okay, too; taking time to herself to make sure she wouldn't yell and throw things was mature. Yet still she repeatedly went over the conversation in her head, driving herself insane with her ricocheting thoughts.

She was so fucking tired of thinking.

After talking with Hayden, she was going to get drunk as fuck.

The headstone was always so cold, she thought when she brushed a couple leaves off the top of it. Even though the temperature was almost seventy, the smooth marble was cold enough to make her wince. Why was everything associated with death cold? The way others processed guilt seemed cold. What was done to the body was heartless and cold. Removing all their fluids and replacing them with a chemical to keep them looking fresh was ridiculous. It was done so the living could view them as they had once been and derive some sort of peace from that viewing. Dark clothing was worn – cold, emotionless black – to signify grief. Flowers bought to give to family members. They would die in days. It was cruel, frigid.

"You're losing it, Iz."

She wondered if Gabriel would mind her visiting. Her mind, her body, felt like it was swirling around the drain, being sucked down.

A glance at her phone told her he wouldn't be done working for another few hours, but maybe just being at his house would keep the darkness away.

For a little while.

●　　●　　●　　●　　●

Gabriel felt like he'd just gone a couple rounds with Rhonda Rousey. He didn't understand how he could be so bone-tired when he hadn't done anything except watch his girlfriend have her body used as a costume by invisible forces.

Ava was currently in the changing room, taking a few moments after effectively blocking spirits in The Interval from overwhelming her. That was according to Daniel, who had stopped the recorder and was currently reading through notes he'd apparently taken from previous sessions.

After a bathroom break, Gabriel was back on the bench with a bottle of water, wondering how much more Ava could take. She was looking better than she had after Hayden's visit (he couldn't quite bring himself to say possession), but he wished she would quit while she was ahead.

"Remember what we discussed this morning on the phone?" Daniel suddenly asked, his voice seeming too loud in the silence of the dojo. "About a word or phrase for protection?"

Gabriel nodded.

"She's going to have a problem with that. Be prepared."

Ava exited the back room and stepped onto the mat, bowing toward the kamidana. She walked to the middle, where they had been working before, and knelt, settling her butt on her heels.

Her eyes were clear now. She didn't look as pale, or as exhausted. She was wearing a fresh, dry uniform and her body didn't look as used as it had before.

Daniel wondered how she would react to the next discussion. He activated the micro recorder and walked to the center of the mat, sitting across from her.

"After this morning's nightmare, I think we need to take certain steps to stop it from happening again," he said.

She glanced up at him. "Controlling my ability will not help my nightmares."

"I understand that. I have a theory about your nightmares, but you have enough on your plate, and we need a solution now. If Gabriel hadn't locked you in the bedroom and called me, who knows what damage you would have done?"

Feeling guilty, Ava looked down at the mat. "I did not mean to break the window."

"The damage I was referring to was you, Ava," Daniel said, and Gabriel saw that affection she had spoken of between father and daughter. "Your fear and aggression are escalating during your dreams. We should consider taking extreme measures to keep you contained so you don't hurt yourself."

She wound her legs into a half lotus position. "What kind of measures?"

"I think you should let me hypnotize you."

Something flashed in her eyes. Gabriel initially thought he'd imagined it, but later, he would realize it was the first sign things were going downhill.

Ava frowned. Her body stilled.

"It would only be to install a kind of subconscious kill switch," Daniel said. "A safe word or phrase. Something Gabriel can say when you're having a nightmare that will snap you out of it. Shut you down physically and mentally."

Her body began stiffening. Muscles in her neck tightened; her head sunk down. Her hands curled into fists. The muscles in her legs compressed, visibly tightening.

"I know you think it will take away your control, Ava, but it would give the control back to you. During an outburst like that, you have no power over yourself or your actions."

She looked over at Gabriel, and he saw betrayal in her eyes. You agreed to this? those unique gray eyes asked. You went behind my back?

He wished he had discussed it with her first, but Daniel suggested he wait until they were all together tonight.

Suddenly, her pupils dilated, filling her eyes, and even the whites changed color so that blackness filled the eye sockets. Gabriel was shocked at the change.

Daniel reached over and touched Ava's hand. She jerked.

"Ava, I won't do anything without your permission."

Slowly, she turned her head to glare at him, and Daniel saw the other in her black eyes.

It snarled.

"You're becoming a pain in my ass, Daniel Ward."

Gabriel leaned forward at the sound of the deeper voice coming from Ava. "What the fuck?"

Keeping his eyes on Ava, Daniel raised a hand to silence him.

Gabriel suddenly remembered hearing the voice before, breaking through Ava's when she told him of how she'd been unable to attend school because she didn't get along with the other children. She had seemed upset by the story and had quickly told him she had to leave.

"This has nothing to do with you," Daniel said to The Monster.

"Ava feels betrayed. It has everything to do with me."

Her head twitched. Placing her right palm behind her on the floor, then her left, she straightened her legs and slid back across the mat, away from Daniel. With her hands at her sides, her eyes never leaving his, she lifted her butt and moved her legs around her arms into a crouch. Gabriel was reminded of a large spider.

"Ava, you're stronger than it is. Remember, it only has power if you let it."

"She's done this before?" Gabriel said, standing.

Ava's head jerked in his direction. Her eyes, impossibly black, glared at him.

"Gabriel, I'm going to need you to sit down and be quiet for a few minutes." Daniel kept his voice calm and his eyes on Ava in case the thing inside her decided to play.

Stunned, Gabriel sat back on the bench, staring at Ava as she regarded him like a stranger. How could Ava's teacher be so calm when something malicious had taken over someone he had come to care about? At least he had known Hayden hadn't meant to hurt Ava. This other thing didn't seem to care.

But Daniel had more experience with this. Gabriel knew he was out of his depth and could only trust the teacher. The lack of control was infuriating, stunning.

"She's not your girl just now, is she?" Daniel said, watching its body language for any signs of attack. When it continued to study Gabriel, Daniel smacked his palm on the mat. The sound was sharp and loud. Its head snapped around to look at him. "She's no longer the weak little child you can control."

As she slowly stood, Ava ran her hands down her chest, her sides, her hips appreciatively. "I've so enjoyed growing up with this body." She gave Gabriel a sideways glance. "Oh, the things we could do if she'd let go of that control a little. I would eat you alive."

The hair on the back of his neck stood on end.

"Ava, you're with people who care about you. You're safe. Come back to us." Daniel stood as well.

The thing inside her sneered. "If you cared so much, you wouldn't go behind her back."

"Fight it, Ava. It lies."

It snarled again. "Such a waste. She could do so many things with this vessel."

It twirled around in a lazy circle, assessing the body.

"She has so much muscle strength, so much agility."

It did a slow back handspring step out, her long, lean body arching and fluid. Switching to cartwheels, it did two in a row followed by three aerials.

"Magnificent."

"It's not your body," Daniel said evenly. "Give it back."

The Monster stopped admiring Ava's body and glared at him. "Take it back."

Stepping toward it, he watched it blink her eyes and shimmer. Somewhere inside that body, Ava was aware. He was sure of it.

"You already know you can't beat me," Daniel said. "Why do you keep trying?"

"It entertains me."

She sprang at him. Gabriel was so startled he jumped. He watched Ava attack her teacher, moving around the mat like a possessed assassin. Daniel didn't hit back, Gabe noticed; he only blocked and evaded her attacks with a resigned patience that told Gabriel this, too, had happened before. Ava was fast, but Daniel was faster. After half a minute, she seemed to stop putting any effort into an attack and spent more time flipping around on the mat.

"Ava, I know you can hear me."

Daniel watched it do several rapid back-handspring step outs in a row. It ran its hands down Ava's body again, more in fascination this time than in a lascivious manner.

"Kick it out."

Her head came up to study him, and he saw her eyes for a moment.

"Huh." Her body jerked. When she spoke, it was Ava's voice. "It is so hard to always be in control."

"This isn't the way to do that. It's using you. It has always used you."

"Everyone uses everyone." Her eyes burned into his. "You took me from one prison only to lock me inside another."

"That wasn't my intention. I wanted you to be able to defend yourself. I didn't want you to feel like a victim."

"You wanted someone to save because you could not save your son."

Gabriel's head snapped up at this. He stared at Daniel, who's expression hadn't changed, but who's eyes held that deep sorrow only recognizable to people that had also suffered loss. How had he missed that?

"That's not you speaking. You're letting it control you."

Ava apologized in Japanese. "I did not mean-"

Her head twisted, her shoulders rising. She grimaced.

"Fight it, Ava."

The look she gave him was one of patient tolerance. When she spoke, her voice almost sounded like Hal from 2001: A Space Odyssey. I can't do that, Dave.

"It is not the same as flipping a coin, Daniel. Give me a moment."

Closing her eyes, she took a deep breath, exhaled. She bent her legs and sank to the floor, hands at her sides with her fingers spread until they found the mat and she settled cross legged. After a moment, she reached her right hand out to the side.

"Will you hold my hand?"

Daniel watched her, curious. She was aware of both his and Gabriel's positions, so he was certain she wasn't talking to them. He and Gabriel studied each other, obviously thinking the same thing.

A moment later, her fingers curled as if they were gripping an object and she rested her hand, palm up, on her leg.

"Thank you," she whispered.

She continued the breathing exercises. At one point her breath stuttered, and her free hand clamped down on her knee. The hand that seemed to hold something clenched. As they watched, Ava nodded, squared her shoulders, loosened her right hand.

"Yes." She nodded again.

She inhaled slowly until her breathing was under control again and resumed her exercises. Her body gradually relaxed.

After five more steady breaths, Ava opened her eyes. "I am ready to be hypnotized, Sensei."

• • • • •

Isabel was surprised to find her brother's vehicle in the driveway but no Gabriel in the garage. His tools were all put away, the machines wiped down, the floor swept. He was done for the day. Although that seemed a little early, Iz was relieved. She really needed the company.

She walked up his porch and turned the knob. The door was locked. What the hell? She found his spare key in the little hidden nook he had created for it. It dawned on her he was probably with Ava, which meant he was too busy for the likes of her. Feeling like an idiot, Isabel returned the key and turned from the door.

The notification on her phone chimed as she walked down the porch steps.

"For fuck's sake, Griffin, take a hint!" she snapped, but she pulled her phone out.

The message was from Gabriel.

> On my way home with Ava. She wanted to know if you'd come over tonight.

Relief hit her like a shock wave, bringing her embarrassingly close to tears. Ava was asking to see her? She sat on the steps, not yet ready to go inside.

She replied to let him know she was already at the house, smiling. Her smile faded as she switched to Griffin's Contact. She began to scroll through the messages he'd left her.

I'm sorry. My head was up my ass this morning.

She scrolled down to the next one.

I'm worried about you.

And the next:

Please come home so we can talk about this.

Followed by:

I don't know what to say to fix this.

Isabel rubbed her forehead. After a moment, she typed a reply:

I don't feel like talking tonight. I'll call you tomorrow.

Digging out Gabriel's spare key again, she let herself into his house and instantly poured a tumbler of whiskey. She missed Griffin terribly, felt as if she had been separated from him for days. And that was why she needed to take a day for herself. She needed to know she could.

Ava's Equinox pulled into the driveway halfway through her first round of whiskey. She prepared an ice water for Ava and pulled a beer out for Gabriel. When they came in, they stayed in the foyer. Iz heard them talking quietly and wondered if this had been a pity invite. Maybe they didn't really want her here, but Gabriel sensed she was having a rough time. He was intuitive in that way.

She carried her whiskey to toward the front door. At the sight of Ava, she froze.

"What the hell happened to her?" she asked, setting her drink on the bench used for taking off boots. She took a step toward them, but Ava raised her head and the look in her eyes made Isabel stop.

Her skin was ashen, her hair hanging limp around her face. She looked like she was barely able to stand up. Both hands were covered in bandages that may have been white at one time, but now were stained with dried blood. She was dressed in baggy black pants and a tee shirt. Gabriel was standing close to her, but he wasn't touching her. A large gym bag was sitting on the floor near the door.

Ava turned back to him. "I need a shower," she said, her voice quiet.

"Do you need help?" Gabriel asked.

Shaking her head, she started toward the stairs. And pulled her tee shirt over her head.

"Oh. Well." Isabel watched her drop the shirt at the bottom of the stairs and start unhooking her bra. "Not shy, is she?"

"Nope."

He knelt beside her gym bag, pulled out a thick uniform top with no button or zipper and set it aside. Giving the bag a quick search, he pulled out a hand towel and set it with the top.

"What's the matter with her?" Isabel asked.

Gabriel stood and nodded toward the kitchen. "She'll be at least half an hour."

They walked down the hall. He noticed the beer on the counter. "Is that for me?"

Nodding, she added a couple fingers of whiskey to her glass. "Why didn't you tell me you guys were busy tonight? Obviously, you don't need my company."

"Thanks for the beer. Ava told me to send you a text. On the drive home, she said she wanted to see you."

He took a long pull on his beer, sighing. What a fucking night.

"She looks sick." Still, Isabel couldn't help but feel a little tug of appreciation that Ava had asked for her.

Gabriel shook his head. "Just exhausted. Usually she has training on Wednesdays, but tonight she and Daniel worked on... ah... it's actually better if she talks to you about that. She said she'll be fine once she takes a shower and has something to eat."

He started rooting through the refrigerator.

"Daniel?" Iz asked, taking a big swallow of alcohol that left her throat burning.

"Her Sensei. He asked me to come to class today. Early this morning she had a nightmare and broke a window in my dining room. That's why the bandages."

He held his hands up, palms facing her.

"No shit?"

"I shit you not. It was a bad nightmare. I had to call Daniel to get her to snap out of it. She does some strange shit when she's sleepwalking, but this was the worst."

"Damn. Sleepwalking's batshit crazy."

Gabriel brought out chicken breasts and fresh green, yellow, and red peppers. "Chop these bad boys up," he said, setting the peppers on the counter in front of Iz. He gave her a cutting board and knife and proceeded to brown the chicken in a skillet on the stove top.

"She does it every night. Usually, she just checks the locks on all the doors, or I find her standing somewhere, staring at nothing. Sometimes she talks in her sleep. This morning, she was in full blown panic mode, breaking stuff, trying to break out of the house."

"Poor thing." Isabel started chopping, munching on an occasional piece of pepper. In another pan, Gabriel grabbed a package of frozen broccoli and tossed it in. He added a little water and set it on to boil.

"Enough about that. How are you doing? How's Griffin?"

"Actually, I should go. You guys obviously have enough on your plate tonight."

Isabel set the knife down.

"I told you, Ava wants you here."

"I heard you guys talking when you first got here. What were you doing, arguing about me being here? I don't want to be here because you feel sorry for me."

"Isabel, you're as stubborn as Ava." He walked over to the counter and picked up the knife, continuing the chopping. "We weren't talking about you. I was trying to get her to let me do her laundry. Her uniform from class. She refuses to let me do anything for her. Who does that sound like?"

He punched her in the shoulder.

"Really?" She glared at him over her drink.

"I swear. It's not all about you." He grinned.

She punched him back.

Needing to lighten the mood, needing to discuss something other than death, he thought about his plans for the weekend.

"I was thinking of having a cookout here on Saturday, inviting the guys and their girlfriends – or spouse, in Tom's case. Interested?"

"Sure. I haven't seen everyone in months. It'll be just me."

Gabriel raised his eyebrow.

"Griffin has to work," Iz said, smirking. "Have they met Ava?"

"Not yet. It'll be kind of a Happy Summer and Meet Ava cookout. Can you pick up a few things between now and then?"

"Sure. The weather's supposed to be beautiful. I feel so... confined."

"Is that why you're not with Griffin tonight?"

Leaning over to grab the whiskey bottle, she poured herself another glass. "I have a life beyond him."

"You're not smiling."

"I never smile."

He nodded, pulling another knife from the block, and handing it to her. "That used to be the case, until you started seeing Griffin. I've seen you smile a lot in the past couple months. I started thinking something was wrong with you."

She smirked.

"It looks good on you."

"Thank you," she said uncertainly. She continued cutting vegetables, deep in thought. She thought of Ava having her cut vegetables the first time she visited and wondered if she would ever be more than a food prepper.

"So?" Gabriel said. "What's going on?"

"I stop smiling for half a second and something has to be going on?" she asked.

"Defensive. Something is definitely going on."

"I'm not defensive." Isabel said, but she frowned as she considered the possibility.

"You're obviously upset about something. The sadness is back in your eyes."

A jarring sensation ran from her stomach to her chest. "My eyes look sad?"

Gabriel paused with the knife halfway through a piece of pepper. For a moment he gazed at her, his expression full of both love and sorrow. "You have the saddest eyes of anyone I've ever known, sis. Except maybe my own."

Her heart kicked up. "Why do you say that?" she asked quietly. The threat of tears stung at the backs of her eyes.

Gabriel shrugged. "Maybe it's just how we are," he said. "Maybe it's because of Hayden. I don't know why, but as far back as I can remember, you've always had this underlying sorrow in your eyes. I recognize it because I see it in the mirror every time I shave. Even when you laugh it's there, buried but always there. Sadness and something else... something I can't put my finger on but it's as strong as the sorrow."

Isabel looked away from him at once, as if she could hide whatever it was by averting her eyes. He turned back to the stove to put the chicken on a plate.

"Anyway, I know you're sad again because even though you're laughing, it's back in your eyes."

"Sorry to disappoint you," she muttered.

She watched him push the peppers off the cutting board into the hot skillet. He moved easily around the kitchen, not particularly enjoying it, but knowing enough to eat well and always have a variety of dishes. He tossed the pepper ends and seeds into the garbage.

"That's not what I meant. What happened with Griffin?"

"I really don't want to talk about it," she said, sighing. She took a big gulp of whiskey, preferring the fire in her throat to the repeated feeling that she was going to cry. She hadn't come over here to fucking cry.

"Fair enough. There she is."

Ava was standing in the doorway. She was wearing yoga pants and a long tee shirt. Her wet hair hung around her face and down her back in long, thick waves. Though she was still pale, her eyes weren't so haunted, and it didn't seem like she was ready to pass out. Her hands were wrapped in fresh, white gauze.

"Hey." Isabel dismounted from the stool and walked toward her for a hug. "Are you feeling better?"

"Keep your hands to yourself, you puny little twig."

Iz stopped, her eyes rounding at the deep voice coming from her friend. "What?"

Ava didn't move. Her head was tilted slightly, and she wasn't looking directly at Isabel. The lack of expression on her face was eerie.

"Isabel, don't touch her." Gabriel made sure everything on the stove would be fine for a couple minutes and turned toward Ava. He held up the glass of ice water.

"Isabel fixed some water for you."

"Well, give her a big old' bag of gold stars."

"What's going on? Why is she talking like that?" Isabel looked at Gabriel, who seemed unnerved but not particularly worried.

Ignoring his sister, Gabriel said, "No one's going to touch you, Ava. I've made dinner. Lots of protein to give you strength. Have a seat."

For several seconds, Ava stood where she was. Her eyes lifted and settled on Isabel's; her pupils were dilated.

"Okay, she's seriously creeping me out." Isabel backed around the breakfast counter, sitting on the stool farthest from Ava.

"The food's almost ready, Ava," Gabriel said, adding teriyaki sauce to the broccoli. "Why don't you take a seat and I'll get you a plate?"

Isabel watched her shuffle to the first stool and climb slowly onto it. She moved as if she was drugged. Reaching across the counter, she pulled the glass of water toward her and drank the entire thing, slowly, deliberately.

Gabriel had loaded a plate with what looked to Iz like enough chicken, peppers, and teriyaki broccoli to feed three people. He set it in front of her with a fork and knife. As he was about to turn to refill her water, her hand flashed out and grabbed his. It was trembling.

He looked down at their hands, up into her eyes.

Isabel watched them, fascinated. She had no idea what was going on, but the communication between them was almost palpable. So much was conveyed without words, so much affection be conveyed with the simplest of touches.

"No one's going to touch you, Ava," Gabriel repeated, his voice calm and patient. "Eat your dinner."

As Isabel watched, Ava's pupils shrank. She blinked.

"Dinner." Now her voice sounded dreamy.

"Yep. I made chicken."

"Chicken."

She released Gabriel's hand, folded her hands, and gave thanks. When she opened her eyes, she picked up her knife and fork and began eating enthusiastically, not waiting for water or everyone else to get their plates.

"What the fuck was that?" Iz said.

"Let her eat," Gabriel said quietly, refilling her glass. "When she's done, you can talk to her."

They ate in silence. Isabel kept sneaking glances at Ava out of the corner of her eye as she tried to eat at least half of her chicken breast and a fist-sized scoop of vegetables. She didn't know what to think. She couldn't think. The look in Ava's eyes had been dangerous, hateful. The voice had caused a chill to slide down Isabel's back.

After a second serving, Ava sighed deeply and pushed her plate back. She closed her eyes, reached out with her right hand, searching, until Gabriel took it, careful not to put too much pressure on the palm. She looked tired but not as distracted. With another sigh, she finished her water and looked directly at Iz.

"What do you want to ask me?"

"Oh. Uh. What just happened?"

"I ate dinner," she said, as if this was the most elementary answer in the world.

"That's not what I meant, obviously." The confusion in Ava's eyes was genuine, Iz thought. "You were talking to me in a weird voice. Your pupils were dilated. Are you on drugs?"

"I do not use drugs."

Isabel looked from her to Gabriel, who was content to let them sort it out.

Ava said, "Explain to me what you are talking about, and I will do my best to answer you."

"Like I said, your eyes. And you just talked to me in a demon voice. You called me a puny twig."

Ava looked at Gabriel for confirmation.

"You don't remember?" he asked gently.

She shook her head. She turned back to Isabel, her expression weary. "Did it hurt you?"

"It?"

"Did I hurt you?" Ava snapped, gripping Gabriel's hand like a vise.

"You didn't touch her," he said. He used his free hand to lightly pat hers. "Settle down. You'll start the bleeding again."

She relaxed. Still looking at Isabel, she said solemnly, "You are my bee eff eff. My best friend forever. We should not have secrets between us."

Raising her chin, she gazed at Gabriel. "You are my mate. We should not have secrets, either."

His eyebrow rose. "We're not bound in blood, Ava. We're still learning about each other. Some things are private."

"You learned part of my ability the other night, but you did not learn all of it."

"Shit's getting' real," Isabel said after a moment of silence. "Pass the whiskey."

Gabriel slid it in her direction. She poured more into her glass. Tomorrow was going to be murder.

"I don't usually invite myself, but in this case, I may need to stay the night. I've already had way too much to drink."

"Yeah, you're not driving," Gabriel agreed. He rubbed his thumb over the top of Ava's hand. "Go on."

"I should start from the beginning." She glanced at Gabriel. "You said I am psychic. That is not entirely accurate, although I understand what you meant.

"I am a mental medium with psychic tendencies. I have clairvoyant and psychometric abilities. Sometimes I experience automatic writing."

"You're a what with what problem?" Isabel asked. "Slow down. Do you know what she's talking about?"

She stared at her brother.

"Ah... somewhat. A medium communicates with spirits-"

"Yeah, I know that part, Einstein," Iz said wryly.

Gabriel ignored her tone and continued. "Clairvoyance is seeing things before they happen. Not sure about psychometry."

"I receive information from touching objects." She turned her attention from Isabel to Gabriel. "Clairvoyance is actually an ability to see things that are not present."

"Isn't that the definition of being psychic?"

Patiently, Ava sipped her drink and tried to convey her knowledge, a knowledge that took years to figure out when she first realized her abilities.

"Mediums can have psychic abilities. Not all psychics have the ability to communicate with spirits."

"That seems to be splitting hairs," Iz mumbled.

Ava nodded. "Humans must have labels for every occurrence in their lives, which makes communication with everyone, living or dead, confusing."

Isabel thought of hers and Griffin's argument and could agree with that.

"And the last thing?" She curled one leg under her butt. "The automatic writing?"

"My hand holds the pen but someone else writes the message."

"Outstanding," Gabriel said, intrigued. "What do you... or what does... whoever write?"

"'I'll tell you a secret.'"

"Great. I'm all ears."

"That is the message. The same phrase, repeatedly."

He considered that with his eyebrow raised.

"There have been other messages, but that is the most common since I moved here."

Isabel wished desperately for the oblivion of too much alcohol, but it wasn't coming. She should have been slurring her words and having trouble staying upright by now. This day had to be at the top of the list for fucking sucking.

"Okay," she said. "Let's pretend I believe all that for a moment. What does that have to do with you snapping at me a few minutes ago? What the fuck did I do to you?"

With a grim expression, Ava said, "Did you try to touch me?"

"I was about to give you a hug when you went all Exorcist on m-"

"I felt threatened. I do not like to be touched."

Isabel stared at her. "I've hugged you every time we get together on Fridays. You've been to my parent's house twice and every single family member hugs you, including me."

"It is quite inconvenient and time consuming," Ava stated, "but I am usually prepared for it. Sometimes after class, I am too tired and hungry. I apologize."

"I don't understand why you have to prepare for a hug after all this time. You've known me for months."

The first time meeting the family, Ava had felt threatened. Isabel understood that, to a point. It was overwhelming to be surrounded by so many people that wanted to engage in close physical contact. But now? After weeks of meeting up on Fridays, Ava seemed to be mellowing out a little. She even returned Isabel's hugs.

Ava stared at her so long, Iz became self-conscious.

"My first instinct is and will always be to defend myself from humans," she said. "As a child, when the abuse was at its worst, I was protected by... something else. I went somewhere far away, and something stood in my place."

Gabriel raised her hand to his mouth, kissed her knuckles.

"I do not remember what I said to you a few minutes ago because I did not say it. Whatever has protected me since childhood said it. Sometimes I remember when it takes over. Most of the time, I do not."

"You don't remember it happening at the dojo tonight?" Gabriel asked.

She shook her head. "I did not know it was happening at all until a few weeks ago, when I... when it first attacked my Sensei."

"But you seemed to be aware of it when you were telling me about breaking the kid's nose in school a few weeks ago," Gabriel said.

"Sometimes it comes to me slowly, and I have time to fight it. After I learned I attacked Sensei without realizing it, I spoke with David. I lost time throughout my childhood when I was upset. I never realized it."

When Gabriel started to pull his hand back, thinking she wanted space, she gripped him fiercely. Her eyes were full of hope. He continued to hold her hand, lacing his fingers with hers.

"Sensei is teaching me how to face it when The Monster comes, but as a child, the pain... the pain..."

She shuddered violently. Gabriel lightly touched her shoulder.

"When it first happened, when Mack raped me the first time, I felt like he had ripped me in half."

The silence was heavy, thick with horror. Isabel tried to swallow and couldn't. Suddenly the whiskey had turned her stomach sour.

"I thought I was dying," Ava continued. "I do not know who The Monster is or where it came from. I only know it allowed me to hide so far inside myself, I did not have to feel what Mack was doing to my body. I think the psychic ability allowed me to form a connection with something on the other side that wanted to protect me."

Tears hit Isabel's arms as she leaned her elbows on the counter, watching her friend. She didn't feel them.

"I do not like losing control, but sometimes The Monster takes over before I know what is happening. I am sorry for the way it spoke to you, Isabel. I do not want to harm you, or anyone. I have always thought it best to limit my exposure to humans to avoid The Monster hurting anyone."

Gabriel quietly stood and entered the kitchen to get himself a tumbler. He detoured to the bathroom to grab a roll of toilet paper for Isabel on his way back. Sitting back down next to Ava, he set the roll in front of Iz, who nodded her thanks.

"I wasn't going to hurt you," she whispered. "I just wanted to give you a hug."

"Part of me is learning that," Ava said carefully. "Most of me still expects an attack."

"Of course, it does." Gabriel slid his hand down her back and was pleased when she pressed against him instead of stiffening. "No one expects you to change overnight."

Irritation flickered over her face. "It has been sixteen years. The man is dead."

Isabel almost laughed with nervous relief. "You're kidding, right? That shit leaves serious emotional scars, Ava. And psychological ones. You're lucky to be alive."

"Yes. I am so very lucky." Contempt laced her tone.

"I'm not sure many kids would have survived what you lived through," Gabriel said.

"I only survived because The Monster took control."

"I don't think so." He brushed her cheek with the back of his knuckles. "I think there was strength to begin with, or it wouldn't have had anything to draw on."

"Now that I do not need it anymore, I cannot get rid of it."

"Your teacher is helping you with that."

"I should not need help," she snapped. "It is inside me; I should be able to handle it."

Yes, she was every bit as stubborn as Isabel, if not more so. He finished his drink and wished there was a way to convince her it was okay to ask for help.

"How about we move this to the deck? It's a beautiful evening."

Gabriel stood, stretching. As Iz passed him, carrying her bottle of whiskey and empty glass, she poked him in the ribs. He jerked, swore under his breath.

"You're evil."

He punched her shoulder. She elbowed him.

Ava watched them wistfully, and loneliness rolled through her so heavy it made her breath catch. Never in her life would she feel as comfortable around another human being as these two felt around each other. Or as comforted. A tear slipped down her cheek. She brushed it away quickly.

"Are you coming?" Isabel asked from the glass door.

"I have to use the restroom first."

When she was alone, Ava hugged herself on her walk to the bathroom. They had convinced her to be their friend, to come out of her carefully shielded world and experience affection, compassion. But to let in those emotions, she had to let in the darkness of human behavior, the sorrow in those mourning loved ones, the rage at how she had been used. Was it worth it? Inside her body, she felt like all those emotions were warring to get out. There were too many all at once and she did not understand how to deal with one emotion, let alone all of them.

She washed her hands, splashed water over her face. As she stepped out of the bathroom, she pressed her hand against the wall across from the doorway to keep from bumping into it.

Instantly, images of her and Gabriel filled her head: her following him toward the kitchen one weekend morning, her wearing a tee shirt and shorts, him wearing only shorts. With a sudden urgency, she jumped on his back and bit his shoulder. He had staggered a little, regained his footing and stepped back, bumping her against the wall. As he turned, he pressed her into the wall so she would not slide down and took her mouth with unrestrained hunger. She had reached between them and gripped him through his shorts. To steady himself, he had pressed his palm against the wall where hers was now.

She had felt like her blood was boiling, she remembered now as her skin began to heat up again. Looking at her hand on the wall, she remembered thinking there were too many layers between them. She'd pulled her shirt over her head and dropped it, attacking his mouth, her hands diving into his hair. There was something so primal about feeling his chest against hers, the wall against her back.

She continued toward the kitchen. Thinking of sex with Gabriel, she absently pressed a hand to her chest. She stopped at the edge of the counter in the kitchen. The first time, he had awakened her with kisses, and she had climbed slowly up from sleep to find herself in his arms. So gentle he had been, so slow and careful. When he thought of that time, he referred to it in his head as making love, not as sex. The phrase confused Ava.

Making love. Two people could not make love. Could they? Love, if the concept existed, either was there or it was not. Ava was not sure it existed.

And when he had taken her against the wall that morning, they had been primal with each other. They yanked clothes off, mouths warring to conquer, and he had driven inside her so hard she still felt wonderfully sore. When he thought about that time (and he thought of it often), he thought of it as banging. Ava did not understand that term either.

"Everything okay?"

Gabriel's voice drifted in from the patio doors in the breakfast room. Ava jumped and was upset she had not heard him open the door.

Swiping her glass of water off the counter, she walked toward him, wondering if her face showed what she had just been thinking about him. He had the sliding door open just enough to lean his body in. The outside lights were on behind him, leaving his face in shadow, but she did not need to see his face to know his blue eyes were steady on hers. He kept his arms outside, braced on either side of the door.

"We can stop talking about it."

So many emotions swirled through her. Feelings, always feelings now, filling her until she felt on fire from the inside out. He was not angry that she had kept The Monster from him. And now he would tell his sister the conversation was over if she was too tired to continue talking about it.

"She should know about Hayden."

"That can wait if you're not up for it."

She reached out, touched the side of his face. Tilting her head, she studied him. Searching his face, she tried to figure out what was going on inside her, what the sensation was that made her insides shake and her head feel light when she was close to him. Was it her connection to Hayden that brought on this odd magnetic pull toward him?

"I am ready."

He backed out of the doorway, gesturing onto the deck.

Twilight was settling in, light purple hugging the horizon. It was too early in the year for fireflies, leaving the yard full of shadows as purple changed to black. The temperature had cooled from earlier, but it was still comfortable enough to enjoy for a little while yet before the full chill of night set in.

Isabel was sitting in a chair by the west railing, the bottle of whiskey on the table next to her, the tumbler in her hand. Gabriel walked to the other two available chairs and paused.

"Do you want this one in the corner, so your back isn't to any doors?"

"'Nobody puts Baby in a corner,'" Iz said, and snickered.

"I am not a baby," Ava said.

Isabel burst into laughter.

Ava did not like how the chairs were set up. There were three, all facing in toward a table, facing toward the house. If she took the corner table so she was not facing any doors, she would be confined.

"You can sit in the corner," she told Gabriel. She handed him her water.

Looking confused, he shrugged and sat. "Now, where w-"

Ava walked to the railing, placed her hands flat on it, and raised herself up. She twisted and set her butt on it without making a sound.

"Jesus," Iz said. "You're going to fall off there. Do you have something against chairs?"

Dangling her feet, Ava regarded her. "I do not fall off anything."

She held her hand out for her water. Gabriel handed it to her, grinning at Isabel. "You should see her perch up there. She looks like a damn eagle."

"Your choice of chair placement is unsavory."

Iz snorted.

"Do you want me to move the chairs around so you can use one?"

"I am fine here."

"You crack me up, Ava." Isabel lifted her glass in a toast.

"Are you coherent?"

"Am I..." Shooting a quick look at Gabriel, she set her drink down. "Yes."

"You will remember what I tell you tonight?"

"Of course."

Ava looked down, wondering if what she said next would complicate her friendship. Would it matter if it did? Had she not wanted an excuse to step back from this friendship even before it started?

Isabel was watching her curiously, her lips curved in a slight smile.

Sitting here, even though Gabriel did not share her ideas about chair placement, was comforting. Training tonight had been exhausting. On the drive home, she wanted a hot shower and to read a book in absolute silence. Instead, she was enjoying the outdoors with her best friend and her mate, having conversations most people could not handle. Was it really so bad?

She mentally prepared herself.

"I have been visited by Hayden since I moved to Langdon seven months ago."

The smile disappeared. For a moment, Isabel's face was completely devoid of expression.

Ava did not say anything more; she let Isabel work through the information on her own.

"You-" Iz shifted in the chair to get more comfortable. "Hayden. Our Hayden?" She pointed to Gabriel, herself, back to Gabriel again.

Ava nodded.

"What does... how... I don't know how to respond to that."

"That reaction is typical."

Gabriel touched Ava's leg. "Are you alright, Iz?"

"No, I'm not alright. Am I supposed to be? How does she visit you? What does that even mean?"

"She appears to me in a Harry Potter nightgown. Her hair is in a single braid. Her eyes are the same color as Gabriel's. Sometimes she-"

Ava stopped abruptly, looked down into her glass. Took a drink.

"What?" Gabriel asked. "What were you going to say?"

"Sometimes she is bleeding. Here."

She pressed her index and middle finger to left temple.

Isabel looked at Gabriel. "Did you know about this?"

"I witnessed some behaviors that made me suspect she was... channeling Hayden." Gabriel rubbed Ava's knee. He needed something stronger than a beer. He motioned for his sister's bottle of whiskey.

The color had drained from Isabel's face. She handed him the bottle almost absently. "What... what types of behaviors?"

"There were things that made me suspect she was psychic – that she was a medium - in general," he said, grabbing the tumbler he'd brought out and pouring the whiskey. "But what sealed the deal is the night I made hot cocoa for us during a storm. She smeared Reddi-wip on my nose and said-"

"'Think fast,'" Iz whispered.

He nodded. Took a drink. It burnt all the way down.

"You believe she sees Hayden?"

Her tone was not full of disbelief or disgust, Ava noticed, but curiosity.

He reached across the table, took her hand. "I believe her."

Isabel looked at Ava, unable to stop the flow of tears. Ava didn't lie. That fact was the one constant in Isabel's life, the one steady fact that she could believe in.

"You are having trouble believing," Ava said. There was no judgment in her expression; it was an observation.

"I..." She couldn't find her breath. "She... do you..." She turned accusing eyes on Gabriel. "Why didn't you tell me?"

"It isn't my ability. It's up to Ava to decide if or when she tells you."

"It has to do with our sister!"

"Who has chosen to communicate with Ava. That leaves the decision up to Ava."

"She would want us to..." The deck suddenly seemed so small. Isabel pushed herself clumsily out of the chair and stepped away from them. Her head was suddenly very heavy.

"I will not find her for you," Ava said evenly.

"This is insane. I don't even know if I believe this." She covered her mouth with both hands.

Why tonight? Why couldn't they tell her this any other night?

"During Easter dinner, Jack noticed my hair had been braided. Your mother said Beth used to braid Hayden's hair the same way. I kept telling everyone I did not braid it, but no one would listen to me."

Turning back to them, Iz shrugged. "So?"

"Hayden braided my hair that day. She does it quite frequently."

"Outstanding," Gabriel said. He could feel energy pulsing off Ava like heat. Her body was vibrating with it.

"It's not outstanding," Iz said, slamming the rest of her whiskey. Shoving a hand through her hair, she pressed her fingers to the bridge of her nose. "Your nut-job girlfriend says she has the ability to talk to our dead sister."

"Careful." Gabriel's voice was steel under the soft tone.

"That is not what you have a problem with," Ava said. "You accepted my ability as soon as I told you because I am your friend, and because Gabriel believes me."

Isabel felt like everything she believed was crumbling. Her life was falling apart, every aspect of it, and she had no rope to hold onto to keep her from plunging over the edge. She pressed her palm to her forehead, feeling the slick sweat gathered there.

"You are upset because you are afraid everything you think and feel is laid open to me, and I will tell Gabriel. You are afraid he would think ill of you if he knew half of the thoughts in your head."

Iz knuckled a tear away and took a drink straight from the bottle of whiskey.

"Is that true?" Gabriel asked Isabel. "You're afraid I'll treat you different because of something you're thinking?"

"But I will never break your trust," Ava continued as if he had not spoken. "Even if I could pick up everything, I would not share what I learned with anyone. Even my mate."

"I cannot read your mind. I can pick up on very strong thoughts, but mostly I pick up on emotions. I have seen Hayden since I moved to Langdon. I do not know why she comes to me."

"She's just now starting to learn to control it," Gabriel offered.

"I told you because I thought you should know."

Iz sat quietly for countless seconds, staring at her glass of whiskey. She was frowning slightly, moving the bottom of the tumbler in a circular motion as she thought. Finally, she set her glass down and stood up.

"So, can I hug you now?"

Ava jumped silently down from the railing. Reaching out, she hugged her friend.

•   •   •   •   •

CHAPTER TWELVE

"Gabe."

The sound of his sister's voice startled him out of sleep immediately. He opened his eyes to darkness and briefly wondered if they were in the woods and he was fourteen years old.

"Gabe. Ava's downstairs."

Isabel. Not Hayden. They had sounded identical as children.

She shook his shoulder.

"I'm awake," he said, and again he was back in that tent with her voice trying to wake him up. Different locations, different situations, but he was still coming out of sleep, and he still heard Isabel's voice. The similarities were uncanny.

He forced himself to roll over and sit up. "Did she say anything?"

"Something about following her through the woods. I don't know who 'she' is. She's naked."

"That's how she sleeps."

He turned on the lamp, rubbing his eyes.

He should get a robe. That would be easier than trying to get her dressed every time. For now, he pulled a small blanket out of the closet and draped it over his arm.

Isabel followed him into the hall.

"She was talking as she went down the stairs. Her voice woke me up. I asked her what she was talking about. I don't think she knew I was there."

"Stay behind me," Gabriel said over his shoulder.

At the bottom of the stairs, he tapped the switch, flooding the foyer with light. Ava was standing parallel to his office door, facing the great room and kitchen. Just standing.

"Ava." Gabriel watched for signs that she heard him: a twitch, a tilt of the head. He saw none. "You're sleepwalking again."

"I cannot find her," she said softly, lifting her hand to rest it on his office door. "I looked, but I cannot find her."

She lightly patted her palm on the door.

"Who are you looking for?"

He came down the last few steps and walked toward her. The door was closed but never locked. Because the room was strictly for business, it was cluttered with his sketches and designs, sometimes tossed on the floor if he was deep into a project. He didn't want the mess of his work available to anyone walking in the front door. However, all client information was in locked cabinets, so locking the door was redundant.

Yet Ava hadn't walked into the office.

"Who are you looking for this time?" he asked. When she didn't answer, he took another step toward her. "Do you need a drink of water?"

"Water," she said dreamily, her hand falling from the door.

"Why don't you go back to sleep, and I'll bring up some more water," he said. "Okay."

She turned and walked into the door. The impact knocked her to the floor in a heap.

"Oh, my God!" Isabel cried.

"Well, that's one way to do it."

Gabriel knelt next to her, gently turning her head to get a look at her face. Red impact marks showed the outline of the bruising to come on the right side of her face, from her eyebrow to her cheek, and more along the inside of her nose.

"You're going to have a nice shiner for that one. Christ, Ava." He couldn't suppress a baffled laugh.

Beside him, Iz punched his arm. "It's not funny!"

Then she snickered.

Ava had no other injuries on her face or body, at least from this little journey. He supposed that was better than blood. Anything was better than screaming in agony or clawing to get out of the house with terror in her eyes.

Picking up the blanket, he draped it over her. He looped his arm under the back of her neck and brought her to a sitting position. He was just about to slip his other arm under her legs when her eyes flew open. She stiffened. Gabriel paused. Ava could do considerable damage so close.

She slowly turned her head, looking toward the great room as she had been when he had found her.

"Hayden."

Hearing her say his dead sister's name still stunned him. Isabel instantly followed her gaze.

"Do you see her, Ava?" Gabe pulled the blanket around to cover her better.

She lifted her arm, pointed toward the kitchen.

"There."

Of course, he couldn't see her, but he so wished he could. He longed to be able to tell her he was sorry for not being able to protect her all those years ago.

"There's nothing there, Ava," Isabel said, her tone filled with disappointment.

"Can you not see her?"

Ava leaned forward and pushed herself to her feet. As she walked toward the kitchen, Isabel scrambled to her feet. Gabriel followed, picking up the blanket Ava had slipped out from under. Gabriel hit the lights when they reached the kitchen. Ava paused at the counter. She turned back to them.

"She bleeds. Here."

She touched her index and middle finger to her left temple as she had earlier. When she pulled her hand away, her fingers were stained with red. Blood trickled down her face.

"I'm going to touch you," Gabriel said, wrapping the blanket around her. He really needed to get a robe for her. He put his fingers on her chin, tilted her head slightly to look at her temple. There was no cut, no mark. Just blood oozing, as if from out of thin air.

"Why are you bleeding, Ava?" he asked, lifting her hand. Her fingertips were smeared with blood.

"It is not my blood. It is Hayden's."

Isabel's stomach turned as she watched Ava's eyes lift to hers. The pupils were huge black circles, seeming to swallow her pale face.

"Can you get me a rag, Iz? Run it under cool water."

Ava's voice was disconnected, her eyes mesmerizing. "The rain was falling. Soft, like whispers. So soft. Even now when it rains that soft, steady rain, it makes you cry."

"Isabel!" Gabriel said sharply. "A cool, damp rag."

She twitched, jerked her eyes away from Ava's. Walked stiffly to the kitchen sink.

"Ava, why is Hayden bleeding?" Gabriel asked, brushing her hair back from her face.

Her head lolled. She blinked.

"Ava, why is Hayden bleeding?" He glanced up as he saw Isabel walking toward them.

"She will not show me. She only shows me the rain, the blood. The river. The rest is in the dark."

Isabel handed Gabriel the rag. He reached up to wipe the blood off Ava's temple... and it faded until it disappeared.

"What the hell?"

Lifting her hand again, he saw her fingers were clean.

"What happened to the blood?" Iz asked.

"I told you it was not my blood."

She shrugged her shoulders, almost causing the blanket to fall off.

Gabriel stepped away from her. "I need to get her some clothes. Make sure she doesn't do anything crazy."

"Because she's been perfectly sane up until now," Iz said dryly.

What am I supposed to do now? she thought, looking at the naked woman in front of her.

Ava's hair was long enough to cover her chest at least, and the blanket was staying on so far, but who knew how long that was going to last? And Ava's eyes were creepy when her pupils were dilated.

"Is... is Hayden still here?" Isabel asked. "Is she in this room?"
Ava nodded.

"She can hear me?"

Ava nodded again. She began to sing, very softly.

> Say say oh playmate,
> Come out and play with me

Isabel felt a shiver. She and Hayden used to sing the song as they played hand clap games. This had been their favorite rhyme. She joined in, surprised she remembered the words.

> And bring your dollies three
> Climb up my apple tree

They both began moving their hands in the pattern Isabel had learned with the song. The blanket slid to the floor but by then, Isabel didn't notice. When Gabriel returned to the kitchen, he found them in the middle of it, clapping in a repeating pattern and singing a nonsensical rhyme.

> Slide down my rainbow
> Into my cellar door

Gabriel watched in fascination as they performed a routine of hand clapping gestures he remembered seeing as a kid. At first Isabel was hesitant but the more she participated, the more she remembered. By the time they reached the final line, Gabriel realized he had watched Hayden and Isabel play that hand clapping game for hours. The repetition had driven everyone in the house insane, until their mother finally threatened to make them wear duct tape over their mouths if they didn't pick a different song. That one had always been their favorite, God knew why. It was rather morbid.

"I haven't played that in years," Iz said.

Gabriel blinked, remembered why he had gone upstairs, and stepped forward with the tee shirt and shorts he'd brought down. He set the shorts on the counter and reached out to help Ava into the shirt.

She slapped him, hard, across the face.

"Oh, damn!" Isabel said.

"Aw, fuck." Gabriel waited for the stars to settle before he said, "Ava, I'm going to touch you."

He waited another moment, then lightly touched her shoulder. Though she didn't slap him, she tilted her head, rolled it back so she was staring at the ceiling, then to the left.

"What is she doing?"

"Christ only knows."

He gently slid the arm holes over her hands, up her wrists.

"You do this every night?"

"Usually twice. Lift your arms, Ava."

She acquiesced and he tugged the shirt down over her head and torso.

"Shadows..." she said softly. "Shadows in the house... shadows everywhere... everyone has a shadow..."

Gabriel leaned down with the shorts and nudged first her right leg, then her left and slid them up around her waist.

"Shadows and darkness and secrets and lies." She raised her right hand, and her middle and ring finger were twitching. "The judge wants his skin back."

"He'll have to wait until tomorrow," Gabriel said. "It's too damn late."

He turned Ava toward the stairs. "Come back to bed."

"Is Hayden still here?" Isabel asked.

"It doesn't matter," Gabriel said shortly. "I'm tired."

Ava put her palm on Isabel's cheek. The gauze was rough against her skin. "She does not sleep like we do, but she rests."

"Come on."

Gabriel pushed her gently toward the stairs, glancing back at Iz.

"She'll probably wake you up again before your alarm goes off. You might want to lock your door."

Isabel followed him up and stood in the doorway while he helped her into the bed. The way he cared for her, being so gentle, making sure she was tucked in with the blankets pulled up to her chin, made Iz realize Ava meant more to him than some casual girlfriend.

"Molly!" Ava called, her eyes glazed, her hand reaching toward the ceiling.

"Which one is Molly?" Gabriel asked, keeping his voice low. He took her hand, pressed his lips to the back of it, and set it on her chest.

"The cook. The cook. The judge's cook. Worked for the family that lived here after Julian killed the judge."

"Tell Molly to keep it down so you can go to bed."

"Go to bed." Her voice was dreamy again, her eye lids drooping.

"If anyone else talks to you, tell them to fuck off."

"Fuck off."

When he stood, he saw Iz was still in the doorway. "Need something?"

"You're really good with her."

They stepped out in the hallway so they wouldn't disturb Ava.

"It's been a lot of trial and error. This isn't the end. She'll probably have another round in an hour or two. She might just check the locks, or she might go through the house like the Tasmanian devil."

"I already left a message at work that I won't be in," Isabel said. "I have a bitch of a hangover anyway. If my sleep gets interrupted again, I can always take a nap later."

She waited a beat. "I didn't realize it was so bad. With Ava, I mean."

He ran a hand through his hair. "I should have warned you. The screaming is the worst, but she hadn't done it for a couple weeks, until this morning."

"How often is she over here?"

"Three or four times a week. On the days she has class, we stay at her place. Tonight, she wanted to come here to hang out with you."

"Why?" When he looked at her sharply, she lifted her eyebrow. "I mean, with all this, why not sleep separately? Why do you put yourself through this?"

He glanced in at Ava, who was lying on her side, facing them. Though her eyes were still slightly open, her breathing was deep and even.

"Can you imagine her thinking she's still five years old, living with a man and woman that terrorize her every chance they get? Reliving the worst period of her life. And then she finally realizes she's awake, only to find out she's alone? I can't make her face it alone."

Isabel swallowed the lump that wanted to rise in her throat.

"Gabriel, you're the best person I've ever known. I love you."

His lips quivered. "I'll remind you of that in a couple hours when she wakes you up again."

•   •   •   •   •

She didn't have to wait two hours.

The shriek had her tearing out of bed and running for the door before she had fully left a dream. She almost ran into Gabriel in the hallway.

"Where is she?" Isabel gasped. Her eyes hadn't yet adjusted to the dark.

"I don't know. She was out of bed before I could stop her."

Something crashed downstairs. Gabriel took the stairs two at a time, Iz following as quickly as she could. He smacked his hand on the switch at the bottom of the stairs, the hallway, the kitchen, turning lights on as he made his way through the house, trying to find Ava. Isabel double checked each room to make sure he hadn't missed her. A quick glance in the great room, with hardly anything in it except the piano, showed her that room was clear. They moved on to the dining room, then the living room.

"Where the fuck is she?" Gabriel muttered.

"Gabe," Isabel said, bumping his arm. She pointed to the southeast corner of the room, where Ava sat huddled, her arms tucked between her chest and her knees. For once, she was still wearing the tee shirt and shorts Gabriel had helped her into earlier.

"Shit." He slowly approached her. "Ava. Wake up, honey."

He was ten feet away from her when she lifted her arm. In her hand was one of Gabriel's biggest butcher knives.

"Fuck me."

"Be careful!" Iz said.

The warning was unnecessary.

"Come back to me, Ava," he soothed. "You're safe."

He inched forward.

Closing her eyes, she wildly swiped the knife left and right. She raised her curled left arm and pressed it against her ear as she blindly struck out with the knife with her right.

"Jesus, Gabe..." Isabel said.

Sweat had gathered at the base of his spine and under his arms. He wiped the back of his hand across his mouth.

Think. Daniel had given him something to say when she was like this, but right now the phrase had completely slipped his mind. It was a simple, two-word phrase that had to be spoken in Japanese, of course. Gabe had practiced in front of Daniel several times in his head during the ride home to make sure he said it right. He'd typed it out phonetically on a note-taking app on his phone... which was charging upstairs on his bedside table.

Yet now, he didn't have a clue what he was supposed to say.

Shit. Shit.

664

Ava let out a low keening sound, her eyes still closed, the hand with the knife raised and ready to strike. Her cheeks were wet with tears.

"Ava, it's Isabel." She crouched down, coming as close as she could without being in stabbing distance. "What's wrong?"

"The Bad People. They came back."

Her lower lip trembled.

"Keep her talking," Gabriel whispered. He walked toward the stairs, giving Ava a wide berth, and jogged up them as quietly as he could.

"Who are The Bad People?"

"I lock the door, but they always get in."

Her body convulsed. Iz stepped forward, instinct telling her to comfort, but Ava's eyes flew open, and she slammed the knife into the hardwood floor. The tip dug in half an inch.

"Okay," Isabel said, easing back. "I'm sorry. I won't hurt you."

Gabriel was coming back. She heard him on the stairs and prayed he knew what to do.

"We're going to help you, Ava. We won't let The Bad People get you."

"They always get in," she whispered. She let go of the knife to cover the sides of her head with both arms now, curling into herself. Rocking, she moved so hard her back knocked against the wall in a steady thumping rhythm.

Gabriel came up beside Isabel with his phone.

"They always find me." Ava's voice was childlike.

She began that keening sound again. Isabel thought that the combination of Ava's wail, her rocking, and that steady thumping was going to drive her insane.

"Ava," Gabriel said firmly, looking at the screen of his phone, "Musha-burui."

Ava stopped rocking immediately. She fell silent. Her arms dropped to her sides. With her eyes still closed, she sat completely still, her muscles relaxed.

"What the fuck did you do to her?" Iz whispered, leaning forward.

Gabriel knelt in front of Ava, setting his phone aside. Holding his breath, he reached out and brushed her hair back from her face. She didn't move.

"Grab my phone."

Lifting Ava, he carried her through the living room, up the stairs, to the master bedroom. Isabel followed silently behind him. She watched from the doorway as she had earlier. He set her gently on the bed, pulling the blankets up around her.

"What did you say to her?" Isabel asked as he wiped the tears from Ava's cheeks. "What was it you said that made her stop?"

"Musha-burui," Gabriel said. "It's a Japanese phrase Daniel told me to use when she's terrified during a nightmare."

"What does it mean?"

"It's the anticipation before an intimidating task. He hypnotized her so when she hears that phrase, she shuts down."

He touched the side of her head. She was breathing deep and even.

Standing, Gabriel took Isabel's arm and walked out into the hallway, as they had earlier. He walked to the railing of the stairs so he could rest his forearms on it.

"I'm going to lock us in the bedroom. I should have thought of it sooner. At least then we won't have to chase her down. We shouldn't hear anything more from her tonight, but if you do, don't freak out if you can't get in."

"You want me to just ignore whatever I hear in there? Assume you have it under control?"

"I've been dealing with it on my own for over a month."

She couldn't argue with that.

"If you need anything, you come get me. Promise?"

He punched her shoulder. "Of course."

Back in the bedroom, he locked the door and turned to find Ava lying on her side, crying again. Her eyes were open, but she wasn't looking at him. Sitting on the edge of the bed, he rested his hand on her head. The tears were coming steadily, though she made no sound. He moved his hand to her shoulder, gave her a reassuring squeeze, but the gesture felt useless.

He stood and walked to his side of the bed. Climbing under the blankets, he turned off the light and pressed his stomach to her back. He wrapped his arm around her, pulling her tighter against him. As the crying became sobbing, she gripped his arm and held on. Her body shook as if the sorrow would rip her apart from the inside out.

Gabriel held on, suddenly engulfed in grief, drowning in it. And he understood he was sharing her emotions; she was feeling them so strongly now that they were pouring out of her and into him. All the terror and hopelessness she'd felt as a child was boiling over, all the suffering, confusion, and yearning for affection was leaking out with every tear drop. The weight of it all crippled him. There was nothing he could do to alleviate her pain.

He held onto her as tight as he could and hoped that was enough.

• • • • •

As usual, she was gone when he woke. He could still smell her. Dragging her pillow to his face, he inhaled deeply. There was something natural about her scent that made him think of summer after a heavy rain. Rolling over, he sat up and looked at the alarm clock. After eight, he thought, so she would have already worked out, showered, eaten breakfast, and left the house to go home to work. And hadn't told him she was leaving.

Pulling on jeans and a tee shirt, he was willing to give her a little slack after the night she'd had. The knife and terror hadn't bothered him as much as the sobbing in bed afterward. That had rattled him more than he cared to admit. For the first time since he had met her, her body had seemed fragile. That iron will he was so impressed by had seemed ready to crack.

The smell of coffee greeted him on the way down the stairs. His mouth watered in anticipation. Everything would come together after his first few sips of coffee. He would be able to think rationally, put things in perspective.

As he was pouring his first mug, he caught a flash in the back yard. Tilting his head to look out the breakfast room window, he saw Ava sprinting along the tree line. He walked toward the deck, watching her run from one end of the trees to the other. The distance was at least half a mile. She was damn fast; no wonder he couldn't keep up with her in the woods. Opening the patio door, he sipped his coffee. It was a good morning when he could drink great coffee and watch a beautiful woman with the grace of a panther.

And she hadn't left, which was why she hadn't told him she was leaving. He'd assumed, yet again, that she wasn't considering what he asked of her instead of the obvious – that she was still at his house. Why had he immediately jumped to the conclusion that she'd ignored his request? Where had the lack of trust come from?

He needed to work on that. She didn't deserve his suspicion.

Another thought hit him: If she'd started working out at her normal time, that put her workout at three to four hours.

Amazed, he leaned on the deck railing with his coffee in his hands, gazing at her. Her long limbs moved fluidly. From this distance, in the clear sunlight, he could see her hair was pinned off her shoulders, but he wasn't quite sure how she had it. He didn't see a ponytail. He hoped she hadn't cut off all that gorgeous dark hair for some reason. Running his hands through it made him feel settled, no matter how his day was going.

Ava was walking toward him. As she neared, her eyes steady on him, he saw the skin around her right eye was bruised in varying shades of purple and red. Her eyelid looked as if she had applied dark plum eye shadow. The rim of the lid was red. Immediately under the eye was fiery and puffy, but her cheek had taken the brunt of it. It started out purple high up and faded to gray halfway down the side of her face.

Those eyes, those strangely beautiful gray eyes, never left his as she stooped just a little to pick up her glass of water and continued up the stairs. Because he stood close enough to the stairs, she walked behind him and stood on his other side, setting her water to the side. Resting her arms on the deck, she kept herself just shy of touching him.

"Good morning," he said, hoping he didn't sound disappointed.

"Good morning."

"Does it hurt?"

She turned her head and he motioned toward his own right eye. She shook her head.

"Have you been exercising all morning?"

She nodded, sipped her drink.

Her hair was done up in that unique way again – one long braid wrapped twice around her head, with a few strands dangling at her temples. It reminded him of a statue on a bridge in Berlin. Beth had sent him a picture of it years ago when she and Jack went to Germany on vacation. She had talked for over an hour about the bridge, the name of which Gabriel couldn't remember now, and how the structure itself was breathtaking but the artwork on it was even more so. She'd taken several pictures of the statue Nike, the goddess known for victory, speed, and strength. The goddess was helping a wounded soldier. She was depicted with wings and a laurel wreath around her head.

Ava was definitely like Nike in her speed, strength, and victory, and instead of a laurel wreath, she wore her hair in this braid get up.

Gabriel could feel something from her, but he wasn't sure what it was. Whatever it was, her body seemed to hum with it.

"I need a shower." Turning away from him, she walked toward the door. When she slid it open, she turned back to him. "Will you join me?"

Surprised, he straightened, studied her. She wasn't asking to save on water or time; she was asking if he would keep her company.

"Sure."

They undressed without speaking. Gabriel wasn't sure what to say. Her mood was baffling him, and she was keeping her expression neutral so he couldn't tell what she was thinking. It was times like this he wished he could borrow some of what she had so he had a clue what the hell to say.

She began pulling pins out of her hair and unwinding it, so he stepped in first. Maybe if he fixed her breakfast, she would feel better. It could be she was only tired from the rough night and needed calories after working out all morning. A nice breakfast with plenty of protein should help her perk up a little.

She stepped into the shower. Her long hair was wavy from the braid and damp from sweat. Gabriel grabbed his bottle of shampoo and moved around her. She eased past him. Backed into the spray. Still not touching. Raising her arms slowly, she took deep breaths as she ran her hands slowly over her face, then her hair, careful not to bump her eye as she soaked her body. He replaced his shampoo bottle with hers and held it out when she opened her eyes.

They switched positions again. When he'd rinsed his hair, he waited for her to finish massaging the shampoo into hers. She slid around him to rinse. Her avoidance of him was second nature to her. Instead of moving onto the body wash, Gabriel reached out and gently took her face in his hands. He was careful not to bump the bruises around her right eye.

Her eyes opened immediately. Her hands, which had been working the shampoo out of the hair she'd piled on the top of her head, slid down to grip his wrists. Water cascaded down her back, her shoulders, sending soap along her body in sudsy streams. Whether she wanted to kiss him or kill him, he wasn't sure. The gray in her eyes was luminescent, curious, but her body was thrumming as it did when she was unsettled.

The toilet flushed from the second bathroom. Gabriel felt his pulse trip, but Ava didn't react. They continued studying each other as they heard Isabel open the bathroom door and walk downstairs.

Gradually, he realized he could no longer feel that vibration from Ava. Her body had settled down, he thought, and maybe her mind as well. They were standing as they had been for the past several seconds, but he no longer felt like he was standing next to an active volcano. Did he have a positive effect on her? Or to be more accurate, had she allowed him to have a positive effect on her?

Lowering his hands to her shoulders, he gave them a squeeze. She broke eye contact and continued rinsing the soap out of her hair. Gabriel reached for the body soap.

The moment was over.

•　•　•　•　•

Fuck.

Head throbbing, mouth dry as sandpaper, Isabel groaned as she poured herself a cup of coffee. Gabriel's first floor had many large windows to let in natural lighting in almost every room – a feature Iz usually appreciated. This morning, the sun was piercing her skull.

"Fuck you, sun."

Her hand gave an involuntary spasm and she spilled coffee on it. "Fuck!" she spat, dropping the carafe back into the coffee maker with a loud clatter. The sound drove straight into her temples. "Cocksucker!"

Wiping the mess up with a paper towel, she glared outside at the offending sun. She picked up her phone and walked to the refrigerator, checking her messages. Griffin had left another one.

> Good morning. Thinking of you and hoping we can talk tonight.

Isabel felt her lips quiver just a little. Setting the creamer on the counter, she typed a message and sent it:

> Morning. Let me know when you're done with work. I'll come over.

She poured creamer in, sipped to evaluate the taste, poured more in. Satisfied, she returned it to the refrigerator and, taking her phone and coffee, rounded the counter and sat on one of the stools.

It was late enough in the morning that he was probably working already, so she might not hear from him until -

"I am THOR, son of ODIN!" her phone proclaimed, letting her know a text message from Griffin had come in.

She smirked.

I'll be early today, 3 PM. What is your favorite flower?

Now she rolled her eyes. Her fingers flew over the buttons on her phone.

I don't need flowers. I'll be there at 3.

She shook her head when he sent her a heart. Then, feeling foolish, she sent one back. Before she became a weepy, star-eyed female in need of rescuing, she turned her phone upside down and took a long drink of her coffee.

Ava appeared. Her right eye was bruised to hell.

"Holy shit."

Isabel stood, started toward her, then stopped. "Right. Sorry."

She sat back on her stool. "How's the eye?"

"Bruised. You may give me a hug."

Iz eyed her warily. "I don't need a pity hug."

"I do not know what that means."

"It means I don't need you to feel sorry for me to get physical affection."

Ava got herself a mug and poured coffee. "You are angry with me."

"I'm angry you think I'm desperate enough to beg for attention, physical or otherwise."

Ava studied her with her strange eyes for several seconds. Isabel took a sip of her coffee to cover her nerves, refusing to break eye contact. She was relieved when Ava turned to get creamer from the refrigerator.

"I do not feel sorry for you, or anyone," Ava said as she fixed her coffee. Almost as an afterthought, she took another mug down from the cupboard and poured coffee into it. She added sugar from the bowl next to the coffee pot.

"I feel an odd sensation…" A little crease appeared between her eyebrows as she lightly touched her fingertips to her chest. "I do not know why, but I feel like a hug would be enjoyable. I understand if you do not want to touch me after my behavior earlier this morning."

Shame flooded Isabel. She stood and walked over to Ava, reaching out. They hugged awkwardly.

That was how Gabriel found them when he entered the kitchen.

"That's precious," he said, keeping one hand behind his back.

"I've got something precious for you," Iz said, raising her middle finger as she walked back to her stool. "Do you have aspirin?"

Gabriel reached into the counter over Ava with his free hand and tossed Isabel a bottle. Ava turned and looked up at him. He was standing close.

"I made you coffee."

She lifted the second mug she had prepared. "Sugar."

Touched, he took a sip. It was exactly right. "Thank you."

He brushed his lips over hers, ignoring the noise Isabel was making as she poured pills into her hand at the breakfast bar. Making his coffee was a sweet gesture, and the timing was perfect.

"I have something for you."

Lines appeared on Ava's brow. "Why?"

"Why not?" He brought his hand out from behind his back.

Ava stared. He had made her nunchucks with carved handle grips out of wood. A tiger was burned into each baton. The detail of the tiger was intricate. It must have been difficult to draw on the thin, round wood, especially with a hot brass tip instead of a pencil. The animal's front paw was extended, so it was over exaggerated and large, with the claws extended. Its mouth was open in a snarl, large canines showing.

"I don't know if you use nunchucks or not," he said, feeling self-conscious about his work for the first time in years. "I wanted to design something for you. Once I learned you studied martial arts, I wanted to use a design that represented your strength and your grace."

She wasn't speaking. She was staring, turning them over in her hands, running her index finger over the animal. Isabel was paying attention now, her interest piqued. Gabriel began to feel insecure the longer Ava went without speaking.

"Ah... I don't know if I crossed cultures with the weapon," he said. "The dojo you train in is traditional Japanese, right? The research I did said nunchucks originated from China. But I wanted to make you something badass, and those..."

Ava lifted her head and Gabriel was shocked to see her eyes were glassy.

"It's martial arts taboo, isn't it? Mixing Japanese and Chinese tradition. I fucked up. I'll make you something else."

He reached out to take them back. Ava was looking down at the tigers again and when Gabriel stepped forward to take them, she planted a hand firmly in his face, her fingers splayed. Isabel smirked.

"Okay," Gabriel said, his voice muffled around Ava's palm. "You're going to have to help me out, Ava, you're giving me mixed signals."

Laying the weapon gently on the counter, she grabbed his shirt and yanked him toward her, wrapping her arms around him. Lifting an eyebrow, he hugged her back, looking at Isabel over her head.

"I guess that means she likes them."

Isabel grinned. She leaned up and picked them up off the counter. "They're beautiful, Gabe."

"They're functional. Don't poke your eye out, kid."

"Funny."

Ava was running the fingertips of one hand up and down his lower back very lightly. When she pulled back, her eyes were intense.

"Sensei teaches several styles of martial arts from cultures in the dojo besides Japanese," she said. "One of the styles I am currently learning is Kung Fu, which is Chinese in origin."

He leaned his forehead against hers, relieved. "I was afraid there was some kind of rivalry between Japanese and Chinese styles, like there is with the Green Bay Packers and the Minnesota Vikings."

"The Shaolin Kung Fu style I am studying based their techniques off five animals to create their defenses. My favorite is the tiger. It is direct and powerful. Sensei said my natural style is the tiger because I have a strong internal force, or chi, which is represented by the tiger. This is a perfect gift."

"Really?" He held her at arm's length.

She nodded. A tear slid just past her eye lid and hovered. "It is a beautiful gift. Thank you."

"You're welcome."

"Ballin'," Iz said, leaning up again so she could set them on the countertop. "What are the other animals?"

"The dragon, the snake, the leopard and the crane. The tiger is the first one I am learning."

Iz watched Ava pick up the chucks. "Have you ever practiced with them?"

Ava walked out of the kitchen, into the great room, where there was a higher ceiling and no furniture to smack into. She began whipping the nunchucks around swiftly, flashing them out in front of her, behind her back, around in a circle above her head, switching from one hand to the other.

Gabriel, who had followed her, nudged Isabel. "I'm dating Bruce Lee."

Iz was gaping. "I think I just peed a little."

Ava was going fast enough that the swinging baton was a blur. She moved around the room as she moved her hands, avoiding the large windows. After forty-five impressive seconds, she stopped with one stick under her arm and her free hand out, fingers splayed, facing Iz and Gabriel, Bruce Lee style.

"Would you like to try?" she asked. Moving her arm, she released the one baton, let it bump against the other, and used her free hand to press the two sticks together. She held them out to Isabel, bending forward slightly in a bow but keeping her eyes on the older woman.

"God, no. I do a fantastic job hurting myself without weapons."

Ava turned to Gabriel and held them out to him.

"I can't follow that act," he said, shaking his head with an amused smile.

She pressed them to her chest in a gesture Gabriel recognized as pure affection. Her gray eyes settled on his.

"Thank you," she repeated.

•   •   •   •   •

Getting yelled at by his manager was the perfect ending to Griffin's rubbish day. Knowing his manager was right to do so, that he had been so distracted he'd needed his superior to knock him back in his place, pissed him off even more. At least he had been pulled into the office instead of being humiliated in front of his team.

He drove Rover through the city gripping the steering wheel until his knuckles ached. He was letting his personal feelings get in the way of his work. Just when he felt he was making progress with Isabel, she shut down or backed away from him. All day he'd tried to figure out what to say to her, to make her understand. Work was not the place for these types of thoughts. His rational mind knew this.

He checked his mail before heading up to his flat to wait for Isabel, hoping his mood wouldn't spoil seeing her.

His door was unlocked. Pushing it cautiously open, he stepped inside to see Isabel pouring whiskey into a tumbler. A glass of wine already sat on the counter. A nice dark red, perfectly fitting his mood.

"Hey," he said softly, closing the door behind him. Just seeing her made his pulse quicken.

She glanced up, and he saw her hesitation in the stiff posture, the wary expression. Her grip tightened on the tumbler. Walking over to the island where she stood, he set his computer bag on one of the stools. Izzie slid his wine over to him but was careful to move her hand away quickly, so their fingers didn't touch. She wasn't ready to forgive him just yet.

"Thank you." He took a sip, then another. Then downed the rest of it. "Do you mind sharing your whiskey tonight?"

Raising her eyebrow, she turned to get another glass. Griffin wanted to reach for her and had to clench his hands to keep them on the counter. He'd missed her scent, her touch, the feel of her against him. One night had felt like a month.

After pouring him a glass and refilling hers, she kept the bottle and walked into the living room. She opened the patio door and disappeared outside, leaving the door open. Griffin waited a moment, then followed her out.

They sat in the chairs for countless seconds, drinking silently. He waited. The sun was out, seeming to contradict the mood. Below them, in the park, joggers were enjoying the trail, kids were storming the playground, and laughter drifted up to where Griffin and Isabel sat.

Finally, he couldn't take it anymore.

"What can I say to make this right, Izzie?" He set the whiskey down. It had upset his stomach, like he knew it would. "This silent treatment is driving me fucking bananas."

"I'm not giving you any treatment," she snapped. "I don't know how to talk to you, how to tell you what's going on in my head."

Running his hand through his hair, he took another drink. "Sorry. I missed you. I'm jumping out of my damn skin."

"It's too fucking happy out here," Isabel said. "I'm going inside."

Hoping he might be able to sit closer to her, he took his drink and followed her back in. She refilled her glass quite full, set the bottle on the coffee table, then sat sideways on the couch so her bare feet were on the cushions facing him. She held her whiskey close to her chest with her knees propped up, closing herself in. Staring into her drink, she swallowed.

"I found out last night that Ava is a medium."

He blinked. That was not where he thought this conversation was going.

"Okay," he said slowly. "What does that have to do with our argument yesterday?"

"Do you believe in the ability?"

"Do I believe she communicates with spirits of the dead?" Griffin blew out a breath. "I'm a little caught off guard for this kind of conversation. There has been research done, some ambiguous scientific leanings. I think the results are still up for interpretation."

"I'm not asking how other people interpret data. I'm asking what you think, what you believe."

He shrugged. "I've never given it any thought. Where is this going?"

"You think you know what's best for me. You think you can save me."

What was happening? Griffin's heart was hammering in his chest. She was shifting subjects, subjects that were not related to each other, not making any sense.

"I think your body is reacting violently to stress, making you sick more often. I think it's been eating away at you for a long time."

"So what if it has?" She was leaving him, going away in her mind. He could see her drifting away as her eyes glazed with a far-off stare. Fingers of panic gripped him, squeezed his throat. He tried to stay calm.

"You should get help for it, talk to someone before your body shuts down completely."

"Because talking will solve all my problems."

Irritation flickered across his face. "No, Isabel, but at least you'll have an outlet for your grief. Letting go of some of that guilt will help you heal."

"Maybe I don't deserve to heal."

"Everyone deserves it."

"You don't know what I fucking deserve." Her hand was shaking when she lifted her glass to drink. She had to steady it with the other one to keep from knocking it against her teeth.

What could he say? Nothing was getting through to her. Everything he said was taken as a personal assault. When he took a moment, he realized she didn't need his advice. She needed him to listen.

Shifting into a more comfortable position on the couch, he gazed at her and waited.

"Hayden woke me up the night she disappeared."

He wanted to reach over and touch her foot, her knee, anything to let her know she was safe. To let her know he cared.

"We always shared a tent. The rule was none of us left the campsite without a buddy. She wanted me to go with her so she could use the bathroom. I was so pissed at her, and so tired. I told her to hold it until morning.

"It had been raining lightly all night. The soft, steady rain that makes people think of Sunday mornings and staying in bed. Even now, when it rains like that, I can't..."

She shuddered softly.

Griffin leaned forward to offer comfort, but she pressed her back against the arm of the couch.

"You don't get to touch me while I'm doing this."

Clenching his fists, he lowered his head, fought for patience.

"You want me to talk, I'm talking. Keep your fucking hands off me."

When he looked at her, she had the tumbler clasped between her hands, her spine rigid. Her expression was devoid of emotion. She didn't think she could get through it without closing herself off, reporting the facts like she was reading a report.

This wasn't how he wanted her to move on from this part of her life. He'd wanted it to be a relief for her to talk, a way to let go of her guilt. He had wanted to be someone she could talk to because she wanted to, not because he was forcing her to.

"I felt her get up and leave. When I crawled to the opening of the tent and looked out, I saw…"

She swallowed.

"What, Izzie?" Griffin asked. "What did you see?"

"Someone in a hoodie walking toward the restrooms. Lightning flashed and I saw it so clearly. A man in a blue hoodie was walking toward the restrooms where Hayden had gone. I was afraid he would see me, so I got back into my sleeping bag and hid, waiting for him to come get me, too. Something about the way he looked, walking at night, his face covered… it was terrifying. I fell asleep waiting. When I woke up the next morning, it all felt like a dream."

"I'm so sorry, Isabel."

"Not sorry enough to leave it alone." She took another drink. Set the glass on the table very deliberately. "By morning, she was gone. If I had gone with her, if I had followed the man in the blue hoodie, she would still be alive."

"You can't know that."

"I do know that. The next day, during the search in the woods, the police found blue threads on a branch where the fabric had torn. They found one of the shoes Hayden put on to go to the restroom. They also found hair, but the rain made DNA testing inconclusive. That's the reason they think she was kidnapped and killed. There was a pedophile just released living within twenty-five miles of the camp site. His hair color matched. They never found him to question him."

"And they never found her body to prove she was dead," Griffin said softly, thoughtfully.

Isabel stared at him. "Pedophiles usually play with their toys until they have no more use for them. He wouldn't have returned her after their play date.

"There was no National Registry for Sex Offenders back then," Iz continued dully. "A pedophile didn't have to contact the local authorities when moving to a new city. If the guy hadn't had previous trouble with the police, they never would have suspected him."

"I'm sorry you lost your sister, Isabel." He set his drink on the table and scooted closer.

"I didn't lose her." She was shaking now, too angry to hold back the tears that had been threatening during this entire conversation. "She's not a cell phone or a wallet. I caused her death."

Her hand came up and covered her mouth. Closing her eyes, she trembled as the agony coursed through her. Griffin rested his palm on her knee.

Instantly, her eyes were open, and she flung his hand off her. "I said don't touch me!"

It seemed to Griffin that all the air had left the room. He couldn't breathe, couldn't find the words to say to ease her pain.

She stood and walked around the coffee table, pacing the length of the rug. Back and forth, her bare feet lost in the thick gray and white marbled material. Her hands were clasped on her elbows, head down, tears streaming.

"Isabel, did you ever tell your family about this, the police?"

She shook her head. "At first, I was in shock. And terrified he would come back for me. Then there was no point. They found the blue material and her shoe, did the search for nearby criminals with histories of violent crimes, and interviewed everyone but the one they couldn't find. King, his name was. Sam King. The case went cold, and what I saw couldn't add anything to the investigation. I couldn't tell height, weight... I couldn't even really tell gender because I never saw the person's face. But it wasn't hard to put the pieces together."

Wiping her cheeks, she leaned down and picked up her glass. A quick swallow and Griffin thought he had watched her finish the equivalent of four drinks. At least. All of them were doubles.

He reached for her hand, but her voice stopped him.

"I hate you."

And there it was, what he had been hoping for all along: a sign that there was still enough of her in there to come out and begin to heal. Isabel couldn't lie worth a damn. The feeling that the world was dropping away beneath his feet faded at once.

"I'll always hate you for making me talk about this."

"Isabel-"

"You said talking about it would make me feel better. You said it would help me let go of some of the guilt I carried with me."

She was shaking again, her eyes boring into his, the shade of green all but black in their sorrow.

"But I don't want to feel better, Griffin. I don't want to let go of the guilt. I want it to eat away at me every day until there's nothing left of this body to put in a coffin. That's what I deserve. For killing my sister."

Back on solid ground emotionally, Griffin stood, taking a step toward her. She took a step back.

"It's not your fault."

He took another step, another, watching her retreat each time.

"You didn't kill your sister. You didn't cause her death. You've no right to take this on yourself."

Her eyes were steady on his. She didn't believe a word he said.

Another step. When she countered, her back hit the bedroom wall.

"I love you, Isabel."

The words startled her, and her eyes shifted. She was thrown off guard.

"I love you for your ability to cuss like a sailor at everyone in the world even though you would be the first to help any one of them if they fell down."

"Shut up." She rubbed her palm over her cheek, absently trying to wipe away tears.

"I love you for your compassion for your sister, even when she treats you like shit because she envies your strength." He eased toward her carefully so she wouldn't bolt.

"Stop it."

"I love you for your honor, taking all the grief and shame your mother throws at you, because you know you're strong enough to handle it and she isn't."

He was so close now he could feel the heat and the anguish pouring off her. He could see her pulse pounding in her neck and her temples, could hear the ragged gasps of her breath.

"Shut up!" She squeezed her eyes shut, tears spilling over.

He rested his hands on her shoulders.

"And I love you because even if you wanted to hate me, you can't. You're not capable of hating. That's not how you're made. I love you, Isabel."

Finally, the dam broke, and she began really crying. Years of internalized mourning poured out in large tears that burned against her cheeks. Her breath hitched. Her hair fell forward, creating a curtain that hid her face from him. When her legs gave out and she began to crumble, Griffin caught her. They sank slowly to the floor together. He leaned back against the entertainment center and held her to him while gut wrenching sobs shook her. Pressing her body hard against him, her head curled against his shoulder, she wailed without shame or restraint.

"It's about bloody time, Izzie," he soothed, stroking her hair. "Well done."

• • • • •

"I'm beginning to think you enjoy getting beat up," Sensei said at class that night.

Kneeling across from her and Vincent on the mat, ready to start warm up exercises, she avoided his raised eyebrows at the bruise covering her eye and half her cheek.

Vincent had already shown his concern, gently touching the skin and examining her face thoroughly before he would drop the subject. Ava was mildly irritated at the attention he gave her; now she was downright livid to have to repeat the story of how it had come to be. In an attempt to gain control over her inconvenient emotions, she pretended to misunderstand her teacher's statement.

"If it is difficult to look at, Sensei, I will wear a mask to class next week."

The muscles in her legs were clenched. She forced herself to concentrate on each one, make it relax. To calm her breathing, to take more air in instead of panting like a wild bull. Averting her eyes, she focused her gaze on the mat. If Sensei looked into her eyes, he would know immediately she was struggling with anger.

"I think you know that's not what I meant." He sat patiently with his legs folded beneath him, his butt resting on his heels, as they all did before training. It was tradition in the dojo.

"Hai, Sensei."

They began with push-ups. Ava hoped the matter was closed. She began to relax to the meditative cadence of his voice as he counted off their push-ups:

"Ichi, ni, san, shi, go, rok, shichi, hachi, kyu, juu…"

The normalcy of the workout, the repetitive, serene tone during each count, eased the stress from her body.

She should have known better.

"So? What happened?" Sensei asked during a brief pause between normal push-ups and doing them on their fingertips.

Trying to unlock her jaw, Ava said as politely as she could, "I do not wish to discuss my personal business."

They began the next set. "Does it have anything to do with what Gabriel was here for last night?"

"Hai, Sensei."

"Then it's also my business."

"Hhmmmmmmmmmmmmm."

The growl came from deep in Ava's throat and filled the dojo. Vincent looked over at her sharply, pausing in the middle of a push up. As he continued counting, Daniel watched Ava's eyes change from dark and outraged to slightly brighter and only moderately pissed off. She sat back in the relaxed state to wait for the next set of push-ups.

The urge to discuss this latest example of control over The Monster was strong, but if he didn't finish the discussion about her bruised eye and make her talk about it, The Monster would consider itself the victor over this small battle.

"Were you sleepwalking again?" he asked.

"Hai, Sensei." The intensity of her eyes was not aimed at him now. She was waiting for it to come back, waiting to have to control it again.

"Relax," Daniel said easily. "You can't spend your life waiting for something that may never happen. Let's do planks. Left side."

They switched exercises.

"You were sleepwalking," he pressed.

"I ran-"

The way she snapped off the end of the word made him glance over at her. She was actually blushing as she lay on her side, propped up on one hand with her feet stacked, the other hand pointed toward the ceiling.

"Gabriel said I ran into a door."

Daniel smirked. Remembered she didn't make jokes. "You're serious."

"Hai, Sensei."

Now she was gritting her teeth again, not from the strain of the exercise. He glanced at Vincent and saw the young man trying to hide a smile.

The only way to keep from laughing was to plow ahead, so he switched to the right side for planks and said, "What about the other matter we discussed last night? The phrase? Was there cause to use that?"

Ava was grateful to move past the door incident. "Hai, Sensei. Gabriel said it worked immediately."

"That's good."

"Hai, Sensei."

"That's very good. Switch."

Later, toward the end of class, Ava and Vincent were in the middle of sparring when she noticed Daniel wave someone into the dojo. He stood and walked toward the entrance. She heard low voices.

Since it did not concern her, she continued with Vincent, enjoying the physical challenge of free style sparring, where they could use any technique, any style, as long as they did not injure each other. This was her favorite exercise, since she had to anticipate Vincent's next move instead of knowing it was going to be the same techniques from the level they were training for. It also reminded her of how many different ways there were to take care of a single problem. Martial arts were simple and straight forward. They did not complicate matters with emotions and drama. If an attack came, the body automatically defended itself.

Her movements with Vincent had always been fluid, natural. They had understood each other from the day she started working with him. The nonverbal communication was intense, precise, and as strong as it had ever been. The connection did not have anything to do with her being psychic. She thought it had to do with her need to survive and his willingness to help her learn how.

Sensei returned to the mat and called out to end the class. They immediately stopped sparring, bowed to each other, and returned to the center of the mat, across from where he was sitting. Ava saw from the corner of her eye that Gabriel had entered the dojo and was waiting for her. She wondered how long he'd been there, watching her with Vincent.

"Your ride's here," Sensei said.

"Hai, Sensei." She thanked him in Japanese, bowing.

He asked if they had any questions on their techniques. Gabriel listened as Ava said something in Japanese and then asked a question. They discussed it at length. Then Vincent asked a question.

The respect in the room loomed like a live thing, a separate entity that bound them all together. After each question was answered, the student thanked the teacher, bowing and showing earnest gratitude for sharing his wisdom. A deep connection bound all three, made them family. Gabriel wondered if the long-term study of martial arts made it that way or if it was something else.

"Vincent, why don't you go ahead and get changed."

Vincent stood and started toward the back.

"Why are you here?" Ava asked Gabriel. "I do not need a ride tonight."

"I was in Madison anyway. I wanted to make sure you were okay to drive."

"I told him to stop by anytime." He turned his attention to Gabriel. "Ava said the phrase worked during a nightmare last night." Daniel added, bumping his fists on his lower legs to get blood circulating in them.

Gabriel nodded. "Immediately."

"I didn't want to get into it too deep with Vincent around," Sensei said to Ava, watching her stretch. "I wasn't sure how much he knew."

"I tell him everything," she said simply. "He should know the phrase in case something happens when I am around him."

She looked at Gabriel. "Isabel should know, too."

He nodded. "She knows. She was awake last night when I had to use it. It's only for the nightmares, right? It doesn't work for that other... thing?"

"The Monster," she said softly. "No. We have not figured out how to stop that yet."

The lack of control over it still upset her, Gabriel noticed. She dropped her eyes from his and continued stretching, performing moves he had seen her do at home.

"You did a good job of that tonight," Daniel said. He turned to Gabriel. "She shut it down pretty fast during class. I think she's getting a grip on it."

Vincent walked out of the back area and Ava stood. She heard Sensei introduce Vincent to Gabriel as she dragged the curtain across the rod and began to undress. Vincent was telling Gabriel he had known Ava since approximately two years after she arrived at the dojo, and they had been training partners ever since. They sounded relaxed. Ava was surprised at how much that mattered to her.

She took off her belt and uniform top. Her tee shirt underneath was damp with sweat. Sparring with Vincent was always a good workout. Sitting on the bench, she took off her tabi and replaced them with socks. She folded everything and put it in her gym bag. Taking small sips of water, she made sure she had everything from her cubby before leaving the changing area.

Vincent was standing next to Sensei on the mats while they talked to Gabriel.

"Ava, can I have a minute before you leave?" Sensei asked, walking back toward her. He glanced over his shoulder at Gabriel. "We'll be just a minute."

They both disappeared into a room just past the mats.

Vincent stepped off the mat, picked up his shoes, and sat at the opposite end of the bench.

"Is she as tired as she looks?"

Gabriel watched him. "I think she's struggling, but she's not going to admit it."

Vincent nodded.

"Daniel hypnotized her the other day to... install a kind of safe phrase for when she's having a nightmare. It stops her from fighting. They both want you to know it, just in case. Musha burui. I think I said it right."

"You did. I doubt I'll have the need for it now but thank you."

Gabriel had a horrible thought. "Did I interrupt something between you two?"

Vincent raised his head, gave him a slow smile. "Ours was not that kind of relationship. Did she not tell you?"

"I wasn't sure if you felt the same way about it."

"Ava and I are very close. We always have been. But that particular aspect of our relationship satisfied a need for her, nothing more. It was the only thing that would release her anger and help her focus so she could keep The Monster out."

Gabriel's stomach clenched. "You're saying she only wanted sex from you when that thing was trying to possess her?"

Vincent returned his gaze with calm deliberation.

"Fuck." He ran a hand down his face.

Make The Monster go away, she'd said that day after their shower, when her voice had begun to change into something carnal. When he refused her, she hadn't been insulted, only fascinated. Then she'd something about sex not "stopping it" or something like that. She must have realized sex wasn't what restrained The Monster. She'd left quickly after that.

"She had urges, which she views as a weakness," Vincent was saying. "But mostly her need for sex was to keep The Monster away. We both knew that."

After her childhood, Gabriel couldn't blame her. Still, to be used that way and not have any regrets...

"You were okay with that?"

Vincent's eyes were very dark. They looked black and emotionless in the fluorescent lighting.

"I love her. Not in the way you do," he added, his tone casual.

Gabriel jerked, shocked. "What makes you say that?"

"The way you look at her." Standing, Vincent turned and leaned against the wall, studying Gabriel as he might a new species. His dark eyes revealed nothing of what he was thinking.

"That doesn't bother you?" Gabriel asked, unnerved. He wanted the conversation to move back to Vincent and Ava, not what he may or may not feel about her. "You don't mind being used that way?"

"Not by her." He glanced toward the changing room.

Gabriel watched those shark eyes, feeling mesmerized. "You put your social life on hold for her."

"Yes. For her."

Unconditional loyalty without question, Gabriel thought. Ava seemed to bring that out in people.

"I can see why she has so much respect for you."

"The feeling is mutual."

Daniel and Ava exited the office and walked across the mat. After a few more minutes of small talk, Gabriel and the students stepped outside. Crossing the parking lot, they stopped at Ava's car.

Gabriel ran his hand down her arm, squeezed her hand. "I'll see you later."

She gave his hand a squeeze in response. "Vincent and I have not spoken in a long time."

"I'll keep myself busy at home," he said, his lips twitching. "It was nice to meet you, Vincent."

Ava barely heard Vincent's response. She kept her hand clasped around Gabriel's when he turned to leave. Her eyes were intense as she watched his face.

"What's wrong?"

"I usually shower at his place," she said softly. "I'm perspiring heavily."

"Yeah, you are." He grinned.

She kept staring.

"What is it?" Touching her shoulder, he began to worry. The little crease had formed between her eyebrows.

"I do not want... I really need to shower."

Gabriel glanced at Vincent, but he was checking his phone. What was the problem?

"Ava, I don't know what you're getting at. Take a shower. I don't expect you to sit around marinating in sweat while you catch up with Vincent."

"But... we are mates..." She tapped her fingers on her chest, then his. She was honestly distressed, he saw.

"It's just a shower, Ava."

"I thought you might be more sensitive because of Rachel."

Hearing her name felt like a slap. Not because it still pained him to hear it, but because he hadn't given her any thought for so long. His ex-girlfriend's name hadn't crossed his mind once in weeks.

"You're not Rachel." How had he ever thought he could settle for someone as shallow and mundane as Rachel? "You would never do that. I trust you."

The gray in her eyes seemed to pulsate. She considered what he said, and finally nodded.

Squeezing her shoulders, he kissed her on the forehead. "I'll see you later?"

Now she seemed thoughtful as she nodded again.

"Don't do anything I wouldn't do," he said, grinning.

"I do many things you do not do," she said, frowning.

"It's a saying, Ava. Have fun."

●　　●　　●　　●　　●

The simplest of movements sent boulders rolling around in her head. Her eyes felt the size of basket balls. Every muscle in her body ached. She had cried so hard her body shook itself into one big bruise. The physical pain wasn't as bad as the remorse she felt.

She was lying on her side. Griffin must have carried her to bed after her breakdown.

Shifting, Isabel let out a startled moan at the sudden ache in her side, gripping the blankets in her fist and tucking them under her chin. A whimper slipped out.

"Shush." Griffin pulled her close and she realized she wasn't gripping the blankets in her fist, but his tee shirt. She tried to loosen her grip, but she couldn't force her hand to let go of him.

"Try some water," he said, leaning over to pick up the glass. He rubbed her back with his other hand.

Curling her legs under her, she pushed herself up. The lamp was on, but he had draped a thin shirt over it, so the light was very dim. Isabel would have started crying all over again at the sweetness of that gesture if she had any moisture left in her body. She hadn't cried that hard since she was a young child. Two years after Hayden's disappearance, she'd decided she wasn't going to be weak anymore and began hardening herself.

She sipped the water. Her stomach was upset. All whiskey and no food made Izzie a sick girl.

"How are you feeling?" Griffin asked.

Squinting, Iz felt the corners of her mouth pull down. "I don't hate you."

He smiled. "I know, Izzie."

His warm hand moved up and down her back, calming her nerves. So much strength and security in those hands. She loved how her skin seemed to wake up in response to his touch.

Taking another drink, she suddenly felt as if she couldn't get enough. She started gulping it down despite her upset stomach, clutching the glass in both hands.

"Take it easy," Griffin said, easing the glass away from her lips. "You're going to make yourself sick."

"Thirsty," she said, breathing heavy, wiping the back of her hand across her mouth.

"I gathered that. Slow it down." He set the glass back on the table.

Isabel nestled against his chest, resting her hand over his heart again. It beat steadily, promising to keep going even when things were tough.

Her body felt hulled out.

"Just breathe," he murmured. He brushed his lips against her hair.

She focused on that, on breathing. In through the nose, out through the mouth. Long, deep breaths that helped to relax her. Feeling the air enter her body, fill her lungs, calm her mind.

Hayden is dead.

On his chest, her hand twitched. Clamped into a fist.

In and out, like the ebb and flow of the tide. Providing life, providing solace.

Hayden will always be dead.

She closed her eyes, turning into Griffin's chest. Her breath hitched.

Everyone dies.

Griffin pulled her against him, resting his chin on the top of her head. His hand was making lazy circles at the small of her back. Their bodies were pressed together comfortably. Isabel could have stayed there the rest of her life.

So why was she unable to catch her breath? Why was her mind racing? She could feel her muscles beginning to contract in anticipation even though they were sore and worn out. Why was she fighting so hard to be upset?

Breathe. In. Out.

Hayden should still be alive. It should have been you that died.

Isabel let out a strangled sob and sat up, reaching out blindly to pull herself toward isolation. Her hands found the bedding and she dragged herself forward like a woman thrashing through quicksand. Griffin looped his arm around her stomach and brought her back to him, holding her against him as she continued to struggle.

"Oh, no you don't," he soothed.

He put his hand on her forehead and pressed her head back against his shoulder.

With his mouth close to her ear, he said, "I won't let you think yourself back into that hole you were in."

Her legs moved, her arms wiggled, but the effort was halfhearted. She was too tired to continue fighting. With a sigh, she collapsed against him.

"It should have been me."

"Shut up."

She had gone very still, and now he couldn't even hear her breathing.

Griffin carefully let go of her forehead and shook his head. "I'm sorry. That's not what I meant. Don't talk about yourself that way."

Trying not to be offended when she instinctively stiffened, Griffin buried his face against her neck. He clamped his arms more tightly around her. He felt like he could crush her bones. She seemed especially frail now, her body as spindly as a newborn filly's.

"You matter to me," he said.

After a few moments, Iz felt her body loosen. Until she thought about returning to work tomorrow. She began to tense again.

"I have to get ready for work," she said, sitting up.

"There you go, getting all tense again." He brushed his hand down her back. Already her muscles were knotting up.

"I think my job is a metaphor for my family." She swung her legs over the side of the bed and waited for the dizziness to pass. Turning to look at him, she continued. "My co-workers, my family members. They just always expect me to be there, to take care of their needs no matter how much they treat me like shit. Oh, damn it, I've turned into a head-shrinker."

Grinning, he leaned up moved closer to her, kissing her on the shoulder. "That's what we call a breakthrough."

"They don't do it to be dicks, right?" Angling her head, her tone was serious again. "Tell me my family doesn't realize they focus their grief on me to be assholes. That they aren't malicious monsters doing that on purpose."

"People rarely realize what they're doing or how it affects others."

She relaxed somewhat. Rubbing his hands up and down her arms, he moved his lips lightly along her skin, from her shoulder to her neck.

"You're trying to distract me."

"Is it working?"

"Yes, but I really need to get ready for work tomorrow. I have to make sure I have an outfit here or I'll have to make a trip to my apartment tonight."

"Quit," Griffin said simply. He lifted her hand, ran his fingers up her palm, laced them with hers, then ran them back down her palm again.

"My bills don't pay themselves," she said, the old sarcasm surfacing for a moment. "They're such assholes that way."

"I'll pay them. Quit your shitty job and take the time to work through this."

"You're sweet, Griffin, but I-"

"Don't be proud." He kissed her neck. "Now's not the time. It's the only way I can help you with this. Let me help you." He pressed his cheek to hers. "I make enough money to support us both. Get out of that soul-sucking place."

Pivoting on the bed, she stared at him.

"You're serious." Her eyes, swollen from tears, were bloodshot but shocked.

"Of course, I am. I think the people at your job and your family are ninety percent of your stress. Get rid of the job, and we'll work on dealing with your family."

"O-okay," she said. "I'll put in my two weeks' notice tomorr-"

"Fuck that. Call in tomorrow and tell them you're done."

"Griffin-"

He took her shoulders, a little rough. "You don't owe that company, or those assholes, anything. They will replace you in a heartbeat and think nothing of it. Call in tomorrow morning and be done with it."

Color had already began seeping into her cheeks as she thought of never returning. Griffin was relieved he could give her peace, even if it lasted only for a little while.

"Okay," she sighed. The weight that had pressed against her chest and rib cage for the past six years had lifted. "Thank you."

He gave her a slow kiss, felt her body begin to relax. Not wanting to take advantage, he pulled back. "You already look better."

"What time is it? I'm so tired. I feel like all I'm doing is sleeping but I'm so tired."

"It's almost eleven. You look exhausted."

He tugged her shirt up, helped her slip out of it. Leaning close, he reached around with both hands, gazing into her eyes as he unhooked her bra and slid the straps down.

"Griffin-"

"I'll get your pjs," he said, taking her shirt and bra and walking toward the closet. "Take off your pants."

He peeled his own shirt off while he was next to the laundry basket. Stripped down to his boxers and brought her tee shirt and shorts into the bedroom. The air left his lungs in a rush.

She was lying in only her panties on her stomach, her head turned toward him, and her arms curled under her against her breasts. The sleek line of her back made his heart dance crazily in his chest. He stood for a moment, just staring.

"What?"

She started to reach for the sheet, self-conscious.

"No, don't."

He crossed the room and sat on the bed, setting her clothes to the side, and resting his hand on her shoulder.

"The way the light hits your skin..."

He trailed a finger down her back...

"It glows. You're so soft."

...and skimmed it gently along her thigh. A shiver ran the length of her flushed body.

"You're a work of art, Izzie."

Snorting, she rolled onto her side. "Yeah, Picasso."

The way you see yourself is twisted and ugly, he thought, not your body. He wished he could convince her of that.

Leaning up, she put her shirt and shorts on. Her face didn't look quite as puffy from the crying jag she'd had earlier, and she wasn't as pale. Sliding down on the bed, she lay on her back and stared at the ceiling.

Griffin kissed her palm, leaned forward, kissed her gently on the lips. He shut off the light and joined her.

"Try to get some sleep."

"If I sleep, I might dream."

"You have to recharge." Griffin rested his hand on her stomach, moved his fingers in a circle. "The dreams will go away. It takes time."

"Promise?" she whispered.

Propped up on his elbow, he kissed her slowly, moving his hand from her stomach to her face. He felt her soften beneath him. Something about the way she lightly touched his arm with her fingertips when he kissed her, as if she couldn't quite believe he was really there, with her, added an extra layer of desire to his already over stimulated system. He had to force himself to pull back mentally and physically.

"Sleep now," he whispered, kissing her forehead.

"Help me sleep."

Iz reached up and touched his face, tried to pull him down to kiss her again. He took her hand and kissed it, gently lay it between them. "Just sleep now."

"Remember the first time you made love to me," she mumbled, already drifting off. "You were so gentle..."

"I'm not likely to forget," he said, stroking her hair.

"Ava," Iz slurred.

"Are we talking in our sleep now?" he asked, smiling. He rubbed her temple softly, kissed her forehead and left his lips there to breathe her in.

"She'll help us."

"That's awfully nice of her. Let's go over there tomorrow and see how's she's doing."

"Yes!"

"I like your enthusiasm."

Isabel fought sleep a few seconds more, her body twitching, before she finally stilled against him. He leaned back, covered her hand with his own.

Letting out a long, shuddering sigh, she muttered, "I love you."

In the dark, he grinned.

"The feeling's mutual, Love."

•　•　•　•　•

Muted songs of the birds coming through the open windows. Barely felt breeze caressing her skin. Blurry, illegible words. The rhythmic scraping of pen on paper as words flowed across the page like magic.

Where was she? some part of her thought vaguely.

Between. Neither here nor there.

Her hand danced across the page, the handwriting loopy and elegant, attempting to get the information down as it had been written decades ago. Someone else had taken control. Ava's eyes were milky white as she stared straight ahead, and her hand continued to write.

The sound of her front door opening went unheard. The male voice calling out to her was muted. She felt like she was underwater, where her vision was murky so she couldn't see more than six inches in front of her and every sound was unclear.

After a quick search on the first floor, Gabriel started up the stairs, calling out to Ava again. Her vehicle was in the driveway, but she might still be working. It was too early for her afternoon bout of exercising, and he didn't hear any sounds from the basement.

He found her in her office, leaned over her desk in a very stiff pose. Her back was board-straight, her arm and neck so precisely angled that she almost looked like a mannequin. She was writing something but moving her entire hand while doing so instead of wresting her palm on the paper.

"Didn't you hear me call you?" he asked, walking toward her.

Without acknowledging him, she continued to write.

"Ava."

While her hand continued writing, her head remained tilted to the side, but she stared straight out the window. Gabriel didn't see ear buds or headphones. She should have heard him.

Curving his hands slightly, Gabriel clapped once. The sound echoed loudly.

Ava's head turned toward him with deliberate reluctance.

"Molly!" she called.

He kept his distance and walked around her until he could see her face. Her eyes were opaque.

"Jesus, Ava."

"Molly," she said again, not as loud as before. "Take Sally out of the library, would you? I have to get this letter written."

Gabriel stepped closer and knelt beside her. "Ava, it's Gabriel."

She rested her hand on his arm. Though her eyes were level with his, she stared right through him. Those eyes, like opal stones, made him shiver.

"Sally, sweetie, Mama's busy. Go with Molly."

She turned back to whatever she was writing. Her gaze returned to the window as her hand began to move.

"Can I read it, Ava?"

The pen paused just a breath above the paper. Without looking down, Ava began speaking in a voice softer and older than hers. Gabriel glanced down at the paper on the desk and saw she was reciting what she had written, word for word:

"Dearest Sir,

I hope this letter finds you well. I have been unable to write sooner, as the arrangements for my mother's funeral took all of my time. I hope I have not offended you in any way.

My sincerest thanks for the flowers you sent to the church on the day of the funeral. I also received the beautiful bouquet at the house the day after. I know my mother would have loved them. Thank you for those as well, and your kind words.

I am forever in your debt for the kindness you -"

Ava blinked. Her hand twitched, but she didn't continue writing.

"Who are you?" Gabriel asked. "Did you used to live in this house?"

Absently, she dropped the pen and raised her fingertips to her temple. She closed her eyes, sighed.

"Molly, I told you to take her out of here. Please. I have a headache just now."

"Is Sally your daughter?"

"I'll tell you a secret."

Something in the room changed. It was suddenly silent. No birds singing, even though the windows were open. No breeze blowing through. No paper rustling. Absolute silence.

When Ava opened her eyes, they were the gray of clouds ready to burst in a storm. They jerked in their sockets as she realized he was there, and her hand was at this throat before he could move. He felt her fingertips gripping and his windpipe closing. The sensation made him gag.

"Ava," he choked.

Her eyes widened. Shoving the chair back, she stood and backed away from him. Her eyes were wide and wild and a little crazy. Gabriel's stomach lurched when he saw her arms raised in defense.

"You're okay. It's just me."

He stood, rubbing his throat. He had only felt the very tips of her fingers, the pressure so light, yet it felt as if his windpipe was being crushed. Clearing his throat, he tried to speak.

"Do you know who I am?"

Her eyes rolled toward him. "Gabriel."

"Gold star for you. How are you feeling?"

She scowled. Dropped her hands. "Agitated. I do not like having my work interrupted."

"Back to normal, then."

He pushed her chair up to her desk. Lifting the letter she had written – that someone had written – he raised an eyebrow at her.

"Your handwriting's very elegant."

Discussion of the incident seemed to be irritating her even further. She snatched the paper from his hand, crumpled it, and tossed it in the garbage can next to her desk.

"It is not my handwriting."

"Is this that... automatic handwriting... you told Iz and I about?"

"Yes."

She was clicking through programs on her computer, shutting down for the day. Gathering papers scattered around her desk to tidy up.

"Fascinating."

"Next time, you can volunteer your body." She waited a beat, pausing with a stack of papers in her hand, then added, "I apologize for injuring your neck."

Using precise movements, she set a mechanical pencil, a red pen, and a blue pen in a pen holder and slid a sticky notepad back from her keyboard. She adjusted the keyboard, studied it, adjusted it more. Glancing over all the items on the desktop, she reached over and made sure the stack of paper was all lined up.

Gabriel was trying unsuccessfully not to smile. She put everything just so, and once it fell out of place, she became annoyed to the point of being rude. It made him want to howl with laughter. Possession didn't upset her because it was an invasion of her body; it upset her because it took up her time.

And that sexy little crease was riding between her eyebrows again.

"Does it hurt?"

Her hand twitched and knocked the mouse a few inches off the mouse pad. "Does what hurt?"

"When you're possessed?"

Leaning down, he lifted her hand and kissed it, his eyes never leaving hers.

696

That little crease was still there, but now it wasn't irritation causing it. She was trying to figure out his motivation for asking.

"It's how I get to know you, Ava," he said. "By asking questions."

"It is not possession, really. It is channeling."

Releasing her hand, he glanced toward the garbage where she had tossed the letter. She had looked pretty damn possessed to him.

"What's the difference?"

"It is hard to explain." She picked up his hand again and put it on the one he had been holding.

Grinning, he rubbed his thumb over the back of her hand. "Is that your not-so-subtle way of telling me you want me to keep holding your hand?"

"I like when you touch me."

She stilled, realizing she had admitted a weakness. Keeping her hand in his, Gabriel slid his other arm around her waist. Their bodies fit together as if they had always been and would always be.

"It's good to hear you say that. I like touching you. Can I get something to drink?"

They walked downstairs. Sunlight was coming in from the large windows on the east and west sides of the house, making the living room a golden chamber of warmth. While Ava went to the kitchen for water, Gabriel wandered around the living room, realizing he hadn't paid much attention to it during his previous visits. They spent more time outside as the weather allowed it. When they were forced to be inside and they stayed here, he would do some work on his computer while she recovered from class. Or they were both in the basement, him using her gym and she her training equipment. He hadn't taken any time to really see how she lived.

A large philodendron sat on the top of a bookcase on the west wall, its vine like leaves spilling over the shelves. Photographs were minimal. There was a five by seven of her and David on the shelf of a bookcase, taken when she was eleven or twelve years old. It showed her holding what he presumed to be the puppy version of Buck, all legs and big paws, while David watched and grinned. Another the same size of Ruth and David sat near the front entry. Another picture he had seen was of David and a very young Ava standing in front of a green 1953 Chevy pickup. That was hanging in the dining room.

And he knew downstairs, in the dojo, she had one of her and Daniel. He had noticed it the morning he found her training. It was a candid shot David had taken several months after she had started training. They were both dressed in their uniforms. Daniel was showing Ava something, and David had caught her expression full on, so intent and ready to learn, while he caught three quarters of Daniel's face at an angle. It was a beautiful picture and showed the start of something that would continue to grow in the years to come.

Ava touched his arm.

Glancing down, he took the glass of water from her. He thought of his conversation with Vincent.

"Listen, I have a question and I'm not exactly sure how to ask it."

Her eyes were intense on his mouth, like a cat's as it watched its prey. She said nothing.

"Right. I was talking with Vincent when you and Daniel were in the other room last night. He said you two..."

Damn. He had to know, but there was no way to talk about this except an awkward way.

"We have had sex." The hungry look in her eyes was replaced with curiosity. "You already knew. I told you."

"No. I mean, yes, I knew. That's not what we were talking about. Not exactly." He ran a hand through his hair. Why was it that talking to her made him feel like an inexperienced teenager? He was eight years older than her, for God's sake. "He said you only had sex with him to keep The... The Monster from possessing you."

Stepping back so she did not have to crane her neck up to study him, Ava tilted her head slightly.

"Intercourse is a stress reliever as well as a physical release. It helps to divert my attention, work off my anger, so my subconscious does not feel the need to summon The Monster."

"You tried to have sex with me once," he said, remembering. "After a shower, you were telling me about fights you were in at school. Your voice kept changing, like it did in the dojo yesterday. You asked me to 'make The Monster go away' and you tried to instigate sex."

"I did not know how else to control it then."

"So, sex with me is a means to an end."

She had been looking down at her coffee table and now her head jerked up, her eyes boring into his.

"No."

Gabriel pondered that, watching her gray eyes darken as she returned his gaze. They had a lot of sex, more than he'd had with any other girlfriend. Had he been the only one enjoying it?

"Do you use sex with me to keep The Monster away?" he finally asked. He didn't want to know. He had to know.

The gray in her eyes softened, lightened, and seemed to swirl in the confines of her eyes. Vulnerability showed there as well.

"N-no."

He took a step toward her and was surprised when she jumped like a child getting caught taking an extra cookie.

Her cheeks flushed. "I want to." Cupping her elbows in her hands, she added, "I have never wanted to before."

"Oh." What else could he say? Because he couldn't think of anything else, he blurted, "Never?"

"I trusted Vincent to educate me when I was curious. My body reacted to his skill and my time with him was not unpleasant. But there was too much..."

She closed her eyes, swallowed with difficulty. When at last she looked at him, her expression was one of resigned hopelessness.

"There was too much damage to enjoy it."

Of course. How could he expect her to enjoy sex when her first introduction to it had been brutal, painful, and physically and mentally damaging? He had waited even when she initiated it, but that one moment when she had been asleep in his arms, he had weakened. All this time had he been fooling himself into thinking they were sharing the pleasure?

"I'm sorry," he said.

"Do not feel sorry for me. I wanted to have sex with you. If we never had sex, I would not have known I could enjoy it."

After all the times she left him speechless, he should have been used to it by now. Yet he stood staring at her, unable to find words once again. She could make him feel heartbroken, confused, guilty, and proud, all in the span of thirty seconds.

"You like having sex with me?" he asked. "It isn't just a... chore?"

"It pleases me," she said, then frowned. "Although you waited so long, I was beginning to wonder what was wrong with you."

He snickered.

"I enjoy the strangest things about you." Her tone was skeptical, as if she thought she might be coming down with something and her judgment was off.

"Like what?" The corners of his mouth twitched.

"Your ability to raise one eyebrow." When he shot it up to amuse her, he thought he saw the beginning of a smile. "I have a detailed understanding of the human body and every muscle in it, but that motion continues to baffle me."

Gabriel sipped his water. What an odd thing to find entertaining, he thought, especially from such a brilliant mind.

"I enjoy your butt."

He choked on the water and began coughing. Raising his eyebrow again, he wiped his mouth with the back of his hand.

"My butt?"

"My interest is completely physical and has no logic. Your butt looks good in jeans. I like how it fits in my hands. I realize the emotion is not helpful in any way, yet I cannot seem to stop feeling it. I like looking at your butt and sometimes I imagine grabbing it at the most inappropriate – what? Why are you laughing at me?"

"It's so strange to hear something so ordinary coming out of your mouth."

Setting his glass on the coffee table, Gabriel pulled her in for a hug. He kissed her forehead.

"Should I keep going?" She slid her hands into his back pockets and squeezed his butt.

"Sure. I have a few minutes before I have to leave for Guy's Night Out. I could use some flattery."

"I like that your hands know how to please me. I do not have to tell you what to do."

He grinned. "It helps that you have an amazing body to explore."

The spark that was in her eyes dampened and she became thoughtful. She tilted her head to the side, gazing at him as she thought of his pleasant attributes.

"Your closeness to Isabel fascinates me. I like watching you two together. You communicate without words in an immensely powerful way."

This wasn't the first time he'd heard that. His parents and Beth had said the same, and many other relatives. Even in school, teachers had noticed that.

"I like your eyes," Ava said, gazing into them like a scientist studying a rare specimen. "You shared them with your sister and now that she is gone, a piece of her still lives on through you. Your mother resents you for it, but I admire it. I am sorry. I should not have said that."

"No." Gabriel tried not to show how shaken he was. "I already knew what you said is true. It's weird to hear it out loud."

"She is wrong." The hint of steel in her voice was comforting. "She is wrong about you, and she is wrong about Isabel. She does not realize that by idolizing one daughter, she will lose another."

He thought about that. His mother had sometimes seemed irritated at Isabel for no reason. Lately, she seemed to snip at her no matter what she said. Had it always been that way and he just hadn't seen it?

He would have to pay attention this Sunday.

"I'll have to get into what I like about you tonight," he said, planting a kiss on her mouth. "I have to go."

"You are going to be late."

"What do you m-"

Ava gave him a shove, knocking him backward onto the couch. Before he regained his breath, she was on top of him, showing him the other parts of him that she liked.

•   •   •   •   •

"Do you think there's anything she can do?" Isabel asked doubtfully. She was tapping her sunglasses on her knee hard enough to dig a trench in her limb. Griffin glanced at her, amused. Her thoughts had been bouncing all over the place since he came home from work, starting with asking how his day had gone and somehow getting on the topic of how Leonardo da Vinci invented scissors before he finally silenced her with a kiss.

"I don't really know what I expect her to fix," she continued. "Shit. I forgot to tell her you were coming. I hope it's okay."

"I don't really know her, but I think if she can help, she will," he said, reaching over and resting his hand on top of hers to still the sunglasses. "You two seem pretty tight."

He pulled into the driveway and Isabel sat up straighter.

"Gabriel's still here. He usually goes to the bar on Fridays."

"Maybe there was a change of plans."

Isabel was already unlatching her seat belt. "He never skips that. Something must be wrong."

She opened the door before he came to a full stop and hopped out, walking quickly toward the front door. Something had happened, she just knew it. Gabriel was in trouble, or they had learned something about Hayden, or maybe something had happened to Ava during a nightmare last night.

Reaching for the door, she squeaked when it opened, and Gabriel almost ran into her.

"Fuck me!" Isabel backed up, stepping on Griffin's foot, and then backing into him.

"Oh. Hey." Gabriel looked bemused.

"Why aren't you at the bar?" Iz asked, looking him over to see if he had any injuries. "What's wrong?"

His hair was disheveled, and he was out of breath. The tee shirt he was wearing looked like it had been left in a basket instead of folded and put in a drawer. His face was flushed.

"What? Nothing. I'm just leaving. Good to see you again, Griffin."

"Gabriel," Griffin said, by way of greeting, giving a knowing nod at his rumpled appearance.

"You're late," Iz pressed, not letting her brother get by her. "You're usually gone by the time I get here. Did something happen to Ava?"

A few somethings, Gabriel thought, trying not to grin.

"She's fine. We're fine. Everybody's fine. I have to go."

Isabel glared at him, then noticed he'd forgotten the button on his jeans. "Oh, for fuck's sake." She gestured toward him. "You missed something."

Unable to hide his grin any longer, he buttoned his jeans and slid past her. "Enjoy your evening."

Iz punched his shoulder. Griffin laughed and followed her into the house.

Ava was in the living room, straightening the cushions on the couch.

"Hey, Ava," Isabel called. She almost kicked a throw pillow and stooped to pick it up. "Are you fucking kidding me? On the couch?"

Without looking at her, Ava moved the lamp back to its original position on the side table. They had nearly knocked it off moments earlier.

"We contained our bodily fluids," she said, bending down to pick her novel up off the floor. She set it on the coffee table. That had been knocked to the floor. She had never lacked control over her body so completely as when Gabriel's hands were on her. Or when he was inside her.

Ugh," Iz groaned, "I did not need to hear that."

Ava turned toward Isabel and saw Griffin. The relaxed expression on her face immediately became guarded. All her attention focused on him.

"Hello, Ava. It's nice to see you again." He noticed the bruising around her eye. "Nice shiner."

He studied her reaction to him. There was no mistaking the intensity of her eyes or the way her body braced at the sight of him. She stopped straightening the room and stood.

"I hope it's okay Griffin came," Iz said, oblivious to Ava's odd behavior. She tossed the pillow onto the couch carelessly. "If you'd rather this be a girl's night, he can come back later and pick me up. I meant to tell you before."

She walked toward the kitchen to get a glass of water. "How's your eye?"

Ava turned so she was fully facing Griffin. Behind him, the dark figure appeared. It shimmered and became more corporeal. The face was the same, the eyes, the strong jaw. Yet something about the thing hovering behind Griffin felt different.

"Do you feel it?" Ava asked. She walked over to Griffin as if mesmerized, lifting her hand and reaching up to the side of his face. Her hand passed by his ear. She kept it there for several seconds.

"Feel what?" Isabel asked. She had two glasses in her hand and had stopped a few feet from Griffin, watching them.

"What do you see, Ava?" Griffin asked, turning his head, and looking behind him. He saw only her hand. She moved her fingers slowly, as if she were trying to get a feel for something.

"You."

Her eyes were dark, so dark and hypnotic as she stood this close. He could see the different shades of gray in them. She lowered her hand but continued to look past him.

"I watched you die."

"What the fuck, Ava?" Iz walked over to the coffee table and set the glasses down. She reached for Griffin's hand. It was cold.

"You did the research," Ava continued. "You wanted to make sure it did not go wrong in any way. You did it, but you watched, too. I do not understand."

She pressed a hand to her forehead.

Isabel watched Griffin stare at Ava, his hand gripping hers. He seemed incapable of speech. Ava was weird all the time, but Griffin could usually talk his way out of any situation. What was going on between them? Something happened when they were together, something tangible that caused tension even though they had never met before Isabel introduced them.

"Do you want me to leave?" Griffin asked, his voice not quite steady. Something about the way Ava stared at him made him feel like ice was coursing through his blood. The hair on the back of his neck was standing on end.

Ava blinked. She took a step back from him, winced. Her head dipped, then shot up.

"I am sorry." Glancing around, she seemed to collect herself. "Hello, Isabel. Hello, Griffin. Isabel, do you want a hug?"

"Oh. I didn't realize..." Isabel stepped toward her and held her arms out. "Sorry, you looked so normal, I didn't realize you were... I mean, not normal... I'll just shut up now."

She hugged Ava briskly before stepping back protectively to Griffin's side.

"Do you require a hug as well, Griffin?"

Eyeing her contemplatively, he said, "Only if you're willing."

Ava awkwardly held out her arms. Griffin stepped into them.

A gunshot sounded right next to her ear, making her rock back on her heels. Guilt filled her. The taste of metal was on her tongue. Salty tears on her cheeks. Blood covered her hands and still more pumped out, all over, covering her shirt, her jeans, her cheek when she pressed it against what was left of his head. A primal cry built in her throat as everything she was drained out of her with the blood draining out of his body.

"Ava? Ava? Are you okay? God, Griffin, she's so pale."

"Get a washcloth and run it under cool water. And a towel."

"Ava?"

"Isabel go, now."

Thudding footsteps that vibrated through her head. It ached, her head, and her ears were ringing. She felt as if her mouth was full of blood.

"I'm sorry," Ava croaked.

"Don't try to talk," Griffin said, feeling her forehead. She was on fire. Her hands were frigid. Her eyes were not quite focused.

"You lost your face." She tried to raise a hand, could not seem to find the strength to lift it.

He paused. "How's that?"

"I'm sorry." She turned her head to the left, the right, her eyes rolling.

"You were a little lightheaded, is all. Do you know what day it is?"

"Friday."

She tried to sit up.

"Easy now." Griffin pressed her down by the shoulders.

"You will not restrain me." Her hands clamped down on his wrists like vises.

"I'm not restraining you. You passed out. Give your body some time to recover."

"Here's the cloth."

Isabel was worried. Ava had made her worry. That upset her because she knew Isabel had enough to worry about.

"Put the towel under her head," Griffin said. He dabbed the cloth over Ava's forehead.

Isabel gently lifted Ava's head and placed the towel on the floor.

"Are you okay?"

"I am fine."

Their hands were conducting emotions, feedback; her head was splitting with the screams of their worry.

She tried to sit up again. Griffin held her arms.

"Restrain me again and you will be the one on the floor."

"Ava, you need to set aside your pride and settle down a minute."

She took a deep breath in, focused her eyes on him. They were full of rage. And blackness.

"It is not pride, you arrogant dumb fuck." The deep, foreign voice of The Monster mixed with hers. She closed her eyes, shook her head. "Back away from her."

"Oh, shit," Iz whispered. Hearing the other voice was always a shock.

"You need-" Griffin started.

"You need to get away from her." Ava's shoulders rose. She twisted like a cat and grimaced. "She – "

Growling, her body shuddered, and she closed her eyes. When she spoke again, her voice was her own.

"I will stay on the floor, but you need to give me space."

Isabel touched Griffin's shoulder before standing and backing away. Reluctantly, he did the same, watching her thoughtfully.

"Okay, we're back, Ava. Everything's okay."

"How the fuck would you know?" The Monster snapped.

"Hey!" Griffin said, taking a step forward.

"Griffin-" Isabel said, but she wasn't fast enough.

Ava instantly used her hands to launch herself forward into a standing position. Her hands were ready to strike, her legs spread in a low stance.

"Griffin," Isabel repeated, "Don't touch her."

"There's no need for her to talk to you like that."

She couldn't help feeling a bit of pride for his chivalry. "It's not Ava talking. Give her a minute."

"Excuse me?"

"Just give her space and let her settle down. She doesn't like to be touched."

She had set her hand on his arm and now she gripped it, tugging him toward the kitchen. "We're going to see what you have for snacks, Ava."

Panting, Ava stood in her stance a few moments longer, her eyes following their progress into the kitchen.

Griffin stared at Izzie as she searched the cupboards for something to munch on. Her entire demeanor had suddenly changed, while he was still trying to figure out what alternate universe he'd just been launched into.

"What the bloody hell is going on?" he asked, glancing back at Ava. She was frozen in the same position, glaring at them. She looked like she was ready to battle an army all by herself. And win.

"I told you she was abused as a child," Iz said casually, finding some black olives in the cupboard. She searched for a bowl to put them in. "She doesn't like to be touched."

"That was a little more complicated than not liking to be touched."

"You're a shrink's son," she said, searching for a can opener. She found an electric one on the bottom of one of the counters. "You know better than most what abuse can do to a person."

She suddenly felt intensely protective over Ava.

"I understand getting defensive," Griffin answered, "I understand learning how to fight so she never has to be a victim again. That doesn't explain her entire personality changing when we were trying to help her."

Isabel held the can of olives over the sink to drain.

"When she was being abused, something came to her that helped her block out the pain. She said she thinks she connected with it because she's psychic. Whatever it was took over during the abuse or she wouldn't have survived it. She calls it The Monster."

"That's absurd."

"You haven't seen the scars all over her body. You haven't been woken up in the middle of the night by her shrieks or had to chase her around the house when she's terrified those assholes are coming after her again."

Griffin watched her cut up little cubes of cheese to go with the olives as if they were discussing their favorite movie on Netflix.

"I understand she may have separated herself mentally to -"

Isabel slammed the knife down on the counter and glared at him. "Could you, for once, not bring your mother's psychological bullshit into a conversation? It's not metaphorical. It's not in her mind. Something takes over her to protect her when she feels threatened. If you don't believe me, go over there and try to touch her again."

Griffin glanced back at Ava, who had finally stepped out of her stance and was sitting on the coffee table. She had her head down between her knees. There was no mistaking her physical reaction. But to believe she was being possessed...

"Izzie-"

"You don't have to believe," she hissed. "But if you touch her, she will knock you on your ass. And I'll break a rib laughing at you. Because not everything can be explained away with psychology and talking about our feelings."

She had arranged the cheese around the bowl of olives on a tray. Lifting the tray, she set it on the counter in front of him with a clatter.

"Have an appetizer."

Turning to wash her hands, she wondered if Ava sensed Griffin's disbelief of her ability, and that was the cause of her disliking him. Every time they were near each other, she became cold. Iz understood not wanting to be touched, and she certainly understood being frustrated with psychobabble. But Griffin hadn't done anything to Ava to warrant her apparent hatred of him. She could at least be civil.

Bringing him for her own support had been a mistake. She should have been stronger.

"This is all a little hard to accept." Griffin popped cheese into his mouth. "Why do you believe so readily?"

"Gabriel believes," she said simply. "And I believe in him."

As she dried her hands, she walked toward the living room. Ava was taking deep breaths. She lifted her head warily as Isabel approached.

"Are you okay?"

Ava nodded, glancing warily at Griffin.

Isabel felt a stab of guilt. "I forgot to explain to him about touching you. I'm sorry."

Ava rubbed at her temples, where a headache was raging.

"I know you don't like him, Ava, but I didn't think it would be such a big deal for him to be here. I wanted him here because I want to ask for your help on something and I really need his support. It was a selfish idea."

Ava was staring at her, head tilted, brow creased. "I have no aversion to Griffin."

"You always tense up when you're around him."

Griffin walked over, picked up the damp wash cloth, and held it out to Ava.

"Thank you." Pressing it to her forehead, she closed her eyes. "What do you want to ask me?"

"We don't have to talk about it now," Iz said. "Did you hit your head when you blacked out? Maybe we should take you to the emergency room."

"That is not going to happen." Ava opened her eyes. "What do you want help with?"

Isabel walked to the couch and sat down, exhaling loudly.

"I feel like..." She glanced at Griffin. Not only did she not want to admit vulnerability in front of him, but she also didn't know what exactly the problem was. What had she been thinking, bringing him here?

"I feel scared all the time, and I'm either pissed off or I cry... fuck." She ran a hand through her hair. "I can't let go of Hayden."

The lack of expression on Ava's face made her feel useless and whiny. The urge to fidget was strong.

"I thought maybe because of your strict discipline you could... help me. You told Beth if she disciplined her body, she could discipline her mind, and be healthier. I'm stuck. I don't know how to get unstuck."

Griffin walked around the coffee table and sat next to her. He picked up her hand and held it in both of his.

When she lifted her gaze, Ava saw a woman at rock bottom. Her eyes were full of torment, exhaustion, self-loathing. Thick gray bands under her eyes showed weeks of restless sleep. She had lost a few pounds and her body was struggling to compensate.

"I can help you," Ava finally said. Her gaze shifted to Griffin. "I can help you, too."

"I'm here for Izzie."

Ignoring him, she turned back to Isabel. "I cannot help you if you think you must defend Griffin from me. I am not his enemy."

"What?" She glanced at him, back at Ava. Her hand instinctively tightened in his.

"All of your attention is focused on my opinion for your mate. You need to let that go. I have no animosity toward him."

"But-"

Ava stood abruptly and stepped sideways between the couch and coffee table until she was in front of Griffin. She sat across from him on the table. His long legs took up more space between the table and the sofa, and she felt slightly encased, but she had no choice at this moment.

"Give me your hand."

"Excuse me?"

"Isabel will not start to work on herself if she perceives there is a threat to you. She is mistaking what I am reading from you as dislike. The only way to show her I harbor no negativity toward you is to solve my confusion."

"And holding my hand will do that?" Griffin asked, obviously skeptical.

"I need to find out why I am reading you," Ava said. She held her hand out.

"Reading me? What does that mean?"

"Someone is trying to communicate with you, and they will not stop until you listen. I have to address the issue. It does not go away on its own."

Griffin rolled his eyes toward Isabel. "Come on."

"You do not have to believe. You only have to want what is best for Isabel. She puts you before herself, always."

Sobering instantly, he reached toward her. Ava took his hand firmly in hers.

She slowed her breathing, focused on his skin. It was warm and dry. A little rough, even though he worked in an office most of the time. Large. Capable of healing Isabel.

She frowned at the stray thought. It was irrelevant to Griffin's story, to whatever was hanging over him that kept drawing him to Ava.

She exhaled with a little more force, willing herself to focus.

These hands had touched Isabel's skin, run up her back, cupped her breasts.

"Uh," she breathed. She twitched. "Your skin is so soft."

"I hardly think that's relevant," Griffin said. He pulled his hand back.

"Not yours," Ava said, opening her eyes and looking at Isabel. "Hers."

Isabel's face turned scarlet.

Ava turned her attention back to Griffin. "Stop thinking about sex and clear your mind."

"I'm a healthy male in my twenties. That's an obvious assumption."

"I do not seek for your approval. Keep your mouth shut and your mind clear until Isabel's stress level decreases."

Plucking his hand up again, she held it firmly. She closed her eyes to block out extra visual stimuli. Turning his hand so it was palm up, she rubbed her thumbs into it. The more tactile the connection, the easier it was for her to link on the spiritual level.

Isabel liked to be kissed just behind her ear, especially on the right side. Ava ground her teeth.

Opening her eyes, she stared at him with narrowed eyes, wondering how mankind had managed to survive so long without wiping its own species out.

"Move closer, Isabel." Her tone was clipped.

Isabel instantly did so, frowning. Ava reached up and touched her behind her right ear lobe. A little shiver ran through Iz.

"She likes when you kiss her right here, especially here, as its more sensitive than the left ear."

Isabel's face looked like a tomato. Ava glared at Griffin.

"I can continue to embarrass her, or you can concentrate for five minutes."

It was his turn to blush. "Sorry, Izzie."

He pulled back from Ava again, balled his hands into fists, closed his eyes. "My mind is wandering. I don't believe in this shit. Sorry."

"Your opinion means nothing to me. You are, however, wasting my time and taking time away that could be used to help her. She is my bee eff eff, so fucking concentrate."

Isabel snorted. "Fuck me, did you just swear, Ava? Like, you, not something possessing you? I'm so proud!"

Ava gave her a glance out of the corner of her eyes.

Thinking of Isabel, wanting to help her, Griffin exhaled. "Can I hold her hand while you're doing this?"

"I need to focus only on you. She will confuse the connection."

She yanked his hand toward her. "Close your eyes. Close them!"

At her command, he instantly shut them. Isabel shut hers out of curiosity.

"Inhale through your nose. Think of inhaling through your nose. A long, deep breath that fills your lungs and makes your stomach expand like a balloon. Yes. Good. Hold it."

His hand twitched in hers. She began running her thumbs over his palms.

"Now exhale through your mouth. Long and slow. Deflate your stomach. Deflate the balloon. Let me hear you push the air out of your lungs."

Her voice was hypnotic, soothing, the way a mother talks to her child as she reads him a story to lull him to sleep. Griffin found his eyes staying closed easily, his body relaxing.

"Inhale again through the nose, long and deep. Fill the balloon, expand your stomach. Hold it."

She continued walking him through breathing for another minute or two.

Then began the breathing exercise on her own, letting herself relax. Concentrating on the feel of his skin against hers, the warmth, how his fingers curled around her hand, she began searching.

"A bathtub."

Griffin jerked, startling Ava, making her jump. Both hands clamped down on his to keep him from moving.

"It means something to you." She opened her eyes to find Griffin staring at her. Her haunted gray eyes stared into his honey-colored ones, stared into him. "You have thoughts of killing yourself."

Sorrow filled her. Her heart was breaking. The grief was as evident on her face as the tone of her skin. Her hands were gripping his so tight his fingertips were starting to lose feeling.

"You're wrong," he managed.

"If I am wrong, why is your heartrate elevated?"

She leaned forward, trying to catch her breath. Instinct had him resting his hand on her shoulder.

"So much blood." She murmured. "I cannot breathe. The blood is everywhere."

Griffin glanced at Isabel. She was worried, and he wanted to comfort her. There was shock in her eyes, and fear. He couldn't stand either. But Ava's presence pulled his attention back to her.

"Griffin," she said, her voice strained. Her eyes were the color of honey. She opened her mouth to speak again.

And blood gushed out.

"Jesus Christ!" Isabel was on her feet instantly but then her feet seemed frozen to the floor.

Ava made a gargling sound in the back of her throat as her head tilted back, her hands releasing his. As she fell back onto the coffee table, Griffin rose and caught her, slipping his hand behind her head so she wouldn't hit it. A ragged cough sent droplets of blood into the air, splattering her lips, his face and shirt. He helped her lie back but she couldn't stay on the table, and she couldn't stay on her back, where strangulation on her own blood was a possibility. He looped his arm under her knees and lifted her, carrying her to the floor where there was more room.

"Towels," he barked, and this time Isabel moved instantly.

Griffin turned Ava onto her side. Thick crimson oozed from her mouth, onto the hardwood floor.

"Griffin," she gargled. Blood was smeared across her teeth. "I'm sorry."

"Christ don't be sorry," he said. "Izzie, call 9-1-1."

"No..."

She tried to lift her head.

"Stay," he snapped. "Do what your bloody told this time."

Isabel rushed back in with an arm full of towels and dumped them on the floor close enough for Griffin to reach them. He started soaking up as much as he could. Iz knelt beside Ava's head and pulled out her cell phone.

"It is..." Ava made a horrible sound in her throat like she was slurping applesauce. "It is not mine."

Too upset to hear her, Iz tried with shaking fingers to unlock her phone. She kept hitting the wrong buttons. Ava's hand reached out and struck hers, sending the phone flying across the floor all the way into the dining room.

"What the fuck did you do that for?" Isabel burst into tears, scrambling across the floor on her hands and knees. The phone was under the table. Ava had smacked her hard. She was halfway across the room when the sound of Griffin's voice stopped her.

"Stop, Isabel."

The tone of his voice, so awestruck yet calm, had her immediately stopping and turning back to look at him.

Ava was sitting up, bracing herself with one hand on the floor and the other holding Griffin's, as much for his support as for her own. There was no trace of blood. Not down the front of her shirt, or all over her mouth and chin. Not on Griffin's face. Not on his shirt. Not all over the floor, as it had been seconds ago.

"What. The. Fuck. What the actual fuck?"

The strength left Isabel and she was thankful to be already on the floor. She slumped forward, staring at them, unable to move. Ava looked mildly tired. Griffin looked like he needed a stint in rehab. Isabel could relate to how Griffin was feeling. Because she wasn't sure she could stand, she slowly crawled back toward them, keeping her eyes on them the entire time.

"Explain that to me," Griffin said. There was barely enough air in his lungs to form the words. "What the fuck just happened?"

"It was not my blood."

"Has this happened to you before?" Iz asked, her heart thundering in her chest so she could barely hear herself. She was so dizzy she felt like she was going to spin off the floor and float away.

"Not exactly."

"Then how the fuck are you so calm?"

She wiped the tears from her cheeks with hands that were still shaking violently.

"Panicking helps nothing."

"Well, how very logical of you."

"You are upset I am not falling apart," Ava said mildly, gazing at her. She leaned over and picked up the nearest glass of water from the table. The taste of blood was still in her mouth.

"I'm pissed off because I thought you were dying, and you don't seem to understand how devastating that is." Isabel hitched in a breath, then another. "I thought you were... fucking... d-dead..."

"Hey," Griffin soothed. Now that he knew Ava was okay, he went to Izzie. She curled into him. The shaking increased, even as she tried to get control over her tears.

He looked at Ava over Isabel's head. "You said it wasn't your blood. What does that mean?"

She had a way of staring at a person until they felt foolish. Tilting her head slowly, her eyes narrowed, and she studied him even more.

"Trying to spare Isabel's feelings is causing her more harm than the truth. I will tell you what I see. I hope it results in complete honesty so she can stop worrying about you and me.

"You either think about ending your life or you will end your life. You will use a Desert Eagle .50 caliber handgun with standard rounds. You will put it in your mouth, angling it down toward the space where your spine meets the base of your skull, because this is the most effective method of self-immolation. It guarantees swift, painless death as it separates the spine from the brain, effectively decapitating you. You will use a bathtub to minimize clean up because you love your family, no matter how difficult they are. You have done extensive research regarding this method. The number four is important."

Griffin's face was white. His eyes had glazed over as Ava spoke. He still heard her, but he couldn't really see her, and her voice sounded like buzzing in his ears. Isabel had raised her head and was staring at Ava. Her arm was curled around Griffin's neck, holding it tightly as she listened to Ava deliver her speech like a child delivering a book report.

Ava's head twitched. She frowned. "Who is Connor?"

· · · · ·

"You're awfully chipper," Tom observed, sitting beside Gabriel in the eerily quiet bar. Most people were out enjoying the late sunset and mild weather.

Gabriel was nodding his head to the music someone had chosen – Led Zeppelin sounded depressing on such a deserted Friday night – and thinking of Ava.

"Twenty bucks says he got laid and that's why he was late to the party," Jeremy smirked.

"Jealous?" Gabriel shot back.

"When do we get to meet this goddess?"

"Shit, that reminds me. I know it's short notice," Gabriel said, "But are you guys free tomorrow afternoon?"

"I can be," Jeremy said. "Shannon, or Denise, or Stephanie... whoever the fuck I'm dating right now is out of town. What's going on tomorrow?"

Tom shook his head as he dug his phone out of his pocket. His fingers began racing over the screen. "I'll check with Abby, see if we have any plans."

Jeremy made a noise and snapped his wrist, pretending to crack a whip. Tom stopped texting just long enough to slug him. Jeremy punched him back, harder.

Gabriel grinned.

"You're smiling," Jeremy said. "Showing teeth and everything. You definitely got laid."

"Did you forget your meds this morning?"

"I just texted Abby," Tom said. He motioned to Karen. "I should be able to let you know in a few minutes."

"So?" he asked, turning back to Gabe. "What's going on Saturday?"

"Isabel and I wanted to have a cookout since the weather's supposed to be nice. I'd like you guys to meet Ava if I can convince her to come."

715

"It's been a while since we've seen Iz. I can't wait to meet Ava. She must be phenomenal to put that look in your eyes."

Gabriel glanced at Tom over his beer bottle. "It's just gas."

Jeremy cracked up.

Karen came over with another round.

"Karen," Jeremy started.

"Careful," Tom said. "He's off his meds and it's hitting him hard."

"I raised three boys," she laughed, setting their drinks down. "I can handle one more."

"Aww, come on, sweetheart, give me some sugar."

Karen considered this, then picked up the jar of sugar, unscrewed the lid, and dumped it all over his lap. Jeremy almost fell out of his chair pushing back from the table.

"Nicely done." Gabriel saluted Karen. When Tom raised his glass in a toast, he clinked his own to it.

"Never mess with a mother," Tom said. "She'll chew you up and spit you out and she'll enjoy every minute of it."

Karen grinned. "I'll go get you a broom and dustpan to clean your mess up."

"But..." Jeremy stood, brushing crystals off his pants. "You made the mess!"

Still laughing, Tom picked up his phone. "Abby just got back to me. Her mom can watch the kids. That woman would kidnap them and raise them as her own if she thought she could get away with it. We'll both be there tomorrow."

"Outstanding."

"Are you going to invite Greg?" Tom asked.

Gabriel finished his beer and set the bottle on the edge of the table. He slid the one Karen had just set down closer. "I texted him."

"Are you going to tell him to leave his bitch at home?"

"Well, shit. Look who decided to show up."

Greg walked toward them, his shoulders hunched, not making eye contact. His hair looked like it hadn't seen a comb in days, and he needed to shave.

"Gregory," Tom said, motioning to an empty chair. "Fancy meeting you here."

"Guys." He nodded somberly. Giving the sugar mess on the floor a glance, he frowned.

"How's it going?" Gabriel asked, keeping his tone cool.

"I feel like a dumbass."

"We've all been there, man," Tom said. "She dump you?"

Karen brought over the broom and dustpan for Jeremy.

"Haven't seen you in here in a while, hon. I missed you. I'll get you a beer." She turned to Jeremy. "Clean up your mess."

Jeremy started sputtering, but Karen shoved the supplies in his hands and spun on her heel, walking back to the counter.

"What did you do to her?" Greg asked.

"I just asked her to give me some sugar," he mumbled. "She thinks she's a comedian."

He began sweeping.

"You coming over tomorrow?" Gabriel wasn't entirely ready to forgive his friend, but he wasn't going to shun him, either.

"I got your text. Thanks for the invite, even with... everything. Yeah, I'll be there. Alone."

"Good for you." Tom leaned over and touched his beer bottle to Greg's. "To good choices."

Greg nodded.

"To good choices," Gabriel repeated, tapping his bottle.

Jeremy glanced up from his position on the floor. "Fuck all of you."

• • • • •

"Who is Connor?" Ava repeated. "When you think of the gun, you think of someone named Connor."

"You're wrong." Griffin's voice was unsteady as he separated himself from Isabel and stood, wiping a hand over his mouth. "I would never kill myself. I know what it does to the people it leaves behind. I need something to drink."

Isabel reached for a glass. "Have some water."

"I need something stronger," he said tightly.

"Ava keeps some whiskey here for me."

Griffin started for the kitchen, but Isabel stood and put her hand on his arm.

"Let me get it."

As he walked stiffly away from the couch to pace by the front window, she poured two glasses of the whiskey Ava had been kind enough to keep here for her. Isabel kept her drinking to a minimum on Friday nights so she could drive home, but she wondered if tonight might be different. She decided to have this one glass and no more so she could drive Griffin home. He looked like he needed to unwind.

Walking back into the living room, she handed him the glass and set the bottle and her glass on the table.

"Are you okay, Ava? Do you need anything?"

Ava had moved to a chair. She was staring at Griffin, frowning, trying to reconcile what her vision had shown her to what little she knew about Griffin and what he had told her.

Absently, she glanced at Isabel and shook her head.

"What did you tell her?"

The tone of Griffin's voice sent a shiver down Izzie's spine. She wouldn't have believed him capable of such fury only a week ago. Taking a sip of her drink, she glanced over her glass at him, ready to defend Ava. She was shocked to see him glaring at her.

"Who, me?" she asked, almost choking on her drink. "What are you talking about?"

"What did you tell her about my brother?" His eyes showed rage so dark she leaned back slightly on the couch.

"I didn't tell her anything about your family."

Anger was taking over her confusion. Who the hell did he think he was, making assumptions and yelling at her?

"Then how did she know details about the gun?"

Setting her glass on the table hard enough that some of the liquid splashed out, Isabel clenched her jaw. "I don't even know details, you ass-hat. I can't give her information I don't have."

Furious, Isabel drew her legs up to her chest. "Asshole."

Griffin ran a hand through his hair. "Fuck."

"Connor is your brother. Why do you see your brother when you hold the gun?" Ava tilted her head, knowing she could get answers more quickly if she just opened her mind to his, if she just searched for the answers herself. Knowing she would never invade him that way.

Isabel only glared when he looked at her.

Griffin opened his mouth, closed it. "I don't. He sees me. My brother committed suicide four years ago."

"You are the one with the gun," Ava insisted. "You are holding it..."

Her voice trailed off as she ran through the visions she had since knowing him. Griffin watched her work through something in her mind, her eyes darting back and forth as if she was watching a movie. Even with what he'd already heard, he needed more proof, he needed to be sure.

"...but you are also trying to stop the one with the gun. You are his twin."

He nodded.

"That is why I see you with the gun and also see you watching."

"You saw something the first time we met, didn't you?" he asked dully. "At Isabel's parent's house? That's why you were acting strange."

She nodded.

"What did you see?"

"Before we continue, you must be sure you want to hear what I have to say."

Without hesitation, Griffin nodded. Everything he had ever believed in had just been wiped clean, the possibilities opened. He was hungry to hear anything and everything even though he wasn't quite ready to accept it yet. He would spend hours, days maybe, sifting through the details before deciding whether to change his mind on his basic beliefs. But for now, this woman seemed to be connected to Connor, and he couldn't turn away from that.

"Tell me everything," he said. He leaned forward and poured himself another drink.

"I first saw him in Isabel's apartment."

Her head snapped up. "What? When?"

"When you found me outside the bookstore. I was sick. You drove me to your apartment until my stomach settled. I saw him then."

"Son of a bitch," Isabel said. "What was he doing at my apartment?"

Ava kept her eyes on Griffin. "I thought he was someone who had once lived there. People... linger. Later I thought he was attached to Isabel because she thought about dying."

Griffin's gaze sharpened on her, then darted to Izzie.

"I thought about... what are you talking about?"

Ava closed her eyes, took a deep breath. She brought the evening to mind, remembering the smells, the sounds, the things she had seen.

"That night, I told you I would not be a good friend. You thought, I'm not contributing to this world anyway. If I died, would anyone notice? Connor took special interest in this."

"Christ, Isabel." Griffin began pacing again.

"I don't remember ever thinking that."

"That is because it was buried very deep. You did not realize you were thinking it at the time."

"When was this?" Griffin asked, staring at Isabel. "Did you know what I'd went through with Connor?"

"Late March." The frown appeared between Ava's brows. "The feeling behind the thought was curiosity. She has no desire to cause you harm."

"They never do."

The bitterness in his voice made Isabel feel very, very cold. She stood slowly. "I need some fresh air."

Ava watched her leave. After the door was shut, she regarded Griffin with cold, hard eyes. "You are grieving and confused, so if Isabel excuses your behavior, I will do the same. To this point. If you speak to her, or about her like that again, I will see you out of my house through whichever exit is closest."

She glanced at the window behind him.

Running a hand through his hair, he paced some more. "I love her."

"That does not give you the right to take your fear out on her."

"Fuck."

She said nothing, only continued to stare at him with her strange eyes.

Blaming Isabel for a subconscious thought was juvenile, he knew. It masked the real problem: his anger at his brother for taking his own life. Blaming those closest was classic human behavior. Knowing that, he had done it anyway, falling prey to his irrational anger.

"Is she suicidal?"

"Why don't you ask her?" Isabel said, shutting the door behind her quietly. "She can speak for herself."

She walked into the living room and stood looking at the floor, her arms crossed over her chest.

"I'm sorry." Griffin set his drink on the nearest bookcase. In two strides he was at her side, taking her hand. "I'm sorry."

His honey-colored eyes were tormented as he relived his grief over his brother's death.

"I'm not suicidal." Isabel kept her hand in his but turned back to Ava. "Keep going."

"At Sunday dinner with your parents, I recognized Griffin because I already saw Connor."

She turned to Griffin. "I did not realize it was you he was attached to. I thought I was seeing you, attached to Isabel. But I heard him first, the night Isabel took me to her apartment. That is why I was sick in the bookstore. I heard him. I think he was trying to show me what it was like the first time he tried to kill himself."

Griffin's hand clenched around Isabel's.

"I tasted alcohol and smelled snow. He was in an attic. The sun was shining through the rafters, and he watched the dust motes as his head grew heavy and the dizziness took over. He kept thinking 'I'm sorry. Don't let him find me.' He did not want your last image of him to be death."

Swallowing, Griffin found he had been holding his breath. He let it out in a whoosh.

"Pills. He took pills. But your grandfather found him and called an ambulance. That is why he chose the method so carefully the second time. To make it instant and definite."

This couldn't be happening. This couldn't possibly be real. People didn't listen to those claiming to communicate with spirits, accepting what they said at face value. Except Ava hadn't claimed to communicate with spirits – Isabel had accidentally let it slip. And Griffin wasn't accepting it at face value. Ava had shown him plenty of evidence to prove she was the real thing.

He walked on shaky legs to the sofa and sat, resting his head in his hands.

How was it that he felt better not knowing? How was it that he couldn't not know now that he had started?

"When you showed up at his apartment months later, you interrupted his second attempt. He tried to make you leave. You refused. He told you not to blame yourself."

Ava watched his eyes. "You do anyway."

She gauged whether she should continue. His face was pale. The emotions warring inside him were suffocating her. The only way to release them, to release him, was to give him the information and let him sort it out in his own time.

"He came to me here."

"Is he..." Griffin motioned toward his chin weakly. His eyes were glassy.

"He is intact," Ava said gently. "Besides showing me his death, he comes to me as he was before he died."

Shuddering, he exhaled. Isabel walked to him, sitting on the arm of the couch, and leaning against him. When her arms circled him in an embrace, he held onto her like a man drowning.

"He looks like you, but it is like seeing a shadow with a face."

"What does that mean?"

"I do not know."

"What the hell kind of medium are you?" he rasped, tightening his grip on Izzie.

"The reluctant kind." Ava stared at him with sinister eyes.

There always came a point in a situation, Ava knew, when a person could no longer handle what was coming at him and simply shut down. She had witnessed it many times throughout her life. Sometimes it was the body that gave up, like when she had stopped the man in the grocery store from hitting on her. Sometimes it was the mind.

Griffin was at that point. His mind was too full of grief and knowledge of his brother's final moments. He was exhausted in every way a person could be.

"I need..." He stood slowly. "This is a lot to take in. I need time to absorb all this. I'm sorry, Izzie, we came here for you."

Blinking, he turned to Isabel. "Will you come with me?"

She stood next to him but looked at Ava. "Thank you for having us tonight, Ava. I'm sorry it was so dark. Can I give you a hug?"

Ava had tucked her feet underneath her butt and was perched on the wingback chair. Her eyes were large and focused, as if she had chugged too many cups of coffee.

"Please do not touch me. I am hypersensitive at the moment."

Iz nodded. "Do you need anything?"

Shaking her head, Ava stared at Griffin and stood slowly. "I wish I could give you the information you are seeking."

He didn't look at her, but he said, "Thank you for telling me what you know. Please excuse my behavior."

• • • • •

Back at his apartment, Isabel watched Griffin fumble with his key before he was able to unlock the door. He hadn't spoken during the ride home. She hadn't tried to engage him. The entire evening had left her feeling numb.

Entering the kitchen, he dropped his keys onto the island and stood, not speaking. Iz was prepared to walk past him, intent on gathering her things and going home. As she was moving toward the bedroom, his voice stopped her.

"I'm sorry."

He sounded so broken. Turning back to him, she wondered how many apologies she had given him. How many times had he forgiven her?

He lifted his head and turned toward her. "I was an asshole. You were just trying to help."

"I'm used to it."

"I'm sorry," he repeated. "I took my grief out on you. It's not your fault."

"I'm tired, Griffin." She started toward the bedroom again. "I'm going home."

"Please stay."

"Why? So you can kick me some more? No thanks. I'm going to bed."

He found her in the walk-in closet, stuffing her dirty clothes into her overnight bag. The overnight bag hadn't been used in weeks because she had been staying here every night. Griffin had cleared a space in the closet for her. The transition had happened so naturally, she hadn't even panicked over it.

Leaning against the doorway, he watched her stack the clothes she wore to work off the little table next to the shoe rack.

"I don't know what else you want from me," he said.

"I can't be what you need me to be right now." Turning to the dresser, she grabbed panties and bras and tossed them into the bag. "I'm too shaken up. I can't be strong and give you what you need."

"What I need you to be is you." He straightened. "That's all I've ever needed. And since you're shaken up, I want you to stay even more. I want to be here for you."

"You shouldn't have to be here for me." Isabel walked past him to her side of the bed, dropping her bag to lean down and unplug her charger. "I should be strong enough to be here for you. And I'm not."

Because the bed was in the way, she was pulling on the cord at an angle. It wasn't budging.

"That doesn't matter. Let's just talk."

"That thing was in my apartment." She stood and whirled on him, her face flushed. "Is that what you want to hear? Is that what you want to discuss? Your dead brother was in my apartment like a creepy stalker, hovering around me, and it makes me sick."

He flinched as if she had struck him.

"Do you blame me for that?"

The shock that flashed over her face released some of the tension in his shoulders.

"No, of course not."

"Then stay. Please. We don't have to talk. Just don't leave me alone tonight."

He didn't blame her for feeling the way she did about his brother. Surprised, grateful, Iz walked around the bed. Her touch was hesitant as she took his hand.

Looking into his amber eyes, she said, "I won't leave you alone."

•　•　•　•　•

CHAPTER THIRTEEN

Like any typical guy, Gabriel was going to wing it when it came to the cookout. Isabel had sent him dozens of texts throughout the week, asking how many would be there, if there were any dietary restrictions, blah, blah. She offered to bring anything he didn't have, which turned out to be almost everything. He had enough meat and a few hot dog buns, condiments, and beer, but the rest Isabel would have to get. So she said. Gabriel thought everyone would be fine with chips and maybe potato salad, and they needed paper plates and cutlery. When he told Isabel those were the only items he thought she needed to pick up, she scoffed.

"You're such a man," she said. "I'll handle it."

Gabriel left Ava beating the shit out of her punching bag to make sure his house was guest ready. She'd been quiet last night and this morning. Not detached; when he reached for her, she didn't shy away from him. But she hadn't said much, and her expression remained thoughtful throughout the morning.

She woke him by fighting in her sleep, a mild interruption compared to the past couple weeks. Kicking her legs and twisting her body, she'd been panting silently when he told her he was going to touch her and tugged her awkwardly into a sitting position so he could slide around behind her. Then he simply held her until she wore herself out.

The second time she sat up, shivering and moaning. Rocking, her hands were listlessly clawing at her throat when he turned on the lamp. A few minutes of holding her, rocking with her, lulled her into submission again. He hadn't used the Japanese phrase either time because he wanted to see if he was enough to calm her down. He had been. The whole evening had been mildly eventful compared to most nights.

Lying on his back, he had settled her on his chest, skin to skin. For a long time, he simply stared at her, running his fingertips up and down her back. She made a sound of contentment. Her body lay snug against his, her breathing evening out. Seeing her so peaceful had allowed him to easily slip back into sleep.

While he waited for Isabel to show up, he cleaned up the kitchen and made sure there were enough chairs on the deck for everyone. He straightened the great room, breakfast room, first floor bathroom, and foyer since guests would see those areas of the house. Not much needed to be done; he paid to have his house cleaned twice a week. Isabel scoffed at that, too.

She showed up a little before noon with bags and bags of items. Gabriel took a moment to give the dogs attention before he helped carry the groceries in.

"Jesus, Iz, is there anything left in the store?" he grumbled.

She slugged him in the shoulder. She packed a harder punch than usual, he noticed, rubbing his shoulder.

Once all the bags were in the kitchen and he had poured her some coffee, he noticed the dull fatigue in her eyes, behind her usual fire.

"What's going on?" he asked, taking items out of the paper sacks, and setting them on the counter. She'd bought enough food to feed Biafra.

"What do you mean?" She was doing the same at the breakfast counter, where she could sit on one of the stools while she worked. Walking around on the grocery store's cement floor for an hour was killing her feet.

"You look tired. Did something happen last night at Ava's?" He noticed the frown on her face even though it disappeared almost as quickly as it emerged.

"What did she say?" Iz asked, keeping her voice carefully neutral.

"Not much. She was exceptionally quiet, even for her."

She began separating the items on the counter to keep her hands busy. "I brought Griffin with me. I wanted to see if Ava could help me... get my shit together."

Avoiding his gaze, she pulled her coffee over to her and wrapped her hands around the mug. She gave him a summary of what had happened while he put the rest of the supplies away. He listened and remained quiet after she was done.

He'd leaned against the counter as she spoke, holding his coffee, and now he studied her with an expression she couldn't read.

"Say something," she finally said. The silence was making her even more twitchy than she was.

"We're like magnets for tragedy, aren't we?" His quiet voice hit her harder than if he had shouted at her.

He had spoken of sadness in her eyes before, a sadness he saw every time he looked in the mirror. She saw it now. How foolish she'd been to think she was the only one suffering. How selfish of her to not see the pain behind his calm blue eyes. Their mother and Beth showed everything on the outside plainly, bursting into tears at every little thing and raging on a whim. For her and Gabriel, their story was in their eyes.

"We should start a club," she said. "I wish I was a guy. You and Griffin deal with it so much better than I do."

"We just hide it better. Most of the time."

Ozzie bumped his nose against Gabriel's leg. He leaned down and rested his hand on his head to let him know he was okay.

Maya set her front paws on the bottom rung of Isabel's stool and raised up, staring at Iz. She let out a whine.

"I'm okay, girl," she soothed, turning, and running her hands down both sides of the dog. The thick fur flowed through her fingers. Something about petting a dog was always therapeutic.

"How's Griffin doing?"

Iz turned back to her coffee. "He's better this morning. He had to go into work today, so I'm glad he didn't look so sick. Last night I thought he was going to throw up."

Gabriel picked up the coffee pot and topped off both their mugs. He grabbed the creamer for Iz. Ozzie, apparently not satisfied that everything was okay, lay in the middle of the kitchen to keep watch.

"Ava said she couldn't help me until I understood she didn't have a problem with him. She kept reading Griffin every time she saw him, but she didn't know why. So, I guess it's my fault he had to relive his brother's suicide last night."

"It would have come out eventually. She was distracted every time she was around him. At least you know it's not because she hates him."

They quietly contemplated that for a few seconds.

"I didn't realize you were having so much trouble about Hayden's disappearance, Iz. You should have told me."

"You have enough going on. It happened to you, too."

"That doesn't matter."

Running a hand through her hair, she raised her head and let out a humorless laugh.

"This is supposed to be a fun day. It will be a fun day. No more deep, existential thoughts. We're going to laugh with your friends, and eat delicious food, and catch up. I've missed everyone."

• • • • •

"This was a bad idea."

Gabriel watched Ava exit her vehicle, set a cloth bag on the hood of it, and kneel to accept Ozzie's unbridled attention. Isabel walked up behind him and nudged him aside so she could see.

"When the hell did you become so cynical? Your friends have met your girlfriends before. She'll be fine."

"She's not my other girlfriends," Gabriel murmured. He felt a rush of heat as Ava stood and walked toward the porch with the bag. Christ, she looked good in jeans, with her hair flowing down her back and the sun framing her entire body. Then again, she looked good in anything.

Or nothing.

She looked up and saw them watching her.

"She's unique," Isabel agreed. She elbowed him in the side. "Your friends accepted me. It'll be fine."

"We all grew up together. They're as much your friends as mine."

"You'll be fine, just fine."

Gabriel opened the inner door as Ava approached. He glanced back over his shoulder at his sister.

"I just don't want another Charity situation. It took Greg over a month to talk to us."

Isabel scoffed. "Ava is not Charity. That bitch needs to step out into traffic."

He smirked.

Ava opened the storm door. Ozzie raced in, banging into Gabriel's legs as he scrambled passed. Gabriel leaned forward as Ava stepped inside, touching her lightly on the shoulder before kissing her on the cheek. "I missed you."

"You saw me this morning." Her blunt tone made him laugh.

Maya followed her in.

"Hi, Ava," Isabel said cautiously.

"Hello."

She surprised Iz by stepping forward and embracing her. It was the first time Ava had initiated a hug. Stunned, Iz raised her hands and rested them on Ava's back.

She raised one eyebrow to Gabriel as she gave her a light squeeze. Ava disengaged herself from Isabel and stepped back.

Gabriel reached for the bag Ava was holding. "Let me take that."

"They will need to be put on the grill for twenty minutes," Ava said, handing it to him.

He glanced in but only saw two large lumps wrapped in foil. "What is it?"

"Grilled Ratatouille. I did not know anyone's dietary needs, so I brought a vegetarian dish."

"I'll put it in the fridge for now," Isabel said, taking it from him and disappearing into the kitchen.

"How was the workout?" Gabriel asked, touching Ava's shoulder again.

He was always touching her in small ways, a hand on the shoulder, his fingertips along her back, his elbow against her side. Her body was getting used to it. She found herself turning into his touch now, craving it, just as she found herself looking forward to Isabel's hugs.

"It improved my strength and endurance."

The corners of his mouth quivered. The lovely smell of her, the scent that was all Ava, was making him want to pull her in and kiss her. The kind of kiss that ended in bed, or on the couch, or against the wall. And the way she was looking at him told him he damn well knew it.

"You smell wonderful."

"Thank you."

He motioned toward the kitchen and walked toward it. "Are you ready to meet my friends?"

"I am familiar with the ritual of meeting new people."

He prepared a glass of ice water, handed it to her. Their fingers brushed briefly as she took it from him. "You're not nervous? About whether or not they'll like you?"

Ava shot him a look of barely contained disgust. "I do not concern myself with the opinions of others."

Isabel grinned. "That's my girl."

"They're good people," Gabriel said, resting his hand on Ava's hip. He brushed his index finger down her temple, where the bruises were turning yellow and just beginning to fade. "That's healing nicely."

"It makes you look bad ass." Isabel was preparing a relish tray, grinning at her.

Gabriel couldn't seem to keep his hands off her. He wondered if he was being too grabby. Trying to be casual, he started to slide his hand down, to remove it from her lower back. Just as casually, she reached behind her and covered his hand with hers. She slid his hand back up to where it started. He raised an eyebrow.

Ava casually tilted her head back toward the foyer.

Maya and Ozzie scrambled for the door. A moment later, Gabriel heard vehicle doors slamming shut.

"They're here. Is Abby coming?" Isabel asked of Tom's wife. She popped a green olive from the relish tray in her mouth. "I haven't seen her in months."

"Yeah, her mom's babysitting the kids." Gabriel glanced at Ava, trying to gauge her emotions. He couldn't read her expression or body language.

"It's going to be a full house." Isabel walked toward the foyer to greet everyone.

Ava was staring at the relish tray. Gabriel touched her shoulder lightly.

"Are you sure you're okay meeting everyone?"

She frowned. Her eyes seemed to lose focus momentarily. When they came back into focus, there was heat in them. "You think I will embarrass you."

"I don't want you to be... overwhelmed."

From the other room came a bark of feminine laughter. Despite the noise, Ava did not take her eyes off Gabriel. She studied him stoically, her eyes unblinking. He felt he could drown in those endless, smokey eyes.

"I do not need to be here." She set her water down. "I am making you uncomfortable."

"I want them to like you. My last relationship... sorry, old habit." He was weary, she saw, as much from his own doubts as from worrying about her.

"She is no longer part of your life. You hold onto something that no longer concerns you."

Gabriel ran a hand down the back of his neck. "I guess I'm still gun shy. I don't want to hurt you."

"You cannot hurt me," she said.

He gazed at her, wondering if she truly believed that, hoping he would never have to find out. He touched her hand. "I'm going to go play greeter. You want to stay here? It'll be a little crowded in the foyer."

She nodded.

Gabriel walked through the great room into the foyer, where Tom and Abby were talking with Isabel. Abby instantly shoved a slow cooker into Tom's hands and threw her arms around Gabriel.

"Gabe! It's been too long!"

"We need to do this more often," Gabriel agreed, wrapping his arms around her.

"You haven't seen the kids since they were babies," she chided. She pulled back. "If you're not careful, they'll be in college the next time you visit."

"I get it."

Tom gave Gabriel a sympathetic look. "You're lucky she's kidding."

"Come into the kitchen," Isabel laughed. "Tom, let's give you a counter to set that on."

"That would be helpful. Abby made enough to feed Ethiopia."

They walked toward the kitchen. Gabriel tried to look over everyone's heads to see where Ava was. He relaxed when he saw her sitting at the breakfast counter, sipping her water. She seemed unfazed by the commotion. Gabriel was surprised that he was so nervous around friends he had known since he was a child, and Ava was perfectly relaxed, having never met them.

Abby was chattering enthusiastically but she stopped as soon as she saw Ava.

"This must be Ava! Ooh, what happened to your eye?" She winced sympathetically and Ava saw the mother in her.

"I injure myself while sleepwalking."

"Goodness. Well, I'm Abby, and this is my husband, Tom. He and Gabriel go way back." She reached her hand across the counter. Ava stared at the outstretched hand for only a second before giving it a firm shake. Then shook Tom's hand when he offered it.

"Nice to meet you," she said, standing. "Would you like something to drink?"

"I'll get their drinks," Isabel said from behind Abby. "You relax. You're a guest, too. Gabe and I are doing all the work today."

A knock at the door made the dogs run into the foyer again. Jeremy called out as he stepped inside.

"I'll go," Isabel said, touching Gabriel's arm. "You get the drinks."

Ava walked around the counter with her glass. Weaving between Abby and Tom without touching them, she poured herself another glass of water. While he opened two beers, Gabriel watched Ava for any signs of distress. So far, she seemed fine, but she had the ability to mask her emotions.

Ava returned the pitcher to the refrigerator. She turned to go back to her seat when she saw Jeremy. Instantly, she recoiled. Gabriel noticed she didn't assume a defensive stance. She wasn't feeling threatened; she was disgusted.

"Well, hello, gorgeous," Jeremy said, grinning at her. "Fancy meeting you here."

"Jeremy, this is Ava," Gabriel said, confused at Ava's reaction. She was bristling.

"This is your girlfriend?" Jeremy said, then laughed. "Holy shit!" He held out his hand. "Jeremy Rowlands. I didn't realize you were spoken for when I hit on you."

"Jesus," Gabriel said, rubbing his forehead. "This is a disaster."

"We were not… together… at the time," she said icily. "My lack of interest in you had nothing to do with my availability." She gave Jeremy's hand a quick, polite shake before taking a deliberate step back.

"Sorry about that," Jeremy said easily to Gabriel. He turned back to Ava, gazing at her face without guile. "That's one hell of a bruise, darling."

Ava's lip raised and Gabriel heard a low snarl.

He felt the fury toward his friend lessen hearing Jeremy had hit on her before she was dating him. Though Jeremy would have no way of knowing

Ava's dating status when he first approached her, Gabriel's initial response had been to slam his fists into his childhood friend.

Ava wove in between bodies like a cat, moving to the other side of the breakfast counter to put plenty of space between herself and everyone else.

"Isabel," Jeremy said, "you get more beautiful every time I see you."

"You're so full of shit, Rowlands," Iz snorted.

"And Abby, my God, nobody will ever convince me you've had three children with that body."

"Save it, Casanova," Abby said, laughing and slapping Jeremy on the shoulder before embracing him.

Isabel began getting drinks for herself and Jeremy. Three different conversations were going on; Gabriel was having one with his sister and one with Abby while Isabel was talking to Tom. Gabriel's house was huge, but Ava felt like she was sinking inside it, melting into the floor to be swallowed up and forgotten. The noise was unnerving. She placed her hands on her ears and tried to shut the clamor out, but her head was hurting. What had made her think she wanted this? She hated crowds.

That she had agreed to do something she hated because she wanted to please Gabriel infuriated her. She never compromised herself for someone else.

He was suddenly standing in front of her, blocking everyone else out of her line of sight.

"How's it going over here?" he asked, placing his large hands over hers. The noise cut out considerably with both their hands covering her ears.

"It is noisy." She squinted.

"Let's go outside. It's a little crowded in here."

Ava thankfully stood. Gabriel rounded the counter and took her hand as he passed by, walking to the patio doors. The dogs burst out as if they had not been outside mere minutes ago. Ava walked to the edge of the patio and rested her elbows on the railing. She covered her ears again, feeling as if every piece of input was overloading her system. Closing her eyes, she took deep breaths.

Gabriel came up beside her. She opened her eyes and lowered her hands.

"I'm sorry about Jeremy. I didn't realize he came onto you."

"You do not control his actions. It was before we..." She struggled to find the right words even as her attention was divided by the noise in the kitchen. She was already getting a headache. "I was not your mate when it happened."

That was something, at least.

"Is it too much?" he asked. "They haven't seen each other in a long time. They're pretty excited and they're trying to fit several months of updates in as quickly as possible."

She took a couple breaths before she answered. "It is like I feel everything from everyone, all at once."

Gabriel's hand barely brushed her lower back. "I shouldn't have put this on you. It's too soon. We don't know each other very well and I rushed this."

"I need a minute."

Wishing he could help somehow, Gabriel pulled away to give her privacy. He was ashamed of himself for trying to flaunt Ava like a muscle car or a new boat. Ava didn't do social, and he had shoved her into the center of a situation she otherwise would have purposely avoided and expected her to act like his version of normal. He liked that she was different. He wanted her to be comfortable, even if that meant he didn't socialize as much.

Ava's arm shot out and she gripped his wrist, surprising him. He turned back.

"I need a minute," she repeated. Her hand slid from his wrist to his hand, clutching it tightly. Her eyes were closed, and she took several deep breaths.

Gabriel stepped back to her side. Surprised she wanted him with her, he covered her hand with both of his and rubbed his thumb over the back of hers.

In time she opened her eyes and nodded. "I am okay."

They walked back into the kitchen.

• • • • •

At first, Gabriel had trouble concentrating on manning the grill. He found his eyes wandering to Ava, watching her help Isabel and Abby set dishes and food out on the deck. Ava, with her long arms, balancing plates on one palm and carrying a serving bowl of food in her other hand as she gracefully moved around Tom and Jeremy to get to the table. Moving with catlike agility around the kitchen and on the deck, between people, always careful not to touch. She was less agitated once people were spread out in smaller groups. Helping set up the food put her even more at ease. She did not like just sitting; helping set up gave her something to do.

How was a man to concentrate when his girlfriend was moving around like a damn ballerina? He tried to focus on grilling the food and his friend's chatter so he wouldn't work himself into a sexual frenzy.

"When was the last time you two spent some time together without the kids?" Isabel asked Abby, putting napkins at each place setting. Abby walked beside her, setting flatware on top of the napkins. Ava set the stack of plates on the table silently. She began setting them at each chair.

Abby paused, thinking. "I don't think Kara was born yet."

"Shit," Isabel said. "That was three years ago."

"I know." Abby laughed.

Ava left them to get more food.

Abby glanced at her. "She's a quiet one."

Isabel nodded. She glanced at Tom and Gabriel, who were talking while Gabriel finished cooking on the grill. Tom was talking, Isabel noted. Gabriel was staring at the door where Ava had just disappeared through, and he seemed to be only half listening to Tom. Jeremy smirked at Gabriel's somewhat dazed expression.

"She had a really bad childhood," Isabel said quietly. "So, if she seems a little strange, I hope you give her the benefit of the doubt."

Abby raised her head, her eyes full of compassion.

"It's not my place to tell her business," Isabel continued as Ava came out with an armload of food. "I just don't want you to think badly of her."

Abby reached over and squeezed her hand. "I don't think that. You're such a good person to look after her, Isabel."

Ava set bowls of food on the table with the efficiency of a seasoned waitress.

"Ava," Abby said brightly, "What kind of work do you do?"

Ava seemed startled by the sudden attention. "Freelance editing." She moved the bowls around to make room for more. Gabriel wanted to run his finger across the wrinkles caused by her intense concentration as she furrowed her brow.

"Do you work from home?"

"Yes." She straightened, satisfied with the placement of the food. All other conversation had stopped as everyone turned their attention to the two women.

"That sounds wonderful. You can work in your pajamas if you want."

Ava stared at her. "I sleep naked." She turned on her heel and walked back into the house.

Abby's eyes widened. Everyone on the deck was silent for a moment before they all burst into laughter. Jeremy clicked his beer bottle to Gabriel's in a toast.

"She's something else," Jeremy said when the women were inside. "I'm sorry again, man. I hit on her, like, two months ago. I didn't even know you were seeing anyone."

"We've only been together a few weeks," Gabriel said. "We weren't dating when you hit on her."

"Still... I feel like I broke a bro code or something."

Gabriel watched the women bring more food out. Isabel plucked two green beans from a bowl and handed one to Ozzie and one to Maya on her way back inside. He felt a surge of pride that Ava hadn't fallen for Jeremy's charm. Only a rare woman refused to succumb to his flirtations, and Ava was definitely rare.

He loved to watch her move in those jeans. The short-sleeved sweater accented her figure perfectly.

Easy, he told himself. Don't get yourself worked up again in front of everyone.

"We're good," he told Jeremy. "Especially since she shut your ass down."

Jeremy grinned. "So hard." He shook his head. "If I tried to pursue her any harder, she would have ground me into hamburger."

Gabriel couldn't help but smile at that. Of course, she would have.

The women exited the house again with glasses, condiments, and serving spoons. Ava straightened and watched a car a couple miles down the road.

"Greg is coming."

As the car drew closer, Gabriel felt his mouth twitch. He got a kick out of her doing that.

"How does she know what car he drives? She must have x-ray vision to see that far away." Tom held a hand up to shield his eyes from the sun.

"Have you already met Greg?" Abby asked Ava.

"No."

She returned to her work at the table.

Everyone else watched Greg as he slowed to turn into the driveway, where he disappeared from their line of sight.

"She seems…" Jeremy started but didn't know how to continue in a polite way.

"Different," Tom offered.

"Yeah. What's her story?"

They were talking low, and Abby and Isabel were busy trying to engage Ava in conversation, but Gabriel had a feeling that Ava knew exactly what was going on between him and his friends.

"You'll have to get that from her," he told Jeremy.

"I don't think she wants to talk to me."

Gabriel gave him a lazy smile. "You have to earn her trust. She doesn't just give it to anyone."

"How did you earn it?" Jeremy asked, honestly curious. "It's pretty obvious she trusts you more than anyone."

How does anyone earn another person's trust? Gabriel thought. Why had Ava decided he was worth trusting?

"I'm still working on it."

"Time to eat," Abby called out.

Tom walked over to her, nuzzling her neck. Gabriel and Jeremy started over toward the table.

"Greg!" Tom called. "Do you need a map to find the patio?"

"I'm getting a drink!" a voice called from the kitchen.

"There's beer out here in the cooler!" Jeremy called. He set his beer on the table.

"Not there," Abby said around Tom's head, dictating where people could sit.

Jeremy lifted his bottle and moved it to the left, watching Abby questioningly. Abby gave him a thumbs up. Jeremy set it down and pulled out his chair.

The patio door opened, and Greg emerged with a bottle of beer. "Sorry I'm late."

"For that, you get the naughty corner, next to Jeremy." Abby pointed.

"Hey!" Jeremy protested.

She gave him a mischievous grin.

Gabriel set the plate of meat down and stood next to Ava. She was at the head of the table, facing the rest of the group. Only Gabriel's expansive yard was at her back.

"Okay?" he murmured.

"Women talk so much," she said, her voice low. She looked slightly dazed.

He let out a bark of laughter. "I won't argue that. Is that where you're sitting?"

She nodded. Gabriel leaned over and pulled out her chair before sitting in his own diagonally across from her.

He was glad to be close to her again. Helping to set up the food, though a simple and everyday task for most people, had somehow seemed sensual when Ava did it. Gabriel's mouth was watering, and not because he was hungry for the burgers and brats.

"Dig i-" Abby started and stopped abruptly. At her silence, everyone followed her gaze and looked at Ava.

She had folded her hands and her head was down with her eyes closed. Though she didn't speak, it was obvious she was praying. Gabriel's and Isabel's heads were tilted down respectfully.

Panic filled Abby's eyes.

After several seconds, Ava lifted her head to see Tom, Abby, Greg, and Jeremy looking at her. She gazed back.

"I'm sorry, Ava," Abby said, looking close to tears. "I didn't realize you're religious."

Ava's brow furrowed. She adjusted her napkin and cutlery around her plate. "I do not believe in organized religion."

"But... you prayed."

"I gave thanks," Ava corrected.

She looked around the table. Everyone was watching her curiously, trying to understand. There was no malice on their faces.

"It reminds me to be grateful each time I avoid hunger."

"Amen to that," Tom said, lifting his beer.

Ava looked at Abby, tilted her head as if listening to something only she could hear. "You want to have another baby."

She leaned over, lifting the bowl of potato salad to set it closer to her plate. Everyone at the table was silent as she plopped a spoonful onto her plate and set the bowl back. Next, she reached for the tongs, setting a burger on her plate.

"Ah... Ava, what did you mean-" Tom started.

"She wants to have one more," Ava said, half-standing to reach the bowl of black olives. "She's been having dreams about a baby crying."

"What are you talking about?" she asked.

"Do not worry," Ava said, motioning absently toward Tom with a serving spoon. "He wants to have another one, too."

Jeremy spit out his beer.

"Thanks, asshole," Tom said, wiping expelled beer off his arm with a napkin. He turned to Ava. "Ava, why did you say Abby and I want a baby?"

She sighed, looking around at the food that was not being passed around. "Because you both do. You both want the same thing, but you are too afraid the other does not want what you want. If you communicated with each other, you would know this. If people are not going to pass food around the table to make serving more efficient, the food should have been set up as a buffet."

After a moment of complete silence, Abby said loudly, "Okay, dig in!"

They began to pile food on their plates and pass the dishes. Initially, no one spoke. The only sounds were the serving spoons against dishes and murmurs of thanks when food was passed. Ozzie instantly was on the deck to make sure no scraps were dropped during the handling of food. Maya walked up and laid down in a corner a few minutes later.

Gabriel kept glancing at Ava, wondering if she would feel comfortable about his friends knowing she was a medium. If she continued to talk as freely as she just had, they would start asking questions, and he would have to say something eventually. He decided he would talk to her about it. She either had to be more careful about the way she talked around them, or he had to be able to explain why she knew things she had no business knowing.

As she always did, Ava dug into her food with enthusiasm. Gabriel noticed Isabel and his friends glancing at Ava as she ate, trying to hide their smiles. Their amusement lightened the mood, and soon conversations were buzzing again.

"Ava, Gabriel said you know karate," Jeremy said, taking a huge bite of his burger.

Ava barely gave him a glance. "I know a lot of things."

"Is that what you used on me when I flirted with you?" he pressed.

Everyone was instantly interested in the conversation.

"No," she said. Her eyes lazily found his. "That was Kung Fu. I was being polite."

"This is the best cookout ever," Isabel said, giggling.

Gabriel couldn't suppress a smile.

"It didn't feel very polite," Jeremy laughed.

Ava studied him in that emotionless way she had perfected. "Neither did having to repeat myself. I responded accordingly."

From Isabel: "Daaammmmnnn!"

Abby playfully slapped Jeremy's shoulder. "Not everyone appreciates being pursued, stud."

"How many... uh... types of fighting do you know?" Tom asked.

"I have studied seven styles of martial arts," Ava said, "but the two I am currently practicing are Ninpo and Kung Fu."

"Two at the same time?" Gabriel was impressed. "Holy shit."

"What made you decide to study martial arts?" Isabel asked.

"I chose not to be a victim. It is difficult to eat when you all are asking so many questions."

Isabel snorted. "We'll lay off."

"Sorry, Ava, you're a very interesting person," Tom said, adding onions to his burger. "We want to find out more about the woman Gabriel is so enamored by."

"Fuck off," Gabriel said mildly.

Tom laughed. "Is there anything you want to ask us?"

Ava was busy stuffing her face. When her mouth was clear, she said, "I know everything I need to know about you."

"How very intriguing," Tom said.

Although they were still curious, Gabriel's friends began chatting with each other to give Ava a break and allow her to eat. Gabriel listened between bites, talking with Isabel, and occasionally throwing in a comment. He noticed Ava seemed to ignore everyone around her while she focused intently on her food, but he would have bet his inheritance that she knew every word that was being exchanged in each conversation.

She eats like a wolf, he thought, fascinated. Always alert to her surroundings but driven only to fuel the machine. Conversation has no place while she's eating.

She didn't inhale her food, but she wasn't hindered by discussion, so she finished before everyone else. Sated, she sat back in her chair and sighed. Gabriel reached over and rested his hand on her knee. She tensed for only a moment, and didn't pull away, but he had an uneasy feeling in his stomach. She hadn't reacted like that to his touch for a while now.

"Who made the grilled vegetable dish?" Abby asked. "This is delicious."

"Ava," Isabel said.

"I can see this being a favorite with the boys, don't you think?" Abby looked at her husband.

"Definitely. I love it. It's a good way to get in our veggies."

"Can I have the recipe, Ava?" Abby asked.

"I can-" Ava shook her head. She blinked in surprise.

Gabriel glanced over at her. "Everything okay?"

"I can get you the -" Grimacing, Ava's head jerked as if she had a sudden headache. Suddenly she sat up in her seat, her hands gripping the arms of the chair so hard her fingers drained of color. The sudden movement startled everyone.

Gabriel could feel the muscles in her leg coiling into stone beneath his hand. "Ava, what's wrong?"

"David."

Her entire body was rigid. Gabriel could hear her breathing in short gasps. Isabel reached out to take her hand, but Gabriel shook his head. "Don't touch her."

"Ava, look at me," he said softly.

Stiffly, as if against her will, she turned her head toward him. Her eyes were out of focus, the pupils dilated until they looked completely black.

"Breathe." His tone was firm enough to snap her attention back to him. She exhaled sharply.

"Is this...?" Isabel asked. She was whispering, as if she thought talking loudly would make things worse.

"What do you need?" he asked Ava.

"David." Her voice sounded mechanical, inhuman.

"Who's David?" Jeremy asked.

Gabriel didn't like how pale Ava had become. If she didn't stop breathing the way she was, she would pass out. "I'll take you to him, Ava. Is he home?"

"He's in Madison," Ava said. She stood so fast she knocked her chair over. Ozzie and Maya, sleeping peacefully a few feet away, jumped to their feet and started barking. Abby let out an involuntary gasp. "He did not tell me. He is here and did not tell me."

"I'll drive you. Ava, calm d-"

But she wasn't listening. Her eyes were glazed over and wherever she was, she couldn't hear him.

Isabel reached for her again.

"Don't touch her!" Gabriel snapped. "She'll think you're attacking her."

"It hurts," Ava choked out, pressing her right hand to her chest. She was having trouble breathing. She leaned over and rested her free hand on the table.

"Oh, honey-" Isabel started, and touched her shoulder before Gabriel could stop her.

Ava swung her right arm in a large outward loop, sliding Isabel's hand off her shoulder and locking her arm. She stepped forward as she struck upward with her open left hand, her fingers splayed like she had claws.

"Ava, stop." Gabriel's voice was quick but calm. He kept it quiet and tried to keep the unease from it. Seeing his sister almost knocked across his deck by his girlfriend had shaken him more than he wanted to admit. Every instinct in him was telling him to defend his sister, but he knew Ava was capable of kicking both their asses. He needed his ass intact to take her where she needed to go.

"Let's go see David. David needs you."

Ava's palm had stopped two inches from Isabel's face. Her claw-like fingers were an inch closer. Isabel's large, round eyes were crossed looking at Ava's hand. Her mouth hung open in a an "O" of surprise. Her arm, interlocked with Ava's, was stiff with pain.

"I told you," Gabriel said, glancing at his sister, "not to touch her."

"Holy shit," Isabel whispered. Her arm was throbbing. Needles of pain shot up into her shoulder. Tears welled in her eyes.

Gabriel walked around the table and stood near Ava, not too close. "We're going to go check on David," he said to the group, not taking his eyes off at Ava. "It may be a while before we're back."

Still poised in a stance, her hand a breath from Izzie's face, Ava turned her head toward Gabriel as if controlled by rusty gears. Her movements were stiff and mechanical. Around them, everyone else had fallen silent. Tension surrounded the table like a bubble.

"Come on," he said gently. "Let Isabel go. She's your friend."

"I didn't mean to hurt you, Ava," Isabel said, tears spilling over her cheeks.

Ava stood a moment longer. Her eyes, as quickly as they had darkened and glazed, suddenly cleared. She blinked, looking at Isabel, looking down at their woven arms. She relaxed and released Isabel's arm.

"I am sorry." She stumbled back a step. Gabriel put his arm out toward her shoulder but didn't touch her.

"Are you okay?" Isabel asked, the tears still fresh on her cheeks.

Ava frowned. She had just injured her friend, yet Isabel was more concerned for her safety. She did not understand. "I... I need to see David."

Gabriel hugged Isabel, leaning in close to her ear. "I'm really sorry. We'll talk when I get back."

She returned the hug, but he could see she was shaken. "Text or call to let me know what's going on as soon as you find out."

He nodded, turned to Ava. "Let's go."

·　·　·　·　·

He drove toward Madison for several minutes in absolute silence. Gabriel wouldn't need directions for several more minutes, until he was closer to the city. He glanced over at Ava often, trying to gauge how she was doing, but he couldn't tell. She was still pale, with smudges of gray under each eye. When he had helped her into his jeep, she had been shivering.

"Where am I going?" he finally asked, glancing at her. "We're twenty minutes from Madison."

She didn't answer. She brought her knees up to her chest, hunching over on the seat.

"Ava, I need to know where David is in Madison."

"Sisters of Faith Hospital," she said, her voice dull.

"What's going on?" It had to be something bad. Something she saw had scared the hell out of her.

"Myocardial infarction."

What the fuck does that mean? In his heightened state of stress, Gabriel's brain wasn't working at full function.

As if she heard the thought, Ava added, "He had a heart attack."

She leaned her forehead against the window and did not speak again.

Fifteen minutes later he pulled into the emergency area parking lot. Ava had her seat belt off and was opening the door before he could stop her.

Reaching out to her, he called her name. She slipped out of the truck, sprinting toward the entrance. "Goddamn it," he muttered, looking for the nearest parking spot. He stopped short of pulling in, leaning over to shut the passenger door so it wouldn't smack into the vehicle next to him before parking.

Inside the hospital, he hurried to the front desk. Ava was nowhere to be seen. He asked for cardiology and sprinted for the elevators. Pressing the buttons on both sides of the hall, Gabriel paced between them, waiting for one to be ready. An old woman with an oxygen tank was waiting with a mask over her face. Gabriel barely gave her a glance. Why was the elevator taking so long? He was about to take the stairs when two bells chimed, indicating two elevators were ready to go up. Gabriel's eyes darted from one to the other, waiting for whichever opened first. They opened simultaneously. He started for the one on the right and stopped when he saw Ava in the one on the left. She was standing in the corner of the elevator, her arms crossed over her chest, eyes staring at the floor. She was pressed against the walls of the elevator as if her life depended on contact with the metal.

Gabriel pivoted and slipped sideways into the elevator on the left as the door was closing. He caught a flash of the old woman with the oxygen mask slowly making her way to the other car.

Staring at the lone figure in the corner, Gabriel had to restrain himself from trying to shake her. "Ava, what the hell were you thinking? You should have waited for me." None of the buttons were lit. He punched the button for the floor to cardiology.

She was still shivering. She didn't look at him, didn't blink. Gabriel slowly reached out with one hand, resting it on her shoulder. When his touch didn't earn him a smack, he brought the other one up to her other shoulder.

"Why are you still in the elevator? Didn't a nurse tell you which room he's in?"

"I did not ask." Her voice was so quiet he had to lean in to hear her.

"What do you mean?"

"I could not…"

Her pale face seemed so vulnerable. Gabriel touched her temple with his fingertips. "That's why I'm here. Let me help you."

For the first time since he met her, Ava gave in. She leaned into him, burying her face against his shoulder. When the elevator stopped and the mechanical voice stated what floor they were on, Gabriel held her. When the door opened, he raised his head and looked at the middle-aged man waiting to step in. The man looked at him, looked at Ava, and gave Gabriel a kind smile.

"I'll take the next one."

The elevator doors closed.

Ava held on.

• • • • •

Even after the food was put away and the dishes were in the dishwasher, Isabel couldn't stop shaking. She had sent the others home after two hours of waiting to hear from Gabriel, promising an update as soon as she received one. The large house was too silent after they left but there was no need for them to be there. If Isabel was to be honest with herself, she didn't want an audience. Her emotions weren't under control lately and if she was going to cry, she wanted to be alone.

She didn't cry.

Her entire body was shaking, but she didn't cry. The dogs followed her everywhere, whining softly, touching their noses to her hand or her leg when she stopped pacing.

To keep herself busy after she dealt with the food and dishes, she decided to tidy up Gabriel's house. It would waste some time, even though he paid to have someone come in and it wasn't dirty. She needed to keep herself busy between now and when Griffin finished working.

When Gabriel called later to say they would still be a while at the hospital, but David was okay, Isabel felt a wash of relief. He told her he didn't need anything; she could leave the dogs and go home if she wanted. Since she was sure they had enough to deal with already, Isabel left a note on his counter and took the dogs back to her parent's house before driving back home. Ava had nightmares every night under normal circumstances. What the hell was going to happen now that she was extremely stressed out? The dogs didn't need to be there for that.

She had tried unsuccessfully to play the guitar. Usually that worked as therapy for her, but her hands were shaking so bad she couldn't keep her fingers from slipping off the strings. Simple chord progressions of songs she had played for years were stumping her. She gave up after twenty minutes.

Now she sat on the sofa with her legs curled under her and a glass of whiskey in her hand. That she was still shaking slightly unnerved her. Strong people didn't shake. If she downed two or three whiskeys, she would probably stop. But she didn't want to stop that way.

Chris Hemsworth bellowed about being Thor from her phone. Isabel jumped. Leaning over to the coffee table, she set her whiskey down and glanced at up her phone. Relief flooded through her when she read Griffin's message.

Getting to his apartment took twenty minutes. She was already starting to feel better, knowing she was going to see him. But she was still shaking, even worse than before.

Just before she raised her hand to knock, Griffin opened the door, startling her.

"Holy balls," she breathed.

He was dressed in crisp white shirt and black slacks. Iz felt a stab of lust so strong she had to stop herself from jumping into his arms and attacking his mouth.

"You look really good," she said.

Griffin reached out, took her wrist, and pulled her close, breathing her in. "It's good to see you. You're gorgeous." He toed the door shut and just held her.

Pulling back, he studied her. "What's wrong?"

"Why do you ask?" she asked, glancing at his mouth so she didn't have to look at his eyes.

"You're shaking. And you won't look at me."

"I'm looking right at you."

"You're looking at my mouth. You avoid my eyes when something's wrong."

A flash of irritation sliced through her, purely out of habit. It cooled almost instantly. How quickly he had picked up on her body language.

"Something happened at the cookout, and it shook me up a little."

"A little?" He set his hands on her shoulders. "Isabel, you're almost convulsing. What's going on?"

She sighed. "I need a glass of wine to tell you. Can I have a kiss first?"

Framing her face in his hands, he bent his head and brushed his lips against hers. The trembling melted away as she let the kiss consume her. For a few moments she was able to let everything go. She felt only his mouth and his hands, the stability of both as they held her. She could have kissed him for hours. Her hands lightly rested on his chest.

When he pulled back at last, she sighed.

"Red or white?" he asked, running his thumb along her lower lip. He gazed into her eyes.

"Whatever you're having." She was sure she looked like a star struck teenager at a rock concert. She watched him walk to the kitchen to pour the wine. "You have a lot of wine."

"I like it," he said. "There's a flavor for every mood."

Observing him choose a wine was almost as calming as the kiss. This was where they had begun; her watching him, admiring him from afar, while they talked about silly things no one else cared about. The last few days, it seemed they'd done nothing but snipe at each other – or, more accurately, she sniped at him – and they had lost that effortless way of being together that she loved. Now everything had shifted back to the way it was supposed to be. Right. The darkness was lifting.

Isabel sat in one of the island stools and enjoyed watching his butt as he bent to reach the small refrigerator. Those pants hugged him in all the right ways.

When he turned around, she had a half smile on her face.

"Were you checking out my ass?" he grinned. He began pouring the wine.

"Yes, yes, I was," she said, lifting her chin. "I won't apologize."

He picked up both glasses and walked to her, giving her another kiss. "Animal. Let's sit on the balcony."

The sun was starting to set. Soft sunlight bathed the balcony in pale yellow. The air was starting to chill, and the sky was sliding into an abstract painting of orange and pink. It was the perfect time of day to sit outside and have a glass of wine. Isabel was going to sit in her own chair but Griffin, after setting the drinks on the table, pulled her down into his lap.

"Oh!" she said. "Okay."

"So," Griffin said, toying with a piece of her hair. "What happened?"

Iz gazed at him. "I'm okay, you know."

"Glad to hear it."

"No, I mean, everyone is fine. We should be focusing on you. You were upset last night."

"What does that have to do with anything?"

"I'm not trying to deflect; I just think what happened last night is more important than my stupid overreaction. Are you okay? Did work go okay?"

"Work was fine. We've almost finished the project we've been working on, so things should slow down a little."

"What about you?"

"I'm better."

His eyes didn't have that lost look anymore, she noticed, and was grateful. She hated seeing him that way, knowing he was in pain and not being able to do anything about it.

"So... do you believe Ava?"

"That she's a medium?" He shifted to get more comfortable, wrapped his arms around her more securely. "She said things that were between Connor and me. I felt... I felt like he was there while she talked about him. Yes, I'm inclined to believe her."

Isabel relaxed against him. "Good. Because if you didn't, telling you about the cookout at Gabe's would be really awkward."

She recounted the meal and Ava's sudden outburst. When she was done, she leaned forward and took too big of a drink of her wine.

"Last night you told me not to touch her."

She nodded.

"Sounds like you've got a grip on what to do for her when she... does her thing."

"I should have known better. When I spent the night, she was sleep walking, and Gabriel told me then not to touch her. So, I should have remembered. But she was in so much pain this time, and I hate seeing people in pain. I tried to hug her, like an idiot and she..."

Isabel shuddered. Her elbow still hurt from Ava's arm lock, and she could still see that clawed hand coming at her so fast, yet as if in slow motion. Had Gabriel not said Ava's name...

"What?" Griffin asked gently. He rubbed his hand on her back. "What happened?"

"She knows a lot of different fighting styles, like karate and... I think she mentioned Kung Fu. She did this thing where she held my arm out-" she straightened her arm, unable to do so fully without it aching, "and she almost... she damn near hit me. If Gabriel hadn't said her name, I think she would have broken my nose or my jaw. It was like she didn't even know it was me at the other end of her hand."

She was shivering again at the memory. Ava's eyes had been like the headlights of a car: cold, uncaring, unseeing. She had been a machine performing a task it was designed to do. She didn't see her friend in front of her.

Griffin pondered it for a few seconds.

"I didn't mean to make her feel she was being attacked. I just hate seeing people in pain. And I know she doesn't like to be touched. I know she was abused as a child. I just reacted, even after Gabriel warned me twice. It was such a stupid thing to do."

"You have the biggest heart of anyone I know," Griffin said, kissing her temple. "If she's worthy of your friendship, she knows that, too. It sounds like she was overreacting because of the state she was in. It seemed to kick her defensive mode into overdrive. It wasn't personal. I know that never helps."

"It does help. I know it, up here." She touched her temple. "You should have seen her eyes, Griffin. There was nothing there. The person I know, as weird as she is... it was like that person wasn't in there anymore."

"Did you talk to her about it when they came back?"

"I left before they came home. I figured they needed time alone so she could deal with everything. Apparently, her foster dad had a heart attack. He's fine, but of course she's shaken up. Gabe texted to let me know they're fine and we'll talk about it later." She laughed. "He apologized. As if it was his fault any more than hers."

Just talking about it again exhausted her. She found herself tensing as she relayed the events. She leaned against his chest and let the dusk envelope her. Griffin ran his hand up and down her back, soothing her.

"Before we all knew each other, Gabriel and I saw her at this restaurant. This whiny woman was giving Ava shit. I think she might have been in Gabe's class. Anyway, she tried to shove Ava and Ava put her in her place. The woman's boyfriend wanted to show how macho he was, so he thought he'd shove Ava around. He was a lot bigger and heavier than her, and she incapacitated him with one punch. It was unbelievable. That could have been me, earlier today."

"But she stopped."

"I don't think... I don't think she would have stopped if Gabriel hadn't said her name. I don't think she knew it was me."

"Was it like last night? When her voice deepened? You said something protects her-"

"I think that's what's bothering me," Iz said. A violent shudder ran through her. "Whatever that is, it wasn't there today. This was all Ava."

She took a drink of her wine. "She's told me so little about her childhood, but Gabe's given me some insight. When she first started training, Gabe said she was like an animal. Her teacher had to hold her down for the first couple weeks. I think I saw that part of her today. The part of her that distrusts, that sees everyone as she must have seen those assholes that abused her."

Griffin was silent. He had no advice to give. Sometimes people just needed to talk.

"I'm glad you're physically unharmed," he said, kissing the top of her head. "How are you doing otherwise? Any better than when you first got here?"

"How was work?" she asked, raising her head. "God, I was so wrapped up in my own problems. I'm sorry."

"Hush," he said, brushing his lips against hers. "Relax." He pressed her head back against his chest. "No work talk."

"Are you sure?"

"Tell me more about the cookout."

"I didn't use anything I've learned from kickboxing," Iz said angrily. "I just stood there. She was going to hit me, and I didn't even raise my hands to protect myself like Jay always says. Well, the one free hand."

Griffin patted her shoulder. "You said she knows multiple styles. How long has she been practicing?"

"I don't know. I think Gabe said since she was seven or eight."

"You've been practicing kickboxing just over a month. You didn't stand a chance against her."

"Everything I've learned went out the window," she insisted. "What good is it to learn if I forget it when I need it?"

He laughed softly. "When you've been doing it long enough, it becomes habit. Your muscles will remember what to do and your body will naturally defend itself. That's according to Jay, by the way; it's not my opinion. Ava started out as awkward as you did."

"Thanks," she said dryly, but she smiled. "I think she was born fighting. You're right. I know you're right. Jay said not to compare myself to the guys in the gym, and I'm sure that goes for anyone outside the gym, too. Thanks for listening to me ramble."

"Anytime." He wrapped his arms around her tightly and rested his cheek against her hair. His warm skin against the cool air felt amazing, like a bonfire on a fall night. Isabel was starting to feel better. The trembling had finally ceased. The knot in her stomach was still there, but it was loosening. Feeling safe in his arms, she relaxed against his body.

●　　●　　●　　●　　●

He couldn't get the image out of his head.

Ava had stepped into the room where David was resting. He looked old and battered, his skin ashen, a shadow of the man Gabriel had met in March. Ava walked stiffly up to the bed. David stirred, his eyes fluttering open.

"I didn't want to worry you," he said softly.

"Papa," Ava sobbed, and leaned into David's faint embrace.

That had been a few hours ago, and now Gabriel sat on his front porch, nursing a beer, and waiting for the storm. Lightning drew jagged lines in the sky a few miles away. The wind was beginning to pick up. That feeling was in the air that always came before a storm; the stillness that hovered no matter how much the wind blew and the quiet that lingered no matter how much thunder growled.

He considered himself able to handle most things. Seeing Ava collapse was not one of them. Even now, it was taking all of his willpower to sit on the porch instead of walking to the bedroom to make sure she was still lying down.

David was going to be fine in a few days. With changes in his diet and new medication, he would reduce his risk for future heart trouble.

Apparently, Madison had better facilities than the area he lived in, so he had set up appointments for a doctor visit and specialist consultations. He had already arranged for his neighbor to take Buck for a few days because he planned to be Madison for the week while he took care of all the appointments he had lined up. It was just dumb luck that he had just checked into a hotel in Madison when the heart attack hit so someone was around to call an ambulance and he was close to a hospital.

That put Ava's mind at ease for why he had been in Madison and hadn't let her know. He told her he had planned to call her as soon as he settled into his room. He just hadn't gotten that far.

There had been a bit of trouble with a nurse at the end of visiting hours. At first, Ava refused to leave David's side. She clutched his hand and sat in the chair next to his bed like a loyal servant. Keeping her face expressionless after that initial sob, she gazed at him without speaking. He mostly slept.

When the nurse, (a middle-aged woman with a name tag that read KELLY) announced visiting hours were over and David needed his rest, Ava simply remained seated with her hand covering his.

"Come on, honey," the tall woman said with absolutely no sympathy in her voice. She lifted David's arm and slid the blood pressure cuff off his arm. "You can come back tomorrow. Visiting hours start at 8:00."

"You don't want to do that," Gabriel said mildly from beside the window, where he had been standing for the past several hours.

Nurse Kelly was rounding the bed, reaching out to put her hand on Ava's shoulder. She turned and looked at him.

"Visiting hours are from 8 AM to 9 PM. You two will have to come back tomorrow."

Gabriel watched Ava gently release David's hand but stay where she was, keeping her eyes on David. It was the only indication she'd heard what was going on around her.

"Ava, do you want to stay?" Gabriel asked.

Her nod was barely perceptible, but he caught it.

She was gathering herself for a confrontation, he knew; though she continued to watch David, her focus was on the nurse in her periphery, and she was very aware of the doorway. Her hands were flat on the hospital bed.

"Look, I don't make the rules, I just inform the families," Nurse Kelly said. "If you don't leave, I'll have to call security."

Those fools wouldn't stand a chance, Gabriel thought.

Keeping one hand on the bed near David's body, Ava stood and fixed her gaze on Nurse Kelly. The woman, roughly two hundred and twenty pounds, took a step back when she looked in Ava's eyes.

David spoke.

"It's okay," he whispered. He gently patted Ava's hand. "Ava, I'm okay. Don't hurt her."

She was still reluctant, but David convinced her they had to monitor him closely and she would be in their way. Ava said her goodbyes and turned to go around the bed. The nurse was standing at the end, watching, looking slightly baffled. As Ava walked around the bed, although there was plenty of room to go around her, she stopped in front of the nurse and stared at her until she backed swiftly out of the way.

They were at Gabriel's house now. It seemed they were waiting, although they would get no more information tonight.

He had to piss. Thankful to have an excuse to check on Ava, he went inside to take care of business and grab another beer. As he stood over the toilet, he hoped David would get a good night of sleep. Gabriel had a feeling his wouldn't be very peaceful.

After he was done, he walked upstairs to the bedroom.

Ava wasn't in bed.

"Shit."

He checked the spare bedroom, but she wasn't there, either. Walking back downstairs, Gabriel checked the restrooms and kitchen with no luck before he caught a shadow on the back patio. The light was on, and he could see Ava standing out there. He didn't expect to see her outside on the deck on such a chilly night. At least she was wearing clothes.

She was leaning on the edge of the deck, facing the expansive back yard into the darkness. She wasn't wearing shoes; one socked foot was draped over the ankle of the other. She didn't open her eyes when Gabriel stood beside her. Her head was tilted up as she smelled the rain coming.

"Can't sleep?" He rested his hand on her back.

Her shoulders rolled and her spine twisted in that way that let him know she didn't want to be touched. Instantly raising his hand, he took a step to the side to give her space.

Her head was still in a fog from seeing David so wounded. Throughout her life, he had always been her constant. Until his strength wavered, she had always expected it to be there.

Frustrated, Ava turned so she was leaning back against the railing of the deck, resting on her elbows. She wished words came more easily to her. He deserved a partner with better communication skills.

"I ruined dinner with your friends," she said. She gazed at him with an expression he couldn't read.

"I let them know what was going on as soon as I knew the details," he said, moving closer to her but being careful not to crowd her. "They understand. They told me to pass along their sympathies."

"I do not want their sympathy." The edge in her voice was coming and going, confusing him. He wasn't sure if she was pissed off, mourning, exhausted, or all three at once.

"What do you want, Ava?" he asked, unable to hide his irritation.

"I would like to try a drink of your beer."

Gabriel gaped at her.

"Why the hell would you want to do that?" he demanded.

"Why not?" she lifted her chin slightly. "I will be twenty-three next Friday. I am well past the legal drinking age."

"I wouldn't call two years well past, and that's not the point. You've made the choice not to drink."

Why was she arguing with every damn thing he said? He tried to remember she had just visited her father in the hospital. Of course her emotions were chaotic. He owed her patience, understanding.

"I will serve myself."

She leaned up from the railing and stalked past him. Gabriel followed her into the house.

"Next Friday's your birthday? Why didn't you tell me?"

"I just told you."

She walked around the island, heading toward the refrigerator.

"Ava, will you stop for a minute?"

Pivoting on her heel, she turned back to him. The transition was so smooth, he almost bumped into her. They stood in the middle of the kitchen as if they were waiting to spar.

"Does Isabel know?"

"Why would she?"

"Friends, boyfriends... mates know each other's birthdays. Isabel especially will want to get you something."

"Something?"

"A gift. She's big on gift giving. I want to get you something, too. I wish you had told me sooner. We should plan something."

"You already made nunchucks. That is a wonderful gift."

Her eyes softened when she mentioned them, and he could see they meant more to her than he initially realized.

Ava suddenly plucked the bottle of beer from his hand. Gabriel watched, shocked, as she tilted it up and began chugging it. He had a good three quarters left, and she was downing it like water.

"What the... Ava... that's not a good...Jesus!" He leaned forward to take the bottle away. Without looking at him, she caught his hand, twisting his wrist and sending a jolt of fire from his fingers to his elbow.

"Your ninja bullshit isn't fair." Despite the pain, he reached over with his other hand.

Ava finished the bottle and handed it to him. She kept his hand in hers but released the lock, so they were simply holding hands. If she were going to give alcohol a try, it would be safer with him around, at least.

"Christ." He held the bottle, looking from it to her.

"May I have another one, please?"

"I don't think that's a good idea. I don't want to be the one influencing you to make bad decisions."

"You do not influence me. I make my own decisions." She dropped his hand and turned back to the refrigerator. "I will get you another as well."

"Ava... You shouldn't just plow through a bunch of alcohol when you've never had any in your system. It's going to hit you hard."

"I will drink this one slower."

"Why do you suddenly want to drink beer?"

"Why not?"

Taking out two bottles, she held one out to him. Gabriel watched her cautiously. Her actions were making him nervous. She was not behaving like herself, but her eyes were clear, and her voice was her own. Nothing was in control of her at the moment.

He opened their bottles with a lighter he took off the top of the refrigerator and touched the neck of his to the neck of hers.

"Here's to new habits," he said, "May they not be too self-destructive."

"New habits," Ava said softly. Her gray eyes gazed at him with a slightly dazed sheen, but she still had an intense expression on her face. "Can we sit in the living room?"

"Sure."

He walked through the dining room, and when he reached the living room, he turned on only one lamp in the corner. It was after eleven and he was ready to chill out. Ava walked to the sofa and sat at one end, setting her bottle on the end table. She ran her hands through her hair. Her body felt fuzzy. Her eyes itched. And her shirt was too damn hot.

"How are you feeling?" Gabriel asked.

He sat on the couch, giving her space.

"I am tired of being in control."

That wasn't what she meant to say. She had meant to tell him she was hot and fuzzy and a little tired. Her thoughts seemed to be floating somewhere above her body.

"Is that why you want to drink? To lose control?"

Blinking slowly, she felt the flush creeping along her skin and imagined her cheeks were full of color. She picked up her bottle and drank more.

"I want... to be normal. I want to let go and not be responsible for one night."

"What's so great about normal?"

Leaning over to scratch her ankle, she glanced at him. "Conformity is all but a necessity in society."

When she shifted, she felt herself continue to lean, as if her head weighed more than her body. Gabriel reached out and grabbed her arm, making her vertical again.

That eyebrow shot up. "I believe the hops are starting to hit you."

Ava leaned toward him to touch his eyebrow and poked him in the forehead instead. The world around her seemed to be moving, as if she were on land and everything else was on the ocean. Her fingertip found his eyebrow the second time and she brushed along the length of it, her lips curving.

"Look at you, smiling," he said softly. He released her arm to skim his thumb over her lower lip. She blinked slowly. "You're going to be so sick tomorrow."

"What do you do when you are drinking?"

Smirking, he watched her tuck her legs up to her chest.

"The same thing I do when I'm not drinking. I only have a beer or two a night, Ava. Sometimes I don't have one at all. I don't use alcohol to hide or get shit faced. I like the flavor of it."

She sipped hers, thinking. "I like this one. It tastes like coffee and chocolate."

"That's because it's a coffee stout. It's from a local brewery. I felt like something different tonight after a hell of a day."

"I am holding you back."

The sudden mournful tone had him pausing with his bottle to his mouth. When he glanced over at her, she was staring at her bottle, her eyes clouded, that little crease between her eyebrows.

"Holding me back from what?" he asked. As far as he could see, his life was going along fine. Better than fine. He earned a decent income doing work he loved, he owned his own house, he was dating a beautiful woman, and lately he was coming to better terms with Hayden's death. What more could a guy ask for?

"Everything. A real life, a good life. You could be with someone who can better show you how she feels, what she thinks. Someone who does not wake you every morning screaming and fighting. I have injured you more than once. I cannot communicate with you. Sometimes I cringe when you touch me. Why would you want to stay with a person like that?"

Gabriel thought of the early morning disruptions, launching him from sleep into a whirlwind of confusion and sometimes combat, depending on the situation. The frustration he often felt when trying to talk with her. How easy it was to misread her intentions when she kept herself at a distance.

Interpreting her moods was difficult when she kept her body language to a minimum and her face devoid of expression. Though he tried not to take it personally, it hurt him deeply when she twisted away from him as if he had raked his hands over an open wound. Yes, being with her was difficult and definitely took a great deal of getting used to.

But those smokey gray eyes settling on his, listening intently to every word he spoke, made him feel he was the only living being in the world. When he held out his hand and she accepted it, he felt humbled and appreciative and proud all at once. She had chosen him. In spite of a disastrous childhood full of abuse and pain, she had chosen him. His were the arms she reached for in those rare moments when she was terrified and searched for comfort instead of fighting. It was uncommon, but it did happen. And he marveled when she curled into his embrace. It made him feel needed and, more importantly, trusted. Having Ava accept him into her life was like being invited to a private tribal ceremony; only the worthy were allowed.

Ava's gaze was all but burning into him. She had finished her beer but at the moment, looked completely sober.

"You communicate just fine, Ava," he said. "We just have to learn each other's language, like any couple. Every relationship has its problems; there's no getting around that. So, you have trouble sleeping. I have a problem holding grudges. Nobody's perfect. I have a pretty damn good life. My business is doing well. I spend a good portion of my time with the woman I love and there's never a dull moment. I happen to be more content now than I have been since my sister died."

She frowned, wondering how that was possible when his life would be so much easier without her.

"I would like another drink."

Standing shakily, she picked up her bottle to take to the kitchen. She was almost to the doorway when she realized what he had said. She turned back to him, her eyes narrowing.

"What did you say?"

"Which part?" he asked, but he couldn't keep his mouth from twitching.

She didn't find the humor. Her body had gone still, as it did when she waited for danger to pass. Dark gray was the color of her eyes now, the stormy gray that meant something was churning in and around her.

"I said I love you. Do you have a problem with that?"

She stood, not blinking, staring at him for several seconds. Her hand rested on the door casing to steady herself from the effects of drinking. Turning away from him without speaking, she disappeared around the corner.

Gabriel grinned, taking a pull on his beer. That had been interesting.

• • • • •

Griffin was on his side with his arm angled and his head resting on his hand. He watched Izzie, who was lying on her stomach, her head turned away from him. She had drawn her arms up and crossed them, using them to cushion her head. The pose showed just a hint of the side of her breast.

"Will Ava still help you, even though I was an asshole last night?" Griffin suddenly asked.

"What?" She turned her head toward him, her eyes soft.

"When she tried to talk to me about Connor. We were there to get help for you, and I buggered it up. Will Ava hold that against you?"

He ran his fingertips over the curve of her shoulder, causing her breath to back up into her throat.

"No." Iz trembled when he trailed his fingers down her back. "That's not her way."

"I'm sorry," he said, leaning over and kissing her shoulder. "I went there to support you. I made a mess of everything."

It was hard to concentrate on the conversation when he was moving his hands and mouth over her. He did it in an almost casual way, the way she would lazily pluck her guitar strings when she didn't really have a specific melody in mind, but her hands wanted to touch. Obviously, she was overreacting; she felt like she was melting beneath his touch, and he was merely keeping his hands busy, like tapping a pen on a desk or bouncing a knee.

"Connor needed you to hear him," she said, trying to focus on last night's visit with Ava. "And Ava needed to know why she kept reading you. It needed to happen."

After a beat, Griffin said, "This is weird to talk about so casually."

"It's kind of a mind fuck in the beginning." She grinned. "We talked about seeing my dead sister as if we were discussing going to a football game. I mean,

Ava takes this all very seriously, but she doesn't shy away from it once you know."

"My parents would think I was not the full quid if I ever tried to tell them any of this."

"God, no," Iz said, widening her eyes. "Anything but 'not the full quid'."

His smile was slow, his eyes full of amusement.

"Have you spoken to them since we had dinner?"

The smile faded. "Mum called when they returned to New York. It's good to have a few states between us."

"Things are still pretty bad between you?"

Running his fingers through her hair, he frowned absently. "They've never been especially good."

"I'm sorry. Do you want to come to Sunday dinner tomorrow with me? My parents aren't perfect, but at least they won't try to control your life."

"I would love to come."

He leaned forward, giving her a deep kiss that made her sigh. "Why don't you move in with me?"

Smiling, her eyes dreamy and her body completely relaxed, she sighed again.

"I'm beat. I think I'll have one last glass of-" She lifted her head and her eyes widened, then narrowed. "What?"

"Move in with me. You're here every night anyway. I love you."

Raising herself up off her stomach, she twisted toward him and sat on her butt, bringing her legs up to her chest. Panic leaped into her throat.

"Whoa. Where the fuck did that come from? We were talking about shitty parents and Sunday dinner."

"And I asked you to move in with me. It's logical, financially sound, but more importantly, I love you and I want you here. I want your scent here on the furniture and your guitar in the corner of the living room. I want you to snarl at me every morning when I wake you up."

"I don't snarl-"

"I want us to learn to cook together so you can swear at our food while you stand at the stove. I want to comfort you if you wake from a nightmare. I want you here, Izzie."

"Well, fuck."

Her arm crossed her chest in a move Griffin recognized as self-preservation. She leaned over the side of the bed to find her shirt.

"Fuck," she repeated in a muffled mutter as she pulled the shirt over her head.

"Why does it make you nervous?" he asked.

"It doesn't, I just-"

"You say 'fuck' a lot when you're nervous."

"Would you stop being so God damn... observant?!"

"You already have a little section of the closet for your clothes. You have a toothbrush, deodorant, and hairbrush here. You're practically living here already."

"But I don't." She pulled the shirt over her head. "I can go to my apartment any time I want."

"So, you have a safety net."

"No. Maybe. So? There's nothing wrong with planning ahead for possible... surprises."

Standing, she snatched her glass of wine off the bedside table and took a gulp. It went down hard. Her eyes watered. Her stomach was doing gymnastics, making her feel like she was going to throw up.

"Why does it scare you?" Griffin asked. "It won't change what we're already doing."

He wanted to touch her, but she needed space. He would give it to her. He wanted to tell her it was no big deal, but her hand was resting on her stomach, shaking, and she needed a moment to gather her thoughts.

"Then why do it? Why mess with what's working?" Setting down her glass, she ran both hands through her hair. "You always do this. I just get comfortable with how things are, and you change everything."

Slowly, thoughtfully, he nodded. "Okay. We'll keep things as they are."

She eyed him suspiciously. "Just like that?"

"If you're not ready, you're not ready."

Still feeling like there was a catch, Iz studied his eyes. They were warm, with no hint of deception. Just acceptance in the honey color she had come to love.

He held out his hand.

She shuffled toward the bed. Reaching out, she took his hand and climbed back in beside him, letting him pull her toward him until she was nestled firmly against his body. Warm and content, she sighed heavily. Griffin ran his hand over her hair. Her heart was slowing down against his chest.

Interlacing her fingers with his, he kissed the back of her hand. The light sensation caused a flutter in her stomach, as it always did.

"I need time to think," she finally said.

He'd started to drift off and the sound of her voice made him twitch.

"About what?" he murmured, kissing the top of her head.

"About moving in with you. I'm not promising anything."

•   •   •   •   •

If he were to be honest with himself, Gabriel didn't know when he realized he'd fallen in love with Ava, but he thought it may have been that first time he had cooked dinner for her. He had been drawn to her from the moment she stood next to him in the grocery store. But the night of the storm, when it was raining so hard and he'd convinced her to stay over in the guest room, she had him. Watching her attempts at being social were endearing. She was fascinating. Then she had punched a hole in his wall, and he had discovered so many things about her: she slept naked, she wandered around during the night and early morning, she had horrible dreams where she sometimes relived her childhood traumas, and she trusted him enough to share a bed with him and know he would not take advantage of the situation.

So many things made her easy to love: her dedication to pushing herself physically and mentally; her misunderstanding of people and their quirks of speech; her unending strength in spite of repeated abuse. But that night what had most drawn him to her was her ability to be both vulnerable and fierce at the same time. She had no control over what her body did while she slept, but it was her mind that held her hostage night after night.

A thud from the other room drew his attention. He stood, making his way toward the kitchen to see what Ava was up to. He found her sitting on the tile floor with two beer bottles sitting in front of her. She looked a little lost sitting there with her legs splayed and her feet turning inward until they were almost touching, like a child playing with blocks.

"Having fun?" Gabriel asked, gazing down at her.

She was plowed. She gazed up at him with bleary eyes and her hand bumped one of the bottles, knocking it over. It spun within the circle of her legs. In an attempt to reach for it, she bumped the other one and sent it toppling over her leg. It clattered onto the floor and rolled across the tile toward the refrigerator.

"Uh oh," she said softly.

"Uh oh," he repeated, grinning. He knelt beside her. "You've got a little party going on down here."

"I cannot feel my arms and legs."

He kissed her on the forehead. "You jumped in with both feet, didn't you?"

Closing her eyes, her head began to dip back. She jerked, blinking.

"I cannot think. I think I like that I cannot think."

"I imagine it's quite a relief for that busy brain of yours. You've endured more in your lifetime than ten women."

"I am afraid," she said mournfully.

Gabriel took her hand and kissed the back of it. "What are you afraid of?"'

Her skin was soft against his cheek. Despite the scent of beer, so unfamiliar coming from the pores of her skin, her base scent was still there, and it filled him with peace.

"He was so small. How did he get so small?"

He didn't need her to tell him she was talking about David lying in the hospital bed.

Pulling her to him, he held her close. "He'll be okay. The doctor said he'll be fine."

A thought occurred to him, and he pulled away from her. "Did you see something different?"

Frowning, she looked at him for several seconds before she realized he meant her psychic ability. She shook her head, which felt the size of Montana. He relaxed and hugged her again.

"Then don't worry. Come to bed, Ava. You're sloshed."

He pulled her to her feet, ignoring the beer bottles for the moment. He would clean up tomorrow.

"You cried when they stopped looking for Hayden," she suddenly said.

Going still, he lifted his head to see her gazing at him with glassy eyes that had dilated slightly. With a smooth move that was opposite the tension he felt inside, he slid his left arm around her back and took her hand with his right.

"Let's go upstairs."

She stumbled. Gabriel instantly tightened his arm around her to keep her from falling.

"Easy," he said, his mouth close to her ear. He helped her gain her footing. The light scent of fresh grass drifted from her. Gabriel inhaled deeply, surrounded himself with her.

"You locked yourself in your room and cried for the first time since she went missing."

The words were like pulsing spikes in his chest.

Placing her arm around his shoulders, he held her close so she wouldn't fall.

"Young Gabriel, lost in his own head," Ava said softly as they moved slowly toward the stairs. Just the smooth texture of her body sent lascivious thoughts through his head. "No one to take his hand and pull him out."

"I turned out okay."

"Why does she refuse to speak to me?"

"I don't know, Ava."

"I am not a very good medium."

He smirked. "You've been fighting it your entire life. You're only now starting to embrace it."

"That is what Sensei says."

Halfway up the stairs, the toe of her boot hit the next step and she tripped, plunging forward. Gabriel tightened his grip and hauled her back up to a standing position. All her natural grace was gone. Her feet moved slowly and dragged across the floor as they made their way to the bedroom. Against his, he could feel the tremors in her body, as if she had some muscular disease.

"You failed your own sister."

Gabriel paused two feet from the doorway. The deep voice, different than Ava's yet somehow echoing her own, was becoming familiar now. The hairs on the back of his neck instantly stood on end.

"You don't deserve her message."

Fury leaped into him. He forced it down, reminding himself Ava wasn't judging him. The thing inside her had control right now.

Slowly, he turned and looked into her eyes.

A void glared back. Blackness filled the spaces that had been Ava's eyes.

"Stop it," Gabriel said, giving her a rough shake. Her head snapped back. The thing inside her smiled slowly.

"You've got it bad for this one," it said, sneering. "It's the sex, isn't it? We've always been good at it. It's all anyone wants from this body."

"Ava," Gabriel said softly, holding her cheek in his palm, "Come back to me."

Although it snarled, he kissed her, putting everything he had into it. With his arm still around her back, he pulled her close against him and tenderly moved his mouth over hers. Her body reacted even as The Monster snarled, and the snarl faded into a soft moan.

When he lifted his head, he saw her eyes were gray. Out of focus and dazed, but gray.

"There you are," he whispered.

"Here I am."

He helped her into the bedroom, where she sat heavily on the bed. Kneeling in front of her, he pulled off her socks. The tremors hadn't stopped; her body was in constant motion as he unbuttoned her jeans and took her hands to help her stand. She watched him pull them slowly down her legs, rest his hand on each leg as she lifted it out of the hole in the fabric, and pull the jeans away. Sitting back down, she continued to watch him as he pulled her shirt over her head.

"You heard them talking but you did not get up," she whispered.

Smelling alcohol on her breath was so foreign. The feeling of surrealism filled him.

He nudged her bra straps off her shoulders.

"You woke up to Hayden and Isabel talking, but you fell back asleep quickly."

Leaning close to her, he reached around to unhook the clasps of her bra. His face was an inch from hers. Her pupils were huge, pulsing orbs.

"You blame yourself for her death," she whispered.

Bringing the bra with him, Gabriel leaned back. He tossed it into the pile with the rest of her clothes. "Sleep now, Ava."

Lifting a quaking hand, she touched her palm to the side of his face. "You think if you had just stayed awake, if you had walked with her, she would not have been taken."

Sharp pain, as fresh as the day it happened, sliced through his chest. He winced. Ava closed her eyes and put her hand to her heart, tears wetting her lashes. Her breath caught.

"Let it be for now."

Gently pushing her back onto the bed, he drew her legs up and tucked her in. The shaking had increased, even as he pulled the blankets up around her chest. Tears were streaming down her temples. Her breath was hitching. He rested his hand against her hair, wishing there was something he could do to calm her down.

Abruptly, her eyes opened. She looked at him solemnly.

"I will help you," she said. She reached out and found his hand with hers. "I will help you find her, if I can."

·   ·   ·   ·   ·

Isabel was curled up on Rover's front passenger seat when Griffin pulled into her parent's driveway for Sunday dinner. She was resting her weight on her elbow, which was propped on the center console, and her legs were tucked up like a doe's. Griffin loved when she did this; it allowed him to rest his arm on the console, so their skin was always brushing together.

"Gabe's already here," she said softly, stretching her legs and sitting up.

"That's Ava's Equinox, yeah?" he asked, parking behind the blue SUV. He left plenty of room in case they wanted to leave before he and Izzie were ready to go.

"Yeah."

She arched her back, placing her palms on the roof of Rover and stretching.

"I don't know why I'm so tired," she said. "Yesterday seemed to go on forever."

He leaned over and gave her breast a squeeze.

Dropping her arms, she gave him a look. "They're not bike horns, you know. They won't honk when you touch them."

Grinning, Griffin leaned over and kissed her, lingering. This time the hand he placed on her breast caressed and enticed, sending a shiver through her. She raised her hand and ran it through his hair.

Maya barked from in front of the garage doors. Iz groaned, remembering where she was. Griffin let the kiss go on another few seconds before he pulled back.

"We should have started that earlier this morning," he murmured. He tugged on a lock of her hair. "Now we have to wait until tonight."

She knew her smile was dopey, but she couldn't help it. She loved him, and it came so easily that she didn't even wonder about it.

Inside, he had barely shut the door behind him before she dragged him across the hall into the laundry room. Shoving her elbow against the door so it swung around, she ravaged his mouth. His hands snaked down to grip her backside, squeezing possessively before he lifted her and set her on top of the dryer.

"I want you all the time," she panted, slipping her hands under his shirt to feel skin. His response was a soft groan. Her mouth returned to his, greedy and impatient. Her hands busily gripped, caressed, clawed, running over his back and sides at a feverish pace.

Nipping her ear lobe, he kissed her behind the ear, sending a shiver through her. His hands were thrust into her hair, urgent yet so gentle, and the rapid breath coming from him was driving her insane.

"Damn, I thought I closed the d-"

The laundry room door swung open, and light filled the room. Griffin froze but stayed pressed against her in case Isabel was exposed in any way. They blinked in surprise.

"Whoa. Sorry, guys." Jack grinned. "I'll come back later."

Iz snorted, her face scarlet.

"No, we're sorry," she said, resting her forehead against Griffin's chest while she tried to catch her breath. He smoothed her shirt.

"Good to see you again, mate," he said, reaching over her head to shake Jack's hand.

"You, too. How's it going?"

Griffin smiled. "Can't complain. Are we in your way?"

"Not yet." Jack stepped around them to the washer. He opened the lid and pulled out a Green Bay Packers hoodie that he held up by the shoulders. A large, dark stain was evident on the chest.

"Damn." He shook his head.

"How did that happen?" Iz asked. She slid off the dryer, moving with Griffin out of Jack's way.

Transferring the ruined shirt to the dryer, Jack pushed buttons and sighed. The dryer rumbled to life.

"Beth spilled coffee on me. I think she did it on purpose so she can steal it."

"Common plot with women," Griffin agreed.

"Hey!" Iz said, punching his arm.

"Have you cooled off enough for a hug?" Jack stepped toward her with his arms out.

The flush returned to her face, but she embraced him.

"We better head to the kitchen or they'll start to wonder if I fell into the washer."

As they moved through the long hall toward the kitchen, Isabel wondered if things would be awkward with Ava. They hadn't exactly ended things on a positive note Friday night.

Griffin rested his hand on the small of her back as they walked. A feeling of calm came over her, starting where he touched and spreading to her hands and feet. Did he have any idea how much she depended on his touch to feel stronger?

In the kitchen, Allie was preparing food. Beth stood near her and was talking quietly. Josh and Gabriel were at the island, quietly discussing something Gabriel was building for his mom. Jack walked to Beth and kissed her on the forehead before sitting at the island table.

She saw Isabel and Griffin and smiled. Looking tired, she came over to give them hugs.

"Hey, sis," she said, her embrace without any strength. "Hi, Griffin. It's good you're here again."

"Glad to be here." He returned the hug, noting the dark patches under her eyes, how he could feel her spine under his fingers.

"Where's Ava?" Iz asked, looking toward the living room.

"Patio," Gabriel said around a slice of Colby cheese. "Don't try to hug her. She feels like shit."

Iz glanced at Griffin. "Is she okay?"

Gabriel grinned. "Yeah, she's just a little hung over. She tied on a good one last night."

"Ava got drunk?" Isabel must have misheard him. "Our Ava had alcohol?"

"It was outstanding."

He pulled her to him and gave her a hug. "She'll be okay, but she doesn't want to be touched. I mean, more than usual."

"Got it."

Iz hugged her father, feeling his kiss on the top of her head and smiling. "Hey, Dad."

"Hey, sweetheart. Glad you're here. Good to see you again, Griffin."

He shook hands while keeping his arm around his daughter. Unsure why he continued to hug her, she squeezed tight, glancing over at Beth. Her sister still looked tired, but something was different about her. Isabel couldn't place what it was.

When her father finally let go, she stared at him.

"What was that for?" she asked.

"You looked like you needed it." He gave her a smile and patted her shoulder.

Isabel moved around the island table to give her mother a hug. She turned back to see what Griffin wanted to drink or if anyone needed a refill. He was no longer in the kitchen.

"What happened to Griffin?"

"He was heading toward the foyer," Josh said. "I think he's going to check on Ava."

"Oh, shit."

Gabriel's attention instantly focused on her. "What's that supposed to mean?"

Snatching two bottles of water from the refrigerator, Iz hurried toward the foyer. "I'll tell you later."

From the foyer, she could see the patio. Ava was standing near the railing with Griffin a couple feet away. She was frowning, and her eyes were half closed; she was probably feeling the effects of the hangover, not glaring at Griffin. The way her shoulders sagged indicated how lethargic she was feeling.

Isabel opened the door and stepped onto the patio. She saw Ava's eyes shift ever so slightly and knew Ava had known where she was the moment she entered the foyer.

"Anyway, I hope you'll forgive my behavior Friday night," Griffin was saying. "It was inexcusable. You were trying to help, and I treated you like garbage."

The frown deepened. "You apologized to me on Friday night."

"I know."

Ava stared at him for a moment, then nodded.

Next to Griffin, Isabel relaxed.

"I appreciate what you told me about my brother. I'm not sure what to do with the information yet, but thank you."

Ava nodded again. Turned her attention to Isabel.

"Hi," Iz said, suddenly feeling shy. "I brought you a bottle of water. Gabe said you're not feeling well."

She held one out by the neck of the bottle so there was no way they would accidentally touch. Ava took it.

"Thank you." She took a drink, eyeing Isabel, and lowered the bottle. "I am sorry I injured your arm yesterday."

"I shouldn't have touched you," Isabel said immediately. "Gabe kept telling me not to."

"You cannot ignore your instinct to help any more than I can ignore my instinct to defend myself."

A comfortable silence settled over them as Ava drank half of the bottle down. Isabel no longer had the feeling that Ava didn't like Griffin. Sure, she'd said she didn't have a problem with him, but Iz thought she was just being polite or that it was a subconscious dislike she hadn't been aware of. Now she knew she had misread Ava's body language. She'd been reading Griffin every time she came into contact with him; now that she knew the circumstances surrounding the readings, she no longer worried he was suicidal.

Which meant Isabel could relax. She didn't have to constantly worry about Ava and Griffin getting along. Ava didn't do anything without a reason. Isabel should have trusted her to begin with.

Ozzie and Maya trotted across the yard and onto the patio. Ozzie's tail wagged enthusiastically, battering Maya's face as she tried to move around him. He pushed against Isabel to get pets. She happily indulged him, then moved onto Maya as Griffin gave Ozzie a companionable pat.

The door to the foyer opened and Gabriel stepped out. "Mom wants a picture." He rolled his eyes.

Isabel groaned. "Hell, no."

Griffin grinned, tugging her toward the door. "Come on, now Izzie, give us a smile."

"That's not going to happen."

She was still grumbling when she slammed the door behind them. Ava winced and closed her eyes. When Gabriel walked over to her, she opened her eyes warily. Not in defense, he noticed, and for that, he was grateful.

"Are you feeling any better?"

He kept his voice low and soft, making her want to curl into him. Alcohol is a depressant; she knew this, and yet her feelings of despair unnerved her still. She felt needy and clingy, though she had kept her distance from everyone today.

Pressing her fingers to her forehead, she shook her head slowly. Then she surprised him by closing the distance between them and standing against him with her head on his shoulder. Hesitantly, he raised his hand and rested it on the back of her neck. When she didn't stiffen, he brought his other hand to her hip.

"The house is restless today," she said absently.

He was unsure what to say to that. In addition to her hangover, he knew she was worried about David. She'd shut down as soon as they left his room at the hospital this morning, her already bleary eyes looking even more haunted than before. David was looking better, so Gabriel wasn't sure why seeing him bothered Ava so much. She insisted she hadn't had any visions of his health getting worse when Gabriel asked. Yet she was quieter than usual, and so pale.

"Mom's waiting," he said.

Ava raised her head. She looked ready to burst into tears. Taking his hand, she allowed him to lead her into the house.

Allie was gathering everyone in the living room in front of the fireplace, where the natural light was best for pictures. She dictated where people needed to stand, arranging her daughters and Jack around her husband, then changing her mind half a dozen times. Griffin watched, amused, as Isabel grumbled through the entire process. Everyone was talking at once.

"Gabriel, it's about time. Get in there," Allie said, pushing him forward. "Griffin, why aren't you standing next to Isabel? You, too, Ava, get in there."

"I thought it was family only," Griffin said, stepping forward. Isabel yanked him toward her.

"If I have to suffer through this bullshit, you do, too."

"Good Lord, you're tall," Allie said. "You'll have to stand behind Isabel, with your arms around – yes! That's perfect! Okay, now I'll move everyone else around you."

Gabriel elbowed Iz and grinned when she elbowed him back. Ava was standing off to the side of Allie, watching without interest as she petted Ozzie. Allie noticed she wasn't in the shot and looked around.

"Ava, what are you doing? Come on, stand over by Gabriel."

Ava did not move. The hand on Ozzie's back stiffened. "I do not like having my picture taken."

Some of the noise died down. Isabel and Gabriel glanced over at Ava.

Allie was fidgeting with her cell phone, trying to get the camera settings exactly right. "Please?" she asked. "Just a few. It's a family tradition."

The look on Ava's face didn't change. "It is not my tradition. I am not your family."

Whoa. Gabriel moved toward her. "Ava?"

The tone of her voice had been angry, cruel. She wasn't purposely callous to people by nature.

When her eyes drifted slowly to rest on him, wandering across the room first as if she was unsure how to use her muscles, she looked at him blandly. There was nothing behind her eyes, as if Ava had stepped outside herself for a moment. But no one else had stepped in to take over.

"Everything okay?"

Blinking slowly, she suddenly looked surprised. She leveled her gaze at Allie.

"I am sorry." She frowned. "I am not feeling well. That is no excuse."

Gabriel held his hand out to her. "Will you come stand by me?"

How was it that no matter what she was thinking or feeling, he could summon her just by reaching for her? She put her hand in his. It seemed to radiate heat, engulfing her hand, making her stomach feel weightless. He drew her to him and tucked a strand of hair behind her ear.

"Is it a headache, Ava? Do you want some aspirin or something?" Allie asked.

"I do not take pills."

Ava turned so she was facing the camera, her shoulder pressed against Gabriel's. Closing her eyes, she leaned her head to the side, so it was resting on his shoulder. He felt her begin her breathing exercises, inhaling and exhaling in long, deliberate breaths. His mother needed to hurry things along; Ava's body was beginning to vibrate with energy.

"What if you have a headache?" Beth asked. She stood on the other side of Isabel, with Jack behind her. She watched her mother and turned, in small degrees, as Allie directed with hand movements.

Without opening her eyes, Ava said, "Then my head aches."

"Don't you believe in modern medicine?" Jack asked, watching Allie's hand movements so he was standing in exactly the right spot. He shifted left, a little more, then right.

"How long is this going to take?" Ava asked, opening her eyes, and lifting her head.

"Mom can be a bit of a perfectionist when it comes to family photos," Gabriel murmured in her ear. "It might take a few minutes."

"I cannot stay in here. It is too busy." She kept her voice low, but he heard the underlying edge in it.

Breaking away from the group, Ava strode across the room and into the foyer. Ozzie followed her, happy to be able to go outside again.

"But we almost have everyone ready," Allie said.

The door to the patio closed hard enough to rattle the windows. Beth and Allie jumped.

"Give us a minute." Gabriel followed Ava. "Get everyone else ready and I'll see if I can get her back in here."

Ozzie was standing at the door, so Gabriel let him inside. Ava was kneeling near the rock wall at the far end of the stone patio that had been built as an extension off the main one. Gabriel walked down the wooden steps, across a brick sidewalk, and down stone steps to reach the more natural courtyard.

"Hey," he said when he was still three feet from her, "What's going on with you?"

"I do not like having my picture taken." Her tone was sharp, and he could hear she was still trying to settle her breathing. "I told her that."

"It's more than that."

Circling around her so she could see him, he knelt, keeping his distance. She had one hand in the mulch bedding and one hovering just above the hosta it was covering.

"This isn't just about a hangover, is it?"

As she turned her head toward him, he saw tears on her cheeks. "Why am I so sad?"

"Alcohol tends to make people emotional," he said, edging closer. "What are you thinking?"

"I just need air. Everyone is so... busy..."

She waved her hands at her temples, as he had seen her do before when there were too many people around her or too many people were talking.

Gabriel thought he understood now what she meant.

"Do you mean loud?" he asked. "Are you hearing everyone's thoughts?"

"It is more like... hearing their emotions. It creates noise in my head. It hurts my ears."

"You don't do very well in crowds, do you?"

"No."

This she said adamantly, and he almost laughed. No wonder. It was like standing in the middle of a mosh pit with everyone pushing from all sides, the yelling and cheering so loud that talking wasn't an option. Damn.

"Is it there all the time, or just sometimes?"

"Sometimes."

She moved her hand over the plant slowly, closing her eyes and breathing. Gabriel gave her several moments of silence. At last, she pulled her hands back and stood.

"What were you doing?"

Brushing her hands together, she gazed at the ground. "Nature calms me. I am ready now."

Back inside, Allie had finally gotten everyone as she wanted them.

"Okay, Ma," Gabriel said, "I hope you know exactly where you want us and make this quick."

"Over there next to Isabel and Griffin. No, a little closer. Ava, standing in front of Gabriel."

His stomach clenched. "She doesn't like anyone-"

To his surprise, she moved two steps over and stood in front of him, clasping his hands and pulling them around her stomach like a seat belt. This was the only time she had trusted him enough to allow him behind her, except when they were in bed. It made his pulse quicken.

"Okay," Allie said, "Josh, move two inches to your right. Your right. Good. Smile everyone."

A blinding flash pierced Ava's eyes and sent agony straight through her temples. She recoiled with a snarl. The back of her head connected with Gabriel's chin as hard as if she would have popped him with her fist.

"Ow, fuck!" he snapped.

"Language!" Allie snapped, then started trying to figure out how to shut the flash off on her phone.

Ava took a step forward, another snarl erupting from her.

"Ava, easy." Gabriel took her by the upper arms without thinking. By the time he realized what he'd done, he expected a strike, and was surprised when she turned without raising her hands. Her eyes were stormy, but the anger wasn't aimed at him.

"Bear with us a little longer," he pleaded, running his thumb down her cheek.

Her eyes shifted. "Your chin is bleeding. I have injured you again."

"'Just a flesh wound,'" he said in an English accent, touching his fingertips to the skin. They came away with very little blood.

Jack laughed.

"That reference is lost on you," Gabriel said, wiping the blood on his pants. "Even if you weren't socially stunted, you wouldn't watch Monty Python. You're female."

"Hey, asshole!" Isabel said, punching his shoulder. "I love those movies!"

"Language!" Allie yelled, but then she figured out her phone and her voice changed instantly. "I got it!"

With a grin, she raised it. "Okay, let's try that again. Smile! I said smile, Ava."

"She doesn't do that."

"Damn it," Allie said as her phone clicked. "Gabriel, I got your lips moving. Hold still everyone."

Another click.

"Isabel, quit snickering at your brother."

Click.

"Jack, come on, be serious."

Click.

"Flipping the bird, Gabriel? Isabel? Are you two still in high school?" She tried to sound stern, but she was smiling.

Click.

Finally, Allie seemed satisfied. "Hold still, I want to make sure I have a good one."

She studied the pictures, frowning, swiping her finger to look at them all.

"Hmm. Smile again everyone."

Isabel and Gabriel rolled their eyes.

"Behave, you two."

Allie took three more pictures rapidly, hoping to get a good one. She looked through them, frowning again.

"Josh, I need to get a new phone. The camera's not working on this one."

He stepped away from the group and came toward her. "What is it doing?"

"Well, everyone looks great except Ava. Her face is blurred. I don't know if this corner of the screen is going out or..."

They played around with it for several seconds. Josh made several 'hmm' and 'huh' noises as he looked through the pictures, checked the settings.

"It's like that in every photo. Only Ava's face is affected."

He held the camera up and zoomed in on her face. She glared at him.

Giving her a warm smile, Josh's demeanor made Ava lessened her glower. He reminded her of David.

"Alright, hon, let's see what's going on here."

He took a picture and studied it. Moved to the right and took another one from a different angle. Took a couple of the group without Ava in them. Frowning, he took a couple with only Gabriel and Ava. Frowning, Josh studied the photos, his fingertips hovering just above the semi-transparent face he saw where Ava's should have been.

"God! Are we done, yet?" Iz complained.

"What's wrong, Dad?" Gabriel asked.

"It can't be," Josh said softly. Beside him, Allie's face had gone pale.

"Dad?" Isabel walked over to them, craning her neck to see a close up of Ava. "Whoa."

The others gathered around the camera, all but Ava, who hung back. She needed to lie down before this headache split her skull wide open and her legs gave up on her.

"Oh, my God," Beth whispered. She covered her mouth with her hand.

Ozzie whined again, tilting his head at the sudden change of attitude in the room.

"Holy shit," Jack said. "Are you guys seeing what I'm seeing?"

"Yeah," Gabriel said. His stomach was tightening, trying to twist itself into a large, painful knot.

Where Ava's face should have been, Hayden's image smiled back at the camera.

• • • • •

"Is it like that with every photo?" Beth asked.

The room was oddly quiet for a Sunday gathering. Gabriel had taken Ava upstairs to lie down in a guest bedroom. Everyone else was sitting at the table, trying to make sense of what they had seen.

Josh nodded. "The images on the phone can't be double exposed like they can with film," he said thoughtfully. "This doesn't make sense."

Isabel didn't have much to say on it, Griffin noticed.

"Has this happened before?" he asked, looking around the table.

"I haven't taken a family picture in quite a while." Allie's hand shook a little when she held her coffee. "This is the first time I've taken any pictures of Ava."

"This must be so hard for you." Griffin's voice was gentle as he watched her struggle. "Having Ava around as a constant reminder of your daughter. Does she channel Hayden often?"

Allie blinked. "What?"

"What are you talking about?" Josh asked.

Isabel opened her mouth, but it was too late.

"You must be frustrated each time Ava communicates with Hayden. I only just found out about her connection to my brother recently. It's difficult to learn things about him four years after he died."

"Griffin-" Isabel started.

"What are you talking about?" Allie echoed, taking her husband's hand. Mistaking her ignorance for grief, Griffin didn't catch her baffled expression.

"I imagine knowing your daughter's spirit is so near, but you can't-"

"Griffin, shut up," Isabel growled.

From the floor near the fireplace, Maya let out a short howl.

"What?" Griffin finally looked at her. Isabel's eyes were huge, her mouth open in shock. He was startled to see she had actually stopped breathing. "They don't know," he said softly.

The shake of her head was barely visible.

Griffin paled and swore softly under his breath. "I apologize. I, ah, was talking out my ass. Forget I said anything."

"Isabel, what's going on?" Josh asked. "What does Ava have to do with Hayden?"

How the hell was she supposed to respond to that? Where was Gabriel? He would know what to do, he had to know. She was frozen in her chair, her entire body rigid. She felt cold deep into her bones.

"I don't know how to answer that." The tremor in her voice scared her. Everything seemed to be falling apart. She stared at her bottle of water. Under the table, she dug her thumb nail into her forearm.

"How about the truth?"

Damn it.

"Ava's a medium," she said, her voice sounding like it was coming from far away. The pain in her arm was real, it was scientific, she could control how little or how much she experienced. It was simple. She dug in harder. "She s-sees Hayden sometimes."

When she swallowed, something in her throat clicked and made her feel like she was choking.

"That's ridiculous." Allie's hand twitched in Josh's. He gave it a gentle squeeze.

"Yes, it is," Iz said. "So, let's move on."

"Isabel," Josh said. His tone made her want to shrink into the floor. It was the voice he used that had, during her childhood, made her sorry she had ever committed whatever childhood crime had warranted punishment.

"What?" she said. "You don't believe me, so there's no point saying anything."

"I don't know what I believe. How long have you known about this?"

"A little while. I've seen her... do things."

"That is the dumbest thing I've ever heard," Beth had been silent up to now, and when she spoke, her voice rasped. "You should be ashamed for talking about Hayden like this."

"I didn't want to talk about shit," Isabel barked. "Dad asked, so I told him. It's not my fault if you don't like what you've heard."

"How often does she... see Hayden?" Jack wanted to know, leaning forward.

Beth glared at him.

"I don't know," Iz said, shifting uncomfortably. Griffin gripped her hand under the table and squeezed. It comforted her less than her nail on her arm. She continued to dig, feeling the sticky wetness of blood against her nail.

"Hayden isn't the only one she communicates with, and she can't fully control it. She's still learning how."

"I'm sorry," Griffin said, squeezing Isabel's hand again. "I assumed you all knew. I can tell you that, as a prior skeptic, she's told me things about my brother that only he and I knew. I believe she is as Isabel says."

A timer went off in the kitchen. Everyone at the table jumped. Allie stood abruptly and hurried to check the food, grateful to get away from the conversation. Beth glared at Isabel and followed her mother.

"Dad," Iz said, "please don't hate me."

He looked at her, surprised. "I don't hate you, sweetheart. I could never hate you." He touched her arm, exhaling slowly. "I just need to get used to the idea."

"You've been with her when she communicates with Hayden?" Jack asked.

"I've been with her when she sees her. Hayden doesn't always speak. Apparently, Ava can't get her to tell her what she wants."

"Interesting," Jack said. He dropped his hand when he felt Ozzie's nose against his leg to give him pets. "Very interesting."

"You believe me?"

"I'm pretty open minded, Iz. Besides, you can't lie worth a shit. I'd know if you were making it up."

He grinned at her.

Isabel felt some of the weight on her chest lighten. It was still hard to breathe, but it was getting easier.

Where the hell was Gabriel?

• • • • •

Ava drifted up from the fog slowly, feeling groggy. She opened her eyes to foreign surroundings: a small room with large floral prints hanging on the walls, white bedding as pure as fresh snow, and a roll top desk with multiple drawers all over it. Most important, however, was Gabriel, who was sitting on the edge of the bed, holding her hand.

How long had she been unconscious? Had he stayed with her the whole time?

Flexing her hand, she curled her fingers around his. He returned the squeeze before rubbing his thumb along the back of her hand. So many emotions were conveyed in that simple gesture. Tears burned at the backs of her eyes.

A soft groan escaped her as she lifted her head. The headache was gone, but she still felt sluggish.

"Nice and easy," Gabriel soothed. He waited for her to get her bearings.

"How long was I asleep?" she croaked.

"About twenty minutes."

He brushed her hair back from her face. "Are you feeling any better?"

"Tired."

"We can leave early if you need to."

She regarded his blue eyes, which were calmly studying her for any signs of pain or another presence. She knew he would leave if she wanted without asking questions. His loyalty to her was fascinating.

Slowly, feeling less dizzy, she sat up.

Buzzing filled her ears, a hundred voices talking. She closed her eyes, inhaled, opened them.

"So many stories."

The voices grew louder. She brought her hands to her ears. Her eyes dilated so quickly it was if they had burst.

"What's going on?" Gabriel kept his voice soft. "What do you see?"

Being so close gave him an intimate view of how large her pupils became, swallowing all color. Although her eyes were rounded, as if in surprise, she seemed to be staring past him, through him, at nothing. Each shallow inhale produced a rasping noise.

"The coyotes came. That's why they couldn't find me."

The voice that came from her was more like a croak, old and hard. Her hands gripped his forearms, her fingers hooked into them like claws.

"I'm right here, Ava."

"Turkey buzzards did the rest. I can feel them picking at my skin."

A moan escaped her. Gabriel reached up and put his hand to her cheek, hoping she knew he was there if she needed him. Could she feel him when she was going through this?

"Take it easy," he said.

Her eyes rolled left, right.

"Look at me. Look at me." He took her face firmly in his hands.

Her hands came up and settled over his. He could hear her breathing very deliberately, fighting for control. The rasp was gone, but she was still struggling. Her wandering eyes found his gaze.

"Just breathe through it, like you did before."

Shaky at first. Her body quivered. "There wasn't much left after a couple days. Just bones with bits of skin on them."

"Breathe," he soothed. He kept her face in his grip, firm but gentle. "There you go."

Each breath became more controlled. Her pupils gradually contracted. Those eyes, wild and out of focus, now homed in on his. Soon they were breathing together, in through the nose, out through the mouth, steady breaths that soothed and brought her back into herself.

"You're gaining control over it."

His eyes, that riveting shade of blue, never left hers. Cautious, she lowered her hands. She no longer heard the voices. The room was just a room, not a historical beacon of unrest.

"You helped me." Her voice was full of shock. No one except David had ever calmed her down before, helped her relax without restraining her.

Gabriel lowered his hands from her face but took her hand in both of his. It was warm, no longer cold and clammy.

"Are you ready to come downstairs or do you need a few minutes?"

Ava stood. She put a hand on the bed to steady herself.

The first thing she noticed when they walked downstairs was that everyone was sitting in the dining room. The second thing she noticed was that everyone stopped talking when she entered the room. Griffin looked at her briefly before his gaze darted away.

"You know," Ava said, her body tensing. They all looked at her, and she could see they believed, however reluctantly. That mattered nothing to her. She turned her furious gaze to Griffin. "You told them?"

Gabriel turned back toward her. "Know what?"

"He thought they already knew," Isabel came to Griffin's defense. "Don't be mad, Ava."

"My apologies," Griffin said. "I'm afraid I've made a dog's breakfast out of this."

Gabriel felt tension building in Ava again and swore under his breath. She had only just begun to settle down.

"Relax," he said sharply. Her eyes jerked to his. "What do they know?"

Without speaking, she kept her eyes on his, trying to control emotions churning inside her. He watched her mentally back away from him as surely as if she had physically distanced herself.

"We just found out about her... ability to see Hayden," Josh said. "Isabel's right; it was completely by accident."

"I'm sure you can understand this is all a little hard to accept," Allie said. She was holding a towel in her hands, wringing it mercilessly.

Ava broke her gaze with Gabriel and turned it on his mother. "I do not require your acceptance or your blessing. Your opinion means nothing to me."

Gabriel's hand, resting on her shoulder, gave her a light squeeze.

"I choose not to inform people of my ability because of the inconvenience it will cause me, not because I am ashamed of it."

"She didn't ask for this." Gabriel watched his mother's face, wondering if she would accept Ava or if he would be forced to make a choice. "She doesn't want anything from us. If being around her is a problem for you, that's a problem for me."

"There's no need to go there," Josh said. "This is a lot to take in. Let's just... enjoy the meal and the visit. Allie, do you need any help in the kitchen?"

Allie held her son's gaze another moment before she looked away and stood. "I think Beth and I can manage."

The tension seemed to ease when they left the room, but silence remained for half a minute before anyone spoke.

"I quit my job," Isabel blurted. Her voice sounded exceptionally loud.

Josh raised his eyebrows. "You finally quit that awful place? Good for you. Tell me all about it."

And just like that, things were back to normal.

• • • • •

There was tension. Everyone felt it. To their credit, Isabel thought, her family did their best to make Ava feel welcome. They tried to engage her in conversation, include her in their discussions so she didn't feel singled out. Isabel knew they weren't sure how to take the news. Had they been told Ava was simply psychic, they might have been eased into it. No one would care if it were true or not. But they were shoved into it, forced to face it, compelled to face the idea of Hayden lingering. That was the part they couldn't run from. Isabel could relate.

Ava answered questions as she always did, oblivious of the odd behavior around her. She did not need to be included. She did not need to feel welcome or join in to be comfortable with herself. Isabel coveted the younger woman's confidence.

As they gathered around the island to dish out food, Isabel watched Ava talk with Jack. He was listening avidly, plating food while she described the dojo to him. He and Griffin were the only two treating her as they always had.

"... thought you should strip naked and dance under the full moon next time you come over," Gabriel was saying.

His elbow bumped her arm. She jumped.

"What?"

Grinning, he added mashed potatoes to his plate. "I said I'm thinking of having the guys to my place again, since the last cookout ended so badly."

"That's a great idea." Her eyes narrowed. "What was that about getting naked and dancing under a full moon?"

He smirked. "I had to get your attention somehow."

She elbowed him. "My fork could stab the tension in the room right now."

Gabriel glanced at Ava, who was listening to something Jack was saying. Beth was on Jack's other side, glancing at Ava occasionally with an expression he couldn't quite interpret. He thought she was a still a little angry about the whole thing, which was surprising. He expected disbelief from her, maybe confusion, but not outright anger.

His parents were waiting for everyone else to get their food first. His dad was pretty mellow, coming around to the idea and trying to keep everyone civil as they adjusted to the possibilities. His mom looked uncertain. Gabriel had expected she would take it the hardest. He just didn't know if she would take it out on Ava. If she did, what that would mean for his relationships with her?

A cell phone rang. All conversation stopped.

"You committed a cardinal sin," Isabel said. "No phones during family time."

Griffin shifted his plate and pulled his phone out of his back pocket, silencing it.

"My apologies."

His eyes had darkened slightly. Iz watched him as they circled the table. "Are you okay?" she asked.

"My mum," he grumbled. "They're in Madison again. I haven't seen this much of them since I was in grade school."

They broke away from the serving line and walked to the dining room table. Both dogs were watching hopefully from the foyer doorway.

"Why are they back again? I thought you said they only came here a few times a year."

She sat down next to him. The wine he had already poured for both of them was a Zinfandel she liked very much. She'd just taken a sip of it when he leaned in and kissed her.

Pulling away from her just enough to speak, he licked his lips. "You taste good."

A fluttering rose from her stomach and seemed to bounce around her rib cage. She smiled.

He sat back in his chair. "My mum is convinced she can talk me into taking over Dad's business. My dad wants to make sure things are okay with us. He doesn't want to leave things bad between us like they were with..."

For a moment, his eyes changed, and she saw deep grief over the loss of his brother. She was so intent on trying to comfort him that she didn't realize Ava had walked in and was standing at her usual place at the head of the table.

Everyone else was sitting down and settling in around her, but Ava barely noticed them. She only noticed his haunted eyes.

"He took your face," she suddenly said.

Griffin looked at her, unblinking. One by one, the conversations around the table stopped until the room was silent. Iz put her hand on Griffin's, but he didn't seem to notice. He was staring at Ava intently.

"Jack, don't touch her," Gabriel said, and Jack lowered the hand he'd raised to touch Ava's shoulder.

"What did you say?" Griffin asked Ava.

"'You took my face,'" she said. Her eyes were huge, black orbs. "That's what you said when you held him. 'You took my face.'"

"Yes." Griffin had to force the word out. "He was my twin brother. I felt I lost half of myself when he died."

Ava lowered her head and closed her eyes tight, dry heaving. "You asked him to stop but he did not, it did not matter anymore that you were there to witness, he did it anyway. 'Connor, what have you done? You bloody fool, what have you done?'"

"Ava, stop it." Isabel's hand was numb in Griffin's. He had gripped hers so hard she felt like her bones were cracking. Tears of pain gathered in her eyes.

"This isn't funny," Beth said. "It's obviously upsetting Griffin."

Gabriel gave her a withering look. "She can't control it. What part of that don't you understand?"

"How convenient."

He stood slowly, glaring at her, then turned to Ava. He felt helpless.

"You heard her scream, 'My baby! What happened to my baby!'" Ava's voice rose until it was as shrill as a whistle. Wrapping her arms around herself, she began rocking her upper body back and forth.

Maya let out a low bark that turned into a short howl. Ozzie whined and stood, pacing the doorway.

"Ava," Isabel wheezed, unable to catch her breath. She rested her other hand on Griffin's thigh, trying to be strong for him, but the pain was making her dizzy. He turned and saw what he was doing and let her go immediately. His arms circled her.

"I'm sorry, Love. I'm so sorry." He delicately picked her hand up and kissed it. "Jesus."

"'You took my face. You took my face. You took my...'" Ava's rocking gradually slowed to a stop. When she opened her eyes, they were opaque. They seemed to have been replaced with two pieces of ice.

Beth and Allie gasped. Josh murmured something too quiet to understand. Jack's mouth hung open in awe. Maya let out a series of yips and short howls, and Ozzie's whines turned into howls to match.

"Are you okay?" Gabriel reached for her, thought better of it. He dropped his hand.

"'I'm sorry, M-Mum,'" she said, but her voice was still very male with an obvious Australian accent. "'I'm so s-sorry I c-couldn't s-stop him.'"

Griffin kissed Izzie's hand again and stood, walking around the table toward Ava.

"Don't touch her when she's like this." Gabriel wondered how many times he would have to tell people before they understood. Or if he should just let Ava pound on everyone and speed things along.

"She won't hit me," Griffin said softly, passing Gabriel and going to Ava.

"How do you know?" Gabriel asked.

"Because I didn't hit my mother."

He touched Ava lightly on the shoulder. To Gabriel's surprise, Ava turned into Griffin's embrace, her hands trapped between them. Her body shook with silent sobs as he held her close, rubbing his hand up and down her back.

"'It's okay,'" Griffin said, as his mother had said to him when she found him holding his shattered brother four years ago. "'It will be okay.'"

Allie wiped a tear away. Whatever Ava was or wasn't, the heartbreak in her voice was real. It was the agony from losing a child that only a mother could know. Beside her, Beth was shaking.

Griffin felt the exact instant Ava came out of it. She stilled in his embrace. The silent sobs stopped immediately, and she held her breath for a moment before letting it out slowly. Her body shuddered violently. Keeping his arms around her, he loosened his grip.

"Are you alright then?" he asked, still looking slightly shaken.

Ava raised her head, leaned back just enough to turn her hands until her palms were on his chest, and firmly pushed him back.

"I am not the one you are worried about."

Without waiting for his reaction, Ava wiped her cheeks and moved toward Gabriel. He raised his eyebrow as she approached. She didn't reach for him, but she stepped up close and simply stood watching him. He brushed a lock of hair from her face and leaned forward until their foreheads touched. Feeling her relax against him, Gabriel was mystified at how much of their communication was body language. Volumes had just been conveyed in those few seconds, and none of it had been spoken.

Griffin had returned to his seat, facing Isabel. He studied her hand to make sure he hadn't sprained it or broken any bones. It was still red from his grip, but she was getting some sensation back, she said.

"Sorry, Love," he murmured. He pressed it gently against his cheek.

"Don't worry about me. How are you doing? It looked like you just relived your brother's suicide."

Nodding, he took a drink of wine. Rubbed a hand down his face. "Jesus."

The silence was broken only by Ozzie's confused whine. He was standing near the hearth, his head cocked, feeling that something was wrong with the humans but unable to figure out what it was.

"Come here, boy," Jack said gently, leaning down to pet him.

Maya was lying in the doorway of the foyer, alert.

Ava abruptly stepped away from Gabriel and sat down. She lowered her head briefly and prayed as everyone around the table watched. When she raised her head, she ignored their stares, picked up her fork, and began eating.

•   •   •   •   •

CHAPTER FOURTEEN

People looked at her differently once they knew. As a young girl, David and Ruth had tried to set up play dates for Ava. They took her to the houses of friends who had young children, attempting to give her a somewhat normal social life. At parks, Ruth tried to encourage her to approach other children and make new friends. She did not know she was different at first. Something always happened to reveal her abilities. She saw a dead member of a kid's family, or she was caught talking to someone only she could see. A bit of information she had no business knowing was shared in passing, causing suspicion. How many curious kids asked their parents why their friend could see Grandma when she was dead before she learned to keep her mouth shut? Their parents told them to stay away, and so they learned to look at her differently, when they looked at her at all. One by one, the children stood a little farther away, and stopped coming over to play, and eventually avoided her altogether. The only people who looked at her the same way after they knew were David and Ruth.

When Gabriel found out, he surprised her by treating her the same as he had before he knew. There was no look of disbelief in his eyes, no doubt. He had simply accepted what she told him. Not many people surprised her, but he continued to do so.

But now his family knew, and they looked at her differently. If she were invited to another Sunday dinner, which she doubted she would be, there would be tension, animosity. A lifelong family tradition would be ruined by her presence. The strain between her and his family would cause issues between them and him. The outcome was inevitable.

Ava silently slipped out of bed the following morning and walked downstairs to dress in the workout clothes she left at Gabriel's. Dawn was not yet beginning; the sky was dark, the moon a half orb still dominating for another hour or more. She drank a full glass of water and put on her shoes. Mornings were still chilly, but she left her jacket inside. She wanted the cold to numb her body and distract her thoughts. She stretched on the deck, trying to ignore the pang of dread building inside her.

I do not care. I do not require their approval.

But she did care about Gabriel's feelings. She did not want to be a cause of stress in his life. She did not want to see his eyes fill with pain at the inevitable choice he would have to make between her and his blood. When he chose his people - and he would, eventually - she would feel betrayed. She had never wanted to care what he thought, and she had not wanted to set herself up for someone to betray her. Why had he insisted on becoming part of her life? Why had she let her guard down? He was a human being, like any other. That he made her want to smile, that she wanted to be a better person because of him, should not matter.

Ava jogged down the steps of the patio and into the grass. She concentrated on her heartbeat and its rhythmic thudding as she jogged across the yard and into the woods. Her body began to warm up. She felt the high of physical exertion settle over her.

She tried to stay focused, but her overactive mind kept returning to the way Gabriel's family members looked at her after they found out. Things would spiral downward from here. Gabriel would begin to resent her for the rift between them. Eventually, he would just end all contact.

It was best that way, she supposed. Life would return to the way it was before, simple and solitary. Could she still be satisfied with that kind of existence?

After two hours of alternating between running and climbing trees on his property, her body was screaming in protest, but her mind still would not shut off. Ava jogged back up the deck stairs and entered the house. She drank a glass of water and started peeling off clothing as she walked upstairs to take a shower.

The water was cool and impersonal, and she fought to mirror its impartiality. Once again, she was alone in it. For a brief time, she had felt part of something. Finally, she was beginning to feel like family to these people, almost as much as she did to David. Now it was going to shatter, all because she was stupid enough to believe she could trust one man's kindness. She wished she had not felt that closeness at all. To have it ripped away was worse than having never felt it.

The needles in her chest finally began to subside. As the water turned cold, Ava let it run over her body for another minute before shutting it off. She dried slowly. Her body was numb. She felt a sorrow flooding her that she couldn't get a grip on. David was injured and now she was going to lose Gabriel and Isabel. Everything was dying around her.

Walking naked into the bedroom, Ava picked out an outfit and turned to leave the room. She wanted to put it on downstairs so she would not wake Gabriel. He was lying sprawled on his stomach, as usual, his face turned away from her. She wanted to run her hands over his back, feel his muscles tense when she touched him. The heat his body radiated felt good against her skin. She would miss it.

Swallowing, she left the room. She waited until she was at the bottom of the stairs to dress. In the kitchen, she made coffee. She sat at the table in the breakfast room as she waited for it to brew. Her eyes wandered to the back yard, trying to find comfort in the beauty of the woods. The trees were full of leaves now, different shades of green that usually pleased her. The large expanse of yard between the deck and woods was lush and dark, with no remnants of the dried, brown death of winter. This was usually her favorite time of year.

Beside her, Sally appeared. The young girl had died in the spare room Gabriel used for various odds and ends. She had died in bed from pneumonia over one hundred and fifty years ago. Now she appeared pale, her shoulder-length blonde hair drab, wearing a thick white night gown that went nearly to her ankles.

Ava felt a small hand on her back. A tear slipped down her cheek. She pushed her hands through her damp hair, resting her head in her hands.

"Morning," Gabriel said from the counter.

Ava startled so hard her elbow smacked into the edge of the table, sending shooting pain up her arm. Disoriented, she rubbed her elbow and sent an accusatory glare at Gabriel.

"Sorry," he said, amused. "You usually know where I am before I do. I thought you heard me come in."

She had been so deep in thought that she had not been aware of his presence. That unnerved her; she would have been unprepared for an attack if there had been one. She angrily wiped her eyes.

Gabriel poured them both a cup of coffee and took the creamer out of the refrigerator. Slipping a spoon into her cup, he carried the bottle of creamer between his arm and chest, and both mugs of coffee over to the table. He set everything down.

Kneeling in front of her, he rested one hand on her knee and the other on the back of the chair. "Are you still worried about David?"

He was going to be released from the hospital soon. Today, after class, they were going for another visit.

Ava shook her head. With his face so close to hers, she could see all the intricate details of his eyes, the specks of dark blue within the other varying shades of blue. Looking into his eyes was like looking into Hayden's. She wanted to help him. She longed to find out what happened to his sister and ease that sorrow she saw in his and Isabel's eyes.

"What's wrong?" He brushed her hair behind her ear. "You look like your heart is breaking."

"I should go. It will be easier." She felt tears threaten again and reigned them in. What was wrong with her? It was a natural reaction to stress, it must be. With David in the hospital and her the addition of psychic training to her physical routine, the stress was too overwhelming. Her body was all raw nerves and exposed emotions. She had to ease back, or she feared she would self-destruct.

"Go where?" Gabriel shifted his weight. "Do you want to visit David this morning instead of later? Visiting hours started at eight."

"No." She was feeling closed in, caged. There was no space to take a step back, assess the situation. She pressed the base of her thumb between her eyebrows. A headache was throbbing there.

"Hey." He rubbed his hand over her shoulder.

How could it feel so comforting and like razor blades on her skin at the same time? Without meaning to, she writhed and shied away from him.

Gabriel instantly stood, giving her space. He picked up his coffee cup and took a sip, studying her. With her head down, her damp, thick hair had fallen over her face. She was on the verge of tears, and that unsettled him more than her reaction to his touch.

Ava had not felt such a loss of control since she was a young child. Gabriel deserved to be with someone that did not recoil at his touch. Someone who could love him and have an enjoyable time with his family and not know things she should have no way of knowing.

"I will just go," she said, horrified to find herself close to sobbing. She could barely catch her breath; she could barely speak. "Thank you for... being kind to me. You deserve better."

She stood, her legs shaky, her heart racing. Fearing she would make a spectacle of herself, she picked up her coffee cup. A simple task like rinsing the cup would give her a moment to compose herself. A job gave her something to focus on.

"Are you breaking up with me?" Gabriel asked, watching her walk to the kitchen.

"It is better this way." She dumped the coffee out. Her hands were shaking. Turning on the faucet, she managed to hitch in a breath.

"Easier, you mean."

When she raised her head, he was surprised to see fresh tears on her cheeks. She swallowed with difficulty. "It is not easy."

"Then don't do it."

"There is no point prolonging the inevitable. People do not accept extrasensory ability." She rinsed the cup and turned off the water. Now she had nothing to do with her hands, but she held onto the mug to give her something to concentrate on. Her hand flexed over the ceramic.

"Is that what this is about?" Gabriel walked to the counter, so he was standing across from her. "Dinner at my parent's last night?"

"I have caused trouble with your family."

"Let me worry about that."

Continuing as if he had not spoken, trying to get through it so she could just leave, Ava had to force the words out. "Once people know, they look at me differently, treat me differently. They... stop touching me... leave..."

"So instead of giving them the chance to come to terms with it, you hide your ability."

She leveled her gaze at him. "Yes."

"You hide yourself, refuse to get close to people. What's the point? They'll turn on you anyway."

"Yes."

"It's better to live on your own, isolated from everyone, so you have no possibility of being hurt ever again, physically or emotionally."

Her chest was hitching. She was unable to gain control of her breathing again. Dizziness almost overcame her, but she fought against it. Damn it, why did he have to make her feel so much? She had been fine without him. Without all of them.

"You're just waiting for every person you've ever known to disappoint you," Gabriel said, walking the length of the kitchen peninsula. He kept his eyes on hers. As he rounded the counter, he slowed. Ava turned to face him. Her grip on the coffee mug was tightening. Her eyes were glassy with tears but beginning to flicker with rage, a dangerous combination.

"Every person disappoints. It is human nature." Her fingertips were turning white where she held the cup.

She was getting more defensive the closer he came. Her eyes set in that way that looked almost mechanical, feral, as if her body was about to react to a threat and the reaction was as natural as breathing. Gabriel supposed for her, after training for so long, it was natural. He stopped a few feet away, not to keep her from feeling threatened but because he thought she was long overdue for what he was sure was coming and he needed a moment to prepare.

"What about Ruth? She took you in, cared for you even though you were never really close to her. Did she let you down?"

Ava recoiled in surprise. "You do not know anything about that."

"How about David? When did he disappoint you? Was it when he legally adopted you to keep you from being moved from one abusive foster home to another? Or every time he treated you as his own flesh and blood?"

Her eyes lit up like liquid fire. She took a step forward and her fury was almost palpable. Gabriel felt it like a shove as she moved toward him.

"He almost died," she moaned, as if the very words caused her agony. The coffee mug shattered in her hand. Shards flew across the counter and littered the floor. Both hands balled into fists. The left hand began dripping blood onto the tile. "He was going to leave me."

Here it comes, Gabriel thought, and hoped he would make it through the storm to be there for the aftermath.

"That would have been a big disappointment," he said, taking a step toward her. "His death would be a real inconvenience for you, wouldn't it?"

Ava shoved him in the chest with her palms, sending him stumbling backward. He regained his footing quickly, knowing the blow was coming and having prepared for it. A handprint in blood appeared smeared across the right side of his chest, glaringly obvious against the white background. The fact that he was still standing told him she was worse off than he thought.

To give himself a few seconds to settle his heartbeat and make sure he didn't bring his own emotion into it, he said wistfully, "Damn. I kind of liked this shirt."

The left side had partial fingerprints smeared on the chest as well. The shirt would have to be tossed, but it was no big deal; it was a cheap tee shirt.

He looked back up at Ava. "That pisses you off, eh? Maybe we're not as inconvenient as you try to tell yourself. I think you actually care about people, and that scares the hell out of you. That even after all the abuse you've endured at the hands of others, you still long to help people. You ache for contact with the outside world, because the alternative is much, much worse."

"I do not need anyone."

She needed just a little push. "You're not a warrior, Ava. You're a whiny little brat who throws a tantrum when she doesn't get her way."

Ava snarled.

"Get some," Gabriel sneered.

She came at him. Not in her usual, graceful way, with every movement fluid. She lunged at him like a rabid dog. Gabriel easily pivoted and grabbed her around the waist. Instead of a well-placed elbow to the jaw or solar plexus, she bucked and kicked recklessly. Gabriel turned his head away and hauled her out of the kitchen, where there was too much to be broken.

Holding her was like trying to cage a lion. She was completely out of control. Because she was faced away from him, and he was carrying her on his hip, her limbs weren't hitting any major targets. He held his hand up beside his head so she couldn't headbutt him.

The largest, most open space was in the center of the living room floor. He plopped them both down and held on. Her feet thrummed on the wood as she tried to find leverage to break free. Her fists flailed. Blood was flowing freely from her hand.

Afraid she would headbutt him and injure them both, Gabriel put his hand on her forehead and forced her head back against his shoulder. An elbow caught him in the side. He let out a grunt but kept a hold of her.

"Having to visit David in the hospital must have really cut into your schedule," he panted against her ear. "He should have planned his heart attack at a time that was more convenient for you."

Her fists were still flying. Suddenly she opened them, into what she had called a tiger claw: her fingers splayed and half-curled, her palms flat. She slammed them down on his thighs.

Bone-deep pain drove into his muscles.

"Outstanding," he ground through his teeth.

But she hadn't done so to hurt him. She was still fighting for purchase with her hands, and when they found his thighs, they gripped his jeans and curled the material into her fists. Wheezing sounds were coming from deep in her chest now.

"Everyone who doesn't conform to your strict discipline is in the way, disposable. You shut them out before they have a chance to let you down."

She let out a sound that was part growl, part sob. "I love him."

Her body became rigid, one last attempt to free herself. She arched her back and raised off the floor like a woman possessed, then collapsed against him. Her body began shaking with gut-wrenching sobs. He released her forehead.

Gabriel let out a sigh of relief. Looking down at her, he turned her so he could embrace her instead of restraining. In her grief, she allowed him to move her easily. Her head dropped heavily to his shoulder, and she wept. Gabriel wrapped his arm around her shoulders and rested his chin on the top of her head. Christ, he hated that sound. All he could do was let her emotions take their course.

"I l-love him and he left m-me," she said, her voice soft but choked with tears.

"Not by choice. He would never leave you by choice."

Her sobs echoed around the room and inside his head. The sensation made him want to scream, but he held onto her. Her arms were around him, her fingers digging into his back. He thought she would never stop. Twenty-two years of agony could never be cried out in one setting.

It took several minutes, but she finally began to wind down. The sobs became quiet weeping, which eventually trickled away. Her body leaned heavily against him in surrender.

He brushed her hair back from her sweaty forehead. He was sitting with his legs splayed, her hunched body between them, his arm slung over her shoulder. Her breath was wheezing and ragged, her throat raw. Her heart was hammering, still raging even though she was too exhausted to fight anymore.

"Everyone leaves." Ava said softly. "You will, too."

"Not by choice," he repeated.

$$\bullet \quad \bullet \quad \bullet \quad \bullet \quad \bullet$$

The air was thick with humidity. Even so early in the morning, each breath was like inhaling steam. Birdsong surrounded her. A few feet away, she heard Mom and Dad preparing coffee and breakfast: the clink of the cast iron skillet on rocks, the hiss of butter heating, the crack of eggs on the lip of the skillet. The smell of bacon cooking over the fire hit her nose, making her stomach growl.

Isabel opened her eyes and found herself staring at the side of the tent. Beige vinyl, with a dark, two-inch mark in the corner. Mud maybe?

Her father murmured something, and her mother laughed. It would be the last time Isabel heard her mother laugh for three years.

Sitting up, Isabel saw she had kicked the sleeping bag away during the night. Still, her tee shirt and shorts were damp. A thin line of sweat coated her upper lip.

Beside her bag, Hayden's was slightly disordered. She must already be awake. Hayden always woke up early. Beth's sleeping bag was also empty but was folded neatly. She had been a real grump during the entire trip.

Isabel rubbed her eyes and climbed out of the sleeping bag. Her parents were finishing up cooking breakfast. They were both smiling. Beth, looking as bored as she always did, was pouting at one end of the table.

"Good morning, Iz," her mother said. "Breakfast is almost ready. Wake Hayden and Gabriel up."

Isabel looked around their camping spot. Hayden wasn't playing on the flat rock that served as a kind of table like she had been yesterday. Isabel shuffled to Gabe's tent. The flaps were opened to let in as much air as possible. Peering inside, she saw her brother lying on his stomach in only his underwear, sideways across his sleeping bag.

"Gabriel," she mumbled. "Breakfast is almost ready."

He shifted slightly, raising his head, and then letting it fall. "I'm awake."

"Where's Hayden?" she asked.

"How should I know? I just woke up."

He was facing away from her. He wouldn't have seen Hayden walk by anyway. Isabel turned and checked their tent again. She walked to the picnic table where her mother was setting out paper plates.

"Mom, I can't find Hayden."

Allie glanced up at her daughter before resuming what she was doing. "What do you mean, honey? Josh, get the salt and pepper!" she called.

"She's not in our tent."

Allie looked around. Josh walked over from the camper with an armful of supplies, including the salt and pepper. He leaned over and kissed Isabel on the top of the head. "Good morning, honey."

"Good morning."

"Was Hayden in there with you?" Allie asked. Iz heard a difference in her mother's voice and felt the first stirrings of unease.

"Nope." He began setting items on the table.

"Maybe in our room?"

"Why would she be in our room?" Josh glanced up, noticing the worry in his wife's voice for the first time. "I'll go check."

"It's okay, Isabel," Allie said carefully, watching her husband walk back to the camper. "Maybe she doesn't feel well so she went to lay down."

But her father returned without her sister.

They searched the woods around them for an hour and met back at the camp site, and that was when her parents finally admitted to themselves that Hayden was missing. That was when Isabel's mother began to scream.

• • • • •

"Please stop screaming please stop screaming..."

Isabel pressed her hands to her ears, trying to block out her mother's shrieks of agony. Rocking back and forth, she mumbled the phrase over and over again. The sound seemed to be a part of her; no matter how hard she pressed her hands to her ears, she could hear it drilling through her head. It went on and on.

Dread sat like a large boulder in her stomach. Iz knew the pain that was coming, the years of depression she would have to endure. The hours of searching, waiting, news coverage, sobbing, outbursts were still to come, and it was worse because she knew the outcome. Hayden would never be found. Isabel would spend horrible hours hiding in alcohol trying to find something she had lost. She would even try to find it in a couple relationships before she gave up. Her mother would begin to resent her and pull away from her, until there a gap so massive between them no bridge would be able to connect the two.

Those failures were all ahead, years and years before anything resembling a normal life was even a glimmer of hope. And still, she would be lacking.

The horror seemed to be a physical thing, restraining her arms, suffocating her, preventing her from escaping the sorrow.

"Isabel," a voice said gently.

"Gabriel?" Had her mother's screaming awoken him? She couldn't seem to force her eyes open. If she did, the horror would be real. She called out to the one constant in her life, the only constant. "Gabe, I can't find her, she's not in the tent..."

A sob escaped her. The dream was still with her. She heard her mother's keening in her head like a fire drill, piercing and horrible. She heard her nine-year-old self sobbing even as her present-self heard her own words repeated.

"Please stop screaming...please stop..." She was crying hard, her throat sore from the effort.

"Isabel, wake up."

Someone was holding her, a hand on her arm and another on her back to stop her from rocking and sobbing. The familiarity of the way she was being comforted tugged at her, helped to bring her closer to the surface of consciousness.

A violent shudder finally shook Isabel fully awake. She found herself sitting up in a bed. Slowly, the dream dissipated, and she pieced together what was going on. She stilled, keeping her hands against her ears, not trusting that the screaming had stopped.

Years had passed since she last had a dream about Hayden's disappearance. Her chest ached. She felt like a stone was resting on it. The bed she was sitting up in was not her own. She jerked around, her arms reaching out to feel something familiar, her eyes straining in the dark room, trying to figure out where she was. The darkness wanted to swallow her. She cried out; a deep sound full of sorrow.

"It's okay," Griffin said, taking her hand and sliding his arm around her shoulders. He drew her against his body. "You're okay. We're in my flat."

She searched with her other hand a moment longer before his words sunk in. Her right hand gripped his shirt, pulling him closer, closer. A shaky breath that was almost another sob burst from her lips.

Griffin's apartment. She was okay. The nightmare was over.

"You should drink-"

"Don't!"

He started to lean over toward the bedside table, but she held his shirt in her fist and kept him tight against her. From her neck to her toes, her body was shivering, and she had no control over it. The feeling was like the knowledge that she was going mad.

Iz quaked for a while against him.

Finally, spent, the strength left her, and she released his shirt. God, she felt as if it had all just happened yesterday. The pain was fresh and sharp.

She pressed her palms to her aching eyes.

"Jesus Christ." She exhaled.

She felt Griffin shift, and a moment later heard the click from the lamp being turned on. Needles pierced her eyes as she lowered her hands, so she closed them until they adjusted to the light. Her face felt cracked and peeling. Trying to breathe was like inhaling dust.

Griffin was watching her. "Here. Water."

He folded her hand around a glass and helped lift it to her mouth. When she started gulping it down, he pulled it back slightly. "Slowly. Slow down."

She was breathing heavily, as a person resurfacing after almost drowning.

"Do you have any whiskey?" she grumbled. Her hands were still shaking.

"Not a good idea, Love," he said gently. He took the water from her.

"I didn't ask if it was a good idea. I asked if you had any."

Griffin should have pulled back – she wouldn't have faulted him if he did – but he didn't. "Of course. Would you like me to get some for you?"

Isabel rubbed her palms on her temples, where a headache was making itself comfortable. "I'm sorry. No, no alcohol."

Good for you, he thought.

"Talk to me." He brushed her hair off her shoulder.

Tears. Her face felt fractured because of the tears drying on them. Why the hell did she have to have this dream now? Why did she have to keep humiliating herself in front of Griffin? The poor guy was going to go into Witness Protection after tonight. Things had been going well. The depression had begun to fall away.

"What's going on up there?" Griffin asked, his voice calm, soothing. He touched her temple with his fingers. "I hear those rusty wheels turning."

"Hayden," she forced out. "I had a dream about the morning I woke up to her missing. My mother started screaming. She didn't stop until the police got there, and an ambulance. I watched her start p-pulling out h-her h-h-hair. I was terrified. I'd never watched someone lose it before. I was crying and Gabriel hugged me, turning me away from her so I couldn't see her."

Slipping back into the memory, Isabel covered her ears with her hands again. Griffin rubbed his hand up and down her back. He hated the way she was shaking, the way all the color had drained from her face.

"They had to g-give her a shot. I still hear her screaming in my head. I'll never stop hearing that sound."

Raising her hands, she watched them twitch. "My h-hands won't stop shaking."

She balled them into fists, then rung them so hard they turned red. Griffin reached over and took one, kissing her knuckles. "Easy now."

"I'm sorry I woke you. I haven't had that dream in years. It came out of nowhere."

"Can I do anything to help?"

Take away memories of my childhood after the age of nine.

She let out a shaky laugh. "Yeah, you can get me some whiskey."

"You don't need to hide in whiskey. You're strong enough to manage this."

"Have you met me?"

Resting his left hand on her shin, he shifted so his leg pressed against hers more firmly. His body was solid, making her feel like she had something sturdy to hold onto when everything else was going to hell around her. Something to keep her tethered to reality.

"I don't want to hide in it... just calm my nerves."

"Oh, well, if a distraction is all you need..." He leaned down and pressed his lips to hers.

Isabel was caught off guard and her mouth responded on instinct. This kiss was gentle but urgent, leaving no room to catch her breath or think. His large palm cupped her face tenderly.

The feel of his hair through her fingers had a calming effect on her. It was soft and slightly curly at the tips. Moving slowly, he engaged her in a soul scorching kiss that had her limbs dissolving, boneless. She didn't realize she had started crying again until he trailed kisses along the tears on her cheek up to her eye.

Griffin rested his forehead against hers. He was always so gentle with her. "I'll make some coffee."

He waited a moment to make sure she was steady before he stood and left the room. Isabel heard a cupboard door opening and shutting, the tap running. A few moments later, the smell of fresh coffee filled her nose.

She raised her knees and set her elbows on them, resting her head in her hands. The headache was growing. Maybe she would talk to Gabriel on Sunday and see if he had dreams about Hayden, too. Had she ever asked him about nightmares? Had it ever occurred to her to ask him?

Griffin returned with two cups of coffee. He handed her one that was lightened with cream. Isabel felt fresh, hot tears start sliding down her cheeks again. Before her shaking hands could spill the liquid and burn herself, he took the mug back and traded it for the box of tissues from the bedside table.

Sniffing, Isabel wiped at her tears. "You're just so sweet. You know exactly how much creamer to put in my coffee."

Griffin rubbed her knee while she composed herself. After a long sigh, she moved to the edge of the bed.

"I need a minute."

She disappeared through the walk-in closet. A moment later he heard the bathroom door shut.

Sipping his coffee, Griffin used his phone to send a text to his boss and waited for a reply.

He thought about everything Izzie had told him so far about Hayden's disappearance. The night before, Hayden had left the tent alone to go to the bathroom. Isabel saw a man in a blue hoodie in the woods, walking toward the public restrooms sometime after Hayden was last seen going in the same direction. Hayden never returned to the tent. The next day, during the search for Hayden, they found material similar to the blue hoodie in proximity to one of Hayden's shoes in the woods. Traces of her blood were also found. That evidence, along with the knowledge that a recently paroled pedophile, Sam King, had moved into the area, had the police looking at the man as a person of interest. When the police were unable to locate the man, their suspicion of him grew, which led the police to the conclusion that it was very likely Hayden had been kidnapped by King on her way to the restroom. He had taken her somewhere and raped her before killing her and disposing of her body. The body had never been found, nor had Sam King.

Isabel had told Griffin that the only thing keeping her sane some days was knowing King wasn't the type to hold onto his victims for hours or days before killing them. Hayden would have been killed instantly after King used her, she had said. The night she told him that was the night she'd lied and told him she hated him for making her talk about Hayden's disappearance.

All in all, he thought she was handling it fairly well. Now, years later, she had a new friend spiritually connected to her sister, a daily reminder that her soul was restless. Yes, Isabel was stronger than she gave herself credit for.

His phone vibrated. Glancing down at it, he brought up the reply his boss had sent – confirmation of what he'd already known. He set his phone on the bedside table and took another long sip of coffee.

When Isabel padded back into the room, she didn't look as pale as she had when she'd first rocketed out of the dream. Her eyes were bloodshot, and she looked exhausted, but she was no longer crying. Griffin thought she must have splashed water on her face; the hair framing it was damp.

She walked to his side of the bed and picked up her coffee. After gulping down one third of the contents, she sighed.

"Shouldn't you be getting ready for work?"

"I took the day off. We're at the beginning of a new project, so nothing's in a rush. The guys – and gal - know what they're doing."

"You didn't do that just because of me, did you?"

Waiting until she set her mug down, he gripped her by the waist and pulled her down into his lap.

"What if I did?"

"You didn't need to do that."

"I know." His mouth skimmed over hers.

"That's sweet. Thank you."

"You're most welcome. How are you doing?"

The emotions the nightmare had evoked shuddered through her again. She closed her eyes on a shallow inhale and opened them on the exhale. Trying to focus on his face to find comfort, she didn't know how to answer that anymore.

"My sister's still dead," she said, and her lower lip trembled.

"Yes, she is. Why don't we go have breakfast, and maybe we can visit Hayden's grave after if you feel up to it," he said softly.

"What?" She pulled away from him to sit up.

"If you need to visit her, I'll go with you to her grave."

"Are we going to stop off at your brother's grave after Hayden's?"

Griffin ran his hand over her hair. "He wasn't buried. He was cremated and his ashes were spread."

"Maybe we can visit where you spread his ashes, then."

"Sure."

Her stomach turned lazily. She'd hoped that mentioning his brother would make him back off, but apparently it wasn't a deterrent. Isabel didn't want to visit the cemetery so soon after such a dark nightmare. To do so was too creepy.

"What's going on up there?" Griffin tugged on a strand of her hair.

Shrugging evasively, she rested her head against his shoulder. "You hardly ever talk about losing him, or the anniversary of his death, or his birthday."

"My birthday is the same as his. Celebrating it is hard, reminds me of what he chose." He kissed the top of her head. "I remember him in my own way. I try not to dwell on his death."

"You don't talk much about his life, either."

He couldn't argue with that.

"So much of our communication was unspoken," he said carefully. "We were very in tune with each other. Sometimes we would go several days without speaking, not realizing it until Mum or Dad mentioned it. I guess... I still feel that connection, even though he's dead. I still talk to him, but it's all in my head."

A violent shiver went through her this time. Griffin raised his hands off her for a moment, watching her.

"Are you alright then?"

"I'm just so cold."

If she could have curled up inside his palms like a newborn kitten, she would have. She reveled in the sensation of his hands moving up and down her arms. Warmth finally began seeping in, chasing away the ice.

"Move in with me."

He murmured it against her temple, so softly she didn't think she'd heard him right. Her body stilled.

"What?"

"I want you to move in here, with me."

Pulling away from him, she stared into his amber eyes, noticing for the first time the different shades in them. There were lighter and darker rings, not all one solid color as she had originally thought. How many times had she gazed into those eyes, and she'd never noticed what seemed like such an obvious detail until now?

"We've been over this." Her tone had no strength, no argument behind it.

"We're going over it again."

"You just gave me the use of a drawer and a few hangers, and now you want me to move in here?"

"If you live here, you can have a whole dresser instead of just a drawer."

"Oh," she breathed. "Alright."

At first, he couldn't read the expression on her face.

"Just like that?"

"Well, my lease isn't up until the end of July, but that gives me time to pack and make arrangements."

His hands continued to move up and down her arms, but he had slowed the pace as he watched her thoughtfully.

"Why are you looking at me like that?"

"I thought... I expected you to protest more."

Giving him a knowing half-smile, she nodded. "You expected me to freak out."

"I thought there was a strong possibility."

"But you asked anyway? You enjoy suffering, don't you?"

"You're worth the risk. I love you, Izzie. I want you here."

Warmth, stronger than any whiskey, grew in her stomach and spread upward. Leaning toward him, Izzie brushed her lips against his. Her hands captured his face as she changed the angle of the kiss and spurred it from affectionate to passionate. Griffin didn't expect the sudden change but willingly followed her, his hands gripping her arms now. The harsh sound of his breath made her smile against his mouth.

Suddenly she pulled back, her eyes wide.

"What's wrong?" he panted.

"I'll need to borrow Rover to move my stuff in here. My car isn't big enough. And I need to buy boxes, and packing tape..."

"Jesus Christ, Isabel," he said, the noise he made somewhere between a laugh and a groan. "Do you really want to think about that now?"

"Sorry."

She snorted as he tackled her back onto the bed.

$$\bullet \quad \bullet \quad \bullet \quad \bullet \quad \bullet$$

By the time he felt it was appropriate to move, Gabriel's legs were starting to fall asleep. He shuffled his weight. Ava didn't stir. Had she fallen asleep? He wouldn't be surprised, after all that. Trying to move her as little as possible, he shifted her in his arms so he could see her face and was startled to find her eyes open.

"Are you okay?" he asked, brushing a lock of hair from her face.

It hurts.

The words flashed in his mind; he heard nothing. He glanced down at her injured hand, which was lying palm up on her leg. Blood had gathered in a thick pool in the palm, making it impossible to see how bad the damage was.

But she hadn't meant her hand. Somehow Gabriel knew this; he didn't understand how, but he felt a deep sorrow and a tightness in his chest that indicated Ava's pain was caused by her love for David, not by her injury.

"I know," he whispered, kissing her forehead. It occurred to him that their nonverbal communication was considerably better than it had been before they started dating. He was picking up on her emotions easier even if she didn't change her facial expressions.

"I need to get a look at that hand. Let's go in the bathroom and see if I have the supplies to fix this up."

Helping her to her feet, trying to get the feeling back into his own, he was careful to avoid bumping her left hand. She kept it cupped so the blood didn't pour out of her palm and followed him to the half bath.

As he cleaned the wound, he periodically glanced at her. She didn't wince or shy away as he used tweezers to pull a couple small chunks of the mug out of the wound. The weary expression on her face never changed as he thoroughly washed her hand with soap and water. His stomach gave a lurch when he saw the extent of the damage. The wound was too deep, with a gaping opening; it required stitches.

He told her he would drive her to the hospital to get it taken care of.

"That is not a possibility."

Angling her hand toward the light as he studied it, he raised an eyebrow. "Ava, I can't fully treat this here. You need medical attention."

"My suturing kit is in my bag."

Turning on the tap, she used her good hand to splash water on her face, wiping away the salty tears she'd shed. Gabriel handed her a towel and watched her dab herself dry.

She insisted on sitting in the breakfast room, where the natural light was the best. Producing a small bag from the backpack she used as a purse, she opened it and methodically set supplies out on the table: a curved needle, thread, a small bottle of clear liquid he assumed was alcohol, a pair of scissors, gauze pads, and another small tool that looked somewhat like a pair of scissors, but with blunt tips.

"Wash your hands. I will instruct you."

She held the small bottle of liquid in her right palm and deftly unscrewed the lid with the thumb and index finger of the same hand. Gabriel realized what she'd said and leaned back.

"What?"

Glancing up at him, she blinked. "I cannot press the skin together or tie the sutures without the use of both hands. You will have to assist."

"Oh, hell no."

"The wound needs to be sutured. There is a risk of infection and improper healing without them."

"Yeah, that's why you need to go to an emergency room," Gabriel said. "You need to see a licensed professional. The kind that took several years of studying and practicing and knows how to do this shit."

"I have the supplies and the knowledge-"

"Ava, I can't stick a needle in your skin."

He suddenly looked pale, and she could see his rapid pulse knocking in the side of his neck.

"I will give you very specific instructions."

"I can't hurt you."

The lines appeared between her eyebrows and Gabriel knew she didn't fully understand the concept. For her, the procedure was as it would be for a doctor; necessary and therefore unemotional. If he ever needed medical attention, she would have no trouble giving it to him because she could emotionally separate herself from him and get the job done. Most people couldn't; it was why people in the medical field weren't supposed to perform procedures on their own families and vets didn't treat their own pets.

"You cannot hurt me," she agreed softly. "I will meditate before you use the needle to minimize the pain, if it will make you feel better."

"Make me feel better? You have a gash in your hand and you're trying to make me feel better?"

He ran his hand down the back of his neck. "If you need me to sterilize, I can do that. I can hand you instruments. I can't jab that damn thing into your skin."

"If I try to do this with one hand, it will be awkward and sloppy. The risk of infection will be greater."

"Let me drive you to the ER."

"I do not-"

"Please."

His eyes had a slightly desperate look to them. Ava studied him for several moments before reluctantly nodding. She picked up the white towel she'd been using to cover the wound and wrapped it around her hand.

An hour and twenty minutes later they still sat in the waiting room, as far away from everyone else as they could get. The place was mostly females with children too young to be in school and older men and women old enough for retirement. This late in the morning, it wasn't too busy. One or two of the children were loud, but Gabriel had heard more obnoxious children and was grateful these ones were somewhat well behaved. Ava sat stiffly, filling out the usual forms in her careful hand before returning the clipboard to the front. She'd picked two chairs up against the wall farthest from the exit. They could see everyone from here, not that any stay-at-home moms or retirees would suddenly go on a killing spree.

One of the doors leading back to the examination and diagnostic rooms swung open. A nurse with a touch pad called Ava's name. Beside him, Ava became even more rigid. She made no indication that she'd heard the woman's voice, except to tighten her fingers on her knees.

She stared straight ahead.

Gabriel leaned forward so he could see her face. "You're up."

She nodded stiffly but remained as she was.

"Do you want me to come with you?" he asked, knowing she would never ask for his help.

Her head barely moved but she bobbed it up and down rapidly several times. For another moment, she stayed seated, until the nurse called her name again. Gabriel touched her shoulder.

"Are you ready?"

Standing, she walked woodenly toward the woman. Gabriel walked beside her but didn't touch her. Somehow, he knew she did not want to be touched right now. The examination was going to be... dicey.

Nina, the nurse's name tag read. She was a stocky, middle-aged woman with curly brown hair and freckles all over her face. She smiled as they approached her.

"Please wait here, sir. She'll be out shortly."

"I'm coming in with her."

The woman glanced at Ava as if she thought Gabriel was abusing her.

"It is in your best interest that he is present," Ava said.

Nina frowned but led them to a height and weight scale. "Please take your shoes off and step on to the scale. You can set your purse on the chair."

"No."

"Excuse me?" Nina was confused as hell. Gabriel would have felt sorry for her if he weren't so amused.

"I am five foot nine inches and weigh one hundred thirty-eight pounds."

"That may be-"

"It is."

"But I still have to take the measurements. Women tend to lie about their weight, especially in front of their boyfriends. I'll make him look away. It'll just take a minute, hon."

"His opinion of my anatomy is of no value to me. I do not lie."

Gabriel snorted. Ava stood where she was, keeping her distance from the woman.

"I'm just doing my job, here," Nina said, shifting her weight from one foot to the other. "We take every patient's height and weight at each visit. It's not personal."

"I gave my measurements. I have not had any weight fluctuation. I did not shrink."

Gabriel snickered.

Nina glared at him. Turning back to Ava, she said, "You can step backward on the scale so you can't see the number, if you're self-conscious about your weight."

"I am not self-conscious about my weight. It is above average for a woman in my age rage and height. I have exceptional muscle tone and my body fat percentile is twenty-one percent. It is my personal choice to refuse being weighed. You should probably know that information if you are a nurse."

Gabriel ducked his head and scratched his forehead to hide his grin. Something about Ava putting a person in her place gave him a kick.

Nina tapped her finger on the touch pad she was holding and turned on her heel.

"Follow me."

In the examination room, she logged into the computer and began typing. She had Ava verify her name and address. Then the fact that she didn't take any prescriptions.

Pulling a blood pressure cuff off a holder on the wall, she asked Ava to roll up her sleeve.

"No."

Nina sighed. "Now what?"

Ava was sitting with two fingers on her left wrist.

"My blood pressure is one-thirty over eighty-six."

"With all due respect-" Nina started, but Ava rested her hands in her lap and stared straight ahead.

"I understand you do not have a baseline to compare my blood pressure. One-thirty over eighty-six is very high for me. My average is one-twelve over seventy-six if you would like to note that in my file."

Nina raised her eyebrows. "Do you know why your blood pressure is so high?"

"I do not like nurses. This room is too small. The cut on my hand has caused my body to pump extra blood to move nutrients to the wound site to begin healing. Please move on. I need to leave this place as soon as possible."

"I need to take your blood pressure," Nina pressed, assuming Ava's dislike of nurses was an attitude problem. "Please roll up your sleeve."

"Ava."

She turned her head to Gabriel, and he cupped his hand under her chin.

"Look at me," he said softly. "Keep looking at me."

He ran his fingertips down her right arm to her hand, moving it toward the nurse. Pushing up her sleeve, he continued to look directly at Ava. From the corner of his eye, he saw Nina staring at the scars on Ava's arm. When the nurse touched her, Ava stiffened. Gabriel ran his thumb over her chin.

"Have you been practicing with the nunchucks I made you?"

Her body was trembling, but she kept her eyes on his and allowed the nurse to slip the cuff around her upper arm. At the sound of the inflation, she blinked rapidly. Gabriel rested his hand on her leg.

Her nod was barely visible.

Nurse Nina slowly released the air from the cuff, mentally counting.

"Do they work? Did I get the measurements right?"

Ava nodded again. Without looking, she reached over and tried to rip the cuff off. Gabriel took her hand and kissed her knuckles.

As Nina was removing the cuff, she shook her head in disbelief. "You were right on the money with your pressure, hon."

She typed more information into the computer.

"Of course, I was."

Glancing at Gabriel, Nina held up a thermometer, the kind that had to go in the ear. She raised her eyebrows.

"She's going to put something in your ear," he said to Ava. "Don't worry about it."

He nodded to the nurse.

"Just let the moment pass." He kept his voice low to soothe. "You will look back at this moment and realize how insignificant it is compared to all the other moments in your lifetime."

Ava's shoulders came up and she twisted in that way she did when she didn't want to be touched.

"I know," Gabriel said. "Just a little longer. Hold still."

Nina entered the reading into the digital file. She took a few moments to type notes into the computer, probably regarding Ava's refusals and bad attitude. The room was silent except for the clacking of the keys.

Ava and Gabriel continued to look at each other. He noticed her breathing had slowed a little and her eyes didn't look quite as wild.

At the computer, Nina was scrolling. She sucked in her breath a couple times and frowned. She was reading Ava's medical history, Gabriel thought. A patient's medical visits are logged and uploaded so they are available to all medical facilities in Wisconsin. Every visit, every injury Ava had ever suffered was documented in the computer, all available anytime her name was entered. Reading through all the details took some time. By the end, Nina had raised a hand to her mouth.

"Oh," she said softly. She took a deep breath and composed herself. Turning back to Ava, she asked in a false cheerful voice, "And what are we seeing you for today?"

Ava pried her eyes away from Gabriel and lifted her hand, taking the towel off. The cut was glaringly obvious in the bright lights.

"Oh, my." Nina seemed to have lost her ability to speak. She turned to the computer to type, and her fingers flew over the keys. "Did you take anything for the pain?"

"No."

"On a scale of one to ten, what is our pain level?"

"Zero."

Nurse Nina looked at her. "Your blood pressure is high, as you said, so I know your body is reacting to pain."

Ava shifted in her seat. Not uncomfortable, Gabriel saw. More like getting ready to launch out of it.

"If I have to explain everything I say twice, this is going to take too long."

Nina sighed. "I can make a note and the doctor can give you something."

"I do not take medication."

Pursing her lips, Nina chose not the argue this time. The young woman would see once the needle went into her skin. "How did that happen?"

Ava gave a brief description of how she had been holding a coffee cup earlier and squeezed it so hard it broke. She did not mention anything about the argument she and Gabriel had been having.

"You must be really strong," the nurse murmured as she clacked away, adding even more notes.

"I am," Ava said without a hint of arrogance.

Finished with the preliminaries, Nina locked the computer and spun around on the stool.

"Okay. I'll let the doctor know you're ready and he'll be in shortly."

"Thank you," Gabriel said, when it became apparent Ava was not going to speak.

When they were alone, he rubbed his thumb over her wrist in a slow, steady pattern.

"How are you doing, Ava?"

It took her a moment to focus on his face. "I do not want to be here."

"I know." He patted her knee. "No one likes hospitals. But you have to get your hand taken care of by someone who knows what they're doing."

The look on her face was baffling him. Her physical reaction was leaving him uneasy. She was shutting down, her body withdrawing into itself. Gabriel wasn't accustomed to seeing her unable to control herself unless she was asleep. He thought any minute she would start slamming herself against the walls like a wild dog.

"Did Ruth die in a hospital? Is that why you're so upset?" He kept his voice casual, trying to set her mind at ease.

"Nurses." She had to force the words out. "Janine was a nurse."

"Oh, fuck."

Realization hit him like a defensive linebacker. Of course. Janine, the foster mother who had stitched Ava up so she could be tortured again and again by Mack. No wonder Ava learned how to take care of herself. She avoided nurses at all costs, and when she had to face them, like when she visited David, she easily became combative.

Framing her face with his hands, he leaned his forehead against hers. "Can you hang in there, just this once?"

She closed her eyes and let out a shuddering breath.

"I'm sorry. I wasn't thinking."

Her skin was cold beneath his lips. All the color had drained from her face. Gabriel made a decision and stood, pulling her to her feet. "Let's go."

Startled, she whipped her head up to stare at him.

"We're leaving," he said, walking toward the door.

The thought of stabbing a needle into her made his stomach turn, but he couldn't stand to see Ava this way. He took her hand and led her toward the sign that pointed toward the lobby.

Nina was glancing at a chart as she walked toward the nurse's station. She glanced up as they passed. "Oh – hey! Dr. Timmons was just finishing up with another patient. He'll only be a couple more minutes."

Gabriel turned back to Ava. "Can you make it to the truck?"

"I will make it."

Her voice was almost inaudible.

"I'll be out in a minute."

He pressed the keys into her good hand and turned back to Nina.

Ava blindly made her way to the doors with the EXIT sign hanging over them. Shoving through them, she ignored everyone sitting in the chairs spaced strategically around the large atrium and headed straight for the door. Her blood was pounding in her ears so loud everything else was muffled. Her heart was slamming against her rib cage, making her chest ache with the force. So focused was she on her destination that she saw only the door, the way outside, the sunshine and the hope and her freedom.

A child stepped into her path, and she plowed into the boy. He was no more than eight or nine, and he flew backwards onto his butt and burst into tears. Ava was knocked back and lost her balance. Instead of falling, she bent at the knees, so she settled into a crouch.

Though she stayed frozen where she was, she assessed the boy's condition and judged him shaken but physically unharmed. She, on the other hand, was stunned. She needed a moment to gather herself.

"What's wrong with you?" a woman cried. Obviously the boy's mother, she ran to him and hovered over him, making a big show of checking him for injuries. "Didn't you see him walking right in front of you?"

She had not, and that was a problem. Losing her focus had caused her to misjudge her surroundings and had put a child's health at risk. These past few weeks she had lost more and more focus, hurting those around her. The only time she seemed completely aware and focused anymore was...

She hated to consider it, but her body was shutting down.

"I cannot do this," she said softly. She felt her will slipping, her desire to shrink inside herself growing.

"Did you say something?" Hover Mom asked, wiping the boy's cheeks with a tissue hard enough to scrape his skin off. "Do you have anything to say for yourself?"

Ava did not answer. She remained kneeling on the floor, the palm of her good hand flat on the carpet, her head down.

"I cannot do this," she repeated, her voice a breathless whisper. "I need your help."

• • • • •

After explaining briefly to Nurse Nina that the abuse she read about Ava suffering in her file had been done by a nurse, Gabriel felt he had eased the tension a little and was leaving on a good note. He hurried toward the waiting room.

He felt like he'd let Ava down, making her come here. Trivializing her reaction before she reminded him about her problem with nurses. She'd become combative with the nurse when she visited David because she was protecting him, but when there was no one to protect but herself, she became almost immobile with fear.

Stepping into the lobby, holding the door open for a nurse and an older woman using a walker, he saw Ava on the floor in a crouched position, facing the exit. A few feet away was a small boy and a woman Gabriel assumed was his mother, trying to calm him down. Instantly, Gabriel was on alert as he walked toward Ava.

A young woman, college-aged, with straight blonde hair several shades lighter than Isabel's, was hurrying over to Ava. She was going to reach Ava before Gabriel.

"Are you okay?" she asked as she reached out.

Ava's head whipped up and she growled at the woman, her body lunging forward as if she meant to bite her. The bellow echoed in the atrium, as loud as a lion's roar.

"Back off!" The Monster thundered, its deep voice echoing just as loud.

The young woman recoiled. Her mouth dropped open.

Everyone in the waiting room stared at Ava. The little boy burst into fresh tears. One receptionist held a phone receiver to her ear, ignoring the person on the other end. Another, in the middle of pointing to a form and explaining something to a new patient, paused in her explanation. She and the new patient gaped at Ava unabashedly. Patients waiting around the lobby had stopped texting, playing games, and checking their emails on their phones to watch the strange woman hunched over on the floor.

Standing, The Monster coldly studied the blonde that tried to help. Her eyes roamed around the room, taking in every person within her line of sight. Those that saw her eyes were baffled or scared. She felt their fear building and felt The Monster gaining strength from their fear.

Letting out a softer growl, she walked out of the building.

Gabriel swore under his breath on his way after her.

By the time he reached his truck, Ava was standing at the back of it, her arms braced on the tailgate. Even from behind her, Gabriel could see she was trembling. He approached her cautiously.

"Ava?"

Slowly, she turned around and leaned back against the truck. Her eyes were slate ovals as she crossed her arms over her chest.

"What happened?"

"She ran into the boy. He'll be fine. He's just scared."

Gabriel hated knowing The Monster was still in control, that Ava didn't feel safe enough yet to gain control and pull it back.

"His mom seemed upset."

"The bitch is overreacting. You humans coddle each other too much."

"Ava's okay now. You can go."

"She asked for my help."

"I don't believe you."

The Monster made Ava's lips curl into a sly smile. "I don't remember requesting your opinion."

"What happened to you?" Gabriel shoved his hands in his pockets, trying not to see Ava as he spoke to the thing inside her. "What made you hate humans so much?"

The Monster was caught off guard by the question. The shift in its eyes surprised Gabriel. He hadn't thought the thing capable of shock.

Gabriel moved forward. Instantly, Ava's right hand was at her side, curled into a fist, ready to strike. She held her left hand out, fingers splayed loosely, prepared to block if a strike came.

He motioned to the truck. "I was going to lower that so we can sit down."

Again, he seemed to have surprised it. Keeping her hands in the ready position, it moved Ava to the side and watched him carefully as he lowered the tailgate and sat down. Ava's arms dropped to her sides. After several moments, she hoisted herself up and sat as far as she could from him at the other end. She leaned back and rested her hands on the truck bed in a casual pose.

"Were you one?" Gabriel asked. When The Monster glanced sharply at him, he added, "A human?"

"That's none of your business."

"I'm curious. You interest me."

"Everyone has a past." Ava's leg swung back and forth over the edge of the tailgate. The dull black ovals that were The Monster's eyes watched people come and go from the hospital's revolving doors.

"Why did you start helping Ava?" Gabriel propped an elbow on his knee. Studying Ava's body language, he noted the stiffening of her muscles again. "That seems to contradict your opinion of humans being weak."

Ava was no longer leaning back on the bed of the truck. She was sitting up straight, frowning down at the towel wrapped around her hand.

"If she was so weak," Gabriel continued, "why didn't you despise her like you despise everyone else?"

Jumping off the tailgate, she gave him a glance from the corner of her eyes. "I'm done talking. I need to take care of this cut so it doesn't get infected. Take her home and help her fix it or fuck off so she can call Vincent."

"I'll help her."

Gabriel slid off the truck and closed the gate. The Monster didn't speak as he drove through Madison, and Gabriel didn't ask any more questions. It wasn't until they were out of the city that he realized Ava's body was tilting toward him. Glancing over, he saw her slump in the seat. Her head dropped, then swiveled toward him.

Hoping The Monster had left her for now, Gabriel continued to drive. He would have to wake Ava up soon enough so she could walk him through suturing her wound.

He wasn't looking forward to performing surgery.

•　•　•　•　•

During the day, with the sun shining and the grass dense and green, Hayden's grave didn't seem quite as dismal as when Isabel usually visited in the evenings. She led Griffin to the stone and rested her hand on the top of it, as was her normal greeting. The stone was cool in spite of the mild temperature. A nearby cedar tree provided shade throughout most of the day.

Isabel dropped her hand and stepped back, sitting in the grass in front of the marker. A moment later, Griffin folded his long legs and joined her.

"She had such beautiful eyes."

The abrupt sound of her voice seemed blasphemous in the serene emptiness of the cemetery. Halfway through a workday, no one else was in the area. The freshly cut lawn was fragrant as they sat quietly looking at the stone with Hayden's name etched into it. A variety of fresh flowers were placed around other headstones, making the area seem too bright, too festive. This was a place of death, not celebration. Why was the sun so damn bright?

"I was so jealous of her eyes," Isabel continued. "Mine are so boring. Green. Yippee. But hers – and Gabriel's – are such a mesmerizing blue. I used to wish I could see her in the mirror every morning like he does, just stare into those eyes, and have something of her left behind. Then maybe I wouldn't have this hole in my chest. What a stupid thing to want. Now I'm glad they aren't blue. Gabriel must be haunted every day of his life."

In fact, he'd told her once that looking in the mirror was like staring at a ghost. Every time he shaved, he tried to avoid eye contact with his reflection.

"You have wonderful eyes," Griffin said, brushing his hand over her leg.

"Really?"

"They remind me of a forest after a heavy rain, all green and fresh."

That seemed to surprise her.

"I especially like watching them when you sing. They go soft, and you relax in a way you rarely do any other time."

A flush lit her cheeks. "Anyway. It was a silly thing to wish for, but I was nine."

"The funeral was the worst," Griffin said, leaning back on his hands and stretching his legs out. He tilted his head up to the sun and closed his eyes. "Everyone kept asking how I was holding up. People break out the worst cliches at funerals. As I walked around, I'd hear people tell others how weird it was to be at Connor's wake but to see someone who looked like him walking around. It was like seeing his ghost, they said. Like I could help that I look like him, that I had chosen to live."

Izzie nodded. Thousands of years of practice, and still mankind was no better equipped to deal with death than he had been at the very start.

"Mom kept staring at me like I had lost Hayden." Her voice was not furious, as Griffin expected it would be. There was too much shock to allow any anger. "Like she had given me one job and I failed at it."

"But you didn't," Griffin assured her, turning his face from the sun, gazing at her. "It wasn't your job to protect her."

Shrugging, she plucked a blade of grass and concentrated on shredding it slowly, precisely.

"Maybe Hayden doesn't know that." Sitting up, Griffin took one of her hands. "Why doesn't she tell Ava what she wants? Why doesn't she talk to us?"

"I don't know, Izzie."

"I don't understand why she came to Ava if she doesn't have anything to say to us. Maybe we're not worth communicating with. Is she punishing us by being just out of reach?"

She didn't expect an answer. There was none.

After a beat, Griffin said, "My family wasn't enough to make Connor stay. I wasn't enough."

Isabel leaned toward him and placed her hands on his cheeks. Her large green eyes were so clear he could imagine himself falling into them. She didn't pretend to know what to say or try to comfort him. She only gazed at him and gently moved her thumbs back and forth along his cheeks.

"We're quite the pair, aren't we?" He raised his hands and lightly gripped her wrists.

"How long did you wait before you spread his ashes?"

Normally a morbid question, it seemed perfectly natural right now as they sat at Hayden's stone and held each other.

"Six months. I couldn't do it before then. I still can't sell Rover."

"Rover's a good boy."

Snorting, he nudged her arm with his elbow. "He's growing on me."

"Mom and Dad waited eight years to have Hayden declared legally dead."

Griffin waited patiently as Izzie pulled away from him, but instead of separating herself as she usually did, she turned and leaned her back against his stomach. He wrapped his arms around her. It was a small gesture, her leaning into him as she talked about her sister, but it meant the world to him. And it was a big step for her.

"They didn't want to let go, you know? I mean, I know seven years is the amount of time before a person can legally be declared dead, but they still couldn't do it. They were barely able to do it after eight."

She leaned forward and shifted, backing her bottom up against his groin, which sent a nice little thrill through him. Her new position seemed to satisfy her, and she seemed more comfortable. "I just kept waiting for her to come home, and then one day, Dad told me he and Mom were filing to have Hayden legally declared dead. Mom was upstairs getting a small bag together of what she wanted buried instead of her body."

"So, you waited eight years to mourn someone you'd lost on that first day," he murmured.

"I suppose so."

They were quiet for a while. A light breeze brought the fragrance of various flowers left by loved ones to them. Somehow sitting here with Griffin made Hayden's grave less ominous. It was simply a piece of stone sitting on a space of lawn in the warm sun. In the past sixteen years, Iz had managed to vilify this plot instead of using it to bring peace, as it was intended.

"Did Connor want you to spread his ashes, or you and your parents?"

Griffin had the feeling she already knew the answer.

"Just me."

"How did your parents take that?"

He curled a lock of her hair around his index finger. "My mum was extremely upset. But his will stated that I was to get his ashes, and what he wanted me to do with them. That's what I did."

"She wanted to keep them."

"Yes."

"He wanted them all spread, nothing left?"

Curling her in close to him, he lowered his head and spoke next to her ear. "Yes."

She didn't answer for so long he thought the conversation was over. Then she asked, "Did you give her some of him anyway? Because she asked?"

"No." His answer was immediate. "She begged me to, but I didn't give in. It was my duty to fulfill his wishes. I couldn't do it right away, but I did it his way when I could."

"I understand not being ready right away. But it's so morbid, holding onto something like that forever. I don't understand how some people can have their relative sitting on the fireplace mantel or hung around their neck like some talisman. It's disgusting."

"It's another denial of death," he said. "And another way to focus their grief and love. People have trouble letting go. I knew I would eventually spread his ashes, and I know that doing it in my own time was okay."

She rested her hands on his legs.

"Griffin?"

"Yes."

"Will you take me to the place you spread Connor's ashes?"

"Of course."

•   •   •   •   •

Daniel knew something was wrong the moment Ava and Gabriel entered the dojo. She bowed and greeted as she always did, but an obvious heaviness hovered over them. When he asked how she was doing, she said that she was doing well and thanked him in Japanese, but her tone was distant. He watched her walk back to put on her uniform before turning to Gabriel.

"You're welcome to hang around, but we train for two and a half hours before we get to the psychic part."

"I'm going to meet with a client, but I'll be back before training is over. Did she tell you about David?"

Daniel nodded. "I visited with him over the weekend. Is that why she's upset? He said he'll be fine with a few changes."

"He's recovering. My family found out about her..." Gabriel shrugged. "Ability. They know she sees my sister. Things are a little tense."

"She met your family?" The surprise was obvious on Daniel's face, as well as the pride.

"A few times now. Hayden is still a sore subject for my mom and sister. I don't know if they accept what they've been told."

He glanced toward the changing room, and Daniel saw an internal struggle. Would the younger man choose Ava, who had never lied to him and would never do anything to hurt him? Or his family, simply because they were his blood? Daniel's paternal instincts wanted to step in and defend Ava, but it wasn't his place. And Ava didn't need defending.

"Also, she has a pretty deep cut on her left palm from breaking a coffee mug," Gabriel said. "She hid it under her hoodie when she came in."

Daniel shook his head, smiling. After all these years, she still tried to downplay injuries so he wouldn't put off her training. The smile disappeared when he saw the look on Gabriel's face.

"What is it?"

"She wanted me to sew her up. I convinced her to go to the ER to get stitches. It didn't go so well."

"Ah. She reacted to the nurse."

"It was bad."

Gabriel shifted, wishing for once that Ava came with a manual, so he knew the right things to do for her, the right things to say.

"She's injured herself more since she's gotten to know me," he said thoughtfully. "I seem to be hazardous to her health."

"I think you're the best thing that's happened to her since David and Ruth took her in."

The statement surprised Gabriel. His eyes shifted to Daniel's, wondering just what he meant by that. Before he could ask, Ava exited the changing room in her uniform and stepped onto the mat. The left sleeve of her top was pulled down passed her hand.

Gabriel glanced at the time on his phone. "I'll be back later."

As the door started to close behind him, he heard Daniel say, "You might as well show me your hand."

Glaring after Gabriel, Ava walked over to Sensei, unwrapping the gauze. It had been packed and wrapped well, so it was protected against light activity. As she carefully unwound the outer bandage, he watched her, wondering how much he should bring up of what Gabriel mentioned.

"Nightmares?" He indicated her hand.

Ava stared at him, then shook her head. "It was another matter, Sensei."

With the bandages stripped away, the wound became clear. It ran the length of her palm. The cut was thick and red from the trauma. The stitches were not as precise as they were on Ava's other injury, and there were small puncture wounds next to the sutures that indicated hesitation to use the needle.

"Did Gabriel do this?" Daniel asked, turning her hand to study the work.

"He became queasy when I handed him the needle. I had to instruct him."

Daniel grinned. "That means he cares about you."

All in all, it wasn't that bad of a job for a first-time surgeon.

"His emotions cost time and may lead to infection of the wound. Had I been able to do it myself, I would not have wasted three hours."

He began to wrap it up again, satisfied that if they kept her training light, she would be okay. Gabriel had also applied butterfly bandages as reinforcements.

"He said he took you to the ER first."

"It was inconvenient," she said stiffly, and he thought he saw her flinch.

"Do you want to talk about it?" He already knew the answer.

Raising her head, she gazed at him. Anyone that didn't know Ava would have thought she was simply studying them, but Daniel knew Ava. She was desperately fighting to contain her fury.

"Why?"

"Gabriel said things didn't go well at the hospital. I thought you might want to discuss it. Obviously, it upset you."

A low grumble emanated from her as if it were oozing out of her very pores. It dragged on for several seconds, during which her eyes never left his.

Returning her gaze, he finished wrapping her wound and secured it.

"What happened is done," she said carefully. "I do not wish to speak of it."

Daniel nodded. As soon as the gauze was fastened to her hand, she nearly yanked it from his grip. Then instantly glanced up at him, surprised at her actions.

He tapped her on the shoulder to let her know they could begin and watched her walk to the other side of the mat.

She knelt gracefully. Eyes large, her expression unsettled, she glanced up at him and quickly away.

Taking a shaky breath, she settled her butt onto her ankles and rested her hands on her knees.

She was relieved when Sensei dropped the matter and began class.

$$\bullet \quad \bullet \quad \bullet \quad \bullet \quad \bullet$$

"You really don't have to do this."

Griffin glanced over at Izzie as he navigated the streets of Madison. They hadn't spoken much since he showed her the lake where he'd spread Connor's ashes. She was sitting at an angle in the seat, her legs drawn up, her hands in her lap. She looked relaxed and very un-Izzie-like.

"Are you uninviting me?"

"No," he said quickly. "It's just... The combination of three things you hate – eating, being in public, and my parents. It's not usually your idea of a fun times."

She didn't bother denying his assessment of her feelings for his parents. "Maybe I want to see your mother's face when she finds out I'm moving in with you."

He chuckled.

The restaurant they pulled into was different than the one Isabel had first met his parents in. It had valet parking. She wondered if Eve Turner had ever parked a car in her life. Iz hated to drive but felt awkward making someone else do a task she was perfectly capable of doing herself.

Inside, a beautiful young hostess walked them to the table where Griffin's parents were already sitting.

"Isabel!"

Griffin's father stood and gave her a kiss on the cheek.

"Oh," she said, not expecting the gesture. "Okay."

"It's so good to see you again." His face lit up and she could see he was being genuine. It mystified her that he enjoyed her company.

"It's good to see you again, too," she answered, just as bewildered to discover she was telling the truth. Griffin had said his mother raised him for most of his childhood, but he seemed to get his personality from his father. Thank God.

"Please, sit down."

He held her chair as she sat and pushed it in for her, another thing that made her feel awkward. How did the person pushing the chair in know how fast or slow to do it? In the movies, they always timed it perfectly. Nathan seemed to know exactly what he was doing.

Griffin had greeted his mother and reached behind Isabel to shake his father's hand. Iz stole a glance at Eve. The older woman was staring at her son, the mask of carefully controlled emotions set on her face. Yet Isabel sensed a sea of affection riding just below the surface, ready to burst. Why did she try so hard to contain it? What would be so bad about showing Griffin how much she loved him?

"Isabel," Eve said, turning her attention away from her son. "It's good to see you."

"Hello."

When they were all seated and their drinks ordered, Nathan made small chat, asking Isabel about her job.

"I quit," she said, sipping her water.

"I see. Congratulations?"

Smiling, she nodded. "I should have done it years ago. My boss is a dick."

An older woman from the next table glanced over at her.

"Was a dick," Isabel amended, remembering she no longer worked there. Then, remembering his character didn't change just because she was unemployed, she added, "Nope, he's still a dick. They didn't find a cure for it that fast."

Griffin hid a grin.

"Everyone believes they deserve more compensation and better treatment than they're getting," Eve said. Her lipstick had left a red mark on her glass of wine.

That's so disgusting, Iz thought. How is leaving that shit smeared on dishes socially acceptable but cigarettes are deemed a filthy habit?

"My wage was great," she said, resting her hand on Griffin's leg. "That's why it took so long for me to leave. The pay was amazing, and I had great benefits, including vacation time. But that didn't matter because I was denied time off. And they refused to adjust my schedule for necessary appointments, even though everyone else in the department was allowed to do it. Not to mention they all spoke to me in a degrading manner meant to make me feel inferior to my coworkers. Much the same way you speak to me, Mrs. Turner. Luckily, your opinion doesn't matter to me, so my self-esteem remains intact."

Isabel thought of Ava as she addressed Griffin's mother and kept her tone cool but neutral. Ava wouldn't take this woman's bullshit, and Iz didn't have to take it, either. Neither, for that matter, did her son.

Griffin's hand squeezed hers under the table. Thinking she'd upset him, she sneaked a glance from the corner of her eye. He grinned and squeezed her hand again.

"I'm sure I don't know what you're referring to," Eve said crisply.

"Why do rich people say that? Is there a handbook you people get at birth with a list of passive aggressive cliches to spit out when someone calls you out on your bullshit?"

Now several people from surrounding tables were glancing their way. One particularly nosy woman frowned at Eve, then turned her glare on Isabel.

"Eat it raw, lady!" Isabel snapped. "If you can't handle an occasional curse, go live in a convent."

Eve looked ready to chew through razor wire.

"Excuse me." The waiter had returned. "Is there anything I can help with?"

"We're ready to order," Nathan said.

After everyone had ordered, Nathan cleared his throat. "So, Isabel, are you looking into sticking with the same field, or trying something new?"

"I've been in the healthcare industry for six years, which will always be a growing industry." Iz ran her index finger up and down the stem of her wine glass. "People will always need healthcare. It's a stable choice."

Nathan raised his eyebrows. "But you're not sure you want to continue with it?"

"I guess I haven't decided yet. I'll probably get something that pays the bills until I figure it out."

Griffin rested his hand on her shoulder and brushed her cheek with his thumb. "You can take your time figuring it out while I pay the bills."

Iz stiffened ever so slightly under his hand. "I pay my own way."

Eve was staring at her son. "What do you mean by that, Griffin?"

He met her gaze. "Isabel is moving in with me."

"Congratulations," Nathan said, smiling at Iz.

Silence settled over the table. Around them, forks scraped against plates and murmurs of polite conversation continued. Griffin kept his hand on Isabel's shoulder, rubbing his fingers along the back of her neck in a slow, drugging rhythm. She glanced at his mother in the hopes that if her head exploded, she would get to witness it.

"Why would you allow that?" Eve asked, moving each piece of her flatware one centimeter to the right.

"I'm not allowing it. I asked her to move in with me."

"Why would you do something so foolish?"

"It's not foolish." Griffin's fingers paused for just a moment before continuing to massage Isabel's neck.

"I think it's wonderful," Nathan said. He lifted his glass toward Isabel. "You obviously make my son very happy, young lady."

"Thank you," she said, blushing. She lifted her glass and touched it to his. "He does the same for me."

Griffin and his mother continued to stare at each other.

"I'm in love with her," he said, and Isabel twitched at the stark honesty in his tone.

Eve's eyes were angry slits as she shifted them to Isabel.

"Don't look at me," she said mildly. She jerked a thumb at Griffin. "He started it."

Their food arrived. Dishes were served and drinks were replenished.

Everyone became too busy fussing over their meals to talk. Griffin ordered a steak, but it was covered with mushrooms and some odd porous yellow stuff. Some kind of whitish-yellow vegetable was cut up beside it.

Nathan had ordered a burger, but even it didn't look normal. It was placed on a weird bun with shredded lettuce and God knows what else and served with some kind of fries hidden under a mountain of what looked like feta cheese and green onions.

Eve's meal had Isabel staring. She couldn't help it. It looked as though a partially cooked egg had fallen onto a piece of stiff toast and broken open, spilling raw yoke. Small chunks of something brown surrounded it. Iz saw spices on the stark white of the egg as well. She didn't realize she had a disgusted expression on her face until Griffin nudged her.

"Are you okay?" he asked. He leaned over so their temples almost touched.

"What the hell is that?" she muttered, unable to look away.

"I believe that's uovo. Poached egg over focaccia bread with chanterelle mushrooms."

"That's nasty."

Griffin scoffed before he could stop himself. "I never acquired the taste."

They watched as Eve speared the concoction with her fork and sliced a piece off with a knife.

"Ugh." Isabel felt queasy. "Of all the ways to eat a dead baby chicken, that way never entered my mind."

Eve set down her knife and fork and fixed them with an icy stare. "I don't know about Isabel, but you weren't raised in a barn, Griffin Nicholas Turner. You're being extremely rude."

Hanging his head, he tried not to smile. "Sorry."

"Sorry," Isabel echoed. She bit her lower lip to keep from laughing.

She turned to her salad, which didn't look ordinary either. It had three distinct types of lettuce, an odd myriad of spices in it, and the house dressing was some vinaigrette with a name a mile long that she couldn't remember. Had this restaurant never heard of romaine lettuce?

Under the table, Griffin kicked her ankle the way Gabriel used to do when they were younger. Waiting for Eve to look away, Isabel returned the kick, satisfied when he grunted in pain.

· · · · ·

Gabriel couldn't stop the guilt he felt about making Ava go to the hospital. She'd gone to appease him, to keep him from having to do something he didn't want to do, and it had cost her dearly. What would have happened if they hadn't left when they did? Would she have assaulted someone? Would The Monster have taken over completely and blasted through bodies until Ava's strength gave out or hospital security tackled her?

Nausea rolled through him.

"Gabriel? Did you hear me?"

He blinked. Patty Meyers was looking at him expectantly. "I'm sorry, Patty. What did you say?"

"I asked if you could get the cabinet done before Memorial Day," she repeated. "I'm having company over and if I had a nice cabinet to show off, I might bring you more clients."

Gabriel estimated the time it would take to make a blueprint, build, and assemble the approximate size of cabinet Patty was looking for, and allow a margin of time for any hiccups that came along. He checked the calendar he used on his phone for scheduling to see when he could fit the project in.

"Sure, I can do that. I'll draw up a few designs and estimates and we can meet again to discuss what you want to go with."

"Thank you, dear, you're a Godsend. And thanks for meeting me in Madison. I know it's a bit of a drive for you. I had to take my sister to her dialysis treatment, or I would have been in Langdon."

"It worked out, Patty. I was in town on other business, anyway. I should have those designs to you by the end of the week."

He closed the notepad he carried around everywhere and stuck it in his jacket pocket.

"She must be a special woman."

"Excuse me?"

"Ava Reid. She must be pretty special to put that far off gaze in those pretty blue eyes of yours." Patty smiled and patted his arm.

"How do you know about us?"

They rarely went out in public, and when they did, it was usually at a secluded park. They weren't hiding their relationship, but they weren't flaunting it.

Chuckling, she touched his shoulder. "Everyone in Langdon knows about you two. We're all so interested in the quiet girl on the outskirts of town that managed to snag the town's longest-running bachelor."

Just what they needed. Gossip.

"Oh, don't worry," Patty said, gathering her purse. "I won't give them anything to chew on. You have a good rest of your evening, Gabriel."

As she walked out of the coffee shop, Gabriel's eyes were aimed in her direction, but he didn't see her. Already, his irritation of meddling neighbors had faded. He wondered if he was making things worse for Ava. Would any of her injuries have happened if he hadn't pushed himself into her life? He didn't know what she did in the early morning hours when he wasn't there to stop her from falling down the stairs or climbing out a window. Maybe not all her scars were from abuse she endured as a child; maybe some were from prior nightmares. Or maybe her nightmares were worse because she was staying at his house or because he was lying next to her. He could be exacerbating her issues.

He left the coffee shop, yanking open his truck door. Drumming his fingers on the steering wheel, he sat for a few moments without starting the engine.

This morning, when he told Ava he wouldn't leave her by choice, he hadn't been blowing smoke. He didn't cut and run when a problem arose, whether it was in a relationship or while working on a stubborn piece of wood in his shop. Each issue deserved the same attention; an innovative approach to find the solution. There was always a solution.

But what if he was the problem?

When he started driving toward the dojo, he wondered what Daniel had meant when he said he thought Gabriel was the best thing that had happened to Ava. How could that be, when she was getting beat to hell and possessed worse now than when they first met?

Was it possible to help her if he was the one harming her? Was she so confused about figuring out all the rules of dating and social interaction that she was causing herself physical harm? Or even worse, that she was distracted and unable to defend herself as easily as she usually could?

In the parking lot, he checked the time. Ava had a little less than half an hour of class. He liked to watch her train and knew his presence didn't affect her. She had a quiet intensity anyway, but once she entered the dojo, it magnified. A parade could march by outside and she would continue without missing a beat.

He walked toward the building with a bottle of water and with the sun at his back. Because of the glare off the large front window, he couldn't see what was going on inside but could hear sharp clacking sounds. Upon opening the door, he fought against every instinct to rush in.

Daniel and Ava were sparring with six-foot staffs. They were moving quickly around the mats in an elegant fight that had Gabriel's instincts pushing him to step in to defend Ava.

Stupid, of course. He would get his ass kicked by both parties if he interfered. Ava clearly did not need defending. That logic didn't stop his instincts from kicking in.

The door closed behind him softly and he stayed where he was to make sure he didn't distract them. They were beautiful. There was no other way to describe what Gabriel saw as he watched his girlfriend and her teacher fight as if their lives depended on it. He didn't know if they were striking at full force. They looked like they were, and the sounds of the clashing wood sounded like they were. They moved smoothly, sliding in and out of stances with such speed it was hard to see where one ended and another began. Their bodies whirled and spun in the air between hits always for a purpose: either to gain strength with the strike or open or close distance between each other. No move was wasted, and though it looked like ballet with sticks, Gabriel could tell that if he were on the wrong side of the staff, it could do severe damage.

This was like breathing for them, Gabriel realized. It wasn't just a hobby, or a workout regimen. This was a way of life they had chosen that affected them in every way.

He also realized that trust was essential to training. Even though the staffs had no sharp edges, they could still injure if used improperly or if a stance were off by even an inch. Ava completely trusted in Daniel not taking advantage or her. She trusted he would never intentionally hurt her. She purposely put herself in a position to get maimed three times a week with only the word of her teacher that he wouldn't take advantage of her.

Holding the staff horizontally with a hand several inches from each end, Daniel thrust his staff forward into Ava's vertical one with a loud crack. The impact lifted her off her feet and knocked her back across the mat. Gabriel again had to fight to keep from interfering. Ava hit the mat on her butt and instantly rolled back over her left shoulder, raising into a crouched position. She held her staff ready but remained where she was, staring up at her teacher from under her lashes.

She didn't look seductive, Gabriel thought, the way women usually used the look. She looked dangerous.

"Good," was all Daniel said.

Nothing in Ava's expression changed but Gabriel could tell the simple word of praise meant everything to her. She thanked her teacher in a monotone, but her body language radiated gratitude and respect.

She stood and they bowed to each other.

"Have a seat, Gabriel."

Gabriel sat on the bench with his water bottle, suddenly thirsty. Watching other people exercise this vigorously was draining.

Setting the staffs aside, they faced each other, bowed, and began sparring again, this time hand to hand. Punches, blocks, kicks, sweeps, all executed fast enough that Gabriel had trouble keeping up as he tried to follow their progress back and forth around the mats. He enjoyed their individual styles. Daniel was intimidating in his confidence yet light on his feet, his power evident behind every move he made. Ava was versatile, her limbs moving like flowing reeds or snapping out like metal rods. Each technique seemed effortless. Her speed was shocking.

Most impressive to Gabriel was what he didn't see. At no time during the showdown did he see evidence of The Monster. Ava was good, she was damn good, but Daniel had over fifteen years of training and life experience on her. Several times he was able to get a good strike in, knocking her back a few feet or dropping her to the floor. Gabriel was watching her closely and never saw that flash of rage in her eyes he was getting used to that indicated The Monster had taken over to protect her. Her breathing remained impossibly steady, without any of the snarling or growling that usually accompanied her uninvited guest. Ava didn't feel threatened even though she was being punched, kicked, and thrown around the mat like a sweaty towel. She had complete trust in her teacher.

In fact, she was enjoying herself. Her eyes were bright with adrenaline, her face flushed with pleasure. Each time Daniel gave her a teeth-jarring punch, she came back at him with renewed vigor. She was proud to take the hit. She basked in the physical aspect of the training. Gabriel had never watched anyone so enthusiastic about a confrontation.

Finally, when there was space between them for more than two seconds, Daniel said something that sounded to Gabriel like "Yah-may" or "Eee may". Ava's body instantly relaxed its rigid combat disposition. It was a subtle change; she stood with her arms at her sides and her eyes lost the intensity they had when she was training. They bowed to each other and returned to where they had started on the mat, kneeling across from each other.

They went through the routine Gabriel recognized from the other night with Vincent: Daniel asked Ava if she had any questions, which they then discussed. Then they said a few words in Japanese and did a little ceremony – Ava had said previously that this was known as "bowing in" or "bowing out". She'd told him the words they said at the beginning and end of every class, but he couldn't remember what they were or what they meant. He supposed that repetition of the routine helped students to learn the language as well as the meaning behind the words.

Daniel then released Ava to go change. He stretched his legs out before him as she stood and walked off the mat.

"Did you have a good meeting with your client?" he asked Gabriel. He folded one leg in and twisted his torso, laying against his outstretched leg to stretch his obliques.

"I got the job."

"You don't seem very happy about it."

"What? No, it's fine. It's good." He unscrewed the cap on his water bottle, screwed it back on.

"Are you worried about what happened today with Ava?"

He nodded. The bench was uncomfortable after thirty minutes of sitting on it. He stood and walked to the door, turned back.

"I shouldn't have taken her to the hospital. But I don't know anything about stitches. I'm not a damn doctor."

He folded his arms across his chest. Staring at the floor, he turned back toward the door and walked to the wall.

"You did a fine job."

"I didn't want to hurt her."

"She has a high tolerance of pain. Gabriel, she's fine."

He stopped and turned to look at Daniel, his eyes full of despair. The kid was beating himself up about it.

"It's my fault she cut her hand in the first place."

"Why don't you start from the beginning, so I know what you're talking about?" Daniel said. "Take off your boots so you can pace on the mat."

Gabriel sat and began fumbling with his laces.

"She tried to break up with me this morning. She thought her connection with Hayden would cause a problem between my family and me. I told her she was taking the easy way out. I kept pushing her, telling her..."

He tucked his boots under the bench, where the students stowed their footwear while they trained.

"What did you tell her?" Daniel coaxed.

Gabriel ran a hand down his face. "I told her she pushes people away because it's easier than caring about them. She was making excuses to avoid getting close to me."

Standing, he stepped onto the mat in his socks and began to pace a larger area.

"I used David and Ruth against her. I just wanted-" Pausing on the mat, he tried to recall how he had justified the things he'd said that morning for her benefit. The morning already felt like it had happened days ago.

"You pushed her so she would break." Daniel curled his legs into the Lotus position. There was no emotion in his voice.

"She was already about to blow a gasket. She was shaking... crying..."

"Did it work?"

"That's where the cut on her hand came in. She crushed a coffee mug. Once she lost it and finally let it all out, she seemed better, until I fucked up and took her to the hospital."

He summarized their visit.

"You couldn't know the extent of her trauma regarding nurses."

"She told me Janine used to fix her so Mack could play with her again." Gabriel couldn't quite stop a wince. "That's how she said it. I knew the history before today."

"Take a seat."

He kept pacing, rubbing his chin absently. Somewhere in the back, he heard a shower running.

"Gabriel, sit."

Snapping out of it, Gabriel walked over and sat across from Daniel, leaving several feet between them like Ava did. He felt strange without his boots on.

"Emotional release, especially for Ava, is physically draining. She was a ball of nerves when David first brought her to me. Now she does whatever it takes to avoid returning to that state. But repression isn't good for anyone."

In the back, the shower stopped.

"She has to learn the difference between control over her emotions and avoiding them," Daniel continued.

He stretched his legs out to his sides until they were almost parallel to Gabriel. He caught the younger man's wince at the ease with which he did the splits and held back a smile.

"As far as her behavior at the ER... from what you said, I think she behaved surprisingly well. She agreed to go, to spare you discomfort. She cares about you. You should be flattered."

"I am," Gabriel admitted.

"Your decision to push her into dealing with her emotions was the correct one."

"How can you tell? She barely said two words to you when she came in."

Smiling, Daniel tucked one leg so he could lean to the side and touch the toes of his foot on the opposite leg, finishing stretching his side muscles.

"She had a very productive class. Her focus was intense, her timing was precise. Her head was clear. It's been several weeks since she's been this present."

They heard shuffling in the back room. Something fell, causing a loud noise. Daniel glanced toward the curtain separating the changing room from the dojo, waiting to see if Ava needed any help. No more noise was heard.

"And distracting her while the nurse took her vitals was a great idea, too," Daniel continued. He switched legs again, stretching his other side to keep himself busy even though he'd already done so. He wanted to keep talking with Gabriel. He didn't want Gabriel to give up on Ava, he realized.

"What?" Gabriel tore his gaze from the curtain.

"What you're doing works. She'd let you know if it didn't."

Thinking about that for a moment, Gabriel nodded.

Ava awkwardly elbowed her way around the curtain, carrying bandages and gauze balanced on her left forearm. She bowed slightly to the kamidana, holding the supplies as level as she could so they wouldn't tumble out of her arms. Keeping her hand turned up to keep the exposed cut from hitting anything, she made her way quickly across the mat toward them.

She apologized in Japanese to them.

"I cannot get my hand wet, so it took me twice as long in the shower."

"Not a problem," Daniel said. "I'll be right back."

Gabriel didn't notice when he walked off the mat. He was watching Ava as she stopped in front of him. Kneeling on the mat, she unceremoniously dumped everything in her arms, trying to hurry. When he reached out to picked up antibiotic ointment, she snatched it up.

"I can do it." Though she all but snarled, Gabriel knew the restricted use of her hand was making her frustrated more than angry.

"I'll be faster," he said.

He held out his hand. Her shoulders sagged slightly but she handed him the tube. He peeled open a cotton swab and squeezed ointment onto the tip.

"You had all these supplies in your bag before you cut your hand, didn't you?"

"Yes."

Only Ava would have a suture kit in her gym bag. She also had one in her Equinox.

As he gently dabbed the skin, he could tell she was watching his face, not his hands.

When he had pierced her skin with the needle earlier, she hadn't flinched once. She guided him through how to sterilize the tools, pull the needle through, and tie the suture thread as if she were instructing medical students. Using a quiet, calm tone, she had not only told him what to do but what her body was doing to heal itself on a cellular level. The hypnotic tone and the way her hand remained steady throughout the procedure had taken his mind off the gruesome aspect, allowing him to get the job done.

He finished with the ointment and set the cotton swab on its wrapper.

Glancing at her, he saw her watching him with that intense gaze she often had.

"How are you doing?" he asked, packing the area with gauze pads as a barrier against any impacts her hand sustained.

"You are doing very well," she said. She glanced down to watch him work. "You are thorough, with exceptional dexterity. I barely feel you."

Daniel walked out from the back. He was now wearing jeans and a tee shirt, his tabi replaced with regular socks. He watched Gabriel wrap Ava's hand slowly, making sure he covered the entire wound, that he didn't wrap it too tight. He studied the look of concentration on Gabriel's face as he worked. The kid was in deep with her.

And what of Ava? Daniel turned his focus on his student. She and Gabriel were both leaning forward so close their foreheads were almost touching. She was watching Gabriel's face curiously.

She's in love with him, Daniel thought.

He wondered if she realized it yet.

Gabriel taped the last of the wrap in place. His hands lingered on Ava's a moment before he released her and began gathering the materials on the mat.

"We're going to try something different today for the psychic session," Daniel said, pulling a set of car keys from his pocket. "Let's go for a ride."

• • • • •

Isabel glanced at the television and thought How does my bra keep ending up on the TV?

"I think I broke a hip," Griffin wheezed.

The sound of his heart thudding against her ear and her own heart pummeling in response was the most beautiful conversation she had ever heard.

They were lying sideways on the bed. Iz was sprawled across Griffin's chest. Where the hell had that come from? She hardly ever instigated sex, and never liked being on top. The position made her feel particularly vulnerable and on display, and she shied away from it.

After a moment, she croaked, "Holy shit."

She'd had at Griffin like a starving dog attacks a discarded scrap of meat. As soon as he entered the apartment, she grabbed onto him, preventing his confused greeting with a kiss so hot he dropped his messenger bag. As she plundered his mouth, she pulled at his shirt and began unbuttoning it. She kept his mouth busy as she hurriedly backed toward the bedroom, so she didn't lose contact with him. Even after his shirt was undone, she gripped it and pulled him with her to the bed.

Now they lay replete with love and satisfaction.

The first attempt to lift her head caused a wave of dizziness to wash over her. Her head fell back to his chest. Griffin ran his hand along the curve of her back with obvious affection. The therapeutic effect of the movement was comforting, but the emotional rewards were much better. Somehow that sliding of his fingertips along her spine made her feel vulnerable and sexy at the same time.

"What..." Griffin cleared his throat, tried again. "What was that for?"

Feeling heat rise into her cheeks, Iz smiled. "Do I need a reason for wanting to have sex with my boyfriend?"

"You're not usually the instigator, Izzie," he said, kissing the back of her hand. "Not that I'm complaining."

"Today is the first time I was able to talk about Hayden without crying or drinking. Or both. I think your mom's warming up a little. It's been a really good day."

"That it has."

"How does my bra keep ending up on the television?"

Griffin turned his head. "Will you look at that?"

Iz shifted, lifting herself until she was straddling him. Her eyes were still dazed. "That's the second time it's ended up there."

He grinned up at her.

"Well..." She glanced around, looking for her panties. "I should go to my place and start packing. Where's my underwear?"

She lifted herself off him and tried to remember at what point he'd ripped them off her, so she had an idea of where to look for them.

"Do you want some help?"

"Yeah, I can't remember if you took them off before or after my bra..."

Laughing, Griffin sat up and watched her. "I meant help packing."

He leaned down and picked up his boxers.

"Oh. Sure."

"We can bring the few boxes we get filled back. Rover can fit quite a few in him, and even some furniture. This will be the first time I've ever spent time in your flat. The last time, it didn't take long for you to wrestle me to get to the coffee shop. I didn't get much time to look around."

"Aha." Iz leaned out into the living room and plucked her panties and jeans off the floor. Yes, he'd dropped them there just after he nearly yanked her out of them, desperate to touch.

Turning back to Griffin, she stepped into panties, tossed the jeans on the bed. "Just think of any trailer trash you've ever seen in a movie, and that's what my apartment looks like. Minus the crystal meth and cigarettes. You're not missing out."

Pulling her bra off the television, she hooked it around her chest, spun it so the cups were at the front, and was looping the straps over her shoulders when she raised her head to find Griffin frowning at her.

"What?"

"You don't even realize you're doing it, do you?"

"What are you talking about?"

She walked to the closet for clean socks. Griffin waited until she was back in the bedroom, fumbling to get one leg of her jeans right side out.

"Putting yourself down. It comes naturally to you."

"I don't even remember what I said."

Sliding into her jeans, she didn't realize he was still studying her until she finished buttoning up, raising her head again. She read the frustration on his face. She walked over to him and stood between his knees.

The simple pleasure of his arms snaking around her and pulling her close made her sigh. She ran her hands through his hair and kissed him, slow and sweet, before pressing his cheek to her belly.

"I'll work on it," she promised.

His arms tightened around her. "You mean everything to me."

"I'll try harder."

His hair was soft against her stomach. Iz liked to run her palm over the top of it, feeling the slight waves brush against her skin. She would do anything for him. If he asked her to run naked down State Street during a full moon, she probably would have.

Slowly, so his body rubbed against hers all the way up, Griffin stood. He pressed his lips to her forehead.

"Thank you."

"You're welcome." She gave him a wicked smile. "Are you going to help me go pack, or are we going to go a second round?"

•　•　•　•　•

Ava hated malls. She hated the music blaring out of most stores that clashed with the music blaring out of the overhead speakers. She hated how people walking in small groups would stand three or four bodies wide, blocking the walkways. The ones that walked slow aggravated her the most. When she was in a mall, she knew which store she was going to, what product she was buying, and where in the store it was located. She didn't want people in the way discussing weekend plans that could have just as easily been discussed in the Food Court, out of everyone else's way.

But the worst part about a mall to Ava was how busy it was in her head. The moment she entered the building, chaos began. Constant, mindless chatter. It filled her head and grew in volume until she felt like her ears were bleeding.

Avoiding touching was nearly impossible during peak hours; people did not look where they were going and often bumped into one another without apology. Ava's head became like a transmitter catching every channel simultaneously.

Sensei knew all this information about her, so when he pulled into the JC Penney parking lot attached to West Towne Mall, she immediately grew suspicious. The muscles in her back and shoulders began to tighten.

"I thought we'd try a different exercise today," Sensei said, turning sideways in his seat so he could speak to both more comfortably.

Gabriel was looking around with an unreadable expression on his face. Ava stayed sitting facing forward in the back center of the seat. Her body was stiff, and she refused to look at Daniel.

"Let's go."

He climbed out of his sedan without waiting to see if they were following.

Because of the mild weather, the parking lot wasn't as full as it was in the winter, when walking outside wasn't an option. Gabriel had seen older people walking around the floors in the mall for exercise on many occasions when a client insisted on meeting in the Food Court for consultations. He was relieved that today was warm enough to encourage outside activities; he had a feeling whatever Daniel had planned wasn't going to be enjoyable.

They followed the teacher into the store.

JC Penney wasn't busy, nor was it the destination. Winding through sections of clothing, purses, and perfumes, Gabriel wished he could watch Ava to see how she was doing without being too obvious. But she was walking several feet behind them. Her usual confident gait was hesitant. Twice when he glanced back, he saw her wince as she passed a group of people. Her head was down, her shoulders hunched, like an abused animal. The closer they came to the entrance into the mall, the slower she walked.

Glancing back at her for the third time, he almost walked into Daniel, who had slowed his pace to match Gabriel's. He moved to the side and kept walking, wondering if they should stop and wait for Ava.

"I'm going to need your help," Daniel said, keeping his voice low.

Gabriel raised an eyebrow. "Sure."

It was very weird to see the man out of his martial arts uniform.

"It's going to be very difficult for Ava to block out the noise in here."

It already is, Gabriel thought, thinking his ears would shatter when a child shrieked from the play area up ahead.

"I need you to help focus her attention."

"Me?"

How the hell could he do that? He already wanted to find the kid that was throwing a fit somewhere down by the Pottery Barn and throttle him.

"She trusts you, and you can help redirect her attention. I need to push her, hard, to get her to block outside stimuli."

"You picked a hell of a place to throw her in," Gabriel muttered.

"That's the point. I've been too gentle with her, and it's costing her. We've been working on this for weeks, and she's still not strong enough to defend herself from a psychic attack."

They reached the entrance to the mall and Gabriel's stomach pitched. Immediately in front of them, in the center aisle, was the play area. Young kids were running around a Thomas the Train engine and crawling over a large smiling toy rotary phone. One kid sat on a cartoon-looking cow; a toddler stood hanging onto a fat pig sitting a few feet from a large red barn that was hollowed out with a slide at one end. Still another kid was jumping on a massive multi-colored xylophone. Thank God that didn't make noise. The entire area was surrounded by a three-foot wall with a bench seat attached to keep the kids somewhat contained and the parents comfortable while they waited.

The noise was head-splitting.

"She's not going to like this," Gabriel groaned.

Daniel gave him a sideways glance. "She doesn't have to. It's your job to make sure she can tolerate it."

They both turned to find Ava several feet behind them, glowering.

Gabriel felt a stab of sympathy for her. In addition to the kid's play area, she would have to deal with the constant traffic of people going in and out of the stores on all four sides of it. She was either going to get this right or The Monster was going to level this end of the mall.

All Gabriel had to do was keep her focused on something other than everything around her.

No pressure.

"Ava, come up here."

She kept her wary eyes on Sensei as she approached him.

"We're going to the Food Court," Daniel said. "Try to block out as much as you can from here to there."

The look she gave him clearly showed she doubted his sanity.

"Just give it a try," Daniel said. "It's not realistic to always practice in total silence in the dojo."

He turned toward Gabriel. "Leave her be for now."

They started toward the Food Court. It was close; a few hundred yards past the Play Area, they turned left. A long, wide hall, filled with more people, kiosks, and businesses on both sides, would lead them to the Court.

Gabriel glanced around, curious. He hadn't been here in so long, at least two dozen stores had changed. He remembered coming here when Beth was still young enough to think it was so cool to hang out with her friends. How old had he been? Eight or nine? She'd been a teenager, so she could go off with her friends while he, Isabel, and Hayden had to stay with Mom and Dad. He never saw what the big deal was. Overcrowded, tiny stores with overpriced products he didn't want. Isabel visibly paled around so many people. To ease her discomfort, he would play games with her while Hayden, ever the socialite, tried on sunglasses or jewelry at a kiosk nearby. Isabel and Hayden were so close in age, yet so different. They were barely nine months apart – when Gabriel was older, he would tease his parents about not being able to wait long after Hayden's birth before they were at it again – but from their personalities, they could have come from different planets.

Hayden had always been daring, expressive, and charismatic, even at so young an age. While eating at a restaurant or waiting in any line, she could strike up a conversation and keep it going with whomever was near her. People found her interesting and wanted to be her friend.

How odd, he thought now, that in life, she couldn't shut up, but now, when they wanted so badly to hear from her, she couldn't seem to find anything to say.

Unlike Hayden, Isabel was an introvert, sarcastic to the point of being caustic, and reserved. Her shyness had cost her numerous friendships simply because people confused her shyness with snobbery. The only time Iz took a break from thinking was when she was with Hayden or Gabriel. Around them, she laughed openly and joined in conversations, which was how she made friends. She was only truly relaxed around her family, so when Hayden went missing, Isabel lost a piece of herself. Gabriel could see it in everything she did.

She didn't want to go out in public anymore. Their parents practically had to drag her out to go to restaurants or to see a movie. On the rare occasion she went out in public, she looked around as if lost. At home, she spent hours sitting on Hayden's bed, writing in notebooks. When she wasn't writing, she lay staring at nothing with a blank expression on her face for several minutes at a time. Gabriel often sat next to her on the bed, holding her hand, so he didn't have time to go to malls.

He hadn't missed much, he thought as he made his way through streams of people going in the opposite direction. Someone walked by loudly chewing bubble gum that smelled like sour apples. Grunting at the overpowering odor, he tried to concentrate. Ava was struggling with all the voices in her head.

They reached the Food Court.

"Outstanding," Gabriel growled.

The vendors lined every wall. Tables and chairs were set up in the main area, making it impossible for Ava to sit with her back to a wall. The smells from various cuisines were overpowering.

Gabriel felt her mentally pull back as clearly as if she was tugging on his shirt.

Daniel scanned the area quickly and walked to a small table near a vendor selling gyros on the west side of the plaza. Not as many people were in that area, and Gabriel immediately saw why. There was no vendor in the outlet between a steakhouse and the gyro place. She could have a wall at her back, and it was a short distance away from the masses. Daniel moved the chairs as close to the empty slot as he could.

Gabriel glanced back at Ava before following Daniel, helping him move the table. He felt the pulling sensation leave his mind and Ava stiffly walked toward them. Her head was down to block out as much sensory input as she could.

"Sit between us," Daniel told Ava, pulling out a chair for her.

She did not like that idea at all. Enclosing her between two people felt too much like being in a cage.

"I know you don't like it," he said, as if he was looking inside her head. He had been reading her mind since she was seven years old. "Do it anyway."

When she sat, her back was rigid and her muscles stiff. She stared out into the atrium with eyes burning intensely, her body pulsing with overwhelming confusion and hostility.

Several vendors had short lines of people waiting to order. The place was getting busier as the day grew later. Gabriel tried to view the scene before him as she did: a myriad of shapes and sizes jumbled together, too many colors bleeding into each other, a constant low hum vibrating in the ears interrupted occasionally by a bark of laughter or a squeal of metal against metal. Christ.

"We can't expect you to keep spirits out of your body if you can't even tune external stimuli out of your head," Daniel said. "You must have control over your body at all times or nothing you learn about communication is relevant."

Sitting next to her, Gabriel felt as if he had wandered too close to a live wire. The hairs on his arms and the back of his neck were standing straight up.

Keeping her gaze straight ahead, she placed her hands flat on the table. Her fingertips curled into the Formica.

"Breathe." Daniel had to raise his voice slightly to be heard over the hum of conversations in the Court, but he kept his tone calm and soothing. "Focus on each breath."

Ava winced when a young woman brayed laughter.

Too loud!

Gabriel and Daniel twitched at the scream inside their heads.

"You must get control over this, Ava," Daniel said. "It is as important as being able to defend yourself from a physical attack. The control must always be there. You have to live it, breathe it. Let it become a habit. Let it become your life. Or your life isn't going to be yours."

Make the noise stop.

Her eyes were huge. Gabriel had never seen them so large. She blinked, and they were black. Blinked again and they were gray. She let out a soft growl.

"Ava."

Daniel leaned forward. She snarled at him, shoving out with her mind. They both felt the sensation, akin to recoil after a gun is fired. It was so strong it pressed them back in their chairs. Lowering her head, Ava closed her eyes and shook it. Her hair fell in a curtain around her face. Her fingers were so tense on the table that her arms were shaking.

"You need to be able to block out everything around you," Daniel continued. "I know you can do it, Ava. You did it as a child when you were brought to me."

Make them all go away.

Lifting her head, she opened her eyes. They were black.

She made a strangled noise in the back of her throat. A tear fell down her cheek.

Looking over her head, Daniel nodded at Gabriel.

Unsure what to do, going with his instincts, Gabriel leaned close to her, careful not to touch. He rested his arm on the table next to her hand so she could see him. With his lips close to her ear, he deliberately inhaled, held it, then exhaled. Again. On the third inhale, she audibly copied his breathing pattern.

"Ava, I'm right here." He lifted his hand and used his middle finger to gently tap the back of her hand twice, so softly he barely made contact, before sliding his fingers under her palm. Her hand relaxed, allowing him to lift it off the table.

Hurts it hurts so loud -

"I know it hurts," he soothed. He moved their hands up by her chin so she could smell him. "You have to let me help you."

He's too strong I can't stop him.

"We'll do this together," Gabriel said. "Listen to my voice."

Using his thumb, he swept it over the back of her hand, back and forth, slowly, rhythmically. He kept his eyes on hers.

An image flashed into his head: Ava as a young child with a heavy chain around her wrist, tethered to a beam in an old, ratty barn. The young girl lunged, the chain tightened, and her arm was yanked out of joint, disfiguring her. She howled, falling to the floor.

Gabriel rubbed his fingers across his forehead, trying to focus. Ava's thoughts were wildly bouncing around. She would never get control this way. Glancing at Daniel, he was sure Ava had projected her memory of being chained in the barn to her teacher, as well.

Gabriel's hand tightened on Ava's. "Pay attention. Kick that bastard out and let's get down to business."

Ava lunged in her seat, snapping her jaws. When she blinked, her eyes returned to the beautiful gray Gabriel had fallen in love with. He said the first thing that came to his mind.

"All this noise is in a room. There are teenagers over at the Chinese place laughing a few hundred yards away. Can you hear them?"

Ava winced.

"And a baby's fussing near the McDonald's. He can't help it; he's just a baby, but it's drilling into your ears right now and you can't concentrate."

Her face crumpled into an expression of despair. She squeezed his hand with bone crushing power.

"And those kids dressed like Marilyn Manson, trying to act like they're so original. Can you hear them? They keep snapping their gum and slamming their hands on the table."

Ava's right hand rose to cover her ear.

"Can you hear all the noise, Ava?" Gabriel asked, keeping her hand in his even as she tried to pull away. Her face was pale. "Close your eyes."

Her eyes rolled in his direction.

"Close them," he demanded. Her eye lids slipped shut.

"All these noises you hear, all the people you see... they're all in the room. You don't have to stay in the room. Nobody's forcing you to be here. All you have to do is walk away."

Ava frowned.

"Close the door and step back."

Her brow furrowed even more.

"Just reach your hand out and push the door closed," Gabriel crooned as if he had done this millions of times. His heart was jackknifing in his chest painfully. He hoped he wouldn't stroke out.

Ava hesitated, then reached up and moved her right hand from right to left as if she was swinging a door shut.

"Good," Gabriel said. "See? It's already quieter. You can barely hear the kids chewing gum. Now walk down the hall with me. The noise is getting quieter."

A shift happened in his head; it was as though he stood looking through a telescope and someone placed a piece of Plexiglass over the lens. He felt nauseous. And suddenly he was standing with her in a hallway, facing a closed door. All around them was gray bleeding into white, making the only things visible the door and walls of a long hallway. He could still hear the chatter around him, the sizzle of the grills the vendors used, the ice falling into plastic cups as customers served themselves sodas. But the noise was a little quieter. A dull ache started in his temples.

He felt Ava reached down and take his hand. She began backing away from the door. Their movements had a weightless quality, slow, the way one floats in dreams.

"As you move away from the room, the sound is getting softer and softer." Gabriel continued, unsure if Ava was ready to keep going on her own. "Just keep walking. The door is further down the hall."

The ache in his head was growing. He clenched his fist on the table, trying to keep focused.

Like a dream, they put more distance between them and the door. Gabriel didn't know what was behind them and didn't care. All that mattered was her ability to visualize separating herself from the clamor in the Food Court.

"The sound is almost gone now. You can barely... see the door. It's disappearing into the gray."

Speaking was getting harder. The pain in his temples was drilling now, making it feel like his eyes were throbbing. Gabriel clenched his jaw and closed his eyes. He didn't know how much more he could take. Someone had taken a hot poker and shoved it into his head, wiggling it around in an attempt to remove his eye.

"We c-can't see the door now," he ground out, "It's gone, and so is the noise. Ava... I can't-"

In the gray, she released his hand and placed her palm on his shoulder, shoving him toward the wall. Fully expecting to hit it, Gabriel raised his hands to brace and found himself back in the Food Court, jerking in his chair. Daniel reached out and grabbed his wrist so he wouldn't topple onto the floor.

"Fuck!" Gabriel managed, glancing around. The brightness of the atrium after the dim hallway hurt his eyes, and his temples were raging war in his head. He pressed his palms to them.

And realized he'd probably broken Ava's concentration.

"Shit."

When he looked up, she was sitting with one arm on the table and one hand in her lap, staring out into the court. Her back was straight but no longer rigid.

"She shoved me out," he said, unable to believe it.

Then he noticed Daniel was sitting across from them, no longer on Ava's other side. He had sat down right in front of Gabriel without Gabriel even realizing it. When the hell had that happened?

"Not bad for her first try," Daniel said, watching Ava. He passed his hand in front of her eyes and received no response. He glanced at Gabriel. "Or yours."

"I didn't do anything. She's the one that dragged me in."

"You showed her how to do it."

He had been winging it. He'd had no idea what he was going to say until he opened his mouth and said whatever came out.

"Instinct is a powerful tool," Daniel said. "You were unresponsive when I switched seats and checked your pulse."

"I didn't see you move," he admitted. "I didn't feel anything. Ava was holding my hand wherever we were, and I felt that, and saw the grey around us."

Daniel nodded thoughtfully, laying two fingers on Ava's wrist to check her pulse for the third time. She didn't react. "She's relaxed. She blocked everything out. Including us."

"Is that a good thing?"

"Eventually, we'll have to work on dialing it back so she can choose what to block and what to let in, but it's a major step. How's your head?"

"Hurts like a bitch."

"Let's bring Ava back, and then we'll see what we can do about your head."

• • • • •

Isabel had to take a deep breath before she opened the door to her apartment. She tried to remember she was leaving it soon, that she was moving to a new, better apartment. A penthouse apartment.

"Are you nervous?" Griffin asked, leaning against the wall next to the door.

"A little." She rubbed her hands down the thighs of her jeans.

"That's ridiculous, Izzie. You should know me better than that."

She nodded. "I should. I do. I definitely do."

Turning her key, she pushed open the door before she could argue with herself anymore.

The space felt lonely. She hadn't been here, really been here in over a month. She'd stopped by a time or two to pick up clothes and clean up a little. The rest of her time was spent at Griffin's.

"It's a cute flat," he said, walking into the kitchen. "There's nothing for you to be embarrassed about."

"It's so quiet," she said. "This place deserves to have someone living here."

"How do you feel about subletting?"

He wandered into the living room, looking at the cabinet Gabriel had built for her with the television sitting on it.

"By the time I found someone willing to do it, my lease would be up," Iz said, opening the glass patio door to let in fresh air. "I'm not exactly social."

"I work with someone looking for a place. I think she'd love this. Do you want me to see if she'll stop by to take a look?"

"Today?" Isabel kicked into the coffee table and stumbled. "Like, now?"

The smile he gave her was both amused and patient. "If she's free. We'll be here packing, anyway."

"Is she an engineer, like you?"

He nodded. "She's on my team."

"She probably wants something a little less..." Pausing, Isabel gave the living room a cursory glance, assessing it.

Then abruptly turned and walked toward the bedroom. Confused, Griffin looked after her. When he heard muffled sounds of items banging around, he walked into the bedroom to see what she was up to.

She was in the tiny walk-in closet, her head covered by clothing hanging in no discernible order.

"Izzie, what are you doing?"

"I'm digging out some boxes." Her voice was faint.

"Come out of there for a minute."

"I'm busy."

"You can take a few seconds to talk to me. I'm not going to have a conversation with your ass."

She stopped moving around. Slowly, she backed out of the closet, careful not to knock clothes off hangers and tip boxes full of her life over. When she stood upright and pivoted toward him, her face was red, and he could see she had teared up a little.

"What's so important that it needs to be discussed this very second?" she asked, a little breathless.

Resting a hand on her shoulder, he used the other to smooth the static out of her wild hair. "What were you going to say? You stopped mid-sentence."

"Nothing." Trying to turn back to the closet, she rolled her eyes when he put his other hand on her shoulder and locked her in place. She let out an exasperated sigh.

"I was going to say she'll probably want something less white-trash," she said. "Then I remembered I told you I would try to stop being self-deprecating, so I shut up. Then I remembered all the memories of the firsts that happened here: the recipe I cooked, and the first time I bought a bottle of whiskey after I turned twenty-one and drank it here with Gabriel. This was my first apartment after I moved away from home. And that made me feel stupid to be sentimental to a shitty place like this when I'm moving into a palace like yours, and I started crying. Like I am now, dammit. And it's stupid to be crying for sentimental reasons over a shit box like this when you're pulling a Pretty Woman on me, taking me from hooker to high class, but I can't help it. So now you know. Are you happy? You made me cry again, talking about it."

"Oh, Izzie." Griffin pulled her in and wrapped his arms around her.

"Fuck you," she pouted, but she hugged him back.

"You have every right to be emotional about leaving."

Sniffing, she felt her tears leaving a wet spot on his shirt. "Your apartment is so much better. I could fit all of my living space into your bathroom."

"That has no bearing in this situation. This was the first place you called home, where you made your own rules. Of course, you're sentimental."

He rubbed her back.

"I appreciate your mindful attempt at curbing your self-deprecation. It means a lot to me."

"I'm working on it."

"I'm not pulling a Pretty Woman on you – whatever that means. I love you. You've always been classy; you just don't know it."

She sniffed again.

"It's a beautiful flat. Lina will love it."

"Yeah?" Pulling away slightly, she looked up at him. "It's really small."

"She's looking more for a space where she can work on her art without being interrupted. This will be more like a studio for her, with a place to sleep when she works too late."

He kissed her damp eyes, her forehead. "If you want to take more time, keep paying rent through July, that's fine. I won't call her."

"No," Isabel said. She broke away from him to get a tissue from her bedside table. "It deserves to have someone in it. I can be out of it by the fifteenth and they'll prorate it for the last half of the month if that works for her."

"That soon?" Griffin raised his eyebrows.

"I don't have much and I'm not working." She smiled, giving him another hug. "Is it too soon for you?"

Chuckling, he gave her an affectionate squeeze. "I was ready for you to move in the morning after I first saw you play at The Raz."

•　•　•　•　•

CHAPTER FIFTEEN

The ball of light woke her from a light sleep. Something bright eased toward her face, stirring her from restless dreams of electricity and knives. Or maybe they were memories. She could no longer tell the difference. The pain was a dull throb in every part of her body, the only thing she knew would always be there.

She blinked, flinching from the glow. The light instantly dimmed.

Wake.

It was not a voice she heard, but a thought in her head. Instinct told her to trust the light as she had before. She sat up, squinting as dried blood kept her eye lids fused together at the corners. The Bad People had beaten her this time, making her eyes big and sore and unable to see much of anything.

Follow me.

Climbing off the dirty mattress that served as her bed, Ava crawled across the stained carpet of the trailer toward the back door, following the ball of light out into the summer night. It was not as bright as it had been in the past; she thought the foggy way she was seeing things was because her eyes were swollen almost shut.

The grass was cool on her bare feet. She was wearing only a thin tee shirt and shorts, but she was warm in the late August heat. Even in the dark, there was no relief from the humidity. A thin layer of sweat collected on her skin almost instantly as she staggered across the yard.

She followed the light into the woods, the skin on her feet hardened from the number of times she came here. Always to hide from the beatings and the touching and the sick laughter. After being led here the first time, she usually came early in the mornings and sometime in the afternoons, when they would pass out from too much drinking and not enough food. The woods smelled of pine, rain, leaves – such welcome fragrances after the stench of pee and alcohol and hot breath.

The light showed her to her usual place. It was a pile of brush and leaves with a small hole for her to crawl into. The first time she'd come here, it had just been a pile of underbrush, something to search for critters if she had been a normal child. But she watched a rabbit rush into it and disappear, and she thought how nice it was to be able to jump into a place so secretive no one knew where she was hiding. So, she pulled away weeds and moved leaves and pushed branches around until she'd made a small hole to sneak into. When she was inside, she pulled the branches down, so it didn't look like there was a deliberate hole.

It was like being in a room made of nature.

Because the brush pile acted as an umbrella, only a few leaves and twigs were on the ground inside. It was cool and damp in there, and so, so dark. The darkness eased the pain in Ava's head, in her eyes. The pleasant smells surrounded her. This place had become her only respite from Mack and Janine.

But the ball of light didn't go inside the thicket right away. It hovered just outside the little nest.

Ava rubbed her sore eye delicately, her little body tired. She slept better when she was out here in the woods. But the light wanted something from her. She waited for answers to come to her, to help her understand.

Someone is coming for you.

Tensing, her entire body going cold, Ava whipped her head around and looked for The Bad People.

The ball of light circled her and swirled around her feet, spiraling up her body.

Not now. Soon. Someone good, and kind, and loving is coming for you. She will take you away from all this. She will take you from The Bad People and give you to The Good People.

Ava did not understand. She did not know what good or kind meant. She did not know love.

The woman who comes for you wears a star. She will help you find a home.

The ball floated into the nest and waited for her to follow, hovering at her shoulder while she curled up on a blanket she had brought out one night.

Sore and worn, Ava curled her hands under her chin and closed her eyes.

Sleep now, came the thought. The light dimmed even more, until it was barely luminescent.

"What is your name?" the girl whispered.

You will not understand until you are much older.

The ball of light floated closer to her and gave her its name.

• • • • •

"Aaron Michael Reid."

Gabriel thought the voice was part of his dream at first. He heard it subconsciously and rose from sleep wondering if it was real or in the dream, which he couldn't remember. For a moment, he lay in bed, listening. He was lying on his back, and he felt the cool breeze from the open window stir the bedding. It was then that he realized he couldn't hear Ava breathing beside him.

"Aaron Michael Reid."

Now he jerked into a sitting position, looking down even though instinct told him Ava wasn't in bed beside him. Quickly standing and dragging on his jeans, he grabbed his phone in case he needed the flashlight on it. The sight of the open balcony door stopped him.

Several thoughts raced through his head, including intruder, but the most prominent one was that Ava had been sleep-walking and toppled right off the balcony. Fear seized him, tightening his chest as he started across the room. It occurred to him only after he began moving that if she'd fallen, he wouldn't be hearing her curious voice. He'd more likely hear her screaming, or nothing at all.

The thought sent a violent shudder through him.

He set his phone on the bed and turned on the lamp.

When he found her, she was standing naked on the balcony, her face tipped up slightly to the sky. Gabriel stepped outside and wished he had put on his shirt. The night was cool and still. He wondered how she could stand out here for who knew how long without shivering.

"Ava?"

"Aaron Michael Reid," she repeated. She didn't turn around. Then: "It was always him."

* * * * *

"Come inside."

Gabriel rubbed his hands up and down his arms. The moon was almost full, casting Ava in a blueish glow that made her look celestial. Her dark hair, reaching almost to her lower back, was in sharp contrast to her pale skin. She seemed to be staring out into the darkness.

Satisfied she wasn't going to plummet to the ground, Gabriel stepped back inside and dragged on the first shirt his hand found in the second drawer of his dresser. He had finally bought a thick robe for these occasions, and he plucked it off the hook next to the bed.

Returning to the balcony, he saw Ava holding her right hand out, palm up.

"What are you doing, Ava?" he asked, not expecting an answer.

"Can you see the light? It is so beautiful." Despite her words, she was still looking up at the sky, not at her hand.

"Wake up," Gabriel said gently, stepping closer. He held the robe an inch from her body, debating whether to attempt to cover her with it.

Ava dropped her hand. Now gooseflesh spread across her body, and she shivered as if feeling the chill for the first time.

"Ava. I'm going to touch you."

He draped the robe over her shoulders and braced for a strike. After a moment, he let out his breath. Tugging lightly on the thick cloth, he turned her until she was facing him.

"You're dreaming."

Maneuvering her was a mistake, but at least she wasn't unprotected against the cold. He'd kept his hands on the lapels of the robe, but he held her loosely now.

"Will you come inside with me?"

The gray of her eyes looked eerily silver with the moon reflecting off them. Her heavy lids made her look like someone out of the Addams Family show. Abruptly, she shivered again, and her posture relaxed.

"Come inside. You were dreaming."

Stiff-legged, she allowed him to lead her through the glass doors. He turned to close and lock them, pulling the curtains across to block most of the light from the moon. When he turned back, she curled into him. His arms automatically came up to embrace her.

Inhaling deeply, she rested her cheek against his chest. "You smell like French toast."

"Come back to bed, Gordon Ramsey."

Turning her toward the bed, he urged her to start walking again.

"Hop on up there."

She broke out in gooseflesh when he pulled away the robe but climbed onto the bed and crawled to her side. Yearning drove into him as he watched the sleek line of her long torso, the curve of her bottom as she moved. He took a moment to hang the robe, hoping to tone down his hormones. When he turned back and she was still sitting up on the bed, he rolled his eyes.

"You're killing me."

She had pulled the bedding over her lower half. Sitting with her head tilted, as if listening to something only she could hear, it was hard to tell if she was awake or asleep. Gabriel sat in bed next to her.

"Who is Aaron Michael Reid?" he asked.

"The light."

"What does that mean?"

Instead of answering, she stared at a place somewhere near the fireplace. She restlessly gathered the bedding in her fists and released it, gathered it and released it. Even when she was obviously uneasy, she was beautiful.

"I love you, Ava."

"That will not stop you from leaving."

For a moment she looked not just uneasy but heartbroken.

Gabriel reached for her hand. Her fingers were cold.

"I won't leave you, Ava."

The expression on her face relaxed.

"Try to get some sleep, okay?" he soothed, rubbing his thumb across the back of her hand. He brought her hand to his lips and kissed her knuckles.

With a sigh, she sank down on the bed.

The true impact of what moving in with Griffin meant didn't hit Isabel until she'd finished unloading her second set of boxes at his apartment. When Griffin was with her, they talked as they worked. On her own, labeling and organizing similar items into boxes took planning, careful packing was structured, and the physical exertion of lifting the boxes kept her mind focused on how to be the most efficient at loading her car with the most boxes for the least effort. She didn't have time to think until he was at work, and she was standing in the kitchen with a bottle of water, looking at the stacks of boxes in the living room.

"Holy fuck."

She set the bottle on the island and clamped her hands to her knees, keeping her head down. Suddenly the apartment, which had looked so incredibly huge before, seemed like a prison cell.

He'd told her she could move his stuff around however she saw fit, but did her cabinet from Gabriel really fit in with his angular furniture and somewhat Frank Lloyd Wright style? Griffin brought warmth to an apartment that would otherwise appear geometric and cool to Isabel. How had she believed for a minute that this would work?

"Fuck."

What would happen in the winter? Would she have to freeze all the time because he liked it too warm? Would he mind if she decorated for holidays? Where would she put the Christmas tree? Did he even celebrate Christmas? Did he believe in God? What was his belief system? What was her belief system? What would she do if they had an argument? Where would she go if she needed space to herself?

This had to stop before she made an irreparable mistake. Friday she was going to meet Lina and discuss the details of subletting, and she couldn't even imagine spending time in the same space during an argument with someone she loved. She'd already chickened out of meeting her at the apartment the other day when she and Griffin were packing. It was too intimidating to be there while a stranger judged it and her belongings. Griffin had suggested instead meeting for dinner, and having Lina look at the apartment on her own.

Get it together, Harris, she snapped at herself. You can do this. You know you do this. It's all in your head.

She grabbed her cell and tapped Griffin's contact.

"Hello, beautiful. Everything okay?"

Just hearing his voice made her heartbeat accelerate. She inhaled sharply.

"Hey."

At first that was all she could say. So many things were rolling around in her head that she couldn't follow.

"What's going on, Izzie?" he asked gently.

"Griffin, I finished that – oh, sorry," a female voice said in the background.

Isabel instantly felt like a moron.

"Set it there and I'll get to it after lunch," Griffin said in a muffled tone. "Sorry about that. What's up? You're in Izzie Land; I can hear the wheels spinning."

"You're busy. I'm sorry to bother you at work."

"I have a few minutes. What's on your mind?"

"Do you celebrate Christmas?" she blurted.

The pause at the other end made her wince.

"Do you... you know... go to any dinners, or decorate your apartment, or... anything?"

"I haven't really," he said slowly. "Well, I've gone to an informal dinner or two. Sometimes a co-worker will invite me. What's this about?"

"Do you object to Christmas decorations?"

"Isabel, did you call to get permission to set up a Christmas tree in May?"

Walking back and forth in the living room, she pressed her palm to her forehead.

"I just realized, you know, looking at all my boxes in your living room, that I have a lot of shit. And I also realized I have no idea what your beliefs are... if you're Jewish or Catholic or... you know... a Satanist. So, I'm not sure if I should bother packing my decorations to bring over. Or if we'll agree on the temperature settings. Some couples argue all the time about the settings on the thermostat. Next thing you know, divorce papers are being served for 'irreconcilable differences."

She was actually panting from lack of oxygen.

"Isabel," Griffin said, and she could hear the smile in his voice, "You can decorate the flat any way you want to."

"You're right; I shouldn't have bothered you at work. I'm an idiot."

"I'm not brushing you off. If I'm busy, I'll tell let you know I don't have time to talk."

She sat on the sofa, each word he spoke making her feel less anxious.

"Bring as much of your stuff as you want. If we need more space, we'll get a bigger flat. Together."

"Okay."

"And Izzie?"

"Yeah?"

"You've been staying at my place for weeks. We haven't argued about the thermostat once."

She considered this. "Right. Of course, you're right. I knew I was overreacting. I knew talking to you would calm me down."

He laughed, lowering her blood pressure several more beats.

She'd stood and was rooting in the refrigerator, trying to figure out if she wanted an orange juice or a water.

A comfortable silence settled between them for two seconds and then he said, "I still hear a squeaky cog in your head, Izzie. What else is bothering you?"

Remembering her bottle of water on the island, she closed the refrigerator door. "It's just a style difference. Yours is kind of cold, with hard lines and -"

"My style is whatever is functional, available to purchase on-line, and subtle." He laughed again. "I can toss it all and we can decorate together with what works for both of us."

When her entire body flushed, she automatically pressed a hand to her heart. Whoa. This was happening. She felt like she was engulfed in a body of light, and her fingertips were going to produce sparks at any moment. Keeping her hand on her heart, she felt its rapid pounding through her shirt. The man knew how to make her heart flutter.

"Did I cover all the bases?" he asked.

"I think that wraps it up," she said softly, barely able to catch her breath. "Except..."

"Except what?"

"I wish you were here. I want to rip your clothes off."

She heard the sound in the back of his throat as he swallowed.

"I could probably take a long lunch or get off early." He cleared his throat. "I mean, come home early."

Smiling, Isabel ran her finger around the rim of her water bottle.

"I'll be waiting."

• • • • •

That night, after training, Gabriel waited on the mats for Ava to finish showering. Daniel was taking a phone call, leaving Gabriel by himself to occupy his time before they discussed psychic phenomena. Because he had never really done it before, he used the time to walk around and study the training area.

It was sparsely decorated. The kamidana – he was finally getting used to the word since he heard it more often when he sat in on Ava's classes – was high on the north wall in the center of the mats. Its contents were similar to those Ava had in her dojo. Moving clockwise, the east wall had a rack of training staffs and wooden swords on it, the entrance into the rest of the facilities, and a utilities closet with a long curtain for privacy. The south wall was clean except close to the front door.

Pictures of elderly Japanese men, all dressed in martial arts uniforms, were hung on the wall so they were the first thing a person saw as he entered the dojo. They hung in simple black frames. Beneath those was a picture of Daniel with an old Japanese man and another of him with a very fit middle-aged man, all kneeling as Ava did at the beginning of every class. Daniel's credentials as a trainer were framed below the photos.

"They are grand masters," Ava said at his shoulder, startling him. He hadn't heard her approach.

"Who is that?"

Gabriel pointed to the picture of Daniel kneeling next to a black man dressed in the same uniform he and Ava wore during class.

"That is Sensei's teacher."

"They look so serious. The same way you look when you're training."

"When training is not taken seriously, people get hurt."

Gabriel hooked his thumbs in his belt loops. "I'm surprised you don't have one of those Japanese symbol tattoos."

Ava pulled her hair back and began threading it into one long braid. "Kanji."

"Bless you," he said dryly.

Giving him a look from the corner of her eyes, she continued with the braid, efficiently weaving with her long fingers.

"Kanji are Chinese symbols used in the Japanese writing system." She backed away from him, walking to her usual place on the mat. "I will never mark my body."

"You're not a fan of tattoos?"

Gabriel turned from the photos at the change in her tone and joined her on the mat.

"I have already been branded."

Her words had the force of a slap.

Again, he had been so careless with his thoughts. Of course, he hadn't forgotten the tattoo the sick fucks had forced on her as a young child; it was hard to forget when he knew her body so intimately. He couldn't run his hands over her without seeing the black symbols on her inner thigh. Early on in their sexual relationship, he'd felt avoiding it would only give its demeaning intent strength. So, when he trailed kisses up her legs, he didn't shy away from the tattoo, nor did he pay extra attention to it. Each time he brushed his lips across the ink, he felt her tense just slightly, and each time he casually moved passed the tattoo.

He decided to do so with the conversation now.

"Have you thought about getting something put over it?" When she turned her gaze on him, affection rolled through him in an unexpected, lazy wave. "Turning it into something positive?"

The way she studied him, without blinking or changing her expression, made him wonder if she understood what he was trying to say.

"I mean, you could have a tattoo artist cover the one your foster parents gave you with something you like."

Her brows met, separated, met again, as she considered the possibility. "I did not consider that option."

"It's just an idea. I think it's less painful than removal."

Gabriel wasn't sure if it was the right move or not. At least it put the way her body looked back in her control.

"I am not afraid of pain."

She seemed to shimmer before him, as if his eyes had to catch up to a reality that had already passed. Her body blurred, and when he blinked, she was looking at the kamidana again and her hair was up in that strange, braided crown she sometimes wore it in.

"Ava," he said, too stunned to realize she seemed paralyzed, "your hair."

"Sorry about that," Daniel said, walking across the mat. He held a bottle of water out to Ava. Without shifting her eyes, her hand came up automatically and took it. Kneeling across from them, he handed another bottle to Gabriel and opened one of his own. "Let's get started. Monday you made great progress on–"

He noted the way Ava was staring at the wall behind him, the way her hand was raised, holding the bottle of water as if she had turned to stone the moment after he had put it into her hand.

"What's wrong?"

Gabriel didn't look away from Ava. "I'm not sure. We were talking about tattoos and she… wavered. I'm not sure how else to describe it. Like watching a monitor blip. She just put her hair in a long braid, but after the blip, it was styled like this."

"Ava?"

Daniel leaned forward, looking into her eyes. Her pupils were not dilated. Nor were they silver. Tilting his head one way, then the other, he saw neither ear was bleeding. She was not having a vision. She was not in The Interval.

"Can you hear me?"

"I can hear you."

Blackness had not filled her eye sockets. Her voice had not deepened. If she was not consumed by The Monster, why wasn't she more responsive?

"What's happening?" Daniel reached toward her and watched her fingers tighten on the bottle of water, indicating she was aware of what was going on around her.

"I think…" Confusion, then surprise flickered across her face. "I think she has something to say."

"Who?" Daniel asked, noticing Gabriel's rigid posture. "Who has something to say?"

Ava's head moved slowly to her left, as if she was following the movement of something or someone from the wall behind Daniel to Gabriel's side. She swallowed.

"Hayden."

·　·　·　·　·

Isabel was still experiencing the repercussions of a bout of long, slow sex. Her thighs felt like partially filled water balloons, all wobbly and quivering. Her stomach was floating around her abdomen, and her tongue was a piece of sandpaper sticking to the roof of her mouth. She tried to say something – she wasn't sure what – and succeeded only in letting out a puff of air. Water. She needed a gallon of water. How much time had passed? Griffin must have spent hours on her, using his mouth and his hands... God, his hands... She had never felt this thoroughly pleasured by a man.

Another aftershock hit and she mewled softly, her thighs squeezing together. She bit her lip as she tried to ride it out. Every muscle below her waist kept flexing and relaxing, giving her odd sensations. Had this happened before? She couldn't remember ever shaking so long after having sex. Her muscles kept seizing and releasing, and the sex had ended at least five minutes ago. And she was so blissfully exhausted.

Griffin rubbed her bare shoulder. "Everything okay, Izzie?"

She was lying with her head on his shoulder, her leg in between his, so when her legs convulsed, they tightened around him. Each time they did, he felt a little more like gloating.

"No. You gave me orgasmic epilepsy."

Grinning, he glanced down at her. Her face was flushed, her mouth still puffy from his assault. She looked thoroughly and adorably tousled.

"It was my pleasure."

He raised her hand and kissed the back of it before settling it back on his chest.

"I have to ask you a favor," he added, and she knew instantly that she needed to panic because the heartrate she felt under her hand accelerated. Her body tensed. Why couldn't he just let her enjoy the moment? So few like this existed.

"Okay." She mentally braced herself.

"When we meet Lina on Friday to discuss you subletting the flat, she wants to bring her boyfriend."

Iz relaxed a fraction. That wasn't so bad.

"And she wants to meet at a bar. She works there a couple nights a week and knows the owner."

That wasn't that great, but it wasn't the end of the world, either. The best thing about bars, for Isabel, was how shitty the lighting was. She felt safely hidden from everyone because no one could see detail in the dark and people were usually too drunk to care.

"Okay," she said slowly. "As long as we can find somewhere to sit that isn't squished in between Bubba the tattooed redneck or Tanya the trailer trash harlot, I should be fine."

Smirking, Griffin toyed with the ends of her hair. "She'll find it amusing that you said that."

"Well, don't tell her that." Iz ran her fingers lightly across his chest. Her legs were quivering less now. Her insides were no longer clenching and releasing.

"It's a classy place." Griffin tugged on her hair. He seemed unable to stop touching it. "It's clean, with good alcohol, and the music isn't too loud."

Oh. So much for hiding in the dark.

Isabel said nothing, closing her eyes and enjoying the moment. She felt herself starting to drift off.

"Is it okay if a couple guys from work come, too?"

Her eyes flew open. From the tone of his voice, this was something he'd already planned to ask her. This was what he knew would upset her, she knew. She tensed again.

"You want me to hang out with a group of your friends?" Raising up, she stared down at him. Panic sank its claws into her throat and began climbing up, making it hard to breathe.

"They've been bugging me to meet you."

"Why?" The utter shock on her face would have been comical if her self-esteem wasn't so low.

"Because they're curious about the woman I'm constantly talking about. And they want to know who is so important that I haven't taken any time for my friends the past two months."

"You fuckshit!"

She shoved off him, leaning over the bed and grabbing her tee shirt off the floor. Yanking it over her head, she glared at him.

"You just spent all that time fucking me to make sure I'd say yes to meeting your damn friends!"

Unperturbed, he gazed at her calmly. "Isabel, you jumped me the minute I opened the door. How exactly is that using sex to get what I want from you?"

Fury turned to bafflement as she realized he was right. Her signature blush lit her cheeks and the tips of her ears. Griffin saw the anger drain from her face.

"Oh, yeah."

Leaning up, he grabbed her around the waist and yanked her back down onto him. She let out a yelp. "You're adorable."

When she opened her mouth to apologize, he smoothly rolled over until she was underneath him and silenced her with a kiss. She giggled.

"I love that sound." He kissed her again. "You've a beautiful laugh."

"You make it easy for me to be happy. I'm sorry. I panicked."

"I know. I'm not asking you to change, Izzie. I don't mind staying in with you most of the time, and I don't mind going out with my friends without you if you don't want to go. But I would like you to meet them. I've been waiting to ask because I know you don't like big groups or public places."

Isabel studied him. His eyes were full of hope. The boyish grin he was giving her, showing his perfect teeth, made her wonder what he'd told his friends that made them interested in meeting her.

She brushed his hair back from his forehead, feeling an overwhelming rush of love for him. She felt like a Lifetime Christmas movie.

"I'd love to meet your friends."

It wasn't a lie. She wanted to make him happy, no matter the cost, and she didn't hate the idea of meeting his friends. The idea just made her nervous.

Yet not as nervous as it once would have, she realized as Griffin gathered her close. Just a few weeks ago, she would have panicked and probably drank until she was completely shit-faced. Or she would have flat-out said no without any room for reconsidering. At least she was making progress.

"Thank you," he murmured, kissing her behind her ear. "This means a lot to me."

She could tell just how much by the way he was holding her against him, like he was drowning, and she was carrying him to shore. His need for her was confusing – how could she possibly contribute to his life? – and yet it felt so good to be the one person he couldn't seem to live without.

"I love you." She wrapped her arms around his neck. "You make me feel important."

"You are important, Izzie. You're everything to me. But you need to slow down on moving your stuff here while I'm at work, or there won't be anything for me to help you with."

She grinned. "You're my reward at the end of the day for working so hard."

• • • • •

"Hayden's here right now?" Gabriel asked. His voice sounded hollow.

Still looking to the left of and slightly above his head, Ava nodded. He turned his head, hoping for a blur, a hunch, anything that would let him know his sister was there. He felt nothing. He saw nothing. Only three people were on the mats.

"What is she doing, Ava?" Daniel asked, watching Gabriel's stricken expression.

"She is touching his shoulder."

"I don't feel anything," Gabriel said softly, his tone full of remorse. "I wish I could feel her."

After a moment of silence, Daniel said, "Ava, what's happening?"

She gave a slight shake of her head. "Her mouth is moving, but I cannot hear her. I can never hear her."

Gabriel felt the energy from Ava again, that strange sensation of emotion emanating from her. Frustration? Anger? He wasn't sure what it was, but the room was filling with it.

"I only heard her when she told me about your son."

"What was different about the time she spoke of my son?" Daniel asked. "Think back to that communication. Were you in a different state of mind? Had you meditated before you spoke with her?"

"Why does she come to me if she refuses to speak?" Ava closed her eyes and pressed her hands to the sides of her head as if Daniel hadn't spoken. "My head hurts."

The lights flickered. Both Gabriel and Daniel glanced at the ceiling, then at the front door as it shook gently in its frame.

"Well, that's new," Daniel said softly.

"Hayden, please talk to us," Gabriel said, staring at the floor with his head turned to the left. "Tell Ava what you need us to hear."

Keeping her eyes closed, Ava let out a long, low growl. Beads of sweat broke out on her forehead.

On the wall, the rack of swords began to vibrate.

"It wants me to let it in."

"Who-" Daniel started.

"The Monster."

Ava opened her eyes and looked at Hayden. The young girl's eyes were wide, darting from the door to the lights to the weapons rack. She backed away from Gabriel.

"Hayden is afraid."

"Is she afraid of The Monster?" Daniel asked. "Can it hurt her somehow?"

Ava lowered her hands from her ears. "I do not know! I do not know the rules."

Her eyes darkened to black, then returned to their natural gray color. Gabriel reached for her shoulder and Ava's head whipped around, fixing him with her gaze. The blackness engulfed her eyes.

"Don't fucking touch her!"

There was no mistaking the deep, guttural yell for anything other than what it was. As soon as The Monster took over Ava, she seemed to take control back. Her eyes resumed their gray color, although they were very dark gray, and she winced in pain. Pressing the heel of her hand to her temple, she looked for Hayden.

The girl took another step back.

"Hayden," Ava said, leaning forward and reaching for her.

Her body was shoved backward across the mats, slamming into the wall on the opposite side of the dojo. She tucked her chin against her chest to avoid hitting her head on the bamboo paneling. The breath was knocked out of her.

Gabriel had reached for her as she began moving. Now he scrambled to his feet and went after her to make sure she was okay. Staying where he was, Daniel waited to see if they needed him. The door abruptly stopped shaking in its frame. The weapons rack slowed its noisy vibration until it stopped completely. The lights went out, then turned on and remained lit.

Ava put her hands flat on the mat on either side of her and looked up. Gabriel was crouched beside her, gazing at her anxiously.

"Are you okay?"

She reached out a shaky hand and gripped his forearm. "I want to go home."

Her voice was a hoarse whisper.

Daniel stood now, walking over to her as Gabriel helped her to her feet. Ava pressed her palm to her temple, where a massive headache had lodged itself like a tumor. The pain was so bad it made her eyes water.

"I know you're tired, Ava, but we should-"

"Some other time," Gabriel snapped. "I need to get her home."

He gently walked her over to the edge of the mat, steadied her as she bowed to the kamidana, and helped her sit on the bench so she could put her shoes back on. While she carefully tied the laces, he glanced at Daniel.

Daniel was still standing by the wall, his expression distant as he contemplated something. His arms were crossed as he studied where Ava had been deposited.

"I'm sorry we have to cut this short," Gabriel said, picking up Ava's gym bag. He took his keys out of his pocket. He hadn't meant to be an asshole to Ava's teacher. Enough was enough for one night.

Daniel raised his head. "I have a couple theories to toss around. We'll discuss them tomorrow after class. Have a good night, both of you."

"Goodnight."

Ava said goodnight in Japanese and bowed as she left the dojo. There was a lot of bowing in Japanese tradition, Gabriel thought as he helped her to his truck. Ava probably preferred it to handshakes because bowing didn't involve touching people.

In the dojo, watching the two from the large front window, Daniel frowned. The Monster came to Ava when it sensed she was in danger or when she felt threatened. She was getting better at warding it off, but it had gone to great lengths to make its presence known just now, to the point of draining all her strength early on in their session. He wondered why it felt threatened by what Hayden had to say.

• • • • •

Friday. Public. People.

Isabel rested her hand on her chin and tried to look casually around the bar. Her stomach was rolling wildly, and her chest felt tight. She tried to ignore both.

Griffin leaned toward her, so his mouth was close to her ear. "You look a little pale."

She tried to smile. "I'm okay."

The response was immediate and insincere.

"Anything I can do to help you relax?"

Take me home!

"I'll be okay," she said aloud, forcing herself to sip her whiskey, not chug it.

Resting his hand on her back, he glanced around. Not many people were here this early in the evening.

"Describe the setting for me," he said to Izzie.

"What?"

"Tell me what you see."

"A bar."

Patiently he straightened in his chair and sampled his wine. "Be specific."

"This is one of your therapies, isn't it? Like reading to dogs or smacking me with pillows."

"Does that bother you?"

"Everything else you've had me do works. I trust you."

That meant more to him than he could put into words. He picked up her hand and squeezed it, taking a moment to make sure his voice was steady.

"Thank you."

Because she saw the sincerity in his eyes and it made her uncomfortable, she glanced around and dove headfirst into the activity.

"Okay. Large space. Bright paint on the walls."

"Mmm hmm. What else?"

Iz took a deep breath and noted the four or five other couples sitting at tables were dressed more like Griffin.

"I'm severely underdressed."

She tugged at her knit top; a simple striped shirt that made her feel slightly less frumpy than when she wore a tee shirt. Griffin had said bar. This was not a simple bar.

"I can't believe I let you talk me into this," she muttered.

"Keep talking," he said, taking her hand so she couldn't pull on her shirt. "What else do you notice here?"

Looking around, Isabel tried to unclench her jaw. Her hand loosed in Griffin's, then tightened around his.

"There's recessed lighting, and natural lighting in the wall of windows on the east, so it's bright and pleasant. Fuck, why did I think I could do this?"

She shifted on the stool.

"Because you can do this."

"The fuck I can."

The central bar was an enclosed rectangle of counters with light-colored marbled tops and wooden stools lined all around it. Large dark lights were suspended above the space, as well as recessed lighting and lights under the counter ledges that brightened and displayed. Isabel couldn't imagine sitting at that bar, being displayed for the rest of the room like a freak.

Two large square pillars stood near the main bar, and shorter counters were set against the pillars to create mini bars. The rest of the area was set up as a dining room, with tables and chairs similar to those Isabel associated with coffee shops: extremely modern and uncomfortable. However, the chairs were surprisingly cozy.

She and Griffin were sitting at a table by the wall of windows, where they would be away from everyone else even as the place filled up. She shouldn't have felt so caged. Squeezing Griffin's hand again, she moved it toward her, then away, restless, constantly moving as her eyes wandered the unfamiliar space looking for a way out.

Iz let out a shuddering breath. She felt her throat closing.

"How many people am I meeting tonight?" she squeaked. "Four? Five? I can't breathe."

"Isabel."

She threw back her drink and signaled to the waitress.

"Fuck." She whispered the word.

"Izzie," Griffin said, shoving his wine glass into her hand, "I'm going to start loading the back of Rover with pillows for when you hold your breath."

She snorted, giggled, and her body naturally took over its normal functions. Feeling lightheaded, she took a sip of his wine. Smiling as the waitress brought her another whiskey, she waited until they were alone again before glancing at Griffin.

"Hardwood floors," she said shortly.

"What?"

"The floors are hardwood," she said, pointing to them. "The décor has hints of Hawaiian influence but isn't overtly tropical. It's... nice. More of a club than a bar. I'm dressed like a fucking hobo."

"You're not-"

She held up her hand to silence him and took a refreshing drink.

"I could get used to this," she said, closing her eyes and breathing in the alcohol.

"Are you going to tease that wine all night or drink it?"

The deep voice startled Isabel and she jerked, her eyes flying open. A middle-aged woman was standing across their table wearing a long, flowing blue skirt and a bright orange sleeveless top that showed tattoos up and down both arms. Her curly chestnut brown hair was pulled back into a loose ponytail. An unfettered smile was on her face, amusement in her eyes, and she had set a cocktail on the counter as if she planned on joining them without being invited.

Isabel narrowed her eyes. "I could tongue-fuck it until the second coming of Christ and it still wouldn't be any of your business."

The woman's brown eyes danced as she shifted them from Isabel to Griffin. "I like her."

"Who the hell are you?" Iz barked.

"Isabel," Griffin said mildly, "I'd like you to meet Lina Hale."

He stood and rounded the counter, giving the older woman a hug and kiss.

Iz turned her glare on him as he returned to his seat. "You couldn't have told me that before I made an ass of myself?"

Lina offered her hand. Isabel humbly shook it.

"You didn't really give him a chance. I'm glad," she added when Isabel reddened. "I want to know the real woman responsible for stealing my second favorite man."

Griffin grinned at her. "I told you she was saucy."

"She's sitting right here." Isabel rubbed her damp palms on her thighs.

He draped his arm around her shoulders and pulled her close, kissing her temple. "Relax, Izzie. My friends will like you just the way you are, or they wouldn't be my friends."

Though she doubted that, Isabel exhaled before taking a gulp of her drink. To think she could do this without being plastered was foolish. She needed to get wasted.

"Where's Adam?" Griffin asked Lina, glancing toward the bar.

"He's finishing up. He'll be over in a few minutes. Adam owns this place," she explained to Iz. "He also bartends."

"Oh." Iz didn't know what else to say.

The woman's nose was a little too big, she thought, but it didn't detract from her being beautiful. The beauty didn't just come from her mahogany hair or flawless skin. It seemed to radiate from her personality.

Iz focused on the tattoos on Lina's arms because it gave her somewhere to look that wasn't in the woman's face. The left wrist had a compass, like the one on Griffin's shoulder, but this one was simpler. It was done all in black and white, attached to a chain that disappeared behind it. At the bottom, a decoration grew from the right side of it and wrapped up around the W and E. Isabel couldn't tell if they were waves or flower petals.

"Griffin said you write music," Lina said, pulling out a stool and sitting.

Despite her slightly thick build – not overweight, just solid – she moved with a grace Isabel could only dream of having. She slid her drink back so she wouldn't knock into it. From the glass, Iz could tell it was some kind of martini. The color was a pale green.

"Griffin has a big mouth," she said, elbowing him in the stomach. He let out a grunt and rubbed his hand up and down her back.

"I love music." Lina sipped her drink. "Adam and I play several instruments between us. It's so expressive."

Isabel was staring at the round wildflower tattoo with yellow and orange petals sitting on the back of Lina's left hand. She'd turned it over after she took a drink, exposing the simple yet beautiful flower, whose stems and leaves grew with reckless abandon and whose petals had come loose to blow across her hand in tiny orange and yellow bits.

"Griffin designed every one of them."

At first, Isabel was so engrossed in the beautiful artwork that she didn't realize she was being addressed. Griffin squeezed her hand.

"What?"

Lina turned her hands slowly to show the ink on both arms. "Griffin designed every tattoo on my body and Adam's."

Does that mean he's seen you naked? Iz thought, feeling like a teenager.

"H-how many do you have?" she asked.

"I don't know the number. They all flow together. But when I look at them, I know when I had each one done and the purpose of all of them. Do you have any?"

Shaking her head, Isabel motioned to the waitress again. "I show my pain in my music."

"It's not just about showing pain. It's about telling a story. For me, anyway. Everyone gets them for different reasons."

A man came up behind Lina and wrapped his well-muscled arms around her shoulders. He was wearing a white tank top, which contrasted with his dark skin and gave Isabel full access to every tattoo on both arms. The left was covered in tribal tattoos, thick, black bands curving around large empty spaces of flesh in between. The patterns were a mix of negative and positive space Isabel vaguely remembered learning about in art class in high school. The right arm was like a tropical forest covered alternately in wild animals and foliage.

But what caught Isabel's attention more than the ink was Lina's immediate reaction to his embrace. Her eyes brightened and her arms came up to return the hug. She turned her head to the side just in time to accept a kiss. Before she saw him, she knew who it was and openly expressed her love.

"Hey, babe," he said in a deep, smooth voice.

His long dreadlocks had swung around when he bent to kiss her, and she pulled on one to tug him closer to her. She smiled against his lips.

"Hello, old soul."

Isabel felt a bizarre stirring inside her chest as she watched them. The man – Adam – looked to be several years younger than Lina. Mid-thirties, Iz guessed, while Griffin had said Lina was in her late forties. Lina didn't look that age, but she projected maturity. How had these two met? How did they stay together with such a gulf of age between them?

"Adam," Griffin said, raising his glass.

Adam walked around the counter and embraced Griffin with a shoulder bump. He whispered something that made Griffin nod. Isabel couldn't hear what they were discussing but she watched them interact. Adam had such a strong presence. Isabel felt the bar around her disappear the closer he came to her.

"You must be Isabel."

What has Griffin told these people about me?

"Hello."

She liked Adam's goatee because it gave her something to look at so she could avoid his eyes.

She held her hand out. Taking it in both of his, he bowed his head slightly. "A pleasure to meet you."

Unsure what to say to that because she didn't know if it would turn out to be a pleasure to know him, she stayed silent.

"Ah, Will and Mark are here," Griffin said, waving.

Isabel was glad to have the attention taken off her. She glanced at the two young men walking toward the table, surprised to find them as shy, or possibly even more shy, than she was.

The one with the copper hair and light blue eyes looked to be her age. He had a medium build and was wearing light khaki pants and a plaid button-down shirt. Iz relaxed a little. He obviously had no fashion sense, which meant he probably wasn't a pretentious asshole.

The younger one had light blond hair and hazel eyes which he kept training exclusively on the floor. On the occasion that he looked up, Isabel thought he looked to be more Ava's age, if he was even old enough to drink. His eyes were large and round and as soon as he saw her looking at him, they returned to the floor.

"Glad I was able to drag you guys out of the lab." Griffin grinned. "Mark, Will, this is Isabel. Isabel, these guys are members of my team at work."

As they dispensed with the pleasantries, Isabel felt herself relaxing even more. She felt oddly protective of these two barely-men she'd just met. They were afraid of their own shadows.

"What can I get you two to drink?" Adam asked, wrapping an arm around each of their shoulders and pulling them in.

They looked uncomfortable at the attention but affectionately hugged Adam back. Will blushed, which contrasted with his pale complexion. They mumbled their orders so softly that Iz couldn't hear what they said.

"Is Will old enough to drink?" She kept her voice low as she turned to Griffin.

"He just turned twenty-two," he grinned.

He looks like a kid, she thought, not that she was much older.

"Why are they here? They're obviously uncomfortable in public."

"Everyone wants to meet you, and they like this place. It's the only bar they feel comfortable in."

Isabel raised an eyebrow. "That's what they look like when they're comfortable?"

Laughing, he wrapped his arm around her shoulder again. "Shut your mind off for a couple hours."

Lina moved over a seat, so she was sitting across from Griffin. She set Adam's drink at the head of the counter. Mark sat next to Lina, putting him across from Isabel, and Will sat beside him. No one was sitting on Isabel's left, which suited her just fine.

Adam came back with a tray of drinks.

"Okay, Lina, another appletini..."

Lina accepted hers and took another one off the tray. She held it out to Iz. "You looked like you were curious to try this. If you don't like it, I'll have another one."

"Thank you." Isabel took the drink, smiling. Turning to Griffin, she said, "I hope you cleaned your dashboard."

He gave her his dazzling smile.

When he smiled like that, it made her want to shove all the drinks off the table and fuck him on top of it.

"Jesus, Izzie, could you say that a little louder?" Griffin asked, accepting the glass of wine Lina passed him. "I don't think they heard you in New York."

"What?"

Lina laughed. "You just said you wanted to fuck Griffin on the top of this table."

876

"I said that out loud?"

Mark was still laughing. Adam winked at her. Will looked like he was going to ignite, his face was flushed a deep red.

"How much have I had to drink?"

"A few sips of my wine and two whiskeys."

"Fuck," she whispered. "I haven't even started. Do you have any duct tape?"

"Kinky," Lina said. "Adam and I have done just about everything on every surface in this place."

She gave him an affectionate rub on the chest.

Mark instantly lifted his hands off the table, making Lina laugh again.

"We disinfected after, obviously. What do you think of the drink?"

To keep more words from pouring out, Isabel threw it back like a shot. It was light and fruity and went down so easily.

"You're supposed to sip it!" Lina laughed.

She laughed so easily, Iz thought. How did she do that? How did she find so much joy, and why was it addictive to feel it with her?

"Oops. I like it. I think. I barely tasted it."

"I'll have Sandra get you another," Adam said, waving the waitress over. He ordered another appletini and whiskey for her. "Anyone else need anything?"

Mark lifted his beer bottle. Will was still nursing his draft.

"Have you ever done karaoke?" Lina suddenly asked, after Sandra moved away.

Iz almost choked on her water. "No. I don't like performing in front of crowds."

"Don't you play at a club on the weekends? I thought Griffin said-"

"I have a gig a couple Saturdays a month." She was talking through gritted teeth. She turned toward Griffin. "You really do talk too much."

"You must be really good if you have a standing gig," Mark said.

"It's a small venue," Isabel said. "They probably don't get a lot of –"

"She is," Griffin interrupted, taking her hand, kissing the back of it. "She's very good."

Feeling like everyone in the bar was looking at her now, Isabel flushed, clenching down on Griffin's hand. The alcohol was burning through her bloodstream, causing her to be feverish as well as furious at Griffin for talking about her music to others. It was her private hobby, something she chose whether or not to share with others.

"I generally know the crowd that shows up on Saturday nights," she said, feeling her chest tighten. "I'm used to them, after years of playing there."

"Maybe we could meet there some Saturday and listen to you." Adam smiled warmly at her, apparently unaware of how that thought made her instantly panic.

"No!" she blurted. "I mean…"

"After a few jam sessions, maybe," Adam said easily. "We can get used to playing together. No pressure, no rush. Just sitting around with our instruments until inspiration hits."

"M-maybe."

She felt a little lightheaded. Everything was moving too fast. She'd just met these people, and now she was committed to playing her guitar with them and inviting them to The Raz?

As the waitress brought another round of drinks, Isabel dove into hers. She was going to need it to get through the rest of the evening after all.

· · · · ·

"Is Greg coming tonight?" Tom asked, tossing a cheese curd into the air and catching it in his mouth. "He isn't back with Charity, is he?"

Jeremy, standing a few feet away, threw a dart. It stuck into the board with a loud thunk. Turning to look at Tom, he shrugged. "I swear to Christ, if he and schizo-bitcho are back together, I'm done with him."

"How are things going with you and Ava?" Tom asked, ignoring Jeremy.

Gabriel's shoulders instantly relaxed. Tom wondered if his friend realized it.

"Good. I've been meeting with her teacher…" he trailed off as he realized he couldn't get into that without revealing Ava's abilities. "It's interesting to watch her train."

They both watched Jeremy squint too hard while he tried to line up his last dart.

"You mean the karate stuff?" Jeremy asked. He dropped darts onto the table. "Your turn."

"Why does everyone say that?" Gabriel swiped the darts up and stood, aiming the first one. "Everything isn't karate. Karate is one style. Ava practices many. Say martial arts since you don't what she's currently practicing."

He whipped the dart harder than he'd intended and it plunged in deep. "She told you at the cookout that she's practicing Kung Fu and Ninpo. Those styles are different than Karate."

"Shit," Jeremy said, taking a drink. "A little touchy, aren't we?"

Gabriel realized he had probably done the same thing when he first met Ava. She'd never said anything, but it had probably driven her nuts. The thought made him smirk.

"Sorry. People use 'karate' like it encompasses every style. That likes using 'ballet' to describe all dancing styles. It annoys me."

"Obviously."

Tom lifted his eyebrows and finished his cheese curds, stacking his plate on top of Jeremy's as Greg walked over.

"There he is."

"Nice of you to show up," Jeremy said, his voice slightly slurred. "You owe me a shot of Patron."

"Okay." Greg looked around for Karen.

"He doesn't need any more shots," Gabriel said, firing another dart at the bullseye. He retrieved his darts and set them on the table.

"I have my designer driver. Designator driver." Jeremy waved his hand and picked up the darts, returning to the board.

"Buy him some cheese curds to soak up some of the alcohol," Tom suggested. "He's going to try to sing on the drive home at the rate he's going."

"Make it two orders," Gabriel said. "I'm hungry."

Karen arrived within seconds to take their order. She picked up bottles of beer and the empty plates. The men ate like starving hyenas.

"Karen!" Jeremy called, even though he was less than five feet away. "When the hell are you going to get a divorce so you and I can make it official?"

Karen glanced at Gabriel. "I knew I shouldn't have handed him those two shots of Patron."

He grinned. "Probably not. In your defense, Tom and I bought them."

Tom laughed when Jeremy's shot hit the board and bounced to the floor. "Well, fuck."

"Mind your mouth or I'll wash it out with soap," Karen said.

"Promises, promises," Jeremy said, giving her a grin. He retrieved his darts. She smiled back.

"Damn," Greg said as Karen walked away to get their order. "You have no shame."

"None," Jeremy agreed. He sat down and took a drink of his beer. "Did one of you order me another shot?"

"No!" Tom and Gabriel said together. They both laughed.

"Holy shit." Jeremy almost dropped his beer.

"You've had way too much to drink already," Tom said. "I'm afraid you'd actually have sex with Karen if she took you up on -"

"No," Jeremy said, smacking Gabriel on the shoulder and pointing.

Ava had stepped into the back room and was glancing around. When she saw them, she walked toward their table. She was wearing a dark dress. That alone was startling. She never wore dresses and Gabriel didn't see any in her closet when he stayed over. The way it hugged her body made every drop of liquid evaporate out of his mouth.

As she neared the table, he could see it was a dark green material with the back hem hanging almost to her ankles and the front hem dipping just below her knees. It was a wrap style that accentuated her cleavage without leaving any of it bare.

Despite how his loins were reacting to her physical appearance, his head was already thinking of a thousand things that could be wrong to make her show up in a bar, especially on Guy's Night Out. His stomach twitched.

He dropped the darts onto the table and stepped forward. "Are you okay?"

"Yes."

Confused, Gabriel glanced sideways. He couldn't help but notice the stares Ava was getting from other patrons, starting with those at the first table she walked by at the bottom of the stairs to the middle-aged men at the table a few feet from Gabriel's group. Jeremy was ogling her. Tom took a long pull on his drink to distract himself from staring. Greg was somewhere in the middle, obviously drawn to her but trying to look discreetly.

"What are you doing here?" Gabriel asked. As an afterthought, he added, "What are you wearing?"

"I want sex."

Jeremy knocked his beer bottle over. Foam sprayed across the table and dripped down the edge. Tom coughed, causing his beer to go down the wrong pipe. He began choking. Greg pounded him on the back several times until Tom waved him away. People were too busy staring at Ava to notice the drama.

Gabriel glanced at his friends again. He was grateful for the dim lighting while his face was crimson.

"Ava... this is Guys Night Out. I get with the guys on Fridays, no matter what."

"But I want sex," she said, louder. The middle-aged guys at the table next to them gaped at her shamelessly. Jeremy was staring at her while he tried to dab up the beer he'd spilled all over the table. He was ineffectually patting the napkin on the only dry piece of table left. Tom's eyes were cartoon huge.

"Sex is something girlfriends do with their boyfriends," Ava said. "We can use the bathroom. It is sufficiently clean. I checked."

"Ava," Gabriel said, half laughing, taking her arm, and turning slightly from the table in an attempt at semi-privacy. The short, fluttering sleeve of her dress brushed against his hand. Jesus, it was silk. "Guys Night Out doesn't get canceled except for medical or family emergencies. We've been doing this since we were kids."

"I will leave after we finish. You can go on with your plans."

Gabriel's face was flushed. The room was starting to buzz again with conversation, and most people had stopped paying obvious attention, but she was talking loud enough that his friends heard every word. He was going to catch hell for this.

He tried to muster some dignity. "I'll be over when I'm done here like I usually -"

"Are you fucking kidding me, Dude?" Jeremy blurted. "You're going to say no to that?"

Helping Jeremy wipe up his mess, Tom let out a bark of laughter and Greg snorted.

"Go get some!" Jeremy said. "We'll still be here when you get back."

Gabriel swore under his breath. He wasn't a teenager who got his rocks off anywhere he could find a closed door anymore. How did he get into this situation?

"I wore this dress for you," Ava said, running her hands down the sides curiously, oblivious to its effect on every male at the table. Jeremy was practically slobbering. "Isabel said not to wear underwear so you would-"

"Alright," Gabriel said, taking her hand and leading her toward the restrooms. The dress flared slightly as she spun around to follow him. He had to admit, it was a beautiful dress. It hugged her in all the right places and left her skin free in others.

Out of habit, Gabriel automatically started for the men's bathroom, but Ava grabbed his shirt and hauled him into the women's. The women's restroom had doors on the stalls. Someone was in the first one. Ava walked to the handicapped compartment on the far end and shoved Gabriel inside. He slammed into the wall on the opposite side, cracking his shoulder on the tile wall.

"Fuck!" he whispered, trying to stifle a laugh.

In the first stall, the person cleared her throat noisily.

Ava locked the stall door and leaned against it. She turned her head to the side as if listening to something he couldn't hear.

Leave us.

The thought was like fire in his head. Gabriel felt a dull stab of pain in his temple. The person in the first stall flushed the toilet and quickly walked to the sinks, washing her hands, and leaving. Her heels clicked rapidly on the tiles.

What in God's name was that? he thought.

He watched Ava as she stepped toward him, the hunter green dress following every move. Her eyes were predatory.

She placed her hands on his pecks and curled them just a little, just enough to grip. Leaning forward until she was only inches from his face, she growled softly. The gray in her eyes was dark with lust.

He slid his hands from her hips to her shoulders.

The door opened and chatter from the bar blasted in. Ava snarled and turned her head slightly at the intrusion.

"Let's go outside," Gabriel murmured.

Ava pushed off him. She unlocked the stall door and flung it open, exiting the restroom. Gabriel strode after her.

The front of the bar was now filled with patrons buzzing with conversation and laughter. Karen yelled something across the room to the cook. One of the other waitresses burst into loud, braying laughter. Gabriel heard none of it. His head was filled with the sound of his own blood pounding as he watched Ava's perfectly sculpted bottom weaving in between groups of people waiting to be served or standing around watching the Brewers game. He noticed they made room as Ava came through.

Outside, free of the overwhelming scents and the bodies, Ava breathed in deeply. She started walking down the sidewalk.

"Where are we going?" Gabriel asked. He couldn't see her Equinox.

"My SUV has ample room for intercourse."

"Well, hallelujah."

From somewhere, she pulled her keys out and unlocked the Equinox remotely. She was walking quickly now; even with Gabriel's longer legs, he was having trouble keeping up. Ava reached back without looking and took his hand.

His blood spiked at the hot feel of her palm against his, the way her dress whispered against her body. Every step closer drove his pulse higher. He wanted more than a few minutes with her – he wanted to spend all night with her.

Two blocks down, she abruptly rounded the corner. The Equinox was parked at an angle next to the bank, just out of the direct glow of a streetlight.

She hit a button on her fob and the rear door opened. The back seats were already folded down. There was no mistaking she had prepared for this eventuality. Knowing she'd covered all her bases sent a stab of lust straight to his loins.

Ava ducked her head and crawled in, giving Gabriel another arousing view of her posterior. He glanced up and down the street, feeling like a teenager out past curfew. Ava's hand shot out and grabbed his shirt. She dragged him into the SUV and on top of her.

"Easy," he laughed, almost driving his head into a window as he overbalanced. She hit a button and the rear door began closing. Before his head stopped spinning, she had dropped the keys and was ravaging his mouth.

He was straddling her, his hands on the floor on either side of her head, and her mouth was busy on his. His blood was boiling; he needed her now, all of her, or his body was going to simply combust. The way her hair spread over the floor of the car was driving him crazy. Her searing full mouth captured his, forcing him to respond, sending jolts of sensation through his body. Her hands were tugging on his hair, keeping their mouths joined as she feasted.

Without warning, she pushed off the floor with her right foot, tipping him off balance. He started rolling off her. She used the momentum to roll over him, slipping her leg over his hip so she was straddling him by the time his back hit the floor. Leaning over so she wouldn't hit her head, she whipped her hair over her shoulder with one arm. She began pulling at his shirt.

The dress flowed around her legs, around him. Gabriel leaned up and helped tug his shirt off. He ran his hands up her thighs. The cool, silky material brushing the backs of his hands contrasted with her feverish skin under his palms. Her body was a torch barely containing the heat. She rested her hands on either side of his head, arching her back so he had full access to her breasts. He obliged by using his teeth to tease the flesh beneath the silk until it strained against the material. Then he began using his hands. The low sounds in her throat were like purrs.

The Equinox was spacious, but he was just over six feet tall. Every time he shifted, he felt he was kicking into something. Ava didn't care. She seemed to forget about her vehicle as her mouth found his again with breath-stealing kisses. Her hair was wild around his face. A flush had risen in her cheeks and her eyes were shiny with lust. Moving her body against him, she lifted her pelvis slightly and ground it against his. The groan came from deep in his throat, seemed to come from his soul. Rising, she looked down at him.

He said her name, framed her face with his hands. She let hers wander over his chest and watched the muscles spasm.

Taking his hand, Ava slid it under her dress, guiding him toward her center. He was amazed at the heat generating there. She kept her eyes, bright and curious, on his as he skimmed his fingertips along her leg toward the heat, slipping away seconds before contact. Her thighs flexed in anticipation. When he ran the backs of his knuckles along her inner thigh, slowly making his way upward, her breath caught. Her eyes darkened as he coaxed and toyed with her. The third time, he brushed against the wet and the hot. She let out a throaty growl, her hands clamping down as she exhaled. Her fingernails bit into his chest and then gripped like tiger's claws.

A grunt escaped as pain shot into him like large, jagged pieces of glass.

Ava instantly relaxed her hands and pressed them flat on the ceiling of the vehicle as her hips pumped against his hand.

Her eyes returned to his, burning with intensity as her breath quickened.

She was a goddess over him. Her hair fell in thick waves down her shoulders. The desperation he felt was mirrored in her eyes, the same need writhing as an animal caged. As he drove her up, he heard each ragged breath as he fought to take his own.

She exhaled sharply a moment before she peaked. There was a ripping sound, and a section of the car's ceiling shredded under her nails. With her hands still poised above her head like Atlas holding the world, her thighs contracted against his hips. She shuddered violently with unbelievable strength.

For a moment, the only sound was her breath panting out.

Then her hands moved to his zipper. Her pupils seemed to be pulsing. As she unzipped and unbuttoned his jeans, he lifted his hips and helped her slide them down. She didn't wait for him. Settling herself over him before his butt hit the vehicle, she paused to take in the sensations bombarding her.

Gabriel's fingers dug into her hips as she began moving, tortuously slow. Never had he been with a woman who possessed so much control of her muscles. She constricted around him, tightly drawing him up inside her. She moved her hips against him.

Resting a hand on his chest, she rose, settled down. She leaned down and took his lips. He could feel her hair tickling his face. Her body was all blazing curves and seductive silk. Leaning up again, she pressed her hands against his chest and began to move steadily.

The world around them seemed to fade into darkness. Gabriel had no concept of time between heartbeats. He only knew the feel of her skin against his, the scent of her around him, filling him until he was all but drowning in it.

Their bodies took what they wanted from each other. Ava began to move faster, closing her eyes as she lost herself. When he heard a loud thump, he looked up to see she had slammed her palm on the window in front of her, bracing herself as she consumed him with wanton greed. The rhythm became more urgent, the air thick with desire. His heart was pounding. His breath was coming in ragged tears that burned his throat and blurred his vision. He felt her let go, felt that unmistakably fierce clenching of her muscles around him again.

As he followed her, he raised up and locked his arms around her, sealing them together as he felt his world ignite.

• • • • •

"Damn," he whispered, still unable to catch his breath.

Ava's head was resting on his shoulder. At some point, they had both fallen back onto the floor of the SUV. Gabriel felt carpet underneath him and silky woman spilling over him. He thought he had never felt anything as wonderful as what he was feeling in this exact moment. His body was sated, his mind relaxed, his emotions... well, he didn't know exactly what his emotions were doing. He didn't care. He felt invincible.

Eventually he would have to return to the bar, and his friends. Eventually seemed like a long way off.

Ava rose above him slowly. Gabriel was amused to see it took an effort on her part. Using her hands, she braced herself on his chest. Her hair was mussed, her face was still flushed.

"Do you like the dress?"

His mouth curved into a smile. "Absolutely. You ripped the ceiling off your car," he added, amazed. Ribbons of fabric hung from the ceiling where her nails had dug in.

She craned her neck to assess the damage. Turning back, she seemed somewhat embarrassed. "I will get a quote for repair on Monday."

That made him grin.

Looking dazed, she studied his face. The gray in her eyes was explosive. Tiny white lines seemed to mix with the gray, giving them the appearance that the irises were constantly in motion. They had never looked that way to him before.

The tips of his fingers grazed from her temple to her jaw. "When we're this close," he said, "sometimes it feels like you're inside my head."

Something shifted in her eyes. She leaned forward and reached past him, pulling a towel from somewhere near the front of the vehicle. She dropped it on his face and picked another one up.

"Ava," he said, moving the towel, "What - hey."

She climbed off him roughly and moved the towel under her dress.

"Why did you pull back?" he asked. He tossed the towel and pulled his pants up.

"You must return to your friends. I have taken up enough of your time."

She tossed her towel on top of his. Somewhere down the street, a car door slammed. Laughter drifted over from another bar. Ava looked around and picked up her keys.

When Gabriel's hand gently rested on her shoulder, she stilled.

"Why did you pull back, Ava?" he repeated. "Why the sudden chill?"

"It was good sex," she said, but her tone uncertain. "You gave me what I came here for."

Gabriel had to bite down on his temper. He clenched a fist to keep it from ripping out upholstery. "So, back off, you have other shit to do? Is that it?"

She finally raised her head and looked at him. "I have already taken time from you and your friends." Her eyes searched his face, confused, but her hands, rubbing the dress material between her fingertips, told him more. "Were you unsatisfied with the sex?"

He snatched his shirt off the wheel well and tugged it on. "Yes, I have a standing commitment to my friends, which they let slide tonight. The sex was phenomenal, as always. That's not the point."

"Do you want to engage in post-coital embracing?" She had moved away from him as he put his shirt on, deliberately putting as much distance as she could between them when his head was covered.

Despite his anger, he almost laughed.

"I'm more concerned with why you're treating me like biological waste when five minutes ago you couldn't keep your hands off me."

He shifted, pulling his shirt down over his jeans. Watching Ava, he saw her raise her hands like she used to in defense. At the last moment, she realized he wasn't coming toward her, and she fidgeted with neckline of her dress with one hand and dropped the other.

Defensive, Gabriel thought. Twitchy. An idea occurred to him.

"Is it because of what I said about you being inside my head?"

Hesitant, she nodded.

"I meant it as a compliment."

"I have no control over what I pick up."

"That's not what I meant. Not everything I say revolves around your ability."

This time when he moved toward her, she remained kneeling. Those dark, amazing eyes studied him, measuring his sincerity. An emotion settled on her face – affection? He brushed a strand of hair back from her temple.

"I've always felt a connection to you, from the moment I saw you." Taking her hand, he kissed her knuckles. "Your ability is not all you are to me. It's just something you can do, like driving a car or doing cartwheels."

She seemed satisfied with what she saw in his eyes and nodded again.

"I really like this dress." He ran his hands down her back, marveling at the feel of her under the satin.

"Isabel helped me pick it out. I do not wear dresses, but she said you would like this."

The eyebrow shot up. "You bought it because you thought I would like it?"

The question embarrassed her, and her cheeks filled with color. To distract her, he brushed his mouth over hers, sending thrills up her spine. He brought his hands around from her back to her hips.

"You bought something you don't normally wear to please me," Gabriel said, enthralled. "That's sweet."

Shifting uncomfortably, Ava's eyes flitted around before settling on his. "It was not entirely altruistic. I benefited from it as well. I wanted sex."

The corner of his mouth lifted. "Is that right?"

"Isabel insisted she buy it for my birthday gift."

His eyes widened. "Today is your birthday. Fuck!"

He slammed his palm onto the roof.

"I'll go tell the guys I have to leave. We should be spending tonight together. I should have taken you out to a fancy dinner, bought you some really nice jewelry…"

"I do not wear jewelry."

Gabriel crawled toward the side door and pushed it open. "I should have gotten a nice suite at a hotel with a pool…"

Ava followed him, frowning. She stood under the streetlight as he paced in a small circle.

"I have my own house. Why do I need a hotel room?"

Stopping, he glanced at her. "Do you like cake? You must like cake. What kind of cake do you like?"

"You are overreacting. I already told you today is my birthday and you have already given me a gift."

"I forgot. I know you told me, and I completely forgot. I'll make it up to you. I'll throw you a party-"

"No!" Ava said sharply, stopping him mid-stride. "No parties."

"No party?"

The fist holding her keys was shaking slightly, though her face was expressionless.

"Only bad girls have parties," she whispered.

He made the decision not to push it. For now.

"No party. What if we had another cookout? The last one was interrupted. You could hang out with my friends. It would be more of another shot at a summer cookout. No presents, no cake."

"Okay."

Taking her shoulders, he stepped in and planted a kiss on her forehead. "I have to get back to the guys. I'll see if we can get everything together for tomorrow afternoon, okay?"

She nodded.

"You're sure you don't want me to come home now? The guys will understand."

"Have fun with your friends," she said, resting her forehead against his. "I will be there when you get home."

• • • • •

"Watch your step," Griffin said, resting a hand on Isabel's shoulder as she stumbled when stepping into the elevator. He pressed the button for the floor to his flat.

Isabel turned into him, resting her head on his shoulder. She was more tired than drunk, but she'd had her fill of alcohol.

"That wasn't too bad, was it?" he asked gently.

"Your friends are nice." She sighed, then yawned. "Gabriel texted me. He wants to have a cookout tomorrow to celebrate Ava's birthday."

"Today. It's after one in the morning."

"Shit." She yawned again.

The elevator dinged and the door opened.

"Do you want to go?"

Nodding against his shoulder, she allowed him to guide her to his door. As he fumbled with the key using his left hand, she moaned softly.

"Gabriel's friends will be there," she said dreamily.

He pushed the door open and shuffled her in. "I thought you didn't like crowds," he said, just to keep her talking. He loved the sound of her voice, especially when she was tired, and it was soft like this.

"We all grew up together. Are you going to come with me?"

He smiled. She wouldn't have brought it up if it wasn't an invitation. But there was no point trying to tell her that when she was out of it.

"I can if you want. Have a seat here."

He guided her to her side of the bed, where she sat down and started pulling off her shirt. Griffin knelt and eased her shoes off.

"Your friends are really nice," she repeated, her eyes heavy.

"They like you." Lifting her feet, he tucked her in and kissed her, sweetly, on the mouth. She smiled. "Maybe we can meet them there again sometime."

"Maybe. I think I might like to have a jam session with Lina and Adam. It would be fun, I think."

"Wow. Look at you, reaching out."

"We'll see."

Picking up her clothes, he tossed them in the basket in the walk-in closet. He stripped down to his tee shirt and boxers and added his own dirty clothes to the basket before turning to get into bed.

Isabel was sitting up, rigid, her hands clasped at her chest protectively. Griffin moved to the bed and climbed in, settling next to her, touching her shoulder.

"What's wrong?"

She blinked. "I have a weird feeling."

"Did you drink too much? Do you need to throw up?"

Shaking her head, she looked around the room as if she was unfamiliar with her location.

"I just feel… weird. Like something's going to happen."

Considering, Griffin rubbed his hand up and down her back. "About your subletting the flat to Lina?"

She shook her head. Her voice was uncertain when she spoke. "It's just a feeling."

"Good or bad?"

"I don't know."

"Maybe it will come to you in a dream."

He pulled her to him and lay back on the bed, tucking her close. She curled against him. In seconds, her breathing had evened out, and she had fallen asleep without any more worry of strange feelings.

● ● ● ● ●

Silence woke him.

For the first time in the history of them sharing a bed, Gabriel woke without being ripped from sleep by a cacophony of noise or an assault from Ava. He opened his eyes to his alarm clock, its blue-white numbers showing it was just past two in the morning. He could hear her steady breathing against his shoulder. He could feel her hand barely touching his side.

Lying on his stomach, he turned his head toward her, wondering why he had awakened. Wondering why she had not.

As his eyes adjusted, he shifted his hand closer so he could curl his fingers around hers. She let out a soft moan and tightened her grip, getting more comfortable beside him. In the dark, he could make out her form and see her hair flowing over her shoulders against her pale skin. He wanted to sit up and turn the light on so he could watch her, but that would wake her up. So often her sleep was interrupted already. He didn't want to be another cause.

Surrendering to the inability to fall back asleep, Gabriel carefully disengaged his fingers from hers and slid to the edge of the bed. Thanking whoever patented memory foam, he eased out of bed without waking Ava and made his way around it to the stairs.

Despite her insistence that he did not get her anything more for her birthday, Gabriel hadn't considered the nunchucks a birthday gift. He wanted to get her something special, or make something for her specifically for her day, even if it was late. It killed him that he had forgotten it, especially when she'd just told him the week before. That he had been busy worrying about her getting drunk for the first time when he found out was of little comfort.

Only bad girls have parties.

The way she looked when she said it unnerved him. Her eyes had widened slightly, her shoulders hunched, and for a moment she looked like a scared little girl awaiting punishment.

What had that been about? Had she never had a birthday party?

He drew a glass of water and added ice to it. In the past few weeks, he'd been drinking a lot of water. It was making him leaner, and his occasional workouts with Ava, added to the daily jogging he had already been doing, was toning his body. When he reached down to scratch his stomach, he was surprised to find it was tight with muscle. He would never be a body builder, nor did he want to be, but he was getting into decent shape.

She'd changed his life so much just by being a part of it. He wished he could give her something that conveyed his love for her. What could he get her that would be a unique, personal gift?

He wondered about it as he filled another glass to set on her bedside table. She went through the liquid incredibly fast, as if she woke up periodically through the night to drink.

Walking back up the stairs with both glasses, he tried to think of anything she'd mentioned needing for the house, or for training, or for her business. Ava liked getting practical gifts because they didn't make her feel so awkward. He could call David tomorrow before the cookout and see if he had any ideas.

A soft sound coming from the bedroom brought him to attention as he reached the second floor. Walking to the doorway, he heard it again. Ava was whimpering. His eyes could make out the furniture in the room. He set her glass of water on her table and moved around to his side of the bed. Turning on the light, he used his body to block as much as he could from her as he watched her.

She was lying on her side, facing him, with her legs drawn up. Her lower lip was quivering. Climbing into bed, he made soothing noises as he neared her.

This is the big one, he thought, waiting for the attack. She was just a little late with the nightmare.

But she didn't strike out. When he gathered her up in his arms and held her close, whispered softly to calm her, she curled against his chest. He was surprised to see tears on her cheeks.

"Hey," he said softly. "Don't cry."

She shivered against him, mumbling incoherently. He pulled her tighter to him.

"What's wrong, Ava? What are you dreaming about?"

Instead of answering, she began whimpering again. She buried her face in his neck, afraid to face whatever it was that was giving her nightmares.

"Oh, Ava." He rocked her gently. "Shush now. I won't let anyone hurt you."

All but climbing into his lap, she was shaking so hard she was almost convulsing. He held her close, trying to figure out what was wrong, trying to warm her frigid body. If this was a nightmare, it was different than her usual full-on scream-fests. She'd never behaved like this before.

"Please, Ava, tell me what's wrong," he pleaded.

When she didn't respond, he rolled onto his side, gently bringing her with him and then rolling her onto her back. He covered her and tried to warm her with his body heat. Pulling the bedding up around them, he leaned up and stared down at her pale, sweaty face.

Tears were drying on her cheeks. Her face was contorted in sorrow. He brushed his thumb across her cheek, wishing he knew what to do for her.

"Ava." He kept his voice firm and steady. "Wake up."

Beneath him, her body stilled. The lines between her eyebrows slowly smoothed.

"Open your eyes."

Gabriel saw confusion and wariness in her expression. She gazed up at him and blinked.

"Hey." Instead of answering, she wrapped her fingers around his hand. His kissed her forehead. "You were having a bad dream."

Her eyes roamed, confirming she was awake, confirming the dream was over. The wariness remained on her face still. Rubbing his thumb on her temple, he searched her eyes for any clues to what she was thinking. He watched her eyes gather tears even as her expression remained as it was. As desperation rocked him, he found himself gripping her tighter than he meant to.

"What can I do?" he whispered.

The answer came not in words or expression, but as a thought echoing around his head that confused him more than it clarified:

Stay.

• • • • •

"This is the perfect day for a cookout."

Abby stood with her eyes closed, her face tilted up to the sky, her arms resting on the railing of Gabriel's deck. Her golden skin seemed to glow against her light brown hair.

Grinning, Tom stepped up behind her and wrapped his arms around her. "That's not all it's perfect for," he murmured.

She giggled.

"Ewww," Greg said.

Isabel glared at him from her seat at the table. "Nobody wanted to see you sucking face with that manipulative, cold-hearted, cu-"

"More iced tea, Izzie?" Griffin interrupted, slipping his hand over her mouth, and kissing her on the cheek.

"Wow," Gabriel said, setting a glass of water down in front of Ava. "Don't hold back, Iz."

She giggled against Griffin's hand. When she spoke, her voice was muffled. "Sorry."

He removed his hand. "Don't make me pull you over my knee."

"Don't make me like it." Her grin was quick and wicked.

"Oh!" Gabriel said, covering his ears and closing his eyes. "I don't want to hear about that."

Griffin laughed.

Ava watched them quietly from her place at the head of the table. Gabriel noticed she liked to watch people, especially when they were touching. Isabel and Griffin weren't overly affectionate in a disgusting way when they were being serious; Griffin often touched her lower back and guided her through a door or hallway, held her hand or touched it when talking to her, and tugged on her hair when he was teasing her. Abby and Tom were similar; he put a hand on Abby's shoulder and his arm around her waist. Ava studied the way each couple touched and how each responded. Platonic physical contact seemed to fascinate her just as much as romantic contact did. Even when his friends had first arrived, after they'd dropped off dishes and everyone was hugging and shaking hands, Ava sat watching as if she would later be quizzed on the social habits of humans.

She seemed to consider hugging as a greeting fascinating, unlike the time-consuming chore it seemed to be when she had to do it.

Now, watching everyone as they settled on the deck with refreshments, she hadn't mentioned this morning's dream, or what had made her upset. Oddly, she'd only woken the one time, not her usual two, and that was only because he'd disturbed her.

"I'm moving in with Griffin," Isabel suddenly blurted.

Conversations stopped. Iz heard Gabriel cough and looked over at him. She couldn't read the expression on his face. Terrified he disapproved, she fidgeted with her hands.

"Jumping right in, are we?" Griffin said, squeezing her side as he nuzzled her temple.

"I'm sorry," she said at once. "I caved under pressure."

"What pressure? Nobody was saying anything!" Greg laughed.

"Her own conscience weighs a ton," Griffin said, grinning. "We were going to say something at dinner tomorrow, Gabriel, but I guess it's out now."

"I wanted you to know first," Isabel said to her brother. "I was hoping at least one person in the family would skip the lecture."

"Why did you think I would lecture you?"

She shrugged.

"It's not because you can't afford your place, is it? Because you're welcome to stay her if you need to."

"He invited me. I thought about it-"

"For weeks," Griffin said with exaggerated horror, earning him an elbow from Izzie.

"And I made the choice. We want to live together."

"You make an adorable couple," Abby said.

"Thanks." Isabel blushed, watching Griffin's fingers weave with hers.

Gabriel studied her and seemed satisfied with what he saw. He nodded. "Good for you, Iz. Congratulations."

"Thanks, Gabe."

"You know, if Mom and Dad come off sounding a little negative, it's because they love you," he said. "They want to make sure you've thought everything through."

She raised her lip and grumbled. "I know."

An uncomfortable silence settled over them. Isabel fidgeted again.

"Why do you hide behind one emotion when you feel another?" Ava suddenly asked.

Everyone looked at her.

"What do you mean?" Gabriel asked.

"People." Ava shifted in her seat, uncomfortable, wanting to separate herself from the crowd of so many bodies. Her skin itched. A throbbing headache was forming at her temples.

"If your parents are worried for you about your decision to move in with Griffin, your mother's response to the fear will manifest as disappointment. She will say things to provoke you, hurtful things that are degrading and meant to make you feel inferior."

"I thought I was the only one that noticed," Iz muttered, wishing she had whiskey to chug down. Or an appletini. Last night, those drinks had gone down like water. All three of them.

"She is hoping that making you feel inferior will make you want her approval. Your need for her approval will stop you from moving in with Griffin to appease her, which will keep you safe, in her opinion."

Abby and Tom had turned from the railing and were watching Isabel, sympathetic. Jeremy was leaning forward, for once ignoring Ava's physical attributes and concentrating on what she was saying. Greg shifted uncomfortably.

"Instead, you will become angry. As you have no problem expressing yourself, you will respond accordingly to your mother's disrespect, then regret it instantly. I have seen this happen in your family dynamic in similar situations. Why not skip all the drama and just tell you they are worried?"

"If you can figure that out," Gabriel said, "You could make a shitload of money."

"Sometimes it's an unconscious reaction," Griffin said, interested in Ava's analysis. She was studying Isabel like one would study a bug under a microscope. "People often speak before they think, especially when their children are involved."

"Sometimes parents just need someone to hate because the child they're stuck with isn't the one they wanted to live. I guess I drew the short straw."

Gabriel looked over at Isabel, his eyes rounded. "Is that what you think?"

"Oh, Isabel," Abby said, moving forward to give her a hug.

She stood abruptly. The legs of the chair ground against the deck surface. "It's not too early to drink, right? I'm going to get some whiskey."

Turning before Griffin could touch her, she quietly disappeared into the house. Ozzie followed her happily until she closed the door. He looked after her, giving a soft whine.

"Come here, Oz," Gabriel said, patting his thigh.

"Shit," Jeremy said.

Gabriel looked at Griffin. "Has she said anything like that to you before?"

He has no idea, Griffin thought. How the fuck does he not know she blames herself for her sister's death? How did he miss their mother blaming Isabel for everything?

Because the people closest to the situations always did, of course. And because people that were hurting didn't show others what they didn't want others to see.

"I think that's a discussion for a different time and place." He gazed mildly at Gabriel, hoping he would take the initiative to bring it up to his sister later. God knew Isabel wouldn't.

Gabriel slid his chair back, but Griffin held up his hand. "I'll see if she's okay. Sorry to get so serious on your birthday, Ava."

She said nothing, just looked thoughtfully out at the tree line.

When he was gone, Greg cleared his throat. "Well... that was... tense."

"So, Ava," Jeremy said. She turned her head and fixed her eyes on him. "Have you had to kick anyone's ass lately?"

• • • • •

"Do you want to talk about it?"

"No," Isabel said immediately, replacing the cap on the bottle of whiskey and leaving it on the counter. She took a large gulp and closed her eyes. With each breath, it felt like she was inhaling pins and needles.

897

"Gabriel doesn't know you blame yourself for Hayden's death, does he?"

"Why the fuck would he?" She took another swig, glanced at the bottle, and unscrewed the cap. "It's my problem, not his."

"I think you have some things you should discuss with him."

"I'm not your patient."

Pushing the bottle back without refilling her glass, Isabel picked up her drink and walked around the island to him. She wound her arm around his neck and gave him a long kiss.

Wary of the sudden change in her demeanor, he gazed down at her.

"I'm sorry," she said. "I know you love me, and that's why you're trying to help. I didn't mean to take it out on you."

He searched her eyes and saw they were clear and bright. She hadn't disappeared into wherever she usually went when she discussed her family. He kissed her forehead.

"Thank you for saying that," he said, kissing her again.

"I'll talk to him after everyone leaves. I'll have him drop me off when we're done if he doesn't mind. I need to talk to him without you around. I'm sorry."

"Don't be. I know it's hard. I think you'll feel better, after."

"I guess we'll see." She shrugged. "I don't want him to think less of me for being too weak to protect Hayden. Come on."

Before he could tell her it wasn't her fault, she was already walking away.

Back on the deck, she sat down and bribed Ozzie with scruff scratches and belly rubs.

"Sorry, baby. Yes, aren't you a good boy? I didn't mean to shut the door in your face." After a few moments of speaking in a silly tone, she glanced up. "Sorry about that. I guess quitting my job and moving are stressing me out more than I thought."

"Do you need help with anything?" Abby asked.

Iz shook her head. "I think taking a break today with friends is the best thing. I need to decompress. So, Ava, did you do anything special for your birthday yesterday?"

"Gabriel and I had very satisfying sex in my Equinox."

Isabel snickered, then started snorting when Gabriel choked on his water. Jeremy laughed so hard iced tea came out his nose. Abby stared at Ava, unsure if she was being serious. Tom looked everywhere except at Ava, and Greg was suddenly interested in reading the ingredients on his soda can.

"Well," Iz said, trying to hide her grin, "that can certainly be special."

"It is." Ava ran her index finger around the rim of her glass carelessly. "Gabriel is very thorough, and his stamina is-"

"How about we change the subject?" Gabriel suggested, leaning forward to take Ava's hand.

"You have nothing to be embarrassed about," she said. "You satisfy me sexually and intellectually-"

"My friends and sister don't need to hear about it."

"Why, Gabriel, you're blushing," Iz said, doing her best impression of a southern accent.

"Fuck off."

"You have no filter at all, do you?" Jeremy asked Ava, his voice filled with awe. "I didn't think I would ever meet someone more direct than Isabel."

"Filter?"

"You say exactly what you think. You have no concept of boundaries within social situations."

"I answered your question," Ava said, looking around the table with her brow furrowed. "If you did not want to know the answer, why did you ask?"

"Most people keep their sex lives private." Gabriel rubbed his thumb over the back of her hand. "They avoid the subject."

The wrinkles between her eyes deepened. "It was the only thing I did for my birthday, besides go shopping with Isabel. She was with me when I shopped, so the only other special thing I did was with you. Why are humans so shy about intercourse? It is a natural activity among most species."

Isabel snorted again.

Tom cleared his throat. "Yes, but there are certain cultural and social practices that are in place to prevent awkwardness regarding taboo subjects like sex. You wouldn't discuss it with your parents, would you?"

"My foster mother was dead before I had any interest in becoming sexually active," Ava said, sipping her water. "When I became curious, I discussed the questions I had about sex with my foster father."

Tom coughed into his drink. Abby glared at him but patted his back.

"Jesus." Jeremy started laughing.

Isabel tried to contain her laughter and instead let out a long snort. She lay her arms flat on the table, one hand on top of the other, and she dropped her head on her hands, her shoulders shaking violently.

Griffin bit the inside of his cheek. "I imagine that was somewhat awkward for him to discuss with you."

"I do not know why," Ava said icily. "I was of legal age to consent. The partner I chose was physically fit, with above average intelligence. I had known him for several years before we became sexually active. I trust him with my life, or I would not have engaged in-"

"Uh, Gabriel, does she always talk like this?" Greg interrupted.

"She's very honest," he said mildly. He leaned back in his chair and stretched his arm across the back of hers. "Things get a little weird when she discusses her previous partner like he was a science experiment, but the honesty is refreshing."

Jeremy gaped. "She discusses the guy she previously banged-"

Gabriel's cool stare stopped him. "Careful."

Jeremy looked at Ava. "You talk to your current boyfriend about your previous boyfriend?"

"We've met," Gabriel said. "He's a good guy."

Isabel was giggling.

"Vincent was not my boyfriend. Gabriel is the first relationship I have ever been in. I am not accustomed to the rules of courtship."

"I don't think my brain can absorb all this," Greg said, pressing his fingers to his temples.

Jeremy cackled. "Did she just say, 'rules of courtship'?"

"What did your foster father say when you asked him about all this?" Abby asked, trying to get the conversation back on some kind of track. Although her husband was no longer coughing, she continued to rub her hand up and down his back absently.

"His face was flushed, and his pulse quickened, but he answered my questions. I had no one else to ask. I had many questions. He has never lied to me. He approved of my choice of partner, although I did not require his approval. I only told him so he would not worry. He is very protective of me because of my childhood. I did not want him to feel the need to place undue stress on himself for my sake."

"I'm sure he did anyway," Abby said, her voice taking on a quality Ava had heard in Ruth's tone sometimes. "Parents worry about their children no matter how safe they are."

"Is your foster father the one that was in the hospital the last time we had a cookout?" Tom asked.

She nodded. "David and Ruth fostered me when I was seven. They later adopted me."

"You seem very close with David." Abby smiled at Ava.

Ava did not know what to say to that, so she kept silent.

"What about your family before that?" Jeremy asked.

Gabriel felt Ava's spine stiffen slightly. He rubbed his fingers over the tense muscles at the back of her neck.

"I had no family before David and Ruth."

"Were you in foster care? Did your birth parents have you up to that point?"

"Jeremy," Gabriel said, his tone warning.

"I spent the first five years of my life moving around foster homes. I had behavioral problems that most homes could not manage. When I was four and a half…"

Gabriel leaned up. "You don't have to talk about this if you don't want to."

Ava gazed at him for a long time. Her eyes were slightly darker than usual. Otherwise, she didn't seem to be reacting.

"You want your friends to get to know me." She turned back to Jeremy. "When I was four and a half, a couple took me in. I stayed with them for over two years, until they tired of me. They left me chained in a barn."

"Oh, my God." Abby clutched Tom's hand. "I'm so sorry."

"They were very abusive." Ava went on as if she hadn't heard. "In the time they had me, they broke seventeen bones in my body."

Abby began crying. Tom immediately held her, touching, trying to comfort, and feeling impotent in his efforts. Greg looked miserably guilty, as if he were somehow responsible. Jeremy was studying his hands, his expression hard and thoughtful.

Gabriel hadn't known all the details, and even after all he had seen, he was still surprised at the depravity Ava had endured. Yet knowing helped clarify the early morning nightmares, the instant suspicion, the unwillingness to touch. Suddenly her behavior didn't seem so erratic; in fact, she seemed to be a very well-adjusted person, considering.

"I broke two bones in my wrist and fractured my collarbone fighting to get away when they chained me in the barn," Ava continued. "That is how I came to David and Ruth."

"Sweet God," Abby whispered. "What a strong, brave child you must have been."

Shifting uncomfortably, Ava lifted her glass. She had not been strong or brave. The Monster had done most of the work for her.

"Please tell me these assholes were executed. Twice." Isabel's hand clenched down hard on Griffin's. He lifted it and kissed it, rubbing it against his cheek to calm her. She was crying now, too, quiet tears that burned all the way down her cheeks.

"Wisconsin doesn't have the death penalty," Jeremy said, gritting his teeth. "Unfortunately."

"They are both dead." Ava stood casually. "I need to refill my water. Does anyone else need a refill?"

"Let's go inside," Gabriel said. "We need to start getting lunch ready anyway, if anyone's still hungry." As they filed into the house, the atmosphere was heavy with tension. Sensing it, the dogs sneaked inside with their heads lowered.

Gabe turned to Ava. "Are you okay?"

"Your friends are entertaining."

"You don't mind discussing your abusive foster parents?"

"Reciting the past does not upset me. You want me to get acquainted with them, and it turns out I appreciate their company more than I thought I would."

Despite the subject matter of the conversation, her eyes were bright and curious. Gabriel was surprised to see she was enjoying engaging with his friends, that she hadn't just said so to appease him.

Shaking his head, he kissed her temple. "You are unique."

They walked into the kitchen to find preparations for the cookout already underway.

"Are you okay to keep talking about this?" Isabel asked, sitting at the island, "or do you want to stop?"

Ava looked mildly confused. "I do not hold onto the past like most humans seem to. You may ask me questions if you like."

"So, you said those fuck knobs are dead," Iz said, pulling out a butcher knife and cutting board. She had contained her tears and was using anger to keep them at bay. "What happened? Jeremy's right: Wisconsin doesn't have a death penalty."

"Janine killed herself while awaiting trial. Mack was stabbed to death a few years into his prison sentence."

"Good," Isabel snapped. "I hope they're both rotting in hell. Bastards."

Jeremy and Gabriel nodded at this.

"What about your birth mother, Ava?" Abby asked softly, dicing up tomatoes. She continued sniffling. "Do you know anything about her?"

"I know she put me up for adoption immediately after giving birth because she was not ready to be a parent. She was young and had her entire life ahead of her. Apparently, my life was an inconvenience."

"Have you ever tried reconnecting with her?" Greg asked, forming ground beef into balls to make hamburger patties.

Ava poured herself another glass of water. "Why would I? She had no use for me when I was born. I have no use for her now."

"But she's your mother." This came from Abby.

Ava stared at her so long Abby became uncomfortable.

"Any mammal can copulate and bear offspring," she said without a drop of emotion. "Doing so does not make it a mother. Ruth and David gave me everything I needed."

"This must a very happy birthday for you," Isabel smirked.

"I would not be here if I did not want to be," Ava said seriously, earning a cackle from Iz.

"Cheers to that," Tom said, raising his glass.

The others joined in.

•　•　•　•　•

They ate and talked of their jobs, their children, and their hobbies. Ava watched them laugh easily as they interacted. How quickly they accepted her into their group, she thought with wonder. Because she was with Gabriel, they enjoyed her without questioning his judgment. They invited her to join their conversations, listened as she spoke, made her feel part of their lives. For the first time in her life, she felt the warmth of friendship.

And she knew that by the end of the day, she would feel the agony of their loss.

•   •   •   •   •

Isabel waved to Jeremy and watched him drive away, exhausted but content. Behind her, Griffin was sturdy and warm against her back. He rubbed his hands up and down her arms, which were cool in the chilly evening air.

"Are you sure you want to talk to him alone? I can hang out without giving input," he said, wrapping his arms around her for warmth.

She curled her hands up around his wrists and rested her head against his chest.

"I need to be able to do it alone, but thank you."

Nuzzling her hair, he inhaled deeply. "Call me if you need me to come back, for any reason."

She turned into his embrace. "I will. I don't know how late I'll be. I guess that depends on how deep we get into it tonight. I may be late, or I may just sleep over, if I'm too tired or we drink a little too much. I'll text you if I'm going to stay over."

Framing her face with his hands, he gave her a long kiss. "It was fun today. You guys are as close as siblings."

She grinned. "We all grew up here. The guys were all in Gabe's class in elementary school, and they've been friends ever since."

He kissed her again. "Good luck with your brother. He'll understand. I'll see you later."

"I love you."

"The feeling's mutual, Miss Harris."

Walking into the house after he left, Isabel sighed and started toward the kitchen. The cookout had been great, as always. She'd missed being with her friends over the colder months. In spite of some of the heavier conversation, things had lightened up and there had been plenty of laughter for the majority of the gathering.

Gabriel was in the kitchen cleaning up as she entered. She automatically began helping, setting leftover burgers into a container.

"Where's Ava?"

He glanced up, gauging her mood as he pulled a beer from the refrigerator. "Bathroom, I think. How's it going?"

She smiled. "I really needed this today. Thanks for pulling it together. Good times."

Grinning, he slid the bottle of whiskey her way. "It was good times. A little heavy at the beginning," he added, raising his eyebrow.

Trying to ignore the knot forming in her stomach, Iz poured herself a drink. "It's no big deal."

"Do you think Mom hates you because Hayden died? Because if you do, that is a big deal."

He set a stack of small tubs in front of her. Setting aside the container of meat, she began transferring the items in the relish tray to the leftover tubs.

"It's my fault she's dead."

Gabriel stopped moving. The words hung in the air like smoke, thick and acidic and stale.

"She woke up to go to the bathroom in the middle of the night and tried to get me to go with her. I was too tired."

"Oh, Iz." He rubbed his hand down the back of his neck, realized he was doing it, and fought to bring his hand down to the counter.

"I was pissed that she'd woken me up, so I went back to bed. I guess she couldn't hold it until morning because she got up again later and left the tent. Our sister was raped and murdered because I couldn't spare five minutes to go with her."

Rubbing his hands over his face, Gabriel turned to the cupboard above the refrigerator and pulled out a bottle of Jägermeister. He pulled two shot glasses from another cupboard and set them on the counter, too hard.

"The only thing you did by not going with Hayden," he said, pouring them each a generous shot, "was keep yourself from getting killed."

They raised their drinks in toast, tapped them twice on the countertop, and took the shots. Isabel sighed.

"Hello, friend," she whispered, skimming her fingertips down the bottle.

Gabriel poured two more shots.

"I looked out when she left," Iz continued, lifting her glass with an arm that felt like a cement pillar, "I saw a man in a blue hoodie walking toward the restrooms."

Again, they raised their drinks, tapped them twice, downed the shots. Gabriel refilled the glasses.

"I was afraid he would come after me, too, so I fell asleep hiding in my sleeping bag. When I woke up, Hayden was missing."

"Again." Gabriel's eyes had taken on a glassy sheen.

They saluted, tapped the counter, drank. Isabel followed her shot with a drink of water to help clear the sickly-sweet taste out of her mouth.

"Mom blames me for Hayden's death because I got her killed."

Iz barely felt her face as the tear slipped down her cheek and couldn't feel her arm to lift a hand and wipe the tear away. She felt hollowed out. She felt free. She was too tired to know if she was relieved or horrified that Gabriel now knew.

"She doesn't know any of this," Iz continued, "I didn't tell anyone except Griffin, because he needled it out of me. But Mom was always closer to Hayden. It's only obvious she'd rather have her here than me."

Gabriel had been leaning forward with his hands on the counter. Now his head came up and he gave her a look so intense she took a step back.

"Don't ever say that. Don't think it."

Feeling another wave of tears, she pulled the relish dish closer and continued putting vegetables into containers. Her moves were terribly slow now, and it took all her concentration to make her hands do what her head was telling them to do. She blinked slowly to try to get her eyes to focus.

"I can't lose you, too, Isabel."

She'd never heard his voice sound so small. Pausing with a handful of black olives dangling over a container, she glanced at him and saw he was staring at her with those faded blue jean eyes. Those beautiful eyes that brought Hayden back into the room every time she looked at him.

"Hayden was older than you, and bigger than you, and the bastard still got her," he said, his voice hoarse. "There's nothing you could have done. He would have taken both of you, and I would have lost two sisters instead of one. I can't lose you."

She walked toward him as he came toward her, embracing her in a fierce hug that took her breath but somehow allowed her to finally breathe after all these years of drowning. He smelled of wood chips and grilled meat, of fresh cut grass and watermelon, and now a little like Jägermeister. He smelled like

Gabriel, her older brother. Her protector. Everything she had kept secret from him was out in the open. The feeling was terrifying and wonderful.

Sighing, she felt light enough to float toward the ceiling if he let go of her.

She mumbled something against his chest.

Stepping back, he looked down at her. "What?"

"I said, I think Ava is having a problem if she's been in the bathroom this long."

He glanced around, noticing she hadn't come back for the first time. Noticing they were alone.

"Where are the dogs?"

Whistling, he walked toward the half bath, calling out to Ozzie and Maya. The door was open, the room empty. As they neared the front door, they heard a sound coming from the living room. It sounded like someone talking.

"Ava?" Isabel called. She nudged Gabriel. "Is someone else still here?"

"Shouldn't be. Just us three." Gabriel instinctively took the lead.

Ozzie and Maya stood between the foyer and the living room. Maya's head was level with her body, her tail down and ears back, her lips drawn back over her teeth. Ozzie, standing behind her, had his body arched up, his tail between his legs and his ears and his eyes pointed down. He was whining and repeatedly licking his lips, terrified.

"Maya," Gabriel said firmly because she was afraid but also ready to fight, "Come here."

She gave another low growl before turning and walking toward him, keeping her eyes on whatever was in the living room. Ozzie instantly followed her. Gabriel took their collars and moved them over to Isabel.

"Keep them here."

He waited until she took their collars before turning back and walking toward the source of their fear.

Only one lamp was on in the living room, a wall sconce near the fireplace. It cast a soft glow over the room. The air seemed particularly chilly in here, and the hair on Gabriel's arms instantly rose. Stepping softly so his boots didn't make noise on the hardwood floor, he walked to the wall and flipped the switch that turned on all the floor lamps.

Ava was sitting on the floor in the half lotus position, her hands dangling off her knees. Her eyes were closed. She was breathing the way she did when she meditated during their sessions with Daniel after her classes. Long, deep breaths that cleared the mind and focused all attention onto one subject. Why had this put the dogs on alert?

Not wanting to disturb her, Gabriel took a step back. Ava opened her eyes. They were milky white.

Behind him, Isabel whispered, "Holy fuck."

Turning back to her, he spat, "Where are the dogs?"

"I put them outside."

He closed his eyes, opened them, and set a hand on her shoulder. "Be quiet. No sudden moves. Sit in one of the recliners and stay there."

She nodded and they walked toward Ava slowly. Iz put her hand on Gabriel's shoulder so he knew she was there. When she reached the recliner, she veered off and sank quietly into the chair.

Ava was in the center of the room. Her back was straight, but she was relaxed. Those odd unblinking eyes were aimed toward Gabriel, but she might as well have been staring right through him. He didn't know if she could see him or not. He didn't know if she was aware of her surroundings.

"Ava?"

Her eyes were freaking him the fuck out. They were as white as opals, glazed. The ground beneath his feet seemed shift the few times he had seen her like this. He took a step toward her cautiously.

"You are not welcome here. I did not call for you."

Pausing, he held his breath. He didn't know how he knew, but something told him she wasn't in the room with him. Who the hell was she talking to?

A thin trickle of blood oozed from her left ear.

"Leave, or I will remove you."

A lightning bolt of unease flashed up his spine at the emotionless tone of her voice, the confidence behind it. It was the tone she had used on the woman in the restaurant the night he and Isabel watched her take down the man with a single punch.

"Should we leave her alone?" Iz whispered.

He shook his head, keeping his eyes on Ava. Keeping his voice low, he said, "She isn't talking to us."

Ava didn't seem to notice their presence. She continued as if they hadn't spoken.

"I am inside The Boundary. No one can enter without my permission."

A sound like thunder echoed in the house. Gabriel looked around the room. Isabel brought her knees up to her chest, hugging her legs. Her eyes were enormous.

"North, south, east, west." As Ava named each direction, a sound like a heavy door slamming echoed around the room. After the fourth, another rumbling sound. The very floor beneath them seemed to vibrate. "Those in The Interval cannot get through the walls of The Boundary unless I invite them. Everyone out."

Gabriel felt dizzy, like he was trying to walk in a building during an earthquake. He walked over to Ava, making sure to keep his distance, and sat facing her, cross legged. He was afraid the nausea would make him sick if he remained standing. What the hell was she doing?

For several moments, Ava was silent. Then: "Come out of the shadows. I called for you."

It was like listening to one side of a telephone conversation. Nothing made sense. Everything was surreal.

"Do not be afraid... He cannot reach you in here... You are safe... I need you to tell me..."

She let out an exasperated sigh.

Gabriel was unsure what to do. Should he touch her? What would she do if she thought he was attacking her?

She was as close to the floor as she was going to get, and she was breathing regularly. She was in complete control, as far as he could see. Gabriel considered this information and decided he shouldn't try to break her out of whatever she was doing.

"Hayden." She said the name loudly, clearly.

Hearing his sister's name jolted Gabriel. Behind him, he heard Isabel's sharp intake of breath. He ran his hand down the back of his neck as questions blasted through his head. Every part of his body was screaming at him to interfere. He had to force himself to stay seated and keep his mouth shut.

For a moment, Ava frowned. Then: "Show me."

She sat very still. Seconds passed. Blood appeared on her left temple and ran down the side of her face. For a moment, her eyelids fluttered, and her body swayed. Just as Gabriel wondered if he would have to catch her, she opened her eyes again. She was still unsteady, but she no longer looked like she was going to fall over.

"Isabel," she whispered.

Gabriel heard the creak of the chair as Isabel shifted and put his hand out to stop her.

"Don't," he said softly. "She's not talking to you. She's not here."

Tears welled in her eyes. Her lower lip began to tremble, and then her entire body. Gabriel watched as tears began running down her cheeks. He was startled to see her lips were turning blue.

"Gabe."

His name left her lips on a sigh. She sucked in a breath as if she only had a limited supply of them.

"I am sorry," she whispered. "I am so sorry."

As if rising from the depths of the ocean, she suddenly reared back, gasping, her fingers scratching at her neck. A gush of water burst from her mouth. Splashing across the floor, it instantly soaked Gabriel's knees and spattered his boots. The faint smell of fish and frogs, moss, and leaves wafted in the air. Ava dragged herself backward across the floor.

Gabriel chased after her. He tried to pry her hands off her skin. Thin red streaks of blood were already rising from the cuts her nails were creating.

Another burst of water erupted from her, this time drenching Gabriel's torso.

I need the door! she yelled in his head. She was leaning back, trying to move away from him.

"Ava, I don't know what that means," Gabriel said, fighting with her hands. Damn it, she was so fucking strong.

She closed her eyes, held her breath. Let it out in a rush. When she spoke, her voice was calmer. Still not completely relaxed, but better than the panic.

"The door is in front of me. All I have to do is open it and-"

A blast of air thrashed across them, whipping Ava's hair around her face. She fell forward into Gabriel's arms. Gasping and coughing, she held onto him, her fingers digging into his arms.

What the almighty fuck was that? Gabriel held her, unsure how to help. The only thing he could do was hold her and let her know he was there for her.

He wasn't sure how long they sat hunched on the floor. He was vaguely aware of Isabel walking up with a stack of towels, dropping some to the floor to soak up the mess and setting two near him for when they were ready to dry themselves off.

Ava gradually regained her breath. She sat up groggily, looking around the room. Her eyes were no longer opal orbs; they had returned to their natural gray color, but they were haunted.

"Do you know where you are?" Gabriel asked, keeping a hand on her elbow.

She nodded. Almost as an afterthought, she said, "I solved the riddle."

He didn't understand that.

"Ava." He brushed her tears away with his thumbs. "What were you doing? Was that a... was that a vision?"

She swallowed. "I did not think it would hurt so much. I did not think it would matter."

It seemed to take some effort, but she forced herself to focus on his face. Her eyes were filled with sorrow. Their ashen depths showed awareness despite her slow responses. Yet she wasn't making sense.

"I should not have allowed myself to become emotionally involved."

"Ava," Gabriel said firmly, giving her a shake. "Tell me what's going on."

"I wanted to give you peace."

"What are you talking about?"

"I felt a part of something today, with your friends," she whispered. She touched his face, loving the way his stubble scraped against her palm. "I wanted to give something back to you."

Closing her eyes, she took a deep breath. "It does not matter; none of it matters. The end is the same. The sorrow remains. Why does she want you to know?"

She shook her head. "How is not as important as you think. The pain will be the same."

Raking her hands through her hair, she pressed her hands to the sides of her head.

"Ava-"

She raised her head. Her eyes were red; Gabriel wasn't sure if it was the vision or from crying. She rose onto her knees and took his face in her hands.

"I don't know what you're talking about," he said, holding onto her arms.

Fiercely trying to understand, he searched her eyes, looking for emotion, understanding, anything that made sense.

She leaned forward and kissed him. It was rough and desperate, and his hands cupped her face before he knew he had moved them. She put all she was into the kiss, knowing it would be her last. When his mind was consumed with her and nothing else, she settled back on her calves.

She was in control of her emotions now, had stamped them down. She was studying him with the kind of professional, emotionless gaze a doctor or police officer would give the relatives of someone that had just died.

"Hayden was not kidnapped."

Gabriel stared. There was nothing else to do. The information was not penetrating deep enough; he heard it but didn't understand it.

Beside them, Isabel had moved to the coffee table and sat, quietly watching. Now she leaned forward with her elbows resting on her knees.

"What did you say?"

"Do you still want to know what happened to her?" Ava asked. Her eyes moved from Isabel's to Gabriel's.

"I thought you didn't know." He was shaking and couldn't seem to stop. A deep, bone-throbbing chill had settled over him.

"She showed me."

She would have done anything to erase the sorrow from his face. To smooth the agony from Isabel's life. Sitting in front of these two people, people she had become so close to, she felt every sharp stab of their grief.

Isabel has eased off the coffee table and was crouched on the floor. Her thoughts were a jumble of disbelief and terror racing around so fast Ava found it hard to focus on any one emotion.

Gabriel was numb. Years of not knowing, of guessing, had exhausted his mind, his spirit. Here was finally the truth he had been looking for, even if he said he had made his peace. Was he ready to face it? He tried to speak and had to clear his throat to continue.

"Is... she's dead, right? She has to be for you to... see her?"

Ava nodded slowly. "She died that night at the campground."

The affirmation was heartbreaking. Even after all those years of knowing, receiving confirmation was difficult to take. Ava watched Gabriel's eyes fill and felt her heart break.

Isabel let out a sob and covered her mouth with the back of her hand. Hot, heavy tears began coursing down her cheeks.

"What happened?" Gabriel rasped. His voice was barely audible.

"She woke in the night," Ava said, trying to keep her voice even. "She had to use the bathroom. Not far from your camp, she stumbled and hit her head. She became disoriented and lost her way in the woods."

"The police said the kidnapper probably hit her to keep her quiet," Gabriel said, shuddering. "Because they found blood on the ground. Some sweatshirt material was found in the area. That's why they thought she was kidnapped."

Ava swallowed hard. "She wandered for over an hour. The rain destroyed most of the evidence. She was cold because of it. She had a concussion. That is why she could not find her way back to the camp site. When she stumbled... too close to the river's edge, she lost her balance and fell in. She drowned."

Tears slipped down Gabriel's cheeks. Which was worse? Kidnapping and torture or fighting for air? Jesus, what was he supposed to do now?

Ava took his face in her hands again. Her voice was soft but confident. "She felt no pain."

"Yeah?" he said, trying to pull away. She held him firmly. "How do you know that?"

"Because she showed me," she whispered.

None of it mattered. Dead was dead. Her peace didn't bring the living peace. Not yet. Maybe not for a long time.

Gabriel broke free this time and stood, backing away. Everyone backed away, eventually. "I need some time to... deal with this."

Ava stood slowly.

She nodded. A feeling was growing inside her, starting in her stomach, and spreading into the rest of her body. Unsure what it was, Ava tried to shut it down before it raged out of control.

Gazing at Isabel, she felt as if a piece of herself had died inside her. Isabel was staring toward the front window, her eyes blank.

"I don't know how to tell my family something like this. Do you... Christ." Gabriel ran a hand down his face. The hand was shaking. "Do you know where her bod...body is?"

"Everywhere. Nowhere. Nature has reclaimed her."

Even though he had asked the question, he was visibly startled at her answer. His face had gone deathly pale. His eyes looked at her from sunken sockets.

"She was still wearing the bracelet Isabel made her the year before she died."

• • • • •

"But I saw…" Isabel choked back a sob. The two people in front of her double, tripled as the tears began falling again. "I saw the man in the hoodie."

"The man you saw had nothing to do with Hayden. Their paths never crossed."

"The police found torn material a few feet from where they found Hayden's shoe…"

"From a camper earlier the day before. The police had a theory based on the little evidence they found. It was never more than that."

"They said Sam King skipped town right after her disappearance. He's a convicted pedophile."

Ava was shivering. Harder than reliving whatever fate had befallen the spirit she communicated with was the denial of the survivors when she told them. She had never hated what she was before, but she hated herself now.

"She drowned, Isabel. No one hurt her."

Gabriel paced in front of the fireplace; his hair shoved up in spikes from where his hands had been raking through it. His heart felt ready to explode.

"Thank you." Isabel's voice shook, but she kept her gaze steady on Ava's as she spoke. "Thank you for telling us what happened to her."

Ava nodded.

They both looked at Gabriel, who was still pacing, still thinking. Over the last ten minutes, he seemed to have aged ten years. His eyes, always hinting at sorrow no matter what his expression was, were now filled with unadulterated grief. They were glassy with tears no longer spilling over. His shoulders were stiff, his hands clenched.

Isabel walked over to him. When he turned back to continue pacing, he jumped, too lost in his own head to expect to see her. She stopped him by resting her hands on his forearms.

"Gabriel."

Wiping his cheeks, he took a deep breath. "I need to be alone with this."

Isabel nodded. Turning back to Ava, she crossed her arms over her chest. "I sing at The Raz tonight. Can you drop me off at Griffin's apartment to get my car?"

The younger woman nodded stiffly.

Turning back to Gabriel, Iz avoided throwing her arms around him.

"Call me if you need anything."

He didn't answer. That bothered her. She wanted to hug him, but he'd pulled away from her when she touched his arms. Never in their lives had he pulled away from her. Forcing herself to remember it wasn't personal, that he was trying to process overwhelming information, she tried to push away the desperation that clawed at her.

All she could do was give him time.

She turned to leave. Touched Ava's arm. "I'll wait in the car."

When it was just the two of them, Gabriel suddenly started toward the door. "I have to let the dogs in."

Ava flinched at the mechanical tone of his voice. He was no longer connected to her. She felt him pull away mentally and fought to stay in control of her emotions. His body was in the room with her, but his mind was not. It had retreated to a place where it could take the information, go over and over it, try to make sense of it, while his body went on performing the necessary functions to continue surviving.

Ava knew that place. It was a prison as much as a refuge; it confined as much as it soothed. It kept the bad out, but it also kept all the thoughts circling around, repeating the lies that kept the prisoner from wanting to leave its sanctuary. So easy to get stuck in that place, to hide while the world went on outside.

Hayden stood in the double doorway, tugging on the end of her braid. Her eyes were wide, her lips trembling. As Gabriel walked through her, she shimmered and disappeared.

Ozzie and Maya charged in the front door, passing Gabriel, and running to Ava. They circled her as she forced herself to walk to the kitchen. Although she did not care if she ever used the dish again, she pulled out the bowl with the recipe she brought to the cookout from the refrigerator. Wasting food was a pet peeve of hers, but she could see herself throwing the entire contents of this bowl into the trash as soon as she was home. Suddenly eating seemed like too much of a chore to ever be able to manage it again.

Gabriel was still standing in the foyer by the front door. His eyes were out of focus, cast at the floor. If she reached for him, Ava knew he would recoil. Her chest ached at the thought that he would turn from her when she reached for him. She suddenly knew exactly how he felt when she did it to him, and shame washed over her, mixing with guilt and sorrow.

She gathered her keys and passed by him on her way out the door. The dogs followed her as far as the porch and stopped. Ozzie whined.

The fleeting thought she caught from Gabriel ripped through her and left her feeling empty.

I will never forgive her for doing this.

•   •   •   •   •

Her entire body was shaking. She did not remember most of the drive to Griffin's apartment, or the drive home. Isabel was wonderfully silent, trapped in her own thoughts, curled in the seat. When they parted ways, she squeezed Ava's hand and didn't bother trying to hide her tears.

At her house, Ava stumbled up the porch stairs, and her hands shook as she tried to unlock the door. She dropped the keys twice before she was finally able to slide the key into the lock.

She had not expected to feel so betrayed. It was a sharp emotion, slicing into her body from all angles, while simultaneously wrapping its hands around her throat and squeezing. Another person's opinion had never mattered to her before. Feeling so much pain from the actions of someone else, especially when those actions were not physical, was illogical. Gabriel had not touched her in anger. He had not even spoken to her harshly. So why was her heart pounding so hard? Why was she so upset?

You do not care. It does not matter.

But she did care. She did not want to, but she did. She thought she could trust him. She wanted to trust him. For the first time in her life, she had opened herself to a man in ways she promised herself she never would. She had allowed him to see her, all of her.

She dropped her purse on the floor and her keys in the little dish on the table just inside the door. She could not stop her hands from shaking. Her eyes were burning. Something inside her chest was trying to claw its way out. Her legs felt wobbly, as if they were made of Play-Doh.

Ava walked to the cupboard to get a glass for water. As she lowered the glass, her hand simply lost its strength, the glass sliding through her fingers and bouncing off the edge of the counter. Shards scattered across the marble and dropped to the linoleum. Her boots crunched over them as she walked to the living room, lowering onto the couch. She curled her right hand and tucked it just under her chin, the way she had done as a child when Mack was slamming around in the kitchen, and she knew he was working his way up to hurting her. It was something she used to do for comfort. She had not done it in years.

Why did he push me away? she thought as a tear rolled across the bridge of her nose. I did nothing wrong. I did not want this. I told him this would happen.

This feeling inside her, this horrible crushing pressure inside was why she had shut herself off. People always failed. It was their nature, their one true dependability; that they could never be depended on.

You have lost nothing, she told herself. You never had anything to lose.

But she had enjoyed spending time with him. The times they spent speaking about profound subjects like martial arts and the psychology of their different upbringings were as precious to her as those they spent in silence, with her reading a book and him sketching out a draft for a project.

She had enjoyed the feel of his hands on her. His mouth had coaxed emotions and reactions from her that she had not known were possible. For the first time, she had felt protected strictly based on his devotion to her, not on her ability to defend herself. The sound of his voice calmed her. One look from his denim blue eyes made her feel important, worthy of inner peace.

Her phone rang from her purse by the door. Shutting her eyes, she covered her ear with her left hand, blocking out the sound.

Blocking out the world.

●　●　●　●　●

CHAPTER SIXTEEN

She quickly learned how to play the game.

Be a good girl. Answer questions about the Bad People that the woman with the star asked. Do not talk about the ball of light or any other voice that spoke to her in her head. Ignore the strange people she saw that no one else seemed to see. Pretend to play with the toys given to her. Lay in the bed when it was dark even if she could not sleep. Pretend she could not remember her dreams when her screams woke others in the night. Stay in the house in the early mornings even when she wanted to be outside, running free, feeling the wind on her face and the ground on her bare feet.

Eventually, she was introduced to a middle-aged couple. His scent was familiar; she did not know that he had visited her while she was unconscious in the hospital. All she knew was that he had kind eyes, his thoughts were calm, and he did not touch her.

• • • • •

Birdsong surrounded her. Robins, blackbirds, and sparrows, their sweet sounds cheerful and constant, interrupted occasionally by the drumming of a tenacious woodpecker. Gradually, she became aware of dirt and leaves and grass beneath her feet. The smell of the woods filled her nose.

Her eyes were open before she rose from sleep. Gritty and dry, she blinked rapidly. The chill of early morning hit her body all at once.

She was standing at the edge of the woods, naked.

Ava took a step back, dazed. The chirping of crickets at her feet stopped.

It was so early the sun had not yet started to rise. Gooseflesh rippled along her entire body.

Turning, she headed back toward the house.

She had not thought of the first few weeks spent with David and Ruth for many years. The dream brought the terror, rage, and agony of her life before him to the surface. And the first stirrings of comfort she experienced as she began to trust him.

As far as nightmares went, this one had been mild.

• • • • •

Gabriel woke to tears on his lashes.

He couldn't remember the dream and didn't want to. Instinctively, he reached across the bed and was sitting up, listening for Ava, before he realized she hadn't spent the night. He had all but kicked her out the night before.

Running a hand through his hair, he swore softly. His sister was dead. There was no hope of running into her on the street one day. There was no way the police would show up on his porch with an unfamiliar grown woman and tell him she was his long-lost sister, and wasn't it a miracle?

She was dead. Gabriel believed it as solidly as if he had watched it happen.

Pulling on a pair of jeans, he grabbed a tee shirt and ambled downstairs. The dogs followed, keeping their distance, feeling the tension.

He had known she was dead. He had prepared himself for this since the day she disappeared, telling himself the likelihood of her return was less than nothing, that getting his hopes up would surely end in disaster. Since he was a child, he had lived his life like she was already dead.

And yet.

Getting the coffee pot going, he leaned against the counter and rubbed both hands down his face. Fuck, it hurt. The shock had worn off sometime during the night, when he had lain in bed, sweating, and kicking around.

He swore again, walking to the patio door to let the dogs out. They ran out quickly, eager to get away from him as fast as they could. He returned to the counter and stared at the brown liquid dripping into the glass carafe.

Ava said Hayden had not felt pain and so what? She still died alone, cold, and wet without her family. There was still no body under the stone in the cemetery. What had the truth about her death afforded him except stealing the hope that one day he might see her again?

How was he going to tell his family? That he must tell them was not a question; they should know Hayden had not been abused and savaged. The way he had gained this information, however, was not something they believed in, and even if they did, how would his mother and Beth react? He was having enough trouble processing it. They were going to be devastated – first, because Ava had the nerve to bring Hayden's disappearance up again, and second, because she knew details of the night she couldn't possibly know, and they would want to believe it was true. And even if they didn't, they would know Gabriel and Iz believed. Emotions would be raw.

Pouring coffee into his mug, he felt as lost he had that morning sixteen years ago, when he found out Hayden was missing.

It was like reliving it all over again.

·   ·   ·   ·   ·

Janine tied off the last stitch and snipped the thread. Her hands were not gentle as she worked. Lying on her stomach on their bed, Ava did her best not to wince, because if Janine was annoyed, Mack might punish her again. She lay still while the older woman pressed a gauze pad to her skin and taped it. A tear slid across her nose and fell onto the blanket beneath her.

When Janine stood, cleaning up the supplies, Ava remained on the bed. She was vaguely aware of the sounds around her: the crinkle of paper being wadded and thrown away, a cupboard door opening and shutting, feet shifting on the floor.

Janine returned with a thin nightgown. She sat Ava up and slid her left arm in the sleeve first so she could move the fabric and keep the arm still. Bunching up the material, she carefully stretched it over Ava's head and moved her right arm through the hole. She pulled the length of the gown down around Ava's hips, humming softly as she worked.

Times like these made the girl wonder how the woman could watch the man do horrible things to her. Sometimes she joined in or told him to do even worse things to her. But now, she was taking care of Ava, cleaning and fixing the slice in her back in an almost caring manner.

The girl was confused by these sudden displays of mercy.

Thundering footsteps sounded on the porch steps. Ava froze. He wasn't supposed to be back until later today. When the door swung open, she curled into a ball on the bed and tucked her hand under her chin.

"All fixed up?" he asked Janine.

She stood. Any softness that may have been here was gone. "I did my best."

Mack gave her a lewd smack on her backside, then gripped, drawing her in for a sloppy kiss.

On the bed, the girl closed her eyes. Hearing them made her feel like gagging. She put her hand to her ear and tried to block out the noise.

"We're leaving," Mack said.

Ava was lifted by her left arm and carried through the trailer. She felt the stitches tear and whimpered. Blood oozed into the gauze pad on her shoulder, thick and warm. She was thrown onto the hard space between them on the seat of the truck, where she kept her eyes closed, her hands covering her ears. The fire in her shoulder made her dizzy, but she didn't say a word. Her body had broken out in a cold sweat, but she was so hot, she just wanted to jump into a bathtub and sink to the bottom of fresh, cold water.

They drove for what seemed like hours. Ava's delirious mind went in and out of consciousness. She barely realized she was pressed up against Janine's thigh. Or that Janine had taken her free hand and squeezed it, letting her know she wasn't alone.

The feeling of falling made her jerk into consciousness and she reached out. Janine was no longer holding her hand. The pungent smell of manure and rotting hay filled her nose. Her body hit a hard cement floor, and everything screamed in pain.

Fury shot through her, and she lunged at Mack. As her teeth sank into his sweaty flesh, he plowed his palm into the side of her head. Bright spots of light flashed behind her closed eyes. Stunned, she sat on the cool floor, unable to resist as he hooked one end of the hand cuffs to her wrist and the other to a heavy chain. He wrapped the chain around a support beam and fixed a padlock to it, so she was tethered.

Gripping her hair and yanking her head up so she was forced to look at him, he sneered at her.

"I'm done with you."

He dropped her head and turned to leave.

With a cry of rage, Ava lurched at him and bit into his calf. Mack howled and twisted around, grabbing her by the back of the nightgown. Yanking her off him, he lifted her above his head, growling at her before tossing her to the ground. Instinct had her throwing her hands out to catch her fall. A loud crack echoed in the barn as her wrist broke. Instead of submitting, she came at him again, jumping at his face this time, digging her fingers into his skin, clawing at his eyes, biting his scalp. At first, he batted at her like she was a mosquito, shocked. Then he gripped her by the shoulders and ripped her off him, throwing her to the floor a second time. There was a softer crunch and a sharp pain exploded next to her neck as a fracture split her collarbone.

Ava was up again, but Mack was walking away, panting. He did not look back. Not as she lunged against the chain, dislocating her shoulder, ripping the rest of the stitches Janine had sewn, not as she continued to fight until her wrist bled, not as the hand cuffs cut into her skin.

He walked away without giving her a second thought.

Thrashing like a rabid dog, Ava burst from the dream with her arms in front of her to ward off an attack. She felt the knife in her hand, the solid weight of it, even as she whipped it left and right. It took several seconds for her already open eyes to register what she was seeing around her.

She was crouched under her kitchen table, slashing out with her biggest kitchen knife. Though she had not done damage to herself during her nightmare, she felt the phantom aches in her wrist and collarbone from where they had been injured in the barn. She dropped the knife and held her wrist in her hand, cradling it to her chest.

I'm done with you.

Mack's words echoed in her head.

She remembered the rage she had felt when she realized he was leaving her in that barn, just dumping her like a piece of garbage. Somehow that had been worse for her than the abuse. She had not understood why, still did not understand why. She only knew that Gabriel leaving felt the same way. Once he had what he wanted from her, he was no longer interested in her.

Her dreams had moved backward this morning, from an almost pleasant memory to a violent reminder of a time when she was at her lowest. She was getting worse.

Growling, Ava lifted the knife and slammed it into the floor, using it to pull herself out from under the table. She stood with it in her hand.

I'm done with you, he had said.

Fine. She was done with him.

She was done with all of it.

•　•　•　•　•

By eleven o'clock Sunday morning, when Isabel hadn't returned his texts or his calls, Griffin was starting to worry. Earlier this morning he saw she had texted him the night before, after he'd fallen asleep waiting for her, letting him know she was okay, but she'd stayed at Gabriel's because she drank too much. She wouldn't be home until today. However, it was getting close to the time they usually left for her parent's house to have dinner, and he still hadn't heard anything from her. Knowing the conversation she'd had planned with Gabriel, Griffin wondered if things had gone horribly wrong.

He told himself he was being paranoid when he texted Gabriel to see if she was still at his house. When two hours passed and Gabriel didn't respond, he felt unease wrap itself around him. Still feeling slightly foolish, he called Allie Harris to "wish her a happy Mother's Day" and make sure dinner was still on. She seemed delighted he'd called and the moment he heard her voice, he knew she was not aware of anything happening between Gabriel and Izzie. The discomfort grew. Griffin didn't think it was likely, but he sent a quick text to Ava to see if Iz had spent the night and received a message back: I dropped her off at her car last night. She said she was playing at The Raz.

Amused at her perfect grammar and punctuation for a text, Griffin thanked her and thought Iz would get a kick out of reading it.

If he ever found her.

Now, a few blocks from her flat, he glanced at the screen of his phone again to make sure Izzie hadn't tried to call or text while he'd been driving. Seeing no indication that she had responded only verified his idea that something was wrong.

He was not being obsessive or controlling, he told himself as he pulled into the car park of her flat. The fact was, Ava had dropped Isabel off at her car last night, and her car was at his flat. Instead of coming in to be with him, she'd taken her car and driven home. She had lied when she sent him the text telling him she was okay. Had she been okay, she wouldn't have run away. Had she played at The Raz or cancelled?

Taking the stairs two at a time, he tried not to run down the hallway to her door. He kept his knock nice and brief.

In a couple days she would be permanently moving in with him. She would wake up with him, brush her teeth with him, read the mail with him. He would be able to listen to her play her guitar-

He raised his hand to knock again but paused when he heard a noise. Her shower was running. Exhaling loudly, relieved, he tried her door. It was unlocked.

Although that unnerved him, he was thankful he was able to enter her apartment since she'd never given him a key. There had never been a reason to; they always stayed at his place. While he waited for her to finish showering, he strolled around the place, checking out the two pieces of furniture she had moved to one corner because she wanted to keep them, a few packed boxes, and the odds and ends she had saved until the last minute in case she needed them.

Her miniature chaos amused him. Almost everything about her amused him, and soon he would have her all to himself.

Glancing toward the bathroom, he wondered what was taking so long. She usually took short, efficient showers unless he joined her and coaxed her into making love.

Suddenly, he realized he didn't smell coffee. It was too early in the day to not smell coffee. Walking to the kitchen, he was surprised to see the machine was off and cool. It didn't look like it had even been turned on yet today. The pot was clean, and a clean mug and spoon sat in front of it. Izzie liked to set her cup on the counter in front of the machine the night before, so it was ready for the next morning.

What was taking her so long in the bathroom?

Griffin decided to make a pot while he continued to wait. He could use some, and if she hadn't had any, she was bound to be a bear. Maybe she had slept in because the conversation with Gabriel ran too late, or he was more upset than Griffin thought he would be, or just because it was a difficult subject to talk about.

Once the pot was done, he poured them both a cup and doctored hers with creamer, stirring it absently as he glanced at the door to the bathroom.

Something was wrong. Isabel didn't take showers over twenty minutes long.

Picking up their mugs, he walked to the door and knocked awkwardly, calling to her.

"It's Griffin. Are you okay in there?"

He heard nothing but the sound of water.

"Isabel, I'm coming in."

After a pause, he opened the door. When he entered the room, he set the cups down on the counter and moved toward the bathtub, pulling the curtain back.

"Didn't you hear m-"

She was huddled in the center of the tub with her back to him, her knees up to her chin, her arms around her legs. Water was pummeling down on her. Griffin reached for her and jerked his hand back. The water was freezing.

"Christ, Izzie."

Standing, he yanked the curtain open and smacked the stopper down so the water gushed from the spigot instead of the shower. He cranked the valves to stop the flow. Suddenly the room was quiet except for the water draining between Isabel's feet and her chattering teeth.

He had no way of knowing how long she'd sat like this, but her skin had a bluish hue, and she was shivering. Tangles of dark blonde hair covered her face, affording him no view of her expression. When he touched her skin, it was arctic.

"Oh, Izzie, what happened?" he murmured, pulling a towel off the rack, and wrapping it around her shoulders. He rubbed his hands up and down her arms and back, willing the blood to flow.

The bathroom was tiny. Griffin kept bumping into the vanity cabinet, the tub, the walls. He grabbed another towel and folded it in half before laying it on the floor. He cupped his hands under Isabel's elbows and raised her to a standing position.

"Come on now," he soothed, directing her out of the tub and onto the towel. "That's the way."

Once she was sitting on the towel on the floor, he left her to find another towel for her hair. It only took a moment of searching - her apartment didn't have much storage space – and he was back, covering her hair and patting it down as he watched her face. He talked about nonsense as he dried her off, things that didn't matter to keep her calm and keep his mind busy so he wouldn't obsess over the fact that she wasn't getting any warmer. The bluish color was fading from her skin, but she was still frigid.

He could do no more in the bathroom. Her body was dry, her hair as dry as it was going to be, and he had to get her warmed up. Lifting her like a bride, he carried her into the bedroom.

She had a full-sized bed, which wouldn't be all that comfortable for his six-foot-three frame, but it was what she had. He lay her down gently, pulled the blankets over her. Walking back to the linen closet, he took two more towels out. He unfolded them and gently lifted her head so he could spread them over her pillow, soaking up any excess water.

Seeing her tears almost undid him. Stripping down to his boxers, he slid under the covers next to her and hugged her tight, using his body heat to try to warm her.

His breath hissed out of him when their skin touched. She was so cold.

"Did you talk to Gabriel?"

He kept his voice soft, his tone soothing. Her body was convulsing against his and she wouldn't hug him back. Her hands were trapped between their chests, limp. She wasn't even trying to get warm.

"Damn it, Isabel, you have to try."

Lifting her leg, he draped it over his so he could settle his groin firmly against hers. He pulled her hand from between them and draped it over his shoulder, drawing their chests together. With another curse, he curled her head down so her face was under his chin. The tip of her nose was an iceberg against his shoulder. Their bodies were interlocked snuggly against each other, tight as puzzle pieces.

"I missed you last night." The only option he had left was to hold her and wait for his body heat to warm her. At least her teeth had finally stopped chattering. "Come back to me, Izzie."

Running his hand over the back of her head in a steady rhythm seemed to calm her, so he continued to do so. And he continued to talk to her because he didn't know what else to do. He told her about the project he and his team were working on, what he did yesterday after he left the cookout, and how he felt waking up this morning to find she was still gone.

By then, she had finally begun to thaw out. She was no longer shaking. Her skin was warming up against his. It occurred to him halfway through his story about his project that he should have given her some coffee to help warm her, but he wasn't sure she could have swallowed it. Instead, the change happened gradually, and when he felt her fingers spread across his back, he felt hopeful. Soon her body was curled around his. She was crying, but she was present.

"Tell me about your talk with Gabriel," he said, brushing her hair back from her forehead. Her eyes were still dull, but they found his after briefly wandering around the room.

"He knows everything," she said softly.

"Is that why you were in the bathtub?"

"I n-needed a sh...shower."

"The water was freezing."

"I... I forgot what I was doing. I must have run out of hot water."

"What did Gabriel say, Isabel? Why were you in the shower so long the water ran cold?"

She shivered and he pulled her against him. Her heart was galloping against his.

"What the bloody hell did he do to you?"

Shaking her head against him, she pulled back. "He didn't do anything. You were right. He understood."

Then why were her eyes so wild? Griffin searched her face.

"Ava told us what happened to Hayden," she whispered.

She told him. By the time she finished, she was shaking again.

"That means she wasn't violated and murdered." Griffin said, rubbing her hand in between both of his. "Ava said she wasn't in pain. That's good, isn't it?"

"It's worse," Isabel said sobbed, struggling to pull away from him.

He wouldn't let her. Gripping her arms, he gave her a quick shake to stop her panicked movements and get her to focus.

"Explain to me how drowning is worse than being raped and murdered."

"I could have saved her!" She beat a limp fist against his chest, dull fury filling her eyes now. "I had an excuse if it was a man that took her. I was a child, there was nothing I could do. But it wasn't. She hit her head and wandered away from camp. If I had been there, I could have led her back and we would have taken her to the hospital. She would still be alive. I killed her!"

Shaking her again, watching her eyes widen in shock, Griffin tightened his grip on her arms.

"Isabel, listen to me."

"Leave me alone."

"Shut up," he snapped. "Listen to me. She's dead. Hayden's dead. It's nobody's fault. There's no one left to blame. Hayden is dead and there's nothing you could have done to stop that from happening."

She froze.

"It's done. It's a fact, a statistic. Nothing you do will change the outcome of what already is. You can either move forward or stay trapped where you are. Do you really want to stay trapped for the rest of your life?"

"It's what I deserve."

"I don't believe that. I don't think Hayden does, either."

She blinked, confused. Tears glistened on her eye lashes.

"You told me, when you found out about Ava's ability, that Hayden started coming to Ava as soon as she moved to Langdon."

Isabel nodded slowly.

"She's been trying to communicate ever since. You've seen it. You've seen her put Ava's hair up in that fancy braid. Does that sound like an upset spirit? Don't you think she would have told Gabriel she was upset with you, if that was how she felt?"

From the shocked look on Izzie's face, he knew she hadn't considered that idea. She blinked again. Her head was throbbing. Her cheeks were chapped from crying.

"She wanted you to know how she died," Griffin said, "because she wanted you to have peace of mind. She made sure Ava told you and Gabriel that she felt no pain, because she wanted you to stop imagining the worst about that night. Those aren't the actions of a vengeful soul. They're the actions of love."

Fresh tears filled Isabel's eyes.

"I don't know how to let her go."

Griffin gathered her up again. This time, she sagged against him.

"You have to want to, first."

• • • • •

Gabriel parked his truck behind Griffin's monstrous Rover and sat for a moment, staring out the windshield. Beside him, Ozzie wagged his tail furiously and tried to thrust his head out the window, stepping on Gabriel's thigh and sending a spear of pain down his leg. He barely noticed. He moved the dog's head out of his face and opened the door, letting them jump down and run around in the yard.

Everything seemed pointless.

Resting his hands on the hood of the truck, leaning over it, he closed his eyes and tried to shut his mind off. It kept racing around in circles, going over the same information repeatedly with the same results. His sister was still dead. What good was the information he'd been given? The body would never be found. Nature had reclaimed her, as Ava said. What good did that do him? She would never get a proper burial. What peace was he supposed to gain from anything Hayden had volunteered? All she had managed to do was open an old wound.

"You're late."

He hadn't heard Isabel come up behind him. Turning toward her, he hoped he looked better than he felt.

"How are you holding up?" he asked. He hadn't shaved and he was due for a haircut. At the moment, he didn't give a fuck that he looked like an escaped mental patient.

Isabel's cheeks were pink and a little dry from crying, but she didn't look too bad. She'd had a rough night but seemed to be better today. She shrugged.

"As good as can be expected. I talked with Griffin. That helped."

"Good."

Ozzie brought over a wet stuffed platypus and dropped it at Isabel's feet. He leaned heavily against her legs, craning his neck to looking at her while she stroked his fur.

"Did you make it to The Raz on time last night?"

She picked up the platypus and heaved it for Ozzie. The dog raced after it happily.

"I didn't go. I couldn't. It's the first show I've ever missed." She kicked the toe of her shoe against the tire. "What about you? How are you doing?"

"I just came to drop the dogs off. I'm not staying."

"Why not?" She took a step toward him, her face full of worry.

Instantly, he stepped back, something he had never done. She felt a stab of rejection. Trying to remember this wasn't about her, she forced herself to take a deep breath.

"I have a couple deadlines for work. Summer's my busiest time."

Iz narrowed her eyes. "Family always comes before work. Always has."

"I can't today."

She studied him for several seconds, feeling odd that she was able to face her family and he wasn't. He was usually the strong one. But his eyes were different, she saw, gazing at them now. There was an emptiness to them that hadn't been there before. An emptiness and a raw anger that made her uneasy. She had seen that look when his friends had to pull him off Stuart after he smacked Rachel.

In an attempt to keep him talking, to persuade him to stay, she said, "I told everyone what really happened to Hayden and how I know."

Raising an eyebrow, he gazed at her. "How'd that go?"

"They were... are... curious. A little skeptical. Probably ready to drink."

Gabriel scoffed.

They watched Ozzie violently shake his head with the platypus in his mouth before trotting toward them, victorious. Maya wandered over and sniffed Isabel's hand.

"I better wish Mom a happy Mother's Day before I go," Gabriel said hollowly, walking toward the side door.

Isabel and the dogs followed. Iz knew there was no changing his mind. He was going through something she couldn't help him with, and she had to let him work through it on his own. She wondered why this latest information was so devastating to him. For her, at least it made some kind of child-like sense: she now felt there had been a greater possibility of saving Hayden if all she'd had to do was lead her back to camp and wake her parents. If Griffin hadn't convinced her to move on, if she chose to continue as she was, she could feel more guilty now that a predator wasn't to blame. That was logical.

But Gabriel hadn't been in a position to help their sister that night, so why was he so upset? The less brutal way she died should have been a relief.

In the kitchen, food was being set out. Gabriel realized just how late he was, and guilt washed over him. He had always put family first, especially on Sundays.

"Gabriel, there you are!" his mother said, pulling off her oven mitts and coming around the island to give him a hug.

She frowned when he instinctively stepped back. Her son wouldn't look at her.

"Happy Mother's Day."

"Thank you, Sweetie." Stopping at the island, she studied his hunched shoulders and scruffy chin. "Where's Ava?"

He winced. "She's not here."

Josh came in from the living room. As he started toward Gabriel, Allie said his name and motioned toward the counter with her head so he would go in the opposite direction. Puzzled, he rounded the island and leaned over to kiss her forehead.

"What's going on?" he asked, keeping his voice quiet.

"Something's wrong," she answered, keeping equally quiet. "Ava's not here and Gabriel wouldn't hug me."

Josh squeezed her shoulder before digging in the refrigerator for a drink.

For the first time, the physical affection seemed unnecessary and cumbersome to Gabriel. He didn't want to be touched. Is this how Ava felt?

"Isabel told us... some interesting things earlier," Josh said, clearing his throat. "Information that is rather hard to accept. But I hope you don't feel Ava's unwelcome."

"I'm not staying," Gabriel said.

From the dining room table, Beth and Jack glanced up. Their Scrabble game lay forgotten as they turned their attention to him.

"Why not?" Jack wondered, standing to get another drink for himself and Beth.

"I have... some things to take care of." Gabriel took a step back toward the door, shoving his hands in his pockets. "I'm busy with work and... shit."

"You've never skipped a Sunday meal," Allie said, looking crushed. "It's Mother's Day."

"I know, Mom, I'm sorry. I just need..."

"Is it because of what Ava told you?" Josh asked, frowning. "About Hayden?"

Gabriel's lack of answer told him all he needed to know.

"Listen, Gabe-"

"I don't want to talk about it." Gabriel took another step back, putting more distance between himself and his family. "Happy Mother's Day, Mom."

"Thank you," Allie said absently, watching her son retreat. After a moment, she glanced at Josh. "He's putting up a wall again."

Her husband nodded. "Just like he did when Hayden first went missing."

Isabel felt Griffin's arms slid around her and leaned back against his chest. She sighed heavily. She had Griffin to pull her out of a very dark hole that was always waiting to consume her. Gabriel had an abyss. When it swallowed him, pulling him out was almost impossible.

•   •   •   •   •

"I tried to call you several times this weekend," Sensei said.

This was said immediately after she bowed to the kamidana and greeted him in Japanese. Ava closed her eyes briefly before opening them and fixing him with a neutral stare.

She apologized in Japanese.

"I was busy, Sensei."

As she took off her boots, he released her to go back and change. Usually, her changing routine took less than two minutes. She stripped off her jeans and socks, put on her uniform pants and top over the tee shirt she usually wore, and slipped her tabi onto her feet. This time, she couldn't seem to get her body moving right. She was slow and clumsy, and it took long enough that Sensei called back and asked if she was okay.

She appeared on the mat, bowed, and apologized. She always seemed to be apologizing lately.

"Where is your head today?" he asked. "You are extremely distracted."

She shrugged helplessly.

Breathing deep, she felt her body shudder. She did not even know where to begin. But she was a fighter, and fighters did not complain about the unfairness of the world. They made changes when they saw wrongs being done.

She knelt on the floor.

Trying a different approach, Daniel said casually, "Last week, you didn't want to discuss what happened Wednesday when Hayden tried to communicate with you. When Gabriel gets here after class, we need to discuss that."

Ava's expression didn't change. "I will no longer be staying late to discuss my psychic ability, Sensei."

Keeping her head down, she waited for warmups to begin. Daniel watched her for a beat, noting the quivering hands, the clenched jaw. He had never seen her try so hard to maintain control.

"Did something happen, Ava?"

"I am ready to train, Sensei."

"Clearly, you are not."

Raising her head slowly, she opened her eyes and he saw the void of The Monster in her sockets. When she blinked, they were gray.

"I no longer want your guidance in my personal life regarding psychic ability," she said carefully. Resting on her thighs, her hands curled into fists, uncurled, curled again. "I appreciate all you have done for me to this point. If you are unwilling to continue training me because of my decision, I understand."

Although they were the width of the dojo apart, he could feel her vibrating with energy, fighting to control something dark and furious that wanted to burst out of her. He was not surprised that The Monster didn't have half the strength of that darkness inside her.

"I will continue training you, Ava. Right now, however, your training consists of discussion, not physical activity."

She exhaled, long and slow. "What would you like to discuss?"

"Something happened this weekend that upset you. Your personal business is just that, until it puts yourself or others in danger."

"You are not afraid of me."

"I will never be afraid of you. That doesn't mean you aren't a threat. The last time you kept this much rage inside, you were seven years old. Where is this anger coming from?"

"I can handle it."

Daniel stretched as he started to stand. "I'm going to call Gabriel to come pick you up. You're not receptive to training like this."

Ava leapt smoothly to her feet, pausing in a crouched position before she straightened her legs and stood. "Gabriel did not drop me off. I trained for years without needing a handler."

"Then stay until you've calmed down, Ava. You know I don't tolerate attitude in the dojo."

"Please, can we just train?" she whispered.

The desperation in her voice pulled at him. There was a time, after he had begun training her, when she had given up completely. For so long she had reacted to trauma, she had no concept of what it was like to have discipline without abuse. She had depended on him to guide her, to feel secure physically and later, emotionally. After weeks of hate-filled fighting, where she came at him with everything her tiny body had, her surrender was absolute.

Her voice showed she was on the brink of that now.

As a child, she'd given up her rage to be ready to accept instruction from him. Today, she had simply given up. But she was fighting to control a deep sadness, something he had not seen in her for years.

"You'll injure yourself if you train like this." Moving toward her, he noted her automatic step back. He regarded her pallid complexion and the bruises under her eyes. "Have you eaten anything today?"

She shook her head.

"Let's get something to eat."

Untying his belt, he folded it and shrugged out of his uniform top. He walked toward the back.

Feeling drugged, Ava stared after him.

Before he closed his door, he called from his office: "Come on, Ava. Change into your people-clothes."

$$\bullet \quad \bullet \quad \bullet \quad \bullet \quad \bullet$$

"That's the last of it," Isabel said. She unhooked her apartment key from the keyring and held it up. "I'll stop by the apartment sometime this week and give this to Lina. She already has one from the office."

"I can give it to her at work."

Iz dropped the key into his hand and stared at the last of the boxes in his living room. She had finished cleaning the old apartment this morning, and Griffin helped her move the furniture and a few boxes she had left after he came home from work. Her mail was forwarded, her banking information and driver's license updated. This was her new address. This was home.

Holy shit.

"Are you okay?" Griffin's hand settled on her shoulder.

Turning to him, she looked a little lost and a lot adorable. The ponytail she'd put her hair up in was failing to keep her hair curtailed, and little strands were escaping on all sides of her face.

"I don't know what I am."

He brushed his lips over hers. "Give yourself time to adjust. And give yourself time to grieve, Izzie."

Her face crumpled, her eyes filling, her mouth curving slightly down. She raised her hands and rested them on his wrists.

"I already knew she was dead. I don't understand why... why it hurts..."

"Just like it did the first time?"

She nodded.

"Because knowing how she died has forced you to confront how you've adjusted your life based on what you thought happened. Now you have to adjust again based on what really happened. Ava's information took you emotionally back to your nine-year-old-self."

She bit her lip, regarding him. "Can't you just say it fucking sucks to lose a sister?"

"If it makes you feel better, yes." He hugged her. "But I don't think rephrasing what's going on in your head is going to make you feel better."

"I had nightmares last night."

Pulling back, he studied her.

"I woke myself up crying. I might wake you up for a while."

"We'll work through it." He tugged on a lock of her hair. "Together."

Nodding, she leaned against his chest, pressing hard so she could feel his heartbeat. She felt that if she could hear his heartbeat, she might someday forget about the one that had stopped beating so many years before.

• • • • •

Daniel watched Ava carefully spear a bite of fish and stare at it for several seconds before setting her fork on the edge of her plate. She picked up her water glass, glancing around the restaurant without seeing anything or anyone in it.

"Happy belated birthday."

He'd told her "Happy Early Birthday" last Thursday afternoon after class. As was her usual reaction, she flushed and thanked him, trying to leave as quickly as possible. Now he was curious to see how she would react.

She flinched when he spoke. As he suspected, something had happened around her birthday.

Recovering quickly, she thanked him in Japanese. She tried to eat the bite of fish she'd cut earlier. It stuck to the roof of her mouth, and she had trouble swallowing it.

"Did you do have a nice birthday?"

"I had sex."

Daniel almost dropped his fork into his salad. "Well, that's... good, I guess."

Dipping her head, she apologized in Japanese. "I am not supposed to discuss such things. I forget the rules and..."

"You're honest, Ava. I've always admired you for that. It catches me off guard sometimes, that's all."

"Honesty is not such a good thing." She stared down at her plate, looking distressed. "It makes people..."

When she didn't finish, Daniel leaned forward. "You can tell me."

The waitress came over with a pitcher of iced water. As she refilled their glasses, she asked if there was something wrong with the food. Ava had turned her head away and continued to poke at her plate.

"The food is fine," Daniel assured the waitress. He gave her a smile. "Thank you."

Setting her fork down, Ava didn't notice when the waitress left. She pushed her plate back.

"Honesty is never wrong." Daniel finished his salad and began on his bowl of mixed fruit. "If someone has a problem with it, the issue is with that person, not you."

She was completely closed off. He was getting nothing from her mentally or emotionally. No snippets of her thoughts, no strange sensations that made

937

his hair stand on end. Everything in her body language was telling him she was on fire – her deliberate breathing, rigid posture, and clenched jaw – but she wasn't letting her thoughts stray enough for him to catch a glimpse of them.

That he was even searching for a psychic connection so effortlessly almost made him want to laugh.

"Did something happen to David?"

Her eyes darted to him. "No."

"Gabriel broke up with you, didn't he?"

Ava's hand jerked and knocked the saltshaker over. Salt spilled across the table as the shaker slid toward the edge. Daniel reached out and caught it just as it fell over the side, setting it back on the tabletop.

He had gone with instinct and blurted out whatever had come to mind. The question had surprised him as much as it surprised Ava.

"Did he give a reason why?"

Ava gathered the salt by cupping her hand and using the outer edge to scrape it all into a pile.

"I am certain it was because I used my ability to tell him how his sister died."

She scooped the salt into her palm and dumped it onto her plate, brushing her hands together. Glancing around the small restaurant, she looked defeated.

"You were finally able to communicate with Hayden?" Daniel said, surprised. "How did you manage that?"

Breathing deeply, she looked at him. "It occurred to me that The Monster is unable to stop Hayden from speaking in The Interval. I spoke with her there."

"I had that same thought last Wednesday. I wanted to talk to you about it Thursday. I thought it might be a safe space. When they're in our realm The Monster can manipulate her physically, I think because it can draw energy from the living."

"Hai, Sensei."

"But if it can possess you, it's also a spirit, so it should have access to The Interval, too. Why can't it get to Hayden there?"

"Because I created The Boundary. You had me create a door to exit The Interval; I created four stone walls to create a barrier between myself and the spirit I wish to speak to. I kick the others out."

"Fascinating." Daniel finished his fruits and thought about that. He was becoming more and more amazed by Ava's ability every time they discussed it.

"And now you think Gabriel deserted you because of your ability?" he asked.

"Hai, Sensei."

"That's quite a theory."

She said nothing at first, but irritation flickered across her face when the waitress returned and asked if they needed boxes. Daniel spoke with the waitress even as he noted Ava's increasing inability to mask her emotions.

As soon as the waitress left, Ava said, "I should not have gotten involved."

"Your solution is to step back and distance yourself. Build walls like you did before you met Gabriel."

She fixed him with an icy glare. "You disapprove."

"I would hate to see you retreat into yourself, especially because of a misunderstanding. Watching you interact with Gabriel, seeing you open up has been... I'm really proud of you, Ava. You've grown a lot. I've always wanted that for you."

Her face reddened at the attention. Daniel had been sparing giving her positive feedback growing up, not because she didn't deserve it or because he was her teacher. He did so because if he gave her too much praise, it embarrassed her. He'd learned early in their relationship that a simple word conveyed his appreciation in her technique, a quiet, "Good" when she had performed correctly was enough.

When she made a mistake, she knew it, because often those who were abused learned to read people very well and gauge their moods. Daniel wasn't abusive but Ava could pick up on the micro changes in his facial expressions when he was about to correct her. And, he now knew, she could also sense it because of her ability. When she first started training, he'd had to come down on her pretty hard about anticipating his moods. She kept stopping when she made a mistake, waiting to be punished. Finally, he told her to continue training, no matter what, until he told her to stop. It was the only way to break the hold Mack and Janine had on her. Mistakes meant punishments in her mind, and Daniel couldn't train her when she was waiting for a punishment at every turn.

The waitress brought the leftover box and the check. Ava reached for it, but Daniel swiped it off the table. The space between her eyebrows creased.

"I asked you to dinner, I'll pay for it." He pulled his wallet out of his back pocket and handed the waitress a card.

They'd had dinner before, and it always amused him how thrown she was to see him out of his uniform. Watching him perform regular tasks and use regular accessories, like a wallet, were often met with long moments of pause and wide stares. His students often forgot he was just a man.

"Why do you think your ability is the reason Gabriel broke up with you?" he asked. He watched Ava dump her leftovers in the takeout box.

He was trying to keep an open mind about the kid. From how Gabriel had treated Ava in the dojo, Daniel didn't believe Ava was reading the situation correctly. Gabriel was crazy about her, and protective of her. That kind of love didn't just stop.

The waitress returned with a slip to sign and thanked them for coming in. Daniel gave her a smile and discretely handed her some bills for a tip. Noticing the generosity of the tip, she thanked him profusely and asked them to come again.

Ava waited for her to leave, impatient. She shouldn't have come out in public when she was in such a foul mood. The waitress was only doing her job, and a good one at that, and Ava's problems weren't her fault. She tried to remove her scowl and thanked the waitress with as much sincerity as she could.

When she left them alone, Ava closed her eyes and took deep breaths to even out her anger while Sensei filled out the receipt and signed it. He finished and set it and the pen at the edge of the table where the waitress would see it.

"Where were we? Oh, I was asking why you thought your ability is the reason Gabriel broke up with you?"

"'I will never forgive her for doing this.'" Ava winced and looked out the window. "That was what he thought after I told him how Hayden really died."

For several seconds, neither said anything. When she looked back at him and saw him staring, she added, "I did not pry. It was an extraordinarily strong thought."

"I know you don't do it on purpose. I wasn't thinking that."

"He was so angry."

She chewed on her lower lip. Daniel reached over and took her hand.

"You love him."

Carefully, she disengaged her hand from his. She was able to conceal every emotion on her face except the deep sorrow.

"The first one's always the hardest."

"I would like to be driven back to my vehicle now, Sensei."

Nodding, Daniel picked up his keys.

He didn't like leaving things so unsettled and hated the idea of leaving her alone when her heart was breaking, but she was a grown woman. He dropped her off in the dojo parking lot. After watching her drive off, he unlocked the school and went inside.

It was going to be a long night.

•   •   •   •   •

As the sun lowered in the western sky, Iz showered in Griffin's spacious bathroom with endless hot water and wonderful pressure. The water drummed on her body, soothing her aches. Griffin had bought her brand of shampoo and conditioner; he even had a bottle of her body soap sitting on one shelf. That he was so considerate stirred something inside her, but she chose his body wash after using her usual products to wash her hair. Something about having the smell of his soap on her made her feel she belonged to him. Not possession, she thought, but a part of something special.

Feeling more relaxed, she dried off thinking about Gabriel.

He'd always been so strong. When Iz woke in the middle of the night crying, he had come into her room and stayed until she fell asleep again. When she didn't feel like talking, he was the one that had sat quietly next to her, not asking questions, not trying to fix her. He just let her be herself and didn't try to fix her. He was always there for her, as immovable as concrete.

Now, she knew he struggled with the details of Hayden's death, and he wouldn't let her be there for him. She'd called several times to let him know she was there if needed. Left messages. None of her attempts at communication had been returned.

Rejection was unavoidable, no matter how many times she told herself it wasn't about her.

She opened the door to the bathroom. Through the walk-in closet, she could see the bedroom illuminated by the bedside lamps and the television screen. The glow was so inviting, the anticipation of burrowing under the blankets and watching mindless entertainment until she fell asleep so relaxing. Pausing in the walk-in closet, she slipped into her tee shirt and panties before continuing to the bedroom.

Griffin was sitting on his side of the bed, leaning back against the headboard with his fingers flying over the keyboard of his laptop. He closed it as soon as she entered the room and glanced up at her.

"Hey. Feel better?" He set the laptop on the floor.

"Much."

Rounding the bed, she glanced at the television as she tucked herself in. He'd turned on the classic Stand By Me but kept the sound low.

"I love this movie," she said, nestling into the blankets and scooting over next to him. "God, 50's music is so great."

"Shit," Griffin suddenly said, leaning back and reaching for the remote. "I didn't realize… we should probably watch something else."

"Why?" Iz sat up.

He fumbled with the remote, dropping it.

She picked it up and held it behind her, frowning as he leaned against her chest trying to reach it. His arms were longer, and he plucked it out of her hand easily.

"Damn it, Griffin, what the hell? This is one of my favorite movies!"

Poised with the remote pointed at the screen, his finger on the button to turn it off, he studied her. "Really?"

"No, I have nothing better to do with my day than lie to you." Her tone dripped with sarcasm, her frown now a full-blown glower. "Why the fuck wouldn't I like it? It's a classic. The soundtrack is brilliant."

"You don't think it… you know… is a little too close to your… past?"

He watched her eyes shift as she considered what he was saying, running through the details in her mind. Four children, camping in the woods, they see a dead body. None of the kids were girls, and none of them died; they spent most of the movie looking for the dead body of one of their classmates. But they did think one thing about the death of the boy (that it would make them famous) and find out it was a totally different situation to look death in the face and have it verified. To know, without a doubt, that someone they knew was dead, ended, never returning.

How had she missed that all these years?

"I never really thought about it," she said slowly, watching Richard Dreyfuss on the screen as he sat alone, remembering his old friend. At the end of the movie, he would be in his office, alone again, typing the story of him and his friends on a computer that looked like it had been dug up from the Cretaceous period. The heartbreaking music would play again, a track that sounded so full of sorrow that every adult understood it told the tale of innocence lost during childhood. The summer any adult could recall and say, "That was the summer everything changed." Isabel knew exactly the summer that happened to her.

"I shouldn't have said anything," Griffin said, reaching for her hand.

"No," she said, dragging her eyes from the screen. "It's not your fault. I never realized it before. You don't have to turn it off."

"Yeah?"

"I still love it. We used to watch it all the time when I was younger. It was one of our favorites on Friday nights with pizza and popcorn."

Griffin returned the remote to the nightstand and shifted so he was lying on his side beside her again. She moved down and laid down on her back.

"That's so sweet to ask," she said, her lips twitching. She reached up and touched his cheek.

Brushing her damp hair from her temple, he leaned down and kissed her firmly. It was instant, hot, bringing her heart to a gallop, making her release a surprised moan. Her body arched, reeling, straining against him.

He pressed his palm to her breast, eliciting another moan that spoke of ache and dark desire. Gripping his arm, she flexed, taut as an arrow ready for flight.

She reached for him, dragging his mouth back to hers as her breath stuttered and stumbled out of her in pants and gasps.

Pulling her shirt up, he gently coaxed it over her head and toss it to the floor. He reached up and gripped his own, yanking it over his head so he could feel her skin against his. He'd wanted to be gentle, make her feel loved, cherished. But he needed her, now. Needed to touch and taste and plunder. As eager as he, her hands explored while her mouth ran over his body.

After, lying with her head cushioned on his shoulder and her body spent from making love, Isabel wondered if she would ever grow tired of touching him. If she closed her eyes as he touched her, she could almost imagine herself as he did. She could sometimes feel beautiful.

She sighed, content, as he ran his fingertips lazily up and down her arm.

"Do you think Connor and Hayden… moved on after they told Ava what they wanted her to tell us?"

"I don't know. I'm not sure what to believe. I was raised Catholic, but since I moved out on my own, I've never strictly adhered to the rules of organized religion. I'd like to believe they've found peace wherever they are."

He was absolutely thrilled, however, that she had brought up her sister's name without him having to pry it out of her, and that she was discussing her without tears or rage.

Her fingertips trailing over his skin, she pondered that. "I want to snuggle and watch classic movies until I doze off. But I should call Ava and see how she's doing."

From what Izzie had told him, Ava was wrecked when she dropped Isabel at her car. It was her nature to worry about others before she settled in for the night.

Griffin ran his hand over her hair. "Maybe if she's up to it, we can drive out there."

"You wouldn't mind?" She sat up, brought the blanket up to cover her chest. "Gabriel was so… devasted. He could barely look at her, Griffin. We've come to mean a lot to her, I could see it in her eyes, and it hurt her to tell us what happened to Hayden."

He patted her thigh. "Give her a call. We'll go see how she's doing, probably run into Gabriel while we're there. I'm sure it's not that bad."

Isabel leaned over and picked up her phone. As she brought up Ava's contact, he took several moments admiring her long, slender torso, letting his hand travel from her shoulder blade to her bottom. She was so beautiful. He was delighted when her lips curved in a smile at his touch.

On the fourth ring, Ava finally answered. Her voice sounded funny.

"Hel-lo, Isabel."

"Hey, Ava. How are you doing?"

She sighed as Griffin's hand travelled the length of her back again. He had wonderful hands.

"It is… early in the evening."

Ava's voice was hard to hear over noise in the background. Was that music?

"Why are you talking funny? Where are you? I hear music in the background."

Glancing up at her, Griffin frowned. He took her free hand and kissed her palm. The tickling sensation it caused made her smile.

"I am at the Shake Your Flirty Feathers on Gammon Road."

"You're at a bar?" She sat up straighter. "Ava, you're at a bar?"

Griffin raised an eyebrow. He kissed the top of her head, rose, and slipped into a pair of boxers. Picking up her underwear, he tossed them to her on his way to the closet. He began to get dressed.

In her ear, Ava's tone became resolute. "My drink arrived. I am going to hang up now."

"Ava-"

The dial tone pulsed in her ear.

"Do we need to go?" Griffin asked from the doorway, pulling his shirt over his head. He grabbed her jeans from the counter and tossed them to her.

"She doesn't drink," Isabel said, quickly putting her underwear on. "She doesn't go to bars. Something is wrong."

•   •   •   •   •

Beer was in no way refreshing or satisfying, but Ava found that she needed strong fruity drinks to mask the taste of alcohol. At first, she tried a shot of whiskey because it was the only other drink she knew of besides beer. She did not like that. How Isabel enjoyed it was inconceivable. Then again, she did not understand the other patrons in the bar drinking beer and laughing loudly, and there seemed to be several of those. Beer smelled and tasted like human sweat; she did not understand how people could consume it in such copious quantities and be so happy.

Even after twenty-three years of living among them, Ava found she did not understand anything about people.

Sitting at the counter, in the corner where it met with the wall so no one could stand behind her, she turned on the stool and tried to figure out what to try next.

She told the bartender she wanted to try something called a sloe gin fizz because it had the word "fizz" in it.

The bartender began mixing her drink. He moved to the wall of alcohol, to the refrigerator, smoothly picking bottles and measuring devices, adding ingredients to a shaker with ice and shaking it. After a few moments, he filled a Collins glass with ice and strained the mixture in the shaker into the Collins glass. He added club soda to the glass, garnishing it with a cherry and lemon wedge.

"Your sloe gin fizz," he said, pulling out a coaster and setting it down in front of her.

Ava had a bill ready and held it out. As he took it, his fingers barely bumped hers.

She was already a little fuzzy from the whiskey, and she learned he was a new father to a baby girl with the same brown eyes. Martina, they had named her, because he and his girlfriend liked the name, and it was close to a feminine version of Matt. They called her Matty for short.

He turned to clean up the bottles he used.

Grinding her teeth, Ava wiped her hand on her jeans as if she could erase the information. She was using cash to make sure she did not spend too much on alcohol, limiting her self-indulgent petulance at least a little. Now she was sorry to have made that choice. Cash transactions heightened the probability of physical contact.

She would not think about that tonight.

Tonight was for drinking, and not worrying. She took a sip of her new drink.

And was surprised to find it delicious. And it was bubbly.

However, the slightly tilted way the world became as she drank it only lasted a few minutes. She stood to use the restroom and felt dizzy, but as she sat back down and ate an order of French fries, the effects had already begun to wear off. She ordered another one as she ate the appetizer, but it just did not take away the bone-deep ache inside her.

Looking at the laminated sheet of paper that served as a drink menu as much as her just-getting-fuzzy eyesight would let her, she frowned. Every description of drink was helpful only if the reader knew something about alcohol. Ava knew only that Gabriel drank beer, Isabel drank whiskey, and Griffin drank wine. Maybe she could try wine. The three of them did not seem to act any different when they drank, but Ava felt funny when she did, and she so longed for that feeling of drifting that freed her from discipline and worry and memories.

"Can I make a suggestion?"

The bartender - Matt, his name is Matt – was watching her, an amused smile on his face. He had short, dark hair and brown eyes.

Ava watched him warily now, blinking to try to make him come into focus. She nodded.

"Let me make you a margherita."

"I do not know what that is."

He grinned. He'd carded her when she came in. It was soon clear she had no experience with alcohol, not because of her age but because she took so long to figure out what she wanted, she pronounced the drink very slowly, and halfway through it, she was already getting tipsy.

"Give it a shot, and if you don't like it, you don't have to drink it."

That seemed fair, so she nodded. He began to make it for her.

She watched him work, fascinated at how quick and easy his movements were. He was as at home behind the bar as she was in the dojo, flawlessly carrying out moves and presenting her with a perfect green product at the end. It was beautiful.

She set a bill on the counter. When he reached for it, her fingertips bumped his and she learned this was his second job, to help with bills and make sure Serena and the baby had everything they needed.

As he went to the register to get change, a man came up to the bar and asked for another Budweiser. Ava could smell light alcohol on him; he had only just begun to drink. Matt nodded at him. He closed the till, reached behind him to the refrigerator for the bottle of beer, and brought it and Ava's change over. Matt reached under the bar and opened the bottle, setting it on the counter.

The man handed Matt a bill, said something Ava did not hear, then tapped another dollar on the counter before walking off toward a group that was conjugating at the pool table.

Ava watched Matt return to the register, appear to make change from the purchase, and put the change and the extra bill the man had given him into a clear jar on the counter with a handwritten sign that read "TIPS".

She instantly felt ashamed.

"Should I be tipping you?"

He grinned again. She was a riot.

"Only if you want to."

Pulling out her wallet, she temporarily forgot about her drink. "You have the new baby to take care of."

His smile faltered. "Have you come in here before?"

Ava paled. "I do not go to bars."

She tried to remember how many drinks she had consumed and what a proper tip would be. Two? Three? She decided it did not matter since he was polite and not trying to engage her in conversation. She pulled two twenties out and stuck them in the tip jar.

Matt's eyes widened. "I think you've had a little too much to drink, there, sweetheart."

Digging in the jar, he started to pull the bills out.

"You need it more than I do," Ava said. She took a sip of the margherita. Winced a little. It was harsh.

He paused, narrowing his eyes. "Do I know you?"

Swallowing, Ava blinked slowly and shook her head. She took another drink, winced, stuck her tongue to the roof of her mouth, and sucked hard while pulling it down, making a loud smacking noise. "It is too tart."

Studying her thoughtfully, Matt cocked his head to the side. "I'm usually a pretty good judge of what drink fits a person," he said. "Do you trust me to give you another one to try?"

She frowned. "You were wrong about the margherita."

"I didn't realize you have such a virgin palette." He took out a tumbler. "Now that I have an idea what you don't like, I have a better idea what you will like."

"I liked the sloe gin fizz, but its effects did not... last long."

Picking up small tongs, he quirked one eyebrow at her, waiting for her response.

The pain was sharp and merciless. Though she continued to breathe, she felt suffocated. Instantly, images of Gabriel filled her head, the sound of his voice filled her ears, and a ball of fire lodged in her throat. She closed her eyes and nodded.

Anything to get rid of this horrible ache that had rooted itself into her heart and wouldn't let go.

"I will be back," she said, sliding off the stool. Her head was beginning to feel like it weighed twenty pounds. Speaking was becoming more difficult.

She walked stiffly toward the bathroom, and when someone bumped into her, she barely heard his rough voice snarl at her to watch where she was going. Passing both male and female doors in the hallway, she stopped just short of the emergency exit. She leaned back against the door and inhaled, forcing herself to concentrate on each breath.

A simple gesture reminded her of Gabriel. Dark hair, a pickup truck, a certain smell, all reminded her of him. Reminded her that whatever she had would be taken from her.

She did not deserve her old life back, and she could not continue living like this. Somehow, she had become a new person, one she did not recognize or know what to do with.

She pulled her phone out of her back pocket and dialed Sensei's number from her Contacts.

"Ava," he said immediately. From the tone of his voice, he thought something was wrong.

But nothing was wrong. She was doing fine.

"I called to tell you I will not be training with you anymore, Sensei," she said, talking slowly to make sure she enunciated every word correctly. "I am paid through the end of the month, so I should not owe you anything."

A long pause followed, and Ava wondered if she had dialed the wrong number. Her head felt funny, and her ears felt like they were full of cotton.

"What is this about, Ava?"

"My decision is not a reflection on your ability to train. You have always been good to me."

"Why stop now?"

Feeling steadier, Ava straightened. "I am no longer worthy of the grace of your instruction."

Someone laughed so loud the sound hurt Ava's ear and she almost dropped her phone.

"What was that?"

Sensei's voice in her ear brought her focus back.

"Someone at the bar was laughing."

"You're at a bar?"

His surprise angered her. She was an adult. All choices she made were her own.

A couple walked in the door and passed the hallway she was in on the way to the counter. The woman was laughing a breathless, cheerful laugh and the man joined in.

"Where are you, Ava?"

"Why?" she demanded. He was not her father.

"Where are you?" he repeated.

"Shake Your F-flirty F-feathers."

"Why are you at a bar?"

She started walking back toward her seat. She covered her free ear as noise from the other patrons grew louder. She had to concentrate on walking a straight line to her spot at the counter.

"I knew I would not be able to sleep," she said into the phone. Sensei did not answer right away.

Over at the pool table, one of the players with a cue yelled at another player. Both were furious at each other, standing mere inches apart. Ava thought one of the guys arguing had been the one that growled at her when they ran into each other moments ago.

She stood at her chair and studied the drink Matt had poured her. She took a tiny sip.

It was sweet, with a heavy orange flavor. There was no bite like the whiskey had; the sugar tamed the alcohol and made it smoother to drink.

"What do you think?" Matt asked, eying her.

She nodded. Her eyes were large and glassy. Matt hoped she was calling someone to come get her. If she wasn't, he was going to have to call a cab. He didn't like doing that without having a way to make sure she made it home safely.

"See? I told you." He wiped the bar off with a damp rag, glancing toward the pool table. The guys were getting a little louder.

"What did who tell you?" Sensei was still talking in her ear.

Annoyed, Ava, frowned. She had called for a certain task, and that task was complete. She was having trouble hearing him anyway with the noise from the two guys getting ready to start using their hands.

"I have told you what I wanted to tell you, Sensei. I wanted to tell you in person instead of sending an e-mail."

"Ava-"

"Dustin, go get a damn beer! You two are acting like children!" A woman yelled from between the men. She shoved the bigger one toward the bar.

As he ambled angrily over, Ava made eye contact.

"I will not need a refund for the remainder of the month," she said absently to Sensei, focusing on the man walking toward the bar.

She ran her eyes lazily up and down his body, sizing him up, and sighed. From the way he carried himself, the argument he'd allowed himself to get into, and the way he glared at her, he was hardly a threat.

"Ava," Sensei said, "Let's talk about this. Take the rest of the week off. Think about what you want to do. We'll meet next week and discuss it."

"What the fuck are you staring at?" The man growled at Ava. There were three stools in between them and he shoved the one next to him to the side so hard it sent them all flying. The one next to hers jerked toward her. Ava reached out and steadied the chair with her palm.

"Mind your temper," she said to the man.

"Leave her alone, Dustin." Matt walked toward the tap, grabbing a cold mug on his way. He glanced at the woman still standing by her stool. She had set her drink down but was still holding the phone.

"I do not want to discuss this, Sensei," Ava said into the phone. She tried to remain calm. Fury was building, making her stomach churn and her heart pound. She felt her blood pulsing and concentrated on its rhythmic thuds in her temples, reminding herself that she did not owe her teacher an explanation.

On the other end of the line, Daniel was hearing bits and pieces of the exchange. He kept the phone to his ear and walked to his door, picking up his keys. The bar was at least ten minutes away.

"He just needs another beer," Matt told Ava uneasily, knowing Dustin was working himself up to pound on someone. In another minute, Matt was going to have to call the cops or dump a bucket of ice on him. "Don't mind him."

"I do not mind anyone," Ava said, keeping her tone emotionless even as her temper continued to flare. As if the mouth breather before her was anything to feel intimidated about. She turned away from the counter. "I have to go, Sensei. I believe I am about to spar."

"Ava-"

She disconnected the call and shoved the phone into her back pocket.

Matt set Dustin's beer down in front of him. "I'll put it on your tab."

He walked back over toward Ava. "That's called an Old-Fashioned," he said, motioning to the drink, "but in Wisconsin we call them 'Brandy Old-Fashioned' because we use brandy instead of whiskey. Now you'll know what to order next time."

"It is good," she said, taking another sip. She finally sat, flicking a disgusted look at Dustin.

Digging into her back pocket to get her wallet, she tilted just a little, her head feeling unbelievably corpulent and unbalanced again.

Matt held his hand up. "Don't worry about it. This one's on me for screwing up the margherita."

"Thank you. I will still give you a good tip."

Matt smiled. "You've already tipped too much for the drinks you've had. Get me on the next one. Can I get you something else, Dustin?"

Ava turned to see Dustin glaring at her, his beer sitting, forgotten, at his elbow.

"I want to know why the fuck you're staring at me. Do I know you?"

"I have no interest in you."

Matt lifted the cordless phone from under the counter, wishing the woman would stop looking at Dustin with that aloof, bored gaze that drilled into him. Didn't she realize she was antagonizing him? Dustin was in the mood to fight, and he didn't care who stepped in his way to take the punch.

"Dustin-"

Ava reached out and gently folded her hand over his, locking it over the phone he was jiggling as a threat to call the cops. She rested it on the top of the bar.

"There is no need," she said softly, still looking at Dustin. "He is no threat to me."

"Oh, really? You think you're so much better than me?" Dustin huffed. He took a step closer.

Ava kept her hand on Matt's but moved her eyes to Dustin's. "You do not want to approach me."

The woman from the pool table started walking over. "Dustin, I swear to God-"

He took another step toward Ava, towering over her. "You think I have to take your shit just because you're a woman? I have no problem hitting women, sister."

Matt's hand tightened on the phone. "Ma'am, he does this once or twice a month. I'll call the cops and he'll cool off in a cell overnight."

Ava squeezed his hand ever so slightly. When she looked at him, her eyes were filled with a calmness he had never seen in any woman's eyes. There was also a sadness there.

"Do not interfere," she said quietly. "Your wife and child need you at home tonight."

She released his hand and remained sitting. Turning back to Dustin, she blinked slowly.

"I am not your sister. Which is fortunate, because I suspect inbreeding, and I would not want to be part of your genetic makeup."

The woman giggled and slapped a hand over her mouth.

"What're you laughing at?" Dustin snapped, glaring at her over his shoulder.

"You humans are all talk." Ava turned back to her drink. "You are not worth the DNA used to create you."

She felt the air from his exhale first because he was already huffing with rage when he came at her. Lifting her drink, she swung it in an arch over his body, keeping it upright, as she moved out of his way. His momentum carried him past her and tumbling into the wall behind her. Ava checked to make sure she hadn't spilled her drink and set it down on the counter.

The woman's eyes were huge. She stared at Ava with her mouth gaping, her purse hanging limply from one hand.

"What is your name?" Ava asked her.

"C-Connie." She turned and stared at Dustin, who was struggling to get to his feet.

"Connie," Ava said sternly. She waited until the woman's eyes locked on hers before continuing. "Go stand with your friends. I do not want you in my way."

Staring at her boyfriend, Connie flinched when Ava snapped her fingers in front of her eyes.

"Get out of my way."

Nodding, keeping her eyes on Dustin, she stumbled back to the pool table. Her friends had stopped their game and were watching.

Let them watch, Ava thought. Let them all watch like vultures waiting for the scraps of the dead.

Dustin finally stood with a shake of his head. "Shit. Caught me off guard."

"Make an effort this time."

Ava moved her head around, causing her neck to crack. She would be disappointed if the desire to fight had already left him.

"I don't want to hurt you," he said, walking toward her. "But your mouth is going to get you in trouble."

"Stop talking and get on with it," Ava said.

"You snotty little-"

He shoved at her shoulder. Before he made contact, Ava pivoted to avoid his jab, causing him to over balance. At the same time, she grabbed his hand and twisted it, bending it back toward him and at an angle. She applied just a little pressure to drive him to his knees. He let out a bellow of pain.

Her phone rang.

Frowning, she used her free hand to answer it.

Isabel greeted her. Ava listened a moment. Below her, Dustin was squirming, trying to find a position that would take the pressure off his wrist. Each time he almost succeeded, she adjusted her position and he groaned in pain. The group from the pool table were inching closer.

"It is... early in the evening." She could not remember what Isabel had said, but she thought that was a sufficient response.

Isabel asked her about being in a bar. She was getting irritated that others thought they could tell her what she could and could not do. She was an adult and could make her own choices. She needed the permission of no one.

Although she had not finished her current drink yet, she said, "My drink arrived. I am going to hang up now."

She needed to get back to business with Dustin and she was tired of people thinking she had to explain herself to them. She hung up and slid her phone back into her pocket.

"Do you want me to call the police?" Matt asked.

Ava shook her head. She released Dustin and stepped back. "I hope you can do better than that. I have not even moved past a white belt."

"You could have broken my wrist, you little bitch!" He stood, unsteady, holding onto a stool.

"Watch your mouth, or I will break your nose," she said in that same bored tone, taking a drink.

The rage was seeping into her, filling her body, spreading into her arms and legs. She flicked her fingers, trying to get rid of excess exergy that made her feel jumpy.

"He's obviously drunk," Connie said, stepping forward. "Come on, Dustin. Let's just go."

Dustin rubbed his wrist and glared at Ava. "Shit, lady, relax. I was just messing with you."

"You should have messed with someone else. I do not have time to waste with your limited intelligence."

"Who the hell do you think you are?" he snarled. He had started to move past her, giving her a wide birth as he joined his friends, but at her comment, he turned back.

"Dustin," one of the other men in the group said, "Come on."

Dustin waved him off. "You think you're better than me?"

Ava leaned back against the counter, so her forearms were resting on the edge. "You invaded my space. You were acting like a fool in front of your friends. To be fair, they encourage your behavior by not speaking against it. Otherwise, you would not continue to behave this way every week until Matt is forced to summon the police."

"Wait a minute-" The guy who had tried to get Dustin to come with them said.

Joel. His name is Joel. He likes Connie, but he does not know she likes him. He thinks she loves Dustin. But he is wrong.

The name and all the information came to her like a curse, a machine she could not turn off. No matter how she tried to block it out, the ability was always a part of her.

"I am done waiting," she snapped at Joel. He stepped back, surprised. "Take your trash and get it out of here so I can finish my drink."

Dustin swore and reached out with both hands to shove her. Ava turned so she was facing him full-on, dropped into the splits, and punched him in the groin. The feeling of his genitalia collapsing beneath her fist was extremely satisfying. She snapped up into a crouched position. As he bent over, she heard the group's collective groan – ooohhhhhh – and Dustin's breathless exhale.

Because she was still angry, and to make sure she had made her point, she drove her fist into his face as she stood the rest of the way up, sending him backward. He stumbled several steps and went down, knocking over a stool and hitting a tall round table, almost sending it crashing to the floor.

"Oh, my God!" Connie said, rushing over to him. She knelt beside him, her hands fluttering around his face as blood gushed from his mouth.

Ava raised her upper lip slightly. She had been aiming for his nose. Part of her was glad she had not broken it; she knew she had provoked the man to attack her and that she was wrong to do so. Part of her was disturbed to find herself so lost that she had severely messed up a simple technique.

She took a step forward, but Joel moved in front of her.

"He's had enough," he said quietly.

For a moment, her eyes seemed to darken, becoming so black the sockets were black as smoke. Joel blinked, stunned. Her eyes were gray; he must have been mistaken.

But the rage was not sated. Someone had to pay for her intense anger, which had entered her when the stupid man thought she would quiver beneath his bigger size and his angry voice. The anger had not left just because the man lay on the floor, wounded.

Ava picked up the nearest bar stool and heaved it. It flew into the wall, splintering at the impact. Joel stared at it. Moments ago, it had been made of thick, sturdy wood, the kind that was made in the fifties and lasted years because it was quality material. This woman had just broken it into toothpicks.

She spun around and kicked a table, knocking it over. The napkin holder skid across the top surface, clattering across the hardwood floor and disappearing under a booth. From the counter, she took another stool and swung it at the next nearest table like a baseball bat, toppling the table and breaking a leg of the stool.

By now, the group with Dustin was watching her warily, keeping their distance.

Good! she thought. It was all she had ever wanted. They had invaded her space, and now she wanted to smash and break and rage until the poisonous energy inside her bled out.

She raised the stool above her head, prepared to shatter it into a million pieces on the floor.

"Ava, stop."

After all these years, the sound of his voice could still cease her body's movement. Ava paused, her chest heaving, her eyes closed. Slowly, she lowered the stool and let it fall to the floor. She knew before she turned that disappointment would be in Sensei's eyes.

But when she turned, all she saw in his eyes was calm. The first thought that flitted through her head was home.

When he was certain she was done, Sensei knelt in front of Dustin to assess his injuries. Connie leaned back to give him room.

Suddenly tired, Ava ran the back of her hand across her mouth and pulled it away to find it bright red.

"Here," Matt said, handing her a clean towel with the end dampened. "I think one of the chairs gave you a bloody lip."

Ashamed of the damage she had caused, at her lack of control, Ava lowered her head and thanked him. He had dipped it in ice water, and it felt wonderful against her stinging lip. Sometime during her fury, she had lost control of a piece of furniture, and it hit her hard enough to bloody her lip. She had not felt the blow. She could have struck someone else, someone not involved. She could have seriously injured an innocent.

"I apologize for my behavior," she started, but Matt held up his hand.

"Usually, Dustin's the one causing damage. Maybe you beat enough sense in him to stop him for a while."

"May I have a glass of water, please?"

He grinned. "I can do that."

Joel wandered over as Ava sat on a stool she had not broken.

"Are you okay?"

"I have sustained worse injuries."

"That's not what I was talking about. You needed to break something. Something pushed you to that point."

Unwilling to get into her personal life to a complete stranger, Ava changed the subject.

Glancing at Joel, she said, "She does not think she deserves you."

He frowned. "Who?"

She flicked her gaze at Connie and back to him.

"Oh, Connie's with Dustin." He stuck his hands in his pockets.

"She is in love with you."

"Really?" He cleared his throat. "I mean... That's not... he's my friend. I would never do that to him."

"If he is really your friend, your happiness will be more important than his jealousy. If he is truly your friend, he will stop acting like a fool every weekend at the bar, embarrassing you and making you clean up after him."

Joel stared at Connie for several seconds.

Ava pressed the cold rag to her lip. The sting was helping to clear her head. "She has loved you for some time now. But she does not think you are interested."

He exhaled slowly. "How could she not know…"

Ava stood abruptly. "Because people never say what they mean. You lie and evade and then are confused when you are misunderstood. Tell her what you feel, or tell her you are not interested. Either way, be done with it."

She walked over to the broken chair. Shoving the cloth in her pocket, she began gathering the larger pieces together.

"Ava? Are you in here?"

The sound of Isabel's voice startled her, and she stood, turning toward the door.

Isabel and Griffin were coming toward her. Isabel's brow was creased, her eyes dark with worry, her hands fidgeting.

"What are you doing here?" Ava asked.

"We were worried about you. Can I give you a hug?"

Ava flinched. "You… you want to hug me?"

"Of course! I always hug you, and since you're drinking, I assume you're going through something, and you need it even more."

Stepping toward her, Ava allowed herself to be hugged. The feel of Isabel's body pressing against her, her arms wrapped around her, shifted something inside Ava and she felt tears stinging the backs of her eyes. She had told Isabel the truth about her dead sister, and Isabel still wanted to be her friend. Ava closed her eyes and held onto her friend a beat longer than she usually did.

Sensei walked over to them. He watched Ava's reaction to the woman hugging her. She seemed ready to break, her hands clutching the person's back as much for comfort as to help hold her steady. Daniel had never witnessed Ava embracing anyone. He certainly had never watched her need to as badly as she did now.

"Sensei," she said, pulling away. She bowed her head, apologizing in Japanese. "How badly have I hurt him?"

They both glanced at the man now leaning against a pool table with his group of friends again. Dustin was holding ice wrapped in paper towels to his lip, his legs bent slightly inward to protect his throbbing groin.

"You mostly hurt his pride. The rest are superficial wounds. His friends convinced him not to press charges since he's usually the one causing problems, and he technically started it."

Ava nodded, keeping her eyes downcast.

"Here's your water," Matt said. "Can I get you guys anything?"

They decided on water for the time being until they figured out if they would be staying.

As Matt filled glasses, everyone introduced themselves.

Ava rested her hands flat on the bar, inhaling deeply. "I am sorry for the trouble. I will clean the mess up if you will get me a broom."

"I'll clean it up. It'll give me something to do while I wait to fill orders. It's dead tonight."

Nodding, she took out her wallet. "Email a copy of the bill for the damages. I will pay for them."

Matt nodded. He could see her hands shaking. "I appreciate that."

She took a business card out of her wallet. "My cell number is on here if you have any questions. I will stop in after I receive the bill to make the payment."

He took the card from her. She felt another jolt.

"She likes to have the bottoms of her feet rubbed."

"Excuse me?"

"Matty." Ava rubbed her forehead. "When she's fussing, she likes to have the bottoms of her feet rubbed. That's how you can get her to go back to sleep."

"How do you know my daughter's name?"

"What?" As if waking, Ava flinched. "I do not know what you are talking about. Thank you for the water."

She turned with her glass and stepped away. Her friends were watching her curiously, he noticed, as if her behavior was not normal.

Matt felt ice water gush all over his hand before he realized the glass he was filling was more than full. He dumped some out, wiped the glass off, and set it aside to fill another.

He had never met the woman before, had barely caught her name from the people that had just arrived, but somehow, she'd known the name of his daughter and that she was having trouble sleeping.

· · · · ·

"Isabel."

Isabel mumbled, the voice not fully registering through the dream she was having.

She was boxing at Jay's, in the ring with a man twice her size, and she was thoroughly kicking his ass. Adrenaline was racing through her, filling each punch with power that sounded like nuclear blasts every time they struck. Jay and Griffin were watching, cheering her on, and

she had become so good that others in the gym had stopped their training to watch her.

"Isabel."

"Damn it, let me finish kicking this guy's ass."

"I don't know how to tell you this, Love, but your best friend is standing naked at the end of the bed."

"What?!"

She sat up, blinking owlishly.

At first, she saw only the outline of a person. Slim and muscular and turned toward the window, the outline was so still, Iz didn't know if she was really seeing someone or if her mind was making it up. Then the figure moved, and Iz almost screamed. Her hand clamped down on Griffin's wrist and she drew in a breath.

"It's okay," he said softly. "It's Ava. She was talking a few minutes ago. You slept right through."

"What was she saying?"

"I have no idea. I think it was Japanese."

"Holy fuck. I should have locked the bedroom door."

After meeting Ava's teacher at the bar, they had decided it would be best if Ava had company overnight. Griffin and Isabel drove to their apartment to get an overnight bag – after almost an hour of trying to convince Ava it wasn't an inconvenience – and then picked her up at Daniel's before driving them all back to Ava's house.

Ava insisted that since she was inconveniencing them, they could use her bed and she would use her couch.

And now she was in the bedroom, obviously naked, as Isabel could see the exact shape of her breasts. She remembered, too late, that Ava not only slept naked, but that she wandered around the house in the middle of the night.

She forgot to warn Griffin.

"Has she done this before?" he asked, trying hard not to stare. Gripping Izzie's hand, he tried to concentrate on her face so his eyes wouldn't wander.

"Every night." She shifted on the bed, leaned over...

And suddenly Griffin was blinded when the room filled with light.

"What the bloody hell are you doing?"

As his eyes recovered from the trauma, he had the perfect view of Ava's profile as she stood a few feet from the window. He caught sight of perfectly sculpted breasts and hips before he slapped his hand over his eyes.

"Why the devil did you do that?"

Isabel rose from the bed and picked up a robe that was draped over a chair in the corner.

"I need to be able to see if she's going to hit me."

She walked slowly toward Ava, trying to remember how Gabriel took care of her when she was sleepwalking.

As she neared the younger woman, she moved around her until she was in front of her. Ava's eyes were open but empty.

"Ava, I'm going to touch you," Iz said firmly.

Testing her response, Iz reached out and pressed her fingertips to Ava's shoulder. Ava tilted her head to the side as if she was listening to something only she could hear.

Satisfied, Iz slid the robe over one arm and across her back, touching as much as she could, running her hand from Ava's shoulder down to her hand so she could lift the hand without breaking contact. She settled the cloth across Ava's shoulders and crossed it, so it covered her chest. Lifting up the belt, she paused.

"Do you want to tie it?" she asked. When she received no response, she tied the belt and stepped back. "All done, Ava."

"Is she decent?"

Griffin's voice drifted over from the bed.

Iz looked over to see his hand still covering his eyes. She giggled. "Yes."

He lowered his hand with a sigh. "You might have warned me she did this every night."

"I forgot. I've only been around her once when it happened, at Gabriel's. I think he said she does it a couple times a night. Or morning, I guess."

Ava lifted her head, so it wasn't tilted anymore. She stepped forward and wrapped her arms around Isabel and rested her chin on Isabel's shoulder. Iz hesitantly hugged her back, wondering why Ava suddenly felt the need for a hug.

"Can she hear us, do you think?"

"Yes," Iz said, waiting for Ava to release her. She turned her head to the side so she could see Griffin as she spoke. "If we don't announce we're going to touch her, she'll defend herself. She's smacked Gabriel."

"You don't have to look like you enjoyed it so much."

Grinning, Iz tried not to laugh. "The look on his face was pretty funny."

The smile slipped from her face. Ava was quivering. When Iz tried to pull back to see what was wrong, Ava kept her arms locked securely around her and shook even harder.

Frowning, Iz rubbed her hand up and down Ava's back. "It's okay," she soothed. "You don't have to be strong all the time."

She glanced at Griffin, unsure what to do.

"Maybe she should stay in here with you," he suggested. "I can take the couch."

Isabel started to nod. Suddenly she froze, her eyes widening.

"What's wrong?"

"You're not Ava," Iz said. She held her hands away from the body she had just been holding.

"What are you talking ab-" Griffin started, and then he heard the low, rumbling chuckle coming from the thing standing in front of Isabel. He stood on the opposite end of the bed, walking around behind Ava. He kept his distance but made himself available in case he was needed.

Slowly unwrapping herself from Isabel, Ava took a step back. But it was not Ava. The eyes were black and emotionless. The belt on the robe had loosened, causing a thin strip of bare flesh to show as the two sides drifted apart.

"What do you want?" Iz asked, wiping her palms on her pajama shorts. She felt dirty.

The Monster chuckled again. "You didn't mind hanging all over your girlfriend when she was all but sobbing on your shoulder."

"I have no problem touching my friends. The way you use Ava disgusts me."

It used Ava's mouth to sneer. "I didn't do anything that sack of flesh didn't ask me to do."

"You took advantage of an abused child. Hooray for you," Isabel snapped, clenching her fists. She wished she could go back in time, to a younger Ava, and show her kindness instead of using her under the guise of friendship.

"You think you know me," it said, taking a step toward her.

Narrowing her eyes, Isabel stood her ground. "I don't give two shits who or what you are. Get out of my friend."

"If you want to keep score," The Monster breathed, "your sister is dead because of you. Who's the monster now?"

Isabel's body moved before she had time to think. She stepped forward and belted Ava in the chin, using her hips to add power, putting everything she had into the punch. She had a moment to see Griffin's eyes widen and then his face disappeared as Ava's body lifted off the floor and she flew backward into Griffin's arms. They were both knocked to the floor.

Isabel held her fists shoulder width apart, staring at them, her jaw hanging open. Beyond her view, Griffin was staring at her, too, ignoring the unconscious, partially naked woman in his arms.

"Holy fuck."

She began to shake.

Griffin was finally coming to his senses. He pulled the robe around Ava and tightened the belt. Lifting her, he carried her to the bed and quickly tucked her in, unable to think of how they were going to explain a bruise. He was grateful no skin had broken open.

"Isabel," he said calmly, walking over to her and taking her by the arms. He had to say her name again before she looked up at him. "I can't believe you just did that."

His voice was full of awe.

Her knees seemed to dissolve. Griffin eased her onto the end of the bed and sat next to her, glancing over at Ava.

"I hit her," Iz said. "She wasn't even in control of herself, and I knocked her out."

"She's fine." He shifted, draping his arm over her shoulder. "What does Gabriel usually do for her when she sleepwalks?"

"He doesn't hit her!"

"Forget about that for a minute." He tried to reign in his exasperation, motivated more by lack of sleep than actual irritation at her. "What did he do the night you stayed over?"

"He was gentle with her. He talked with her and led her back to bed. But she was her when it happened. He didn't have to deal with the other thing the night I stayed over."

Iz climbed into bed next to Ava, watching her sleeping form.

"I wonder why Daniel told us not to call Gabriel last night to pick her up." Griffin sat on the edge of the bed next to Iz. "Has Gabriel said anything to you?"

"No. I haven't talked to him since last night."

"Did something happen between them? Is that why Ava was at the bar?"

Isabel shrugged. Reaching out, hesitant, she touched Ava's shoulder. Ava let out a soft sigh.

"We might have to call him if she wakes up again. For now, I think you've taken care of the problem."

She blushed. "I didn't mean to."

Grinning, he gave her a squeeze. "It was great, Izzie. You knocked that thing right out of her."

"Ava might not see it that way," she mumbled.

"I'll go sleep on the couch. Come get me if you need me."

He leaned up and kissed her, lingering a bit.

"Yeah... okay."

$$\bullet \quad \bullet \quad \bullet \quad \bullet \quad \bullet$$

Lightning bugs flashed intermittently across the front yard. The sound of crickets carried up the side of the house to the roof, where Gabriel sat outside his bedroom window. There was no breeze, making the early morning cool but not unpleasant.

He felt none of it. On another day, he might have listened to the insects and watched the light show and found peace. But not now. Now, he thought the darkness brought loneliness, hopelessness.

What had Hayden felt in those last moments of her life? Had the song of crickets terrified her as she wandered the woods, trying to find her way back to the people she loved? Had she cried?

Rubbing his hand down his face, he lifted his other hand to drink and found not a beer but a glass of water. That surprised him. He thought he'd come out here with a beer in his hand. After he took a drink, he shifted his position and found his body was incredibly stiff. How long had he been sitting out here? He had come out around midnight, according to his alarm clock. His glass of water was almost empty, but he didn't remember drinking. All he remembered was thinking of Hayden.

Suddenly, another memory hit him: a freezing day in March, when he had gone to visit Hayden's grave. Ava had been there, looking so depressed. She had told him she was taking a walk when he asked her what she was doing at the grave but hadn't explained why she stopped at that particular grave. And she had looked around, almost... almost as if she saw something he did not.

The night he found out she was psychic, she told him Hayden had led her to the grave. She had tried to read him; she had told him. That night at the grave she had held his hand, he remembered, taking off her glove so their skin was touching.

What had she finally said?

I cannot help you. It is in the dark.

Apparently, no information was coming through to her that night.

But they had talked and being with her had soothed some of the ache in his heart for his sister.

For some reason, this year had been especially hard on him during Hayden's birthday, and he'd said as much to Ava that night in the cemetery. And she'd said something so strange, something that he'd thought about off and on in the past two months because it was so out of place in their conversation.

She had said, It is because of me. My presence has made it more difficult for you to grieve.

He didn't understand it then or now. Even after getting to know her so intimately, there was still so much of her that was a mystery to him. Why would his grief for his sister have anything to do with Ava?

His mind was frantically searching all his discussions with her, all the times he spent with her, trying to find the hidden meaning in the odd things she said. His first time bringing her to the dojo, Hayden had spoken through her. I miss you, she had said. Water had poured from her mouth like a geyser... water that smelled of the river. And she had also said-

Gabriel jerked as the details resurfaced.

It was the river, Gabe.

She had been trying to tell him she'd drowned. It seemed so painfully obvious now, but at the time he didn't understand what she was talking about.

And Ava had been caught in the middle.

He was in love with her, that much he knew, even if he didn't know how to show it right now. Even if he couldn't speak, and he couldn't look at her, and he couldn't be with her, he knew what he felt.

That will not stop you from leaving.

The thought made his hand twitch. The glass of water almost tumbled out of his hand. Blinking, Gabriel frowned. Where had that come from?

He'd heard it in Ava's voice. A memory... she had said it once, not so long ago...

She had awakened him from yet another dream to find her standing on the balcony. This one hadn't been a nightmare, but she had woken him up by repeating the full name of a boy. When he asked her who it was, she had said something incoherent. He never found out what the name meant.

What stuck with him, however, was what she said after. He had told her he loved her. And she had said -

That will not stop you from leaving.

"Fuck."

He tipped the glass up only to find he had already finished his water.

She had known this was going to happen. Maybe not the circumstances of his leaving her alone, but she had known he would bail on her long before he'd known he was capable of it. Yet she stayed. She could have cut her loses and ditched him before he could hurt her, but she chose to stay, knowing he would inevitably leave her.

"Christ, Ava, why did you tell me about Hayden? You knew I couldn't handle it," he mumbled, furious with himself. He ran a hand through his hair.

He wanted to put his fist through a wall.

A sudden, sharp cry shot through his head like a railroad spike. The sound was piercing, raising the hair on the back of his neck, and reverberating through his skull. The glass slid from his hand and clattered to the roof, rolling down the shingles until it hit the metal gutter with a loud clanging ring.

Holding his head in his hands, Gabriel ground his teeth and tried to block out the sound of Ava's scream in his head.

•　•　•　•　•

His first thought was Isabel.

Almost immediately, he realized the scream he was hearing was not her voice.

Thrashing around, Griffin crashed to the floor and began stumbling around as he tried to come to his senses in the foreign dark room. Nothing was around him to give him points of reference – no bedside table, no walk-in closet, no flat screen television. The scream was coming from everywhere and nowhere, further disorienting him. At last, he hit a wall and his hands fumbled to find a light switch.

Except it wasn't a wall. It was a bookcase.

Ava's house. He was at Ava's house, in the living room. He took a moment, took a breath, and tried to figure out where he was. The scream stopped abruptly. As his eyes adjusted, he saw the outline of the Douglas fir outside the window and knew he was standing on the west wall of the room. The nearest source of light was a lamp behind him – on the table beside the couch, where he had begun.

He turned around, and by the dim light of what he guessed was early morning, inched back toward the couch. Feeling his way, he found the lamp and pulled the cord, shutting his eyes and turning his head away. The blackness behind his closed eyes brightened. Giving himself a five count, he eased his eyes open and looked around.

The kitchen, dining room, and living room seemed to be empty except for him. Isabel and Ava should be upstairs in Ava's room. He thought the scream had sounded closer than that, but he couldn't be sure his memory was accurate. He had been asleep when he heard it. If he'd actually heard it.

Moving toward the stairs, his adrenaline spiking, he paused when he felt a chill move across his ankles. He turned to find the front door open. Ava had checked the locks twice before they'd all said good night.

He walked cautiously toward the door. A yard light illuminated Rover in the driveway. Crouched against the pole of the yard light was Ava. Even as his mind registered what he was seeing, she screamed again, lowering her head between her arms as if she were throwing up on the ground.

Griffin hurried outside, bypassing the stairs, and jumping off the porch. He crouched next to her quivering body and reached out to put his hand on her shoulder. He had almost made contact when he remembered Isabel's warning. He snatched his hand back.

"Ava?"

He had to speak up to be heard. She wasn't crying, exactly, but she was close to it, her breath coming in short gasps and pants. She was wearing the robe Isabel had put on her earlier and he thanked God for that. The belt had come undone, and it was spread around her body like the train of a wedding dress.

"Ava, what are you doing out here?"

She gave no indication she'd heard him, only continued to heave, and shake until Griffin thought her heart would break.

"Give me your hand." He was trying not to shiver himself. It was bloody cold out here in a tee shirt and shorts. "Let's go inside."

The sniffling abruptly stopped.

Slowly, Ava lifted her arm. Her hand was limp, with bits of grass clinging to it.

"That's the way."

Griffin set his hand under hers, pressing palm to palm, and was surprised when Ava simply wrapped her fingers around his. An owl called from somewhere in the woods. Griffin felt Ava's fingers twitch against his hand at the sudden noise.

"Let me help you stand."

He set his other hand on her back and eased her up, focusing on her head so he wouldn't be tempted to look at the swath of naked body showing where the robe was open. She kept her head down, making her hair fall forward, so he couldn't see her face.

"Can you do me a favor, Ava? Can you close your robe for me and tie your belt around your middle?"

Reaching down, she did as he asked.

"Thank you. Come inside with me."

He took her hand again to help her navigate the porch stairs. When she finally lifted her head, he saw her eyes were open but glazed; she wasn't aware of her surroundings.

"Here's the first step," he said, pausing in front of it.

She raised her foot. As it settled on the stair, she tilted her head slightly to the right and raised her right hand as if offering it to someone else. Then she continued up the stairs.

Griffin watched her carefully, mesmerized by her condition, shuffling across the porch to keep her from stumbling. He had his right hand on her back again, and even through the fabric he could feel heat radiating from her body.

"Is someone else here with us, Ava?"

She nodded.

"Who is it?" Griffin opened the door and held it open with his body so she could get in.

"Connor."

He almost dropped her hand. "My brother?"

"He watches over you."

Stopping in the living room, Griffin debated what to do. Should he take her back upstairs? The safest route was straight to the couch to sleep. According to Isabel, she would probably sleep through now until morning. But it felt wrong to have her sleep on the couch in her own home.

Ava turned her head to the right again.

"I do not do that anymore."

Studying her, Griffin watched her appear to listen for a few seconds before she said, "I am done with that."

"What are you talking about?" he asked.

"I am not talking to you." She leaned against him, shying away from whatever she saw to her right. "I am not talking to anyone."

Griffin thought of Isabel finally admitting to him that Ava had told her and Gabriel what had really happened to Hayden.

"You think bad things happen when you communicate with spirits."

"I know they do." She pulled away from him and stepped back, cupping her hands under her elbows.

"Would you like to go back to bed?"

"I am not tired. And they are not... quiet."

"How about we sit down and talk, then?"

Hesitating, her eyes hooded and glassy, she turned toward the couch and then simply stood. Griffin set his hand on her back and guided her to sit.

"I'm going to get you a glass of water."

When he came back, she had curled up on the end of the couch, her long legs drawn up by her chest. Her arms were wrapped around her legs and her head was resting on her knees at an angle. Griffin sat next to her.

"I have your water here."

He reached out, bumping her hand with the glass. She took the glass and sipped pensively.

"Did you have a nightmare? Is that why you were outside?"

She didn't look at him directly; her eyes remained unfocused somewhere over his right knee. Clutching the glass of water between her hands, she remained silent.

"Why is Connor here?" he asked, trying to keep his voice steady. "Is there something else he wants me to know?"

Her hands stiffened around the glass.

"I do not do that anymore."

"You don't want to help people?"

She looked stricken. "I have not helped anyone. I only make things worse."

Pursing his lips, he nodded slowly. "How people take the information is beyond your ability. All you can do is tell them what the spirits want you to tell them."

"I can stay away," Ava whispered. "It hurts too much when it is all around me."

"Your empathy gets in the way of the message. That's noble, Ava, to care about the people who are left grieving. But it's not on you. Your gift is to relay the message, not to control the outcome."

"I hate it."

"Even so. It is yours."

It was all advice he could have given himself. His knowledge of how the mind processed emotions wasn't always a gift and he didn't always want it, but he had the ability, and it was up to him to help people with it. Regardless of how they took it. He could no longer walk away from it than he could leave an injured grandma on the sidewalk with her groceries dumped all around her.

"Connor does not like the tension between your mother and you. It is what drove a wedge between her and him. He does not want the same for you."

The sudden change of subject took him a few seconds to process. "I've tried everything to make things right between us."

Ava took a drink and held out her glass. Griffin took it, setting it on the coffee table, and watched her curl up again and place her hands over her ears.

"People claim to love. They use your love for them against you." She winced. "Stop talking to me!"

She began rocking.

"What is he saying, Ava?" Griffin asked. He was curious about what his brother was saying, but he also wanted to help this woman so obviously tortured by her experiences. Finding out that the well-being of his friend meant more to him than messages from his dead brother stupefied him.

She inhaled deeply. "He smells of paint and turpentine. He painted his death many times."

Griffin jerked. He hadn't even told Izzie about Connor's paintings. They were locked away, so he hadn't thought of them in months. Even his parents didn't know about the suicide paintings. Griffin had taken them before he and his parents had gone through the rest of his belongings.

Ava shut her eyes and twisted her head, her hands still covering her ears. "I do not want to hear them anymore. Make them stop."

"I'm sorry, Ava, I don't know how."

He heard footsteps on the stairs and glanced up to see Isabel, wide-eyed and blinking, looking around the living room. She had something in her hand.

"Hey, Izzie."

Moving carefully around Ava, he walked over and wrapped his arms around Isabel.

"Did we wake you up?"

He felt her shake her head against his chest. "I had to go to the bathroom and Ava wasn't in bed. What's going on?"

"She was outside screaming."

Pulling back, she searched his face. "I didn't wake up to her screaming?"

His lips twitched. "You sleep like the… ah… dead. Come sit down. She's having a rough time."

He led her to the couch. As she neared it, she reached out. "Ava, it's Isabel. Here's my hand."

She brushed the backs of her fingers against Ava's knee and kept the contact as she moved around to sit next to her on the couch. Griffin continued past her and sat, resting his arm on the back of the couch, and rubbing his other hand up and down Isabel's back.

"I brought your shirt and shorts down."

She held them out, pressing them against Ava's elbow. She lowered her hands from her ears and took the clothing, staring straight ahead for a moment. Unsure if she understood what they were, Iz was just about to explain to her when Ava draped her legs over the couch and slipped off her robe, tugging her shirt on.

"Bollocks, she's got no sense of… anything…." Griffin floundered, almost poking himself in the eye getting his hands up to cover his face.

Iz snorted. She pulled the robe away and draped it over the back of the couch. Ava stood and pulled her shorts on. When she sat down again, she sat close to Iz. She raised her hands to cover her ears again.

"Are they keeping you awake, Ava?" Iz asked, draping her hand over the younger woman's ankle so they were continually touching.

Frowning, Ava moved her hands by her ears. "They are busy."

"Who are they?" She glanced over her shoulder. "Do we know?"

"Connor is one of them." Griffin's hand ceased its rubbing on her back. "Apparently, he's not done yet."

Raising an eyebrow, Iz shifted slightly so she could look at his face easier. "He's still here?"

"They are all still here." Ava's eyes were rolling, and she was blinking rapidly, making Isabel's stomach turn. "Where else would they be?"

Her tone indicated this should have been obvious.

"What about… you know, heaven or whatever? Don't they move on, go to the bright light, once they've said what they need to say?"

Ava sighed, as if she had explained this concept so many times, she was tiring of it. "The human concept of heaven and hell is up and down. It is a finality to you. In reality, the spirit, or energy, exists on a different plane than ours. They will continue on as they did before they came to me."

"What about finding peace?" Griffin asked.

"What of it?"

"How do they find peace if they're stuck watching this world constantly?"

"Nothing is more liberating than shedding the human form. It is not so hard to see the horrors of this world when you are only a visitor."

"Weird," Isabel said.

Ava rubbed her forehead. "Will you sing?"

"What? I don't have my guitar."

"I just want to sleep."

Iz thought for a few seconds, then began to sing. Griffin watched her hand move back and forth along Ava's ankle, following the rhythm of the song. She had picked the song, "Imagine" by John Lennon, slowing it down a little and keeping her voice soft.

Ava's eyes were still unfocused, but they had stopped rolling and she was no longer blinking. They were aimed somewhere past Isabel and Griffin, out the window maybe, or maybe she was looking at something not visible to anyone but her.

Finally, her eyelids started to droop. In a move that surprised both Griffin and Iz, she leaned forward and curled up with her head on Isabel's lap. Glancing at Griffin, Iz began to stroke Ava's hair the way Gabriel used to when she was crying.

"You're safe now," Iz whispered, drawing her fingers through Ava's hair in long, slow strokes. "The voices are far away."

"Far away," Ava mumbled, curling her hand under her chin. "Good night, Isabel."

"Good night, Ava. You'll sleep better now."

"Good night, Griffin."

Touched, Griffin reached over and covered her hand with his. "Good night, Love."

"Good night, Connor."

Silence was the only answer.

•   •   •   •   •

Gabriel threw himself into his work because that's what he did. When he still wasn't sleeping at four in the morning, he went to his workshop and finished the cabinet his father wanted for his mother and the bookcase for another client. There was paperwork to do, invoices to send out and calls to make regarding payment, but when he was restless, he needed to work with his hands. He had finished drawing and designing to set the groundwork for the next project he had contracted for, so he started measuring and cutting to get rid of the energy.

He could easily take a leave of absence due to a family emergency. Most of his clients were by word-of-mouth. They were loyal, compassionate, and most importantly, understanding of the loss of Hayden. If he updated his messaging service and website to show he was on leave for family business, most would assume it had something to do with his "lost sister, poor thing" and soon the entire town would know.

Pausing just long enough to take a sip of strong coffee, Gabriel looked at his diagram to double check measurements. He'd measured twice, as he always did, yet he still cut the board half an inch too short. Swearing, he tossed the piece toward the corner. The echoing thud as it hit others in the pile was gratifying. He started over.

What did he think he would do if he took some time off? Sit around and mope? Think endless, restless, thoughts that circled in his head, driving him crazy? He didn't run from his problems. He promised Patty Meyers a cabinet – more like a sideboard, really, as it turned out – before the fourth of July. He had promised products to other clients, with deadlines he should be able to keep. He wasn't about to give up now.

Knowing the details of Hayden's death wasn't the same as finding out she was dead. He had no excuse for taking bereavement time. There would be no funeral, no closure.

There was only an empty feeling inside that could never be filled.

•   •   •   •   •

In the woods on her property, Ava had her feet propped up on a fallen log and was doing pushups to the sound of birds and insects singing.

She had awakened to find herself curled on the couch with Isabel. As she moved Isabel's hand off her head and stood, she saw Griffin behind her, his head resting on his arm on the back of the couch. Isabel was slumped against him, but her hand had remained on Ava's. She had a vague memory of someone caressing her hair, as if in a dream.

Upstairs, she dressed for a workout and quietly left the house to so she wouldn't wake everyone to her pounding on the body bag or striking the mook yan jong. They had been kind to her, sensing she was upset and showing up at the bar. Even kinder, they had driven her all the way home and stayed with her when she had not been sure her actions would remain honorable.

Had they heard her scream in the night and come down to comfort her? Is that why they had all been asleep on the couch?

Now she lost herself in the natural sounds and smells of the woods as she switched from elevated pushups to pull ups, using a sturdy tree branch. Sweat glistened on her skin. The familiar surge of adrenaline coursed through her. All of her focus was centered on her body as she pushed it, hard, to perform.

Don't you need me anymore?

Flinching, she dropped to the ground. The unwelcomed voice surrounded her, echoing off the trees. She bit back a snarl and began lunges. Each time she stepped forward and knelt, she threw a punch, because she did not believe parts of her should remain motionless when other parts were moving.

Haven't I been there when no one else was?

She ignored the voice. Discipline the body and you will discipline the mind. She continued with the lunges.

Everyone leaves you eventually, but I never will. I have been with you from the beginning.

"Go away. You are dead."

A chuckle echoed in the branches above her. Ava lifted her head and looked around, trying to find its source. What was it when it wasn't inside her? What form did it take?

She had never thought to question its source. It came to her as a child, and as a child, she had accepted it as an authority on how to take care of her problems. Now she was curious.

"What is your name?"

Standing, she took a moment to catch her breath. She stretched her arms while she waited.

The Monster was silent. The woods had gone silent as well; the birds were no longer singing, and the insects had stopped their constant noise. Continuing to stretch, she listened intently.

"You are a coward."

For the next two hours she pushed herself more than she usually did, reveling in the sweat, the focus, the structure of physical exertion. She used the trees and her own body instead of weights and machinery. Being forced to work out in the openness of the outdoors allowed her to immerse herself nature, which she was always more comfortable in, and delve deeper in thought as she worked.

At last she finished up with her four-mile run and headed back toward the house in a walk that allowed her to cool down.

Her body was sated. Her mind was numb. Working out allowed her the ability to think of nothing, so she took the time to empty her mind.

She didn't need to worry about what happened next. She had survived on her own before, and she would do it again.

●　　●　　●　　●　　●

After a few minutes of acquainting himself with Ava's kitchen, Griffin had all the fixings to make a pot of coffee. He set it up, then set about finding coffee cups for himself and Izzie.

She stumbled in from the couch a few minutes later despite his best efforts to lay her down and cover her with a blanket. Rubbing her hand over her cheek, she squinted at him.

"Good morning, Beautiful."

Sliding onto a breakfast bar stool across from him, she sighed heavily.

"'Morning."

"Your coffee should be ready in a couple minutes."

"Thank you." She tried to smile but moving her facial muscles that much this early in the morning was too much to ask for. "Is Ava upstairs?"

"I haven't seen or heard her."

She looked worried. Sliding back off the stool, she padded upstairs. A few moments later, she came back down.

"She isn't up there."

She walked to the front door, checking the porch. Back inside, she brought her phone from the living room into the kitchen. When she brought up Ava's Contact, they heard the default trilling of a cell phone coming from the dining room table.

"She doesn't have her phone with her."

Isabel walked to the table, where a legal pad of paper was sitting next to the phone. Thinking Ava may have left them a note indicating where she had gone, she glanced down at the pad and froze.

The page was filled with hastily scribbled writing that looked nothing like Ava's penmanship. The author had pushed so hard onto the pad while writing that the letters pressed through several consecutive pages. At some points, the tip of the pen had ripped through the paper.

"What do you have there?"

Isabel yelped at Griffin's voice directly behind her.

"Hey," he said, resting his hands on her shoulders. "What's wrong?"

She touched the page, feeling how deep the ink was pressed into the page, how furious the writer must have been when writing it.

"Look at this," she whispered.

Standing behind her, he read over her shoulder.

FUCKING BITCH YOU'LL BOW TO ME FUCKING CUNT DEAD WHORE YOU WILL PAY FOR LOCKING ME OUT NEVER LEAVE NEVER LET GO YOU'LL BEG FOR MY HELP YOU SELFISH BITCH I OWN YOU UNGRATEFUL BRAT I'LL WATCH YOU SCREAM WATCH YOU DIE

"Bugger," Griffin breathed.

The entire page was filled with similar malignancy and threats. He reached around Isabel's arm and lifted the top page to discover what she had: some ink that had torn through and the hard impressions from the rage of the writer.

"Did our Ava write this?"

Isabel stepped away from it. Something about looking at the writing, about being near it, made her feel ill. She wanted to get as far away from it as possible.

"It's not her handwriting, but she mentioned automatic writing as part of the psychic tendencies." He hadn't found the coffee cups when she interrupted him, so she pulled out two and set them on the counter. "Her hand holds the pen but someone else writes the message is how she put it. Or something like that."

She pulled a spoon from the drawer to doctor her coffee and creamer from the refrigerator.

"That wasn't there last night before we went to bed. She did it sometime during the night or early this morning."

At the knock at the door, she almost dropped the bottle of creamer on the table.

Griffin stood, covering her hand with his. "Try to relax."

"Right."

As he went to answer the door, Isabel took a deep breath and tried unsuccessfully to stop her mind from filling with questions. Was Ava aware when someone else was making her write a message? If she wasn't, how did it make her feel to come out of it and see those horrible words on the page? To feel violated inside and out.

And what the hell was she going to do when Isabel told her she had punched her in the face this morning because she was insulted? Iz wasn't looking forward to that conversation.

"Good morning, Isabel."

Daniel, Ava's teacher, was standing in the dining room with Griffin.

She took a deep breath and tried to stop her mind from wandering. "Hello. Would you like some coffee?"

"Water, please."

She was glad to keep herself busy getting a glass of water. Having tasks helped her slow down.

"If you're looking for Ava, she's missing."

"Missing?"

Griffin poured himself a cup of coffee and sat on one of the stools at the counter. "We can't find her," he explained. "When we woke up, she was gone."

Daniel checked his watch. "She's probably working out."

Isabel set the glass in front of him. "She isn't in the basement."

"She prefers to be outside as much as possible. She's probably in the woods."

Sighing, Iz stirred her coffee, visibly relieved. "I hope so."

"Did you have a bad night?"

Surprised, Isabel looked sharply at him. "My night was fine. She's the one with the nightmares."

She leaned back against the counter, thinking.

Daniel watched her. He sat on a chair next to Griffin, who seemed relaxed in spite of Isabel's agitation. Ava had made two more friends, and they seemed to care greatly for her. For that, he was grateful. In the little amount of time he had spent with them, they seemed loyal and willing to do anything to keep her safe. Last night they'd shown up because Ava was in the type of place she didn't usually go to, and her voice sounded funny. Obviously, Isabel was intelligent as well as compassionate.

"So-" he started and was interrupted by the front door opening.

Ava strolled in sweating and stretching her arms over her head as she walked toward the stairs. Everyone turned to look at her. Without acknowledging them, she crossed her arms at the hem of her shirt and pulled it up, twisting it off as she reached the bottom of the stairs. She tossed the shirt to the floor and began unhooking her bra as she ascended.

"Bloody hell, that woman has no sense of social etiquette," Griffin muttered, averting his eyes.

Daniel had to admit it had taken him by surprise.

"I hope she doesn't do that after class," Iz said.

"No," Daniel said, shaking his head. "She only showers at the dojo when we work on her psychic ability after class. Ava's like a daughter to me, so that was extremely awkward."

They heard the shower start upstairs.

"So, how long have you been... doing martial arts?" Isabel asked, refilling her cup. She was glad she needed more creamer so she could turn her back on Daniel while her face was red with humiliation. Her attempts at conversation were pathetic.

"I've been training since I was fourteen. Almost twenty-four years."

"Wow."

Returning to the counter, she poured creamer thoughtfully.

"Have you considered trying it?" he asked.

"Me? Oh, no... I couldn't..."

"Why not?"

She stirred her coffee absently. "I'm not that... noble."

"You showed up last night for a friend in need. That's noble. But nobility isn't a prerequisite for learning martial arts."

Upstairs, the shower had stopped.

"Ava doesn't need anyone." Isabel cupped her elbows in her hands and glanced toward the stairs. "Least of all, me."

"She likes her independence," Daniel agreed. "But everyone needs friends. Ava thinks very highly of you."

Iz raised her eyebrow.

"I think you would benefit from learning martial arts, whether you come to my school or Ava teaches you. It would help build your confidence."

"She could use that." Griffin spoke for the first time in several minutes.

"Quiet, you." She smiled at him.

"Why are you here, Sensei?"

Isabel yelped at the sound of Ava's voice. She stood at the entrance to the kitchen, clothed in yoga pants and a sleeveless shirt, her wet hair hanging down around her shoulders. Her eyes were dull.

"I wanted to make sure you're okay."

"I am fine."

"Is that why it hurt to put on a shirt?" Daniel asked.

"I put the shirt on to satisfy you.

She walked around Iz to get a coffee cup. As she reached for the carafe, her arm brushed against Isabel's and she stilled. Her eyes widened. With her other hand, she reached across her own arm and gripped Isabel's arm like a vise, her fingers digging into the flesh.

For a moment she was frozen, her pupils dilated and her hand clenching Iz so hard it hurt. She closed her eyes and yanked her hand away, backing up until her butt hit the counter. Her eyes flew open.

"You struck me?"

"I didn't mean to." Isabel stiffened. "It wasn't really you –"

"You struck me," Ava repeated, rubbing her hand on chin. "You knocked me out. That takes a great deal of strength."

"I'm sorry."

Griffin leaned over and took her hand, squeezing it.

"Do not be," Ava said thoughtfully as she filled her mug. "It was an impressive strike."

"It certainly surprised me," Griffin said, squeezing her hand again and grinning.

"It's not funny." Isabel set her coffee cup down too hard, splashing a little onto her hand. "I've never done anything like that before."

"Care to fill me in?" Daniel asked, noting Isabel's dark red flush.

Griffin rubbed his thumb over the back of her hand.

"Ava was sleepwalking this morning," she said, gripping his hand as if her life depended on it. "The Monster paid a visit, being his usual charming self."

"Izzie clocked him a good one," Griffin said proudly. "Knocked Ava off her feet."

"That is impressive."

"She was off her game." Trying and failing to keep her voice cold, Isabel broke away from Griffin and walked to the counter on the other side of the sink, looking for food. "I never would have been able to do that if she was awake."

"Your ability embarrasses you," Ava said, studying her.

"I lost my temper." She kept her back to them, moving to the refrigerator when she didn't find anything interesting in the cupboards. She pulled out a carton of eggs and a pound of turkey bacon. Turning back, she set everything on the counter and started looking for cookware.

"Do you have a hangover?" she asked, changing the subject. "You were pretty drunk last night."

Ava sipped her coffee. "My head hurts."

"That'll happen. I hope you don't mind me cooking breakfast for everyone."

Instead of answering, Ava leaned forward and opened a cupboard door where the skillets were kept.

"Thank you." Iz continued to keep busy, hoping the conversation would stay off of her.

"What made you feel like drinking, Ava?" Daniel asked.

Standing back at the coffee pot so she was out of Isabel's way, she leveled her gaze at him. "I do not need permission to imbibe."

"You certainly don't. But it's out of character. I'm worried about you. So are your friends."

She said nothing to this, only fixed her stare on the floor. Her grip on the coffee mug tightened.

"Did our conversation upset you?"

Griffin watched her silently stare for several seconds, ignoring the soft noises as Isabel prepared breakfast, and wished he knew how to take that horrible sadness from Ava's eyes. For the first time since he had met her, she looked broken, defeated, and it wasn't because she was in the grip of a nightmare.

She lifted her eyes to Daniel slowly and the emotion reflected in them was immobilizing. Slowly, deliberately, she set her coffee cup on the counter.

"I wanted... to stop feeling."

Daniel nodded sympathetically. "Did it work?"

"Hai, Sensei. Until you showed up."

"I'm sorry I ruined your pity-party." He turned to Griffin. "I think I'll have some coffee after all."

Griffin leaned forward and picked up the carafe. When he stood to get another cup, Daniel set his hand on his arm and stood.

"I'll get it."

Ava stood frozen as Daniel moved around her. The fury emanating from her was palpable. Griffin poured more coffee into his own cup to distract himself from the tension mounting and noticed Izzie was being extra quiet.

"I'm going to slide in here and get some milk," Daniel said, setting his hand on Isabel's shoulder as he moved passed her and opened the refrigerator. As he reached in for the milk, he leaned toward her ear. "She'll be okay."

He patted her shoulder.

Ava hadn't moved when he walked back to the counter and added milk to the coffee Griffin had poured for him. As he returned the milk to the refrigerator, she took a spoon from the drawer and whipped it at him, sending it flying across the room with the precision of a knife. Daniel turned just before it reached his head and brought his palms together over it, stopping it less than an inch from his nose. Isabel exhaled.

"Fuck me," Griffin muttered.

Walking back to the counter, Daniel dropped the spoon into the cup and returned to his seat. He calmly stirred the milk into his coffee.

"Is this about Gabriel?" he asked.

Isabel dropped the fork she'd been using to beat eggs in a glass bowl, the sound echoing sharply in the room.

"What happened with Gabriel?" she asked.

"Our relationship is not your business," Ava growled, glaring at her. She turned to Daniel. "Or yours."

"You picked a fight in a bar last night using the training I've given you. I'm responsible for my students."

Her eyes flashed, the dull black filling the void of her sockets briefly. "You are not my father."

Closing her eyes, she took a deep breath. She shook her head and exhaled, a puff of air that sounded more like exhaustion than anger. When she opened her eyes, they were gray. Troubled, but gray.

"He was drunk. He was looking for a fight."

The excuse sounded weak even to herself.

"You baited him."

Isabel backed away from the counter. "Maybe we should go, Griffin."

"Yes. Go." The Monster sneered at her. "Everyone leaves."

Iz looked desperately into those smoldering black eyes. "You like driving everyone away, don't you? You want her all to yourself."

The thing inside Ava made her lean back against the counter with a hand on the marble at each side.

"It doesn't take much to make you run away, Isabel Harris."

"Isabel." Daniel stood slowly. "Come stand by me."

Griffin shifted but Daniel rested his hand on his arm to keep him seated. "Come over here."

Ava turned her head to look at him.

Isabel inched toward him, trying to be as invisible as she could. He moved around the island and stood so he was flush with the counter, facing Ava. As Iz moved closer, he reached out, taking her hand, and guiding her behind him. Griffin slid his arms around her waist, unsure what to do. He wasn't sure if their presence was helping or hindering.

"If you want to leave," Daniel said, keeping his gaze on Ava, "now is the time to do it."

"Ava's in there somewhere," Iz couldn't keep the tremor from her voice. "I want to help her, if I can."

"She needs all the support she can get."

Ava's eyes flashed. When she spoke, her tone was hers again, listless and ~~Fr~~iends are liabilities."

Ignoring her, Isabel spoke to Daniel. "I don't want to be in the way."

"Then stay where you are and move if I tell you to move. Griffin, are you still with us?"

"I'm here." His grip tightened on Isabel.

"Good." He rolled his neck, stretching the muscles. "Ava, can you hear me?"

"She's done listening to you." Ava straightened with exaggerated slowness.

As she took a step toward Daniel, Iz watched him prepare for an attack, though she saw no change in his posture or expression. How could that be? That she was suddenly aware he looked ready to fight, yet he hadn't so much as moved his hands or hardened his eyes?

The tension in the room was so thick she could chew it. Ava and Daniel were nonchalantly at a standoff, and Isabel was so terrified she filled the room with doubt and frustration.

Griffin's hand squeezed hers. From his expression, she could tell he wasn't sure how it was going to end, but he was confident everything was going to be okay. How could he be so sure?

Startled, she squeezed his back.

"Ava, listen to my voice."

Her lip raised in a snarl.

"If you're upset, we'll help you deal with it. Don't let it handle your problems for you."

"I'll deal with all of you," The Monster snapped. "None of you have been there for her the way I have."

"Possession isn't the same as friendship," Iz said.

The Monster turned Ava's head to study her thoughtfully. "Friendship. Concern. You use pretty words to describe the same means of control."

"You're wrong. I'm sorry." She glanced at Daniel, but he nodded and mouthed, keep going. Focusing on Ava, trying to remember her friend was in there somewhere, she said, "Real friends don't manipulate each other."

A dark, hateful chuckle rumbled from Ava's mouth. "You don't really believe that. You manipulate your man every time you tell him you are fine. And you," it said, narrowing its eyes at Griffin. "You play on her emotions like she plays her guitar strings. You pluck and strum until you get what you want from her, all the while claiming to do it out of love."

"Shut up," Griffin said, tightening his grip on Isabel. "We don't twist love the way you do."

"Don't let it get to you," Daniel said. "Its power comes from your emotions."

"Aren't you the enlightened one?" it sneered. "You've become so wise since your family abandoned you, Daniel."

Ava picked up her coffee and sipped slowly, savoring the flavor.

"For all your flaws, you people sure know how to make a good cup of coffee."

Isabel barked out laughter and quickly slapped her hand over her mouth. The Monster smiled in Ava's body and raised her mug for another sip.

"What's your name?" Iz asked, and her voice had softened. "How did you die?"

"What does it matter?"

"Does Ava know what happened to you? Is that why she lets you control her? Because she feels sorry for who you used to be?"

Her lip curled in disgust. "I don't need her pity, or yours. I don't need anyone. We don't need anyone. We were fine by ourselves. Your brother had to butt in and ruin everything."

"I know you're in there, Ava." Iz stepped around Daniel, leaving herself exposed. "We care about you. Please don't shut us out. Gabriel is grieving, but he loves you. He'll find his way back."

"He's had sixteen years to grieve," The Monster spat. "The circumstances are different, but the outcome is the same. That whiny little brat is still dead."

Isabel took a step forward. "Talk about my sister again, and I'll knock your ass into next week."

She was aware of nothing else around her. Griffin and Daniel had faded into the background. She didn't hear the birds through the open windows or the occasional sputter from the coffee pot. The only thing she was aware of was whatever was wearing Ava's body right now, manipulating her and convincing her she had no one in the world but it as a companion. Iz remembered the way Griffin had brought her out of her depression, how he had held on even when she fought against him.

"I love you, Ava," she said, taking another step forward. Ava flinched. "I need you here. Can you hear me?"

She reached out and was surprised to find her hand steady as she waited to see if Ava would take it.

The thing inside Ava made her snarl.

"We all love you, Ava," Daniel said. He stood just behind Isabel. "We're all here for you."

She backed against the counter, pressing her body against it to put as much distance as she could between her and the people standing in front of her.

Griffin joined them, resting a hand on Isabel's shoulder. "We won't let anything happen to you, Ava. We're your family."

"She doesn't need you." But The Monster's voice sounded uncertain.

A knock at the door startled them. Daniel, Isabel, and Griffin turned to the front screen door and saw David standing outside. Ava frowned.

"Come in, David," Daniel said, walking over to greet him. The men shook hands.

"What's going on? You said she was in trouble."

"You called him?" The Monster yelled, slamming Ava's fist onto the counter hard enough to make her coffee cup jump. The floor seemed to shift underneath them momentarily.

Isabel and Griffin turned back to her, but Griffin kept his body between the two women. Her eyes were flashing between angry gray and oily black. Isabel felt the hairs on her arms and the back of her neck rise. From the look on Griffin's face, he'd felt it, too. On the counter, the spoons and coffee mugs were vibrating.

"She's spiraling," Daniel said softly.

David instantly entered the kitchen. Isabel and Griffin moved aside and watched as he studied Ava calmly.

"They should not have called you," The Monster said, keeping Ava's head tilted down at an angle. The submissive posture was shocking after the arrogance Isabel was used to.

"Get the hell out of my daughter." David moved closer, so if he reached out, he could touch her. But he held off for now. "You get out of my daughter and leave her alone."

The Monster raised Ava's head and shied away from him. Its voice was small, defeated. "I protect her."

"When she was a child. She's not a child anymore."

"She doesn't want to feel the pain. She doesn't want... to feel..."

She lifted her hand to run fingers along the neckline of her shirt. In a pose that David recognized from her childhood, she tucked her hand under chin. He used to find her that way after a nightmare, huddled under her bed, folded into herself with her hand curled at the base of her neck, her chin resting on it.

"Ava," he said gently, taking her shoulders, "Stop hiding."

She blinked. The smokey black turned to gray, back to black.

"We are unlovable," The Monster said. "We have to stick together."

But its voice was fading, its eyes dissolving behind Ava's gray irises more often now. Whatever energy had previously filled the room was leaving. Isabel no longer felt the odd static that made her hair raise and her back itch with dread.

"I'm sorry for whatever happened to you," David said, lowering his head until he made eye contact with The Monster's and then holding it. "But you are not unlovable. Neither is she."

"Why did he hurt us?"

"Come here."

David enveloped Ava in a hug. "I don't know why people hurt each other, but it wasn't your fault."

"I tried to help her. I only wanted to help."

"I know you did." He patted her back.

Tears slipped down Ava's cheeks, though her expression didn't change. The Monster's eyes, glazed with exhaustion, saw nothing in the room around it. It held onto David and silently cried.

Isabel watched, surprised to find herself feeling sorry for whatever was inside Ava. It hadn't meant to hurt anyone. It had been lonely and scared, and probably abused, and Ava must have felt like a kindred spirit to it. Now, she and Griffin and Gabriel were threatening its bond with her.

"What is your name?" she asked. "Why did you come to Ava?"

The Monster lifted its eyes and studied her warily. "Robbie."

"What happened to you, Robbie?"

David eased back and turned toward Isabel, Griffin and Daniel, but slid his arm around Ava's shoulder. As the thing inside Ava spoke, the deep, distorted voice came and went, disintegrating as a new voice emerged; a quieter, male voice no one had heard before.

987

"My father was a mean man. He liked to hurt my mama and me. I promised myself that one day, I would be big enough to protect my mama from him. But I never could. He beat her to death with a crowbar."

Griffin tightened his grip on Isabel's hand when she gasped.

David rubbed his hand up and down Ava's arm.

Robbie blinked Ava's eyes. They were no longer black pools that took up her entire socket. Nor were they gray. Isabel was startled to see they were a deep, chocolate brown.

"I couldn't save her," Robbie said, his breath hitching.

"It wasn't your job to save her," David said, brushing Ava's hair from her forehead.

Her body was sweating, exhausted. Her skin was pale.

"My father took her body away and I never saw her again."

The voice that came from her lips was no longer distorted. It was only the voice of a young boy, filled with sorrow.

"When my father came back, he beat me with a hammer."

She touched the back of her neck. It came away red with blood.

"I didn't realize I was dead until I saw my father burning everything of mine and my mothers. He just erased us from his life. How can a person do that? Just pretend their family never happened?"

No one had an answer to that.

"My father's name was Malcolm Redding."

David's head whipped around at the sound of the name.

"Do you recognize the name?" Daniel asked.

"Malcolm Redding was killed in 2006 by an inmate in Columbia Correctional Institute. He was in prison for child abuse and murder. He never used his full name. He went by his nickname, Mack."

"You mean... Mack that fostered Ava before she came to you?" Isabel asked. Her legs wanted to buckle.

David nodded.

Ava shuddered violently. He hugged her closer.

"You found Ava because she was being abused by your father." Iz felt her stomach turn.

"I took her pain away. It was all I could give her."

Isabel wiped tears off her cheek and cautiously moved forward. "You saved her, Robbie. She doesn't need you to save her anymore."

She took Ava's hand in both of hers. The blood she had wiped from the back of her neck was gone, as if its power to be seen held only as long as the memory was recalled.

"But she needs a friend. You can still be that for her."

"I chased her friend away."

"What friend?" Griffin asked.

"Let's move this to the living room," David said. "She needs to sit down."

Isabel was grateful. She wasn't sure her legs would hold her much longer.

After David helped Ava to the couch, when she was hugging a pillow with her knees up to her chest, Griffin repeated his question from the recliner in the corner. Iz sat on his lap, and he ran his hand up and down her back.

"The light. It came to her one night when Mack was abusing her. I was trying to take her pain away, but she was panicking. Someone brought the light. The light is kind. I thought it was weak, like I was. I thought Ava should be hard, or she wouldn't survive."

Her hand searched the cushion beside her. David took her hand and squeezed it.

"She didn't know who it was then. Now she calls the light Aaron Michael Reid."

David sat back, stunned.

"David?" Daniel didn't like how pale his friend had become. "Who is Aaron?"

"My son."

Ava's head turned to study David with those odd brown eyes that weren't hers.

"Ruth and I lost a baby before we took Ava in. We never told her... we never told anyone. It was late, in her second trimester. We knew the gender, gave him a name... and then, he was just... gone. Ava only found out about him a few weeks ago."

An uncomfortable silence settled in the room. David wiped his eyes and patted Ava's leg. Standing, he walked to the kitchen.

Isabel set her coffee on the table beside the chair and picked up a tissue to wipe her tears and blow her nose. She glanced back at Griffin.

"Am I getting too heavy?" Though she kept her voice low, it sounded too loud in the silence.

Giving her a small smile, he shook his head. He lifted her hand and brushed his lips against the knuckles.

David returned with a tray with a bottle of root beer, the pot of coffee, and the bottle of creamer on it. "Anyone need a refill?"

As everyone prepared their coffees, Ava sat on the couch listlessly. David set the tray on the coffee table and sat next to her.

"How are you doing, kiddo?"

"We are tired."

"Why won't she come back to us?" Iz asked, shifting on Griffin's lap. "Why is Ava still hiding?"

"She's not," Robbie answered. "She's letting me talk."

"Can she hear us?"

He nodded. "She is aware of what's going on around this body."

Using her body, he leaned forward to pick up his coffee mug, lifted it to his nose, and inhaled deeply.

"I miss the sense of smell the most, I think. It triggers memories the quickest and makes them stronger. I have good memories of coffee."

He sipped it thoughtfully. "The Woman smelled like coffee."

"What woman?" Daniel asked.

"The woman who cared for Ava."

David frowned. "You mean Ruth."

"She didn't call her that, but yes, your wife. Time does not exist in The Interval. I only notice it from the eyes of a host. After Ava was living with you for a while," Robbie said, looking at David, "she didn't need me anymore. She found peace. But I stayed near her. She had a family. I began to feel... something for The Woman."

Ducking Ava's head, Robbie tugged on her ear before looking up at David again. "I began to feel something... for you."

"We became your family."

Isabel's heart ached when Ava's head nodded. "I had nowhere else to go."

He turned his attention to Daniel. "As you taught her to control her anger, she locked me out. For years, she had other outlets.

"The next time she called, she was older. The Wo- Ruth was sick, and Ava started to withdraw. As Ruth's health deteriorated, she called for me more and more."

Sighing, Robbie wrapped Ava's arms around her legs. "By the time of the funeral, I was the one in attendance. We both mourned her."

"She wore sunglasses all day," Daniel murmured, remembering. He had attended for David's and for Ava's sake. "I never saw her eyes. She never spoke. I had no idea."

"Ava processes everything differently, so I didn't think anything of it." David ran a hand down his face.

"For months, she didn't know what to do with her grief, so she hid inside herself. I protected her. Her grief for Ruth lasted many months. When it was at its worst, she... let me take over."

"Why didn't she come to me?" David asked absently, mostly to himself.

"She didn't want to burden you with it," Daniel said. "She knew you were grieving and didn't want to add to it."

"I would have-"

David rubbed his damp eyes and nodded. That was so typical of Ava, setting aside her own grief to care for him. His daughter, who couldn't tell him she loved him but would fight an army to the death to save his life. His daughter, who needed him now.

"I will not hurt her anymore," Robbie said, and then Ava's body gave a stuttering sigh before she sagged against the back of the couch.

David leaned forward and caught her as she began to tilt toward him. "I've got you," he murmured.

He eased out from under her and turned, gently laying her on the couch. Tucking a pillow under her head, he pulled the throw blanket off the back of the sofa and spread it over her limp body. He lifted an eyelid and was relieved to see a gray iris underneath.

"She'll be out for a little while now." He ran his hand over her hair with obvious affection. "I'm going to stay with her."

Isabel stood, gathering Griffin's and her mugs, and setting them on the tray David had brought in.

"Thank you both for staying with her last night."

"Of course," Griffin told David, as Iz continued to set creamer, spoons, and everything else on the tray. "It was... not the best circumstances, but nice to meet you."

"I'll get those, dear," David said, laying a calloused but gentle hand on Isabel's arm. "You look exhausted."

She gazed into his kind eyes and understood instantly why Ava was so close to him.

"Is she going to be okay?"

He patted her arm. "She'll be fine. You took good care of her."

"My brother broke her heart," she blurted. Tears burned her eyes and she felt foolish crying in front of a stranger. "She told us what really happened to Hayden when we were kids and he abandoned her."

"Come on, now." David pulled her to him in an embrace. He ran his hand over her hair as he had for Ava. "You're not responsible for your brother's actions."

After a few moments, Iz leaned back and pulled a couple tissues from the box David offered.

"Ava didn't fall apart because of her relationship with Gabriel," he said, setting the box back on the coffee table. "Her heart is broken because he's in pain, because he misses Hayden. And because she has people that she cares about now. You've opened her heart to so much by being her friend."

"We broke her." Iz sniffled.

"You made her whole. It just takes time for her to get used to the overwhelming emotions."

"I think she preferred to be friendless and impartial. All the touchy-feely shit is too much for her."

"She's stronger than she thinks. And she has all of you to support her. She just has to get used to asking for help now that it's there and offered."

"Come on, Izzie," Griffin said. "She needs to rest, and I need a shower before work."

"Thanks for filling me in," David said after they'd left. He watched Ava sleeping peacefully. "She hasn't told me everything that's been happening."

In one of the recliners, Daniel rested his elbows on his knees. "She quit training."

David narrowed his eyes.

"I don't know how serious she was, as she was drunk off her ass when she told me, but she told me she quit, and she didn't show up at class yesterday."

David sat on the edge of the coffee table. "When you called last night, you said she started a bar fight?"

"She let him make the first move, but my instinct tells me she baited the guy into it. She didn't deny it."

"I should have checked in on her. I knew she was getting close to Gabriel; I know she's not as emotionally mature as others her age. And she was asking me about blackouts she had as a child. I should have known she was taking too much on."

"Ava doesn't let people know anything she doesn't want them to know. Vincent said she hasn't spent any time with him outside class. She's pulling away."

"I'm going to stay with her for a few days." David stood and picked up the tray Isabel had tidily filled with the remnants of everyone's coffee. "I won't always be here for her. I need to be while I still can."

Daniel followed him to the kitchen. "We've been working on her ability, David. She's gotten control over it, for the most part. She called to Hayden and was able to use her ability to help her friends communicate with their sister. This morning she gave The Monster... Robbie... permission to communicate through her. He didn't take her over like he used to. Her first successes just happened to be connected to people she was emotionally invested in. That would be hard on anyone."

"I'm so used to her not needing me, I didn't notice the signs when she did. She started a bar fight, for God's sake."

"She didn't do any permanent damage," Daniel assured him. "She let off some steam. Most of the damage was done to property, which she's going to pay for."

Agitated, David gathered the utensils and put them in the dishwasher. As he was turning to pick up the coffee mugs, he caught movement from the corner of his eye. Ava was rising from the couch. He glanced at Daniel and back to Ava to make sure the conversation about her was over for now. She walked slowly into the kitchen, getting herself a glass of water. Her movements were sluggish.

"I will clean up," she said to David as he set the cups in the dishwasher.

"I've got it." He didn't mean for his tone to be so sharp, and he could tell by the way her body stiffened that she caught it. She walked around the island and sat two stools down from Daniel.

"How do you feel?" Sensei asked her.

"Irritated by my irresponsible behavior." She gazed into her glass of water as if it held the secret of life.

He gave her a wry smile. "You're allowed an occasional mistake, Ava. Everyone makes them."

She said nothing to that, only turned her head and stared out the window. A hundred yards from the side of the house were three old birch trees growing so close together that they looked like they came from one trunk. She watched the hypnotic way the hummingbirds darted around the red feeders she hung out there.

"Where's Buck?" she suddenly asked David without turning from the window.

"The neighbor's watching him for a few days while I stay with you."

With her brow furrowed, she turned to him.

"I don't want any arguments," he said firmly. He started cleaning up the materials Isabel had taken out to make breakfast.

Ava studied her glass of water. All the fight had left her.

"I'm going to head out," Daniel said, standing. "Give me a call when you want to talk, Ava."

Avoiding his eyes, she nodded.

"Good to see you again, David." He shook the older man's hand. "Thank you for calling me."

"Sensei…"

Turning back, he watched Ava slide off the stool at the breakfast bar, her head lowered.

"I…" She swallowed, licked her lips. "I would like to continue to train with you, starting Monday, if that is acceptable."

He studied her for several seconds before nodding. "Of course, Ava."

David watched him leave. From the corner of his eye, he saw Ava run her finger along a pattern in the marble counter.

"I have to work." She hesitated, balancing her butt on the edge of the stool and chewing on her lower lip.

"I'll keep myself busy."

She winced at that.

"Go about your day as if I'm not here." Finished cleaning, David walked to the island and rested his hand over hers.

"I was going to tell you about the light."

"Why didn't you?" David couldn't keep the irritation out of his voice. "He was my son."

She silently stared into her glass of water.

"Are you jealous of him?"

Now she jerked her head up. "I have no reason to be jealous of him. He is dead."

The flash of pain on David's face made her feel ashamed of the blunt indifference in her tone.

"I cannot catch my breath," she said, unable to keep her voice from rising. "Everything is moving so fast. I never expected to have friends. I never wanted to get involved with people. I am confused."

He kept forgetting what it was like for her, going from a nonexistent social life to being flooded with friends, a boyfriend, new experiences in public. Add to that, working with Daniel on her psychic ability, and it was no wonder her head was spinning.

"Of course you are."

Walking around the island, he sat on the stool next to her. He rested his arm on the counter, studying her with his patient eyes.

"I want it to go away. I want to be left alone, like before."

"Do you?"

Dropping her head, she took a moment to think about it. "It is difficult enough, holding onto what I am, without being distracted by relationships. I do not want to injure people."

"I believe that." David took her slender hands in his large, calloused ones.

"I have something inside me that scares everyone and makes them sad. I can physically harm anyone I meet. I cannot even speak without being insulting. No part of me is made for this world."

"Oh, Ava."

He brought her hands to his forehead, sighing. When he lifted his head, his eyes were raw with emotion.

"Don't you understand how much you mean to the people around you?"

Uncomfortable, her eyes darted away from his.

"Can't you feel how much I love you?"

She leaned back.

"Don't run from it, Ava." He tightened his grip on her hands. "Your teacher was here this morning because he loves you. Your friends stayed with you because they care about you. Why does that scare you?"

"You will all leave. Everyone leaves. I cannot take it."

"Oh, baby."

He pulled her into his arms. At first her body remained rigid, resisting his embrace. Her heart was thudding against her rib cage so hard he felt it against his own chest. Then she let out a soft little sigh and melted into him. Her head dropped to his shoulder.

"I love you so much, Ava."

She nodded against him. It wasn't the same as saying it back, but it was one step closer.

• • • • •

He spent the rest of the week with her. During that first day, between the morning's gathering and dinner that evening with just him, the urge to feel offended at his keeping a constant eye on her quickly dissipated. An odd feeling settled inside her. She needed her independence and loved having her own home. But not having David within easy driving distance for months, with only a visit or two since she moved to Langdon, made her realize how much she had missed him. It was strange to realize the ache she felt, the feeling as if a piece of her was missing, was the loss of weekly visits with David. She had not been aware of his impact in her life until he was reintroduced to it.

One night, as they sat together silently, she had felt a rush of such intense emotion coming from him. When she looked over at him, he was studying her intently. She didn't know what prompted his feelings and he had not brought the subject up.

Tonight, as they had every night this week, they sat on her porch in the fading light of sunset. She had bought two padded chairs for the front porch, because they were more comfortable for guests. He sat in one of them and she perched on the railing, her glass of water on the table between the two chairs. With a root beer in his hand, he gazed out at the quiet evening, watching the lightning bugs flicker over the grass.

"I think I might buy a house that's closer to Langdon," he said after almost an hour of silence.

He couldn't see her eyes in the pastels of sunset, so he couldn't figure out what she thought of the idea.

"It's not because I think you're incapable of taking care of yourself," he added softly.

"You are going to sell the farm?" she finally asked. She shifted so she sat on the railing, her legs dangling.

"Would that bother you?"

Considering that possibility took a few moments. The farm had been where she grew up. Her formative years were spent there; those years she had learned that not all men were monsters, that some women had kind voices and hands, that love existed in many forms even if she did not think herself capable of feeling it. She had grown and changed and learned to thrive on that farm. She had always been a survivor, but without her life with David and Ruth, she did not think she would have been able to accept friendship or experience the connections she felt with Gabriel and his family.

As she sat thinking about what it meant to her, all she could feel was… thankful. She appreciated the time she had spent there. Having the space and solitude it provided had given her a real home and the freedom to heal at her own pace. But it was time to move on. Having David closer would mean she could see him more often. It meant if he were in trouble, she would be close enough to help him.

That meant more to her than a building and some land.

"I miss you."

The admission surprised them both. David couldn't see her blushing in the twilight, but he heard it in her tone.

"I miss you, too."

Ava turned so she was leaning back against the post, stretching her crossed legs out along the railing. They used to sit outside in the evenings at the farm, too. More often than not, they sat silently. They could do this anywhere.

"The farm is too big for me now," David continued. "I don't need all that space anymore. I'm too old to keep up with the house and all the land. All I need is a little place to take walks with Buck."

"Langdon is within fifteen minutes of several beautiful parks."

He nodded. "It is a nice little town. I don't want you to feel crowded if I decide to move to the area."

Sliding off the railing, she sat on the chair beside him and picked up her glass. "I do not own the town. You are free to purchase a house wherever you want."

Grinning, he wondered how he had managed to keep so much distance between them for so long. She'd had apartments not far from the farm since she was eighteen, none more than a few minutes away. When she chose the house in Langdon, he'd been proud of her for finding a place that seemed to suit her needs perfectly. Sure, she was an hour away, but that wasn't much of a drive.

It wasn't until the first weekend she hadn't visited that he began to feel the loss. She hadn't lived with him for four years by then but suddenly, the silence and the knowledge that she wouldn't be there for weekly visits made the house seem too big. He heard every creak of the roof, every tree branch against a window. Even Buck wandered the house looking for her.

But he wasn't going to tell her that and make her feel guilty. She had her own life. Being surrounded by memories of Ruth and the familiar smells of the farm had helped, but neither was a substitute for Ava's company.

"I realize, that," he said now. "I'm asking if it would bother you to have me so close."

He took a small sip of his root beer. It was almost empty. He wanted a second bottle, but the immense heartburn it would cause was more than he wanted to pay for a little extra flavor. "You moved away, in part, to get space away from me."

Her head whipped around; her eyes narrowed. "I did not choose Langdon because I wanted distance between us. I almost declined a very fair offer because of the distance."

"You were going to pass up on a house that suited you..."

"Because of the restrictions it would put on our visits," Ava finished. "In the end, I had to consider my needs above my wants. I needed a house that accommodated an indoor area for training, plenty of land for training on the days I did not want to train indoors, and distance between myself and all others. I needed to keep everyone safe."

"I don't think you have to worry about that anymore."

"No," she said thoughtfully. "I do not think The Mon-" She frowned, trying to get used to the idea of calling him by anything other than what she had known him as for sixteen years. "I do not think Robbie will injure anyone now."

"I hope he's found peace." David watched her yawn behind her hand. "I hope you've found peace."

Unsure how to answer that, Ava said, "I still have nightmares. I hope I did not wake you the past few nights."

"I haven't heard a thing. I thought maybe you were doing better."

"I locked myself in my bedroom so I would not walk around the house in the night."

"You don't have to lock yourself in your room," David said, distress in his voice. "I handled your nightmares for ten years, remember."

"I sleep naked."

"Oh… well. Yes, I suppose that would be awkward."

After a few moments, David stood. "I'm going to call Harley and see how Buck's doing."

Ava listened to the insects' songs getting into full swing as night settled fully around her.

Was Gabriel at the bar with his friends, as was his usual custom on Friday nights? Was he able to do even that?

Shaking her head, she was startled to feel the sting of tears at the thought of him. He was full of so much sorrow, and there was nothing she could do about it.

She lifted her feet onto the seat of the chair, hugging her legs and resting her chin on her knees. How could she be expected to help people speak to their loved ones, when she did not even understand people while they were alive? Nothing about humans made sense to her.

David came back out onto the porch with a glass of milk. "Buck's playing with Harley's grandbaby. What's wrong?"

He sat next to her and leaned forward, setting a hand on her arm.

Frowning, she lifted her head.

"You're crying, Ava."

Surprised, she pressed her palm to her cheek.

Her tears were hot against her skin.

●　●　●　●　●

"What is with you?" Jeremy asked, setting his pool cue back in the rack a little too hard. The other sticks rattled from the force. "You've been in a funk all damn night."

"It's been a real blast being around you, too, Fuckstick," Gabriel snarled, dropping into a chair next to Tom.

"You weren't even trying at pool. Usually you whip my ass."

"You haven't said ten words all night," Tom said, eyeing the beer Gabriel had been nursing. He had been distracted for two hours now, not drinking, not joining in the conversations, not cracking jokes. He might as well not have physically been here at all.

"Jeremy talks enough for the both of us."

"If you're not getting laid, it's no reason to shit all over me," Jeremy complained, reaching for an onion ring.

"Why don't you go fuck yourself?" Gabriel flicked his wrist, sending the basket of appetizers flying across the table, scattering onion rings and cheese curds to the floor.

"What the fuck, man?" Jeremy yelled.

"Jesus, Gabe," Greg said softly. "What the hell is the matter with you?"

Running a hand down the back of his neck, Gabriel stood and rounded the table, kneeling to clean up his mess. The fury was gone as quickly as it had come, leaving him hulled out and feeling guilty.

"Sorry."

"I'll get that, hon," Karen said as she set the tray of beers on the table.

"It's my mess," he mumbled.

He waited until he had cleaned every curd and ring up and she had left before he said, "I found out what happened to Hayden the summer she disappeared."

No one at the table spoke for a full thirty seconds. Gabriel set the basket of ruined food on the empty table next to theirs and returned to his seat. He took a long pull on his drink.

"What happened?" Tom asked.

"Did they find her?" Greg asked.

"Holy fuck," Jeremy exhaled.

"She was never kidnapped." Gabriel curled his hand into a fist and pressed it to his thigh, afraid he would lash out again. "She was on her way to the restrooms when she fell and hit her head, giving her a concussion. She wandered too close to the river and…"

"Jesus." Jeremy motioned for Karen. When she looked over, he mimed taking shots and held up four fingers.

"Ah... Were there... did they find..." Tom shifted in his seat. "Did the police contact you...?"

"Not exactly."

Gabriel seemed to wrestle for several moments.

"Fuck it." Finishing his beer, he slid it back and wiped his mouth. "Ava's been communicating with Hayden since she moved to Langdon."

Another silence descended, this time with three pairs of eyes the size of saucers staring at Gabriel. He would have laughed if he had any humor left in him.

"I'm sorry," Jeremy said, "Did you just say Ava's been communicating with your dead sister?"

"Yeah, that's what I said. Ava's psychic. At the cookout, she wasn't having a seizure, she was having a vision of her foster father having a heart attack."

"What..." Greg looked around the table as if he could find some answer in the salt and pepper shaker. "What..."

"Honestly, I don't give a fuck if you guys believe her or not. I believe her. You've known me my whole life. If you don't trust me with this, there isn't anything left for us to talk about."

Karen, sensing the tension surrounding the table, quietly dropped off their shots and left.

Tom picked up his shot and held it at eye level. "To Hayden, the best little sister I never had."

The rest of them picked up their shot glasses.

"To Hayden," they echoed. They tapped their shot glasses on the table twice, and they drank.

Greg winced and stuck his tongue out. "I hate tequila."

"So," Tom said, looking at Gabriel, "Why don't you start over from the beginning?"

● ● ● ● ●

She recognized the sound of his truck long before the headlights turned down her driveway.

Ava sat up straight in the chair, unable to relax her muscles. Beside her, David glanced out into the night.

"I was going to going to bed," he said, as the truck eased toward the house, "but I can stay up for a bit if you want."

She turned to look at him and she looked so damn vulnerable that he was reminded of when she was sixteen and he had taught her how to dance. She'd learned about school dances and was curious but appalled by them. David had tried to explain why they were a tradition and what their significance were in a young person's life. The dance moves were easy for her to learn; she had been training for almost half her life by then, and dexterity was second nature. But she had never managed to relax when allowing the man to lead. The glow a young lady or a woman had while dancing with a gentleman had not reached her eyes as it had when he danced with Ruth. She had a look of confused panic on her face. This is not a useful skill to me, that look had said. I have no idea what to do with this information.

She had that same look on her face now.

Gabriel's truck stopped and she found herself feeling edgy. Before she could respond to David, Gabriel got out of the truck and walked forward. He stopped at the bottom of the steps to the porch.

"Hello, Gabriel," David finally said, when it was obvious no one else was going to speak.

"Hello, Mr. Reid. I'm sorry to visit so late."

David struggled briefly between an urge to laugh and his instinct to defend his daughter. "Call me David, please. I was just getting ready to turn in."

He reached over and squeezed Ava's hand, surprised when she held on like she was drowning for a moment before releasing him.

"Goodnight, kids."

He heard their murmured responses behind him and hoped for the best. He liked Gabriel. Even more, he loved seeing Ava light up at the mention of the kid's name. She was more relaxed around him... as relaxed as she could get. Only an idiot would miss how much she cared about him. But because of what had been done to her as a child, she wasn't forgiving by nature. They had to figure things out for themselves.

Left without someone to guide her, Ava did not know what to do. She stood and took a step toward the stairs, then stopped and simply stood, staring at him. Some light shone from the kitchen, giving his body a bluish hue.

She fidgeted with her hands. She hated not knowing what to do.

"Can I come up?" Gabriel asked, shoving his hands into his pockets.

After a moment, she nodded once. He tried not to feel insulted when she stepped back as he ascended, her eyes watching him warily.

"Do you want to come inside?" She thought that was what a good host would offer.

"Let's stay out here for now."

While he sat where David had been sitting, she leaned back against the railing.

"Why are you here?" she asked.

"I'm sorry I didn't handle what you told me very well." He leaned forward in the chair and rested his elbows on his knees. "I thought... I thought I had a grip on how this thing with you worked. And I thought I'd dealt with Hayden's death years ago."

Ava stood rigidly, staring at him, taking shallow breaths.

"I thought I just needed to think about it for a night, just take a little time to breathe. But a night turned into the next day and the next night and now it's been damn near a week. I didn't mean to leave you hanging."

"You did not."

Surprised, he stood. "I didn't?"

"You made your intent clear before I left Saturday night."

Frowning, he took half a step toward her. She took a step to the side, away from him.

"I didn't really say anything."

"Not with your mouth."

"What are you talking about?"

"I heard you." She absently touched her temple. Did he think she would forget? Did he think she would move on, and they could act like nothing had ever happened?

"You heard my thoughts?"

"You were upset. They were hard to miss."

Feeling defensive, unwilling to risk him accusing her of invading his privacy, she snapped it at him more forcefully than she meant to.

"What did I think?"

"You thought, 'I will never forgive her for doing this.'"

Realization dawned on him, and he felt simultaneously foolish and relieved. "Did you think I broke up with you?"

She frowned. "You told me to leave."

In his haste to convince her she hadn't taken what he meant correctly, he lost some of the defeated look about him. Even with only a little kitchen light, she could see his eyes were more open and were scanning her for hints of her mood in her body language. Even his spine had straightened.

"For the night. I needed time to deal with what you told me."

"I refuse to be with someone who does not accept me for who I am."

"I've always accepted you. You invented this barrier between us and blamed it on your ability."

"I did not invent the thought in your head."

She was more comfortable with anger than with sorrow or confusion; she took two steps away and then turned back to him. Sighing, she rested her hands on the railing.

"No, but you were wrong to assume I meant you when I thought it."

Turning her head slowly, she studied him.

"Who else would you mean?"

"Hayden." Gabriel took a cautious step toward her. She didn't back away this time, but her eyes were narrowed and full of suspicion. "She shouldn't have put you in that position."

Dropping her shoulders, she turned to him, surprised.

"You wanted to know what happened to her." Her eyes roamed his face, searching, trying to understand.

"She should have told me herself. Written through me, or come to me in a dream, or written in some spilled sugar, or whatever the hell ghosts do to get people's attention. She didn't need to use you to do it."

Ava said nothing. She tilted her head, studying him in that odd way, trying to make sense of what he was saying. No one had ever made her consider it that way. In anything she had read about psychic ability, all the responsibility landed on the medium. Fiction books and movies portrayed psychics as being duty-bound to helping spirits. No one ever discussed the possibility that the spirits were going about it the wrong way.

"I shouldn't have put you in the middle," Gabriel continued. "I'm sorry. I'll say it one million times if it will take that betrayed look off your face. I need you."

Leaning back against the railing, she clenched and unclenched her fists.

"You left me."

"I know. I didn't mean to."

"I hate you." Her voice cracked.

"That's okay."

"No, it is not. I do not like feeling this way."

"I'm sorry."

"Stop saying that!"

She slammed her palms into his chest, forcing him back a step. The backs of his legs hit the bench and he overbalanced, sitting down with a hard thump. He did not get up. He stayed sitting like a chastised puppy that had been caught chewing on a favorite shoe.

Running a hand through her hair, she leaned against the railing again, resting her chin on her chest.

"You said you would not leave me by choice," she said, and he heard the tears in her voice.

"I know."

"You lied to me."

"I didn't..."

Her head whipped up and she glared at him.

Shrugging, he searched for the right words. "I never thought... anything in my life would affect me like that. I didn't know I had any grief left for Hayden."

As she watched, he kept his head low and rubbed his forehead. He abruptly stood. "I wanted you to know I'm sorry, and I love you, and I hope you can forgive me."

Pulling his keys out of his pocket, he started toward the stairs.

Panic seized her. "You are leaving?"

"Do you want me to stay?"

When she didn't answer, he turned back. So many emotions warred against each other on her face: confusion, anger, fear, pain, bewilderment.

"I do not know what I want."

"I don't give up, Ava."

She tilted her head, studying him.

"I won't ever end it unless there's no hope of fixing things between us. When I asked you to be with me, I meant for the long haul."

At her continued silence, he added, "Just so you're clear in the future if you think I'm breaking up with you."

He made it to the bottom step before she whispered, "Please stay."

Turning back, he squinted against the light glowing around her body as she stood at the top of the stairs.

"Did you say something?" he asked.

"Do not go."

He raised his foot to walk back up the steps and she automatically stepped back toward the front door. Her hands were fidgeting.

"I'm sorry I took so long," he said hoarsely.

Slowly, keeping his eyes on hers, he took another step, and another, even when she backed up again. Her instinct was to keep her distance, but he could see she wanted to reach out to him. Unlike when he'd first met her, this time he had given her a reason to mistrust him. He had known what breaking her loyalty meant and had done it anyway. Now he had to earn it back.

At the top of the stairs, he gave her a moment before he took another step toward her. After a moment of warily eying him, she took a half step toward him. He reached out and was pleased when she allowed him to draw his fingers down her arm without flinching.

"I missed you."

He kept his voice light, like his touch. He could finally see her beautiful eyes, though there was still too much distance between their bodies. They could be fused together, and it wouldn't be close enough for him.

Wondering what she was thinking, he tried to get some clue from her expression, but it was carefully neutral.

"Did you miss me?" he asked, his mouth curving. Being coy wasn't her nature; she was still struggling with a flood of emotions but hiding it better now.

"Yes."

To admit it gave her such an odd feeling. As if something heavy had been lifted off her chest.

With a little step he was against her, wrapping her in an embrace and resting his chin on the top of her head. She had not realized the extent of her loneliness until he touched her. For once her body greedily soaked up every sensation instead of warring with her to break away. She shuddered violently.

Suddenly she realized her hands were pinned between their chests.

Shoving herself back, she felt Gabriel's arms immediately loosen, but he said firmly, "Take it easy."

The shortness of breath that had started was already easing up. She slid her hands around his waist, gripping him fiercely, and rested her head on his shoulder. They stood together for countless minutes, refamiliarizing themselves with each other's scent. Ava did not know how long they stayed there, but she thought she may have dozed a little with the smell of sawdust and grass surrounding her. When he murmured something, she drifted up.

Pulling away, she gazed up at him.

"Do you want me to leave, or can I stay the night?"

"I want you to stay," she said, glancing inside. "We have to be quiet."

Giving her a wry smile, he took her hand and allowed her to lead him inside.

"I feel like a teenager again."

He watched her lock the door, check it. She turned back to him.

"I went to a bar to get drunk last night."

Raising his eyebrow, he followed her a couple steps into the living room and watched her shut off lamps. He moved toward the stairs as she turned off the kitchen light. Remaining silent so he didn't disturb David, he waited until they were in Ava's bedroom and she had shut the door before he asked her about the bar. They kept their voices low.

"I was in the mood to hit something," she said, still standing at the door.

"Did you start a fight?"

"I encouraged one." She pulled her shirt off and draped it over her arm. "Then I ended it."

It was then Gabriel noticed she had installed a deadbolt on the door. She pulled a chain from around her neck, took it off, and locked the deadbolt. She used another key in the keyhole. Walking to her dresser, tossing her shirt in the laundry sorter as she went, she took a small box from one of the drawers and put the keys inside. She buried the box underneath the clothing in that drawer.

"You lock yourself in at night?"

"I do not want to wake David. He has been staying all week."

"Why?"

Gabriel took off his shirt, dropping it on the floor beside the bed.

"He thought I was in trouble." Ava undressed the rest of the way, separating her clothing, and tossing it into the laundry sorter. She seemed to think about her answer. "I was in trouble. My behavior has been erratic."

She walked to her side of the bed and sat, pulling the bedding around her. The linens were freshly laundered; she had been unable to bear smelling him as she stiffly waited for sleep to come each night without him. The first night, lying with her head on his pillow, she had found herself crying as his scent surrounded her. Although she had fought it, her mind kept replaying the moment she told him about Hayden, the way the tears had slipped over his lids so easily, as if they were waiting for the slightest nudge to push them. She had curled into a ball, wrapping herself in the bedding, until it was obvious she would not be able to fall asleep. Stripping the bed, she had lain atop the mattress until just before dawn, when she began her workout.

Watching him join her in bed now, she felt a staggering sense of relief.

The next morning, after sleeping alone, she had taken the bedding the basement to be laundered and put fresh sheets on bed, ones she had never used while Gabriel had stayed here. She did not want to smell him and give herself one more reason to have a nightmare.

But the ache for him was bone deep, exhausting.

Ava caught herself frowning as she thought of the long nights without him. How she had woken from her nightmares, sweating and terrified, her hands reaching... Every night this week, she had awakened to find her arms outstretched, her hands searching for something to hold onto. Someone to hold onto. She had exploded from memories of abuse only to find herself huddled in her closet or under her bed, reaching, reaching.

He plunged his hands into her hair so abruptly he startled a gasp from her. Dragging her head back, his mouth took hers urgently, making her head spin before she had time to put up any defenses. Fire churned low in her belly and spread outward, so she had to brace herself or fall against him.

"God, I missed you." He pressed his forehead to hers, his breath ragged.

Surprised by the flood of emotions she felt in his touch, heard in his words, she rested her hands on his wrists, unsure what else to do.

"Let me hold you."

Gabriel eased back onto his side, drawing her down with him. He kept his hands cupped around her face and gazed into her eyes. Moaning, Ava fought the comfortable haze that had settled over her as they held each other.

"Come to Sunday dinner with me tomorrow."

"David is here."

"He can come, too. I want to be with you."

He drew her even closer, tucked her head on his shoulder. They were pressed so tightly together, she could feel his pulse thudding against her neck, chest, and inner thigh. The sound of his breath was slightly distressed.

"I will ask him if he wants to go."

"I'm sorry," he repeated, holding tighter. "I didn't mean to hurt you."

"I did not know you could."

Rubbing her hand up and down his back seemed to ease his remorse, and she liked touching him, so she continued to do so. She liked that he slept without a shirt. He had started doing so after the first time they had sex. Feeling the different points of her skin against his fascinated her. Easing his grip on her, he lay gazing at her again in a way that made her feel he could see into her soul.

"You're tired."

She nodded. "So much has happened this last week. It has been overwhelming."

Rubbing his thumb along her cheek, he shifted. "Between us? Or did something else happen?"

Sighing, she told him about going to the bar, being friendly with the bartender but still socially inept, and calling Sensei to quit training. As quickly as she could, she told him about Sensei, Isabel, and Griffin showing up, then Isabel and Griffin driving her home and staying the night so she would not be alone. Gabriel listened patiently, touching her hair, or holding her hand. When she came to the part where Isabel knocked her out, he smirked, looking impressed. She finished by telling him about David showing up and discovering who The Monster really was.

Going over it again was almost as exhausting as living it. Ava's eyelids were heavy when she was done. Her voice was starting to rasp.

"Jesus." He brought her hand to his mouth and kissed her knuckles. "I'm glad David was with you this week. That's a lot to deal with."

She leaned up and looked at the clock on her bedside table. "I want to sleep." Falling back onto the pillow, she pressed her hand to her forehead. "I wish I could have one night without nightmares."

"Tell your nightmares to go fuck themselves so you can get a good night's sleep."

Her brow furrowed, making him smile. "I do not think that is how it works."

"How do you know, if you haven't tried it?" He ran his finger over the wrinkles between her eyebrows.

Leaning over, she shut off the lamp, rolling over and scooting against him so her back fit to his stomach. They settled against each other, listening to the rhythm of their breathing in the silence of the house.

"I love you, Ava."

He heard her soft intake of breath, the pause where she held it, filling the room with silence.

Squeezing his hand, she said, her voice quiet, "Love."

And Gabriel understood it was her way of saying she loved him.

•　•　•　•　•

Standing at the island with her hands flat on the counter, Isabel chewed on her lower lip and glared at the note Griffin had left in his beautiful handwriting. It was early in the morning – too early for her to be awake, but she couldn't get back to sleep – and somehow, they had run out of coffee.

"How the fuck did we run out of coffee?" she fumed, her knuckles turning white under the pressure she was putting on them. "We don't run out of coffee!"

She slammed her palm on the counter.

The notification sound on her phone loudly announced she had received a text message from Griffin. Glancing over, she snatched her phone from the counter and opened the text.

On my way back with coffee. Hang in there.

Doing her best to unlock her jaw, Iz rested her elbow on the counter and pressed her forehead into her palm. The knock on the door had her head whipping back up again.

"What the actual fuck?" She was still grumbling to herself when she opened the door.

Eve and Nathan stood in the doorway, waiting expectantly. Nathan smiled warmly, but Eve's eyes narrowed when she saw Isabel instead of her son at the door.

"You've got to be fucking kidding me," Iz growled.

"Excuse me?" Eve slowly raked her eyes up and down Isabel.

"What are you doing here at –" Iz looked at the clock on the wall as she opened the door wider and walked back toward the kitchen, "- seven fifteen in the morning?"

"What are you doing here this early?" Eve asked, walking stiffly behind her.

"I live here."

"It's good to see you, Isabel," Nathan said warmly, opening his arms cautiously.

Isabel edged suspiciously into his embrace. "You, too, Mr. Turner."

"Call me Nathan, please."

"I'll call you Nathan when you bring me coffee. Griffin isn't here right now."

"Where is he?" Eve asked, not bothering to keep the irritation out of her tone. "We would like to speak to him."

"I'd like an IV drip of Columbian dark roast, so I guess we're both fucked. Can I get you anything to drink?" Iz didn't bother hiding her irritation, either. Given the choice, she would have stayed away from humans until her attitude was better, but since they'd invaded her space, they would take what she gave them or leave.

"How long will he be?" Eve asked.

Nathan shot her a look, which she pretended not to see.

Isabel stretched lazily and settled into a chair at the island. "We didn't synchronize our watches. Did he know you were coming?"

"No, we were going to surprise him." Nathan pulled a stool over diagonally from her and sat, giving her a smile.

"Did you want something to drink?" Iz asked again, because he was being so nice, and he was trying not to impose.

"I'll see what he has. What you have, I guess, since this is your home now. If you don't mind." He stood again, looking in the refrigerator. "What about you? Did you just get up? Do you want something to drink?"

"I'm waiting for Griffin to bring home coffee," she said, running her fingertips along the top of the counter. After a moment, she added, "I guess I'll take a water. Thank you."

Nathan tossed her one. "Do you want anything, honey?"

When Eve only gave him a cold stare, Isabel wondered how she had thawed out enough to produce twin boys.

"Can you call him and see how long he's going to be?" she asked, setting her designer bag on the counter with a prissy thump. "There are other things we could be doing."

"I'm not his damn secretary. If you don't call to say you're visiting, don't expect us to drop everything to conform to your schedule." Isabel twisted the cap off her water and blurted, "Why are you always bugging him? When I first met Griffin, he said you guys only visit once or twice a year."

Flushing, she muttered, "Sorry."

She chugged some water to keep her mouth busy. To her surprise, Nathan burst out laughing.

"You say exactly what you're thinking."

"Noticed that, did you?" Her lips twitched at the sound of his laughter. It was contagious.

He sat down again, grinning. "I love that about you, Isabel."

"Most people are put off by it." She forced herself not to look at his wife.

"There are decisions to be made for after I'm no longer around to run my business. We've been trying to get Griffin to take it over so we can keep it in the family. Normally, we don't visit Wisconsin often."

"He made it clear he doesn't want to run your business," Iz said, trying not to squeeze her water bottle until it burst.

"Yes, he did." Nathan was looking at her with an expression she couldn't read, and it made her uncomfortable. "So how are you settling in? It doesn't look any different than when you didn't live here."

"That's because I only had a couple pieces of furniture I needed to bring with me for sentimental reasons. I like it the way it is. Someday, maybe we'll go out and buy new stuff that fits us both. Or not."

"You're truly one of a kind, Isabel." Nathan gave her the smile that Griffin had inherited.

The door opened, and Griffin came in.

"Izzie, before you kick me in the balls, I brought a peace offer–" He stopped when he saw his parents. Clearing his throat, he finished weakly, "Mum. Dad. What are you doing here?"

Isabel shot to her feet and rounded the island, standing on her toes and wrapping her hand around the back of his neck as she gave him a deep, stirring kiss. With her other hand, she took one of the to-go coffee containers from the drink carrier and twisted it until it eased out from the biodegradable holder.

Griffin slid his free arm around her waist, momentarily forgetting his parents as his heart kicked into overdrive and his hormones leaped to attention.

"I love you," she breathed, her lips brushing against his.

She stepped back, looking dreamily at the hot beverage cup, and lifted it to her nose. She inhaled deeply, sighing as the aroma filled her nostrils. The first drink was like liquid heaven sliding down her throat.

"I love you, too," he said, giving her an amused smile.

He held up the bag of coffee grounds he had picked up at the store. "Do either of you want coffee?" he asked his parents. The sight of them brought his libido to a screeching halt.

"I'll have some," his dad said. He took the bag from Griffin and gave him a brief hug. "Have a seat and enjoy yours. I'll make a pot."

Griffin took his out of the holder and set it on the counter while he showed his dad where the supplies to make the coffee were.

Once his dad seemed to have everything, Griffin sat next to Izzie, relieved to see she didn't appear at all bothered by his parents. Either she knew the visit was a casual one, or she cared so much about her coffee that his parents could burst into flames and she wouldn't care. Either was possible this early in the morning.

"What brings you two here?"

"We need to settle some things with the business," Nathan said, measure coffee into the filter.

Griffin felt his back stiffen. Sundays were for dinner with Isabel's family. Besides, he had no interest in going over this argument yet again. They'd been after him for months, and nothing he said was getting through.

"No," Isabel barked suddenly, making him jump.

Following her gaze, he saw his father getting ready to put the scoop back into the bag of coffee. Nathan paused and was waiting to see what Izzie wanted.

"That wasn't enough coffee. Add more."

She twirled her index finger in a horizontal circle like a director motioning to "keep filming".

Grinning, Nathan added another scoop, slowly dipped the scoop in the bag again, and when Isabel put her hand out flat in a "stop" gesture, pulled out a partial scoop. She gave him a thumbs up and a nod as she drank her current cup.

Griffin leaned forward and kissed the top of her head. Whatever was going on, he had her. Nothing else mattered. His coffee forgotten, he wrapped his hands around her waist and rested his chin on her shoulder.

"Isabel has been keeping us company while we waited for you," Nathan continued, grinning.

Her eyes weren't as squinty as they had been now that she had caffeine in her. The color in her cheeks had blossomed, and she was moving more like a person and less like a walking corpse. She was starting to wake up.

Griffin raised his eyebrows.

"I was a complete bitch," she said abruptly, "but I would have stayed away from people until I was tolerable to be around. They intruded on my morning. I'll be better now that I have coffee."

Nathan walked back to the chair he had pulled over to sit near Isabel and sat again now that the coffee amount had been settled.

"We came over unannounced," he said. "You look like you've just woken up. A little crankiness is expected."

Griffin kissed Isabel's shoulder. His father was being incredibly understanding; Isabel was a monster in the mornings on her best days. Today she'd had no coffee and her home had been invaded with company too early in the morning.

Her home, Griffin thought, hugging her tighter. Our home.

"There are some details we need to go over," Nathan continued.

"Mum, are you going to sit?" Griffin asked, rubbing Izzie's hip. He wanted his parents to leave so he could nibble on the place behind her ear that drove her crazy.

"I'll stand." Her voice was cooler than usual.

Griffin thought she looked more sad than angry, although she was using anger to hide it.

"Look, Dad, I already told you-"

Nathan held up a hand. "You don't want the business. I know. But you're my son. A father passes his legacy to his son. There are many reasons for this. To keep the business in the family, to keep the family name and reputation going, but also to make sure his son is taken care of. Connor is gone, and you're my only heir."

Eve made a sound and turned abruptly, walking into the living room. She cupped her elbows in her hands. Nathan waited until she was standing near the large window at the far end of the room before he continued.

"I'm proud of the business I built. But my real pride is in my family. As long as you're taken care of, Griffin, that's all I've ever wanted. You mentioned you wanted to start your own business someday."

Feeling suddenly emotional, Griffin cleared his throat. "Eventually, yes."

"I would rather use the proceeds from my business to help you start your own company than demand you work at my company and be miserable the rest of your life."

"Starting my own business is still at least two years off, maybe more," Griffin said.

"Hopefully, my death is, too." Nathan smiled. "There's a young man at the office that I have in mind for taking over when I retire. I think he'll take the business in a good direction and keep the integrity of what I tried to build. But I want to provide for you and your mother first, and I wanted to make sure you know the offer was yours first if you wanted it. I don't want any resentment. There's been enough of that in our family over the years."

Griffin nodded. Isabel laced her fingers with his across her stomach.

"So, we're clear: you don't want the business?" Nathan asked.

"No, Dad. I'm sorry, but I don't."

"Don't apologize for having your own dream. I just want to make sure, like I said. I'll hand things over to my protégé over the next few years, but a percentage of the company's earnings will be set aside for you and your mother. When you're ready, you'll have what you need to start your own business. I wanted to make sure you know where things stand before we leave. It's going to be a while before we visit again, but the paperwork will be drawn up today and my office will send you copies of everything."

Nathan stood. "It was nice to see you again, Isabel. It's always a pleasure."

Isabel stood, accepting the hug when he offered it because the coffee had kicked in and she remembered she really did like him. Griffin accepted a hug as well, grateful but awkward because their family had never been especially affectionate.

"I'm proud of you, Griffin," Nathan said. "I don't say that enough."

"Thanks, Dad."

Eve walked briskly over and gave Griffin a brief hug. Before he could raise his arms, she pulled back. "I love you. Sometimes you're just so hard to look at."

She pulled him against her again, this time pressing his head to her shoulder. She was over a foot short than he was, so he had to stoop to accommodate her, but he hugged her for several moments.

"I have something for you," he said when she pulled back. His voice caught.

He walked into the bedroom. They heard him moving things around in the walk-in closet.

"I suppose I should thank you," Eve said, her face turned toward the bedroom doorway. "You've made my son happier than he's been in a long time."

She turned and leveled her gaze on Isabel. Iz held her gaze but thought that was a strange thing to say. Griffin seemed so together, so at peace with himself and his life. He had brought Isabel happiness, not the other way around.

He returned with a roll of paper Isabel had never seen before. Holding it out to his mother, he said, "Connor had trouble with self-portraits, but on his good days, he could use me as a guide."

Eve unrolled the paper slowly. It was an eleven by fourteen pencil drawing of Nathan, Eve, Connor, and Griffin, so detailed it looked like he had traced over a photograph. Nathan stood behind Griffin, his hand on his son's shoulder. Isabel could tell it was Griffin because he was slightly thinner than the other young man in the drawing. Eve stood behind a kneeling Connor, her arm draped around his chest. They were all smiling. Connor had signed the bottom corner in a loopy script similar to Griffin's handwriting but all his own. Above it, he had written a message:

I never meant to take your smile.

"Oh," Eve sighed, her hands shaking. She fumbled with the drawing, rolling it up, holding it to her chest. Closing her eyes, she let a single tear slip down her cheek.

"Thank you for this." She opened her eyes and smiled at Griffin, and Iz was startled at the warmth the expression brought to her face. Was this the way she was before her son killed himself? For the first time, Isabel saw Eve as beautiful, as a mother. As a person.

Griffin nodded.

"Well, we have a few things to get done," Nathan said. He walked over to Eve and placed his hand on the small of her back. Instead of becoming rigid, as she usually did, Eve leaned back into it. "Maybe if you have some time this evening or tomorrow, we can have dinner before we leave."

"I'd like that," Griffin said, glancing at Isabel. "We have dinner with her family on Sundays but-"

"Tomorrow, then?" Eve asked, looking at Isabel hopefully.

"Sure." Iz suddenly found herself wanting to accommodate this woman. The feeling made her uncomfortable. She didn't want to feel pity for Griffin's mother. Isabel found harsh feeling so much easier to deal with: bitterness, fury, contempt.

When they had left, Isabel and Griffin stood in the kitchen, letting the silence build as they tried to make sense of what had just happened. Iz hopped onto the counter and sipped her coffee.

"Menopause," she suddenly said.

Griffin twitched. "What?"

"Maybe she's going through menopause. I hear the mood swings are brutal."

Instead of shrugging it off, he walked over to her, a thoughtful expression on his face. He nudged her knees apart and stood between her legs. Lowering his head to her shoulder and resting his arms along the outside of her legs, he stood silently for several seconds before Isabel realized he was crying.

She rested her hands on his shoulders. "Are you okay?"

Pulling back, he nodded. She reached up and took his face in her hands, wiping his tears.

"My mum hasn't hugged me in a long time." He rubbed his hands up and down her thighs. "It was nice to hug her again."

• • • • •

"Ava."

The voice called to her from far away as she drifted up from sleep. She felt a tickle on her shoulder. Lips skimmed against her skin.

Before she could stop it, a soft moan had escaped, and she pressed back against Gabriel's stomach. His hand slid around to cup her breast.

And she realized she was still in bed. While morning sun shone bright against her eyelids.

She rose into a sitting position, blinking in confusion. Disoriented, she shied away from the sunlight piercing the cracks between the curtains. Her head was throbbing, her mouth as dry and gritty as sandpaper. She did not understand where she was.

"Ava." Gabriel's hand bumped her elbow. She jerked, knowing her body was overreacting but unable to stop herself. Every color was too bright, every birdsong too loud, every touch too sharp against her skin. Even the smells filling her nose were different than they had been the past few mornings.

"Hey!" The authority in his voice stopped her head from spinning, slowed her thoughts. She froze.

"Breathe. You're in your own bed."

"What happened?"

"Nothing. You slept through the night."

"What?!"

"Dammit, stop struggling. You act like you've never done that before." At the baffled look she gave him out of half-opened eyes, his voice softened. "You're kidding."

"I do not joke."

"You've never slept through the night? Ever?"

She shook her head. Her eyes were adjusting to the light, and she was able to open them a little more. As far back as she could remember, she had awakened in the darkness and her eyes had gradually adjusted as the sun rose.

"Well, shit."

She pressed her hand to the base of her throat. Why was her mouth so dry? How long had she slept?

"Here."

Brushing the glass of water against her elbow, he settled back on his pillow as she drank. She caught him watching her when she finished and handed the glass back.

"Why are you staring at me?"

"Because I love watching you. Because I love you."

He picked up her hand and rubbed the back of it against his cheek.

"Love," she said uncertainly.

Giving her a lopsided smile, he tugged her down and gave her a kiss. "You should move in with me."

She jolted against his mouth. Pulling back, she stared at him, her gray eyes wide.

"What did you say?"

"Move in with me." He laced his fingers with hers. "My house is bigger and has more land."

Frowning, she looked down at the bedding. He couldn't tell what she was thinking.

"You're worried I'll leave you again?"

Leaning up, he scraped his teeth along her shoulder. The sensation caught her attention. She turned to watch him. "No."

"What, then?"

Releasing her hand, he slid his fingertips up her thigh, along her side, and brushed against the side of her breast. He heard the catch of her breath.

She closed her eyes. "I need room for a dojo."

"I have a basement."

He moved his hand slowly down her flat stomach. "And I'll clear out the catch-all bedroom, so you have an office."

"That is kind of you."

"I wasn't joking when I said I'm in this for the long haul."

"I cannot give you children."

Her gaze was solemn and, for the first time since he'd met her, troubled at the thought of not bearing children.

He rested his forehead against hers. "All I need is you. That's all I'll ever ask of you."

She tilted her head, her eyes roaming the bedspread.

"What are you thinking about? What's making you hesitate?"

She frowned. "I am not hesitating. David is considering moving to Langdon. I am curious if he would find my house satisfactory. It is small, with enough land for Buck. I would have to disclose Anton's occasional disturbance. If I move in with you, David can live here."

"Is that a yes?" Gabriel sat up and clutched her hand. "You want to move in with me?"

"Yes." Ava drew the blankets back and draped her legs over the edge of the bed.

"Where are you going?" He barely caught her hand in time to keep her from standing.

"I need to see if David needs anything before I begin training."

"Just like that? Yeah, you'll move in with me, and by the way, David, do you have enough toothpaste?"

Ava gave him a patient look. "He uses the same toothpaste as I do. I have a full tube."

"That's not the point." In spite of her inability to grasp sarcasm, she made him laugh. "It's exciting that we'll be living together. Why don't we hang out with David instead? It won't kill you to skip one day of training. I want to tell him the good news."

Walking to the dresser, she pulled on a pair of cotton panties. She turned back to him as she spoke. "You may talk to him while I train."

"Don't you train for hours?"

"Two hours every morning, one hour in the afternoon, and one hour in the evenings, unless I have class with Sensei. Then it's two."

"Take a break, Ava."

"I need to at least run." She slipped a tee shirt over her head. "Excess energy is not good for me."

He raised his brow. "I can wear you out."

Her lips curved.

"Is that a smile?" His sexual innuendo was superficial; he didn't feel comfortable having sex with her father in the house. He stood and pulled on yesterday's jeans and tee shirt. "It's a good day when I can make you smile."

Turning back to her, he found her directly in front of him and jumped. "Jesus."

She was wearing yoga pants and a thin baggy tee shirt she favored for running, and she looked amazing. She studied him intently, as if she could find the answers to all her questions in his face.

"What is it?" he asked when it was clear she wasn't going to speak.

"Love."

He liked the soft way she said the word, as if saying it too loud would make it shatter.

Wrapping his arms around her, he kissed the top of her head. "I love you, too."

• • • • •

They were silent during most of the drive to Isabel's parent's house. Griffin turned on the stereo but kept it low, and Iz sang softly as she stared out the window. When they were just outside of Langdon, she turned the radio off.

"Are you going to keep Rover?"

Griffin glanced at her from the corner of his eye. "I've thought about it. I'm still not sure. I don't have a lot of Connor's stuff left, so it's kind of become a keepsake."

She nodded absently.

"Why?"

"I think you should. It's very roomy and it smells like him."

"It smells like Rover?"

"It smells like Connor."

"How do you know? You never met my brother."

He turned Rover into the Harris driveway and pulled up by the garage. Beth and Jack were already there. He took off his seatbelt and turned sideways in his seat.

"Because it doesn't smell like you."

Iz reached out and touched the dashboard, her eyes soft with affection.

They entered a house full of wonderful smells. Ozzie hurried over to them as they walked into the kitchen. Maya stood a short distance away, sniffing the air.

"Gabriel didn't take the dogs yesterday?" Iz asked her mother, who was standing at a counter, writing in a small notebook, with Beth standing next to her. They seemed to be concentrating on something.

"Nope." Josh wrapped his arm around Iz and gave her a squeeze. "We're keeping the dogs on the weekends from now on. They're getting older, and don't travel as well, and he has his own life."

She narrowed her eyes. He's running from his life, she thought. He's a coward.

"How's my favorite youngest daughter?" Josh continued.

She raised her eyebrow. "Funny. You should do standup."

He grinned, reaching over her easily to shake Griffin's hand. "Good to see you again, Griffin."

"I'm glad to be invited, Mr. Harris. Your wife is a wonderful cook."

Allie looked up from whatever she was writing. "That's a sweet thing to say. You're welcome any time, Griffin."

"And call me Josh. Mr. Harris makes me feel old."

They began their ritual hugging.

"Where's Jack?" Isabel asked, realizing he was missing.

"He's upstairs fixing their desktop," Beth said. "Again." She hurried back to whatever she and Allie had been working on and closed the notebook. Looking guilty, she walked to her purse and tucked the notebook inside.

Left out, as always, Iz thought, and felt the sting of tears. Why do I even come to these things?

Jack came in, smiling when he saw her and Griffin. Another round of hugs went around the room. Isabel felt a little less depressed. Griffin had made progress with his parents. That was something to be happy about.

"How are you doing, kid?" Jack asked, gazing down at her as he held onto her after he hugged her.

"I'm still here."

"I'm glad." He squeezed her shoulder as he let her go.

"At least somebody is," she mumbled, walking to the refrigerator. "Griffin, do you want something to drink?"

"Water, please." He'd noticed her instant mood change and wished he had what she needed to mend her relationship with her mother and sister.

There's time, he thought. He never thought his parents would let up about his refusal to take over the family business, yet today they had made serious progress. And they had hugged him, something they had stopped doing since Connor died. He hadn't realized how much he missed it until he felt his Dad's

1022

embrace, and his mother's small hands pull him against her. If his parents could change, anything was possible.

Isabel had set a bottle of water in front of him and was walking toward the library.

"Where are you going?"

"I'm going to tune my guitar."

"Can't that wait? You just got here." Allie opened the oven to check the prime rib, but Iz had already left the room.

Griffin quietly slipped from the room and found Isabel at a window in the library, staring into the side yard. He wrapped his arms around her.

"What's going on in that sexy head of yours?"

To his surprise, she sniffed. "Nothing."

"Hey." He turned her around to face him. "What's wrong?"

"I'm fine." She wiped her cheek. "It's been a long week."

"I'm sure your mother has pillows around here somewhere," he said, turning to see if there were any in the room.

That brought half a smile to her lips. "I don't need a pillow fight. I'll come back in a minute."

He gave her a long, hard look with his beautiful golden eyes. "I don't like that they upset you so much."

She waved him off with a flick of her hand. "I'm being petty. Mom and Beth are up to something. I feel left out. It's stupid to keep expecting something different."

"They're very close."

"That's how it's been since Hayden died. I really should get over it."

He leaned his forehead against hers. "I wish I could make them see what a wonderful person you are."

She smirked. "No need to get carried away."

Drawing her in, he gave her a fierce hug.

"There you guys are," Josh said from the doorway. "Gabriel's here. Who wants to help with manual labor? He has a cabinet he needs help carrying in."

Griffin offered.

"I need to talk to Gabriel first," Isabel said, stalking out of the room. She marched up to the island, where he had just disengaged from a hug with Beth.

"What the fuck's the matter with you?"

"Isabel!" Allie snapped. The black olive she was about to eat was forgotten. She continued to hold it, halfway between picking it up out of the tray and putting it in her mouth.

Ignoring her, Isabel punched Gabriel's shoulder. Surprised by her strength and anger, he stepped away from Beth so he wouldn't get knocked into her.

"You broke up with Ava just because you can't handle what she told us about Hayden?"

"I didn't-" he started.

"What kind of pansy-ass mama's boy are you?"

"Isabel Erin Harris, that's enough!" Allie took a step toward them.

"You broke her heart!" she continued, punching him the shoulder again. The strike wasn't playful, and her little knuckles seemed to drive straight to his bone. "She trusted you. You know it's hard for her to trust people and you fucked her over anyway. How could you?"

Gabriel's eyes were unreadable as he quietly studied her.

The toilet just outside the kitchen flushed and Iz froze, trying to figure out who could be in the bathroom. Everyone was accounted for. A few moments later, she heard the door open, and Ava stepped into the kitchen.

"What are you doing here?" Isabel asked.

"Isabel," Gabriel said calmly, "I didn't break up with Ava, which I explained to her yesterday. She misunderstood me."

The silence in the room hung like cigarette smoke in a bar for several seconds.

"Oh." Iz shrugged, the fury immediately gone. "Never mind then. Good to see you."

She punched him in the shoulder again, playfully this time. He raised his eyebrow but pulled her in for a hug.

"How are you doing?" Allie asked, walking over to him, and spreading her arms.

"I'm fine." He returned the hug but rolled his eyes and grinned at Iz over her head.

"You were really upset last weekend."

"I'm not now." Stepping back, he squeezed her shoulders. "I have to get Dad's present for you out of the truck. I need Griffin and Jack."

"I'm getting a present?"

"I will help," Ava said, ready to leave the crowded room. The energy was palpable, humming like the occupants of an angry hornet's nest. Her mind was buzzing.

"You haven't said hello to everyone," Allie replied, opening her arms. She started toward Ava, motioning for her to come closer.

"Time to run," Gabriel said to Jack and Griffin.

Even with three people out of the room, it still seemed too small. Ava braced herself for Allie's hug and raised her hands to place them lightly on the woman's back. There seemed to be no animosity in her, in spite of the previous tension after the family found out Ava was communicating with Hayden.

"My turn," Beth said, walking up behind her mother.

Even as Allie backed away and Beth moved forward, Ava realized the crackling energy was coming from Beth. She took a step back and rammed into the counter, hard.

"That looked like it hurt." Allie's tone was sympathetic. "Are you okay?"

"I am sorry," Ava said, stepping forward and hesitantly reaching out for Beth. "I…"

She did not finish as Beth wrapped her arms around her, and everything in her mind went blank.

She saw darkness. It was so black it made her moan. Without realizing it, she had stepped back, gripping Beth's hand with mechanical strength.

"Ava, you're hurting my hand." Beth tried to pull away, but Ava's grip was unyielding. And her eyes were like pools of ink, her pupils so large they seemed to consume her face.

"What's wrong?" Isabel walked around the island so she could see her face. "Oh. It's happening."

"What's happening?" Allie asked.

"What do you see, Ava?" Iz asked, ignoring her mother.

Instead of trying to pry the death grip off her sister's wrist, she slid her hand along Beth's lower arm, brushing it against Ava's fingers and hand.

"Darkness," Ava said, twitching at Isabel's touch. But she didn't strike out, and that was good. "It is so dark I cannot sense if I have a body."

Isabel skimmed her hand over the top of Ava's, keeping her touch light.

"Ava, can you take my hand instead of Beth's? You're hurting her."

"But I can… I feel…"

She released Beth's hand to place her own hand on her chest, over her heart. Patting herself lightly, she tapped out a quick, steady rhythm.

"A heartbeat." Her eyes came into focus. She stared at Beth with intense, clear eyes. "A child's heartbeat. You are pregnant."

Beth's jaw dropped open. At first, nothing came out. Then: "There's no way you could know that. I haven't…"

She turned to her mother. "Did you tell her?"

"I've been in the kitchen this whole time. She just got here."

"Jack." Beth turned back to Ava and aimed accusatory eyes at her. "He told you."

Ava held her gaze. "I have not spoken to Jack since I was last here, thirteen days ago."

There was noise from the living room as the men tried to fit the cabinet Gabriel had made through the door. They were chatting and laughing, unaware that two rooms away, tension was mounting.

"How did you know?"

"You know how." Ava refused to look away.

"Is it true?" Isabel asked.

Beth glanced at her. "I haven't been to the doctor, but I've had three positive pregnancy tests."

"That's good, right?" Iz temporarily forgot about Ava.

"I'm not far enough along to be too excited yet. Only a few weeks. I… don't want to… get my hopes up."

"I can still congratulate you, can't I?"

Beth gave her a little smile. "Sure. I was going to say something at dinner anyway."

"That's delicious."

Iz gave her a hug and was thankful to feel more substance over her sister's bones. She'd noticed more color in her cheeks as well, and her eyes weren't quite so empty.

When they parted, Beth's eyes had misted over.

"I did not mean to ruin your announcement." Ava shifted uncomfortably, backing away from the energy flickering around the bodies.

Before anyone could answer, she hurried toward the living room to see if the guys needed help with the furniture.

"That's wild," Beth finally said. "I thought I had kind of accepted what she could do, but to have her touching me while she did it... that was... surreal."

Unsure what to say, Iz busied herself getting some water. If they were preoccupied with Ava's ability, they wouldn't ask too many questions. She had put off telling her family she moved in with Griffin. Too much had been going on. It took days to process what had really happened to Hayden and to relive her loss. She didn't understand it, but she couldn't deny the horrible ache in her heart that mirrored how she felt when Hayden first disappeared. Then Ava was at the bar...

"Isabel? Is everything okay?"

She shook herself out of her thoughts and looked up at her mother. "Fine."

"How are things going with you? Have you found a job? Do you need help with rent, or any other bills?"

"No," she said softly. "I moved in with Griffin."

"You what?"

"Wow," Beth said, dropping the sweet red pepper she had been cutting and sitting down at the island. "Tell me everything."

"It's a huge apartment," Iz said, feeling like she had when she was younger and her sisters sat with her up in one of their rooms, talking and giggling with some stupid movie in the background. "His shower is heavenly."

"You did what?" Allie repeated, setting a spoon down a little too hard.

"I moved in with Griffin. We spend all our time there anyway." Iz turned back to Beth. "There's a gorgeous balcony just off the bedroom, and the kitchen is almost as big as my old apartment."

Beth took her hand and squeezed it. "He's so adorable. And he seems to really love you."

"He does." Iz blushed. "He sees me."

"Isabel, stop ignoring me. Tell me what's going on." Allie stopped pulling clean dishes out of the dishwasher and leaned on the island.

"I told you. I moved in with Griffin. What else is there to say?"

"Why didn't you tell me?"

Uneasiness flipped in Isabel's stomach.

"I was going to, but everything with Hayden happened and it didn't seem like the right time. What's the big deal? It makes more sense to pay one rent and we love each other."

"How do you know if you love him? You've barely dated before now."

Whose fault is that? Iz thought angrily. I didn't want to get close to anyone because of you.

"That's between Griffin and I." She squeezed Beth's hand. "I'm going to see if Gabriel needs any help."

In the living room, they had set the cabinet near the fireplace, where everyone could see it. It was gorgeous, with rich dark wood tones and perfect crafting. The guys were standing around admiring it. Ava stood to the side. The dogs paced around it, sniffing the new scents it emitted.

"You're a genius, Gabe," Josh said, shaking his head. "That is perfection."

"Thanks, Dad. I burned my name into the inside of the top drawer on the right. Mom will probably get a kick out of that."

Josh gave him a hug. "She'll love it. I'm going to go get her."

He hurried to the kitchen, finding Allie bent over a notebook with Beth again. It took some coaxing, but she finally followed him back to the living room.

She went ballistic when she saw the cabinet. She cried, kneeling down, and opening every door. Inhaling loudly, she took in the cedar smell and smiled.

"I love it. Thank you so much."

Giving Josh a huge hug, she turned to Gabriel.

"Oh, no." He back away.

"Gabriel, give your mother a hug." She stalked him, coming closer. Reluctantly, he held his arms out.

"Dad asked me to do it," he explained. "It's my job."

"I love it," she repeated. She wrapped her arm around each of their necks and pulled them in to kiss them noisily on the cheek. "I love you guys!"

Gabriel lifted his eyebrow at Iz, who lifted hers back.

"Is the food going to be a while, hon?" Josh asked. "Can we sit and chat?"

Allie checked her watch. "About fifteen minutes. Then I have to get back in there."

They sat around the fireplace, where the new cabinet was easily seen from each seat. Gabriel sat next to Ava on the sofa, linking his fingers with hers. She had been quiet, watching at a distance but not joining in, since they arrived. Her demeanor wasn't unfriendly, just wary, and Gabriel thought she was waiting to see how his family was adjusting to the news of Hayden's death. It must be hard for her to have that information, not knowing what to do with it, unable to predict how family members or friends would react to hearing it.

But if anyone was strong enough to handle it, Ava was.

"Are you sure you're okay, Gabriel?" Allie asked.

"Mom, I'm fine," he tried to keep the exasperation out of his tone. "Let's move on."

"So... Isabel, have you found another job?" Josh asked.

Beside Griffin, Izzie stiffened.

"She moved in with Griffin," Allie said, her voice clipped.

"Congratulations!" Josh said, giving her a big smile. Then he looked unsure. "Right? It's because you want to, not because you can't afford your apartment?"

"Why does everyone think that?" Iz curled her hand into a fist. "Is it so hard to believe Griffin would ask me to move in with him because he loves me?"

"Of course not," Josh said immediately. "I just wanted to make sure you know you could come to us if you needed help. If you're happy, I'm happy, honey."

"Thank you," she said pointedly.

Ozzie came over and rested his head on her lap. She laid her free hand on the top of his head. Dogs were simpler. They didn't judge. They accepted everything in stride and all they wanted in return was love and maybe a table scrap.

Griffin set his hand on top of her fist and gently pried her fingers open. "I'm in love with your daughter, Mr. and Mrs. Harris," he said. "I want her living with me."

"You're so young," Allie said.

"We were younger than they are when we were married," Josh said. "And we had two kids."

"Speaking of kids...," Beth said, looking at Gabriel, "I'm pregnant. You're going to be an uncle."

"I'm going to..." He was stunned into silence. Glancing at Isabel, his eyes widened when she shrugged.

"I accidentally found out a few minutes ago. Ava read her."

His eyes darted to Ava. She shifted uncomfortably beside him. "I did not mean to ruin the announcement."

Turning back to Beth, he wet his lips. "No shit? You're having a baby?"

Beth nodded. Her eyes were glistening, but she couldn't stop grinning. "It finally happened."

Gabriel stood and crossed the room, kneeling in front of the chair she was sitting in. Pulling her forward, he wrapped his arms around her.

"That's outstanding, sis." He leaned back. "What happened? Did you make an appointment to see–"

"I took Ava's advice, actually," Beth said, glancing over as Ava ran her finger around the rim of her bottle of water. "I'm planning meals, so I remember to eat regularly. I made an exercise routine and I've stuck to it. I'm taking Yoga. It's really helping me get in touch with myself. It sounds cliché, I know, but I feel... I feel like I know myself again."

"You look so much better," Iz said honestly. "You aren't so pale and thin. You were starting to look like someone with an eating disorder. No offense."

"None taken." Beth laughed. "I know I looked horrible. I wasn't eating more than a few bites a day, if that much. I had no appetite. I was letting this baby thing consume me. I wasn't sleeping, I quit my job... Everything I was as a person was gone."

Jack ran his hand down his wife's hair.

She looked at Ava, blushing.

"I thought about what you said at dinner on Easter, Ava."

Ava raised her eyes and studied Beth, silent.

"When you talked about destroying my body. I thought about that a lot. I was trying so hard to force something to happen that should be beautiful. When I couldn't make it happen, I punished my body for failing. After what you said at Easter, I..."

She lightly tapped her fingers against her chest, unsure how to verbalize everything that had happened to her that day. Ozzie came over and drove his nose into her stomach, snorting curiously.

"What did you say at Easter?" Josh asked, looking from one woman to the other. "What did I miss?"

"She told me I can't control whether or not my body is capable of having children." Beth blinked, sending tears down her cheek. Smiling, she gently pushed Ozzie's nose away from her stomach. "But there are things I can control. It made me realize that I had no chance of taking care of a child if I couldn't even take care of myself."

"Is that why you left early that night?" Allie frowned at Ava, remembering everything that had happened, the way Ava's braided hair had shocked her so much she had to leave the room because it reminded her of Hayden. When she returned, Jack and Beth had left.

Beth nodded. "I want to thank you, Ava, for telling me the truth, even if I wasn't ready to hear it then."

Ava tilted her head, curious. Maya had wandered over closer to her and sat a few inches away, accepting the hand Ava rested on her neck.

"I don't know if exercising, eating, and finally sleeping had anything to do with being able to conceive, but it's definitely been better for me. My stress levels dropped considerably. The headaches have been less frequent and less severe."

"I didn't know you were having headaches," Iz said.

"They were horrible migraines. They're almost gone now, and I'm not using any medication. I feel like a new person."

She rested her hand on her stomach, which hadn't yet begun to swell.

"I sound like one of those empowerment idiots that sell wellbeing for five thousand dollars a seminar," Beth said, laughing. She looked at Isabel. "I'll stop rambling."

"No, it's great. You look so much better, healthier. You've wanted a baby for so long. I'm really happy for you, Beth."

"Thank you. I've probably been a monster."

"Oh, yeah." Isabel said, and she, Beth, and Gabriel laughed.

Ava had been quiet during conversation. Gabriel stood and returned to her side. Her long, thick hair was done up in that crown-like braid again. She seemed distracted.

"Has it really sunk in yet?" Iz asked. "Have you given any thought to baby names?"

Beth shrugged, trying to appear nonchalant, but she was clearly excited. "Mom and I started making general lists."

That's what they were collaborating over when I walked in, Iz thought. The notepad Beth had slid into her purse was a list of names they were considering. Another activity they felt Isabel wasn't good enough to participate in. The pain that realization caused ripped through her. Would she even be allowed to hold her niece or nephew, or did they think she would fuck that up, too?

Griffin saw the flicker of hurt cross Izzie's face and clenched his teeth. Were they seriously that obtuse, or did they push her away to punish her?

Ozzie, feeling the tension, pushed his head against Isabel's legs and wagged his tail. She ran her hands up and down his neck.

"So, Isabel," Josh said, grinning, "When are you and Griffin going to give us grandkids?"

"I'm never having kids," Isabel snapped, so vehemently that Griffin tossed a worried glance at her. Her hands were frozen in Ozzie's coat. Her jaw was set as she returned his stare. "I'm not. If you want kids, find someone else."

"Hey," he said, reaching for her, "Easy. He was just joking."

"It's not a joke to me." She jerked away from him. Ozzie scooted across the floor. "I will never be a mother. If that's a problem for you, now's the time to say so."

"Listen... I didn't mean to start anything..." Josh said, shifting uncomfortably.

"It's fine." Iz adjusted on the sofa so there was distance between her and Griffin.

"Why don't you want kids, Iz?" Gabriel asked, honestly shocked. He rubbed his hand across Ozzie, who had leaned hard against his leg, unsure of Isabel's sudden change of mood. "You'd be an outstanding mother."

"Because I don't want to hurt them. I don't want to have favorites. I would never let any of my children feel like I blame one for letting another one die."

The silence in the room was amplified by the unnaturally loud ticking of the grandfather clock.

Griffin was surprised to see Isabel's cheek was wet, but her jaw was clenched, and her eyes were hard. He stared at her, baffled. She hesitantly turned to look at him. The fire left her eyes and she looked embarrassed.

"I guess I should have told you that up front in case you want a family. I won't hold it against you if you've changed your mind about me moving in with you."

"You're all I want, Isabel." Griffin said firmly.

Josh cleared his throat. Jack was leaning forward in his seat, frowning. Beth had begun crying as well, but Iz wasn't sure if they were sympathy tears or if her hormones were playing hell with her emotions already.

Standing abruptly, Isabel pivoted toward the kitchen. "I'm going to… I need more water."

Ozzie followed her into the kitchen at a distance.

Allie started to speak several times and couldn't. Finally, she was able to ask, "Does Isabel think I blame her for Hayden's death?"

"No," Griffin said, unable to hide the anger in his tone. "She knows you do."

•　•　•　•　•

"What? Why?" Allie asked, pressing her hand to her chest. "I've never said -"

"You don't need to say it. You treat her like you blame her. Every time you look at her, she sees the accusation in your eyes. I can see it, and I don't even know you."

"That's right, you don't, and I don't think you can make an assumption-"

"He's right," Gabriel interrupted his mother. "I thought Iz was overreacting when she told me you blame her. I can't believe I didn't see it."

"Isabel ties herself up in knots every time we come here," Griffin said, rage building with every word. "In fact, this is the last time we'll be here for dinner. She's not putting up with this anymore."

"Whoa, now, let's not make rash decisions," Josh said, trying to keep emotions from spiraling out of control. "I'm sure this is just a misunderstanding-"

Griffin lifted his bottle of water so he wouldn't punch something. "It's not a misunderstanding. She can't have a conversation without putting herself down. It's as natural as breathing to her. If she'd known at least one person was on her side, one person in her entire family backed her up, she might actually feel welcome at these dinners."

"We've always been on her side," Josh said, heat igniting his eyes.

"Really? Because anytime she and Beth get into it, Allie automatically takes Beth's side, even when she's wrong. And I don't hear anyone speak up when Allie rides your daughter for swearing. The disgust is so thick in your wife's voice, I'm surprised she doesn't choke on it."

"Now, look-"

"Why am I the one getting attacked?" Allie stood, walking to the fireplace, and putting her back to everyone. "Where did all this come from?"

The heart, Griffin thought. And it's about time.

Isabel walked into the room with a bottle of water but stayed between the dining room and living room, wary of coming back in. Ozzie leaned against her leg. With the open concept of the house, she'd heard everything. The shock of Griffin standing up for her had her tears drying on her cheeks. Knowing she could walk out the door and not return, that she could follow Griffin and step away from her family without feeling any guilt, had lifted the cement blocks that had been sitting on her chest for years. Griffin would support her no matter what choice she made.

"You're not being attacked," he said, trying to find a way to help them improve instead of being condescending. His protective instinct toward Isabel made it difficult. "The rest of the family automatically adjusted to compensate for your grief years ago. No one wants to confront a mother who lost her daughter."

"You seem to have no trouble doing it," Beth murmured.

"That's because Allie isn't my priority, Isabel is. I choose Isabel over anyone. She doesn't deserve to be the scapegoat. Hayden's death is no more Isabel's fault than it was any of yours."

"Is this true, Isabel?" Josh asked. "Do you feel like your mother blames you for Hayden's death?"

Thinking carefully, trying to choose her words in a way that would convey her feelings without sounding vindictive, she swallowed the hot ball that seemed to be lodged in her throat. Griffin's words had touched her deeply. Speaking was almost impossible.

"I don't know if you mean to shut me out," she said softly. Her eyes filled but didn't spill over. "You don't include me in anything. You cook and garden with Beth. And now you have the baby to plan for. You've already started to, without me. I feel like less of a person after I leave here every Sunday."

Allie was crying openly now. "And that's my fault."

Iz realized that even though her isolation was caused partly by her mother's and Allie's closeness, Beth had never purposely pushed her away from what they were doing. It had always been her mother separating them. Beth was too caught up in conceiving a child the past few years to pay any attention to Isabel's petty feelings of desertion. They sniped at each other, but what siblings didn't?

She shrugged. "Everything I do seems to piss you off. The way I talk, my decision to stay single, now moving in with Griffin. You don't like my choice of alcohol. I don't cry enough when we visit Hayden's grave because I'm not wailing like you and Beth."

Griffin watched Allie's eyes dart away from her daughter's as she considered what she was saying.

"Look, nothing will change if I'm not here," Iz continued. "What does it matter to you, if I'm always excluded?"

A clock on the wall ticked loudly for several seconds.

"When I spend time with Griffin, he actually enjoys my company." Iz took a breath, feeling dizzy. Being able to speak after so long was tiring.

"I'm sorry, Iz," Gabriel said, standing and walking to her. "I didn't know." He crushed her in a hug, careful not to step on Ozzie.

"You're the only reason I kept coming." She pressed her face against his tee shirt.

"Why didn't you come to us about this?" Josh asked.

"She was nine when Hayden disappeared." Griffin appreciated Gabriel's apology but stayed close to Izzie. "She didn't know she had a choice for things to be any better."

"What was I going to say?" Isabel asked, turning her head so she could be heard. "I couldn't criticize Mom for hating me when I blamed myself for Hayden's death."

"Oh, Isabel," Beth came over and wrapped her arms around her and Gabriel. "It wasn't your fault."

"I know that, now."

"I couldn't let her think-" Allie blurted, then shook her head. She snatched a tissue from a box on the coffee table and dabbed at her eyes.

"You should tell her."

Everything stopped when Ava spoke. She had been quiet until now, watching the emotions unfold, trying not to drown in their sorrow and grief. When she saw movement beside Allie, she narrowed her eyes. The small figure standing beside the woman shimmered, looking up at her mother.

"Who should tell who what?" Gabriel asked, stepping back from Iz.

Ava raised her arm and pointed to Allie.

Everyone turned to the older woman, who had picked up a framed photo from the mantel. Tears were streaming down her face as she looked at the last family photo that had been taken before that August camping trip when everything turned to shit.

Beside Ava, Maya was watching Allie. She let out a long moan that turned into a low howl.

"What are you talking about?" Josh asked.

"Allie does not blame Isabel for Hayden's death," Ava explained. She glanced at Griffin. "She was wrong to think her mother did."

"Bullocks. I can't tell you how many times Isabel has pushed me away because she doesn't want to get close to anyone," he said, moving to the edge of the sofa. "How long it took me to break down the barriers she put up-"

"I do not mean Isabel," Ava said. "I mean Hayden."

"What?" He snapped the word out unintentionally; he was so frustrated with the entire family avoiding dealing with Allie's bullshit that his temper slipped out. He wished Izzie would come back to sit with him. But he was also relieved to see Beth and Gabriel standing with their sister.

Ava focused on Isabel. "Like you, like Griffin, Hayden thought your mother blamed you for her death." She turned to Allie. "But you do not, do you? You should tell her the truth."

Allie was so pale. When she turned back to face the people in the room, she held a trembling hand to her mouth. Josh had left the room without anyone noticing, leaving her alone. She gave a barely visible shake of her head.

"I can't," she whispered.

Maya stood and walked over to Allie, stopping when there was still some distance between them. She let out a soft chuff.

Ava tilted her head, studying Allie. Her eyes darted to the place beside her. Hayden was frowning at her mother now. After a moment, Ava turned to Gabriel and Isabel.

"That morning at the campsite, the initial shock of losing a child hit her, and her body shut down. They had to give her a sedative and take her to the hospital."

"Did you tell her that?" Beth asked Gabriel. She walked back to sit next to Jack.

Gabriel shook his head.

"How do you know that?" Beth asked.

Josh returned with a glass of wine, which he handed to his wife silently.

"Because I hear her scream in the mornings sometimes." Ava remembered being launched from sleep several times from a scream filled with such horror that her entire day had felt dismal. That late winter morning she watched the rabbit in the yard, a scream had caused her to wake. Anytime that scream woke her, she would feel the emptiness of loss but did not understand why. Until now.

"I cannot always tell the difference between my screams and those of the people in the visions I am given in dreams," she said, gazing at Allie with remorse, "but yours are always followed by sobbing."

Gabriel squeezed Isabel's hand before he made his way back to the sofa to sit beside Ava. He rested his hand on her shoulder.

Allie paced the length of the fireplace, shaking her head silently. Maya watched her, moaning and chuffing.

"When you woke after the sedative, you were confused. You thought Isabel was the missing child."

"This is pointless," Allie said angrily. "It was bad enough to live through it the first time."

"Hayden has been showing me pieces of that day for months," Ava responded. "It is not pointless to her."

"So what if Mom thought I was missing?" Iz asked. "Why does that matter?"

Ava glanced at the area near the fireplace and nodded before focusing on Isabel.

"Your mother was relieved when Josh told her you were safe. The guilt in her eyes is not from hating you for living," Ava continued. "The guilt is because she was relieved when she found out the missing child was Hayden, not you."

Iz scoffed. "Horseshit. Why would she be relieved that Hayden was missing instead of me?"

"Because you are her baby. She loves all her children, but you are her youngest, the one she is most protective over."

"She has a hell of a way of showing it," Iz snapped. Her mouth was dry in spite of the water she had been drinking all morning.

"Humans overcompensate to atone for their sins. Your mother believes a lifetime of negative behavior toward you can compensate for one action she committed while under duress." Ava glanced at Allie, then back at Isabel.

Isabel looked doubtful until her mother spoke.

"I didn't mean to think it," Allie said softly. She'd stopped pacing. She closed her eyes as more tears welled. "What kind of mother wishes harm to one daughter at the cost of another?"

Isabel was stunned into silence. Everything she'd thought the past sixteen years had been false, a misunderstanding. Over a decade wasted because of miscommunication.

"The food!" Allie said suddenly. Her eyes widened.

Maya let out a muffled bark of alarm.

"I checked on the prime rib," Josh said. "It's fine. This is more important."

He stayed by her instead of returning to his seat.

Isabel was holding her bottle of water in both hands. She kept drumming the fingers of her right hand on it, unable to stay still.

"Ava, you said Hayden also thought Mom blames me for her death. How did you know she felt that way?"

Ava glanced to the right of Allie's body. "I could see it in her eyes. The same way I can see now that she no longer believes it."

•   •   •   •   •

"She's here?" Jack, who had been silent until now, looked around the room.

Ava glanced at him, nodded.

"Does she hate me?" Allie couldn't seem to get her voice above a whisper.

Maya and Ozzie whined in solidarity.

"No." Ava's answer was immediate. "She is your daughter."

"Then why is she still here?" Josh asked, moving his head around, as if he would catch a glimpse of her shadow.

Ava sighed. Her tone was dry when she said, "Because McDonald's is closed."

In spite of her recent tears, Isabel snorted, startling Ozzie. "Ava's learning sarcasm. My work here is done."

Ava closed her eyes and took a deep breath, holding it for several seconds before she let it out. When she regarded Josh, her expression was less hostile.

"I apologize. Common misconceptions irritate me. I keep forgetting you are ignorant on this subject. In addition, you have a personal connection that makes being objective more difficult. I should be more understanding to your situation."

She rubbed her forehead. Before she could continue, Griffin took over.

"We've already had this conversation with her," he explained. "Apparently there's no 'going' anywhere, in the traditional way people think of their loved ones 'going to a better place'. Whatever the afterlife is, the location of spirits overlaps ours. They exist all around us, just not in a realm most people can see."

"People need to move on, not spirits," Ava said. "Their business is done."

"Oh." Josh wasn't sure what else to say to that.

"But she does want you to fix your relationship with Isabel if you can," Ava said, staring hard at Allie. "You are both still alive. The time to reconcile is now."

Allie's shoulders sagged. "I never meant for you to think you were less than anyone else. Everything got so messed up so fast. I don't know what to say."

As she turned into Josh and he gave her a firm squeeze, she tried to hold back more tears. She was so damn tired of crying.

"Don't bother saying anything," Isabel said tightly. "Griffin's right. We won't be coming back."

"Isabel, come on," Josh said.

Allie raised her head. "You're not even going to give me a chance?"

"You've had sixteen years of chances," Iz snapped. "You felt guilty for a random thought about Hayden, made when you were doped up, and you took it out on me all this time. Do you have any idea how fucked up that is?"

Whining, Ozzie trotted over to Jack and sat beside him, resting his head on his knee.

"It wasn't a… conscious decision," Allie said. It sounded lame even to her. "I just wanted Hayden to know that I loved her, wherever she was. I wanted her to know… I never wished her harm."

"So you worshipped her and acted like I was the one that got her killed. All to please a ghost you didn't believe existed until a few days ago." Iz felt dizzy with rage. Her heart was knocking around in an unusual rhythm; her insides felt like they were floating around untethered, and her head was pounding. "Do you have any idea what that does to a kid?"

"Isabel-" Josh started.

"And you!" she yelled, turning on her father. "You should have stood up for me. You're my father. You were supposed to protect me."

She closed her eyes and tilted her head back, curling her hands into fists at her sides.

"Fuck ALL OF YOU!" she yelled.

Maya let out a howl. Ozzie stood, raised his head, and started whining. Jack tried to soothe him.

Sitting next to Ava, Gabriel set a hand on her knee. He said nothing. His head was down. Ava could feel the shame coming off him in thick waves.

It was emanating from all of them, so powerful it was suffocating her. She felt her body being squeezed all over and tried to draw in a deep breath. It was like inhaling through wet cloth. She willed herself to see it through, to take whatever emotions this reckoning was causing and keep going, for Isabel's sake. It was what a friend would do, she was sure.

Griffin stood and walked over to Isabel, pulling her into his arms. She kept her eyes closed as she stiffly accepted the hug for several moments, then raised her arms to hug him back.

Beth and Allie were crying. Even Josh's and Jack's eyes were glassy with tears.

Ava looked from one family member to the next, studying each reaction with her head tilted. Hayden had moved from Allie's side and was standing next to Isabel now. Her hand was on Isabel's elbow.

Griffin lifted his head and looked at Izzie. She opened her eyes. Gave him a tired but relieved smile.

"That was several years of therapy crammed into a very short amount of time," he murmured.

Gabriel looked at his sister. "I should have protected you."

"You were a kid, just like me," she said. "It wasn't your job. And you," she added, looking at Jack, "Unfuck you. You've always been nice to me."

He tried to hide his smile.

Griffin stepped to the side, so he was facing the rest of the family, but he glanced down at Izzie.

"Are you ready to go?" he asked, draping his arm on her shoulder.

"Please don't go, Isabel," Allie said. She'd plucked several tissues from the box to blow her nose and they were scattered in little balls at her feet. She held one in her hand for wiping her eyes. Her nose was red, her cheeks raw. Seeing her mother so vulnerable took away the invincible quality Isabel had always associated with her, reducing the all-powerful, omniscient manipulative monster to a mere mortal, cowering under an unbearable amount of pain and guilt.

How had she ever been trapped under this woman's insecurity?

"I'm so sorry." Allie sniffed. "I can't undo the past sixteen years. All I can do is ask you to forgive me and try as hard as I can to do better. I don't want to lose you. Can that be enough?"

Iz thought about all the times she had come over and felt isolated because her mother and Beth were so close. All the times she seemed to interrupt a private conversation between the two and they refused to include her in anything they were discussing. And especially every time her mother had growled at her to stop swearing as if Iz was a lesser person because she talked differently.

She glared at her mother, and Allie seemed to know she was not going to forgive her. She looked dejected.

"Not even close," Isabel said.

Allie's lower lip trembled, but she nodded her acceptance to Isabel's decision.

Isabel ran her hands through her hair, took a deep breath, let it out.

"But it's a start."

· · · · ·

Ava.

The voice, warm and strong as it had always been, called to her as she slept. She sat up stiffly. The smell of rain greeted her from the open windows. In the distance, thunder was barely audible. The wind was just starting to pick up. She was unaware of the coming storm, as she was unaware of Gabriel sleeping next to her.

Draping her legs over the bed, her unfocused eyes staring at some point across the room, Ava sat for a moment. Hayden appeared at her side. When she set her hand on top of Ava's, Ava sighed.

Cupping her hand against the side of Ava's head, Hayden whispered in her ear. Ava leaned forward and brushed her fingers along the hardwood floor until she felt cloth. She lifted the tee shirt Gabriel had given her and slipped into it, then stood and put on her shorts.

When the voice called out to her again, she followed it without fear. She walked to her bureau, her hand skimming over the underwear in the top drawer until her fingers found the necklace with the keys. Carrying them to the door, she stared straight ahead as Hayden guided her hand to stick the key in and turn, releasing her from her bedroom. She slipped the necklace over her head as she exited the room.

Down the stairs she walked, not feeling the hardwood floors under her feet or the banister sliding under her palm. Only hearing, hearing the voice call to her. Hayden held her hand and guided her to keep her from bumping into anything.

The drive to follow the voice grew as she reached for the front door. She brought her hand up and used one hand to jangle the knob while the other patted the wood. The door shook but did not open.

She had to get out. She had to find the owner of the voice.

Endless seconds later, Hayden guided her hand to the deadbolt. The lock clicked loudly, and Ava pulled the door open. She crossed the porch and would have walked right off the steps if Hayden hadn't reached out and set her hand on Ava's chest.

She saw nothing, though her eyes were open.

No longer hearing the voice, she stood at the top of the steps and swayed slightly. Nature was singing around her: crickets and mosquitos and tree frogs all rehearsing their nightly musical numbers. The rough wood beneath her feet was cold. Goosebumps layered her entire body. The smell of freshly mown grass registered somewhere in her subconscious.

The smell of coffee made her nostrils flare. The bench seat under the front window was no longer empty. Ava turned slowly until she was facing the figure.

"Hello, Ava."

Ava's heart all but stopped.

"Have a seat."

Ava tilted her head. Even asleep, her body reacted to the sound of the woman's voice. Tears welled in her eyes. She began shivering.

The visitor patted the bench beside her twice. The scent of coffee intensified.

"Sit down, kiddo."

Ava walked to the bench. She turned, her movements jerky, until the backs of her legs bumped against the edge of the bench, then sat on the soft cushion.

Opening her mouth, she was only able to emit a hollow exhalation. Words refused to come.

"Ava, I didn't come to you sooner because you needed to figure some things out for yourself. You may hate me for that, and I'm sorry."

Finally, Ava turned to look at the figure. The tears in her eyes refused to drop, causing everything to appear blurry. Thunder rumbled, closer now. Ava felt as if the storm was inside her, building pressure in her chest. The wind had grown stronger, too, lifting her hair when it gusted.

After all these years, after all the questions, she was unable to find the words when she was given the chance to face the one spirit she had looked for since she was a teenager.

The person next to her usually wore jeans and a tee shirt because she spent most of her time outside working with plants. Now she was wearing a navy dress.

It was the dress she had been buried in.

Ruth Reid had short, chestnut hair, just starting to turn gray. She kept it short because when she worked in one of her gardens or did the landscaping on the property, she needed to keep her hair out of her way. She smelled of coffee, with a hint of the earth she always worked in. In the years Ava had known her, Ruth had spent most of her time with her hands in the dirt, tending to one plant or another. That Ava loved nature because it reminded her of Ruth had never occurred to her.

Around them, the storm was coming closer, growing louder. Lightning momentarily brightened the porch, illuminating the two figures on the bench. A crack of thunder bellowed around them, shaking the entire house.

Ava reached out toward her foster mother, then withdrew her hand quickly. The woman's soft brown eyes regarded her warmly.

"People need to grieve for their loved ones," Ruth continued. "It's part of moving on. Grief is different for you. Seeing me so soon after my death wouldn't have let you accept it."

"It has been seven years." Ava clenched her hands into fists. A flash of rage propelled her from the bench. She leaned against a post on the railing, surprised at her own anger.

"You weren't ready."

"I wanted to show you to David." Ava felt tears build again. The pressure in her chest had become intense, pushing against her ribcage painfully. "I wanted to take away his pain."

"I know." Lightning briefly lit her features. "But you can't. It's part of healing."

Thunder cracked as if to emphasis her point.

"I searched for you every day."

"I know."

Rain began to softly fall around them. To Ava, the drops hitting the ground sounded like an ethereal shhhhh. With another bark of thunder, the rain fell harder, splattering Ava with fat drops as the wind pushed it. She stepped away from the railing just enough to keep dry.

"You never came to me." The anger was replaced with a longing so profound she wanted to crumble to the floor. Where was this crippling emotion coming from? "I called to you, and you never came."

"I've watched you every day."

"You never came," Ava repeated, her frustration growing. "I wanted to help David. He was lost without you."

"Grief is harder for those like you. It takes longer for those with your abilities to let go."

"I wanted to help David." The petulance in her tone almost made her wince.

Ruth gazed at her patiently. "You're not angry at me for not coming to you all these years. You're angry because I died."

The fury was back. "You left us. David was sad. The M-monster came back."

Lightning broke through the clouds, setting the sky ablaze and casting Ava's face in an expression of fury she did not bother trying to control.

"The body stopped working. I never left. You know that Ava, better than anyone."

"You l-left us," she insisted. Her fists shook at her sides with nowhere for the energy to go. "You left m-me."

"Oh, baby," Ruth sighed, holding her arms out. "Come here."

Ava walked hesitantly to her, dropping to her knees, and burying her head in the folds of the navy dress. She did not cry, but the intensity of the passion raging through her made her body shake. Ruth leaned over and began rubbing her back in a slow, soothing motion. She had done the same when Ava was sick as a child. Comfort spread through Ava as the storm raged around them.

Minutes later, as the thunder and lightning began to die down, Ava's nerves had gone from unstable to raw to numb. Her body gradually stopped shuddering.

"Come sit beside me, baby."

Sniffling, Ava stood and settled on the bench. She felt hollowed out. Ruth pulled her against her like she would a little child she was reading a bedtime story to.

"You know, I always I thought you hated me." She smiled slightly at the look of horror on Ava's face. Tilting her head, she widened her smile. "It's funny, how much people allow their emotions to get in the way of things."

"I am sorry I never needed you."

Ava wished she had at least pretended to be less independent, so Ruth could feel wanted. She had never meant to hurt the woman by being self-sufficient.

"You did need me, Ava. You needed my love, and I gave it to you freely. Dave and I loved all the children we fostered over the years. But you were my only daughter."

Raising her head, Ava stared into Ruth's eyes and saw the truth. Tears slipped down her cheeks.

"Mama," Ava said, her tone filled with awe.

Ruth leaned down and kissed her forehead. "It's time for me to go."

Ava reached out to touch her forearm, but her fingertips slipped through. Ruth was losing substance, fading as the storm passed.

Panic wanted to envelop her, made her want to beg Ruth to stay, but she willed it away.

"I'm never far, Ava. I'll see you again."

For a moment, her body was as obscure as a reflection in a window. Then she was gone.

"Love," Ava whispered, dropping her head.

She rested her hands on the bench where Ruth had been sitting. The wood was cool, with no indication that anyone had been there at all.

· · · · ·

That was how Gabriel found her when he burst outside moments later. He charged out onto the porch, yelling her name, and swung around when he caught sight of her out of the corner of his eye.

He'd awakened as the storm was dying down and found her missing. Putting on jeans and a tee shirt in anticipation of a struggle, he hadn't expected to go outside until he reached the bottom of the stairs and saw the front door open. Without pausing to put on shoes, he rushed out, flipping on the porch light as he opened the screen door.

Relief flooded over him when he saw her sitting on the bench. She was in an odd position, her upper body turned so she was facing him with her hands resting on the seat. But her legs were facing forward.

When she lifted her head, he saw her eyes had that dead gaze in them that indicated she was sleepwalking.

Gabriel walked slowly over to the bench, passed in front of her, and sat next to her on her other side, careful not to touch her.

"You need to wake up, hon."

Ava sat up and turned until she was facing forward again. She dropped her hands into her lap and sat with her back stiff.

"Let me touch you," Gabriel said, testing her by placing his fingers on her shoulder. When she didn't react, he slid his hand down her arm and gently took her hand. "Did the storm wake you?"

She shook her head. "She called to me."

"Who?" She didn't answer, so he said, "Let's get you back to bed."

He slipped his arm under her legs and lifted her as gently as he would a child. Walking inside, he used his hip to push the door shut. He turned back and turned the lock in the door handle. As he carried her up the stairs, he glanced down at her. Lightning no longer lit his way, but he'd turned on the lamp on his bedside table and a soft glow spilled down from his bedroom.

Her head rested against his shoulder. She had fallen asleep again – or at least she was no longer semi-conscious. Her hand was curled against his chest.

A flash of silver showed the chain of keys around her neck that was supposed to be in the top drawer of her dresser.

So much for keeping her locked in the room.

It occurred to him that he hadn't been awakened earlier in the morning. This was the first he'd left the room to find her, and as he lay her gently on the bed, his alarm clock showed him it was nearing three in the morning. Usually, she was on her second nightmare by now.

Maybe finding out who The Monster really was had helped with the nightmares, or maybe she was telling the spirits to give her a break during the night like he suggested. Either way, she was sleeping better. She looked more rested the past couple mornings. As far as he could tell, this sleepwalking trek hadn't been a nightmare exactly. Wandering around, even outside, was still better than shrieking and fighting until she injured herself.

He carefully lifted the chain from her neck and locked the bedroom door.

As he pulled the bedding up around her, she stirred. Lifting her dark lashes, she gazed at him.

"I saw her," she whispered.

"Who?" Gabriel sat on the side of the bed, resting his hand on her hip above the blankets.

"I saw her," she repeated.

He was surprised to hear tears in her voice.

Thunder grumbled, soft and far away now. Though it was moving on, the storm had been intense. Like Ava, he thought. She was like a thunderstorm contained in human skin.

"Who did you see, Ava?"

"Ruth."

"She came to you." It wasn't a question.

Her eyes were full of curiosity as she nodded.

Without taking his eyes off her, Gabriel shifted and climbed over her. She was fully awake now, but he still felt hesitant to straddle her and leave his testicles exposed. He quickly moved to his side of the bed and pivoted until he was sitting. He set the keys in the drawer of the bedside table. Hopefully, if she tried to get to them again, she would make enough noise to wake him up.

Punching his pillow to get some life back into it, he tilted it against the headboard and leaned back.

He held his hand out. She willingly took it and curled against him. They listened to the storm, Gabriel brushing his hand down her hair.

Rain was still striking the windows, but the thunder and lightning were moving away. Ava kept her hand pressed to Gabriel's chest, feeling his steady heartbeat, listening to his breath. He trailed his fingertips up and down her arm in a slow rhythm.

"Did you wake up before this?" he asked, tilting his head to look down at her.

She shook her head against him.

"You're wearing clothes."

"Hayden told me to put them on."

He thought about that. "Have you had a nightmare since we went to bed last night?"

Again, she shook her head.

"You didn't have any nightmares?" He sat up straighter.

Leaning away from him so she could see his face, she frowned. "I woke up to Ruth calling me. I have slept through until morning these past two nights."

"That's great." He tucked her hair behind her ear and rested his palm against her cheek. "What are you doing differently?"

"I told the spirits you said to fuck off while I am sleeping."

He gave her his half smile. Sliding his hand down her arm, he gripped her hand. "Good for you."

He moved down so he was lying on the bed.

"I did not use those exact words." She lay next to him, pulling the bedding up over them both.

"Whatever you said must have worked."

Shifting so she could press against him, she draped her arm across his chest. She slid her leg up until it was across his thighs. Nestled in and sighed deeply. A long yawn reminded her it was still too early in the morning to get out of bed and start her exercises. When his arms encircled her and filled her with comfort, she made a content sound and sighed.

"Love," she whispered, her unique way of telling him she loved him.

Gabriel pressed her tighter against him and kissed the top of her head again.

"I love you back," he murmured.

He leaned over and turned off the lamp. In the darkness, they held each other as they drifted off to sleep.

Around them, the spirits were silent, for the moment at peace.

Keisha Cones
November 23, 2020

CPSIA information can be obtained
at www.ICGtesting.com
Printed in the USA
BVHW051935200323
660576BV00002B/1

9 798887 290157